Published in 1984, **David A. Gemmell**'s first novel, *Legend*, has become a classic. His most recent Drenai and Rigante books have all been published by Bantam Press, and his latest novels, *Hero in the Shadows*, *Ravenheart* and *Stormrider*, have been *Sunday Times* bestsellers.

Now widely acclaimed as Britain's king of heroic fantasy, David Gemmell lives in East Sussex.

G000232058

www.booksattransworld.co.uk

DRENAI TALES VOLUME III

The Legend of Deathwalker
Winter Warriors
Hero in the Shadows

DAVID A. GEMMELL

BANTAM PRESS

LONDON • NEW YORK • TORONTO • SYDNEY • AUCKLAND

TRANSWORLD PUBLISHERS
61–63 Uxbridge Road, London W5 5SA
a division of The Random House Group Ltd

RANDOM HOUSE AUSTRALIA (PTY) LTD
20 Alfred Street, Milsons Point, Sydney,
New South Wales 2061, Australia

RANDOM HOUSE NEW ZEALAND LTD
18 Poland Road, Glenfield, Auckland 10, New Zealand

RANDOM HOUSE SOUTH AFRICA (PTY) LTD
Endulini, 5a Jubilee Road, Parktown 2193, South Africa

Published 2002 by Bantam Press
a division of Transworld Publishers

Copyright © David A. Gemmell 2002

THE LEGEND OF DEATHWALKER
Copyright © David A. Gemmell 1996

WINTER WARRIORS
Copyright © David A. Gemmell 1997

HERO IN THE SHADOWS
Copyright © David A. Gemmell 2000

A catalogue record for this book is available from the British Library.
ISBNs 0593 050681 (cased)
0593 049187 (tpb)

Typeset in 11½/13pt Sabon by Falcon Oast Graphic Art Ltd.

Printed in Great Britain by
Mackays plc, Chatham, Kent

1 3 5 7 9 10 8 6 4 2

CONTENTS

THE LEGEND OF DEATHWALKER

Introduction

Of all the characters I have created over the years, none has touched my heart in the same way as Druss the Axeman. He was loosely based on my stepfather, Bill Woodford, a big man, with hands so large I could, as an adult, slip his signet ring over my thumb. Druss was then – and is now – an idealized portrait of Bill. Huge, uncompromising, loyal, and courageous to the death.

Every time I come to write a story featuring Druss I feel a great warmth and a sense of discovery. It is not unlike returning to a favourite place and reaching out to touch the timbers, or staring over the hills.

Back in 1995 I was about to join a new publisher. They had optimistically commissioned six books over a four-year period. I had happily banked a cheque from them. The problem was I didn't have a single idea, let alone six novels.

One night I had given a talk to a group of writers and a young man approached me. He asked whether there would be any more Druss books. I said it was unlikely since Druss had first appeared, in *Legend*, as an old hero who died valiantly. His earlier life had been covered some years later in *The First Chronicles of Druss the Legend*. The young man listened attentively and then said, 'How did he get the name Deathwalker from the Nadir?'

Not a question I could answer. I simply didn't know. Then he added, 'Was he fighting against the Nadir or for them?'

'For them?' I queried.

He laughed. 'Well, I always think of him as an equal-opportunities killer. He doesn't exactly serve nations. It's more about causes, isn't it?'

On the drive home along the south coast I started to think about Druss and his life. The young man was right. Druss didn't get carried away with jingoism. If he felt something was right he would fight for it, regardless of the odds. He was, as the Americans would say, a natural maverick. He lived by an iron code, which meant tackling evil wherever he found it.

This code was largely down to a saying my mother, Olive, had taught me as a child: 'Every little bit of good that I may do, let me do it now, for I may not pass this way again.'

Druss's version was naturally more muscular, but the results were the same.

I still had no story, but then I rarely do when I begin a book. One of my editors, Steve Saffel of Del Rey, tears his hair out in frustration at my writing methods. He sends me e-mails asking for plot details to be used in marketing. I write back saying, 'I'm only 30,000 words in and I have no idea where it's going.' I sometimes feel that I can hear the echoes of his screams.

So I sat down to write a new Druss novel. I began it with Druss and his long-time friend Sieben heading into the lands of the Gothir.

I still remember that first day. It was raining hard, and there was a distant rumble of thunder out over the sea. I typed, 'The moon hung like a sickle blade over Dros Delnoch . . .'

A great feeling of homecoming swept over me.

DG
2002

Prologue

The moon hung like a sickle blade over Dros Delnoch and Pellin stood quietly staring down at the Nadir camp in the lunar light below. Thousands of warriors were gathered there, and tomorrow they would come screaming across the narrow strip of blood-stained ground, hauling their ladders, carrying their grappling irons. They would be baying for battle and death, and just like today the sound would terrify him, seeming to penetrate his skin like needles of ice. Pellin was more frightened than he had ever been in his young life, and he longed to run, to hide, to throw away his ill-fitting armour, and race south to his home. The Nadir kept coming, wave after wave, their raucous battle cries sending their hatred ahead of them. The shallow wound in his upper left arm was both throbbing and itching. Gilad had assured him this meant that it was healing well. But it had been a taste of pain, a bitter promise of worse pain to come. He had watched comrades writhing and screaming, their bellies opened by serrated swords . . . Pellin fought to push the memories away. A cold wind began to blow from the north, bunching dark rain-clouds before it. He shivered, and remembered his warm farmhouse with its thatched roof and large stone-built fireplace. On cold nights like this one he and Kara would lie in bed, her head resting on his shoulder, her left leg warm on his thighs. They would lie together in the soft red glow of the fading fire, and listen to the wind howling mournfully outside.

Pellin sighed. 'Please don't let me die here,' he prayed.

Of the twenty-three men who had volunteered from his village, only nine were left. He gazed back at the rows of sleeping defenders, lying on the open ground between Walls Three and Four. Could these few hold the greatest army ever assembled? Pellin knew they could not.

Returning his gaze to the Nadir camp, he scanned the area close to the mountains. The Drenai dead, stripped of armour and weapons, had been thrown there, and burnt. Oily black smoke had drifted over the Dros for hours afterwards, bringing with it the sickly and nauseating smell of roasting flesh. 'It could have been me,' thought Pellin, remembering the slaughter as Wall Two fell.

He shivered. Dros Delnoch, the mightiest fortress in all the world: six walls of rearing stone, and a broad keep. Never had she been conquered by an enemy. But then never had she faced an army of such numbers. It seemed to Pellin that there were more Nadir than there were stars in the sky. The defenders had fallen back from Wall One after bitter fighting, for it was the longest and therefore the hardest to hold. They had crept back in the night, surrendering the wall without further losses. But Wall Two had been taken at great cost, the enemy breaching the defences and sweeping forward to encircle the defenders. Pellin had barely made it back to Wall Three, and remembered the acid taste of fear in his throat, and the terrible shaking of his limbs as he hauled himself over the battlements and sank to the ramparts.

And what was it all for, he wondered? What difference would it make if the Drenai enjoyed self-rule, or government by the Warlord, Ulric? Would the farm yield any less corn? Would his cattle sicken and die?

It had all seemed such an adventure twelve weeks ago, when the Drenai recruiting officers had arrived at the village. A few weeks of patrolling these great walls, and then a return home as heroes.

Heroes! Sovil was a hero – until that arrow pierced his eye, ripping it from the socket. Jocan was a hero as he lay screaming, his blood-covered hands seeking to hold his entrails in place.

Pellin added a little coal to the iron brazier and waved at the sentry thirty paces to the left. The man was stamping his feet against the cold. He and Pellin had swapped places an hour before, and soon it would be his turn to stand by the brazier. The knowledge of heat soon to be lost gave the fire an even greater significance, and Pellin stretched out his hands, enjoying the warmth.

A huge figure moved into sight, stepping carefully over the sleeping defenders and making his way towards the ramparts. Pellin's heart began to beat faster as Druss strode up the steps.

Druss the Legend, the Saviour of Skeln Pass, the man who had battled his way across the world to rescue his wife. Druss the Axeman, the Silver Slayer. The Nadir called him Deathwalker, and Pellin now knew why. He had watched him fighting on the battlements, his terrible axe cleaving and slaying. He was not mortal; he was a dark god of war. Pellin hoped the old man would stay away from him. What could a novice soldier find to say to a hero like Druss? To Pellin's great relief the Legend stopped by the other sentry, and the two men began to talk; he could see the sentry moving nervously from foot to foot as the old warrior spoke to him.

It struck him then that Druss was the human embodiment of this ancient fortress, unbeaten and yet eroded by time; less than he was, but magnificent for all that. Pellin smiled as he remembered the Nadir herald giving Druss the ultimatum of surrender or die. The old hero had laughed. 'In the north,' he said, 'the mountains may tremble when Ulric breaks wind. But this is Drenai land and to me he is just another pot-bellied savage who couldn't wipe his arse without a Drenai map tattooed on his thigh.'

Pellin's smile faded as he saw Druss clap the other sentry on the shoulder and move on towards him. The rain had eased, and the moon shone bright once more. Pellin's hands began to sweat and he wiped the palms on his cloak. The young sentry stood to attention as the Legend approached him, striding along the ramparts, his axe shining silver in the bright moonlight. Pellin's mouth was dry as he stood, fist clenched against his breastplate, to salute him. 'Relax, laddie,' said Druss, laying the mighty axe on the ramparts. The old warrior stretched his huge hands to the brazier, warming them, then sat with his back to the wall, beckoning the youth to join him. Pellin had never been this close to Druss, and he saw now the lines of age etched deep into his broad face, giving it the look of ancient granite. The eyes were bright and pale, though, beneath heavy brows, and Pellin found he could not stare into them. 'They'll not come tonight,' said Druss. 'Just before first light they'll rush in. No war cries; it will be a silent assault.'

'How do you know that, sir?'

Druss chuckled. 'I'd like to tell you that my vast knowledge of

13

war leads me to that conclusion, but the answer is more simple. The Thirty predict it, and they're a canny bunch. Normally I have little time for wizards and such, but these lads are great fighters.' He lifted his black helm clear of his head and ran his fingers through his thick white hair. 'Served me well, this helm,' he told Pellin, twirling it so that moonlight shone upon the silver axe motif on the brow. 'And I don't doubt it will do its job tomorrow.'

At the thought of the battle to come Pellin cast a nervous glance over the wall, to where the Nadir waited. From here he could see many of them lying in their blankets, close to hundreds of camp-fires. Others were awake, sharpening weapons or talking in small groups. The young man turned and ran his gaze over the exhausted Drenai defenders lying on the ground behind the ramparts, wrapped in their blankets, trying to snatch a few hours of precious, refreshing sleep. 'Sit down, laddie,' said Druss. 'You can't worry them away.'

Resting his spear against the wall the sentry sat. His scabbard clanged against the stone, and clumsily he swivelled it. 'I cannot get used to wearing all this armour,' said Pellin. 'I trip over the sword all the time. I am not much of a soldier, I fear.'

'You looked every inch the soldier three days ago on Wall Two,' said Druss. 'I saw you kill two Nadir, then fight your way back to the ropes on this wall. Even then you helped a comrade who had a wound in his leg – you climbed below him, supporting him.'

'You saw that? But there was so much confusion – and you were in the midst of the battle yourself!'

'I see many things, boy. What is your name?'

'Pellin . . . Cul Pellin,' he corrected himself. 'Sir,' he added swiftly.

'We can dispense with the formalities, Pellin,' Druss told him amiably. 'Here tonight we are just two veterans sitting quietly waiting for the dawn. Are you frightened?'

Pellin nodded and Druss smiled. 'And do you ask yourself, Why me? Why should I be standing here facing the might of the Nadir?'

'Yes. Kara didn't want me to go with the others. She told me I was a fool. I mean, what difference will it make if we win or lose?'

'In a hundred years? None at all,' said Druss. 'But all invading armies carry their own demons with them, Pellin. If they break through here they will sweep across the Sentran Plain bringing fire and destruction, rape and slaughter. That's why we must stop them. And why you? Because you are the man for the role.'

'I think I am going to die here,' said Pellin. 'I don't want to die. My Kara is pregnant and I want to see my son grow, tall and strong. I want . . .' He stumbled to silence as the lump in his throat blocked further speech.

'You want what we all want, laddie,' said Druss softly. 'But you are a man, and men must face what they fear or be destroyed by it.'

'I don't know if I can. I keep thinking of joining the other deserters. Creeping south in the night. Going home.'

'Then why haven't you?'

Pellin thought for a moment. 'I don't know,' he said lamely.

'I'll tell you why, boy. Because you look around and you see the others who must stay, and fight all the harder because you are not standing by your post. You are not a man to leave others to do your work for you.'

'I'd like to believe that. Truly I would.'

'Believe it, laddie, for I am a good judge of men.' Suddenly Druss grinned. 'I knew another Pellin once. He was a spear-thrower. A good one, too. Won the Gold in the Fellowship Games when they were held in Gulgothir.'

'I thought that was Nicotas,' said Pellin. 'I remember the parade when the team came home. Nicotas carried the Drenai flag.'

The old man shook his head. 'That feels like yesterday,' said Druss, with a wide grin. 'But I am talking about the Fifth Games. I would guess they took place around thirty years ago – long before you were a gleam in your mother's eyes. Pellin was a good man.'

'Were they the Games you took part in, sir? At the court of the Mad King?' asked the sentry.

Druss nodded. 'It was no part of my plan. I was a farmer then, but Abalayn invited me to Gulgothir as part of the Drenai delegation. My wife, Rowena, urged me to accept the invitation; she thought I was growing bored with life in the mountains.' He chuckled. 'She was right! We came through Dros Delnoch, I remember. There were forty-five competitors, and around another hundred hangers-on, whores, servants, trainers. I have forgotten most of their names now. Pellin I remember – but then he made me laugh, and I enjoyed his company.' The old man fell silent, lost in memories.

15

'So how did you become part of the team, sir?'

'Oh, that! The Drenai had a fist-fighter named . . . damned if I can remember. Old age is eating away at my memory. Anyway he was an ill-tempered man. All the fighters brought their own trainers with them, and lesser fighters to spar with. This fellow . . . Grawal, that was it! . . . was a brute, and he disabled two of his sparring partners. One day he asked me to spar with him. We were still three days from Gulgothir and I was *really* bored by then. That's one of the curses of my life, lad. Easily bored! So I agreed. It was a mistake. Lots of the camp women used to watch the fighters train, and I should have realized that Grawal was a crowd-pleaser. Anyway, he and I began to spar. At first it went well, he was good, a lot of power in the shoulders but supple too. Have you ever sparred, Pellin?'

'No, sir.'

'Well, it looks the same as a genuine fight, but all the punches are pulled. The purpose of it is to increase the speed of the fighter's reflexes. But then a group of the camp women turned up, and sat close by us. Grawal wanted to show the women how tough he was, and he let rip with a combination of blows at full power. It was like being kicked by a mule and I have to admit that it irritated me. I stepped back and told him to ease up. The fool took no notice – and then rushed me. So I hit him. Damned if his jaw didn't break in three places. As a result the Drenai had now lost their one heavy fighter, and I felt honour bound to take his place.'

'What happened then?' asked Pellin as Druss eased himself to his feet and leaned over the ramparts. The faint light of pre-dawn was showing in the east.

'That story had better wait until tonight, laddie,' said Druss softly. 'Here they come!'

Pellin scrambled to his feet. Thousands of Nadir warriors were streaming silently towards the wall. Druss bellowed a warning and a bugler sounded the alert. Red-cloaked Drenai defenders came surging from their blankets.

Pellin drew his sword, his hand trembling as he gazed on the rushing tide of men. Hundreds were carrying ladders, others held coiled ropes and grappling hooks. Pellin's heart was hammering now. 'Sweet Missael,' he whispered. 'Nothing will stop them!' He took a backward step, but then Druss laid his huge hand on the boy's shoulder.

'Who am I, laddie?' he asked, his ice-blue eyes holding to Pellin's gaze.

'W . . . what?' stammered Pellin.

'Who am I?'

Pellin blinked back the sweat that trickled into his eyes. 'You are Druss the Legend,' he answered.

'You stand by me, Pellin,' said the old man grimly, 'and we'll stop them together.' Suddenly the axeman grinned. 'I don't tell many stories, laddie, and I hate it when they're interrupted. So when we've seen off this little sortie I'll stand you a goblet of Lentrian Red, and tell you the tale of the Gothir God-King and the Eyes of Alchazzar.'

Pellin took a deep breath. 'I'll stand with you, sir,' he said.

Chapter One

As the huge crowd bayed for blood, Sieben the Poet found himself staring around the vast colosseum, its mighty columns and arches, its tiers and statues. Far below on the golden sand of the arena two men were fighting for the glory of their nations. Fifteen thousand people were shouting now, the noise cacophonous like the roaring of some inchoate beast. Sieben lifted a scented handkerchief to his face, seeking to blot out the smell of sweat that enveloped him from all sides.

The colosseum was a marvellous piece of architecture, its columns shaped into statues of ancient heroes and gods, its seats of finest marble covered by cushions of down-filled green velvet. The cushions irritated Sieben, for the colour clashed with his bright blue silken tunic inset with shards of opal on the puffed sleeves. The poet was proud of the garment, which had cost a suitably enormous amount of money from the best tailor in Drenan. To have it beggared by a poor choice of seat covering was almost more than he could stand. Still, with everyone seated, the effect was muted. Servants moved endlessly through the crowd, bearing trays of cool drinks, or sweetmeats, pies, cakes, savoury delicacies. The tiers of the rich were shaded by silken coverings, also in that dreadful green, while the very rich sat in red-cushioned splendour with slaves fanning them. Sieben had tried to change his seat and sit among the nobility, but no amount of flattery nor offers of bribes could purchase him a place.

To his right Sieben could just see the edge of the God-King's balcony, and the straight backs of two of the Royal Guards in their silver breastplates and white cloaks. Their helms, thought the poet, were particularly magnificent, embossed with gold and crested with white horsehair plumes. That was the beauty of the simple colours, he thought, black, white, silver and gold were rarely upstaged by upholstery – no matter what the colour.

'Is he winning?' asked Majon, the Drenai ambassador, tugging at Sieben's sleeve. 'He's taking a fearful battering. The Lentrian has never been beaten, you know. They say he killed two fighters last spring, in a competition in Mashrapur. Damn, I bet ten gold raq on Druss.'

Sieben gently lifted the ambassador's fingers from his sleeve, brushing at the bruised silk, and forced his gaze away from the wonders of the architecture to focus briefly on the combat below. The Lentrian hit Druss with an uppercut, then a right cross. Druss backed away, blood seeping from a cut over his left eye. 'What odds did you get?' asked Sieben.

The slender ambassador ran his hand over his close-cropped silver hair. 'Six to one. I must have been mad.'

'Not at all,' said Sieben smoothly, 'it was patriotism that drove you. Look, I know ambassadors are not well paid, so I will take your bet. Give me the token.'

'I couldn't possibly . . . I mean he's being thrashed out there.'

'Of course you must. After all Druss is my friend, and I should have wagered on him out of loyalty.' Sieben saw the glint of avarice in the ambassador's dark eyes.

'Well, if you are sure.' The man's slim fingers darted into the pearl-beaded leather pouch at his side, producing a small square of papyrus bearing a wax seal and the amount wagered. Sieben took it and Majon waited with hand outstretched.

'I didn't bring my purse with me,' said Sieben, 'but I will hand over the money tonight.'

'Yes, of course,' said Majon, his disappointment obvious.

'I think I'll take a walk around the colosseum,' said Sieben. 'There is so much to see. I understand there are art galleries and shops on the levels below.'

'You don't show much concern for your friend,' said Majon.

Sieben ignored the criticism. 'My dear ambassador, Druss fights because he loves to fight. Generally one saves one's concern for the poor unfortunates he faces. I will see you later at the celebrations.'

Easing himself from his seat Sieben climbed the marble steps, making his way to the official gambling booth. A gap-toothed cleric was sitting inside the recess. Behind him stood a soldier, guarding the sacks of money already wagered. 'You wish to place a wager?' asked the cleric.

'No, I am waiting to collect.'

'You have bet on the Lentrian?'

'No. I bet on the winner. It's an old habit,' he answered, with a smile. 'Be so good as to have sixty gold pieces available – plus my original ten.'

The cleric chuckled. 'You bet on the Drenai? It will be a cold day in Hell before you see a return on that investment.'

'My, I do think I sense a drop in the temperature,' Sieben told him with a smile.

In the heat of the arena the Lentrian champion was tiring. Blood was seeping from his broken nose and his right eye was swollen shut, but even so his strength was prodigious. Druss moved in, ducking beneath a right cross and thundering a blow to the man's mid-section; the muscles of the Lentrian's stomach were like woven steel. A punch smashed down on to Druss's neck and he felt his legs buckle. With a grunt of pain he sent an upper-cut into the taller man's bearded chin and the Lentrian's head snapped back. Druss hammered an overhand right that missed its mark, cracking against the man's temple. The Lentrian wiped blood from his face – then hit Druss with a thundering straight left, followed by a right hook that all but spun Druss from his feet.

The crowd was baying now, sensing the end was close. Druss tried to move in and grapple – only to be stopped by a straight left that jarred him to his heels. Blocking a right he fired home another uppercut. The Lentrian swayed but did not fall. He countered with a chopping blow that took Druss behind the right ear. Druss shrugged it off. The Lentrian's strength was fading, the punch lacked speed and weight.

Now was the moment! Druss waded in, sending a combination of punches to the Lentrian's face: three straight lefts followed by a right hook that exploded against the man's chin. The Lentrian spun off balance, tried to right himself – then fell face first to the sand.

A sound like rolling thunder went up, booming around the packed arena. Druss took a deep breath and stepped back, acknowledging the cheers. The new Drenai flag, a white stallion on a field of blue, was hoisted high, fluttering in the afternoon breeze. Striding forward, Druss halted below the Royal balcony and bowed to the God-King he could not see.

Behind him two Lentrians ran out and knelt beside their fallen champion. Stretcher-bearers followed and the unconscious man was carried from the arena. Druss waved to the crowd, then walked slowly to the dark mouth of the tunnel which led through to the bathhouses and rest areas for the athletes. The spear-thrower Pellin stood grinning at the tunnel entrance. 'Thought he had you there, mountain man.'

'It was close,' said Druss, spitting blood from his mouth. His face was swollen and several teeth had been loosened. 'He was strong. I'll say that for him.'

The two men walked on down the tunnel, emerging into the first bathhouse. The sound from the arena was muted here, and around a dozen athletes were relaxing in the three heated pools of marble. Druss sat down beside the first. Rose petals floated on the steamy surface of the water, their fragrance filling the room. The runner, Pars, swam across to him. 'You look as if a herd of horses has run across your face,' he said.

Leaning forward Druss placed a hand on top of the man's balding head and propelled him down beneath the surface. Pars swam clear and surfaced several yards away; with a sweep of his hand he drenched Druss. Pellin, stripped now of his leggings and tunic, dived into the pool.

Druss peeled off his leggings and slid into the warm water. The relief to his aching muscles was instant and for some minutes he swam around the pool then he hauled himself clear. Pars joined him. 'Stretch yourself out and I'll knead the aches away,' he said. Druss moved to a massage table and lay face down, where Pars rubbed oil into his palms and began to work expertly on the muscles of his upper back.

Pellin sat down close by, towelling his dark hair, then draping the white cloth over his shoulders. 'Did you watch the other contest?' he asked Druss.

'No.'

'The Gothir man, Klay, is awesome. Fast. Strong chin. That plus a right hand that comes down like a hammer. It was all over in less than twenty heartbeats. Never seen the like, Druss. The Vagrian didn't know what hit him.'

'So I heard,' Druss grunted as Pars's fingers dug deep into the swollen muscles of his neck.

'You'll take him, Druss. What does it matter that he's bigger, stronger, faster, and better-looking?'

'And fitter,' put in Pellin. 'They say he runs for five miles every day on the mountains outside the city.'

'Yes, I forgot fitter. Younger, too. How old are you, Druss?' asked Pars.

'Thirty,' grunted Druss.

'An old man,' said Pellin, with a wink at Pars. 'Still, I'm sure you'll win. Well . . . fairly sure.'

Druss sat up. 'It is good of you youngsters to be so supportive.'

'Well, we are a team,' said Pellin. 'And since you deprived us of Grawal's delightful company we've sort of adopted you, Druss.'

Pars began to work on Druss's swollen knuckles. 'More seriously, Druss, my friend,' said the runner, 'your hands are badly bruised. Back home we'd use ice to bring the swelling down. I should soak them in cold water tonight.'

'There's three days before the final. I'll be fine by then. How did you fare in your race?'

'I finished second – and so will contest the final at least. But I'll not be in the first three. The Gothir man is far better than I, as are the Vagrian and the Chiatze. I cannot match their finish.'

'You might surprise yourself,' said Druss.

'We're not all like you, mountain man,' observed Pellin. 'I still find it hard to believe that you could come to these Games unprepared and fight your way to the final. You really are a legend.' Suddenly he grinned. 'Ugly, old and slow – but still a legend,' he added.

Druss chuckled. 'You almost fooled me there, laddie. I thought you might be showing some respect for me.' He lay back and closed his eyes.

Pars and Pellin strolled away to where a servant stood holding a pitcher of cold water. Seeing them coming, the man filled two goblets. Pellin drained his and accepted a refill, while Pars sipped his slowly. 'You didn't tell him about the prophecy,' said Pars.

'Neither did you. He'll find out soon enough.'

'What do you think he'll do?' asked the bald runner.

Pellin shrugged. 'I have only known him for a month – but somehow I don't think he'll want to follow tradition.'

'He'll have to!' insisted Pars.

Pellin shook his head. 'He's not like other men, my friend. That Lentrian should have won – but he didn't. Druss is a force of nature, and I don't think politics will affect that one jot.'

'I'll wager twenty gold raq you are wrong.'

'I'll not take that bet, Pars. You see, I hope for all our sakes that you are right.'

From a private balcony high above the crowd, the giant, blond fighter Klay watched Druss deliver the knockout blow. The Lentrian carried too much weight on his arms and shoulders, and though it gave him incredible power the punches were too slow . . . easy to read. But the Drenai made it worthwhile. Klay smiled.

'You find the man amusing, my Lord Klay?' Startled, the fighter swung round. The newcomer's face showed no expression, no flicker of muscle. It is like a mask, thought Klay – a golden Chiatze mask, tight and unlined. Even the jet-black hair, dragged back into the tightest of pony-tails, was so heavily waxed and dyed that it seemed false – painted on to the over-large cranium. Klay took a deep breath, annoyed that he could have been surprised on his own balcony, and angry that he had not heard the swish of the curtains, nor the rustle of the man's heavy ankle-length robe of black velvet.

'You move like an assassin, Garen-Tsen,' said Klay.

'Sometimes, my Lord, it is necessary to move with stealth,' observed the Chiatze, his voice gentle, melodic. Klay looked into the man's odd eyes, slanted as spear points. One was a curious brown, flecked with shards of grey; the other was as blue as a summer sky.

'Stealth is necessary only when among enemies, surely?' ventured Klay.

'Indeed so. But the best of one's enemies masquerade as friends. What is it about the Drenai that amuses you?' Garen-Tsen moved past Klay to the balcony's edge, staring down into the arena below. 'I see nothing amusing. He is a barbarian, and he fights like one.' He turned back, his fleshless face framed by the high, arched collar of his robe.

Klay found his dislike of the man growing, but masking his feelings he considered Garen-Tsen's question. 'He does not *amuse* me, Minister. I admire him. With the right training he could be very good indeed. And he is a crowd-pleaser. The mob always love a plucky warrior. And, by Heaven, this Druss lacks nothing in courage. I wish I had the opportunity to train him. It would make for a better contest.'

'It will be over swiftly, you think?'

Klay shook his head. 'No. There is a great depth to the man's strength. It is born of his pride, and his belief in his own invincibility; you can see it in him as he fights. It will be a long and arduous battle.'

23

'Yet you will prevail? As the God-King has prophesied?' For the first time Klay noticed a slight change in the Minister's expression.

'I should beat him, Garen-Tsen. I am bigger, stronger, faster, and better trained. But there is always a rogue element in any fight. I could slip, just as a punch connects. I could fall ill before the bout and be sluggish, lacking in energy. I could lose concentration, and allow an opening.' Klay gave a wide smile, for the Minister's expression was now openly worried.

'This will not happen,' he said. 'The prophecy will come true.'

Klay thought carefully before answering. 'The God-King's belief in me is a source of great pride. I shall fight all the better for it.'

'Good. Let us hope it has the opposite effect on the Drenai. You will be at the banquet this evening, my Lord? The God-King has requested your presence. He wishes you to sit alongside him.'

'It is a great honour,' answered Klay, with a bow.

'Indeed it is.' Garen-Tsen moved to the curtained doorway, then he swung back. 'You know an athlete named Lepant?'

'The runner? Yes. He trains at my gymnasium. Why?'

'He died this morning, during questioning. He looked so strong. Did you ever see signs of weakness in his heart? Dizziness, chest pain?'

'No,' said Klay, remembering the bright-eyed garrulous boy and his fund of jokes and stories. 'Why was he being questioned?'

'He was spreading slanders, and we had reason to believe he was a member of a secret group pledged to the assassination of the God-King.'

'Nonsense. He was just a stupid boy who told bad-taste jokes.'

'So it would appear,' agreed Garen-Tsen. 'Now he is a dead boy, who will never again tell a bad-taste joke. Was he a very talented runner?'

'No.'

'Good. Then we have lost nothing.' The odd-coloured eyes stared at Klay for several seconds. 'It would be better, my Lord, if you ceased to listen to jokes. In cases of treason there is guilt by association.'

'I shall remember your advice, Garen-Tsen.'

After the Minister had departed Klay wandered down to the Arena gallery. It was cooler here, and he enjoyed walking among the many antiquities. The gallery had been included on the Arena plans at the insistence of the King – long before his diseased mind

24

had finally eaten away his reason. There were some fifty stalls and shops here, where discerning buyers could purchase historical artefacts or beautifully made copies. There were ancient books, paintings, porcelain, even weapons.

People in the gallery stopped as he approached, bowing respectfully to the Gothir Champion. Klay acknowledged each salutation with a smile, and a nod of his head. Though huge, he moved with the easy grace of the athlete, always in balance and always aware. He paused before a bronze statue of the God-King. It was a fine piece, but Klay felt the addition of lapis lazuli for the pupils too bizarre in a face of bronze. The merchant who owned the piece stepped forward. He was short and stout, with a forked beard and a ready smile. 'You are looking very fine, my Lord Klay,' he said. 'I watched your fight – what little there was of it. You were magnificent.'

'Thank you, sir.'

'To think your opponent travelled so far only to be humiliated in such a fashion!'

'He was not humiliated, sir, merely beaten. He had earned his right to face me by competing against a number of very good fist-fighters. And he had the misfortune to slip on the sand just as I struck him.'

'Of course, of course! Your humility does you great credit, my Lord,' said the man, smoothly. 'I see you were admiring the bronze. It is a wonderful work by a new sculptor. He will go far.' He lowered his voice. 'For anyone else, my Lord, the price would be one thousand in silver. But for the mighty Klay I could come down to eight hundred.'

'I have two busts of the Emperor; he gave them to me himself. But thank you for your offer.'

Klay moved away from the man and a young woman stepped before him. She was holding the hand of a fair-haired boy of around ten years of age. 'Pardon me, Lord, for this impertinence,' she said, bowing deeply, 'but my son would dearly like to meet you.'

'Not at all,' said Klay, dropping to one knee before the boy. 'What is your name, lad?'

'Atka, sir,' he replied. 'I saw all your fights so far. You are . . . you are wonderful.'

'Praise indeed. Will you watch the final?'

'Oh, yes, sir. I shall be here to see you thrash the Drenai. I watched him too. He almost lost.'

'I don't think so, Atka. He is a tough man, a man of rock and iron. I wagered on him myself.'

'He can't beat you though, sir. Can he?' asked the boy, his eyes widening as doubt touched him.

Klay smiled. 'All men can be beaten, Atka. You will just have to wait a few days and see.'

Klay stood and smiled at the blushing young woman. 'He is a fine boy,' said the Champion. Taking her hand he kissed it, then moved away, pausing to study the paintings on the far wall. Many were landscapes of the desert and the mountains, others depicted young women in various stages of undress. Some were of hunting scenes, while two, which caught Klay's eyes, were of wild flowers. At the far end of the gallery was a long stall, behind which stood an elderly Chiatze. Klay made his way to the man, and studied the artefacts laid out so neatly. They were mostly small statuettes, surrounded by brooches, amulets, bracelets, bangles and rings. Klay lifted a small ivory figurine, no more than four inches tall. It was of a beautiful woman in a flowing dress. There were flowers in her hair, and in her hand she held a snake, its tail coiled around her wrist.

'This is very lovely,' he said.

The small Chiatze nodded and smiled. 'She is Shul-sen, the bride of Oshikai Demon-bane. The figurine is close to a thousand years old.'

'How can you tell?'

'I am Chorin-Tsu, Lord, the Royal Embalmer – and a student of history. I found this piece during an archaeological survey near the site of the fabled Battle of Five Armies. I am certain that is no less than nine centuries old.' Klay lifted the figurine close to his eyes. The woman's face was oval, her eyes slanted; she seemed to be smiling.

'She was Chiatze, this Shul-sen?' he asked.

Chorin-Tsu spread his hands. 'That depends, Lord, on your perspective. She was, as I told you, the wife of Oshikai, and he is considered the father of the Nadir. It was he who led the rebel tribes from the lands of the Chiatze, and fought his way to the lands now ruled by the Gothir. After his death the tribes roamed free, warring upon one another, even as now. So, if he was the first Nadir, then Shul-sen was . . . what? Nadir or Chiatze?'

'Both,' said Klay. 'And beautiful too. What happened to her?'

The Chiatze shrugged, and Klay saw sorrow in the dark, slanted eyes. 'That depends on which version of historical events you happen to believe. For myself I think she was murdered soon after Oshikai's death. All the records point to this, though some stories have her sailing to a mythic land beyond the sea. If you are of romantic leanings perhaps that is the story you should cling to.'

'I tend to hold to the truth where I can,' said Klay. 'But in this case I would like to believe she lived happily somewhere. I would guess we will never know.'

Chorin-Tsu spread his hands once more. 'As a student I like to think that one day the mists will be opened. Perhaps I might find some documentary evidence.'

'If you do so, let me know. Meanwhile I shall purchase this figurine. Have it delivered to my house.'

'You wish to know the price, Lord?'

'I am sure it will be a fair one.'

'Indeed it will, sir.'

Klay turned away, then swung back. 'Tell me, Chorin-Tsu, how is it that the Royal Embalmer runs a stall of antiquities?'

'Embalming, Lord, is my profession. History is my passion. And as with all passions they must be shared to be enjoyed. Your delight in the piece brings me great pleasure.'

Klay moved on, through the gallery arch and through to the Hall of Cuisine. Two guards opened the door to the beautifully furnished dining room of the nobility. Klay had long since lost any sense of nervousness upon entering such establishments, for despite the lowliness of his birth his legend was now so great among the people that he was considered higher than most nobles. There were few diners present, but Klay spotted the Drenai ambassador, Majon, engaged in a heated discussion with a fop in a bejewelled blue tunic. The fop was tall and slim, and very handsome, his hair light brown and held in place by a silver headband adorned with an opal. Klay approached them. Majon did not at first notice the fighter, and continued to rail at his companion.

'I do think this is unfair, Sieben, after all you won . . .' At that moment he saw Klay and instantly his face changed, a broad smile appearing. 'My dear chap, so good to see you again. Please do join us. It would be such an honour. We were talking about you only moments ago. This is Sieben the Poet.'

'I have heard your work performed,' said Klay, 'and I have read, with interest, the saga of Druss the Legend.'

The poet gave a wolfish smile. 'You've read the work, and soon you'll face the man. I have to tell you, sir, that I shall be wagering against you.'

'Then you will forgive me for not wishing you luck,' said Klay, sitting down.

'Did you watch today's bout?' asked Majon.

'I did indeed, ambassador. Druss is an interesting fighter. It seems that pain spurs him to greater efforts. He is indomitable, and very strong.'

'He always wins,' said Sieben happily. 'It's a talent he has.'

'Sieben is particularly pleased today,' put in Majon icily. 'He has won sixty gold pieces.'

'I won also,' said Klay.

'You bet on Druss?' asked Sieben.

'Yes. I had studied both men, and did not feel the Lentrian had the heart to match your man. He also lacked speed in his left, which gave Druss the chance to roll with the punches. But you should advise him to change his attacking stance. He tends to duck his head and charge, which makes for an easy target with an uppercut.'

'I'll be sure to tell him,' promised Sieben.

'I have a training ground at my house. He is welcome to use it.'

'That is a very kind offer,' put in Majon.

'You seem very confident, sir,' said Sieben. 'Does it not concern you that Druss has never lost?'

'No more than it concerns me that I have never lost. Whatever else happens, one of us will surrender that perfect record. But the sun will still shine, and the earth will not topple. Now, my friends, shall we order some food?'

The air was fresh and clean, and a slight wind whispered across the fountain pool, cooling the air as Sieben and Druss climbed the steep path to the summit of the highest hill in the Grand Park. Above them the sky was the glorious blue of late summer, dotted with thick white clouds drifting slowly from the east. Shafts of sunlight in the distance, breaking clear of the clouds, suddenly illuminated a section of the eastern mountains, turning them to deep shadowed red and gold, glowing like jewels in torchlight. And just as swiftly the wandering clouds blocked the sun, the golden rocks returning to grey. Druss gazed longingly at the mountains, remembering the smell of the pine and the song of the stream in his own high homeland. The clouds drifted on, and the sun shone down on the far mountains once more. The sight was beautiful, but Druss knew there would be no pine forests there. To the east of Gulgothir were the Nadir steppes, an enormous stretch of desert, dry, harsh and inhospitable.

Sieben sat beside the fountain, trailing his hand in the water. 'Now you can see why this is called the Hill of the Six Virgins,' he said. At the centre of the pool was a statue of six women, exquisitely carved from a single block of marble. They stood in a circle, each leaning forward and extending their arms, as if in entreaty. Behind and above them was the figure of an old man, holding a huge urn from which came the fountain, spilling out over the white statues and flowing down to the pool. 'Several hundred years ago,' continued Sieben, 'when a raiding army from the north surrounded Gulgothir, six virgins were sacrificed here to appease the Gods of War. They were ritually drowned. After that the Gods favoured the defenders, and they beat off the attack.'

Sieben smiled as he saw Druss's pale blue eyes narrow. The warrior's huge hand came up and idly tugged at his square-cut black beard – a sure sign of his growing irritation. 'You don't believe in appeasing the Gods?' asked Sieben innocently.

'Not with the blood of the innocent.'

'They went on to win, Druss. Therefore the sacrifice was worthwhile, surely?'

The axeman shook his head. 'If they believed the sacrifice would appease the Gods, then they would have been inspired to fight harder. But a good speech could have done that.'

'Supposing the Gods *did* demand that sacrifice, and therefore *did* help win the battle?'

'Then it would have been better lost.'

'Aha!' exclaimed Sieben triumphantly, 'but if it had been lost a far greater number of innocents would have been slain: women raped and murdered, babes slain in their cribs. How do you answer that?'

'I don't feel the need to. Most people can smell the difference between perfume and cow-dung; there's no need for a debate on it.'

'Come on, old horse, you're not stretching yourself. The answer is a simple one – the principles of good and evil are not based on mathematics. They are founded on the desire of individuals to do – or not to do – what is right and just, both in conscience and law.'

'Words, words, words! They mean nothing!' snapped Druss.

'The desire of individuals is what causes most evils. And as for conscience and law, what happens if a man has no conscience, and the law promotes ritual sacrifice? Does that make it good? Now stop trying to draw me in to another of your meaningless debates.'

'We poets live for such *meaningless* debates,' said Sieben, battling to hold back his anger. 'We tend to like to stretch our intelligence, to develop our minds. It helps to make us more aware of the needs of our fellows. You are in a sour mood today, Druss. I would have thought you would have been delirious at the thought of another fight to come, another man to bash your fists against. The Championship, no less. The cheers of the crowd, the adoration of your fellow-countrymen. Ah, the blood and the bruises and the endless parades and banquets in your honour!'

Druss swore and his face darkened. 'You know I despise all that.'

Sieben shook his head. 'Part of you might, Druss. The best part loathes the public clamour, yet how is it your every action always leads to more? You were invited here as a guest – an inspirational mascot, if you like. And what do you do? You break the jaw of the Drenai Champion – then take his place.'

'It was not my intention to cripple the man. Had I known his chin was made of porcelain, I would have struck him in the belly.'

'I am sure you would like to believe that, old horse. Just as I am sure I do not. Answer me this, how do you feel as the crowd roars your name?'

'I have had enough of this, poet. What do you want from me?'

Sieben took a deep, calming breath. 'Words are all we have to describe how we feel, what we need from one another. Without them how would we teach the young, or express our hopes for future generations to read? You view the world so simplistically, Druss, as if everything was either ice or fire. That in itself matters not a jot. But like all men with closed minds and small dreams you seek to mock what you can never comprehend. Civilizations are built with words, Druss. They are destroyed by axes. What does that tell you, *axeman*?'

'Nothing I did not already know. Now, are we even yet?'

Sieben's anger fell away and he smiled. 'I like you, Druss, I always have. But you have the most uncanny power to irritate me.'

Druss nodded, his face solemn. 'I am not a thinker,' he said, 'but nor am I stupid. I am a man like so many others. I could have been a farmer, or a carpenter, even a labourer. Never a teacher, though, nor a cleric. Intellectual men make me nervous. Like that Majon.' He shook his head. 'I have met a great number of ambassadors and they all seem identical: easy, insincere smiles and gimlet eyes that don't miss a thing. What do they believe in? Do they have a sense of honour? Of patriotism? Or do they laugh at us common men, as they line their purses with our gold? I don't know much, poet, but I do know that men like Majon – aye, and you – can make all I believe in seem as insubstantial as summer snow. And make me look foolish into the bargain. Oh, I can understand how good and evil can come down to numbers. Like those women in the fountain. A besieging army could say, "Kill six women and we'll spare the city." Well, there's only one right answer to that. But I couldn't tell you why I know it is right.'

'But I can,' said Sieben, his anger fading. 'And it is something, in part at least, that I learned from you. The greatest evil we can perpetrate, is to make someone else do evil. The besieging army you speak of is actually saying: "Unless you commit a small evil act, we will commit a great one." The heroic response would naturally be to refuse. But diplomats and politicians are pragmatists, Druss. They live without any genuine understanding of honour. Am I right?'

Druss smiled and clapped Sieben's shoulder. 'Aye, poet, you are. But I know that without turning a hair you could argue the opposite. So let us call an end to this.'

'Agreed! We will call it even.'

Druss switched his gaze to the south. Below them lay the centre of Old Gulgothir, a tightly packed and apparently haphazard jumble of buildings, homes, shops and workplaces, intersected by scores of narrow alleyways and roads. The old Keep Palace sat at the centre, like a squat, grey spider. Once the residence of kings, the Keep Palace was now used as a warehouse and granary. Druss looked to the west and the new Palace of the God-King, a colossal structure of white stone, its columns adorned with gold leaf, its statues – mostly of the King himself – crowned with silver and gold. Ornate gardens surrounded the palace, and even from here Druss could see the splendour of the royal blooms and the flowering trees. 'Have you seen the God-King yet?' asked the warrior.

'I was close to the Royal Balcony while you were toying with the Lentrian. But all I saw were the backs of his guards. It is said he has his hair dyed with real gold.'

31

'What do you mean *toying*? The man was tough, and I can still feel the weight of his blows.'

Sieben chuckled. 'Then wait until you meet the Gothir Champion, Druss. In combat the man is not human; it is said he has a punch like a thunderbolt. The odds are nine to one against you.'

'Then maybe I'll lose,' grunted Druss, 'but don't wager on it!'

'Oh, I won't be wagering a copper coin this time. I've met Klay. He is unique, Druss. In all the time I have known you I never met another man I thought could best you in combat. Until now.'

'Pah!' snorted Druss. 'I wish I had a gold raq for every time someone has told me another man was stronger, or faster, or better, or more deadly. And where are they now?'

'Well, old horse,' answered Sieben coolly, 'they are mostly dead – slain by you in your endless quest to do what is good and pure and right.'

Druss's eyes narrowed. 'I thought you said we were even.'

Sieben spread his hands. 'Sorry. Couldn't resist it.'

The Nadir warrior known as Talisman ducked into the alleyway and loped along it. The shouts of his pursuers were muted now, but he knew he had not lost them . . . not yet. Emerging into an open square, Talisman paused. There were many doors here – he counted six on each side of the square. 'This way! This way!' he heard someone shout. The moonlight shone brightly on the north and west walls as he ran to the south of the square and pressed his back against a recessed doorway. Here, in his long, black hooded cloak, he was all but invisible in the shadows. Talisman took a deep breath, fighting for calm. Absently his hand strayed towards his hip, where his long hunting-knife should have been. Silently he cursed. No Nadir warrior was allowed to carry weapons inside any Gothir city. He hated this place of stone and cobbles, with its seething masses and the resultant stench of humanity. Talisman longed for the open expanse of the Nadir steppes. Awesome mountains beneath a naked, burning sky, endless plains and valleys, where a man could ride for a year and never see another soul. On the steppes a man was *alive*. Not so here in this rats' nest of a city, its foul, polluted air carrying the bowel-stink of human excretions, thrown from windows to lie rotting in the alleyways, alongside other garbage and waste.

A rat scuttled over his foot but Talisman did not move. The enemy were close. *Enemy?* These scum from the poorest quarter of Gulgothir could hardly be considered worthy of the title. They were merely filling time in their worthless existence by hunting a Nadir tribesman through their vermin-infested streets; enjoying a transient moment of entertainment to brighten their poverty-stricken lives. He cursed again. Nosta Khan had warned him of the gangs, telling him which areas to avoid, though Talisman had barely listened. But then he had never visited a city as large as Gulgothir, and had no idea how easily a man could become lost within its warrens.

The sound of running feet came to him, and his hands clenched into fists. If they found him here they would kill him.

'Did you see where he went?' came a guttural voice.

'Nah! What about down there?'

'You three take the alley, we'll cut through Tavern Walk and meet you in the square.'

Drawing his hood around his face, leaving only his dark eyes showing, Talisman waited. The first of the three men ran past his hiding place, then the second. But the third glanced in his direction – and spotted him. Talisman leapt forward. The man lunged with a knife, but Talisman side-stepped and hammered his fist into the attacker's face. The man stumbled back as Talisman darted to the left and sprinted into another alleyway.

'He's here! He's here!' shouted the attacker.

Ahead was a wall around eight feet high. Talisman jumped, curling his fingers over the top and scrambling up. Beyond was a moonlit garden. Dropping to the grass, he ran to a second wall, and scaled this also. On the other side was a narrow road; landing lightly he loped along it, his anger mounting. It shamed him to run from these soft, round-eyed Southerners.

He came to an intersection and cut to the north. There was no sound of pursuit, but he did not relax. He had no idea where he was, all of these foul buildings looked the same. Nosta Khan had told him to seek out the home of Chorin-Tsu, the Embalmer, which was on the Street of Weavers in the north-west quarter of the city. But where am I now? thought the tribesman.

A tall man moved from the shadows, a rust-pitted knife in his right hand. 'Got you, you little Nadir bastard!' he said. Talisman gazed into the man's cruel eyes and his anger rose, cold and all engulfing.

'What you have found,' said Talisman, 'is death.'

Knife-hand raised, the man ran in and stabbed down towards Talisman's neck. But Talisman swayed to the right, his left forearm sweeping up to block the attacker's wrist. In the same flowing movement his right arm came up behind the man's shoulder, then with a savage jerk he brought his weight down on the knife-arm – which snapped at the elbow. The man screamed and dropped the knife. Releasing him Talisman swept up the blade, ramming it to the hilt between the man's ribs. Dragging back on his victim's greasy hair, Talisman's dark eyes fixed on the terrified face. 'May you rot in many Hells,' whispered the Nadir, twisting the knife-blade. The mortally wounded man's mouth opened for one last scream of pain – but he died before he could draw breath.

Releasing the body, Talisman wiped the knife clean of blood on the man's filthy tunic and moved on into the darkness. All was silent here. Walls towered on both sides of him, decorated with lines of shuttered windows. Talisman emerged on to a wider alley, no more than sixty yards long, and saw glimmering lights from the windows of a tavern. Hiding the knife beneath his hooded cloak he walked on. The tavern door opened and a big man with a square-cut black beard stepped into sight. Talisman approached him.

'Your pardon, Lord,' said the Nadir, the words tasting like acid upon the tongue, 'but could you direct me to the Street of Weavers?'

'Laddie,' said the man, slumping drunkenly to an oak bench, 'I'd be surprised if I could find my own way home. I'm a stranger here myself and have been lost in this city maze more than once tonight. By Heaven, I don't know why anyone would want to live in such a place. Do you?'

Talisman turned away. At that moment the men who had been pursuing him came into sight, five at one end of the alley and four at the other. 'We're going to cut your heart out!' shouted the leader, a fat, balding ruffian. Talisman drew his knife as the first five attackers rushed in. Movement came unexpectedly from Talisman's left! His eyes flickered towards it. The drunken stranger had risen to his feet and appeared to be trying to move the oak bench. No, not move it, Talisman realized, but lift it! It was so incongruous and bizarre a moment that he had to jerk his eyes from the scene in order to face his attackers. They were close now – three armed with knives, two with cudgels of lead. Suddenly the heavy oak bench hurtled past Talisman like a spear. It struck the gang leader full in the face, smashing his teeth and punching him from his feet, then spun off into the others sending

34

two of them to the ground. The remaining two men leapt over the bodies and ran in close. Talisman met the first, blade to blade, then hammered his elbow into the man's chin. The attacker fell face first to the cobbles. As he struggled to rise Talisman kicked him twice in the face; at the second kick the man groaned and slumped unconscious to the ground.

Talisman swung – but the last assailant was vainly struggling in the iron grip of the stranger, who had lifted him by neck and groin and was holding him suspended above his head. Spinning on his heel, Talisman saw the four remaining attackers edging forward from the other end of the alley. The stranger ran towards them, gave a grunt of effort and hurled his hapless victim straight into them. Three went down – but struggled to their feet. The stranger stepped forward.

'I think that's enough now, lads,' he said, his voice cold. 'So far I haven't killed anyone in Gulgothir. So gather your friends and go on about your business.'

One of the men moved carefully forward, peering at the stranger. 'You're the Drenai fighter, aren't you? Druss?'

'True enough. Now be on your way, lads. The fun is over – unless you've an appetite for more?'

'Klay will beat you to a bloody pulp in the final, you bastard!' Without another word the man sheathed his knife, and turned to his comrades. Together they helped the injured from the alley, having to carry the leader who was still unconscious. The stranger turned to Talisman. 'An ugly place,' he said, with a broad grin, 'but it does have its delights. Join me in a jug?'

'You fight well,' said Talisman. Glancing round he could see the attackers milling at the mouth of the alley. 'Yes, I'll drink with you, Drenai. But not here. My feeling is they will talk amongst themselves until their courage returns – then they will attack again.'

'Well, walk with me, laddie. The Gothir gave us lodgings – which I believe are not far from here – and there's a jug of Lentrian Red that has been calling my name all evening.' Together they moved west, out on to the main avenue leading to the colosseum. The attackers did not follow.

Talisman had never been inside so luxurious a lodging, and his dark, slanted eyes soaked in the sights – the long oak-panelled staircase, the wall hangings of velvet, the ornate cushioned chairs, sculpted and gilded, the carpets of Chiatze silk. The huge warrior called Druss led him up the stairs and into a long corridor. Doors were set on both sides at every fifteen paces. The stranger paused at one of them, then pressed a bronze latch and the door slid open to reveal a richly furnished apartment. When Talisman peered in, his first sight was of a six-foot-long rectangular mirror. He blinked, for he had seen his reflection before, but never full-length nor quite so clearly. The stolen black cloak and tunic were travel-stained and dust-covered, and his jet-black eyes gazed back at him with undisguised weariness. The face he gazed upon – despite being beardless – looked far older than his eighteen years, the mouth set in a grim, determined line. Responsibility sat upon him like a vulture, eating away at his youth.

Stepping closer to the mirror, he touched the surface. It looked like glass. But glass was virtually transparent – how then did it reflect so wonderfully? Peering closer, he examined the mirror and on the bottom right edge he saw what appeared to be a scratch. Dropping to his knee he stared at it, and found that he could look through the scratch at the carpet beyond the mirror. 'They paint the glass with silver somehow,' said Druss. 'I don't know how it is done.'

Turning from the mirror, Talisman walked into the room. There were six couches covered with polished leather, several chairs, and a long, low table upon which was set a jug of wine and four silver goblets. The room was as large as the home tent of his father – and that housed fourteen! Twin doors on the far side opened on to a wide balcony, which overlooked the colosseum. Talisman padded across the lush carpets and out on to the balcony. The Great Arena was surrounded by tall brass poles, on which stood burning lamps casting a red light on the lower half of the coliseum. It was almost as if the enormous structure was on fire. Talisman wished that it was – and this entire city with it!

'Pretty, is it not?' asked Druss.

'You fight there?'

'Just once more. The Gothir Champion, Klay. Then I'm going home to my farm, and my wife.'

Druss passed his guest a goblet of Lentrian Red and Talisman sipped it. 'All the flags flying from so many nations. Why? Are you all planning a war?'

'As I understand it,' said Druss, 'it is the opposite. The nations are here for the Fellowship Games. They are supposed to encourage friendship between the nations, and trade.'

36

'The Nadir were not invited to take part,' said Talisman, turning from the window and re-entering the main room.

'Ah, well, that's politics, laddie. I neither understand nor condone it. But even if they did wish to invite the Nadir – to whom would the invite be sent? There are hundreds of tribes, mostly at war with one another. They have no centre – no leader.'

'That will change,' said Talisman. 'A leader is prophesied, a great man. The Uniter!'

'I hear there have been many so-called Uniters.'

'This one will be different. He will have eyes the colour of violet, and will bear a name no Nadir has ever chosen. He is coming. And then let your world beware!'

'Well, I wish you luck,' said Druss, sitting back on a couch and raising his booted feet to the table. 'Violet eyes, eh? That'll be something to see.'

'They will be like the Eyes of Alchazzar,' said Talisman. 'He will be the embodiment of the Great Wolf in the Mountains of the Moon.'

The door opened and Talisman spun to see a tall, handsome young man enter. His fair hair was tied back in a tight pony-tail, and he wore a cloak of crimson over a long blue tunic of opal-adorned silk. 'I hope you've left some of that wine, old horse,' the newcomer said, addressing Druss. 'I'm as dry as a lizard's armpit.'

'I must be going,' said Talisman, moving towards the door.

'Wait!' said Druss, rising. 'Sieben, do you know the whereabouts of the Street of Weavers?'

'No, but there's a map in the back room. I'll fetch it.' Sieben returned moments later and spread the map on the low table. 'Which quarter?' he asked Talisman.

'North-west.'

Sieben's slender finger traced the map. 'There it is! Beside the Hall of Antiquities.' He glanced up at Talisman. 'You leave here by the main entrance and continue along the Avenue until you come to the Statue of the War Goddess – a tall woman carrying a long spear; there's a hawk on her shoulder. You bear left for another mile until you see the Park of Poets ahead of you. Turn right and keep going until you reach the Hall of Antiquities. There are four huge columns outside, and a high lintel stone upon which is carved an eagle. The Street of Weavers is the first on the right, past the hall. Would you like me to go over it again?'

'No,' said Talisman. 'I shall find it.' And without another word the Nadir left the room.

As the door closed Sieben grinned. 'His gratitude overwhelms me. Where do you meet these people?'

'He was involved in a scuffle and I gave him a hand.'

'Many dead?' enquired Sieben.

'None, as far as I know.'

'You're getting old, Druss. Nadir, was he not? He's got a nerve walking around Gulgothir.'

'Aye, I liked him. He was telling me about the Uniter to come, a man with the Eyes of Alchazzar, whatever that means.'

'That is fairly simple to explain,' said Sieben, pouring himself a goblet of wine. 'It's an old Nadir legend. Hundreds of years ago three Nadir shamen, men of great power – reputedly – decided to create a statue to the Gods of Stone and Water. They drew magic from the land and shaped the statue, which they called Alchazzar, from the stone of the Mountains of the Moon. It was, I understand, in the form of a giant wolf. Its eyes were huge amethysts, its teeth of ivory . . .'

'Get to the point, poet!' snapped Druss.

'You have no patience, Druss. Now bear with me. According to the legends the shamen drew all the magic from the land, placing it within the wolf. They did this so that they could control the destiny of the Nadir. But one of the shamen later stole the Eyes of Alchazzar and suddenly the magic ceased. Robbed of their Gods, the Nadir tribes – peaceful until then – turned upon one another, fighting terrible wars which continue to this day. There! A nice little fable to help you to sleep.'

'So what happened to the man who stole the Eyes?' asked Druss.

'I have no idea.'

'That's what I hate about your stories, poet. They lack detail. Why was the magic trapped? Why did he steal the Eyes? Where are they now?'

'I shall ignore these insults, Druss, old horse,' said Sieben, with a smile. 'You know why? Because when word got out that you were ill, your odds against Klay lengthened to twelve to one.'

'Ill? I have never been ill in my life. How did such a rumour start?'

Sieben shrugged. 'I would . . . guess it was when you failed to attend the banquet in the God-King's honour.'

'Damn, I forgot about it! You told them I was sick?'

'I don't believe I said sick . . . more . . . injured. Yes, that was it. Suffering from your injuries. Your opponent was there and he asked after you. Such a nice fellow. Said he hoped the prophecy did not affect your style.'

'What prophecy?'

'Something about you losing the final,' said Sieben airily. 'Absolutely nothing to worry about. Anyway you can ask him yourself. He has invited you to his home tomorrow evening – and I should be grateful if you would accept.'

'You would be grateful? Do I take it there is a woman involved in this?'

'Now that you mention it, I did meet a delightful serving-maid at the palace. She seems to think I'm some kind of foreign prince.'

'I wonder how she formed that opinion,' muttered Druss.

'No idea, old lad. However, I did invite her to dine with me here tomorrow. Anyway I think you'll like Klay. He's witty and urbane, and his arrogance is carefully masked.'

'Oh, yes,' grunted Druss. 'I like him already.'

Chapter Two

The house on the Street of Weavers was an old grey stone Gothir building, two storeys under a roof of red terracotta tiles. However, the rooms inside had been redesigned after the fashion of the Chiatze. No square or rectangular rooms remained, the walls now flowed in perfect curves: ovals or circles, or circles upon ovals. Doors and door frames followed these lines; even the heavy, square-framed Gothir windows, so bleak and functional from the outside, had been decorated on the interior frames with exquisitely sculpted circular covers.

In the small central study Chorin-Tsu sat cross-legged on an embroidered rug of Chiatze silk, his deep brown eyes staring unblinking at the man kneeling before him. The newcomer's eyes were dark and wary, and though he was kneeling – as was customary in the presence of one's host – his body was tense, and ready. He reminded Chorin-Tsu of a coiled snake, very still but ready to strike. Talisman flicked his gaze to the rounded walls, the reliefs of sculpted, lacquered wood and the delicate paintings in their lacquered frames. His gaze flowed over the works of art, never pausing to examine them. Swiftly he returned his attention to the little Chiatze. Do I like you? wondered Chorin-Tsu, as the silence lengthened. Are you a man to be trusted? Why did destiny choose you to save your people? Without blinking Chorin-Tsu studied the young man's face. He had a high brow, which often denoted intelligence, and his skin was closer to the gold of the Chiatze than the jaundiced yellow of the Nadir. How old was he? Nineteen? Twenty? So young! And yet he radiated power, strength of purpose. You have gained experience beyond your years, thought the old man. And what do you see before you, young warrior? A wrinkled ancient – a lantern whose oil is almost gone, the flame beginning to stutter? An old man in a room of pretty pictures! Well, once I was strong like you, and I had great dreams also. At the thought of those dreams his mind wandered briefly, and he came to with a start and found himself staring into Talisman's jet-black eyes. Fear touched him fleetingly – for now the eyes were cold and impatient.

'Be so kind as to show me the token,' said Chorin-Tsu, speaking in the southern tongue, his voice barely above a whisper. Talisman reached into his tunic and produced a small coin stamped with the head of a wolf. He offered it to the old man, who took it with trembling fingers, leaning forward to examine it. Talisman found himself staring at the small white braid of hair on the crown of Chorin-Tsu's otherwise shaven head. 'It is an interesting coin, young man. Sadly, however, anyone can possess such a piece,' said the embalmer, his breath wheezing from him. 'It could have been taken from the true messenger.'

Talisman gave a cold smile. 'Nosta Khan told me you were a mystic, Chorin-Tsu. You should, therefore, have little difficulty judging my integrity.'

There were two shallow clay cups of water set upon a silk rug. The young Nadir reached for one, but the old man waved a hand and shook his head. 'Not yet, Talisman. Forgive me, but I shall tell you when to drink. As to your point, Nosta Khan was not speaking of psychic powers. I was never a true mystic. What I have been, all my life, Talisman, is a student. I have studied my craft, I have examined the great sites of history, but most of all I have studied men. The more I studied the race, the better I understand its foibles. But the curious thing about study, when conducted with an open mind, is that it makes one smaller. But, forgive me, philosophy is not a Nadir preoccupation.'

'Being savages, you mean?' answered the Nadir, without rancour. 'Perhaps I should therefore leave the answer to the priest-philosopher Dardalion, who said, "Every question answered leads to seven other questions. Therefore to a student the gathering of knowledge merely increases the awareness of how much more there is still to know." Will that suffice, Master Embalmer?'

Chorin-Tsu masked his surprise, and bowed deeply. 'Indeed it will, young man. And I pray you will forgive this old one for such rudeness. These are heady days and I fear my excitement is affecting my manners.'

'I take no offence,' said Talisman. 'Life is harsh upon the steppes. There is little opportunity for a contemplative existence.'

The old man bowed again. 'I do not wish to compound my rudeness, young sir, but I find myself intrigued as to where a Nadir warrior would come upon the words of Dardalion of the Thirty.'

'It is said that a little mystery adds spice to a relationship,' Talisman told him. 'However, you were talking about your studies.'

Chorin-Tsu found himself warming further to the young man. 'My studies also involve astrology, numerology, the casting of runes, the reading of palms, the fashioning of spells. And yet there remain so many things to baffle the mind. I shall give you an example.' From his belt he pulled an ivory-handled throwing-knife, which he pointed towards a round target set on the wall some twenty paces away. 'When I was younger I could hurl this blade into the golden centre of that target. But now – as you see – my fingers are gnarled and bent. Do it for me, Talisman.' The young Nadir caught the tossed blade. For a moment he weighed it in his hand, feeling the balance. Then he drew back his arm and let fly. The silver steel shimmered in the lantern light, and flashed across the room to lance home into the target. It missed the gold by a finger's breadth. 'The target is covered with small symbols. Go and tell me the symbol that the blade pierced,' ordered Chorin-Tsu.

Talisman rose and walked across the room. The target had been decorated with curious Chiatze hieroglyphs, traced in gold paint. He did not recognize most of them. But the knife-blade had pierced an oval, at the centre of which was a delicately drawn talon, and this image he understood. 'Where did it strike?' called Chorin-Tsu. Talisman told him.

'Good, good. Come and rejoin me, my boy.'

'I have passed your test?'

'One of them. Here is the second. Drink from one of the cups.'

'Which one contains the poison?' asked Talisman.

Chorin-Tsu said nothing and Talisman stared at the cups. 'Suddenly I am not thirsty.'

'Yet you must drink,' Chorin-Tsu insisted.

'Tell me the purpose of the game, old one. Then I shall decide.'

'I know you can throw a knife, Talisman, this I have seen. But can you *think*? Are you worthy to serve the Uniter – to bring him to our people? As you rightly surmise, one of the cups contains a deadly poison. Death will follow if it even touches your lips. The other contains nothing but water. How will you choose?'

'There is insufficient information,' said Talisman.

'You are wrong.'

Talisman sat quietly, his mind working at the problem. He closed his eyes, recalling every word spoken by the old man. Leaning forward he lifted the left-hand cup, twirling it in his fingers; then the right. Both were identical. Transferring his gaze to the rug he gave a rare smile. It was embroidered with the same set of symbols as the target. And below the left-hand cup was the oval and the talon. Lifting the cup, he tasted the water. It was sweet and cool.

'Good, you are observant,' said Chorin-Tsu. 'But is it not amazing that you should have thrown the knife to the exact symbol, when there were twelve others to strike?'

'How did you know I would strike it?'

'It was written thus in the stars. Nosta Khan knew it also. He knew it through his Talent, whereas I knew it through study. Now, answer me this: What is the third test?'

Talisman took a deep breath. 'The talon was the mark of Oshikai Demon-bane, the oval the symbol of his wife, Shul-sen. When Oshikai wished to wed Shul-sen her father set him three tasks, the first was one of marksmanship, the second concerned intelligence, the third . . . required a sacrifice. Oshikai had to slay a demon, who had been his friend. I know no demons, Chorin-Tsu.'

'As with all myths, my boy, they serve a purpose beyond the richness of the tales. Oshikai was a reckless man, given to great rages. The demon was merely a part of himself, the wild and dangerous side of his personality. Shul-sen's father knew this, and wanted Oshikai to pledge himself to love her till the end of his days – never to harm her, never to put her aside for another.'

'What has this to do with me?'

'Everything.' Chorin-Tsu clapped his hands together. The door opened and a young Chiatze woman entered. She bowed to both men, then knelt and touched her head to the floor at Chorin-Tsu's feet. Talisman gazed at her in the candlelight. She was exquisitely beautiful, with raven-dark hair and wide, almond-shaped eyes. Her mouth was full, her figure trim within a white silk blouse and long satin skirt.

43

'This is Zhusai, my grand-daughter. It is my wish that you take her with you on your quest. It is also the wish of Nosta Khan, and your father.'

'And if I refuse?'

'No more will be said. You will leave my home and journey back to the tents of your people.'

'And my quest?'

'Will continue without my aid.'

'I am not ready for a wife. I have dedicated my life to the pursuit of revenge and the Day of the Uniter. But even were I to consider marriage, then as the son of a chieftain it would be my right to choose my own woman. It would certainly be my wish that she be Nadir. I have great respect for the Chiatze – but they are not my people.'

Chorin-Tsu leaned forward. 'Leaders have no rights; that is one of the great secrets of leadership. However, you miss the point, young man. Zhusai is not to be your wife. She is pledged to the Uniter; she will be the Shul-sen to his Oshikai.'

'Then I do not understand,' admitted Talisman, relieved. 'What sacrifice is required of me?'

'Do you accept Zhusai into your custody? Will you protect her with your life?'

'If that is required, so be it,' promised Talisman. 'Now what is the sacrifice?'

'Perhaps there will be none. Zhusai, show our guest to his room.' The young woman bowed once more, then rose silently and led Talisman from the chamber.

At the end of a short corridor Zhusai opened a door and stepped inside. Rugs were set around the room, and blankets had been spread upon the floor. There were no chairs, nor ornaments. 'This is your room,' she said.

'Thank you, Zhusai. Tell me, have you ever been into the desert?'

'No, Lord.'

'Does the prospect of our journey cause you concern? We will be travelling through hostile lands and there will be many dangers.'

'There is only one danger I fear, Lord,' she said.

'And that is?' As he asked the question he saw a gleam appear in her eyes, and a tightening of the muscles of her face. In that moment the quiescent, agreeable Chiatze girl-child disappeared, replaced by a hard-eyed woman. Then, just as suddenly, the girl-mask fell back into place.

'It is best not to speak of fears, Lord. For fear is akin to magic. Good night. Sleep well.'

The door closed behind her.

Sieben's laughter was rich, the sound filling the room, and the Drenai ambassador reddened. 'I think you'll find that this is no subject for humour,' he said coldly. 'We are talking here about international diplomacy, and the whims of individuals have no place in it.' The poet sat back and studied the ambassador's thin face. His steel-coloured hair was carefully combed and delicately perfumed, his clothes immaculate – and very costly. Majon wore a white woollen cloak, and a blue silk tunic edged with gold. The ambassador's fingers toyed with his crimson neck scarf and the ceremonial brooch – a silver horse rearing – that denoted his rank. The man was angry, and allowing it to show. This, Sieben decided, was a calculated insult. Diplomats were masters of oily charm, their expressions endlessly amiable when dealing with superiors. 'Do you disagree?' asked Majon.

'I rarely *disagree* with politicians,' Sieben told him. 'It seems to me that the worst of you could convince me that a horse turd tastes like a honey-cake. And the best would leave me believing that I alone in all the world had failed to enjoy its flavour.'

'That is a highly insulting remark,' snapped Majon.

'I do apologize, ambassador. It was meant as a compliment.'

'Will you seek to convince him – or not? This matter is of the highest importance. I swear, by the memory of Missael, that we could be talking of war!'

'Oh, I don't doubt that, ambassador. I saw the God-King, remember?' Majon's eyes widened and he swiftly raised his hand to his mouth, holding a finger to his lips in warning. Sieben merely grinned. 'An inspired leader,' he said, with a wink. 'Any ruler who would sack a politician and raise his pet cat to ministerial rank has my support.'

Majon rose from his chair and walked to the door, opening it and peering out into the corridor. Swinging back into the room he stood before the poet. 'It is not wise to mock any ruler – most especially when in the capital city of such a man. The peoples of the Drenai and the Gothir are at peace. Long may it remain so.'

'Yet in order to ensure that peace,' said Sieben, his smile fading, 'Druss must lose against Klay?'

'Put simply, that is indeed the situation. It would not be . . . appropriate . . . for Druss to win.'

'I see. You have little faith, then, in the God-King's prophecy?'

Majon poured himself a goblet of wine and sipped it before answering. 'It is not a question of faith, Sieben; it is simply politics. The God-King makes a prophecy at this time every year. They come true. There are those who believe that, since his prophecies generally concern the actions of men, the men themselves ensure their accuracy. Others simply accept that their ruler is divine. However, in this instance the point is academic. He has predicted that Klay will take the gold. If Druss were to win it would be seen as an insult to the God-King, and interpreted as a Drenai plot to destabilize the administration. The consequences of such an action could be disastrous.'

'I suppose he could put his cat in charge of the army and attack Dros Delnoch. A terrifying prospect!'

'Is there a brain inside that handsome head? The army you speak of numbers more than fifty thousand men, many of them battle-hardened by war against Nadir tribes and Sathuli raiders. But that is not the point. Here in Gothir there are three main factions. One faction believes in the divine right of the Gothir to conquer the world. The other seeks to conquer the world without concerning themselves with the question of divine rights. You understand? For reasons best known to themselves, each faction hates the other. This nation stands constantly on the brink of civil war. While they are thus fighting among themselves, the Drenai are free from the appalling cost of resisting an invasion.'

'Cost? Are we talking coin here?'

'Of course we are talking coin,' said Majon, his irritation flaring. 'Mobilization of men, training, new armour, swords, breastplates. Food for the recruits. And where do we find the recruits? The land. Peasants and farmers. When they are soldiers, who gathers the crops? The answer is that many fields are left unharvested. What happens to the price of grain? It soars. And, at the end, what has been achieved? The fortress will hold, and the men will go home to find their taxes have risen to pay for the war. Fifty thousand trained soldiers angry at the government.'

'You didn't mention the dead,' said Sieben softly.

'A good point. The threat of disease from corpses, the costs of burial. Then there are the cripples, who become an endless drag upon the benevolence of the state.'

'I think you have made your point, ambassador,' put in Sieben. 'Your humanity does you credit. But you mentioned three factions, and you have described only two.'

46

'Lastly there is the Royal Guard – ten thousand men, the elite of the Gothir army. They placed the God-King on the throne after the last Insurrection – and they keep him there. Neither of the other two factions is yet powerful enough to be guaranteed victory *without* the support of the Guards. Therefore everyone stands frozen, unable to move. Ideally that situation should be encouraged to continue.'

Sieben laughed. 'And meanwhile a madman sits on the throne, his reign punctuated by murder, torture and enforced suicides?'

'That is a problem for the Gothir, Sieben. Our concern is the Drenai, of which there are also close to three thousand living in Gothir lands whose lives would be forfeit if any general hostilities were announced. Merchants, labourers, physicians – aye, and diplomats. Are their lives without meaning, Sieben?'

'Smoothly done, Majon,' said Sieben, clapping his hands. 'And now we come to the horse-turd-honey-cake. Of course their lives have meaning. But Druss is not responsible for them, nor for the actions of a madman. Don't you understand, ambassador? Nothing you – or the God-King – can do will change that. Druss is not a stupid man, yet he sees life very clearly. He will go out and face Klay, and give everything he has to win. There is nothing anyone could say that would induce him to do less. Nothing at all. All your arguments here would be meaningless. Druss would say that whatever the God-King chooses to do – or not to do – is up to his own conscience. But even more than that, Druss would refuse for one very simple reason.'

'And that is?'

'It wouldn't be right.'

'I thought you said he was intelligent!' snapped Majon. 'Right, indeed! What has *right* to do with this? We are dealing with a . . . sensitive and . . . unique ruler . . .'

'We are dealing with a lunatic who, if he wasn't King, would be locked away for his own safety,' responded Sieben.

Majon rubbed his tired eyes. 'You mock politics,' he said softly. 'You sneer at diplomacy. But how do you think we hold the world at peace? I'll tell you, Sieben. Men like me travel to places like this, and we're fed those horse-turd cakes of yours. And we smile, and we say how nourishing they are. We move in the space between other men's egos, massaging them as we walk. We do this not for gain, but for peace and prosperity. We do it so that Drenai farmers, merchants, clerics and labourers can raise their families in peace. Druss is a hero; he can enjoy the luxury of

47

living his own life and speaking his own truths. Diplomats cannot. Now will you help me to convince him?'

Sieben rose. 'No, ambassador, I will not. You are wrong in this – though I give you the benefit of the doubt as to your motives.' He walked to the door and turned. 'Perhaps you've been eating those cakes too long. Perhaps you have acquired a taste for them.'

Behind the panelled walls a servant slipped away to report the conversation.

Garen-Tsen lifted the hem of his long purple robe and stepped carefully down the worn stone steps to the dungeon level. The stench here was great, but the tall Chiatze closed his mind to it. Dungeons were supposed to stink. Prisoners dragged into such places were assailed by the gloom, the damp and the awful smell of fear. It made interrogation that much more simple.

In the dungeon corridor he paused and listened. Somewhere to his left a man was crying, the noise muffled by the heavy stone of his cell. Two guards stood by. Garen-Tsen summoned the first. 'Who weeps?' he asked.

The guard, a fat, bearded man with stained teeth, sniffed loudly. 'Maurin, sir. He was brought in yesterday.'

'I will see him after speaking to the Senator,' said Garen-Tsen.

'Yes, sir.' The man backed away and Garen-Tsen walked slowly to the interrogation room. An elderly man was seated there, his face blotched and swollen, his right eye almost shut. Blood had stained his white under-tunic.

'Good morning, Senator,' said Garen-Tsen, moving to a high-backed chair which a guard slid into position for him. He sat opposite the injured man, who glared at him balefully. 'I understand that you have decided to remain uncooperative?'

The prisoner took a deep, shuddering breath. 'I am of the royal line, Garen-Tsen. The law expressly forbids torture.'

'Ah, yes, the law. It also expressly forbids plotting to kill the King, I understand. And it frowns upon conspiracies to overthrow the rightful government.'

'Of course it does!' snapped the prisoner. 'Which is why I would never be guilty of such dealings. The man is my nephew; you think I would plan to murder my own blood kin?'

'And now you add heresy to the charges,' said Garen-Tsen mildly. 'The God-King is never to be referred to as *a man*.'

'A slip of the tongue,' muttered the Senator.

'Such slips are costly. Now, to matters at hand. You have four sons, three daughters, and seven grandchildren, fourteen cousins, a wife, and two mistresses. Let me be frank with you, Senator. You are going to die. The only question that remains is whether you die alone, or with your entire family.'

All colour drained from the prisoner's face – but his courage remained. 'You are a vile devil, Garen-Tsen. There is an excuse for my nephew, the King – poor boy – for he is insane. But you – you are an intelligent, cultured man. May the Gods curse you!'

'Yes, yes, I am sure they will. Shall I order the arrest of your family members? I do not believe your wife would relish the atmosphere of these dungeons.'

'What do you desire from me?'

'A document is being prepared for your signature. When it is completed, and signed by you, you will be allowed to take poison. Your family will be spared.' Garen-Tsen rose. 'And now you must excuse me. There are other traitors awaiting interrogation.'

The old man looked up at the Chiatze. 'There is only one traitor here, you Chiatze dog. And one day you will be dragged screaming to this very room.'

'That may indeed prove true, Senator. You, however, will not be here to see it.'

An hour later Garen-Tsen rose from his scented bath. A young manservant applied a hot towel to his wet body, gently rubbing away the drops of water clinging to the golden skin. A second servant brought a phial of scented oil which he massaged into Garen-Tsen's back and shoulders. When he had finished, a third boy stepped forward carrying a fresh purple robe. The Chiatze raised his arms and the robe was expertly settled in place. Two ornate slippers were laid on the rug at his feet. Garen-Tsen slipped his feet into them, and walked to his study. The ornate desk of carved oak had been freshly polished with beeswax, scented with lavender. Three inkwells had been placed there and four fresh white quill pens. Seating himself in a padded leather chair, Garen-Tsen took up a quill and a virgin sheet of thick paper and began his report.

As the noon bell was struck in the courtyard beyond, there came a tap at his door. 'Enter!' he called. A slim, dark-haired man moved to the desk and bowed.

'Yes, Oreth, make your report.'

'The sons of Senator Gyall have been arrested. His wife

committed suicide. Other family members have fled, but we are hunting them now. The wife of the noble Maurin has transferred funds to a banker in Drenan: eighty thousand gold pieces. His two brothers are already in the Drenai capital.'

'You will send a message to our people in Drenan. They must deal with the traitors.'

'Yes, sir.'

'Anything else, Oreth?'

'Only one small matter, sir. The Drenai fighter, Druss. It seems he will probably attempt to win. His ambassador will try to persuade him but the fighter's friend, Sieben, maintains he will not be convinced.'

'Who do we have following the fighter?'

'Jarid and Copass.'

'I have spoken to Klay and he says the Drenai will prove a tough opponent. Very well, arrange to have him waylaid and cut. Any deep wound will suffice.'

'It might not be so simple, Lord. The man was engaged in a fracas recently and thrashed several robbers. It may be necessary to kill him.'

'Then kill him. There are far more important matters needing my attention, Oreth. I have little time for consideration of such tiny problems.' Lifting his quill, Garen-Tsen dipped it into an inkwell and began once more to write.

Oreth bowed and backed away.

Garen-Tsen continued to work for almost a full hour. The words of the Senator, however, continued to echo through his mind. *And one day you will be dragged screaming to this very room.* Such an event was – at present – extremely likely. As of this moment Garen-Tsen was perched on the very top of the mountain. The hold, however, was precarious, for his position of eminence depended entirely upon a madman. Laying aside his quill, he contemplated the future. So far, mainly through his own efforts, both rival factions remained in balance. Such harmony could not be maintained for much longer – not with the King's illness proceeding at such a terrifying rate. Soon his insanity would become too difficult to control and a blood-bath would surely follow. Garen-Tsen sighed.

'On top of the mountain,' he said aloud. 'It is not a mountain at all, but a volcano waiting to erupt.'

At that moment the door opened and a middle-aged soldier stepped inside. He was powerfully built, and wore the long, black

50

cloak of the Royal Guard. Garen-Tsen's odd-coloured eyes focused on the man. 'Welcome, Lord Gargan. How may I be of service?'

The newcomer moved to a chair and sat heavily. Removing his ornate helm of bronze and silver, he laid it on the desk top. 'The madman has killed his wife,' he said.

Two Royal Guards led Chorin-Tsu into the grounds of the palace. Two more came behind, carrying the trunk in which lay the objects and materials necessary to the trade of the embalmer. The old man's breath was wheezing from him as he hurried to keep up. He asked no questions.

The guardsmen led him through the servants' halls, and up a richly carpeted stairway into the warren of royal apartments. Skirting the fabled Hall of Concubines the Guards entered the Royal Chapel, bowing before the golden image of the God-King. Once through the rear of the chapel they slowed, as if to make less noise, and Chorin-Tsu took this opportunity to regain his breath. At last they came to a double-doored private chamber. Two men were waiting outside; one was a soldier with a forked beard the colour of iron, the second was the purple-garbed First Minister, Garen-Tsen. He was tall and wand-thin, and his face bore no expression.

Chorin-Tsu bowed to his countryman. 'May the Lords of High Heaven grant you blessings,' said Chorin-Tsu, speaking in Chiatze.

'It is unseemly and discourteous to use a foreign language in the Royal Chambers,' admonished Garen-Tsen, in the Southern tongue. Chorin-Tsu bowed once more. Garen-Tsen's long fingers tapped at the second knuckle of his right hand. Then he folded his arms, his index finger touching his bicep. Chorin-Tsu read the sign language: *Do what is required and you will live!*

'My apologies, Lord,' said Chorin-Tsu. 'Forgive your humble servant.' Bringing his hands together he bowed even lower than before, touching his thumbs to his chin.

'Your skills are needed here, Master Embalmer. No-one else will enter this room until you have completed your . . . craft. You understand?'

'Of course, Lord.' The guardsmen placed Chorin-Tsu's trunk by the door. Garen-Tsen opened the door just wide enough for the elderly Chiatze to enter, dragging the trunk behind him.

Chorin-Tsu heard the door close behind him, then gazed

around the apartments. The rugs were of the finest Chiatze silk, as were the hangings around the royal bed. The bed itself had been exquisitely carved, then gilded. Every item in the room spoke of riches and the extremes of wealth only monarchs could afford.

Even the corpse . . .

She was hanging by her arms from golden chains attached to rings in the ceiling above the bed, and blood had drenched the sheets below her. Chorin-Tsu had seen the Queen only twice before – once during the parade at her wedding, and then, two weeks ago, when the Fellowship Games began. In her new role as Bokat, Goddess of Wisdom, she had blessed the opening ceremony. Chorin-Tsu had seen her closely then. Her eyes had seemed vacant, and she slurred the words of the Blessing. Now he moved to a chair and sat, staring at the still body.

The old man sighed. Just as at the Games Ceremony, the Queen was wearing the Helm of Bokat, a golden headpiece with flaring wings and long cheek-guards. Chorin-Tsu was not well versed in Gothir myths, but he knew enough. Bokat was the wife of Missael, the God of War. Their son, Caales, future Lord of Battle, sprang fully grown from his mother's belly.

But that was not the myth that inspired this insanity. No. Bokat had been captured by the enemy. The Gods of the Gothir had gone to war, the world burning from the flame arrows of Missael. Bokat had been taken by one of the other gods, and hung from chains outside the Magical City. Her husband, Missael, was warned that if he attacked she would be the first slain. He had taken his bow and shot her through the heart, then he and his companions rushed forward, scaling the walls and slaying all within. When the battle was over he drew the arrow from his wife's breast, and kissed the wound. It healed instantly and she awoke, and took him in her arms.

Here in this room someone had tried to duplicate the myth. The blood-covered arrow was lying on the floor. Wearily Chorin-Tsu climbed to the bed, loosening the bolts that held the golden chains to the slender wrists of the dead Queen. The body fell to the bed, the helm rolling clear and striking the floor with a dull clang. The Queen's blond hair fell free, and Chorin-Tsu noticed that the roots were a dull, mousy brown.

Garen-Tsen entered, and the two men spoke in sign.

'The God-King tried to save her. When the bleeding would not stop he panicked and sent for the Royal Physician.'

'There is blood everywhere,' said Chorin-Tsu. 'I cannot perform my arts upon her in these conditions.'

'You must! No-one will be allowed to know of this . . .' Garen-Tsen's fingers hesitated . . . 'this stupidity.'

'The physician is dead, then?'

'Yes.'

'As I will be when my work is done.'

'No. I have arranged for you to be smuggled from the palace. You will flee to the south and Dros Delnoch.'

'I thank you, Garen-Tsen.'

'I will have a chest left outside these apartments. Place all the . . . soiled linen within it.' 'How long will you need to prepare her?' he concluded, aloud.

'Three hours, perhaps more.'

'I shall return then.'

The Minister left the room and Chorin-Tsu sighed. The man had lied to him; there would be no escape to the south. Putting the thought from his mind, Chorin-Tsu moved to the trunk by the door and began to remove the jars of embalming fluid, the cutters and the scrapers, setting them out neatly on a table by the bed.

A gilded panel at the rear of the apartment slid open. Chorin-Tsu dropped to his knees, averting his gaze – but not before he had seen the gold paint on the royal face, and the dried blood on his lips from when he had kissed the wound on his wife's breast.

'I shall awaken her now,' said the God-King. Moving to the body he knelt and pressed his lips to hers. 'Come to me, sister-wife. Open your eyes, Goddess of the Dead. Come to me, I command you!'

Chorin-Tsu remained on his knees, eyes closed. 'I command you!' shouted the God-King. Then he began to weep and for long moments the sobbing continued. 'Ah,' he said suddenly. 'She is teasing me, she is pretending to be dead. Who are you?'

Chorin-Tsu jerked as he realized the King was addressing him. Opening his eyes, he looked up into the face of madness. The blue eyes shone brightly within the mask of gold; they were friendly, and gentle. Chorin-Tsu took a long slow breath. 'I am the Royal Embalmer, sire,' he said.

'Your eyes are slanted, but you are not Nadir. Your skin is gold, like my friend, Garen. Are you Chiatze?'

'I am, sire.'

'Do they worship me there? In your homeland?'

'I have lived here for forty-two years, sire. Sadly, I do not receive news from my homeland.'

'Come, talk to me. Sit here on the bed.'

Chorin-Tsu rose, his dark eyes focusing on the young God-King. He was of medium build and slender, much like his sister. His hair was dyed gold, and his skin was painted the same colour. His eyes were a remarkable blue. 'Why is she not waking? I have commanded it.'

'I fear, sire, that the Queen has . . . moved to her second realm.'

'Second? Oh I see, Goddess of Wisdom, Queen of the Dead. Do you think so? When will she come back?'

'How could any mortal man predict such a happening, sire? The gods are far above mere mortals like myself.'

'I suppose that we are. I think you are correct in your assumption, Embalmer. She is ruling the dead now. I expect she will be happy. A lot of our friends are there to serve her. Many, many. Do you think that's why I sent them all there? Of course it was. I knew Bokat would return to the dead, and I sent lots of her friends ahead to welcome her. I only pretended to be angry with them.' He smiled happily and clapped his hands. 'What is this for?' he asked, lifting a long, brass instrument with a forked end.

'It is an . . . aid to me, sire, in my work. It helps to . . . make the object of my attentions remain beautiful always.'

'I see. It is very sharp, and wickedly hooked. And why all the knives and scrapers?'

'The dead have little use for their internal organs, sire. They putrefy. For a body to remain beautiful they must be removed.' The God-King stood and wandered to where Chorin-Tsu's chest stood open by the door. He peered inside, then lifted out a glass jar in which were stored many sets of crystal eyes.

'I think I shall leave you to your craft, Master Embalmer,' he said brightly. 'I have many matters to attend to. There are so many of Bokat's friends who will want to follow her. I must prepare their names.'

Chorin-Tsu bowed deeply, and said nothing.

Sieben was wrong. When Majon broached the subject of the prophecy with Druss, there was no immediate refusal. The Drenai warrior listened, his face impassive, his cold, pale eyes expressionless. As the ambassador concluded, Druss rose from his chair. 'I'll think on it,' he said.

'But, Druss, there are so many considerations that . . .'

54

'I said I'll think on it. Now leave.' The coldness of the warrior's tone cut through Majon like a winter wind.

During the late afternoon Druss, dressed casually in a wide-sleeved shirt of soft brown leather, woollen leggings and knee-length boots, walked through the city centre, oblivious to the crowds surging around him: servants buying supplies and wares for their households, men gathered around inns and taverns, women moving through the marketplaces and shops, lovers walking hand in hand in the parks. Druss weaved his way among them, his mind focused on the ambassador's plea.

When slavers had attacked Druss's village and captured the young women – Rowena among them – Druss had instinctively followed the raiders, hunting them down. That had been right! There were no moral or political questions to be addressed.

But here and now it was all blurred. 'There would be honour in such a decision,' Majon had assured him. And why? Because thousands of Drenai lives would be saved. Giving in to the wishes of a madman, suffering humiliation and defeat? This was honour?

Yet to win could mean, at worst, a terrible war. Was winning a fight worth such a risk, Majon had asked. For the satisfaction of pounding a man to the ground?

Druss crossed the Park of Giants and cut to the left, through the Arch of Marble and on towards the low Valley of the Swans in which Klay's house was situated. Here were the homes of the rich, the roads lined with trees, the houses elegantly designed, the grounds boasting small lakes and fountains or beautifully sculpted statues set around winding paths which ran through immaculately tended gardens.

Everything spoke of money, enormous amounts of gold. Druss had been raised in mountain communities where homes were built of rough-cut timber sealed with clay; places where coin was as rare as a whore's honour. Now he stood gazing at palace after palace of white marble, with gilded pillars, painted frescoes, carved reliefs, each topped with red terracotta tile or black Lentrian slate.

Walking on, he sought out the home of the Gothir Champion. Two sentries stood before the high, wrought-iron gates; both men wore silver breastplates, and were armed with short swords. The house was imposing, though not as ostentatious as the other homes nearby. It was square-built with a sloping red-tile roof, and boasting no ornate columns, no frescoes, nor paint work.

The home of the Champion was of simple white stone. The main door was set beneath a stone lintel, and the many windows were functional, displaying no coloured glass, no leaded figures, no ornamentation at all. Much to his own annoyance Druss found himself liking the man who owned the house, which was set amidst gardens boasting willow and beech.

There was one gesture to the dramatic. A statue of the fighter, almost twice life-size, was set upon a pedestal at the centre of a well-tended lawn. Like the house it was of white stone, unpainted and unadorned, and showed Klay with his fists raised defiantly.

For a while Druss stood on the broad avenue outside the gates. A movement in the shadows caught his eye and he saw a small boy crouched by the bole of an elm tree. Druss grinned at him. 'Waiting for a glimpse of the great man, are you?' he asked amiably. The boy nodded, but said nothing. He was painfully thin and scrawny, his eyes deep-set, his face pinched and tight. Druss fished in the small pouch at his belt, producing a silver coin which he tossed to the urchin. 'Go on with you. Buy yourself some food.'

Catching the coin the child stowed it in his ragged tunic – but remained where he was.

'You really want to see him, don't you? Even hunger can't draw you away? Come with me then, boy. I'll take you in.' The child's face brightened instantly and he scrambled forward. Standing he was even thinner than he had appeared, his elbows and knees seeming swollen larger than biceps or thighs. Beside the huge form of the Drenai fighter he appeared no more than a frail shadow.

Together they walked to the gates, where the sentries stepped forward, blocking the way.

'I am Druss. I have been invited here.'

'The beggar boy hasn't been invited,' said one of the guards. Druss stepped in close, his cold gaze locking to the man's eyes, their faces only inches apart. The guard stepped back, trying to create space between himself and Druss, but the Drenai followed him and the man's breastplate clanged against the gate. 'I invited him, laddie. You have a problem with that?'

'No. No problem.'

The sentries stepped aside, pushing open the wrought-iron gates. Druss and the boy moved slowly on. The axeman paused to gaze at the statue, then once more scanned the house and the grounds. The statue was out of place here, at odds with the natural contours of the garden. As he approached the house an elderly servant opened the main door and bowed.

'Welcome, Lord Druss,' he said.

'I am no Lord – nor would ever wish to be. This child was waiting in the shadows for a glimpse of Klay. I promised him a closer look.'

'Mmm,' said the old man. 'I think he could do with a meal first. I'll take him to the kitchen. My master is waiting for you, sir, in the training grounds at the rear of the house. Just follow the hallway; You cannot miss it.' Taking the boy by the hand the old man moved away.

Druss strode on. In the grounds behind the house there were some twenty athletes engaged in training, or sparring. The area was well designed, with three sand circles, punching-bags, weights, massage tables, and two fountains supplying running water. At the far end was a deep pool where Druss could see several men swimming. The setting was simple and he warmed to it, feeling the tension drain from him. Two men were sparring in one of the sand circles while a third, the colossal Klay, stood close by watching intently. In the fading sunlight Klay's short-cropped blond hair shone like gold. His arms were folded and Druss noted the powerful muscles of his shoulders and back, and the way his body tapered to waist and hips. Built for speed and power, thought Druss.

'Break away!' ordered Klay. As the fighters moved apart the Gothir Champion stepped into the circle. 'You are too stiff, Calas,' he said, 'and that left hand moves like a sick turtle. I think your training is out of harmony. You are building weight in your shoulders and arms, which is good for power, but you are ignoring the lower body. The most deadly punches are powered by the legs, the force flowing up through the hips and *then* to the shoulders and arms. When it reaches the fist the impact is like a lightning bolt. Tomorrow you will work with Shonan.' Swinging to the other man he laid a hand on his shoulder. 'You have great skill, boy, but you lack instinct. You have courage and style, but not the heart of a fighter. You see with your eyes only. Shonan tells me your spear-work is excellent. I think we will concentrate on that for the time being.' Both men bowed and moved away.

Klay swung and saw Druss. He gave a broad smile and walked across the training area, his hand extended. A head taller than Druss, he was broader across the shoulders. His face was flat, no sharpness to the bones upon brow or cheek. It was unlikely that a blow would split the skin above or below his eyes, and his chin was square and strong. He had the face of a natural fighter. Druss shook his hand. 'This is what a training area should be,' said Druss. 'It is very fine. Well considered.'

The Gothir fighter nodded. 'It pleases me, though I wish it were bigger. No room for spear-throwing, or hurling the discus. My trainer Shonan uses a field close by. Come, I will show you our facilities.' There were four masseurs at work, skilfully kneading and stretching the muscles of tired athletes, and a bathhouse with two heated pools set back from the training area. For some time the two men wandered the grounds, then at last Klay led Druss back into the house.

The walls of Klay's study were covered with drawings and paintings of the human form, showing muscle structures and attachments. Druss had never seen the like. 'Several of my friends are physicians,' said the Gothir fighter. 'Part of their training involves the dissection of corpses, and the study of the workings of the human body. Fascinating, is it not? Most of our muscles appear to work in an antagonistic fashion. For the biceps to swell, the triceps must relax and stretch.'

'How does this help you?' asked Druss.

'It enables me to find balance,' said Klay. 'Harmony, if you will. Both muscles are vital, one to the other. Therefore it would be foolish to develop one at the expense of the other. You see?'

Druss nodded. 'I had a friend back in Mashrapur, a fighter named Borcha. He would have been as impressed as I am.'

'I have heard of him. He trained you and helped you to become a champion. After you left Mashrapur, he was the first fighter in Circle history to regain his championship. He retired six years ago, after losing to Proseccis in a bout that lasted for almost two hours.'

A servant brought a jug and filled two goblets. 'Refreshing,' observed Druss, as he drank.

'The juices of four fruits,' said Klay. 'I find them invigorating.'

'I prefer wine.'

'They say red wine feeds the blood,' agreed Klay, 'but I have always found it inhibits full training.' For several heartbeats the men sat in silence, then Klay leaned back on his couch. 'You are wondering why I invited you here, are you not?'

'I had thought it was an attempt at intimidation,' said Druss. 'Now I do not believe that.'

'That is gracious of you. I wanted you to know that I was

dismayed to hear of the prophecy. It must be galling for you. I know that I always find it hateful when politics intrudes on what should be honest competition. Therefore I wanted to set your mind at rest.'

'How do you plan to do that?'

'By convincing you to fight to win. To give it your very best.'

Druss leaned back and looked hard at the Gothir Champion. 'Why is it,' he asked, 'that my own ambassador urges me to an opposite course of action? Do you wish to see your King humbled?'

Klay laughed. 'You misunderstand me, Druss. I have watched you fight. You are very good, and you have heart and instinct. When I asked Shonan how he saw us both, he said, "If I had to put all my money on a fighter it would be you, Klay. But if I had to have someone fight for my life, it would be Druss." I am an arrogant man, my friend, but it is not an arrogance born of false pride. I know what I am, and I know what I am capable of. In some ways, as my physician friends tell me, I am a freak of nature. My strength is prodigious, but my speed is extraordinary. Stand up for a moment.'

Druss did so, and Klay positioned himself an arm's length away. 'I shall pluck a hair from your beard, Druss. I want you to block me, if you can.' Druss readied himself.

Klay's hand snapped forward and back, and Druss felt the sting as several hairs were torn clear. His own arm had barely moved in response. Klay returned to his couch. 'You cannot beat me, Druss. No man can. *That* is why you must not concern yourself with prophecies.'

Druss smiled. 'I like you, Klay,' he said, 'and if there was gold to be won for plucking hairs, I think you'd win. But we can talk about that after the final bout.'

'You will fight to win?'

'I always do, laddie.'

'By Heavens, Druss, you are a man after my own heart. No give in you, is there? Is this why they call you the Legend?'

Druss shook his head. 'I made the mistake of befriending a saga poet. Now everywhere I go he makes new stories, each more outlandish than those that came before. What astonishes me is that they are believed. The more I deny them, the more widespread is the belief they are true.'

Klay led Druss back outside into the garden training area. The other athletes had gone now, but servants had lit torches. 'I know the feeling, Druss. Denial is seen as modesty. And people like to believe in heroes. I once lost my temper during training and I struck a stone statue with the blade of my hand. Broke three bones. There are now a hundred men who claim the power of my blow shattered the statue into a thousand pieces. And there are at least twenty more who swear they saw it done. Will you stay and dine with me?'

Druss shook his head. 'There's a tavern I passed coming here. I smelt a spiced meat dish being prepared, and have had a taste for it ever since.'

'Were the windows of the place stained blue?'

'Yes. You know it?'

'It's called The Broken Sword and has the finest chef in Gulgothir. I wish I could join you, but I have business to discuss with my trainer, Shonan.'

'I would have been glad of the company. My friend, Sieben, is entertaining a lady at our quarters, and would not relish the sight of me arriving home early. Perhaps after tomorrow's final?'

'That would be pleasant.'

'By the way, you have a guest. An urchin I found waiting outside. I would be grateful if you treated him kindly, and offered him a word or two.'

'Of course. Enjoy your meal.'

Chapter Three

Kells licked his fingers, then tore another chunk of dark bread with which to scour the bowl for the last of the stew. The old servant chuckled. 'It's all right, boy, there is more where that came from.' Lifting the pot from the stove he ladled the bowl full. Kells's pleasure was undisguised. Taking up his spoon, he attacked the stew with renewed gusto and within moments it had vanished. He belched loudly.

'I am Carmol,' said the old servant, holding out his hand.

Kells looked at it, then reached out with his own grimy palm. Carmol shook hands. 'I think this is the point where you tell me your name,' he said.

Kells looked up into the old man's face. It was heavily lined, especially around the eyes, which were blue and merry. 'Why?' There was no insolence in Kells's tone, merely innocent enquiry.

'Why? Well, it is considered polite when two people share a meal. It is also the way friendships begin.' The old man was friendly, and his smile was not sly.

'I am called Fastfinger,' said Kells.

'Fastfinger,' echoed Carmol. 'Is that what your mother calls you?'

'No, she calls me Kells. But everyone else calls me Fastfinger. The stew is very good. And the bread is soft. Fresh. I've had fresh bread and I know the taste.' Kells climbed down from the bench and belched again. The kitchen was warm and cosy, and it would have been nice to curl up on the floor beside the stove and sleep. Yet he could not, for his mission was not yet complete. 'When can I see . . . the Lord Klay?'

'What is your business with him?' enquired Carmol.

'I have no business with him,' said Kells. 'I have no business. I am . . . a beggar,' he announced, thinking it sounded better than thief, or cut-purse.

'So you have come to beg?'

'Yes, to beg. When can I see him?'

'He is a very busy man. But I can give you a coin or two – and another bowl of stew.'

'I don't want coins . . .' He stumbled to silence, his brow furrowing. 'Well, I *do* want coins from you, but not from him. Not from the Lord Klay.'

'Then what do you want?' asked Carmol, sitting down at the bench.

Kells leaned in close. It could surely do no harm to tell the Lord Klay's servant of his mission? The old man might even prove an ally. 'I want him to lay his hands on my mother.'

The old man laughed suddenly, which embarrassed Kells; this was no subject for laughter and his eyes narrowed. Carmol saw his expression and his smile faded. 'I am sorry, boy. You took me by surprise. Tell me why you require such . . . such an act from my master?'

'Because I *know* the truth,' said Kells, dropping his voice. 'I haven't told anyone, the secret is safe. But I thought that he could spare a little magic for my mam. He could make the lump go away. Then she could walk again, and laugh. And she could work and buy food.'

There was no smile on Carmol's face now. Tenderly he laid his hand on Kells's shoulder. 'You . . . believe the Lord Klay has magic?'

'He is a god,' whispered Kells. The old man was silent for a moment, but Kells watched him closely. His face softened, and he looked worried. 'I swear I won't tell anyone,' said the boy.

'And how did you come by this intelligence, young Kells?'

'I saw him perform the miracle – last year it was. My mam had one of her . . . friends with her, so I was sitting in the alley mouth under cover. There was a storm raging and the lightning was fierce. I saw the flash of it in the alley, and I heard the loud crack as it struck nearby. A body came hurtling by me – and cracked into the wall. I ran out. It was Tall Tess; she's my mam's partner, and she works the Long Avenue. She must have been coming home. The lightning hit her, it did. Killed her dead. I felt her neck and there was no thumping in the veins. I pushed my ear to her breast, and the heart was stopped. Then a carriage came by. I run swift back into the darkness – for fear they'd think I killed her. Then Lord Klay jumps down from the carriage and goes to her. He feels for the thumping, and listens for her heart. And then he did it.' Kells felt his breathing quicken at the memory, his heart beating fast.

'What did he do?' asked Carmol.

'He bent over her and kissed her! I couldn't believe my eyes. He kissed a dead woman. Full on the lips – like a lover. You know what happened then?'

'Tell me.'

'She groaned – and come back from the dead. That's when I knew. I said nothing, not even to Tess. She had burns on her feet, and one earring had melted to her skin. But even she don't know as how she was dead.'

The old man sighed. ''Tis a powerful tale, boy. And I think you should speak with the Lord Klay. Sit here, and I will see if he can spare you a moment or two. There is some fruit there. Help yourself to whatever you can eat.'

Kells needed no second invitation. Even before Carmol had left the room the boy had grabbed two ripe oranges and several bananas. These he devoured at speed, washing them down with fruit juice he discovered in a stone jug.

This was bliss! Fine food – and a miracle for his mam!

It was a good day's work. Sitting down by the warm stove, Kells thought about what he would say to the god, how he would explain that his mother was sick and could not work. She was not lazy-sick. When the first lump appeared on her breast she had continued to work the Short Avenue, even though dizziness often caused her to faint during the labour. As the lump grew harder and more unsightly some of her clients had turned away from her, and she was forced to work longer hours, many of them in the alleys where business was brisk and conducted in darkness. But then came the second lump on the side of her neck – big as one of the oranges he had just eaten. Nobody wanted to pay for her favours then. Her colour had changed too, ghost grey her face was now, with dark rings under the eyes. And thin! Terrible thin, despite all the food Kells stole for her.

All this he would tell the god – and He would make it right.

Not like that surgeon Tall Tess paid for. Five silver coins he took – and he did nothing! Oh, he felt the lumps, and moved his hands over the rest of her body. Dirty skike! Then he whispered to Tess and shook his head a lot. Tess cried after that, and spoke to mam. Mam cried too.

Kells lay down by the fire and dozed.

He awoke suddenly, and found the god leaning over him. 'You are tired, boy,' said the god. 'You may sleep if you wish.'

'No, Lord,' said Kells, rising to his knees. 'You must come with me! Me mam is sick.'

Klay nodded, then sighed. 'Carmol has told me what you saw; it was not a miracle, Kells. One of my physician friends taught me the trick. The shock of the lightning stopped her heart. I blew air into her lungs, then massaged the heart. There was no magic, I swear it.'

'She was dead! You brung her to life!'

'But without magic.'

'You won't help me, then?'

Klay nodded. 'I'll do what I can, Kells. Carmol has gone to fetch the physician I spoke of. When he returns, we'll go to your mother and see what can be done.'

Kells sat quietly in the corner as the grey-haired physician examined Loira. The old man's fingers pressed gently at the lumps, then probed her belly and back and loins. All the time the dying woman was groaning, semi-delirious; only the pain keeping her conscious. Her red hair was lank and greasy, her face pale and glistening with sweat. But even now she looked beautiful to Kells. He listened as the physician spoke to Klay, but he did not understand the conversation. Nor did he need to. The sepulchral tones conveyed it all. She was dying – and there was no god to lay his hands upon her. Anger rose as bile in Kells's throat. He swallowed it down as hot tears flowed to his cheeks, streaking the dirt. Blinking rapidly, he fought for control. Tall Tess stood by the opposite corner, her skinny arms crossed. She was still wearing the tattered red dress that denoted her calling.

'We need to get her to the hospice,' he heard the physician say.

'What is that?' asked Kells, pushing himself up from the floor.

The old surgeon knelt before him. 'It is a place the Lord Klay paid for, where people in great pain can spend . . . can be when their sickness is too great to heal. We have medicines there to take away the pain. You may come too, young man. You can sit with her.'

'She's going to die, isn't she?'

Klay placed his hand on Kells's skinny shoulder. 'Aye, boy.

There is nothing we can do. Eduse is the finest physician in Gulgothir. No-one knows more than he.'

'We can't pay for it,' said Kells bitterly.

'It is already paid for – by the Lord Klay,' said Eduse. 'It was built for those who have nothing. You understand? The Lord Klay . . .'

'He needs no lecture about me, my friend. I am far less than he believed, and no amount of words will take away his disappointment.' Leaning over the bed, he lifted the woman, cradling her head against his chest.

The sick woman groaned again and Tess moved to her, stroking her head. 'It's all right, my little dove. We'll look after you. Tess'll be there, Loira. And Kells.'

Klay carried Loira to the black carriage and opened the door. Kells and Tess scrambled in. Klay laid the now unconscious woman on a padded seat and sat beside her. The physician, Eduse, climbed up alongside the driver. Kells heard the slap of reins on the backs of the four horses, then the carriage lurched forward. His mother awoke and cried out in pain and Kells felt his heart would burst.

The journey did not take long, for the hospice was built close to the poor quarter, and Kells followed as Klay carried her inside the white-walled building. Orderlies in long white tunics rushed forward to help, laying Loira on a stretcher and covering her with a thick blanket of white wool. Eduse led them down a long corridor to a room as large as any Kells had ever seen. The north and south walls were lined with pallet beds, in which lay the sick and the dying. Many people were moving around the room – orderlies dressed in white, visitors arriving to see relatives or friends, physicians preparing medicines. The stretcher-bearers carried his mother the length of the room and out into another corridor, coming at last to a small room some twelve feet long. They transferred Loira to one of the two narrow beds, both covered in fresh white linen, then covered her with a blanket. After the orderlies had gone Eduse produced a phial of dark liquid. Lifting Loira's head he poured the liquid into her mouth. She gagged, then swallowed. Some of the medicine dribbled to her chin. Eduse dabbed at it with a cloth, then eased her head back to the pillow.

'You may sleep here with her, Kells,' said Eduse. 'You too,' he told Tess.

'I can't stay,' she said. 'Have to work.'

'I'll pay your . . . wages,' said Klay.

65

Tess gave him a gap-toothed grin. 'That's not it, lovely man. If I'm away from my patch some other whore will take my trade. I need to be there. But I'll come here when I can.' Stepping in close she took Klay by the hand, raising it to her lips and kissing it. Then she swung away, embarrassed, and left the room.

Kells walked to the bedside and took his mother's hand. She was sleeping now, but the skin was hot and scaly to the touch. The boy sighed and sat down on the bed.

Klay and Eduse walked from the room. 'How long?' he heard Klay ask, his voice little more than a whisper.

'Difficult to say. The cancers are very advanced. She could die in the night – or last another month. You should get home, you've a fight tomorrow. I saw the Drenai fight – you'll need to be at your best.'

'I shall be, my friend. But I'll not go home yet. I think I'll take a stroll. Get some air. You know, I have never wanted to be a god. Not until tonight.'

Kells heard him move away.

Jarid was a careful man, a thinker. Few understood this – for what they saw was a large, round-shouldered, shambling bear of a man, slow of speech – and therefore dim-witted. This was a misconception which Jarid did not seek to change. Far from it. Born in the slums of Gulgothir, he had learned fast that the only way for a man to prosper lay in outwitting his fellow men. The first lesson to be learned was that morality was merely a weapon used by the rich. There was – and never would be – an ultimate right or wrong. All life was theft in one form or another. The rich called their thefts taxes, and a king could steal a nation by invasion and conquest and men would proclaim it a glorious victory. Yet a beggar could steal a loaf of bread and the same men would label it larceny, and hang the man. Jarid would have none of it. He had killed his first man just after his twelfth birthday, a fat merchant whose name he could no longer remember. He had stabbed him in the groin, then slashed his purse clear of its retaining belt. The man had screamed loud and long, the sound following Jarid as he sped through the alleyways. The money had bought medicines for his mother and sister, and food for their shrunken bellies.

Now, at forty-four, Jarid was an accomplished killer. So accomplished that his skills had come to the attention of the State, and his work was now paid for out of public funds. He had even been allotted a tax number, the ultimate symbol of citizenship, giving him the right to vote in local elections. He had a small house in the south-east quarter, and a housekeeper who also warmed his bed. Far from rich, Jarid was still a long way from the urchin thief he had once been.

From his position in the alleyway he had watched Druss enter The Broken Sword tavern, and had followed him inside, listening as he ordered his meal and noting the tavern maid telling him that the house was almost full and that the food would take a little time to prepare.

Jarid had left the tavern and run to where Copass waited; he gave the man his orders and stood back in the shadows, waiting. Copass soon returned with a dozen men, tough capable fighters mostly armed with knives and clubs. The last man carried a short crossbow. Jarid took the thin faced bowman by the arm and led him away from the others, then he spoke to him in a low voice. 'You don't shoot unless all else fails. You will be paid whether you loose a bolt or no. Your target is a black-bearded Drenai in a dark leather shirt – you will have no trouble picking him out.'

'Why don't I just kill him as he appears in the doorway?'

'Because I am telling you not to, half-wit. He is the Drenai Champion. It will suit our purposes if he is merely injured – you understand?'

'Whose purposes are we talking about?'

Jarid smiled. 'Large sums have been wagered on tomorrow's fight. If you wish, I shall speak the name of my master. Know, however, that once I have done so I will take your neck in my hands and snap the bones beneath. Your choice. You wish to know?'

'No. I understand. But *you* have to understand that if your men fail then I'll be sending a bolt into the darkness at a moving target. I can't guarantee I won't kill him! What happens then?'

'You'll still get paid. Now take up your position.' Swinging to the others, Jarid gathered them in a tight group and spoke, his voice scarcely above a whisper. 'The Drenai is a fearsome fighter, very powerful. Once any of you have planted a knife in his upper body, shoulders, chest or arm, the rest of you must break away and run. You understand? This is not a fight to the death; a deep wound is all we require.'

'Begging your pardon, sir,' said a lean man with missing front teeth, 'but I've bet on Klay. Won't that bet be voided if the Drenai can't fight?'

Jarid shook his head. 'The bet would be on Klay taking gold. If the Drenai doesn't fight then the gold is automatically given to Klay.'

'What if a knife goes too deep and he dies?' asked another man.

Jarid shrugged. 'All life is a game of chance.'

Moving away from the men he ducked into an alley, then cut left across a section of waste ground, ducking into a shadowed doorway. Tall Tess was standing by a broken mirror, her red dress unfastened at the breast and pushed down to her hips. She was sponging cool water to her naked upper body.

'It's hot tonight,' she said, grinning at Jarid. He did not return the smile but stepping in close he grabbed her arm, twisting it painfully. Tess cried out.

'Shut up!' he ordered. 'I told you no other clients tonight, my girl. I like my women fresh.'

'There haven't been any, lovely man,' she said. 'I had to run from the hospice, all the way. That's why I'm sweating!'

'Hospice? What you talking about, girl?' Releasing her arm he took a step back. Tess rubbed at her scrawny bicep.

'Loira. They took her in today. Klay come for her. Took her in his carriage, he did. It was wonderful, Jarid. All dark wood, lacquered black, and padded leather seats and cushions of satin. And she's in a bed now, with linen so white it could have been spun from clouds.'

'I didn't know Klay was one of her marks?'

'He wasn't. Her snipe, Fastfinger, went and begged him to help. And he did. So Loira's being looked after now, with medicines and food.'

'You'd better be telling me the truth, girl,' said Jarid huskily, moving in close and cupping his hand to Tess's sagging breast.

'I'd never lie to you, lovely man,' she whispered. 'You're my darling. My only darling.' Tess slid her hand downwards and allowed her mind to drift. Everything now was performance, and so mind-numbingly familiar was every move that she no longer needed to think. Instead, as she moaned and touched, teased and caressed, Tess was thinking about Loira. It seemed so wrong that a woman should be laid on such clean sheets merely to die. Many was the time that she and Loira had been huddled together under a thin blanket on cold winter nights, when the freezing winds had kept marks from the street. Then they had spoken of such luxuries as all-day fires, down-filled pillows and quilts, blankets of

68

softest wool. And they had giggled and laughed, and cuddled in close for warmth. Now poor Loira had the kind of sheets she had dreamt of – and would never know it. One day soon she would die, and her bowels would open and gush out their contents on those clean, white sheets.

The pounding of the man's hips increased in power and speed. Instantly Tess began to moan rhythmically, arching her thin body up against his. His breathing was hoarse in her ear, then he groaned and sank his weight down upon her. Curling her arm around him, she stroked the nape of his neck. 'Ah, you are a wonder, lovely man. You are my darling. My only darling.'

Jarid heaved himself from her, pulled his leggings up from around his ankles and rolled to his feet. Tess smoothed down her red dress and sat up. Jarid tossed her a full silver piece. 'You want to stay for a little, Jarid? I have some wine.'

'No, I have work to do.' He smiled at her. 'It was good tonight.'

'The best,' she assured him.

Chapter Four

Druss finished his meal and pushed away the wooden platter. The meat had been good – lean and tender, covered with savoury spices and a rich, dark gravy. Yet despite the quality of the meal he had barely tasted it. His thoughts remained confused, and melancholy. Meeting Klay had not helped. Damn it, he liked the man!

Druss lifted his tankard and swallowed half the contents. The ale was thin, but refreshing, and brought back memories of his youth and the beer brewed in the mountains. He had grown to manhood among common folk; men and women of simple pleasures who worked from first light to dusk, and lived for their families, battling to put enough bread on the table. Often on summer evenings they would gather in the communal hall and drink ale, sing songs and swap stories. Not for them the great questions of politics, the compromises, the betrayals of ideals. Life was hard, yet uncomplicated.

He had been torn from that life when the renegade Collan led an attack on the village, slaughtering the men and the older women, and taking the young girls captive to be sold as slaves.

Among them had been Druss's wife, Rowena, his love and his life. He had been felling trees, high in the timber-line, when the attack took place. He had returned to the ruins of the village and set off after the killers, and he had found them.

Druss slew many of the raiders, and freed the girls, but Rowena was not with them; Collan had taken her to Mashrapur and sold her to a Ventrian merchant. In order to earn money for passage to Ventria, Druss had become a fighter in the sand circles of Mashrapur. And moment by bone-crunching moment the young farmer had changed, his natural strength and ferocity honed until he became the most feared fighter in the city.

At last he journeyed on, in the company of Sieben and the Ventrian officer Bodasen, joining in the Ventrian Wars and fast earning a deadly reputation. The Silver Slayer, they called him, for his deeds with the shining double-headed axe, Snaga.

Druss fought in a score of battles, and hundreds of skirmishes. Many times he was wounded, yet always he emerged triumphant.

When, after many years, he found Rowena and brought her home, he truly believed that his wanderings and his battles were blood-dreams of the past. Rowena knew differently. Day by day Druss grew more morose. He was no longer a farmer, and could find no pleasure in tilling the earth or tending his cattle. A little more than a year had passed when he journeyed to Dros Delnoch to join a militia force formed to counter raids by Sathuli tribesmen. Six months later, with the Sathuli forced back into the mountains, he returned home with fresh scars and fond memories.

Closing his eyes, he recalled Rowena's words on the night he returned from the Sathuli campaign. Sitting on the goatskin rug before a log fire, she had reached out and taken his hand. 'My poor Druss. How can a man live for war? It is so futile.'

He had seen the sorrow in her hazel eyes, and struggled to find an answer. 'It is not the fighting alone, Rowena. It is the comradeship, the fire in the blood, the facing of fear. When danger threatens I become . . . a man.'

Rowena sighed. 'You are what you are, my love. But it saddens me. There is great beauty here – bringing food from the earth, watching the sun rise over the mountains and the moon's reflection dancing upon the lakes. There is contentment, and joy. Yet it is not for you. Tell me, Druss, why did you cross the world for me?'

'Because I love you. You are everything to me.'

She had shaken her head. 'If that were true you would have no desire to leave me and go wandering in search of war. Look around you at the other farmers. Do they rush off to battle?'

Druss rose and strode to the window, pushing the shutters wide and staring out at the distant stars. 'I am not like them any more. I do not know if ever I was. I am a man fitted for war, Rowena.'

'I know,' she said sadly. 'Oh, Druss, I know . . .'

Draining his tankard now, Druss caught the eye of a blonde serving-maid. 'Another!' he called out, waving the tankard in the air.

'Just a moment, sir,' she answered him. The tavern was almost full, the atmosphere bright and noisy. Druss had found a booth in the corner of the room, where he could sit with his back to the wall and watch the crowd. Usually he enjoyed the gently chaotic rhythms of a tavern, the mix of laughter, conversation, the clattering of plates, the clinking of tankards, the shuffling of feet and the scraping of chairs. But not tonight.

The maid brought him a second tankard of ale; she was a buxom girl, full-breasted and wide-hipped. 'Did you enjoy your meal, sir?' she asked, leaning forward with her hand on his shoulder. Her fingers stroked up into his short-cropped, dark hair. Rowena often did the same thing, when he was tense or angry. Always it soothed him. He smiled at the girl.

'It was a meal fit for a king, lass. But I didn't enjoy it as I should. Too many weighty problems that I haven't the brain to solve.'

'You need to relax in the company of a woman,' she said, her fingers now stroking his dark beard.

Taking her hand, he gently moved it away from his face. 'My woman is a long way from here, girl. But always she is close to my heart. And pretty as you are, I'll wait to enjoy her company.' Dipping into the pouch at his belt, Druss drew out two silver pieces. 'The one is for the meal, the second for you.'

'You are very kind. If you change your mind . . .'

'I won't.'

As she moved away, Druss felt a cold draught upon his cheek.

In that instant all sound died away. Druss blinked. The serving-maid was standing statue-still – her wide skirt, which swished as she walked, motionless. All around him the diners and revellers were frozen in their places. When Druss flicked his gaze to the fire, the tongues of flame were no longer dancing between the logs but standing steady, the smoke above them hanging solid in the chimney. And the normal smells of a tavern, roasted meats, wood-smoke, and stale sweat – had disappeared, to be replaced by the sickly-sweet odour of cinnamon and burning sandalwood.

A small Nadir dressed in a tunic of goat's hair stepped into sight, weaving his way through the silent revellers. He was old, but not ancient, his thinning black hair greasy and lank. Swiftly he crossed the room and seated himself opposite Druss. 'Well met, axeman,' he said, his voice soft, almost sibilant.

Druss looked deep into the man's dark, slanted eyes and read the hatred there. 'Your magic will need to be very strong to stop me reaching across and snapping your scrawny neck,' he said.

The old man grinned, showing stained and broken teeth. 'I am not here to bring you harm, axeman. I am Nosta Khan, shaman to the Wolfshead tribe. You aided a young friend of mine, Talisman; you fought alongside him.'

'What of it?'

'He is important to me. And we Nadir like to repay our debts.'

'I have no need of repayment. There is nothing you can offer me.'

Nosta Khan shook his head. 'Never be too sure, axeman. Firstly, would it surprise you to know that even now there are a dozen men waiting outside, armed with clubs and knives? Their purpose is to prevent you fighting the Gothir Champion. They have been told to cripple you if they can, and kill you if they must.'

'It seems everyone wants me to lose,' said Druss. 'Why do you warn me? And don't insult me with talk of repayment. I can see the hatred in your eyes.'

The shaman was silent for a moment, and when he spoke his voice was rich with both malice and a sense of regret. 'My people need you, axeman.'

Druss gave a cold smile. 'It cost you to say that, did it not?'

'Indeed it did,' admitted the little man. 'But I would swallow burning coals for my people, and telling a small truth to a Round-eye is a pain I can live with.' He grinned again. 'An ancestor of yours aided us in the past. He hated the Nadir; yet he helped my grandfather in a great battle against the Gothir. His heroism brought us closer to the days of the Uniter. He was known as Angel, but his Nadir name was Hard-To-Kill.'

'I've never heard of him.'

'You Round-eyes disgust me! You call us barbarians, yet you know not the deeds of your own ancestors. Pah! Let us move on. My powers are not limitless, and soon this stinking tavern will return with all its foul noise and stench. Angel was linked to the Nadir, Druss. Linked by blood, held by destiny. So are you. I have risked my life in many Fever-dreams, and always your face floats before me. I do not know, as yet, what role you have to play in the coming drama. It may be small, though I doubt it. But

73

whatever it is, I know where you must be in the coming days. It is necessary that you travel to the Valley of Shul-sen's Tears. It is five days' ride to the east. There is a Shrine there, dedicated to the memory of Oshikai Demon-bane, the greatest of Nadir warriors.'

'Why would I wish to go there?' asked Druss. '*You* say it is necessary, but I do not think so.'

The shaman shook his head. 'Let me tell you of the Healing Stones, axeman. There is said to be no wound they cannot mend. Some even claim they can raise the dead. They are hidden at the Shrine.'

'As you can see,' said Druss, 'I have no wound.'

The little man averted his eyes from Druss's gaze, and a secretive smile touched his weatherbeaten features. 'No, you have not. But much can happen in Gulgothir. Have you forgotten the men who wait? Remember, Druss, five days' ride due east, in the Valley of Shul-sen's Tears.'

Druss's vision swam and the noise of the tavern covered him once more. He blinked. The tavern maid's skirt swished as she walked. Of the shaman there was no sign.

Draining the last of his ale, Druss pushed himself to his feet. According to the shaman a dozen men waited outside; rogues hired to prevent him fighting Klay. He gave a deep sigh and moved to the long trestle bar. The tavern-keeper, fat of belly and red of face, approached him. 'Another ale, sir?'

'No,' said Druss, placing a silver coin on the bar. 'Loan me your club.'

'My club? I don't know what you mean.'

Druss smiled and leaned forward conspiratorially. 'I've never met a tavern-keeper yet, friend, who did not keep a weighted club at hand. Now, I am the Drenai fighter, Druss, and I am told there is a gang outside – waiting for me. They seek to stop my fight with Klay.'

'I've got money on that,' muttered the innkeeper. 'Now look, lad, why don't you just come with me and I'll take you downstairs to the ale cellar? There's a secret door that will allow you to sneak past them all.'

'I don't need a secret door,' said Druss patiently. 'I need to borrow your club.'

'One day, lad, you might realize that it is more sensible to avoid trouble. No-one is invincible.' Reaching down, he produced an eighteen-inch truncheon of black metal which he laid on the bar. 'The outer casing is iron,' he said, 'but the inner is lead. Return it when you are done.' Druss hefted the weapon; it was twice as heavy as most short swords. Sliding it up the right sleeve of his shirt he eased himself through the crowd. As he opened the door, he saw several big men standing outside. Dressed in shabby tunics and leggings, they looked like beggars. Switching his gaze to the right he saw a second group gathered close by. They stiffened as he appeared and for a moment no-one moved. 'Well, lads,' said Druss, with a broad grin. 'Who wants to be first?'

'That would be me,' answered a tall man with a shaggy beard. He had wide, powerful shoulders, and despite his grimy clothing was no beggar, Druss knew. The skin of his neck was white and clean, as were his hands. And the knife he carried was of Ventrian steel; weapons like that did not come cheap. 'I can tell by your eyes that you're frightened,' said the knife-man, as he moved in. 'And I can smell your fear.'

Druss stood very still and the man suddenly leapt forward, his knife flashing towards Druss's shoulder. With his left forearm Druss blocked the thrust, and in the same movement sent a left hook exploding against the man's chin; he hit the cobbles face first and did not move. Opening his fingers, Druss allowed the truncheon to slide from his sleeve. Figures darted from the shadows and he charged into them, turning his shoulder into the first and cannoning him from his feet. The truncheon hammered left and right, hurling men from their feet. A knife-blade grazed the top of his shoulder. Grabbing the wielder by his tunic he head-butted the man – smashing his nose and cheekbone – then spun him into the path of two more attackers. The first fell clumsily, landing on his own knife; as the blade tore into his side his screams rent the air. The second backed away. But more men gathered: eight fighters, all with weapons of sharp steel. Druss knew they were no longer thinking of crippling him; he could sense their hatred, and the blood-lust surging within them.

'You're dead meat, Drenai!' he heard one of them shout as the group edged forward.

Suddenly a voice boomed out. 'Hold on, Druss, I'm coming.'

Druss glanced to his left to see Klay charging from the mouth of a nearby alley. As the giant Gothir hurtled into them the men, recognizing him, scattered and ran. Klay walked over to Druss. 'Such an exciting life you lead, my friend,' he said, with a broad grin.

Something bright flashed towards Druss's face and in that one terrifying moment he saw so many things: the moonlight shining on the dagger-blade, the thrower, a look of triumph on his dirty face – and Klay's hand snaking out with impossible speed, catching the hurled knife by the hilt to stop the blade mere inches from Druss's eye.

'I told you, Druss, speed is everything,' said Klay.

Druss let out a long, deep breath. 'I don't know about that, laddie, but you saved my life and I'll not forget it.'

Klay chuckled. 'Come on, my friend, I need to eat.' Throwing his arm around Druss's shoulder, he turned towards the tavern. In that moment a black-feathered crossbow bolt slashed across the open ground to plunge into the back of the Gothir Champion. Klay cried out and collapsed against Druss. The axeman staggered under the weight, then saw the bolt low in the fighter's back. Gently he lowered him to the ground. Scanning the shadows for signs of the attacker, he saw two men running away. One carried a crossbow and Druss longed to give chase, but he could not leave the wounded Klay.

'Lie still – I'll fetch a surgeon.'

'What's happened to me, Druss? Why am I lying down?'

'You've been struck by a crossbow bolt. Lie still!'

'I cannot move my legs, Druss . . .'

The interrogation room was cold and damp, fetid water leaving a trail of slime on the greasy walls. Two bronze lanterns on one wall put out a flickering light, but no heat. Seated at a crudely fashioned table, upon which he could see bloodstains both old and new, Chorin-Tsu waited patiently, gathering his thoughts. The little Chiatze said nothing to the guard, a burly soldier in a grubby leather tunic and torn breeches, who stood with arms folded by the door. The man had a brutal face and cruel eyes. Chorin-Tsu did not stare at him, but gazed about the room with clinical detachment. Yet his thoughts remained with the guard. I have known many good, ugly men, he thought, and even a few handsome, evil men. Yet one had only to look at this guard to recognize his brutality – as if his coarse and vile nature had somehow reached up from within and moulded his features, swathing his eyes in pockets of fat, set close together above a thick pock-marked nose and thick, slack lips.

A black rat scurried across the room and the guard jumped, then kicked at it, missing wildly. The creature vanished into a hole by the far corner of the wall. 'Bastard rats!' hissed the guard, embarrassed that he had allowed himself to be startled in front of the prisoner. 'You obviously like 'em. Good! You'll be living with them soon enough. Have 'em running all over you then, biting your skin, leaving their little fleas to suck your blood in the dark.'

Chorin-Tsu ignored him.

Garen-Tsen's arrival was sudden, the door whispering open. In the lantern light the Minister's face glowed with a sickly yellow sheen, and his eyes seemed unnaturally bright. Chorin-Tsu offered no greeting. Nor, as should have been Chiatze custom in the presence of a Minister, did he rise and bow. Instead he sat, his expression calm and impassive.

Dismissing the guard, the Minister sat down opposite the little Chiatze embalmer. 'My apologies for the inhospitable surroundings,' said Garen-Tsen, speaking in Chiatze. 'It was necessary for your safety. You did wonderfully well with the Queen. Her beauty has never been so radiant.'

'I thank you, Garen-Tsen,' answered Chorin-Tsu coolly. 'But why am I here? You promised I would be freed.'

'As indeed you will be, countryman. But first let us talk. Tell me of your interest in Nadir legends.'

Chorin-Tsu stared at the slender Minister, holding his gaze. It was all a game now, with only one ending. I am to die, he thought. Here, in this cold, miserable place. He wanted to scream his hatred at the monster before him, to rage and show defiance. The strength of feeling surprised him, going against all Chiatze teaching, but not a trace of his inner turmoil showed upon his face as he sat very still, his expression serene. 'All legends have a basis in fact, Garen-Tsen. I am a student of history and it pleases me to study.'

'Of course. But your studies have been focused in recent years, have they not? You have spent hundreds of hours in the Great Library, studying scrolls concerning Oshikai Demon-bane and the Legend of the Stone Wolf. Why is that?'

'I am indeed gratified by your interest – though puzzled as to why a man of your status and responsibilities should concern himself with what is, after all, no more than a hobby?' countered Chorin-Tsu.

'The movements and interests of all foreign nationals are scrutinized. But my interest goes beyond such mundane matters. You are a scholar, and your work deserves a wider audience. I would be honoured to hear your views on the Stone Wolf. But since time is pressing, perhaps it would be best if you merely outlined your findings concerning the Eyes of Alchazzar.'

Chorin-Tsu gave an almost imperceptible bow of his head. 'Perhaps it would be better to postpone this conversation until we are both sitting in more comfortable apartments.'

The Minister leaned back in his chair and steepled his fingers under his long chin. When he spoke his voice was cold. 'Spiriting you away will be both costly and dangerous, countryman. How much is your life worth?'

Chorin-Tsu was surprised. The question was vulgar, and considerably beneath any high-born Chiatze. 'Far less than you would think, but far more than I can afford,' he replied.

'I think you will find that the price is well within your reach, Master Embalmer. Two jewels, to be precise,' said Garen-Tsen. 'The Eyes of Alchazzar. It is my belief that you have located their hiding-place. Am I wrong?'

Chorin-Tsu remained silent. He had known for many years that death would be his only reward, and had believed himself prepared for it. But now, in this cold, damp place his heart began to beat in panic. He wanted to live! Looking up, he met the reptilian gaze of his countryman. Keeping his voice steady, he said, 'Let us, for the sake of argument, assume that you are correct. In what way would sharing this information prove of benefit to this humble embalmer?'

'Benefit? You will be free. You have the sacred word of a Chiatze nobleman – is that not enough?'

Chorin-Tsu took a deep breath and summoned the last of his courage. 'The word of a Chiatze nobleman is indeed sacred. And in the presence of such a man I would not hesitate to surrender my knowledge. Perhaps you should send for him, so that we may conclude our conversation.'

Garen-Tsen's colour deepened. 'You have made the most unfortunate error, for now you will have to make the acquaintance of the Royal Torturer. Is this what you truly desire, Chorin-Tsu? He will make you speak; you will scream and babble, weep and beg. Why put yourself through such agony?'

Chorin-Tsu considered the question carefully. All his long life he had cherished Chiatze teaching, most especially the laws governing the subjugation of self to the rigours of an iron etiquette. This alone was the foundation of Chiatze culture. Yet here he sat seeking an answer to a question no *true* Chiatze would dream of asking. It was obnoxious and invasive – indeed the kind of question only a barbarian would utter. He looked deeply into Garen-Tsen's eyes. The man was waiting for an answer. Chorin-Tsu sighed and, for the first time in his life, spoke like a barbarian.

'To thwart you, you lying dog,' he said.

The ride had been long and dry, the sun beating down on the open steppes, the strength-sapping heat leaving both riders and ponies near to exhaustion. The rock pool was high in the hills, beneath an overhang of shale and slate. Few knew of its existence, and once Talisman had found the dried bones of a traveller who had died of thirst less than fifty feet from it. The pool was no more than twenty feet long and only twelve wide. But it was very deep, and the water winter-cold. After tending to the ponies and hobbling them, Talisman threw off his jerkin and tugged his shirt over his head. Dust and sand scraped against the skin of his arms and his shoulders. Kicking off his boots he loosed his belt, stepped out of his leggings and walked naked to the pool's edge. The sun beat down upon his skin, and he could feel the heat of the rock beneath his feet. Taking a deep breath, he launched himself out over the sparkling water in an ungainly dive that sent up a glittering spray. He surfaced and swept his sleek black hair back from his face.

Zhusai sat, fully clothed, by the poolside. Her long, black hair was soaked with sweat, her face streaked with dust, and her pale green silk tunic – a garment of bright, expensive beauty back in Gulgothir – was now travel-stained and dirt-streaked.

'Do you swim, Zhusai?' he asked her. She shook her head. 'Would you like me to teach you?'

'That is most kind of you, Talisman. Perhaps on another occasion.'

Talisman swam to the poolside and levered himself to the rock beside her. Kneeling, she leaned over the edge, cupping her hands to the water and dabbing her fingers to her brow and cheeks. In the two days they had been together Zhusai had not initiated a conversation. If Talisman spoke she would respond, with typical Chiatze politeness and courtesy. Replacing her wide straw hat to her head, she sat in the stifling heat without complaint, her eyes averted from him.

'It is not difficult to swim,' he said. 'There is no danger, Zhusai, for I shall be in the pool with you, supporting you. Also it is wondrously cool.'

Bowing her head, she closed her eyes. 'I thank you, Lord

Talisman. You are indeed a considerate companion. The sun is very hot. Perhaps you should dress now – or your skin will burn.'

'No, I think I will swim again,' he told her, jumping into the pool. His understanding of the Chiatze people was limited to their methods of warfare, which were apparently ritualistic. According to Gothir reports many campaigns were conducted and won without bloodshed, armies manoeuvring across battlefields until one side or the other conceded the advantage. It helped not at all with his understanding of Zhusai. Rolling to his back, Talisman floated on the cool surface. Her good manners, he realized, were becoming hard to tolerate. He smiled, and swam to the pool's edge, hooking his arm to the warm stone.

'Do you trust me?' he asked her.

'Of course. You are the guardian of my honour.'

Talisman was surprised. 'I can guard your life, Zhusai, to the best of my ability. But no-one but you can guard your honour. It is something no man – or woman – can *take*. Honour can only be surrendered.'

'As you say, so must it be, Lord,' she said meekly.

'No, no! Do not agree for the sake of courtesy, Zhusai.' Her eyes met his and for a long moment she did not speak. When she did her voice was strangely different, still lilting and soft, yet with an underlying confidence that touched a chord in Talisman.

'I fear my translation of your title was not sufficiently exact. The *honour* you speak of is essentially a male concept, born in blood and battle. A man's *word*, a man's *patriotism*, a man's *courage*. Indeed, this form of honour can only be surrendered. Perhaps "guardian of my virtue" would suffice. And though we could enter a fine philosophical debate on the meaning of the word *virtue*, I use it in the sense that a male would apply to a woman – most especially a Nadir male. I understand that among your people a raped woman is put to death, while the rapist is merely banished.' She fell silent and averted her eyes once more. It was the longest speech he had heard from her.

'You are angry,' he said.

She bowed and shook her head. 'I am merely hot, my Lord. I fear it has made me indiscreet.'

Levering himself from the pool, he walked to the hobbled ponies and pulled a clean shirt and leggings from his saddle pack. Once dressed, he returned to the seated woman. 'We will be resting here today and tonight.' Pointing to the south section of the pool, he told her, 'There is a shelf there, and the water is no more than four feet deep. You may bathe there. So that you may have privacy, I shall walk back down the trail and gather wood for tonight's fire.'

'Thank you, Lord,' she said, bowing her head.

Pulling on his boots, Talisman looped an empty canvas bag over his shoulder. Slowly he walked back up the trail, stopping short of the crest and scanning the steppes below. There was no sign of other riders. Above the crest the heat was searing and intense. Talisman walked slowly down the hillside, pausing to gather sticks which he dropped into the bag. Desert trees and bushes grew here, their roots deep into the dry earth, their arid existence maintained by the few days of heavy rain in what passed for winter here. Fuel was plentiful and soon his bag was crammed full. He was just starting back up the slope when he heard Zhusai cry out. Throwing the bag to one side, Talisman sprinted up the trail and over the crest. Zhusai, her arms thrashing wildly, had slipped from the shelf and her head sank below the surface.

Talisman ran to the pool's edge and dived after her. Below the surface he opened his eyes to see that Zhusai, still struggling, was sinking some twenty feet below him. Bubbles of air were streaming from her mouth. Talisman dived towards her, his fingers hooked into her hair and, twisting in the water, he kicked out for the surface. At first he did not rise and panic touched him. She was too heavy. If he hung on to her they would both drown! Looking round, he saw the shelf from which she had slipped; it was no more than ten feet to his left. The surface must be close, he thought. Zhusai was a dead weight now and Talisman's breath was failing. But he hung on – and kicked out with renewed force. His head splashed clear of the water. Taking a great lungful of air, he dragged Zhusai to the shelf and heaved her body on to it. She rolled in the shallow water, face down. Talisman scrambled alongside her and, with his feet on solid rock, lifted her to his shoulder and climbed from the pool. Laying her down on her stomach he straddled her and pushed down against her back. Water bubbled from her mouth as again and again he applied pressure. Suddenly she coughed – then vomited. Talisman stood, then ran to her pony and unfastened her blanket. Zhusai was sitting up as he returned. Swiftly he wrapped the blanket around her.

'I was dying,' she said.

'Yes. But now you are alive once more.'

81

For a moment she was silent, then she looked up at him. 'I would like to learn to swim,' she told him.

Talisman smiled. 'Then I shall teach you – but not today.'

The sun was setting, and already it was cooler. Talisman rose and fetched the bag of wood. When he returned Zhusai had dressed in a blue tunic and leggings, and was now washing the dust from their travel-stained clothes. In a wide niche in the rock wall Talisman lit a fire above the ashes of a previous blaze. Zhusai joined him, and together they sat for some time in comfortable silence.

'Are you a student of history, like your grandfather?' he asked her.

'I have assisted him since I was eight years old, and many times since I have travelled with him to the sacred sites.'

'You have been to Oshikai's Shrine?'

'Yes, twice. It was once a temple. My grandfather believes it is by far the oldest building in all the Gothir lands. Oshikai is said to have been carried there after the Battle of the Vale. His wife was with him when he died; thereafter they named it the Valley of Shul-sen's Tears. Some visitors claim you can still hear her weeping, if you sit close to the Shrine on cold winter nights. Did you hear her weeping, Lord Talisman?'

'I have never been there,' admitted the warrior.

'Forgive me, Lord,' she said swiftly, bowing and closing her eyes. 'I fear my words, which were intended lightly, have caused offence.'

'Not at all, Zhusai. Now tell me of the Shrine. Describe it for me.'

She glanced up. 'It is three years since last I was there. I was fourteen and my grandfather gave me my woman-name, Zhusai.'

'What was your child name?'

'Voni. It means Chittering Rat in the Chiatze tongue.'

Talisman chuckled. 'It has a . . . similar . . . meaning in Nadir.'

'In Nadir it means Windy Goat,' she said, tilting her head and giving a smile so dazzling that it struck him between the eyes with the power of a fist. He blinked and took a deep breath. Before that smile her beauty had seemed cold and distant, leaving Talisman untroubled by their journeying together. But now? He felt curiously short of breath. When he had saved her from drowning he had not been unduly affected by her nakedness. Now, however, the memory of her golden skin shone in his mind, the curve of her hips and belly, the large dark nipples on her small

82

breasts. He realized Zhusai was speaking to him. 'Are you well, Lord?'

'Yes,' he replied, more tersely than he had intended. Rising, he walked away from the bemused girl, moving up the trail to sit on a rock close to the crest. Her smile shone in his mind, and his body ached for her. It was as if a spell had been cast. Nervously he glanced back down to the fire where Zhusai was sitting quietly. She is not a witch, he thought; no, far from it. She was simply the most beautiful woman Talisman had ever known.

And he was honour bound to take her to another man.

Chorin-Tsu had spoken of sacrifice.

Talisman knew now what it meant . . .

Zhusai sat quietly by the small fire, a multi-coloured blanket wrapped around her shoulders. Talisman slept nearby, his breathing deep and steady. When one of the ponies moved in its sleep, hoof scraping on stone, Talisman stirred but did not wake. She gazed down on his face in the moonlight. He was not a handsome man, nor an ugly one. Yet you are attractive, thought Zhusai, remembering the gentle touch as he laid the blanket around her shoulders, and the concern in his eyes as she had recovered from the terrifying experience in the water. During her seven years in the company of her grandfather Zhusai had met many Nadir tribesmen. Some she had liked, others she had loathed. But all were frightening, for there was a ferocity lurking close to the surface of the Nadir personality, a terrible hunger for blood and violence. Talisman was different. He had strength, and a power not often found in one so young. But she sensed he had no love of cruelty, no lust for blood letting.

Zhusai added the last of the fuel to the fire. The night was not cold, but the little blaze was comforting. Who are you, Talisman? she wondered. Talisman was Nadir – of that there was no doubt. And he was past the age of manhood. Why then did he carry no Nadir name? Why *Talisman*? Then there was his speech. The Nadir tongue was guttural, with many sounds created from the back of the throat, which usually made for clumsiness when they spoke the softer language of the round-eyed Southerners. Not so with Talisman, whose speech was fluent and well modulated. Zhusai had spent many months among the Nadir as her grandfather travelled widely, examining sites of historical interest. They were a brutal people, as harsh and unyielding as the steppes on which they lived. Women were treated with casual cruelty.

Zhusai sat back and considered the events of the day.

When Talisman had stripped himself and dived into the water, Zhusai had been both outraged, and wonderfully stirred. Never had she seen a man naked. His skin was pale gold, his body wolf-lean. His back, buttocks and thighs were criss-crossed with white scars: the marks of a whip. While the Nadir were cruel to women, they rarely whipped their children, and certainly not with enough force to leave the marks that Talisman bore.

There was no question about it, Talisman was an enigma.

'He will be one of the Uniter's generals,' her grandfather had told her. 'He is a thinker, yet also a man of action. Such men are rare. The Nadir will have their day of glory with men such as he.'

His zeal had confused Zhusai. 'They are not our people, Grandfather. Why should we care?'

'Their origins are the same, little one. But that is not the whole reason. The Chiatze are a rich, proud nation. We pride ourselves on our individuality and our culture. These Round-eyes are the true savages, and their evil soars far beyond our comprehension. How long before they turn their eyes to the Chiatze, bringing their wars, their diseases, their foulness to our homeland? A united Nadir nation would be a wall against their invasion.'

'They have never been united. They hate one another,' she said.

'The one who is coming, the man with violet eyes, he has the power to draw them together, to bind up the wounds of centuries.'

'Forgive my slow-wittedness, Grandfather, but I do not understand,' she said. 'If he is already coming – if it is written in the stars – why do you have to spend so much time studying, travelling and meeting with shamen? Will he not rise to power regardless of your efforts?'

He smiled and took her small hands into his own. 'Perhaps he will, Voni. Perhaps. A palm reader can tell you much about your life, past and present. But when he looks into the future he will say, "This hand shows what *should* be, and this hand shows what *could* be." He will never say "this hand shows what *will* be." I have some small talent as an astrologer. I know the man with violet eyes is out there somewhere. But I also know what dangers await him. It is not enough that he has the courage, the power, the charisma. Great will be the forces ranged against him. He exists, Zhusai. One special man among the multitude. He *should* rise to rule. He *could* change the world. But *will* he? Or will the enemy find him first, or a disease strike him down? I cannot sit and wait. My studies tell me that somehow I will prove to be the catalyst in the coming drama, the breath of wind that births the storm.'

And so they had continued their travels and their studies, seeking always the man with the violet eyes.

Then had come the day when the vile little shaman, Nosta Khan, had arrived at their home in Gulgothir. Zhusai had disliked him from the first; there was about him an almost palpable sense of evil and malice. He and her grandfather had been closeted together for several hours, and only when he had gone did Chorin-Tsu reveal the full horror of what was to be. So great was the shock that all Chiatze training fled from her, and she spoke bluntly.

'You wish me to marry a savage, Grandfather? To live in filth and squalor among a people who value women less than they value their goats? How could you do this?'

Chorin-Tsu had ignored the breach of manners, though Zhusai could see he was stung – and disappointed by her outburst. 'The savage – as you call him – is a special man. Nosta Khan has walked the Mist. I have studied the charts, and cast the runes. There is no doubt; you are vital to this quest. Without you the days of the Uniter will pass us by.'

'This is your dream – not mine! How could you do this to me?'

'Please control yourself, grand-daughter. This unseemly display is extremely disheartening. The situation is not of my making. Let me also say this, Zhusai: I have cast your charts many times, and always they have shown you are destined to marry a great man. You know this to be true. Well, that man is the Uniter. I know this without any shade of doubt.'

Under the moon and stars, Zhusai gazed down at Talisman. 'Why could it not have been you?' she whispered.

His dark eyes opened. 'Did you speak?'

She shivered. 'No. I am sorry to have disturbed you.'

He rolled to his elbow, and saw that the fire was still burning. Then he lay down and slept once more.

When she awoke she found that Talisman's blanket, as well as her own, was laid across her. Sitting up, she saw the Nadir sitting cross-legged on the rocks some distance away, his back to her. Pushing the blankets aside, she rose. The sun was clearing the peaks, and already the temperature was rising. Zhusai stretched, then made her way to where Talisman sat. His eyes were closed, his arms folded to his chest, palms flat and thumbs interlinked.

Zhusai's grandfather often adopted this position when meditating, usually when he was trying to solve a problem. Silently Zhusai sat opposite the warrior.

'Where are you now, Talisman?' she wondered. 'Where does your restless spirit fly?'

He was a small boy who had never seen a city. His young life had been spent on the steppes, running and playing among the tents of his father's people. At the age of five he had learned to tend the goats, and to make cheese from their milk, to stretch and scrape the skins of the slaughtered animals. At seven, he could ride a small pony and shoot a bow. But at twelve he was taken from his father by men in bright armour who journeyed far beyond the steppes, all the way to a stone city by the sea.

It had been the first real shock of Talisman's life. His father, the strongest and bravest of Nadir chieftains, had sat by in silence as the round-eyed men in armour came. This man who had fought in a hundred battles had said not a word, he had not even looked his son in the eye. Only Nosta Khan had approached him, laying his scrawny hand on Talisman's shoulder. 'You must go with them, Okai. The safety of the tribe depends upon it.'

'Why? We are Wolfshead, stronger than all.'

'Because your father orders it.'

They had lifted Okai to the back of a tall horse, and the long journey began. Not all Nadir children were fully taught the tongue of the Round-eye, but Talisman had a good ear for language and Nosta Khan had spent many months teaching him the subtleties. Thus it was that he could understand the shining soldiers. They made jokes about the children they were gathering, referring to them as dung-puppies. Other than this, they were not unkind to their prisoners. Twenty-four days they travelled, until at last they came to a place of nightmare which the Nadir children gazed upon with awe and terror. Everything was stone, covering the earth, rearing up to challenge the sky; huge walls and high houses, narrow lanes, and a mass of humanity continually writhing like a giant snake through its marketplaces, streets, alleys and avenues.

Seventeen Nadir youngsters, all the sons of chieftains, were brought to the city of Bodacas in that late summer. Talisman-Okai remembered the ride through the city streets, children pointing at the Nadir, then baying and screeching and making gestures with their fingers. Adults too stood and watched, their faces grim. The cavalcade came to a stop at a walled structure on the outskirts of the city, where the double gates of bronze and iron were dragged open. For Okai it was like riding into the mouth of a great dark beast, and fear rose as bile in his throat.

Beyond the gates was a flat, paved training area, and Okai watched as young men and older boys practised with sword and shield, spear and bow. They were dressed identically in crimson tunics, dark breeches and knee-length boots of shining brown leather. All exercise ceased as the Nadir youngsters rode in with their escort.

A young man with blond hair stepped forward, his training sword still in his hand. 'I see we are to be given proper targets for our arrows,' he said to his comrades, who laughed loudly.

The Nadir were ordered to dismount, then led into a six-storey building and up a seemingly interminable winding stair to the fifth level. Here was a long, claustrophobic corridor leading to a large room in which, behind a desk of polished oak, sat a thick-set warrior with a forked beard. His eyes were bright blue, his mouth wide and full-lipped. A scar ran from the right side of his nose, curving down to his jawbone. His forearms too showed the scars of close combat. He stood as they entered.

'Get in two lines,' he ordered them, his voice deep and cold. The youngsters shuffled into place. Okai, being one of the smallest, was in the front line. 'You are here as janizaries. You do not understand what that means but I will tell you. The King – may he live for ever – has conceived a brilliant plan to halt Nadir raids, both now and in the future. You are here as hostages so that your fathers will behave. More than that, however, you will learn during your years with us how to be civilized, what constitutes good manners and correct behaviour. You will learn to read, to debate, to think. You will study poetry and literature, mathematics and cartography. You will also be taught the arts of war, the nature of strategy, logistics and command. In short you are to become cadets, and then officers in the great Gothir army.' Glancing up, he addressed the two officers who had led the boys into the room. 'You may go now and bathe the dust of travel from your bodies. I have a few more words to say to these . . . cadets.'

As the officers departed and the door clicked shut, the warrior moved to stand directly before the boys, towering over Okai. 'What you have just heard, you dung-eating monkeys, is the *official* welcome to Bodacas Academy. My name is Gargan, the Lord of Larness, and most of the scars I carry come from battles with your miserable race. I have been killing Nadir scum for most of my life. You cannot be taught, for you are not human; it would be like trying to teach dogs to play the flute. This foolishness springs from the addled mind of a senile old man, but when he dies this stupidity will die with him. Until that blessed day work hard, for the lash awaits the tardy and the stupid. Now get downstairs where a cadet awaits you. He will take you to the quartermaster who will supply you with tunics and boots.'

Talisman was jerked back to the present as he heard Zhusai move behind him. He opened his eyes, and smiled. 'We must move with care today. This area is, your grandfather tells me, controlled by a Notas group called Chop-backs. I wish to avoid them if I can.'

'Do you know why they are called Chop-backs?' she asked him.

'I doubt that it is connected with the study of philanthropy,' he said, moving past her to the ponies.

'The study of philanthropy?' echoed Zhusai. 'What kind of a Nadir are you?'

'I am the dog who played the flute,' he told her, as he tightened the cinch of his saddle and vaulted to the pony's back.

They rode through most of the morning, halting at noon in a gully to rest the horses and eat a meal of cold meat and cheese. No riders had been seen, but Talisman had spotted fresh tracks, and once they had come across horse-droppings that were still moist. 'Three warriors,' said Talisman. 'They are ahead of us.'

'That is most disconcerting. Is it not possible that they are merely travellers?'

'Possible – but not likely. They are not carrying supplies, and they are making no effort to disguise their tracks. We will avoid them if we can.'

'I have two throwing-knives – one in each boot, Lord,' she said, bowing her head. 'I am skilled with them. Though, of course,' she added hurriedly, 'I have no doubt that a warrior such as yourself can easily kill three Notas.'

Talisman absorbed the information. 'I shall think on what you have said, but I hope there will be no need for bloodshed. I will try to talk my way through them. I have no wish to kill any Nadir.'

Zhusai bowed again. 'I am sure, Lord, you will devise a suitable plan.'

Talisman pulled the cork from the water canteen and took a

sip, swishing the warm liquid around his mouth. According to Chorin-Tsu's map, the closest water was half a day to the east; that was where he intended to camp, though it occurred to him that the Notas were probably thinking along similar lines. He passed the canteen to Zhusai and waited while she drank. Then he took the canteen to the hobbled ponies and, wetting a cloth, cleaned the dust and sand from their nostrils. Returning to Zhusai, he squatted down before her. 'I accept your offer,' he said. 'But let us be clear: you will use your knife only upon my explicit command. You are right-handed?' She nodded. 'Then your target will be the furthest man to your left. If we meet the Notas you must draw your knife surreptitiously. Listen for the command. It will be when I say your name.'

'I understand, Lord.'

'There is one other matter we must settle. Chiatze politeness is legendary, and well suited to a world of silk-covered seats, vast libraries and a ten-thousand-year civilization. Not so here. Put from your mind thoughts of guardian and ward. We have just established our battle plan, and are now two warriors travelling together in a hostile land. From now on it would please me to have you speak less formally.'

'You do not wish me to call you Lord?'

Talisman looked into her eyes and felt his mouth go dry. 'Save that honorific for your husband, Zhusai. You may call me Talisman.'

'As you command, so be it . . . Talisman.'

The afternoon sun beat down upon the steppes, and the ponies plodded on, heads down, towards the distant mountains. Although the land looked flat and empty, Talisman knew there were many hidden gullies and depressions and the three Notas could be in any one of a hundred different hiding places. Narrowing his eyes, Talisman scanned the shimmering heat-scorched landscape. There was nothing to be seen. Loosening his sabre, he rode on.

Gorkai was a killer and a thief. Usually – but not exclusively – in that order. The sun beat down upon him, but not a bead of sweat shone on his flat, ugly face. The two men with him both wore wide-brimmed straw hats, protecting head and neck from the merciless heat, but Gorkai gave no thought to the heat as he waited for yet another victim. Once he had aspired to be more than a thief. He had longed to possess his own goat herd, and a string of fine ponies sired from the hardy stallions of the north passes. Gorkai had dreamt of the day when he could afford a second wife, even though he had not yet won his first. And further to this, on those evenings when his imagination took flight, he saw himself invited to sit among the Elders. All of his dreams were like remembered smoke now, merely an acrid aftertaste upon the memory.

Now he was Notas – no tribe.

As he sat in the blazing sunshine, staring out over the steppes, he had no dreams. Back at the camp the nose-slit whore who waited for him would expect some pretty bauble before bestowing upon him her favours.

'You think they turned off the trail?' asked Baski, crouching alongside him. The horses were hobbled in the gully below, and the two men were part hidden behind the overlapping branches of several *sihjis* bushes. Gorkai glanced at the stocky warrior beside him.

'No. They are riding slowly, conserving the strength of their ponies.'

'We attack when he comes into view?'

'You think he will be easy to take?' countered Gorkai.

Baski cleared his throat and spat, then he shrugged. 'He is one man. We are three.'

'Three? You would be wise not to consider Djung in your estimate.'

'Djung has killed before,' said Baski. 'I have seen it.'

Gorkai shook his head. 'He is a *killer*, yes. But we are facing a *fighter*.'

'We have not seen him yet. How do you know this, Gorkai?'

The older man sat back on his haunches. 'A man does not have to know birds to see that the hawk is a hunter, the pigeon his prey. You understand? The sharpness of the talons, the wicked curve of the beak, the power and speed of the wings. So it is with men. This one is careful, and wary, avoiding areas of ambush, which shows he is skilled in the ways of the raid. Also he knows he is in hostile territory, yet he rides anyway. This tells us he has courage and confidence. There is no hurry, Baski. First we observe, then we kill.'

'I bow to your wisdom, Gorkai.'

A sound came from behind and Gorkai twisted round to see Djung scrambling up the slope. 'Slowly!' hissed Gorkai, 'you are making dust!'

90

Djung's fat face adopted a sulky expression. 'It cannot be seen from any distance,' he said. 'You worry like an old woman.'

Gorkai turned away from the younger man. There was no need for further conversation. Djung had a gift for stupidity, an almost mystic ability to withstand any form of logic.

There was still no sign of the riders and Gorkai allowed his mind to relax. Once he had been considered a *coming man*, a voice for the future. Those days were far behind now, trodden into the dust of his past. When he was first banished he had believed himself unlucky, but now, with the near-useless gift of hindsight, he knew this was not so. He had been impatient, and had sought to rise too far, too fast. The arrogance of youth. Too clever to recognize its own stupidity.

He was just seventeen when he took part in the raid on the Wolfshead tribe, and it was Gorkai who captured thirty of their ponies. Suddenly rich, he had learned to swagger. At the time it seemed that the Gods of Stone and Water had smiled upon him. Looking back he saw that it was a gift laced with poison. Capturing two ponies would have helped him find a wife; ten would have gained him a place among the elite. But thirty was too many for a young man and the more he swaggered, the more he became disliked. This was hard for a young man to understand. At the midsummer gathering he made an offer for Li-shi, the daughter of Lon-tsen. Five ponies! No-one had ever offered five ponies for a virgin.

And he was rejected! The flush of remembered shame stained his cheeks even now. Before all he was humiliated, for Lon-tsen gave his daughter to a warrior who offered only one pony and seven blankets.

Angry beyond reason, Gorkai had nursed his humiliation, fanning it into a hatred so strong that when the plan came to him he saw it as a blindingly brilliant scheme to restore his shattered pride. He had abducted Li-shi, raped her, then returned her to her father. 'Now see who desires Gorkai's leavings,' he told the old man. Nadir custom was such that no other man would marry her. Nadir law decreed that her father would either have to give her to Gorkai, or kill her for bringing shame to her family.

They had come for him in the night, and dragged him before the Council. Once there he witnessed the execution of the girl, strangled by her own father, and heard the words of banishment spoken by the Elders.

Despite all the killing since, he still remembered the girl's death with genuine regret. Li-shi had not struggled at all, but had turned her eyes upon Gorkai and watched him until the light fled from her and her jaw fell slack. Guilt remained with him. A stone in the heart.

'There they are,' whispered Baski. Gorkai forced the memories away and narrowed his eyes. Still some distance away, the man was riding just ahead of the woman. This was the closest they had been. Gorkai narrowed his eyes and studied the man. A bow and quiver were looped over his saddle-horn, and a cavalry sabre was scabbarded at his waist. The man drew rein some sixty paces from Gorkai. He was young, and this surprised Gorkai; judging by the skill he had shown so far, the Notas leader had expected him to be a seasoned warrior in his thirties.

The woman rode alongside the man and Gorkai's jaw dropped. She was exquisitely beautiful, raven-haired and slender. But what shook him was the resemblance to the girl he had once loved. Surely the gods were giving him a chance to find happiness at last? The sound of rasping steel broke the silence and Gorkai swung an angry glance at Djung, who had drawn his sword.

Out on the steppes the rider swung his mount, cutting to the left. Together he and the woman galloped away.

'Idiot!' said Gorkai.

'There are three of us. Let's ride them down,' urged Baski.

'No need. The only water within forty miles is at Kall's Pool. We will find them.'

Talisman was sitting back from the fire when the three riders rode in to the camp he had prepared some two hundred yards from Kall's Pool. It was yet another rock tank, fed in part by deep wells below the strata. Slender trees grew by the poolside, and brightly coloured flowers clung to life on the soft mud of the water's edge. Zhusai had wanted to camp by the water, but Talisman had refused, and they had built their fire against a rock wall in sight of the water. The girl was asleep by the dying fire as the riders made their entrance, but Talisman was wide awake with his sabre drawn and resting on the ground before him. By his side was his hunting-bow, three arrows drawn from the quiver and plunged into the earth.

The riders paused, observing him as he observed them. In the centre was a thickset warrior, his hair close-cropped, a widow's peak extending like an arrowhead over his brow. To his right was a shorter, slimmer rider with burning eyes, and to his left was a fat-faced man wearing a fur-rimmed iron helm.

The riders waited but Talisman made no move, nor did he speak. At last the lead rider dismounted. 'A lonely place,' he said softly. Zhusai woke and sat up.

'All places are desolate to a lonely man,' said Talisman.

'What does that mean?' asked the warrior, beckoning his comrades to join him.

'Where in all the Land of Stone and Water can a Notas feel welcome?'

'You are not very friendly,' said the man, taking a step forward. The other two moved sideways, hands on their sword-hilts.

Talisman rose, leaving the sabre by his feet, his hands hanging loosely by his sides. The moon was bright above the group. Zhusai made to rise, but Talisman spoke to her. 'Remain where you are . . . Zhusai,' he said. 'All will be well in a little while.'

'You seem very sure of that,' said the widow-peaked leader. 'And yet you are in a strange land, and not among friends.'

'The land is not strange to me,' Talisman told him. 'It is Nadir land, ruled by the Gods of Stone and Water. I am a Nadir, and this land is mine by right and by blood. You are the strangers here. Can you not feel your deaths in the air, in the breeze? Can you not feel the contempt that this land has for you? Notas! The name stinks like a three-day dead pig.'

The leader reddened. 'You think we chose the title, you arrogant bastard? You think we wanted to live this way?'

'Why are you talking to him?' snarled the fat-faced warrior. 'Let's be done with him!' The man's sword snaked from its leather scabbard and he ran forward. Talisman's right hand came up and back, the knife-blade slashing through the air to hammer home into the man's right eye, sinking in to the ivory hilt. The warrior ran on for two more paces, then pitched to his left, striking the ground face first. As the second warrior leapt forward, Zhusai's knife thudded into the side of his neck. Blood bubbled into his windpipe. Choking, he let go of his sword and tore the knife clear, staring down at the slender blade in shock and disbelief. Sinking to his knees he tried to speak, but blood burst from his mouth in a crimson spray. Talisman's foot flipped the sabre into the air and he caught it expertly.

'Your dead friend asked you a question,' he told the stunned leader. 'But I would like to hear the answer. Why *are* you talking to me?'

The man blinked, and then suddenly sat down by the fire. 'You are right,' he said. 'I can feel the contempt. And I am alone. It was not always thus. I made a mistake, born of pride and foolishness and I have paid for it these last twenty years. There is no end in sight.'

'What tribe were you?' asked Talisman.

'Northern Grey.'

Talisman walked to the fire and sat opposite the man. 'My name is Talisman and I live to serve the Uniter. His day is almost upon us. If you wish to be Nadir again, then follow me.'

The man smiled and shook his head. 'The Uniter? The hero with violet eyes? You believe he exists? And if he did, why would he take me?'

'He will take you – if you are with me.'

'You know where he is?'

'I know what will bring us to him. Will you follow me?'

'What tribe are you?'

'Wolfshead. As you will be.'

The man stared gloomily into the fire. 'All my troubles began with the Wolfshead. Perhaps they will end there.' Glancing up, he met Talisman's dark gaze. 'I will follow you. What blood oath do you require?'

'None,' said Talisman. 'As you have said it, so shall it be. What is your name?'

'Gorkai.'

'Then keep watch, Gorkai, for I am tired.'

So saying Talisman laid down his sabre, covered himself with a blanket and slept.

Zhusai sat quietly as Talisman stretched himself out, his head resting on his forearm; his breathing deepened. Zhusai could scarcely believe he would do such a thing! Nervously she glanced at Gorkai, reading the confusion in the man's expression. Moments before, this man and two others had ridden in to the camp to kill them. Now two were dead, and the third was sitting quietly by the fire. Gorkai rose and Zhusai flinched. But the Nadir warrior merely walked to the first of the corpses, dragging it away from the camp; he repeated the action with the second body. Returning, he squatted before Zhusai and extended his hand. She glanced down to see that he was holding her ivory-handled throwing-knife. Silently she took it. Gorkai stood and gathered firewood before settling down beside the fire. Zhusai felt no need of sleep, convinced that the moment she shut her eyes this killer would cut Talisman's throat, then abuse and murder her.

The night wore on, but Gorkai made no movement towards her or the sleeping Talisman. Instead he sat cross-legged, deep in thought. Talisman groaned in his sleep, and spoke suddenly in the tongue of the Gothir. 'Never!' he said.

Gorkai glanced at the woman, and their eyes met. Zhusai did not look away. Rising, Gorkai gestured her to walk with him. He did not look back but strode to the ponies and sat upon a rock. For a while Zhusai made no move to follow, then, knife in hand, she followed him.

'Tell me of him,' said Gorkai.

'I know very little.'

'I have watched you both. You do not touch; there is no intimacy.'

'He is not my husband,' she said coldly.

'Where is he from? Who is he?'

'He is Talisman of the Wolfshead.'

'Talisman is not a Nadir name. I have given him my life, for he touched upon my dreams and my needs. But I need to know.'

'Believe me, Gorkai, you know almost as much as I. But he is strong, and he dreams great dreams.'

'Where do we travel?'

'To the Valley of Shul-sen's Tears, and the tomb of Oshikai.'

'Ah,' said Gorkai, 'a pilgrimage, then. So be it.' He rose and took a deep breath. 'I too have dreams – though I had all but forgotten them.' He hesitated, then spoke again. 'Do not fear me, Zhusai. I will never harm you.' Gorkai walked back to the fire and sat.

Zhusai returned to her blanket.

The dawn sun was hidden by a thick bank of cloud. Zhusai awoke with a start. She had been determined not to sleep, but at some point in the night had drifted into dreams. Talisman was up and talking to Gorkai. Zhusai opened their pack and re-kindled the fire, preparing a breakfast of salted oats and dried meat. The two men ate in silence, then Gorkai gathered the wooden platters and cleaned them in the pool. It was the work of a woman or a servant, and Zhusai knew it was Gorkai's way of establishing his place with them. Zhusai placed the platters within the canvas pack and tied it behind her saddle. Gorkai helped her mount, then handed her the reins of the other two ponies.

Talisman led the way out on to the steppes, Gorkai riding beside him. 'How many Notas raid in this area?' Talisman asked.

'Thirty,' answered Gorkai. 'We . . . they call themselves Chop-backs.'

'So I have heard. Have you been to Oshikai's tomb?'

'Three times.'

'Tell me of it.'

'It is a simply carved sarcophagus set in a building of white stone. Once it was a Gothir fort, now it is a holy place.'

'Who will be guarding it now?'

Gorkai shrugged. 'Hard to say. There are always warriors from at least four tribes camped close by. A blind priest sends messages to each, telling them when they may take up their duties. He also tells them when to return to their own lands, and at such times other tribes send warriors. It is a great honour to be chosen to guard the resting place of Oshikai. The last time I was there the Green Monkey tribe patrolled the tomb. Waiting were the Northern Greys, the Stone Tigers, and the Fast Ponies.'

'How many in each group?'

'No more than forty.'

The clouds began to break, and the burning sun shone clear. Zhusai lifted a wide-brimmed straw hat from the pommel of her saddle and tied it into place. The shifting dust dried her throat, but she resisted the urge to drink.

And the trio rode on through the long day.

Chapter Five

The riots lasted three days, beginning in the poorest section and spreading fast. Troops were called in from surrounding areas, cavalry charging into the rioters. The death toll rose, and by the end of the third day some four hundred people were reported killed, and hundreds more injured.

The Games were suspended during the troubles, the athletes advised to remain in their quarters, the surrounding area patrolled by soldiers. As darkness fell Druss stared gloomily from the upstairs window, watching the flames leap from the burning buildings of the western quarter.

'Madness,' he said as Sieben moved alongside him.

'Majon was telling me they caught the crossbow man and hacked him to pieces.'

'And yet the killing still goes on. Why, Sieben?'

'You said it yourself: madness. Madness and greed. Almost everyone had money on Klay, and they feel betrayed. Three of the gambling houses have been burned to the ground.' Outside a troop of cavalry cantered along the wide avenue, heading for the riot area.

'What is the news of Klay?' asked Druss.

'There is no word, but Majon told me he has many friends among the physicians. And Klay is a rich man, Druss; he can afford the best.'

'I would have died,' said Druss softly. 'A knife was flashing towards my eye. In that moment I could do nothing. His hand moved like lightning, poet. I have never seen anything like it. He plucked the blade from the air.' Druss shook his head. 'I still do not believe it. Yet moments later a coward's bolt had smashed him to the ground. He'll not walk again, Sieben.'

'You can't say that, old horse. You are no surgeon.'

'I know his spine was smashed. I have seen that injury a score of times. There's no coming back from it. Not without . . .' He fell silent.

'Without what?'

Druss moved away from the window. 'A Nadir shaman came to me – just before the fight. He told me of magical gems to heal any wound.'

'Did he also try to sell you a map to a legendary diamond mine?' asked Sieben, with a smile.

'I'm going out,' said Druss. 'I need to see Klay.'

'Out? Into that chaos? Come on, Druss, wait till morning.'

Druss shook his head.

'Then take a weapon,' Sieben urged. 'The rioters are still looking for blood.'

'Then they had better stay away from me,' snarled Druss, 'or I'll spill enough of it to drown them all!'

The grounds were deserted and the gates open. Druss paused and stared at the broken statue lying on the lawn. It looked as if the legs had been shattered by hammers. The neck was sheared away, the head lying on the grass, its stone eyes staring unseeing at the black-bearded warrior standing in the gateway.

Druss gazed around him. The flower-beds had been uprooted, the lawn churned into mud around the statue. He strode to the front door, which was open. No servants greeted him as he moved through to the training area. There was no sound. The sand circles were empty of fighters, the fountains silent. An old man came in sight, carrying a bucket of water; he was the servant who had looked after the beggar boy. 'Where is everyone?' asked Druss.

'Gone. All gone.'

'What of Klay?'

'They moved him to a hospice in the southern quarter. The scum-sucking bastards!'

Druss wandered back into the main building. Couches and chairs had been smashed, the curtains ripped down from the windows. A portrait of Klay had been slashed through, and the place smelt of stale urine. Druss shook his head in puzzlement. 'Why would the rioters do this? I thought they loved the man.'

The old man set down the bucket, righted a chair and slumped down. 'Oh aye, they loved him, until his back broke. Then they hated him. People had wagered their life savings on him. They heard he was involved in a drunken brawl and that all bets were dead. Their money gone, they turned on him. Turned on him like animals! After all he'd won for them – done for them. You know,' he said, glancing up, his ancient face flushed with anger, 'the hospice they carried him to was built from money donated by Klay. Many of the people who came here and screamed abuse had been helped by him in the past. No gratitude. But the worst of them was Shonan.'

'Klay's trainer?'

'Pah!' spat the old man. 'Trainer, handler, owner? Call him what you will, but I call him a blood-sucking parasite. Klay's gone now – and so has his wealth. Shonan even says that this house belongs to him. Klay, it seems, had nothing. Can you believe that? The bastard didn't even pay for the carriage that took Klay to the hospice. He will die there penniless.' The old man laughed bitterly. 'One moment he was the hero of the Gothir – loved by all, flattered by all. Now he is poor, alone and friendless. By the gods, it makes you think, doesn't it?'

'He has you,' said Druss. 'And he has me.'

'You? You're the Drenai fighter, you hardly knew him.'

'I *know* him and that is enough. Can you take me to him?'

'Aye, and gladly. I'm finished here now. I'll gather my gear and meet you at the front of the house.'

Druss strolled through to the front lawn. A group of about a dozen athletes were coming through the gate and the sound of laughter pricked Druss's anger. At the centre of the group was a bald-headed man wearing a gold torque studded with gems. They stopped by the statue and Druss heard a young man say, 'By Shemak, that monstrosity cost over 3,000 raq. Now it is just rubble.'

'What's past is past,' said Gold Torque.

'So what will you do now, Shonan?' asked another.

The man shrugged. 'Find another fighter. It will be hard, mind, for Klay was gifted. No doubt about that.'

The old man moved alongside Druss. 'Doesn't their grief move you to tears? Klay supported them all. See the young blond one? Klay paid off his gambling debts no more than a week ago. Just over a thousand raq. And this is the way they thank him!'

'Aye, they're a shoddy bunch,' said Druss. Striding across the lawn, he approached Shonan.

The man grinned at Druss. 'How fall the mighty,' he said, pointing to the statue.

'And the not so mighty,' said Druss, his fist thundering into the man's face and catapulting him from his feet. Several of the athletes surged forward but Druss glared at them – and they stopped in their tracks. Slowly they backed away and Druss moved to the fallen Shonan. Both the man's front teeth had been smashed through his lips, and his jaw was hanging slack. Druss ripped the gold torque from his neck and tossed it to the old man. 'This might pay a bill or two at the hospice,' he said.

'It will that,' agreed the old man. The athletes were still standing close by. Druss pointed to the young man with long blond hair.

'You, come here.' The man blinked nervously, but then stepped forward.

'When this piece of offal wakes, you tell him that Druss is going to find him again. You tell him that I expect Klay to be looked after. I expect him to be back in his own house, with his own servants, and with money enough to pay them. If this is not done I will come back and kill him. And after that I will find you, and I will rip your pretty face from your skull. You understand me?' The young man nodded and Druss swung to the others. 'I have marked all you maggots in my mind. If I find that Klay wants for anything I shall come looking for each of you. Make no mistake: if Klay suffers one more ounce of indignity you will all die. I am Druss and that is my promise.'

Druss walked away from them, the old man alongside him. 'My name is Carmol,' said the servant, with a broad grin. 'And it is a pleasure to meet you again!'

Together they walked across the riot-torn city. Here and there bodies could be seen lying by the wayside, and the smell of burning buildings wafted to them on the wind.

The hospice was sited in the centre of the poorest quarter, its white walls out of place among the squalid buildings that surrounded it. The riots had begun near here, but moved on days since. An elderly priest showed them to Klay's room, which was small and clean with a single cot bed placed beneath the window. Klay was asleep when they entered and the priest brought two chairs for the visitors. The fighter awoke as Druss sat beside the bed.

'How are you feeling?' asked the Drenai.

'I've known better days,' answered Klay, forcing a smile. His face was grey beneath his tan, his eyes sunken and blue-ringed.

Druss took hold of the fighter's hand. 'A Nadir shaman told me of a place to the east where there are magical jewels to heal any wound. I leave tomorrow. If they exist, I shall find them and bring them to you. You understand?'

'Yes,' said Klay, despair in his voice. 'Magical jewels to heal me!'

'Do not give up hope,' said Druss.

'Hope is not on offer here, my friend. This is a hospice and we come here to die. Throughout this building there are people waiting for death, some with cancers, others with lung rot, still more with wasting diseases for which there are no names. There are wives, husbands, children. If such jewels exist, there are other more deserving cases than mine. But I thank you for your words.'

'They are not just words, Klay. I am leaving tomorrow. Promise me you will fight for life until my return.'

'I always fight, Druss. That's my talent. The east, you say? That is Nadir heartland, filled with robbers and thieves, and deadly killers. You wouldn't want to meet them.'

Druss chuckled. 'Trust me, laddie. They wouldn't want to meet me!'

Garen-Tsen stared down at the body of the embalmer – his face twisted in death, frozen in mid-scream, eyes wide and staring. Blood had ceased to flow from the many wounds, and the broken fingers twitched no longer.

'He was a tough one,' said the torturer.

Garen-Tsen ignored the man. The information gleaned from the embalmer had been far from complete; he had held something back to the end. Garen-Tsen stared at the dead face. You knew exactly where they were, he thought. Through his years of study Chorin-Tsu had finally pieced together the route taken by the renegade shaman who had originally stolen the Eyes of Alchazzar. The man had ultimately been found hiding in the Mountains of the Moon, and he was slain there. Of the Eyes there was no sign. He could have hidden them anywhere, but a number of incidents suggested they were concealed in – or near – the tomb of Oshikai Demon-bane. Miraculous healings were said to have taken place there: several blind men regained their sight; a cripple walked. In themselves these *miracles* meant nothing.

Tombs of heroes or prophets always attracted such claims, and being Chiatze Garen-Tsen well understood the nature of hysterical paralysis or blindness. Even so, it was the only indication as to the whereabouts of the jewels. The problem remained, however, that the tomb had been surreptitiously searched on at least three occasions. No hidden jewels had been found.

'Dispose of it,' Garen-Tsen ordered the torturer and the man nodded. The University paid five gold coins for every fresh corpse – though this one was in such a wretched state he would probably receive only three.

The Chiatze minister lifted the hem of his long velvet robe and walked from the chamber. Am I clutching at leaves in the wind? he wondered. Can I send troops to Shul-sen's Valley with any surety of success?

Back in his own rooms, he emptied his mind of the problem and pored over the reports of the day. A secret meeting at the home of the Senator Borvan, an overheard criticism of the God-King in a tavern on Eel Street, a scuffle at the home of the fighter Klay. The name Druss caught his eye, and he remembered the awesome Drenai fighter. He read on, skimming through the reports and making notes. Druss's name figured once more; he had visited Klay in the hospice that morning. Garen-Tsen blinked as he read the small script. *The subject made reference to healing jewels, which he would fetch for the fighter . . .*' Picking up a small silver bell, Garen-Tsen rang it twice. A servant entered and bowed.

An hour later the informant was standing nervously before Garen-Tsen's desk. 'Tell me all that you heard. Every word. Leave nothing out,' ordered Garen-Tsen. The man did so. Dismissing him the Chiatze walked to the window, staring out over the towers and rooftops. A Nadir shaman had told Druss of the jewels, and he was heading east. The Valley of Shul-sen's Tears was in the east. Chorin-Tsu's daughter was riding east with the Nadir warrior Talisman.

He rang the bell once more.

'Go to Lord Larness,' he told the servant, 'and say that I must meet with him today. Also have a warrant drawn up for the arrest of the Drenai fighter, Druss.'

'Yes, Lord. What accusation should be logged against him?'

'Assault on a Gothir citizen, leading to the man's death.'

The servant looked puzzled. 'But, Lord, Shonan is not dead; he merely lost some teeth.' Garen-Tsen's hooded eyes fastened to the man's face and the servant reddened. 'I will see to it, Lord. Forgive me.'

The haggle had reached the crucial point, and Sieben the Poet steeled himself for the kill. The horse-dealer had moved from politeness to polite disinterest, to irritation, and now he was displaying an impressively feigned anger. 'This probably just looks like a horse to you,' said the dealer, patting the beast's steel-dust flanks, 'but to me Ganael is a member of my family. We love this horse. His sire was a champion, and his dam had the speed of the east wind. He is brave and loyal. And you insult me by offering the price normally paid for a sway-backed nag?'

Sieben adopted a serious expression, and held to the man's grey-eyed gaze. 'I do not disagree with your description of this . . . gelding. And were it five years younger I might be tempted to part with a little more silver. But the horse is worth no more than I have offered.'

'Then our business is concluded,' snapped the dealer. 'There are many noblemen in Gulgothir who would pay twice what I am asking of you. And I only offer you this special price because I like you, and I feel that Ganael likes you too.'

Sieben glanced up at the steel-dust and looked into the gelding's eye. 'He has a mean look,' he said.

'Spirited,' said the dealer swiftly. 'Like me, he doesn't suffer fools gladly. But he is fearless and strong. You are riding into the steppes. By Heaven, man, you will need a horse with the power to outrun those Nadir hill ponies.'

'Thirty pieces is too much. Ganael may be strong, but he is also verging on the old.'

'Nonsense. He is no more than nine . . .' As the dealer spoke Sieben raised a quizzical eyebrow. '. . . well, perhaps nearer ten or eleven. Even so, he has years of service left in him. His legs are strong, and there is no weakness in the hoof. And I'll re-shoe him for the steppes. How does that sound?'

'It would sound very fine – at twenty-two pieces of silver.'

'Gods, man, have you come here merely to insult me? Did you wake this morning and think, "I'll spend the day bringing an honest Gothir businessman to the threshold of heart failure?" Twenty-seven.'

'Twenty-five – and you can throw in the old mare in the furthest stall, and two saddles.'

The dealer swung round. 'The mare? Throw in? Are you trying

103

to bankrupt me? That mare is of the finest pedigree. She . . .'

' . . . is a member of the family,' put in Sieben with a wry smile. 'I can see she is strong, but more importantly she is old and steady. My friend is no rider and I think she will suit him. You will have no buyers for her – save for prison meat or glue. The price for those mounts is one half-silver.'

The dealer's thin face relaxed and he pulled at his pointed beard. 'I do happen to have two old saddles – beautiful work-manship, equipped with bags and canteens. But I couldn't let them go for less than a full silver each. Twenty-seven, and we will grip hands upon it. It is too hot to haggle further.'

'Done,' agreed Sieben. 'But I want both horses re-shod and brought to me in three hours.' From his pouch he took two silver pieces and passed them to the man. 'Full payment will be upon receipt,' he said.

After giving the dealer the address, Sieben strolled out into the marketplace beyond. It was near deserted, mute testimony to the riots that had taken place here last night. A young whore approached him, stepping from the doorway of a smoke-blackened building. 'Do you seek delight, Lord?' she asked him. Sieben gazed down; her face was young and pretty, but her eyes were world-weary and empty.

'How much?'

'For a nobleman like you, Lord, a mere quarter-silver. Unless you need a bed, and that will be a half.'

'And for this you will delight me?'

'I will give you hours of pleasure,' she promised. Sieben took her hand and saw that her fingers were clean, as was the cheap dress she wore.

'Show me,' he said.

Two hours later he wandered back into the House of Lodging. Majon was sitting by the far window, composing a speech he was to make at the Royal Funeral tomorrow. He glanced up as Sieben entered, and laid aside his quill. 'We must talk,' he said, beckon-ing Sieben to join him.

The poet was tired, and already regretting his decision to join Druss on his journey. He sat on a padded couch and poured him-self a goblet of watered wine. 'Let us make this swift, ambassador, for I need an hour's sleep before I ride.'

'Yes, the ride. This is not seemly, poet. The Queen's funeral is tomorrow and Druss is an honoured guest. To ride out now is an insult of the worst kind. Especially following the riots – which began over Druss, after all. Could you not wait for a few days at least?'

Sieben shook his head. 'I am afraid we are dealing here with something you don't understand, ambassador. Druss sees this as a debt of honour.'

'Do not seek to insult me, poet. I well understand the notion. But Druss did not ask for this man's help, and therefore is in no way responsible for his injury. He owes him nothing.'

'Amazing,' said Sieben. 'You prove my point exactly. I talk of honour and you speak of transactions. Listen to me . . . a man was crippled trying to help Druss. Now he is dying and we cannot wait any longer. The surgeon told Druss that Klay has perhaps a month to live. Therefore we are leaving now, as soon as the horses are delivered.'

'But it is all nonsense!' roared Majon. 'Magical jewels hidden in a Nadir valley! What sane man would even consider such . . . such a fanciful tale? I have been researching the area you plan to visit. There are many tribes raiding in those parts. No convoys passed through there – unless heavily guarded. There is one particular group of raiders known as Chop-backs. How do you like the sound of that? You know how they got their name? They smash the lower spines of their prisoners and leave them out on the steppes for the wolves to devour.'

Sieben drained his wine, and hoped his face had not shown the terror he felt. 'You have made your point, ambassador.'

'Why is he *really* doing this?'

'I have already told you. Druss owes the man a debt – and he would walk through fire to repay it.'

As Sieben rose, Majon also stood. 'Why are you going with him? He is not the brightest of men, and I can . . . just . . . understand his simplistic view of the world. But you? You have wit and rare intelligence. Can you not see the futility of this venture?'

'Yes,' admitted Sieben. 'And it saddens me that I can, for it merely highlights the terrible flaws of what you call intelligence.'

Back in his room, Sieben bathed and then stretched himself out on his bed. The delights the whore had promised had proved to be ephemeral and illusive. Just as all the delights of life Sieben had ever sampled. Lust followed by a gentle sorrow for all that had been missed. The ultimate experience, like the myth of the ultimate woman, was always ahead.

Why are you going with him?

Sieben loathed danger, and trembled at the thought of approaching fear. But Druss, for all his faults, lived life to the full, relishing every breath. Sieben had never been more alive than when he had accompanied Druss on his search for the kidnapped Rowena, in the storm when the *Thunderchild* had been hurled and tossed like a piece of driftwood, or in the battles and wars when death had seemed but a heartbeat distant.

They had returned in triumph to Drenan, and there Sieben had composed his epic poem, *Druss the Legend*. It was now the most widely performed saga in all the Drenai lands, and had been translated into a dozen languages. The fame had brought riches, the riches had bought women, and Sieben had fallen back with astonishing speed into a life of idle luxury. He sighed now and rose from the bed. Servants had laid out his clothes – leggings of pale blue wool, and soft thigh-length riding-boots of creamy beige. His puff-sleeved shirt was of blue silk, the wrists slashed to reveal grey silk inserts decorated with mother of pearl. A royal blue cape completed the ensemble, fastened at the neck with a delicate braided chain of gold. Once dressed, he stood before the full-length mirror and looped his baldric over his shoulder. From it hung four black sheaths, each housing an ivory-hilted throwing-knife.

Why are you going with him? It would be fine if he could say, 'Because he is my friend.' Sieben hoped there was at least a semblance of truth in that. The reality however was altogether different. 'I need to feel alive,' he said, aloud.

'I have purchased two mounts,' said Sieben, 'a fine thoroughbred for myself and a cart-horse for you. Since you ride with all the grace of a sack of carrots, I thought it would be fitting.'

Druss ignored the jibe. 'Where did you get the pretty knives?' he asked, pointing at the ornate leather baldric slung carelessly over Sieben's shoulder.

'Pretty? These are splendidly balanced weapons of death.' Sieben slid one from its sheath. The blade was diamond-shaped and razor-sharp. 'I practised with them before I bought them. I hit a moth at ten paces.'

'That could come in handy,' grunted Druss. 'Nadir moths can be ferocious, I'm told.'

'Ah, yes,' muttered Sieben, 'the old jokes are the best. But I should have seen that one staggering over the horizon.'

Druss carefully packed his saddle-bags with supplies of dried

106

meat, fruit, salt, and sugar. Fastening the straps, he dragged a blanket from the bed and rolled it tightly before tying it to the saddle-bags. 'Majon is not best pleased that we are leaving,' said Sieben. 'The Queen's interment is tomorrow, and he fears the King will take our departure at this juncture as an insult to his dearly departed.'

'Have you packed yet?' asked Druss, swinging the saddle-bag to his shoulder.

'I have a servant doing it,' said Sieben, 'even as we speak. I hate these bags, they crumple the silk. No shirt or tunic ever looks right when produced from one of these grotesqueries.'

Druss shook his head in exasperation. 'You're bringing silk shirts into the steppes? You think there will be many admirers of fashion among the Nadir?'

Sieben chuckled. 'When they see me, they'll think I'm a god!'

Striding to the far wall Druss gathered up his axe, Snaga. Sieben stared at the awesome weapon, with its glittering butterfly blades of shining silver steel, and its black haft fashioned with silver runes. 'I detest that thing,' he said, with feeling.

Leaving the bedroom, Druss walked out into the main lounge and through to the entrance hall. The ambassador Majon was talking to three soldiers of the Royal Guard, tall men in silver breastplates and black cloaks. 'Ah, Druss,' he said smoothly. 'These gentlemen would like you to accompany them to the Palace of Inquisition. There's obviously been a mistake, but there are questions they would like to ask you.'

'About what?'

Majon cleared his throat and nervously swept a hand over his neatly groomed silver hair. 'Apparently there was an altercation at the house of the fighter Klay, and someone named Shonan died as a result.'

Druss laid Snaga on the floor, and dropped the saddle-bags from his shoulder. 'Died? From a punch to the mouth? Pah! I don't believe it. He was alive when I left him.'

'You will come with us,' said a guard, stepping forward.

'Best that you agree, Druss,' said Majon soothingly. 'I am sure we can . . .'

'Enough talk, Drenai,' said the guard. 'This man is wanted for murder, and we're taking him.' From his belt the guard produced a set of manacles and Druss's eyes narrowed.

'I think you might be making a mistake, officer,' said Sieben. But his words came too late as the guard stepped forward – straight into Druss's right fist, which cannoned from his jaw. The officer pitched to his right, his head striking the wall, dislodging his white-plumed helm. The other two guards sprang forward. Druss felled the first with a left hook, the second with a right uppercut.

One man groaned, then all was still. Majon spoke, his voice trembling. 'What have you done? You can't attack Royal Guards!'

'I just did. Now, are you ready, poet?'

'Indeed I am. I shall fetch my bags and then I think it best we quit this city with all due speed.'

Majon slumped to a padded chair. 'What will I tell them when they . . . wake?'

'I suggest you give them your discourse on the merits of diplomacy over violence,' said Sieben. Gently he patted Majon's shoulder, then ran to his apartments and gathered his gear.

The horses were stabled at the rear. Druss tied his saddle-bags into place, then clumsily hauled himself into the saddle. The mare was sixteen hands and, though sway-backed, was a powerful beast. Sieben's mount was of similar size but, as he had told Druss, the horse was a thoroughbred, steel-grey and sleek.

Sieben vaulted to the saddle and led the way out into the main street. 'You must have hit that Shonan awfully hard, old horse.'

'Not hard enough to kill him,' said Druss, swaying in the saddle and grabbing the pommel.

'Grip with your thighs, not your calves,' advised Sieben.

'I never liked riding. I feel foolish perched up here.'

There were a number of riders making for the Eastern Gate, and Druss and Sieben found themselves in a long convoy threading through the narrow streets. At the gates soldiers were questioning each rider and Sieben's nervousness grew. 'They can't be looking for you already, surely?' Druss shrugged.

Slowly they approached the gates. A sentry walked forward. 'Papers,' he said.

'We are Drenai,' Sieben told him. 'Just out for a ride.'

'You need papers signed by the Exit Officer of the Watch,' said the sentry, and Sieben saw Druss tense. Swiftly he reached into his pouch and produced a small silver coin; leaning over the saddle, he passed it to the soldier.

'One feels so cooped up in a city,' said Sieben, with a bright smile. 'An hour's ride in open country frees the mind.'

The sentry pocketed the coin. 'I like to ride myself,' he said.

'Enjoy yourselves.' He waved them through and the two riders kicked their mounts into a canter and set off for the eastern hills.

After two hours in the saddle Sieben drank the last of his water and stared about him. With the exception of the distant mountains, the landscape was featureless and dry.

'No rivers or streams,' said the poet. 'Where will we find water?' Druss pointed to a range of rocky hills some miles further on. 'How can you be sure?' asked the poet. 'I don't want to die of thirst out here.'

'You won't.' He grinned at Sieben. 'I have fought campaigns in deserts and I know how to find water. But there's one trick I learned that's better than all the others.'

'And that is?'

'I bought a map of the water-holes! Now let's walk these horses for a while.'

Druss slid from the saddle and strode on. Sieben dismounted and joined him. For a time they walked on in silence.

'Why so morose, old horse?' asked Sieben, as they neared the outcrop of rocks.

'I've been thinking of Klay. How can people just turn on him like that? After all he did for them.'

'People are sometimes vile creatures, Druss, selfish and self-regarding. But the real fault is not in them, but in us for expecting better. When Klay dies they'll all remember what a fine man he was, and they'll probably shed tears for him.'

'He deserves better,' grunted Druss.

'Maybe he does,' agreed Sieben, wiping sweat from his brow with a perfumed handkerchief. 'But when did that ever matter? Do we get what we deserve? I do not believe so. We get what we can win – what we can take, whether it be employment, or money, or women, or land. Look at you! Raiders stole your wife; they had the power to take, and they took her. Sadly for them you had the power to hunt them down, and the sheer determination to pursue your love across the ocean. But you didn't win her back by luck, or by the whim of a capricious deity. You did it by force of arms. You might have failed for a hundred reasons, illness, war – the flight of an arrow, the flash of a sword-blade – a sudden storm at sea. You didn't get what you deserved, Druss, you got what you fought for. Klay was unlucky. He took a bolt that was meant for you. That was your good luck.'

'I don't argue with that,' said Druss. 'Yes, he was unlucky. But they tore down his statue, and his friends robbed and then deserted him – men he had supported, aided, protected. That's what I find hard to swallow.'

Sieben nodded. 'My father told me that a man is lucky if in his life he can count on at least two good friends. He always maintained that a man with many friends had to be either rich or stupid, and I think that is largely true. In all my life I have had only one friend, Druss, and that is you.'

'Do you not count your women?'

Sieben shook his head. 'Everything with them has always been transactional. They require something of me, I require something of them. We each supply the other. They give me the warmth of their bodies and their yielding flesh; I give them the incredible expertise of the perfect lover.'

'How can you call yourself a lover when love is never present in your encounters?'

'Don't be a pedant, Druss. I am worth the title. Even accomplished whores have told me I'm the best lover they ever had.'

'How surprising,' said Druss, with a grin. 'I'll wager they don't say that to many men.'

'Mockery does not suit you, axeman. We all have our skills. Yours is with that appalling weapon, mine is in love-making.'

'Aye,' agreed Druss. 'But it seems to me my weapon ends problems. Yours causes them.'

'Oh, very droll. Just what I need as I walk through this barren wilderness, a lecture on morals!' Sieben stroked the neck of the steel-dust gelding then stepped into the saddle. Lifting his hand he shaded his eyes. 'It is all so green. I've never seen a land that promised so much and gave so little. How do these plants survive?'

Druss did not answer. He was trying to hook his foot into the stirrup, but the mare began walking in circles. Sieben chuckled and rode alongside, taking the mare's reins and holding her steady while the axeman mounted. 'They are deep-rooted,' said Druss. 'It rains here for a full month every winter. The plants and bushes soak it in, then battle to survive for another year. It is a hard land. Harsh and savage.'

'Like the people who dwell here,' said Sieben.

'Aye. The Nadir are a fierce people.'

'Majon was telling me about a group called Chop-backs.'

'Renegades,' said Druss. 'They call them Notas, no tribe. They are outcasts, robbers and killers. We'll try to avoid them.'

'And if we can't?'

Druss laughed. 'Then you can show me your skills with the pretty knives!'

Nosta Khan sat in the shade of an overhanging rock, his scrawny left hand dipped in the cool waters of the rock pool. The sun was high overhead now, the heat beyond the shade pitiless, relentless in its power. It caused Nosta Khan no distress. Neither heat nor cold, nor pain nor sorrow could touch him now. For he was a Master of the Way – a shaman.

He had not desired this mystic path. No, as a young man he had dreamed the dreams of all Nadir warriors: many ponies, many women, many children. A short life filled with the savage joy of battle and the grunting, slippery warmth of sex.

It was not to be. His Talent had denied him his dreams. No wives for Nosta Khan, no children to play at his feet. Instead he had been taken as a boy to the Cave of Asta Khan, and there had learned the *Way*.

Lifting his hand from the water he touched it to his brow, closing his eyes as several drops of cold water fell to the wrinkled skin of his face.

He was seven years old when Asta took him and six other boys to the crest of Stone Hawk Peak, to sit in the blazing sunshine dressed only in breech-clouts and moccasins. The old shaman had covered their heads and faces with wet clay and told them to sit until the clay baked hard and fell clear. Each child had two reed straws through which to breathe. There was no sense of time within the clay, no sound and no light. The skin of his shoulders had burned and blistered, but Nosta had not moved. For three blazing days and three frozen nights he sat thus within that tomb of drying clay.

It did not fall clear and he had longed to lift his hands and rip it away. Yet he did not . . . even when the terror gripped him. What if the wolves came? What if an enemy were close? What if Asta had left him here to die because he, Nosta, was not worthy? Still he sat unmoving, the ground beneath him soiled with his urine and excrement, ants and flies crawling over him. He felt their tiny legs upon his skin and shivered. What if they were not flies, but scorpions?

Still the child did not move. On the morning of the fourth day, as the sun brought warmth and pain to his chilled yet raw flesh, a section of the clay broke clear, allowing him to move the muscles of his jaw. Tilting his head, he forced open his mouth. The

111

two reed straws dropped away, then a large chunk of baked clay split above his nose. A hand touched his head and he flinched. Asta Khan peeled away the last of the clay.

The sunlight was brutally bright and tears fell from the boy's eyes. The old shaman nodded. 'You have done well,' he said. They were the only words of praise he ever heard from Asta Khan.

When at last he could see, Nosta looked around him. He and the old man were alone on Stone Hawk Peak. 'Where are the other boys?'

'Gone. They will return to their villages. You have won the great prize.'

'Then why do I feel only sadness?' he asked, his voice a dry croak.

Asta Khan did not answer at first. He passed a water skin to the boy and sat silently as he drank his fill. 'Each man,' he said at last, 'gives something of himself to the future. At the very least the gift is in the form of a child to carry his seed onward. But a shaman is denied that pleasure.' Taking the boy by the hand, he led him to the edge of the precipice. From here they gazed down over the plains and the distant steppes. 'See there,' said Asta Khan, 'the goats of our tribe. They worry about little, save to eat, sleep and rut. But look at the goat-herder. He must watch for wolves and lions, for the flesh-eating worms of the blowfly, and he must find pastures that are safe, and rich with grass. Your sadness is born of the knowledge that you cannot be a goat. Your destiny calls for more than that.'

Nosta Khan sighed and once more splashed his face with water. Asta was long dead now, and he remembered him with little affection.

A golden lioness and three cubs came into sight on the trail. Nosta took a deep breath and focused his concentration.

The rearing rocks are part of the body of the Gods of Stone and Water, and I am one with the rocks.

The lioness moved warily forward, her great head sniffing the air. Satisfied that her family was safe she edged to the pool, the cubs gambolling behind her. The last of the cubs leapt upon the back of one of the others and commenced a play fight. The lioness ignored them and drank deeply. She was thin, her pelt patchy. When she had drunk her fill, she moved into the shade and lay beside Nosta Khan. The cubs followed her, nuzzling her teats. One scrambled over Nosta Khan's bare legs, then settled down in the old man's lap with its head resting on his thigh.

Reaching out, he laid his hand on the lioness's broad head. She did not flinch. Nosta Khan allowed his mind to float free. High above the hills he floated, scanning the folds and gullies. Less than a mile to the east he found a small family group of *ochpi*, wild mountain goats with short curved horns. There was a male, three females, and several young. Returning to his body, Nosta touched the lioness with his spirit. Her head came up, nostrils flaring. There was no way she could pick up the scent from this distance, with the wind against her, but Nosta Khan filled her mind with the vision of the *ochpi*. The lioness rose, scattering the cubs, then she loped away. At first the cubs remained where they were, but she gave a low growl and they ran after her.

With luck she would feed.

Nosta sat back, and waited. The riders would be here within the hour. He pictured the axeman, his broad, flat face and deep, cold eyes. Would that all these Southerners could be so easily manipulated, he thought, remembering his spirit meeting in the tavern. Once outside it had been so easy to mesmerize the crossbow man and command him to shoot down the Gothir fighter. Nosta recalled with pleasure the flight of the bolt, the sickening impact, and the intense shock of the crossbow man when he realized what he had done.

The threads were drawing together well now, but there was so much still to weave. Nosta rested his body and his mind, floating in half-sleep in the warmth.

Two riders came into view. The shaman took a deep breath and focused, as he had when the lioness came to the pool. He was a rock, eternal, unchanging, save to the slow eroding winds of time. The lead rider, a tall, slim young man with fair hair, dressed in garish silks, dismounted smoothly, holding firm to the reins, preventing the steel-dust gelding from reaching the cool water. 'Not yet, my lovely,' he said softly. 'First we must cool you down.' The second rider, the black-bearded axeman, lifted his leg over the saddle pommel and jumped down. His mount was old, and more than tired. Laying his axe to the ground Druss unbuckled the saddle, hauling it clear of the mare's back. She was lathered in sweat and breathing heavily; he wiped her down with a cloth and tethered her next to the tall gelding in the partial shade of the east side of the pool. The fair one moved to the pool and stripped off his clothing, shaking off the dust and folding it neatly. His body was pale as ivory, smooth and soft. No warrior this, thought Nosta Khan as the young man dived into the water.

113

Druss gathered his axe and moved to the shade where Nosta Khan sat. Squatting down he cupped his hands and drank, then splashed water to his thick dark hair and beard.

Nosta Khan closed his eyes and reached out to touch Druss's arm and read his thoughts. An iron grip closed around his wrist and his eyes flared open. Druss was looking directly at him.

'I have been waiting for you,' said Nosta, fighting for calm.

'I do not like men creeping up on me,' said the axeman, his voice cold. Nosta glanced down at the pool and the tension eased from him. The Spell of Concealment had not failed him, Druss had merely seen the reflection of his hand upon the water. Druss released his grip and drank once more.

'You are seeking the Healing Jewels, eh? That is good. A man should stand by his friends in their darkest moments.'

'Exactly where are they?' asked Druss. 'I do not have much time. Klay is dying.'

'I cannot tell you *exactly*. They were stolen several hundred years ago by a renegade shaman. He was hunted and stopped to rest at the Shrine of Oshikai; after that he was found and killed. Despite the most severe torture he refused to reveal the hiding-place. I now believe they are hidden at the Shrine.'

'Then why have you not searched for them?'

'I think he placed them within the tomb of Oshikai Demonbane. No Nadir may defile that sacred object. Only a . . . foreigner . . . would desecrate it.'

'How much more are you concealing from me, little man?'

'A great deal,' admitted Nosta. 'But then there is much that you do not need to know. The only truth that is of value to you is this: the jewels will save the life of your friend, and return him to full health.'

Sieben emerged from the water and padded across the hot stones to the shade. 'Ah, made a friend, I see,' he said, as he sat beside the shaman. 'I take it this is the old man who spoke to you in the tavern?' Druss nodded and Sieben extended his hand. 'My name is Sieben. I am the poet. You may have heard of me.'

'I have not heard of you,' said Nosta, ignoring the outstretched hand.

'What a blow to one's vanity,' said Sieben, with an easy smile. 'Do you have poets among the Nadir?'

'For what purpose?' asked the old man.

'Art, joy, entertainment . . .' Sieben hesitated as he saw the blank look of incomprehension on the old man's face. 'History!'

114

he said suddenly. 'How is your history retained among the tribe?'

'Each man is taught the history of his tribe by his mother, and the history of his family by his father. And the tribe's shaman knows all their histories, and the deeds of every Nadir hero.'

'You have no art, no sculptors, actors, painters?'

Nosta Khan's coal-dark eyes glittered. 'Three in five Nadir babies die in infancy. The average age of death among Nadir men is twenty-six. We live in a state of constant war, one with another, and in the meanwhile being hunted for sport by Gothir noblemen. Plague, pestilence, the constant threat of drought or famine – these are matters which concern the Nadir. We have no time for *art*.' Nosta Khan spat out the last word as if the taste upon his tongue was offensive.

'How excruciatingly dull,' said Sieben. 'I never felt sorry for your people – until now. Excuse me while I water the horses.'

Sieben rose and dressed. Nosta Khan swallowed down his irritation, and returned his gaze to Druss. 'Are there many like him in the South lands?'

Druss smiled. 'There are not many like him anywhere.' Reaching into his pack, he produced a round of cheese wrapped in muslin and some dried beef. He offered a portion to Nosta Khan, who refused. Druss ate in silence. Sieben returned and joined him. When they had completed the meal, Druss yawned and stretched out in the shade; within moments he was asleep.

'Why do you travel with him?' Nosta Khan asked Sieben.

'For the adventure, old horse. Wherever Druss goes one is sure to find adventure. And I like the idea of magical jewels. I'm sure there'll be a song or a story in it.'

'On that we will agree,' said Nosta Khan. 'Even now two thousand Gothir warriors are being marshalled. Led by Gargan, the Lord of Larness, they will march to the Shrine of Oshikai Demon-bane and lay siege to it, with the intention of killing everyone there, and taking the jewels as a gift to the madman who sits upon the throne. You are riding into the eye of the hurricane, poet. Yes, I am sure there will be a song in it for you.'

Nosta relished the fear that showed in the young man's soft eyes. Stretching his scrawny frame, he struggled to his feet and walked away from the pool. All was moving as he had planned, yet Nosta felt uneasy. Could Talisman marshal the Nadir troops to withstand Larness? Could he find the Eyes of Alchazzar? Closing his eyes Nosta let his spirit fly to the east, soaring over the mountains and dry valleys. Far below he saw the Shrine, its curved white walls shining like a ring of ivory. Beyond it were the tents of the Nadir guardians. Where are you, Talisman? he wondered.

Concentrating on the face of the young man, he allowed his spirit to drift down, drawn by the pull of Talisman's personality. Opening the eyes of his spirit, Nosta Khan saw the young Nadir warrior breasting the last rise before the valley. Behind him came the Chiatze woman, Zhusai. Then a third rider came in sight, leading two ponies. Nosta was surprised. Floating above this stranger he reached down, his spirit fingers touching the man's neck. The rider shivered and drew his heavy coat more closely about his powerful frame.

Satisfied, Nosta drew back. In the one instant of contact he had witnessed the attempted attack on Talisman and the girl, and Gorkai's conversion to the cause of the Uniter. It was good; the boy had performed well. The Gods of Stone and Water would be pleased.

Nosta flew on, hovering over the Shrine. Once it had been a small supply fort, its walls boasting wooden parapets but no towers. Less than twenty feet high, they had been constructed to keep out marauding tribesmen – not two thousand trained soldiers. The west-facing gates were rotting upon their hinges of bronze, while the west wall had crumbled at the centre, leaving a pile of rubble below a V-shaped crack.

Fear touched Nosta Khan with fingers of dread.

Could they hold against Gothir Guards?

And what of Druss? What role would the axeman play? It was galling to see so much, and yet know so little. Was his purpose to stand, axe in hand, upon the walls? In that moment a fleeting vision flickered in his mind: a white-haired warrior standing upon a colossal wall, his axe raised in defiance. As suddenly as it had come, it faded away.

Returning to his body Nosta took a deep, shuddering breath.

By the pool the poet was sleeping alongside the giant axeman.

Nosta sighed, and walked away into the east.

Talisman sat on the highest wall staring out over the Valley of Shul-sen's Tears. The sun was bright, and yet here a light breeze was blowing, robbing the heat of its withering power. In the distance the mountains looked like banks of dark storm clouds hugging the horizon, and overhead two eagles were circling on the thermals. Talisman's dark eyes scanned the valley. From this southern wall of Oshikai's resting place he could see two camps. At the first a long horse-hair standard, bearing the skull and horns of a wild ox, was planted before the largest tent. The thirty warriors of the Curved Horn tribe were sitting in the fading sunshine cooking their evening meals. Three hundred paces to the west was a second series of goat-hide tents; the standard of the Fleet Ponies was pitched there.

Out of sight on the northern side of the Shrine were two more camps, of the Lone Wolves and the Sky Riders, each guarding a compass point near the resting-place of the greatest Nadir warrior. The breeze died away and Talisman strolled down the rickety wooden steps to the courtyard, making his way to a table near the well. From here he could see where the west wall had crumbled away at the centre. Through the jagged hole he could just make out the distant tree line of the western hills.

This place is rotting away, he thought, just like the dreams of the man whose bones lie here. Talisman was fighting to control a cold, gnawing anger deep in his belly. They had arrived last night just in time to witness a sword duel between two Nadir warriors, which ended in the sudden and bloody disembowelling of a young man from the Fleet Ponies tribe. The victor, a lean warrior wearing the white fur wrist-ring of the Sky Riders, leapt upon the dying man, plunging his sword into his victim's neck, see-sawing the blade through the vertebrae, tearing the head from the shoulders. Blood-drenched, he had surged to his feet, screaming his triumph.

Talisman had heeled his pony on through the gates. Leaving Gorkai to tend the mounts, he had walked across the courtyard to stand before the Shrine entrance.

But he did not enter, he could not enter. Talisman's mouth was dry, his stomach knotted with fear. Out here in the bright moonlight his dreams were solid, his confidence unshakeable. Once through that door, however, they could disappear like woodsmoke.

Calm yourself! The Shrine has been plundered before. The Eyes will be hidden. Step inside, and pay homage to the spirit of the hero.

Taking a deep breath, he moved forward and pushed open the ancient wooden door. The dust-covered room was no more than thirty feet long, and twenty wide. Wooden pegs were hammered into the walls, but nothing hung from them now. Once Oshikai's armour had been displayed here, his breastplate and helm, and

117

Kolmisai, the single-bladed hand-axe which had felled a hundred foes. There had been tapestries and mosaics, detailing his life and his victories. Now there were only bare and empty walls. The Shrine had been ransacked hundreds of years ago. They had, so Nosta Khan informed him, even opened the coffin and torn off the fingers of the corpse to get to the golden rings worn by Oshikai. The chamber was bleak, the stone coffin resting on a raised platform at the centre. The coffin itself was unadorned, save for a square of black iron set into the stone. Upon it, in raised letters, were the words:

Oshikai Demon-bane – Lord of War.

Talisman laid his hand on the cold stone of the coffin lid. 'I live,' he said, 'to see your dreams return. We will be united again. We will be Nadir, and the world will tremble.'

'Why do the dreams of men always lead to war?' asked a voice. Talisman spun to see that sitting in the shadows was an old blind man wearing a grey robe and cowl. He was stick-thin, and hairless. Taking hold of his staff, he levered himself to his feet and approached Talisman. 'You know,' he said, 'I have studied the life of Oshikai, sifting through the legends and the myths. He never wanted war. Always it was thrust upon him. That was when he became a terrible enemy. The dreams you speak of were mostly of finding a land of promise and plenty where his people could grow in peace. He was a great man.'

'Who are you?' asked Talisman.

'I am a priest of the Source.' As the man stepped into the beam of moonlight coming through the open western window, Talisman saw that he was Nadir. 'I live here now, writing my histories.'

'How does a blind man write?'

'Only the eyes of my body are blind, Talisman. When I write I use the eyes of my spirit.'

Talisman shivered as the man spoke his name. 'You are a shaman?'

The priest shook his head. 'I understand the *Way*, though my own path is different. I cast no spells, Talisman, though I can heal warts and read the hearts of men. Sadly I cannot alter them. I can walk the paths of the many futures, but do not know which will come to pass. If I could, I would open this coffin and raise the man within. But I cannot.'

'How is it that you know my name?'

'Why should I not? You are the flaming arrow, the messenger.'

'You know why I am here,' said Talisman, his voice dropping to a whisper.

'Of course. You are seeking the Eyes of Alchazzar, hidden here so many years ago.'

Talisman fingered the dagger at his belt, and silently drew it. 'You have found them?'

'I know they are here. But they were not left for me to find. I write history, Talisman; it is not for me to create it. May the Source give you wisdom.'

The old man turned away and walked to the sunlit doorway where he stood for a moment, as if waiting. Then his voice sounded once more. 'In at least three of the futures I have seen, you struck me down as I stood here, your dagger deep in my back. Why did you not do so in this one?'

'I considered it, old man.'

'Had you committed the deed you would have been dragged from this chamber, your arms and legs tied with ropes attached to the saddles of four ponies. You would have been ripped apart, Talisman. That also happened.'

'Obviously it did not, for you still live.'

'It happened somewhere,' said the old man. Then he was gone.

Talisman followed him into the light, but he had vanished into one of the buildings. Seeing Gorkai drawing water from the well, he strolled across to him. 'Where is Zhusai?'

'The woman sleeps,' said Gorkai. 'It looks as if there will be another fight today. The head of the boy who was killed now sits atop a pole at the Sky Rider camp. His comrades are determined to punish this insult.'

'Stupidity,' said Talisman.

'It seems to be in our blood. Maybe the gods cursed us.'

Talisman nodded. 'The curse came when the Eyes of Alchazzar were stolen. When they are returned to the Stone Wolf, then we shall see a new day.'

'You believe this?'

'A man must believe in something, Gorkai. Otherwise we are merely shifting grains of sand, blown by the wind. The Nadir number in their hundreds of thousands, perhaps in millions, and yet we live in squalor. All around us there is wealth, controlled by nations whose armies do not exceed twenty thousand men. Even here the four tribes guarding the Shrine cannot live in peace.

Their purpose is identical – the Shrine they protect is of a man who is a hero to all Nadir – yet they stare at each other with undisguised hatred. I believe that will change. We will change it.'

'Just you and I?' asked Gorkai softly.

'Why not?'

'I have still seen no man with violet eyes,' said Gorkai.

'You will. I swear it.'

When Druss awoke Nosta Khan had gone. It was approaching dusk and Sieben was sitting by the poolside, his naked feet resting in the cool water. Druss yawned and stretched. Rising, he stripped off his jerkin, boots and leggings and leapt into the pool, where the water was welcomingly cool. Refreshed, he climbed out and sat beside the poet. 'When did the little man leave?' he asked.

'Soon after you fell asleep,' Sieben told him, his voice flat.

Druss looked into his friend's face, and saw the lines of tension there. 'You are concerned about the two thousand warriors heading for the Shrine?'

Sieben bit back an angry retort. 'Concerned does not quite cover it, old horse. I see it doesn't surprise you, though.'

Druss shook his head. 'He told me he was repaying a debt because I helped his young friend. That is not the Nadir way. No, he wanted me at the Shrine because he knew there would be a battle.'

'Oh, I see, and the mighty Druss the Legend will turn the tide, I suppose?'

Druss chuckled. 'Perhaps he will, poet. Perhaps he will not. Whatever the answer, the only way I'll find the jewels is if I go there.'

'And what if there are no magical jewels? Suppose he lied about that also?'

'Then Klay will die, and I will have done my best.'

'It is all so simple for you, isn't it?' stormed Sieben. 'Black and white, light and dark, pure or evil? Two thousand warriors are going to ransack that Shrine. You won't stop them. And why should you even try? What is it about Klay that has touched you so? Other men have suffered grievous wounds before now. You have seen comrades cut down beside you for years.'

Druss stood and dressed, then he wandered to the horses and unhooked a sack of grain from the saddle pommel. From his pack he took two feed-bags and looped them over the ears of the mounts. Sieben joined him. 'They say a grain-fed horse will out-run anything fed on grass,' said Druss. 'You are a horseman, is that true?'

'Come on, Druss, answer my question, damn you! Why Klay?'

'He reminds me of a man I never knew,' answered Druss.

'Never knew! What does that mean?'

'It means that I must try to find the jewels, and I don't give a damn about two thousand Gothir whoresons, or the entire Nadir nation. Leave it there, poet!'

The clatter of hooves sounded on the trail and both men swung towards the source of the noise. Six Nadir warriors, riding in single file, approached the pool. They were dressed in goatskin tunics and wore fur-rimmed helms. Each carried a bow and two short swords. 'What do we do?' whispered Sieben.

'Nothing. Water-holes are sacred places and no Nadir will fight a battle at one. They'll merely water their horses, then leave.'

'Then what?'

'Then they'll try to kill us. But that is a problem for another time. Relax, poet, you wanted adventure. Now you'll have it.'

Druss strolled back to the shade and sat down beside the fear-some axe. The Nadir affected to ignore him, but Sieben could see them cast furtive glances in his direction. Finally the leader – a middle-aged, stocky warrior with a thin, wispy beard – came and sat opposite him.

'You are far from home,' he said, speaking haltingly in the Southern tongue.

'Yet I am at ease,' replied Druss.

'The dove is rarely at ease in the home of the hawk.'

'I am not a dove, laddie. And you are no hawk.'

The man rose. 'I think we will meet again, Round-eye.' He strolled back to his companions, vaulted to the saddle and led the riders on towards the east.

Sieben sat down beside Druss. 'Oh, well done, old horse. Always best to appease an enemy who outnumbers you three to one.'

'There was no point. He knows what he must do. As do I. You wait here with the horses; get them saddled and ready.'

'Where are you going?'

'East a little way. I want to see what sort of trap they will set.'

'Is this wise, Druss? There are six of them.'

Druss grinned. 'You think it would make it fairer if I left my axe behind?' With that he gathered up Snaga and set off up and

121

over the rocks. Sieben watched him go, then settled down to wait. Darkness came swiftly in the mountains and he wished he had thought to gather dead-wood back along the trail. A fire would be a welcome friend in this desolate place. The moon was bright, however, and Sieben wrapped himself in his blanket and sat deep in the shadows of the rock wall. Never again, he thought. From now on I'll welcome boredom with open arms and a mighty hug!

What was it Druss had said about Klay? *He reminds me of a man I never knew?* Suddenly it came clear to Sieben. Druss was speaking of Michanek, the man who had loved and wed Rowena back in Ventria.* Like Druss Michanek was a mighty warrior, and a champion among the rebels opposed to Prince Gorben. And Rowena, robbed of her memory, had grown to love him, had even attempted suicide when she learned of his death. Druss had been there as Michanek faced the elite of Gorben's Immortals. Alone he had killed many, until at last even Michanek's prodigious strength failed him, sapped from his body in the gushing of blood from a score of wounds. As he died, he asked Druss to look after Rowena.

Once, when visiting Druss and his lady at their farm in the mountains, Sieben had walked with Rowena across the high meadows. He had asked her then about Michanek and she smiled fondly. 'He was like Druss in many ways, but he was also gentle and kind. I did love him, Sieben, and I know Druss finds that hard to bear. But they took my memory from me. I did not know who I was, and remembered nothing of Druss. All I knew was that this huge man loved me and cared for me. And it still saddens me to know that Druss had a part in his death.'

'He didn't know Michanek,' said Sieben. 'All he had dreamed of through those long years was finding you and bringing you home.'

'I know.'

'Given the choice between the two men, who would you have chosen?' asked Sieben suddenly.

'That is a question I never ask myself,' she told him. 'I merely know that I was fortunate to be loved by, and to love, both of them.'

Sieben had wanted to ask more, but she touched a finger to his lips. 'Enough, poet! Let us go back to the house.'

A cold wind blew around the rock pool now and Sieben wrapped his cloak more tightly about him. There was no sound,

* *First Chronicles of Druss the Legend*

save for the wind whistling through the rocks, and Sieben felt terribly alone. Time passed with a mind-numbing lack of speed and the poet dozed several times, always waking with a start, terrified that hidden Nadir assassins were creeping up on him.

Just before the dawn, with the sky brightening, he heard the sound of hooves on stone. Scrambling to his feet he drew one of his knives, dropped it, gathered it and stood waiting. Druss came into sight leading four Nadir ponies and Sieben walked out to meet him. There was blood on Druss's jerkin and leggings. 'Are you hurt?' asked Sieben.

'No, poet. The way is now clear – and we have four ponies to trade.'

'Two of the Nadir got away?'

Druss shook his head. 'Not the Nadir, but two of the ponies broke loose and ran off.'

'You killed all six?'

'Five. One fell from the cliff as I was chasing him. Now let us be moving on.'

Chapter Six

Just before midnight Talisman entered the tomb of Oshikai Demon-bane. While Gorkai stood guard outside the door, the Nadir warrior crept inside and placed four small pouches on the ground before the coffin. From the first he poured a small amount of red powder; then, with his index finger, he formed it into a circle no bigger than his palm. Faint moonlight shining through the open window made his task more easy. From the second pouch he took three long dried leaves, which he rolled into a ball and placed in his mouth, under his tongue. The taste was bitter and he almost gagged. Taking a tinder-box from the pocket of his goatskin tunic, he struck a flame and held it to the red powder, which flared instantly with a crimson light. Smoke billowed up. Talisman breathed it in, then swallowed the ball of leaves.

He felt faint, dizzy, and as if from a great distance he heard the sound of soft music, then a sigh. His vision blurred, then cleared. Upon the walls of the shrine there were flickering lights that made his eyes water. He rubbed them with finger and thumb, and looked again. Shimmering in place beneath the pegs on the wall was the armour of Oshikai Demon-bane – the breastplate with its one hundred and ten leaves of hammered gold, the winged helm of black iron, set with silver runes, and the dread axe, Kolmisai. Talisman slowly scanned the chamber. Beautiful tapestries decorated the walls, each showing an incident from the life of Oshikai – the hunt for the black lion, the razing of Chien-Po, the flight over the mountains, the wedding to Shul-sen. This last was a spectacular piece, a host of ravens carrying the bride to the altar

124

while Oshikai stood waiting with two demons beside him.

Talisman blinked and battled to hold his concentration against the waves of narcotics coursing through his blood. From the third pouch he took a ring of gold, and from the fourth a small finger-bone. As Nosta Khan had commanded, he slid the ring over the bone and placed it before him. With his dagger he made a narrow cut in his left forearm, allowing the blood to drip upon the bone and the ring. 'I call to thee, Lord of War,' he said. 'I humbly ask for your presence.'

At first there was nothing, then a cool breeze seemed to blow across the chamber, though not a mote of dust was disturbed. A figure began to materialize over the coffin. The armour of gold flowed over him, the axe floating down to rest in his right hand. Talisman almost ceased to breathe as the spirit descended to sit cross-legged opposite him. Though broad of shoulder, Oshikai was not huge, as Talisman had expected. His face was flat and hard, the nose broad, the nostrils flared. He wore his hair tied back in a tight pony-tail, and he sported no beard or moustache. His violet eyes glowed with power, and he radiated strength of purpose.

'Who calls Oshikai?' asked the translucent figure.

'I, Talisman of the Nadir.'

'Do you bring news of Shul-sen?'

The question was unexpected and Talisman faltered. 'I . . . I know nothing of her, Lord, save legends and stories. Some say she died soon after you, others that she crossed the oceans to a world without darkness.'

'I have searched the Vales of Spirit, the Valleys of the Damned, the Fields of Heroes, the Halls of the Mighty. I have crossed the Void for time without reckoning. I cannot find her.'

'I am here, Lord, to see your dreams return to life,' said Talisman, as Nosta Khan had ordered. Oshikai seemed not to hear him. 'The Nadir need to be united,' continued Talisman. 'To do this we must find the violet-eyed leader, but we do not know where to look.'

The spirit of Oshikai gazed at Talisman, then sighed. 'He will be found when the Eyes of Alchazzar are set in their rightful sockets. The magic will flow back into the land, and then he will be revealed.'

'I seek the Eyes, Lord,' said Talisman. 'They are said to be hidden here. Is this true?'

'Aye, it is true. They are close by, Talisman of the Nadir. But you are not destined to find them.'

125

'Then who, Lord?'

'A foreigner will take them. More than this I will not tell you.'

'And the Uniter, Lord. Can you not tell me his name?'

'His name will be Ulric. Now I must go. I must keep searching.'

'Why do you search, Lord? Is there no Paradise for you?'

The spirit stared at him. 'What Paradise could there be without Shul-sen? Death I could bear, but not this parting of souls. I will find her, though it take a dozen eternities. Fare you well, Talisman of the Nadir.'

Before Talisman could speak the figure was gone. The young Nadir warrior rose unsteadily and backed to the door.

Gorkai was waiting in the moonlight. 'What happened in there? I heard you speak, but there was no answer.'

'He came, but he could not help me. He was a soul in torment, seeking his wife.'

'The witch, Shul-sen. They say she was burned alive, her ashes scattered to the four winds and her spirit destroyed by sorcery.'

'I have never heard that story,' said Talisman. 'Among others we were taught that she crossed the sea to a land where there was no nightfall, and there she lives for ever in the hope that Oshikai will find her.'

'It is a prettier tale,' admitted Gorkai, 'and both would explain why the Lord of War cannot find her. What will we do now?'

'We will see what tomorrow brings,' said Talisman, striding off to the rooms Gorkai had found for them. There were thirty small chambers set within the main building, all constructed for the use of pilgrims. Zhusai had spread her blankets on the floor beneath the window, and pretended to be asleep as Talisman entered. He did not go to her, but pulled up a chair and sat staring out at the stars. Unable to bear the silence any longer, she spoke.

'Did the spirit not come to you?' she asked.

'Aye, he came.' Slowly he told her the full story of Oshikai's search for Shul-sen, and of the two legends told of her passing.

Zhusai sat up, holding the blanket around her. 'There are other stories of Shul-sen – that she was thrown from a cliff high on the Mountains of the Moon; that she committed suicide; that she was turned into a tree. Every tribe has a different tale. But it is sad that he cannot find her.'

'More than sad,' said Talisman. 'He said that without her could be no Paradise.'

'How beautiful,' she said. 'But then he was Chiatze, and we are a people who understand sensitivity.'

'I have found in my life that people who boast of their sensitivity are sensitive only to their own needs, and utterly indifferent to the needs of others. However, I am in no mood to argue the point.' Taking up his blanket, he lay down beside her, and slept. His dreams, as always, were filled with pain.

The lash cut deep into his back, but he did not cry out. He was Nadir, and no matter how great the pain he would never show his suffering to these *gajin* – these round-eyed foreigners. The whip he had been forced to make himself, the leather wound tightly around a wooden handle, then sliced into thin strips each tipped with a small pellet of lead. Okai counted each stroke to the prescribed fifteen. As the last slashing swipe lanced across his bleeding back, he allowed himself to slump forward against the stake. 'Give him five more,' came the voice of Gargan.

'That would exceed the regulations, my Lord,' answered Premian. 'He has received the maximum allowed for a cadet of fifteen.' Okai could scarce believe that Premian had spoken up for him. The House Prefect had always made clear his loathing of the Nadir boys.

Gargan spoke again. 'That regulation is for human beings, Premian, not Nadir filth. As you can see, he has not suffered at all. Not a sound has he made. Where there is no sense, there is no feeling. Five more!'

'I cannot obey you, my Lord.'

'You are stripped of your rank, Premian. I had thought better of you.'

'And I of you, Lord Gargan.' Okai heard the lash fall to the floor. 'If one more blow is laid upon this young man's back I shall report the incident to my father at the palace. Fifteen strokes was bad enough for a misdemeanour. Twenty would be savage beyond belief.'

'Be silent!' thundered Gargan. 'One more word and you will suffer a similar punishment, and face expulsion from this academy. I'll not tolerate disobedience, nor insubordination. You!' he said, pointing at a boy Okai could not see. 'Five more lashes if you please.'

Okai heard the whisper of the lash being swept up from the floor, and tried to brace himself. Only when the first blow fell did he realize that Premian had been holding back. Whoever now held the lash was laying on with a vengeance. At the third stroke a groan was torn from him, that shamed him even more than the punishment,

127

but he bit down hard on the leather belt between his teeth and made no further sound. Blood was running freely down his back now, pooling above the belt of his leggings. At the fifth stroke a great silence fell upon the hall. Gargan broke it. 'Now, Premian, you may go and write to your father. Cut this piece of offal down.'

Three Nadir boys ran forward, untying the ropes that bound Okai. Even as he fell into their arms he swung to see who had wielded the whip, and his heart sank. It was Dalsh-chin, of the Fleet Ponies tribe.

His friends half carried him to the infirmary, where an orderly applied salve to his back and inserted three stitches into a deeper cut on his shoulder. Dalsh-chin entered and stood before him. 'You did well, Okai,' he said, speaking in the Nadir tongue. 'My heart swelled with pride for you.'

'Why then did you make me cry out before the *gajin*?'

'Because he would have ordered five more had you not, and five more still. It was a test of will, and one which might have killed you.'

'You stop talking in that filthy language,' said the orderly. 'You know it is against the rules, and I won't have it!'

Dalsh-chin nodded, then reached out and laid his hand on Okai's head. 'You have a brave heart, young one,' he said, in the southern tongue. Then he turned and strode from the room.

'Twenty lashes for defending yourself,' said his closest friend Zhen-shi. 'That was not just.'

'You cannot expect justice from *gajin*,' Okai told him. 'Only pain.'

'They have stopped hurting me,' said Zhen-shi. 'Perhaps it will be better for all of us from now on.'

Okai said nothing, knowing that they had stopped hurting his friend because Zhen-shi ran errands for them, cleaned their boots, bowed and scraped, acted like a slave. As they mocked him he would smile, and bob his head. It saddened Okai, but there was little he could do. Every man had to make his own choices. His own was to resist them in every way, and yet to learn all that they could teach. Zhen-shi had not the strength for this course; he was soft, and remarkably gentle for a Nadir boy.

After a short rest in the infirmary, Okai walked unaided to the room he shared with Lin-tse. From the Sky Rider tribe, Lin-tse was taller than most Nadir youths, his face square and his eyes barely slanted. It was rumoured that he had *gajin* blood, but no-one said this to his face. Lin-tse was short of temper, and long on remembered wrongs. He stood as Okai entered. 'I have brought you food and drink, Okai,' he said. 'And some mountain honey for the wounds upon your back.'

'I thank you, brother,' replied Okai formally.

'Our tribes are at war,' said Lin-tse, 'and therefore we cannot be brothers. But I respect your courage.' He bowed, then returned to his studies.

Okai lay face down on the narrow pallet bed and tried to block the hot pain that flowed from his lacerated back. 'Our tribes are at war *now*,' he said, 'but one day we will be brothers, and the Nadir will sweep down upon these *gajin* and wipe them from the face of the earth.'

'May it be so,' responded Lin-tse. 'You have an examination tomorrow, do you not?'

'Yes. The role of cavalry in punitive expeditions.'

'Then I shall question you upon the subject. It will help to shield your mind from the pain you are suffering.'

Talisman awoke just before the dawn. Zhusai still slept as silently he rose and left the room. In the courtyard below the blind Nadir priest was drawing water from the well. In the half light of the pre-dawn the man looked younger, his face pale and serene. 'I trust you slept well, Talisman?' he enquired as the Nadir approached.

'Well enough.'

'And were the dreams the same?'

'My dreams are my concern, old man, and should you wish to live to complete your history, you would be advised to remember my words.'

The priest laid down the bucket and sat on the lip of the well, his pale opal eyes glinting in the last of the moonlight. 'Dreams are never secret, Talisman, no matter how hard we try to protect them. They are like regrets, always seeking the light, always shared. And they have meaning far beyond our understanding. You will see. Here in this place the circle will be complete.'

The priest carried the bucket to a nearby table and, with a copper ladle, slowly began to fill clay water pots that hung on slender ropes from the beams of the porch. Talisman walked to the table and sat. 'What are these histories you write?' he asked.

'They mostly involve the Chiatze and the Nadir. But I have become fascinated by the life of Oshikai. Do you know the origin of the name *Nadir*?'

Talisman shrugged. 'In the southern tongue it means the point of greatest hopelessness.'

'In Chiatze it means the cross-roads of death,' said the priest. 'When Oshikai first led his people out of Chiatze lands a great army followed them, seeking to exterminate what they perceived as his rebel force. He met them on the plain of Chu-chien, and destroyed them. But two more armies were closing in upon him, and he was forced to lead his people across the Ice Mountains. Hundreds died, many more lost fingers and toes, arms and legs, to the terrible cold. As they cleared the frozen passes they emerged on to the terrible desert of salt beyond. The despair was almost total. Oshikai called a meeting of his Council. He told them that they were a people born in hardship and danger, and that they had now reached their nadir. From that moment he changed their name. Then he addressed the multitude, and told them that Shul-sen would lead them to water, and that a land full of promise would await them beyond the salt desert. He spoke of a dream, where the Nadir grew and prospered from shimmering sea to snow-topped peaks. That is when he gave them the verse all Nadir children learn as they suck their mothers' milk:

'Nadir we,
youth born,
axe wielders,
blood letters,
victors still.'

'What happened to Shul-sen?' asked Talisman. The priest smiled as, laying down his bucket once more, he sat at the table.

'There are so many tales, most embroidered upon, some mere fancy, others crafted with such mystical symbolism that they become meaningless. The truth, I fear, is more mundane. It is my belief that she was captured by Oshikai's enemies and slain.'

'If that were so, then he would have found her.'

'Who would have found her?'

'Oshikai. His spirit has searched for her for hundreds of years, but he has never found her. How could that be?'

'I do not know,' admitted the priest, 'but I will think on it. How is it you know these things?'

'Accept merely that I know,' answered Talisman.

'We Nadir are a secretive people, and yet also curious,' said the priest, with a smile. 'I will return to my studies and consider the question you pose me.'

'You claim to walk the many paths of the future,' said

Talisman. 'Why can you not walk the single path of the past and see for yourself?'

'A good question, young man. The answer is simple. A true historian must remain objective. Anyone who witnesses a great event immediately forms a subjective view on it, for it has affected him. Yes, I could go back and observe. Yet I will not.'

'Your logic is flawed, priest. If the historian cannot observe events, he must then rely on the witness of others who, by your own words, can offer only a subjective view.'

The priest laughed aloud and clapped his hands together. 'Ah, my boy! If only we had more time to talk. We could debate the hidden circle of deceit in the search for altruism, or the lack of evidence for the non-existence of a supreme being.' His smile faded. 'But we do not have the time.'

The priest returned the bucket to the well and walked away. Talisman leaned back and watched the majesty of the dawn sun rising above the eastern peaks.

Quing-chin emerged from his tent and into the sunlight. A tall man, with deep-set eyes and a solemn face, he stood enjoying the warmth of the sun on his face. He had slept without dreams, and had woken feeling refreshed and ready for the sweet taste of revenge, his anger of yesterday replaced by a cold, resolute sense of purpose. His men were seated in a circle nearby. Quing-chin lifted his powerful arms above his head and slowly stretched the muscles of his upper back. His friend Shi-da rose from the circle and brought him his sword. 'It is sharp now, comrade,' said the smaller man, 'and ready to slice the flesh of the enemy.' The other six men in the circle rose. None were as tall as Quing-chin.

The sword-brother of Shanqui, the warrior slain by the Sky Rider champion, moved before Quing-chin. 'The soul of Shanqui waits for vengeance,' he said formally.

'I shall send him a servant to tend his needs,' quoted Quing-chin.

A young warrior approached the men, leading a dappled pony. Quing-chin took the reins from him and swung into the saddle. Shi-da handed him his long lance decorated with the dark, double twist of horse-hair that denoted a blooded warrior of the Fleet Ponies, and a black helm of lacquered wood rimmed with fur. Pushing back his shoulder-length dark hair, Quing-chin donned the helm. Then touching heels to the pony's flanks he rode from the camp, and out past the white walls of Oshikai's resting place.

Men were already moving around the camp of the Sky Riders, setting their cook-fires, as Quing-chin rode in. He ignored them all and headed his pony towards the furthest of the eighteen tents. Outside the entrance a lance had been plunged into the ground and set atop the weapon was the head of Shanqui. Blood had dripped to the ground below it, and the flesh on the dead face was ashen grey.

'Come forth,' called Quing-chin. The tent flap was pulled open and a squat warrior stepped into view. Ignoring Quing-chin, he opened his breeches and emptied his bladder on the ground. Then he looked up at the severed head.

'Here to admire my tree?' he asked. 'See, it is blooming already.' Most of the Sky Riders had gathered around the two men now, and they began to laugh. Quing-chin waited until the sound had died down. When he spoke his voice was cold and harsh.

'It is perfect,' said Quing-chin. 'Only a Sky Rider tree would have rotting fruit upon it.'

'Ha! This tree will have fresh fruit today. So sad you will not be able to admire it.'

'Ah, but I shall. I will tend it myself. And now the time for talk is past. I shall await you in the open, where the air is not filled with the stench of your camp.'

Tugging on the reins, Quing-chin galloped his pony some two hundred paces to the north. The twenty-eight warriors of the Fleet Ponies had already gathered there, sitting their mounts in silence. Within moments the thirty Sky Riders rode out, forming a line opposite Quing-chin and his men.

The squat Sky Rider, long lance in hand, heeled his pony forward, then swung to the right and galloped some fifty yards before savagely hauling on the reins. Quing-chin rode his pony between the lines of the two tribes, then turned and raised his lance. The squat warrior levelled his lance and kicked his mount into a run, charging at Quing-chin. The Fleet Ponies leader remained motionless as his opponent closed the gap between them. Closer and closer came the Sky Rider, until at the last possible moment Quing-chin jerked the reins and barked out a command. His pony bunched its muscles and sprang to the right. In the same heartbeat Quing-chin lifted his lance over his pony's head and rammed it to the left. The move was intended to spear the opposing rider through side and belly, but the Sky Rider had dragged back on his reins more swiftly than Quing-chin had anticipated, and the lance slammed into the neck of his opponent's pony which stumbled and fell, dragging Quing-chin's lance from his hand. The Sky Rider was thrown clear and spun in the air to land heavily on his back. Quing-chin leapt from his mount and ran forward, drawing his sword. The Sky Rider rolled to his feet, still groggy from the fall, but even so he drew his own blade and blocked the first cut. Quing-chin closed in, his left foot lashing out into the Sky Rider's unprotected knee. The Sky Rider jumped back and half fell. Quing-chin followed in, sending his sword in a vicious cut that ripped open the other man's jerkin and sliced up across his left cheek, tearing the flesh and sending a spray of blood into the air. The Sky Rider screamed in pain and attacked. Quing-chin blocked a belly thrust, spun on his heel and hammered his left elbow into the Sky Rider's blood-covered face. The man was hurled from his feet, but he scrambled up as Quing-chin closed in; he was fast, and sent a lightning thrust at Quing-chin's face. The taller man swayed aside, the blade slicing his ear lobe. His own sword flashed out in a neck cut that was too low, the blade cleaving into the Sky Rider's left shoulder. The squat warrior stumbled forward, but swung just in time to block a second blow aimed at his neck. The two warriors circled one another more warily now, respect growing between them. Quing-chin had been surprised by the man's speed, and the Sky Rider, blood pouring from the wounds to his shoulder and face, knew he was in desperate trouble.

Quing-chin darted forward to feint a cut to the throat. The Sky Rider's sword swept across to block but his speed betrayed him. The block was too fast. Quing-chin's blade plunged into the man's upper chest, but at the moment of impact the Sky Rider hurled himself backwards so that Quing-chin's sword penetrated no more than two inches before the blade was ripped clear. The Sky Rider fell, rolled and staggered to his feet.

'You are very skilled,' he said. 'I shall be proud to add your head to my tree.' His left arm was hanging useless now, blood streaming over his hand and dripping to the ground. In that instant Quing-chin experienced a moment of regret. Shanqui had been an arrogant, boastful young man, who had challenged this warrior and had died for it. And now, according to Nadir custom, Quing-chin would send this man's soul to serve him for eternity. He sighed.

'I too feel pride,' he said. 'You are a man among men. I salute you, Sky Rider.'

The Sky Rider nodded . . . then ran forward into the attack. Quing-chin swayed aside from the desperate thrust, slamming his own blade into the man's belly and up through the heart. The Sky Rider fell against him, his head falling to Quing-chin's shoulder as the dying man's knees gave way. Quing-chin caught him as he fell and lowered him to the ground. With a shuddering sigh the Sky Rider died.

This was the moment. Kneeling beside the body, Quing-chin drew his knife. The two lines of riders waited, but Quing-chin rose. 'I will not take this man's eyes,' he said. 'Let his friends bear him away for burial.'

Shi-da leapt from his pony and ran to him. 'You must, brother! Shanqui must have the eyes in his hand, or he will have no servant in the Netherworld!'

A Sky Rider nudged his pony forward, then dismounted alongside Quing-chin. 'You fought well, Dalsh-chin,' he said.

The Fleet Ponies warrior turned at the sound of his childhood name, and looked into the sorrowful eyes of the Sky Rider. Lin-tse had changed little in the two years since they had left the Bodacas Academy; he was broader in the shoulder now, and his head had been shaved clean save for a short braid of dark hair at the crown. 'It is good to see you again, Lin-tse,' he said. 'It saddens me that it should be on such an occasion.'

'You talk like a Gothir,' said Lin-tse. 'Tomorrow I will come to your camp. And when I have killed you I will take your eyes, and give them to my brother. You will serve him until the stars are ground to dust.'

Back at his own tent, Quing-chin stripped off his blood-stained jerkin and knelt upon the ground. In the two years since he had left the Bodacas Academy he had fought to re-establish his Nadir roots, aware that his own people felt he was somehow tainted by his years among the Gothir. He had denied it, even to himself, but today he knew that it was true.

Outside he heard the riders returning with the head of Shanqui, but he remained in the tent, his thoughts sombre. The rituals of the revenge-duel differed from tribe to tribe, but the principles remained the same. Had he cut out the eyes of the Sky Rider and placed them in the dead hand of Shanqui, then the spirit of the Sky Rider would have been bonded to Shanqui for eternity. The belief was that the Sky Rider would be blind in the Void, unless Shanqui loaned him the use of his eyes. This would ensure obedience. Now Quing-chin had broken the ritual. And to what purpose? Tomorrow he must fight again. If he won, another warrior would challenge him.

His friend Shi-da entered the tent, and squatted down before him. 'You fought bravely,' said Shi-da. 'It was a good fight. But tomorrow you must take the eyes.'

'The eyes of Lin-tse,' whispered Quing-chin. 'The eyes of one who was my friend? I cannot do this.'

'What is wrong with you, my brother? These are our enemies!'

Quing-chin rose. 'I shall go to the Shrine. I need to think.'

Leaving Shi-da, he ducked under the tent flap and stepped out into the sunshine. The body of Shanqui, wrapped in hide, had been left within yards of his tent. The right hand of the corpse had been left exposed, the fingers clawed and open. Striding to his dappled pony, Quing-chin mounted and rode to the white-walled Shrine.

In what way did they poison my Nadir spirit? he wondered. Was it the books, the manuscripts, the paintings? Or perhaps the teachings concerning morality, or the endless discussions on philosophy? How can I know?

The gates were open and Quing-chin rode inside and dismounted. Leaving his pony in the shade, he strode towards the Shrine.

'We shall make them suffer, as Zhen-shi suffered,' said a voice. Quing-chin froze. Slowly he turned towards the speaker.

Talisman stepped from the shadows and approached the taller man. 'It is good to see you again, my friend,' he said.

Quing-chin said nothing for a moment, then he gripped Talisman's outstretched hand. 'You gladden my heart, Okai. All is well with you?'

'Well enough. Come, share water and bread with me.'

The two men strolled back to the shade, where they sat beneath a wooden awning. Filling two clay cups with cool water from a stone jug, Talisman passed one to Quing-chin. 'What happened in the fight this morning?' he asked. 'There was so much dust I could see nothing from the walls.'

'A Sky Rider died,' said Quing-chin.

'When will such madness end?' asked Talisman sadly. 'When will our eyes be opened to the real enemy?'

'Not soon enough, Okai. Tomorrow I fight again.' He looked into Talisman's eyes. 'Against Lin-tse.'

*

135

Lin-tse sat on a rock sharpening his sword, his face impassive and his anger masked. Of all the men in the world, the last he wished to kill was Dalsh-chin. Yet such was his fate, and a true man never whined when the Gods of Stone and Water twisted the knife! The whetstone slid along the sabre's edge and Lin-tse imagined the silver steel blade slicing through Dalsh-chin's neck. He swore softly, then stood and stretched his back.

At the last there had only been four Nadir janizaries at the Academy – himself, Dalsh-chin, the miserable Green Monkey boy, Zhen-shi, and the strange one from the Wolfshead, Okai. Some of the others had fled, most had simply failed their examinations miserably – much to the delight of Gargan, Lord Larness. One had been hanged after killing an officer; another had committed suicide. The experiment – as Lord Larness intended – had been a failure. Yet much to the Gothir general's chagrin four Nadir youngsters had consistently passed the examinations. And one – Okai – excelled above all other students including the general's own son, Argo.

Lin-tse scabbarded his sword and walked out on to the steppes. His thoughts turned to Zhen-shi, with his frightened eyes and his nervous smile. Tormented and abused, he had fawned around the Gothir cadets, especially Argo, serving him like a slave. 'Grinning Monkey', Argo called him and Lin-tse had despised the youth for his cowardice. Zhen-shi carried few scars, but then he was everything the Gothir boys had been taught to expect of a barbarian – subservient and inferior to the civilized races.

Yet he had made a mistake – and it had cost him his life. In the end-of-year examinations he had outscored all but Okai. Lin-tse still remembered the look on Zhen-shi's face when the results were announced. At first his delight was obvious but then, as he gazed at Argo and the others, the full horror of his plight dawned on him. Grinning Monkey had beaten them all. No longer did they see him as an object of scorn or derision. Now he became a figure of hate. Little Zhen-shi had withered under their malevolent gazes.

That night Zhen-shi had plunged from the roof, his body crushed to pulp on the snow-covered cobbles below.

It was winter, the night harsh and cold, ice forming on the insides of the glass windows. Yet Zhen-shi had been dressed only in a loincloth. Hearing the scream as he fell, Lin-tse had looked out of the window and saw his scrawny body leaking blood to the snow. He and Okai had run out with scores of other boys, and stood over the corpse. The body bore the red weals of a lash on the back, buttocks and thighs. The wrists were also bleeding.

'He was tied,' said Lin-tse. Okai did not answer; he was staring up at the gable from which Zhen-shi had fallen. The rooms on that top level were reserved for the senior cadets from noble families. But the nearest window was that of Argo. Lin-tse followed Okai's gaze. The blond-haired son of Gargan was leaning on his window-sill, and gazing down with mild interest on the scene below.

'Did you see what happened, Argo?' someone shouted.

'The little monkey tried to climb the roof. I think he was drunk.' Then he leaned back and slammed shut his window.

Okai turned to Lin-tse and the two boys walked back to their room. Dalsh-chin was waiting for them. Once inside they squatted on the floor and spoke Nadir in low voices.

'Argo sent for Zhen-shi,' whispered Dalsh-chin, 'three hours ago.'

'He was tied and beaten,' said Okai. 'He could not stand pain, and therefore must have also been gagged. Otherwise we would have heard the screams. There will be an inquiry.'

'It will find,' said Lin-tse, 'that Grinning Monkey, having consumed too much alcohol in celebration of his success, fell from the roof. A salutary lesson that barbarians have no tolerance for strong drink.'

'That is true, my friend,' said Okai. 'But we will make them suffer – as Zhen-shi suffered.'

'A pleasing thought,' said Lin-tse. 'And how will this miracle be accomplished?'

Okai sat silently for a moment. Lin-tse would never forget what followed. Okai's voice dropped even lower: 'The re-building work on the north tower is not yet complete. The labourers will not return for three days. It is deserted. Tomorrow night we will wait until everyone is asleep, then we will go there and prepare the way for vengeance.'

Gargan, Lord of Larness, removed his helm and drew in a deep breath of hot desert air. The sun was beating down, shimmering heat hazes forming over the steppes. Twisting in the saddle, he glanced back along the column. One thousand lancers, eight hundred infantry Guardsmen and two hundred archers were moving slowly in line, dust rising in a cloud around them. Gargan tugged on the reins and cantered back along the column, past the

137

water-wagons and supply carts. Two of his officers joined him and together they rode to the crest of a low hill where Gargan drew rein and scanned the surrounding landscape.

'We will make camp by that ridge,' said Gargan, pointing to a rocky outcrop some miles to the east. 'There is a series of rock pools there.'

'Yes, sir,' answered Marlham, a grizzled, white-bearded career officer coming close to mandatory retirement.

'Put out a screen of scouts,' Gargan ordered. 'Any Nadir seen should be killed.'

'Yes, sir.'

Gargan swung to the second officer, a handsome young man with clear blue eyes. 'You, Premian, will take four companies and scout the marshes. No prisoners. All Nadir are to be treated as hostiles. Understand?'

'Yes, Lord Gargan.' The boy had not yet learned how to keep his feelings from showing in his expression.

'I had you transferred to this force,' said Gargan. 'Do you know why?'

'No, Lord Gargan.'

'Because you are soft, boy,' snapped the general. 'I saw it at the Academy. The steel in you – if steel there is – has not been tempered. Well, it will be during this campaign. I mean to soak the steppes in Nadir blood.' Spurring his stallion, Gargan galloped down the hillside.

'Watch yourself, my boy,' said Marlham. 'The man hates you.'

'He is an animal,' said Premian. 'Vicious and malevolent.'

'All of that,' Marlham agreed. 'He always was a hard man, but when his son disappeared . . . well, it did something to him. He's never been the same since. You were there at the time, weren't you?'

'Aye. It was a bad business,' said Premian. 'There was to be an inquiry over the death of a cadet who fell from Argo's window. On the night before the inquiry Argo vanished. We searched everywhere; his clothes were gone, as was a canvas shoulder-pack. We thought at first that he had feared being implicated in the boy's death. But that was ridiculous, for Gargan would have protected him.'

'What do you think happened?'

'Something dark,' said Premian. With a flick of the reins he moved away, returning to the rear of the column and signalling his junior officers to join him. Swiftly he told them of their new

138

orders. The news was greeted with relief by the two hundred men under his command, for it would mean no more swallowing the dust of the column.

While the men were being issued with supplies, Premian found himself thinking back to his last days at the Academy, that summer two years ago. Only Okai remained of the original Nadir contingent, his two comrades having been sent home after failing the toughest of the pre-final examinations. Their failure had concerned Premian, for he had worked with them and knew their mastery of the subjects was no less proficient than his own. And he had passed with a credit. Only Okai remained – a student so brilliant there was no way he could fail. Even he, however, had barely scraped a pass.

Premian had voiced his concerns to the oldest – and best – of the tutors, a former officer named Fanlon. Late at night, in the old man's study, he told Fanlon he believed the youths were unfairly dismissed.

'We speak much of honour,' said Fanlon sorrowfully, 'but in reality it is in short supply. It always was. I was not allowed to take part in the judging of their papers; the Lord Larness and two of his cronies marked them. But I fear you are correct, Premian. Both Dalsh-chin and Lin-tse were more than capable students.'

'Okai was allowed to pass. Why?' asked Premian.

'He is exceptional, that one. But he will not be allowed to graduate; they will find a way to mark him down.'

'Is there no way we can help him?'

'Tell me first, Premian, why you would wish to? You are not friends.'

'My father taught me to loathe injustice,' answered Premian. 'Is that not enough?'

'Indeed it is. Very well then, I shall help you.'

On the day of the finals, upon entering the examination room, each cadet was handed a small numbered disc taken from a black velvet sack held by the Chief Prefect, a tall, spindly youth named Jashin. Each disc was wrapped in paper to prevent the number being seen by the Prefect. It was a ritual intended to ensure no preferential treatment could be given to any student during the examinations; cadets would merely write the number of their disc at the top of their papers. At the close of the examination the gathered papers would be taken to the judges, who would mark them immediately.

Premian stood in line behind Okai, and noticed that Jashin's fist was already clenched as he delved into the bag before handing the Nadir boy his disc. Premian followed Okai into the examination room, where desks had been set out in rows.

The examination lasted three hours and involved, firstly, establishing a logistical formula and a strategy for supplying an invading army of twenty thousand men, conducting a campaign across the Ventrian Sea; and secondly, constructing a letter of advice to the commanding officer of the expedition, outlining the hazards he must expect to face during his invasion of Ventria.

Premian felt exhausted by the close, but was fairly certain he had performed well. The questions were based on a real campaign of two centuries earlier led by the legendary Gothir General, Bodacas, after whom the Academy was named. Happily, Premian had studied the campaign fairly recently.

As the cadets trooped out, Premian saw General Gargan enter the room along with the other judges. Premian avoided eye contact and sought out Fanlon. The elderly tutor poured the cadet a goblet of watered wine, and the two of them sat for a while in silence by the upper window overlooking the bay.

The afternoon wore on and finally the Keep bell sounded. Premian joined the other students streaming towards the main hall to hear the results.

Gargan and the senior tutors stood on the raised stage at the south end of the hall as the two hundred senior cadets filed in. This time Premian looked squarely at the general, who was now wearing the full armour of his rank, gilded breastplate and the white cloak of a senior Guards officer. Behind him, set on wooden stands, were scores of shining sabres. When the cadets had taken up their positions, Gargan moved to the front of the stage.

His voice thundered out. 'One hundred and forty-six cadets have passed the final examination and will receive their sabres this day,' he said. 'A further seventeen passed with credit. One cadet gained an honour pass. Thirty-six failed, and leave this honoured place bearing the shame earned by their slothful behaviour. In the time-honoured tradition we will begin with the passes, and progress to the honour-cadet. As your disc number is called, move forward.'

One by one the cadets moved forward and handed in their discs, receiving their sabres and bowing to their tutors, before marching to the back of the hall and standing in rank.

The credit students followed. Premian was not among them, nor was Okai. Premian's mouth was dry; he was standing close to the stage and staring up at Gargan. 'Now,' said Gargan, 'we come to the Honour Student – the cream of the Academy, and a man whose martial skills will help to maintain the glory of Gothir.' Turning, he took the last sabre from the stand. Its blade was shining silver steel, its hilt embellished with gold. 'Step forward, number seventeen.'

Okai marched from the ranks and up the short wooden steps as whispers began all around the hall. Premian focused on Gargan's broad face; the man's eyes widened, and Premian saw his jaw twitch. He stood silently, staring with undisguised hatred at the young Nadir.

'There has been a mistake,' he said at last. 'This cannot be! Fetch his paper!'

There was silence in the hall as the Chief Prefect ran from the stage. Minutes passed and no-one moved or spoke. The Chief Prefect returned and handed the sheaf of papers to Gargan, who stood and studied them. Fanlon stepped forward. 'There is no question as to the handwriting, Lord Gargan,' he said softly. 'These are Okai's papers. And I see that you marked them yourself. There can be no mistake.'

Gargan blinked. Okai stepped forward, hand outstretched. Gargan stared at him, then looked down at the sabre in his own trembling hands. Suddenly he thrust the sabre at Fanlon. 'You give it to him!' he hissed. And he strode from the stage.

The elderly tutor smiled at Okai. 'This was well-merited, young man,' he said, his voice carrying to all in the hall. 'For five years you have endured much, both in physical hardship and emotional cruelty. For what it is worth – and I hope it is something – you have my respect and my admiration. I hope that when you go from here you will carry with you some fond memories. Would you like to say a few words to your fellow cadets?'

Okai nodded. Stepping forward, he stood and ran his gaze over the assembled cadets. 'I have learned much here,' he said. 'One day I will put that knowledge to good use.' Without another word he walked from the stage, and out of the hall.

Fanlon followed him from the stage and approached Premian. 'I shall appeal on your behalf and have your papers re-examined.'

'Thank you, sir. For everything. You were right about the discs. I saw Jashin's fingers were closed as he dipped his hand into the bag; he already had a disc ready for Okai.'

'Jashin will be in serious trouble,' said Fanlon. 'Lord Gargan is not a forgiving man.'

Later that day Premian was summoned to Gargan's study. The general was still in his armour, and his face was grey. 'Sit down, boy,' he said. Premian obeyed. 'I am going to ask you a question, and I put you on your honour to answer it with truth.'

'Yes sir,' answered Premian, with a sinking heart.

'Is Okai a friend of yours?'

'No, sir. We rarely speak; we have little in common. Why do you ask, sir?'

For a long moment Gargan stared at him, then he sighed. 'It does not matter. It broke my heart to see him take the sabre. However, that is of no interest to you. I called you here to tell you there has been an error in the marking. You have gained a credit pass.'

'Thank you, sir. How . . . did it happen?'

'It was an honest mistake, and I hope you will accept my apologies for it.'

'Of course, sir. Thank you, sir.'

Premian had left the study and returned to his room, where at midnight he was awakened by a tapping at the door. Rising, he lifted the latch. Okai stood there; the Nadir was fully dressed for travel. 'You are leaving? But the prize-giving is not until tomorrow.'

'I have my sabre,' said Okai. 'I came to thank you. I had thought Gothir honour was all sham. I was wrong.'

'You have suffered here, Okai, but you emerged triumphant and I admire you for it. Where will you go now?'

'Back to my tribe.'

Premian held out his hand and Okai shook it. As the Nadir turned away Premian spoke: 'Do you mind if I ask a question?'

'Not at all.'

'When we were at the burial of your friend, Zhen-shi, you opened the coffin and pressed a small package into his hand. There was blood on it. I have often wondered what it was. Is it part of some Nadir ritual?'

'Yes,' said Okai. 'It gave him a servant in the next life.'

With that Okai walked away.

Three days later, after continuing complaints of a bad smell coming from behind a wall in the new section of the north tower, labourers dug out several blocks of stone. Behind them they found a rotting body, from which the eyes had been cut out.

Chapter Seven

Nuang Xuan was a wily old fox, and he would never have brought his people into Chop-back territory had fortune not ceased to smile upon him. Shading his eyes he scanned the surrounding land, pausing at the pinnacles of rock to the west. His nephew Meng rode alongside. 'Are they the Towers of the Damned?' he asked, keeping his voice low so as not to invoke the spirits who dwelt there.

'They are indeed,' Nuang told the boy, 'but we will not be going close enough for the demons to strike us.' The boy reined his pony round, galloping back to the little convoy. Nuang's gaze followed him. Fourteen warriors, fifty-two women and thirty-one children; not a great force with which to enter such lands. But then who could have supposed that a Gothir cavalry force would be so close to the Mountains of the Moon? When Nuang had led the raid on the Gothir farmers of the marches, seeking to seize horses and goats, he had done so in the knowledge that no soldiers had been stationed there for five years. He had been lucky to escape with fourteen men when the Lancers charged. More than twenty of his warriors had been hacked down in that first charge, among them two of his sons and three nephews. With the cursed *gajin* following his trail, he had no choice but to lead the remnants of his people into this cursed place.

Nuang kicked his pony into a run and rode to the high ground, squinting against the morning sun and studying the back trail. There was no sign of the Lancers. Perhaps they too feared the Chop-backs. Yet why had they been so close to the marches? No

143

Gothir force ever entered the eastern flat lands, save in time of war. Were they at war with someone? The Wolfshead perhaps, or the Green Monkeys? No, surely he would have heard from passing merchants and traders.

It was a mystery, and Nuang disliked mysteries. Once more he glanced at his small company – too small now to build his clan into a full tribe. I will have to lead them back to the north, he thought. He hawked and spat. How they would laugh when Nuang begged for re-admittance to the tribal grounds. Nuang No-luck, they would call him.

Meng and two of the other young men galloped their ponies up the rise. Meng arrived first. 'Riders,' he said, pointing to the west. '*Gajin*, two of them. Can we kill them, Uncle?' The boy was excited, his dark eyes gleaming.

Nuang swung his gaze to where Meng pointed. At this distance, through the heat haze, he could barely make out the riders, and just for a moment he envied the eyes of the young. 'No, we will not attack yet. They may be scouts from a larger force. Let them approach.'

Heeling his pony he rode down to the flat lands, his fourteen warriors alongside him, fanning out in a skirmish line. Summoning Meng, he said, 'What do you see, boy?'

'Still only two, Uncle. *Gajin*. One has a beard and wears a round black helm and a black jerkin with silver armour on the shoulders; the other is yellow-haired and carries no sword. He has knife-sheaths on his chest. Ah!'

'What?'

'The black-bearded one carries a great axe, with two shining blades. They ride Gothir horses, but are leading four saddled ponies.'

'I can see that myself now,' said Nuang testily. 'Go to the rear.'

'I want my part in the kill, Uncle!'

'You are not yet twelve, and you will obey me or feel my whip across your buttocks!'

'I'm almost thirteen,' contradicted Meng, but reluctantly he dragged on his reins and backed his pony to the rear of the group. Nuang Xuan waited, his gnarled hand resting on his ivory-hilted sabre. Slowly the two riders closed the distance until Nuang could see their features clearly. The fair-haired *gajin* was very pale, his manner betraying his nervousness and fear, his hands gripping the reins tightly and his body stiff in the saddle. Nuang flicked his gaze to the axeman. No fear could be seen in this one.

Still, one man and a coward against fourteen? Surely now Nuang's luck had changed? The riders drew rein just ahead of the group and Nuang took a deep breath, ready to order his men to the attack. As he did so he looked at the axeman, and found himself staring into the coldest eyes he had ever seen – the colour of winter storm clouds, grey and unyielding. A nagging doubt struck him and he thought of his remaining sons and nephews, many of whom already carried wounds as their bloody bandages bore witness. The tension grew. Nuang licked his lips and prepared once more to give the signal. The axeman gave an almost imperceptible shake of his head; then he spoke, his voice deep and, if anything, colder than his stare. 'Think carefully about your decision, old one. It seems that luck has not favoured you recently,' he said. 'Your women outnumber your men by, what, three to one? And the riders with you look bloodied and weary.'

'Perhaps our fortune has changed,' Nuang heard himself say.

'Perhaps it has,' agreed the rider. 'I am in a mood for trade. I have four Nadir ponies, and a few swords and bows.'

'You have a fine axe. Is that also for trade?'

The man smiled; it was not a comforting sight. 'No, this is Snaga, which in the Old Tongue means the Sender, the blade of no return. Any man who wishes to test her name need only ask.'

Nuang felt the men around him stirring. They were young and, despite their recent losses, eager for battle. Suddenly he felt the full weight of his sixty-one years. Swinging his horse, he ordered his men to prepare for a night camp close to the towers of rock, and sent out riders to watch for signs of any enemy force. He was obeyed instantly. Turning back to the axeman, he forced a smile. 'You are welcome in our camp. Tonight we will talk of trade.'

Later, as dusk fell, he sat at a small fire with the axeman and his companion. 'Would it not be safer within the rocks?' asked the black-bearded warrior.

'Safer from *men*,' Nuang told him. 'They are the Towers of the Damned and demons are said to stalk the passes. An ancient sorcerer is entombed there, his devils with him. At least, that is how the stories tell it. Now, what do you desire in exchange for those scrawny ponies?'

'Food for the journey, and a guide to take us to the next water, and then on to the Shrine of Oshikai Demon-bane.'

Nuang was surprised, but his expression remained neutral. What would *gajin* seek at the Shrine? 'That is a difficult journey, and perilous. These are the lands of the Chop-backs. Two men and a guide would be . . . tempting . . . prey.'

'They have already been tempted,' the axeman told him. 'That is why we have ponies and weapons to trade.'

Bored by the continued bartering, Sieben stood and wandered away from the fire. The Nadir clan had pitched their tents in a rough circle and erected wind-screens between them. The women were cooking over small fires, the men sitting in three small groups sharing jugs of *lyrrd* – a liquor fermented from rancid goat's milk. Despite the fires and the screens the night was cold. Sieben moved to the horses and unstrapped his blanket, tossing it carelessly over his shoulders. When he had first seen the Nadir riders he had assumed that death would be swift, despite the awesome power of Druss. Now, however, reaction had set in and he felt an almost overwhelming sense of fatigue. A young Nadir woman rose from a cooking-fire and brought him a wooden bowl of braised meat. She was tall and slim, her lips full and tempting. Sieben forgot his weariness instantly as he thanked her and smiled. She moved away without a word, and Sieben's eyes lingered on her swaying hips. The meat was hot and heavily spiced, the flavour new to him, and he ate with relish, returning the bowl to where the woman sat with four others. He squatted down among them. 'A meal fit for a prince,' he told her. 'I thank you, my lady.'

'I am not your lady,' she said, her voice flat and disinterested.

Sieben flashed his best smile. 'Indeed, no, which is my loss I am sure. It is merely an expression we . . . *gajin* use. What I am trying to say is: Thank you for your kindness, and for the quality of your cooking.'

'You have thanked me three times, and dog is not difficult to prepare,' she told him, 'as long as it has been hung until the worms appear in the eye-sockets.'

'Delightful,' he said. 'A tip I shall long remember.'

'And it mustn't be too old,' she continued. 'Young dogs are better.'

'Of course,' he said, half rising.

Suddenly she cocked her head and her eyes met his. 'My man was killed,' she said, 'by Gothir Lancers. Now my blankets are cold, and there is no-one to stir my blood on a bitter night.'

Sieben sat down again more swiftly than he had intended. 'That is a tragedy,' he said softly, looking deep into her almond-shaped eyes. 'A beautiful woman should never suffer the solitude of a cold blanket.'

'My man was a great fighter; he killed three Lancers. But he rutted like a dog on heat. Fast. Then he would sleep. You are not a fighter. What are you?'

'I am a scholar,' he said, leaning in to her. 'I study many things – history, poetry, art. But most of all I study women. They fascinate me.' Lifting his hand he stroked his fingers through her long dark hair, pushing it back from her forehead. 'I love the smell of a woman's hair, the touch of skin upon skin, the softness of lips upon lips. And I am not fast.'

The woman smiled and said something in Nadir to her friends. All the women laughed. 'I am Niobe,' she told him. 'Let us see if you rut as well as you talk.'

Sieben smiled. 'I've always appreciated directness. But is this allowed? I mean, what of the . . .' He gestured towards the men at the camp-fires.

'You come with me,' she said, rising smoothly. 'I wish to see if what they say about *gajin* is true.' Reaching out, she took his hand and led him to a night-dark tent.

Back at the leader's fire, Nuang chuckled. 'Your friend has chosen to mount the tiger. Niobe has fire enough to melt any man's iron.'

'I think he will survive,' said Druss.

'You want a woman to warm your blankets?'

'No. I have a woman back home. What happened to your people? It looks as if you've been mauled.'

Nuang spat into the fire. 'Gothir Lancers attacked us, they came from nowhere on their huge horses. Twenty men I lost. You spoke with great truth when you said fortune has not favoured me. I must have done something to displease the Gods of Stone and Water. But it does no good to whine about it. Who are you? You are not Gothir. Where are you from?'

'The lands of the Drenai, the far blue mountains to the south.'

'You are far from home, Drenai. Why do you seek the Shrine?'

'A Nadir shaman told me I might find something there to help a dying friend.'

'You take a great risk to help this friend; these are not hospitable lands. I considered killing you myself, and I am among the more peaceable of my people.'

'I am not an easy man to kill.'

'I knew that when I looked into your eyes, Drenai. You have

seen many battles, eh? Behind you there are many graves. Once, a long time ago, another Drenai came among my people. He too was a fighter; they called him Old-Hard-To-Kill and he fought a battle against the Gothir. Years later he came to live among us. I was told these stories when I was a child; they are the only stories I have heard of Drenai. His name was Angel.'

'I have heard the name,' said Druss. 'What more do you know of him?'

'Only that he was wed to the daughter of Ox-skull, and they had two sons. One was tall and handsome, and did not look like Angel, but the other was a powerful warrior. He married a Nadir maiden, and they left the tribe to journey south. That is all I know.'

Two women came and knelt beside them, offering bowls of meat to the men. A short series of keening cries came from the tent of Niobe, and the women laughed. Druss reddened and ate his meal in silence. The women moved away. 'Your friend will be a tired man come the dawn,' said Nuang.

Druss lay quietly looking up at the stars. He rarely found sleep difficult, but tonight he was restless. Sitting up, he threw back his blanket. The camp was silent, the fires faded to glowing ash. Nuang had offered him the shelter of his own tent, but Druss had refused, preferring to sleep in the open.

Gathering his axe and helm and silver-skinned gauntlets, he stood and stretched. The night was cold, and a chill breeze whispered under the wind-breaks stretching between the tents. Druss was uneasy. Pushing his helm into place and pulling on his gauntlets, he silently strode through the camp, easing himself past a stretched canvas wind-break and out on to the open steppes. A sentry was sitting by a creosote bush, a goatskin cloak drawn about him. As Druss approached him he saw it was the slender boy, Meng, whom Nuang had introduced as his youngest nephew. The youth looked up, but said nothing.

'All quiet?' asked Druss. The boy nodded, obviously ill at ease.

Druss strolled on towards the towers of black rock, and sat down on a boulder some fifty feet from the boy. By day the steppes were hot and inhospitable, but the cold magic of the night gave the land a sense of brooding malevolence that spoke of nameless horrors stalking the shadow-haunted rocks. The eyes played tricks upon the brain. Gnarled boulders became crouching demons that seemed to shimmer and move, and the wind hissing over the steppes became a sibilant voice, promising pain and death. Druss was not oblivious to this lunar sorcery. Pushing such thoughts from his mind he gazed up at the moon and thought of Rowena, back on the farm. He had tried so hard, during the years since the rescue, to make her feel loved, needed. But deep down there was a gnawing pain in him that he could not ignore. She had loved the warrior Michanek, and he had loved her. It was not jealousy that hurt Druss, it was a deep sense of shame. When the raiders had stolen her so many years before, Druss had set out to find her with a single-minded determination that would brook no opposition. He had journeyed to Mashrapur and there, to gain enough money for passage to Ventria, had become a fist-fighter. After that he had crossed the ocean, engaged in battles with corsairs and pirates and had joined the demoralized army of Prince Gorben, becoming his champion. All this so that he could find Rowena, and rescue her from what he perceived as a life of abject slavery.

At the last, though, he had learned the truth. Her memory lost to her, she had fallen in love with Michanek, and was a respected and loved wife, living in luxury, happy and content. Yet knowing this, Druss had still fought alongside the soldiers who destroyed the city in which she lived, and butchered the man she loved.

Druss had watched Michanek stand against the best of the Immortals, and had seen them fall back in awe as he stood bleeding from a score of wounds, a dozen assailants dead around him.

'You were a man, Michanek,' whispered Druss, with a sigh. Rowena had never once shown bitterness for his part in Michanek's death. Indeed, they had never spoken of the man. Out here in this lonely wilderness Druss realized that this was wrong. Michanek deserved better. As did Rowena – sweet, gentle, Rowena. All she had wanted was to marry the farmer Druss would have become, build a house and raise children. Druss had been a farmer once, but never could be again. He had tasted the joys of battle, the exhilarating narcotic of violence, and not even his love for Rowena could keep him chained to the mountains of home. And as for children? They had not been blessed. Druss would have liked a son. Regret touched him, but he swiftly blocked it from his mind. His thoughts drifted to Sieben, and he smiled. We are not so different, he thought. We are both skilled in a dark sterile art. I live for battle without need of a cause, you live for sex without thought of love. What do we offer this tormented world? he wondered. The breeze picked up and Druss's restlessness increased. Narrowing his eyes, he scanned the steppes. All was silent. Standing, he walked back to the boy. 'What do the riders report?' he asked.

'Nothing,' replied Meng. 'No sign of *gajin* or Chop-backs.'

'When is the next change of watch?'

'When the moon touches the tallest peak.'

Druss glanced up. That would be soon. Leaving the boy, he strolled out once more, his unease growing. They should have camped within the rocks, and to Hell with fears of demons! A rider came into sight; he waved at Meng and then cantered into the camp. Minutes later his replacement rode out. Another rider came in, then another. Druss waited for some time, then returned to the boy. 'Were not four sent out?'

'Yes. I expect Jodai is sleeping somewhere. My uncle will not be pleased.'

The breeze shifted. Druss's head came up and he sniffed the air. Grabbing the boy by his shoulder, he hauled him to his feet. 'Wake your uncle, *now*! Tell him to get everyone back into the rocks.'

'Take your hand off me!' Feebly the boy lashed out but Druss dragged him in close. 'Listen to me, boy, death is coming! You understand? There may be no time left. So run as if your life depended on it, for it probably does.'

Meng turned and sprinted back towards the camp. Druss, axe in hand, stared out at the seemingly empty steppes. Then he too turned and loped back to the camp. Nuang was already moving as Druss ducked under the wind-break. Women were hastily gathering blankets and food, and shushing the children into silence. Nuang ran to Druss. 'What have you seen?' he asked.

'Not seen, *smelt*. Thickened goose-grease. The Lancers use it to protect the leather on their mounts, and also to prevent rust on their chain-mail. They have hidden their horses, and they are close.'

Nuang swore and moved away. As Sieben emerged from a tent, looping his knife baldric over his shoulder, Druss waved to him, pointing to the rocks some hundred paces away. Leaving their tents, the Nadir opened a gap in the wind-breaks and ran across the open ground. Druss saw the remaining warriors leading the ponies into a deep cleft in the rocks. Taking up the rear he moved behind the column. A running woman fell and Druss helped her to her feet. She was carrying a baby, and also holding the hand of a toddler. Druss swept the boy into his arms and ran on. There were only a handful of Nadir women still short of the rocks when fifty Lancers emerged from a nearby gully. On foot they charged, blades bright in the moonlight.

Passing the toddler to his terrified mother, Druss hefted Snaga and turned to face the advancing soldiers. Several of the Nadir warriors had scrambled high in the rocks and they sent black-shafted arrows into the enemy. But the Gothir Lancers were well armoured, with breastplates, chain-mail and full-faced helms. Each carried a round buckler strapped to his left forearm. Most of the arrows bounced harmlessly clear, save for one which took a man deep in the thigh. He stumbled and fell, his white horse-hair-plumed helmet falling clear. 'Shoot low!' yelled Druss.

The entrance to the rocks was narrow and Druss backed into it. The first three Lancers ran in to the cleft and with a roar he leapt to meet them, smashing Snaga through the helm of the first, and killing the second with a reverse cut that smashed his hip and tore open his belly. The third tried to bring his sabre to bear, but the blade bounced from Druss's black helm. Snaga sang out, thundering against the man's chain-mail neck-guard. The mail was well made, and prevented the blades from reaching the skin, but the sheer weight of the blow drove the links against the man's neck, smashing his spine to shards. More soldiers ran in. The first tried to block the sweep of the axe with his iron-reinforced wooden buckler, but the silver blades sliced it cleanly, half severing the arm beneath. With a scream of pain the man fell, tripping two men behind him. The narrow opening would allow only three to attack at any one time, and the rest of the Lancers milled behind the entrance. From above, the Nadir hurled rocks down upon them and sent shafts into unprotected legs.

Druss hacked and cut, the mighty axe drenched in blood . . .

And the Lancers fell back. A man groaned at Druss's feet; it was the soldier with the half-severed arm. Kneeling, Druss dragged the soldier's helm clear and seized the wounded man's hair. 'How many in your force?' asked the axeman. 'Speak and you live, for I'll let you go back to your friends.'

'Two companies. I swear it!'

'Get up and run, for I cannot answer for the archers above.'

The man stumbled out into the open, and began to run. Two arrows bounced from his breastplate, a third nailing home into the back of his thigh. Gamely he limped on, and managed to reach his comrades.

Two companies . . . fifty men. Druss glanced down at the

bodies he could see. Seven were dead by his axe, several more had been struck by shafts and would not fight again. That still left around forty – not enough to storm these rocks, but enough to pin them down until a second force could be sent for.

Three young Nadir climbed down to where he stood and began to strip the dead of armour and weapons. Nuang clambered down also. 'You think they will pull back?'

Druss shook his head. 'They will look for another way in. We must get further back into the rocks, otherwise they'll find a way to get behind us. How many were in the group that attacked you on the marches?'

'No more than a hundred.'

'Then the question remains: Where are the other two companies?'

Suddenly the Lancers charged again. The Nadir youngsters ran back and Druss stepped forward. 'Come in and die, you whoresons!' he bellowed, his voice booming and echoing in the rocks. The first of the Lancers sent his sabre in a hissing arc towards Druss's throat, but Snaga flashed up to shatter the blade. The soldier hurled himself back, cannoning into two of his comrades. As Druss leapt at them, they turned and fled.

Nuang, sword in hand, appeared alongside Druss. Flames leapt up from the Nadir camp and Nuang cursed, but Druss chuckled. 'Tents can be replaced, old man. It seems to me that your luck has changed for the better.'

'Oh, yes,' said Nuang bitterly. 'I leap with joy at this change of fortune!'

Niobe lay on her stomach, staring down into the narrow cleft of black, basaltic rock. 'Your friend is a very great fighter,' she said, pushing her raven hair back from her face.

Sieben hunkered down beside her. 'That is his talent,' he admitted, annoyed at her admiring tone and the way her dark, almond-shaped eyes were focused on the axeman below.

'Why did you not fight alongside him, po-et?'

'My dear, when Druss starts swinging that dreadful axe the last place you want to be is beside him. Anyway, Druss always likes the odds to be against him. Brings out the best in him, you know.'

Niobe rolled to her elbow and gazed into his eyes. 'Why is it you are no longer frightened, po-et? When we ran in here you were trembling.'

'I don't like violence,' he admitted, 'especially when it is directed towards me. But they won't follow us in here. They are

Lancers, heavily armoured; they are trained for cavalry charges on open ground. Their boots are metal-reinforced and high-heeled to keep the feet in the stirrups. They are entirely unsuited to scrambling over volcanic rock. No, they will pull back now, and try to catch us in the open. Therefore, for the moment, we are safe.'

She shook her head. 'No-one is safe here,' she told him. 'Look around you, po-et. These black rocks are part of the Towers of the Damned. Evil dwells here. Even now there may be demons creeping towards us!'

Sieben shivered, but even in the fading moonlight he could see the amused gleam in her eyes. 'You don't believe that for a moment,' he said.

'Perhaps I do.'

'No, you are just trying to frighten me. Would you like to know why the Nadir believe there are demons here?' She nodded. 'Because this area is – or once was – volcanic. It would have spewed fire, poisoned ash and red-hot lava. Travellers close by would have heard great rumblings below the earth.' He swung round and pointed to the twin towers rearing towards the brightening sky. 'Those are just cones of hollow, cooled lava.'

'You don't believe in demons?' she asked him.

'Aye,' he said sombrely, 'I do. There are beasts which can be summoned from the Pit – but they are like puppy-dogs when compared with the demons every man carries in his heart.'

'Your heart has demons in it?' she whispered, eyes widening.

'Such a literal people,' he said, shaking his head and rising. Swiftly he climbed down to where Druss was waiting with Nuang and several Nadir. He noted wryly how the Nadir stood close to the axeman, hanging on his words and grinning as he spoke. Only hours before they had been lusting to kill him. Now he was a hero to them. A friend.

'What ho, old horse!' Sieben called and Druss swung towards him.

'What do you think, poet? Have we seen the last of them?'

'I believe so. But we had better find another way out of these hills. I wouldn't want to be caught by them on open ground.'

Druss nodded. Blood was staining his jerkin and beard, but he had cleaned his axe blades.

The dawn sun glinted above the distant mountains and Druss strode to the mouth of the cleft. The Lancers had pulled back in the darkness, and were nowhere in sight.

153

For another hour the Nadir waited nervously in the rocks, then several of them crept down to the smoking ruins of their camp, gathering what possessions had not been lost to the fires.

Nuang approached Druss and Sieben. 'Niobe tells me you believe the rocks are safe,' he said, and Sieben explained once more about volcanic activity. Nuang did not look impressed, his dark flat face expressionless and his eyes wary.

Druss laughed. 'Given a choice between demons we haven't seen and Lancers we have, I know what I'd choose.'

Nuang grunted, then cleared his throat and spat. 'Does your axe kill demons?'

Druss gave a cold smile and hefted Snaga, holding the blades close to Nuang's face. 'What it can cut it can kill.'

Nuang gave a broad smile. 'I think we will walk the Hills of the Damned,' he said.

'Never a dull moment with you, Druss,' muttered Sieben. As Druss clapped him on the shoulder, he glanced down at the blood-smeared hand. 'Oh, thank you. Just what a blue silk shirt needs, a spot of drying blood!'

'I'm hungry,' Druss announced, swinging away with a grin. Taking a handkerchief from the pocket of his leggings Sieben dabbed at the offending mark, then followed the axeman back into the rocks. Niobe brought him food, cold meat and goat's cheese, and sat beside him as he ate.

'Is there any water?' he asked.

'Not yet. The *gajin* destroyed all but one of our barrels. Today will be dry and hot. That is a pretty shirt,' she added, reaching out and stroking the silk, her fingers lingering over the mother-of-pearl buttons at the neck.

'I had it made in Drenan,' he told her.

'Everything is so soft,' she murmured, stroking her hand down over his woollen leggings, and resting her palm on his thigh. 'So soft.'

'Raise your hand any higher and it won't stay soft,' he warned her. Glancing up at him she raised one eyebrow, then slid her hand along the inside of his thigh. 'Ah,' she said, 'how true.'

'Time to be moving, poet!' called Druss.

'Your timing is impeccable,' replied Sieben.

For two hours the convoy moved into the black hills. There was no vegetation here, and walls of dark, volcanic rock reared above them. Silently the group pushed on, the Nadir casting fearful glances around them. Even the children remained quiet.

No-one rode, for the footing was treacherous. Towards midday the ground gave way under a pony which fell, its left front leg snapping. It thrashed around until a young Nadir warrior leapt upon it, slicing open its throat; blood gushed to the rocks. The women moved forward, dragging the pony clear of the hole and butchering it. 'Fresh meat tonight,' Niobe told Sieben.

The heat was intense now, so strong that Sieben had ceased to sweat and felt his brain was shrivelling to the size of a walnut. By dusk the exhausted party had reached the centre of the hills, and they made camp beneath one of the twin towers. For more than an hour Sieben had been lusting after a drink of water from the one remaining barrel, and he queued with the warriors for a single cup. The taste was beyond nectar.

Later, just before sunset, he wandered away from the camp and climbed the jagged rocks towards the west-facing summit. The climb was not difficult, but it was tiring. Even so Sieben had a need to get away from the others, to find solitude. At the peak he sat down and stared out over the land. White clouds dotted the sky, peaceful and serene, and the setting sun was falling behind them, bathing the distant mountains in golden light. The breeze here was deliciously cool, the view extraordinary. The far mountains lost their colour as the sun sank lower, becoming black silhouettes like storm clouds gathering at the horizon, the sky above them turning mauve, then grey-silver and finally pale gold. The clouds also changed colour, moving from pristine white to coral red in a sea of royal blue. Sieben leaned back against a rock and soaked in the sight. At last the sky darkened and the moon appeared, bright and pure. Sieben sighed.

Niobe clambered up to sit alongside him.

'I wanted to be alone,' he said.

'We are alone,' she pointed out.

'How stupid of me. Of course we are.' Turning from her he gazed down into the cone of the tower. A shaft of moonlight broke through the clouds and illuminated the core.

Niobe's hand touched his shoulder. 'Look at the ledge down there,' she said.

'I am in no mood for sex, my pretty. Not at this moment.'

'No, look! At the far end of the ledge.' His gaze followed her pointing finger. Some twenty feet below and to the right there was – or what appeared to be – an entrance carved into the rock.

'It is a trick of the light,' he said, peering down into the cone.

'And there,' she said, 'steps!' It was true. At the far end of the ledge a series of steps had been cut into the wall of the cone.

'Go and fetch Druss,' he commanded.

'That is where the demons live,' she whispered, as she walked away.

'Tell him to bring a rope, torches and a tinder-box.'

Niobe stopped and looked back. 'You are going down there? For why?'

'Because I am a naturally curious man, my darling. I want to know why anyone would carve an opening on the inside of a volcano.'

The moonlight was brighter now, as the clouds dispersed, and Sieben edged around the crater, moving closer to the ancient steps. Immediately above the first of them there were rope grooves in the soft rock. The steps themselves had either been hacked with great speed, or had weathered badly – perhaps both, he thought. Leaning over the rim he pushed his fingers against the first step. The rock crumbled away at his touch. Under no circumstances would these steps any longer support the weight of a man.

Druss, Nuang and several Nadir warriors climbed up towards him. Niobe was not with them. The old Nadir chieftain leaned over the rim and stared at the rectangular entrance below. He said nothing. Druss squatted down beside Sieben. 'The girl says you want to go down there. Is that wise, poet?'

'Perhaps not, old horse. But I don't want to spend the rest of my life wondering about it.'

Druss peered down into the cone. 'That's a long way to fall.'

Sieben gazed down into the black depths. The moonlight, though bright, did not reach the bottom of the cone. 'Lower me down to the ledge,' he said, hanging on to the last of his courage. There was no way now that he could withdraw. 'But don't release your hold when I reach the ledge. The rock crumbles like salt crystals and the ledge may not support me.' Tying a rope around his waist, and waiting until Druss looped it over his huge shoulders, he swung out over the rim. Slowly Druss let out the rope until Sieben's feet touched the ledge, which was solid and strong.

Now he stood before the entrance. There was no doubt it had been carved by men. Strange symbols had been etched into the rock, swirls and stars surrounding what appeared to be the outline of a broken sword. Just inside the entrance a series of iron bars had been cemented into the black rock; these were now red with rust. Sieben gripped one of them and pulled hard, but it did not budge.

'What is happening?' called Druss.

'Come down and see. I'll untie the rope.'

Moments later Druss, holding a lighted torch, joined him. 'Stand back,' said the axeman, handing the torch to Sieben and removing his rope. Taking a firm grip with both hands, Druss wrenched at the first of the bars. With a grinding groan it bent in the middle, then ripped away from the surrounding rock. Druss hurled it over his shoulder and Sieben heard it clanging and bouncing down the walls of the cone. Two more bars were prised loose in the same fashion. 'After you, poet,' said Druss.

Sieben eased himself through the gap in the bars and held up the torch. He found himself standing in a small, round chamber. Turning, he saw two chains hanging from the ceiling. Druss appeared alongside him, and approached the chains, from one of which something dangled. 'Bring the torch closer,' ordered the axeman and Sieben did so.

The chain held a dried and withered arm, which had torn loose from the shoulder as the corpse decayed. Lowering the torch, Sieben gazed down at the long-dead, almost mummified body. The flickering torchlight shone on a long dress of decaying white silk, still strangely beautiful in this dark and gloomy setting.

'It was a woman,' said Druss. 'Someone entombed her here alive.'

Sieben knelt by the corpse. Glints of light came from the sunken eye-sockets and he almost dropped the torch. Druss peered closer. 'The whoresons put out her eyes with nails of gold,' he said. Touching the corpse's head, he turned it. Gold also glinted in the ear canals on both sides. Sieben wished Niobe had never seen the ledge. His heart sank with sorrow for this long-dead woman and her terrible suffering.

'Let's get out of here,' he said softly.

At the rim they told Nuang what they had seen. The old leader sat silently until they had finished. 'She must have been a great sorceress,' he said. 'The swirls and the stars on the entrance show that spells were cast there to chain her spirit to this place. And the nails would stop her hearing or seeing in the world of spirit. It is likely they also pierced her tongue.'

Sieben rose and retied his rope. 'What are you doing?' asked Druss.

'I'm going back, old horse.'

'For why?' queried Nuang. Sieben gave no answer, but swung himself once more over the rim.

Druss grinned at him as he took up the rope. 'Ever the romantic, eh, poet?'

'Just hand me the torch.'

Once more in the chamber, Sieben knelt by the corpse and forced himself to push his fingers deep into the dry eye-sockets, drawing out the nails of gold. They came away cleanly, as did the longer nail in the right ear. The left was wedged deep and Sieben had to loosen it with a knife-blade. As he opened the mouth of the corpse the jaw fell clear. Steeling himself, he lifted clear the last golden nail. 'I do not know,' he said softly, 'if your spirit is now free, lady. I hope that it is.' As he was about to rise he saw a glint of bright metal within the rotted folds of the woman's dress. Reaching down, he lifted it; it was a round medallion, ringed with dark gold. Holding it up to the light he saw that the centre was tarnished silver and raised with a relief he could not make out. Pocketing it, he walked back out to the ledge and called out to Druss to haul him up.

Once back in the camp Sieben sat in the moonlight polishing the medallion, bringing back its brightness. Druss joined him. 'I see you found a treasure,' said the axeman, and Sieben passed it to him. On one surface was the profile of a man, on the obverse a woman. Around the woman's head were words in a language Sieben did not recognize.

Druss peered at it. 'Perhaps it was a coin – a king and queen,' he said. 'You think the woman was her?'

Sieben shrugged. 'I do not know, Druss. But whoever she was, her murder was administered with the foulest cruelty. Can you imagine what it must have been like? To be dragged to that soulless place and to have your eyes put out? To be left hanging and bleeding while death crept up with agonizing lack of speed?'

Druss handed the medallion back to him. 'Perhaps she was a terrible witch who ate babies. Perhaps her punishment was just.'

'Just? There is no crime, Druss, for which that punishment was just. If someone is evil, then you kill them. But look what they did to her. Whoever was responsible took delight in it. It was so carefully planned, so meticulously executed.'

'Well, you did what you could, poet.'

'Little enough, wasn't it? You think I freed her spirit to see, to talk, to hear?'

'It would be good to think so.'

Niobe moved alongside them and sat next to Sieben. 'You have great tension, po-et. You need love-making.'

Sieben grinned. 'I think you are entirely correct,' he said, rising and taking her by the hand.

Later, Niobe sleeping beside him, Sieben sat in the moonlight thinking about the woman in the tomb. Who was she and for what crime had she been executed? he wondered. She was a sorceress, of that there was no doubt. Her killers had gone to great lengths – and greater cost – to destroy her.

Niobe stirred beside him. 'Can you not sleep, po-et?'

'I was thinking about the dead woman.'

'For why?'

'I don't know. It was a cruel way to die, blinded, chained and left alone in a volcanic cave. Brutal and vicious. And why did they bring her here, to this desolate place? Why hide the body?'

Niobe sat up. 'Where does the sun go to sleep?' she asked. 'Where are the bellows of the winds? Why do you ask yourself questions you cannot answer?'

Sieben smiled and kissed her. 'That is how knowledge is gained,' he said. 'People asking questions for which there are no immediate answers. The sun does not sleep, Niobe. It is a great ball of fire in the heavens, and this planet is a smaller ball spinning round it.' She looked at him quizzically, but said nothing. 'What I am trying to say is that there are always answers even if we cannot *see* them right away. The woman in that cave was rich, probably high-born, a princess or a queen. The medallion I found has two heads engraved upon it, a man and a woman. Both have Nadir or Chiatze features.'

'Show me.'

Sieben took the medallion from his pouch and dropped it into her hand. The moonlight was bright, and Niobe studied the heads. 'She was very lovely. But she was not Nadir.'

'Why do you say that?'

'The writings on the *lon-tsia*. They are Chiatze; I have seen the symbols before.'

'Can you read what it says?'

'No.' She passed it back to him.

'What did you call it? A *lon-tsia*?'

'Yes. It is a love gift. Very expensive. Two would have been made for the wedding. The man is her husband, and her *lon-tsia* would have been worn with the man's head facing inward, over

159

her heart. He would wear his in the reverse way, her head upon his heart. Old Chiatze custom – but only for the rich.'

'Then I wonder what happened to her husband.'

Niobe leaned in close. 'No more questions, po-et,' she whispered. 'I shall sleep now.' Sieben lay down beside her. Her fingers stroked his face, then slid over his chest and belly.

'I thought you said you wanted sleep?'

'Sleep is always better after love-making.'

By the afternoon of the following day the group came to the last outcrop of rocks before the steppes. Nuang sent out scouts, and the last of the water was doled out to the women and children. Druss, Nuang and the boy, Meng, climbed the rocks and scanned the bleak, apparently empty steppes. There was no sign of any enemy.

After an hour the scouts returned to report that the Lancers had moved on. The riders had followed their tracks to a waterhole in a deep gully, which had been drunk dry and was now deserted.

Nuang led his weary people to the hole, and there made camp. 'They have no patience, these *gajin*,' he told Druss as they stood beside the mud-churned water-hole. 'It is a seep, and yet they allowed their horses to ride into it. Had they waited and taken only a little water at a time, it would have fully nourished both men and mounts. Now? Ha! Their horses will have barely wet their tongues, and will be useless to them by sunset.'

Several of the Nadir women began digging in the mud and the gravel below, slowly clearing the hole. Then they sat back and waited. After an hour the small seep began to fill.

Later Nuang sent out scouts once more. They returned an hour before dusk. Nuang spoke to them, then moved to where Druss and Sieben were saddling their horses. 'The *gajin* have cut to the north-west. My men saw a great cloud of dust there. They rode as close as they dared – and saw an army on the march. For why is an army here? What is here for them to fight?'

Druss laid his huge hand on the old man's shoulder. 'They are riding for the Valley of Shul-sen's Tears. They seek to pillage the Shrine.'

'They want Oshikai's bones?' asked the old man, incredulously.

'How far is it to the Shrine?' Druss asked.

'If you take two spare mounts and ride through the night to the north-east, you will see its walls in two days,' said Nuang. 'But the *gajin* will not be far behind you.'

'May your luck be good,' said Druss, holding out his hand. The Nadir leader nodded, and shook hands.

Sieben moved away to where Niobe stood. 'I hope we meet again, my lady,' he said.

'We will or we won't,' she said, and turned away from him. The poet walked to his horse and vaulted to the saddle. Druss mounted the mare and, leading two spare ponies, the two men left the camp.

Even before Nosta Khan's arrival at the Shrine, news of the Gothir invasion had reached the four camps. A rider from the Curved Horn tribe came in, his pony lathered in sweat. Galloping to the tents of his own people, he leapt from the saddle. A cavalry group had attacked two Curved Horn villages, slaughtering men, women and children. Thousands more soldiers were heading towards the valley, he said.

The leader of the Curved Horn contingent, a middle-aged warrior named Bartsai, sent for the other leaders and they gathered at noon within his tent: Lin-tse of the Sky Riders, Quing-chin of the Fleet Ponies, and Kzun, the shaven-headed war chief of the Lone Wolves. They sat in silence as the rider told of what he had seen – a Gothir army on the march, killing all Nadir in their path.

'It makes no sense,' said Kzun. 'Why have they made war upon the Curved Horn?'

'And why is their army heading for this valley?' put in Lin-tse.

'Perhaps more importantly,' said Quing-chin, 'we should be asking ourselves what we intend to do. They are less than two days from us.'

'Do?' queried Bartsai. 'What can we do? Do you see an army around you? We have fewer than one hundred and twenty men.'

'We are the guards of the Sacred Shrine,' said Lin-tse. 'Numbers mean nothing. Were we but four, we should fight.'

'You speak for yourself!' snapped Bartsai. 'I see no point in throwing away our lives. If there are no warriors here then the *gajin* will pass by the Shrine. There is nothing here for them, save the bones of Oshikai. No treasures, no plunder. Therefore we keep the Shrine safe by fleeing.'

'Pah!' sneered Lin-tse. 'What more could be expected from a Curved Horn coward?'

Bartsai surged to his feet, snatching a curved dagger from his belt as Lin-tse reared up, reaching for his sabre. Quing-chin jumped between them. 'No!' he shouted. 'This is madness!'

'I will not be insulted in my own tent,' shouted Bartsai, glowering at the taller Lin-tse.

'Then do not talk of flight,' said Lin-tse, slamming his sabre back into its scabbard.

'What else is there to talk of?' asked Kzun. 'I do not wish to run from *gajin*. Neither do I wish to throw away the lives of my men needlessly. I have no love for the Curved Horn, but Bartsai is a warrior who has ridden in many battles. He is no coward. Neither am I. What he says is true. Whatever their purpose, the *gajin* are looking to kill Nadir. If there are none of us here, they must move on. We should draw them further into the steppes, away from water. Their horses will die there.'

The tent-flap opened and a small man stepped inside. He was old and wizened, and wore a necklace of human finger-bones.

'Who are you?' asked Bartsai warily, aware from the bones that the man was a shaman.

'I am Nosta Khan.' Moving forward he sat between Kzun and Bartsai. Both men moved sideways, making more room for him. 'You now know the threat facing you,' said the shaman. 'Two thousand Gothir warriors, led by Gargan Nadir Bane, are marching upon this holy place. What you do not know is why, but I shall tell you. They come to destroy the Shrine, to raze the walls, take the bones of Oshikai and grind them to dust.'

'For what purpose?' asked Kzun.

'Who can read the minds of the *gajin*?' said Nosta Khan. 'They treat us like vermin, to be destroyed at their whim. I care nothing for their reasons, it is enough that they are coming.'

'What do you advise, shaman?' asked Lin-tse.

'You must appoint a war leader, and resist them with all your might. The Shrine must not fall to the *gajin*.'

'Stinking round-eyed vermin!' hissed Kzun. 'It is not enough that they hound us and kill us. Now they wish to desecrate our holy places. I will not suffer this. The question is, which of us should lead? I do not wish to sound arrogant, but I have fought in thirty-seven battles. I offer myself.'

'Hear me,' said Quing-chin softly. 'I respect every leader here, and my words are not intended to cause insult. Of the men here in this tent only two could lead, myself and Lin-tse, for we were both trained by the *gajin* and we well know the ways of the siege.

162

But one among us here is a man who understands the strategies of *gajin* warfare better than any other.'

'Who is this . . . hero?' asked Bartsai.

Quing-chin turned towards Lin-tse. 'Once he was named Okai. Now he is called Talisman.'

'And you believe this man can lead us to victory?' put in Kzun. 'Against a force twenty times our number?'

'The Sky Riders will follow him,' said Lin-tse suddenly.

'As will the Fleet Ponies,' added Quing-chin.

'What tribe is this man from?' Bartsai asked.

'Wolfshead,' Lin-tse told him.

'Then let us go to him. I wish to see him myself before I commit my men to him,' said Bartsai. 'In the meantime I will send out riders, for there are many Curved Horn villages close by. We will need more fighters.'

Zhusai had endured a troubled night, with strange dreams filling her mind. Men were dragging her through a twisted landscape, chaining her in a dark, gloomy chamber. Names were screamed at her: 'Witch! Whore!' Blows struck her face and body.

She had opened her eyes, her heart hammering in panic. Jumping from her bed she had run to the window, throwing it open and breathing deeply of the cool night air. Too frightened to return to sleep, she had walked out into the open yard before the Shrine. Talisman and Gorkai were sitting there as she approached and Talisman rose. 'Are you well, Zhusai?' he asked, taking her arm. 'You are very pale.'

'I had a terrible dream but it is fading now.' She smiled. 'May I sit with you?'

'Of course.'

The three of them had discussed the search for the Eyes of Alchazzar. Talisman had checked the Shrine Room thoroughly, scanning walls and floor for hidden compartments, but there were none. Together with Gorkai he had even lifted the stone coffin lid and examined the dried bones within. There was nothing to be found, save a *lon-tsia* of heavy silver bearing the heads of Oshikai and Shul-sen. He had left it with the bones and carefully replaced the lid.

'Oshikai's spirit told me the Eyes were hidden here, but I cannot think where else to look,' said Talisman.

Zhusai stretched herself out beside the men, and drifted to sleep . . .

A slim man with burning eyes pushed his face into her own, biting her lip until it bled. 'Now you die, witch, and not before time.' She spat in his face.

'Then I shall be with my love,' she said, 'and will never have to look upon your worthless face again!' He struck her then, savagely, repeatedly. Then he grabbed her hair.

'You'll never see him this side of eternity.' Holding up his hand he showed her five small golden spikes. 'With these I shall put out your eyes, and pierce your ear-drums. The last I will drive through your tongue. Your spirit will be mine, throughout time. Chained to me, as you should have been in life. Do you want to beg? If I cut you loose will you fall down on your knees and swear loyalty to me?'

Zhusai wanted to say yes, but the voice that came from her mouth was not hers. 'Swear loyalty to a worm? You are nothing, Chakata. I warned my Lord of you, but he would not listen. Now I curse you, and my curse will follow you until the stars die!'

Her head was dragged back. His hand came up, and she felt the glittering spike push into her eyeball . . .

With a cry of pain, Zhusai woke to find Talisman sitting beside her bed. 'How did I get here?' she asked.

'I carried you. You began speaking in Chiatze. It is not a tongue with which I am familiar; it changed your voice incredibly.'

'I had the dream again, Talisman. It was so real. A man . . . many men . . . took me to a dark chamber, and there they put out my eyes. It was horrible. They called me a witch and a whore. They had . . . I think . . . murdered my husband.'

'Rest,' said Talisman. 'You are distraught.'

'I am distraught,' she agreed, 'but . . . I have never experienced a dream like this one. The colours were so sharp, and . . .' Gently he stroked her head and, exhausted, she slept again. And this time there were no dreams.

When she awoke she was alone, and bright sunlight filled the room. There was a jug of water and a basin on a table by the window. Rising from the narrow bed she took off her clothes, filled the basin, added three drops of perfume from a tiny bottle and washed her face and upper body. From her pack she took a long tunic of white silk; it was crumpled, but clean. Once dressed, she washed the clothes she had been wearing the previous day and laid them over the window-sill to dry. Bare-footed she left the room, walked down the narrow wooden stairs and emerged into the courtyard below.

Talisman was sitting alone, eating a breakfast of bread and cheese. Gorkai was grooming the ponies on the other side of the courtyard. Zhusai sat beside Talisman and he poured her a goblet of water. 'Did you dream again?' he asked her.

'No.' He is bone-tired, she thought, his eyes dull. 'What will you do now?' she asked him.

'I know . . . believe . . . the Eyes are here, but I cannot think where else to look.'

Five men came walking through the open gates. Zhusai's heart sank as she recognized Nosta Khan, and she stood and moved back into the shadows. Talisman's face was impassive as the men approached. The first of the men, a shaven-headed warrior with a gold earring, halted before him. 'I am Kzun of the Lone Wolves,' he said, his voice deep and cold. His body was lean and hard, and Zhusai felt a flicker of fear as she gazed upon him. His posture was challenging as he stood looming over Talisman. 'Quing-chin of the Fleet Ponies claims you are a war leader to follow. You do not look like a war leader.'

Talisman rose and stepped past Kzun, ignoring him. He walked to a tall, solemn-faced warrior. 'It is good to see you, Lin-tse,' he said.

'And you, Okai. The Gods of Stone and Water have brought you here at this time.'

A burly, middle-aged man stepped forward. 'I am Bartsai of the Curved Horn.' Dropping into a crouch, he extended his right arm with palm upward. 'Quing-chin of the Fleet Ponies speaks highly of you and we are here to ask of you a service.'

'Not yet we don't,' snapped Kzun. 'First let him prove himself.'

'Why do you need a war leader?' asked Talisman, directing his question at Lin-tse.

'Gargan is coming with an army. The Gothir seek to destroy the Shrine.'

'They have already attacked several Nadir camps,' added Quing-chin.

Talisman walked away from the group, and sat cross-legged on the ground. Three of the others followed and sat around him. Kzun hesitated, then joined them. Gorkai moved across the courtyard and stood, arms folded across his chest, behind Talisman.

'How many men in the Gothir army?' Talisman asked.

'Two thousand,' said Nosta Khan. 'Lancers and foot soldiers.'

'How long before they arrive?'

'Two days. Perhaps three,' Bartsai answered.

'And you intend to fight?'

'Why else would we need a war leader?' asked Kzun.

For the first time Talisman looked the man in the eye. 'Let us be clear, Kzun of the Lone Wolves,' he said, no anger in his voice, 'the Shrine is ultimately indefensible. A sustained assault by two thousand men will take it . . . eventually. There is no hope here of victory. At best we could hold for a few days, perhaps a week. Look around you. One wall has already crumbled, and the gates are useless. All the defenders would die.'

'Exactly what I said,' put in Bartsai.

'Then you advocate flight?' Kzun asked.

'At this moment I am not advocating anything,' said Talisman. 'I am stating the obvious. Do you intend to fight?'

'Yes,' said Kzun. 'This is the one place sacred to all Nadir. It cannot be surrendered without a fight.'

Lin-tse spoke up: 'You know the ways of the Gothir, Okai. You know how they will fight. Will you lead us?'

Talisman rose. 'Go back to your warriors. Tell them to assemble here in one hour; I will speak with them.' Leaving them sitting there Talisman walked across the courtyard and climbed to the east-facing parapet. Bewildered, the leaders rose and left the Shrine. Nosta Khan followed Talisman.

Zhusai stood quietly by the wall as Gorkai approached her. 'I don't think we will live to see the day of the Uniter,' he said grimly.

'And yet you will stay,' she said.

'I am Wolfshead,' he told her, proudly. 'I will stay.'

On the wall Nosta Khan came alongside Talisman. 'I did not foresee this,' said the shaman.

'It does not matter,' Talisman told him. 'Win or lose, it will speed the day of reckoning.'

'How so?'

'Four tribes will fight together. It will show the way we must follow. If we succeed, then the Nadir will know the Gothir can be beaten. If we fail, then the sacrilege they commit upon this Shrine will bind the tribes with chains of fire.'

'Succeed? You said we would all die.'

'We must be prepared for death. But there is a chance, Nosta. They have no water, so we must guard the wells, denying them

166

access. Two thousand men will require two hundred and fifty gallons of water a day; the horses three times that. If we deny them
water for more than a few days, the horses will start to die. Then
the men . . .'

'Surely they will have thought of that?' argued Nosta Khan.

'I doubt it. They will expect to take the Shrine within a day.
And here there are three deep wells.'

'Can you hold them with a hundred men – and guard the wells
and water-holes outside?'

'No, we need more warriors. But they will come.'

'From where?' asked the shaman.

'The Gothir will send them,' Talisman told him.

Chapter Eight

Talisman sat alone on the parapet, cross-legged, arms out-stretched, eyes closed and face upwards to the blazing sun. There were so many ambitions he had longed to achieve, the foremost of them to ride into the city of Gulgothir beside the Uniter; to see the Gothir humbled, their high walls brought down and their army in ruins. Anger flooded him and for a while he allowed the richness of the emotion to rage within his veins; then, slowly, he calmed himself. What he had told Nosta Khan was true. The Battle for the Shrine would unite the tribes as never before. Even were he to die here – which was probable – the effect would be to speed the day of the Uniter.

He had told the tribal leaders that victory was impossible. This also was true. Yet a general who fought with defeat in mind would surely lose. Slowing his breathing and calming his heart, Talisman floated above the sense of rage and frustration. Two armies were about to meet. Put aside thoughts of numbers, and examine the essentials. He saw again Fanlon's panelled study back at the Bodacas Academy, and heard the old soldier's voice whisper across the years. 'The responsibility for a martial host lies in one man. He is its spirit. If an army is deprived of its morale, its general also will lose heart. Order and confusion, bravery and cowardice, are qualities dominated by the heart. Therefore the expert at controlling his enemy frustrates him, and then moves against him. Aggravation and harassment will rob the enemy of his heart, making him fearful, affecting his ability to plan.'

Talisman pictured Gargan and once again anger flickered. He waited for it to pass. The Lord of Larness had failed against him once, when all the odds were in his favour. Can I make him do so again? wondered Talisman.

The man was full of hate, yet still a mighty general and a warrior of courage – and when calm he was not stupid. The secret then was to steal away his calm, allowing his hatred to swamp his intellect.

Opening his eyes, Talisman rose and stared out to the west. From here he could see where the enemy would camp, at the foot of the dry hills, where there would be shade for their horses in the afternoon. Would they surround the Shrine? No. They would have Lancers patrol the area.

Sitting on the wall, he gazed in at the buildings and walls of the Shrine. There was the resting-place of Oshikai, with its flat roof, a two-storied dwelling beside it with ten rooms, built for pilgrims. Beyond that there was the fallen ruin of an old tower. Three of the twenty-foot walls surrounding the buildings were still strong, but this west-facing barrier with its long V-shaped crack was the weak spot – this was where the main attack would come. Gargan would send archers to pin down the defenders, and foot soldiers armed with trench tools to tear at the crack, opening it out. Then sheer force of numbers would carry the Gothir inside.

Talisman walked down the stone steps and along the base of the wall, halting below the damaged section. Given enough men and enough time he could repair it – or at worst, reinforce it with rocks from the fallen tower.

Men and time. The Gods of Stone and Water had robbed him of both.

Through the gates rode Kzun and his Lone Wolves. Talisman stripped off his shirt, dropping it to the dust, then once more climbed the steps to the parapet. Quing-chin followed with the Fleet Ponies contingent, then Lin-tse and his Sky Riders. The last to arrive was Bartsai of the Curved Horn. The Nadir warriors sat on their ponies in silence, their eyes on Talisman on the wall above them.

'I am Talisman,' he said. 'My tribe is Wolfshead, my blood Nadir. These lands are ruled by the Curved Horn. Let the leader Bartsai join me upon this wall.' Bartsai lifted his leg over the pommel of his saddle and jumped to the ground; he walked up the steps to stand beside Talisman. Drawing his knife, Talisman

169

drew the blade across the palm of his left hand. Blood welled from the wound. Holding out his arm, he watched as the red drops fell to the ground below. 'This is my blood which I give to the Curved Horn,' he said. 'My blood and my promise to fight unto death for the bones of Oshikai Demon-bane.' For a moment longer he stood in silence; then he called the other leaders forward. When they had joined him he gazed down on the waiting riders. 'At this place far back on the river of time Oshikai fought the Battle of the Five Armies. He won and he died. In the days to come the Nadir will speak of our struggle as the Battle of the Five Tribes. They will speak of it with pride in their hearts. For we are warriors, and the sons of men. We are Nadir. We fear nothing.' His voice rose. 'And who are these men who ride against us? Who do they think they are? They slaughter our women and our children. They pillage our holy places.' Suddenly he pointed at a rider of the Curved Horn. 'You!' he shouted. 'Have you ever killed a Gothir warrior?' The man shook his head. 'You will. You will slash your sword into his throat, and his blood will pour out on to the land. You will hear his death scream, and see the light fade from his eyes. So will you. And you! And you! Every man here will get the chance to pay them back for their insults and their atrocities. My blood – Nadir blood – stains the earth here. I shall not leave this place until the Gothir are crushed or withdrawn. Any man who cannot make the same oath should leave now.' Not one of the riders moved.

Lin-tse stepped up alongside Talisman. With a curved dagger he cut his left hand, then raised it high. One by one the other leaders joined them. Kzun turned to Talisman, stretching out his bloody hand, and Talisman gripped it. 'Brothers in blood!' declared Kzun. 'Brothers unto death!'

Talisman strode to the edge of the parapet. Drawing his sabre he looked down on the riders. 'Brothers unto death!' he shouted. Swords hissed into the air.

'Brothers unto death!' they roared.

The blind priest sat in his quarters, listening as the roar went up. The dreams of men, he thought, revolve always around war. Battle and death, glory and pain. Young men lust for it, old men talk of it fondly. A great sadness settled on him and he slowly moved around the room, gathering his papers.

Once he too had been a warrior, riding the steppes on raids, and he remembered well the heady excitement of battle. A small part of him wished he could remain with these young men, and smite the enemy. But a very small part.

There was only one real enemy in all the world, he knew. Hatred. All evil was born of this vile emotion. Immortal, eternal, it swept through the hearts of men of every generation. When Oshikai and his armies had reached these lands hundreds of years before, they had found a peaceful people living in the lush south lands. After Oshikai's death they had subjugated them, raiding their villages and taking their women, sowing the seeds of hatred. The seeds had grown and the southerners had fought back, becoming more organized. At the same time the Nadir had splintered into many tribes. The southerners became the Gothir, and their remembrances of past iniquities made them hate the Nadir, visiting upon them the terror of the killing raids.

When will it end? he wondered.

Slowly he packed his manuscripts, quills and ink into a canvas shoulder-bag. There was not room for all of them, and the others he hid in a box below the floorboards. Hoisting the pack to his back, he walked from the room and out into a sunlit morning he could not see.

The riders had returned to their camps and he heard footsteps approaching. 'You are leaving?' asked Talisman.

'I am leaving. There is a cave a few miles to the south. I often go there when I wish to meditate.'

'You have seen the future, old man. Can we beat them?'

'Some enemies can never be overcome,' said the priest, and without another word he walked away.

Talisman watched him go. Zhusai came to him, and wrapped a linen bandage around his wounded hand. 'You spoke well,' she said admiringly. Reaching out, he stroked his hand through her dark hair.

'You must leave this place.'

'No, I shall stay.'

Talisman gazed on her beauty then, the simple white tunic of silk shining in the sunlight, the sheen of her long, black hair. 'I wish,' he said, 'that you could have been mine.'

'I am yours,' she told him. 'Now and always.'

'It cannot be. You are pledged to the Uniter. To the man with violet eyes.'

She shrugged. 'So says Nosta Khan. But today you united five tribes and that is enough for me. I stay.' Stepping in to him, she took his hand and kissed the palm.

171

Quing-chin approached them. 'You wished to see me, Talisman?'

Zhusai drew away, but Talisman caught her hand and lifted it to his lips. Then he turned, and beckoned Quing-chin to follow him. 'We must slow their advance,' he said, leading the warrior to the breakfast table.

'How so?'

'If they are still two days from us they will make one more night camp. Take ten men and scout the area. Then, when they are camped, scatter as many Gothir horses as you can.'

'With ten men?'

'More would be a hindrance,' said Talisman. 'You must follow the example of Adrius – you remember your studies with Fanlon?'

'I remember,' said Quing-chin, with a wry smile. 'But I didn't believe it then.'

'Make it true now, my friend, for we need the time.'

Quing-chin rose. 'I live to obey, my general,' he said, speaking in Gothir and giving the Lancers' salute. Talisman grinned.

'Go now. And do not die on me – I need you.'

'That is advice I shall keep close to my heart,' the warrior promised.

Next Talisman summoned Bartsai. The Curved Horn leader sat down and poured himself a cup of water. 'Tell me of all the water-holes within a day's ride of here,' he said.

'There are three. Two are small seeps. Only one would supply an army.'

'That is good. Describe it to me.'

'It is twelve miles to the east, and high in the mountains. It is very deep and cold, and is full even in the driest seasons.'

'How easy is it to approach?'

Bartsai shrugged. 'As I said, it is high. There is only one path to it, snaking up through the passes.'

'Could wagons reach it?'

'Yes, though the trail would have to be cleared of large rocks.'

'How would you defend it?'

'Why would I defend it?' countered Bartsai. 'The enemy is coming here!'

'They will need water, Bartsai. It must be denied them.'

Bartsai grinned, showing broken teeth. 'That is so, Talisman. With fifty men I could hold the trail against any army.'

'Fifty cannot be spared. Pick twenty – the finest you have.'

'I will lead them myself,' said Bartsai.

'No, you are needed here. As the Gothir approach, other Curved Horn riders will come to the Shrine and they will look to you for leadership.'

Bartsai nodded. 'This is true. Seven came in last night, and I have men scouting for others.' The older man sighed. 'I have lived for almost fifty years, Talisman. And I have dreamt of fighting the Gothir. But not like this – a handful of men in a rotting shrine.'

'This is only the beginning, Bartsai. I promise you that.'

Kzun heaved another rock into place and stepped back, wiping sweat from his face with a grimy hand. For three hours he and his men had been moving stone blocks from the ruined tower and packing them against the west wall, just below the crack, creating a platform that Talisman had ordered to be twenty feet long, ten feet wide and five feet tall. It was back-breaking work, and some of his men had complained. But Kzun silenced them; he would suffer no whining before the other tribesmen.

He glanced to where Talisman was deep in conversation with the long-faced Sky Rider, Lin-tse. Sweat dripped into his eyes. He hated the work, for it reminded him of the two years he had spent in the Gothir gold-mines to the north. He shivered at the memory, remembering the day when he had been dragged in ankle-chains to the mouth of the shaft and ordered to climb down. They had not removed the chains, and twice Kzun's feet had slipped and he had hung in darkness. Eventually he had arrived at the foot of the shaft where two guards carrying torches had been waiting. One smashed a fist into Kzun's face, propelling him into the wall. 'That's to remind you, dung-monkey, to obey every order you hear. Instantly!' The fifteen-year-old Kzun had struggled to his feet and looked up into the man's bearded, ugly face. He saw the second blow coming, but could not avoid it. It split his lips and broke his nose. 'And that is to tell you that you never look a guard in the eyes. Now get up and follow.'

Two years in the dark followed, with weeping sores on his ankles where the chains bit, boils upon his back and neck, and the kiss of the whip when his weary body failed to move at the speed the guards demanded. Men died around him, their spirits broken long before their bodies surrendered to the dark. But Kzun would not be broken. Every day he chipped at the tunnel walls with his pick of iron, or a short-handled shovel, gathering up baskets of rock and hauling them back to the carts drawn by blind ponies. And every sleep time – for who could tell what was day and what was night? – he would fall to the ground upon the order and rest his exhausted body on the rock of the ever-lengthening tunnel. Twice the tunnel at the face collapsed, killing miners. Kzun was half-buried in the second fall, but dug himself clear before the rescuers came.

Most of the slave workers around him were Gothir criminals, petty thieves and house-breakers. The Nadir contingent were known as 'picked men'. In Kzun's case this meant that a troop of Gothir soldiers had ridden in to his village and arrested all the young men they could find. Seventeen had been taken. There were mines all over the mountains here, and Kzun had never seen his friends again.

Then, during a shift, a workman preparing support timbers broke the tip of his file. With a curse he strode back down the tunnel, seeking a replacement. Kzun picked up the tip; it was no longer than his thumb. Every sleep time for days and days he slowly filed away at the clasps of his ankle-chain. There was always noise in the tunnels, the roaring of underground rivers, the snoring of sleepers whose lungs were caked with dirt and dust. Even so Kzun was careful. Finally, having worked evenly on both clasps, the first gave way. Feverishly Kzun filed the second. This too fell clear. Rising, he made his way back down the tunnel to where the tools were stored. It was quieter here, and a man wearing chains would have been heard by the guards in the small chamber by the shaft. But Kzun was wearing no chains. Selecting a short-handled pick, he hefted it clear of the other tools and padded silently to the guards' chamber. There were two men inside; they were playing some kind of game, involving bone dice. Taking a deep breath Kzun leapt inside, swinging his pick into the back of the first man – the iron point driving through the rib-cage and bursting from his chest. Releasing the weapon, Kzun drew the dying man's knife and hurled himself across the table at the second guard. The man surged to his feet, scrabbling for his own knife, but he was too late. Kzun's weapon punched into his neck, down past the collar-bone and into his heart.

Swiftly Kzun stripped the man, then climbed into his clothes. The boots were too big, and he hurled them aside.

Moving to the shaft, he began to climb the iron rungs set into the stone. The sky was dark above him, and he saw the stars shining clear. A lump came to his throat then. Climbing more slowly, he reached the lip of the shaft and warily looked out. There was

174

a cluster of buildings beyond, where they milled the ore, and a barracks for the guards. Scrambling clear, Kzun walked slowly across the open ground. The smell of horse came to him on the night breeze, and he followed it to a stable.

Stealing a fine horse, he rode from the settlement and out into the clean, sweet air of the mountains.

Returning to his village, he found that no-one recognized him as the young man taken only two years before. He had lost his hair, and his skin and face had the pallor of the recently dead. The teeth on the right side of his mouth had rotted away, and his once powerful body was now wolf-lean.

The Gothir had not come for him. They took no names of the Nadir 'picked men', nor had any record of which village they had raided to capture him.

Now Kzun heaved another slab of old stone into place and stepped back from the new wall. It was just under four feet high. A beautiful woman appeared alongside him, carrying a bucket of water in which was a copper ladle. She bowed deeply, and offered him a short scarf of white linen. 'It is for the head, Lord,' she said, formally.

'I thank you,' he replied, not smiling for fear of showing his ruined teeth. 'Who are you?' he asked, as he tied the scarf over his bald head.

'I am Zhusai, Talisman's woman.'

'You are very beautiful, and he is most fortunate.'

She bowed again and offered him a ladle of water. He drank deeply, then passed the bucket to his waiting men. 'Tell me, how is it that Talisman knows so much of the ways of the Gothir?'

'He was taken by them as a child,' answered Zhusai. 'He was a hostage. He was trained at the Bodacas Academy – as were Quing-chin and Lin-tse.'

'A janizary. I see. I have heard of them.'

'He is a great man, Lord.'

'Only a great man would deserve someone like you,' he said. 'I thank you for the scarf.'

With a bow she moved away and Kzun sighed. One of his men made a crude comment, and Kzun rounded on him. 'Not one more word, Chisk, or I will rip your tongue from your mouth!'

'How do you read the other leaders?' asked Talisman.

Lin-tse let the question hang for a moment, marshalling his thoughts. 'The weakest of them is Bartsai. He is old. He doesn't

175

want to die. Quing-chin is as I remember him, brave and thoughtful. I am grateful to Gargan. Had he not been marching here with his army I would have been forced to kill Quing-chin. It would have scarred my soul. Kzun? The man has a demon within him. He is unhinged, Talisman, but I think he will stand tall.'

'And what of Lin-tse?'

'He is as you knew him. My people call me the Man with Two Souls. I do not think it is true, but the years at Bodacas changed me. I now have to *try* to be Nadir. It is worse for Quing-chin. He killed my best fighter – and refused to take his eyes. I would not have done that, Talisman, but I would have wished to. You understand?'

'I understand,' said Talisman. 'They took from us. But we also took from them. We will put it to good use here.'

'We will die here, my friend,' said Lin-tse softly. 'But we will die well.'

'Brothers unto death,' said Talisman. 'And perhaps beyond. Who knows?'

'Now what orders do you have for me, general?'

Talisman looked into Lin-tse's dark, brooding eyes. 'It is important that we begin this venture with a victory – no matter how small. Gargan will come with the main van of the army. Ahead will be several companies of Lancers. They will reach us first, and I want you and your Sky Riders to bloody them. Bartsai tells me there is a narrow pass twelve miles west. When the Lancers reach it, attack them – not head on, but with arrows. Then run – back through the pass. You will have most of today and early tomorrow to prepare your surprises. Bring back spoils if you can.'

Lin-tse nodded. 'You are thinking of Fecrem and the Long Retreat.'

'I am indeed. As I said, a victory is important. What is vital, however, is that you take no unnecessary risks. If there are more than three companies, do not engage them. Your thirty men are irreplaceable.'

Lin-tse rose. 'I will do my utmost, general.'

'Of that I have no doubt. You have the coolest head, Lin-tse. That is why I chose you for this mission.'

Lin-tse's expression did not change. Without a word he strode away. Gorkai stepped forward. 'He is a hard man, that one,' he observed.

'A man of stone,' agreed Talisman. 'Where is Zhusai?'

'She went into the Shrine to pray.'

Talisman followed and found her standing by the stone sarcophagus. It was cool in the shadowed chamber and he stood for a moment, watching her. She turned towards him and smiled. 'It is so quiet here,' she said.

'I saw you give the scarf to Kzun. Why did you do it?'

'He is a dangerous man, and one who might . . . question your orders.'

'A man that gold could not buy – and you won him with a piece of linen. You are a surprising woman, Zhusai.'

'There is nothing I would not do for you, Talisman. You will forgive me for being forward, but time is precious, is it not?'

'It is,' he admitted, moving to her side. She took his hand and held it to her breast.

'Have you been with a woman?' she asked him.

'No.'

'Then there is much for us both to discover.' Drawing her to him, he touched his lips to hers. The scent of her hair filled his nostrils, the taste of her mouth swamped his senses. He felt dizzy and weak, and drew back from her. 'I love you, my Talisman,' she whispered.

For just those fleeting seconds he had forgotten the perils that awaited them both. Now realization struck him like a fist. 'Why now?' he asked, pulling away.

'Because that is all there is,' she said. Swinging to the sarcophagus, she ran her hand over the iron plate. 'Oshikai Demon-bane, Lord of War,' she read. 'He was beset by enemies when he wed Shul-sen. And they had so little time, Talisman. They were together only four years. But great was their love. Ours will be as great. I know it. I feel it, here in this place. And if we die we shall walk hand in hand through the Void. I know this too.'

'I do not want you to die,' he said. 'I wish I had never brought you here. I wish it with all my heart.'

'And I am glad you did. You will win, Talisman. Your cause is just. The evil comes from the Gothir.'

'It is a touching sentiment, Zhusai. And one which I wish were true. Sadly, the good do not always conquer. I must go, for there is much to do.'

'When you have done all that you can, and the night grows long, come to me, Talisman. Will you do that?'

'I will come to you,' he promised.

*

177

The sky was black with crows and vultures as Druss and Sieben came over a ridge and down into a shallow valley. Below them were some forty goathide tents. Bodies were strewn everywhere, under a writhing mass of carrion birds. Elsewhere small desert dogs tugged at rotting flesh.

'Sweet Heaven,' whispered Sieben, pulling back on the reins.

Druss touched heels to the mare and rode down the hillside. Leading their extra ponies, Sieben followed him. Vultures too fat to fly spread their wings and waddled away from the horses. The stench of death caused the horses to shy away from the scene, but the riders forced them on. At first Sieben just stared ahead, trying not to look at the bodies. There were children there, and women – some huddled together, others slain as they ran. A brown dog edged into a flapping tent, then yelped and ran away. Druss dragged on the reins.

'Why are we stopping?' asked Sieben. Druss dismounted, passing the mare's reins to the poet. Axe in hand, he strode to the tent and, ducking down, moved inside. Sieben sat on his horse and forced himself to view the scene. It was not hard to see what had happened here. The killers had attacked late in the evening, as the cook-fires were under way. The Nadir had fled in all directions, but had been cut down with ruthless efficiency. Several of the bodies had been mutilated, beheaded or dismembered.

Druss emerged from the tent and moved to the horses, lifting clear a water canteen. 'There's a woman inside,' he said. 'She's alive, but only just. She has a babe.'

Sieben dismounted and tethered the horses to a tent-pole. The Gothir mounts were skittish and nervous of the dogs and vultures, but the Nadir ponies stood by calmly. Swiftly he hobbled the horses with lengths of rawhide, then joined Druss. Inside the tent lay a naked young woman, a terrible wound in her belly and side. Blood had drenched the brightly coloured blankets on which she lay. Her eyes were open, but her mouth was hanging slack. Druss raised her head, holding the canteen to her lips; water dribbled over her chin, but she managed to swallow a little. Sieben gazed at the wound; it was deep, the blade having completely pierced her body. The babe, part hidden beneath a pile of furs, was whimpering softly. Druss picked it up, and held it to the woman's swollen breast. It began to suck, weakly at first. The woman groaned and moved her arm around the child, drawing it in to her.

'What can we do?' asked Sieben. Druss's cold eyes met his. The axeman said nothing. When Sieben reached up to stroke the woman's face, her dead eyes stared at him. The babe continued to feed.

'This one they kept for rape,' said Druss. 'What a pack of mongrels!'

'May they rot in Seven Hells,' said Sieben. The babe ceased to suck and Druss lifted it to his broad shoulder, supporting its head and gently rubbing its back. Sieben's eyes were drawn to the woman's swollen nipple. Milk and blood were seeping from it.

'Why, Druss?' he asked.

'Why what?'

'Why did they do it? What was the purpose?'

'I am not the man to ask, poet. I have seen the sack of cities, and watched good men become evil as they are fired by rage and lust and fear. I don't know why they do it. The soldiers who did this will go home to their wives and families and be good husbands and fathers. It is a mystery to me.'

Wrapping the naked babe in a blanket, he carried him out into the sunlight. Sieben followed him. 'Will they write it as a victory, do you think?' asked Sieben. 'Will they sing songs about this raid?'

'Let's hope there are some women with milk in their breasts at the Shrine,' said Druss. Sieben freed the horses and held the babe until Druss had mounted. Passing the child to the axeman, he stepped into the saddle of the gelding.

'He fed on milk and blood,' said Sieben. 'He drank from the dead.'

'But he lives,' said Druss. 'He breathes.'

The two rode on. Druss lifted the blanket over the top of the infant's head, shielding him from the bright sun. The child was asleep now. Druss could smell the newness of life upon him, the creamy scent of milk-fed breath. He thought of Rowena, and her longing for such a child to hold at her own breast.

'I will be a farmer,' he said suddenly. 'When I get home, I shall stay there. No more wars. No more vultures.'

'You believe that, my friend?' asked Sieben.

Druss felt the sinking of his heart. 'No,' he said.

They rode on across the burning steppes for another hour, then transferred the saddles to the two Nadir ponies. The baby awoke and cried for a while. Druss tried to calm him, then Sieben took him. 'How old is he, do you think?' the poet asked.

'Perhaps a month. Two – I don't know.'

Sieben swore and Druss laughed. 'Anointed you too, has he?'

'During my short, eventful life I have learned many things, Druss, old horse,' he said, holding the babe at arm's length. 'But I never thought I would have to worry about urine stains on silk. Will it rot the fabric, do you think?'

'We can only hope not.'

'How does one stop them crying?'

'Tell him one of your stories, poet. They always put me to sleep.'

Sieben cradled the babe close, and began to sing a gentle song about the Princess Ulastay and her desire to wear stars in her hair. He had a good voice, strong and melodic. The Nadir child rested its head against his chest and was soon asleep. Towards dusk they saw a dust-cloud ahead, and Druss led them off the trail and into a small gully. Two companies of Lancers rode by above them, heading west, their armour bright, the helms gleaming red in the fading sunshine. Sieben's heart was hammering fast. The babe murmured in his arms, but the sound did not carry above the drumming of hoofbeats.

Once they had passed, Druss headed north-east.

With the dying of the sun the air grew cooler, and Sieben felt the warmth of the child in his arms. 'I think he has a fever,' he told Druss.

'All babies are hot,' said Druss.

'Really? I wonder why.'

'They just are. By Heavens, poet, do you have to question everything?'

'I have a curious mind.'

'Then set it to work on how we are going to feed the child when he wakes. He looks a lusty infant to me, and his cries are likely to travel far. And we are unlikely to meet friends out here.'

'That's it, Druss. Always try to finish on a comforting note.'

Gargan, Lord of Larness, waited patiently as his manservant, Bren, unbuckled the heavy breastplate and removed it. The flesh around his middle had spread since last he had worn it, and the freedom of release caused him to sigh with pleasure. He had ordered new armour last month, but it was not ready when Garen-Tsen told him of the jewels, and the need for speed.

Bren unfastened the thigh-plates and greaves and Gargan sat down on a canvas chair and stretched out his legs. The nation was sliding into the pit, he thought bitterly. The emperor's

180

madness was growing daily, and the two factions were hovering in the shadows. Civil war loomed. Madness!

And we are all caught up in it, he realized. Magical jewels indeed! The only magic that counted was contained in the swords of the Royal Guards, the shining points of the Royal lances.

What was needed now was an outside threat to pull the Gothir nation together. A war with the tribes would focus the minds of the people wonderfully. It would buy time. The Emperor had to go. The question was when, and how, and who would replace him? Until that day, Gargan would have to give the factions something else to think about.

Bren left the tent, returning with a tray of wine, butter, cheese and bread. 'The captains wish to know when you will see them, my Lord,' he said. Gargan looked up at him. The man was getting old, worn out.

'How many campaigns have you served with me?' asked Gargan.

'Twelve, my Lord,' answered Bren, cutting the bread and buttering three slices.

'Which do you remember most fondly?'

The old man paused in his preparations. 'Gassima,' he said.

Pouring the wine into a silver goblet, Bren added water and passed it to his general. Gargan sipped it. Gassima! The last civil war, almost twenty-five years ago now. Outnumbered, Gargan had led a retreat across the marshes, then swung his force and launched an attack which ought to have been suicidal. On his giant white stallion, Skall, he had thundered into the heart of the enemy camp and killed Barin in hand-to-hand combat. The war was won on that day, the civil war ended. Gargan drained his wine and handed the goblet to Bren, who refilled it.

'That was a horse, by Missael! Feared nothing. It would have charged into the fires of Hell.'

'A mighty steed,' agreed Bren.

'Never known another like him. You know the stallion I ride now? He is of the blood of Skall, his great-grandson. But he does not have the same qualities. Skall was a prince of horses.' Gargan chuckled. 'Mounted three mares on the day he died – at the ripe age of thirty-two. I have only wept twice in my life, Bren. The first was on the death of Skall.'

'Yes, my Lord. What shall I tell the captains?'

'One hour from now. I have letters to read.'

'Yes, my Lord.' Leaving the meal on the table, Bren stepped

back through the tent-flap. Gargan stood and poured a third goblet of wine; this time he added no water. The mail riders had caught up with the vanguard of the army at dusk and there were three letters for him. He opened the first, which bore the seal of Garen-Tsen. Gargan tried to focus on the spidery script. Lifting a lantern from its pole, he lowered it to the desk. His eyes were not what they were. Nothing is what it was, he thought.

The letter told of the funeral of the Queen, and how Garen-Tsen had smuggled the King from the city, having him taken to the Winter Palace at Siccus. The factions were beginning to speak openly now in the Senate about 'a need for change'. Garen-Tsen urged a speedy end to the campaign, and a swift return to the capital.

The second letter was from his wife. He scanned it: four pages containing little of interest, detailing small incidents from the household and the farms. A maidservant had broken an arm, falling from a chair as she cleaned windows, a prize foal had been sold for a thousand raq, three slaves had fled the North Farm, but had been recaptured in a local brothel.

The last letter was from his daughter, Mirkel. She had given birth to a baby boy and she was calling him Argo. She hoped Gargan could see him soon.

The old soldier's eyes misted.

Argo. Finding his mutilated body had been like a knife blow to the heart, and Gargan could still feel the pain of it. He had known all along that allowing Nadir filth to attend the Academy would lead to disaster. But never had he remotely considered the possibility that it would lead to the death of his own son. And what a death to suffer!

Anger and sorrow vied in him.

The old Emperor had been a wise man, ruling well in the main. But his later years had seen a rise in confusion, a softening of his attitudes. It was for this man that Gargan had fought at Gassima. I gave you that crown, he thought. I placed it on your head. And because of you my son is dead.

Nadir janizaries! A foul and perditious idea. Why was it the old man could not see the stupidity of it? The Nadir were numberless, and dreamed only of the day when a Uniter would draw them together into one unstoppable army. And yet the Emperor had wished the sons of their chiefs to be trained in the ways of Gothir warfare. Gargan could still scarcely believe it.

The day when Okai had been the prize student was a grim one

to recall. What was worse was to know that the man who walked up to the dais was the murderer of his son. He had him close then; he could have reached out and torn away his throat.

Gargan reached for the jug – and hesitated. The captain would be here soon, and strong drink was no aid to planning.

Rising from the table, he rubbed at his weary eyes and stepped outside the tent. Two guards came to attention. Gargan stared out over the camp-site, pleased with the orderly placing of tents, the neatness of the five picket lines. The ground had been well cleared around the camp-fires, dug over and wetted down, so that no spark could land upon the tinder-dry grass of the steppes.

Gargan walked on, scanning the camp for signs of disorderliness or complacency. He found none, save that one of the latrine trenches was dug in an area where the prevailing wind would carry the stench back into the camp. He noted it in his mind. Two Nadir heads had been tied to a pole outside one tent. A group of Lancers were sitting around a camp-fire close by. When Gargan strode up, the men leapt to their feet, saluting smartly.

'Bury them,' said Gargan. 'They are attracting flies and mosquitoes.'

'Yes, sir!' they chorused.

Gargan returned to his tent. Sitting down at the table, he took quill and ink and wrote a short letter to Mirkel, congratulating her and stating his hope and his intention to be with her soon. 'Take good care of little Argo,' he wrote. 'Do not rely on wet-nurses. A child draws much from his mother's milk, taking in not only nourishment but also spirit and courage. One should never allow a babe of noble birth to suckle at a common breast. It dissipates character.'

Travelling carefully, using dry gullies and low terrain, Quing-chin and his nine riders avoided the Gothir patrols. As darkness fell they were hidden to the south of the Gothir encampment. His friend, Shi-da, crept alongside him as he knelt behind a screen of dry bushes, scanning the camp.

The night breeze was picking up, blowing from the south-east. Shi-da tapped Quing-chin's shoulder. 'It is done, my brother.'

Quing-chin settled back on his haunches. The breeze was picking up. 'Good.'

'When?' asked Shi-da, eagerness showing on his young face.

'Not yet. We wait until they settle for the night.'

'Tell me of Talisman,' said Shi-da, settling down alongside him. 'Why is he the chosen one? He is not as strong as you.'

'Strength of body counts for nothing in a general,' said Quing-chin. 'He has a mighty heart, and a mind sharper than a dagger.'

'You also have a great heart, my brother.'

Quing-chin smiled. The boy's hero-worship was a source of both irritation and delight. 'I am the hawk, he is the eagle. I am the wolf, he is the tiger. One day Talisman will be a war leader among the Nadir. He will lead armies, little brother. He has a mind for . . .' He hesitated. There was no Nadir word for *logistics*. 'A mind for planning,' he said, at last. 'When an army marches it must be supplied. It needs food and water and, just as important, it needs information. It takes a rare man to be able to plan for all eventualities. Talisman is such a man.'

'He was at the Academy with you?'

'Yes. And at the last he was the Honour Student, beating all others.'

'He fought them all?'

'In a way.' Behind them a pony whinnied and Quing-chin glanced back to where the others were hidden. 'Get back to them,' he said, 'and tell Ling that if he does not control his pony better than that I shall send him back in disgrace.'

As the boy eased himself back from the gully's crest Quing-chin settled down to wait. Fanlon had often said that a captain's greatest gift was patience – knowing when to strike, and having the nerve to wait for the right moment.

As the air cooled the wind would increase. So too would the moisture, caused by the change in temperature. All these factors combined to make good timing essential. Quing-chin looked out at the enemy camp, and felt his anger rise. They were not in defensive formation, as was required when in enemy territory. There was no outer perimeter of fortifications. They had constructed the encampment according to the regulations for a peace-time manoeuvre: five picket lines, each with two hundred horses, the tents set out in squares by regiment. How arrogant they were, these *gajin*. How well they understood Nadir mentality.

Three Gothir scouts came riding from the east. Quing-chin ducked down below the crest until they had passed. They were talking as they rode, and laughing. Tomorrow there would be no laughter; they would be biting upon a leather strap as the whip lashed their backs.

184

Quing-chin carefully made his way down the slope to where his men were waiting. Tinder and brush had been packed into a net of twine, and tied to a long rope. 'Now is the time,' he said.

Shi-da stepped forward. 'May I ride the fire?' he asked.

'No.' The boy's disappointment was intense but Quing-chin walked past him, stopping before a short, bow-legged warrior. 'You have the glory, Nien,' he said. 'Remember, ride south for at least a quarter of a mile before releasing the rope. Not too fast, then double back along the line.'

'It will be done,' said the man. Swiftly they mounted and rode to the top of the gully. Quing-chin and two others leapt from their saddles and, using tinder-boxes, lit the tinder bundle tied behind Nien's pony. Flames licked up, then roared into life.

Nien kicked his horse and set off at a slow trot across the dry grass of the steppes. Fire flickered behind him, and dark oily smoke spiralled up. The wind fanned the blaze, and soon a roaring wall of flames swept towards the Gothir camp.

'Might I enquire, sir, the purpose of this mission?' asked Premian, as he and the other ten senior officers gathered in Gargan's tent.

'You may,' said the general. 'Our intelligence reports show that a Nadir uprising is planned, and it is our duty to see that it does not happen. Reports have been gathered and compiled showing that the Curved Horn tribe have been mustering for a major raid on the lands around Gulgothir. We shall crush this tribe; it will send a message to other Nadir chieftains. First, however, we shall march to the Shrine of Oshikai and dismantle it stone by stone. The bones of their hero will be crushed to powder and scattered upon the steppes.'

The veteran Marlham spoke up. 'But surely, sir, the Shrine is a holy place to all the tribes. Will this not be seen by all the leaders as provocation?'

'Indeed it will,' snarled Gargan. 'Let them know, once and for all, that they are a slave race. Would that I could bring an army of forty thousand into the steppes. By Shemak, I would slay them all!'

Premian was tempted to speak again, but Gargan had been drinking and his face was flushed, his temper short. He was leaning on the desk, the muscles of his arms sharp and powerful in the lantern light, his eyes gleaming. 'Does any man here have a problem with this mission?'

The other officers shook their heads. Gargan straightened and moved round the desk, looming over the shorter Premian. 'How about you? As I recall you have a soft spot for these scum.'

'I am a soldier, sir. It is my duty to carry out all orders given to me by a superior officer.'

'But you don't agree with them, do you?' sneered Gargan, pushing his bearded face so close to Premian's that the officer could smell the sour taste of wine upon the other's breath.

'It is not my place to disagree with policy, sir.'

'Not my place,' mimicked Gargan. 'No, sir, it is not your place. Do you know how many tribesmen there are?'

'No, sir.'

'No, sir. Neither do I, boy. Nor does any man. But they are numberless. Can you imagine what would happen if they joined together, under one leader? They would sweep over us like a tide.' He blinked and returned to his table, sitting heavily on the canvas chair which groaned under the sudden weight. 'Like a tide,' he mumbled. Sucking in a great breath, he fought to overcome the wine in his system. 'They must be humbled. Crushed. Demoralized.'

A commotion began outside, and Premian heard men shouting. With the other officers he left the tent. A wall of flame was lighting the night sky, and smoke was swirling around the camp. Horses began whinnying in fear. Premian swung his gaze around the camp. The fire would sweep right over it. 'The water wagons!' he yelled. 'Harness the wagons!' Premian began to run across the camp to where the twenty wagons had been drawn up in a square. Each carried sixteen barrels. A man ran by him in panic and Premian grabbed his shoulder. 'Fetch horses for the wagons,' he said, his voice ringing with authority.

'Yes, sir,' replied the soldier, saluting. He moved away. Premian saw a group of soldiers trying to gather their belongings from a communal tent. 'Leave them,' he shouted. 'If the wagons go up, we'll all die. You three get to the picket line. Fetch horses. The rest of you start dragging these wagons into line for harness.'

The flames were licking at the edge of the camp now. Hundreds of men were trying to beat out the fires using blankets and cloaks, but Premian saw that it was pointless. Soldiers came running back, leading frightened horses. A tent caught fire. The first of the wagons was harnessed and a soldier climbed to the driving board and lashed out with the reins. The four horses leaned in to the harnesses and the wagon lurched forward.

A second wagon followed; then a third. More men came to help. Premian ran to the nearest picket line. 'Cut the rest of the horses loose,' he told a soldier standing by. 'We'll round them up tomorrow!'

'Yes, sir,' responded the man, slashing his knife through the picket rope. Premian grabbed the reins of the nearest horse and vaulted to its bare back. The beast was panicked, and reared, but Premian was an expert horseman. Leaning forward, he patted the horse's long neck.

'Courage, my beauty,' he said. Riding back to the wagons, he saw that a further six had been harnessed and were moving east away from the line of fire. More tents were ablaze now, and smoke and cinders filled the air. To the left a man screamed as his clothes caught fire. Several soldiers threw him to the ground, covering him with blankets, smothering the flames. The heat was intense now, and it was hard to breathe. Flames were licking at the last of the wagons, but two more were harnessed.

'That's it!' yelled Premian at the struggling soldiers. 'Save yourselves!'

The men mounted the last of the horses and galloped from the burning camp. Premian turned to see other soldiers running for their lives. Several stumbled and fell, and were engulfed by flames. He swung his horse – and saw Gargan walking through the smoke. The general looked bewildered and lost. 'Bren!' he was shouting. 'Bren!'

Premian tried to steer his horse to the general, but the beast would not move towards the flames. Dragging off his shirt Premian leaned forward, looping it over the horse's eyes and tying it loosely into place. Heeling the now blind stallion forward, he rode to Gargan.

'Sir! Mount behind me!'

'I can't leave Bren. Where is he?'

'He may already be clear, sir. If we stay any longer we'll be cut off!'

Gargan swore, then reached up to take Premian's outstretched hand and, with the practised ease of a skilled horseman, he swung up behind. The young officer kicked the stallion into a gallop across the burning steppes, swerving around the walls of flame that swept towards the north-west. The heat was searing, and Premian could hardly see through the smoke as the horse thundered on, its flanks scorched.

At last they outran the fire and Premian dragged the exhausted stallion to a stop. Leaping from its back, he turned and watched the camp burn.

Gargan slid down beside him. 'You did well, boy,' he said, placing his huge hand on Premian's shoulder.

'Thank you, sir. I think we saved most of the water wagons.'

The stallion's flanks were charred and blistered, and the great beast stood shivering now. Premian led him to the east, where the main body of soldiers had gathered.

Slowly, as the fire died away in the distance, men began making their way back to the camp, searching through the wreckage. By dawn all the bodies were recovered. Twenty-six men and twelve horses had died in the flames. All the tents had been destroyed, but most of the supplies had survived; the fire had passed too quickly to burn through all the sacks of flour, salt, oats and dried meat. Of the nine water wagons left behind, six had caught fire and were now useless, though most of the barrels containing the precious water were saved. Only three had split their caulks.

As the early-morning sun rose above the blackened earth of the camp-site, Gargan surveyed the wreckage. 'The fire was set in the south,' he told Premian. 'Find the names of the night sentries in that section. Thirty lashes per man.'

'Yes, sir.'

'Less destruction than we might have expected,' said the general.

'Yes, sir. Though more than a thousand arrows were lost, and around eighty lances. I'm sorry about your manservant. We found his body behind the tent.'

'Bren was a good man. Served me well. I took him out of the line when the rheumatic ruined his sword arm. Good man! They'll pay for his death with a hundred of their own.'

'We've also lost six water wagons, sir. With your permission I will adjust the daily ration to allow for the loss, and suspend the order that every Lancer must be clean-shaven daily.'

Gargan nodded. 'We'll not get all the horses back,' he said. 'Some of the younger ones will run clear back to Gulgothir.'

'I fear you are correct, sir,' said Premian.

'Ah, well. Some of our Lancers will have to be transferred to the infantry; it'll make them value their mounts more in the future.' Gargan hawked and spat. 'Send four companies through the pass. I want reports on any Nadir movements. And prisoners. Last night's attack was well executed; it reminds me of Adrius

188

and the winter campaign, when he slowed the enemy army with fire.'

Premian was silent for a moment, but he saw that Gargan was staring at him, awaiting a response. 'Okai was Wolfshead, sir. Not Curved Horn. In fact, I don't believe we had any Curved Horn janizaries.'

'You don't know your Nadir customs, Premian. Four tribes guard the Shrine. Perhaps he is with them. I hope so. I would give my left arm to have him in my power.'

The moon was high above the Valley of Shul-sen's Tears, and Talisman, weary to the bone, took a last walk to the battlements, stepping carefully over sleeping Nadir warriors. His eyes were gritty and tired, his body aching with unaccustomed fatigue as he slowly climbed the rampart steps. The new wooden platform creaked under his feet. In the absence of nails the planks had been tied into place; but it was solid enough, and tomorrow it would be more stable yet, as Bartsai and his men continued their work upon it. The fighting platform constructed by Kzun and his Lone Wolves was nearing completion. Kzun had worked well, tirelessly. But the man worried Talisman. Often during the day he would walk from the Shrine compound and stand out on the steppes. And now he was not sleeping with his men, but outside back at the former Lone Wolves camp.

Gorkai strode up to join him. On Talisman's instructions, the former Notas had worked alongside Kzun's men throughout the day. 'What did you find out?' asked Talisman, keeping his voice low.

'He is a strange one,' said Gorkai. 'He never sleeps inside his tent; he takes his blankets out and spreads them under the stars. He has never taken a wife. And back in Curved Horn lands he lives alone, away from the tribe; he has no sword brothers.'

'Why then was he placed in command of the Tomb Guards?' asked Talisman.

'He is a ferocious fighter. Eleven duels he has fought – he has not been cut once. All his enemies are dead. His men hate him, but they respect him.'

'What is your evaluation?'

Gorkai shrugged, and scratched at the widow's peak on his brow. 'I don't like him, Talisman, but if I was faced with many enemies I would want him by my side.' Talisman sat down on the rampart wall and Gorkai looked at him closely. 'You should sleep.'

'Not yet. I have much to think on. Where is Nosta Khan?'

'In the Shrine. He casts spells there,' said Gorkai, 'but he finds nothing. I heard him curse a while back.'

Gorkai gazed along the wall. When first he had seen the Shrine he had thought it small, but now the walls – at sixty paces each – looked ridiculously long. 'Can we hold this place?' he asked suddenly.

'For a time,' said Talisman. 'Much depends on how many ladders the enemy have. If they are well equipped, they will sweep over us.'

'A thousand curses on all of them,' hissed Gorkai.

Talisman grinned. 'They will not have enough ladders. They would not have expected a siege. And there are no trees to hack down here to make them. We have close to two hundred men now, fifty per wall should they try to attack on all sides. We will hold them, Gorkai – at least for some days.'

'And then what?'

'We live or die,' answered Talisman, with a weary shrug.

Far away to the south-west the sky began to glow a dull, flickering red. 'What is that?' asked Gorkai.

'With luck it is the enemy camp burning,' said Talisman grimly. 'It will not slow them overmuch, but it will rob them of their complacency.'

'I hope many die.'

'Why do you stay?' asked Talisman.

Gorkai looked puzzled. 'What do you mean? Where else would I be? I am Wolfshead now, Talisman. You are my leader.'

'I may have led you to a path of no returning, Gorkai.'

'All paths lead to death, Talisman. But here I am at one with the Gods of Stone and Water. I am Nadir again, and that has meaning.'

'Indeed it does. And I tell you this, my friend, it will have more meaning in the years to come. When the Uniter leads his armies the world will tremble at the sound of the name Nadir.'

'That is a pleasant thought to take to my bed,' said Gorkai, with a smile.

Just then both men saw the figure of Zhusai emerge from the sleeping quarters. She was dressed only in a shift of white linen and she walked slowly, dreamily, towards the gates. Talisman ran down the steps, closely followed by Gorkai, and they caught up with her on the open steppes. Gently Talisman took her by the arm. Her eyes were wide open and unblinking. 'Where is my Lord?' she asked.

'Zhusai? What is wrong?' whispered Talisman.

'I am lost,' she said. 'Why is my spirit chained in the Dark Place?' A tear formed and fell to her cheek. Talisman took her in his arms and kissed her brow.

'Who speaks?' said Gorkai, taking Zhusai's hand.

'Do you know my Lord?' she asked him.

'Who are you?' asked Gorkai. Talisman released his hold and turned towards the warrior. Gorkai gestured him to silence and stepped before the woman. 'Tell me your name,' he said.

'I am Shul-sen, the wife of Oshikai. Can you help me?'

Gorkai took her hand and kissed it. 'What help do you require, my Lady?'

'Where is my Lord?'

'He is . . .' Gorkai fell silent and looked to Talisman.

'He is not here,' said Talisman. 'Do you recall how you came here?'

'I was blind,' she said, 'but now I can see, and hear and speak.' Slowly she looked around. 'I think I know this valley,' she said, 'but I do not remember the buildings here. I tried to leave the Dark Place, but there are demons there. My spells have no effect. The power is gone and I cannot leave.'

'And yet you have,' said Gorkai. 'You are here.'

'I do not understand,' she said. 'Am I dreaming? Someone called me, and I awoke here. These clothes are not mine. And where is my *lon-tsia*? Where are my rings?'

Suddenly she jerked as if struck. 'No!' she cried. 'It is drawing me back. Help me! I cannot abide the Dark Place!' Wildly she reached out, grabbing Talisman's arm, then she went limp and fell against him. Her eyelids fluttered and Zhusai looked up at Talisman. 'What is happening, Talisman?' she asked.

'What do you remember?'

'I was dreaming. You remember? The woman in the cave? She was walking hand-in-hand with a man. Then the sun died away, and walls of black rock formed around us . . . her. All light faded until the darkness was absolute. The man was gone. I . . . she . . . tried to find a door in the rock, but there was none. And there were moans and snarls coming from close by. That is all I can remember. Am I going mad, Talisman?'

'I do not think so, my Lady,' said Gorkai softly. 'Tell me, have you ever seen visions?'

'No.'

'Have you ever heard voices, though there was no-one near?'

'No. What are you saying?'

'I believe the spirit of Shul-sen is somehow drawn to you. I don't know why. But I do know you are not insane. I have seen spirits, and spoken with them. It was the same with my father. What we have just experienced here was no dream-walking. Your voice was different, as was your manner. You agree, Talisman?'

'This is beyond my understanding,' admitted the Nadir leader. 'What must we do?'

'I do not know what we can do,' said Gorkai. 'You told me that Oshikai is searching for his wife, and now we know that Shul-sen is also seeking him. But their world is not ours, Talisman. We cannot bring them together.'

The moon vanished behind a bank of clouds, plunging the steppes to darkness. A man cried out in the distance, and Talisman saw a light hastily struck, and a lantern flickered to life outside the tent of Kzun.

Chapter Nine

The blind Nadir priest, Enshima, sat silently on the edge of the rocks overlooking the steppes below. Behind him, at the hidden spring, some two dozen refugees – mostly older women and young children – sat forlornly in the shade. He had seen the distant fire in the night, and felt the passing of souls into the Void. The priest's pale blue robes were dust-stained, and his feet were sore and bleeding from walking upon the sharp, volcanic rock that blighted this area of the mountains.

Silently Enshima offered up a prayer of thanks for the ragged band of Curved Horn who had reached the spring two days before. They had been part of a larger group attacked by Gothir Lancers, but had managed to flee to higher ground where the heavily armed horsemen could not follow. Now they were safe for the moment. Hungry, bereaved, desolated, but safe. Enshima thanked the Source for their lives.

Releasing the chains of his spirit Enshima soared high above the mountains, gazing down on the vast emptiness of the steppes. Twelve miles to the north-west he could see the tiny battlements of the Shrine, but he did not fly there. Instead he scanned the land for the two riders he knew would soon be approaching the spring.

He saw them riding out of a gully some two miles from the rocks in which his body sat. The axeman was leading two horses while the poet, Sieben, rode at the rear, carrying the babe wrapped in its red blanket. Floating closer to the lead rider, he looked closely at the man. Riding a sway-backed mare, he was dressed in a jerkin of black leather with shining silver shoulder-guards, and carrying a huge, double-headed axe.

The route they were taking would lead them past the hidden spring. Enshima floated closer to the poet. Reaching out with his spirit hand, he touched the rider's shoulder.

'Hey, Druss,' said Sieben. 'You think there might be water in those rocks?'

'We don't need it,' said the axeman. 'According to Nuang the Shrine should be no more than around ten miles from here.'

'That may be true, old horse, but the child's blanket is beginning to stink. And I would appreciate the opportunity to wash some of my clothes before we make our grand entrance.'

Druss chuckled. 'Aye, poet, it would not be seemly for you to arrive looking any less than your glorious best.' Tugging the reins to the left, Druss angled towards the dark, volcanic rocks.

Sieben rode alongside him. 'How will you find these healing jewels?' he asked.

The axeman pondered the question. 'I expect they are in the coffin,' he said. 'That would be usual, would it not?'

'It is an old shrine. I would think it would have been pillaged by now.'

Druss was silent for a moment, then he shrugged. 'Well, the old shaman said they were there. I'll ask him about it when I see him.'

Sieben gave a wry grin. 'I wish I had your faith in human nature, Druss, my friend.'

The mare's head came up, nostrils quivering, and she quickened her pace. 'There is water, right enough,' said Sieben. 'The horses can smell it.'

They climbed the narrow, twisting trail, and as they reached the crest two ancient Nadir warriors stepped out ahead of them. Both were carrying swords. A small priest in robes of faded blue appeared and he spoke to the old men, who grudgingly backed away. Druss rode on, dismounting by the spring and casting a wary eye over the group of Nadir sitting close by.

The priest approached him. 'You are welcome at our camp, axeman,' he said. The man's eyes were blind, their pupils of smoky opal. Laying Snaga against a rock, Druss took the baby from Sieben and waited as the poet swung down.

'This child needs milk,' said Druss. The priest called out a name and a young woman came forward, moving hesitantly. Taking the child from Druss, she walked back to the group.

'They are survivors from a Gothir raid,' said the priest. 'I am Enshima, a Priest of the Source.'

'Druss,' said the axeman. 'And this is Sieben. We are travelling . . .'

'To the Shrine of Oshikai,' said Enshima. 'I know. Come, sit with me for a while.' He walked away to a cluster of rocks by the spring. Druss followed him, while Sieben watered the horses and refilled their canteens.

'A great battle will be fought at the Shrine,' said Enshima. 'You know this.'

Druss sat down beside him. 'I know. It does not interest me.'

'Ah, but it does, for your own quest is linked to it. You will not find the jewels before the battle begins, Druss.'

The axeman knelt by the spring and drank. The water was cool and refreshing, but it left a bitter aftertaste on the tongue. Looking up at the blind man, he said, 'You are a seer?'

'For what it is worth,' agreed Enshima.

'Then can you tell me what this damned war is about? I see no sense in it.'

Enshima gave a rueful smile. 'That question presupposes there is sense to any war.'

'I am not a philosopher, priest, so spare me your ruminations.'

'No, Druss, you are not a philosopher,' said Enshima amiably, 'but you are an idealist. What is this war about? As with all wars it is about greed and fear; greed in that the Gothir are rich and desire to stay that way, and fear in that they see the Nadir as a future threat to their wealth and position. When has a war been fought over anything else?'

'These jewels exist, then,' said Druss, changing the subject.

'Oh, they exist. The Eyes of Alchazzar were crafted several hundred years ago. They are like amethysts, each as big as an egg, and each imbued with the awesome power of this savage land.'

'Why will I not find them before the battle?' asked Druss, as Sieben came up and sat alongside.

'Such is not your destiny.'

'I have a friend in need of them,' said Druss. 'I would appreciate your help in this matter.'

Enshima smiled. 'It gives me no pleasure to withhold help from you, axeman. But what you would ask of me I shall not give you. Tomorrow I will lead these people deep into the mountains, in the hope – vain though it may be – that I can keep them alive. You will journey to the Shrine, and there you will fight. For that is what you do best.'

'You have any bright words of comfort for me, old man?' asked Sieben.

The old man smiled and, reaching out, patted Sieben's arm. 'I was set a problem, and you helped solve it, for which my thanks. What you did, back in the death chamber, was a pure and good act, for which I hope the Source blesses you. Show me the *lontsia*.' Sieben fished into his pocket and produced the heavy silver medallion. The old man held it up before his face and closed his wood-smoke eyes. 'The male head is that of Oshikai Demonbane, the female that of his wife, Shul-sen. The script is Chiatze. A literal translation would be *Oshka-Shul-sen – together*. But it really means *spirit-entwined*. Their love was very great.'

'Why would anyone want to torture her so?' asked Sieben.

'I cannot answer that, young man. The ways of evil men are lost to me; I have no understanding of such barbarity. Great magic was used, in order to cage Shul-sen's spirit.'

'Did I free her?'

'I do not know. A Nadir warrior told me that the spirit of Oshikai has been searching for her through the endless dark valleys of the Void. Perhaps now he has found her. I hope so. But as I said, the spells were very great.'

Enshima returned the *lon-tsia* to Sieben. 'This too has had a spell cast upon it,' he said.

'Not a curse, I hope,' said the poet, holding the medallion gingerly.

'No, not a curse. I think it was a Hide-spell. It would have masked it from the eyes of men. It is quite safe to carry, Sieben.'

'Good. Tell me – you said the man was Oshikai, and yet the name upon it is Oshka. Is that a short form?'

'There is no *i* in the Chiatze alphabet. It is written as a small curved stroke above the preceding letter.'

Sieben pocketed the medallion and Enshima rose. 'May the Source guard you both,' he said.

Druss strode away and mounted the mare. 'We leave you the two ponies,' he said.

'That is most kind.'

Sieben paused beside the old man. 'How many defenders at the Shrine?'

'I expect there will be fewer than two hundred when the Gothir arrive.'

'And the jewels are there?'

'Indeed they are.'

196

Sieben swore, then he smiled sheepishly. 'I was rather hoping they weren't. I am not at my best in battles.'

'No civilized man is,' said the priest.

'So why are the jewels hidden there?' asked Sieben.

Enshima shrugged. 'They were crafted several hundred years ago, and set in the head of a stone wolf. A shaman stole them. Obviously he wanted the power for himself. He was hunted and hid the jewels, then he tried to escape over the mountains. But he was caught, tortured and killed near where you found the bones of Shul-sen. He did not reveal the hiding-place of the Eyes.'

'The story makes no sense,' said Sieben. 'If the jewels were imbued with great power, why did he leave them behind? Surely he could have used their power against his pursuers?'

'Do the deeds of men always, as you say, make sense?' countered the priest.

'After a fashion,' argued Sieben. 'What kind of power did the Eyes possess?'

'That is difficult to say. Much would depend on the skill of the man using them. They could heal all wounds, and breach any spell. They were said to have powers of regeneration and replication.'

'Could their power have hidden him from his pursuers?'

'Yes.'

'Then why did he not use it?'

'I am afraid, young man, that will remain a mystery.'

'I hate mysteries,' said Sieben. 'You said regeneration. They could raise the dead?'

'I meant regeneration of tissue – as in deep wounds, or diseases. It was said that an old warrior became young again after being healed by them. But I think that is a fanciful tale.'

Druss pushed himself to his feet. 'Time to move on, poet,' he said.

A young Nadir woman approached them, carrying the baby. Silently she offered it to Sieben. The poet stepped back. 'No, no, my dear,' he said. 'Fond as we are of the little tyke, I think he is better off here, with his own people.'

Talisman walked along the narrow wooden ramparts of the north wall, testing the strength of the structure, examining the ancient beams that held them in place. They seemed solid. The parapets were crenellated, allowing for archers to shoot through the gaps. But each Nadir warrior carried only about twenty arrows, and these would be exhausted by the end of the first charge. The enemy would be loosing shafts, and these could be gathered. Even so, this would not be a battle won by archery. Gazing around, he saw Kzun directing building operations below the broken wall. A solid fighting platform had been constructed there. The Lone Wolves leader was still sporting the white scarf Zhusai had given him. Kzun saw him watching, but did not wave. Quing-chin was working with a team on the gates, smearing animal fat to the hinges, trying to free them. How long since they have been closed? Talisman wondered. Ten years? A hundred?

Bartsai and ten of his men were working on the parapet of the eastern wall, where a section of ramparts had given way. Floorboards had been ripped from nearby buildings to be used in the repairs.

Quing-chin climbed the ramparts and gave a Gothir salute. 'Make that the last Gothir tribute to me,' said Talisman coldly. 'It does not amuse the tribesmen.'

'My apologies, brother.'

Talisman smiled. 'Do not apologize, my friend. I did not mean to scold. You did well last night. A shame they saved their water wagons.'

'Not all of them, Talisman. They will be on short rations.'

'How did they react when disaster struck?'

'With great efficiency. They are well led,' said Quing-chin. 'We almost killed Gargan. I was watching from a rise and I saw him stumbling around in the flames. A young officer rode in and rescued him – it was the same man who saved the wagons.'

Talisman leaned on the parapet staring out over the valley. 'Much as I hate Gargan, it must be said that he is a skilled general. He has his own chapter in Gothir history books. He was twenty-two when he led the charge that ended the civil war, the youngest general in Gothir history.'

'He's not twenty-two now,' said Quing-chin. 'He is old and fat.'

'Courage remains, even when youth has faded,' Talisman pointed out.

'There is great venom in the man,' said Quing-chin, removing his fur-fringed helm and running his fingers through his sweat-streaked hair. 'An abiding malice that burns him. I think it will rage like last night's blaze when he learns that you are the leader here.'

'With luck you will be proved correct. An angry man rarely makes rational decisions.'

Quing-chin moved to the ramparts and sat down. 'Have you thought about who will lead the fighters at the water-hole?'

'Yes. Kzun.'

Quing-chin looked doubtful. 'I thought you said the Curved Horn were to guard it?'

'They will. Under Kzun.'

'A Lone Wolf? Will they stand for it?'

'We will see,' said Talisman. 'Get your men to gather heavy rocks and stones, and place them around the battlements. We should have some missiles to hurl down upon the infantry as they try to scale the walls.'

Without another word Talisman walked away, climbing down from the wall and approaching Bartsai, who had stopped repair work while his people rested and drank from the well. 'You have chosen your fighters?' he asked.

'I have. Twenty as you ordered. We could make it more now. Another thirty-two warriors have come in.'

'If the well is as you described it, then twenty should be enough. Have the men come to me here. I wish to speak with them.'

Bartsai moved away and Talisman walked to where Kzun and his men were putting the last touches to the fighting platform. The top had been covered with wooden planks from the old tower. Talisman climbed to it and gazed through the jagged crack. 'It is good,' he said, as Kzun moved alongside.

'It will do,' said Kzun. 'Is this where you wish my men and me to fight?'

'Your men, yes. But not you. Appoint a leader for them. I want you to take command of the Curved Horn at the well.'

'What?' Kzun reddened. 'You want me to lead those frightened monkeys?'

'If the Gothir take the well, they will take the Shrine,' said Talisman, his voice low and even. 'It is the very heart of our defence. Without water the enemy will be forced to all-out attack; if we can hold them for long enough they will start to die. With water they have a dozen options; they could even starve us out.'

'You don't have to convince me of the importance, Talisman,' snapped Kzun. 'But why should I lead Curved Horn? They are soft. My own men could hold the well. I can trust them to fight to the death.'

'You will lead the Curved Horn,' said Talisman. 'You are a fighting man and they will follow you.'

Kzun blinked. 'Just tell me why. Why me?'

'Because I order it,' said Talisman.

'No, there is more. What is it you are hiding from me?'

'There is nothing,' lied Talisman smoothly. 'The well is vital and it is my judgement that you are the best man to lead the defence. But the well is on Curved Horn lands and they would feel insulted should I ask another tribe to defend it.'

'You think they will not feel insulted when you name me as their leader?'

'That is a risk that must be taken. Come with me now, for they are waiting for us.'

Bartsai was furious, but he bit back his anger as he watched Kzun lead the warriors out through the gates. The nagging chest pain was back – a dull, tight cage of iron around his upper ribs. He had looked forward eagerly to the fight at the well. There were many escape routes open. He and his men would have defended it well, but also slipped away to safety should the need have arisen. Now he was trapped here in this rotting would-be fortress. Talisman approached him. 'Come, we must talk,' he said. A fresh pain stabbed at him as he looked at the younger man.

'Talk? I have had enough of talk. If the situation were not desperate I would challenge you, Talisman.'

'I understand your anger, Bartsai,' said Talisman. 'Now hear me: Kzun would have been useless in the siege. I have watched him pacing this compound, and seen his lantern flickering throughout the night. He sleeps in the open. Have you noticed that?'

'Aye, he's a strange one. But what makes you think he should lead *my* men?'

Talisman led Bartsai to the table in the shade. 'I do not know what demons plague Kzun, but it is obvious he fears confinement. He does not like the dark, and he avoids enclosed spaces. When the siege begins we will all be confined here. I think that would have broken Kzun. But he is a fighter, and will defend the well with his life.'

'As would I,' said Bartsai, not meeting Talisman's eyes. 'As would any leader.'

'We all carry our own fears, Bartsai,' said Talisman softly.

'What does that mean?' snapped the Curved Horn leader, reddening. Anxiously he looked up into Talisman's dark, enigmatic eyes.

'It means that I also fear the coming days. As do Quing-chin, Lin-tse and all the warriors. None of us want to die. That is one reason why I value your presence here, Bartsai. You are older and more experienced than the other leaders. Your calm and your strength will be of great importance when the Gothir attack.'

Bartsai sighed, and the pain subsided. 'When I was your age I would have ridden a hundred miles to be at this battle. Now I can feel the cold breath of Death upon my neck. It turns my bowels to water, Talisman. I am too old, and it would be best if you did not rely on me too much.'

'You are wrong, Bartsai. Only the stupid are fearless. I am young, but I am a good judge of men. You will stand, and you will inspire the warriors around you. You are Nadir!'

'I don't need pretty speeches. I know my duty.'

'It was not a speech, Bartsai. Twelve years ago, when Chopbacks raided your village you led a force of twenty men into their camp. You scattered them, and recovered all the lost ponies. Five years ago you were challenged by a young swordsman from the Lone Wolves. You were stabbed four times, but you killed him. Then, though wounded, you walked to your pony and rode away. You are a man, Bartsai.'

'You know a great deal about me, Talisman.'

'All leaders must know the men who serve them. But I only know this of you because your men brag of it.'

Bartsai grinned. 'I'll stand,' he said. 'And now I had better get back to the work on the ramparts. Otherwise I'll have nothing to stand on!'

Talisman smiled and the older man walked away. Nosta Khan came out of the Shrine building and walked across the compound. Talisman's good mood evaporated as the shaman approached. 'There is nothing there,' said Nosta Khan. 'I have cast search spells, but they fail. Perhaps Chorin-Tsu was wrong. Perhaps they are not there at all.'

'The Eyes are here,' said Talisman, 'but they are hidden from us. The spirit of Oshikai told me that a foreigner was destined to find them.'

Nosta Khan spat upon the dust. 'There are two coming, Druss and the poet. Let us hope one of them will prove to be the man of destiny.'

'Why is Druss coming here?' asked Talisman.

'I told him the Eyes would heal a friend of his who was wounded in a fight.'

'And will they?'

'Of course – though he'll never have them. You think I would allow the sacred future of the Nadir to rest in the hands of a *gajin*? No, Talisman. Druss is a great warrior. He will be of use to us in the coming battle, after that he must be killed.'

Talisman looked closely at the little man, but said nothing. The shaman sat down at the table and poured himself a cup of water. 'You say there is a *lon-tsia* inside the coffin?'

'Yes. Silver.'

'That is curious,' said Nosta Khan. 'The Shrine was plundered centuries ago. Why would the thieves leave a silver ornament behind?'

'It would have been worn next to the skin,' observed Talisman, 'underneath his shirt. Perhaps they missed it. The shirt then rotted away, which is why I found it.'

'Hmm,' murmured Nosta Khan, unconvinced. 'I think a spell was placed upon it, which has faded with time.' His glittering dark eyes fixed on Talisman's face. 'Now let us talk about the girl. You cannot have her, Talisman; she is pledged to the Uniter and you are not he. From his line will come the great men of the future. Zhusai will be his first bride.'

Talisman felt a tight knot in his belly, and his anger rose. 'I do not want to hear any more prophecies, shaman. I love her as I love life. She is mine.'

'No!' hissed Nosta Khan, leaning in close. 'The welfare of the Nadir is your first concern – indeed it is your *only* concern. You want to see the day of the Uniter? Then do not meddle with his destiny. Somewhere out there,' said Nosta Khan, waving his thin arm in the air, 'is the man we wait for. The strands of his destiny are interwoven with that of Zhusai. You understand me, Talisman? You cannot have her!'

The young Nadir looked into Nosta Khan's dark eyes and saw the malice lurking there. But more than that, he saw the little man was genuinely frightened. His life, even more than Talisman's, was devoted to one end, the coming of the Uniter.

Talisman felt as if a stone had replaced his heart. 'I understand,' he said.

'Good.' The little shaman relaxed and gazed around at the

warriors working on the walls. 'It looks impressive,' he said. 'You have done well.'

'Are you staying with us for the battle?' asked Talisman coldly.

'For a while. I shall use my powers against the Gothir. But I cannot die here, Talisman; my work is too important. If the defence fails I shall leave. I shall take the girl with me.'

Talisman's heart lifted. 'You can save her?'

'Of course. Though let me speak plainly, Talisman. If you take away her virtue I shall leave her behind.'

'You have my word, Nosta Khan. Is it good enough for you?'

'Always, Talisman. Do not hate me, boy,' he said sadly. 'There are too many who do. Most of them have justification. It would hurt me for you to be among them. You will serve the Uniter well, I know this.'

'You have seen my destiny?'

'Yes. But some things are not to be spoken of. I need rest now.' The shaman walked away, but Talisman called him back.

'If you have any regard for me, Nosta Khan, you will tell me what you have seen.'

'I have seen nothing,' said Nosta Khan, without turning round. The little man's shoulders sank. 'Nothing. I do not see you riding with the Uniter. There is no future for you, Talisman. This is your moment. Relish it.' Without looking back he moved away.

Talisman stood for a moment, then turned towards the sleeping quarters and made his way up the stairs to Zhusai's room. She was waiting for him, her long black hair sleekly combed and shining with perfumed oil. As he entered she ran across to him, throwing her arms around his neck and kissing his face. Gently he pulled away from her, and told her the words of the shaman.

'I don't care what he says,' she told him. 'I will never feel for another man what I feel for you. Never!'

'Nor I for any woman. Let us sit together for a while, Zhusai. I need to feel the touch of your hand.' He led her to the small bed. She took his hand and kissed it, and he felt the warmth of her tears falling to his skin. 'When all else fails,' he whispered, 'Nosta Khan will take you from here to a place of safety. He has great magic and he will lead you through the Gothir. You will live, Zhusai.'

'I don't want to live without you. I will not leave.'

Her words touched Talisman, but they also made him fearful. 'Do not say that, my love. You have to understand that, for me, your safety would be like a victory. I could die happy.'

'I don't want you to die!' she said, her voice breaking. 'I want to be with you, somewhere deep in the mountains. I want to bear your sons.'

Talisman held her close, breathing in the perfume of her hair and skin, his fingers stroking her face and neck. He could find no words, and a terrible sadness smote him. He had thought his dreams of Nadir unity were more important than life itself. Now he knew differently. This one, slender woman had shown him a truth he had not known existed. For her he could almost betray his destiny. Almost. His mouth was dry, and with a great effort he released his hold on her and stood. 'I must go now,' he said.

She shook her head and rose alongside him. 'No, not yet,' she told him, her voice controlled. 'I am Chiatze, Talisman. I am trained in many things. Remove your shirt.'

'I cannot. I gave my word to Nosta Khan.'

She smiled then. 'Take off your shirt. You are tense and weary, your muscles knotted. I shall massage your shoulders and neck. Then you may sleep. Do this for me, Talisman.'

Shrugging off his goatskin jerkin, he doffed his shirt, unbuckled his sword-belt and sat back on the bed. She knelt behind him, her thumbs working at the knots in his muscles. After a while she ordered him to lie down on his stomach. He did so, and she rubbed perfumed oil into his back. The scent was delicate, and Talisman felt his tension flowing from him.

When he awoke she was lying beside him under a single blanket. Her arm was resting on his chest, her face next to his on the pillow. The dawn sun was shining through the window. Lifting her arm, Talisman eased himself from the bed and stood. She awoke. 'How are you feeling, my Lord?' she asked him.

'I am well, Zhusai. You are very skilled.'

'Love is magic,' she said, sitting up. She was naked, the sunlight turning her skin to gold.

'Love is magic,' he agreed, dragging his gaze from her breasts. 'You did not dream of Shul-sen?'

'I dreamed only of you, Talisman.'

Pulling on his shirt and jerkin he looped his sword-belt over his shoulder and left the room. Gorkai was waiting below.

'Two riders coming,' he said. 'Could be Gothir scouts. One carries a great axe. You want them dead or alive?'

'Let them come. I have been expecting them.'

*

204

Druss reined in the mare before the western wall and stared hard at the jagged crack that ran down it. 'I have seen better forts,' he told Sieben.

'And friendlier welcomes,' muttered Sieben, staring up at the bowmen who stood on the ramparts, aiming down at them. Druss grinned and tugged on the reins and the mare walked on. The gates were old and half-rotted, but he could see that the hinges had been recently cleaned of rust. The ground was scored under both gates in deep semi-circles, showing they had been closed recently.

Touching heels to the mare, he rode into the compound and dismounted. He saw Talisman walking towards him. 'We meet again, my friend,' he said. 'No robbers this time hunting you?'

'Two thousand of them,' Talisman told him. 'Lancers, infantry and archers.'

'You had better set some men to soak those gates,' said Druss. 'The wood is dry. They'll not bother to smash them. They'll set fire to them.' The axeman cast his experienced eye over the defences, impressed with what he saw. The ramparts had been restored, and a fighting platform raised beneath the crack in the western wall. Rocks and boulders were set on each rampart, ready to be hurled down on advancing infantry. 'How many men do you have?'

'Two hundred.'

'They'll need to be fighters.'

'They are Nadir. And they are defending the bones of the greatest Nadir warrior of all time. They will fight. Will you?'

Druss chuckled. 'I love a good fight, boy. But this one isn't mine. A Nadir shaman told me there were jewels here – healing jewels. I need them for a friend.'

'So I understand. But we have not found them yet. Tell me, did this shaman promise you the jewels?'

'Not exactly,' admitted Druss. 'He just told me they were here. Do you mind if we search?'

'Not at all,' said Talisman. 'I owe you my life, it is the least I can do.' He pointed to the main building. 'That is the Shrine of Oshikai Demon-bane. If the jewels are anywhere they are hidden there. Nosta Khan – the shaman you spoke of – has searched with spells, but he cannot find them. For myself I summoned the spirit of Oshikai, but he would not divulge their whereabouts. Good luck, axeman!'

Hoisting his axe to his shoulder, Druss strode across the

compound with Sieben beside him. The Shrine was dimly lit, and the axeman paused before the stone sarcophagus. The chamber was dust-covered, and empty of adornments.

'It has been plundered,' said Sieben. 'Look at the pegs on the wall. Once they would have carried his armour and his battle flag.'

'No way to treat a hero,' said Druss. 'Any idea where to look?'

'Inside the sarcophagus,' said Sieben. 'But you'll find no jewels there.'

Druss laid his axe aside and moved to the coffin. Grasping the stone lid, he tensed his muscles and heaved. The stone groaned and grated as he slid it aside. Sieben looked in. 'Well, well,' he said.

'Are they there?'

'Of course they are not there,' snapped Sieben. 'But the corpse is wearing a *lon-tsia* exactly like the one we found on the woman.'

'Nothing else?'

'No. He has no fingers, Druss. Someone must have hacked them away to get at his rings. Put the lid back.'

Druss did so. 'What now?' he asked.

'I will think on it,' said the poet. 'There is something here that is not right. It will come to me.'

'Make it soon, poet. Otherwise you may find yourself at the centre of a war.'

'A charming thought.'

The sound of horses' hooves came from the compound. Druss walked to the door and stepped into the sunlight. Sieben followed him in time to see Nuang Xuan leap from his pony, his people streaming in through the gates behind him.

'I thought you were heading away from here,' called Druss. The Nadir leader hawked and spat.

'So did I, axeman. But some fool set a fire in our path and we had no choice but to flee from it. When we tried to cut across to the east we saw a column of Lancers. Truly the Gods of Stone and Water hate me.'

'You're still alive, old man.'

'Pah, not for much longer. Thousands of them, there are – all heading this way. I will let my people rest for tonight.'

'You are a bad liar, Nuang Xuan,' said Druss. 'You have come here to fight – to defend the Shrine. It is no way to change your luck.'

206

'I ask myself, is there no end to Gothir malice? How does it benefit them to destroy that which we hold dear?' He drew in a deep breath. 'I shall stay,' he said. 'I will send the women and children away, but I and my warriors will stay. And as for luck, axeman, to die defending a sacred place is a privilege. And I am not so old. I think I will kill a hundred by myself. You are staying, yes?'

'It is not my fight, Nuang.'

'What they are planning to do is evil, Druss.' He gave a sudden, gap-toothed grin. 'I think you will stay too. I think the Gods of Stone and Water brought you here so that you could watch me kill my hundred. Now I must find the leader here.'

Sieben walked to where Niobe was standing in the shade. She was carrying a canvas pack, which she had dropped to the ground at her feet. Sieben smiled. 'Missed me?' he asked.

'I am too tired for love-making,' she said tonelessly.

'Ever the Nadir romantic,' said Sieben. 'Come, let me get you some water.'

'I can fetch my own water.'

'I am sure that you can, my lovely, but I would cherish your company.' Taking her hand he led her to the table in the shade. Stone jugs had been filled with water and there were clay cups upon the table. Sieben filled one and passed it to her.

'Do men serve women in your land?' she asked.

'One way or another,' he agreed. Niobe drained the cup and held it out to him, and Sieben re-filled it.

'You are strange,' she said. 'And you are no warrior. What will you do here, when the blood spills?'

'With luck I won't be here when the fighting starts. But if I am . . .' He spread his hands. 'I have some skill with wounds,' he told her. 'I will be the Fort Surgeon.'

'I too can stitch wounds. We will need cloth for bandages, and much thread. Also needles. I will gather these things. And there must be a place for the dead, otherwise they stink, bloat, split and attract flies.'

'How nicely phrased,' he said. 'Shall we talk about something else?'

'Why for?'

'Because the subject is . . . demoralizing.'

'I do not know this word.'

'No,' he said. 'I don't think you do. Tell me, are you frightened at all?'

'Of what?'

'Of the Gothir.'

She shook her head. 'They will come, we will kill them.'

'Or be killed by them,' he pointed out.

She shrugged. 'Whatever,' she said grimly.

'You, my dear, are a fatalist.'

'You are wrong. I am of the Lone Wolves,' she said. 'We were to be Eagle Wing tribe, under Nuang. Now there are not enough of us, so we will become Lone Wolves again.'

'Niobe of the Lone Wolves, I adore you,' he said, with a smile. 'You are a breath of fresh air in this jaded life of mine.'

'I will only wed a warrior,' she told him sternly. 'But until a good one approaches me I will sleep with you.'

'What gentleman would spurn such a delicate advance?' he said.

'Strange,' she muttered, then walked away from him.

Druss strolled across the compound. 'Nuang says he's tired of running. He and his people will stay here and fight.'

'Can they win, Druss?'

'They look like a tough bunch, and Talisman has done well with the defences.'

'That doesn't answer the question.'

'There is no answer,' Druss told him. 'Only odds. I wouldn't bet a half-copper on their holding for more than a day.'

Sieben sighed. 'Naturally this does not mean we'll do something sensible – like leave?'

'The Gothir have no right to despoil this Shrine,' said Druss, a cold look in his grey eyes. 'It is wrong. This Oshikai was a hero to all the Nadir. His bones should be left in peace.'

'Excuse me for stating the obvious, old horse, but his tomb has already been plundered and his bones hacked around. I think he's probably past caring by now.'

'It is not about him, it's about them,' said Druss, indicating the Nadir. 'Despoiling the Shrine robs them of their heritage. Such a deed has no merit. It is born of spite and I can't abide such things.'

'We're staying, then?'

Druss smiled. 'You should leave,' he said. 'This is no place for a poet.'

'That is a tempting thought, Druss, old horse. I may just do that – as soon as we sight their battle flags.'

Nuang called out to Druss and the axeman strode away. As

Sieben sat at the table, sipping water, Talisman walked across to him and sat down.

'Tell me of the friend who is dying,' he said. Sieben explained all that he knew about the fight that had left Klay crippled, and Talisman listened gravely.

'It is right,' he said, 'that a man should risk all for friendship. It shows he has a good heart. He has fought in many battles?'

'Many,' said Sieben bitterly. 'You know how a tall tree attracts lightning during a storm? Well, Druss is like that. Wherever he is battles just seem to spring up around him. It really is galling.'

'Yet he survives them.'

'That is his talent. Wherever he walks, Death is close behind.'

'He will be most welcome here,' said Talisman. 'But what of you, Sieben? Niobe tells me you wish to be our surgeon. Why should you do this?'

'Stupidity runs in my family.'

Lin-tse sat on his pony and scanned the pass. To his right rose the sheer red rock-face of Temple Stone, a towering monument to the majesty of nature, its flanks scored by the winds of time, its shape carved by a long-forgotten sea that had once covered this vast land. To Lin-Tse's left was a series of jagged slopes, covered with boulders. The enemy would have to pass along the narrow trail that led down beside Temple Stone. Dismounting, he ran up the first slope, pausing at several jutting rocks. With enough men, and enough time, he could dislodge several of the larger boulders and send them hurtling down on to the trail. He thought about it for a while.

Running back to his pony, he vaulted to the saddle and led his small company on, deeper into the red rocks. Talisman needed a victory, something to lift the hearts of the defenders.

But how? Talisman had mentioned Fecrem and the Long Retreat – that had involved a series of lightning guerrilla raids on enemy supply lines. Fecrem was Oshikai's nephew, and a skilled raider. Red dust rose in puffs of clouds beneath the ponies' hooves and Lin-tse's throat was dry as he leaned in to his mount, urging the stallion up the steep slope. At the crest he paused, and dismounted once more. Here the trail widened. A long finger of rock jutted from the left, leaning towards a cluster of boulders on the right. The gap between was about eighteen feet. Lin-tse pictured the advancing line of Lancers. They would be travelling slowly, probably in a column of twos. If he could make them move faster at this point . . . Swinging in the saddle, he scanned the back trail. The slope behind him was steep, but a skilled horseman could ride down it at a run. And the Lancers were skilled. 'Wait here,' he told his men, then dragged on the reins. The pony reared and twisted, but Lin-tse heeled him into a run and set off down the slope. At the bottom he drew up sharply. Dust had kicked up behind him, like a red mist over the trail. Lin-tse angled to the right and moved on more cautiously. Away from the trail the ground was more broken, leading to a crevice and a sheer drop of some three hundred feet. Dismounting again, he moved to the lip of the chasm, then worked his way along it. At the widest point there was at least fifty feet between the two edges, but it narrowed to ten feet where he now knelt. On the other side the ground was angled upwards, and littered with rocks. But this led to a wider trail, and Lin-tse followed it with his eyes. It would take him down to the western side of Temple Stone.

He sat alone for a while, thinking the plan through. Then he rode back to his men.

Premian led his hundred Lancers deep into the red rock country. He was tired, his eyes bloodshot and gritty. The men behind him rode silently in columns of twos; all of them were unshaven, their water rations down by a third. For the fourth time that morning Premian held his arm in the air, and the troops reined in. The young officer, Mikal, rode alongside Premian. 'What do you see, sir?' he asked.

'Nothing. Send a scout to that high ground to the north-east.'

'There is no *army* facing us,' complained Mikal. 'Why all these precautions?'

'You have your orders. Obey them,' said Premian. The young man reddened and wheeled his horse. Premian had not wanted Mikal on this mission. The boy was young and hot-headed. Worse, he held the Nadir in contempt – even after the fire at the camp. But Gargan had overruled him; he liked Mikal, and saw in him a younger version of himself. Premian knew that the men did not object to the slow advance into enemy territory. The Royal Lancers had all fought Nadir warriors in the past, and in the main were canny men who would sooner suffer discomfort in the saddle than ride unawares into an ambush.

One fact was sure: the man who planned the raid on the camp would not have only one string to his bow. Premian had not ridden these lands before, but he had studied the exquisite maps in the Great Library at Gulgothir, and knew that the area around Temple Stone was rich with hiding-places from which archers could attack his troops or send boulders hurtling down upon them. Under no circumstances would he lead his men headlong into the enemy's arms. Sitting on his mount, he watched as the scout rode to the high ground. The man reached the top and then waved his arm in a circular motion, indicating the way was clear. Premian led his four companies forward once more.

His mouth was dry. Fishing in his saddle-bag, he produced a small silver coin which he put into his mouth to encourage saliva. The men would be watching him, and if he drank then so would they. According to the maps there was no major water supply in this region, though there were several dry river-beds. Often solid digging produced small seeps which would at least give the horses a drink. Or there might be hidden rock tanks of which the cartographers were unaware. Premian kept watch for bees, who never strayed far from water. So far he had seen nothing. Nor had the horses reacted to the shifting of the hot winds; they could scent water from great distances.

Premian summoned his Master Sergeant, Jomil. The man was close to fifty, and a veteran of Nadir campaigns. Heeling his horse alongside Premian he gave a crisp salute. His grizzled face looked even older now, with its two-day growth of silver bristles. 'What do you think?' he asked the man.

'They're close,' answered Jomil. 'I can almost smell them.'

'Lord Larness requires prisoners,' said Premian. 'Relay that to the men.'

'A reward would be pleasant,' suggested Jomil.

'There will be one, but do not announce it. I want no recklessness.'

'Ah, but you are a careful man, sir,' Jomil said, with a grin.

Premian smiled. 'That is what I would like my grandchildren to say as I sit with them in the cool of an autumn garden. "He was a careful man."'

'I already have grandchildren,' Jomil told him.

'Probably more than you know.'

'No *probably* about it, sir.' Jomil returned to his men, passing the word concerning prisoners. Premian lifted the white horse-hair-plumed helm from his head and ran his fingers through his sweat-streaked blond hair. Just for a moment the wind felt cool as the sweat evaporated, then the oppressive heat began again. Premian replaced the helm.

211

Ahead the trail twisted and Temple Stone came into sight. Shaped like a giant bell, it reared up majestically towards the sky. Premian found it an impressive sight, and wished that he had the time to sketch it. The trail steepened towards a crest. Summoning Mikal, he told him to take his company of twenty-five to the crest and wait for the main body to follow. The young man saluted and led his men away to the east. Premian scowled. He was riding too fast – did he not understand that the horses were tired, and that water was scarce?

Mikal and his men reached the crest – just in time to see a small group of four startled Nadir warriors running for their ponies. The Lord Gargan had said he wanted prisoners, and Mikal could almost hear the words of praise the general would heap upon him. 'A gold raq for the man who captures one!' he shouted, and spurred his mount. The gelding leapt forward. The Nadir scrambled to their mounts and kicked them into a run, sending up clouds of red dust as they galloped down the slope. The ponies were no match for Gothir horses, and it would be a matter of only moments before Mikal and his men reached them. Drawing his sabre, Mikal squinted against the dust and leaned in to the neck of his mount, urging it to greater speed. The Nadir rounded a bend in the trail . . . he could just make them out through the dust-cloud. His horse was at full gallop, his men bunched behind him as he rounded the bend. He saw the Nadir slightly to the left; their horses bunched and jumped, as if over a small fence.

In that terrible moment Mikal saw the chasm yawning before him like the mouth of a giant beast. Throwing himself back in the saddle, he hauled savagely on the reins – but it was too late. The gelding, at full gallop, leapt out over the awesome drop and then tipped head-first, flinging Mikal from the saddle. He fell screaming towards the distant rocks.

Behind him the Lancers had also dragged on their reins. Seven fell immediately after him, the others milling at the edge of the crevice. Fifteen Nadir warriors, shouting at the tops of their voices, rose from hiding-places in the rocks and ran towards the riders. The startled horses bolted, sending ten more Lancers plunging to their deaths. The remaining eight men jumped from their saddles and turned to fight. Outnumbered and demoralized, with the chasm behind them and nowhere to run, they were hacked down swiftly and mercilessly. Only one Nadir warrior was wounded – his face gashed, the skin of his cheek flapping against his chin. Gathering the Gothir horses, and the helms of the fallen men, they rode swiftly back down the trail.

Premian and his three companies topped the crest moments later. Jomil rode down and found the bodies. Returning to his captain, he made his report. 'All dead, sir. Most of them appear to have ridden over a cliff. Their bodies are scattered on the rocks below. Some good men lost, sir.'

'Good men,' agreed Premian, barely keeping the fury from his voice. 'Led by an officer with the brains of a sick goat.'

'I heard your order to him, sir. You told him to wait. You're not to blame, sir.'

'We'll detour down to the bodies and bury them,' he said. 'How many do you think were in the attacking party?'

'From the tracks, no more than twenty, sir. Some of the Nadir were riding ahead of our boys. They jumped the gorge at a narrow point.'

'So, twenty-six men dead for the loss of how many of the enemy?'

'Some were wounded. There was blood on the ground where they hid their ponies – maybe ten of them.'

Premian gave him a hard look. 'Well, maybe one or two,' Jomil admitted.

It took more than three hours to detour to the foot of the chasm. By the time the Gothir troops reached the bodies it was almost dusk.

The eighteen corpses had all been stripped of armour and weapons, and beheaded.

Chapter Ten

Sieben stood and gazed around at the old storehouse. Niobe and other Nadir women had cleaned it of dust, dirt and ancient cobwebs, and five lanterns had been set in brackets on the walls. Only one was lit now and he used its flickering light to study the layout of this new hospital. Two barrels full of water had been set at the northern end of the large, square room, placed close to the two long tables the Nadir had carried in earlier. Sieben examined the tools set there – an old pair of pliers, three sharp knives, several curved needles of horn and one long straight needle of iron. He found that his hands were trembling. Niobe moved silently alongside him. 'Is this all you need, po-et?' she asked, laying a small box filled with thread upon the table.

'Blankets,' he said. 'We'll need blankets. And food bowls.'

'Why for food bowls?' she asked. 'If a wounded man has strength to eat, he has strength to fight.'

'A wounded man loses blood, and therefore strength. Food and water will help rebuild him.'

'Why do you tremble?'

'I have assisted surgeons three times in my life. Once I even stitched a wound in a man's shoulder. But my knowledge of anatomy . . . the human body . . . is severely limited. I do not, for example, know what to do with a deep belly wound.'

'Nothing,' she said, simply. 'A deep belly wound is death.'

'How comforting! I could do with honey. That is good for wounds, especially when mixed with wine; it prevents infection.'

'No bees, po-et. No bees – no honey. But we have some dried

214

lorassium leaves. Good for pain, and for dreams. And some *hakka* roots to ward off the blue-skin demons.'

'Blue-skin demons? What are they?'

'Truly you know little of wounds. They are the invisible devils who creep in through the open flesh and turn it blue, so it stinks and men die.'

'Gangrene. I see. And what does one do with these *hakka* roots?'

'We make poultice and lay it over the wound. It smells very bad. The demons avoid it.'

'And what cures do you have, my lady, for trembling hands?' he asked her.

She laughed and slid her hand over his belly and down. 'I have big cure,' she said. Curling her left arm around his neck, she drew down his head and kissed him. He felt the warmth and sweetness of her tongue upon his. Arousal swept through him.

She pulled away. 'Now look at your hands,' she said. They were no longer trembling. 'Big cure, yes?'

'I can offer no argument there,' he said. 'Where can we go?'

'Nowhere. I have much to do. Shi-sai will be in labour soon, and I have promised to help when the waters break. But if you have trembling hands in the night, you may come to me by the north wall.'

Kissing him once more, she spun away from his embrace and walked from the room. Sieben took a last look at the hospital, then blew out the lantern and made his way to the compound. Some work was still being done in the moonlight, repairing the ramparts beside the crack in the west-facing wall. Elsewhere Nadir warriors were sitting around camp-fires. Druss was talking to Talisman and Bartsai on the ramparts above the gates.

Sieben thought of joining them, but realized he did not want to listen to more talk of battles and death. His mind flickered to Niobe. She was unlike any woman he had ever known. When first he had seen her he had thought her to be mildly attractive – certainly no more than that. Up close, her laughing eyes had made him re-appraise her. Even so she would pale against the beauties who had shared his bed. Yet each time he made love to her it seemed her beauty grew. It was uncanny. All his previous lovers were drab by comparison. As he was thinking, two Nadir warriors approached him. One of them spoke to him in Nadir.

'Sorry, lads,' he said, with a nervous smile. 'I don't understand the language.' The taller of the two, a ferocious-looking man with narrow, malevolent eyes, pointed to his companion and said, 'This one have big pain.'

'Big pain,' echoed Sieben.

'You doctor. Fix it.' Sieben glanced down at the second warrior. The man's face was grey, his eyes sunken and his jaws clenched. 'We go in,' muttered the first man, leading his friend into the new hospital. With a sinking heart Sieben followed them and, re-lighting the lantern, he led them to the table. The small warrior tried to tug off his faded crimson shirt, but groaned as he did so. The taller man dragged the garment clear, and in the flickering light Sieben saw a growth on the man's spine the size of a small apple. The area all around it was red, swollen and angry. 'You cut,' said the taller man.

Sieben indicated that the warrior should lie down on the table; then he reached out and, with great care, touched the swelling. The man stiffened, but made no sound. The lump was rock-hard. 'Fetch the lantern,' Sieben ordered the taller man. The warrior did so, and Sieben peered more closely at the growth. Then taking the sharpest of the knives, he drew in a deep breath. He had no idea what the growth was – it looked like a giant boil, but for all he knew it might be a cancer. What was certain was that he had no choice of action, burdened as he was by the expectations of both men. Touching the point of the knife to the lump, he pressed down hard. Thick yellow pus exploded from the cut, and the skin peeled away as if from a section of rotten fruit. The warrior cried out, the sound strangled and inhuman. Laying aside the knife, Sieben gripped the lump and squeezed it. More pus – this time mixed with blood – oozed from the cut, covering his fingers. The wounded man sighed and relaxed on the table. Sieben moved to a water barrel and filled a wooden bowl, cleaning his hands and wrists. Then he returned to the warrior. Fresh blood was oozing from the three-inch cut and flowing down to the wood of the table. With a wet cloth Sieben cleaned the wound, then ordered the man to sit up while he applied a wedge of cloth to it, strapping it in place with a bandage around the man's waist. The patient spoke in Nadir to his companion; then without another word both men walked from the building.

Sieben sat down. 'Not at all, it was my pleasure,' he said, not loud enough to be heard by the departing warriors.

Once more extinguishing the lantern, he left the building by a side door and found himself standing close to the main entrance to the Shrine. With Niobe otherwise occupied, and with nothing else to do, Sieben pushed open the door and stepped inside.

Something about the place had been nagging at him from the subconscious, but he could not bring it to the surface. His eyes were drawn to the blackened iron plate on the stone coffin. The symbols upon it were Chiatze, part alphabet, part hieroglyph, and Talisman had told him what they said:

Oshikai Demon-bane – Lord of War

Kneeling before it, Sieben scanned the symbols. They were deeply engraved into the iron, and they told him nothing. Irritated that he could not solve the problem, he left the Shrine and climbed to the ramparts of the north wall, where he sat on the parapet in the moonlight gazing out over the distant mountains. His thoughts turned once more to Niobe and her beauty, and he listened a while in vain for the birth sounds of the newborn. Be patient, he told himself. Fishing the lon-tsia from his pocket, he looked at the profile of the woman embossed there. She too was beautiful. Turning the coin over, he looked down at the image of Oshikai. 'You're causing a lot of trouble for someone who's been dead for ten centuries,' he said.

Then it hit him . . .

Rising, he climbed down the steps and returned to the Shrine, squatting down before the iron plate. Checking Oshikai's name against the embossing of the *lon-tsia*, he saw that the name on the plate boasted two extra and identical symbols. Peering more closely, he saw that the engraving of each was deeper than that of the other symbols.

'What have you found?' asked Talisman, from the doorway. The slender Nadir leader moved forward and knelt beside the poet.

'Is this the original plate?' Sieben asked. 'Was it made by Oshikai's followers?'

'I would imagine so,' said Talisman. 'Why?'

'What are these symbols?'

'The Nadir letter *i*.'

'But the Chiatze had no such letter,' said Sieben. 'Therefore the name-plate is either not original, or it has been altered.'

'I don't understand your point,' said Talisman.

Sieben sat back. 'I don't like mysteries,' he said. 'If this is original there would be no *i*'s. If it is not, why is it in the Chiatze tongue? Why not fully Nadir?'

Moving forward on his knees, Sieben laid his hands on the

plate, pressing a finger into each of the engraved symbols. Something gave way under his pressure, there was a dull clunk from within and the name-plate fell clear. Behind it was a shallow niche cut into the coffin, and within this lay a small pouch of hide. Talisman pushed Sieben aside and grabbed the pouch. As he pulled it open the hide split and the contents fell to the dusty floor. There were two knuckle-bones stained with black symbols, a small coil of braided hair and a piece of folded parchment. Talisman looked disappointed. 'I thought you had found the Eyes of Alchazzar,' he said.

Sieben lifted the parchment and tried to open it, but it broke into pieces under his fingers. 'What are these objects?' he asked.

'A shaman's medicine bag. The knuckle-bones are used in spells of prophecy, the hair is that of the shaman's greatest enemy. The parchment? I do not know.'

'Why would it be placed here?'

'I don't know,' snapped Talisman. Reaching down, Sieben picked up the knuckle-bones.

The world spun. He cried out, but was dragged down into the dark . . .

Shocked by his sudden collapse, Talisman knelt over the still figure of the blond Drenai and placed his index finger on the pulse point of the neck. The heart was beating, but incredibly slowly. Roughly he shook Sieben's shoulders, but there was no response. Rising, he ran from the Shrine. Gorkai was sitting on the ground, sharpening his sword with a whetstone. 'Fetch Nosta Khan and the Drenai axeman,' commanded Talisman, then returned to where Sieben lay.

Druss arrived first. 'What happened?' he asked, kneeling beside his friend.

'We were talking, and he collapsed. Is he subject to fits?'

'No.' Druss swore softly. 'His heart is barely beating.' Talisman glanced at the axeman, and noted the fear on his broad, bearded face. Nosta Khan arrived, and Talisman saw his gimlet eyes fasten to the sagging name-plate on the coffin.

'The Eyes . . . ?' he asked.

'No,' said Talisman, and told him what they had found.

'You fool!' hissed Nosta Khan. 'I should have been summoned.'

'It was just a medicine pouch. There were no jewels,' Talisman responded, feeling his anger rise.

'It is the medicine pouch of a *shaman*,' snapped Nosta Khan. 'A spell has been placed upon it.'

'I touched it also, and nothing has happened to me,' argued Talisman.

The little shaman knelt beside Sieben, prying open the fingers of his right hand. The knuckle-bones lay there, but now they were white and pure – the black symbols having transferred to the skin of Sieben's palm. 'But the bag split,' said Nosta Khan, 'and it was not you who lifted the Seeing Bones.'

The axeman rose, towering over Nosta Khan. 'I do not care who is at fault,' he said, his voice dangerously even, his pale eyes glittering. 'What I want is for you to bring him back. *Now!*'

Sensing danger, Nosta Khan felt a moment of panic as he looked into the axeman's cold eyes. Placing his hand over his heart, he whispered two words of power. Druss stiffened and groaned. The spell was an old one, and shackled the victim in chains of fiery pain. Any attempt on Druss's part to move would bring colossal agony and a subsequent loss of consciousness. Now, thought Nosta Khan triumphantly, let this Drenai *gajin* feel the power of the Nadir! The shaman was about to speak when Druss gave a low, guttural growl. His eyes blazed and his hand snaked out, huge fingers grabbing Nosta Khan by the throat and lifting him into the air. The little man kicked out helplessly, as through a sea of pain Druss spoke: 'Lift the . . . spell, little man . . . or . . . I'll snap . . . your neck!' Talisman drew his knife and jumped to the shaman's defence. 'One more move and he dies,' warned the axeman. Nosta Khan gave a strangled gasp, and managed to speak three words in a tongue neither Druss nor Talisman recognized. Druss's pain vanished. Dropping the shaman, he stabbed a finger into the little man's chest. 'You ever do anything like that again, you ugly dwarf, and I'll kill you!'

Talisman could see the shock and terror on Nosta Khan's face. 'We are all friends here,' he said softly, sheathing his knife and stepping between Nosta Khan and the menacing figure of Druss. 'Let us think of what is to be done.'

Nosta Khan rubbed his bruised throat. He was astonished, and could barely gather his thoughts. The spell had worked, he *knew* this. It was not possible that a mortal man could overcome such agony. Aware that both men were waiting for him to speak, he forced himself to concentrate and lifted the white knuckle-bones, holding them tightly in his fist. 'His soul has been drawn out,' he said, his voice croaking. 'The medicine pouch belonged to

Shaoshad the renegade. He was the shaman who stole the Eyes – may his soul be for ever accursed and burn in ten thousand fires!'

'Why would he hide it here?' asked Talisman. 'What purpose did it serve?'

'I do not know. But let us see if we can reverse his spell.' Taking Sieben's limp hand in his own, he began to chant.

Sieben fell for an eternity, spinning and turning, then awoke with a start. He was lying beside a fire, set at the centre of a circle of standing stones. An old man was sitting by the small blaze. Naked, but with a bulging bag hanging from one thin shoulder, he had two long wispy beards growing from both sides of his chin, and reaching his scrawny chest; his hair was shaved on the left side of his head, and gathered into a tight braid on his right.

'Welcome,' said the old man. Sieben sat up and was about to speak when he noticed with horror that the speaker had been mutilated. His hands had been cut off, and blood was seeping from the stumps.

'Sweet Heavens, you must be in great pain,' he said.

'Always,' agreed the man, with a smile. 'But when something never passes, remaining constant, it becomes bearable.' Shrugging his shoulder he let the bag fall, then reached into it with his mangled, bleeding arms. From the bag he produced a hand, which he held carefully between the stumps. Gripping it with his knees, he held his mutilated right arm to the severed wrist. The limb jerked, and the hand attached itself to the wrist. The fingers flexed. 'Ah, that is good,' said the man, reaching into the bag and producing a left hand which he held in place over his left wrist. This too joined, and he clapped the hands together. Then he removed his eyes and dropped them into the bag.

'Why are you doing this to yourself?' asked Sieben.

'It is a compulsion engendered by sorcery,' said the stranger amiably. 'They were not content to merely kill me. Oh, no! Now I can have my hands or my eyes, but never both at the same time. If I try – and I have – then the pain becomes unbearable. I have great admiration for the way the spell was cast. I did not think it would last this long. I managed to counter the curse upon my ears and tongue. I see you found my medicine pouch.'

The fire flickered down, but the old man gestured with his hands and the flames sprang to new life. Sieben found himself staring at the man's empty eye-sockets. 'Have you tried using just one hand and one eye?' he asked.

'Is there something about me that suggests I am an idiot? Of course I have. It works . . . but the pain is too awesome to describe.'

'I have to tell you that this is the worst dream I've ever had,' said Sieben.

'No dream. You are here.' Sieben was about to question him when a low, inhuman growl came from beyond the stones. The old man's hand came up and blue forked lightning flashed from it, exploding between the stones with a loud crack. Then there was silence. 'I need my hands, you see, to survive here. But I cannot go anywhere without my eyes. It is a sweetly vile punishment. I wish I had thought of it myself.'

'What was that . . . thing?' asked Sieben, craning round to peer between the stones. There was nothing to be seen. All was darkness, deep and final.

'Difficult to know. But it did not mean us any good. I am Shaoshad.'

'Sieben. Sieben the Poet.'

'A poet? It is long since I savoured the delicious sounds of exquisite wordplay. But I fear you will not be with me long, so perhaps another time . . . Tell me how you found my pouch.'

'The use of the Nadir letter *i*,' Sieben told him.

'Yes. It was a joke, you see. I knew no Nadir would see it. Not given to jokes, the Nadir. They were searching for the Eyes of Alchazzar. Eyes and *i*'s. Good, isn't it?'

'Most amusing,' agreed Sieben. 'I take it you are not Nadir?'

'In part. Part Chiatze, part Sechuin, part Nadir. I want you to do something for me. I cannot offer you anything, of course.'

'What do you require?'

'My medicine pouch. I want you to take the hair and burn it. The knuckle-bones must be dropped into water. The parchment is to be shredded and scattered to the air, the pouch itself buried in the earth. Can you remember that?'

'Hair burnt, knuckles drowned, paper scattered, pouch buried,' said Sieben. 'What will that do?'

'I believe the release of my elemental power will end this cursed spell and give me back my hands and my eyes. Speaking of which . . .' He lifted the eyes from the bag and slid them back in their sockets. Holding his arms over the bag, he released his hands, which fell from the wrists. Immediately blood began to flow. 'You are a handsome fellow and you have an honest face. I think I can trust you.'

221

'You are the man who stole the Eyes of Alchazzar,' said Sieben.

'Indeed I am. A rare mistake it was. Still, the man who never made a mistake never made anything, eh?'

'Why did you do it?'

'I had a vision – false as it has so far turned out. I thought I could bring the Uniter to my people five centuries early. Arrogance was always my downfall. I thought to use the Eyes to raise Oshikai from the dead. To regenerate his body and summon his soul. Well, I did summon his soul.'

'What happened?'

'You will scarcely credit it. I still have difficulty believing it myself.'

'I think I know,' said Sieben. 'He wouldn't accept life without Shul-sen.'

'Exactly. You are a bright fellow. Can you guess what happened next?'

'You set off to find her body – that's why you were caught so close to her resting place. What I don't understand is why you did not use the power of the jewels.'

'Ah, but I did. That is why I was caught and killed.'

'Tell me,' whispered Sieben, fascinated . . .

He groaned and opened his eyes. Nosta Khan was leaning over him and Sieben swore. Druss grabbed his arm, hauling him to his feet. 'By Heavens, poet, but you gave us a scare. How are you feeling?'

'Miffed!' said Sieben. 'A moment longer and he would have told me where he hid the jewels.'

'You spoke to Shaoshad?' said Nosta Khan.

'Yes. He told me why he took them.'

'Describe him.'

'A man with a curious beard, who has detachable hands and eyes.'

'Aha!' shouted Nosta Khan happily. 'The spell holds, then. Does he suffer?'

'Yes, but he is taking it rather well. Can you send me back to him?'

'Only by cutting out your heart and casting seven spells upon it,' the shaman told him.

'I'll take that as a no,' said Sieben.

From outside came the cries of a new-born infant and Sieben smiled. 'I hope you'll all excuse me. This has been a wearying experience and I need some rest.' Stooping, he gathered the hair, knuckle-bones, pouch and shreds of parchment.

'What are you doing with those?' asked Nosta Khan.

'Souvenirs of an interesting experience,' he said. 'I shall show them to my grandchildren and brag about my visit to the Underworld.'

Zhusai was afraid, though not with a simple fear, like the thought of dying. It was worse than that, she realized. Death was but another doorway, but this was a kind of extinction. At first her dreams of Shul-sen had been merely that – curiously unpleasant visions she suffered when sleeping. But now she was hearing voices whispering in her subconscious, and her own memories were becoming vague and blurred. Not so the memories of another life – a life as consort to the renegade chieftain Oshikai Demon-bane. These were becoming sharper, more distinct. She remembered the ride through the long hills, making love in the grass in the shadow of Jiang-shin, the Mother of Mountains, wearing her dress of white silk on the day of the wedding in the White Palace of Pechuin.

'Stop it!' she cried, as the memories seemed to engulf her. 'It is not me. Not my life. I was born in . . . in . . .' But the memories would not come. 'My parents died. I was raised by my grandfather . . .' For a moment the name was lost to her. Then: 'Chorin-Tsu!' she shouted triumphantly. Talisman entered the room, and she flew to him. 'Help me!' she begged him.

'What is wrong, my love?'

'She is trying to kill me,' sobbed Zhusai. 'And I cannot fight her.'

Her almond eyes were wide open, fear radiating from them. 'Who is trying to kill you?' he asked her.

'Shul-sen. She wants my life . . . my body. I can feel her within me, her memories swamping me.'

'Calm yourself,' he said soothingly, taking her to the bed and sitting her down. Moving to the window Talisman called out to Gorkai, who came running up the stairs. Talisman told him of Zhusai's fears.

'I have heard of this,' said Gorkai grimly. 'Spirit possession.'

'What can we do?' asked Talisman.

'Find out what she wants,' Gorkai advised.

'Supposing she just wants me?' asked Zhusai. 'My life?'

'Why have you not spoken to your own shaman?' asked Gorkai. 'His knowledge is greater than mine in these matters.'

'I won't have him near me,' said Zhusai, her voice breaking. 'Not ever. I don't trust him. He . . . would want her to kill me. She is Shul-sen, the Mother of the Nadir people. A witch. She has power and he would seek to use it. I have nothing.'

'I have not the skill to deal with this, Talisman,' said Gorkai. 'I can cast no spells.'

Talisman took hold of Zhusai's hand. 'Then it must be Nosta Khan. Fetch him.'

'No!' shouted Zhusai, struggling to rise. Talisman held her tightly, pulling her in to his chest.

'Trust me!' he urged her. 'I would let no harm come to you. I will watch Nosta Khan carefully. If there is danger, I will kill him. Trust me!'

Her body jerked in a wild spasm, and her eyes closed momentarily. When they opened all fear was gone. 'Oh, I trust you, Talisman,' she said softly. He felt her shoulder draw back, and some sixth sense made him pull away from her – just in time to see the knife-blade. Throwing up his right arm he blocked the blow, and slammed his left fist into her jaw. Her head snapped back and she slumped to the bed. Retrieving his knife from her limp hand, he flung the weapon across the room.

Nosta Khan entered. 'What happened here?' he asked.

'She took my knife and tried to kill me. But it was not Zhusai. She is possessed.'

'Your servant told me. The spirit of Shul-sen seeks release. You should have come to me before, Talisman. How many more secrets do you keep from me?'

Without waiting for an answer he moved to the bed. 'Tie her hands behind her back,' he ordered Gorkai. The warrior glanced at Talisman, who gave a curt nod. Using a slender belt of cord Gorkai lashed her wrists together, then he and Nosta Khan lifted her, propping her back against the bed pillows. From an old pouch that hung at his belt, Nosta Khan drew a necklace of human teeth which he tied around the unconscious woman's neck. 'From this moment,' he said, 'no-one is to speak.' Placing his hand upon her head, he began to chant.

It seemed to the two watching men that the temperature in the room was dropping, and a cold wind began to blow through the window.

The chant continued, the sound rising and falling. Talisman did not know the language used – if language it was – but the effect within the room was astonishing. Ice began to form on the

224

window-frame and walls, and Gorkai was shivering uncontrollably. Nosta Khan showed no sign of discomfort. He fell silent, then drew his hand back from Zhusai's brow. 'Open your eyes,' he commanded, 'and tell me your name.'

The dark eyes slid open. 'I am . . .' A smile formed. 'I am she who was blessed above all women.'

'You are the spirit of Shul-sen, wife to Oshikai Demon-bane?'

'I am she.'

'You are dead, woman. There is no place for you here.'

'I do not feel dead, shaman. I can feel my heart beating, and the rope around my wrists.'

'The form is one you have stolen. Your bones lie in a chamber of volcanic rock. Or do you not remember the night of your death?'

'Oh, I remember,' she said, her lips thinning, her eyes glittering. 'I remember Chakata and his spikes of gold. He was human then. I can still feel the pain as he slowly pushed them home, deep enough to blind but not to kill. I remember. Oh, yes, I remember it all. But now I am back. Release my hands, shaman.'

'I shall not,' said Nosta Khan. 'You are dead, Shul-sen – as your husband is dead. Your time is gone.'

She laughed then, the sound filling the room. Talisman felt the terrible cold bite into his bones. Beside him Gorkai could scarcely stand, and was now trembling and shaking. The laughter died away. 'I am a witch with great powers. Oshikai knew that and he used me well. I know from the memories of the girl that you are facing an army, shaman. I can help you. Release me!'

'How can you help?'

'Release me, and you will know.'

Talisman's hand crept to his knife scabbard, but it was empty. Reaching out, he pulled Gorkai's knife clear of its sheath. The woman turned her dark eyes on him. 'He means to kill you,' she told Nosta Khan.

'Do not speak – either of you!' warned the shaman. Turning to the woman, he began to chant. She winced, then her lips drew back in a bestial snarl. One word of power she spoke. Nosta Khan was hurled from the bed, striking the wall just below the window. He rolled to his knees, but her voice sounded once more and, flung back, his head cracked against the window-sill and he sank to the floor, unconscious.

The woman looked at Gorkai. 'Release me,' she said. On stumbling legs Gorkai tottered forward.

'Stand where you are!' ordered Talisman. Gorkai gave a cry of pain, but he forced himself to halt. Sinking to his knees, he groaned and fell face forward to the floorboards.

'So,' she said, looking at Talisman, 'you are a man of power. Your servant obeys, despite the pain he feels. Very well, you may release me.'

'Did you not love Oshikai?' he asked suddenly.

'What? You question my devotion, you ignorant peasant?'

'It was an honest question.'

'Then I shall answer it: Yes, I loved him. I loved his breath upon my skin, the sound of his laughter, the glory of his rages. Now release me!'

'He searches for you still,' Talisman told her.

'He died a thousand years ago,' she said. 'His spirit is in Paradise.'

'Not so, lady. I spoke with him, when first I came here. I summoned his spirit. The first question he asked was, "Do you bring news of Shul-sen?" I told him there were many legends, but that I did not know what had happened to you. He said: "I have searched the Vales of Spirit, the Valleys of the Damned, the Fields of Heroes, the Halls of the Mighty. I have crossed the Void for time without reckoning. I cannot find her." And as for Paradise, he said: "What Paradise could there be without Shul-sen? Death I could bear, but not this parting of souls. I will find her, though it take a dozen eternities."'

She was silent for a moment, and the feral gleam faded from her eyes. 'I know you speak the truth,' she said, 'for I can read the hearts of men. But Oshikai will never find me. Chakata drew my spirit to the Dark Place, where it is guarded by demons who once were men. Chakata is there, but no human would recognize him now; he taunts me and tortures me whenever he wills. Or at least he did, before I made my escape. I cannot go to Oshikai, Talisman. If I died here I would be drawn back to the Dark Place.'

'Is that where you have sent Zhusai?' he asked her.

'It is. But what is her life compared with mine? I was a queen. I will be again.'

'Then you will leave Oshikai searching for an eternity, risking his soul in the terrors of the Void?'

'I can do nothing there!' she shouted. By the window Nosta Khan was stirring, but he remained silent. Gorkai too lay very still, scarcely breathing.

'Where is this Dark Place?' asked Talisman. 'Why can Oshikai not find it?'

'It is not a part of the Void,' she said tonelessly. 'Do you understand the nature of the Underworld? The Void is set between two levels. In the simplest terms, it sits between Paradise and Giragast, Heaven and Hell. The Void is the place in between where souls wander, in search of final rest. Chakata chose to trap me in the dark centre of Giragast, the pit at the centre of the lakes of fire. No human soul would travel there voluntarily, and Oshikai would know of no reason why I would be there. He trusted Chakata. He would never have guessed the depth of the man's lust, nor the heights of his treachery. But if he were to know, then he would die the second death, the lasting death. There is no way a single warrior – not even one as mighty as my Lord – could pass the demon-haunted passageways. Nor conquer the creature Chakata has become.'

'I will go with him,' promised Talisman.

'You? What are you? Just a child in a man's body. How old are you, child? Seventeen? Twenty?'

'I am nineteen. And I will walk with Oshikai across the Void, to the Gates of Giragast.'

'No, it is not enough. I see that you are brave, Talisman. And you are quick and intelligent. But to pass those gates takes something more. You are asking me to risk my soul in everlasting darkness and torment, and the soul of the man I love. The mystic number is Three. Do you have a warrior here who could match Oshikai? Is there one who would walk the Void with you?'

'I will,' said Gorkai, pushing himself to his feet.

Her eyes fixed him, holding to Gorkai's gaze. 'Another brave one. But not skilled enough.'

Talisman strode to the window and leaned out over the sill. Below Druss, stripped of his jerkin, was washing himself at the well-side. The Nadir leader called out to him, beckoning him. Throwing his jerkin over his shoulder, Druss strolled to the building and climbed the stairs. As he entered, his pale blue eyes scanned the room. Gorkai was still upon his knees, and Nosta Khan was sitting below the window with a trickle of blood running from broken skin over his temple. He saw that Zhusai was tied, and said nothing.

'This man has walked the Void,' said Talisman, 'in search of his wife. He found her.'

'I can read his thoughts, Talisman. He has no loyalty to the

Nadir. He is here seeking . . .' She stared hard at Druss. ' . . . healing stones for a dying friend. Why would he risk the terrors of the Giragast? He does not know me.'

Talisman swung to Druss. 'This is not Zhusai,' he said. 'Her body is possessed by the spirit of Shul-sen. To free her, I must send my spirit into the Void. Will you travel with me?'

'As she said, I came here to find the jewels the shaman spoke of,' said Druss, 'and he lied to me. Why should I do this?'

Talisman sighed. 'There is no reason that I can offer you, save that the woman I love is now trapped in that dark and vile place. And Oshikai, our greatest hero, has been searching for a thousand years to find the spirit of his wife. He does not know where to look. I can tell him, but Shul-sen says the journey would see his soul extinguished. Two men cannot fight the demons there.'

'And three can?' asked Druss.

'I cannot answer that,' Talisman told him. 'She will not release the spirit of Zhusai unless I can find a man to match Oshikai. You are the only one here who has built a legend. What more can I say?'

Druss eased past him and moved to the bound woman. 'How did you die?' he asked.

'Chakata put golden spikes in . . .' She hesitated and her eyes flared wide. 'You! You and your friend released me. I see it now, back in the chamber. He came back and removed the spikes. He found my *lon-tsia*.'

Druss stood and looked Talisman in the eyes. 'If I go with you, laddie, I want your word on something.'

'Name it!'

'You will let me use the jewels to save my friend.'

'Is that not why you are here?' hedged Talisman.

'Not good enough,' said Druss, making for the door.

'Very well. You have my word. When we find the jewels, I will hand them to you and you may take them to Gulgothir.'

'No!' shouted Nosta Khan. 'What are you saying?'

Talisman held up his hand. 'But I want your pledge to return them as soon as your friend is healed.'

'It will be done,' said Druss.

'Come to me, blackbeard,' said Shul-sen, and Druss returned to the bed and sat. She looked deep into his eyes. 'Everything I am, or could ever be, is in your hands now. Are you a man I can trust?'

'I am,' he said.

'I believe you.' Turning her gaze to Talisman she spoke again. 'I shall return to the Dark Place, and free the soul of Zhusai. Do not fail me.'

Her eyes closed, then flickered. A long, broken sigh came from her throat. Talisman ran to the bedside, untying the cord that bound her wrists. Her eyes opened, and a scream formed. Talisman hugged her to him. 'It is all right, Zhusai. You are back with us!'

Nosta Khan moved to the bedside, and placed his hand upon her head. After a moment he said: 'She has returned. This is Zhusai. I shall now cast spells to prevent any re-entry. You did well, Talisman, to deceive her.'

'I did not deceive her,' replied the Nadir coldly. 'I shall fulfil my part of the bargain.'

'Pah! That is insane. An army is marching upon us and the destiny of the Nadir rests in your hands. This is no time to play the man of honour.'

Talisman walked to the far wall and picked up his dagger. Slowly he moved towards Nosta Khan. 'Who is the leader here?' he asked softly, his voice cold.

'You are, but . . .'

'Yes, I am, you miserable worm. I am the leader. You are *my* shaman. I will tolerate no further disobedience. I do not *play* at honour. It is what I am. My word is iron. Now and ever more. We will go now to the Shrine. You will summon Oshikai, then do what you must to send Druss and myself into the Void. Is that clear, shaman?'

'It is clear, Talisman.'

'Not Talisman to you!' thundered the warrior. 'Now is it clear?'

'It is clear . . . my Lord.'

'Why do you hold to my hand, po-et?' asked Niobe, as she and Sieben walked the ramparts of the western wall. Sieben, his passion spent during the last two hours with her, gave a weary smile.

'It is a custom among my people,' he said, lifting her fingers to his lips and kissing them. 'Lovers often walk hand-in-hand. It is, perhaps, a spiritual joining; or at least a touching that proclaims a couple are lovers. It is also considered pleasurable. Do you not like it?'

'I like feeling you inside me,' she said, withdrawing her hand and sitting back on the battlements. 'I like the taste of your tongue upon mine. I like the many delights your hands can conjure. But I like to feel free when I walk. Hand-holding is for mother and small child. I am not your child.'

Sieben chuckled, and sat back admiring the way the moonlight made her long hair shine. 'You are a delight to me,' he said. 'A breath of fresh air after a lifetime in musty rooms.'

'Your clothes are very pretty,' she noted, reaching out and stroking the blue silk of his shirt. 'The buttons contain many colours.'

'Mother-of-pearl,' he said. 'Exquisite, aren't they?' On an impulse he pulled the shirt over his head and stood bare-chested on the wall. 'Here. It is yours.'

Niobe giggled, then removed her own shirt of faded green wool. Sieben stared at her full breasts, and saw that the nipples were erect. Arousal flared afresh within him. Stepping forward he reached out to caress her. Niobe jumped back, holding the blue silk shirt to her body. 'No,' she said. 'First we talk.'

'Talk? What do you want to talk about?'

'Why no wife for you? Your friend has wife. And you are old.'

'Old? Thirty-four is not old. I am in the prime of my life.'

'You have balding patch at the crown. I have seen it.'

Sieben's hand swept up to his blond hair, pushing his fingers through to the scalp. 'Balding patch? It can't be.'

Her laughter pealed out. 'You are peacock,' she said. 'Worse than woman.'

'My grandfather had a full head of hair to his death at ninety. Baldness does not run in our family.'

Niobe slipped into the blue shirt and then moved alongside Sieben, taking his arm and pulling his hand from his hair.

'So why no wife?'

'It was a joke about the hair, yes?'

'No. Why no wife?'

'That's a difficult question.' He shrugged. 'I have known many beautiful women, but none I would wish to spend my life with. I mean, I like apples, but I wouldn't want to live on a permanent diet of them.'

'What is apples?'

'Fruit. Er . . . like figs.'

'Good for bowels,' she said.

'Exactly. But let's move on from that, shall we? What I'm trying to say is that I like the company of many women. I am easily bored.'

'You are not strong man,' she said, sadness in her voice. 'You are frightened man. Many women is easy. Make children is easy. Life with them, help to raise them, that is hard. Watch babies die . . . that is hard. I have had two husbands. Both die. Both good men. Strong. My third will be also strong. Many babies, so some will survive.'

Sieben gave a wry smile. 'I tend towards the belief that life holds more than making strong babies. I live for pleasure, for sudden bursts of joy. For surprises. There are enough people making babies and eking out their boring lives in the harshness of deserts, or the green splendour of mountains. The world will not miss my children.'

She considered his words thoughtfully. 'My people came over the tall mountains with Oshikai. They made babies, who grew proud and strong. They gave their blood to the land, and the land nurtured their young. For a thousand years. Now there is me. I owe it to my ancestors to bring life to the land, so that in a thousand years to come there will be those with the blood of Niobe and her ancestors. You are good lover, po-et. You bring many joy-trembles in your love-making. But joy-trembles are easy; I can do that for myself. I feel great love for you. But I will not wed frightened man. I have seen strong warrior of the Curved Horn. He has no wife. I think I will go to him.'

Sieben felt her words hit him like a blow to the belly. But he forced a smile. 'Of course, lovely one. You go and make babies.'

'You want shirt back?'

'No. It suits you. You look . . . very fine.'

Without a word she left him there. Sieben shivered as a cold breeze touched his bare skin. What am I doing here? he wondered. A Nadir warrior with short hair and a pronounced widow's peak climbed to the ramparts and, ignoring Sieben, stood staring out to the west.

'A pleasant night,' remarked Sieben.

The man turned and stared at him. 'It will be a long night,' he said, his voice deep and cold.

Sieben saw a candle-flame flickering through the window of the Shrine. 'Still searching,' he said.

'Not searching,' said the man. 'My Lord, Talisman, and your friend are journeying to Giragast.'

'I fear something has been lost in the translation,' said Sieben. 'Giragast isn't a place, it is a myth.'

'It is a place,' said the man stubbornly. 'Their bodies are lying on the cold floor, their souls have gone to Giragast.'

Sieben's mouth was suddenly dry. 'Are you saying they are dead?'

'No, but they are going to the place of the dead. I do not think they will come back.'

Sieben left the man and ran to the Shrine. As the Nadir had said, Druss and Talisman were lying side by side on the dusty floor. The shaman, Nosta Khan, was sitting beside them. On top of the stone coffin was a lighted candle, marked with seven lines of black ink.

'What is happening?' he asked the shaman.

'They go with Oshikai to rescue the witch, Shul-sen,' whispered Nosta Khan.

'Into the Void?'

'Beyond the Void.' Nosta Khan glanced up at him, his eyes dark and malevolent. 'I saw you scatter the parchment to the winds. Did you also throw the knuckle-bones into the well?'

'Yes. And I burnt the hair and buried the pouch.'

'You *gajin* are soft and weak. Shaoshad deserved his punishment.'

'He wanted to bring Oshikai and Shul-sen back to life, to unite the Nadir,' said Sieben. 'That does not seem so terrible a crime.'

Nosta Khan shook his head. 'He wanted power, and fame. Oh, he could have raised the body, and perhaps even infused it with the soul of Oshikai. But the body would have needed the magic of jewels constantly; he would have been a slave to Shaoshad. Now, thanks to his arrogance, we have no jewels and the power of the land is lost to us. And *gajin* like you treat us as vermin. His lust for power sentenced us to five hundred years of servitude. He should have been left to rot for eternity.'

Sieben sat down alongside the shaman. 'Not a forgiving people, are you?'

Nosta Khan gave a rare smile. 'Our babies die in childbirth. Our men are hunted down like animals. Our villages are burnt, our people slaughtered. Why for should we forgive?'

'So what is the answer, old man? For the Nadir to mass into a huge army and hunt down the *gajin* like animals, burning their villages and towns, and slaughtering their women and children?'

'Yes! That is how it will begin. Until we have conquered the world, and enslaved every race.'

'Then you will be no different from the *gajin* you despise. Is that not so?'

'We do not seek to be different,' replied Nosta Khan. 'We seek to be triumphant.'

'A charmingly honest point of view,' said the poet. 'Tell me, why are they travelling through the Void?'

'Honour,' said Nosta Khan admiringly. 'Talisman is a great man. Were he destined to live he would make a fine general for the Uniter.'

'He is going to die?'

'Yes,' said Nosta Khan sadly. 'I have walked the many futures but he is in none of them. Now be silent, for I have much work to do.'

From his pouch Nosta Khan removed two small, dry leaves, which he placed under his tongue. Raising his hands, bony fingers spread wide, he closed his eyes. The bodies of Druss and Talisman began to glow, radiating lights of many colours – purple around the heart, bright white pulsing from their heads, red from the lower torso, white and yellow from the legs. It was an extraordinary sight. Sieben remained silent until Nosta Khan sighed and opened his eyes.

'What did you do to them?' whispered the poet.

'Nothing,' answered Nosta Khan. 'I have merely made their life force visible. He is a powerful man, this Druss. See how the energy of his *zhi* dwarfs that of Talisman? And Talisman is greater than most men.' Sieben gazed at the glowing figures. It was true. The radiance around Druss extended to almost three feet, while Talisman's flickered no more than a foot from his torso.

'What is this . . . *zhi*?' asked Sieben.

Nosta Khan was silent for a moment. 'No man fully understands the mystery,' he said. 'The energy flows around the human body, bringing life and health. It flickers and changes when disease strikes. I have seen old men with the rheumatic in their arms where the *zhi* no longer flows. And I have seen mystic healers transfuse their own *zhi* into the sick, making them healthy again. It is connected in some way to the soul. After death, for example, the *zhi* flares to five times its size. This happens for three days. Then, in a heartbeat, it is gone.'

'But why have you chosen to make it visible?'

'Their souls have gone to a place of untold dangers, where they will be fighting demons. Each cut they take, each wound they suffer, will affect the *zhi*. I will watch, and when they come close to death I hope to be able to draw them back.'

'You mean you are not certain of your ability to do this?'

'In Giragast there is no certainty,' snapped Nosta Khan. 'Imagine a fight here. A soldier is wounded in the arm; he suffers, but lives. Another man is struck to the heart; he dies instantly. Such can happen in the Void. I can see the wounds they suffer there. But a death blow will extinguish the *zhi* in an instant.'

'But you said the *zhi* flares for three days after death,' Sieben pointed out.

The glow around Druss seemed just as strong, though Talisman's *zhi* was weaker now. Sieben settled himself down against the wall. It was so like Druss to volunteer a trip to Hell. What is it about you, my friend? he thought. Why do you revel in such unnecessary risks? Is it that you think you are immortal? Or do you believe the Source has blessed you above other men? Sieben smiled. Maybe he has, he thought. Maybe there *is* something indestructible in your soul. Talisman's body spasmed, bright green flaring within his *zhi*. Druss too shuddered, his fists clenching.

'They are in a battle,' whispered Nosta Khan, moving to his knees with hands outstretched. Talisman's *zhi* flickered and faded, the glow dying away. Nosta Khan shouted three words, the sound harsh and discordant. Talisman's back arched, and he groaned. His eyes opened wide, and a strangled cry came from his lips. His arm swept out, as if still holding a sword.

'Be calm!' cried Nosta Khan. 'You are safe.' Talisman rolled to his knees, his face drenched in sweat. He was breathing heavily.

'Send . . . send me back,' he said.

'No. Your *zhi* is too weak. You will die.'

'Send me back, damn you!' Talisman tried to rise, but slumped to his face in the dust.

Sieben ran to him, helping him to sit up. 'Your shaman is right, Talisman. You were dying. What happened there?'

'Beasts, the like of which I have never seen! Huge. Scaled. Eyes of fire. We saw nothing for the first days of travel. Then we were attacked by wolves. Great creatures, almost the size of ponies. We killed four. The rest fled. I thought they were bad enough. But, by the Gods of Stone and Water, they were puppies compared with what followed.' He shivered suddenly. 'How many days have I been gone?'

'Less than two hours,' Sieben told him.

'That is not possible.'

'Time has no meaning in the Void,' said Nosta Khan. 'How far did you get?'

'We made it to the Gates of Giragast. There was a man there. Oshikai knew him – a small shaman, with a twin-forked beard.' Talisman turned to Sieben. 'He said to thank you for the gift. He will remember it.'

'Shaoshad the Cursed,' hissed Nosta Khan.

'Cursed he may be, but we would never have mastered the demons at the Gates without him. Druss and Oshikai are . . . colossal. Never have I seen such power, such controlled rage. When the scaled beasts came I thought we were finished. Oshikai attacked them, with Druss beside him. I was already wounded and scarce able to move.' His hand moved to his side, seeking a wound. He smiled. 'I feel so weak.'

'You need to rest,' said Nosta Khan. 'Your *zhi* is diminished. I will cast healing spells over you as you sleep.'

'They cannot succeed. More demons everywhere.'

'How were they when you left?' asked Sieben.

'Druss has a wound in his thigh and his left shoulder. Oshikai is bleeding from chest and hip. I last saw them enter a black tunnel. The little man, Shaoshad, was leading them. He was holding a stick, which burst into flame like a torch. I tried to follow them . . . but then I was here. I should never have agreed to Shulsen's request. I have killed Druss, and destroyed the soul of Oshikai.'

'Druss is still strong,' said Sieben, pointing to the glowing aura around the axeman. 'I've known him a long time, and I'd wager on him returning. Trust me.'

Talisman shivered again. Nosta Khan covered his shoulders with a blanket. 'Rest now, Talisman,' he told the younger man. 'Let sleep wash away the weakness within.'

'I must wait,' he said, his voice slurred with weariness.

'Whatever you wish, my Lord,' whispered Nosta Khan. As Talisman lay down, Nosta Khan began to chant in a low voice. Talisman's eyes closed. For long minutes the chant continued, then at last the shaman lapsed into silence. 'He will sleep for many hours,' said the old man. 'Aya! But my heart is filled with pride for him. He is a warrior among warriors. Aye, and a man of honour!'

Sieben glanced at Druss's body. The glow was fading. 'You had better fetch him back,' he said.

'Not yet. All is well.'

Druss eased his huge frame against the black rock-face, then slumped to his knees. His strength was all but gone, and blood the colour of milk was flowing from numerous wounds in his upper body. Oshikai laid his golden axe on a rock and sat down. He too was sorely wounded. The tiny shaman, Shaoshad, moved to Druss, laying his skinny hand on a deep cut on Druss's shoulder. The wound closed instantly.

'Almost there,' said the little man. 'One more bridge to cross.'

'I don't believe I could move another step,' said Druss. Shaoshad touched all his wounds and one by one the milky ichor ceased to flow.

'One more bridge, Drenai,' repeated Shaoshad, moving to Oshikai and treating his wounds also.

'Did Talisman die?' Oshikai asked the shaman, his voice weak.

'I do not know. But he is here no longer. Either way he cannot help us. Can you go on?'

'I will find Shul-sen,' said Oshikai stubbornly. 'Nothing shall stop me.'

Druss gazed around the awesome black cavern. Towering stalagmites rose towards the high, domed ceiling, met there by colossal stalactites – like two rows of fangs in a vast maw. One of the surviving bat creatures was still in view, crouching high on a ledge above them. Druss stared up into its baleful red eyes. The bodies of its comrades lay scattered on the cavern floor, their grey wings outstretched and broken. The survivor made no move to attack. The journey here had been long and terrifying, across a landscape unlike any to be found in the world of flesh. Druss had walked the Void once before, to bring Rowena back from the dead. But then he had walked the Road of Souls, a veritable garden of delights when compared with this journey. The land obeyed no laws of nature that Druss understood. It shifted and changed endlessly under a slate-grey sky; cliffs suddenly rearing from a desolate plain, showering boulders the size of houses down from the sky. Chasms would appear, as if an invisible plough was tearing at the dead soil. Black and twisted trees would sprout into forests, their branches reaching out to claw like talons at the flesh of the travellers. Some time ago – it could have been days or hours – they had descended into a gorge, the floor of which was festooned with what appeared to be discarded helms of rusted iron. Lightning lit the sky endlessly, casting hideous shadows around them. Talisman was in the lead when the helms began to shake. The earth parted, and long-buried warriors erupted from the black earth. The skin of their faces had rotted away, and maggots clung to the flesh beneath. Soundlessly they advanced. Talisman had beheaded the first, but taken a deep wound from a second. Druss and Oshikai charged, their axes slicing into corrupt flesh.

The battle was long, and hard. Shaoshad blasted globes of explosive fire into the awful ranks, and the air stank with the smoke of burning flesh. At the last Druss and Oshikai stood back to back gazing round at the mound of corpses. Of Talisman there was no sign.

On the far side of the gorge they had entered a tunnel, which led into the heart of the highest mountain Druss had ever seen. In a cavern at its centre they had fought off a frenzied attack from the demonic bats. 'Tell me,' said Druss to Shaoshad, 'that there are no more guardians. That would please me greatly.'

'Plenty more, axeman. But you know what they say,' he added with a mischievous grin, 'nothing worth while ever comes easy, yes?'

'What can we expect?' asked Oshikai.

'The Great Bear guards the bridge. After that I know not. But there is one who will remain. That is Chakata. He it was who murdered Shul-sen in a manner most foul. He is here . . . in one form or another.'

'Then he is mine,' said Oshikai. 'You hear me, Druss? He is mine!'

Druss looked across at the stocky figure in his shattered golden armour. 'No argument from me, laddie.'

Oshikai chuckled and moved across to sit beside Druss. 'By the Gods of Stone and Water, Druss, you are a man I would be proud to call brother. I wish I had known you in life. We could have downed a dozen flagons of wine, and filled the night with boasting.'

'The wine sounds good,' said Druss, 'but I never was much of a boaster.'

'It is an acquired skill,' agreed Oshikai. 'I always found that a story sounds better if a multiple of ten is added to the enemy. Unless of course it was known that there were, say, only three. Then they become giants.'

'I have a friend who understands that very well,' said Druss.

'Is he a fine warrior?'

Druss looked into Oshikai's violet eyes. 'No, a poet.'

'Ah! I always took a poet with me, to record my victories. I am no mean braggart myself, but when I listened to his songs of my deeds I felt put to shame. Where I would speak of slaying giants, he would sing of subduing the gods themselves. Are you feeling rested?'

'Almost,' lied Druss. 'Tell me, little man,' he said to Shaoshad, 'what is this Great Bear you spoke of?'

'The Guardian of the Bridge of Giragast. It is said to be eight feet tall; it has two heads, one of a bear with sharp fangs, the other of a snake. The snake spits venom, which will burn through all armour. Its talons are as long as a short sword, and sharper than spite. It has two hearts, one high in the chest, the other low in the belly.'

'And how do you propose we pass this beast?'

'My magic is all but spent now, but I shall cast one more Hide-spell, to mask Oshikai. Then I shall rest here, and await your return.'

Oshikai rose and laid his hand on the little man's shoulder. 'You have served me well, Shaoshad. I am a king no longer; but if there is justice in this vile realm, you will be rewarded. I am sorry that my refusal of your offer led to your death.'

'All men die, Great King. And my own actions led to my death. I bear no ill-will towards any. But if . . . when . . . you reach Paradise, speak a word on my behalf to the Gatekeeper there.'

'I shall.' Taking up his golden axe, Kolmisai, the warrior turned to Druss. 'Are you ready now, my brother?'

'I was born ready,' grunted Druss, forcing himself to his feet.

'You will see the bridge about a hundred paces that way,' said Shaoshad. 'It spans the Abyss of Fire. If you fall it will be for an eternity, then the flames will devour you. The bridge is wide at the start, maybe fifty feet, but then it narrows. You must draw the bear to you on to the wide section, to allow Oshikai to slip past.'

'No,' said Oshikai, 'we will face it together.'

'Trust me, Great King, and follow my bidding. When the bear dies Chakata will know you are coming. Then he will slay Shulsen. It is vital that you cross the bridge to the Dark Place before that.'

'In the meantime I dance with the bear and try not to kill it?' queried Druss.

'Delay for as long as you can,' advised Shaoshad, 'and do not look into its eyes. You will see only death there.' The shaman closed his eyes and raised his hands. The air around Oshikai crackled with bright, flickering lights. The Great King's image faded, becoming translucent and then transparent. Then it was gone.

Shaoshad opened his eyes, then clapped his hands with glee. 'Arrogant I may be,' he chortled, 'but skilled am I!' His smile faded and he turned to Druss. 'When you approach the bridge

Oshikai must be close behind you. Otherwise the bear will sense both spirits. Once the beast is engaged, Great King, you must slip by him and run. Make no sound. Do not call out for Shul-sen – you will sense her when she is close.'

'I understand,' came the voice of Oshikai. 'You move on, Druss, and I will follow.'

Taking up his axe, Druss led the way. His legs were heavy, his arms weary. Never in his life, not even in his years in the prison dungeon, had he felt such a sense of physical weakness. Fear rose strong within him. His foot struck a stone, and he stumbled.

The sound of wings beating came to him. Swivelling, he saw the last of the bat creatures swooping down towards him, its black wings wide, its grey-taloned hands outstretched. Snaga flashed up, smashing through the thin neck – but not before the talons had scored across his face, ripping open his cheek. The creature's body struck him, toppling him from his feet. He felt the hand of Oshikai grasp him by the wrist, hauling him upright.

'You are exhausted, my friend,' said Oshikai. 'Rest here. I will try to slip by the bear.'

'No, I will see it through,' grunted Druss. 'Do not concern yourself for me.'

He staggered on, rounding a bend in the black cavern. Ahead of them an awesome bridge arced across a chasm. Druss stepped on to it, and glanced over the edge. It seemed to him that he was staring down into infinity. It made him dizzy, and he swiftly stepped back on to the black stone. Holding Snaga in both hands, he walked on. From here he could not see the far side of the bridge. 'It must be miles across,' he whispered, a sense of despair filling him.

'One step at a time, my friend,' said Oshikai.

Druss stumbled on through a haze of bone-numbing exhaustion. A cold wind blew across the chasm, and Druss could smell acrid smoke upon it. On he struggled, forcing his body through each weary step.

After what seemed like hours they reached the mid-point of the bridge. The far side could now be seen, a towering hill of black rock set against a slate-grey sky. A figure moved upon the bridge and Druss narrowed his eyes, straining to see it. It moved slowly on its hind legs, mighty arms stretched wide. As it neared, Druss saw that Shaoshad's description was correct in every detail: two heads, one a bear, the other a serpent. What Shaoshad had not conveyed was the sense of evil that radiated from the demon. It struck Druss like the numbing claws of a winter blizzard, colossal in its power, dwarfing the strength of Man.

The bridge had narrowed here to less than ten feet wide. The creature coming slowly towards them seemed to fill the gap.

'May the Gods of Stone and Water smile upon you, Druss!' whispered Oshikai.

Druss stepped forward. The beast gave a terrible roar, thunder deep and deafening. The wall of sound struck the axeman like a blow, pushing him back.

The beast spoke: 'We are the Great Bear, devourers of souls. Your death will be agonizing, mortal!'

'In your dreams, you whoreson!' said Druss.

'Bring him back!' shouted Sieben. 'You can see he is dying!'

'In a good cause,' said Nosta Khan. Sieben looked at the little man, and saw the malevolence in his eyes.

'You treacherous cur!' he hissed, scrambling to his feet and launching himself at the man. Nosta Khan threw up his right hand and needles of fire sliced into Sieben's head. He screamed and fell back, yet even through the pain he scrabbled for the knife at his hip. Nosta Khan spoke a single word and Sieben's arm froze.

'Don't do this to him,' begged Sieben. 'He deserves better.'

'Deserve has nothing to do with it, you fool. He chose to walk in Hell; I did not force him. But he has not yet accomplished what he set out to do. If he dies, so be it. Now be silent!' Sieben tried to speak, but his tongue clove to the roof of his mouth. The pain subsided, but he was unable to move.

The beast spoke, the voice issuing from both heads: 'Come to me and know death, Druss!'

Druss hefted his axe and moved forward. With astonishing speed the Great Bear dropped to all fours and charged. Snaga flashed up, then down with sickening force, plunging between the two heads, smashing through bone and sinew. The beast's body struck the axeman hard, hurling him from his feet. Losing his grip on his axe, Druss skidded across the bridge on his back, his legs slipping over the chasm. Rolling to his belly he scrabbled at the black stone, halting his slide, then hauled himself back on to the bridge. The Great Bear had reared up now, black blood gouting from between its heads. Druss surged upright, charging the beast. A taloned arm swept down, ripping through his jerkin and

240

scoring his flesh with the pain of fire. Reaching up, he grabbed Snaga's haft and wrenched the weapon clear. Blood spurted over his face, burning like acid. The snake mouth opened, spewing a stream of venom that covered his jerkin, bursting into flame. Ignoring the pain, Druss hammered Snaga into the snake neck, severing it. The head fell clear, bouncing on the black stone as smoke spewed from the mutilated neck. The Great Bear lashed out once more, Druss was thrown clear and he landed heavily, but rolled to his feet with axe in hand. The beast tottered forward. The venom on Druss's jerkin burnt through to the flesh beneath and, with a cry of rage and pain, he threw himself at the mortally wounded guardian. The talons swept down, but the speed of Druss's charge carried him under the blow and his shoulder hit the beast in the chest. The Great Bear staggered back, then fell from the bridge. Druss crawled to the edge, watching the body spiral down and down.

Sinking to the black stone, Druss rolled to his back. Exhaustion overtook him, and he longed for the bliss of sleep. 'Do not close your eyes,' came the voice of Shaoshad. Druss blinked and saw the little man kneeling beside him. Shaoshad touched his slender hands to Druss's wounds and the pain subsided. 'Sleep here is death,' said the shaman.

Oshikai ran on, crossing the bridge at speed and reaching the other side just as the Great Bear fell into the chasm. Ahead of him the black hill beckoned. Swiftly he scaled the flanks of the hill, his thoughts reaching out to Shul-sen. At first there was nothing, but then, ahead, he saw a rectangular black stone doorway set into the hillside. And he felt the presence of Shul-sen's spirit beyond it. Oshikai pushed hard, but the door did not give. Stepping back, he struck the stone with his golden axe. Sparks flew from the stone, and a gaping crack appeared. Twice more Oshikai thundered Kolmisai against the stone. On the third stroke, the door fell into four pieces.

Beyond it was a dark tunnel. As Oshikai stepped forward, a black lion with eyes of bright fire came hurtling out of the darkness. Kolmisai leapt to meet it, the axe-blade ripping into the creature's chest, and with a terrible cry it fell to Oshikai's left. The King swung and slashed the axe through its thick neck, beheading it. Lifting the head by the mane, Oshikai strode forward. The eyes of bright fire were fading now, but still they cast a dim light on the walls of the tunnel.

Oshikai moved on. A whisper of movement came from his left. Spinning towards the sound, the King threw the demon-head. Huge, serpentine jaws snapped down upon it, the bones of the skull splitting, brains oozing out through the rows of crocodile teeth in the long snout. The lizard beast opened its jaws and shook its head, spitting out the broken skull. In that moment Oshikai leapt forward to smash Kolmisai into the thick, scaled head, the golden blade shearing through the bone. The beast slumped to the ground, gave one low groan, and died.

In darkness now, Oshikai moved forward with one hand on the wall. 'Shul-sen!' he called. 'Can you hear me?'

'I am here,' came her voice. 'Oh, my Lord, is it you?' The sound came from ahead and to the left. Oshikai crossed the tunnel floor and found a sleek doorway. Blindly he struck at it; the door splintered and gave way. All was pitch darkness as he stepped into the room beyond.

A slender hand touched his face. 'Is it truly you?' she whispered.

'Truly,' he answered, his voice thick with emotion. His left arm drew her to him, and dropping his head he held her close, his limbs shaking. 'My love, the soul of my heart,' he whispered. Their lips touched, and he felt Shul-sen's tears mingle with his own. For a moment only he forgot everything, the perils and the dangers still to come.

Then, from the tunnel, came sounds of stealthy movement. Taking her hand, Oshikai backed out through the doorway. The sounds were coming from his right. Oshikai turned left and, still holding to Shul-sen, moved on deeper into the tunnel. After a while the floor began to rise. Higher and higher they climbed. A faint light could be seen above them now, seeping through a crack in the rocks of the hillside.

Oshikai paused in his flight and waited.

A lion beast with eyes of flame padded into sight, and with a great roar it charged. Oshikai leapt to meet it, Kolmisai sweeping down and cleaving through its skull. The beast sagged to the ground.

Oshikai climbed to the crack in the rocks, and struck it with his axe. The crack opened to two feet wide, stones falling from it and showering the King. A boulder was lodged in the crack and, stretching up, he pushed at it. The boulder rolled clear. Climbing through the gap, he turned and reached down for Shul-sen. The mossy ground beneath him shivered. Oshikai was thrown to his left and almost lost hold of his axe. What he had taken to be moss below his feet quivered and lifted from the earth, and he was thrown into the air. The whole of the hillside seemed to shudder, as two immense wings unfolded. The brow of the hill rose up, becoming the head of a giant bat. Oshikai clung to the wing as the colossal creature rose into the air. Higher and higher it flew, out over the bridge and the bottomless pit. Oshikai sunk his fingers deep into the fur, and hung on. The head of the bat twisted round and its huge mouth opened. Within the darkness of its maw there shone a face that he recognized.

'How do you like my new form, Great King?' sneered Chakata. 'Is it not magnificent?'

Oshikai did not answer, but began to crawl towards the creature's neck. 'Shall I tell you how many times I have enjoyed Shul-sen? Shall I describe the pleasures I have forced her to undergo?' The King moved closer. The face of Chakata smiled. The bat banked suddenly and Oshikai began to fall – then lashed out with his axe, burying it deep into the black wing. Slowly he hauled himself closer to the neck, dragging the axe clear and hammering it again through the fur, inching his way towards his enemy.

'Don't be a fool, Oshikai!' shouted Chakata. 'If you kill me, you will fall with me. You will never see Shul-sen again!'

Slowly, inexorably the King moved on. The bat flipped over into a backward dive, then rolled and beat its wings trying to dislodge the tiny figure. But Oshikai clung on. Closer and closer he came to the head. The bat's jaws snapped at him, but he rolled wide of them. Dragging clear his axe, he dealt a mighty blow to the creature's neck. Black blood gouted from the wound. Twice more he struck. Suddenly the bat's wings folded, and the body began to plummet towards the bridge far below. Oshikai continued to hammer his blade into the half-severed neck, cleaving through bone and sinew. The head fell clear, the dead beast spiralling down towards the pit.

Determined not to die alongside such vermin, Oshikai threw himself from the corpse.

Far below the naked Shul-sen had clambered free of the tunnel, and she stood now watching the epic battle in the grey skies above. Now free of the spells Chakata had woven, she felt her power returning. Instantly she clothed herself in shirt and leggings of silver silk, and a cloud-white cloak. Pulling her cloak from her shoulders, she spoke the Five Words of the Eleventh

Spell. Then she hurled the cloak high into the air. It flew on, spinning wildly, a wheel of white cloth glistening against the smoke-grey sky.

Shul-sen stood with hand outstretched, directing the cloak with all the power she could muster. The dead creature that had once been Chakata plunged down into the abyss. Oshikai continued to fall, but the cloak soared up towards him, enveloping his body. For a moment only the fall was halted, but then he plunged on with the cloak around him. Shul-sen cried out, the cloak flared open and Oshikai's rapid descent slowed. The cloak floated down to the bridge and Oshikai jumped clear. Shul-sen ran down the hillside towards him, arms outstretched. Dropping his axe he went to meet her, drawing her in to a tight embrace. For a long moment he held her thus, then drew back, and she saw tears upon his cheeks.

'I have searched for so long,' he said. 'I had begun to believe I would never find you.'

'But you did, my Lord,' she whispered, kissing his lips and the tear-stained cheeks.

For a long time they stood, holding each other close. Then he took her hand and led her to where Druss lay on the bridge. Oshikai knelt beside him. 'By all that is sacred, I never met a man like you, Druss. I pray that we meet again.'

'Not here, though, eh?' grunted Druss. 'Perhaps you could choose somewhere more . . . hospitable?'

Two glowing figures appeared on the bridge, with light blazing around them. Druss squinted and shaded his eyes as the figures came closer. There was no threat from them, and Oshikai rose to meet them.

'It is time,' came a gentle voice.

'You can take us both,' said Oshikai.

'No. Only you.'

'Then I will not come.'

The first of the glowing figures swung towards the woman. 'You are not ready, Shul-sen. You carry too much that is dark within you. All that was good came from your union with this man; the only selfless acts you committed were for him. Twice now he has refused Paradise. This third refusal will be final . . . we will come for him no more.'

'Give me a moment with him,' she said. 'Alone.'

The glowing figures floated away some fifty paces. Shul-sen approached Oshikai. 'I will not leave you,' he said. 'Not again.'

Reaching up, she cupped her hand around his neck, drawing his head down into a long, lingering kiss. When at last they separated she stroked his handsome face, and gave a wistful smile. 'Would you deny me Paradise, my love?' she asked him.

'What do you mean?'

'If you refuse them now, you will never see the Land of Heavenly Dreams. And if you do not, then how can I? By refusing them you sentence us to walk the Void for ever.'

Drawing her hand to his lips, he kissed her fingers tenderly. 'But I have waited so long for you. I could not bear another parting.'

'And yet you must,' she said, forcing a smile. 'We are united, Oshikai. We will be again. But when next I see you it will be under blue skies, beside whispering streams. Go now – and wait for me.'

'I love you,' he said. 'You are the stars and moon to me.'

Pulling away from him, she turned to the glowing figures. 'Take him,' she said. 'Let him know joy.' As they drew closer, she looked hard into the shining face of the first of the men. 'Tell me, can I earn a place beside him?'

'What you have done here is a step towards it, Shul-sen. You know where we are. The journey will be long, and there will be many calls upon you. Travel with Shaoshad. He too has much to learn.'

The second of the men floated alongside Druss, laying a golden hand upon his body. All wounds closed, and Druss felt new strength coursing through him.

Then, in an instant, they were gone, and Oshikai with them. As Shul-sen fell to her knees, her long, dark hair falling over her face, Shaoshad moved to her side. 'We will find him, my Lady. Together. And great will be the joy when we do.'

Shul-sen gave a deep, shuddering sigh. 'Then let us be away,' she said, rising to her feet. Druss rose also.

'I wish I could help you,' he said.

Taking his hand, she kissed it. 'I knew you were the one,' she told him. 'You are like him in so many ways. Go back now to the world you know.'

Her hand touched his head, and darkness swallowed him.

Chapter Eleven

Druss awoke to see the dawn sunlight shining through the window of the tomb. Never had he been happier to witness the birth of a new day. Sieben moved alongside him, and Nosta Khan edged forward, blocking the sunlight. 'Speak!' said the shaman. 'Did you succeed?'

'Aye,' muttered Druss, sitting up. 'They were united.'

'Did you ask about the Eyes of Alchazzar?'

'No.'

'What?' stormed the shaman. 'Then what was the purpose of this insane journey?'

Ignoring him, Druss stood and walked to where Talisman lay sleeping. Laying a huge hand on the young man's shoulder, Druss called to him. Talisman's dark eyes opened. 'Did we win?' he asked.

'We won, laddie, after a fashion.' Quietly Druss told him about the appearance of the angels, and the second separation.

Talisman pushed himself to his feet. 'I hope she finds him,' he said, and walked from the building, followed by Nosta Khan.

'Their gratitude brings a tear to my old eyes,' said Sieben sourly.

Druss shrugged. 'It is done. That is what counts.'

'So, tell me all.'

'I don't think so, poet. I want no songs about this.'

'No songs – you have my word of honour,' lied the poet.

Druss chuckled. 'Maybe later. For now I need some food, and a long, slow drink of cool water.'

'Was she beautiful?'

'Exceptionally. But she had a hard face,' said Druss, striding away. Sieben followed him out into the sunlight as Druss stood, gazing up at the rich blue of the sky. 'The Void is an ugly place, devoid of colour save for the red of flame, and the grey of stone and ash and sky. It is a chilling thought that we must all walk it one day.'

'Chilling. Absolutely,' agreed Sieben. 'Now the story, Druss. Tell me the story.'

Above them on the ramparts, with Gorkai and Nosta Khan beside him, Talisman gazed down at Druss and the poet. 'He should have died there,' said Nosta Khan. 'His life force was almost gone. But it surged back.'

Talisman nodded. 'I have never seen the like,' he admitted. 'Watching Druss and Oshikai together, battling demons and monsters . . . it was awesome. From the moment they met they were like sword brothers, and when they fought side by side it seemed they had known each other for an eternity. I could not compete, shaman. I was like a child among men. And yet I felt no bitterness. I felt . . . privileged.'

'Aye,' whispered Gorkai, 'to have fought beside Oshikai Demon-bane is privilege indeed.'

'Yet we are no closer to the Eyes,' snapped Nosta Khan. 'A great warrior he may be, but he is a fool. Shaoshad would have told him had he but asked!'

'We will find them, or we won't! I'll lose no more sleep over it,' said Talisman. Leaving the shaman, he moved down the rampart steps and crossed the open ground to the lodging house.

Zhusai was asleep in the bed and Talisman sat beside her, stroking her hair. Her dark eyes opened, and she gave a sleepy smile. 'I waited until Gorkai told me you were safe; then I slept.'

'We are all safe,' he told her, 'and Shul-sen will haunt you no more.' He fell silent. Sitting up, she took his hand, and saw the sorrow in his eyes.

'What is it, Talisman? Why so sad?'

'Their love lasted an eternity,' he said, his voice low. 'Yet for us there will be no joining. All my life I have longed to help the Uniter band our people together. I thought there was no greater cause. You fill my mind, Zhusai. I know now that when the Uniter takes you I will not be able to follow him. I could not.'

'Then let us defy the prediction,' she said, taking him in her arms. 'Let us be together.'

Gently but firmly he took hold of her arms, drawing away from her. 'I cannot do that either. My duty forbids it. I shall tell Nosta Khan to take you away from here. Tomorrow.'

'No! I will not go.'

'If you truly love me you will, Zhusai. I need to clear my mind for the battle ahead.' Rising, he left her and returned to the compound. For the next hour he toured the fortifications, checking the repairs to the ramparts. Lastly he sent Quing-chin and three riders to scout for the enemy.

'Do not engage them, my friend,' he told Quing-chin. 'I need you here when the battle begins.'

'I will be here,' the warrior promised. And he rode from the fort.

Gorkai approached Talisman. 'You should take the woman,' he said softly.

Talisman turned on him angrily. 'You were listening?'

'Yes. Every word,' agreed Gorkai amiably. 'You should take her.'

'And what of duty? What of the fate of the Nadir?'

Gorkai smiled. 'You are a great man, Talisman, but you are not thinking this through. We won't survive here, we are all going to die. So if you wed her, she will be a widow in a few days anyway. Nosta Khan says he can spirit her away. Good. Then the Uniter will wed your widow. So how will destiny be changed?'

'What if we win?'

'You mean what if the puppy-dog devours the lion?' Gorkai shrugged. 'My view on that is simple, Talisman. I follow you. If the Uniter wants my loyalty, then let him be here fighting with us! Last night you united Oshikai and Shul-sen. Look around you. There are men here of five tribes. You have united them – that's enough of a Uniter for me.'

'I am not the man prophesied.'

'I do not care. You are the man that's *here*. I am older than you, boy, and I have made many mistakes. You are making one now, regarding Zhusai. True love is rare. Take it where you find it. That is all I have to say.'

Druss sat quietly on the ramparts, gazing around at the defenders as they continued their work on the walls, carrying rocks to hurl down on advancing infantrymen. There were now just under two hundred fighting men, the bulk of them refugees from the Curved Horn. Nuang Xuan had sent his people to the east, but several women remained behind, Niobe among them. The old man waved at Druss, then climbed the broken steps to the ramparts. He was breathing heavily when he reached the top. 'A fine day, axeman,' he said, drawing in a deep breath.

'Aye,' agreed Druss.

'It is a good fort now, yes?'

'A good fort with old gates,' said Druss. 'That's the weak spot.'

'That is my position,' said Nuang, his face devoid of expression. 'Talisman has told me to stand among the defenders at that point. If the gate is breached we are to fill it with bodies.' He forced a smile. 'A long time since I have known such fear – but it is a good feeling.'

Druss nodded. 'If the gate is breached, old man, you will find me beside you.'

'Ha! Then there will be plenty killing.' Nuang's expression softened. 'You will be fighting your own people again. How does this sit with you?'

Druss shrugged. 'They are not my people, and I do not go hunting them. They are coming for me. Their deaths are on their own heads.'

'You are a hard man, Druss. Nadir blood, maybe.'

'Maybe.' Nuang saw his nephew, Meng, below and called out to him. Without a word of farewell the old man strolled back down the steps. Druss transferred his gaze to the west and the line of hills. The enemy would be here soon. He thought of Rowena, back at the farm, and the days of work among the herds, the quiet of the nights in their spacious cabin. Why is it, he wondered, that when I am away from her I long for her company, and when I am with her I yearn for the call to arms? His thoughts ranged back to his childhood, travelling with his father, trying to escape the infamy of Bardan the Slayer. Druss glanced down at Snaga, resting against the battlement wall. The dread axe had belonged to his grandfather, Bardan. It had been demon-possessed then, and had turned Bardan into a raging killer, a butcher. Druss, too, had been touched by it. Is that why I am what I am? he thought. Even though the demon had long since been exorcized, still its malice had worked on him through the long years when he searched for Rowena.

Not normally introspective, Druss found his mood darkening. He had not come to the lands of the Gothir for war, but to take part in the Games. Now, through no fault of his own, he was waiting for a powerful army, and desperate to find two healing jewels that would bring Klay back to health.

'You look angry, old horse,' said Sieben, moving alongside him. Druss looked at his friend. The poet was wearing a pale blue shirt, with buttons of polished bone. His baldric was freshly polished, the knife-handles gleaming in their sheaths. His blond hair was newly combed, and held in place by a headband at the centre of which an opal was set.

'How do you do it?' asked Druss. 'Here we are in a dust-blown wilderness, and you look as if you've just stepped from a bath-house?'

'Standards must always be maintained,' said Sieben, with a broad grin. 'These savages need to see how civilized men behave.'

Druss chuckled. 'You lift my spirits, poet. You always have.'

'Why so gloomy? War and death are but a few days away. I would have thought you would have been dancing for joy.'

'I was thinking of Klay. The jewels aren't here, and I can't keep my promise to him.'

'Oh, don't be too sure of that, old horse. I have a theory – but we'll say no more of it until the time is right.'

'You think you can find them?'

'As I said, I have a theory. But now is not the time. Nosta Khan wanted you to die, you know, and you almost did. We cannot trust him, Druss. Nor Talisman. The jewels are too important to them.'

'You are right there,' grunted Druss. 'The shaman is a loath-some wretch.'

'What's that?' exclaimed Sieben, pointing to the line of hills. 'Oh, sweet Heaven, they are here!'

Druss narrowed his eyes. A line of Lancers in bright armour were riding single file down the hillside. A cry went up on the walls and warriors ran from the compound to take their places, bows in hand.

'They are riding ponies,' muttered Druss. 'What in Hell's name . . . ?'

Talisman and Nosta Khan came alongside Druss. The riders beyond broke into a gallop and thundered across the plain with their lances held high. On each lance was a spitted head.

'It is Lin-tse!' shouted Talisman. The Nadir defenders began to cheer and shout as the thirty riders slowed to a canter and rode along the line of the wall, lifting their lances and showing their grisly trophies. One by one they thrust the lances into the ground, then rode through the newly opened gates. Lin-tse jumped from his pony and removed the Gothir helm. Warriors streamed from the walls to surround him and his Sky Riders.

Lin-tse began to chant in the Nadir tongue. He leapt and danced, to wild cheering from the warriors. On the battlements above Sieben watched in fascination, but could understand none of the words. He turned to Nosta Khan. 'What is he saying?'

'He is telling of the slaughter of the enemy, and how his men rode the sky to defeat them.'

'Rode the sky? What does it mean?'

'It means the first victory is ours,' snapped the shaman. 'Now be silent so I can listen.'

'Irritating man,' muttered Sieben, sitting back alongside Druss.

Lin-tse's story took almost a quarter of an hour to complete, and at the close the warriors swept in around him, lifting him shoulder-high. Talisman sat quietly until the roar of noise died down. When Lin-tse was lowered to the ground, he walked to Talisman and gave a short bow. 'Your orders were obeyed,' he said. 'Many Lancers are dead, and I have their armour.'

'You did well, my brother.'

Talisman strode to the rampart steps and climbed them, swinging back to stare down at the gathered men. 'They can be beaten,' he said, still speaking Nadir. 'They are not invincible. We have tasted their blood, and we will taste more. When they come to despoil the Shrine we will stop them. For we are Nadir, and our day is dawning. This is but the beginning. What we do here will become part of our legends. The story of your heroism will spread on the wings of fire to every Nadir tribe, every camp and village. It will bring the Day of the Uniter closer. And one day we will stand before the walls of Gulgothir, and the city itself will tremble before us.' Slowly he raised his right arm, with fist clenched. 'Nadir we!' he shouted. The warriors followed him, and the chant was taken up.

> 'Nadir we,
> youth born,
> blood letters,
> axe wielders,
> victors still.'

'Chills the blood, rather,' observed Sieben.

Druss nodded. 'He's a clever man. He knows there are disasters to come, and he's filling them with pride at the outset. They'll fight like devils for him now.'

'I didn't know you could understand Nadir?'

'I can't . . . but you don't need to be a linguist to understand what's happening here. He sent out Lin-tse to blood the enemy. To give them a victory. To bond them together. He's probably just told them they are all heroes, and that together they can withstand any force. Something like that.'

'And can they?'

'No way to judge, poet. Not until the first deaths. A fighting force is like a sword-blade. You can't test it until it has passed through fire.'

'Yes, yes, yes,' said Sieben irritably, 'but apart from the warlike analogies, what is your feeling? You know men. I trust your judgement.'

'I don't know *these* men. Oh, they are ferocious, right enough. But they are not disciplined – and they are superstitious. They have no history of success to fall back upon, to lift them in the dark hours. They have never defeated the Gothir. Everything depends on the first day of battle. Ask me again if we survive that!'

'Damn, but you are gloomy today, my friend,' said Sieben. 'What is it?'

'This is not my war, poet. I have no *feeling* for it, you know? I fought alongside Oshikai. I *know* that it doesn't matter a damn to him what happens to his bones. This is a battle over nothing, and nothing will be achieved by it, win or lose.'

'I think you may be wrong there, old horse. All this talk of a Uniter is important to these people. You say they have no history of success to fall back upon – well, perhaps this will be the first for them.' Sieben hoisted himself to the wall and sat looking at his friend. 'But you know all this. There's something more, isn't there, Druss? Something deeper.'

Druss gave a wry smile, then rubbed his huge hand over his black beard. 'Aye, there is. I don't like them, poet. It is that simple. I have no affinity with these tribesmen. I don't know how they think, or what they feel. One thing is for damned sure, they don't think like us.'

'You like Nuang, and Talisman. They are both Nadir,' Sieben pointed out.

'Yes, I know. I can't make sense of it.'

Sieben chuckled. 'It's not hard, Druss. You are Drenai, born and raised – the greatest race on earth. That's what they told us. Civilized men in a world of savages. You had no trouble fighting alongside the Ventrians, but then they are like us, round-eyed and tall. We share a common mythology. But the Nadir are descended from the Chiatze and with them we share nothing that is obvious. Dogs and cats, Druss. Or wolves and lions if you prefer. But I think you are wrong to believe they don't think like us, or feel like us. They just show things differently, that's all. A different culture base.'

'I am not a bigot,' said Druss defensively.

Sieben laughed. 'Of course you are, it is bred into you. But you are a good man, Druss, and it won't make a damn bit of difference to the way you behave. Drenai teachings may have lodged in your head, but you've a fine heart. And that will always carry you through.'

Druss relaxed, and felt the tension flow from him. 'I hope you are right,' he said. 'My grandfather was a butchering killer; his atrocities haunt me still. I never want to be guilty of that kind of evil. I never want to be fighting on the wrong side. The Ventrian War was just, I believe that, and it meant something. The people now have Gorben as a leader, and he is as great a man as I ever met.'

'Perhaps,' said Sieben doubtfully. 'History will judge him better than you or I. But if you are concerned about this current . . . vileness, put your mind at rest. This is a Shrine, and here lie the bones of the greatest hero the Nadir have ever known. This place means something to all their people. The men who are coming serve a mad Emperor, and they seek to despoil this place for no other purpose than their desire to humiliate the tribes, to keep them in their place. The Source knows how I hate violence, but we are not on the wrong side in this, Druss. By Heaven, we're not!'

Druss clapped him on the shoulder. 'You're beginning to sound like a warrior,' he said, with a wide grin.

'Well, that's because the enemy haven't arrived yet. When they do, you'll find me hiding in an empty flour barrel.'

'I don't believe that for a moment,' Druss told him.

In a small room alongside the makeshift hospital, Zhusai sat quietly as Talisman and Lin-tse discussed the raid. The two men were physically very different; Lin-tse was tall, his solemn face showing his mixed-blood ancestry – the eyes only barely slanted, the cheek and jaw-bones heavy. His hair too was not the jet-black of the Nadir, but tinged with auburn streaks. Talisman, his hair drawn back into a tight pony-tail, looked every inch the Nadir warrior – his skin pale gold, his face flat, the dark eyes expressionless. And yet, thought Zhusai, there was a similarity that was not born of the physical; an aura almost that spoke of brotherhood. Was it, she wondered, the shared experience in the Bodacas Academy, or the desire to see the Nadir free and proud once more? Perhaps both, she thought.

'They will be here tomorrow afternoon. No later,' said Lin-tse.

'There is nothing more we can do. The warriors are as ready now as they will ever be.'

'But will they hold, Talisman? I have never heard much that is good of the Curved Horn. And as for the Lone Wolves . . . well, they seem nervous without their leader. And I see the groups do not mix at all.'

'They will hold,' Talisman told him. 'And as for what you have heard of the Curved Horn, I wonder what they have heard of the Sky Riders. It is not our custom to think well of tribal enemies. Though I note you have not mentioned the Fleet Ponies. Could that be because our friend Quing-chin leads them?'

Lin-tse gave a tight smile. 'I take your point. The axeman looks like a fighting man.'

'He is. I have walked the Void with him, my friend, and believe me he is awesome to behold.'

'Even so I feel uncomfortable with a *gajin* within the walls. Is he a friend?'

'To the Nadir? No. To me? Perhaps. I am glad that he is here. He has an indomitable feel about him.' Talisman stood. 'You should go and rest, Lin-tse. You have earned it. I wish I could have seen you and your men leap the chasm. Truly you were Sky Riders in that moment. Men will sing of it in years to come.'

'Only if we survive, general.'

'Then we must, for I would like to hear that song myself.'

Lin-tse rose and the two men gripped hands. Then Lin-tse bowed to Zhusai and left the room. Talisman slumped back to his seat.

'You are more tired than he,' Zhusai admonished him. 'It is you who needs to rest.'

Talisman gave a weary smile. 'I am young and full of strength.'

Zhusai crossed the room and knelt beside him, her arms resting on his thighs. 'I will not go with Nosta Khan,' she said. 'I have thought long on this. I know it is the custom for a Nadir father to choose the husband for his daughter, but my father was not Nadir and my grandfather had no right to pledge me. I tell you this, Talisman, if you make me leave then I shall wait for news of you. If you die . . .'

'Do not say it! I forbid it!'

'You can forbid me nothing,' she told him quietly. 'You are not my husband; you are my guardian. No more. Very well, I shall not say it. But you know what I will do.'

Angrily he grabbed her shoulders, lifting her. 'Why are you torturing me in this way?' he shouted. 'Can you not see that your safety would give me strength; give me hope?' Relaxing in his arms, she sat down on his lap. 'Hope? What hope for Zhusai with you dead, my love? What would the future hold? Marriage to an un-named man with violet eyes? No, not for me. It will be you, or no-one.'

Leaning forward she kissed him, and he felt the soft warmth of her tongue on his lips. His mind screamed at him to pull away from her, but arousal swept over him and he drew her close, returning the kiss with an ardour he had not known he possessed. His hand slid over her shoulder, feeling the softness of her white silk shirt and the flesh beneath. His palm followed the contours of her body, down over her left breast, the hardness of the nipple causing him to slow, and stroke it between thumb and forefinger.

He did not hear the door open, but felt the warm flow of air from outside. Drawing back, he swung his head to see Nuang Xuan. 'This a bad time, hey?' said the old warrior, with a wink.

'No,' answered Talisman, his voice thick. 'Come in.' Zhusai rose, then leaned forward and kissed his cheek. He watched her walk from the room, following the sway of her slender hips.

Nuang Xuan sat down awkwardly on the wooden chair. 'Better to sit Nadir fashion on the floor,' he said, 'but I don't want to be looking up at you.'

'What do you require of me, old one?'

'You wish me to guard the gate – but I desire to stand alongside Druss on the wall.'

'Why?'

Nuang sighed. 'I think I will die here, Talisman. I do not object to this, for I have lived a long time. And I have killed many men. You doubt me?'

'Why would I doubt you?'

'Because it's not true,' said Nuang, with a wicked grin. 'I have killed five men in my life: three in duels when I was young, and two Lancers when they attacked us. I told the axeman I would kill a hundred on the walls. He said he would keep count for me.'

'Only a hundred?' queried Talisman.

Nuang smiled. 'I have not been feeling well.'

'Tell me the real reason you wish to stand beside him,' said Talisman.

Nuang's old eyes narrowed, and he took a deep breath. 'I have seen him fight and he is deadly. Many *gajin* will die around him. If I am there, men will see me fight. I cannot reach a hundred, but it will seem like it to those watching. Then, when they sing the songs of this defence, my name will live on. You understand?'

'Nuang and the Deathwalker,' said Talisman softly. 'Yes, I understand.'

'Why do you call him that?'

'He and I walked the Void. It is a good name for him.'

'It is very fine. Nuang and the Deathwalker. I like this. Can it be so?'

'It can. I shall also watch you, old man, and keep count.'

'Ha! I am happy now, Talisman.' Nuang stood and rubbed his buttocks. 'I don't like these chairs.'

'The next time we talk, we will sit on the floor,' promised Talisman.

Nuang shook his head. 'Not much talking left. The *gajin* will be here tomorrow. Is your woman staying here?'

'Yes.'

'As it should be,' said Nuang. 'She is very beautiful and sex with her will aid you in the times ahead. Bear in mind, however, that her hips are very small. The first birth for such women is always hard.'

'I will bear that in mind, old one.'

Nuang strode to the door. He stopped there for a moment, then looked back at Talisman. 'You are very young. But if you live you will be a great man – I know these things.'

Then he was gone.

Talisman moved to a second door at the back of the room and emerged into the hospital. Sieben was spreading blankets on the floor, and a young Nadir woman was sweeping the dust from the room.

'All ready here, general,' said Sieben brightly. 'Plenty of thread and sharp needles. And bandages – and the most disgusting-smelling herbs I've ever come across. I would think the threat of them alone will have wounded men rushing back to the walls.'

'Dried tree fungus,' said Talisman. 'It prevents infection. Do you have any alcohol?'

'I do not have the skill to operate. There will be no need to get men drunk.'

'Use it for cleaning wounds and implements. This also helps to prevent infection.'

'Maybe you should be the surgeon,' said Sieben. 'You seem to know a lot more than I do.'

'We had lessons on military surgery at Bodacas. There were many books.'

As Talisman walked away, the Nadir woman approached him. Not conventionally pretty, she was devastatingly attractive. She moved in close. 'You are young for a general,' she said, her breasts touching his chest. 'Is it true what they say about you and the Chiatze woman?'

'What do they say?'

'They say she is pledged to the Uniter, and that you cannot have her.'

'Do they? And if it is true, how does that concern you?'

'I am not pledged to the Uniter. And no general should have to worry about both heads, above and below. It is said there is not enough blood in any man to fill both heads at the same time. Perhaps you should empty one, so that the other may function?'

Talisman laughed aloud. 'You are one of Nuang's women . . . Niobe?'

'Yes. Niobe,' she said, pleased that he remembered her name.

'Well, Niobe, I thank you for your offer. It is a great compliment and it has lifted my spirits.'

'Is that a no or a yes?' she asked, bemused.

Talisman smiled, then swung away and walked out into the sunlight. As Niobe turned back to Sieben, the poet chuckled.

'By Heavens, but you are a brazen hussy. What happened to the warrior you had your pretty eye on?'

'He has two wives, and one pony,' she said. 'And bad teeth.'

'Well, don't despair, there are almost two hundred others to choose from.'

She looked at him, then cocked her head. 'There is no-one here. Come, lie with me.'

'There are men, my darling, who would feel hurt and humiliated to be second choice to a man with one pony and bad teeth. I, on the other hand, have no qualms about accepting such a graceless offer. But then the men of my family have always had a weakness for attractive women.'

'Do all the men in your family talk so much?' she asked, untying the cord belt and letting fall her skirt.

'Talking is the second-best talent we have.'

'What is the first?' she asked him.

'Sarcasm as well as beauty, sweet one? Ah, but you are an enchanting creature.' Stripping off his clothes, Sieben spread a blanket on the floor and drew her down upon it.

'You will have to be quick,' she said.

'Speed in matters of the loins is a talent that seems to have escaped me. Thankfully,' he added.

Kzun felt a roaring sense of exultation as he watched the two wagons burning. Leaping over the boulders he ran down to where a Gothir wagon driver, shot through the neck, was trying to crawl away. Plunging his dagger between the man's shoulders, Kzun twisted it savagely; the man cried out, then began to choke on his own blood. When Kzun rose up and let out a blood-curdling cry, the Curved Horn warriors rose from their hiding-places and ran down to join him. The wind shifted, acrid smoke burning Kzun's eyes. Swiftly he loped around the blazing wagons and surveyed the scene. There had been seven wagons in all, and a troop of fifteen Lancers. Twelve of the Lancers were dead – eight peppered with arrows, four slain in fierce hand-to-hand fighting. Kzun himself had killed two of them. Then the Gothir had turned the remaining wagons and fled. Kzun had longed to ride after them, but his orders were to remain at the pool, denying it to the enemy.

The Curved Horn men had fought well. Only one had a serious wound. 'Gather their weapons and armour!' shouted Kzun, 'then move back into the rocks.'

A young man, sporting a Lancer's white plumed helm, approached him. 'Now we go, hey?' he said.

'Go where?' countered Kzun.

'Where?' responded the man, mystified. 'Away before they come back.'

Kzun walked away from him, back up the boulder-strewn slope to the pool. Kneeling there, he washed the blood from his naked upper body. Then, removing the white scarf from his head, he dipped it into the water before re-tying it over his bald dome. The warriors gathered behind him.

Kzun stood and turned to face them. Scanning their faces, he saw the fear there. They had killed Gothir soldiers. Now more would come – many more. 'You want to run?' he asked them.

A slender warrior with greying hair stepped forward. 'We cannot fight an army, Kzun. We burned their wagons, hey? They will come back. Maybe a hundred. Maybe two. We cannot fight them.'

'Then run,' said Kzun contemptuously. 'I would expect no more from Curved Horn cowards. But I am of the Lone Wolves, and we do not run. I was told to hold this pool, to defend it with my life. This I shall do. While I live not one *gajin* will taste of the water.'

'We are not cowards!' shouted the man, reddening. An angry murmur rose up among the warriors around him. 'But what is the point of dying here?'

'What is the point of dying anywhere?' countered Kzun. 'Two hundred men wait at the Shrine of Oshikai, ready to defend his bones. Your own brothers are among them. You think they will run?'

'What would you have us do?' asked another warrior.

'I don't care what you do!' stormed Kzun. 'All I know is that I will stand and fight.'

The grey-haired warrior called his comrades to him and they walked away to the far side of the pool, squatting in a rough circle to discuss their options. Kzun ignored them. A low groan came from his left, and he saw the wounded Curved Horn warrior sitting with his back against the red rock, his blood-covered hands clenched over a deep belly wound. Kzun lifted a Lancer helmet and dipped it into the pool, then carried it to the dying man. Squatting down, he held the helmet to the warrior's lips. He drank two swallows, then coughed and cried out in pain. Kzun sat down beside him. 'You fought well,' he said. The young man had hurled himself upon a Lancer, dragging the soldier from his horse. In the fight that followed the Lancer had drawn a dagger and rammed it in the Nadir's belly. Kzun had rushed to his aid and slain the Lancer.

The sun rose above the red cliffs, shining down on the young man's face, and Kzun saw then that he was no more than fifteen years old. 'I dropped my sword,' said the warrior. 'Now I am going to die.'

'You died defending your land. The Gods of Stone and Water will welcome you.'

'We are not cowards,' said the dying boy. 'But we . . . spend so much of our lives . . . running from the *gajin*.'

'I know.'

'I am frightened of the Void. If . . . I wait . . . will you walk with me into the dark?'

Kzun shivered. 'I have been in the dark, boy. I know what fear is. Yes, you wait for me. I shall walk with you.' The youngster gave a tired smile, then his head fell back. Kzun closed the boy's eyes and stood. Spinning on his heel, he walked across to the far side where the warriors were still arguing. They looked up as he approached. Pushing through the circle, he stood at its centre. 'There is a time to fight,' he said, 'and a time to run. Think back over your lives. Have you not run enough? And where will you go? How far must you run to avoid the Lancers? The fighters at the Shrine will become immortal. How far must you run to escape the haunting words of their song?

'The enemy can fight only so long as they have water. This is the only deep pool. Every day that we deny them water gives our brothers a further chance of victory, and in this we become part of the Great Song. I am a man with no friends, no sword brothers. My youth was stolen from me in the Gothir mines, working in the dark, my body covered in sores. I have no wife, no sons. Kzun can make no gifts to the future. When I am dead, who will mourn for me? Not one. The blood of Kzun runs in no living creature. The Gothir put my spirit in chains, and when I slew the guards and freed my body my spirit remained, trapped in the dark. I think it is there still, living in the black filth, hiding in the dark tunnels. I could not . . . cannot . . . ever feel the sense of belonging that is at the heart of all we are. All that is left to me is a desire to see the Nadir – my people – walk straight and free. I should not have called you cowards, for you are all brave men. But your spirits too have been chained by the *gajin*. We are born to fear them, to run from them, to bow our heads. They are the masters of the world. We are vermin upon the steppes. Well, Kzun believes this no longer. Kzun is a lost and bitter man,' he said, his voice breaking. 'Kzun has nothing to lose. Your comrade back there is dead. He asked me if I would walk into the dark with him; he said his spirit would wait for me. I knew then that I would die here. I am ready for that. Perhaps I will be reunited with my spirit? But I will meet him on the dark road. And we will walk together into the Void. Any man among you who is not ready to do the same should leave now. I will not send him on his way with curses. Here is where Kzun stands. Here is where he will fall. That is all I have to say.'

Kzun walked back through the circle and on up into the rocks overlooking the steppes. The wagons were no longer burning, but smoke was rising still from the charred wood. Vultures had begun to tear at the corpses. Kzun squatted down in the shadows; his hands were trembling and fear rose in him, bringing bile to his throat.

An eternity in the dark beckoned and Kzun could imagine no greater terror. He glanced up at the clear blue sky. What he had told them was true – that when he died not one living creature upon the surface of the steppes would mourn for him. He had nothing save a scarred, hairless body and rotting teeth to show for his life. In the mines there were no luxuries like friendship. Each man struggled alone. When he was free, the legacy of the years in the dark haunted him still. He could no longer abide sleeping in tents with others, but needed the clean open air and the wondrous taste of solitude. There had been one woman he had yearned for, but he had never spoken of it. By then Kzun was a warrior with many ponies, and could have bid for her. He had not, and had watched in sick despair as she wed another.

He felt a hand upon his shoulder. The warrior with the greying hair squatted down beside him. 'You say you have no sword brothers. Now you have. We will stand with you, Kzun of the Lone Wolves. And we will walk the dark road with you!'

For the first time since he had been dragged to the mines Kzun felt the rush of hot tears to his cheeks. He bowed his head, and wept unashamedly.

Gargan, the Lord of Larness, reined in his massive grey stallion and leaned forward on the high pommel of his saddle. Ahead lay the buildings housing the Shrine of Oshikai Demon-bane. Behind him his troops waited: the eight hundred infantry standing in patient lines of four, the two hundred archers flanking the foot soldiers, while the Royal Lancers, in four columns of two hundred and fifty, fanned out on both sides. Gargan stared hard at the white walls, noting the V-shaped crack in the first. Shading his eyes the warrior scanned the defenders, seeking out the vile face of Okai. But at this distance they were all a blur.

Gargan's hands opened and closed, gripping the pommel so tightly that his knuckles shone white against the tan of his skin.

'I will take you, Okai,' he whispered. 'I will put you through ten thousand torments before you die.'

Raising his arm, Gargan called out for the herald. The young man rode alongside him. 'You know what to say. Do it! And try to stay out of bowshot. These savages have no understanding of honour.'

The soldier saluted and then rode his black gelding at a run towards the walls, drawing up in a cloud of red dust. The gelding reared and the herald's voice rang out. 'Know this, that the Lord Gargan, with the full authority of the God-King, has come to visit the Shrine of Oshikai Demon-bane. The gate will be opened within the hour, and the traitor Okai, known now as Talisman, will be brought before the Lord Gargan. If this is done, no harm will be offered to those within the Shrine.' He paused, allowing his words to sink in, then he called out again. 'If this is not done the Lord Gargan will have to consider all men inside the compound as traitors. The army will surround them and take them captive. Every man will have his hands cut off, his eyes put out, before being hanged. You will all walk the Void blind and maimed. These are the words of the Lord Gargan. You have one hour.'

Swinging his horse, the young Lancer rode back to the column.

Premian rode alongside Gargan. 'They'll not surrender, sir,' he said.

'I know,' replied Gargan.

Premian looked up into the general's hard face, seeing the glint of triumph there. 'We have only thirty ladders left, sir. An assault on the walls will be costly.'

'That's what soldiers are paid for. Prepare the camp, and send out fifty Lancers to patrol the surrounding country. We'll launch the first attack at dusk. Concentrate on the broken wall and then torch the gates.'

Gargan turned his horse and rode back through the men, while Premian ordered the troops to stand down and prepare camp. Gargan's tent had been destroyed in the fire, but a new one had been constructed from canvas sacking and cloth that had survived the blaze. The general sat his stallion as soldiers erected the tent, then dismounted and strode inside. His chairs had been destroyed but the pallet bed had survived. Gargan sat down, glad to be out of the blazing sun. Removing his plumed helm and unbuckling his breastplate, he stretched out on the bed.

A rider from the city had arrived the previous afternoon. There was great unrest in Gulgothir, according to the message from

Garen-Tsen, but the secret police had arrested scores of nobles, and the situation was under control at the moment. The God-King was in hiding, guarded by Garen-Tsen's minions. Gargan was urged to complete his mission with all speed and return as soon as possible.

Well, he thought, we should take the Shrine by dawn. With luck he could be back in Gulgothir in ten days.

A servant entered the tent, bringing a goblet of water. When Gargan sipped it, the water was hot and brackish. 'Send Premian and Marlham to me,' he told the man.

'Yes, sir.' The officers arrived, saluted, then removed their helms, holding them under their arms. Marlham looked terribly tired, the iron-grey stubble on his cheeks adding ten years to him. Premian, though much younger, also looked weary, with dark rings under his pale blue eyes.

'How is morale?' Gargan asked the older man.

'Better now we are here,' he said. 'The Nadir are not known for their defensive abilities. Most of the men believe that once we have reached the ramparts they will run.'

'Probably true,' said Gargan. 'I want Lancers ringing the walls. They must not be allowed to escape – not one of them. You understand me?'

'I understand, sir.'

'I do not believe they will run,' put in Premian. 'They will fight to the death. This Shrine is their one great holy place.'

'That is not the Nadir way,' sneered Gargan. 'You don't understand these vermin – cowardice is built into them! You think they will care about Oshikai's bones once the arrows fly and cold steel scores their flesh? They won't.'

Premian drew in a deep breath. 'Okai will. He is no coward. He is a trained tactician – the best we ever saw at Bodacas.'

Gargan surged to his feet. 'Do not praise him!' he roared. 'The man murdered my son!'

'I grieved for your loss, general; Argo was a friend of mine. But that evil deed does not change Okai's talents. He will have banded those men together and he understands discipline and morale. They won't run.'

'Then let them stand and die,' shouted Gargan. 'I never yet met any ten Nadir who could outfight a single Gothir swordsman. How many men do they have? Two hundred. By dusk we'll have twice that many infantry storming the walls. Whether they stand or run is immaterial.'

'They also have the man, Druss,' said Premian.

'What are you saying? Is Druss a demi-god? Will he cast mountains down upon us?'

'No, sir,' said Premian evenly, 'but he is a legend among his own people. And we know, to our cost, that he can fight. He slew seven of our Lancers when they attacked the renegade camp. He is a fearsome warrior, and the men are already talking about him. No-one relishes going up against that axe.'

Gargan looked hard at the young man. 'What are you suggesting, Premian? That we go home?'

'No, sir. We have our orders, and they must be carried out. All I am saying is that we should treat them with a little more respect. In an hour our infantry will assault the walls. If they believe – wrongly – that the defence will be no more than token they will be in for a terrible surprise. We could lose a hundred men before dusk. They are already tired and thirsty; it would mean a bitter blow to morale.'

'I disagree, sir,' said Marlham. 'If we tell them that the assault will be murderous, then we risk instilling a fear of defeat in them. Such fears can prove self-fulfilling prophecies.'

'That's not what I am saying,' insisted Premian. 'Tell them the defenders are ready to lay down their lives, and that the battle will not be easy. *Then* impress upon them that they are Gothir soldiers, and no-one can stand against them.'

Gargan returned to the bed, where he sat in silence for several minutes. At last he looked up. 'I still think they will run. However, it would be a foolhardy general who did not allow for a margin of error. Do it, Premian. Warn them and lift them.'

'Yes, sir. Thank you, sir.'

'When the hour is up, release the prisoner. Send him towards their walls. When he is close enough for the defenders to see him, have three mounted archers cut him down.'

Premian saluted and replaced his helm.

'No words of condemnation, Premian?' asked Gargan.

'No, sir. I have no taste for such things, but the sight of him will unnerve the defenders. Of that there is no doubt.'

'Good. You are learning.'

Sieben gazed out at the Gothir army, and felt the cold touch of panic in his belly. 'I think I'll wait in the hospital, old horse,' he told Druss.

The axeman nodded. 'Probably best,' he said grimly. 'You'll soon have plenty to do there.'

On unsteady legs, Sieben walked from the ramparts. Nuang Xuan approached Druss. 'I stand with you,' he said, his face pale, his eyes blinking rapidly.

Around twenty Nadir were standing silently close by. 'What tribe are you?' Druss asked the nearest, a young man with nervous eyes.

'Lone Wolves,' he answered, licking his lips.

'Well,' said Druss good-naturedly, his voice carrying to the other men on the western wall. 'This old man with me has pledged to kill a hundred Gothir soldiers. I am to keep count. I don't want any of you Lone Wolves to get in his way. Killing a hundred takes great concentration!'

The young man swung to look at Nuang. Then he grinned. 'I kill more than him,' he said.

'That sounds like a wager in the offing,' said Druss. 'What is your name?'

'I am Chisk.'

'Well, Chisk, I have a silver piece that says when dusk falls old Nuang will have outscored you.'

The man looked downcast. 'I have no silver with which to gamble.'

'What have you got?' the axeman asked.

The Nadir warrior fished deep into the pocket of his filthy goatskin jacket, coming up with a small round charm inset with lapis lazuli. 'This wards off evil spirits,' he said. 'It is worth many pieces of silver.'

'I expect it is,' agreed Druss. 'You want to pledge it?'

The man nodded. 'I bet I kill more than you too,' said the Nadir.

Druss laughed and patted the man's shoulder. 'One bet per man is enough, lad. Any of you other Lone Wolves want to wager?'

Warriors pushed forward, offering ornate belts, curved daggers and buttons of carved horn. Druss accepted all offers.

A burly warrior with deep-set eyes tapped him on the arm. 'Who counts?' he asked 'No-one can watch us all.'

Druss smiled. 'You are all heroes,' he said, 'and men to trust. Count for yourselves. Tonight, when the enemy has skulked back to his camp, we'll get together and see who has won. Now get back to your positions. The hour is almost up.'

Nuang stepped in close. 'I think you lose a lot of silver, axe-man,' he whispered.

'It's only money,' said Druss.

Talisman joined Druss. 'What is the commotion here?' he asked. Several of the warriors gathered around him, speaking in Nadir. Talisman nodded and gave a weary smile. 'They think you are a great fool,' he told Druss.

'It's been said before,' the axeman admitted.

Three riders came from the enemy camp, one of them dragging a prisoner. As they came closer they swerved their horses; the prisoner fell heavily, and struggled to rise.

'It is Quing-chin,' said Talisman, his voice flat, his expression unreadable.

The prisoner's hands had been cut off, the stumps dipped in black pitch. The rider leading him cut free the rope; Quing-chin stumbled on, turning in a half-circle.

'He has been blinded also,' whispered Nuang.

Several of the Nadir on the walls cried out to the maimed man. His head came up and he staggered towards the sound. The three riders let him approach, then notched arrows to their bows and galloped towards him. One arrow struck him low in the back, but he did not cry out. A second arrow plunged between his shoulder-blades. Quing-chin fell then, and began to crawl. A horseman drew reins alongside him, sending a third shaft deep into his back.

An arrow flew from the ramparts, falling well short of the riders.

'No-one shoot!' bellowed Talisman.

'A hard way to die,' whispered Nuang Xuan. 'That is what the enemy promises for all of us.'

'This was their moment,' said Druss, his voice cold and bitter. 'Let them enjoy it. In a little while we will have *our* moment. They will not enjoy that!'

A drum sounded in the enemy camp and hundreds of infantry-men began to move towards the western wall, the sun bright upon their silver breastplates and helms. Behind them came two hundred archers, arrows notched to the strings.

Druss swung to Talisman, who had drawn his sabre. 'No place here for you, general,' he said softly.

'I need to fight,' hissed Talisman.

'Just what they'd want. You are the leader, you cannot die in the first attack – the blow to morale would be savage. Trust me. Leave the wall. I won't let it fall.'

Talisman stood for a moment, then rammed his sabre back in its scabbard and turned on his heel.

'Right, lads,' shouted Druss. 'Keep your heads down, for they'll pepper us with arrows at first. Spread yourselves and put away your swords. When the ladder men reach the walls we'll pelt the whoresons with rocks. Then use daggers – they're better for the close work. Save the long blades for when they've reached the ramparts.'

The lines of infantry slowed, just out of bowshot. Druss knelt and watched the archers run through their ranks. Hundreds of shafts slashed through the air. 'Get down!' he yelled, and all along the wall the Nadir defenders ducked behind the crenellated battlements. Druss glanced back to the compound. Talisman and the reserve force of twenty men, led by Lin-tse, were out in the open as the shafts soared over the wall. One man was struck in the leg; the rest ran back to the cover of the lodging building. Out on the plain the infantry began to move, slowly at first and then, as they closed upon the wall, they raised their round shields before them and broke into a charge. Nadir arrows slashed at them and several men fell. The Gothir archers sent volley after volley over the heads of the infantry. Two Nadir bowmen were cut down.

The ladder-bearers reached the western wall. Druss knelt, wrapped his arms around a boulder as large as a bull's head and, with a grunt, heaved it to the battlements. A ladder thudded against the wall. Gripping the boulder between his hands, Druss hoisted it above his head and sent it sailing out over the wall. Seven men were on the ladder as the boulder struck the first, smashing his skull to shards. The huge rock hit the shoulder of the third man, snapping his collar-bone; he fell, dislodging three others. Rocks and stones rained down on the attackers, but they pushed on.

The first man reached the ramparts, his shield held above his head. Chisk ran forward, ramming his dagger through the man's eye, and with a choking cry he fell.

'One for Chisk!' shouted the Nadir. Two more men reached the ramparts. Druss leapt to his right, sending Snaga crashing through a wooden helm, and braining the second man with a reverse sweep. Nuang jumped forward, thrusting his dagger at the head of a climbing soldier. The blade gashed the man's forehead but he stabbed out with his own short sword, catching Nuang on the left wrist and scoring the flesh. Snaga crashed down on the man's shoulder, splitting his breastplate. Blood gushed from the wound and the climber fell away.

To Druss's left four Gothir soldiers had forced their way to the ramparts, forming a fighting wedge that allowed more men to reach the walls unopposed. Druss charged the group, Snaga sweeping down in a murderous arc. One man was cut down instantly; Druss shoulder-charged a second, spinning him from the ramparts to fall head first to the compound below; a third went down to a terrible blow which caved in his ribs. The fourth thrust his sword at Druss's belly. Nuang's blade hacked down, parrying the thrust, then swept up to slash through the soldier's neck. Dropping his sword, the Gothir soldier staggered back with blood pumping from his severed jugular.

Dropping his axe, Druss grabbed the dying man by throat and groin and heaved him high into the air. Spinning, he hurled the body at two more soldiers as they cleared the ramparts; both were thrown back from the walls. Nuang ran forward to plunge his sword into the open mouth of a bearded soldier who had just reached the top of the ladder. The blade smashed through the man's palate, emerging from the back of his neck. The sword was torn from Nuang's grasp as the man plummeted to the ground.

Druss swept up a short sword lying on the ramparts and tossed it to the old man. Nuang caught it expertly.

All along the western wall the Nadir struggled to block wave after wave of attackers.

Below, Talisman stood with Lin-tse and twenty warriors, trying to judge the best moment to launch fresh troops into the fray. Beside him Lin-tse waited with sword drawn. The defence was briefly breached: five soldiers hacking and cleaving a path to the steps. Lin-tse started forward, but Talisman called him back. Druss had attacked the men, cutting three down in as many heartbeats.

'He is terrifying,' said Lin-tse. 'Never have I seen the like.'

Talisman did not reply. The Lone Wolves were fighting like demons, inspired by the ferocious skills of the black-garbed axeman. On the other walls Nadir warriors watched in awed admiration.

'They are coming for the gates!' shouted Gorkai. 'They have fire buckets and axes.'

Talisman lifted his arm to show that he had heard, but made no move. More than a dozen of the defenders on the western wall were wounded. Five fought on, several others struggled down the steps, making their way to the hospital.

'Now!' he told Lin-tse.

The tall Sky Rider leapt forward, sprinting up the steps.

Axes thudded into the gate and Talisman saw Gorkai and the men of the Fleet Ponies hurling rocks over the battlements. Smoke seeped through the ancient wood. But, as Druss had suggested, they had soaked the gates every day and the fires quickly died away.

Talisman signalled to Gorkai to send back ten men to stand with him.

The battle raged on. Druss, covered in blood, stormed along the ramparts, leaping down to the fighting platform and scattering the Gothir warriors who had forced a way over the battlements. Talisman committed his ten men to help, then drew his sword and followed them in. He knew Druss was right about the crushing blow there would be to morale if he died. Equally, his men had to see him fight.

Climbing to the platform, he swept his sabre through the throat of a charging Gothir soldier. Two more ran at him. Druss smashed his axe through the shoulder of the first; then the old man, Nuang Xuan, gutted the second.

The Gothir fell back, taking their ladders with them.

A great cry went up from the Nadir. They jeered and waved their swords over their heads.

Talisman called Lin-tse to him. 'Get a count of the injured, and have the more seriously wounded men carried to the hospital.'

The Lone Wolves gathered around Druss, clapping him on the back and complimenting him. In their excitement they were speaking Nadir, and Druss understood not a word of it. He turned to the stocky Chisk. 'Well, laddie,' he said. 'How many did you kill?'

'I don't know. But it was many.'

'Did you beat this old man, do you think?' asked Druss, throwing his arm around Nuang's shoulder.

'I don't care,' shouted Chisk happily. 'I kiss his cheek!' Dropping his sword, he took the surprised Nuang by the shoulders and hugged him. 'We showed them how Nadir fight, eh? We whipped the *gajin* dogs.'

Nuang grinned, took a step, then fell to the ground with a surprised look on his face. Chisk knelt down beside him, dragging open the old man's jerkin. Three wounds had pierced Nuang's flesh and blood was flowing freely.

'Hold fast, brother,' said Chisk. 'The wounds are not bad. We get you to the surgeon, though, hey?' Two Lone Wolves helped Chisk to carry Nuang across to the hospital.

Druss strode from the wall to the well, drawing up a bucket of clear, cool water. Pulling an old cloth from his belt, he sponged the blood from his face and jerkin, then emptied the bucket over his head.

From the battlements came the sound of laughter. 'You could do with a bath too, you whoresons!' he shouted. Dropping the bucket back into the well, he drew it forth again, then drank deeply. Talisman joined him. 'We killed or wounded seventy,' said the Nadir leader. 'For the loss of nine dead and fifteen wounded. What next, do you think?'

'The same again, but with fresh troops,' said Druss. 'And before dark too. My guess is there will be at least two more attacks today.'

'I agree with you. And we will hold – I know that now.'

Druss chuckled. 'They're a fine bunch of fighters. Tomorrow it will be the gates – a concerted attack.'

'Why not tonight?'

'They haven't learned their lesson yet,' said Druss.

Talisman smiled. 'You are a good teacher, axeman. I am sure they will learn before the day is over.'

Druss took another long drink, then pointed to a group of men working at the base of the old tower. They were separating blocks of granite and hauling them clear of the rubble. 'What is the purpose of that?' asked the axeman.

'The gates will fall,' said Talisman, 'but we will have a surprise for the first troops to get through!'

Nuang Xuan lay quietly on the floor with his head on a pillow stuffed with straw, a single blanket covering him. The stitches in his chest and shoulder were tight, his wounds painful, yet he felt at peace. He had stood beside the axeman, and had killed five of the enemy. Five! Across the room a man cried out. Nuang carefully rolled to his side, seeing that the surgeon was stitching wounds in a man's belly; the wounded warrior thrashed out and Niobe grabbed his arms. Waste of time, thought Nuang, and within moments the injured man gave a gurgling cry and was still. The surgeon swore. Niobe dragged the corpse from the table, and two men carried a freshly wounded man to take his place.

Sieben pulled open the man's jerkin. He had been cut across the chest and deep into the side; the sword had broken off above the hip. 'I need pliers for this,' said Sieben, wiping a bloodied hand across his brow, leaving a smear of crimson. Niobe handed him a rusty pair and Sieben dug his fingers into the wound, feeling for the broken blade. Once he had it, he pushed the pliers against the split flesh and with a great wrench dragged the iron clear. Elsewhere in the room two other Nadir women were applying stitches or bandages.

Nosta Khan entered, looked around and then moved across the room, past Nuang and into the small office beyond.

Nuang could just make out the conversation that followed. 'I leave tonight,' came the voice of the shaman. 'You must prepare the woman.'

'She stays,' said Talisman.

'Did you not understand what I said about destiny?'

'It is you who are without understanding,' roared Talisman. 'You do not know the future, shaman. You have had glimpses, tantalizing and incomplete. Despite your powers you cannot locate Ulric. How hard should it be to find a violet-eyed leader? You cannot find the Eyes of Alchazzar. And you did not warn me they would take Quing-chin. Go from here if you must. But you travel alone.'

'You fool!' shouted Nosta Khan. 'This is no time for betrayal. Everything you live for hangs in the balance. If I take her, she lives. Can you understand that?'

'Wrong again, shaman. If you take her, she will kill herself – she has told me this and I believe her. Go. Seek out the man with violet eyes. Let him build on what we accomplish here.'

'You will die here, Talisman,' said Nosta Khan. 'It is written in the stars. Druss will escape, for I have seen him in the many futures. For you there is no place.'

'Here is my place,' responded Talisman. 'Here I stand.'

The shaman said more, but Nuang did not hear it for the voices within were suddenly lowered.

Niobe knelt beside Nuang handing him a clay cup full of *lyrrd*. 'Drink, old father,' she said. 'It will put strength back into your ancient bones.'

'Ancient they may be, but my blood runs true, Niobe. Five I killed. I feel so strong I could even survive a night with you.'

'You were never that strong,' she said, patting his cheek. 'Anyway Chisk told us you killed at least a dozen.'

'Ha! Good men, these Lone Wolves.'

Rising, she moved back to the table. Taking a fresh cloth, she wiped the blood and sweat from Sieben's brow. 'You are working good,' she said. 'No mistakes.'

From outside came the screams of wounded men and the clash of swords. 'It is vile,' he said. 'All vile.'

'They say your friend is a god of battle. They call him the Deathwalker.'

'The name suits him.'

The doors opened and two men were carried inside. 'More bandages and thread,' he told Niobe.

Outside on the walls Druss relaxed; the enemy had pulled back for the second time. Chisk came alongside him. 'You hurt, Deathwalker?'

'The blood is not mine,' Druss told him.

'You are wrong; your shoulder bleeds.'

Druss glanced down to the gash in his jerkin. Blood was leaking from it. Doffing the jerkin he examined the cut beneath, which was no more than two inches long, but deep. He swore. 'You hold this damned wall till I get back,' he said.

'Till the mountains crumble to dust,' promised Chisk. As Druss walked away he added, 'But you don't take too long, hey?'

Inside the hospital Druss called out to Niobe and she ran across to him. 'Don't bother Sieben with it,' he said. 'It's no deeper than a dog-bite. Get a needle and thread for me; I'll do it myself.'

She returned with the implements and a long stretch of bandage. The wound was just below the collar-bone and Druss fumbled his way through the stitching, drawing the lips of the gash together.

'You have many scars,' said Niobe, staring at his upper body.

'All men get careless,' he told her. The wound was beginning to throb now. Pushing himself to his feet, he strode from the room and out into the fading sunlight. Behind the gates some thirty warriors were manhandling blocks to form a semi-circular wall. The work was back-breaking and slow, yet no word of complaint came from them. They had erected a rough hoist and pulley on the ramparts, and the blocks of granite were being hauled into place, blocking the gates. Suddenly the pulley gave way and a huge block fell, hurling two men to the ground. Druss ran over to where they lay. The first was dead, his skull crushed, but the other man was merely winded. Pulling the corpse aside the other warriors continued with their work, their faces grim. The blocks were being laid four deep, forming a curved wall eight feet wide.

'They'll get a nasty shock as they come through,' said Lin-tse, striding down the rampart steps to join Druss.

'How tall can you get it?'

'We think twelve feet at the front, ten at the back. But we need a stronger hoist bar and supports.'

'Tear up the floorboards in the upper lodging-rooms,' advised Druss. 'Use the cross joists.'

Returning to the wall, Druss put on his jerkin and silver-skinned gauntlets. Talisman's man, Gorkai, joined him. 'The Curved Horn will stand with you for the next attack,' he said. 'This is Bartsai, their leader.' Druss nodded, then reached out and shook hands with the stocky Nadir.

'Well, lads,' he said, with a wide smile, 'do you fight as well as the Lone Wolves?'

'Better,' grunted a young warrior.

'Would you care to make a wager on that, laddie?'

Chapter Twelve

The moon was bright as Talisman and Lin-tse watched the Gothir carrying away their dead and wounded. The stretcher-bearers worked with great efficiency and no little courage, coming in close to the walls to pick up the wounded. The Nadir did not loose shafts at them. Talisman had forbidden it – not for any reason of mercy, but simply because every wounded Gothir soldier needed to be tended and fed, and that would help to exhaust the enemy's supplies. The Nadir dead had been wrapped in blankets and placed in the cool of the Shrine.

'They lost sixty-four, with another eighty-one wounded,' said Lin-tse gleefully. 'Our losses are less than a third of that.'

'Twenty-three dead,' said Talisman, 'and nine wounded who will not fight again.'

'That is good, eh?'

'They outnumber us ten to one. Five to one for casualties is not good enough,' Talisman told him. 'However, as Fanlon used to say, the worst always die first – those with the least skill, or the least luck. We did well today.'

'The Lancers are not riding out,' observed Lin-tse.

'Their mounts are thirsty and tired,' said Talisman, 'as indeed are the men. Their wagons went out again this morning. They have not returned; Kzun is still holding them away from the pool.'

Lin-tse moved to the edge of the battlements. 'I wish we could bring in Quing-chin's body,' he said. 'It saddens me to think of his spirit wandering blind and maimed.'

Talisman did not reply. Two years before, the three Nadir warriors had sought revenge for the death of their comrade. They had found satisfaction in kidnapping and killing the son of Gargan; he too had been blinded and maimed. Now the circle of violence had swung once more, and Quing-chin's body lay as cold testimony to the cruel reality of revenge. Talisman rubbed at his eyes.

The smell of scorched wood drifted to him. The gates had come under two attacks, the Gothir using oil in an attempt to burn a way through. This had failed, and some twenty Gothir soldiers had paid with their lives. Talisman shivered.

'What is wrong, brother?' asked Lin-tse.

'I do not hate them any longer,' Talisman told him.

'Hate them? The Gothir? Why?'

'Do not misunderstand me, Lin-tse. I will fight them, and – if the Gods of Stone and Water permit – I will see their towers crumble and their cities fall. But I cannot hold to hate any longer. When they killed Zhen-shi, we lusted for blood. Do you remember the terror in Argo's eyes as we gagged him and carried him out?'

'Of course.'

'Now his father nurses the hatred and it hangs like a bat at his throat, ready to be passed on.'

'But his father began it with his hatred of all Nadir,' argued Lin-tse.

'Precisely. And what caused it? Some Nadir atrocity back in his own youth? My dream is to see the Nadir united, every man standing tall and proud. But I will never again hate an enemy.'

'You are tired, Okai. You should rest. They will not come again tonight.'

Talisman walked away along the ramparts. Nosta Khan had gone, and no man had seen him drop from the walls. He had tried to reach Zhusai, but had found Gorkai standing guard at her door.

Even as he thought of her, Talisman saw her walking across the compound. She was wearing a white blouse of shining silk, and silver-grey leggings. She waved and moved to him, throwing her arms around his neck.

'We are together, now and always,' she said.

'Now and always,' he agreed.

'Come. I have perfumed oil in my room, and I will ease away your fatigue.' Taking him by the hand, she led him back to her room.

Druss and Sieben watched them from the ramparts of the western wall. 'Love in the midst of death,' said Druss. 'It is good.'

'Nothing is good here,' snapped Sieben. 'The whole business stinks like a ten-week fish. I wish I had never come.'

'They say you are a great surgeon,' said Druss.

'A fine seamstress, more like. Eleven men died under my hands, Druss, coughing up their blood. I cannot tell you how sick I am of it. I hate war and I hate warriors. Scum of the earth!'

'It won't stop you singing about it, if we survive,' Druss pointed out.

'What is that supposed to mean?'

'Who is it who tells of the glory, the honour and the chivalry of war?' asked Druss, softly. 'Rarely the soldier who has seen the bulging entrails and the crows feasting on dead men's eyes. No, it is the saga poet. It is he who feeds young men with stories of heroism. How many young Drenai men have listened to your poems and songs and lusted for battle?'

'Well, that is a neat twist,' said Sieben. 'Poets are to blame now, are they?'

'Not just poets. Hell's teeth, man, we are a violent race. What I am saying is that soldiers are not the scum of the earth. Every man here is fighting for what he believes in. You knew that – before the killing started. You'll know it again when it has stopped.'

'It will never stop, Druss,' said Sieben sadly. 'Not as long as there are men with axes and swords. I think I had better get back to the hospital. How is your shoulder?'

'Stings like the devil.'

'Good,' said Sieben, with a tired smile.

'How is Nuang?'

'Resting. The wounds were not mortal, but he won't fight again.'

As Sieben walked away Druss stretched himself out on the ramparts. All along the wall exhausted Nadir warriors were sleeping. For many it would be the last sleep they ever enjoyed.

Maybe for me, thought Druss. Perhaps I will die tomorrow.

Perhaps not, he decided. And drifted into a dreamless sleep . . .

Gargan walked among the wounded, talking to the survivors and offering praise for their heroism. Returning to his tent, he summoned Premian. 'I understand the Nadir are still denying us water,' he said. 'How many defend the pool?'

'That is hard to say, sir. The trail up to the pool is narrow, and our men are coming under attack from warriors hidden in the rocks. No more than thirty I would say. They are led by a madman who wears a white scarf upon his head; he leapt twenty feet from a tall rock and landed on the officer's mount, breaking its back. Then he killed the rider, wounded another and sprinted back into the rocks.'

'Who was the officer?'

'Mersham, sir. Newly promoted.'

'I know his family. Good stock.' Gargan sat down on his pallet bed; his face was drawn and strained, his lips dry. 'Take a hundred men and wipe them out. The water here is all but gone, and without more we are finished. Go now, tonight.'

'Yes, sir. I have had men digging at the bend of the dry stream to the east and we have uncovered a seep. It is not large, but it will fill several barrels.'

'Good,' said Gargan wearily. The general stretched himself out on the bed and closed his eyes. As Premian was about to leave, he spoke again. 'They killed my son,' he said. 'They cut out his eyes.'

'I know, sir.'

'We will not attack before mid-morning. I need you back with water by then.'

'Yes, sir.'

Sieben crossed the compound and quietly woke Druss. 'Follow me,' he whispered. Druss rose and the two men moved down the rampart steps and across the open ground to the Shrine. It was dark within and they stood for a moment, allowing their eyes to adjust to the faint moonlight coming through the single window. The Nadir dead had been placed against the north wall, and already the smell of death clung to the air. 'What are we doing here?' whispered Druss.

'I want the healing stones,' said Sieben. 'No more dead men under my hands.'

'We've already searched this place.'

'Yes, and I think we have already seen them. Lift the lid.' Moving to the stone coffin Druss pushed at the lid, slowly easing it to one side to make enough room for Sieben to push his arm inside. His fingers touched dry bones and the dust of decayed garments. Swiftly he moved his hand upward until he reached the skull. Closing his eyes and concentrating, he searched below the fractured jaw until his fingers touched the cold metal of Oshikai's *lon-tsia*. Pulling it free, he brought it out into the pale moonlight.

'Now you have a pair,' said Druss. 'So what?'

'Shaoshad came here to ask Oshikai to agree to be regenerated. Oshikai refused, unless Shul-sen could be with him. How then did he set about finding her?'

'I don't know,' said Druss, holding his patience. 'I do not understand magic.'

'Bear with me, my friend, and look at the evidence. Both Oshikai and Shul-sen wore *lon-tsia*. Oshikai's tomb has already been plundered, but no-one found the medallion. Why? The blind priest told me a Hide-spell had been placed upon the *lon-tsia* worn by Shul-sen. It is reasonable to suppose that a similar spell was cast upon that worn by Oshikai. Now, I believe Shaoshad lifted the spell on this one,' he said, holding up the *lon-tsia*. 'Why? In order to help him locate Shul-sen. Talisman's man, Gorkai, told me the *lon-tsia* of the rich were blessed with many spells. I think that in some way Shaoshad used this medallion to find the other. You follow me?'

'No, but I am hanging in,' said Druss wearily.

'Why did he not have the stones when he was caught?'

'Will you stop asking me questions for which there are no answers?' Druss snapped.

'It was rhetorical, Druss. Now don't interrupt any more. According to Gorkai, a search spell is like a tracker dog. I think Shaoshad imbued Oshikai's medallion with the power of one of the stones, and sent the other in search of Shul-sen's *lon-tsia*. Then he tried to follow the spirit trail. That is why he was caught between here and where we found Shul-sen's remains.'

'And where does this leave us?' asked Druss.

Sieben fished in his pocket, producing the second *lon-tsia* which he held close to the first. 'It leaves us with this,' he said triumphantly, clapping his hands and pushing the two medallions together.

Nothing happened . . .

'It leaves us with what?' asked Druss.

Sieben opened his hands. The two *lon-tsia* glittered in the moonlight and he swore. 'I was sure I was right,' he said. 'I thought if they were brought together the stones would appear.'

'I am going back to sleep,' said Druss, spinning on his heel and striding from the room.

Sieben pocketed the medallions, and was about to follow when he realized the coffin was still open. He swore again and grasped the lid, straining to drag it back into place.

'So close, my friend,' came a whispered voice, and Sieben swung to see the tiny, glowing figure of Shaoshad sitting cross-legged on the floor. 'But I did not hide the Eyes within the *lon-tsia.*'

'Where, then?' asked the poet. 'And why did you hide them at all?'

'They should never have been made,' said Shaoshad, his voice edged with sorrow. 'The magic was in the land, but now it is barren. It was an act of colossal arrogance. As to why I hid them – well, I knew I risked capture. There was no way I would allow the Eyes to be retaken. Even now it saddens me to know they must surface once more.'

'Where are they?'

'They are here. You were mostly right – I did use the power to locate Shul-sen's tomb, and I did indeed imbue her *lon-tsia* with enough power to regenerate her. Watch – and be suitably impressed!'

The two *lon-tsia* medallions rose up from Sieben's palm and floated across to the stone coffin, hovering just in front of the inscribed name-plate. 'Can you guess?' asked the spirit of the shaman.

'Yes!' said Sieben, moving forward and retrieving the floating medallions. Holding them up before the engraved word *Oshikai*, he pressed them side on into the two *i* indentations. Both *lon-tsia* disappeared. A violet glow radiated from within the coffin. Sieben rose and peered inside. Two jewels now rested in the eye-sockets of the skull of Oshikai Demon-bane. Reaching inside, he drew them out; both were the size of sparrow's eggs.

'Tell no-one you have them,' warned Shaoshad, 'not even Druss. He is a great man, but he has no guile. If the Nadir find out they will kill you for them; therefore do not use their powers too obviously. When treating the wounded, stitch them and bandage them as before, then concentrate on the healing. You will not need to produce the jewels. If you keep them hidden on your person, the power will still flow through you.'

'How will I know how to heal?'

Shaoshad smiled. 'You do not need to know – that is the beauty of magic, poet. Simply place your hands over the wound and *think* it healed. Once you have done this you will understand more.'

'I thank you, Shaoshad.'

'No, poet, it is I who thank you. Use them wisely. Now replace the lid of the coffin.'

Sieben took hold of the stone and, as he did so, glanced down. Just for a moment he saw the *lon-tsia* of Oshikai gleaming among the bones, then it faded. Dragging the lid back into place, he turned to Shaoshad. 'He wears it once more,' said the poet.

'Aye, as it should be, hidden again by a Hide-spell. No-one will plunder it. The other has returned to the resting-place of Shul-sen.'

'Can we win here?' asked Sieben, as the shaman's image began to fade.

'Winning and losing is entirely dependent on what you are fighting for,' answered Shaoshad. 'All men here could die, yet you could still win. Or all men could live, and you could lose. Fare you well, poet.'

The spirit vanished. Sieben shivered, then thrust his hands in his pocket, curling his fingers around the stones.

Returning to the hospital, he walked silently among the ranks of wounded men. In the far corner a man groaned and Sieben moved to his side, kneeling beside the blanket on which he lay. A lantern flickered brightly on the wall, and by its light Sieben looked at the man's gaunt face. He had been stabbed in the belly, and though Sieben had stitched the outer flap of the wound the bleeding was deep and internal. The man's eyes were fever-bright. Sieben gently laid a hand on the bandages and closed his eyes, seeking to concentrate. For a moment nothing happened; then bright colours filled his mind, and he saw the torn muscles, the split entrails, the pooling blood within the wound. In that instant he knew every muscle and fibre, the attachments, the blood routes, the sources of pain and discomfort. It was as if he was floating inside the wound. Blood flowed from a gaping gash in a twisting purple cylinder . . . but as Sieben gazed at it, the gash closed and healed. Moving on he sealed other cuts, his mind flowing back from the depths of the wound, healing as he went. At last he reached the outer stitches and here he stopped. It would be wise to let the man feel the pull of the stitches when he woke, he thought. If any wound was utterly healed, the secret of the stones would be out.

The warrior blinked. 'It is taking me a long time to die,' he said.

'You are not going to die,' Sieben promised him. 'Your wound is healing, and you are a strong man.'

'They pierced my guts.'

'Sleep now. In the morning you will feel stronger.'

'You speak the truth?'

'I do. The wound was not as deep as you believe. You are healing well. Sleep.' Sieben touched the man's brow; instantly his eyes closed and his head lolled to one side.

Sieben made his way to every wounded man one by one. Most were sleeping. Those who were awake he spoke softly to, and healed. At the last he came to Nuang. As he floated within the old man's injuries he found himself drawn to the heart, and here he found a section so thin it was almost transparent. Nuang could have died at any time, he realized, for his heart – under strain – could have torn itself apart like wet paper. Sieben concentrated on the area, watching it thicken. The arteries were hard, the inner walls choked and narrow; these he opened and made supple.

Withdrawing at last, he sat back. There was no feeling of weariness in him, rather a sense of exultation and rare delight.

Niobe was asleep in another corner of the room. Placing the jewels in a pouch he hid them behind a water cask, moved to Niobe and lay down beside her, feeling her warmth against him. Drawing a blanket over them both, he leaned over and kissed her cheek. She moaned and rolled in to him, whispering a name that was not his. Sieben smiled.

She awoke then, and raised herself up on one elbow. 'Why you smile, po-et?' she asked him.

'Why not? It is a fine night.'

'You wish to make love?'

'No, but I would appreciate a hug. Come close.'

'You are very warm,' she said, snuggling alongside him and resting her arm on his chest.

'What do you want from life?' he whispered.

'Want? What is there to want? Apart from a good man and strong babies?'

'And that is all?'

'Rugs,' she said, after thinking for a few moments. 'Good rugs. And a fire-bucket of iron. My uncle had a fire-bucket of iron; it heated the tent on the cold nights.'

'What about rings and bracelets, items of gold and silver?'

'Yes, those too,' she agreed. 'You will give these to me?'

'I think so.' Turning his head, he kissed her cheek. 'Amazing as it might seem, I have fallen in love with you. I want you with me. I will take you to my own land and buy you an iron fire-bucket and a mountain of rugs.'

'And the babies?'

'Twenty if you want them.'

'Seven. I want seven.'

'Then seven it will be.'

'If you are mocking me, po-et, I will cut out your heart.'

Sieben chuckled. 'No mockery, Niobe. You are the greatest treasure I ever found.'

Sitting up she looked around the large hospital. 'Everyone is sleeping,' she said suddenly.

'Yes.'

'I think some must have died.'

'I don't believe so,' he told her. 'In fact I am sure that is not the case – just as I am sure none will wake for several hours. So let us return to your earlier offer.'

'Now you want love-making?'

'Indeed I do. Maybe for the first time in my life.'

Master Sergeant Jomil pressed his thick fingers to the cut on his face, trying to stem the flow of blood. Sweat trickled into the shallow wound, the salt stinging him, and he cursed. 'You are slowing down, Jomil,' said Premian.

'Little bastard almost took my eye out . . . sir,' he added.

The bodies of the Nadir defenders were dragged from the rocks and laid in a line away from the pool. The fourteen Gothir dead had been wrapped in their cloaks, the bodies of the six slain Lancers tied across the saddles of their mounts, the infantry buried where they had fallen.

'By the Blood of Missael, they put up a fight, didn't they, sir?' said Jomil.

Premian nodded. 'They were fighting for pride and love of land. There is no greater motivation.' Premian himself had led the charge up the slope, while the infantry stormed the rocks. Weight of numbers had carried the day, but the Nadir had fought well. 'You'll need stitches in that face wound. I'll attend to it presently.'

'Thank you, sir,' replied Jomil, without enthusiasm.

Premian grinned at him. 'How is it that a man can face swords, axes, arrows and spears without flinching, yet be terrified of a small needle and a length of thread?'

'I get to whack the buggers with the swords and axes,' said

Jomil. Premian laughed aloud, then moved to the poolside. The water was deep, clear and cool. Kneeling, he cupped his hands and drank deeply, then rising, he walked to the line of Nadir dead. Eighteen men, some of them little more than boys. Anger churned inside him: what a wasted exercise this was. What a futile little war! Two thousand highly trained Gothir soldiers marching through a wasteland to sack a Shrine.

Yet something was wrong, Premian could feel it. An invisible worry nagged at his subconscious. An infantry soldier approached him and saluted. The man had a bloody bandage around his scalp.

'Can we start cook-fires, sir?' he asked.

'Yes, but move further into the rocks. I don't want the smoke to spook the wagon horses when they arrive. It'll be hard enough getting them up the slope.'

'Yes, sir.'

Premian walked to his horse and took needle and thread from his saddle-bag. Jomil saw him and cursed under his breath. Only two hours past dawn, and already the heat was formidable, radiating from the red rocks. Premian knelt by Jomil's side and eased the flap of skin into place over his right cheekbone. Expertly he stitched the wound. 'There,' he said, at last, 'now you'll have a fine scar to bewitch the ladies.'

'I already have more than enough scars to brag of,' grumbled Jomil. Then he grinned. 'You remember that battle outside Lincairn Pass, sir?'

'Yes. You received an unfortunate wound, I recall.'

'I don't know about unfortunate. The ladies love the story about that one. Not sure why.'

'Buttock wounds are always a source of great merriment,' said Premian. 'As I recall, you were awarded forty gold crowns for bravery. Did you save any of it?'

'Not a copper of it. I spent most of it on strong drink, fat women and gambling. The rest I wasted.' Premian glanced back at the Nadir dead. 'Something bothering you, sir?' asked Jomil.

'Yes . . . but I don't know what.'

'You expected there to be more of them, sir?'

'Perhaps a few.' Premian strolled to the line of dead warriors, then called out to a young Gothir Lancer. The man ran to his side. 'You were involved in the first attack. Which of these is the leader?' The Lancer gazed down at all the faces.

'It is hard to say, sir. They all look alike to me, vomit-coloured and slant-eyed.'

'Yes, yes,' said Premian irritably. 'But what do you remember of the man?'

'He had a white scarf over his head. Oh . . . and rotting teeth. I remember that. They were yellow and black. Vile.'

'Check the teeth of the dead,' ordered Premian. 'Find him for me.'

'Yes, sir,' replied the man, without enthusiasm.

Moving back to Jomil, he reached out, taking the man's extended hand and hauling him to his feet. 'Time to work, sergeant,' he said. 'Get the infantry out on the slope. I want all the boulders pushed from the trail. We've fourteen wagons on the way, and it will be bad enough trying to get them up the slope without needing to negotiate them through a maze of scattered rocks.'

'Yes, sir.'

The Lancer returned from his examination of the corpses. 'He's not there, sir; he must have run off.'

'Run off? A man who would leap from rock twenty feet high and launch himself into a group of Lancers? A man who could inspire his warriors to die for him? Run off? That is most unlikely. If he is not here then . . . sweet Karna!' Premian swung on Jomil. 'The wagons; he has gone after the wagons!'

'He can't have more than a handful of men,' argued Jomil. 'There are fourteen drivers, tough and armed.'

Premian ran to his horse and stepped into the saddle. Calling out to two of his officers, he ordered them to gather their companies and follow him. Kicking the horse into a run, he left the pool and galloped out on to the slope. As he breasted the rise he saw the smoke more than a mile to the south. At full gallop he pushed the gelding hard. Behind him came fifty Lancers.

It was a matter of minutes before they rounded a bend in the trail and saw the burning wagons. The horses had been cut free, and the bodies of several of the drivers could be seen with arrows jutting from their chests. Premian dragged his exhausted mount to a halt and swiftly surveyed the scene. Smoke was billowing around the area, stinging the eyes. Five wagons were burning.

Suddenly he saw a man with a blazing torch run through the smoke. He was wearing a white head-scarf. 'Take him!' bellowed Premian, kicking his horse forward. The Lancers swept out around him, riding through the oily smoke.

A small group of Nadir warriors were desperately trying to fire the remaining wagons. As the thunder of hoofbeats reached them over the roaring of the flames they dropped their torches and ran for their ponies.

The Lancers tore into them, cutting them down.

Premian swung his horse, just as something dark came launching at him from a blazing wagon. He instinctively ducked as a white-scarfed Nadir warrior cannoned into him, sending him hurtling from the saddle. They hit hard and Premian rolled, scrabbling for his sword. But the man ignored him and, taking hold of the saddle pommel, vaulted to the gelding's back. Drawing his sabre the Nadir charged the Lancers, hacking and cutting. One man fell from his mount with his throat slashed open, a second pitched to his left as the flickering blade pierced his face. A lance ripped into the Nadir's back, half lifting him from the saddle. Twisting savagely, he tried to reach the Lancer. Another soldier heeled his horse forward, cleaving his longsword into the man's shoulder. The Nadir, dying now, sent one last lunge at the sword-wielder, the blade piercing his arm. Then he sagged to his right. The gelding reared, throwing him to the ground with the lance still embedded deep in his back. He struggled to rise and groped for his fallen sabre; blood was bubbling from his mouth and his legs were unsteady. A rider closed in on him, but he lashed out, his sword cutting the horse's flanks. 'Get back from him!' shouted Premian. 'He's dying.'

The Nadir staggered and turned towards Premian. 'Nadir we!' he shouted.

A Lancer spurred his horse forward and slashed his sword down at the man. The Nadir ducked under the blow and leapt forward to grab the Lancer's cloak, dragging him down into the path of his own sabre which sliced up into the man's belly. The Lancer screamed and pitched from the saddle. Both men fell to the ground. Soldiers leapt from their mounts and surrounded the fallen Nadir, hacking and cleaving at his body.

Premian ran forward. 'Get back, you fools!' he yelled. 'Save the wagons!'

Using their cloaks, the Lancers beat at the flames, but it was useless. The dry timbers had caught now and the fires raged on, unstoppable. Premian ordered the five remaining wagons pulled clear, then sent out riders to gather the wagon horses which, having picked up the scent of water, were walking slowly towards the pool. Ten of the drivers were also found, hiding in a gully, and were brought before Premian. 'You ran,' he said, 'from seven Nadir warriors. Now half our wagons are gone. You have put the entire army in peril by your cowardice.'

'They came screaming out of the steppes, in a cloud of dust,' argued one man. 'We thought there was an army of them.'

'You will take your places on the remaining wagons, see them loaded and the water delivered back to the camp. Once there, you will face the Lord Gargan. I don't doubt your backs will feel the weight of the lash. Now get out of my sight!'

Swinging away from them, Premian thought through the mathematics of the situation. Five wagons with eight barrels each. Some fifteen gallons could be stored in each barrel. In these conditions a fighting man needed, minimally, around two pints of water per day. By this rough estimate he calculated that one barrel could supply sixty men with water. Forty barrels would be barely enough for the men, let alone the horses. And horses for only one day . . . From now on there would need to be a constant shuttle between the camp and the pool.

Still, he reasoned, it could have been worse. Had he not reacted when he did, all the wagons would have been lost. But the thought did not cheer him. Had he left a guard force with them in the first place, the Nadir attack would have failed.

His thinking was interrupted by the sound of savage laughter and the hacking of sword-blades. The white-scarfed Nadir leader had been beheaded and dismembered. Furious, Premian ran into the jeering group. 'Stand to attention!' he bellowed, and the men shuffled nervously into a line. 'How dare you?' stormed Premian. 'How dare you behave like savages? Can you have any idea what you look like at this moment? Would any of you wish to be seen by your loved ones, prancing about and waving the limbs of a dead warrior above your heads. You are Gothir! We leave this . . . barbarity to lesser races.'

'Permission to speak, sir?' asked a lean soldier.

'Spit it out.'

'Well, the Lord Gargan said all Nadir were to have their hands cut off, didn't he, sir?'

'That was a threat made to frighten the Nadir, who believe that if they lose a limb they will be devoid of that limb throughout eternity. It was not a threat, I believe, that the Lord Gargan intends to carry out in reality. I may be wrong in this. But here and now, I am in command. You will dig a grave for that man, and place his limbs alongside him. He was my enemy, but he was brave and he gave his life for a cause he believed in. He will be buried whole. Am I understood?'

The men nodded. 'Then get to it.'

Jomil approached Premian and the two walked away from the surly group. 'That wasn't wise, sir,' said Jomil, keeping his voice low. 'You'll get the name of a Nadir-lover. Word'll spread that you're soft on the enemy.'

'It doesn't matter a damn, my friend. I shall be resigning my commission the moment this battle is over.'

'That's as maybe, sir – but, if you'll pardon my bluntness, I don't think the Lord Gargan was making an idle threat. And I don't want to see him putting you on trial for disobedience.'

Premian smiled and looked into the old soldier's grizzled face. 'You are a fine friend, Jomil. I value you highly. But my father told me never to be a part of anything that lacked honour. He once said to me that there was no greater satisfaction for a man than to be able to look in a mirror while shaving, and be proud of what he saw. At this moment I am not proud.'

'I think you ought to be,' said Jomil softly.

It was three hours after noon and still the enemy had not attacked. The foot soldiers were sitting in the camp, many of them using their cloaks and swords to form screens against the harsh heat of the blazing sun. The horses of the Lancers were picketed to the west. Most stood forlornly with heads down, others had sunk to the ground for want of water.

Shading his eyes, Druss saw the five water wagons returning and gave a low curse under his breath. Gothir soldiers ran to the wagons, surrounding them.

Talisman climbed to the ramparts and stood beside Druss. 'I should have sent more men with Kzun,' he said.

Druss shrugged. 'As I recall, they set out last night with fourteen wagons. Your man did well. There'll be scarce enough water in those wagons and they'll not last a day. The horses alone need more than those wagons will supply.'

'You've been in sieges before?' asked Talisman.

'Aye, laddie. Too many.'

'Then what is your appraisal?'

'I think they'll throw everything at us. They can't play a waiting game. They have no engineers to mine the walls; they have no battering ram to smash the gates. I think they'll send in every man they have, Lancers and foot. They'll storm this wall by sheer weight of numbers.'

'I think not,' said Talisman. 'It is my belief that they will try a three-pronged attack. This western wall will take the brunt, but I think they will also try to breach the gates, and one other wall. They will try to stretch us. Only if that fails will they risk the final assault.'

'We'll know soon enough,' said Druss. 'If they do what you surmise, how will you combat it?'

Talisman smiled wearily. 'Our options are limited, Druss. We just hold as best we can.'

Druss shook his head. 'You've got to assume some of their soldiers will get through to the ramparts, and perhaps down into the compound itself. Our reaction to that will be crucial. Gut instinct tells a man to tackle the nearest enemy, but in that situation such instincts are liable to prove fatal. If a wall is breached the first option must be to seal the breach. The men already inside are a secondary consideration.'

'What do you suggest?'

'You already have a small reserve force ready to fill in the gaps. Draw more men to it, and split them into two groups. If the enemy take a section of wall, one group must join the defenders to win it back. The second group can attack those who have penetrated inside. We only have one outer perimeter. There is nowhere to fall back to, so these ramparts must be held. No defender must leave his post on them, no matter what he sees in the compound below. The walls, Talisman! Nothing else matters.'

The young Nadir nodded. 'I take your point, axeman. It will be relayed to the men. Did you know that the tribes have been drawing lots to see which group should have the privilege of standing beside you today?'

Druss chuckled. 'So that's what they were doing? Who did I get?'

'The Sky Riders. They are greatly pleased. It is rare for a *gajin* to be so popular.'

'You think so?' Druss hefted his axe. 'I'm usually popular at times like this. Could be the song of the soldier, could it not? When war and the fear of war comes upon people, they revere the warrior. Once it has passed he is forgotten, or reviled. It never changes.'

'You don't sound bitter about it,' Talisman pointed out.

'I don't get bitter at the falling of the sun, or the cold north

288

wind. They are facts of life. I once took part in a raid that rescued a score of rich farmers from Sathuli tribesmen. Oh, they waxed eloquent about how heroic we were, how they would honour us always. There was a young soldier with us who lost an arm that day. He was from their town. Within six months he and his family had almost starved to death. Facts of life.'

'And did they die?'

'No. I went back to the Sentran Plain and spoke to the leader of the farmers. Reminded him of his obligations.'

'I am not surprised that he listened,' said Talisman, looking into Druss's cold blue eyes. 'But you will not find that with us. Nadir memories are long. You are the Deathwalker; your legend will live on with us.'

'Legends. Pah! I have enough of legends. If I had half the courage of a farmer I would be at home with my wife, looking after my lands.'

'You have no sons?'

'None. Nor will have,' said Druss coldly. 'No. All I will leave behind are those damned legends.'

'Some men would die for your fame.'

'A lot of men have,' observed Druss.

The two warriors stood in silence for a while watching the Gothir surrounding the water wagons. 'You regret being here?' Talisman asked.

'I try not to regret anything,' replied Druss. 'There's no point in it.' Twenty Sky Rider tribesmen trooped up to the ramparts, standing by quietly as the two men spoke. Druss glanced at the first, a hawk-faced young man with brown eyes. 'Were you one of those who leapt the chasm?' he asked him.

The man gave a wide grin and nodded.

'I would like to hear about that,' said Druss. 'Later, when we've seen off the Gothir, you can tell me of it.'

'I shall, Deathwalker.'

'Good. Now gather round, my boys, and I'll give you a few tips about siege warfare.'

Talisman left the ramparts. As he reached the compound below he could hear laughter coming from the men around Druss. Lin-tse joined him. 'I should be there, Talisman. With my men on the wall.'

'No.' Talisman told him to pick forty warriors from among the other tribes. 'You will lead the first group, Gorkai the second.' Then he outlined Druss's battle plan for a wall breach defence.

A young warrior moved past them, heading for the north wall. Talisman called him back. 'What is your name?' he asked.

'Shi-da, general.'

'You were a friend of Quing-chin's?'

'I was.'

'I saw you wounded yesterday – in the belly and chest.'

'It was not as deep as I feared, general. The surgeon has healed me. I can fight.'

'There is no pain?'

'Aye, there is pain. The stitches are tight. But I will stand with the Fleet Ponies, general.'

'Let me see the wound,' said Talisman, leading the man to the shade and sitting him on the table set there. Shi-da doffed his goatskin jerkin. There was blood on the bandage wrapped around his waist. The young warrior started to unravel it but Talisman stopped him.

'The wound is bound well. Do not disturb it. Fight well today, Shi-da.'

The young man nodded, his face grim, then walked away.

'What was that about?' asked Lin-tse.

'Every one of the wounded is back on the walls today,' said Talisman. 'Truly the poet is a fine surgeon. I saw Shi-da struck – I would have sworn the blade passed almost all the way through him.'

'You think he has found the Eyes of Alchazzar?' whispered Lin-tse.

'If he has, then I will take them.'

'I thought you said that Druss needed them?'

'Druss is a fighting man I admire above all others. But the Eyes belong to the Nadir. They are part of our destiny and I cannot allow them to be taken by *gajin*.'

Lin-tse laid his hand on Talisman's arm. 'If we survive here, my brother, and if Sieben has the jewels, you know what will happen if you try to take them. Druss will fight for them. He is not a man to be frightened by weight of numbers. We will have to kill him.'

'Then we will kill him,' said Talisman, 'though it would break my heart to do so.'

Talisman poured water from a stone jug, drained the clay cup and walked away with Lin-tse to the newly built wall around the gates. Niobe stepped from the shadows behind them and made her way to the hospital.

Sieben was sitting with Zhusai. They were laughing together, and Niobe was surprised to find a ripple of anger within herself at the sight of them. The Chiatze woman was slim and beautiful, her clothes of white silk adorned with mother of pearl. Niobe was still wearing Sieben's blue silk shirt, but it was stained now with the blood of the wounded and with sweat from her own tired body. Sieben saw her, and a broad smile showed on his handsome face. He walked across the deserted room and hugged her. 'You are a vision,' he said, kissing her.

'Why is she here?' asked Niobe.

'She has offered to help with the wounded. Come, say hello.'

Taking Niobe by the hand, he led her to Zhusai. The Chiatze woman looked nervous under Niobe's piercing gaze as Sieben introduced them.

'I should have offered help before,' said Zhusai to Niobe. 'Please forgive me.'

Niobe shrugged. 'We need no help. The po-et is very skilled.'

'I am sure that he is. But I know much of the tending of wounds.'

'She will be valuable,' put in Sieben.

'I do not want her here,' said Niobe.

Sieben was surprised, but he masked it and turned to Zhusai. 'Perhaps, my lady, you should change your clothes. Blood will ruin that fine silk. You can return to us when the battle has started.'

Zhusai gave a short bow of her head and walked from the room.

'What is the matter with you?' Sieben asked Niobe. 'Are you jealous, my dove?'

'I am not a dove. And there is no jealousy. Do you not know why she is here?'

'To help. That is what she said.'

'You are in much danger, po-et.'

'From her? I do not think so.'

'Not just from her, fool. Every Nadir knows the story of the Eyes of Alchazzar, the purple jewels of power. Talisman thinks you have found them and so do I. There were men dying here yesterday who are now standing on the walls.'

'Nonsense. They were . . .'

'You don't lie to me!' she snapped. 'I hear Talisman. He says that if you have the jewels he will take them, he says that they will kill Druss if he interferes. You give jewels to Talisman – then you are safe.'

Sieben sat down on the newly scrubbed table. 'I can't do that, my love. Druss made a promise to a dying man, and Druss is a man who lives by his word. You understand? But I won't keep them, I promise you that. If we survive here – which is doubtful at best – I will take them to Gulgothir and heal Druss's friend. Then I will return them to Talisman.'

'He will not allow it. That is why he sent the woman; she will watch you like a snake. You heal no more dying men, po-et.'

'I have to. That is what the power is for.'

'This is no time to be weak. Men die in battle. They go to the earth, they feed the land. You understand?' She looked deep into his blue eyes and knew she was not convincing him. 'Fool! Fool!' she said. 'Very well. Keep them alive. But do not heal them so much that they walk from here. You hear what I say?'

'I do, Niobe. And you are right. I can't risk Druss being killed for them.' He smiled and, reaching out, pushed his fingers through her dark hair. 'I love you. You are the light in my life.'

'And you are a trouble to me,' she said. 'You are no warrior, and you are soft like a puppy. I should have no feelings for a man like you.'

'But you do, don't you?' he said, drawing her in to an embrace. 'Tell me!'

'No.'

'You are still angry with me?'

'Yes.'

'Then kiss me and feel it fade.'

'I don't want it to fade,' she said, pulling away.

Outside a battle horn sounded. 'It begins again,' sighed Sieben.

The Gothir infantry formed into three groups of about two hundred men. Druss watched them carefully. Only two of the groups contained ladder-bearers. 'The third group is going for the gates,' he said, to no-one in particular.

Behind the infantry more than five hundred Lancers waited on foot in two lines, their lances discarded and their sabres in their hands. A slow drumbeat sounded and the army moved forward, slowly. Druss could feel the fear in the men around him.

'Don't think of numbers,' said Druss, 'all that counts is the number of ladders – and they have fewer than thirty. Only thirty men can reach the wall at any time; the rest will be milling around below, useless. Never be cowed by numbers alone.'

'Do you not know fear, axeman?' asked Nuang Xuan.

Druss turned and grinned. 'What are you doing here, old man? You are wounded.'

'I am as tough as a wolf, as strong as a bear. How close am I to my hundred?'

'By my reckoning you need more than ninety more.'

'Pah, you obviously miscounted.'

'Stay close to me, Nuang,' said Druss softly. 'But not too close.'

'I will be here at day's end, and the Gothir dead will be a mountain,' promised Nuang.

Archers ran through the enemy lines sending scores of shafts at the defenders, who ducked down below the battlements. No-one was struck. The drum-beat quickened, and Druss could hear the sound of running men drowning out the drums. Ladders clattered against the wall and a man to Druss's left started to rise but Druss dragged him down. 'Not yet, laddie. The archers are waiting.'

The warrior blinked nervously. Druss knelt for ten more heart-beats, then launched himself upright, the great axe shining in the sunlight. As he reared up, a Gothir warrior reached the top of the ladder and Snaga thundered down to smash the man's skull.

'Climb and die!' roared Druss, sending a reverse cut into the bearded face of a second warrior.

All around him the Nadir were hacking and slashing at the attackers. Two Gothir soldiers reached the ramparts, but were cut down instantly. A Nadir warrior fell with an arrow jutting from his temple.

On the wall above the gate, Talisman watched as Druss and the Sky Riders fought to contain the western ramparts. The second Gothir force had swung to the north wall, where Bartsai and his Curved Horn were battling to hold them.

Axes smashed into the gates, splintering the ancient wood. Nadir defenders threw rocks down upon the enemy soldiers milling below, but the sounds of tearing wood continued.

'Be ready!' Talisman warned the men of the Fleet Ponies. Notching arrows to their bows, they knelt on the ramparts and the newly built curved wall inside the gates. In that moment Talisman felt a fierce pride surge through him. These men were Nadir, his people! And they were fighting together against the common enemy. This is how it should be, thought the young man. No more slavelike obedience to the cursed *gajin*. No more running from the threat of their Lancers, their punitive raids, their slaughters.

Suddenly the gates were breached and scores of men pushed

through, only to be confronted by an eight-foot wall.

'Now! Now! Now!' yelled Talisman. Arrows lanced into the crowded mass below. So closely packed were they, with others pushing from behind, that few Gothir could raise their shields. Shafts tore into them and rocks pelted them. As Talisman strained to lift a jagged boulder, two men helped him and they pitched the stone over the ramparts and down into the death pit. Panicked now, the Gothir fought to retreat, trampling their own wounded.

Talisman gazed down with grim satisfaction at the thirty or more bodies. An arrow flashed past his face, and he ducked. Enemy archers were now crowding around the breached gates, shooting up at the defenders. Two Nadir warriors fell, their chests pierced.

'Stay down!' shouted Talisman. As ladders suddenly clattered against the wall behind him, he swore. With archers shooting at them from the rear, and an assault from the front, the section would be hard to hold.

Throwing himself flat, Talisman squirmed to the edge of the ramparts, calling down to the bowmen on the curved wall. 'Ten of you pin down the archers,' he commanded. 'The rest to me!'

Ignoring the threat of arrows, Talisman surged upright and drew his sabre. Three men appeared at the ramparts. Leaping forward, he plunged his sabre into the leading man's face, spearing his open mouth.

In the compound below, Gorkai waited with twenty men. Sweat dripped from his face as he watched Talisman and the Fleet Ponies men battling against the warriors swarming over the ramparts. 'I should go to him,' he told Lin-tse.

'Not yet, brother. Stand firm.'

On the north wall, Bartsai and his men fell back as the Lancers gained the ramparts. With an awful suddenness the defending line broke and a dozen enemy soldiers broke clear, swarming down the rampart steps and into the compound.

Lin-tse and his men charged to meet them. Gorkai transferred his sabre to his left hand and wiped his sweating right on his leggings. The men of the Curved Horn were on the verge of breaking, and Gorkai prepared himself to rush to their aid.

At that moment, seeing the danger, Druss ran along the ramparts of the western wall and leapt the yawning gap to the northern ramparts, his huge form crashing into the attackers and scattering them. The silver blades of his axe cut into the enemy ranks. His sudden appearance galvanized the Curved Horn into renewed ferocity, and the Gothir were forced back.

Lin-tse had lost eight men, but the twelve Gothir Lancers were reduced now to four, fighting in two pairs back to back. Two more Nadir fell before Lin-tse and his men cut the Lancers down.

Gorkai swung to watch Talisman. The line was holding, but more than ten Nadir were dead and the attack was no more than minutes old. Some wounded men were making their way to the hospital, others lay where they had fallen, trying to stop the flow of blood with their hands.

Lin-tse and the remainder of his men moved back to stand alongside Gorkai's group. The tall Nadir chief glanced at Gorkai. Blood was flowing from a wound in his face. 'You can tackle the next breach,' he said, forcing a smile.

Gorkai did not have long to wait. Talisman's men were swept aside as a section of the battlements gave way, and Talisman himself took a spear thrust into the chest. Gorkai screamed a battle cry and led his men forward, hurtling up the rampart steps two at a time. Talisman gutted the spearman, dragged the broken spear from his chest and then fell. Gorkai leapt across his body as more Gothir soldiers made it to the ramparts.

Talisman's vision was blurring, and he felt a great dizziness sweep over him. I cannot die, he thought. Not now! Struggling to his knees, he scrabbled for his sabre. Darkness loomed but he fought against it.

Gorkai and his men re-took the battlements, forcing the Gothir back. Blood was bubbling from Talisman's chest, and he knew a lung was punctured. Two men took him by the arms, hauling him to his feet. 'Get him to the surgeon!' ordered Gorkai.

Talisman was half helped, half carried to the hospital building. He heard Zhusai cry out as he was brought in. Desperately trying to focus, he saw the face of Sieben above him . . . then he passed out.

The Gothir had given up their assault on the northern wall and Druss, his helm struck from his head, jumped the gap in the ramparts and rejoined the Fleet Ponies. Nuang Xuan, wounded again in the chest and arms, was sitting slumped by the wall.

The Gothir fell back.

Druss knelt down by the old Nadir leader. 'How goes it?' he asked.

'More than a hundred,' said Nuang. 'I think I have killed all the Gothir there are, and what you see outside are merely ghosts.'

Druss rose and scanned the defences. The north wall had only eighteen defenders still standing. Around him on the western ramparts there were some twenty-five Sky Riders. Above the gates he counted thirty, including Talisman's man, Gorkai. In the compound below Lin-tse had fewer than a dozen men. Druss tried to add the numbers together, but lost them in a sea of weariness. Taking a deep breath, he re-counted.

Fewer than a hundred defenders were visible to him, but the bodies of Nadir dead lay everywhere. He saw the Curved Horn leader Bartsai lying on the ground below the ramparts, three dead Gothir around his corpse.

'You are bleeding, Deathwalker,' said a Sky Rider.

'It is nothing,' replied Druss, recognizing the hawk-faced young man he had spoken to earlier.

'Take off your jerkin,' said the youngster.

Druss groaned as he eased the ripped and near ruined leather from his huge frame. He had been cut four times around the shoulders and upper arms, but there was a deeper wound under his right shoulder-blade. Blood had pooled around his belt.

'You need stitches, hey,' the Nadir told him. 'Or you bleed to death.'

Druss leaned on the ramparts and stared down at the Gothir forces, who had moved back out of bowshot.

'Take the old man with you,' said the Nadir, grinning. 'He fights so well he shames us all.'

Druss forced a grin and hauled Nuang Xuan to his feet. 'Walk with me a while, old man.' Turning to the Nadir warrior, he said, 'I'll be back before you know it.'

Talisman felt the pain of his wounds recede, and found himself lying on a bare hillside under a grey sky. His heart hammered in panic as he recognized the landscape of the Void. 'You are not dead,' came a calm voice from close by. Talisman sat up, and saw the little sorcerer Shaoshad sitting beside a flickering blaze. The tall figure of Shul-sen stood beside him, her silver cloak gleaming in the firelight.

'Then why am I here?' he asked.

'To learn,' said Shul-sen. 'When Oshikai and I came to the land of the steppes we were touched by its beauty, but more than this we were called by its magic. Every stone carried it, every plant grew with it. Elemental power radiated from the mountains, and flowed in the streams. The Gods of Stone and Water, we called them. You know what gives birth to this magic, Talisman?'

'No.'

'Life and death. The life forces of millions of men and animals, insects and plants. Each life comes from the land, then returns to the land. It is a circle of harmony.'

'What has this to do with me?'

'Not so much with you, my boy, as with me,' put in Shaoshad. 'I was one of the Three who robbed the land of its magic. We drew it forth and invested it in the Eyes of Alchazzar; we made the land barren; we sought to redirect the random magnificence of the energy, to focus it on behalf of the Nadir. In doing so we destroyed the link between the Nadir and the Gods of Stone and Water. Our people became increasingly nomadic, feeling no love for the earth beneath their feet or the mountains that towered above them. They became split and divided, isolated from one another.'

'Why are you telling me this?' asked Talisman.

'Why do you think?' responded Shul-sen.

'I do not have the Eyes. I thought the poet might, but I think now he is merely a skilled surgeon.'

'If you had them, Talisman, would you do what is right for the land?' asked Shaoshad.

'And what is that?'

'Return to it what was stolen.'

'Give up the power of the Eyes? With them I could bring all the tribes together into one unstoppable army.'

'Perhaps,' admitted Shul-sen, 'but without love of land, what would they fight for? Plunder and rape, revenge and murder? And this army you speak of – it would be filled with men whose lives are but a fraction of a beat in the heart of eternity. The land is immortal. Give it back its magic and it will repay you a thousandfold. It will give you the Uniter you dream of, it will give you Ulric.'

'And how do I do this?' he whispered.

'It is not as deep as you thought,' said Sieben as Druss lay on the table, feeling the poet's fingers probing at the wound in his back. Indeed there was little pain now, except from the ragged stitches.

'You are a revelation to me,' said Druss, grunting as he sat up, the stitches pulling tight. 'Who would have thought it?'

'Who indeed? How is it going out there?'

'The big attack is to come . . . soon,' answered Druss. 'If we hold that off . . .' His voice tailed away.

'We are going to lose, aren't we?' asked Sieben.

'I think so, poet – though it hurts me to say it. Is Talisman dead?'

'No, he is sleeping. His wounds were not as bad as we feared.'

'I'd better get back to the wall.' Druss stretched his back. 'Amazing,' he said. 'I feel as if I've slept for eight hours. I can feel the strength flowing through me. Those poultices you use have great power – I'd be interested to know what's in them.'

'Me too. Niobe prepares them.'

Druss shrugged on his jerkin and buckled his belt. 'I am sorry I brought you to this,' he said.

'I'm a free man who makes his own decisions,' Sieben told him, 'and I am not sorry at all. I met Niobe. Sweet Heaven, Druss, but I love that woman!'

'You love all women,' said Druss.

'No. Truly, this is different. And what is more incredible is that, given the choice, I would not change a single thing. To die not having known true love must be terrible.'

Nuang approached them. 'Are you ready, axeman?'

'You are a tough old goat,' Druss told him, and together they returned to the battlements. Sieben watched them for a moment, then moved back among the wounded men. He caught Niobe's eye and smiled as she pointed to where Zhusai was sitting beside Talisman, holding the sleeping man's hand. The Chiatze girl was weeping. Sieben crossed the room, settling down beside her.

'He will live,' he told her softly.

She nodded dumbly.

'I promise you,' he said, gently laying his hand on Talisman's chest.

The Nadir warrior stirred, and opened his eyes. 'Zhusai . . .?' he whispered.

'Yes, my love.'

He groaned and struggled to rise. Sieben helped him to his feet. 'What is happening?' he asked.

'The enemy are gathering for another charge,' said Sieben.

'I must be there.'

'No, you must rest!' insisted Zhusai.

Talisman's dark eyes turned to Sieben. 'Give me more strength,' he said.

The poet shrugged. 'I cannot. You have lost a lot of blood and you are weak.'

'You have the Eyes of Alchazzar.'

'I wish I did, old horse – I'd heal everybody here. By Heaven, I'd even raise the dead.'

Talisman looked closely at him, but Sieben met his stare with blank equanimity. Placing his arm over Zhusai's shoulder, Talisman kissed her cheek. 'Help me to the wall, my wife,' he said. 'We will stand upon it together.'

As they moved off, Sieben heard a small voice whisper in his ear. *'Go with them.'* He swung round, but there was no-one close. The poet shuddered, and stood where he was. *'Trust me, my boy,'* came the voice of Shaoshad.

Sieben walked out into the sunlight, then ran to catch Talisman and the woman. Taking the warrior's other arm he helped him up the rampart steps to the western wall.

'Well, they're gathering again,' muttered Druss.

On the plain beyond, the Gothir were once more in fighting ranks, waiting for the drum-beat signal. All along the wall weary Nadir defenders also waited, swords ready.

'Must be more than a thousand of them,' said Sieben, feeling the onset of terror.

The drum-beat sounded, and the Gothir army began to move.

Zhusai stiffened, and drew in a sharp breath. *'Put your hand on her shoulder,'* ordered Shaoshad. When Sieben reached out and gently touched Zhusai, he felt the power of the stones flow from him, like a dam bursting. She released her hold on Talisman and moved to the ramparts.

'What are you doing, Zhusai?' hissed Talisman.

She turned to him and gave a dazzling smile. 'She will return,' said the voice of Shul-sen.

The woman climbed to the top of the ramparts and raised her arms. Overhead the sun – brilliant in a clear blue sky – shone down now on the woman in blood-stained clothes. The wind picked up, stirring her raven-dark hair. Clouds began to form with astonishing speed – small white puffballs that swelled and grew, darkening down and obscuring the sun. The wind roared, buffeting the defenders. Blacker and blacker grew the sky, then a clap of thunder burst above the Shrine. Lightning forked down, exploding in the midst of the Gothir army. Several men were hurled from their feet. Jagged spears of dazzling light flashed into the enemy force, while thunder rolled across the heavens.

The Gothir broke and ran, but still the lightning tore into them, catapulting men into the air. The fierce wind brought the smell of burning flesh to the stunned defenders. The Gothir horses uprooted their picket ropes and galloped away. On the plain men were tearing off their armour and hurling aside their weapons – to no avail it seemed. Sieben saw a man struck, his breastplate exploding. Those close to him were punched to the ground, where their bodies went into spasm.

Then the sun broke through the clouds and the woman in white turned and stepped back to the ramparts. 'My Lord is in Paradise,' she told Talisman. 'This is a debt repaid.' She sagged against Talisman, who held her close.

On the plain more than half the Gothir force was dead, many others suffering terrible burns.

'They'll not fight again,' said Gorkai, as the clouds dispersed.

'No, but *they* will,' muttered Druss, pointing to a line of cavalry breasting the hills and riding down towards the shattered Gothir camp.

Sieben's heart sank as more than a thousand men came into sight, riding in columns of twos.

'Who would have my luck?' said Nuang bitterly.

Chapter Thirteen

Premian rolled to his belly and pushed his blistered hands into the cold mud. Lightning had struck three men close to him. They were unrecognizable now. He staggered to his feet, his legs unsteady and dizziness swamping him. The dead and dying were everywhere, and the living staggered around as if drunk.

Some way to his left Premian saw the Lord Gargan sitting beside his dead horse. The man looked old now, and sat with his head in his hands. Premian had been wearing no armour – Gargan had stripped him of his rank, and had sentenced him to thirty lashes for disobedience – but the lack of metal on his frame had saved him during the lightning storm.

Slowly he made his way to the general. Half of Gargan's face was blistered and black. He looked up as Premian approached, and the younger man had to mask his horror at the sight. Gargan's left eye was gone, and blood flowed from the empty socket.

'All finished,' mumbled the general. 'The savages have won.' Premian knelt by him and took his hand, unable to think of anything to say. 'They murdered my mother,' said Gargan. 'I was five years old. She hid me under some sacking. They raped and murdered her. And I watched. I . . . wanted to help her. Couldn't. Just lay there and wet myself with fear. Then my son . . .' Gargan drew a long shuddering breath. 'Fetch me a sword.'

'You don't need a sword, my Lord. It is over.'

'Over? You think it is over? It will never be over. Them or us, Premian. Now and for ever.' Gargan sagged to his right. Premian

301

caught him and lowered him to the ground. 'I can hear horses,' whispered the general. And he died.

Premian glanced up to see the line of cavalry moving towards him and he stood as they approached. A cavalry general rode up and glanced down at the dead Lord of Larness.

'I had orders for his arrest and immediate execution,' he said. 'It is just as well he is gone. I had a great respect for him.'

'Arrest? On what charge?' Premian asked.

'Who are you?' responded the general.

'Premian, sir.'

'Ah, good. I am also carrying orders for you. You are to take command of the Lancers and return to Gulgothir.' Swinging in his saddle, he surveyed the chaos. 'Your force will not be a large one, I fear. What happened here?'

Swiftly Premian told him. Then: 'Does the attack continue, sir?' he asked.

'The sacking of a Shrine? Great Heavens, no! What an utter waste of good men. I can't think what possessed Gargan to lead such a lunatic venture.'

'I believe he was under orders, sir.'

'All orders are changed now, Premian. We have a new Emperor. The madman is dead – killed by his own Guards. There is sanity once more in Gulgothir.'

'Praise the Source for that,' said Premian, with feeling.

Upon the walls of the Shrine Druss, Talisman and the defenders watched a rider move slowly from the devastated camp. He was wearing no armour, and his silver hair shone in the sunlight.

'Shemak's Balls, it's Majon!' said Sieben. 'He rides that horse with all the grace of a carrot sack.'

'Who is Majon?' asked Talisman, his face grey with the pain of his wounds.

'The Drenai ambassador. Best advise your men not to shoot at him.' Talisman relayed the order as Majon rode closer; his long face was pinched and tight, and Druss could see the fear in the man.

'Ho, Druss!' called Majon. 'I am unarmed. I come as a herald.'

'No-one is going to hurt you, ambassador. We'll lower a rope for you.'

'I am quite comfortable here, thank you,' he replied, his voice shaking.

'Nonsense,' Druss called out. 'Our hospitality is well known, and my friends here would think themselves insulted if you didn't join us.'

A rope was lowered and the ambassador dismounted. Removing his sky-blue cape, which he draped over his saddle, he took hold of the rope and was hauled to the ramparts. Once there Druss introduced him to Talisman. 'He's one of the kings among the Nadir,' said Druss. 'An important man.'

'Delighted to meet you, sir,' said Majon.

'What words do you bring from the enemy?' countered Talisman.

'There are no enemies here, sir,' Majon told him. 'The . . . battle is over. The cavalry force you see before the walls was sent to arrest the renegade Gargan. The general, Cuskar, has asked me to assure you that all hostilities are now at an end, and that the Shrine will not be despoiled by any Gothir soldier. Equally, you and all your men are free to go. Your actions against the renegade Gargan will not be seen as crimes against the new Emperor.'

'New Emperor?' put in Druss.

'Yes, indeed. The madman is dead – killed by two of his Guards. There is a new order now in Gulgothir. The scenes in the city were wonderful to behold, Druss. Dancing and singing in the streets, no less. The new Emperor's government is being led by a minister of rare culture and breeding: his name is Garen-Tsen and it seems he has been working behind the scenes for some time in order to overthrow the God-King. A charming man, with a great understanding of diplomacy. Already we have signed three trade agreements.'

'You mean we won?' said Sieben. 'And we are all going to live?'

'I believe that puts the facts succinctly,' said Majon. 'One small matter, Druss, my friend,' added the ambassador, drawing the axeman away from the others. 'Garen-Tsen asked me to mention the matter of some jewels said to be hidden here.'

'There were no jewels,' said Druss bitterly. 'Just old bones and new deaths.'

'You . . . er . . . searched the coffin, did you?'

'Yes. Nothing. It's all a myth.'

'Ah, well. It matters not, I am sure.' Returning to Talisman, the ambassador bowed again. 'The general Cuskar has brought three surgeons with him. He has asked me to offer you their services for your wounded.'

'We have a good surgeon, but thank the general for his

kindness,' said Talisman. 'In return for such goodwill, do tell the general that if he brings his water wagons to the walls I will see that the barrels are filled.'

Druss and Gorkai lowered Majon to the ground. The ambassador mounted his horse, waved once, then cantered back to the Gothir camp.

Talisman sank back to the ramparts. 'We won,' he said.

'That we did, laddie. But only just.'

Talisman held out his hand. 'You are a man among men, Deathwalker,' he said. 'On behalf of my people, I thank you.'

'You should get back to the hospital,' said Druss, 'and let our *fine* surgeon tend to you.'

Talisman smiled and, with the support of Zhusai and Gorkai, made his way down the rampart steps. In the compound below the Nadir had formed into loose groups, talking excitedly about the battle. Lin-tse watched them dispassionately, but in his eyes there was sadness.

'What is wrong?' asked Sieben.

'Nothing a *gajin* could see,' said the warrior, walking away.

'What was he talking about, Druss?'

'They are all with their own tribesmen. The mixing has ended. They came together for this one battle, and now they are drawing apart again – the way of the Nadir perhaps.' Druss sighed. 'Ah, but I am weary, poet. I need to see Rowena again, to breathe the air of the mountains. By Heavens, it would be nice to smell the sweet breeze coming over the long grass and the pine meadows.'

'It would indeed, Druss, old horse.'

'First we must return to Gulgothir. I want to see Klay. We'll rest for a couple of hours, then ride out.'

Sieben nodded. 'Niobe is coming with us. I'm going to marry her, Druss – give her babies and an iron fire-bucket!'

Druss chuckled. 'I expect it will be in that order.'

Sieben returned to the hospital where Talisman was sleeping soundly. In the small office he found a strip of parchment, a quill pen and an inkwell that was almost dry. Adding a little water to the ink, he penned a short message upon the parchment. When the ink was dry he folded the parchment into four and walked back into the larger room. Kneeling by Talisman, he slid the message under a fold of the bandage around his chest and used the power of the Eyes of Alchazzar to heal the Nadir leader.

One by one he visited all the wounded, leaving them all asleep, their wounds vanished.

At the last he stood in the doorway and looked back, satisfied. Many men had died defending this Shrine, but there were others, Talisman among them, who would have died had it not been for him. The thought pleased the poet.

He glanced up at the battlements, where Druss was stretched out asleep. Sieben climbed the rampart steps and healed him also.

Lin-tse and his Sky Riders were dismantling the wall around the gates. Sieben sat upon the walls watching them. The sky was a glorious blue, and even the hot breeze tasted good upon the tongue.

I am alive, he thought. Alive and in love. If there is a better feeling in all the world, I have yet to taste of it, he decided.

Chapter Fourteen

Okar, the fat gatekeeper at the hospice, cursed as the pounding on the front door continued. Rolling from his pallet bed, he pulled on his leggings, stumbled along the corridor and dragged back the bolts. 'Be quiet!' he ordered, as he dragged open the thick door. 'There are sick people here trying to sleep.'

A huge man with a thick black beard stepped into the doorway, seized him by the arms and hoisted him into the air. 'They won't be sick for much longer,' he said, with a wide grin. Okar was not a small man, but the giant lifted him and moved him aside as if he were a child.

'You must forgive my friend,' said a slim, handsome man, 'but he is very excitable.'

A young woman followed the two men inside. She was Nadir, and strikingly attractive.

'Where do you think you are going?' asked Okar, as the group made their way up the stairs. They did not reply, and he hurried after them. The Abbot was waiting at the top of the stairs; still in his night robe, a candle-holder in his hand, he blocked their way.

'What is the meaning of this intrusion?' asked the Abbot sternly.

'We've come to heal our friend, Father Abbot,' said the giant. 'I kept my promise.'

Okar waited for the harsh words that he was sure would follow. But the Abbot stood in silence for a moment, his expression unreadable in the flickering candle-light. 'Follow me,' he said softly, 'and please be silent.'

The Abbot led the way through the first ward, and on to a small office in the western part of the building. Lighting two lanterns, he sat down at a desk littered with papers. 'Now explain,' he said.

The giant spoke first. 'We found the healing stones, Father. And they work! By all that's holy, they work! Now take us to Klay.'

'That is not possible,' the Abbot told him, and he sighed. 'Klay passed from this life three days after you left. He is buried in a simple grave behind the gardens. A stone has been fashioned for him. I am truly sorry.'

'He promised me,' said Druss. 'He promised me he would live until my return.'

'It was a promise he could not keep,' said the Abbot. 'The bolt that struck him was tainted with some vile substance and gangrene set in almost immediately. No man could have withstood the deadly effect.'

'I can't believe it,' whispered Druss. 'I have the stones!'

'Why is it so hard for you warriors to believe?' snapped the Abbot. 'You think the world revolves around your desires. Do you honestly believe that nature and the laws of the universe can be changed by your will? I have heard of you, Druss. You crossed the world to find your lady. You have fought in many battles, you are indomitable. But you are a man of flesh and blood. You will live, and you will die – just like any other man. Klay was a great man, a man of kindness and understanding. His death is a tragedy beyond my ability to describe. Yet it is part of the cycle of life, and I do not doubt that the Source received him with joy. I was with him at the end. He wanted to leave you a message, and we sent for pen and ink, but he died very suddenly. I think I know what he wanted to ask you.'

'What?' asked Druss, numbly.

'He told me of the boy, Kells, and how he had believed that Klay was a god who could lay his hands upon his mother and heal her. The boy is still here. He sat with Klay, holding to his hand, and he wept bitter tears when the fighter died. His mother still lives. If the stones have the power you say then I think Klay would want you to use their power on her.'

Druss said nothing but sat slumped in his chair, staring down at his hands. Sieben stepped forward. 'I think we can do a little better than that, Father. Take me to the boy.'

Leaving Druss alone in the office, Sieben, Niobe and the Abbot walked silently through the hospice, coming at last to a long, narrow room in which twenty beds were set against the walls, ten on each side. Kells lay curled up and asleep on the floor by the first bed; a tall thin woman was sleeping in a chair beside him. Within the bed, her face pale in the moonlight from the high window, lay a wasted, dying figure, the skin of her face drawn tightly around her skull – no flesh visible, black rings beneath her eyes.

Sieben knelt by the boy, lightly touching his shoulder. Kells came awake instantly, his eyes flaring wide in fear. 'It is all right, boy. I come with a gift from the Lord Klay.'

'He is dead,' said the child.

'But I bring his gift anyway. Stand up.' Kells did so. The movement and the voices awoke the thin woman in the chair.

'What is happening?' she asked. 'Is she gone?'

'Not gone,' said Sieben. 'She is coming home.' To the boy he said, 'Take your mother's hand,' and Kells did so. Sieben leaned forward and laid his own palm on the dying woman's fevered brow. The skin was hot and dry. The poet closed his eyes, and felt the power of the stones flowing through him. The woman in the bed gave a weak groan and the Abbot moved in closer, looking down in wonder as her colour deepened and the dark rings beneath her eyes slowly faded. The bones of her face receded as the wasted muscles of her cheeks and jaw swelled into health. Her hair, which had been dry and lifeless, now shone upon the pillow. Sieben took a deep breath and stepped back.

'Are you an angel of the Source?' asked the thin woman.

'No, just a man,' said Sieben. Kneeling down by the boy, he saw the tears in his eyes. 'She is healed, Kells. She sleeps now. Would you like to help me heal all these others?'

'Yes. Yes, I would. The Lord Klay sent you?'

'In a manner of speaking.'

'And my mother is going to live?'

'Aye. She is going to live.'

Together Sieben and the boy moved from bed to bed, and when the dawn sun rose over Gulgothir the sounds of laughter and unfettered joy came from within the walls of the hospice.

It was all lost on Druss, who sat alone in the drab office, his feelings numbed. He could help hold a fortress against all the odds, but could not prevent the death of a friend. He could cross the ocean and fight in a hundred battles. He could stand against any man alive, yet Klay was still dead.

Rising from his chair, he moved to the window. The dawn sun had filled the gardens beyond with colour – crimson roses growing around the white marble fountain, purple foxgloves amid carpets of yellow flowers beside the curving paths. 'It is not fair,' said Druss aloud.

'I cannot recall anyone saying that it would be,' came the voice of the Abbot.

'That bolt was meant for me, Father. Klay took it for me. Why should I live and he die?'

'There are never answers to such questions, Druss. He will be remembered with great fondness, by a great many people. There will even be those who will revere his memory enough to try to emulate him. We are none of us here for very long. Would you like to see his stone?'

'Aye. I would.'

Together the two men left the office and walked down the rear stairwell to the gardens. The air was sweet with perfume, the sun bright in the morning sky. Klay's grave was beside a dry-stone wall, beneath an ancient willow. A long, rectangular slab of white marble had been set into the earth, and upon it were carved the words:

Any good that I may do, let me do it now, for I may
not pass this way again.

'It is a quote from an ancient writing,' said the Abbot. 'He did not ask for it, but I thought it was fitting.'

'Aye, it is fitting,' agreed Druss. 'Tell me, who is the woman Klay wanted saved?'

'She is a prostitute; she works the southern quarter, I understand.'

Druss shook his head and said nothing.

'You think a whore is not worth saving?' the Abbot asked.

'I would never say that,' Druss told him, 'nor would I think it. But I have just come from a battle, Father, where hundreds of men lost their lives. I have returned here – to find a great man dead. And at the end of it I have ensured that one more whore will work the southern quarter. I'm going home,' said Druss sadly. 'I wish I had never come to Gulgothir.'

'If you hadn't, then you would not have known him. And that would have been your loss. My advice is to hold to the memory of what he was, and think about him as you live your own life.

There may come a time when you will draw upon those memories, in order to achieve some good for others – just as he would have done.'

Druss took in a deep breath, glanced down once more at the simple grave, then turned away. 'Where is my friend? We should be leaving soon.'

'He and his wife are gone, Druss. He said to tell you he will meet you on the road – he is returning the stones to a man named Talisman.'

Talisman, Gorkai and Zhusai rode up the dusty rise, cresting the slope and pulling back on the reins of their weary ponies. Below them, spreading right across the valley, were the tents of the Northern Wolfshead.

'We are home,' said Talisman.

'Now perhaps, my general,' said Gorkai, 'you can tell me why we have ridden so hard?'

'This is the Day of the Stone Wolf. All the captains of every Wolfshead tribe are gathered here. At noon there is a ceremony in the High Cave.'

'And you must be there?'

'Today I will stand before my people and take my Nadir name. That right was denied me when I returned home from the Academy; some of the Elders believed I had been tainted by Gothir education. Nosta Khan named me Talisman, and said that I would keep that name until I found the Eyes of Alchazzar.'

'What name will you now choose, my love?' asked Zhusai.

'I have not yet decided. Come, let us ride.' And Talisman led the trio down into the valley.

High on the hillside, from the mouth of a huge cave, Nosta Khan watched them. His emotions were mixed. He could sense the presence of the Eyes, and knew that Talisman had fulfilled his quest. This alone was cause for rejoicing, for with the power restored to the Stone Wolf the Day of the Uniter was infinitely closer. Yet there was anger too, for Talisman had disobeyed him and had despoiled the woman. Even now she was pregnant, and almost lost to the cause. There was only one answer, and it saddened Nosta Khan. Talisman, for all his strength and skill, had to die. After that there were herbs and potions to rob Zhusai of the babe. Perhaps then all could proceed as it should.

Rising, he turned from the sunlight and entered the cave. It was huge and spherical, great stalactites hanging like spears from the domed ceiling. The Stone Wolf had been carved from the rock of the rear wall centuries before and it sat now, its great jaws open, its sightless eyes waiting for a return to the light.

Today, at noon, the Eyes would shine again – albeit briefly. They were too powerful to be left in the stone sockets, prey to whatever thief had the wit or the courage to steal them. No. From now on the Eyes of Alchazzar would be carried on the person of Nosta Khan, shaman to the Wolfshead.

Three acolytes entered the cave, bearing bundles of oil-soaked torches which they placed in rusting brackets on the walls around the Stone Wolf.

Nosta Khan strolled back into the sunlight and watched the steady stream of men moving purposefully up the hillside. 'Light the torches,' he commanded the acolytes.

Returning to the Stone Wolf, he squatted down before it and closed his eyes, focusing his powers. More than forty leaders would be here today; not one of them had violet eyes, but after the ceremony he would question all of them. The Uniter was out there, somewhere on the steppes. With the power of the Eyes, Nosta Khan would find him.

The leaders trooped into the cave and sat in a wide semi-circle some twenty feet back from the Stone Wolf. Each leader had his own champions with him, chosen warriors. These stood behind their warlords with their hands upon their sword hilts, ready for any treachery. Truly, thought Nosta Khan, we are a divided people.

When all the leaders were present Nosta Khan rose. 'This is a great day,' he told the assembly. 'What was lost has been returned to us. This is the first day of the Uniter. The Eyes of Alchazzar have been found!'

A gasp went up from the crowd, followed by a stunned silence. 'Step forth, Talisman,' commanded the shaman.

Talisman rose from the centre of the group and made his way through the ranks to stand beside the shaman. 'This is the man who led the defenders at the Shrine of Oshikai Demon-bane. This is the man who inflicted defeat upon the *gajin*. Today, with pride, he will take his Nadir name, and be remembered for all time as a great Wolfshead hero.' Turning to Talisman, he said, 'Give me the Eyes, my boy.'

'In a moment,' said Talisman. The young warrior turned to the assembly. 'The Shrine of Oshikai stands,' he said, his voice ringing out. 'It stands because Nadir warriors aimed straight and

311

stood tall. Here in this place I praise Bartsai, leader of the Curved Horn, who died defending the bones of Oshikai. Here in this place I praise Kzun of the Lone Wolves, who was slain leading Curved Horn warriors in defence of our holiest Shrine. Here in this place I praise Quing-chin of the Fleet Ponies, who was maimed and butchered by the *gajin*. Here in this place I praise Lin-tse of the Sky Riders. And I bring a new warrior to the ranks of the Wolves. Come forward, Gorkai.'

Gorkai rose and marched to the front. Across his shoulder he carried a long hammer with a head of heavy iron. 'This is Gorkai, who was Notas, and is now Wolfshead.

'Nosta Khan has told you that the Day of the Uniter is close, and he is right. It is time to put aside the stupidity of the past. Look at you all! You are Wolfshead, and yet you sit here with your champions behind you, fearing the brothers who sit beside you. Rightly fearing them! For given the chance there is not one of you who would not slay the other in order to rule. Each man here is an enemy. It is folly of the worst kind. While the Gothir wax rich, we starve. While the Gothir raid our villages, we plan wars among ourselves. Why is this? Were we born stupid?

'Centuries ago, wise men of the Nadir committed an act of appalling stupidity. They drew the magic from the land and set it in these,' he said, drawing the Eyes of Alchazzar from the pocket of his goatskin jerkin. The jewels shone in the torchlight as he raised them up.

'The power of the steppes and the mountains,' he said. 'The magic of the Gods of Stone and Water. Trapped here . . . with these purple jewels any man here could be khan. He could be immortal. I saw their power. I was struck down at the Shrine, pierced through the body, yet I have no scar.'

All eyes were upon the jewels now, and he felt the lust in every gaze.

'The Eyes of Alchazzar!' he shouted, his voice echoing around the cavern. 'But does any man here believe that Bartsai or Kzun or Quing-chin died so that one petty Wolfshead leader could command the magic of the Gods of Stone and Water? Is any one of you worthy to wield this power? If he is here, let him stand now and tell us why he deserves this honour!'

The leaders glanced one to another, but no-one moved.

Talisman spun on his heel and walked to the Stone Wolf. Reaching up he pressed the stones back into the eye-sockets. Then turning once more he gestured to Gorkai, who threw the long hammer through the air. Talisman caught it.

'No!' screamed Nosta Khan.

Talisman took one step back, then swung the hammer in a mighty blow, the iron connecting with the stone brow and shattering the wolf's head. In that moment the jewels flared in a blinding blaze of purple light, engulfing Talisman and filling the cavern. Lightning crackled between the stalactites and a great rumble, like distant thunder, caused the cavern floor to tremble and groan.

Dust fell from the ceiling, the purple light shining upon the motes like a thousand jewels hanging in the air. As the dust settled and the light faded, Talisman dropped the hammer and stood staring at the ruins of the Stone Wolf. Of the Eyes of Alchazzar there was no sign.

'What have you done?' screamed Nosta Khan, rushing at him and grabbing his arm. Talisman turned and the shaman gasped and fell back, his jaw slack, his eyes blinking rapidly.

Gorkai moved forward . . . and stopped. Talisman's eyes had changed, as if the blazing purple light of the jewels had lodged there, glittering in the torchlight. No longer dark, they shone with violet light.

'Your eyes . . .' whispered Gorkai.

'I know,' said Talisman.

Moving past the stunned shaman, Talisman stood before the awed leaders.

'Today I take my Nadir name,' he said. 'Today Talisman is no more. He died as the magic returned to the land. From this day, I am Ulric of the Wolfshead.'

Dros Delnoch

Thirty years later

Druss the Legend sat beside the young soldier, Pellin, and chuckled as he concluded his tale. 'So, in the end,' he said, 'we did it all for a young whore! Sieben didn't seem to mind; he had Niobe, and he took her home and bought her a fabulously ornate firebucket. She was a good woman – outlived him by ten years. He wasn't faithful to her – I don't think Sieben knew what faithful meant. He was loyal though, and I guess that counts for something.'

The surgeon, Calvar Syn, moved alongside the axeman. 'The boy is dead, Druss,' he said.

'I know he's dead, damn you! Everyone dies on me.' Tenderly he patted Pellin's still warm hand, then rose from the bedside. 'He fought well, you know. He was frightened, but he didn't run. He stood his ground like a man should. You think he heard any of my story?'

'It is hard to say. Perhaps. Now you should get some rest. You're no youngster.'

'Aye, that is the advice from Rek and Hogun and all the others. I'll rest soon enough. We all will. They've all gone, you know – all my friends. I killed Bodasen myself, and Sieben fell at Skeln.'

'What about Talisman? Did you ever see him again?'

'No. I expect he died in one of Ulric's battles.' Druss forced a laugh and ran his gnarled hand over his silver beard. 'He would have been proud to see the tribes now, though, eh? Battling before the walls of Dros Delnoch? All the tribes united?'

314

'Get some rest, old man,' ordered Calvar Syn. 'Otherwise tomorrow you may be in one of these beds and not sitting alongside it.'

'I hear you, surgeon.'

Taking up his axe, Druss strolled out into the moonlight and made his way to the ramparts, staring out over the awesome camp of the Nadir which filled the pass for as far as the eye could see.

Three of the six great walls had fallen, and Druss stood now by the gate towers of Wall Four. 'What are you thinking, old horse?' asked Bowman, moving out of the shadows.

'Ulric said his shaman warned that I would die here . . . by this gate. It seems as good a place as any.'

'You won't die, Druss. You're immortal – all men know this.'

'What I am is old and tired,' said Druss. 'And I knew before I came here that this would be my last resting-place.' He grinned. 'I made a pact with death, boy.'

Bowman shivered, and changed the subject. 'You liked him, didn't you? Ulric, I mean. What else did he say to you?'

Druss did not answer. Something about the meeting with Ulric had been bothering him, but he had not yet figured it out.

He never would . . .

Several days later, alone in his tent, Ulric was also thinking about the axeman, remembering their last meeting on the killing ground between Walls One and Two. The sun was bright in the sky and the enemy had fallen back from Eldibar, Wall One.

Ulric had walked out on to the killing ground and spread a purple rug upon the ground. A jug of wine, a plate of dates and some cheese were brought forward by one of his men, and the Great Khan had sat waiting.

He had watched as Druss was lowered from the ramparts of Wall Two. He looked old, his beard shining silver in the sunlight. Will you remember me, Druss? he thought. No, how could you? The fresh-faced, dark-eyed young man you knew thirty years ago is now a violet-eyed, battle-scarred warrior. As the axeman approached Ulric found his heart hammering. In Druss's hand was the terrible weapon, Snaga, which had wreaked such a heavy toll at the Shrine of Oshikai. Will you use it on me? wondered Ulric. No, he realized. As always, Druss would be the man of honour.

'I am a stranger in your camp,' said the old man.

'Welcome, stranger, and eat,' said Ulric, and Druss sat cross-legged opposite him. Slowly Ulric unbuckled his lacquered black breastplate and removed it, laying it carefully at his side. Then he removed his black greaves and forearm straps. 'I am Ulric of the Wolfshead.'

'I am Druss of the Axe.' The axeman's pale blue eyes narrowed as he stared at the Great Khan. Was recognition flickering? Ulric wondered. Tell him! Speak to him now. Voice your gratitude.

'Well met! Eat,' bade Ulric.

Druss took a handful of dates from the silver platter before him and ate slowly. He followed this with goat's milk cheese and washed it down with a mouthful of red wine. His eyebrows rose, and he grinned.

'Lentrian Red,' said Ulric. 'Without poison.'

Druss grinned. 'I'm a hard man to kill. It's a talent.'

'You did well and I am glad for you.'

'I was grieved to hear of the death of your son. I have no sons, but I know how hard it is for a man to lose a loved one.'

'It was a cruel blow,' said Ulric. 'He was a good boy. But then all life is cruel, is it not? A man must rise above his grief.'

Druss was silent, helping himself to more dates.

'You are a great man, Druss. I am sorry you are to die here.'

'Yes, it would be nice to live for ever. On the other hand, I am beginning to slow down. Some of your men have been getting damn close to marking me – it's an embarrassment.'

'There is a prize for the man who kills you – one hundred horses, picked from my own stable.'

'How does the man prove to you that he slew me?'

'He brings me your head and two witnesses to the blow.'

'Don't allow that information to reach my men. They will do it for fifty horses.'

'I think not! You have done well. How is the new Earl settling in?'

'He would have preferred a less noisy welcome, but I think he is enjoying himself. He fights well.'

'As do you all. It will not be enough, however.'

'We shall see,' said Druss. 'These dates are very good.'

'Do you believe you can stop me? Tell me truly, Deathwalker.'

'I would like to have served under you,' said Druss. 'I have admired you for years. I have served many kings. Some were weak, others wilful. Many were fine men, but you . . . you have the mark of greatness. I think you will get what you want eventually . . . but not while I live.'

'You will not live long, Druss,' said Ulric gently. 'We have a shaman who knows these things. He told me that he saw you standing at the gates of Wall Four – Sumitos, I believe it is called – and the grinning skull of Death floated above your shoulders.'

Druss laughed aloud. 'Death always floats where I stand, Ulric! I am he who walks with Death. Does your shaman not know your own legends? I may choose to die at Sumitos. I may choose to die at Musif. But wherever I choose to die, know this: as I walk into the Valley of Shadows I will take with me more than a few Nadir for company on the road.'

'They will be proud to walk with you. Go in peace.'

A movement came at the tent flap, jerking Ulric's mind back to the present. His lieutenant, Ogasi, son of the long-dead Gorkai, stepped inside. Fist to chest, he saluted his khan. 'The cairn is ready, Lord,' said the warrior.

Ulric took a deep breath and then walked out into the night.

The body of Druss the Legend lay upon the cairn, his arms folded across his chest, his great axe held in his dead hands. Ulric felt the jolt of inner pain as he gazed upon the cairn, and the sick empty suffering of bereavement followed. Druss had killed the Nadir champion Nogusha in single combat. Nogusha, however, had smeared poison upon his sword-blade. When the next attack came the old warrior had already been dying in agony, yet still he had fought, his great axe dealing death, until at last, ringed by Nadir warriors, he was cut down.

'Why are we doing this honour for him, Lord?' asked Ogasi. 'He was *gajin* and our enemy.'

Ulric sighed. 'He fought beside your father and me at the Shrine of Oshikai. He helped to bring the magic back to the land. Without him there would have been no Nadir army. Perhaps no future for our people.'

'The more fool him, then,' observed Ogasi.

Ulric quelled the rush of anger he felt. Ogasi was brave and loyal, but he would never understand the greatness of men like Druss the Legend.

'It was my honour and my privilege to stand beside him,' said Ulric. 'He was a man who always fought for what he believed in, no matter what the odds. I know you hate the *gajin*, Ogasi. But Druss was special, he transcended race. A long time ago he and I walked the Void to save the soul of Shul-sen, and to reunite her

317

with the spirit of Oshikai. Yes, he fought us. But there was no malice in him. He was a great man, and – for a time – my friend. Do him honour for my sake.'

'I will, Lord,' said Ogasi. The warrior was silent for a moment, then he smiled. 'By the Gods of Stone and Water, but he could fight, hey?'

'Yes,' said Ulric softly. 'He could fight.'

WINTER WARRIORS

Introduction

As I've said before, Druss was an idealized version of my step-father Bill. He was Bill seen through the rose-tinted eyes of childhood. As I got older, Bill's flaws became more apparent. He was still a great and wonderful man, but he had – as we all do – his darker side.

Born in 1915 and raised in a country that believed it was God's chosen nation, he had an antipathy towards foreigners. In short he was racist. Towards the end of his life many of his friends were black, and yet he held to his convictions despite all evidence to the contrary.

I once sat with him and, one by one, named all of his black friends. Finally I said, 'So which of them even comes close to fitting your ideas of black people?'

'The ones I don't know,' he said.

To be fair to Bill, he was also the man who ran out into a darkened street when a gang of white thugs stabbed a black woman. He scattered them, picked her up and carried her into our house. My mother called an ambulance and set about staunching the blood streaming from the woman's back.

Even so, Bill's dark side confused me as a young man. I tried to deal with it in stories. After *The Legend of Deathwalker*, the next Drenai novel was *Winter Warriors*. A group of old heroes are culled from the army and sent off into retirement. On their way home they are drawn into a mighty battle of good versus evil.

One of the heroes was a man called Bison. Once again he was Bill, the real Bill. Harsh and uncompromising, racist and

321

self-deluding. He was also a man of incredible courage, who would stand by his friends no matter what the odds.

I found in the creation of Bison a genuine understanding of what made Bill the complex man he was.

Many years ago, as a child, I came home from Sunday school confused by the lesson we had learned. It was about being struck on the right cheek and then offering the left to be hit as well. I couldn't begin to get to grips with this.

Bill said, 'It's easy, son. Often you get into a row with a mate. He might pop you. Since he's a mate you don't want to get into a fight with him. So you turn the other cheek, see? It gives him the chance to cool down. Then you can let it go.'

'But what if he hits you on that other cheek?'

'Then you punch his bloody lights out. You don't ever let anybody get away with that. That would be taking the piss.'

Druss would understand that, I think.

Though I expect the Pope might raise an objection or two.

DG
2002

Chapter One

The night sky over the mountains was clear and bright, the stars like diamonds on sable. It was a late winter night of cold and terrible beauty, the snow hanging heavy on the branches of pine and cedar. There was no colour here, no sense of life. The land lay silent, save for the occasional crack of an overladen branch, or the soft, whispering sound of fallen snow being drifted by the harsh north wind.

A hooded rider on a dark horse emerged from the tree line, his mount plodding slowly through the thick snow. Bent low over the saddle he rode on, his head bowed against the wind, his gloved hands holding his snow-crowned grey cloak tightly at the neck. As he came into the open he seemed to become a focus for the angry wind, which howled around him. Undaunted he urged the horse on. A white owl launched itself from a high treetop and glided down past the horse and rider. A thin rat scurried across the moonlit snow, swerving as the owl's talons touched its back. The swerve almost carried it clear.

Almost.

In this frozen place *almost* was a death sentence. Everything here was black and white, sharp and clearly defined, with no delicate shades of grey. Stark contrasts. Success or failure, life or death. No second chances, no excuses.

As the owl flew away with its prey the rider glanced up. In a world without colour his bright blue eyes shone silver-grey in a face dark as ebony. The black man touched heels to his tired mount, steering the animal towards the woods. 'We are both tired,' whispered the rider, patting the gelding's long neck. 'But we'll stop soon.'

Nogusta looked at the sky. It was still clear. No fresh snow tonight, he thought, which meant that the tracks they were following would still be visible come dawn. Moonlight filtered through the tall trees and Nogusta began to seek a resting place. Despite the heavy, hooded grey cloak and the black woollen shirt and leggings he was cold all the way to the bone. But it was his ears that were suffering the most. Under normal circumstances he would have wrapped his scarf around his face. Not a wise move, however, when tracking three desperate men. He needed to be alert for every sound and movement. These men had already killed, and would not hesitate to do so again.

Looping the reins over his pommel he lifted his hands to his ears, rubbing at the skin. The pain was intense. Do not fear the cold, he warned himself. The cold is life. Fear should come only when his body stopped fighting the cold. When it began to feel warm and drowsy. For death's icy dagger lay waiting within that illusory warmth. The horse plodded on, following the tracks like a hound. Nogusta hauled him to a stop. Somewhere up ahead the killers would be camped for the night. He sniffed the air, but could not pick up the scent of woodsmoke. They would have to light a fire. Otherwise they would be dead.

Nogusta was in no condition to tackle them now. Swinging away from the trail he rode deeper into the woods, seeking a sheltered hollow, or a cliff wall, where he could build his own fire and rest.

The horse stumbled in deep snow, but steadied itself. Nogusta almost fell from the saddle. As he righted himself he caught a glimpse of a cabin wall through a gap in the trees. Almost entirely snow covered it was near invisible, and had the horse not balked he would have ridden past it. Dismounting Nogusta led the exhausted gelding to the deserted building. The door was hanging on one leather hinge, the other having rotted away. The cabin was long and narrow beneath a sod roof, and there was a lean-to at the side, out of the wind. Here Nogusta unsaddled the horse and rubbed him down. Filling a feedbag with grain he looped it over the beast's ears, then covered his broad back with a blanket.

Leaving the horse to feed Nogusta moved round to the front of the building and eased his way over the snow that had piled up in the doorway. The interior was dark, but he could just make out the grey stone of the hearth. As was customary in the wild a fire had been laid, but snow had drifted down the chimney and half covered the wood. Carefully Nogusta cleaned it out, then relaid the fire. Taking his tinder box from his pouch he opened it and hesitated. The tinder would burn for only a few seconds. If the thin kindling wood did not catch fire immediately it might take him hours to start a blaze with knife and flint. And he needed a fire desperately. The cold was making him tremble now. He struck the flint. The tinder burst into flame. Holding it to the thin kindling wood he whispered a prayer to his star. Flames licked up, then surged through the dry wood. Nogusta settled back and breathed a sigh of relief, and, as the fire flared, he looked around him, studying the room. The cabin had been neatly built by a man who cared. The joints were well crafted, as was the furniture, a bench table, four chairs and a narrow bed. Shelves had been set on the north wall. They were bare now. There was only one window, the shutters closed tight. One side of the hearth was filled with logs. An old spider's web stretched across them.

The empty shelves and lack of personal belongings showed that the man who had built the cabin had chosen to move on. Nogusta wondered why. The construction of the cabin showed a neat man, a patient man. Not one to be easily deterred. Nogusta scanned the walls. There was no sign of a woman's presence here. The builder had been a man alone. Probably a trapper. And when he had finally left – perhaps the mountains were trapped out – he had carefully laid a fire for the next person to find his home. A considerate man. Nogusta felt welcome in the cabin, as if greeted by the owner. It was a good feeling.

Nogusta rose and walked out to where his horse was patiently waiting. Removing the empty feedbag he stroked his neck. There was no need to hobble him. The gelding would not leave this place of shelter. The stone chimney jutted from the wooden wall of the cabin here, and soon the fire would heat the stones. 'You will be safe here for the night, my friend,' Nogusta told the gelding.

Gathering his saddlebags he returned to the cabin and heaved the door back into place, wedging it against the twisted frame. Then he pulled a chair up to the fire. The cold stones of the hearth were sucking almost all the heat from the fire. 'Be patient,' he told himself. Minutes passed. He saw a woodlouse run along a log as the flames licked up. Nogusta drew his sword and held the blade against the wood, offering the insect a way of escape.

The woodlouse approached the blade, then turned away from it, toppling into the fire. 'Fool,' said Nogusta. 'The blade was life.'

The fire was blazing now and the black man rose and removed his cloak and shirt. His upper body was strongly muscled and heavily scarred. Sitting down once more he leaned forward, extending his hands to the blaze. Idly he twirled the small, ornate charm he wore around his neck. It was an ancient piece, a white-silver crescent moon, held in a slender golden hand. The gold was heavy and dark, and the silver never tarnished. It remained, like the moon, pure and glittering. He heard his father's voice echo down the vaults of memory: 'A man greater than kings wore this magic charm, Nogusta. A great man. He was our ancestor and while you wear it make sure that your deeds are always noble. If they remain so you will have the gift of the Third Eye.'

'Is that how you knew the robbers were in the north pasture?'

'Yes.'

'But don't you want to keep it?'

'It chose you, Nogusta. You saw the magic. Always the talisman chooses. It has done so for hundreds of years. And – if the Source wills – it will choose one of your own sons.'

If the Source wills . . .

But the Source had not willed.

Nogusta curled his hand around the talisman, and stared into the fire, hoping for a vision. None came.

From his saddlebag he took a small package and opened it. It contained several strips of dried, salted beef. Slowly he ate them.

Adding two logs to the fire he moved to the bed. The blankets were thin and dusty and he shook them out. Away from the blaze he shivered, then laughed at himself. 'You are getting old,' he said. 'Once upon a time the cold would not have affected you this way.'

Back at the fire once more he put on his shirt. A face came into his mind, sharp featured and with an easy, friendly smile. Orendo the Scout. They had ridden together for almost twenty years, serving first the old king and then his warrior son. Nogusta had always liked Orendo. The man was a veteran, and when you gave him an order you knew it would be carried out to the letter. And he had a heart. Once, several years back, Orendo had found a child lost in the snow, unconscious and half dead from the cold. He had carried him back to camp, then sat with him all night, warming blankets, rubbing the boy's frozen skin. The child had survived.

Nogusta sighed. Now Orendo was on the run with two other soldiers, having murdered a merchant and raped his daughter. She too had been left for dead, but the knife had missed her heart, and she had lived to name her attackers.

'Don't bring them back,' the White Wolf had told him. 'I want them dead. No public trials. Bad for morale.' Nogusta had looked into the old man's pale, cold eyes.

'Yes, my general.'

'You want to take Bison and Kebra with you?' asked the general.

'No. Orendo was Bison's friend. I'll do it alone.'

'Was Orendo not your friend also?' said Banelion, watching him closely.

'You want their heads as proof that I killed them?'

'No. Your word is good enough for me,' said Banelion. That was a source of pride to Nogusta. He had served Banelion now for almost thirty-five years – almost all his adult life. The general was not a man given to praise, but his men served him with an iron loyalty. Nogusta stared into the fire. It had been more than a surprise when Orendo had betrayed him. But then Orendo was being sent home. Like Bison and Kebra. And even the White Wolf himself.

The king wanted the old men culled. The same old men who had fought for his father, saving the Drenai when all seemed lost. The same old men who had invaded Ventria, smashing the emperor's armies. Paid off and retired. That was the rumour. Orendo had believed it, and had robbed the merchant. Yet it was hard to believe he had also taken part in the rape and attempted murder of the girl. But the evidence was overwhelming. She said he had not only been the instigator of the rape, it had been he who had plunged the knife into her breast.

Nogusta stared moodily into the fire. Had the crime shocked him? A good judge of men he would not have thought Orendo capable of such a vile act. But then all those years ago he had learned what *good* men were capable of. He had learned it in fire and blood and death. He had learned it in the ruin of dreams and the shattering of hopes. Banking up the fire he moved the bed closer to the hearth. Pulling off his boots he lay down, covering himself with the thin blankets.

Outside the wind was howling.

He awoke at dawn. The cabin was still warm. Rising from the bed he pulled on his boots. The fire had died down to glowing embers. He took a long drink from his canteen, then put on his cloak, hefted his saddlebags, and went out to the gelding. The back stones of the hearth were hot, the temperature in the lean-to well above freezing. 'How are you feeling, boy?' he said, stroking the beast's neck. The gelding nuzzled his chest. 'We'll catch them today, and then I'll take you back to that warm stable.' Back in the cabin he put out the remains of the fire, then laid a fresh one in its place, ready for any other weary traveller who came upon it. Saddling the gelding he rode out into the winter woods.

Orendo stared gloomily at the jewels, purple amethysts, bright diamonds, red rubies, sparkling in his gloved hand. With a sigh he opened the pouch and watched them tumble back into its dark interior.

'I'm going to buy a farm,' said the youngster, Cassin. 'On the Sentran Plain. Dairy farm. I've always loved the taste of fresh milk.' Orendo's weary eyes glanced up at the slim young man and he said nothing.

'What's the point?' countered Eris, a thickset bearded warrior with small dark eyes. 'Life's too short to *buy* hard work. Give me the whorehouses of Drenan and a fine little house high on the Sixth Hill. A different girl every day of the week, small, pretty and slim hipped.'

A silence grew among them, as each remembered the small, pretty girl they had murdered back in the city of Usa. 'Looks like we're clear of snow today,' said Cassin, at last.

'Snow is good for us,' said Orendo. 'It covers tracks.'

'Why would anyone track us yet?' asked Eris. 'No-one saw us at the merchant's house, and there's no roll-call until tomorrow.'

'They'll send Nogusta,' said Orendo, leaning forward to add a chunk of wood to the fire. It had been a cold night in the hollow and he had slept badly, dreaming awful dreams of pain and death. What had seemed a simple robbery had become a night of murder and shame he would never forget. He rubbed his tired eyes.

'So what?' sneered Eris. 'There's three of us, and we're not exactly easy meat. If they send that black bastard I'll cut his heart out.' Orendo bit back an angry retort. Instead he rose and stepped towards the taller, heavier man.

'You have never seen Nogusta in action, boy. Pray you never do.' Stepping past the two younger men Orendo walked to a nearby tree and urinated. 'The man is uncanny,' he said, over his shoulder. 'I was with him once when we tracked four killers into Sathuli lands. He can read sign over rock, and he can smell a trail a hound would miss. But that's not what makes him dangerous.' Orendo continued to urinate, the water coming in slow, rhythmic spurts, sending up steam from the snow. He had endured trouble with his bladder for over a year now, needing to piss several times a night. 'You know what makes him dangerous?' he asked them. 'There is no bravado in him. He moves, he kills. It is that quick. When we found the killers he just walked into their camp and they were dead. I tell you it was awesome.'

'I know,' came the tomb-deep voice of Nogusta. 'I was there.'

Orendo stood very still, a feeling of nausea flaring in his belly. His water dried up instantly and he retied his leggings and turned very slowly. Eris was lying flat on his back, a knife through his right eye. Cassin was beside him, a blade in his heart. 'I knew they'd send you,' said Orendo. 'How did you find us so fast?'

'The girl lived,' said Nogusta.

'I thank the Source for that,' said Orendo, with a sigh. 'Are you alone?'

'Yes.' The black man's sword was sheathed, and there was no throwing knife in his hands. It does not matter, thought Orendo. I don't have the skill to best him.

'I'm glad. I wouldn't want Bison to see me now. Are you taking me back?'

'No. You will remain here, with your friends.'

Orendo nodded. 'Seems a shame to end a friendship this way, Nogusta. Will you take back our heads?'

'The White Wolf told me my word was good enough.'

Orendo felt a trickle of hope. 'Look, man, I was only the look out. I didn't know there was going to be murder. But it happened. There are enough jewels in that pouch to give us a life . . . a real life. We could buy a palace with them, you and me.' Nogusta shook his head. 'You could just tell them you killed me. And keep half the jewels.'

'That is what I will tell them. For you will be dead. You were not the look out,' said Nogusta, sadly. 'You raped the girl, and you stabbed her. You did this. You must pay for it.'

Orendo moved to the fire, stepping over the bodies of his companions. 'They were sending me home,' he said, kneeling down and pulling off his gloves. The fire was warm and he held his hands out to it. 'How would you feel? How does Bison feel?' He glanced up at the tall warrior. 'Ah, it is different for you, isn't it? The champion. The blade master. You're not quite as old as us. No-one's told you you're useless yet. But they will, Nogusta. The day will come.' He sat down and stared into the flames. 'You know, we had no intention of killing the merchant. But he struggled and Eris stabbed him. Then the girl ran in. She had been sleeping, and she was wearing a transparent shift. I still can hardly believe it happened. The room went very cold. I remember that, and I felt something touch me. Then I was filled with rage and lust. It was the same for the others. We spoke about it last night.' He looked up at Nogusta. 'I swear to you, Nogusta, that I believe we were possessed. Maybe the merchant was a sorcerer. But there was something evil there. It affected us all. You know me well. In all the years we have fought together I have never raped a woman. Never.'

'But you did three nights ago,' said Nogusta, moving forward, and drawing his sword.

Orendo lifted a hand. 'If you will permit me I will do the deed myself?'

Nogusta nodded and squatted down on the other side of the fire. Orendo slowly drew his dagger. For a moment he considered hurling it at the black man. Then the image of the girl came to his mind, and he heard her voice begging for life. Swiftly he drew the sharp blade across his left wrist. Blood flowed instantly. 'There is a bottle of brandy in my saddlebag. Would you get it?'

Nogusta did so and Orendo drank deeply. 'I am truly sorry about the girl,' said the dying man. 'Will she recover?'

'I don't know.'

Orendo drank again, then tossed the bottle to Nogusta. The black man took a deep swallow. 'It all went wrong,' said Orendo. 'Never put your trust in kings. That's what they say. It was all so glorious in those early days. We knew where we were. The Ventrians invaded us and we fought back. We knew what we were fighting for.' Blood was pooling on the snow now. 'Then the boy-king convinced us we should invade Ventria, to force the emperor to end the war. No territorial ambitions, he said. Justice and peace were all he wanted. We believed him, didn't we? Now look at him! Emperor Skanda, would-be conqueror of the world. Now he's going to invade Cadia. But he has no territorial ambitions. Oh no . . . the bastard!' Orendo lay back and Nogusta moved around the fire to sit alongside him. 'You remember that boy I saved?' asked Orendo.

'Yes. It was a fine deed.'

'You think it will count for me? You know . . . if there is a paradise?'

'I hope so.'

Orendo sighed. 'I can't feel the cold now. That's a good thing. I've always hated the cold. Tell Bison not to judge me too hard, eh?'

'I am sure that he won't.'

Orendo's voice was slurring, then his eyes flared open. 'There *are* demons,' he said, suddenly. 'I can see them. There are demons!'

He died then, and Nogusta rose, collected the pouch of jewels and walked to his horse.

He glanced up at the sky, which was blue, clear and bright. Not a trace of cloud.

Stepping into the saddle he gathered the other three mounts and headed back for the city.

There were demons in the air over the city of Usa, shroud-pale and skinny, their talons long, their teeth sharp. Ordinary eyes could not see them, and they seemed to pose no threat to ordinary folk.

Why then are they here? thought Ulmenetha. Why do they hover close to the palace? The large priestess pushed her thick fingers through her short cropped blond hair. Rising from her bed she poured water into a bowl and washed her face. Refreshed she silently opened the connecting door and stepped through into the queen's bedroom. Axiana was asleep, lying on her back, one white slender arm curled around a satin pillow. Ulmenetha smiled. Only a few years before that arm had, in the same manner, cuddled a stuffed toy – a woollen lioness with only one glass eye.

Now Axiana was a child no longer.

Ulmenetha sighed. Despite her bulk the priestess moved silently across the royal bedroom, casting an affectionate look at the pregnant Axiana. The queen's face shone in the moonlight, and, in sleep, Ulmenetha could just discern the child she had grown to love. 'May your dreams be rich and joyful,' she whispered.

Axiana did not stir. The fat priestess reached the window balcony and stepped out into the moonlight. Her white-streaked blond hair shone like silver beneath the stars, and her voluminous nightdress of white cotton shimmered, as if turned to silk. There was a marble-topped table set on the balcony, and four chairs. Easing herself down she untied her rune pouch and placed it on the table. Ulmenetha gazed up at the night sky. All she could see with the eyes of her body were the stars, shining bright. To her left a crescent moon seemed to be balancing precariously on the uppermost tower of the Veshin temple. Closing the eyes of her body, she opened the eyes of her spirit. The stars remained, brighter and clearer now, robbed of the twinkling illusion caused by human astigmatism and the earth's atmosphere. Tall mountains could clearly be seen on the far-away face of the crescent moon. But it was not the night sky Ulmenetha wished to see.

Above the palace three scaled forms were hovering.

For weeks now their malevolent presence had kept her chained to her flesh, and she longed to fly free. But the last time she had tried they had come for her, screeching across the sky. Ulmenetha had barely made it back to her body.

Who had summoned them, and why?

Closing her eyes she loosened the draw-string of her rune pouch and reached inside, her fingers stroking the stones within. They were smooth and round and flat, and for a while she continued to stir them. At last one stone seemed to call for her, and she drew it from the pouch. Painted upon it was a cracked goblet. Ulmenetha sat back.

The Broken Flagon was a stone signalling mistrust. At best it warned of caution in dealings with strangers. At worst it signalled treachery among friends.

From the pocket of her white dress she produced two leaves. Rolling them into a ball she placed them in her mouth and began to chew. The juices were acrid and bitter. Pain lanced into her head and she stifled a groan. Bright colours danced now on the edge of her vision, and she pictured the Broken Flagon, holding to the image and freeing her mind of conscious thought.

A silver serpent slithered up and around the flagon, slowly crushing it. The flagon suddenly shattered, the pieces exploding outward, ripping through the curtain of time. Ulmenetha saw a tree-shrouded hollow and four men. Axiana was there. Ulmenetha saw herself kneeling beside the queen, a protective arm around her shoulder. The four men were warriors, and they had formed a circle around Axiana, facing outward ready to fight off some unseen threat. A white crow was hovering over them all, his wings beating silently.

Ulmenetha sensed a colossal evil, about to sweep over the

332

hollow. The vision began to fade. She struggled to hold the image, but it collapsed in upon itself and a fresh scene unfolded. A camp-fire beside a dark frozen lake stretching between high mountains. A man – a tall man – sitting with his back to the lake. Behind him a dark, taloned hand reached up through the ice, then a demonic form pulled itself clear. It was colossal and winged and stood blinking in the moonlight. The great wings spread wide and the demon floated closer to the man at the camp-fire. It extended an arm. Ulmenetha wanted to cry out, to warn him, but she couldn't. The talons rammed into the back of the seated man. He reared up and screamed once, then slumped forward.

As Ulmenetha watched the demon began to shimmer, his body became black smoke, which swirled into the bloody wound in the dead man's back. Then the demon was gone, and the body of the man rose. Ulmenetha could not see his face, for he was hooded. He turned towards the lake and raised his arms. Through the surface of the ice a thousand taloned hands rose up to salute him.

Once more the vision faded and she saw an altar. Upon it, held with chains of iron, was a naked man with a golden beard. It was Axiana's father, the murdered emperor. A voice spoke, a soft voice, which she felt she should recognize, but it was blurred somehow, as if she were listening to a distant echo. 'Now,' said the voice, 'the day of Resurrection is at hand. You are the first of the Three.' The chained emperor was about to speak when a curved dagger sliced into his chest. His body arched.

Ulmenetha cried out – and the vision disappeared. She found her gaze focused now only on the bare, moonlit wall of the royal bedchamber.

The visions made no sense. The emperor was not sacrificed. Having lost the last battle he had fled with his aides. He had been slain, so it was said, by officers of his own guard, men disgusted by his cowardice. Why then should she see him sacrificed in this way? Was the vision symbolic?

The incident at the lake of ice was equally nonsensical. Demons did not live below ice.

And the queen would never be in a wood with a mere four warriors. Where was the king and his army? Where were the royal guards?

'Dismiss the visions from your mind,' she told herself. 'They are flawed in some way. Perhaps your preparation was at fault.'

Axiana moaned in her sleep and the priestess rose and moved to the bedside. 'Be still, my pet,' she whispered, soothingly. 'All is well.'

But all was not well, Ulmenetha knew. Her *lorassium* visions were certainly mysterious, and might indeed be symbolic. They were, however, never false.

And who were the four men? She summoned their faces to her mind. One was a black man, with bright blue eyes, the second a huge bald man, with a white, drooping moustache. The third was young and handsome. The fourth held a bow. She remembered the white crow and a shudder went through her.

This was one sign she could read without interpretation.

The white crow was Death.

Kebra the Bowman dropped a small golden coin into the palm of the outraged innkeeper. The fat man's anger faded instantly. There was no feeling in the world quite so warming as that of gold against the skin. The seething anger at the thought of broken furniture and lost business receded into minor irritation. The innkeeper glanced up at the bowman, who was now survey-ing the wreckage. Ilbren had long been a student of human nature, able to read a man swiftly and accurately. Yet the friend-ship of Kebra and Bison remained a mystery. The bowman was a fastidious man. His clothes were always clean, as were his hands and skin. He was cultured and softly spoken, and he had a rare talent for creating space around himself, as if he disliked crowds and the closeness of bodies. Bison, on the other hand, was an un-cultured oaf and Ilbren despised him. The sort of man who would always drink two more flagons of ale than he could handle, and then became aggressive. Innkeepers loathed such customers. Bison's saving grace, however, was that to reach the last two flagons he could drink an inn dry, and would make every effort to do so. This naturally created large profits. Ilbren wondered how Kebra could tolerate such a friend.

'He did all this?' asked Kebra, shaking his head. Two long bench tables had been smashed, and several chairs were lying in pieces on the sawdust-covered floor. The far window had been smashed outward, and shards of broken glass still clung to the lead frame. An unconscious Ventrian officer was being tended by the window, and two other victims, common soldiers, were sit-ting near the doorway, one still bleeding from a gashed cheek, the other holding his bandaged head in his hands.

'All this and more. We have already swept away the broken crockery and two bent pots, which cannot be used again.'

'Well, at least no-one is dead,' said Kebra, his voice deep and sombre, 'so we must be grateful.'

The innkeeper smiled and lifted a flagon of wine, gesturing the grey clad bowman to join him at a nearby table. As they sat down he looked closely at Kebra's face. Deeply lined, as if carved from stone, Kebra looked every inch his fifty-six years. The bowman rubbed his tired eyes. 'Bison's like a child,' he said. 'When things go against him he loses control.'

'I do not know how it started,' said Ilbren. 'The first I knew of trouble was when I saw that officer flying through the air. He hit that table there, and cracked it clean through.'

Two Ventrian soldiers came in carrying a stretcher. Tenderly they lifted the unconscious man onto it, and carried him out. A Drenai officer approached Kebra. He was a veteran, and well known to the bowman as a fair man. 'You'd better find him fast!' he warned Kebra. 'The wounded man is an officer on Malikada's staff. You know what the penalty will be if he dies.'

'I know, sir.'

'Gods, man! As if we haven't enough trouble with the cursed Ventrians as it is, without one of our men cracking the skull of one of their officers.' The Drenai swung to the innkeeper. 'No offence meant, Ilbren,' he said.

'Oh, none taken I am sure,' replied the Ventrian, with just a trace of sarcasm. The officer wandered away.

'I am sorry for the trouble, Ilbren,' said Kebra. 'Do you know where Bison went?'

'I do not know. He is old enough to know better than to wreak such . . . such devastation.' The innkeeper filled two goblets, passing one to Kebra.

'This has not been a good day for him,' said Kebra, softly. 'Not a good day for any of us.' He sipped the wine, then laid the goblet down.

Ilbren sighed. 'I heard of the king's decision. We all have. For what it is worth I shall miss you.' He smiled. 'I will even miss Bison.' He stared at the white-haired archer. 'Still, war is for young men, eh? It is way past the time when you should have settled down with a wife and raised sons.'

Kebra ignored the comment. 'Which way did Bison go?'

'I did not see.'

Kebra moved away, stepping past the injured men in the doorway. 'It was just a bad joke,' said the soldier with the bandaged head. 'Then he went berserk.'

335

'Let me guess,' said Kebra. 'Something about his age, was it?'

The young soldier looked suddenly sheepish. 'It was just a joke,' he repeated.

'Well, I'm sure Bison didn't take it too seriously.'

'How can you say that?' stormed the second soldier. 'Look what he did to my face.' Blood was still seeping from his swollen cheekbone, and his right eye was closed tight, purple swelling distending the eyelid.

'I can say it because you are still alive, boy,' said Kebra, coldly. 'Did anyone see where he went?'

Both men shook their heads and Kebra stepped out into the fading winter sunlight. Across the square market traders were packing up their wares, and children were playing by the frozen fountain, scooping snow and fashioning balls which they hurled at one another. A tall black man in a long dark cloak moved through the crowd. The children stopped to watch him. Then one child moved silently behind him, a snowball in his raised hand.

'Not a wise move, child,' said the black man, without looking back. 'For if you throw it I shall be obliged to –' suddenly he swung around '– cut off your head!' Terrified the boy dropped the snowball and sprinted back to his friends. The black man chuckled and strode on to where Kebra waited.

'I take it he was not at the barracks,' said Kebra. Nogusta shook his head.

'They have not seen him.'

The two men made an incongruous pair as they walked off together, Nogusta black and powerful, Kebra wand slim, white-haired and pale. Cutting through the narrow streets they reached a small eating house overlooking the river. They took a table by the fire and ordered a meal. Nogusta removed his cloak and the sheepskin jerkin he wore below it and sat down, holding his hands out to the blaze. 'I, for one, will be pleased to say farewell to this frozen country. Why is Bison so depressed? Does he not have three wives waiting for him back home?'

'That's enough to depress anyone,' replied Kebra, with a smile.

They ate in companionable silence and Nogusta added another log to the fire. 'Why is he depressed?' he asked again, as they finished their meal. 'There must come a time when a man is too old for soldiering, and we are all way past that. And the king has offered every soldier a pouch of gold, and a scrip to give them land when they return to Drenan. The scrip alone is worth a hundred in gold.'

Kebra thought about the question. 'There was a time,' he said, 'when I could outshoot any archer alive. Then, as the years went by, I noticed I could no longer see quite as clearly. When I turned fifty I could no longer read small script. That was when I began to think of going home. Nothing lasts for ever. But Bison is not a thinker. As far as he is concerned the king has just told him he is no longer a man. And he is hurting.'

'There is some pain for all of us,' said Nogusta. 'The White Wolf will be leading almost two thousand men home. Every one of them will feel some sense of rejection. But we are alive, Kebra. I fought for the king's father – as you did – and I have carried my sword through thirty-five years of warfare. Now I am tired. The long marches are hard on old bones. Even Bison must admit to that.'

Kebra shook his head. 'Bison admits to nothing. You should have seen his face when they called the roll. He could not believe he had been chosen. I was standing beside him. You know what he said? "How can they send me back with all the old men?" I just laughed. For a moment I thought he was joking. But he wasn't. He still thinks he's twenty-five.' He let out a soft curse. 'Why did he have to hit a Ventrian? And what if the man dies?'

'If he dies they will hang Bison,' said Nogusta. 'Not a pleasant thought. Why did he hit the man?'

'He made a joke about Bison's age.'

'And the others?'

'I have no idea. We'll ask him when we find him. The officer was one of Malikada's men.'

'That makes it worse,' said Nogusta. 'He might demand a hanging, regardless. He's a hard man.'

'The White Wolf would never allow it.'

'Times are changing, Kebra. The White Wolf is being sent home with the rest of us. I doubt he has the power to oppose Malikada.'

'A pox on Bison,' snapped Kebra. 'He's always been trouble. You remember when he and Orendo stole that pig . . . ?' The bowman's voice faded away. 'I'm sorry, my friend, that was crass.'

Nogusta shrugged. 'Orendo took part in a rape and a murder. It saddens me that he is dead, but he was the victim of his own actions.'

'Strange, though,' said Kebra. 'I am a fair judge of men and I would never have believed Orendo capable of such an act.'

'Nor I. Where shall we look for Bison?' asked Nogusta, changing the subject.

Kebra shrugged. 'He was drunk when he thrashed those men. You know Bison. After a fight he'll look for a woman. There must be two hundred whorehouses within walking distance. I do not intend to spend the night scouring them.'

Nogusta nodded, then he gave a wide grin. 'We could try just one, though,' he said.

'For what purpose? The odds against finding him are enormous.'

Nogusta leaned forward and placed his hand on his friend's shoulder. 'I was not thinking of *finding* Bison,' he said. 'I was thinking of soft skin and a warm bed.'

Kebra shook his head. 'I think I'll return to the barracks. I have a warm bed there.'

Nogusta sighed. 'Bison refuses to get old, and you refuse to stay young. Truly, you white men are a mystery to me.'

'Life would be dull without mysteries,' said Kebra.

After Nogusta had gone he ordered another flagon of wine, then made the long walk back to the barracks. The room he shared with Nogusta and Bison was cold and empty. Bison's bed was unmade, the blankets in a heap on the floor beside it. The Senior Cul no longer made inspections, and without the threat of punishment Bison had reverted to slovenly behaviour.

Nogusta's bed was tidily made, but he had left a tunic upon it.

Kebra's pallet was immaculate, the blankets folded into a square, topped by the pillow, the undersheet pulled tight, the corners overlapped with a perfect horizontal fold. Kebra moved to the hearth and lit the fire. He had cleaned out the ash and re-laid it that morning, the kindling placed with perfect symmetry.

Just about now Nogusta would be lying beside a fat, sweating whore. He would be, perhaps, the twentieth man she had opened her legs for that day. Kebra shuddered. It was a nauseating thought.

Silently he padded out to the bath house. The boilers had not been lit and the water was cold. Even so Kebra undressed and immersed himself, scrubbing at his body with soap. There were no clean towels on the rack. Angry now he searched through the large laundry basket and dabbed at his cold body with the cleanest of the used towels.

The collapse of discipline unnerved the bowman. Carrying his clothes he returned to the room and sat, shivering, in front of the fire. Then he took a nightshirt from his chest and slipped it on. It was crisp and clean and he could smell the freshness of the cotton. It eased his mind.

Ilbren's words haunted him. 'It is way past the time when you should have settled down with a wife and raised sons.'

Kebra felt the weight of the words, like a stone on his heart.

Most of Palima's customers thought of her as a whore with a golden heart. This was a view she cultivated, especially as she grew older, with age and the laws of gravity conspiring to ravage her features. The truth was more stark: Palima's heart *was* like gold, cold, hard and well hidden.

She lay now on her bed, staring at the hulking figure by the window. Bison was well known to her, a generous giant, un-hindered by imagination or intellect. His needs were simple, his demands limited, his energy prodigious. For a year now – ever since the Drenai had taken the city – he had come to her at least once a week. He paid well, never troubled her with small talk or promises, and rarely outstayed his welcome.

This night was different. He had come to her bed and had cuddled her close. Then he had fallen asleep. Bison usually paid with a single silver coin upon leaving. Yet tonight he had given her a gold half *raq* just after he arrived. Palima had tried to rouse him – not usually a difficult feat. But Bison was in no mood for sex. This did not concern Palima. If a man wanted to pay for a hug with gold she was more than happy to oblige. He had slept fitfully for two hours, holding her close. Then he had dressed and moved to the window. Bison had been standing there in the lantern light for some time now, a huge man, with great sloping shoulders and long, powerful arms. Idly he tugged at his bristling white, walrus moustache and stared out at the night dark square below.

'Come back to bed, lover,' she said. 'Let Palima work her magic.'

'Not tonight,' he told her.

'What is wrong?' she asked. 'You can tell Palima.'

He turned towards her. 'How old do you think I am?' he asked, suddenly.

Sixty-five, if you're a day, she thought, staring at his bald head and white moustache. Men were such children. 'Maybe forty,' she told him.

He seemed satisfied with the answer, and she saw him relax.

'I'm older than that, but I don't feel it. They're sending me home,' he said. 'All the older men are going home.'

'Don't you want to go home?'

'I was one of the first to join the White Wolf,' he said. 'Back when Drenan was beset on all sides and the king's army had been all but destroyed. We beat them all, you know. One after another. When I was a child my country was ruled from afar. We were just peasants. But we changed the world. The king's empire stretches for –' he seemed to struggle for a moment with the mathematics. '– thousands of miles,' he concluded lamely.

'He is the greatest king who ever lived,' she said, softly, hoping that was what he wanted to hear.

'His father was greater,' said Bison. 'He built from nothing. I served him for twenty-three years. Then the boy-king for another twenty. Twenty-six major battles I've fought in. There. Twenty-six. What do you think of that?'

'It's a lot of battles,' she admitted, not knowing where the conversation was leading. 'Come back to bed.'

'It's a lot of battles, all right. I've been wounded eleven times. Now they don't want me any more. Eighteen hundred of us. Thank you and goodbye. Here's a bag of gold. Go home. Where's home, eh?' With a sigh he moved to the bed, which creaked as his huge frame settled upon it. 'I don't know what to do, Palima.'

'You are a strong man. You can do anything you want. Go anywhere you want.'

'But I want to stay with the army. I'm a front ranker! That's what I am. That's what I want.'

Sitting up she cupped his face in her hands. 'Sometimes – most times – we don't get what we want. Rarely do we even get what we deserve. We get what we get. That's it. Yesterday is gone, Bison. It will never come again. Tomorrow hasn't happened yet. What we have is now. And do you know what is real?' She took his hand in hers and lifted it to her naked breast, pressing his fingers to her flesh. '*This* is real, Bison. *We* are real. And at this moment *we* are all there is.'

His hand fell away, then he leaned down and kissed her cheek. He had never done that before. In fact she couldn't remember the last time a man had kissed her cheek. Then he rose. 'I'd better be getting back,' he said.

'Why not stay? I know you, Bison. You'd feel better afterwards. You always do.'

'Aye, that's true. You are the best, you know. And I speak from a lifetime of having to pay for it. But I have to go. I'll be on charges. The Watch is probably looking for me.'

'What have you done?'

'Lost my temper. Tapped a few soldiers.'

'Tapped?'

'Well, maybe more than tapped. One of them laughed at me. Ventrian scum! Said the army would be better off without the greybeards. I picked him up and threw him like a spear. It was really funny. But he landed on a table and broke it with his head. That upset the Drenai soldiers who were eating there. So I tapped them all.'

'How many were there?'

'Only five or so. I didn't really hurt no-one. Well, not badly.' He grinned. 'Well, not *very* badly. But I'll be on charges.'

'What kind of punishment will you get?'

'I don't know . . . ten lashes.' He shrugged. 'Twenty. No problem.'

Palima climbed from the bed and stood naked before him. 'How did it feel when you were *tapping* them?' she asked.

'It was . . . good,' he admitted.

'You felt like a man?'

'Yes. I felt young again.'

Her hand slid down over his leggings. 'Like a man,' she whispered, huskily. She felt him swell at her touch.

'And how do you feel now?' she asked him.

He let out a long sigh. 'Like a man,' he said. 'But they don't want me to be one any more. Goodbye, Palima.'

Without another word he walked out into the night.

Palima watched him from the window. 'A pox on you and all your kind, Drenai,' she whispered. 'Go away and die!'

Banelion, the legendary White Wolf, gathered his maps and carefully placed them inside a brass bound chest. Tall and lean, his long white hair tied at the nape of the neck, the general's movements were swift and precise, as he packed the chest with the expertise of a lifetime soldier. Everything neatly in its place. The maps were stacked in the order they would be needed during the 1400 mile journey to the western port. Alongside them were notes listing the names of tribes and their chieftains, way stations, fortresses and cities along the route. As with everything else he undertook the journey home would be planned meticulously.

Across from the broad desk a young officer in full armour of gold and bronze stood watching the general. The old man glanced up and gave a swift grin. 'Why so sad, Dagorian?'

The young man took a deep, slow breath. 'This is wrong, sir.'

'Nonsense. Look at me. What do you see?'

Dagorian stared at the white-haired general. Leathered by desert sun and winter winds, the White Wolf's face was seamed and wrinkled. Beneath bristling white brows his eyes were pale and bright – eyes that had seen the fall of empires, and the scattering of armies. 'I see the greatest general who ever lived,' said the younger man.

Banelion smiled. He was genuinely touched by the officer's affection, and thought momentarily of the boy's father. The two were so unalike. Catoris had been a cold, hard man, ambitious and deadly. His son was infinitely more likeable, loyal and steadfast. The only virtue he shared with his father was courage. 'Ah, Dagorian, what you should see is a man two years past seventy. But you are looking at what was, boy. Not what is. I will be honest with you, I am disappointed. Even so I do not believe the king is making a mistake. Like me the soldiers who first marched against the Ventrian Empire are growing old now. Eighteen hundred men over fifty. Two hundred of those will not even see sixty again. The king is only thirty-five, and he wants to cross the Great River and conquer Cadia. All reports suggest that such a war will last five years or more. The army will have to cross deserts and mountains, wade rivers thick with crocodiles, hack their way through jungles. Young men will be needed for such an enterprise. And some of the older men are yearning for home.'

Dagorian removed his black and gold helm, and absently brushed his hand over the white horsehair plume. 'I don't doubt you are right about the older men, sir. But not you. Without you some of the battles would have been . . .' The White Wolf raised his finger to his lips, the movement sharp and swift.

'All my battles have been fought. Now I will go home and enjoy my retirement. I will breed horses, and watch the sun rise over the mountains. And I will wait for news of the king's victories, and I will celebrate them quietly in my home. I have served Skanda, as I served his father. Faithfully and well, and to the best of my considerable abilities. Now I need a little fresh air. Walk with me in the garden.'

Swinging a sheepskin cloak around his shoulders Banelion pushed open the doors and strode through to the snow-covered garden. The paved path could no longer be seen, but the statues

342

that lined it pointed the way. Crunching the snow underfoot the two men walked out past the frozen fountain. The statues were all of Ventrian warriors, standing like sentries, spears pointed towards the sky. The older man took Dagorian's arm and leaned in close. 'It is time for you to learn to curb your tongue, young man,' he said, keeping his voice low. 'Every whisper spoken inside the palace is reported to the king and his new advisers. The walls are hollow, and listeners write down every sentence. You understand?'

'They even spy on *you*? I cannot believe it.'

'Believe it. Skanda is no longer the boy-king who charmed us all. He is a man, ruthless and ambitious. He is determined to conquer the world. And he probably will. If his new allies are as trustworthy as he thinks.'

'You doubt the Prince Malikada?'

Banelion grinned and led the young man around the frozen lake. 'I have no reason to doubt him. Or his wizard. Malikada's cavalry are superbly disciplined, and his men fight well. But he is not Drenai, and the king puts great faith in him.' On the far side of the lake they came to a stone arch, beneath which was a bust of a handsome man, with a forked beard, and a high sloping brow. 'You know who this is?' asked Banelion.

'No, sir. A Ventrian noble of some kind?'

'This is the general, Bodasen. He died three hundred and fifty years ago. He was the greatest general the Ventrians ever had. He it was – with Gorben – who laid the foundations of their empire.'

The old man shivered and drew his cloak more tightly about him. Dagorian stared hard at the white stone of the bust. 'I have read the histories, sir. He is described as a plodding soldier. Gorben was said to have led the army to victory.'

Banelion chuckled. 'As indeed has Skanda. And in the months to come you will hear the same of me. That is the way of the world, Dagorian. The victorious kings write the histories. Now let us go back, for this cold is eating into my bones.'

Once back inside Dagorian banked up the fire and the general stood before it, rubbing his hands. 'So tell me,' he said, 'have they found Bison yet?'

'No, sir. They are scouring the whorehouses. The man with the cracked skull has regained consciousness. The surgeons say he will not die.'

'That is a blessing. I would hate to hang old Bison.'

'He's been with you from the first, I understand.'

343

'Aye, from the first, when the old king was merely a young prince, and the kingdom was in ruins. Days of blood and fire, Dagorian. I would not want to live them again. Bison is – like me – a relic of those days. There are not many of us left.'

'What will you do when we find him, sir?'

'Ten lashes. But don't tie him to the post. That'll hurt his dignity. He'll stand there and hold to it. His back will bleed, and you'll not hear a sound from him.'

'I take it you like the man.'

Banelion shook his head. 'Can't stand him. He has the strength of an ox, and the brains to match. A more irritating, undisciplined wretch I have yet to see. But he symbolizes the strength, the courage and the will that has brought us across the world. A man to move mountains, Dagorian. Now you best get some rest. We'll finish in the morning.'

'Yes, sir. Can I fetch you some mulled wine before you retire?'

'Wine does not sit well with me these days. Warm milk and honey would be pleasant.'

Dagorian saluted, bowed and left the room.

Chapter Two

Regimental discipline was observed in ritual fashion. Every one of the 2000 men of the regiment, in their armour of black and gold, stood in a giant square around the barracks ground. At the centre the twenty senior officers waited, and, seated on a dais behind them was the White Wolf. He wore no armour, but was dressed in a simple tunic of grey wool, black leggings and boots. Around his shoulders was a hooded sheepskin cloak.

The morning was bright and clear as Bison was led out. The lumbering giant had been stripped to the waist, and Dagorian suddenly understood the man's bizarre nickname. His head was totally bald, but thick, curling hair grew from his neck and over his massive shoulders. More like a bear than a bison though, thought Dagorian. The young officer's dark gaze flickered to the men walking with Bison. One was Kebra, the famed bowman, who had once saved the king's life, sending a shaft through the eye of a Ventrian lancer. The other was the blue-eyed black man, Nogusta, swordsman and juggler. Dagorian had once watched the man keep seven razor sharp knives in the air, then, one by one send them flashing into a target. They walked straight and tall. Bison cracked a joke with someone in the first line.

'Silence!' shouted an officer.

Bison approached the whipping-post and stood beside the lean, hawk-faced soldier who had been ordered to complete the sentence. The man looked ill at ease, and was sweating despite the morning cold.

'You just lay on, boy,' said Bison, amiably. 'I'll hold no grudge for you.' The man gave a weak, relieved smile.

'Let the prisoner approach,' said the White Wolf. Bison marched forward and saluted clumsily.

'Have you anything to say before sentence is carried out?'

'No, sir!' bellowed Bison.

'Do you know what is special about you?' asked the general.

'No, sir!'

'Absolutely nothing,' said the White Wolf. 'You are an undisciplined wretch and the clumsiest man ever to serve under me. For a copper coin I'd hang you and be done with it. Now get to the post. This cold is chilling my bones.' So saying he lifted the sheepskin hood over his head and pulled the cloak around him.

'Yes, sir!' Bison spun on his heel and marched back to the post, reaching up and taking hold of the wood.

The man with the whip untied the thong binding the five lashes and cracked it into the air. Then he shrugged his shoulders twice and took up his position. His arm came back.

'Hold!' came a commanding voice. The soldier froze. Dagorian turned to see a small group of men striding onto the barracks ground. They were all Ventrian officers wearing golden breastplates and sporting red capes. At the centre was the Prince Malikada, the king's general, a tall, slender nobleman, who had been chosen to replace the White Wolf. Beside him was his champion, the swordsman, Antikas Karios. A fox and a cobra, thought Dagorian. Both men were slim and graceful, but Malikada's power was in his eyes, dark and brooding, gleaming with intelligence, while Antikas Karios radiated a physical strength, built on a striking speed that was inhuman.

Malikada strode to the dais and bowed to the general. His hair was jet black, but his beard had been dyed with streaks of gold, then braided with gold thread. Dagorian watched him closely.

'Greetings, my lord Banelion,' said Malikada.

'This is hardly the time for a visit,' said Banelion. 'But you are most welcome, Prince.'

'It is *exactly* the time, General,' said Malikada, with a wide smile. 'One of my men is about to be disciplined incorrectly.'

'One of *your* men?' enquired the White Wolf, softly. Dagorian could feel the tension in the officers around him, but no-one moved.

'Of course one of my men. You were present when the king – glory be attached to his name – named me as your successor. As I recall you are now a private citizen of the empire about to head for home and a happy retirement.' Malikada swung round. 'And this man has been accused of striking one of my officers. That, as I am sure you are aware, under Ventrian law, is a capital offence. He shall be hanged.'

An angry murmur sounded throughout the ranks. Banelion rose. 'Of course he shall hang – if convicted,' he said, his voice cold. 'But I now change his plea to not guilty and – on his behalf – demand trial by combat. This is *Drenai* law, set in place by the king himself. Do you wish to deny it?' Malikada's smile grew wider, and Dagorian realized in that moment that this was exactly what the Ventrian wanted. The swordsman, Antikas, was already removing his cloak and unbuckling his breastplate.

'The king's law is just,' said Malikada, raising his left arm and clicking his fingers. Antikas stepped forward, drew his sword and spun it in the sunlight. 'Which of your . . . former . . . officers will face Antikas Karios? I understand your aide, Dagorian, is considered something of a swordsman.'

'Indeed he is,' said Banelion. Dagorian felt fear rip into him. He was no match for the Ventrian. He swallowed down the bile rising in his throat, and fought to keep his emotions from his face. Glancing up he saw Antikas Karios staring at him. There was no hint of a sneer, or mockery of any kind. The man simply stared. Somehow it made Dagorian feel even worse. Rising from his seat Banelion gestured for Nogusta to come forward. The black man approached the dais, saluted, then bowed. 'Will you defend the honour of your comrade?' asked the White Wolf.

'But of course, my general.'

Dagorian's relief was intense, and he reddened as he saw a slight smile appear on the face of the Ventrian swordsman.

'This is not seemly,' said Malikada, smoothly. 'A common soldier to face the finest swordsman alive? And a black savage to boot? I think not.' He turned to a second Ventrian officer, a tall man with a long golden beard, crimped into horizontal waves. 'Cerez, will you show us your skills?'

The man bowed. Wider in the shoulder than the whip lean Antikas, Cerez had the same economy of movement and catlike grace found in all swordsmen. Malikada looked up at Banelion. 'With your permission, General, this student of Antikas Karios will take his place.'

'As you wish,' said Banelion.

Nogusta stepped forward. 'Do you wish me to kill the man, or merely disarm him, General?'

'Kill him,' said Banelion. 'And do it swiftly. My breakfast is waiting.'

Both men removed their armour and upper clothing and strode out bare-chested into the centre of the barracks ground. Nogusta lifted his sword in salute. Cerez attacked immediately, sending out a lightning thrust. Nogusta parried it with ease. 'That was discourteous,' whispered Nogusta, 'but I will still kill you cleanly.'

Their blades clashed as Cerez charged forward, his curved sword flashing with bewildering speed. But every thrust or cut was parried by the black man. Cerez dropped back. Dagorian watched the contest closely. The Ventrian was younger by thirty years, and he was fast. But there was not an ounce of fat on Nogusta's powerful frame, and his vast experience enabled him to read his opponent's moves. Dagorian flicked a glance at Antikas Karios. The champion's dark, hooded eyes missed nothing, and he leaned in to whisper something to Malikada.

The two warriors were circling one another now, seeking an opening. The action had been fast, and the black man, though skilful, was visibly tiring. Cerez almost caught him with a sudden riposte, the blade slashing close to Nogusta's cheek. Suddenly Nogusta appeared to stumble. Cerez lunged – and in that moment realized he had been tricked! Nimbly spinning on his heel, all signs of fatigue vanished, Nogusta swayed away from the blade, his own sword slicing through his opponent's golden beard and biting deep into his throat. Cerez stumbled forward, falling to his knees, blood gushing from the wound. Dropping his sword he tried to stem the rush of life from his severed jugular. Slowly he toppled forward, twitched once, then was still. Nogusta strode back across the barrack-square and bowed to the White Wolf. 'As you commanded, Lord, so was it done.'

Ignoring the furious Malikada the White Wolf rose. 'The prisoner is not guilty,' he said, his voice clear and firm. 'And since this is my last moment among you all, let me thank you for the service you have given the king, while under my command. Those among you chosen to retire will find me camped on the flat ground to the west of the city. We will be ready for departure in four days. That is all. Dismissed!'

As he stepped from the dais Malikada moved in close. 'You have made an enemy this day,' he whispered. The White Wolf paused, then met the prince's hawk-eyed gaze.

'An infinitely better prospect than having you for a friend,' he said.

*

The king's birthday was always celebrated with extravagant displays; athletics competitions, boxing matches, horse races, and demonstrations of magic to thrill the crowds. Spear-throwing, archery, sword bouts, and wrestling were also included, with huge prizes for the winners in all events. This year promised even greater extravagances, for it was the king's thirty-fifth birthday, a number of great mystical significance to Drenai and Ventrian alike. And the event was to take place in the Royal Park at the centre of Usa, the ancient capital of the old Ventrian Empire. The city was older than time, and mentioned in the earliest known historical records. In myth it had been a home for gods, one of whom was said to have raised the royal palace in a single night, lifting mammoth stones into place with the power of his will.

Hundreds of huge tents had been pitched in the meadows at the centre of the thousand-acre Royal Park, and scores of carpenters had been working for weeks building tiered seating for the nobility.

The tall towers of the city were silhouetted against the eastern mountains as Kebra the Bowman leaned on a new fence and stared sombrely out towards where the archery tourney would be held. 'You should have entered,' said Nogusta, passing the bowman a thick wedge of hot pie.

'To what purpose,' answered Kebra, sourly, placing the food on the fence rail and ignoring it.

'You are the champion,' said Nogusta. 'It is your title they will be shooting for.'

Kebra said nothing for a moment, transferring his gaze to the snow-topped peaks away to the west. He had first seen these mountains a year ago, when Skanda the king, having won the Battle of the River, had ridden into Usa to take the emperor's throne. Cold winds blew down now from these grey giants and Kebra shivered and drew his pale blue cloak closer about his slender frame. 'My eyes are fading. I could not win.'

'No, but you could have taken part.' The words hung in the cold air. A team of thirty workers moved to the king's pavilion and began to raise wind-shields of stiffened crimson silk around it. Kebra had seen the pavilion constructed on many occasions, and recalled, with a stab of regret, the last time he had stood before it, receiving the Silver Arrow from the hand of the king himself. Skanda had given his boyish grin. 'Does winning ever get boring, old lad?' he had asked.

'No, sire,' he had answered. Turning to the crowd he had

raised the Silver Arrow, and the cheers had thundered out. Kebra shivered again. He looked up into the black man's pale, unreadable eyes. 'I would be humiliated. Is that what you want to see?'

Nogusta shook his head. 'You would not be humiliated, my friend. You would merely lose.'

Kebra gave a tired smile. 'If I had entered most of the Drenai soldiers would have bet on me. They would lose their money.'

'That would be a good reason to decline,' agreed Nogusta. 'If it were truly the reason.'

'What is it you want from me?' stormed Kebra. 'You think there is a question of honour at stake here?'

'No, not honour. Pride. False pride, at that. Without losers, Kebra, there would be no competitions at all. There will be more than a hundred archers taking part in the tourney. Only one will win. Of the ninety-nine losers more than half will know they cannot win before they draw the first shaft. Yet still they will try. You say your eyes are fading. I know that is true. But it is distance that troubles you. Two of the three events require speed, skill and talent. Only the third is shot over distance. You would still be in the top ten.'

Kebra stalked away from the fence. Nogusta followed him. 'When the day comes that you don't wish to hear the truth from me,' he said, 'you merely have to say.'

The bowman paused and sighed. 'What is the truth here, Nogusta?'

The black man leaned in close. 'You demean the championship by refusing to take part. The new champion will feel he has not earned the title. In part, I fear, this is why you have declined.'

'And what if it is? He will still earn a hundred gold pieces. He will still be honoured by the king, and carried shoulder high around the Park.'

'But he will not have beaten the legendary Kebra. I seem to recall your delight fifteen years ago when you took the Silver Arrow from the hands of Menion. He was as old as you are now when he stood against you in the final. And you beat him finally only when it came to the distant targets. Could it be that his eyes were fading?'

Bison strolled over to where they stood. 'Going to be a great day,' he said, wiping crumbs from his white moustache. 'The Ventrian sorcerer, Kalizkan, has promised a display no-one will ever forget. I hope he conjures a dragon. I've always wanted to see a dragon.' The bald giant looked from one man to the other. 'What is it? What am I missing here?'

350

'Nothing,' said Nogusta. 'We were just involved in a philosophical debate.'

'I hate those,' said Bison. 'I never understand a word. Glad I missed it. By the way I've entered the wrestling. I hope you two will be cheering for me.'

Nogusta chuckled. 'Is that big tribesman taking part this year?'

'Of course.'

'He must have thrown you ten feet last year. It was only luck that you landed head first, and thereby avoided injury.'

Bison scowled. 'He caught me by surprise. I'll take him this year – if we're matched.'

'How many times have you entered this competition?' asked Kebra.

'I don't know. Almost every year. Thirty times, maybe.'

'You think you'll win this time?'

'Of course I'll win. I've never been stronger.'

Nogusta laid his hand on Bison's massive shoulder. 'It doesn't concern you that you've said the same thing for more than thirty years? And yet you've never even reached the quarter-finals.'

'Why should it?' asked Bison. 'Anyway, I did reach the quarters once, didn't I? It was during the Skathian campaign. I was beaten by Coris.' He grinned. 'You remember him? Big, blond fellow. Died at the siege of Mellicane.'

'You are quite right,' said Nogusta. 'Coris was beaten in the semifinal. I remember losing money on him.'

'I've never lost money on the king's birthday,' said Bison, happily. 'I always bet on you, Kebra.' His smile faded and he swore. 'This will be the last year when you pay off all my winter debts.'

'Not this year, my friend,' said Kebra. 'I'm not entered.'

'I thought you might forget,' said Bison, 'so I entered you myself.'

'Tell me you are joking,' said Kebra, his voice cold.

'I never joke about my debts. Shouldn't you be out there practising?'

The crowds were beginning to gather as Dagorian strolled out onto the meadow. He was uncomfortable in full armour, the gilded black and gold breastplate hanging heavy on his slim shoulders. Still, he thought, at least I don't have to wear the heavy plumed helm. The cheek guards chafed his face and, despite the padded cap he wore below it, the helm did not sit right. Once when the king called out to him Dagorian had turned

351

sharply and the helm had swivelled on his head, the left cheek guard sliding over his left eye. Everyone had laughed. Dagorian had never wanted to be a soldier, but when your father was a hero general – and, worse, a dead hero general – the son was left with little choice.

And he had been lucky. The White Wolf had taken him on to his staff, and spent time teaching the youngster tactics and logistics. While Dagorian did not enjoy soldiering he had discovered he had a talent for it, and that made a life of campaigning at least marginally tolerable.

The preparations for the king's birthday were complete now, and within the hour the crowds would begin to surge through the gates. The sky was clear, the new day less cold than yesterday. Spring was coming. Only in the evenings now did the temperature drop below freezing. Dagorian saw the three old warriors talking by the fence rail. He strolled across to where they stood. As he approached, Kebra the Bowman strode away. He looks angry, thought Dagorian. The black swordsman saw Dagorian approach and gave a salute.

'Good morning to you, Nogusta,' said the officer. 'You fought well yesterday.'

'He does that,' said Bison, with a wide, gap-toothed grin. 'You're the son of Catoris, aren't you?'

'Yes.'

'Good man,' said Bison. 'You could always rely on the Third Lancers when he was in command. He was a hard bastard, though. Ten lashes I got when I didn't salute fast enough. Still, that's the nobility for you.' He swung to Nogusta. 'You want more pie?' The black man shook his head and Bison ambled away towards one of the food tents.

Dagorian grinned. 'Did he just praise my father, or insult him?' he asked.

'A little of both,' said Nogusta.

'An unusual man.'

'Bison or your father?'

'Bison. Are you entered in any of the tournaments?'

'No,' said the black man.

'Why not? You are a superb swordsman.'

'I don't play games with swords. And you?'

'Yes,' answered Dagorian. 'In the sabre tourney.'

'You will face Antikas Karios in the final.'

Dagorian looked surprised. 'How can you know that?'

Nogusta lifted his hand and touched the centre of his brow. 'I have the Third Eye,' he said.

'And what is that?'

The black man smiled. 'It is a Gift – or perhaps a curse – I was born with.'

'Do I win or lose?'

'The Gift is not that precise,' Nogusta told him, with a smile. 'It strikes like lightning, leaving an image. I can neither predict nor direct it. It comes or it . . .' His smile faded, and his expression hardened. Dagorian looked closely at the man. It seemed he was no longer aware of the officer's presence. Then he sighed. 'I am sorry,' he said. 'I was momentarily distracted.'

'You saw another vision?' asked Dagorian.

'Yes.'

'Did it concern the sabre tourney?'

'No, it did not. I am sure you will acquit yourself well. Tell me how is the White Wolf?' he asked, suddenly.

'He is well, and preparing plans for the return home. Why do you ask?'

'Malikada will try to kill him.' The words were spoken softly, but with great authority. The black man was not venturing an opinion, but stating a fact.

'This is what you saw?'

'I need no mystic talent to make that prediction.'

'Then I think you are wrong,' said Dagorian. 'Malikada is the king's general now. Banelion does not stand in his way. Indeed he will be going home in three days, to retire.'

'Even so his life is in danger.'

'Perhaps you should speak to the general about this?' said Dagorian, stiffly.

Nogusta shrugged. 'There is no need. He knows it as well as I. Cerez was Malikada's favourite. He believed him to be almost invincible. Yesterday he learned a hard lesson. He will want revenge.'

'If that is true will he not seek revenge against you also?'

'Indeed he will,' agreed Nogusta.

'You seem remarkably unperturbed by the prospect.'

'Appearances can be deceiving,' Nogusta told him.

As the morning wore on Nogusta's words continued to haunt the young officer. They had been spoken with such quiet certainty that the more Dagorian thought of them, the more convinced he became of the truth they contained. Malikada was not known as

353

a forgiving man. There were many stories among the Drenai officers concerning the Ventrian prince and his methods. One story had it that Malikada once beat a servant to death for ruining one of his shirts. As far as Dagorian knew there was no evidence to support the tale, but it highlighted the popular view of Malikada.

Such a man would indeed nurse a grudge against Banelion.

With at least another two hours before the start of his duties Dagorian decided to seek out the general. He loved the old man in a way he had never learned to love his own father. Often he had tried to work out why, but the answer escaped him. Both were hard, cold men, addicted to war and the methods of war. And yet with Banelion he could relax, finding words easy and conversation smooth. With his father his throat would tighten, his brain melt. Clear and concise thoughts would travel from his mind to his mouth, appearing to become drunken on the way, spilling out – at least to himself – as stuttering gibberish.

'Spit it out, boy!' Catoris would yell, and the words would dry up, and Dagorian would stand very still, feeling very foolish.

In all his life he could only recall one moment when his father had shown him affection. And that was after the duel. A nobleman named Rogun had challenged Dagorian. It was all so stupid. A young woman had smiled at him, and he had returned the compliment. The man with her stormed across the street. He slapped Dagorian across the face, and issued a challenge.

They had met on the cavalry parade-ground at dawn the following day. Catoris had been present. He watched the fight without expression, but when Dagorian delivered the killing stroke he ran forward and embraced him clumsily. He remembered the incident now with regret, for instead of returning the embrace he had angrily pulled clear and hurled his sword aside. 'It was all so stupid!' he stormed. 'He made me kill him for a smile.'

'It was a duel of honour,' said his father, lamely. 'You should be proud.'

'I am sick to my stomach,' said Dagorian.

The following day he had entered the monastery at Corteswain, and pledged his life to the Source.

When his father died at Mellicane, leading a charge that saved the king's life, Dagorian had known enormous grief. He did not doubt that his father loved him, nor indeed that he loved his father. But – apart from that one embrace – the two of them had never been able to show their affection for one another.

Shaking off the memories Dagorian approached the gates, and saw the crowds waiting patiently outside. They parted and cheered as the Ventrian sorcerer, Kalizkan, made his entrance. Tall and dignified, wearing robes of silver satin, edged with golden thread, the silver-bearded Kalizkan smiled and waved, stopping here and there to speak to people in the throng. Six young children stayed close by him, holding to the tassels of his belt. He halted before a young woman, with two children. She was wearing the black sash of the recently widowed, and the children looked thin and undernourished. Kalizkan leaned in close to her, and lifted his hand towards the cheap tin brooch she wore upon her ragged dress. 'A pretty piece,' he said, 'but for a lady so sad it ought to be gold.' Light danced from his fingers, and the brooch gleamed in the sunlight. Where it had sat close to the dress the sheer weight of the new gold made it hang down. The woman fell to her knees and kissed Kalizkan's robes. Dagorian smiled. Such deeds as this had made the sorcerer popular with the people. He had also turned his vast home into an orphanage in the northern quarter and spent much of his free time touring the slum areas, bringing deserted children to his house.

Dagorian had met him only once – a brief introduction at the palace, with twenty other new officers. But he liked the man instinctively. The sorcerer gave a last wave to the crowd and led his children into the park. Dagorian bowed as he approached.

'Good morning to you, young Dagorian,' said Kalizkan, his voice curiously high pitched. 'A fine day, and not too cold.'

The officer was surprised that Kalizkan had remembered his name. 'Indeed, sir. I am told you have prepared a wondrous exhibition for the king.'

'Modesty forbids me to boast, Dagorian,' said Kalizkan, with a mischievous grin. 'But my little friends and I will certainly attempt something special. Isn't that right?' he said, kneeling down and ruffling the blond hair of a small boy.

'Yes, uncle. We will make the king very happy,' said the child.

Kalizkan pushed himself to his feet and smoothed down his silver satin robes. They matched the colour of his long thin beard, and highlighted the summer sky blue of his eyes. 'Well, come along, my children,' he said. With a wave to Dagorian the tall sorcerer strode on.

Dagorian moved out through the gates, and along the highway to where the horses of the officers were stabled. Saddling his chestnut gelding he rode out to where the White Wolf was

355

camped, west of the city walls. The camp itself was largely deserted, since most of the men would be at the celebrations, but there was a handful of sentries, two of whom were standing outside Banelion's large, black tent. Dagorian dismounted and approached the men.

'Is the general accepting visitors?' he asked. One of the sentries lifted the tent flap and stepped inside. He returned moments later.

'He will see you, Captain,' he said, saluting.

The sentry lifted the flap once more and Dagorian ducked into the tent. The White Wolf was sitting at a folding table, examining maps. He was looking frail and elderly. Dagorian hid his concern and gave a salute. Banelion smiled. 'What brings you here today, my boy? I thought you had duties in the Park.'

Dagorian quietly told him of the conversation with Nogusta. The White Wolf listened in silence, his expression unreadable. When the young man had finished he gestured him to a chair. Banelion sat quietly for a moment, then leaned forward. 'Do not take this amiss, Dagorian, but I want you to forget about the warning. And let us make our goodbyes now, for you must not come close to me again.'

'You think it is true, sir?'

'True or false it must not affect you. You are remaining behind, and will serve Malikada as you served me – with loyalty and honour.'

'I could not do that if he was responsible for your death, my general.'

'I am no longer *your* general. Malikada is!' snapped Banelion. His face softened. 'But I am your friend. What is between Malikada and myself is for me to concern myself with. It has no bearing on your dealings with the king's general. We are not talking friendship here, Dagorian, we are talking politics. More than this we are talking survival. I can tolerate an enemy like Malikada. You cannot.'

Dagorian shook his head. 'You talk of honour, sir? How could I honour the man who murdered my friend?'

'Try to understand, boy. Two years ago Malikada was leading an army that killed Drenai soldiers. He faced the king in two battles and did his best to kill him. When the last city fell we all expected Malikada to be executed. Skanda chose to make him his friend. And he has proved a remarkable ally. That is Skanda's great talent. Half the army he leads used to be his enemies. That is why he took the empire, and why he will hold it. Three of

Skanda's closest friends were killed by Malikada and his men – including your father. Yet Skanda honours him. If Malikada manages to have me killed it will not matter to the king, for I am yesterday, Malikada is today. Let it not matter to you either.'

The White Wolf fell silent. Dagorian reached out and took the old man's hand. 'I am not the king. I am not even a soldier by choice. And I cannot think as you would wish me to. All I want is to see you live.'

'Many men have tried to kill me, Dagorian. I am still here.' Banelion rose. 'Now go back to the celebrations.'

Dagorian moved to the tent entrance and turned. 'Thank you, sir, for all you have done for me.'

'And you for me,' said Banelion. 'Farewell.'

Outside the tent Dagorian summoned the sentries to him. Both were older men, their beards flecked with silver. 'The general's life is in danger,' he told them, keeping his voice low. 'Watch carefully for strangers. And if he leaves the camp for any reason make sure someone is close to him.'

'We know, sir. They'll not get to him while we live,' said the first.

Dagorian stepped into the saddle and rode back through the city. Leaving his horse at the stables he joined the last of the crowd surging through the open gates. He had been gone for more than an hour, and many of the events had already begun. Threading his way through the throng he made his way to the king's pavilion and rejoined the guards.

The wrestling was under way. More than forty pairs of fighting men were grappling, and the crowd was cheering loudly. Dagorian saw the giant Bison hurl an opponent out of the circle. Far to the left the archery tournament had also begun. Two hundred bowmen were shooting at straw-filled targets.

Dagorian glanced at the nobles seated around the king. Malikada was sitting beside Skanda. The king looked magnificent in his armour of polished iron. Unadorned it gleamed like silver. Skanda laughed and gestured towards one of the wrestling bouts. Dagorian's eyes did not follow where the king pointed. His gaze remained fixed on Skanda's profile. The king was a handsome man, his golden hair, streaked now with silver, shone in the sunlight like a lion's mane. This was the man who had conquered most of the world. Beside the powerful figure of Skanda the Ventrian prince Malikada seemed almost frail. Both men were laughing now.

357

Two rows behind the king sat the pregnant queen, Axiana. Serene and exquisitely beautiful she seemed to have no interest in the proceedings. The daughter of the Ventrian emperor deposed by Skanda she had been taken in marriage to cement Skanda's claim to the throne. Dagorian wondered if the king loved her. A ridiculous thought, he chided himself. Who could not love Axiana? Dressed in white, her dark hair braided with silver thread, she was – despite the advanced state of her pregnancy – an arresting vision of beauty. Her gaze suddenly turned to Dagorian, and he looked away, guiltily.

The smell of roasting meats drifted out from the huge tent behind the pavilion. Soon the tourneys would be suspended for an hour for the nobles to eat and drink. Dagorian moved back to check the guards around the tent. Sixty spearmen were waiting there. They stood to attention as the young officer approached. 'Take your places,' he commanded. All but four of the men filed out around the tent. Dagorian led the last group to the entrance behind the pavilion.

'Tie your chin strap,' he ordered one of the men.

'Yes, sir. Sorry, sir.' Passing his spear to a comrade the man hastily tied the thongs.

'Remain silent and at attention until the last of the guests return to the pavilion. You are the King's Guards. Your discipline is legendary.'

'Yes, sir!' they chorused.

Dagorian stepped into the tent. Food tables had been set all around the huge enclosure, and a score of servants waited, bearing trays on which goblets of wine had been set. Dagorian gestured the servants forward, and they moved in two lines to flank the entrance. Trumpets sounded from the Park. Dagorian moved behind the first line of servants and waited. Within moments the king and queen entered, followed by Skanda's generals and nobles.

Immediately the silent tension within the tent disappeared, as wine was served and the guests made their way to the food tables. Dagorian relaxed, and allowed himself to gaze on the wonder that was Axiana. Her eyes were dark blue, the colour of a sunset sky, just after the sun had fallen. They are sad eyes, he thought. In his young life Dagorian had never given much thought to the status of women, but now he wondered just how the queen had felt when ordered to marry the man who took her father's empire. Had she and her father been close? Had she sat upon his knee as a child and tugged his long beard. Had he doted upon her? Pushing such thoughts from his mind Dagorian was about to leave when a young Ventrian officer approached him. The man gave a slight, almost contemptuous, bow. 'The Prince Malikada would like a word with you, sir,' said the man.

Dagorian eased his way to where Malikada waited. The Ventrian prince was dressed in a black tunic, embroidered with a silver hawk at the shoulder, and his beard was now braided with silver wire to match it. He gave a friendly smile as Dagorian approached and extended his hand. His grip was firm and dry. 'You were Banelion's aide, and I understand you accomplished your tasks with dedication and efficiency.'

'Thank you, sir.'

'I have my own aide, Dagorian, but I wanted you to know that I appreciate your talents, and that I will bear you in mind for promotion when a suitable position arises.'

Dagorian bowed, and was about to step away when the prince spoke again. 'You were fond of Banelion?'

'Fond, sir? He was my general,' replied Dagorian, carefully. 'I respected him for his great talents.'

'Yes, of course. In his time he was a formidable foe. But now he is old and spent. Will you serve me with the same dedication?'

Dagorian found his heart beating faster. He looked into Malikada's dark, cold eyes, and saw again the fierce intelligence there. There would be no point in trying to lie to this man directly. He would read it immediately. Dagorian's mouth was dry, but his words when they came were spoken steadily. 'I am dedicated to the king's service, sir. You are the king's general. Any order you give me will be carried out to the best of my ability.'

'That is all one can ask,' said Malikada. 'Now you may go. Antikas Karios will take over your duties here.' With that he smiled and swung away.

Dagorian turned, and almost collided with the heavily pregnant queen. 'My apologies, my lady,' he stuttered. She gave him a distant smile and moved past him. Feeling like a dolt Dagorian left the tent and wandered back to the open park.

Thousands of people were wandering across the grass, or sitting on blankets and eating prepared lunches. Soldiers and athletes were practising for their events, horse trainers were running their mounts, stretching them for the races ahead. Dagorian looked around for the king's horse, Starfire. It was always entered in the races, and never failed. But, as he scanned the horses he saw that the giant black gelding was not among the mounts being exercised. He strolled to one of the handlers and enquired of the horse.

'Lung rot,' said the man. 'It's a damn shame. Still he's getting old now. Must be eighteen if he's a day.'

Dagorian was saddened to hear it. Every Drenai child knew of Starfire. Bought by the king's father for a fabulous sum it had carried Skanda into all his major battles. Now it was dying. Skanda must be heartbroken, he thought.

Relieved to be free of his duties he wandered back to the officers' rest area and stripped off his armour, ordering a young Cul to return it to his quarters. Then he strolled out to enjoy the festivities. The prospect of becoming Malikada's aide had been an odious one, and he was grateful that the task had been taken from him. I should have gone home with the White Wolf, he thought, suddenly. I hate soldiering. While his father had been a living hero Dagorian had attended the Docian Monastery at Corteswain, studying to become a priest. He had been happy there, his lifestyle humble and almost serene.

Then his father had died, and the world changed.

Moving through the crowd he saw Nogusta sitting on the grass, Bison stretched out beside him. The bald giant had a swollen eye and a purple bruise on his cheekbone. Dagorian joined them. 'How are you faring?' he asked Bison.

'Quarter-finals,' said the giant, sitting up and stifling a groan. 'This is my year.'

Dagorian saw the vivid bruises and the man's obvious fatigue, and masked his scepticism. 'How long before your next bout?'

Bison shrugged and looked to Nogusta. 'An hour,' said the black man. 'He's fighting the tribesman who beat him last year.'

'I'll take him this time,' said Bison, wearily. 'But I think I'll take a nap first.' Lying back the giant closed his eyes. Nogusta covered him with a cloak and rose.

'You saw the general?' he asked Dagorian.

'I did.'

'He advised you to stay away from him.'

'You have a great gift.'

Nogusta smiled. 'No, that was just common sense. He is a wise man. Malikada is not so wise. But that is often the way with ambitious men. They come to believe in tales of their own destiny. Everything they desire, so they believe, is theirs by right. Chosen by the Source.'

360

'The Source is given credit and blame for many deeds,' said Dagorian. 'Are you a believer?'

'I would like to be,' admitted Nogusta. 'It would certainly make life more complete if one could believe in a grand plan for the universe. If we could be certain that evil men would receive judgement. However, I fear that life is not so simple. Wise men say that the universe is in a state of constant war, a battle between the Source and the forces of chaos. If that is true then chaos commands the most cavalry.'

'You are a cynic,' said Dagorian.

'I think not. I am just old and have seen too much.'

The two men sat down beside the sleeping Bison. 'How is it that a black man serves in the army of Drenan?' asked Dagorian.

'I am a Drenai,' answered Nogusta. 'My great-grandfather was a Phocian seaman. He was captured at sea and the Drenai made a slave of him. He was freed after seven years and became an indentured servant. Later he returned to his homeland and took a wife, bringing her back to Drenan. Their first son did the same, bringing my grandmother back to our estates in Ginava.'

'Estates? Your family have done well.'

'My people had a talent with horses,' said Nogusta. 'My great-grandfather bred war mounts for the old king's cavalry. It made us rich at the time.'

'But you are rich no longer?'

'No. A Drenai nobleman became jealous of our success, and fostered stories about us among the local villagers. One night a child went missing. He told them we had taken her for an obscene sacrifice. Our house was burned to the ground, and all my family slaughtered. The child, of course, was not there. It transpired she had wandered into the mountains and fallen down a steep slope. Her leg was broken.'

'How is it you were not killed with your family?'

'I went out to find the child. When I got back with her it was all over.'

Dagorian looked into Nogusta's strange blue eyes. He could read no emotion there. 'Did you seek justice?' he asked. Nogusta smiled.

'Twelve villagers were hanged.'

'And the nobleman?'

'He had friends in very high places and was not even arrested. Even so he fled to Mashrapur, and hired four swordsmen as his permanent bodyguards. He lived in a house behind high walls, and rarely came out in public.'

'So he was never brought to justice?'

'No.'

'What became of him? Do you know?'

Nogusta looked away for a moment. 'Someone scaled his walls, slew his guards and cut his heart out.'

'I see.' For a while both men sat in silence. 'Are you pleased to be going home?' asked Dagorian.

The black man shrugged. 'I am tired of constant war. What does it achieve? When the old king took arms against the emperor we all felt the cause was just. But now . . . ? What has Cadia ever done to us? Now it is about glory and building an everlasting name. The Ventrian Empire once boasted a thousand universities, and hospitals for the sick. Now it is bled dry and all the young men want to fight. Yes, I am ready to go home.'

'To breed horses?'

'Yes. Many of my father's horses escaped into the high country. There will be a sizeable herd by now.'

'And will Bison go with you?'

Nogusta laughed aloud. 'He will sign on with a mercenary regiment somewhere.' His smile faded. 'And he will die in a small war over nothing.'

The winter sun was high now, its pale warmth melting the patches of snow.

'I wanted to be a priest,' said Dagorian. 'I thought I heard the call. Then my father was killed and my family informed me it was my duty to take his place. From a priest to a soldier . . . there's a leap!'

'Once there were warrior priests,' said Nogusta. 'The Thirty. There are many legends of them.'

'There has been no temple since the War of the Twins,' said Dagorian. 'But the order had slipped a long way by then. One of my ancestors fought alongside the Thirty at Dros Delnoch. His name was Hogun. He was a general of the Legion.'

'I only know about Druss and the Earl of Bronze,' admitted Nogusta.

'That's all anyone remembers. I sometimes wonder if he even existed at all . . . Druss, I mean. Or was he just a combination of many heroes?'

'Don't say that to Bison. He swears he is of Druss's line.'

Dagorian gave a wry chuckle. 'Almost every soldier I know claims Druss as an ancestor. Even the king. But the simple fact is that most of the earliest stories tell us Druss had no children.'

Trumpets sounded and Dagorian looked up to see the royal party moving back to their seats. Nogusta woke Bison.

'Almost time, my friend,' he said.

Bison sat up and yawned. 'That was all I needed,' he said. 'Now I'm ready. How's Kebra doing?'

'He didn't take part in the elimination event,' said Nogusta. 'As reigning champion he can come in for the final stages, the Horse, the Hanging Man, and the Distance.'

'He'll win,' said Bison. 'He's the best.'

'Place no money on him, my friend,' said Nogusta, lightly touching the centre of his forehead.

'Too late,' said Bison.

Dagorian strolled to a food tent and purchased a wedge of meat pie, which he ate swiftly, then returned to the meadow. He saw Bison engaged in a furious contest with a massive opponent. Bison was bleeding from cuts above both eyes, and seemed to be suffering. His opponent charged in, ducking to grab Bison's leg and up-end him. But the Drenai warrior skipped back, then dived onto the tribesman's back. Both men rolled, but Bison had a neck lock in place. Robbed of air the tribesman was forced to submit. Bison rose, staggered, then sat down. Nogusta ran to his side, helping Bison from the circle. Men were cheering now, and clapping Bison on the back.

Dagorian moved forward to offer his congratulations when a giant of a man stepped in front of him. 'You will be easy meat, old man,' he told Bison. 'Look at you! You're exhausted.' Dagorian saw anger in Bison's eyes, but Nogusta half dragged him away. The young officer followed them.

'Who was that?' he asked Nogusta.

'The Ventrian champion, Kyaps,' said the black man.

'I'll . . . whip . . . him too,' muttered Bison.

Dagorian moved to Bison's left and between them he and Nogusta half carried Bison to a bench seat. The big man slumped down. 'Semifinals, eh?' he said, spitting blood to the grass. 'Just two more and I'll be champion.'

'When is the next bout?' asked Dagorian.

'They are preparing for it now,' said Nogusta, massaging Bison's huge shoulders.

'I think he should withdraw,' said the officer.

'Don't worry about me,' said Bison, forcing a grin. 'I'm just acting like this to fool them all.'

'It's certainly fooling me,' said Nogusta, drily.

363

'Have faith, black man,' grunted Bison, heaving himself to his feet. The Ventrian champion was waiting for them. He tied his long dark hair into a pony-tail and gave a wide smile as the older man entered the circle. At the sound of the drum Bison surged forward, to be met with a kick to the chest that halted him in his tracks. A chopping elbow opened a huge cut on his cheek, then Kyaps ducked down, threw an arm between Bison's legs and heaved him high, hurling him out of the circle. The old man landed hard. He lay still and did not move. Nogusta and Dagorian moved to his side. He was out cold. Nogusta felt for a pulse. 'Is he alive?' asked Dagorian.

'Yes.'

After some minutes Bison stirred. He tried to open his eyes, but one was swollen shut. 'I guess I didn't win,' he mumbled.

'I guess you didn't,' agreed Nogusta. Bison smiled.

'Still, I earned some money,' he said. 'I only bet myself to make the semis. Ten to one they offered.'

'It'll cost you what you won to have your face mended,' Nogusta told him.

'Nonsense. You can stitch the cuts. They'll be fine. I'm a fast healer.' He sat up. 'I should have entered the boxing,' he said. 'I would have won that.'

The two men helped him to his feet. 'Let's go see Kebra win,' said Bison.

'I think you should have another nap,' advised Nogusta.

'Nonsense. I feel strong as an ox.'

As they were about to move off Kyaps strolled across to where they stood. He was a full head taller than Bison. 'Hey, old man,' he said. 'The next time you see me you kiss my boots. Understand?'

Bison chuckled with genuine humour. 'You have a big mouth, child,' he told him.

Kyaps leaned forward. 'Big enough to swallow you, you Drenai scum!'

'Well,' said Bison, 'swallow this.' His fist smashed into Kyaps' chin, and Dagorian winced as he heard the snapping of bone. The Ventrian champion hit the grass face first and did not move. 'See,' said Bison. 'I should have entered the boxing. I'd have won that.'

Chapter Three

Kebra the bowman was relaxed, his mind focused, his emotions suppressed, all thoughts of Bison's actions forgotten. Anger would not be an ally now. Archery required calm concentration and great timing.

He had entered the tourney in the fifth stage with only twenty archers left. The target, thirty paces away, was a straw man, with a round red heart pinned to the chest. Kebra had struck the heart ten times with ten shafts, giving him 100 points. The Ventrian bowman standing to his right had hit nine, and two other men had seven.

These four alone moved on to the sixth stage.

The crowd among the competitors was swelling now, and once again Kebra could feel the old excitement coursing through him. He had watched the other three competitors, and only the stocky Ventrian posed any real danger. But the man was being unsettled by the mainly Drenai crowd, who jeered and shouted as he took aim.

The next event was one of Kebra's favourites. He had always enjoyed the Horse, for it was the closest the tourney could offer to combat shooting. Led by running soldiers four ponies bearing figures of straw tied to the saddle would pass before the bowmen. Each archer was allowed three shafts. There was a larger element of luck in this event, as the horses would swerve, causing the straw figures to sway in the saddle. But the crowd loved it. And so did the Drenai champion.

Kebra stood waiting, one shaft notched to the string, two others stuck in the ground before him. He glanced at the four ostlers, watching them eke out the guide ropes. A trumpet sounded. The men ran forward, exhorting the ponies to follow them. Three obeyed immediately, the fourth hanging back. Kebra drew back on the string, sighting carefully, allowing for the speed of the first horse. He loosed the shaft. Without waiting to see it strike home he ducked down and notched a second arrow. Coming up smoothly he shot again at the second target. An angry roar went up from the crowd. Kebra ignored the impulse to see what had caused it and brought his bow to bear. The last pony, an arrow jutting from its flank had reared up and was fighting the rope. It broke loose and galloped towards the king's pavilion. Kebra loosed his last shaft, and watched as it arced towards the panic-stricken pony. The arrow punched home in the back of the straw man.

Angry jeers turned to a roar of applause at the strike. Several men ran out onto the meadow and gathered the wounded pony, which was led away. The man whose arrow caused the wound was disqualified.

Only then did Kebra have a chance to check his score. All three shafts had scored. Another thirty points.

The Ventrian archer, a small, chubby man, turned to him. 'It is an honour to see you shoot,' he said. He held out his hand. 'I am Dirais.' Kebra accepted the handshake. He glanced at the scoreboard, held aloft by a young cadet. The Ventrian was ten points behind him. The other archer, a slim, young Drenai, was a further twenty points adrift.

A dozen soldiers moved out onto the meadow, dragging a wheeled, triangular scaffold, 20 feet high, across the grass. As they were setting it into place Kebra saw the king and Malikada striding out from the pavilion, coming towards them.

Skanda gave a wide grin and clapped Kebra on the shoulder. 'Good to see you, old lad,' he said. 'That last shot reminded me of the day you saved my life. A fine strike.'

'Thank you, sire,' said Kebra, with a bow. Malikada stepped forward.

'Your legend is not exaggerated,' he said. 'Rarely have I seen better bowmanship.' Kebra bowed again. Skanda shook the young Ventrian's hand.

'You are competing with the finest,' he told Dirais. 'And you are acquitting yourself well. Good luck to you.' Dirais gave a deep bow.

Malikada leaned in close to the Ventrian. 'Win,' he said. 'Make me proud.'

The king and his general moved back and the last three archers faced the Hanging Man.

A figure of straw was hung from the scaffold. A soldier dragged the figure back, then released it to swing like a pendulum between the supports. The young Drenai stepped up first. His first shaft struck the straw man dead centre, but his second hit a support pole and glanced away. His third missed the Hanging Man by a whisker.

Next came Dirais, and the Hanging Man was swung back once more. It seemed to Kebra that it was given an extra push by the Drenai soldiers, and was moving at greater speed. And the Drenai soldiers in the crowd began again to jeer and shout in an effort to unsettle the Ventrian. Even so the chubby archer hammered his first two shafts into the dummy. His third also struck a support pole.

Kebra stepped up. The figure was swung again, this time more sedately. For the first time anger flared in the bowman. He did not need this advantage. Even so he did not complain, and, calming himself, sent three arrows into the target. The applause was thunderous. He glanced towards Dirais, and saw the fury in the man's dark eyes. It was bad enough for him to be facing the Drenai champion without such partisan efforts from the officials.

The young Drenai archer was eliminated, and now came the final test. Two targets were set up thirty paces distant. They were the traditional round targets, with a series of concentric circles, each of a different colour, surrounding a gold circle at the centre. The outer rim was white, and worth two points. Within this was blue, worth five, then silver worth seven, and lastly gold for ten.

Kebra shot first, and struck gold. Dirais equalled him. The targets were moved back ten paces. This time Kebra only managed blue. Dirais, despite the increased jeering struck gold once more.

With only two shafts left Kebra was leading by 175 points to 160. Keep calm, he told himself. The targets were lifted and carried back another ten paces. The colours were a distant blur to Kebra now. He squinted hard and drew back on the string. The crowd was silent. He loosed, the shaft arcing gracefully through the air to thud home into the white. There were no cheers from the crowd now. Dirais took aim and struck gold once more – 177 points to 170, with only one shaft left.

The targets were moved back again. Kebra could only dimly make out the outline. He rubbed his eyes. Then, taking a deep breath he took aim at the target he could barely see – and let fly!

He did not know where the shaft landed, but heard one of the judges shout: 'White!' He was relieved to have hit the target at all – 179 points to 170.

Dirais would need gold to win. Kebra stepped back. The crowd were shouting now at the top of their voices.

Please miss, thought Kebra, wanting the championship more than he had ever wanted anything in his life. His chest felt tight and heavy, and his breathing was shallow. He glanced at the crowd, and saw Nogusta. Kebra tried to force a smile, but it was more like a death's head grin.

Dirais stood up to the mark, and drew back on the string. He stood, rock steady. Kebra's heart was pounding now. What were the odds on a man striking three golds in a row? A minor fluctuation in the breeze, a slight imperfection in the shaft or the flights. The gold was no bigger than a man's fist, and the distance was great: sixty paces. During his best days Kebra would have hit only four in five at this distance. And this Ventrian was not as skilled as I once was, he thought. What, three in five? Two in five? Sweet Heaven, just miss!

Just as Dirais was about to loose his final shaft a white dove flew up out of the crowd in a frantic flurry. His concentration momentarily lost he shot too quickly, his arrow punching home into silver. Kebra had won.

Strangely there was no joy. The crowd was cheering wildly but Kebra looked at Nogusta. The black man was standing very still. Dirais turned away, offering no congratulation. Kebra took him by the arm. 'Wait!' he commanded him.

'For what?' asked the Ventrian.

'I want you to shoot again.' Dirais looked puzzled, but Kebra drew him to the line.

'What is happening here?' asked one of the judges.

'Someone released that dove deliberately,' said Kebra. 'I have asked Dirais to shoot again.'

'You cannot ask this,' said the judge. 'The last shaft has been fired.' The king moved through the crowd, and the judge explained what had happened. Skanda approached Kebra.

'Are you sure this is what you want?' he asked, his good humour vanished, his face hard and cold. 'It makes no sense.'

'I have been champion for fifteen years, sire. I have beaten every man who stood beside me at the line. I beat them with skill. The jeering was unpleasant, but a true champion rises above that. The dove, however, is a different matter. Such a sharp and flurried movement would have unsettled anyone. It was a deliberate act to sabotage the man's chances. And it succeeded. I ask you, sire, to let him shoot again.'

Suddenly Skanda grinned, and for a moment he looked like the boy-king again. 'Then let it be so,' he said.

The king climbed to a fence rail and stood above the crowd. 'The champion has requested that his opponent be allowed to shoot one more arrow,' he bellowed. 'And there will be silence when he does so.' He leapt down and signalled Dirais.

The young Ventrian notched his shaft and sent it unerringly into the gold.

Kebra's heart sank. Ventrian soldiers swarmed forward and hoisted Dirais into the air. Kebra stood by silently. The king approached him. 'You are a fool, man,' he whispered. 'But the deed was not without merit.'

Skanda handed him the Silver Arrow, and Kebra waited until the celebrations had died down. The Ventrians lowered Dirais and the small archer stepped up and bowed deeply before Kebra. 'This is a day I shall remember all my life,' he said.

'As shall I,' Kebra told him, presenting the arrow. The little man bowed again.

'I am sorry your eyes let you down.' Kebra nodded and swung away.

No-one approached him as he stalked from the meadow.

Stunned and disbelieving Bison watched him go. 'Why did he do that?' he asked, dabbing at his wounded cheek with a blood-soaked cloth.

'He is a man of honour,' said Nogusta. 'Come, it is time that wound was stitched.'

'What has honour to do with paying my debts?'

'I fear it would take too long to explain,' the black man told him. Taking him by the arm he led the bewildered Bison to a medical tent. Nogusta borrowed a sickle shaped needle and a length of thread and carefully drew the folds of the cheek wound together. Altogether ten stitches were needed. Blood slowly seeped between them. The cuts above Bison's eyes were shallow, and needed no stitches. Already scabs were forming there and the trickle of blood had ceased.

'He really let me down,' grumbled Bison. 'He let us all down.' Dagorian, who had stood by in silence moved alongside the giant.

'You are not being fair on him,' he said, softly. 'It was an act of greatness. The Ventrian was being barracked and jeered. And someone did release that dove in order to throw his aim.'

'Of course he did,' said Bison. 'I paid him to do it.'

Dagorian's expression changed, becoming cold. 'You make me ashamed to be a Drenai,' he said. Turning away Dagorian left the two warriors.

'What's wrong with him?' enquired Bison. 'Has the world gone mad?'

'You are an idiot sometimes, my friend,' said Nogusta. 'Perhaps you should go back to the barracks and rest.'

'No. I want to see Kalizkan's magic. There might be a dragon.'

'You could ask him,' said Nogusta, pointing to a section of open lands between the tents. The silver garbed wizard was sitting on a bench, surrounded by children.

'I don't think so,' said Bison, doubtfully. 'I don't like wizards much. I think I'll collect my winnings and get drunk.'

'What about your debts?'

Bison laughed. 'We're leaving next week. They'll never follow me back to Drenan.'

'Is the word *honour* just a sound to you?' asked Nogusta. 'You have built up credit on trust. You gave your word to repay. Now you will become a thief whose word cannot be trusted.'

'What's put you in such a foul mood?' asked Bison.

'You would not understand if I carved the answer on your simian forehead,' snapped the black man. 'Go and get drunk. A man should always stick to what he does best.' Leaving Bison he walked across the meadow, threading his way through the crowd.

Antikas Karios approached him as he passed the king's pavilion. The swordsman gave a thin smile. 'Good morning to you,' he said. 'That was a clever trick you used against Cerez. I had warned him in the past about arrogance. I will not have to warn him again.'

Nogusta was about to move on, but the Ventrian stepped into his path. 'The king would like you to entertain his guests before the races.' Nogusta nodded and followed the officer towards the front of the pavilion. Skanda saw him coming and gave a broad smile, then turned to say something to Malikada. Nogusta approached the king and gave a deep bow. 'My congratulations on your birthday, sire,' he said.

Skanda leaned forward. 'I have told Prince Malikada of your skill with knives. I fear he doubts my word.'

'Not at all, majesty,' said Malikada, smoothly. Skanda clapped him on the shoulder, then rose. 'What can you show us today, my friend?' he asked Nogusta. The black man called for one of the archery targets to be brought up. While this was being done a sizeable crowd began to gather. Nogusta removed five throwing knives from the sheaths stitched to his baldric, then spread the blades in his left hand.

'Is the target large enough?' asked Malikada, as the 6 foot high target was placed within 10 feet of the black man. The Ventrian officers around him laughed at the jest.

'I will make it smaller, my lord,' said Nogusta. 'Perhaps you would care to stand in front of it?' Malikada's smile froze in place. He glanced at the king.

'Either you or me, old lad,' said Skanda.

Malikada rose and walked to the front of the pavilion, where a soldier opened the gate for him. He strode out to the target and turned, his dark eyes staring intently at Nogusta. 'Do not move, my lord,' said Nogusta.

The black man spun a razor sharp knife in the air, then caught it. He repeated this with the other blades, throwing each one higher than the last. Then, while one was still in the air, he sent up another, then another, until all five were spinning and glittering in the sunlight. There was absolute silence now as the crowd waited in tense expectation. Still spinning the knives Nogusta slowly backed away until he was ten paces from where Malikada stood at the target.

The Ventrian prince watched the whirling blades. He seemed relaxed, but his eyes were narrowed and unblinking. Suddenly Nogusta's right arm shot forward. One of the knives slashed through the air, punching home in the target no more than an inch from Malikada's left ear. The Ventrian jerked, but remained where he was. A bead of sweat began at his temple, trickling down his right cheek. Nogusta was juggling once more with the four remaining blades. Another knife thudded home alongside Malikada's left ear. The third and fourth slammed into the target alongside his arms.

Nogusta caught the last knife then bowed deeply to Skanda. Led by the king the crowd burst into applause.

'You want to risk the blindfold?' asked Skanda, 'or is that the end of the display?'

'Let it be as you desire, sire,' said Nogusta.

The king looked across at Malikada. 'What do you think, my friend? Would you like to see him throw blindfolded?'

Malikada gave an easy smile but stepped away from the target. 'I accept that his skills are remarkable, majesty, but I have no wish to stand before a blind man with a throwing knife.' The crowd laughed and applauded the prince, who returned to the pavilion.

'I'd like to see it,' said Skanda, moving down the steps and vaulting the gate. He strode to the target and stood before it. 'Don't let me down, old lad,' he told Nogusta. 'It's bad luck for a king to be killed on his birthday.'

Antikas Karios moved alongside Nogusta. He was holding a black silk scarf, which he folded to create a blindfold. This he tied over Nogusta's eyes. The black man stood for a moment, statue still. Then spun on his heel, making a complete circle. The throwing knife flashed through the air. The crowd gasped. For just a moment they believed it had slammed into the king's throat. Skanda lifted his hand, touching his finger to the ivory hilt which was nestling alongside his jugular. Nogusta pulled clear the blindfold. Skanda stepped up to him. Applause and cheers rang out.

'Just for a moment there you had me worried,' said the king.

'You take too many chances, sire,' Nogusta told him.

Skanda grinned. 'That is what makes life worth living.' Without another word he turned back to the pavilion. Nogusta gathered his knives and sheathed them, then made his way back through the crowd.

Three men followed him at a discreet distance.

As Nogusta had predicted Dagorian won his way through to the final of the sabres, and there met Antikas Karios. The Ventrian was faster in the strike than any man Nogusta had ever seen, his blade a shimmering blur. Three times in swift succession he pierced Dagorian's defences, lightly touching his sabre to the padded chest guard. The contest was short, and embarrassingly one sided.

With the contest over Dagorian waited courteously while Antikas Karios received the Silver Sabre then faded back into the crowd. Nogusta tapped him on the shoulder. 'You fought well,' said the black man. 'Your arm is swift, your eye good, but your narrow stance let you down. Your feet were too close together. When he attacked you were off balance.'

'Even so he is the most formidable swordsman I have ever seen,' said Dagorian.

'He is deadly,' agreed Nogusta.

'Do you think you could have beaten him?'

'Not even at my best.'

Dusk was closing in and the crowd began to mill at the

meadow. Kalizkan strode out alone to the centre of the field. As the sky darkened he raised his slender arms. Bright light shone from his fingers, spraying up into the air in vivid parallel flashes. The crowd applauded. In the sky the lights became a sea of stars, flowing together to form a male face, crowned with horns. This was the Bat-god, Anharat. Other divine faces glowed into view, gods and goddesses from Ventrian mythology. The faces spun in the air, creating a colossal circle of light that filled the sky. Lastly a white horse and rider could be seen, galloping between the stars. It came closer and closer. The rider was a handsome man, his armour glowing, his sword held high. He rode to the centre of the circle of gods, and reared his horse. Then he pulled off his helm, and the crowd roared to see it was Skanda. The king of kings to whom even the gods showed obeisance. Applause rang out. The image shimmered for several seconds, then the eldritch stars broke up once more, flowing over the heads of the crowd, and lighting the way to the three exit gates.

The carriages of the nobles had been drawn up outside the pavilion. The king and Malikada rode together, Skanda waving to the people as the carriage made its slow way to the gates. Then the crowd was allowed to leave. Nogusta bade farewell to the young Drenai and wandered away.

Night fell upon the meadow, and workmen moved in to dismantle the tents and the pavilion.

A lone wagon pulled up outside the tent of Kalizkan, and four men climbed from it. Furtively they glanced around, to be sure they were not overlooked. Then they entered the tent, and removed the blood-drenched bodies of six young children.

Nogusta was troubled as he made his way through the city streets. The crowd was thinning now, many stopping at ale houses and taverns, or moving through to the lantern lit night markets and the whores who plied their trade there. Nogusta was uneasy – and it was not the three men following who made him so. He had become aware of them earlier in the day. No, it was the talisman he wore. Sometimes a year could pass without a vision. Yet today he had experienced three, bright, vivid scenes. The first he had outlined to Dagorian. The second he had withheld, for it showed the young man fallen and bleeding upon a bridge of stone. But the third was altogether more mysterious; he was facing someone wearing black armour. His enemy was not human, and when their swords clashed lightning leapt up from

373

the blades. And there was something else. The shadow of huge wings descending towards him. Nogusta shivered. He had experienced the vision during Kalizkan's magical display, and wondered if somehow the sorcery had affected the talisman, causing a false vision. He hoped so.

He glanced up into the night sky and shivered. The last of the winter could be felt now that the sun had gone down, and the temperature was barely above freezing. Lifting his head he scented the night, the city smells, hot food, spicy and rich, smoke from wood fires, the musty human scents left by the crowd. The last vision had left him on edge. It was like the night before a battle, when the air is charged with tension.

Pausing in the Lantern Market he stopped at a stall and examined the wares, glazed pottery and necklaces of jade. He glanced back the way he had come. Two of the assassins were engaged in conversation. The third he could not see. Swiftly he scanned the crowd. Then he saw him, some way ahead, in a shadowed doorway.

Nogusta had no wish to kill these men. They were merely obeying the orders of their commander. But it would not be easy to evade them. A woman approached him. She was young and blonde, her face and lips painted. He smiled at her and she took his arm, leading him into an alley. A narrow flight of stairs led to a small room and a grimy bed. Nogusta paid her, then opened the window and stared down. The three assassins were waiting in the shadows.

'Is there another way out of here?' Nogusta asked the girl.

'Yes.' She pointed to a curtain. 'Through there, along the corridor, and down into the back streets. Why?'

'Thank you,' he said, opening his pouch and tossing her a silver coin. He was about to leave when she opened her dress and lay back on the bed, moonlight gleaming from her full breasts, her ivory belly and her pale thighs. Nogusta chuckled. Let them wait in the cold, he thought.

And moved to the girl.

An hour later he slipped through the curtain, along the corridor and out into the night.

The feeling of unease was still strong upon him, and he had long ago learned to trust his instincts. He smiled as he remembered the lion. It had been a night like this, cold and bright. He had awoken, nostrils flaring, aware of danger. Armed with only a knife the fourteen-year-old Nogusta had slipped from his room and out into the night. His father's horses had been uneasy, and they stood in a tight group, watching warily. The lion had burst from the undergrowth, and leapt the paddock fence. In one movement Nogusta had hurled his knife. It slammed into the lion's side. With a startled roar it turned on the boy. Nogusta had sprinted towards the barn, knowing the lion would catch him. But then Palarin, the lord of the herd, a huge black stallion of seventeen hands charged the lion, rearing up and lashing out with his hooves. The sudden attack made the lion swerve, but then he continued after the boy. Nogusta made it to the barn, grabbed a pitchfork, and turned just in time. The lion leapt, impaling itself on the twin blades. In its dying rage it lashed out, snapping the pitchfork and slashing Nogusta's chest, breaking three ribs.

He smiled at the memory. Never as good with horses as his brothers he had, for a time at least, been the hero who saved the herd. It was a good memory. Palarin had sired many fine warhorses, and from his line came the king's great war mount, Starfire.

Yet, like me, even he is getting old now, thought Nogusta, with a sigh. And he had been missing from the afternoon races. The rumour was that Starfire was ill. Nogusta decided to seek out the horse tomorrow, and see what treatment had been recommended.

He moved off into the back streets, enjoyed a meal at a small tavern, then headed for the barracks. He had no doubt the men, having lost him, would be waiting there. How he would handle the situation would depend entirely on their skill. If they were clumsy he would disable them, but if they were skilful he would have to kill them. This thought was not a happy one. In truth Nogusta had seen enough killing in his life, and wanted nothing more than to return to the high mountains and find the descendants of the herd. It would, he thought, at least make some sense of the remainder of his life. His thoughts turned to Skanda. The man was brave and adored by his troops. He was charismatic and intelligent. Yet there was something missing in him, some cold empty place untouched by human warmth. Despite this Nogusta liked him. Who could not? The man was capable of immense generosity. Yet equally he could be suddenly vain and jealous, and act with incredible malice. Perhaps all kings are this way, thought Nogusta. Perhaps it is the nature of powerful men.

The sky was clear, the moon and stars bright as he made his way through the back streets. The smell of freshly baked bread from the barracks kitchens wafted to him on the breeze, and he slowed his walk. Some thirty paces ahead the street intersected the Avenue of Light. Across the avenue, past the statues of the emperors was the old barracks building. Nogusta halted. Three men, armed with knives or short swords, were waiting somewhere ahead. Three men he had never met, who had been ordered to kill him. He did not hate them. They were merely soldiers obeying orders.

Yet neither was he prepared to die. Taking a deep breath he strode out onto the Avenue of Light. Lanterns were placed on tall poles along both sides of the Avenue, the bronze statues of the emperors gleaming like gold.

Nogusta moved out into the open and walked across the broad paved road. As he skirted the statue of the ancient king, Gorben, two men sprinted from the shadows. Both carried knives. Nogusta let them come. As the fastest man approached him Nogusta spun to one side, then launched a kick into the man's kneecap. The strike was not perfect, but the assassin was hurled from his feet. Nogusta ignored him and leapt to meet the second man, knocking aside the knife arm and hammering a right hook to the man's chin. He too spun to the ground, but rolled to his feet immediately. The first man was sitting in the road, unable to stand on his twisted knee. But he hurled his knife. Nogusta swayed aside from the blade, which flashed harmlessly by to clatter against the base of Gorben's statue. The second assassin attacked again, this time more warily. Nogusta stood very still, encouraging the man to move in close. He did so with a sudden rush. Nogusta grabbed his wrist and dragged him into a savage head butt which smashed the man's nose. He groaned and sagged against the black warrior. Nogusta spun him then slammed the edge of his palm against the assassin's neck. The man fell without a sound. The third man had not shown himself.

Nogusta walked on. The barracks gate was only thirty paces ahead now. Nogusta glanced back. The Ventrian with the injured knee had hobbled to his comrade and was sitting beside him. The black man moved into the shadow of the gate arch. A whisper of movement! Nogusta dived forward just as a knife sliced the air above him. The assassin was fast and leapt upon Nogusta before he could rise. Nogusta's elbow slammed back into the man's ribs, bringing a grunt of pain. The black man swivelled and sent a straight left into the Ventrian's face. The man lashed out, his fist cracking against Nogusta's cheek. Nogusta's head thumped against the stone walkway. Bright stars exploded before his eyes and Nogusta felt a wave of dizziness threatening to engulf him. For a while the two men grappled, and the older warrior felt his strength draining away. The assassin drew a second knife. With the last of his strength Nogusta hit him in the throat with stiffened fingers. The man gagged and reared up. Nogusta grabbed him by his shirt and threw him to one side. Rolling to his feet the black warrior kicked the assassin under the chin, catapulting him backwards. He moved in for a second strike, but his opponent was unconscious.

Breathless and exhausted Nogusta slumped to a bench seat under the arch. It would have been less effort to kill them all, he thought.

Hooded and cloaked against the night winds Ulmenetha walked slowly up the winding path towards the white marble temple that crowned the hill. She was tired, her calves burning as she reached the open gates. There was a time, back in Drenan, when she would have run this hill for the sheer pleasure of it. In the days of her youth she had been slim and fast, and physical exertion had been a joy that lifted her spirits. Not now. Now it was a chore to drag her overweight frame up such an incline. Panting she sat herself down on the steps of the temple entrance and waited for her hammering heart to slow down.

A young priest in white robes walked by her, bowing as he passed.

Heaving herself to her feet she entered the building, curtsying towards the High Altar. Dipping her finger into a stone bowl full of holy water she traced a circle upon her brow then walked to the back of the temple, seating herself in an alcove beneath a wreath of elegantly carved vines.

Another priest, a tall, balding young man with a prominent nose and a weak chin, saw her there and approached. 'What do you seek, mother?' he asked her. 'The Oracle Voice is not present.'

'I need no Voice,' she told him.

'Then why are you here at this late hour?' He was wearing the grey robes of a Senior Brother and his blue eyes looked world-weary and bored.

'Are you a Seer?' she asked him.

'Sadly, no, mother. I am still a student in such matters. But I have hopes that one day the curtain will part for me. What encouragement do you seek?'

'I seek a place without demons,' she told him. Instantly his face changed, and he made the sign of the Protective Horn.

'Such a word should not be used here,' he admonished her, his voice less friendly.

She smiled. 'If not here, then where? Never mind,' she added, seeing his confusion. 'Is there one among your order who is a Seer?'

'There was one,' he told her. 'Father Aminias. But he died last week. We were all saddened, for he was a fine man.'

'Was he ill?'

'No. He was attacked while out on his pastoral duties. A madman, it seems. He was screeching at the top of his voice, and he stabbed poor Aminias many times before he was dragged away.'

'And there is no-one else?'

'No, mother. Such Gifts are becoming increasingly rare, I think.'

'And yet they are ever more important,' she said, pushing herself to her feet.

'You spoke of . . . unholy beings. Why was that?' His blue eyes were suddenly fearful. Ulmenetha shook her head.

'You do not have the power to help me,' she said.

'Even so, mother, I would be grateful if you would enlighten me.'

Ulmenetha was silent for a moment. She looked at the grey robed priest. Her first impression had been of a weak man, but as she looked more closely she felt she might have mistaken sensitivity for weakness. And she desperately needed someone to confide in. Ulmenetha took a deep breath, and sat down once more. 'Someone is summoning demons,' she said, at last. 'They are everywhere, and growing in number. I have the eyes to see them, but not the wit to discern their purpose.' The balding priest sat down beside her.

'Father Aminias said the same thing,' he told her. 'It was his belief that a great spell was being wrought. But I cannot see these . . . these creatures. And I know not how to combat them. Nor even if I should try.' He gave a wan smile. 'Who are you, mother?'

'I am the Priestess Ulmenetha, the companion of Axiana the queen.'

'And what did you hope to achieve here?'

'I sought answers. I have had three visions, and can make no sense of any of them.' She told him of the four warriors and the white crow, of the demon in the lake, and of the sacrifice of the emperor. He listened in silence.

'I have never been blessed with your Gift,' he said, 'but what I have been given is the Gift of Discernment. Your visions are true ones. This I know. You saw three scenes. Three is a number of great power among mystics, and your experience is not unique.

What you saw is called a *kiraz*. The first scene concerns the *cause* of the problem. The second illuminates how the problem will *manifest* itself. The third is more complex. It always reveals the protagonists, but also often reveals a clue to the *solution* of the problem. Now let us examine them in detail. The Demon of the Lake – the *cause* – is more of a symbolic vision. It came out of the ice, you say. If I read it correctly the lake is a symbol for a gateway between its world and ours. You say it flowed like smoke into the body of a man. This is a man being possessed. But more than that it is a man being possessed after having been slain. What we have is a demon inhabiting a corpse. This demon must therefore be a most powerful creature. He now dwells in the world of men. He it is who has summoned the creatures you see over the city. It is his purpose that must be discerned.

'As to the emperor being sacrificed . . . this is not a symbol. There were many rumours when he was slain, and the body was never recovered. But the voice you heard was interesting. "The day of Resurrection is at hand. You are the first of the Three." Once again we have the number three. But what is to be resurrected? And who are the other two? This is the *manifestation* of the problem. Three are to be sacrificed in order for the Demon to achieve his purpose. One is already slain.

'Now to the scene in the forest. You and the queen stand protected by a few soldiers. Three old men and a youngster are all that stand between you and a terrible evil. The clue here, I believe is the person you are protecting. Axiana is obviously one of the Three. It makes sense, since her father was the first. Perhaps there is something in the bloodline that the Demon requires.' He smiled and spread his hands. 'I can tell you no more, Ulmenetha.'

'Should I try to find these soldiers?'

He shook his head. 'What you saw is what will be, whether you seek them out or not.'

'You did not mention the white crow,' she pointed out.

'No,' he said, sadly. 'Nor did I need to. You know what that means.'

'Aye, I know,' she said, wearily. She gazed around the temple, unwilling to leave its quiet sanctuary. On the wall above the High Altar was carved the symbol of Emsharas, the slender hand holding a crescent moon. 'I thought this to be a Source temple,' she said. 'It is unusual to find the crescent moon in such a place.'

'You perceive Emsharas to be a creature of evil?'

'Was he not, according to legend, a demon?' she asked.

'He was indeed one of the Windborn, a spirit being. The name "demon" is a description devised by man. We have here in this temple many of the oldest scrolls in existence, and even some legends engraved on gold foil. I have studied them over the years. I have come to admire Emsharas, and I believe he was Source driven. Did your studies include the legends of the Demon Wars?'

'Very briefly,' she told him. 'Thousands of years ago Emsharas and his brother, Anharat, were enemies. Emsharas joined the human armies of the Three Kings, and banished all demons from the world. That is the sum total of my knowledge.'

'In truth that is probably the sum total of all our knowledge,' he said. 'But you notice the figure three appearing again? It is of great mystical significance. However, he did not merely banish demons from the world. All the creatures of the Windborn vanished as a result of the Great Spell.'

'And now they are coming back,' she said.

'It would appear so,' he agreed.

Banelion summoned his twenty senior officers soon after dawn. All were veterans, many of them men who had served with him for more than thirty years. They were survivors, tough and lean, hard eyed and iron willed. They stood to attention around him, filling the tent. No-one could ever have accused the White Wolf of sentimentality, and yet, as he looked into their faces, he felt an acute sense of family. These men had been his brothers, his sons. He had raised them, and trained them, and led them across the world. Now he was taking them home, to a retirement few desired, but all deserved.

Banelion rarely looked into mirrors. He had lost that vanity at sixty. But now, looking at these men he felt the weight of his years. He could remember them all as they had been, bright eyed, fresh of face, their hearts burning to serve – aye and to save – the country of their birth.

'There will be no easing of discipline,' he told them. 'We will have eighteen hundred men with us, all private citizens now. But I will not lead an unruly mob back to Drenan. Every man who travels with us will sign on for the journey as a soldier, subject to my discipline and under my orders. Any who do not wish to do so will be turned away. The payment will be one half silver per man per month, to be paid out of my own treasury. Officers will receive five full silvers. The payment will be made upon landing at Dros Purdol. Any questions?'

There were many, and for more than an hour he discussed the logistics of the journey with the officers, then dismissed them.

Alone once more he sat down on his pallet bed and spent a further half-hour planning for the problems he expected upon the journey. Satisfied he had covered most of the areas of possible delay he finally allowed his mind to dwell on the immediate danger posed by the threat of Malikada.

Despite what he had told Dagorian about the king, and his lack of concern over the fate of his oldest general, the White Wolf knew that Malikada was unlikely to send Ventrian assassins to kill him. Such a move would cause uproar in the army, and affect the king's plan to march on Cadia. That march would begin in three days. If the White Wolf was murdered Skanda would be forced to call for an inquiry. No, Malikada's attempt would be more subtle. A Drenai might be paid to kill him, a man known to harbour resentment against Banelion. And there were plenty of those, common soldiers who had suffered under the lash for minor infringements of discipline, junior officers who felt they had been overlooked for advancement, senior officers who had suffered public rebuke. Then there were men stripped of their rank for incompetence. Banelion smiled. If Malikada offered enough money he could be trampled to death under a stampede of men anxious to earn it.

Banelion poured himself a goblet of water. But if the murderer was taken alive and questioned under torture such a payment would come to light, and that would throw suspicion back upon Malikada, no matter who he hired to make the transaction. The White Wolf dismissed the idea. It was too unsubtle for the Ventrian fox.

What then? Banelion lifted the goblet to his lips. He hesitated, and stared down at the clear liquid. Poison would be the likeliest answer. Not a cheerful prospect, he thought, putting down the goblet. From now on he would eat at the communal kitchen, standing in line with the rest of his men.

Satisfied he had considered every possibility for attack he relaxed.

He was wrong.

Chapter Four

The old barracks building was three hundred years old, built to house the Immortals, the Emperor Gorben's élite regiment. At the time of its construction it was one of the wonders of the world. Famous artists and sculptors had been summoned from all over the empire to paint its ceilings, and sculpt the masterpieces that surrounded it. Now most of the statues had been removed, and shipped to Drenan, or sold to collectors to raise money for the king's wars. The painted ceilings and walls were chipped, cracked and faded. Most of the Drenai soldiers of the king's new army were housed in the north of the city, in three new barracks.

Here, off the Avenue of Light, the old building was slowly surrendering to the ravages of time and lack of care. Already there were plans to demolish it, and erect a colosseum. But for now it remained the temporary quarters of the old men being sent home. Discipline was already non-existent, and there were no guards at the gates, no bugle call to announce the dawn, no officers to oversee drills or exercises.

Nogusta shivered as he walked across the deserted parade-ground and on into the east wing where he shared a room with Bison and Kebra.

Once upon a time architects from all over the world visited this barracks, to marvel at its design. Now it was a dying place, full of decaying memories no-one wanted to share.

Wearily Nogusta climbed the stairs. There were no lanterns here now, the interior lit only by the shafts of moonlight spearing

382

through the high windows of each landing. Slowly Nogusta made his way to the fourth floor.

Kebra and Bison were sitting in stony silence within the room. Nogusta guessed the question of winter debts had been discussed. He moved past his comrades towards a blazing fire in the hearth. Its warmth was comforting.

Nogusta removed his black shirt and allowed the heat to bathe his upper body. The gold and silver charm he wore glittered in the firelight. Something cold touched his back, like the whisper of a frozen wind. He stood and turned, expecting to see the door or the window open. But they were closed tight.

'Did you feel that breeze?' he asked the silent men. They did not answer him. Kebra was sitting on his bed, his face stony, his pale eyes glaring at Bison. Suddenly an icy chill enveloped the room, the heat from the fire dying away. Nogusta stared at the flames, which were high and bright. No warmth came from them. The only heat he could feel was radiating from the crescent moon charm upon his breast. It glowed with a bright light. In that moment a terrible fear settled on the black man, for he knew why the charm was glowing.

Bison surged to his feet with a menacing growl. 'You slagging traitor!' he shouted at Kebra. His huge hand snatched his sword from its scabbard. The slender bowman drew a curved dagger and rose to meet him.

'No!' shouted Nogusta, leaping towards them. The sound of his voice, deep and powerful, cut through the tension. Kebra hesitated. But Bison moved in for the kill. 'Bison!' yelled Nogusta. For a moment only the giant hesitated. His eyes were glittering strangely, and his mouth was frozen into a snarl.

'Look at me! Now!' bellowed Nogusta. Bison paused again. The cold was now almost intolerable, and Nogusta began to shiver uncontrollably. Bison turned towards him, his eyes distant. 'Take my hand,' said Nogusta, reaching out. 'Do it for friendship, Bison. Take my hand!'

Bison blinked, and his expression softened for an instant. Then his anger blazed again. 'I'm going to kill him!'

'Take my hand first, then do what you must,' urged Nogusta. For a fraction of a moment he thought Bison would refuse, but then the big man reached out. Their fingers touched, their hands gripped. Bison let out a long, shuddering sigh and fell to his knees. Kebra leapt at him. Nogusta caught the movement at the last moment. Dragging Bison back he leapt between them, his left hand snaking out to grab Kebra's wrist. The bowman's face was twisted into an evil grimace, his pale eyes bulging. Nogusta hung on to the knife wrist. 'Be calm, Kebra,' he said. 'Be calm. It is Nogusta. It is your friend, Nogusta.'

Kebra's twisted face relaxed, the madness ebbing away. He shuddered and dropped the knife. The room grew warmer. Nogusta released his grip on the two men. Kebra sagged to the bed.

'I . . . I don't know what came over me,' said Bison. He stumbled towards Kebra. 'I'm sorry,' he said. 'Truly.' Kebra said nothing. He merely sat and stared at the floor.

The glowing light of Nogusta's charm faded, leaving only the simple silver crescent and the golden hand which held it.

'We have been attacked,' he said, softly. 'You are not at fault, Bison. Nor is Kebra.'

The white-haired bowman glanced up. 'What are you talking about?'

'Sorcery. Did you not feel the cold in the room?' Both men shook their heads. Nogusta pulled up a chair and sat. Kebra and Bison were staring at him now. He touched the crescent charm. 'This is what saved us.'

'Have you gone mad?' asked Kebra. 'It was just rage, that's all. Bison kept on and on about me losing the tournament. We just got angry.'

'Can you really believe that?' asked Nogusta. 'You have been friends for thirty years. Never have you drawn weapons against each other. I urge you to trust me on this, my friends. Orendo told me the same thing. He said when they were in the merchant's house a terrible cold came upon the room, and they became full of rage and lust. That's when they killed and raped. He said there were demons in the air. I did not believe him. I believe him now. Do you remember how you felt when you ran at Bison?'

'I wanted to cut his heart out,' admitted Kebra.

'And you believe now that it was really what you wanted?'

'It felt real *then*,' said Kebra. He shook his head and wiped his hand across his face. 'What did you mean about the charm saving us?'

'Simply that. It is a "ward charm". A talisman. It has been in my family for generations.'

'It was glowing when you reached out for me,' said Bison. 'It shone like a huge diamond.'

'I saw that,' said Kebra. 'But, gods, man, who would want to use sorcery against us?'

'Malikada perhaps. Had I not been wearing the charm my rage would have surged also. We could have killed each other.'

'Well, let's kill Malikada,' said Bison.

'Good idea,' said Kebra. 'Then we'll grow our magic wings and fly away free over the mountains.'

'Well, what then?' asked the giant.

'We leave the city,' said Nogusta. 'We won't travel with the White Wolf. We'll head south into the mountains until the army marches on the Cadian border, then we'll join the other returnees.'

'I don't like the idea of running away,' said Bison.

'As I recall,' said Kebra, drily, 'I once saw you racing like a sprinter to get out of the way of a flash flood. And are you not the man who had his arse scarred while fleeing from that lioness outside Delnoch?'

'That was different,' argued Bison.

'No it wasn't,' said Nogusta. 'Malikada is the king's general. We cannot fight him. It would be like fighting a storm or, indeed, a flash flood. Pointless. Added to which we do not know for sure that this was Malikada's work. No, the safest and most sensible plan is to leave the city. In two days the army marches and Malikada will have other problems to consider. He will forget about us.'

'What will we do in the mountains?' asked Bison.

'Hunt a little meat, pan for gold in the streams, perhaps,' Nogusta told him.

'Gold. I like the sound of that,' said Bison, tugging on his white walrus moustache. 'We could get rich.'

'Indeed we could, my friend. Tomorrow I will purchase horses and supplies.'

'And pans for the gold,' Bison reminded him.

The giant moved to his own bed and pulled off his boots. 'I still say you shouldn't have let that Ventrian shoot again,' he said.

Kebra looked up at Nogusta and shook his head. Then he smiled. 'I would feel a lot better if I didn't agree with him,' he said. 'I still can't believe I did it.'

'I can, my friend. It was noble,' said Nogusta, 'and no more than I would expect from you.'

Ulmenetha took hold of the iron chains, leaned back upon the swinging wicker chair and gazed out over the distant mountains. She could feel them calling to her, like a mother to a lost child. In the mountains of her home she had known great happiness. There was ancient wisdom there, and serenity radiated from the eternal peaks. These were not her mountains, but they called nonetheless. Ulmenetha resisted the pull and turned her attention to her immediate surroundings. The roof garden of the late emperor's palace was a wondrous place in summer, its terraces ablaze with colour, and filled with the scent of many perfumed flowers. High above the city it seemed an enchanted place. In winter it was less so, but now, with spring but days away, the yellow and purple polyanthuses were flowering, and the cherry trees were thick with blossom, gossamer thin petals of faded coral. Sitting here alone in the bright sunshine thoughts of demons seemed far away, like a child's dream in a darkened bedroom. Ulmenetha had enjoyed her early childhood. Wrapped in love, and full of joy, she had played in the mountains, living wild and free. The memory lifted her, and – just for a moment – she felt like a child again. Ulmenetha swung the chair around and around on its iron chains. Then she let go and watched the mountains spin before her eyes. She giggled and closed her eyes.

'You look foolish,' said Axiana, sternly. 'It does not become a priestess to play on a child's swing.'

Ulmenetha had not heard the queen's approach. She leaned forward, her feet thumping to the ground, halting the swing. 'Why do you say that?' she asked. 'Why is it that so many people believe that religion and joy have little in common?'

Ulmenetha eased her large frame upright and walked with the pregnant queen to a wide bench seat beneath the cherry trees. Already they were rich with blossom of coral and white. 'There is no dignity in such behaviour,' the young woman told her. Ulmenetha said nothing for a moment. Axiana settled herself down, her slender hands over her swollen belly. You never laugh, child, thought Ulmenetha, and your eyes radiate sorrow.

'Dignity is much overrated,' she said, at last. 'It is a concept, I think, devised by men to add gravitas to their strutting.' A flicker of a smile touched Axiana's beautiful face. But it passed as swiftly as a noonday shadow. 'Men are ridiculous creatures,' continued the priestess, 'arrogant and vain, insensitive and boorish.'

'Is this why you became a priestess? To avoid contact with them?'

Ulmenetha shook her head. 'No, dear heart. I had a jewel among men. When I lost him I knew there would never be another.' She took a deep breath and stared out over the southern mountains. She could just make out three riders heading into the high country.

'I am sorry, Ulmenetha,' said the queen. 'My question brought you sadness.'

'Not at all,' the priestess assured her. 'It brought me remembered joy. He was a fine man. He spent two years trying to woo me, and became convinced that if he could beat me to the top of Five Rise mountain I would marry him.' The queen looked mystified. 'I used to run through the mountains. I was slimmer then, and I could run for ever. No man could best me on the longer races. Vian tried for two years. He trained so hard. That's when I grew to love him.'

'And did he beat you?'

'No, but he won me. Good days.' They lapsed into silence for several minutes, enjoying the warmth of the morning sun.

'What is it like to be in love?' asked Axiana. Ulmenetha felt sadness swell in her, not for the love she had lost, but for the lovely young woman at her side. How sad it was that a woman only weeks from giving birth should still wonder about love.

'Sometimes it arrives like a flash flood, but at other times it grows slowly until it becomes a great tree. Perhaps it will be that way for you and the king.'

Axiana shook her head. 'He thinks nothing of me. I am an ornament of no more worth than any of the other ornaments he owns.'

'He is a great man,' said Ulmenetha, aware of the shallowness of her response.

'No, he is not. He is a great killer and destroyer. Men worship him as if he were a god, but he is not. He is a plague, a cancer.' The words were not spoken with passion, but with a quiet resignation that somehow added to their power.

'He has a good side,' said Ulmenetha. 'His people love him, and he is often generous. And I have seen him weep. When he was younger and it was thought that Starfire was lame, he was inconsolable.'

'Inconsolable?' queried Axiana. 'He did not appear inconsolable when Starfire went to the tannery. I understand they use the hides for furniture, the meat for food, and the hoofs and bones for glue. Is that right?'

'You must be mistaken, my pet.'

'I am not mistaken. I heard him on his birthday. All the older horses – including Starfire – were sold. The money received went into the war chest. The man is without a soul.'

'Do not speak this way, dear heart,' whispered Ulmenetha, feeling a sudden chill.

'No-one can hear us. There are no secret passages in the garden, no hollow walls for clerics to hide behind with their quill pens. Skanda cares only for war, and he will never be satisfied. The world could fall to him and he would know only despair, for there would be no more battles to fight. So, tell me, Ulmenetha, about love.'

The priestess forced a smile. 'There is an old legend. I am rather partial to it. In the beginning the old gods created a herd of perfect animals. They had four legs, four arms and two heads. And they were blissfully happy. The gods looked upon this perfection of happiness and grew jealous. So one day the Chief of the Gods cast a mighty spell. And in an instant all the animals were ripped in half and scattered across the world. Now each of the beasts only had one head, two arms and two legs. And they were destined for ever to search the earth for their other halves, seeking that perfect fit.'

'That is a vulgar story,' chided Axiana.

A young, female servant approached them and curtsied deeply. 'You have a visitor, my lady,' she said. 'The Lord Kalizkan.' Axiana clapped her hands together in delight.

'Send him out to us,' she said.

Moments later the tall wizard made his entrance. He was wearing robes now of sky blue satin, and a matching wide-brimmed hat of stiffened silk. Sweeping off the hat he made an elaborate bow. 'And how is the queen today?' he asked, with a wide, enchanting smile.

'I am well, sir. All the better for seeing you.' Ulmenetha rose and offered the wizard her seat. He gave her a dazzling smile and sat beside the queen. Ulmenetha moved back to allow them privacy and returned to her seat in the swinging chair. It was a pleasure to see Axiana in such high spirits. Kalizkan was good for her, and Ulmenetha liked him. The wizard leaned in close to the queen and the two talked for some time. Then Axiana called out. 'Come here, Ulmenetha, you must see this!'

The priestess obeyed and stood before the white-bearded wizard. 'What is your favourite flower?' he asked her.

'The high mountain lily,' she told him.

'The white lily with blue stripes?'

'Yes.'

Kalizkan reached down and lifted a handful of dirt. Then his pale eyes narrowed in concentration. A tiny stem appeared in the dark earth, then grew, putting out slender leaves. A bud appeared and opened slowly, exposing long white petals, striped with the blue of a summer sky. Reaching out he offered her the flower. Ulmenetha's fingers touched it, and it became smoke, dispersing on the breeze. 'Is that not wonderful?' said Axiana.

Ulmenetha nodded. 'You have a great talent, sir,' she said.

'I have studied long and hard,' he told them. 'But it pleases me to bring pleasure to my friends.'

'Is your orphanage prospering, Kalizkan?' asked the queen.

'It is, dear lady, thanks to the kindness of the king and your good wishes. But there are so many more children living on the streets, close to starvation. One wishes one could help them all.'

As the two talked on, oblivious to Ulmenetha, the priestess found herself once more thinking of the demons in the air. Quietly she made her way back to the swinging chair and settled her back against the cushions. The sun had reached noon and was shining down with painful brightness. She closed her eyes – and a thought came to her.

Demons had no love of bright light. Perhaps now she could soar unobserved.

With a last look at the chatting couple she took a deep breath, reaching for the inner calm that precipitated flight. Then she released her spirit and fled towards the sun like an arrow. High above the city she floated, and gazed down. The roof garden was tiny now, the size of her thumbnail, the river flowing through the city no more than a thin web-thread of glistening blue and white. No demons were flying now, but she could see them in the shadows, under the eaves of buildings. There were hundreds of them. Perhaps thousands. They were writhing over the city like white maggots on rotting pork.

Three detached themselves from the shadows of the palace, and swept up towards her, their talons reaching out. Ulmenetha waited, frozen in terror. They closed upon her, and she could see their opal eyes and their sharp teeth. There was nowhere to run. They were between her and the safety of her flesh.

A shining figure of bright light appeared alongside her, a sword of flame in his hands. Ulmenetha tried to look into his face, but the brilliance of the light forced her to turn away. The demons veered away from him. A voice whispered into her mind. It was strangely familiar. 'Go now, swiftly!' he urged her.

Ulmenetha needed no urging. With the demons fallen back she fled for the sanctuary of her flesh.

She swept over the roof garden and saw the queen sitting beside . . . sitting beside . . .

The eyes of her body flared open, and a strangled cry burst from her lips. Axiana and Kalizkan moved swiftly to her side. 'Are you well, Ulmenetha?' asked Axiana, reaching out to stroke her friend's cheek.

'Yes, yes. I had a bad dream. So stupid. I am sorry.'

'You are trembling,' said Kalizkan. 'Perhaps you have a fever.'

'I think I will go inside,' she said, 'and lie down.'

She left them there and returned to her own room alongside the queen's apartments. Her mouth was dry and she poured a cup of water and drank deeply. Then she sat down and tried to picture what she had seen in the roof garden.

The image had been fleeting, and she found that the more she concentrated upon it the less clear it became.

Silently she returned to the roof garden, pausing in the doorway, unseen. From here she could see the kindly wizard and the queen sitting together. Closing the eyes of her body she gazed upon them both with the eyes of spirit.

Her heart hammered, and she began to tremble once more.

Kalizkan's face was grey and dead, his hands only partly covered in flesh. Bare bone protruded from the ends of his fingers. And as Ulmenetha looked more closely she saw a small maggot slither out from a hole in the wizard's cheek and drop to the shoulder of his blue satin robes.

Backing away she returned to her room, and prayed.

Dagorian stood in the centre of the small room. Blood had splashed to the white walls, and the curved dagger that caused the terrible wounds had been tossed to the floor, where it had smeared a white goatskin rug. The body of the old woman had been removed before Dagorian arrived, but the murderer was still sitting by the hearth, his head in his hands. Two Drenai soldiers stood guard over him.

'It seems fairly straightforward,' Dagorian told Zani, the slender Ventrian official. 'In a rage this man killed his mother. There are no soldiers involved. No threat to the king. I do not see why you called me to the scene.'

'You are the Officer of the Watch for last night,' said Zani, a small man, with close cropped dark hair and a pronounced widow's peak. 'We are to report all cases of multiple killings.'

'There was more than one body?'

'Yes, sir. Not here, but elsewhere. Look around you. What do you see?'

Dagorian scanned the room. Shelves lined the walls, some bearing jars of pottery, others bottles of coloured glass. On the low table beside the hearth he saw a set of rune stones, and several papyrus charts of the heavens. 'The woman was a fortune-teller,' he said.

'Indeed she was – and a good one, by all accounts.'

'This is relevant?' asked Dagorian.

'Four such people were killed last night in this quarter of the city alone. Three men and a woman. Two were murdered by customers, a third by his wife, and this woman by her son.'

Dagorian crossed the room and opened the back door, stepping out into the narrow garden beyond. The Ventrian followed him. The sun was bright in the sky, the warmth welcome. 'Did the victims know one another?' asked Dagorian.

'The son told me he knew one of the dead.'

'Then it remains coincidence,' concluded Dagorian.

The Ventrian sighed and shook his head. 'Twenty-seven in the last month. I do not think coincidence will stretch that far.'

'Twenty-seven fortune-tellers?' Dagorian was astonished.

'Not all were fortune-tellers. Some were mystics, others priests. But their talent was the common factor. They could all walk the path of Spirit. Most could read fragments of the future.'

'Not very well, apparently,' Dagorian pointed out.

'I disagree. Come, let me show you.' Dagorian followed the small Ventrian back to the door. Zani pointed to recent scratches upon the wood, in the shape of an inverted triangle, with a snake at the centre. 'All the entries to the room bear this sign. It is part of a ward spell, protective sorcery. The old woman knew she was in danger. When we found her she was clutching an amulet. This too was a protective piece.'

'Protection against *sorcery*,' said Dagorian, patiently. 'But she wasn't killed by sorcery, was she? She was murdered by her son. He admits to the crime. Does he claim he was demon possessed? Is that his defence?'

'No,' admitted Zani. 'But perhaps it ought to be. I have spoken to the neighbours. He was devoted to his mother. And even he no longer knows why his rage exploded.'

Dagorian approached the distraught young man sitting by the hearth. 'What do you recall of the crime?' he asked him. The man looked up.

'I was sitting in my room, and I just got angrier and angrier. The next thing I knew I was here . . . in this room. And I was stabbing, and stabbing . . .' He broke down and hid his face in his hands.

'What made you angry?'

It seemed at first that the young man had not heard the question, but the sobbing subsided and he wiped his eyes with the sleeve of his shirt. 'I can't remember now. I really can't.'

'Why did your mother make the ward signs on the doors?'

'She was frightened. She wouldn't see any customers and she wouldn't come out of the room. We were running out of money. I think, maybe, that's why I got angry. We couldn't afford fuel, and my room was so cold. So terribly cold.' He began to sob once more.

'Take him away,' Dagorian told the soldiers. They lifted the man to his feet and marched him from the house. A small crowd had gathered outside. Some of them shouted abuse at the prisoner.

'There is something very wrong here,' said Zani.

'Send me the details of the other crimes,' Dagorian told him. 'I will look into them.'

'You think you will solve the mystery in a day?' asked Zani. 'Or will you not be marching with the army tomorrow?'

'I leave tomorrow,' said Dagorian. 'But still I wish to see the reports.'

Leaving the house he mounted his horse and rode back to the new barracks. Once there he waited for the reports, read them carefully, then requested a meeting with his immediate superior, the Ventrian swordsman Antikas Karios.

He was kept waiting outside the Ventrian's office for an hour, and when he was at last ushered inside, he saw Antikas walk in from the garden beyond, where he had been exercising. Stripped to the waist he was sweating heavily. A servant brought him a towel. Antikas sat down behind the broad desk and drank a cup of water. Then he towelled his dark hair. The servant moved behind him with a brush and a jar of oil. Lightly he massaged the Ventrian's scalp, before brushing his hair back and tying it in a pony-tail. With a flick of his hand Antikas dismissed the man, then turned his dark eyes on Dagorian.

'You wished to see me?'

'Yes, sir.' Swiftly he told the officer of the spate of murders, and the concerns of the official Zani that some orchestrated campaign of killing might be under way.

'Zani is a good man,' said Antikas. 'He has been a city official for fourteen years, and served with distinction. He has a fine mind. What is your opinion?'

'I have read the reports, sir. In each case the killers have been apprehended, and confessed, without torture. But I do share Zani's concern in one respect.'

'And that is?'

'Twenty-seven mystics in sixteen days. And, according to the reports, every one of them was living in fear.'

Antikas rose from his desk, crossed the room and took a fresh shirt from a drawer. Shaking the rose petals from it he pulled it over his head. Then he returned to the desk. 'You are a good swordsman,' he said. 'Your moves are well executed.'

'Thank you, sir,' said Dagorian, confused by the change of subject.

'It is your footwork that lets you down.'

'So Nogusta told me, sir.'

'Yes,' said Antikas, with a cold smile. 'If he were twenty years younger I would challenge him. He is exceptional.' Antikas sat down and took a second drink from the water cup. 'I see from your dossier that you were training for the priesthood.'

'I was, sir. Until my father died.'

'Yes, a man must uphold family honour. Did your teaching incorporate mysticism?'

'Only briefly, sir. But no sorcery.'

'I think you will find that these crimes are based on rivalry among petty wizards. Even so, such actions cannot be tolerated. Find out which mystics are still alive. The true source of the murders will be one of those.'

'Yes, sir, I will try, but I cannot do this in a day.'

'Indeed so. You will remain here. I will send for you when we have crossed the Great River.'

'Yes, sir. Is this a punishment, sir?'

'No. Merely an order.' Antikas began to shuffle papers on his desk, but Dagorian stood his ground. 'There was something else?' he asked.

'Yes, sir. I was wondering if the Lord Kalizkan could help us. His powers are great, and it would save time.'

'The Lord Kalizkan is busy preparing spells to aid the king in his coming battle with the Cadians. But I will convey your request to him.' Dagorian saluted crisply and took one step back, before spinning on his heel and marching to the door. The Ventrian's voice halted him. 'Trust me, Dagorian, you will never need to *ask* if I am punishing you. You will *know*.'

Dagorian and Zani rode to three addresses in the north of the city, each said to be the home of an astrologer or seer. All were empty. Neighbours were unable to supply information. The fourth address was a house in a rich area called Nine Oaks. The houses here stood in several acres of landscaped gardens, with fountains and walkways meandering through cultivated woodland.

The two men rode their horses through the woods, coming at last to a tall house, the outer walls faced with blocks of green marble. No servant moved out to greet them as they made their way to the front of the building. Dagorian and Zani dismounted and tied the reins of their mounts to a hitching rail.

The main doors were locked and barred, the green wooden shutters of the windows closed tight. A one-eyed old man wearing a green patch and pushing a wheelbarrow came into sight, moving slowly across the garden. He stopped as he saw them. Dagorian approached him. 'We are looking for the master of the house,' he said.

'Gone,' the old man told him.

'Gone where?'

'Just gone. Had all his valuables packed into three wagons and left.'

'When was this?'

'Four days ago. No . . . five now.'

Zani moved alongside the old man. 'What is your name?'

'I am Chiric, the head gardener. The only gardener now, come to think of it.'

'Did your master seem troubled?' asked Dagorian.

'Aye, that would be one word to describe it. Troubled.'

'What other words might you use?' put in Zani.

The old man gave a crooked grin. 'I might say terrified.'

'Of what?' queried Dagorian. Chiric shrugged.

'Don't know and don't care. Spring's coming and I've too much planting to do to worry about what frightens the likes of him. Can I go now?'

'In a moment,' the Ventrian told him. 'Do you live in the house?'

'No. Got a small cabin back in the woods. Warm and snug. Suits me, anyway.'

'Has anything strange happened here recently?' asked Dagorian.

The old man gave a dry, rasping laugh. 'Strange things happen here all the time. That's the way with wizards. Coloured lights, flashes of fire. Groups of them used to come round. They'd chant late into the night. Then he asks me why the hens have stopped laying. Asked me to join in one night. Said they were one short of some mystic number. No thank you, said I.'

'What was it that terrified him?' persisted Dagorian.

'Do I get paid for all this information?' asked Chiric. 'If not I've got better things to do than stand around jawing all day.'

Zani's anger overflowed. 'You could spend a few weeks in the Watch dungeons,' he said, 'for obstructing officers of the king. How does that sound?'

Dagorian stepped in swiftly, dipping his hand into his money pouch and producing a small silver coin. The old man pocketed it with incredible speed, then cast a surly glance at Zani. 'Labourers get paid,' he said. 'That's why they labour. Anyway, you were asking about his fear. Well I was away for a few days last month. My youngest got wed to a farmer from Captis. When I got back some of the servants had gone. And the master had bought three big black wolfhounds, teeth like knives. Hated the bastards, I did. I asked Sagio about it . . .'

'Sagio?' put in Zani.

'My under gardener. Good lad. He quit too – afterwards! Anyways, he said that the master wouldn't come out of the house. Claimed someone had put a death spell on him. He spent days and days in his library poring over scrolls and the like. And always the dogs were padding around the house. Then, last week, the dogs attacked him. Went mad by all accounts. He managed to lock himself in the library. When he came out the dogs had torn each other to pieces. Blood everywhere. I had to clear it up. Well, me and Sagio had to clear it up. Still, horrible it was. But then if you're going to keep wild dogs you've got to expect trouble, haven't you. I reckon it was the cold got to 'em. Marble houses, pah! Can't keep them warm, can you? Room they were in was freezing.'

'And he left the city?'

'The same day. You should have seen him.' Chiric chuckled. 'He was covered in charms and talismans. And he was chanting all the way to the coach and four. You could still hear him as it drove through the gates.'

Dagorian thanked the man and walked back to his horse. Zani came alongside. 'What now, Drenai?'

'We break in,' said Dagorian, moving to one of the shutters on the ground floor and drawing his sword.

'Hey, what are you doing?' shouted the old man.

'We are officers of the king,' Zani told him. 'You are welcome to observe our investigation. But if you seek to hinder us I will keep my promise about that dungeon.'

'It was only a question,' grumbled Chiric, grasping the handles of his wheelbarrow. Clearing his throat the old man spat on the path, then trundled the wheelbarrow off towards the woods.

Dagorian slid his sabre between the shutters and lifted the bar beyond. It fell clear with a hollow thud. Opening the shutters Dagorian sheathed his blade and climbed inside. The interior was gloomy and he opened two other windows. Zani clambered into the building. 'What are we looking for?' he asked. Dagorian spread his hands.

'I have no idea.' They were standing now in a beautifully decorated sitting-room, with seven sofas and a splendid mosaic floor and painted walls. Passing through it they entered a hall, and searched the rooms beyond. The furniture throughout was expensive. The library was shelved from floor to ceiling, the shelves bent under the weight of books, scrolls and parchments. The north wall was still blood-stained, as was the pale green carpet.

'I hope Chiric is a better gardener than a cleaner,' said Zani.

A door at the back of the library led to a study. This too had shelves on all four walls, most of them bearing glass jars, filled with viscous liquids. In one floated a human hand, in another a small, deformed foetus. Others contained organs. There was a large cupboard set into the western wall. Dagorian opened it. More jars were stored here, this time filled with herbs. The Drenai officer scanned them, finally selecting one and carrying it to a narrow desk, upon which was a human skull, resculpted into a container for two ink wells. Dagorian placed the jar on the desk and broke the wax seal around the lid.

'What is it?' asked Zani.

'*Lorassium* leaves. They have great healing powers, but

lorassium is essentially a heavy narcotic used by mystics to aid their visions.'

'I have heard of it. It is very expensive.'

The young Drenai officer sat down, dipped his hand into the jar, pulling two leaves from it. They were a dark, lustrous green, and a heady scent filled the air. 'What are you doing?' asked Zani.

For a moment Dagorian said nothing, then he looked up at the Ventrian. 'There is a force working here that is outside the realm of normal human senses. We could stumble around the city for days and never find the answer. Perhaps it is time to use the eyes of the spirit.'

'Are you versed in these things?'

'Not entirely. But I know the procedure.'

Zani shook his head. 'I know nothing of sorcery – nor do I wish to. But there have been a lot of deaths, Drenai. I think the risk is too great for one who only – as you openly admit – knows the *procedure*. I think it might be wiser to take the problem to the Lord Kalizkan. There is no greater wizard than he.'

'I have already set that in motion, Zani,' said the officer. 'But arrogance compels me to try to solve this mystery myself.'

As he finished speaking he rolled the two leaves and placed them in his mouth.

Bright colours flashed before his eyes, and a sharp pain lanced from his neck, down his arms and into his fingers. Calming himself Dagorian began to recite in his mind the Mantra of Dardalion, the simplest of the Three Levels. He felt as if he were floating inside his own body, twisting and turning. But there was no release, and he did not soar free as he had hoped. Slowly he opened his eyes. Zani's blue tunic was shining now with ethereal lights and dancing colours. A bright aura flickered around the man. Dagorian realized that it was not the tunic which was shining, but the man himself. Over his heart there was violet light, tinged with red, which deepened into maroon over his belly. This then was the aura mystics spoke of. How beautiful it was. He looked at Zani's round face. Honesty, loyalty and courage shone there, and he had a vision of the Ventrian sitting in a small room, three children playing at his feet. A young woman was close by, plump and raven haired. She was smiling.

Transferring his gaze he glanced at the walls. Ward spells had been placed over the windows and the doors, and these he could see now, glowing faintly red. Turning in the chair he looked out of the east window at the shadowed garden. He blinked. A face was staring in, a ghost white face, with large dark, protruding eyes and a lipless mouth. The skin was scaled like a fish, the teeth sharp as needles. Other faces clustered around it, and a long skinny arm pushed into the room. The ward spell flared and the arm was hastily withdrawn.

'There are demons at the window,' he said, huskily, his words echoing inside his head.

'I see no demons,' said Zani, his voice trembling.

'Yet they are there.'

'It is getting cold in here,' said Zani. 'Can you feel it?'

Dagorian did not answer. Rising from the desk he walked to the inner door and looked out into the library and the stairs beyond. White forms were floating close to the ceiling, others were huddled together away from the sunlight lancing through the western windows.

Fear touched the officer. There were scores of them.

They flew at him, their talons lashing out. The pain was great and he stumbled back. 'What is it?' shouted Zani.

In panic Dagorian ran for the front door. The demons were covering him now, tearing at him. He screamed aloud, blundered into the door, then scrabbled for the handle. It was locked. He fell to his knees, the pain indescribable. Zani grabbed his arm, hauling him to the western window. Bright light bathed him, and the demons withdrew. Zani helped him climb out into the garden. Dagorian stumbled out to the grass, then fell and rolled to his back under the shadows of the trees.

White, translucent forms dropped from the branches above, talons and teeth ripping at his face. Wildly he thrashed his arms at them, but his fingers passed through them.

A shining sword of fire swept out. The demons fell back. A voice whispered to him. 'The Prayer of Light! Recite it you fool, or you will die here.'

Pain and terror were blocking Dagorian's memory. The voice spoke again. 'Say it with me: Oh Lord of Light, Source of All Life, be with me now in this hour of peril and darkness . . . Say it aloud!'

Dagorian began to recite the prayer. The demons withdrew, but hovered close by, their dark malevolent eyes glaring at him.

Rising to his knees Dagorian watched them. Slowly the power of the *lorassium* began to fade, and with it his spirit sight. The demons became more and more translucent, until, at last, they appeared no more than shapeless wisps of wood smoke. Then they were gone.

Safe now he stared down at his arms and hands, amazed that there was no blood. The talons had ripped into him so many times. He slumped back exhausted. 'What happened here?' whispered Zani. 'What were you struggling against?'

Dagorian did not answer. The *lorassium* did not merely increase visual powers, but also enhanced perception and cognitive skills. As the effects faded he fought to hold to the impressions he had gained, even during his panicked flight.

The demons were not sentient – at least not in a way any human could understand. They were . . . the word 'Feeders' came to his mind. Yes, that was it. Like a hungry pack they sought to devour . . . what? What was the source of his pain? It was not physical, and yet it would have killed him. The *lorassium* was almost gone now, and he struggled to hold to the knowledge he had gained. Though not sentient the creatures had a purpose that was *beyond* their own desires. Their violence was *directed*.

The sun was setting behind the mountains. Soon the dark would come. Fear rose again in Dagorian. 'We must get away from here,' he said.

Chapter Five

Moonlight glistened on the outer skin of the White Wolf's tent, turning its flanks to silver. Inside the old man opened the map casket, and began searching through it. A brazier full of hot coals filled the tent with warmth, and two glowing lanterns cast flickering shadows on the inner walls.

Finding the map he was looking for the old man straightened. His lower back ached, and he stretched his arms high, trying to loosen his muscles. The cold struck him then, bitter as a winter blizzard. With a groan he turned towards the brazier of coals. No heat came from them now. He sat on the pallet bed, suddenly weary, dropped the map upon the thin mattress and reached out his hands towards the fire. The hands were old and liver spotted, the knuckles large with rheumatism.

Depression grew in him. Once I was young, he thought. He remembered his first battle in the old king's re-formed army. He had fought all day, with never a hint of fatigue. And that night he had bedded two of the camp women, one after the other. He glanced down at his thin, wrinkled legs, the loose skin slack over withered muscles. You should have died years ago, he said to himself.

The cold grew more intense, but he had ceased to feel it.

The depression deepened into a bleak despair, formed of regret for what had passed, and a chilling fear of all that was to come; incontinence and senility. What would he do back in Drenan? Hire servants to change his soiled bed linen, and to wipe away the drool that dripped from his mouth. Perhaps he would not see the disgust on their faces. Then again, perhaps in moments of clarity, he would.

The old man drew his dagger and laid the blade upon his wrist. Clenching his fist he saw the arteries stand out. Swiftly he sliced the dagger blade across them. Even the blood that flowed was weak and thin, pumping out to stain the leather cavalry kilt, flowing on over his thighs and down into his boots.

He sat very still, remembering the glory days, until at last he toppled from the bed.

The fire flared, and heat began once more to permeate the tent.

After some minutes the tent flap was opened and two men stepped inside.

The first man ran to the body and knelt beside it. 'Sweet Heaven,' he whispered. 'Why? He was in good spirits when you sent him for the map, my lord. And he won heavily on the king's birthday. He was talking about his home near Dros Corteswain, and his plans for the farm. This makes no sense.'

The White Wolf stood silently, his pale gaze scanning the interior of the tent. Upon the folding table was a goblet and a jug, that had contained water. Now it was filled with melting ice. Condensation had also created a sheen of ice on the tent walls.

Banelion masked his anger. The possibility of a sorcerous attack had not occurred to him, and he cursed himself for his stupidity.

'I don't understand,' said the grey-bearded officer, kneeling by the corpse. 'Why would he kill himself?'

'Why does anyone kill themselves?' countered Banelion. 'Have the body removed.'

Dagorian and Zani stabled their mounts. The ride had been a silent one, and now, as they walked through the dusk shadowed streets, the little Ventrian moved in close to the taller officer. 'I think you should tell me what happened back there,' he said.

The Drenai warrior nodded, then led Zani to a small tavern just off the Market Square. It was almost empty and they took a window table. Dagorian ordered wine, added a little water, then sipped the drink. 'There were demons,' he said, at last, keeping his voice low. 'Scores of them. Perhaps hundreds. They filled the house – all except for the room with the ward spell. They tore at me with talons and teeth. I thought my flesh was being ripped from my bones.'

'But there were no wounds. Perhaps it was just the drug.'

Dagorian shook his head. 'There were wounds, Zani. I can still feel them. They were tearing at my spirit – my soul, if you like. They were even outside, in the trees. Worse, I sensed they were everywhere. They are probably here even now, in the shadows of the ceiling, by the walls.'

Zani glanced around nervously. But he could see nothing. 'What were they like?' Dagorian described them, their bone-white faces and bulging eyes, their sharp teeth and talons. Zani shivered. It sounded like the ravings of a madman – which Zani would have infinitely preferred to be true. But they were investigating more than a score of bizarre murders, and everything Dagorian described had the ring of truth to it. Even so it was wildly beyond Zani's understanding. The Drenai officer fell silent. Zani spoke again, keeping his voice low. 'What does all this mean, Drenai?'

'I do not know. It is far beyond what I was taught. But there was something else. I was rescued by a shining figure with a sword of fire. He it was who made me recite the holy verses.'

'A shining figure,' repeated Zani. 'An angel, you mean?'

Dagorian saw scepticism swell once more in the Ventrian's expression. 'I am sorry, Zani. Were I you I would also be deeply suspicious. Is the man mad? Did the *lorassium* merely swell his delusions?' Zani relaxed and smiled. 'Well, the man is not mad. But he is frightened. And he does have a theory, of sorts.'

'That, at least, sounds promising,' said Zani.

'All the people killed – or fled – were seers. They could *see* the demons.'

'Which means?'

'Think of an army on the march in enemy territory. The scouts are the eyes. Therefore the first objective is to kill the scouts. The army is now blind.'

'But these demons cannot kill. They did not attack me. And once the drug wore off you were also safe.'

'They cannot kill *directly*. But they can influence emotions. That much I was taught back at the Temple. If their malevolence is directed by a power magus they can inspire great malice and hatred. That is the key to the killings. The boy who killed his mother, the dogs who attacked their master. All of them.'

'I know little of demons – and I wish I knew less,' said Zani. 'But what I do know is that this is far beyond my talents. We must consult Kalizkan.'

'Before this morning I would have agreed with you,' said Dagorian. 'I will think on it.'

'What is there to think about? He is the greatest sorcerer in the empire.'

'I know. That is what worries me.'

'You make no sense.'

'I have read stories about sorcerers summoning demons. In ones or twos. Here we have hundreds. Only the greatest of the magi could even consider such a spell. A sorcerer of such power would not be unknown. He would be famous, rich and powerful. Is there another such sorcerer in Usa?'

Zani's face darkened. 'I have met Kalizkan many times,' he said, coldly. 'He is a fine man, and much admired. He rescues children from the streets. He is kind and greatly loved. To speak of him summoning demons is a slander. And I'll hear no more of it. I think the drug addled your senses, Drenai. I suggest you return to the barracks and rest. Perhaps tomorrow you will be clear headed again.'

The Ventrian pushed back his chair and strode for the door. Dagorian made no attempt to call him back. If the situation were reversed he too would be sceptical. Zani reached the door, pulled it open and stepped outside. Dagorian heard him scream. The Ventrian officer stumbled back into the tavern, blood pumping from a terrible wound in his throat. Three dark-clad warriors moved inside. They were hooded and masked. The first thrust a sword deep into Zani's belly. The other two ran at Dagorian. The Drenai warrior up-ended the table in their path, slowing them, then drew his own blade. A sword lunged for his throat. Dagorian swayed aside and launched an overhand cut that chopped deep into his opponent's neck, slicing through the bone beneath. He was dead before he hit the floor. As his sabre came clear Dagorian leapt backwards. The second assassin's sword sliced air. Bringing up his sabre in a reverse cut Dagorian slashed the blade into the assassin's arm. It cut deep. The man screamed and dropped his sword. The killer who had stabbed Zani threw a knife, which missed Dagorian and clattered against the far wall.

The man with the wounded arm scrambled back and ran for the door. His companion hesitated – then joined him, and the two escaped into the night. Dagorian ran to Zani, but the little Ventrian, lying in a spreading pool of blood, was dead.

Anger rose in the Drenai officer, and he ran from the tavern, trying to catch the killers.

The streets were dark now, and there was no sign of them. Sheathing his sabre he returned to where the bodies lay. The tavern keeper approached him. 'I have sent for the Watch,' he said. Dagorian nodded and moved to the rear of the room, where the dead assassin lay. Flipping the body with his foot he knelt down and wrenched away the mask and hood. The man was unknown to him. He heard a soft curse from the tavern keeper and swung round.

'You know this man?'

The tavern keeper nodded dumbly. 'He has been in here several times – usually in uniform.'

'Who is he?'

'I don't know his name. But he's an aide to Antikas Karios.'

For the third time that afternoon Nogusta signalled a halt to rest the horses. The two mares ridden by Kebra and Bison did not need rest, but Nogusta's huge black gelding was breathing heavily and sweat bathed its flanks. Nogusta stroked its sleek neck. 'Do not be downhearted, Great One,' he whispered, soothingly. 'You have been ill, and you need time to regain your strength.' The black man led him through the stand of pine and up the last rise. On the crest he paused and gazed down at the verdant valley below.

'I still can't believe it,' said Bison, moving alongside Nogusta. 'Sold for his hide! There must have been a mistake.'

'No mistake. He has a lung infection, and the king decided he was no longer of use.'

'But this is Starfire. He's been the king's warhorse for years. The king loves this horse.'

'Beware the love of kings,' said Nogusta, coldly. 'Starfire is like us, Bison. He's at least eighteen years old, and not as strong and fleet as once he was. Skanda had no more use for him. So he was sold for hide and meat and glue.'

'If he's useless why did you buy him?'

'He deserved better.'

'Maybe he did, but what will you do when he drops dead?' argued Bison. 'I mean . . . look at the state he's in! Horses don't survive lung rot.'

'The diagnosis is wrong. There is no wasting of the muscles. It is just an infection and he will improve in the mountain air. But if he does die it will be under the sky, free and proud, among friends who care for him.'

404

'He's just a horse,' persisted Bison. 'Do you really think he cares?'

'I care.' Taking up the reins Nogusta started the long walk down into the valley. Bison and Kebra rode ahead and by the time the black warrior led the warhorse to level ground his two companions had made camp beside a stream. Bison had collected dry wood for a fire and Kebra had unpacked pots and plates for the evening meal.

Nogusta unsaddled the black gelding, let him roll, then groomed him. The horse was huge, almost eighteen hands, with a strong, arched neck and a beautiful back. A white blaze, in the shape of a star, adorned his brow. 'Rest now, my friend,' said Nogusta. 'The grass here is good.' The weary gelding plodded onto the meadow and began to crop grass.

'This is a fine place,' said Kebra. 'Good farming land. If I was twenty years younger I'd build here.'

As dusk deepened jack rabbits began to appear. Kebra shot two, skinned and cleaned them, adding the fresh meat to the broth.

Nogusta wrapped himself in his cloak and sat with his back to a tree. It was peaceful here, and the view was majestic. Snow-crested mountains broke the line of the horizon, and folds of hills and valleys lay before them. Away to the east he could see a deep forest part bathed in mist. To the west a lake glimmered blood red in the dying sunlight. Kebra was right. It was a place to build on, and he imagined a wide, low house, with windows that looked out on the mountains. Horses and cattle would prosper here. He gazed lovingly upon the mountains. What were the works of Man, when set against these giants of nature? he wondered. Man's evil seemed small here, tiny and insubstantial. The mountains cared nothing for the whims of kings and princes. They were here before Man, and they would outlast him, surviving perhaps even when the sun failed and eternal darkness fell upon the planet.

Kebra brought him a plate of food and the two men sat in companionable silence, eating their meal. Bison finished his swiftly, then took a flat pan and headed off upstream to search for gold.

'He'll find nothing,' said Kebra. 'There is no gold here.'

'It will keep him occupied,' said Nogusta, sadness in his voice. 'You still expect us to be followed?'

Nogusta nodded. 'Malikada is not a forgiving man. He will

send men, and I will kill them. And for what? One man's arrogance.'

'We might be able to avoid them,' offered Kebra. Nogusta took a deep breath and pushed himself to his feet.

'Maybe. I have had no fresh visions to tell me otherwise. But death is coming, Kebra. I can smell it.' Kebra did not reply. Nogusta was rarely wrong about these things.

Starfire moved closer to the two men. His breathing was still ragged. Nogusta moved smoothly to his feet and stroked the gelding's long neck. 'Bison could be right,' said Kebra. 'Trying to escape pursuit upon a sick horse does not seem to make a great deal of sense.'

'He has been poorly stabled,' said Nogusta. 'My father knew about these things. He always soaked the straw, and ensured the stables were clean. And Starfire has not been exercised.'

'That's not my point,' said Kebra, softly.

'I know, my friend. It is not sensible.' He grinned. 'But I would do it again.'

Ulmenetha watched from the roof gardens as the army marched from the city. Four thousand Drenai foot soldiers, in ranks of threes, and three thousand Ventrian cavalry in columns of twos. Behind them were the wagons, bearing supplies, or dismantled siege engines and ballistae. Word had reached Usa that the Cadian army was on the march and Skanda was eager to meet them.

The king had not bothered to visit Axiana, but had sent a farewell message via Kalizkan. Ulmenetha had avoided the wizard, keeping to her rooms until he had gone. Now she stood high above the cheering crowds as Skanda rode from the city. The populace were scattering rose petals before his horse, and he was waving and smiling.

Amazing, thought Ulmenetha. A few years ago he had been an invading foreigner, feared by all. Now, despite the endless battles and the destruction of empire, he was a hero to them. He was a god.

She wondered idly whether it would have been different had he been ugly. Could a man with an ugly face command such devotion? Probably not. But then Skanda was not ugly. He was handsome and tall, golden haired, with a winning smile and enormous charm. We are so stupid sometimes, she decided. Last year Skanda had donated 10,000 *raq* to the city orphanage – one hundredth of the amount he spent on his wars. Yet the people loved him for it. It was the talk of the city. In the same month a respected holy man had been accused of trying to seduce a young priestess. He was savagely condemned and banished from Usa. This also was the talk of the city. Such extremes, thought Ulmenetha. All the holy man's life work was dust following one misguided action. People scorned him. Yet the greatest killer in the empire could win love by giving away a tiny portion of the money he had plundered from the city treasury.

Ulmenetha sighed. Who could understand it?

As the last of the soldiers left the city she wandered back through the upper levels of the palace, and down to the long kitchens. Servants were sitting around with little to do and Ulmenetha helped herself to a second breakfast of cheese and eggs, followed by bread and a rich red strawberry preserve.

While eating she listened to the chatter among the servants. They were talking about a young Drenai officer who had gone insane, and stabbed to death a Ventrian official and an officer from the staff of Antikas Karios. Soldiers were scouring the city for him. Others had ridden south to see if he had tried to join the men marching home with the White Wolf. Returning to the upper levels she sought out Axiana. The queen was sitting on her balcony, a wide-brimmed hat shielding her face from the spring sunlight. 'How are you feeling today?' asked Ulmenetha.

'I am well,' answered Axiana. 'Kalizkan wants me to move into his home. He wishes to be close when the boy is born.'

Ulmenetha felt a sudden chill in her heart. 'What answer did you give him?' she asked.

'I said I would think on it. Did you hear about Dagorian?'

'Dagorian?'

'The handsome young officer who always stares at me. I told you about him.'

'I remember. What has he done?'

'They say he went mad and killed some people. I find it hard to believe. He has such gentle eyes.'

'Looks can be deceptive,' said Ulmenetha.

'I suppose so. I have been to Kalizkan's house. It is very comfortable. He has wonderful gardens. And he is so amusing. You like him too, don't you?'

'I have always enjoyed his company,' admitted Ulmenetha. 'But I think you should stay here.'

'Why?' asked Axiana, looking up. Ulmenetha was at a loss to

explain her remark. She was not even tempted to tell the queen of what she had seen on the roof garden.

'His house is overrun by shrieking children,' she said, finally, 'and most of his servants are male. I think you would be more at your ease here.' She saw Axiana's expression harden. 'But it is your decision, my lady. Whatever you think best.'

Axiana relaxed and smiled. 'You are probably right. I shall consider your advice. Will you do something for me?'

'Of course.'

'Find out what happened with Dagorian.'

'It may be too gruesome,' argued Ulmenetha.

'Even so.'

'I shall do it immediately,' said Ulmenetha.

With Antikas Karios and his staff gone from the city Ulmenetha walked the two miles to the offices of the Militia who were seeking the renegade officer. There a thin cleric, with deep-set eyes, told her of the murder of Zani. She asked what investigation the two men were working on, and was told it involved a series of murders. She pressed for further details.

'What is your interest here, lady?' asked the cleric, suspiciously.

'I am the queen's midwife, and she herself asked me to ascertain the facts. The young officer is known to her.'

'I see.' The man's expression changed instantly, and he gave an oily smile. 'Can I fetch you a chair?'

'No, I am fine. You were about to tell me the details of their investigation.'

He leaned forward across the broad counter that separated them. 'The papers relating to their case are no longer here, lady,' he said, lowering his voice. 'They were transferred to the offices of Antikas Karios. But I can tell you that the investigation involved the killing of mystics. I spoke to Zani about it myself. He was convinced there was more to the murders than was immediately apparent.'

'I see. And where was Zani killed?'

He gave her the address of the tavern, and once more Ulmenetha trekked across the city. It was noon before she reached the tavern, which was already full. Easing her way through the throng she sought out the innkeeper, but was told that he was visiting his family to the west of the city. Further inquiries were useless in the noise and the hustle. She found a seat at the back of the tavern, and ordered a lunch of roast chicken, followed by several pieces of freshly baked fruit pie and cream.

Then she sat quietly, waiting for the midday rush to ease. She stayed in the tavern for almost two hours, and when the crowd dissipated she summoned a serving maid.

'Were you here when the murders took place?' she asked. The girl shook her head.

'Did you want more food?' she enquired.

'Yes. Another slice of pie. Were any of the serving maids here that night?'

'Yes. Dilian.'

'Is she here today?'

'No. She went away with Pavik.'

'Pavik?'

'The tavern keeper,' answered the girl, moving away.

Moments later a thick set woman in her early fifties strode to where Ulmenetha sat. 'Why are you pestering my staff?' she asked, belligerently, her large arms folded across her ample bosom. 'And why should you be interested in the whereabouts of my husband?'

'I am investigating the murders,' said Ulmenetha. The woman gave a scornful laugh.

'Oh, I see. Now the army has gone the city police have turned power over to you, eh? Is that right, you fat cow?'

Ulmenetha gave a sweet smile. 'Perhaps you would prefer to answer my questions in the city dungeon, you raddled slut. One more foul word from you and I shall send the Watch to arrest you.' Ulmenetha spoke the threat softly, and with quiet confidence, and the power of the words lanced through the woman's bluster.

'Who are you?' she asked, licking her lips.

'Sit down,' ordered Ulmenetha. The woman sank to the seat opposite.

'I have been sent here by someone in a very high place – someone who could cause you great harm. Now tell me all you know of the killings.'

'I wasn't here. My husband saw it all.'

'What did he tell you?'

'This is not fair,' whined the woman. 'We've been told what to say. And we've said it. We've done our duty, Pavik and me. We don't want to be involved in . . . in politics.'

'Who told you what to say?'

'Someone in a very high place who could do me considerable harm,' spat the woman, regaining some of her courage.

Ulmenetha nodded. 'I understand your fear,' she said. 'And you are quite right in your desire to avoid becoming enmeshed in the intrigues of the nobility. But you have already told me much.'

'I've told you nothing.'

Ulmenetha looked into the woman's frightened eyes. 'You have told me that your husband lied about the murders. Therefore I must assume that the officer, Dagorian, did not commit them. This means that you have accused an innocent man of a crime. Whatever the intrigue you are now facing the death penalty.'

'No! Pavik told the truth to the first man. Absolutely the truth. Then this other man came and made him change his story. Then he told Pavik to leave the city for a few days.'

'This other man has a name?'

'Who are you?'

'I dwell at the palace,' said Ulmenetha, softly. 'Now, give me the name.'

'Antikas Karios,' whispered the woman.

'What really happened that night?'

'The policeman, Zani, was murdered as he left the tavern. Then three men tried to kill the Drenai. He slew one, wounded another, and they fled. That's all I know. But please, for pity's sake, tell no-one I told you. Say you heard it from someone in the tavern that night. Will you do that?'

'Indeed I will. You say your husband and the serving maid have left the city. Do you know where they went?'

'No. Antikas Karios sent a carriage for them.'

'I see. Thank you for your help.' Ulmenetha rose. The woman pushed herself to her feet and grabbed the priestess by the arm.

'You won't say. You promise!'

'I promise.'

Ulmenetha left the tavern. She glanced back once to see the woman's fearful face at the window.

She will never see her husband again, thought Ulmenetha.

When Dagorian left the tavern that night he ran back to his rooms at the new barracks, changed his clothing, leaving his armour, breastplate and greaves behind, gathered what money he had saved and walked away into the city night.

The death of Zani had been shocking enough, but to discover that the assassins had been sent by Antikas Karios was a bitter blow. Dagorian knew that his life was in far greater peril than he had feared. Antikas Karios had no reason to order him killed,

410

and this meant that the order must have come from Malikada himself. And, as Banelion had pointed out, Dagorian did not have the power to withstand such an enemy.

Worse, the whole poisonous business was undoubtedly linked to the deaths of the mystics, and the demons over Usa. It was therefore likely that he would be hunted on two fronts, on one side by swords, on the other by sorcery.

Dagorian had never been more frightened. He had no plan, save to make his way to the oldest quarter of the city. Here he could hide among the multitudes of the poor and the dispossessed, the beggars and thieves, the whores and the urchins. It was the most densely populated quarter, with narrow streets and twisting lanes, dark alleyways and shadowed arches.

It was close to midnight as Dagorian lay down in the doorway of an old warehouse. He was desperately tired and close to despair.

A figure emerged from the moon shadows. Dagorian pushed himself to his feet, his hand on his knife hilt.

In the moonlight he could see the man was not an assassin, but a beggar, dressed in rags. The man approached him cautiously. He was painfully thin, and his skeletal face was pitted with old sores. 'Spare a copper coin, sir, for an unfortunate victim of the war?'

Dagorian relaxed and was about to reach into his money pouch, when the man sprang forward, a rusty knife in his hand. Dagorian swayed aside, blocking the knife arm and sending a right cross to the beggar's chin. The man fell heavily against the warehouse door, striking his head on the wooden frame. Dagorian wrestled the knife from his grasp, and flung it to one side. The man sank to his haunches.

'Give me your clothes,' said the officer, removing his own cloak and shirt.

The man blinked in the moonlight, and stared up at the Drenai with a look of incomprehension. 'Your clothes, man. I need them. In return you get this fine cloak.'

Slowly the beggar peeled off his wretched coat and the soiled shirt he wore beneath it. 'And your footwear,' said Dagorian. 'You may keep your breeches. I think I'd rather hang than wear them.' The man's body was fish white in the moonlight, his chest and back criss-crossed with old scars – the marks of many whips.

The officer donned the clothing and the coat, then sat down and pulled on the man's boots. They were of cheap hide, the soles as thin as paper.

'You're the one they seek,' said the beggar, suddenly. 'The killer Drenai.'

'The first part is right,' Dagorian told him.

'You won't pass for a beggar. You're too clean. Well scrubbed. You need to lie low for a few days, let your hair get greasy, and get some dirt under your fingernails.'

'A pleasant thought,' responded the Drenai. Yet he knew the man was right. He looked at the beggar, who had made no attempt to clothe himself, despite the chill of the night. He is waiting for me to kill him, thought Dagorian, suddenly. And that is what I should do. 'Get dressed and be on your way,' he said.

'Not very bright, are you?' said the beggar, pulling on the fine blue woollen shirt, and giving a gap-toothed grin.

'You'd prefer it if I slit your throat?'

'It's not about preference, boy. It's about survival. Still, I'm grateful.' The beggar rose, and swung the black cloak around his thin shoulders. 'You'd better start thinking about a hiding place. If you can stay clear of them for a couple of days they'll believe you escaped from the city. Then you can make a move.'

'I do not know the city,' admitted Dagorian.

'Then good luck to you,' said the beggar. Holding the boots in his left hand he moved to where his knife lay and picked it up. Then he was gone.

Dagorian moved away, ducking down a dark alley. The man was right. He needed a place to hide. But where could a man hide from the powers of sorcery?

He felt the rising of panic, and quelled it. The White Wolf had taught him much, but the most valuable lesson was that, when in peril, keep a cool head. 'Think fast if you have to – but always think!' Dagorian sucked in a deep, calming breath, and leaned against a wall. Think! Where can the powers of sorcery be held at bay? In a holy temple. He considered travelling to one of the many churches, but that would mean asking for sanctuary. The building may be holy, but he would be putting his life in the hands of the monks. And – even if they did not betray him – he would be risking their lives. No, that was not an option. Where else then? At the home of a friendly sorcerer, who could place ward spells around him. But he knew no sorcerers – save Kalizkan.

Then a thought struck him. The old woman who had been killed by her son. She had laid ward spells on all the doors of the inner room.

Dagorian carried on walking, trying to get his bearings. The old woman had lived in the northern section of the old quarter. He glanced at the sky, but there were thick clouds and he could see no stars. He walked on for an hour. Twice he saw soldiers of the Watch, and ducked into the shadows.

At last he reached the woman's house. Moving to the rear he scaled a wall and entered the building. There were no windows in the back room and Dagorian lit a lantern. Blood still stained the walls, and the rune stones remained scattered on the table. He glanced at the two doors. Both bore the carved triangle and the snake.

Hoping that the ward spells were still active he blew out the lantern and moved to a narrow bed in the corner.

Sleep came instantly.

He was sitting in a cave, and a fire was burning. He felt hot and confused. 'Be calm, child,' came a familiar voice. He tried to place it, and remembered the shining figure who had rescued him at the wizard's house.

'What am I doing here?' he asked, sitting up and looking around. The cave was empty, and when the voice spoke again, he realized it was coming from the blazing fire.

'You are not here. There is no here. This is a place of spirit. Your body lies in the woman's hovel. It was a good choice. They will not find you.'

'Why do you not show yourself?'

'All in good time, child. Have you put together the clues? Do you even begin to understand what is happening?'

'No. All I know is that Malikada wishes me dead.'

'Malikada cares nothing for you, Dagorian. You are an incidental in a great design. Kalizkan – or the creature that calls itself Kalizkan – is a Demon Lord, of enormous power. He seeks to cast the Spell of the Three Kings. If he succeeds the world will be changed beyond the recognition of man. It will become as it once was. The demons will be flesh once more, and the two worlds will become one.'

Dagorian raised his hand. 'Stop for a moment. This is making my head spin. The two worlds? What is the meaning?'

'Aeons ago the creatures we call demons lived among us. Shape-Shifters, blood-drinkers, were beings. We were at war with them for a thousand years. Then three kings came together, and with the aid of a mighty wizard they changed the world, banishing the demons to another place, a grey realm of spirit. Sorcerers

413

can still summon demons using blood magic, opening the gateways for fleeting heartbeats. But when the spell is done the demons return to the grey. Kalizkan seeks to repeat the Spell of the Three Kings.'

'And he can do this?'

'It has already begun, child. The Ventrian emperor was the first to be sacrificed. But the spell requires three deaths, each of kings, and each king to be mightier than the last. When the final death blow is delivered the world will be cursed as it was in time past. The drinkers of blood will return.'

'Three kings? Then they will try to kill Skanda. I must get to him.'

'You cannot. His death is but hours away, and on the fastest horse you could not reach the army within a day. By this time tomorrow the Drenai army will be destroyed, and Skanda will be strapped to the altar.'

'Sweet Heaven! There must be something I can do.'

'You can save the third king.'

'There is no king greater than Skanda.'

'There is his unborn son. If destiny allows him to live he will be a greater man than his father. But Kalizkan plans to destroy him.'

'I could not get into the palace. They are searching for me everywhere.'

'If you do not then all is lost.'

Dagorian awoke in a cold sweat. As he saw the solid walls of the house relief swelled within him. It was a dream. He laughed at his foolishness, and fell asleep once more.

Wrapped in his cloak against the night cold Nogusta leaned back against the tree and fed another stick to the fire. Bison was snoring softly, the sound strangely comforting in the quiet of the night. Nogusta drew one of his ten diamond-shaped throwing knives from the black baldric draped across his chest and idly twirled the blade through his fingers. The silver steel gleamed in the moonlight.

Ushuru would have loved this place of high, lonely beauty, the vast expanse of the mountains, the wildness of wood and forest. She would have been happy here. *We* would have been happy here, he corrected himself.

Time had not eased the grief. Perhaps he had not wished it to. His mind flew back, ghosting over the years, seeing again the

414

huge living-room. They had all been laughing and joking, sitting around the hearth. His father and his two brothers had just returned from Drenan, where they had negotiated a new contract with the army for a hundred horses, and the celebrations were in full flow. He could still see Ushuru sitting on the couch, her long legs drawn up beneath her. She was crafting a dream-deceiver for Nogusta's youngest nephew. A web of twisted horse hair, woven around a sapling circle that would hang over his bed. Nightmares were said to be drawn to the deceiver, and trapped in the web, leaving the sleeper free of torment. The twenty-year-old Nogusta moved to her side, placing his arm over her shoulder. Lightly he kissed her cheek.

'It is a fine piece of work,' he told her.

She smiled. 'It will confuse the sleep demons.'

He grinned. She had learned the western tongue well, but her translations were always too literal. 'Do you miss the lands of Opal?' he asked her, in the ancient tongue.

'I would like to see my mother again,' she told him. 'But I am more than content.'

She continued to weave the web. 'Of what does Kynda dream?' he asked her.

'Fire. He is surrounded by fire.'

'He burned his fingers last week at the forge,' Nogusta told her. 'Children learn by such painful mistakes.' Even as the thought came to him a bright picture formed in his mind. A small child tumbling down a steep slope. As she fell her foot became trapped under a jutting tree root, snapping her leg. Nogusta stood.

'What is it, my love?' asked Ushuru.

'A child hurt in the hills. I'll find her.'

He kissed her once more, this time upon the lips, then left the house. The memory burned at him now with exquisite pain. He had been twenty years of age, and would never kiss her again. The next time he saw her, less than ten hours distant, she would be a corpse, her beauty destroyed by knives and fire. Kynda's nightmares would have come true, flames roaring through his bedroom.

But this he did not know as he set out to find the village child. When he came upon her she was unconscious. Freeing the child he splinted the leg then carried her back to the village. He had been surprised to find no search parties, and it was just after dawn when he entered the village from the north.

A crowd surged out from the meeting hall as he approached.

The girl was awake now. Her father – Grinan the baker – ran forward. 'I fell down, daddy,' she said. 'I hurt myself.' Nogusta saw that the baker's shirt was smeared with soot. He thought it strange. Grinan took his daughter from Nogusta's arms. Then he saw the splint.

'I found her by Sealac Hollow,' said Nogusta. 'Her leg is broken, but the break is clean. It will mend well.'

No-one spoke. Nogusta knew the villagers had little love for his family, but even so their reaction was strange, to say the least. Then he saw that a number of the men in the crowd also had scorch marks upon their clothes.

From the back of the crowd came Menimas, the nobleman. He was a tall thin man, with deep-set dark eyes, and a moustache and beard trimmed to a perfect circle. 'Hang him!' he said. 'He is a demon worshipper!'

At first the meaning of the words did not register. 'What is he saying?' Nogusta asked Grinan. The man avoided his eyes. He looked down at his daughter.

'Did this man take you away, Flarin?' he asked her.

'No, daddy. I fell down in the woods. I hurt my leg.'

Menimas stepped forward. 'He has bewitched the child. Hang him, I say!' For a moment no-one moved, then several men ran at Nogusta. He downed two of them with a left and right combination, but weight of numbers overpowered him and he was wrestled to the ground. They bound his arms and dragged him to the oak on the market square. A rope was thrown over a high branch, and a noose fastened around his neck.

He was hoisted up, the rope burning into his throat. He heard Menimas scream: 'Die, you black bastard!' Then he passed out.

Somewhere within the darkness he became aware of sensation; warm air being forced into his lungs. He could feel the flow of it, his chest rising to accommodate it. Then he felt the warmth of a mouth upon his own, pushing more air into his starved lungs. Gradually other sensations followed; a burning pain on the skin of his throat, the cool of the ground beneath his back. Strong hands pushed down upon his chest, and he heard a commanding voice. 'Breathe, damn you!'

The warm air had stopped flowing now, and Nogusta, growing short of oxygen, sucked in a huge, juddering, breath.

He opened his eyes to find himself lying on the ground, staring up at the leaves of the oak. The rope still hung from a thick branch, but it had been hacked in two. The face of a stranger swam into sight. Nogusta tried to speak, but his voice was a croak. 'Say nothing,' said the grey-eyed man. 'Your throat is bruised, but you will live. Let me help you stand.' Nogusta struggled to his feet. There were soldiers in the square, and twelve villagers were standing by under guard.

Nogusta touched his throat. The noose still hung there. He lifted it clear. The skin below was raw and bleeding. 'I . . . rescued . . . a child,' he managed to say. 'And . . . they attacked me. I . . . don't know why.'

'I know why,' said the man. Turning to Nogusta he laid a slender hand on his shoulder. 'Last night these people burned your home. They killed your family.'

'My family? No! It cannot be!'

'They are dead, and I am sorry for your loss. I cannot tell you how sorry. The killers believed . . . were led to believe . . . that your family kidnapped the child for . . . some blood rite. They are simple and stupid people.'

The pain in his throat was forgotten now. 'They didn't kill them all? Not all of them?'

'Yes. All of them. And though it will not bring them back you will see justice now. Bring the first!' he ordered. It was the baker, Grinan.

'No, please!' he shouted. 'I have a family. Children. They need me!'

The pale-eyed soldier stepped in close to the pleading man. 'Every action a man takes has consequences, peasant. This man also had a family. You have committed murder. Now you will pay for it.' A woman outside the ring of soldiers screamed for mercy, but a noose was placed over Grinan's head and he was hauled into the air, his feet kicking out.

One by one the twelve villagers with fire-blackened clothes were brought forward and hanged.

'Where is Menimas?' asked Nogusta, as the last man died.

'He fled,' said the soldier. 'He has friends in high places. I doubt he will be convicted.'

Leaving the village to bury its dead the soldiers and Nogusta returned to the burnt-out estate. Nogusta was in deep shock now, his mind swimming. The seven corpses had been wrapped in blankets and laid out in a row before the ruins. One by one he went to them, opening the shrouds, and staring down at the dead. The child Kynda was unmarked by fire, and his tiny hand was clutching the dream-deceiver made by Ushuru. 'Smoke killed him,' said the officer.

One by one Nogusta dug the graves, refusing all offers of help.

When they were all buried the pale-eyed officer returned. 'We have rounded up some of your horses. The rest escaped into the mountains. The tack room was largely intact and I have had a horse saddled for you. I need you to come with me to the garrison to make a report on the . . . incident.'

Nogusta did not argue. They rode for most of the day, and camped that night at Shala Falls. Nogusta had spoken to no-one during the ride. Now he lay within his blankets, his emotions numbed. It was as if he could feel nothing. He kept seeing Ushuru's face, and her smile.

Two of the soldiers were talking nearby, their voices low. 'Did you see it?' said one. 'It was horrible. I've never seen the like. Don't want to again. Made me feel sick.'

Even through the numbness Nogusta felt grateful for the sympathetic reaction in the soldier.

'Yes, it was gross,' said his companion. 'The White Wolf blowing air into a black man's mouth! Who'd believe it?'

Even now – more than thirty years later – Nogusta felt a cold anger rising in him at the memory. Still, anger is a better emotion than sorrow, he thought. Anger is alive and can be dealt with. Sorrow is a dead creature and sits like a weight that cannot be released.

He rose and wandered away into the trees, gathering more dead wood for the fire. You should sleep, he told himself. There will be killers coming. You will need all your strength and skill.

Returning to the fire he fed it then settled down under his blanket, his head resting on his saddle.

But sleep would not come, and he rose again. Bison groaned and woke. Pushing back his blanket the giant pushed himself to his feet and stumbled to a nearby tree, where he urinated noisily. Retying his leggings he turned and saw Nogusta sitting by the fire.

'Didn't find any gold today,' he said, squatting down beside the black man.

'Maybe tomorrow.'

'You want me to keep watch?'

Nogusta grinned. 'You never could keep watch, Bison. By the time I lie down you'll be asleep.'

'I do find it easy to sleep,' admitted Bison. 'I was dreaming about the Battle at Purdol. You, me and Kebra on the wall. Have you still got your medal?'

'Yes.'

'I sold mine. Got twenty *raq* for it. Wish I hadn't now. It was a good medal.'

'You can have mine.'

'Can I?' Bison was delighted. 'I won't sell it this time.'

'You probably will, but it doesn't matter.' Nogusta sighed. 'That was the first great victory. It was on that day we realized the Ventrians could be beaten. I remember it rained all that day, lightning in the sky, thunder over the sea.'

'I don't remember much about it,' admitted Bison. 'Except that we held the wall and the White Wolf supplied sixty barrels of rum for the army.'

'I think you drank most of it.'

'That was a good night. All the camp whores gave it away for free. Have you slept?'

'Not yet,' said Nogusta.

Bison tugged at his white walrus moustache. He could see his friend was unhappy, but did not have the courage to broach the subject. Nogusta and Kebra were both *thinking* men, and much of what they spoke of sailed high above Bison's head. 'You ought to sleep,' said Bison, at last. 'You'll feel better for it.' At the thought of sleep he yawned. Then he wandered back to his blankets. Nogusta settled down again and closed his eyes.

In that moment he experienced a sudden vision. He saw ten riders moving slowly across green hills, white-topped mountains behind them. Nogusta looked at the riders. The sun was high, the ten riders hooded against its glare. They rode into a wood. One of them pushed back his hood and removed a helm of black iron. His hair was long, and ghost white, his face grey, his eyes blood red. An arrow flashed from the trees. The rider threw up his hand, and the shaft sliced through it, driving on to pierce the flesh of his face. He dragged it clear. Both wounds healed instantly.

The vision changed. Suddenly it was night, and two moons hung in the sky, one a crescent, the other full. And he saw himself standing by the tree line on a hillside beneath alien stars. A woman was walking towards him. It was Ushuru. And she was smiling.

This vision also faded, and Nogusta found himself floating high above a plain. He saw the Drenai infantry commit themselves to an attack on the Cadian centre. Skanda was leading the charge. As the Cadians reeled back a trumpet sounded and Skanda signalled to Malikada for the cavalry to attack the right.

But Malikada did not move, and the cavalry remained, holding to the hill.

Nogusta could see the despair in Skanda's eyes; the disbelief and the dawning realization of betrayal and defeat.

And then the slaughter began.

Nogusta awoke in a cold sweat, his hands trembling. Bison and Kebra were asleep, and the dawn light was creeping above the mountains. Pushing aside his blankets the black warrior rose soundlessly. Kebra stirred and opened his eyes.

'What is wrong, my friend?'

'Skanda is dead. And we are in peril.'

Kebra pushed himself to his feet. 'Dead? That cannot be.'

'He was betrayed by Malikada and the Ventrians. They stood by while our comrades were slaughtered.' Slowly, remembering every image, he told Kebra of his visions.

The bowman listened in silence. 'The betrayal and the battle I can understand,' he said, when Nogusta had finished. 'But demonic riders with eyes of blood? What is that supposed to mean? It can't be real, can it? Any more than walking with Ushuru beneath two moons.'

'I do not know, my friend. But I think the riders will come. And I will face them.'

'Not alone you won't,' said Kebra.

Chapter Six

All her life Ulmenetha had known many fears. Her mother's sickness and death had filled her with a terror of cancer that caused awful nightmares, and left her trembling in her bed, her face and body bathed in cold sweat. Small, scurrying rodents inspired a sense of dread in her, leaving her incapable of movement. But most of all the death of her beloved Vian had made her fear love itself, and to run for the sanctuary of the convent.

She sat now in her room, staring up at the stars, contemplating the nature of fear.

For Ulmenetha terror began the moment control was lost. She had been powerless when her mother was dying. She could only watch in silent anguish as the flesh shrivelled away and the spirit fled. As a consequence Ulmenetha had worried over Vian, making sure he ate well, and was always dressed in warm clothes when the winter winds blew. He had laughed at her coddling. Ulmenetha had been preparing an evening meal when word reached her he was dead. While searching for a lost sheep he had slipped on the ice and fallen from the high ridge. There was nothing she could have done to prevent it, but that did not stop the guilt from eating its way into her soul. It was she who had urged him to find the sheep. Guilt, remorse and sorrow had overwhelmed her.

So she had run from her fears, and even taken the extra precaution of becoming fat, in order that men would no longer find her attractive. All this so that she would never again suffer the true terrors of life.

Yet here she was, sitting in a palace bedroom, with the demons closing in.

What can I do? she asked herself. The first answer, as always, was to run, to leave the palace and make the long journey back to Drenan and the convent. The thought of running, putting these fears behind her, was immensely seductive. She had money, and could book passage on a caravan to the coast, and then take a ship to Dros Purdol. Sea air on her face. The thought of flight brought calm to her mind.

Then she pictured Axiana's face, the large, childlike eyes, and the sweet smile. And with it the memory of Kalizkan's rotting, maggot-ridden flesh.

I cannot leave her! The panic began again. What can you do against the power of demons, whispered the voice of flight. You are a fat priestess with no arcane skills. Kalizkan is a sorcerer. He could blast your soul from your overweight body. He could consign you to the Void. He could send assassins to plunge their knives into your obese belly!

Ulmenetha rose from her chair and moved to the table by the window. From a drawer she took a silver-rimmed oval mirror and held it up to her face. For years she had avoided mirrors, hating the bloated image they portrayed. But now she looked beyond the flesh, and deep into the grey eyes, recalling the girl who had run the mountain paths – the girl who had run for joy and not for fear.

At last calm, her mind set, she returned the mirror to the drawer. First she must tell Axiana of her discoveries concerning Dagorian. The officer was innocent, and the true villain, she was sure, was Kalizkan. Then realization struck her. Kalizkan was not the enemy. Kalizkan was dead! Something had taken over the body; something powerful enough to cast a sweet and reassuring spell, enchanting all who came into contact with it.

If she were to tell Axiana the simple truth the queen would think her mad. How then to convince her of the perils that lay in wait?

You must walk with care down this road, she warned herself.

Gathering her thoughts she was about to find Axiana when a servant tapped at her door. Ulmenetha called for her to enter. The girl stepped inside and curtsied.

'What is it, child?'

'The queen wishes you to prepare your belongings. They will be taken to Kalizkan's house in the morning.'

Ulmenetha fought for calm. 'Is the queen in her apartments?'

'No, my lady. She left this afternoon. The Lord Kalizkan came for her.'

At noon on the second day Dagorian found his hunger overriding his caution. Leaving his sabre behind, but hiding his hunting knife beneath the beggar's rags, he left his hiding place and risked the short walk to the market. The sun was bright in a clear sky, the market square packed with people. Easing his way through the crowd he stopped at a meat stall, where a spit of beef was being turned over a charcoal grill. The cook looked at him sourly, but Dagorian produced two copper coins and the man cut several thick slices, placing them on a wooden platter. The smell of the roasting meat was divine. It was almost too hot to hold and Dagorian burned his fingers. He blew on the meat, then tore off a chunk. It was exquisite. Juices ran down his stubbled chin. The cook's expression softened. 'Good?' he enquired.

'The best,' agreed Dagorian.

A commotion began at the far end of the market place. Instantly alert Dagorian prepared to run. Had he been spotted? Were they coming for him? The crowd milled, and word spread like a fire through dry brush. An old man pushed his way through them, coming to the stall.

'The army's been crushed,' he told the cook. 'The king is dead.'

'Dead? The Cadians are coming here?'

The old man shook his head. 'Apparently Prince Malikada forced them back across the river. But all the Drenai perished.'

The crowd surged around Dagorian, everyone talking. Skanda dead? It was unthinkable.

His hunger gone he felt sick with anguish. Turning from the stall he stumbled back into the crowd.

Everywhere people were talking, theorizing, wondering. How had Malikada repulsed the Cadians? How could all the Drenai have been wiped out, and yet Malikada's force remain intact? Dagorian was a soldier – albeit a reluctant one – and he knew the answer.

Treachery.

The king had been betrayed.

Sick at heart he made it back to the seer's home and slumped down in a chair.

The dream came back to him. Two kings slain. The third – the unborn child – in terrible danger.

What can I do, he thought? I am alone, trapped at the centre of a hostile city. How can I get to the queen? And even if I can how do I convince her of the danger she is in. He recalled trying to tell Zani of his fears concerning Kalizkan. The little man had rounded on him instantly. The sorcerer was probably the most popular man in the city, loved by all for his good works.

Dagorian took a deep breath. A phrase his father used came to his mind. 'If a man has a boil on his arse, you don't heal it by lancing the foot.'

Strapping his sabre belt to his waist Dagorian opened the back door, walked through the small garden, and out onto the crowded streets.

Kalizkan's house was an old one, originally built for Bodasen, the general who had led the Immortals in the time of Emperor Gorben. The façade was of white marble, inlaid with statues, and fronted by four tall columns. The building was three storeys high, with more than a hundred rooms, the grounds around it beautifully landscaped, with flowering trees and willows clustered on the banks of a small lake.

A high wall surrounded the estate, and a wrought-iron double gate ensured privacy for the master of the house.

Ulmenetha's carriage drew up outside the gate, and a soldier climbed down to open it. The carriage moved on, coming to a halt before the marble steps leading to a high, arched doorway. A second soldier opened the door of the carriage and Ulmenetha stepped down.

'Stay with me until I have spoken to the queen,' Ulmenetha told the two soldiers. Both bowed. They were strong men, tall and broad shouldered, and the priestess felt more comfortable knowing they were to be close.

She strode up the marble steps and was about to knock when the door opened. A hooded man stood in the shadows beyond. She could not see his face clearly.

'What is it you want?' he asked her, his voice deep, and curiously accented.

Ulmenetha was unprepared for such a cold greeting, and she bridled. 'I am the queen's companion, and here at her invitation.' The hooded man said nothing for a moment, then he stepped aside. Summoning the soldiers Ulmenetha walked inside. Curtains were drawn everywhere, and the interior was gloomy.

'Where is the queen?' she demanded.

'Upstairs . . . Resting,' replied the man, after a moment's thought.

'Which rooms?'

'Go to the top of the stairs and turn right. You will find them.'

Turning to the soldiers she said: 'Wait here. I will be down presently.'

There was the smell of strong perfume in the air, cloying and strangely unpleasant, as if it masked some dank, underlying odour. Ulmenetha began to climb the wide, red-carpeted staircase. Her footfalls raised dust on the carpet and she shivered. Fear was strong in her now. This gloomy, shadow-haunted place was cold and unwelcoming. Glancing back she saw the soldiers standing by the open door, sunlight streaming through and shining on their armour. Fortified by the sight she walked on. Ulmenetha was breathing heavily by the time she reached the top of the stairs. There was a gallery here, the walls covered with old paintings, most of them landscapes. She noticed one of them was torn. She shivered again. This was no place for Axiana!

Reaching the first of the doors she found it was locked. A large key was still in the lock and she turned it. The door opened, the dry hinges creaking.

Dressed in a gown of blue and white satin Axiana was sitting on a couch in front of a barred window. She looked startled as Ulmenetha entered.

'Oh!' she cried, running to Ulmenetha and throwing her arms around the priestess's shoulders. 'Take me away from here! Now. This is an awful place!'

'Where are your servants?' asked Ulmenetha.

'He sent them away. The hooded man. He locked me in! He locked me in, Ulmenetha! Can you believe it?' The priestess stroked the queen's hair.

'There are soldiers downstairs to bring you home. I shall send them to you to fetch your belongings.'

'No. Never mind them. Leave them. Let us just go!'

Taking the queen by the hand Ulmenetha returned to the gallery.

She glanced down. One of the soldiers was leaning against the far wall, the other sitting in a chair. The hooded man was standing by the door, which was now closed.

'The queen wishes her clothes to be packed, and the chests taken to the carriage,' said Ulmenetha, supporting Axiana to the first of the steps. Her words hung in the dusty air. The soldiers did not respond.

'The queen must remain here,' said the hooded man. 'It is the will of my lord.'

'You men! Come here!' called Ulmenetha. Still there was no movement. It was not that they had ignored her, she realized with horror. They had not heard her. Both remained still and silent. Axiana gripped her arm.

'Get me away from here!' she whispered.

Ulmenetha continued to walk down the stairs. Halfway down she saw a glint of metal in the standing soldier's throat. It was a knife hilt and it had pinned him to the wooden panelling beyond. Transferring her gaze to the seated man, she saw that he too was dead. The queen saw it too.

'Sweet Heaven,' whispered Axiana. 'He has killed them both.'

The hooded man advanced to the foot of the stairs. 'Take the queen back to her room,' he ordered. Ulmenetha's right hand, hidden until now in the folds of her voluminous white dress, came into sight. Even in the gloomy half-light the blade of the hunting knife shone bright.

'Get out of my way,' she told the hooded man. He laughed and continued to climb the stairs.

'You think to frighten me, woman? I can taste your fear. I will feed upon it.'

'Feed on this!' said Ulmenetha. Her hand shot up in an underarm throw which sent the blade slamming into the hooded man's throat. He stumbled, then righted himself, dragging the knife clear. Black blood gushed to the front of his dark tunic, streaming down his chest. He tried to speak, but the words were drowned in a bubbling dark froth. Ulmenetha waited for him to fall.

But he did not. He continued to advance. Axiana screamed. Ulmenetha pushed her back up the stairs, then swung to meet the threat from below. The flow of blood from his ruined throat had now drenched the man's dark leggings, but still he came on.

In that moment the priestess knew what she was facing. A demon clothed in human flesh. And yet there was no fear in her, no rising panic. For this was no disease, to slip past her guard and kill her mother, no icy ledge to rob her of her husband. This was flesh and bone, and seeking to harm a girl that she loved like a daughter.

She was calmer than at any time she could remember, her mind focused, her senses sharp.

Closer and closer he climbed. Ulmenetha waited until he raised the knife, then leapt forward, hammering her foot into his chest. He was catapulted back, his body arching in the air. His head struck the stair, his neck snapping. The body crashed to the floor.

Ulmenetha was not surprised as he struggled to his feet, his head flopping grotesquely to his shoulder. The hood had fallen away to reveal a pale, ghostly face, with a lipless mouth and protruding, blood-red eyes.

'Run, Axiana!' shouted the priestess, pointing to the gallery on the left and the far door. Axiana stood rooted to the spot. Tearing her gaze from the advancing man Ulmenetha moved swiftly to the queen, grabbing her arm and hauling her along the gallery. The far door was locked, but, as with Axiana's rooms, there was a key. Opening the door she pulled the key clear, pushed Axiana through, then locked the door behind them. A fist thundered against the door panel, causing it to vibrate. Twice more it struck, and a long, narrow crack appeared in the panelling.

'How do we get out?' asked Axiana, the tremble of panic in her voice.

Ulmenetha had no idea. The house was like a warren, and the corridor in which they stood had many doors, but no obvious stairway to take them back to ground level. 'This way,' said Ulmenetha, moving along the darkened corridor, and through two more doors. There were no keys here, and from far behind them the women heard a splintering crash.

Ulmenetha looked around. They were in a dormitory, a dozen beds on both sides of the room. All the beds were empty. The priestess moved to a window and dragged back the heavy curtains. The window was barred. Light filled the room now, and she could see several toys on the dusty floor, and by the far wall was a straw-filled doll, looking forlorn against the bare, dusty boards. 'Keep moving,' she told the queen. At the far end of the dormitory was another door. It was held shut by a locking bar between two brackets. Ulmenetha lifted the bar clear and pulled open the door. Within was a second dormitory.

Three children sat huddled against the far wall. A red-headed boy of around fourteen or fifteen stepped in front of the two girls, a small knife in his hand. He was painfully thin, and Ulmenetha could see open sores on his skinny arms. One of the girls moved forward. Perhaps a year older than the boy she was also waif thin, and dressed in rags, but she held a long piece of jagged wood, torn from one of the beds. Together they formed a protective shield in front of the youngest child, a small blonde girl of around four.

'Come any closer and we'll kill you,' said the waif with the jagged wooden spear.

There was no other exit from the room.

A floorboard creaked behind them. Ulmenetha swung to see the broken-necked man moving, knife in hand, across the dormitory.

Reaching down she took up the long wooden bar that had secured the door. As the demonic creature approached she rushed at him, swinging the wood like a club. He took the force of the blow on his shoulder. His arm snapped up, his fist cannoning into Ulmenetha's face. Thrown back she lost control of the wooden club and it clattered to the floor. The demon was upon her. Leaping back she avoided his first thrust, and scrambled over a bed. His red eyes stared at her, but as he moved forward the head lolled on the broken neck. He staggered. Then gripped the head with his left hand, dragging it by the hair until the eyes focused once more on the priestess. Then he advanced.

The young red-headed boy leapt at the creature, slashing at his face with the knife blade. The demon swatted him aside. As he did so the waiflike girl crept up behind him and thrust the splintered wood into his back. He arched up. Ulmenetha crouched down, swept up the wooden bar, and charged forward, using it as a ram which hammered into his chest, hurling him into the far wall. As he struck the wall it seemed to Ulmenetha that his chest exploded. She blinked – and saw that the makeshift spear used by the girl had been driven through his back, tearing a huge hole in his chest. The body slid down the wall, then pitched forward to the boards.

Immediately the room was filled with the stench of rotting meat, and Ulmenetha saw maggots writhing through the dead flesh. The waif girl put her hand to her mouth and gagged.

'Let us get out of here,' said Ulmenetha. 'Quickly.'

Despite her revulsion Ulmenetha gathered her knife from beside the rotting corpse and, taking the shocked queen by the arm, led her back along the corridor, out onto the gallery, and down the stairs. The red-headed boy picked up the four-year-old and followed.

Not knowing where to go Ulmenetha moved down a set of

stairs to what she thought must be the ground floor. A locked door barred her way at the bottom. A large key was hanging on a rusted hook. Lifting it clear she opened the door and stepped inside. Light was streaming in from two windows on the far side of the chamber, and shining down onto a sea of small bodies, carelessly heaped around a blood-drenched altar. The sight froze her blood. Though never having been blessed with the gift of a child Ulmenetha's maternal instincts were powerful, and the sight of so many murdered children filled her with an aching sadness.

Closing her eyes against the horror Ulmenetha stepped backwards, just as the pregnant queen was about to enter. 'There is no way through,' said Ulmenetha. 'We must go back the way we came.'

A cold and terrible fury grew in her as she led the group back up the stairs. There must have been over a hundred children in that chamber, a hundred lives ended in torment and terror. This was evil on a scale Ulmenetha could scarcely imagine.

Moving back to the landing she came to the broken door and emerged onto the gallery above the front door. A tall figure stepped from the shadows. Axiana screamed, and Ulmenetha swung round, the knife flashing up and stabbing out. The blade was parried, then a calm voice spoke. 'I am no danger, lady. I am Dagorian.'

Ulmenetha looked into his face, recognizing it from her *lorassium* vision. Fear surged again in her. The scene in the woods, four men – three old, one young – protecting the queen from a hidden evil. Dagorian was the young man from the dream. 'Why are you here?' demanded Ulmenetha.

'I came to kill Kalizkan.'

'He is with the army,' said Ulmenetha. 'Now let us get out of this dreadful place.'

The sun was shining outside and the queen's carriage was still there, the driver stretched out asleep on the grass. Ulmenetha looked up at the bright, clean, blue of the sky with a gratitude she could scarce believe.

As the group approached the coachman yawned and stretched. Seeing the queen he scrambled to his feet and bowed.

'At your bidding, your highness,' he said.

'Take us to the palace,' ordered Ulmenetha.

Helping the queen into the carriage she glanced back at the two girls and the boy. All three were badly undernourished, clothed in rags. 'Get in,' she ordered them.

'Where you taking us?' asked the boy, suspiciously.

'Somewhere safer than this,' Ulmenetha replied.

They crowded in, followed by Dagorian. As the carriage moved away the young officer leaned in close to Ulmenetha. 'There is nowhere safe in the city,' he said, keeping his voice low.

'What do you suggest?'

'We must get to the coast, and find a ship. And we must do it before Malikada returns. We should head for the mountains.'

'There are forests there,' whispered Ulmenetha.

'You fear forests?' he asked, surprised by her reaction.

'The white crow will be there,' she told him. He was confused, but she turned away from him.

As the carriage made its way along the broad avenues Axiana saw the crowds milling. 'What is happening?' she asked. 'Why is everyone gathering so?'

'They have heard the news, highness. They are wondering what will happen to them now,' Dagorian explained.

'The news? What news?' she asked, mystified. Dagorian blinked, and transferred his gaze to Ulmenetha. She too was none the wiser.

The officer rubbed his hand over his stubbled jaw. 'I am truly sorry, your highness. But word has reached the city that our army was defeated by the Cadians.'

'That is not possible,' said Axiana. 'Skanda is the greatest warrior alive. You must be mistaken. This is just a rumour.'

Dagorian said nothing, but his gaze met that of Ulmenetha. The queen was looking out of the window again. Ulmenetha mouthed a question.

'The king?'

Dagorian shook his head. 'Then we must brave the forest,' said Ulmenetha.

Irritation crept into Malikada – a small, dark cloud in the clear blue sky of his joy. He stood on the hillside gazing down on the Drenai dead. Stripped now of armour and weapons, gone was their arrogance and their might. They were merely pale corpses, ready to be rolled into the huge pit being dug by Ventrian soldiers.

It was Malikada's moment of triumph. The army which had destroyed the empire of his ancestors was now ruined. He had always known revenge would be sweet, but had never guessed just how exquisite the taste would be.

Yet it was marred.

He swung to the swordsman, Antikas Karios. 'Now we will rebuild Ventria,' he said. 'And we will burn away the Drenai presence.'

'Yes, my lord,' replied Antikas, dully.

'What is wrong with you, man? Do you have the toothache?'

'No, my lord.'

'Then what?'

'They fought well and bravely, and it does not sit well with me that we betrayed them.'

Malikada's irritation flared into anger. 'How can you talk of betrayal? That would be their perspective. We fought them, you and I. We risked our lives to prevent Skanda's victories. The old emperor was weak and indecisive, and yet we stood by him. We served him faithfully and well. At the last Skanda conquered us. We had two choices, Antikas. You remember that? We could have died, or we could have gone on fighting a different kind of war. We both chose the latter. We have remained true to our own cause. We are not traitors, Antikas. We are patriots.'

'Perhaps so, Lord. But this leaves a bad feeling in my stomach.'

'Then take your stomach elsewhere,' stormed Malikada. 'Go! Leave me to my pleasure.' Antikas bowed and walked away. Malikada watched the swordsman. He moved with such grace. The deadliest bladesman Malikada had ever seen, and yet, beneath it all, it now transpired, he was soft and weak! He had always envied Antikas, yet now he felt only contempt.

Malikada forced the image of the man from his mind, picturing again the moment when Skanda had signalled the charge. Oh, how he wished he could have been closer, to see the expression on the bastard's face, to witness the realization that he was doomed, that Malikada was ending his dreams of empire. Oh, how that must have eaten into Skanda's soul.

Irritation flared again within him. When Skanda had been dragged unconscious from the battlefield Kalizkan had refused permission for Malikada to witness the sacrifice. He would like to have seen that; to see the living heart cut from the body. A truly magnificent moment it would have been to stand over the king, their gaze locked together, watching the death agony, feeling Skanda's dying hatred. Malikada shivered with pleasure at the thought.

But then Kalizkan was a secretive man. Malikada had not been allowed to watch the old emperor's sacrifice either.

The corpses were being tumbled into the pit now, and covered with oil and dry wood. As the flames spread and black smoke spiralled up Malikada turned away. It was almost noon, and he needed to see Kalizkan. This was only the beginning. There were other Drenai garrisons along the coast, and there was still the problem of the White Wolf.

Also there was the question of Malikada's coronation. Emperor Malikada! Now that had a fine sound. He would order Kalizkan to create an even greater illusion in the night skies over Usa – something that would dwarf the display Skanda had enjoyed.

He strolled back through the Ventrian camp towards the cliffs beyond. Red dust rose up around him as he walked, staining his highly polished boots. The cave entrance was dark, but he could see lantern light further inside. Stepping into the cave he felt a momentary fear. Kalizkan had become so withdrawn lately, and had ceased to treat him with his customary respect. Malikada had allowed the discourtesy, for he needed the man. His spells and his wizardry had been vital.

Had been vital.

The thought struck him that he no longer needed Kalizkan.

I need no-one, he realized. But I shall keep him with me. His skills will be more than useful when it comes time to invade the lands of the Drenai. But first there is Axiana. I shall wait until she has birthed the child, see it strangled, and then wed her myself. Who can then deny me the crown?

His good humour restored he continued on his way.

The body of Skanda was laid on a stone altar, the chest cut open. A linen cloth had been laid over his face. Kalizkan was sitting by a small fire, his blue satin robes stained with blood.

'Did he scream as he died?' asked Malikada.

Kalizkan rose. 'No, he did not scream. He cursed you with his last breath.'

'I would like to have heard that,' said Malikada.

There was a foul odour in the cave, and Malikada pulled a perfumed handkerchief from his pocket, holding it to his nose. 'What is that smell?' he asked.

'It is this form,' said Kalizkan. 'It has served its purpose, and is now rotting. And I have no wish to waste my enhanced powers sustaining it any longer.'

'Form? What are you talking about?'

'Kalizkan's body. It was already dying when I inhabited it. That

432

was why he summoned me. To take away his cancer. I took him instead. His arrogance was overwhelming. How could he think to control Anharat, Lord of the Night?'

'You are making no sense, wizard.'

'On the contrary, Malikada. It all makes perfect sense, depending, of course, upon your perspective. I listened to your conversation with the swordsman. You were quite right. It is all a question of perspectives. Skanda believed you betrayed him, whereas you and I know you remained true to the one cause you believed in, the restoration of the Ventrian throne. Naturally with you to sit upon it. I, on the other hand, have no interest in the throne. And I have also remained true to my cause – the restoration of my people to the land which was once theirs by right and by force of arms.'

Malikada was suddenly frightened. He tried to back away, but found that his legs would not obey him. The perfumed handkerchief dropped from his fingers, and his arms fell uselessly to his sides. He was paralysed. He tried to shout for help, but, as his mouth opened, no sound came forth.

'I don't suppose,' said the creature within Kalizkan, 'that you are interested in my cause, save that to tell it will extend your life by a few moments.' The body of the wizard seemed to shimmer, and Malikada found himself gazing upon a rotting corpse. Half the flesh of the face had disappeared, the other half was grey-green and maggot infested. Malikada tried to shut his eyes, but even that was lost to him. 'My people,' said Kalizkan, 'lost a war. We were not killed. We were banished, to a grey, soulless world alongside your own. A world without colour, without taste, without hope. Now, thanks in small part to you, Malikada, we have the chance to live again. To feel the cold, heady night winds upon our faces, to taste the sweet joys that spring from human fear.'

Kalizkan came closer, and reached out his hand. Talons sprouted from the fingers. 'Oh yes, Malikada, let your terror flow. It is like wine, soft upon the tongue.' With an agonizing lack of speed the talons slowly pierced Malikada's chest.

'And now you can help me complete my mission. The queen, you see, has escaped from my home, and I need your form in order to use your men to hunt her down.'

The fierce pain of fire flowed through Malikada, searing its way across his chest, down into his belly, and up the spinal cord, exploding into his brain. It was an agony beyond enduring, and Kalizkan shivered with pleasure at it.

The talons ceased their probing as they closed around Malikada's heart. 'If I had more time,' said Anharat, 'I would hold you like this for some hours. But I have no time. So die, Malikada. Die in despair. Your world is ruined, and soon your people will be food for the Windborn.' The Ventrian's corpse twitched. The rotting body of Kalizkan fell to the floor.

Within Malikada now the demon stretched out his new arms. Kalizkan's body burst into flames.

Stepping back the new Malikada strode to the cave entrance. Lifting his hand he focused his concentration on the rocks above him. Dust filtered down, the rocks groaned. Malikada stepped into the sunlight.

And the cave ceiling crashed down behind him, blocking the entrance.

He strode down to where his men were waiting, pausing only to sniff the smoke rising from the great pyre. There was a delicious sweetness to it.

Back at his tent he summoned Antikas Karios. The swordsman bowed low.

'Go to the city and find the queen,' said Malikada. 'Protect her until my arrival.'

'Yes, my lord. Protect her from whom?'

'Just make sure she is there when I arrive.'

'I shall leave immediately, my lord.'

'Do not fail me, Antikas.'

An angry look came into the swordsman's deep, dark eyes. 'When have I ever failed you, cousin?'

'Never,' replied Malikada, 'and now is not the time to start.'

Antikas said nothing for a moment, but the demon within Malikada felt the swordsman's piercing gaze. Coolly he cast a small spell, which radiated from him, surrounding Antikas. The swordsman relaxed.

'It will be as you command,' he said.

'Take spare horses and ride all night. Be there before the dawn.'

The carriage moved slowly through the city streets. Crowds were everywhere now, and as dusk deepened, the riots began in the poorer quarters of the city. Several buildings were set afire. 'Why do they do this?' asked Axiana, watching the distant smoke, and hearing the far-off screams. 'What purpose does it achieve?'

Dagorian shrugged. 'That is hard to explain, your highness.

Some people are in a state of panic. They fear the Cadians will descend on them with fire and sword. Others know that with the army destroyed they are free to commit crimes they would otherwise have been punished for. They see the disaster as an opportunity to obtain wealth they could not hope to earn. I do not know all the reasons. But there will be many deaths tonight.'

The carriage pulled into the palace grounds, where it was stopped by an officer of the guards, and a squad of spear men. The man opened the door, saw the queen, and bowed low.

'Thank the Source you are safe, your highness,' he said. She gave him a wan smile, and the carriage moved on.

Inside the queen's apartments Axiana sank to a couch, resting her head on a satin pillow, and fell asleep. Ulmenetha began to gather clothes for the queen, packing them carefully into an ornate wooden chest. Then she went with the children to the deserted kitchens, where she gathered food: sides of ham, some hard cheese wrapped in muslin, and several small sacks of flour, sugar and salt. The children sat close by, gorging themselves on bread and preserves, washed down with fresh milk. Ulmenetha paused and watched them.

'What happened in that orphanage?' she asked the red-headed boy.

His bright blue eyes were suddenly fearful, but his expression remained set and hard. 'Children died,' he said. 'Everybody said Kalizkan was kind. You could be sure of a meal there. Lots of my friends had already gone. We went there ten days ago.' The boy closed his eyes and took a deep breath. 'Most of my friends were dead by then, but I didn't know. They used to take them underground, but you could still hear the screams.' He opened his eyes. 'I don't want to talk about it.'

'I understand,' said the priestess. Moving opposite the children she sat down. 'Listen to me. We are leaving the city. Tonight. You can come with us if you wish, or you can stay in Usa. It is up to you.'

'Where are you going?' asked the older girl, her deep, dark eyes holding to Ulmenetha's gaze.

'We will try to find a way to the coast, and then a ship to Drenan. It is a long way, and I think it will be a perilous journey. You may be safer here.'

'I am Drenai,' said the girl. 'Or at least my father was Drenai. I will come with you. There is nothing here for me. I do not want to stay.'

'You won't leave me here!' wailed the small blonde child, taking hold of the girl's hand.

'I won't leave you, little one. You can come with us.'

'Why should we go?' asked the boy. 'I can steal food for all of us.'

Reaching out she ran her fingers through his tangled red hair. 'Maybe in Drenan you won't have to steal food. We could live in a house.'

The boy swore. 'Who's going to give us a house, Pharis? Nobody *gives* anyone anything. You get nothing for nothing. That's the way of it.'

'You found food for me, Conalin. And you looked after Sufia when she was sick. You got nothing in return.'

'You're my friends and I love you. That's different. How do you know you can trust this fat woman?'

The girl looked up again into Ulmenetha's eyes. 'She came to rescue her friend. And she fought the beast. I trust her.'

'Well, I don't want to go,' said the boy, stubbornly.

'If you don't come, who will protect little Sufia?' she said.

'Oh, please come with us, Con,' pleaded Sufia. 'Please!'

He sat silently for a moment, then stared up at Ulmenetha, his eyes angry. 'Why should we trust you?' he asked her.

'I can offer no reason, Conalin. Save that I never lie. And I promise you this: If we reach Drenan safely the queen will buy you a house.'

'Why should you? You owe us nothing.'

'That is not true. Your bravery, and that of your sister, helped to kill the . . . beast, as you call it. Had you not helped me I would have been killed.'

'She's not my sister. She's Pharis, my friend. And if she and Sufia are going, I'll come too. But I don't believe you about the house.'

'Wait and see,' said Ulmenetha. 'Now let's find some sacks for supplies, and fill them. We don't want to be hungry when we reach the mountains.'

Back in the apartments the queen was asleep on the couch, and Dagorian had swapped his beggar's rags for one of Skanda's grey woollen tunics. It was emblazoned with a rearing white horse at the shoulder. He stood now on the balcony, watching the glow from the fires in the western quarter.

The rioting would die down during the night, and their best chance of escape lay in the hour before dawn, when the rioters were asleep, and the soldiers of the Watch were busy with the aftermath of the chaos.

Escape?

How long before the pursuit began? And how fast could they travel? The queen was heavily pregnant, the child due within days. She could not ride a horse at speed. The threat of miscarriage was too great. That meant taking a wagon. Hard-riding horsemen would catch them within hours.

Perhaps it would be wiser to try to reach Banelion. The White Wolf and his men could not be further than a few days' ride to the west.

He dismissed the idea. That would be the enemy's first thought. And anyway what could a few hundred old men do against Malikada's Ventrian army? Joining Banelion would merely serve a death warrant on more Drenai soldiers.

What then?

Some deception was necessary. Something that would give them time.

He heard the queen give out a soft moan in her sleep and moved back into the apartment. Sitting down beside her he gently took her hand. 'I will defend you with my life,' he whispered.

Ulmenetha watched him from the doorway. He was holding her hand with great tenderness and she realized, in that moment, that the young man was in love with Axiana. Sadness touched her. In a just world they would have met two years ago, when both were free. Even if she returned his love Axiana was carrying the heir to the throne of two nations. Her life would remain ruled by men of power. And they would never sanction a marriage to a junior officer like Dagorian.

Clearing her throat she stepped into the room, the children following her, bearing sacks of supplies.

'What now?' she asked Dagorian.

Releasing the queen's hand he rose. 'Are the children coming with us?' Ulmenetha nodded. 'Good,' he said. 'We will need a wagon and extra horses. I will find them. The queen must be disguised. No silks nor satins. No jewellery. We will leave the city as a poor family, fleeing from the riots. There will be many such over the next few days. With luck we will pass unnoticed among them. This will slow down the pursuit.'

'What can I do while you are fetching a wagon?'

'Find maps of the mountains. There will be many box canyons, broken trails, and treacherous areas. It would be helpful if we could plan a route, and not move blindly on faith alone.'

Swirling a dark cloak around his shoulders Dagorian left them. The youngest child, Sufia, was exhausted, and Pharis led her to a couch, where she lay down and fell asleep. Leaving the children in the apartment Ulmenetha took a lantern and made her way to the Royal Library on the ground floor. There were thousands of books here, and hundreds of scrolls. She searched for some time through the index, locating three ancient maps of the mountains, and also a traveller's diary that told of the trek from Usa to Perapolis in the south. If the Source was with them they would be following this route for at least part of the way.

Returning to the apartment she found the red-headed boy, Conalin, sitting on the balcony. Pharis and Sufia were cuddled together on the couch, fast asleep. She covered them with a blanket then moved to Axiana. The queen stirred, opened her eyes, and smiled sleepily. 'I had a terrible dream,' she said.

'Rest, my lady. You will need your strength in the morning.' Axiana closed her eyes.

Ulmenetha walked out onto the balcony. The western quarter of the city was ablaze, and she could hear distant screams. 'Are you not tired?' she asked Conalin.

'I am strong,' he said.

'I know that. But even the strong need sleep.'

'They are killing one another,' he said, gesturing towards the distant flames. 'Robbing, looting, raping. Slaughtering the weak.'

'Does it sadden you?'

'It is what the weak are for,' he said, solemnly. 'That is why I shall never be weak.'

'How did you come to meet Pharis and the child?'

'Why do you want to know?' he demanded.

'I am making conversation, Conalin. If we are to be friends we need to know one another. That is the way of things. What is Pharis's favourite food?'

'Plums. Why?'

She smiled. 'That is part of knowing a friend. When you go out to steal food you will look for a plum for Pharis, because you know she likes them. Knowing is good among friends. So where did you meet?'

'Her mother's a whore who worked Merchant Alley. I first saw Pharis there. Two summers ago. Her mother was drunk, and lying in the gutter. Pharis was trying to lift her, to get her home.'

'And you helped?'

'Yes.'

'Why did you do that?'

'What do you mean?'

Ulmenetha shrugged. 'You were helping the weak, Conalin. Why did you not just rob her and walk away?'

'That's what I was going to do,' he snapped. 'I saw her lying there and I knew she'd have coin from the men she'd doxied. But then Pharis came along. She saw me standing there and she said, "Take her arm." So I did. Anyway, that's how we met.'

'What happened to the mother?'

Now it was his turn to shrug. 'She's still around. She sold Pharis to a whorehouse. Where rich men like to fondle young girls. I took her away from that. I climbed through the rear window one night, and I got her out.'

'That was very brave of you.' He seemed pleased at the compliment and his hard face relaxed. As it did so he looked younger, and terribly vulnerable. Ulmenetha wanted to reach out and stroke his tangled red hair, to draw him to her. He spoke again.

'Had to pick the lock on her room. And all the while the Breaker was asleep in a chair next to it.'

'The Breaker?' she enquired.

'The leg-breaker. The man who watches out for the girls. Well, they say he watches out for them, but if a girl won't do what she's told he bashes them.' He grinned suddenly. 'I bet he was in real trouble the following morning.'

'And what about Sufia?'

'We found her in that wizard's house. She was hiding under a bed. She was the last of them. Why was he killing children?' he asked her.

'He was, I believe, making blood magic,' said Ulmenetha. 'It is a vile practice.'

'There's a lot of them,' he said, softly. 'Vile practices.'

'Tell me about you,' she said.

'No,' he said, simply. 'I don't talk about me. But you are right, I am tired. I think I'll sleep now for a while.'

'I'll wake you when Dagorian gets back.'

'You won't have to,' he assured her.

Out on the streets the rioting continued unabated. Dagorian had avoided the guards by climbing over the palace wall, and dropping down onto the broad Avenue of Kings. From here he could see several bodies, sprawled in death. Rioters moved into sight, swilling looted wine. Keeping to the shadows he moved down the Avenue, then darted across it to one of the wide roads leading to the Merchants' Acre. Here, he knew, were the hauliers who daily distributed the merchants' wares to shops, homes and market stalls in the city.

He reached the first to find the buildings engulfed by flames, and could see wagons burning on the open ground beyond. Anger swept through him, threatening to engulf his mind. He wanted to draw his sword and run at the rioters, hacking and slashing. His fingers closed around the hilt of his sabre. A voice whispered into his mind, cold and calm, dispelling the fury.

'Do not let them possess you, Dagorian. They are everywhere.'

Dagorian leaned back against a wall, his hands shaking with the aftermath of rage. 'Who are you?' he whispered.

'A friend. You remember me? I came to you when the demons were rending your soul. And again at the home of the murdered seer.'

'I remember.'

'Know this, then, child: The city is possessed, and the demons are feasting on rage and murder. Every hour they grow stronger. By tomorrow no-one will be able to resist them. Do not succumb. Think clearly and coolly. I will be with you, though I will not speak again. Now find a wagon!'

The officer moved away from the wall, and ducked down a narrow alley. Smoke, thicker than any fog, hung in the air, burning his lungs. Holding his cloak over his face Dagorian ran on. The sounds of screaming came from all around him now, from the burning buildings where people were trapped, from the alleyways, where victims had been cornered.

Anger touched him again, but he fought it down.

He came to the wide gates of a second haulier. They had been burst open and a group of men and women carrying torches were running around the yard, setting the wagons ablaze. Others had thrown torches into the stables, igniting the straw inside. Horses were whinnying in terror. Cutting across the yard Dagorian opened the stable doors, ran inside, freeing all but two of the horses. Panic stricken the freed beasts galloped into the yard, scattering the rioters.

Moving to the remaining two horses Dagorian calmed them as best he could and led them from the stable. Fear was strong upon

440

them, but they were used to the sure touch of their handlers, and they accepted Dagorian's authority. In the yard he tethered them to a wagon untouched by the rioters. The traces and brasses used to hitch the horses were laid over the back of the wagon. Dagorian moved to them.

A rioter ran forwards, tossing a torch to the wagon seat. Dagorian spun on his heel and sent a thundering right cross to the man's jaw. He fell without a sound. Hurling the torch aside he moved to the traces. A whoosh of burning air seared across the yard as flames burst through the stables' wall. The horses reared. Once more Dagorian tried to calm them, stroking their long necks, whispering soothing words. The heat was intense and the rioters moved away. Dagorian hitched the horses and climbed to the driver's seat. Releasing the brake he took up the whip and cracked it. The horses surged into the traces and the wagon moved forward. But to exit the yard they had to drive past the burning stables and the horses faltered, unwilling to face the flames again.

In the back of the wagon were several empty sacks. With his dagger he sliced two strips from one of them. Leaping to the ground he blindfolded the horses. Back in the driver's seat he cracked the whip. Reluctantly the team moved on. He could feel them faltering again as the heat swelled, but lashed them both with the whip and shouted at the top of his voice. The horses powered into the traces and the wagon rolled past the burning building and out into the road beyond.

Swinging them to the right he took them at speed down towards the Avenue of Kings.

Another mob was gathered there, but they scattered as the wagon bore down on them. One man ran forward and leapt at him. His face was a twisted mask of hatred, his eyes staring wide. Dagorian lashed out with his foot, kicking the attacker in the chest, and pitching him to the street. Up ahead a group of men tried to block his way, but the horses were galloping now, and would not be stopped. A hurled knife thudded into the backrest behind him, but then he was clear of them, and the palace gates were in sight.

They were open. And no guards could be seen.

Dagorian drove through, then dragged on the reins, hauling the horses to a stop.

Jumping down he struggled with the wrought-iron gates, pulling them closed.

They would not hold firm against a mob, he knew. Mounting the wagon again he drove it to the main doors.

The sky was lightening as he ran into the building, and up the long, winding staircase. The queen was awake now, and dressed in a simple woollen gown of blue, edged with white cotton.

'We must go quickly,' said Dagorian. 'The mob will soon be here.'

'Go? Where should I go? I am the queen. They will not harm me,' said Axiana. 'They are my people and they love me.' Her slender fingers touched the sleeve of her gown. 'And I will not wear this revolting outfit. It scratches my skin.'

'A mob does not know of love,' said Dagorian. 'They are outside killing each other, raping and looting. It will not be long before they realize that true riches can be found here.'

'My cousin Malikada will be back soon. He will protect me,' said Axiana.

'Please, my dove,' urged Ulmenetha, 'trust me! Your life is in danger, and we must flee the city.'

'The nobility are not given to panic, Ulmenetha. And certainly not in the face of peasant unrest.'

'It is not merely *unrest*,' Dagorian told her. 'The mobs are possessed.'

'Possessed? That cannot be!'

'It is true, highness. I swear it. I discovered the demons while investigating a series of murders. I believe Kalizkan summoned them. I have seen mobs before, and I have been out there among those demented people. There is a difference, believe me.'

'You are saying this to frighten me,' insisted Axiana.

Ulmenetha approached the queen. 'What he says is true, my dove. I have known about these demons for some time. I also know that Kalizkan is a walking corpse. He too is possessed. You saw the creature at his house. It was a *zhagul*. A dead man. I think we should listen to Dagorian and follow him to the mountains.'

'I will not!' insisted Axiana, drawing back, her eyes fearful. 'Malikada will protect me. I will tell him of Kalizkan's evil and he will punish him.'

Ulmenetha stepped in close and put her hands on Axiana's shoulders. 'Be calm,' she said, softly. 'I am here. All will be well.' Her right hand lifted, as if to stroke the queen's brow. Dagorian saw a blue light radiate from her palm. Axiana fell forward into Ulmenetha's arms. The priestess lowered her to a couch. 'She will sleep for several hours,' she said.

'You are a sorceress?' whispered Dagorian.

'I am a priestess!' she snapped. 'There is a difference. The little magic I know is used for healing. Now carry her down – and be careful with her.'

Dagorian lifted Axiana to his arms. Despite her pregnancy she was not heavy and he carried her to the wagon, lifting her to the tailboard. Ulmenetha settled her down, rolling an empty sack for a pillow, and covering her with a blanket. Pharis and Sufia scrambled aboard, and Conalin climbed to the driver's seat. Dagorian stepped up to sit beside him.

Dagorian drove the wagon to the royal stables, and there saddled a warhorse of some seventeen hands. 'Can you drive the wagon?' he asked Conalin. The boy nodded.

'Good. Then I will clear a way to the East Gate. If I go down do not stop. You understand?'

'Oh, I won't stop,' said Conalin. 'You can count on that.'

'Then let's go.'

The Avenue of Kings was deserted now, and eerily quiet. Dagorian led the way, the sound of his horse's hoof beats like slow beating war drums. He drew his sabre and scanned the Avenue. There was not a sign of life.

The dawn sun cleared the mountains.

The wagon moved on. After half a mile they saw a group of men sitting quietly by the roadside. They were blood smeared, their clothing stained by smoke. They looked up at the wagon, but made no hostile moves. Their eyes were dull, and they seemed weary beyond reckoning.

Dagorian sheathed his sabre.

They reached the gate and found themselves waiting in a line of some twenty wagons and coaches, all filled with fleeing families and their possessions. The gate arch was narrow, and it was taking time to manoeuvre the wagons through. A group of riders arrived from outside the city, but could not pass, and Dagorian heard the beginnings of an angry exchange.

Dismounting he tethered his horse and was about to climb onto the wagon when he heard the voice of Antikas Karios, ordering a wagon driver to draw his vehicle aside. Ducking down below the wagon he waited until the group cleared the gate, and thundered their mounts towards the palace.

The wait now to leave the city seemed interminable. Two impatient drivers moved forward at the same time. One of the horses reared, and lashed out at the opposing team. Both drivers leapt down and began a heated argument. Dagorian's patience snapped. Vaulting to the saddle he rode to the shouting men. Drawing his sabre he held the blade to the neck of the first. 'Back off,' he said, 'or I'll gut you like a fish!' The argument died instantly. The man scrambled back to his wagon and hauled on the reins, reversing his team. Swinging in the saddle Dagorian shouted to Conalin. 'Drive through!'

And then they were out onto open ground.

Conalin headed the horses up the long slope towards the mountains. Dagorian rode alongside, constantly looking back, expecting at any moment to see pursuers galloping after them. 'Give them a touch of the whip!' he ordered Conalin. The boy did so and the horses broke into a run. In the back of the wagon Ulmenetha was thrown to one side. The child Sufia began to cry. Ulmenetha gathered her close. 'There is nothing to fear,' she said, soothingly. The horses were breathing heavily as they reached the crest of the hill, dropping down on the other side. Out of sight of the city Dagorian ordered Conalin to slow down and continue following the road south and west.

The officer rode back to the rise and dismounted. Minutes later he saw Antikas Karios and his men leave the city. For one dreadful moment he thought they were heading in pursuit, but they turned due west along the merchant road.

How long before they realized their mistake? An hour? Less?

Back in the saddle he caught up with the wagon. Axiana was conscious now, and sitting silently, staring out over the mountains. Dagorian hitched his horse to the wagon and climbed aboard. 'We have lost them for now,' he told Ulmenetha. 'Where are the maps?'

Ulmenetha passed him the first. It was an old, dry scroll, which he carefully unrolled. The city depicted was vastly smaller than the metropolis Usa had become, but the mountain roads were clearly marked. They formed part of a trade route to the ghost city of Lem, 200 miles south. Built around the wealth of nearby silver mines – which had failed more than 200 years ago – Lem was now an abandoned series of ruins. Dagorian studied the map carefully. They would travel south for just over a hundred miles, then swing to the west for another 70 miles, crossing the Carpos mountains and picking up the coast road to Caphis. It was not the nearest of the ports, but the route was less well travelled, and should help them avoid the dangers of bandits and rebel tribesmen. Merchants were constantly harassed by such bands around the closest port, Morec.

A secondary factor in choosing Caphis, but nonetheless important, was that Malikada was likely to expect them to head for Morec, the intended destination of the White Wolf and his men.

He showed the route to Ulmenetha. She peered at the map. 'What do the symbols mean?' she asked him, tapping the scroll with her finger.

'They are a form of shorthand taken from High Ventrian. This one, which looks like the head of a ram, is a pictorial representation of three letters, N.W.P. It stands for no winter passage.'

'And the figures?'

'Distance between set points, using not the mile, but the Ventrian league. These will not be precise.'

'How far must we travel?' asked Pharis.

'Perhaps two hundred and fifty miles, much of it over rough country. We have no spare horses, so we will have to move with care, conserving the animals as best we can. With luck we will be in Caphis within a month. It is but a short trip then across the sea to Dros Purdol – and home!'

'Whose home?' asked Axiana, suddenly. Dagorian looked across at the queen. Her face was pale, her dark eyes angry. 'It is not my home. My home was raided by Drenai savages from across the sea. These same savages saw my father slain, and forced me to wed their leader. Is Axiana going home? No, she is being kidnapped and taken *from* her home.'

The officer was silent for a moment. 'I am sorry, your highness,' he said, at last. 'I am one of those Drenai savages. But I would willingly give my life for you. I have brought you from the city because you are in danger. Kalizkan is a monster. And, for purposes which I do not fully understand, desires to kill the child you carry. He and Malikada are in league. Of that I have no doubt. Malikada delivered your father to him. Kalizkan killed him. Now Malikada's treachery has seen Skanda similarly murdered. If it is in my power to bring you safely to Drenan then I shall. After that you will be free. You will be fêted as the queen, and, if it is possible, an army will bring you back to Ventria and establish you once more upon the throne.'

Axiana shook her head. 'How can you be so naive, Dagorian? You think the Drenai nobility will care about me? I am a foreigner. You think they will support my child? I think not. He will die, poisoned or strangled, and some other *Drenai* nobleman will take the throne. That is the way it will be. You say Malikada delivered up my father. I can believe that. He loathed him, thought him weak, and blamed him for the losses against Skanda. You say he betrayed Skanda. This I can also believe, for he hated him. But he has always loved me. He is my cousin and would do nothing to harm me.'

'And the babe you carry?' asked Ulmenetha.

'I care nothing for him. He is a poisoned gift from Skanda. Let them take him. And as for you, Dagorian, return to your horse. I find your company repulsive.'

The words hurt him, but he stood, untied the reins of his mount and stepped into the saddle. Ulmenetha gathered up the map. 'You are wrong, highness,' she said, softly.

'I need to hear no words from you, traitress.'

A dry chuckle came from Conalin. He glanced back at Ulmenetha. 'You save her from the beast and she calls you names. Gods, how I hate the rich.'

Axiana made no reply, but stared out over the snow-capped mountains, her face set, her expression unreadable. She wanted to apologize to Ulmenetha, to say that the words were spoken in anger. Ingratitude was not one of Axiana's weaknesses. She knew that the priestess had risked her life to save her from the undead creature in Kalizkan's house. More than this, she knew that Ulmenetha loved her, and would never willingly see her come to harm.

But Axiana was frightened. Raised at court, her every whim catered to instantly, the events of the past two days had been deeply shocking to her. In the space of forty-eight hours she had been locked in a dank room, witnessed violent death, heard of her husband's murder, and was now in a creaking wagon, heading into the wild lands. She felt as if her mind was unravelling. Kalizkan, whom she had trusted and been fond of, was now revealed as a mass murderer, a child-killing beast. The Source alone knew what he had planned for her. She shuddered.

'Are you cold, my dove?' Ulmenetha asked her. Axiana nodded dumbly. The priestess moved to her, laying a blanket over her shoulders. Tears welled in Axiana's eyes. The wagon lurched over a rut in the road and Axiana half fell into Ulmenetha. The priestess caught her. Axiana rested her head against Ulmenetha's shoulder.

'I'm sorry,' she whispered.

446

'I know, child.'

'The baby is due soon. I am very frightened.'

'I will be here. And you are strong. Everything will be all right.'

Axiana took a deep breath, then sat upright. She could see Dagorian riding ahead, scanning the trail. They were heading towards a forest that covered the flanks of the hills like a buffalo robe. Axiana glanced back. The city of Usa could no longer be seen behind them.

The dark-haired Pharis took a red apple from a food sack, and offered it to Axiana. The queen accepted it with a smile, then looked at the girl. She was terribly thin and undernourished, but her face was pretty, her eyes large and brown. Axiana had never been this close to a commoner. She studied Pharis's thin dress. It was impossible to say what colour it had once been, for it was now a drab, lifeless grey, torn at the shoulder, the hip and the elbow, and badly frayed at the wrists and the neck. It would not have been used as a cleaning rag in the palace. Reaching out she touched the material. It was rough and dirty. Pharis drew back, and Axiana saw her expression change. The girl swung away and moved back to sit with Sufia.

At that moment the child within her moved. She gave a little cry. Then she smiled. 'He kicked me,' she said. Ulmenetha gently placed her hand over Axiana's swollen belly.

'Yes, I can feel him. He's lusty and anxious for life.'

'Can I feel him?' asked little Sufia, scrambling back on her hands and knees. Axiana gazed down into her bright blue eyes.

'Of course,' she said. Taking the child's small, grimy hand, she placed it over her stomach. For a moment there was no movement, then the baby kicked again. Sufia squealed with delight.

'Pharis, Pharis, come feel!' she cried.

Pharis looked up and met the queen's gaze. Axiana smiled and held out her hand. Pharis moved to her, and the baby obediently kicked once more.

'How did it get in there?' asked Sufia. 'And how will it get out?'

'Magic,' said Ulmenetha, swiftly. 'How old are you, Sufia?' she added, changing the subject. The child shrugged.

'I don't know. My brother Griss said he was six. And I'm younger than Griss.'

'Where is your brother?' asked Axiana, stroking Sufia's greasy blond hair.

'The wizard man took him away.' She was suddenly frightened. 'You won't let him take me away, will you?'

'Nobody will take you away, little one,' said Conalin, fiercely. 'I'll kill any who try.'

This pleased Sufia. She looked up at Conalin. 'Can I drive the wagon?' she asked.

Pharis helped her clamber over the backrest, and Conalin sat her on his lap, allowing her to hold the reins.

Axiana bit into the apple. It was sweet, wondrously sweet.

They had just reached the trees when they heard the sound of thundering hoof beats. Axiana glanced back. Five horsemen were cresting the rise behind them.

Dagorian galloped back to the wagon, his sabre gleaming in his hand.

Chapter Seven

Vellian had been a fighting man for fifteen of his twenty-nine years, and had served Malikada and Antikas Karios for twelve of them. He had joined the Ventrian army for the Great Expedition; the invasion of Drenan, and the righting of ancient wrongs. Every Ventrian child knew of Drenai infamy, their broken treaties, their territorial impudence, and their killing, centuries before, of the Great Emperor Gorben.

The invasion was to have put right all past wrongs.

That, at least, was how it was sold to the fourteen-year-old Vellian when the recruiting officers arrived at his village. There was no greater honour, they said, than serving the emperor in a just cause. They made extravagant promises about wealth and glory. The wealth did not interest Vellian, but thoughts of glory swept through him like a powerful drug. He signed that day, without seeking permission from his parents, and rode away to smite the savages and seek his fame.

Now he rode a weary horse on the Old Lem road, and all his dreams were dust.

He had watched the Drenai army in their hopeless battle against the Cadians and had felt the enormous weight of shame. None of the junior officers had known of Malikada's plan, and they had waited, swords drawn, for the signal to attack. The Drenai centre had fought bravely, driving a wedge into the Cadian ranks. The battle was won. Or it would have been, had the Ventrian cavalry moved in on the signal and attacked. Every man saw the signal, and some even began to move forward. Then Malikada had shouted: 'Hold firm!'

Vellian had at first believed it to be part of some subtle, superior plan worked out between Skanda and Malikada. But as the hour wore on, and the Drenai died in their thousands, the truth revealed itself. Malikada, a man he had served loyally for almost half his life, had betrayed the king.

There was worse to come. Skanda was taken alive, and delivered to a cave high in the mountains, where the wizard Kalizkan waited. He was taken inside and sacrificed in some foul rite.

For the first time Vellian considered desertion. He had been raised to value honour and loyalty and the pursuit of the truth. He believed in these things. They were at the heart of any civilized nation. Without them there was anarchy, chaos, and a rapid descent into the dark.

There was no honour in betrayal.

Then Antikas Karios had come to him, ordering him to gather his Twenty and follow him to Usa to protect the queen. This duty, at least, was honourable.

They had found the city in flames, bodies on the streets, and the palace deserted. No-one knew where the queen was hiding. Then Antikas questioned a group of men on the Avenue of Kings. They had seen a wagon leave the palace. A red-headed boy was driving it, and a soldier was riding beside it. There were women in the wagon, and it was heading towards the west gate.

Antikas had split the Twenty into four groups, and sent Vellian to the south.

'I may not come back, sir,' he told him. 'I have a desire to leave the army.'

Antikas had pondered the statement, then he gestured Vellian to follow him, and rode away from the other soldiers. 'What is wrong?' Antikas had asked him.

'I would say just about everything,' Vellian told him, sadly.

'You are referring to the battle.'

'To the slaughter, you mean? To the treachery.' He expected Antikas to draw his blade and cut him down, and was surprised when the officer laid a hand upon his shoulder.

'You are the best of them, Vellian. You are brave and honest, and I value you above all other officers. But you betrayed no-one. You merely obeyed your general. The weight of responsibility is his alone. So I say this to you: Ride south and if you find the queen bring her back to Usa. If you do not find her then go where you will with my blessing. Will you do this? For me?'

'I will, sir. Might I ask one question?'

'Of course.'

'Did you know of the plan?'

'I did – to my eternal shame. Now go – and do this last duty.'

An hour of hard riding followed, and then Vellian saw the wagon. As the men had said it was being driven by a youth with red hair. A child was sitting on the seat with him, and in the rear of the wagon were three women.

And one was the queen.

The soldier with them had drawn his sabre.

Keeping his hands on the reins Vellian rode his horse down the slope, and halted before the rider. His men rode alongside him. 'Good morning,' he said. 'I am Vellian, sent by the General Antikas Karios to fetch the queen back to her palace. The city is quiet now and the army will be returning before tomorrow to fully restore order.'

'An army of traitors,' said Dagorian, coldly. Vellian reddened.

'Yes,' he agreed. 'Now return your sabre to its scabbard and let us be on our way.'

'I don't think so,' said Dagorian. 'The queen is in great danger. She will be safer with me.'

'Danger from whom?' asked Vellian, unsure as to how to proceed.

'The sorcerer, Kalizkan.'

'Then put your fears at rest, for he is dead, killed in a rock fall.'

'I don't believe you.'

'I am not known as a liar, sir.'

'Neither am I, Vellian. But I have pledged my life to protect the queen. This I will do. You ask me to turn her over to you. Did you not pledge your life to protect her husband the king?' Vellian said nothing. 'Well,' continued Dagorian, 'since you failed in that I see no reason to trust you now.'

'Do not be a fool, man. You may be as skilled as Antikas himself with that sabre, but you cannot beat five of us. What is the point then of dying, when the cause is already lost?'

'What is the point of living without a cause worth dying for?' countered Dagorian.

'So be it,' said Vellian, sadly. 'Take him!'

The four riders drew their sabres. Dagorian gave out a yell and slapped the flat of his sabre on his horse's flanks. The beast leapt forward, straight into the group. One horse went down, two others reared. Swinging his mount Dagorian slashed his sabre across the shoulder of the nearest rider. The blade sank deep, then

451

sang clear. Vellian stabbed at him, but Dagorian parried the thrust, sending a counter strike that sliced across Vellian's chest, cutting through his tunic and opening a shallow wound.

A rider moved in behind Dagorian, his sabre raised.

An arrow pierced the man's temple, pitching him from the saddle.

Then Nogusta came galloping into sight. Dagorian saw his arm go back, then snap forward. A shining blade flashed through the air, sinking deep into the throat of a second rider. Vellian attacked Dagorian, but his blade was parried. Dagorian's return cut missed him, but in swaying back Vellian almost lost his balance. His horse reared, hurling him to the ground. He landed heavily, and was stunned for a moment. Struggling to his knees he gathered his sabre and looked around him. All four of his men were dead.

Dagorian dismounted and approached him. Vellian stood his ground. From the trees came two other warriors, a bald giant with a white moustache, and an archer Vellian recognized as Kebra, the former champion. 'It seems,' said Vellian, 'that the roles are now reversed.'

'I have no wish to kill you,' said Dagorian. 'You may travel with us as our prisoner. You will be released when we reach the coast.'

'I think not,' said Vellian. 'How could I fail to follow so bold an example.'

Leaping forward he launched an attack. Their blades clashed, again and again. Just for a moment he felt he could win, but then a murderous riposte from Dagorian sent a spasm of fire through Vellian's chest. The sabre slid clear and the Ventrian sank to the ground.

He was lying now on the grass, looking up at the blue sky. 'I would also have protected the queen with my life,' he heard himself say.

'I know.'

For Axiana the rest of the day had a dreamlike quality, both real and unreal. The lurching of the wagon over the narrow forest trail, and the smell of damp earth, and green leaves, were strong and vital. But as she gazed about her at the faces of her companions she felt a curious sense of detachment. Apart from little Sufia they all seemed so tense, their movements sharp, their eyes frightened. Well, not all, she realized, her gaze settling on the black warrior. There was no fear in those strange blue eyes.

Dagorian rode silently alongside the wagon, occasionally swinging in the saddle to study the back trail. There was little to be seen, for they were deep in the forest now, the trail snaking through the trees. Yet still he looked. The other three also rode silently. Twice the black man left the group, riding the huge gelding back along the trail. The other two had placed themselves on either side of the wagon, only dropping back when the trail narrowed, and the trees closed in.

Axiana remembered the bowman, Kebra. He it was who had lost the tournament, and caused Skanda such anger. And the other fellow – Kebra called him Bison – was a hulking brute with a drooping white moustache.

The queen had never before been in a forest. Her father had often hunted here. He had killed lion and bear, deer and elk. She recalled seeing the trophies from her window. The bodies had looked so sad, slung upon the back of the wagon.

Bear and lion.

The thought did not frighten her. All fear had gone now. She was floating in harmony, living in the moment.

'How are you feeling?' asked Ulmenetha, placing her hand on the queen's arm. Axiana looked down at the hand. It was an impertinence to touch her, and yet she felt no anger.

'I am well.' Sunlight broke through the clouds, and speared through a gap in the trees ahead, slanted columns of gold illuminating the trail. 'How pretty,' said Axiana, dreamily. She saw the concern in Ulmenetha's eyes, but did not understand it. 'We should be getting back to the city,' she said. 'It will be dark soon.'

Ulmenetha did not reply, but moved in, drawing her close and cuddling her. She settled her head on Ulmenetha's shoulder. 'I am very tired.'

'You rest, my dove. Ulmenetha will look after you.'

Axiana saw the five horses tied to the rear of the wagon, and her body tensed. Ulmenetha held her close. 'What is wrong?' asked the priestess.

'Those horses . . . where did we get them?'

'We took them from the soldiers who attacked us.'

'That was just a dream,' said Axiana. 'No soldiers would attack me. I am the queen. No soldiers would attack me. No-one would lock me away. There are no walking dead men. It is all a dream.' She began to tremble and felt Ulmenetha's hand touch her face. Then she slid gratefully into darkness.

When she opened her eyes she saw bright stars in the sky. She

453

yawned. 'I dreamt I was in Morec,' she said, sitting up. 'I grew up there. In the spring palace overlooking the bay. I used to watch the dolphins there.'

'Was it a nice dream?'

'Yes.' Axiana looked around. The trees were shadow-haunted now, and the temperature was dropping. Here and there, in sheltered hollows, the snow still lay on the ground. 'Where are we?'

'I'm not sure,' replied Ulmenetha. 'But we will be making camp soon.'

'Camp? Are we camping?'

'Yes.'

'Is there no house close by?'

'No,' said Ulmenetha, softly. 'No house. But it will be safe.'

'From bears and lions,' said Axiana, trying to sound authoritative.

'Yes, highness.'

Dagorian rode alongside the wagon and climbed to the driver's seat. 'Hold tight,' he said, taking the reins from Conalin. 'We are leaving the trail.' The wagon lurched to the right and down a shallow slope. Ulmenetha held on to Axiana. Dagorian drove the wagon down to a shallow stream. Kebra and Bison rode their horses across to where the black man waited. There was a fire burning against the cliff wall. The weary horses splashed into the stream and Dagorian cracked the whip twice as the wagon was slowly hauled across. Once on the other side he turned the team and applied the brake.

Ulmenetha helped the queen to climb down, and led her to the fire. There were flat rocks close by and Axiana sat upon one of them. Kebra lit a second fire and began to prepare a meal. The children gathered firewood. Everyone seemed so busy. Axiana gazed up at the towering cliff wall. There had been cliffs like this in Morec. She had climbed one once, and her mother had scolded her dreadfully. Suddenly she remembered the Royal Guards who had ridden up to the wagon earlier. What had happened to them? Why had they gone away? She was about to ask Ulmenetha, but then she caught the aroma of meat and spices coming from the pot on the camp-fire. It smelt delicious!

Rising she walked to the fire. The bowman, who was kneeling beside the pot, glanced up. 'It will be ready soon, your highness.'

'It smells wonderful,' she said. She wandered to the moonlit stream, then along the banks, captivated by the glittering lights on the smooth stones beneath the water. They shone like gems. Alone now she sat down by the waterside, and remembered sitting on the beach in Morec, her feet in the water. Her nurse used to sing a song to her there, a song about dolphins. Axiana tried to remember it. She laughed as the lines came back to her, and began to sing.

'How I long to be,
such a queen of the sea,
to follow the ocean, always in motion,
and always so wonderfully free.'

The bushes rustled alongside her and a huge form reared up, towering over her. Axiana clapped her hands and laughed happily. The bear was so large, and, unlike the sad carcasses her father had brought back, so full of life. The bear gave a deep, rumbling growl.

'Do you not like my song, Bruin?' she said.

She felt a strong hand upon her arm, and looked up to see the black warrior beside her. He was holding a burning torch in his left hand. Gently he drew her to her feet. 'He is hungry, highness, and in no mood for song.'

Slowly he backed away, drawing the queen with him. The bear spread his paws wide and lumbered through the bushes towards them. 'He is coming with us,' said Axiana, brightly. The black man moved carefully in front of her, holding out the burning torch. To her left she saw Kebra the Bowman, a shaft notched to the bow string.

'Do not shoot,' said Nogusta.

Bison and Dagorian moved in from the right. Bison was also holding a torch. The bear's great head moved from side to side. 'Be off with you!' shouted Bison, darting forward. Surprised by the movement the bear dropped to all fours and ambled away into the darkness.

'He was so big,' said Axiana.

'Indeed he was, highness,' the black man told her. 'Now let us return to the fire.'

The stew was served upon pewter plates and Axiana ate with relish. She asked for wine, and Ulmenetha apologized for forgetting to bring any. Instead she drank a cup of water from the stream. It was cool and pleasant. Ulmenetha prepared a bed for her beside the fire. Dagorian made a small hollow for her hip beneath the blankets. Resting her head on a rolled blanket pillow Axiana lay quietly listening to the conversation around the fire. She heard the words. The child, Sufia, was asleep beside her, the boy Conalin sitting watching over her.

'I saw a bear today,' Axiana told him, sleepily.

'Go to sleep,' said the boy.

Bison added a log to the fire as Kebra collected the pewter plates and carried them to the stream for cleaning. The giant cast a furtive glance at Nogusta, who was sitting quietly, his back to the cliff wall. Dagorian and Ulmenetha were whispering to one another, and Bison could not make out the words. Bison was confused by the events of the day. Nogusta had woken them early, and they had set off back towards the city. 'The queen is in danger,' was all the black man had said, and the ride had been fast, with no time for conversation. Bison was not a rider. He hated horses. Almost as much as he hated sleeping on the ground in winter, he realized. His shoulder ached, and he had a deep, nagging pain in his lower back.

Bison glanced towards where the queen was sleeping, the children stretched out alongside her. None of this made any sense to the giant. Skanda was dead – which served him right for putting his faith in Ventrians and sending all the best soldiers home. But this talk of wizards and demons and sacrifices made Bison uncomfortable. It was a known fact that men couldn't fight demons.

'What are we going to do?' he asked Nogusta.

'About what?' countered the black man.

'About all this!' said Bison, gesturing towards the sleepers.

'We'll take them to the coast and find a ship bound for Drenan.'

'Oh, really? Just like that?' snapped Bison, his anger growing. 'We've probably got the entire Ventrian army on our heels and demons to boot. And we're travelling with a pregnant woman who's lost her mind. Oh . . . and did I mention the fact that we're also saddled with the slowest wagon in Ventria?'

'She hasn't lost her mind, you oaf,' said Ulmenetha, icily. 'She is in shock. It will pass.'

'She's in shock? What about me? I was kicked out of the army. I'm not a soldier any more. That was a shock I can tell you. But I haven't started singing to bears yet.'

'You are not a sensitive seventeen-year-old girl, heavily pregnant,' said Ulmenetha, 'who has been torn from her home.'

456

'I didn't tear her from her home,' objected Bison. 'She can go back for all I care. So can you, you fat cow.'

'What do you suggest, my friend?' asked Nogusta, softly.

The question threw Bison. He was not used to being asked for opinions, and he didn't really have one. But he was angry at the fat woman for calling him an oaf. 'We ought to ride on. She's not Drenai, is she? None of them are.'

'I am,' said Ulmenetha, her voice edged with contempt. 'But then that is not the issue, is it?'

'Issue? What's she talking about?' Bison demanded.

'This isn't about nationalities,' said Dagorian. 'The demons desire to sacrifice the queen's child. You understand? If they succeed the world will slide down into horror. All the evils we know from legends, the Shape-Shifters, the Hollow Tooths, the Krandyl . . . all will return. We must protect her.'

'Protect her? There are four of us! How are we going to protect her?'

'The best way we can,' said Nogusta. 'But you do not have to stay, my friend. Your life is free. You can ride away. You are not held here by chains.'

The conversation was heading along a path Bison didn't like. He had no wish to leave his friends, and was surprised that Nogusta would even suggest it. 'I can't read maps,' he objected. 'I don't even know where we are now. I want to know *why* we should stay with her.'

Kebra returned to the fire, and carefully stowed away the clean plates. Then he sat down beside Bison. He said nothing, but his expression was one of amusement.

'*Why* we should stay?' stormed Dagorian. 'What kind of a question is that from a Drenai warrior? Evil threatens to kill a child. Never mind that the child is the heir to the throne, and that his mother is the queen. When evil threatens good men stand against it.'

Bison hawked and spat into the fire. 'Just words,' he said, dismissively. 'Just like all that high sounding bull that Skanda used to spout before battles. Justice and right, forces of Light against the Dark tyranny. And where did it get us, eh? Army's gone, and we're sitting in a cold forest waiting to be struck down by demons.'

'He is quite right,' said Kebra, with a wink to Nogusta. 'There is no point in arguing the issue. I don't much care about wealth and glory. Never did. The thought of getting back to Drenan and

457

attending parades and banquets in my honour means nothing to me. And I do not need to live in a palace, surrounded by beautiful women. All I require is a simple farm on a nice plot of land. And I'll best achieve those dreams by heading for the coast on a fast horse.'

'My point exactly,' said Bison, triumphantly. Then he faltered. 'What was that about wealth?'

Kebra shrugged. 'Meaningless baubles. But you can imagine the kind of reception given to the small band of heroes who rescued the queen? Showered with gold and praise. Probably given a commission in the avenging army that would return to Ventria. Who needs it? You and I will head for Caphis tomorrow. We'll sail home quietly and retire. You can have a place on my farm.'

'I don't want to live on a farm,' insisted Bison. 'I want to be in the . . . what did you call it? . . . the avenging army.'

'You probably can,' Kebra assured him. 'You could dye your moustache black and pretend to be forty again. Now I'm for bed. It's been a long and tiring day.'

Rising from the fire he strolled to his blankets. 'Would they really give us riches and fame?' Bison asked Dagorian.

'I fear so.'

'They'd probably write songs about you,' said Nogusta.

'A pox on songs! Can't buy a whore with a song. But can we fight demons, Nogusta? I mean, can we actually beat them?'

'Have you ever seen me lose?' countered Nogusta. 'Of course we can beat them.'

'Then I think you are right,' said Bison. 'Can't let evil get its own way. I'm with you.' Pushing himself to his feet he walked back to his blankets and lay down. Within moments he was snoring softly.

'Sweet Heaven, he makes me sick,' said Dagorian.

'Don't judge him so harshly,' Nogusta told him. 'Bison is not a complex man, but he has a little more depth than you give him credit for. He may have trouble with the concepts, but the realities are different. You will see. Now you get some sleep. I'll take the first watch. And I'll wake you in around three hours.'

When Dagorian had gone Ulmenetha moved alongside Nogusta. 'Do you believe we can make it to the coast?' she asked him.

'Do you believe in miracles?' he countered.

Nogusta sat alone, enjoying the solitude. There was no real need to keep watch. They could do nothing if attacked here, save fight

458

and die. But he had always enjoyed forest nights, the wind whispering in the leaves, the filtered moonlight, and the sense of eternity emanating from the ancient trees around him. Forests were never silent. Always there was movement; life. Bison's gentle snoring drifted to him and he smiled. Dagorian and Ulmenetha had gazed at the giant scornfully when he decided to travel with them for the wealth and the glory. Nogusta knew better. Bison needed an excuse for heroism. Like all men of limited intelligence he feared being tricked or manipulated. There was never any doubt that he would journey with them. Kebra had known this, and had given Bison the excuse he needed. The giant would stand beside his friends against any foe.

Do you believe in miracles? Nogusta had asked Ulmenetha.

Well, a miracle would be needed, he knew. Lifting Dagorian's map he turned it towards the fire. The symbols stood out well in the flickering light. Some 20 miles to the south was the line of the River Mendea. Three fords were marked. If they could reach the first by late tomorrow they would have a chance to cross the water and lose themselves in the high country. After that there was another 70 miles of rugged terrain. Old forts were indicated along the southern route, but these would be deserted now. There might be villages along the way, from which they could obtain supplies. But probably not. This was inhospitable land. Then they would reach the plains, and face a further 150 miles west to the coast. Even with the five spare horses it would be a month of hard, slow travel. We cannot make such a journey undetected, he realized. Despair struck him.

Ruthlessly he suppressed the emotion. One step at a time, he cautioned himself. First the river.

'Why are you doing this for us?' Ulmenetha had asked him.

'It is enough that I do,' he told her. 'It needs no explanation.'

He thought about it now, recalling the dread day he had arrived home to find his family murdered, seeing their bodies, carrying them to graves he dug himself. He had buried them, and with it had buried his dreams and theirs. All their hopes and fears had been consigned to the earth, and a part of him had remained there with them, in the cold, worm-filled ground.

He glanced around the camp. Ulmenetha was asleep in the wagon. Nogusta liked the priestess. She was a tough woman, and there was no give in her. Rising he walked round the fire and stood over the sleeping children. Conalin was a sullen boy, but there was steel in him. The two girls were cuddled together under one blanket. The child, Sufia, had her thumb in her mouth, and was sleeping peacefully.

Nogusta walked to the edge of the camp. Through a break in the trees the black silhouette of the mountains could be seen against the dark grey of the sky. He heard Kebra approach.

'Can you not sleep?' he asked the bowman.

'I slept for a while. But I am getting too old to enjoy cold nights on bare earth. My bones object.'

The two men stood in silence, breathing in the cold, clean air of the night. Then Kebra spoke. 'The riders we killed were carrying around three days of supplies. They may not be missed for a while.'

'Let us hope so.'

'I'm not afraid of dying,' said Kebra, softly. 'But I am afraid.'

'I know. I feel it too.'

'Do you have a plan?' asked the bowman.

'Stay alive, kill all enemies, reach the coast, find a ship.'

'Things always look brighter when you have a plan,' said Kebra.

Nogusta smiled, then his expression hardened. The black man ran his hand over his shaved head. 'The forces of evil are gathering, and all hope rests in the hands of three old men. It almost makes me believe in the Source. The sense of humour here is cosmic.'

'Well, my friend, I *do* believe. And if I had to pick three old men to save the world I'd make the same choice He did.'

Nogusta chuckled. 'So would I, but that just makes us *arrogant* old men.'

For two days Antikas Karios searched to the west. Now he and his fifteen men rode weary horses into Usa. The men were no less tired and sat slumped in their saddles. They had removed their bronze helms and hung them from the pommels of their saddles. Their clothes were travel stained, their white cloaks grimy. Antikas was faced with two unpalatable truths. First that the fleeing group must have headed south, and secondly that Vellian had either betrayed him, or was dead. The latter was surely unlikely. Dagorian was a highly skilled swordsman, but he could not have defeated five veteran soldiers.

Antikas recalled the notes he had read concerning the young officer. The son of a hero general Dagorian had never wished to be a soldier. In fact he had trained for two years to be a priest.

According to the reports pressure from his family had led him to enlist in his father's regiment. These facts alone would have meant little to most men, but to the sharp mind of Antikas Karios they revealed a great deal. To become a priest required not only immense commitment and belief, but a willingness to put aside all desires of the flesh. Such a decision could not be taken lightly, and once taken would clothe a man in chains of iron. But Dagorian had shrugged off those chains following 'pressure from his family'. His commitment to his god, therefore had been less than his commitment to his kin. This showed either a weak personality, or a man destined always to put the needs of others before his own desires. Or both.

Antikas had not been concerned when Malikada ordered the officer's death. Nor had he been unduly surprised when Dagorian bested the assassins. But his actions since were mysterious. Why had he kidnapped the queen? And why had she, apparently, gone willingly with him?

The tall chestnut he was riding stumbled on the wide avenue, then righted itself. Antikas patted its neck. 'Soon you can rest,' he said.

It was nearing dusk as they approached the palace gates. A pall of smoke hung over the western quarter of the city, and there was no-one on the streets. Sending his riders to the barracks to tend their mounts and get some rest Antikas rode through the gates of the palace. Two sentries were standing to attention as he passed. Guiding his horse to the stable he dismounted. There were no stable hands in sight. This irritated Antikas and he unsaddled the gelding and rubbed him down with a handful of dry straw. Then he led him to a stall. Antikas filled the feedbox with grain, drew a bucket of water from the stable well and covered the gelding's back with a blanket. He deserved more, and Antikas was irritated that no ostlers were present. But then why should they be? he thought. There are no other horses in the stables.

Antikas was tired, his eyes gritty through lack of sleep, but he went in search of Malikada. Rather than face the long walk back to the main doors he cut in through the kitchen entrance, thinking to order a meal sent to his rooms. Here too there was no sign of life. The place was deserted. As he moved on he saw piles of unwashed, food-encrusted dishes and noticed that the pantry door was open, the shelves empty. It made no sense. At dusk the kitchens should have been bustling with servants preparing the evening meal.

Climbing the narrow winding stair to the first floor he emerged into a wide, richly carpeted corridor, and walked on, past the library, to the ornate staircase leading to the royal apartments. After his experience at the stables and kitchens he was not surprised to find no sign of servants, and none of the lanterns had been lit. The palace was gloomy, and lit only by the fading light of the dying sun streaming through the tall windows.

He had just begun to believe Malikada was staying at the barracks when he saw two sentries at the door of what had been Skanda's apartments. Antikas strode towards them. Neither offered him the customary salute. He paused to admonish them, then heard Malikada's voice call out from beyond the door. 'Come in, Antikas.'

Antikas entered and bowed. Malikada was standing at the balcony, his back to him. The swordsman was momentarily confused. How had Malikada known he was outside?

'Speak,' said Malikada, without turning.

'I am sorry to report that the queen has gone, my lord. But I will find her tomorrow.'

Antikas expected an angry outburst, for Malikada was a volatile man. He was surprised, therefore, when his cousin merely shrugged. 'She is on the Old Lem road,' said Malikada. 'She is travelling with four men, her midwife, and three youngsters. One of the men is the officer, Dagorian. I will send men after her tomorrow. You need not concern yourself further.'

'Yes, Lord. And what of the other matters?'

'Other matters?' asked Malikada, dreamily.

'Getting messages to our garrisons on the coast, dealing with the White Wolf, rooting out Drenai sympathizers. All of the plans we have been discussing for months.'

'They can wait. The queen is all important.'

'With respect, cousin, I disagree. When the Drenai learn of Skanda's death they could mount a second invasion. And if the White Wolf is allowed to escape . . .'

But Malikada was not listening. He stood on the balcony, staring out over the city. 'Go to your room and rest, Antikas. Go to your room.'

'Yes, Lord.'

Antikas left the room. Once more there was no salute from the guards, but he was too preoccupied now to take issue with them. He needed a change of clothing, a meal, and then rest. His own apartment was small, a tiny bedroom and a modest sitting-room with two couches and no balcony. He lit two lanterns then stripped off his armour and the dust-stained tunic beneath, filled a bowl with water from a tall jug and washed his upper body. He would have preferred a hot, perfumed bath, but, without servants, it was unlikely that the bath-house boilers were working.

Where had the servants gone? And why had Malikada not gathered more?

Clothing himself in a fresh tunic and leggings he sat down and, out of habit, polished his breastplate, helm and greaves, which he then hung on a wooden frame. The room began to grow cold. Antikas strode to the window, but it was tightly shut. He thought of lighting a fire, but hunger was gnawing at him. The temperature dropped even further. Antikas swung his sword belt around his waist and left the room. The corridor was infinitely warmer. How curious, he thought.

Behind him, within the room, the water in his washing bowl froze, and ice patterns formed on the windows.

Leaving the palace he crossed the Avenue of Kings. Canta's Tavern was but a short walk, and the food there was always good.

When he arrived he found the doors locked, but he could hear signs of movement within. Angry now he hammered his fist on the wood. All movement inside ceased. 'Open up, Canta! There is a hungry man out here,' he called.

He heard the bolts being drawn back. The door swung open. Within were two men. One, the owner, Canta, a short, fat, balding man with a heavy black moustache, had a kitchen knife in his hand, the other man was holding a hatchet. 'Come in quickly,' said Canta. Antikas stepped inside. They slammed shut the door and bolted it.

'What are you afraid of?' asked Antikas. The men looked at one another.

'How long have you been back in the city?' asked Canta.

'I just rode in.'

'There have been riots,' said the tavern keeper, dropping his knife to a table and slumping down. 'Riots like you've never seen. People hacking and stabbing their neighbours. Last night the baker murdered his wife and ran along the street with her head in his hands. I saw it with my own eyes, Antikas, through the window slats. There is madness everywhere. Tomorrow I'm getting out.'

'And what of the Militia?' asked Antikas.

'They're out there with them, burning and looting. I tell you, Antikas, it beggars belief. By day everything is quiet, but when the sun goes down the nightmare begins again. There is a great evil at work here. I feel it in my bones.'

Antikas rubbed his weary eyes. 'The army is back now. They will restore order.'

'The army is camped a mile from the city,' said the other man, a stocky figure with a greying beard. 'The city is defenceless.'

The tavern was gloomy and dark, lit only by a fading log fire in the hearth. 'Do you have any food?' asked Antikas. 'I have not eaten since yesterday.'

Canta nodded and moved away to the kitchen. The other man sat opposite the swordsman. 'There is sorcery here,' he said. 'I think the city is dying.'

'Nonsense,' snapped Antikas.

'You haven't seen it, man. Outside. After dark. I have. I'll not forget it. The mob becomes possessed. You can see it in their eyes.'

'That is the way with mobs,' said Antikas.

'Maybe it is, soldier. But yesterday . . .' his voice tailed away. The man rose and walked away to the fire, slumping down beside it and staring into the flames. Canta returned with a plate of cold beef and cheese and a jug of watered wine.

'It is the best I can offer,' said Canta. Antikas reached for his money pouch. 'Don't concern yourself with that,' said Canta. 'Take it as a gift.'

The sound of sobbing came from the hearth. Antikas looked at the weeping man with distaste. Canta leaned in close. 'Last night he killed his wife and daughters,' whispered the innkeeper. 'And he loved them dearly. He came to me this morning, covered in blood. He could not believe what he had done.'

'He will be arrested and hanged,' said Antikas, coldly.

'Wait until you've lived through the night before making judgements,' advised Canta.

Antikas did not reply. Slowly he ate the meal, savouring the taste of the cold beef and the texture of the smoked cheese. At last replete he sat back. A stair board creaked. Antikas glanced up and saw a tall, thin priest, in robes of white, moving down the stairs. 'He has been here two days,' said Canta. 'He says little, but he is mightily afraid.'

The priest acknowledged Antikas with a curt nod and moved past him to sit at a table at the far wall.

'What is he doing at a tavern?' asked Antikas.

'He says that this place was built on the ruins of a shrine, and that demons will avoid it. He is leaving with us tomorrow.'

Antikas rose and moved across the room. The priest glanced up. He had a thin, ascetic face, with a prominent nose and a receding chin. His eyes were pale and watery. 'Good evening to you, Father,' said Antikas.

'And to you, my son,' answered the priest.

'What is it you fear?'

'The end of the world,' said the priest, his voice dull and toneless.

Antikas leaned forward on the table, forcing the man to meet his gaze. 'Explain,' he ordered him.

'Words are useless now,' said the priest, once more averting his gaze. 'It has begun. It will not be stopped. The demons are everywhere, and growing stronger each night.' He lapsed into silence. Antikas found it hard to suppress his irritation.

'Tell me anyway,' he said, sitting down on the bench seat opposite the man.

The priest sighed. 'Some weeks ago Father Aminias, the oldest of our order, told the Abbot he had seen demons over the city. He maintained the city was in great danger. Then he was murdered. A few days ago a woman came to me in the temple. She was a priestess, and midwife to the queen. She had been blessed with a *kiraz* – a threefold vision. I spoke with her, and tried to interpret it. After she had gone I began to study the ancient scrolls and grimoires in the temple library. There I came upon a prophecy. That prophecy is being fulfilled now.'

'What are you saying?' persisted Antikas. 'You think the sun will fall from the sky, that the oceans will rise up and destroy us?'

'Nothing so natural, my son. Both the old emperor and Skanda were, I believe, descended from the line of three ancient kings. These kings, and a wizard, fought a war long ago. It was not a war against men. There are few details of it now, and those that remain are hopelessly distorted, and full of bizarre imagery. What is clear, however, is that it was a war against non-humans – demons, if you like. All the ancient tomes tell of a period when such creatures walked among us. The three kings ended that period, banishing all demons to another world. There are no details now of the spell that was wrought, but one of the tomes tells of the patterns of planets in the sky that awesome night. A similar pattern is in the heavens now. And I believe – with utter certainty – that the demons are returning.'

'Tomes, stars, demons – I understand none of this, priest,' snapped Antikas. 'Offer me proofs!'

'Proofs?' The priest laughed aloud. 'What proofs would be sufficient? We are in a city being torn apart every night by those possessed. The prophecy talks of the Sacrifice of Kings. The priestess told me her vision showed the old emperor was killed in such a manner. Now Skanda is dead. You are a soldier. Were you there when his army was destroyed?' Antikas nodded. 'Was he slain on the battlefield, or taken to a secret place, and then killed?'

'It is not my place to discuss these things,' said Antikas. 'But, for the sake of argument, let us assume he was. What do you take it to mean?'

'It means the fulfilment of prophecy. Two of three kings sacrificed. When the third dies the gateways will open, and the demons will be back among us. In the flesh.'

'Pah!' snorted Antikas. 'And there your argument falters, for there is no third king.'

'Not so,' said the priest. 'In the words of the prophecy the sacrifices will consist of an owl, a lion and a lamb. The owl represents wisdom and learning. The old emperor was, as you will recall, a learned man, who founded many universities. Skanda, may his soul burn, was a ravening lion, a destroyer. The third? A lamb is a newborn creature. A child, therefore, or a babe. I am not a seer. But I do not need to be, for I saw Queen Axiana recently, and her child is soon due. He will be the third king.'

Antikas leaned back in his chair and drew in a long breath. 'You speak of spells and grimoires, but only one man had such power. Kalizkan. And he is dead. Killed in a rockfall.'

'I do not speak of men,' said the priest. 'No *man* could summon such magic. I knew Kalizkan. He was a caring man, thoughtful and sensitive. Two years ago he came to the temple to be healed of a terrible cancer. We could not help him. He had but days to live. He spent two of those days studying ancient texts in our library. After the visit of the priestess I studied those same texts myself. One of the spells contained there was of a merging. If a sorcerer had enough power – so it maintained – he could draw a demon into himself for the purposes of prolonging his life. Shared immortality.' The priest fell silent, then sipped water from a pewter tankard. Antikas waited patiently. The priest spoke again. 'We were all surprised when Kalizkan continued to survive. But he did not come to the temple again, nor visit any holy place. It is my belief – though I can offer you no further proofs – that Kalizkan, in a bid to heal himself, allowed his body to be possessed. But either the promise of the spell was a lie, or Kalizkan was not powerful enough to withstand the demon. Whatever, I think Kalizkan died long ago. And, if I am right, no rockfall would have killed him.'

'And yet it did,' insisted Antikas.

The priest shook his head. 'The Demon Lord would merely have found another host. You say he died in a rockfall. Was there one survivor who walked away unscathed?'

Antikas pushed back his chair and rose. 'I have heard enough of this nonsense. Your brains are addled, priest.'

'It is my sincere hope that you are right,' the priest told him.

From outside came the sound of wailing. Scores of voices joined in. Antikas shivered, for the sound was unearthly.

'It begins again,' said the priest, closing his eyes in prayer.

Despite his apparent dismissal of the priest Antikas was deeply troubled. He had served Malikada for more than fifteen years, and had shared his hatred of the Drenai invaders. And while he had never fully condoned the treachery that led to the destruction of the Drenai army, he had seen it as the lesser of two great evils. However, the events of the past few days had concerned him, and now, with the added weight of the priest's words, doubt began to gnaw at him.

Malikada had escaped the rockfall which killed Kalizkan, and from that moment had seemed changed. He was colder, more controlled. That, in itself, meant nothing. Yet he had also lost interest in strengthening his grip on the empire. Killing Skanda was but a step towards freeing Ventria from the grip of the Drenai. There were garrisons all over the land, many of them containing Drenai units. And the sea lanes were patrolled by Drenai ships. Both he and Malikada had planned this coup for months, and both had been acutely aware of the dangers of Drenai reprisals. Yet now Malikada showed complete disinterest in the grand design. All he seemed to want was Axiana.

Antikas crossed to the fire. The wife-killer was sitting silently, staring at the flames through eyes red-rimmed from weeping. Outside they could hear hundreds of people moving through the streets. Canta crept across the room. 'Stay silent,' he whispered. 'Make no movement.'

Antikas moved to the shuttered window, and listened. People were gathering together, and he could hear a babble of voices. There were no words to be understood, though they seemed to be speaking to one another in strange tongues. Antikas shivered.

Suddenly a spear smashed through the shutters, passing inches from Antikas's face. He leapt back. An axe blade smashed the wood to shards and he found himself staring at a sea of faces, all twisted into fearsome grimaces, their eyes wide and staring. At that moment Antikas knew the truth of the priest's words. These people were possessed.

Behind him Canta screamed and fled for the stairs. Antikas drew his sabre and stood his ground. The axeman grabbed the window-sill and began to haul himself across the threshold. His face changed, his expression softening. He blinked. 'In the name of Heaven, help me!' he shouted, dropping his axe to the floor. A knife was plunged through his back and the body was dragged from the window. The mob did not advance, but stood, staring with hatred at the lone swordsman standing inside. Then they drew back and moved away down the street.

The priest approached Antikas. 'A long time ago there was a shrine here. The remains of the altar can still be found at the rear of the cellar. Great and holy spells were once cast here. They cannot enter.'

Antikas sheathed his sabre. 'What are *they*?'

'The Entukku. Mindless spirits who live to feed. Some say they are born from the souls of the evil dead. I do not know whether that be true. But they swim in the air all around us now, like sharks, feasting on the dark emotions of the possessed. Usa is a feeding ground, and faces extinction.'

'What can be done, priest?'

'Done? Nothing.'

Antikas swung on the man, grabbing his white robes at the neck and hauling him close. 'There is always something!' he hissed. ' So think!'

The priest sighed. Antikas released him. 'Are you a believer?' asked the priest.

'I believe in my skills and my sabre.'

The priest stood for a moment, staring out into the darkness. 'You cannot kill the Demon Lord,' he said, 'for he is immortal. You could destroy the host body, but he would find another. And his strength is growing. You saw the mob. A few days ago the Entukku could merely inspire men to acts of violence. Skanda's death gave them the ability to possess hosts utterly. How can you fight such power with a sabre? Were you to step outside this door the demons would descend upon you and then the great Antikas Karios would be running with the mob, screaming and killing.'

Antikas considered his words. 'That may be so, priest,' he said, at last, 'but you say his power is derived from the murder of kings. What happens if he fails to kill the third?'

'How can he fail? Who can withstand demons?'

Antikas stepped in close to the man. The words he used were softly spoken, but the priest blanched. 'If I hear another negative phrase from you I will hurl you from this window, and out into the night. Do you understand me?'

'In the name of mercy . . . !' wailed the priest. Antikas cut him short.

'I am not known as a merciful man, priest. Now answer the question. What if the third king eludes the demons?'

'I am not sure,' answered the priest. 'The power he is using is derived from the previous sacrifices. Such power, though great, is finite. If he does not complete the third sacrifice in time then he will – I believe – be drawn back into his own world.'

'What do you mean, in time?'

'The pattern of the heavens is the clue. There are times when the strength of a spell is made immeasurably more powerful if cast with the right conjunction of planets. I believe this to be the case now.'

'And how long does that give us?'

'That is hard to estimate, for I am no astrologer. But no more than a month. That is for sure.'

Canta returned from his hiding place upstairs. He and the man by the fire up-ended a table, lifting it into place against the shattered window. Antikas lit several lanterns. 'What are you doing?' asked Canta, fearfully.

'They cannot pass the portals of the tavern,' said Antikas, 'so let us have some light.' He gestured to the priest to join him and returned to the table. 'I need to get to my horse before dawn,' he said. 'Have you a spell to aid me?'

The priest shook his head. 'My skills were not suited to magick.'

'What then, pray, are your skills?'

'I am a healer.'

469

Antikas cursed, then lapsed into thought. They were silent for several minutes. Then the swordsman glanced up. 'You say this place is holy. What makes it so?'

'I told you. It was once a shrine.'

'Yes, yes. But what remains here to keep it holy. Was a spell cast?'

'Yes, many spells. They are held in the stone of the walls, and the wood of the beams.'

'Therefore, if we were to move the shrine to another place, that would also be holy?'

'I believe so.'

'Come with me,' ordered Antikas, rising and lifting one of the lanterns from its wall bracket. Together the two men moved through to the back of the tavern. Finding the door to the cellar Antikas moved down the steps. It was cold below ground, and he threaded his way past barrels of beer, wine and spirit. 'Where is the altar?' he asked.

'Over here,' said the priest, leading him to a block of stone some 3 feet high. The shape of a bull had been carved on the front of the stone, the image all but weathered away. On each side was a sculpted hand, holding a crescent moon. These too had been eroded by time. Antikas left the priest holding the lantern and returned upstairs.

Gathering the axe dropped by the first of the mob he moved back to the cellar.

'What are you going to do?' asked the priest. Antikas swung the axe, bringing it crashing down on the altar. Twice he struck, then a fist-sized section broke away. Dropping the axe he took up the stone.

'You say that spells are held in the stone. Perhaps this will shield me from the demons.'

'I cannot say that for sure,' said the priest. 'What you have is a tiny fragment.'

'I have no choice but to try, priest. The queen is in the mountains, guarded by only four men.'

'And you think a fifth will make a difference?'

'I am Antikas Karios, priest. I always make a difference.'

Tucking the rock into his tunic Antikas returned to the upper room. Moving to the upturned table which blocked the window he peered out into the street. All was silent. His mouth was dry, his heart beating fast. Antikas Karios feared no living man, but

470

the thought of the demons waiting threatened to unman him. Placing his hand on the table he prepared to draw it aside.

'Don't go out there!' pleaded Canta, echoing the voice in Antikas's own heart.

'I must,' he said, wrenching the table aside and climbing to the sill.

The night breeze was cool on his skin, and he leapt lightly to the ground. Behind him the others hastily drew back the table. Antikas ran across the street, ducking into an alley. He had gone no more than a hundred paces when the attack came. The temperature around him plummeted, and he heard whispers on the breeze. They grew louder and louder, filling his ears like angry hornets. Pain roared inside his head. Inside his tunic the rock grew warmer. Antikas staggered and almost fell. Anger surged – but as it did he felt the cold seep into his brain. Voices were hissing at him now in a language he had never heard, and yet he knew what they were saying. 'Give in! Give in! Give in!'

He lurched against the side of a building and fell to his knees. The pain from striking the cobbles cut through the discordant shrieking inside his mind. He focused on it – and on the heat from the rock against his skin.

He wanted to rage against the invasion, to scream. But some deeper instinct overrode his emotions, urging him to stay calm, to fight coolly. Yet he felt like he was drowning in this sea of voices – at one with them, sharing their hunger for blood and pain and death.

'No,' he said, aloud. 'I am . . .' For a moment there was panic. Who am I? Scores of names surged through his mind, shouted by the voices within. He fought for calm. 'I am . . . Antikas Karios. I am ANTIKAS KARIOS!' Over and over, like a mantra, he said his name. The voices shrieked louder still, but with less power, until they receded into dim, distant echoes.

Antikas pushed himself to his feet and ran on. The shrieking of human voices could be heard now, some distance to his left. Then to his right. Then ahead.

Unable to possess him the demons were gathering their human forces to cut him off.

Antikas paused and looked around. To his left was a high wall, and, close by, a wrought-iron gate. He ran to it, and climbed the gate, stepping out onto the wall some 15 feet above the ground. Nimbly he moved along it, to where it joined the side of a house. There was an ivy covered trellis here and Antikas began to climb.

471

Below him a mob gathered, shouting curses. A hurled hammer crashed against the wall by his head. He climbed on. A piece of rotten wood gave way beneath his foot, but he clung on, drawing himself towards the flat roof. He heard the creaking of the iron gate below, and glanced back. Several of the mob were climbing the wall.

Easing himself onto the roof Antikas gazed around in the moonlight. There was a door to the building. Moving swiftly to it he forced it open. As he entered the stairwell beyond he heard the sound of boots upon the stairs. With a soft curse he backed out onto the roof, and ran to the edge of the building.

Some 60 feet below was a narrow alleyway. He glanced at the roof opposite, gauging the distance. Ten feet at least. On the flat he could make the jump with ease, but there was a low wall around the rooftop.

Pacing his steps he moved back to the door then turned and ran at the wall. He leapt, his left foot striking the top and propelling him out over the alleyway. For one terrifying moment he thought he had misjudged his leap. But then he landed and rolled on the opposite rooftop. The hilt of his sabre dug into his side, tearing the skin. Antikas swore again. Rising he drew the blade. The golden fist guard was dented, but the weapon was still usable.

The door on the second roof burst open and three men ran out. Antikas spun towards them, the sabre slicing through the throat of the first. His foot lashed out into the knee of the second, spinning the man from his feet. The third died from a sabre thrust to the heart. Antikas ran to the doorway and listened. There was no sound upon the stairs, and he moved down into the dark, emerging into a narrow corridor. There were no lanterns lit, and the swordsman moved forward blindly, feeling his way. He stumbled upon a second stair and descended to the first level. Here there was a window with the curtains drawn back, and faint moonlight illuminated a gallery. Opening the window he clambered out, and dropped the 10 feet to the garden below.

Here there was a lower wall, no more than 8 feet high. Sheathing his sabre he leapt, curling his fingers over the stone and hauling himself to the top. The street beyond was empty.

Antikas silently lowered himself to the cobbles and ran on.

Emerging onto the Avenue of Kings he raced across the street towards the palace. The mob erupted from alleyways all around him, shrieking and baying. Ducking he sprinted for the gates. The two sentries stood stock still as he approached, showing no sign of alarm. Antikas reached them just ahead of the mob, and realized he could go no further. Angry now he spun to face them.

But they had halted just outside the gates and were now standing silently, staring at him.

The sentries still had not moved, and Antikas stood, breathing heavily, his sabre all but forgotten.

Silently the mob dispersed, moving back into the shadows on the opposite side of the Avenue.

Antikas approached the first of the sentries. 'Why did they not attack?' he asked.

The man's head turned slowly towards him. The eyes were misted in death, the jaw hanging slack. Antikas backed away.

Reaching the stable he moved to the stall where he had left his horse. The beast was on its knees. He noticed someone had changed the blanket with which he had covered the beast. His had been grey, this was black. Opening the stall door he stepped inside.

The black blanket writhed, and scores of bats fluttered up around him, their wings beating about his face.

Then they were gone, up into the rafters.

And the horse was dead.

Angry now Antikas drew his sword and headed for the palace. The priest had said he could not kill the Demon Lord, but, by all the gods in Heaven, he would try. The rock grew warm against his skin, and a soft voice whispered into his mind.

'*Do not throw away your life, my boy!*'

Antikas paused. 'Who are you?' he whispered.

'*You cannot kill him. Trust me. The babe is everything. You must protect the babe.*'

'I am trapped here. If I leave the palace the mob will hunt me down.'

'*I will guide you, Antikas. There are horses outside the city.*'

'Who are you?' he repeated.

'*I am Kalizkan, Antikas. And all this pain and horror is of my making.*'

'That is hardly a recommendation for trust.'

'*I know. I am hoping that the power of truth will convince you.*'

'My choices appear limited,' said Antikas. 'Lead on, wizard!'

High in the palace the Demon Lord raised his arms. Over the city the Entukku, in ecstasy and bloated with feeding, floated aimlessly above the buildings. The Demon Lord's power swept

473

over them, draining their energies. They began to wail and shriek, their hunger increasing once more.

Stepping back from the window the Demon Lord began to chant. The air before him shimmered. Slowly he spoke the seven words of power. Blue light lanced from floor to ceiling, and a pungent odour filled the room. Where a moment before had been a wall, decorated with a brightly coloured mural, there was now a cave entrance, and a long tunnel.

Faint figures of light moved in the tunnel, floating towards him. As they came closer the Demon Lord held out his hands. Black smoke oozed from his fingers and drifted down the tunnel. The light figures hovered and the smoke rose up around them. The lights faded, but the smoke hardened, taking shape.

Ten tall men emerged, wearing dark armour and full-faced helms. One by one they strode into the room. The Demon Lord spoke a single harsh word and the tunnel disappeared.

'Welcome to the world of flesh, my brothers,' said the Demon Lord.

'It is good to feel hunger again,' said the first of the warriors, removing his helm. His hair was ghost white, his eyes grey and cold. His face was broad, the lipless mouth wide.

'Then feed,' said the Demon Lord, raising his hands. This time a red mist flowed from his hands, and floated across the room. The warrior opened his mouth, displaying long, curved fangs. The red mist streamed into his open mouth. The others removed their helms and moved in close. One by one they absorbed the mist. As they did so their bone-white faces changed, the skin blushing red. Their eyes glittered, the grey deepening to blue and then, slowly, to crimson.

'Enough, my brother,' said the first warrior. 'After so long the taste is too exquisite.' Moving to a couch he sank down, stretching out his long, black-clad limbs.

The Demon Lord's arms dropped to his side. 'The long wait is almost over,' he said. 'Our time has come again.' The others seated themselves and remained silent.

'What is it you require of us, Anharat?'

'In the mountains to the south there is a woman. She carries the child of Skanda. It will be born soon. You must bring it to me. The Spell of Three must be completed before the Blood Moon.'

'She is guarded well?'

'There are eight humans with her, but only four warriors, and three of these are old men.'

474

'With respect, brother, such a mission is demeaning. We are all Battle Lords here. The blood of thousands has stained our blades. We have feasted on the souls of princes.'

'It was not my intention,' said the Demon Lord, 'to offer insult to the Krayakin. But if we do not take the babe then all will be lost for another four thousand years. Would you rather I entrusted this task to the Entukku?'

'You are wise, Anharat, and I spoke hastily. It will be as you order,' said the warrior. Raising his hand he made a fist. 'It is good to feel the solidity of flesh once more, to breathe in air, and to feed. It is good.' His blood-filled eyes gazed on the body of Malikada. 'How long before you can let fall this decaying form? It is ugly to the eye.'

'Once the sacrifice is complete,' Anharat told him. 'For now I need this obscenity around me.'

A shimmering began in the air around Anharat, and the hissing of many voices. Then it faded.

'These humans are so perverse,' said Anharat. 'I ordered one of my officers to rest in his room. Now he is fleeing the city in a bid to save the queen and her child. It seems he went to a tavern and a priest spoke to him.'

'He understands magick, this officer?' asked the warrior.

'I do not believe so.'

'Then why have the Entukku failed to seize him?'

'There are spells around the tavern, ancient spells. It is not important. He will afford you some pleasure, for he is the foremost swordsman in the land. His name is Antikas Karios, and he has never lost a duel.'

'I shall kill him slowly,' said the warrior. 'The taste of *his* terror will be exquisite.'

'There is one other of the group to be considered. His name is Nogusta. He is the last of the line of Emsharas the Sorcerer.'

The warrior's eyes narrowed, and the others tensed at the sound of the name. 'I would give up eternity,' said the warrior, 'for the chance to find the soul of Emsharas the Traitor. I would make it suffer for a thousand years, and that would not be punishment enough. How is it that one of his line still lives?'

'He carries the Last Talisman. Some years ago one of my disciples inspired a mob to destroy him and his family. It was a fine night, with great terror. Pleasing to the eye. But he was not there. Many times I have tried to engineer his death. The

Talisman saves him. That is why he must be considered with care.'

'He is one of the old ones guarding the woman?'

'Yes.'

'I do not like the sound of it, Anharat. It is not a coincidence.'

'I do not doubt that, at all,' said Anharat. 'But does it not show how far the enemy has fallen in power that his only defence is a group of old men? All but one of his priests here are slain, his temples deserted, his forces routed. He has become to this world a pitiful irrelevance. Which is why it will pass to us before the Blood Moon.'

'Is this tavern far?' asked the warrior.

'No.'

The warrior rose and put on his helm. 'Then I shall go and feast myself upon the heart of this priest,' he said.

'The spells are strong,' warned Anharat.

The warrior laughed. 'Spells that would drain the Entukku are as wasp stings to the Krayakin. How many other humans are there?'

'Only two.'

The warrior gestured and two of his fellows stood. 'The milk of the Entukku was good, but flesh tastes sweeter,' he said.

The wagon lurched as one of the rear wheels hit a sunken rock. The weary horses sagged against their traces. Conalin tried to back up the team, but the horses stood their ground. Bison swore loudly and dismounted. Moving to the rear of the wagon he grabbed two spokes of the wheel. 'Give them a touch of the whip,' he ordered. Conalin cracked it above the horses' backs. They surged forward. At the same time Bison threw his weight against the wheel and the wagon bumped over the rock. The giant fell sprawling to the trail, the wheel narrowly missing his arm.

The women in the wagon – save Axiana – laughed as he rose, mud on his face. 'It's not funny!' he roared.

'It is from where I'm sitting,' said Ulmenetha. Bison swore again and trudged back to where Kebra was holding the reins of his mount.

'This trail is too narrow,' he said, heaving himself into the saddle. 'I don't think we've made more than twelve miles today. And already the horses are exhausted.'

'Nogusta says we'll change the team again when we reach the flatlands.'

Bison was not mollified. He glanced back to the spare mounts they had taken from the dead lancers. 'They are cavalry mounts. They're not bred to pull wagons and they tire easily. Look at them! They were ridden hard even before we took them, and they are exhausted also.'

It was true, and Kebra knew it. The horses were all weary. Somewhere soon they would have to rest them. 'Let's move on,' he said.

The wagon finally crested a high hill and emerged from the forest. Far off to the south they could see the glittering ribbon of the River Mendea, and beyond it soaring mountain peaks, snow crested and crowned by clouds. 'We'll not make the river by dark,' said Kebra.

'I could carry the cursed wagon faster than these horses can pull it,' said Bison.

'You are in a foul mood today,' observed Kebra.

'It's this damned horse. Every time I go up, he goes down. He goes up, I come down. He's treating my arse like a drum.' Another squeal of laughter came from the wagon, this time from little Sufia, who repeated the phrase in a sing-song voice.

'His arse is a drum! His arse is a drum!'

Ulmenetha scolded her, gently, but was unable to keep the smile from her face.

'I'll ride your horse if you drive the wagon,' said Conalin.

'Done!' said Bison, happily. 'Heaven knows I'm no rider.'

Dagorian came riding up the trail. 'About a mile further the road widens,' he said. 'There is even a paved area. It is overgrown now, but it will help us earn back a few miles.'

Bison climbed to his place at the driving seat and sat upon a folded blanket. 'Ah, but that is good,' he murmured, settling himself down and taking up the reins. Kebra saw the boy was having difficulty reaching the stirrup of Bison's mount and edged closer, holding out his hand. Conalin spurned it and clumsily hauled himself up. Kebra dismounted and adjusted the stirrups.

'Have you ever ridden, lad?' he asked.

'No, but I am a fast learner.'

'Grip with your thighs, not your calves. And trust the horse. He knows what he's doing. Come, I'll give you a lesson.' Swinging into the saddle he moved out over the rise and slowly rode down to the flat land below. Glancing back he saw Conalin holding the reins at chest level as the horse picked its way down the slope. At the base of the hill Kebra drew alongside Conalin, showing him the basics of guiding the mount.

'We'll try a trot,' he said. 'You must get in rhythm with the horse. Otherwise you'll end up like Bison, and it will play a tattoo on your buttocks. Let's go!'

Kebra's mount moved smoothly into a trot. Behind him Conalin was being bounced around in the saddle. His horse slowed. 'Don't haul on the reins, lad. That's his signal to stop.'

'I'm no good at this,' said the red-head, his face flushing. 'I'll go back to the wagon.'

'Nothing good ever comes easy, Conalin. And I think you are doing fine. A born horseman.'

'Truly?'

'You just need to get used to the horse. Let's try again.'

As the wagon trundled down the slope the two riders set off once more. For a while Conalin felt his spine was being bruised, but then, suddenly and without warning, he found the rhythm and the ride became a delight. The sun broke through the clouds, and the tightness in his stomach faded away. He had lived his life in the squalor of the city, and had never before seen the glory of the mountains. Now he rode a fine horse, and the breeze was fresh against his skin. He found in that moment a joy he had never known. He gave Kebra a wide grin. The bowman smiled and rode in silence beside him. At the tree line they swung their mounts.

'Now for a little canter,' said Kebra. 'Not too much, for the horses are tired.'

If trotting had been a joy, the ride back to the wagons was a delight Conalin would treasure all his life. The rags he wore were forgotten, as were the sores on his back. Today was a gift no-one could take away from him.

'You ride so well – like a knight!' Pharis told him as he drew alongside the wagon.

'It's wonderful,' he told her. 'It's like . . . it's like . . .' He laughed happily. 'I don't know what it's like. But it's wonderful!'

'You won't be saying that by this evening,' warned Bison.

Dagorian rode with them for the next hour, then headed off towards the south to find a place to camp.

As the sun began to slide towards the western mountains Nogusta came galloping up from the rear. 'There is no sign of pursuit yet,' he told Kebra. 'But they are coming.'

'We won't reach the river by tonight. The horses are tired,' said the bowman.

'As am I,' admitted Nogusta.

They rode on, and as dusk deepened they came across Dagorian, camped beside a small lake. He had lit a fire and the weary travellers climbed down from the wagon to sit beside it. Kebra and Conalin unsaddled the horses, wiping their backs with dried grass. Kebra showed the boy how to hobble the mounts, then they left them to graze and unhitched the wagon team. Conalin was moving stiffly and Kebra grinned at him. 'The muscles on the inside of your thighs have been stretched,' he said. 'You'll get used to it. Did you enjoy the ride?'

'It was all right,' said Conalin, nonchalantly.

'How old are you, lad?'

The boy shrugged. 'I don't know. What does it matter?'

'At your age I don't think it does. I am fifty-six. *That* matters.'

'Why?'

'Because my dreams are all behind me. Do you swim?'

'No. And I don't want to learn.'

'It is almost as fine a feeling as riding a horse. But it is up to you.' Kebra strolled away to the lake side and stripped off his clothing. The water was cold as he waded out. Then he dived forward and began to swim with long easy strokes. Conalin wandered to the water side and watched him in the fading light. After a while Kebra swam back and climbed out of the water. He shivered and dried himself with his tunic, which he then stretched out on a rock. Pulling on his leggings he sat down beside the boy.

'I don't dream,' said Conalin, suddenly. 'I just sleep and then wake up.'

'Those are not the dreams I spoke of. I meant the dreams we have for life, things we wish for ourselves, like a wife and family, or riches.'

'Why are they behind you? You could have these things,' said the boy.

'Perhaps you are right.'

'My dream is to wed Pharis, and to fear nothing.'

The sky darkened to crimson as the sun dropped behind the western peaks. 'It would be nice to fear nothing,' admitted Kebra. Bison strolled up and draped a blanket around Kebra's shoulders.

'Old men like you should beware of the cold,' said Bison, walking on and dipping a cup into the water. He drank noisily.

'Why did he say that?' asked Conalin. 'He looks old enough to be your father.' Kebra chuckled.

'Bison will never be old. You look at his bald pate and his

479

white moustache and you see an old man. Bison looks in a mirror and sees a young man of twenty-five. It is a gift he has.'

'I don't like him.'

'I agree with you. I don't like him much either. But I love him. There's no malice in old Bison, and he'd stand by your side against all the armies of the world. That's rare, Conalin. Believe me.'

The boy was unconvinced, but he said nothing. Out on the lake the splintered reflection of the moon lay broken upon the water, and to the west the lake gleamed blood red in the dying sun. Conalin glanced up at the silver-haired bowman. 'Will I ride tomorrow?' he asked him.

Kebra smiled. 'Of course. The more you ride the better you'll get.'

'It feels safer on a horse,' said Conalin, gazing out over the lake.

'Why safer?'

'The wagon is so slow. When they catch us we'll not be able to escape in a wagon.'

'Maybe they won't catch us,' said Kebra.

'Do you believe that?'

'No. But there's always hope.' Conalin was pleased that the man had not tried to lie to him. It was a moment of sharing that made the boy feel like an equal.

'What will you do when they come?' asked Conalin.

'I'll fight them. So will Nogusta and Bison. It's all we can do.'

'You could ride away on your fast horses,' Conalin pointed out.

'Some men could, but we're not made that way.'

'Why?' asked the boy. It was such a simple question, yet, at first, Kebra was unable to answer it. He thought about it for a while.

'It is hard to explain, Conalin. You start by asking yourself what makes a true man. Is it his ability to hunt, or to farm, or to breed stock? In part the answer is yes. Is it his capacity to love his family? In part the answer is also yes. But there is something else. Something grand. It seems to me that there are three instincts which drive us on. The first is self-preservation – the will to survive. The second is tribal. We have an urge to belong, to be a part of a greater whole. But the third? The third is what counts, boy, above all things.'

Ulmenetha moved silently alongside them and removed her shoes. Sitting down she rested her feet in the water.

'What is the third thing?' asked Conalin, angry that they had been interrupted.

'That is even harder to explain,' said Kebra, who was also disconcerted by the arrival of the priestess. 'The lioness would willingly give her life to save her cubs. That is her way. But I have seen a woman risk her life for someone else's child. The third instinct compels us to put aside thoughts of self-preservation for the sake of another life, or a principle, or a belief.'

'I don't understand,' said Conalin.

'You should ask Nogusta. He would explain it better.'

Ulmenetha turned towards them. 'You don't need it explained, Conalin,' she said, softly. 'When you rescued Pharis it was that third instinct which came into play. And when you stood in that room in Kalizkan's house and fought against the beast.'

'It is not the same. I love Pharis and Sufia. But I do not love the queen. I would not risk death to save her.'

'It is not about her,' said Kebra. 'Not specifically, anyway. It is about many things: honour, self-worth, pride . . .' he lapsed into silence.

'Would you die for me?' asked Conalin, suddenly.

'I'm hoping not to die for anyone,' said Kebra, embarrassed. Swiftly he rose and walked back to the camp.

'Yes, he would,' said Ulmenetha. 'He is a good man.'

'I don't want anyone dying for me,' the boy told her. 'I don't want it!'

Chapter Eight

Nogusta and Dagorian were sitting by the fire, studying the maps Ulmenetha had supplied. Bison was stretched out alongside them, his head resting on his arm. 'When are we going to eat?' he grumbled. 'My stomach thinks my throat's been cut.'

'Soon,' promised Nogusta. He turned back to Dagorian, and spread a second map on the ground beside the fire. The map was of etched leather, the hide stained white. Once there had been many colours, denoting woods, mountains and lakes. But these were badly faded now, and some of the etching had worn away. Even so the scale was good and both men could just make out the symbols showing the positions of forest roads and river crossings. 'I would think we are close to here,' said Nogusta, indicating an etched spear on the top right-hand corner of the map. 'The outer edge of the Forest of Lisaia. According to the map there are three bridges. Two questions arise: Are they still there, and, if they are, what effect will the spring floods have upon them? I have seen bridges under water at this time of year in the mountains.'

'I'll ride ahead and scout them tomorrow,' said Dagorian. The young man stared down at the map. 'Once we reach the high country beyond we will have to leave the wagon.' Nogusta nodded. The only other route was to journey all the way to the ghost city of Lem, and then take the coast road. This would add 80 miles to the journey. In the distance a wolf howled. The sound hung eerily in the air. Dagorian shivered.

Nogusta smiled. 'Contrary to popular belief wolves do not attack men,' he said.

'I know. But it chills the blood nonetheless.'

'I was bitten by a wolf once,' said Bison. 'On the arse.'

'One can only pity the wolf,' said Nogusta.

Bison chuckled. 'It was a she-wolf and I got too close to her cubs, I guess. She chased me for half a mile. You remember? It was back at Corteswain. Kebra did the stitching. I had a fever for four days.'

'I remember,' said Nogusta. 'We all drew lots and Kebra lost. He says the sight haunts him to this day.'

'Left a nasty scar,' said Bison. Rolling to his knees he dropped his leggings. 'Look at that!' he said, pointing his buttocks towards Dagorian. The officer laughed aloud.

'You are quite right, Bison. That's one of the ugliest things I've ever seen.' Bison hauled up his leggings and buckled his belt. He was grinning broadly.

'I tell all the whores it's a war wound from a Ventrian spear.' He swung towards Kebra. 'Are we going to eat or starve to death?' he bawled.

Some way back, sitting with her back to a tree, Axiana accepted a cup of water from Pharis. The slim, dark-haired girl squatted down before the queen. 'Are you feeling better now?' she asked.

'I am hungry,' said Axiana. 'Fetch me something from the wagon. Some fruit.'

Pharis was delighted to obey. The order made her a servant of the queen, an honourable role, and she was determined to fulfil it well. She ran to the wagon and rummaged in the food sacks. Little Sufia was sitting there, unmoving, her eyes staring up at the sky.

'What are you looking at?' asked Pharis.

The little girl took a deep breath. 'Fetch Nogusta,' she said, her voice cool and distant.

'He's talking to the officer. I'd better not disturb him.'

'Fetch him now,' said Sufia. Pharis looked hard at the little girl. 'What is wrong?'

'Do it now, child, for time is short.' Pharis felt goose-flesh upon her arms, and backed away.

'Nogusta!' she called. 'Come quickly!' The black warrior ran across to the wagon, followed by Dagorian and Kebra.

'What is it?' he asked. Pharis simply pointed to the small blonde child. She was sitting cross-legged facing them, her face serene, her blue eyes bright.

'The wolves are coming,' said Sufia. 'Draw your swords! Do it now!' Although the voice was that of the child, the words were spoken with great authority.

Suddenly the queen screamed.

A huge grey wolf padded from the trees, then another. And another.

One raced forward, straight at Bison, who was sitting beside the fire. The giant reared up and, as the gleaming fangs darted towards his throat, hammered a blow to the wolf's face. The beast spun away, rolled, and attacked again. As it leapt Bison grabbed it by the throat and hurled it at the pack. Nogusta grabbed Pharis and threw her onto the wagon, then drew his sword as a wolf leapt for him. The blade flashed in the moonlight, slashing through the beast's neck. Kebra was hurled to the ground as another beast lunged at him. One of the horses screamed and went down. Dagorian lanced his blade through the chest of a huge grey male, then swung towards Axiana. She was sitting by the tree, and not one of the beasts approached her. Conalin and Ulmenetha had waded into the lake, and one of the beasts was swimming out towards them. Another wolf leapt. Dagorian jumped backwards, the fangs snapping at his face. Thrusting up his sword he plunged it into the wolf's belly. On the ground beside him, his left hand gripping the fur of a wolf's throat, Kebra plunged his dagger again and again into the side of the beast. The wolf slumped down over him.

On the back of the wagon Sufia stood and raised her arms over her head, bringing her hands slowly together. She was chanting as she did so. Blue fire formed around her fingers. Her right arm snapped forward, pointing to the lake. A ball of fire flew from her hand, exploding against the back of the swimming wolf. It thrashed about, flames licking over its fur. Then it swam away.

Her left hand dropped and the fire flew down into the earth beside the wagon, flaring up with a tremendous flash. The wolf pack scattered and ran back into the forest.

Dagorian felt a pain in his arm. He glanced down to see blood dripping from a bite to his left forearm. He could not recall being bitten. Bison walked over to where he stood. His left ear was sliced open, blood streaming to his thick neck.

Five wolves were dead in the camp-site.

Kebra pushed the body of the dead wolf to one side and rose unsteadily. For a moment no-one spoke. 'Wolves don't attack

484

people, you said,' Bison pointed out to Nogusta. Lifting his hand to his blood-covered ear he swore.

'They do if the Entukku inspire them,' said the voice of Sufia. Ulmenetha and Conalin waded ashore and approached the wagon. Pharis was sitting against the food sacks, her knees drawn up. She was staring fearfully at the child.

'Who are you?' asked Nogusta. Sufia sat down, her little legs dangling over the tailboard.

'I am a friend, Nogusta. Of that you can be sure. I helped Dagorian back in the city, when the demons were upon him. And I rescued Ulmenetha when she sat upon the palace roof and saw the monster. I am Kalizkan the Sorcerer.'

For a moment no-one spoke. 'You are the cause of this terror,' said Nogusta, coldly.

'Indeed I am. But it was done unwittingly, and no-one feels more grief than I. But time is too short to explain. I cannot stay in this child's form for long, for it would damage her mind. So listen to me now. The enemy has sent a force against you the like of which you will never have seen. They are called the Krayakin. They are supreme warriors, but they are not immortal. Blades can cut them, but not kill them. They fear only two things, wood and water.' The child turned to Kebra. 'Your arrows can kill them, if you pierce heart or head. The others of you must fashion weapons of wood, stakes, spears, whatever you can.'

'How many are there?' asked Nogusta.

'There are ten, and they will be upon you before you reach the river.'

'What more can you tell us?' asked Dagorian.

'Nothing now. The child must return. I will help you where I can. But death calls me and the power of my spirit is fading. I cannot remain among the living for much longer. But trust me, my friends. I will return.'

Sufia blinked and rubbed her eyes. 'Why is everyone staring at me?' she said, her eyes filling with tears.

'We were wondering if you were hungry, little one,' said Kebra. 'What shall I cook for you?'

Bakilas, Lord of the Krayakin, reined in his mount. The five men lay sprawled in death, and the parallel lines of the wagon tracks could be seen disappearing into the forest. Bakilas dismounted and examined the ground around the dead men. Removing his black, full faced helm he winced as sunlight speared against his skin. Swiftly he scanned the tracks. Replacing his helm he moved to his horse and stepped into the saddle.

'The soldiers caught up with the wagon here, and were met by a single rider. They spoke to him, and then there was a fight. At this point other men joined in, having ridden from the forest. The battle was brief. One of the soldiers fought a hand to hand duel and was killed cleanly.'

'How do you know they spoke first, brother?' asked Pelicor, the youngest of the Krayakin. As well as the black armour and helm he was hooded against the sunlight.

Bakilas swung in the saddle. 'One of the soldiers' horses urinated on the grass. You can still see the stain. It was standing still at the time.'

'It is still conjecture,' muttered Pelicor.

'Then let us see,' said Bakilas. They rode their horses in a circle around the dead men, then Bakilas pointed to one of the corpses. 'Rise!' he commanded. The body of Vellian twitched and slowly rose from the grass. The ten riders focused upon it. The body spasmed, the air around it shimmering.

Images formed in the minds of the Krayakin; scenes drawn from the decaying brain of the slain soldier. They saw, through the dead man's eyes, the wagon and its occupants, and watched as the young officer rode to meet them. The conversation they heard was fragmented, and they honed their concentration.

'Good morning, I am Vellian, sent . . . Karios . . . palace. The city . . . restore order.'

'An army . . . traitors.'

'Yes. Now . . . sabre . . . scabbard and let . . . way.'

'I don't think so . . . great danger . . . safer with me.'

There followed a sudden fracture in the image and the Krayakin saw a brief intrusion of other memories, of a young woman running on the grass.

'The corruption has gone too far,' said Pelicor. 'We cannot hold the line.'

'We can,' said Bakilas, sternly. 'Concentrate!'

Once more they saw the young officer facing the soldiers. The man Vellian was speaking. 'Do not be a fool, man. You may be as skilled as Antikas himself with that sabre, but you cannot beat five of us. What is the point then of dying, when the cause is already lost?'

'What is the point of living without a cause worth dying for?' countered the officer.

The Krayakin sat silently as the scene played itself out, the young officer attacking, then being joined by a black rider and a silver-haired bowman. As Bakilas had already said the battle was brief, and the Krayakin analysed the skills of the victors.

The body slumped back to the grass. 'The young man is fast, and sure,' said Bakilas. 'But the black man is a master. Speed, subtlety and strength, combined with cunning and ferocity. A worthy opponent.'

'Worthy?' snapped Pelicor. 'He is human. There are no worthy opponents among them. Only sustenance. And he will supply little.'

'So angry, brother? Are you not enjoying this return to the flesh?'

'Not yet,' said Pelicor. 'Where are my armies? Where is the glory to be found here, on this miserable mountain?'

'There is none,' admitted Bakilas. 'The days of Ice and Fire are long gone. But they will return. The volcanoes will spew their ash into the sky, and the ice will return. It will be as it was. But first we must bring the mother and babe to Anharat. Be patient, brother.'

Bakilas touched spurs to his horse and rode for the forest.

The sunlight was less harsh in the shelter of the trees and Bakilas once more removed his helm, his white hair flowing free in the slight breeze, his grey eyes scanning the trail. Pelicor was not alone in lusting after the days of Ice and Fire. He too longed for them. Marching with the armies of the Illohir, scattering the humans, feasting on their terror and sucking their souls from their skulls. Heady days!

Until Emsharas had betrayed them.

It remained a source of pain that would never ease. Yet even with Emsharas's treachery the Battle of the Four Valleys could have been won, should have been won. The Krayakin had led the counter charge, and had smashed the enemy right. Bakilas himself had almost reached the Battle Standard of the human king, Darlic. Above the battle Anharat and Emsharas had fought on the Field of Spirit, and, just as Bakilas breached the spear wall around Darlic, Anharat had fallen. The dark cloud of ash shielding the Illohir from the harsh, deadly light of the sun, had been ripped apart. Illohir bodies withered in their tens of thousands, until only the Krayakin remained. Ten thousand of the greatest warriors ever to stride the earth. The humans had turned on them with renewed ferocity, their Storm Swords – enchanted by the traitor, Emsharas – had ripped into Krayakin flesh. By the end of the day only 200 Krayakin remained in the flesh to flee the field. The rest were Windborn once more.

The days of Illohir dominance on earth were over.

In the weeks that followed the Krayakin were harried and tracked down, until only ten survivors remained.

Then Emsharas had evoked the Great Spell, and all the remaining creatures of the Illohir, demons and sprites, wood nymphs, trolls and warriors, were cast into the grey hell of Nowhere. Existing without substance, immortal without form, the Illohir floated in a soulless sea. Only memory survived, memories of conquest and glory, of the sweet wine of terror, and the sustenance it supplied.

Nothing in all of existence could surpass the joys the Krayakin had known. Bakilas himself had once adopted human form, and had partaken of all the pleasures known to Man. Food and drink, drugs and debauchery. All were pitiful when compared to the tasting of souls. A faint memory stirred, and he remembered Darela. What he had felt for her was frightening. They had touched hands, then lips. Unused to human frailty Bakilas had been drawn into a relationship with the woman that left his senses reeling. With the last of his strength he had returned to the caverns of the Illohir and resumed his Krayakin form. Then he journeyed back to the village and drank Darela's soul. He had thought that would end her spell over him.

But he had been wrong. The memory of their days together came back again and again to haunt him.

The Krayakin rode in silence for several hours. The smell of death was strong upon the wind as they rode down a short slope and emerged by the shores of a glittering lake. Keeping to the shadows of the trees Bakilas took in the camp-site. There were five dead wolves upon the ground, and a sixth body by the waterline. Bakilas dismounted and lifted his hood into place. Then he walked out into the sunshine. Pain prickled his skin, but he ignored it. At the centre of the camp the grass was singed in a circle of around five feet in diameter. Removing his black gauntlet he reached out and touched the earth. His hand jerked back. Pulling on his gauntlet he returned to the shadows.

'Magick,' he said. 'Someone used magick here.'

Tethering their mounts the Krayakin sat in a circle. 'Anharat did not speak of magick,' said Mandrak, at just under 6 feet tall, the smallest of the warriors. 'He spoke only of three old men.'

'How strong was it?' asked Drasko, next to Bakilas the eldest of the group.

'By the power of four,' he answered. 'The wolves must have been possessed by the Entukku and the wizard used the light of *halignat*. Only a master could summon such power.'

'Why should the wolves have been possessed?' asked Pelicor.

Bakilas felt his irritation rise. 'Study was never a strength of yours, brother. Had they been merely wolves then any bright flash of light would have dispersed them. *Halignat* – the Holy Light – is used only against the Illohir. It would have hurled the Entukku back to the city – and perhaps beyond. Those closest to the flash might even have died.'

'If there is such a wizard,' said Drasko, 'why did we not sense his presence before now?'

'I do not know. Perhaps he is using a mask spell unknown to us. Whatever, we must proceed with more caution.'

'Caution is for cowards,' said Pelicor. 'I have no fear of this wizard, whoever he may be. His spells may vanquish the Entukku, but they are little more than mind-maggots. What spells can he hurl against the Krayakin?'

'We do not know,' said Bakilas, struggling to remain patient. 'That is the point.'

Bakilas strode to his horse and stepped into the saddle. Mandrak rode beside him as they set out after the wagon. 'He has always been impatient,' said Mandrak.

'It is not his impatience which offends me – but his stupidity. And he is a glutton. I have always abhorred that trait.'

'His hunger is legendary,' admitted Mandrak.

Bakilas did not reply. They had reached the end of the tree line, and the bright sun scorched his face. Putting on his helm he pulled up his hood and spurred his mount onwards. The brightness hurt his eyes, and he longed for the onset of night, the freshness of the breeze, the dark, cold beauty of the star-filled sky.

Their mounts were tired as they reached the base of a tall hill. Bakilas examined the trail. The fugitives had stopped here to change the horses, and the occupants of the wagon had walked up the hill. Two women and a child. He rode on. One of the women had picked up the child and carried it. A heavy woman, whose imprints were deeper than the rest.

Spurring his mount up the hill he rode over the crest, and saw the tracks wending away into another wood. He was grateful for the promise of shadow.

Did they know they were being followed? Of course they did. No-one could hope to spirit away a queen without pursuit. Did they know they were being followed by the Krayakin? Why should they not, since a wizard was amongst them? Bakilas thought hard about the wizard. Drasko's point had been a good one. Why could they not sense the presence of his magick? The air should be thick with it. Closing his eyes Bakilas reached out with his senses.

Nothing. Not a trace of sorcery could be detected. Even a mask spell would leave a residual taste in the air. It was worrying. Anharat had always been arrogant. It was his arrogance that led to the defeat of the Illohir at the Battle of the Four Valleys. What had he said? How far had the enemy fallen that he could rely on only three old men. It could be viewed quite differently. How mighty was the enemy that all he *needed* were three old men. He thought of the black warrior. Such a man was not built for retreat. Somewhere along this trail he would seek to attack his pursuers. It was the nature of the man.

They approached the trees with caution, swords drawn, then entered the wood.

There was no attack. For another hour they followed the wagon tracks. They were fresher now, the edges of the wheel imprints clean and sharp.

Bakilas drew back on the reins. The wagon tracks turned off from the road and vanished into the trees. There was thick undergrowth beyond the tree line, and the wagon had crushed bushes and saplings beneath it. Why would they take such a difficult trail? Bakilas removed his helm and sniffed the air.

Mandrak moved alongside his leader. 'Can you smell it?' he asked. Bakilas nodded. Humans could never surprise the Krayakin, for human glands secreted many scents, oozing from their pores in the disgusting sweat that bathed them. Of all of his brothers Mandrak's sense of smell was the most keen. Bakilas drew rein and scanned the tree line and the bushes beyond, careful not to let his gaze dwell on two of the hiding places he had identified.

'Three men are hidden there,' said Mandrak.

'I have identified two,' whispered Bakilas.

'One is behind the large oak overhanging the rise, another is crouched behind a bush just below it. The other one is further back. Yes . . . with the horses.'

'Why are we stopping?' asked Pelicor.

490

'Remove your helmet, and you will know,' Bakilas told him, his voice low.

Pelicor did so. Like his brothers his hair was white, but his face was broad and flat, the eyes small and set close together. His nostrils flared, and he smiled. 'Let me take them, brother. I am hungry.'

'It might be wiser to circle them,' offered Mandrak. 'Cut off their means of escape.'

'There are three of them!' snapped Pelicor. 'Not thirty. How can they escape us? Come let us put an end to this dismal mission.'

'You wish to take them alone, Pelicor?' asked Bakilas.

'I do.'

'Then by all means charge. We will await your victory.'

Pelicor replaced his helm, drew his longsword and slashed his spurs into the horse's flanks. The beast reared then galloped into the trees. Just beyond the trail the black warrior stepped from behind a tree. Pelicor saw him and dragged on the reins. The warrior was holding a slim knife by the blade.

'You think to hurt me with that?' yelled Pelicor, spurring the horse once more.

The warrior's arm came back, the knife flashed forward, missing the charging rider. The blade slammed into a small wedge of wood, beside the trail, slicing through a length of stretched twine. A young tree, bent like a bow, snapped upright. Three pointed stakes lashed to it slammed into Pelicor's chest, smashing through his black armour, breaking his ribs and spearing his lungs. The horse ran on. The body of the Krayakin warrior hung in the air twitching.

Bakilas heard a whisper of movement. Flinging up his arm he took the arrow through his gauntleted hand. The arrow head sliced through the limb and buried itself in the pale flesh of his face, cutting his tongue. The wood of the shaft burned like acid. At first he tried to pull the arrow loose from his cheek, but the barbs caught against the inner flesh. With a grunt he pushed the shaft through his other cheek, snapped off the head, then drew the arrow clear of his face and hand. The wounds began to heal instantly. But where the wood had touched him the soreness continued for some time.

'They have run,' said Mandrak. 'Do we give chase?'

'Not through the woods. There will be other traps. We will catch them upon the road . . . very soon.'

Bakilas rode to where Pelicor hung from the stake. His eyes were open, his body in spasm.

'Help me,' he whimpered.

'Your body is dying, Pelicor,' said Bakilas, coldly. 'And soon you will be Windborn again. We can taste your fear. It is most exquisite. Drasko, Mandrak and myself fed only recently. Therefore our brothers shall draw sustenance from what remains of your form.'

'No . . . I . . . can . . . heal.'

Bakilas shivered with pleasure at the increase in fear emanating from the impaled warrior. Like the others Pelicor had endured thousands of years in the torment that was Nowhere. The thought of returning to it filled him with horror. 'Who would have thought you could be capable of such intense terror, Pelicor. It is almost artistic,' said Bakilas.

Bakilas drew back, and the remaining six Krayakin moved in with daggers drawn.

Dagorian moved out onto the old bridge, testing each step. The ancient boards beneath his feet were 10 feet long, 18 inches wide, and 2 inches thick. They creaked ominously as he moved out upon them. Less than 12 feet wide the bridge spanned just over 100 feet. Below it the swollen river rushed on down the mountains, white water surging over massive rocks, and sweeping on to a rumbling fall some 2 miles down river. If he fell through he would be swept to his death. No man could swim in such a torrent.

The boards were nailed to huge cross beams set every 9 feet, and gaping cracks showed between them. Dagorian was sweating heavily as he moved out over the river. Since the attack by the wolves his fears had been growing, preying on his mind. Doubt had crept in, and with it a fierce longing to live. To be free of his duty. Only his sense of honour held him to this doomed quest, and even this was fraying. You should have stayed in the temple, he thought, as he moved carefully out over the rotting boards. Nogusta had ordered him to get the wagon across, if possible. He glanced back to where the others waited. They were all looking at him, including the queen. Carefully he moved on to the safety of the far bank.

There was still no way to be sure the bridge would take the weight of the wagon.

Moving swiftly back to where the others waited he instructed them to walk with care, keeping to the stone reinforced rail.

Ulmenetha took Axiana by the arm and led her out onto the bridge. Pharis followed with Sufia. Conalin remained with the wagon.

'Get across, boy,' ordered Dagorian.

'I can drive it,' insisted Conalin.

'I don't doubt your skill. I just don't want to see you die.' The boy was about to argue, but Dagorian shook his head. 'I know you have courage, Conalin, and I respect it. But if you want to help me then lead the spare horses across. I will follow when you are safe on the far bank.'

Conalin climbed down and moved to the rear of the wagon. Dagorian took his place, gathered up the reins, and waited. The boy moved out past him. 'Talk to them as you walk,' advised Dagorian, 'for the rushing water will frighten them.'

The boy was halfway across when one of the boards suddenly moved. A horse reared, but Conalin stepped in close, whispering to it, stroking its long neck. Dagorian looked on admiringly. Conalin continued on his way. Upon reaching the far side he turned and waved. Dagorian flicked the reins and the team moved out onto the bridge. The horses were nervous and, keeping his voice low and even, Dagorian encouraged them. Underneath the wagon the boards groaned. One split, but did not give way. Dagorian was sweating as they reached the centre of the bridge. The rushing of the water below sounded thunderous now. One of the horses slipped, but righted itself.

Then a board cracked, and the wagon lurched. For a sickening heartbeat Dagorian thought he was about to be pitched into the river. He sat very still for a moment, his heart thudding in his chest, then carefully climbed down. The left rear wheel was halfway through the boards, being supported only by the jutting axle head. Dagorian let out a soft curse. Putting both hands under the tailboard he struggled to lift it clear. It did not move a hair's breadth.

'They're coming!' shouted Conalin. Dagorian swung to see Nogusta, Kebra and Bison. They were galloping their horses, riding hard and fast. Nogusta reached the bridge first, dragging on the reins. Then he leapt from the saddle and led the giant black gelding out onto the bridge. Kebra and Bison followed his lead. There was no room for them to pass.

Bison tossed his reins to Kebra and strode to where Dagorian stood at the rear of the wagon. 'Get back in the driver's seat,' said the giant, 'and give them a lash when I call.'

493

'It won't move,' said Dagorian.

'Riders!' yelled Conalin.

The warriors of the Krayakin breasted the slope, and, swords drawn, rode for the bridge. Dagorian scrambled up to the wagon. Bison grabbed the wheel. 'Now!' he shouted. The giant heaved, and the wagon rose. At the same time Dagorian lashed the reins across the backs of the team. The wagon lurched forward. Bison was hurled from his feet, but rolled clear of the iron shod wheel.

Dagorian lashed the backs of the team and the wagon picked up speed. Nogusta and Kebra came running behind.

The child Sufia climbed into the wagon as it reached the bank. In a high-pitched voice she chanted something in an alien tongue.

The Krayakin had reached the bridge, and two of them set off across it.

A ball of flame flew from Sufia's hand, striking the bridge. A column of fire reared up, and the bridge began to blaze. One of the Krayakin backed his horse to safety, but the second spurred his mount, riding through the blaze. Bison ran at the charging horse, waving his arms and shouting at the top of his voice. The beast reared. Bison hurled himself forward, ducking under the flailing hoofs. Throwing up his arms Bison clamped his hands to the horse's chest and pushed with all his strength. The horse toppled back hurling its rider into the flames. The boards gave way. Horse and warrior crashed through to the roiling river below. Fingers of fire swept along the boards. Bison's leggings caught alight. Spinning on his heel the giant ran, panic stricken, to the bank. Nogusta and Kebra leapt upon him, hurling him to the ground. They tried to beat out the flames on Bison's burning clothing, but to no avail. Then Sufia stepped forward and held out her hand. The fire leapt from Bison to the child's waiting fingers, where it vanished. Bison tore off his leggings. His flesh was badly burned on the left thigh. Sufia moved to him, dropping to her knees. Her tiny hand reached out. Bison winced as her fingers touched the blistered flesh of his thigh. Then, as if a cool breeze was whispering over the burn, all pain ceased. She lifted her hand. The burn was gone.

'Such small magick is still left to me,' said the voice of Kalizkan. The body of the child settled down against Bison, her blond head resting on his chest. 'Let her sleep,' said Kalizkan. Bison carefully lifted the sleeping child and carried her to the wagon, where he laid her down and covered her with a blanket.

Ulmenetha approached the giant warrior. 'That was a brave act,' she said, 'to charge a mounted knight. I must say you surprised me.'

Bison turned to her and gave a wide, gap-toothed grin. 'If you'd like to thank me properly we could move further back into the bushes.'

'Now, that reaction *doesn't* surprise me,' she said. With a withering glance at his naked lower body she added: 'And find some fresh leggings. There are ladies present.'

'That's when I normally need it,' he said, still grinning.

Swinging away the priestess walked back to where Axiana and Pharis were sitting together. From the wagon Conalin grinned at the old man. 'Women,' said Bison, 'who can understand them?' Conalin shrugged.

'I don't,' he admitted. 'But I know enough to realize that she doesn't like you.'

'You think so?' asked Bison, genuinely surprised. 'What makes you believe that?'

Conalin laughed aloud. 'Perhaps I'm wrong.'

'I think you might be,' agreed Bison.

Black smoke was rising from the blazing bridge, and Nogusta strode to the bank, staring across the river to where the eight remaining Krayakin warriors waited. Dagorian joined him. 'There are other bridges,' he said. 'But we have gained a little time.'

The Krayakin divided into two groups. Four warriors rode down river towards the west, the other four heading east.

'We have had more luck than we deserve,' said Nogusta, softly.

'What happened back in the forest?'

'We killed one. But only because the leader wanted him dead. They are deadly foes, Dagorian. More terrible than any I have faced before.'

'And yet two are dead, and we have suffered no losses.'

'Not yet,' whispered Nogusta.

Dagorian shivered suddenly. He glanced at the black warrior. 'What have you seen with that Third Eye of yours?'

'Do not ask,' advised Nogusta.

Ulmenetha's spirit rose above the campsite, hovering in the night air. The moon was bright, the sky clear over the mountains. From here she could see Nogusta, sitting alone on a hillside. Close by Kebra was talking to Conalin. Axiana, Pharis and Sufia were asleep in the wagon. Bison sat alone by the camp-fire, finishing the last of the stew prepared by Kebra.

There was freedom here in this astral solitude, and Ulmenetha gloried in it. There were no demons over the forest, no Entukku with their slashing talons. She allowed herself to rise further, the moonlit forest shrinking below her. Ulmenetha flew north, over the ruined bridge, intending to seek out the Krayakin.

A glowing form materialized in the air alongside her. This time she could make out a face. It was that of a young man, golden haired and handsome. 'It is not wise,' he said, 'to journey far. The Krayakin will be able to see you, and they can summon the Entukku to attack you.'

'I need to know how close they are,' said Ulmenetha.

'The group heading east will lose two days. Those heading west will cross the river at Lercis, forty miles from here. They will not catch up with you by tomorrow.'

'Why is this happening to us, Kalizkan? What did you do?'

'It is not safe here, lady. Return to your body and sleep. We will talk again in a place of sanctuary.'

The figure vanished.

Ulmenetha flew back to the camp-site, and there hovered for a while, enjoying a last taste of freedom.

Back within her body she settled down, covering herself with a blanket. Sleep came easily, for she was very tired.

She became aware of the smell of honeysuckle, and opened her eyes to see a small garden. A latticework arch was close by, red and cream honeysuckle growing up and through it. There were flower beds full of summer plants, blazing with colour in the sunlight. Ulmenetha looked around, and saw a small cottage, with a thatched roof. She recognized it instantly. It was her grandmother's house.

The door opened, and a tall man stepped out. He was silver-haired and silver-bearded, and dressed in a long robe of silver satin. Kalizkan bowed. 'Now we can talk,' he said.

'I preferred you as the golden-haired young man,' said Ulmenetha.

Kalizkan chuckled. 'I must admit to you, lady, that he is a conceit. I never was golden haired, nor handsome . . . save in the spirit form. Were you ever as you appear now? So slim and innocent.'

'Indeed I was. But those days are long gone.'

'Not here,' said Kalizkan.

'No, not here,' she agreed, wistfully.

'So what would you have me tell you?'

'All of it.'

Kalizkan led her to a wooden bench beneath the honeysuckle arch, and they sat down in the shade. 'I was dying,' he said. 'Cancer was spreading through me. For more than ten years I used my magick to hold it at bay, but as I grew older my powers began to fade. I was frightened. Simply that. I studied many ancient grimoires, seeking spells to prolong my life, but always avoiding blood magick. Finally I sank to that. I sacrificed an old man. I told myself he was dying anyway – which he was – and I was only robbing him of a few days of life. He came willingly for I offered to create a pension for his widow.' Kalizkan lapsed into silence. Then he spoke again. 'The deed was an evil one, though I tried to convince myself otherwise. I thought of all the good I could still do if I lived. I reasoned that a small evil was acceptable, if it led to a greater good.' He smiled ruefully. 'Such is the path to perdition. I summoned a Demon Lord and sought to control him, ordering him to heal me. Instead he possessed me. With the last of my strength I hurled my spirit clear. From that day to this I have watched all the good I have done in my life eroded and stained by the evils he used my form to commit. All my children were sacrificed. And now thousands are dead, and the city of Usa is in torment.

'There is little I can do now to set matters right. My powers are limited – aye, and fading. Death calls me and I will not be here to see the end.

'But what I can do in the time that remains is teach you, Ulmenetha. I can instruct you in the magick of the land. I will teach you to use *halignat* – the holy fire. I will show you how to heal lesser wounds.'

'I have never been adept at such skills,' she said.

'Well now you must learn,' he told her. 'I can no longer use the child. She is malnourished and her heart is weak. It almost failed when I burned the bridge. I will not have another innocent life upon my hands.'

'I cannot do it,' said Ulmenetha. 'I cannot learn in a day!'

'Where we sit is not governed by *time*, Ulmenetha. We are floating in the open heart of eternity. Trust me. What you take from here will be vital to the safety of the child and the future of the world.'

'I do not want such responsibility. I am not . . . strong enough.'

'You are stronger than you think!' he said, forcefully. 'And you will need to be stronger yet.'

Angry now, Ulmenetha rose from the bench. 'Bring Nogusta here. Teach him! He is a warrior. He knows how to fight!'

He shook his head. 'Yes, he is a warrior. But I do not need someone who knows how to kill. I need someone who knows how to love.'

The night air was cold, but Conalin, a blanket round his shoulders, sat in quiet contentment alongside Kebra. The bowman did not speak, and this, in itself, pleased Conalin. They were together in silence. Companions. Conalin flicked a glance at Kebra's profile, seeing the moonlight glinting on the old man's white hair.

'What are you thinking?' asked the boy.

'I was remembering my father.'

'I didn't mean to disturb you.'

'I'm glad you did,' said Kebra. 'They were not pleasant memories.' He turned to the boy. 'You look cold. You should sit by the fire.'

'I am not cold.' The open sores on his arms and back were troubling him. Pushing up his sleeve he scratched at the scabs on his arm. 'What will you do if you reach Drenan?'

'I'll try my hand at farming. I own a hundred acres in the mountains close to the Sentran Plain. I'll build a house there. Maybe,' he finished, lamely.

'Is that what you really want?'

Kebra gave a rueful smile. 'Perhaps not. It is a dream. My last dream. The Sathuli have a blessing which says: May all your dreams – but one – come true.'

'Why is that a blessing? Would not a man be happier if all his dreams came true?'

'No,' said Kebra, shaking his head, 'that would be awful. What would there be left to live for? Our dreams are what carry us forward. We journey from dream to dream. At this moment your dream is to wed Pharis. If that dream comes true, and you are happy, you will want children. Then you will dream for them also. A man without dreams is a dead man. He may walk and talk, but he is sterile and empty.'

'And you have only one dream left? What happened to all the others?'

'You ask difficult questions, my friend.' Kebra lapsed into silence. Conalin did not disturb it. He felt a great warmth within, that all but swamped the cold of the night. My friend. Kebra had called him, my friend. The boy stared out over the silhouette of the mountains and watched the bright stars glinting around the moon. There was a harmony here, a great emptiness that filled the soul with the music of silence. The city had never offered such harmony, and Conalin's life had been an endless struggle to survive amid the cruelty and the squalor. He had learned early that no-one ever acted without selfish motives. Everything had a price. And mostly Conalin could not afford it.

Nogusta strolled towards where they sat. Conalin felt his irritation rise. He did not want this moment to be disturbed. But the black warrior moved silently past them and down to the camp-site.

'Is he your best friend?' asked Conalin.

'Best friend? I don't know what that means,' Kebra told him.

'Do you like him better than Bison?'

'That's easier to answer,' said Kebra with a smile. 'After all, nobody *likes* Bison. But no, he's not a *better* friend.' Reaching down he plucked two grass stems. 'Which of these stems is better?' he asked Conalin.

'Neither. They are just grass.'

'Exactly.'

'I don't understand.'

'Neither did I when I was young. In those days I thought that anyone who smiled at me was a friend. Anyone who offered me food was a friend. The word had little real meaning. But true friendship is rarer than a white raven, and more valuable than a mountain of gold. And once you find it you realize there is no way to grade it.'

'What did he do to become your friend? Did he save your life?'

'Several times. But I can't answer that question. I really can't. No more, I think, could he. And now my tired old bones need sleep. I will see you in the morning.'

Kebra rose and stretched his back. Conalin stood and they walked back to the camp-site. Bison was asleep by the fire, and snoring loudly. Kebra nudged him with his foot. Bison grunted and rolled over.

Conalin added sticks to the dying fire and sat watching the flames flicker as Kebra settled down alongside Bison. The bowman spread his blanket over his lean frame, then came up on one elbow. 'You are a bright lad, Conalin,' he said. 'You can be whatever you want to be, if your dreams are grand enough.'

For a while Conalin sat quietly by the fire. Dagorian emerged from the bushes and strolled to the wagon. The young officer looked tired, his movements heavy with weariness. Conalin watched him take an apple from a food sack and bite into it. Seemingly unaware of the boy Dagorian strolled back to the fire, pausing to gaze down on the sleeping figure of Axiana. Pharis was lying beside her, little Sufia cuddled in close. Dagorian stood silently for a moment, then sighed and joined Conalin by the dying blaze. Bison began to snore again. Conalin rose and prodded the giant with his foot, exactly as Kebra had done. Obligingly Bison rolled over, and the snoring ceased.

'Neatly done,' said Dagorian, reaching out and adding the last of the fuel to the fire. Conalin did not reply. Rising he left his blanket and wandered to the tree line, gathering dry sticks and twigs. He was not tired now, for his mind was full of questions, and the only man he would trust to answer them was asleep. He made several trips back to the fire, and was pleased to see Dagorian settle down in his blankets.

Conalin walked to the nearby stream and drank, then moved out away from the camp, strolling through the moonlit woods. The night breeze rustled in the leaves, but there was no other sound. The day's drama seemed far away now, an incident from another life. Then he remembered the big man running at the mounted knight, ducking under his horse and hurling the enemy back into the flames. He knew what Ulmenetha had meant when she said she was surprised. Conalin had not expected such a rare display of courage from the obscene old man. Yet the others had not been surprised. Conalin walked on, oblivious to his surroundings. The night air was full of new scents, fresh and vibrant and utterly unlike the musty stink of the city. He came to a break in the trees, and saw a moonlit meadow. Rabbits were feeding on the grass, and he paused to watch them. It seemed strange to see these creatures so full of life. His only previous experience of them was to see them hanging by their hind legs in the market place. Here, like him, they were free.

A dark shadow swept over the meadow, and a great bird swooped low over the feeding rabbits. They scattered, but the bird's talons slashed across the back of one fleeing rabbit, bowling it over. Before it could rise the bird was upon it, gripping it tight, its curved beak tearing the life from its prey.

Conalin watched as the hawk fed.

'That is unusual,' said a voice. Conalin leapt like a startled deer, and swung round, fists raised. Nogusta was standing beside him. The boy's heart was pounding. He had not heard the black man approach. Nogusta appeared not to notice Conalin's reaction. 'Hawks usually feed on feather,' he said. 'They need to be wedded to fur by a falconer.'

'How can they survive on feathers?' asked Conalin, anxious to seem unperturbed by the warrior's silent approach.

Nogusta smiled. 'Not literally feathers. It means they generally feed on other birds, pigeon and – if the hawk is clever enough – duck. This hawk probably escaped his handler and returned to the wild.'

Conalin sighed. 'I thought the rabbits were free here,' said Conalin.

'They are free,' said Nogusta.

'No. I meant really free. Free from danger.'

'Nothing that walks, flies, swims or breathes is ever free from danger. Speaking of which you should not stray too far from the camp.'

Nogusta turned and walked away into the darkness. Conalin caught up with him. 'If you do save the queen,' he said, 'what reward will you get?'

'I don't know. I haven't given it any thought.'

'Will you become rich?'

'Perhaps.'

They reached the edge of the camp and Nogusta paused. 'Go and get some rest. We will have to push hard tomorrow.'

'Is that why you are doing this?' persisted Conalin. 'For the reward?'

'No. My reasons are far more selfish.'

Conalin took a step towards the camp. Then another question occurred to him and he swung round. But Nogusta was nowhere to be seen.

Gathering his blankets Conalin lay down beside Pharis. There was so much here that he didn't understand. What could be more selfish than labouring for a personal reward?

Life in the city had been brutally hard, and Conalin had been alone for much of his young life. Even so he felt he understood the nature of human existence. Happiness was a full belly, joy was having enough food for a full belly tomorrow, and love was a commodity mostly associated with money. Even his love of Pharis was ultimately selfish, for Conalin gained great pleasure from her company. It was that pleasure, he believed, which led

501

him to yearn for her. Like the men and women who gathered at the Chiatze House, and smoked the long pipe, paying for pleasure dreams, and returning again and again, with haunted eyes and shrinking purses.

Conalin had no recollection of his parents. His first memories were of a small room, packed with children. Some of them were crying. All of them were filthy. Conalin had been tiny then, perhaps three or four years of age. He recalled the baby, lying on a soiled blanket. He remembered prodding it with his finger. It did not move. The lack of movement had surprised him. A fly had landed on the baby's open mouth, and slowly walked over the blue lips. Some time later a tall man had removed the baby.

Conalin couldn't remember the man's face. It had seemed so high and far away. But he remembered the legs, long and thin, encased in loose-fitting black leggings. His time in the house of gloom had not been happy, for his belly was rarely full, and there were many beatings.

After that there had been several homes. One, at least, had been warm and comfortable. But the price of that warmth had been too high, and he pushed the memories away.

Life on the streets had been better.

Conalin had even begun to think of himself as a wise man. He knew where to steal his breakfast, and could always find a warm, safe place to sleep, even in the depths of harsh winters. The soldiers of the Watch could never catch him, and his troubles with the street gangs had largely ended when he had killed Cleft-tongue. The gangs avoided him then, for Cleft-tongue had been feared, and anyone who could kill him in one-to-one combat was not to be trifled with. Conalin remembered the fight without any pleasure. He hadn't wanted to kill anyone. All he desired was to be left alone. But Cleft-tongue would have none of it. 'You steal on my patch, you pay rent,' he had said. Conalin had ignored him. Then, one night, the burly youth had come at him with a knife. Conalin was unarmed and had run. He recalled the laughter which followed him on his flight. Angry he had stolen a butcher's cleaver, and returned to where the gang had settled down for the night, in a deserted alleyway. He had walked up to where Cleft-tongue sat, called his name, and, as the youth turned, hit him in the temple with the cleaver. The blade had sunk deep, far deeper than Conalin had intended. Cleft-tongue died instantly.

'Now leave me alone,' Conalin told the others.

They had done so.

Unable to sleep Conalin pushed back his blanket and rose, walking to a nearby tree and urinating. Then he moved to the remains of the fire and added some of the twigs he had gathered earlier. With a stick he located the last glowing area of coals and, for some minutes, tried to blow them to fresh life. Finally admitting that the fire had died he sat back.

That was when he noticed the glow on the far side of the camp, a soft white light that was bathing the body of the sleeping priestess. Conalin watched it for some time, then he moved to Kebra's side and woke the bowman.

'What is it, lad?' asked Kebra, sleepily.

'Something is wrong with the priestess,' said Conalin. Kebra sat up, then pushed back his blankets. Dagorian awoke, saw the glowing light, and, with Conalin and Kebra, walked over to where Ulmenetha lay. The light was stronger now, almost golden. It was radiating from her face and hands. Kebra knelt beside her.

'She is burning up,' said the bowman. Conalin looked closer. Sweat was running from the woman's fat face, and her silver and blond hair was drenched. Kebra tried to wake her, but to no avail. The light around her grew brighter, and small white flowers blossomed around her blankets, writhing up through the grass. A heady scent filled the air, and Conalin could hear faraway music, whispering in his mind. Kebra drew back the blanket that covered the priestess. Only then did they see that she was floating some inches above the ground.

Nogusta moved alongside them, kneeling down and taking Ulmenetha's hand. The glowing light swelled, and flowed up along Nogusta's arm, bathing him in light. Releasing her hand he leapt backwards.

'Is she under attack?' asked Dagorian.

'No,' said Nogusta. 'This is not blood magick.'

'What should we do?' put in Kebra.

'Nothing. We will cover her and wait.'

Conalin peered down at the priestess's glistening face. 'She is getting thinner,' he whispered. It was true. Sweat was coursing over her body, and her flesh was receding.

'She'll die if this carries on,' said Kebra.

'What is happening to her is not of an evil origin,' said Nogusta. 'If it were I would sense it through my talisman. I do not think she will die. Cover her.'

Conalin lifted the blanket over Ulmenetha. As he did so his

hand touched her shoulder. Once more the light flowed, bathing him. An exquisite feeling of warmth and security filled him. His back itched and tingled, and he moaned with pleasure. Dizziness overcame him and he fell back to the grass. Pulling off his filthy shirt he gazed down at his arms. The open sores had vanished, and his skin glowed with health. 'Look!' he said to Kebra. 'I am healed.'

The bowman said nothing. Reaching out he also touched the priestess. The light flowed over him. Bright lights danced behind his eyes, and it seemed, at first, as if he was looking through a sheen of ice, distorting his view. Slowly the ice melted, and he found himself staring at the distant mountains, their peaks sharp and clear against the new dawn. He too sat back. 'I can see!' he whispered. 'Nogusta, I can see! Clearly!'

As the dawn rose, streaking the sky with gold, the light around Ulmenetha faded away, and her body slowly settled down upon the carpet of white flowers.

Her eyes opened, the last of the golden light shining from them. 'We cannot reach the coast,' she said. 'The Demon Lord is marching his army across the mountains, and the way to the sea is closed to us.'

Nogusta knelt beside her. 'I know,' he said, wearily.

Ulmenetha tried to sit, but sagged back exhausted. Her lips were dry. Nogusta ran to the wagon, returning with a water skin and a cup. Helping her to sit he held the cup to her lips. She drank sparingly. 'We must try . . . to reach . . . the ghost city,' she said. 'Now let me rest.' Nogusta lowered her to the ground. She fell asleep instantly.

'What did she mean?' asked Kebra. 'The sea is our only hope.'

'We would never reach it. The Krayakin are less than a day behind us, and the Ventrian army is moving across the mountains. Three thousand men are on the march, and more than two hundred cavalry have been sent to cut us off from the coast.'

Kebra knew the strength of Nogusta's Third Eye and he sat silently for a moment, absorbing the information. 'What then can we do?' he asked. 'We cannot fight an army, and we cannot escape it. Is our plan merely to run until we are exhausted – like an elk tracked by wolves?'

'Who is being tracked by wolves?' asked Bison, rising from his blankets and walking across to join them. Before Nogusta could explain the situation to him the giant saw the sleeping priestess.

504

'Kreya's Tits!' he exclaimed. 'Look at her! She's thin as a spear. What have I missed?'

'A great deal, my friend,' said Kebra. Slowly he explained the events of the last few minutes, the glowing around the priestess, the healing of his eyes, and the sores on Conalin's back and arms, and lastly, the news of the march of the Ventrian army. Bison ignored the last news.

'She healed you? What about my ear? It hurts like the devil. You could have woken me up. What kind of a friend are you?' He dropped to his knees beside the priestess and shook her shoulder. Ulmenetha did not stir. 'Well, this is nice,' said Bison, glancing up at Kebra. 'So far I've been bitten by wolves, burnt by magick and kicked by a horse. And you get your eyes healed. Is that fair?'

'Life is not fair, Bison,' said Kebra, with a smile. 'As any one of your large number of wives would testify.' His smile faded. 'The question is what are we going to do?' At that moment Axiana cried out. Beside her Pharis awoke and moved to her side.

'What is it, my lady?' she asked.

'I think . . . the baby is coming,' said Axiana.

Axiana was frightened, and called for Ulmenetha. The black warrior, Nogusta, moved to her side. 'She cannot come to you now,' he said, taking the queen's hand. 'She is sleeping, and cannot be woken.' Fear turned to panic in Axiana.

'The baby is coming! I need her!' Her face spasmed as fresh pain seared through her.

'Move aside, man,' said Bison, dropping to his knees beside the frightened girl.

'I don't want you!' shouted Axiana, horrified. 'Not you!'

Bison chuckled. 'As I've just been told, life isn't fair. But I've birthed babes before, and a large number of horses, cows and sheep. So you'll just have to trust me.' He turned to Nogusta. 'I want you to make a screen around her. Give us some privacy. And you, girl,' he told Pharis, 'can help me.' Bison drew back the blanket covering the queen. Her gown was wet. 'The water's broken,' he said. He looked across at Nogusta. 'Could we get a little urgency going here?'

Nogusta nodded and rose. Nogusta and Dagorian cut long branches from nearby trees, then stripped them of leaves. Plunging them into the earth around the queen they tied blankets to them, creating a roofless tent around her. Several times she cried out. Pharis emerged and moved to the stream, filling a bowl with water, and returning to the tent.

Little Sufia sat in the doorway of the tent, staring wide eyed into the interior. Conalin walked over to her, lifting her into his arms and carrying her to the wagon. The child was nervous and frightened. 'They are hurting her,' she said, her eyes brimming with tears.

'No they are not,' said Conalin, soothingly. 'A baby is coming. It's inside her, and it is going to come out.'

'How did it get inside her?' asked Sufia.

'It grew from a very small seed,' said Conalin. 'And now it is ready to live.'

A long shriek came from the tent. Sufia jumped. 'Why is she hurting?' Sufia began to cry. Kebra walked to the wagon. 'It is all right,' he said, ruffling the child's blond hair.

'She wants to know why the queen is in pain,' said Conalin.

'Well,' began Kebra, uneasily, 'she's . . . slim in the hips and –' Sufia's bright blue eyes were locked to Kebra's gaze. '– and . . .' He swung and called for Nogusta. 'The child has some questions,' he said, brightly.

'Answer them,' said Nogusta, walking away towards the stream.

'Thank you so much,' Kebra called after him. He turned back to Sufia. 'I can't really explain,' he told the child. 'Childbirth is sometimes painful, but soon the queen will be well, and you will be able to see the baby boy. That will be nice, won't it?'

The queen shrieked once more, and Sufia dissolved into tears.

Kebra moved away and began to prepare breakfast. Sitting beside the stream Nogusta and Dagorian talked in low voices. 'Does Bison know what he's doing?' asked the young officer.

'Yes. Believe it or not many of the camp whores request Bison when they are ready to deliver.'

'I can't think why.'

'Maybe he fathered most of the children,' ventured Nogusta. 'But I believe she is in safe hands.'

'Safe hands? How safe are any of us?'

Nogusta heard the fear in the young man's voice. He was concerned, for he had noticed the growing tension in the officer ever since the wolf attack. 'Nothing has changed since you rescued the queen,' he said.

'I didn't rescue her – Ulmenetha did that. And the children. I just came later. And we would all have been killed had you not arrived to kill the lancers. I don't feel that I have been of any real use.' Dagorian sighed. 'I am not like you, Nogusta. Nor the others. You are tough men. The stuff of heroes. I . . .' he faltered. 'I am just a failed priest.'

'You do yourself a disservice,' said Nogusta. Dagorian shook his head.

'You remember when you warned me about an attempt on Banelion's life? I went to him, as I told you.'

'Yes. He advised you to stay away from him. That was good advice.'

'Maybe it was – but a hero would have disobeyed him. Don't you see? I was glad to be relieved of responsibility. I thanked him and I left. Would you have done so?'

'Yes,' said Nogusta.

'I don't believe you.'

'I wouldn't lie to you, Dagorian.'

'But would you have felt relief?'

'You are torturing yourself unnecessarily,' said the black man. 'What is really at the heart of this?'

'I am afraid.' He looked into Nogusta's face. 'What is it that you have seen? I need to know.'

'You do not *need* to know,' Nogusta assured him. 'And it would serve no purpose to tell you. This gift I have is like a sharp sword. It can save a life, or it can take it. At this moment you and I are alive, and we have a mission. All we can do is try to stay alive. What I have seen, or not seen, is irrelevant.'

'That is simply not true,' said Dagorian. 'The future is not set in stone. You could, for example, have seen me walking on a particular cliff top. The ground gives way and I fall to my death. But if you warn me I will not walk on that cliff top. Then I will live.'

Nogusta shook his head. 'I told you once before that the gift is not that precise. I do not choose what to see.'

'I just want to know whether I will survive,' said Dagorian. 'Have you seen that, at least?'

'Ultimately no-one survives,' hissed Nogusta. 'That is the way of life. We are born, we live, we die. All that counts is the manner in which we live. And even that does not count for long. History will forget us. It forgets all men eventually. You want certainty? *That* is certainty.'

'I fear I may be a coward,' said Dagorian. 'I might run from this mission.'

'You will not run,' said Nogusta. 'You are a man of courage and honour. I know you are afraid. So you should be – for so am I. Our enemies are great in number, and our friends are few. Yet we will do what we must, for we are men, and the sons of men.'

The queen cried out again. Dagorian jerked at the sound, then pushed himself to his feet and walked from the camp.

For more than an hour the group waited, and there was little sound from within the roofless tent. Then Bison emerged, wandered to the fire and ate some of the hot oats Kebra had prepared for breakfast. The bowman approached him.

'What is happening?' asked Kebra.

'She is resting a little,' the giant told him.

'How soon will she have the child?'

Bison shrugged. 'The water sac has burst and the baby is on its way. How long? I don't know. Another hour. Perhaps two or three. Maybe more.'

'That's not very precise,' snapped Kebra. 'I thought you were an expert in this.'

'Expert? A few times doesn't make you an expert. All I know is that there are three stages to birthing. The first is under way. The baby is moving.'

'And the second?'

'The contractions will become more severe as the child enters the birth canal and on into the vagina.'

Kebra smiled. 'That's the first time I've ever heard you use the correct term.'

'I'm not in the mood for jokes at the moment,' said Bison. 'She's a slim girl, and this is the first child. There's likely to be a lot of torn flesh. And I know little of what to do if anything goes wrong. Has anyone tried again to wake the priestess?'

'I'll sit by her,' promised Kebra.

'You do that. Smack her face. Pour water on her. Anything.'

'As soon as she wakes I'll send her to you.'

Bison rose and ambled back to the tent. Kebra moved to the sleeping priestess. She was no longer bathed in sweat. Her skin was clear and firm, and Kebra was surprised to see how pretty she was now that the excess flesh was gone. And she looked so much younger. He had thought her to be in her forties, but now he saw she was – despite the grey in her blond hair – at least ten years younger. He took her hand and squeezed her fingers. 'Can you hear me, lady?' he said. But she did not stir.

The morning wore on, the sun climbing towards noon. Nogusta, normally so cool and in control, was pacing the camp. Once he approached the tent and called out to Bison. The response was short, coarse and to the point. Nogusta strode to the stream. Kebra, still unable to wake the priestess, joined him there.

'We are losing the time we gained at the bridge,' said Nogusta. 'If this goes on much longer the enemy will be upon us.'

'Bison doesn't know how long the labour will last. It could be hours yet.'

Nogusta suddenly smiled. 'Would you want Bison as the midwife to your first-born?'

'It is a ghastly thought,' admitted Kebra.

Chapter Nine

No nightmare ever suffered by Axiana had been worse than this. Her dress removed, her bare feet pressing into the damp earth, her lower back a rhythmic sea of pain, she squatted like a peasant beneath an open sky. Her emotional state had been fragile ever since the horror of the events at the house of Kalizkan, and everything since had conspired to fill her with terrible fear. Her husband was dead, her life as a royal princess a diminishing memory. All her life she had been pampered, never knowing hunger or poverty; the heat of summer kept from her by servants with peacock fans, the cold of winter barred from the palace by warm fires and fine clothes of wool.

Only days ago she had been sitting in a padded satin chair amid the splendour of the royal apartments, servants everywhere. And despite her husband's disdain of her, she had been the queen of a great empire.

Now, naked and frightened, she squatted in a forest, racked with pain, and waiting to birth a king in the wet and the mud.

Beside her the giant, Bison, was supporting her weight. His ugly face was close to hers, and when she turned her head she could feel the coarseness of his bristling moustache against the skin of her face. His left hand was rubbing gently across the base of her spine, easing the pain there. Back in Usa Ulmenetha had showed her the satin covered birthing stool, and quietly explained all the processes of birth. It had almost seemed an adventure then. Fresh pain seared through her and she cried out.

'Don't breathe too fast,' said Bison. His gruff voice cut through her rising panic. The contractions continued, the rhythm of pain rising and falling. The girl, Pharis, lifted a cup to Axiana's lips. The water was cool and sweet. Sweat dripped into Axiana's eyes. Pharis wiped it away with a cloth.

Cramp stabbed through her right thigh. She reared up against Bison and screamed. 'My leg! My leg!' Lifting her easily he turned her to her back, leaning her against a fallen tree. Kneeling beside her his huge hands began to rub at the muscles above her knee. Pharis offered her more water. She shook her head. The humiliation was colossal. No man but her husband had ever seen her naked, and on that one night she had bathed in perfumed water and waited in a room lit with the light of three coloured lanterns. The light now was harsh and bright, and the ugly peasant was rubbing her thighs with his huge calloused hands.

And yet, she thought suddenly, he cares! Which is something Skanda never did.

Axiana remembered the night the king had come to her. He cared nothing that she was a virgin, untutored and unskilled. He had made no attempt to ease her fears, nor even arouse her. There had been no pleasure in the act. It had been painful and – thank the Source – short lived. He had not said a word throughout, and when he had finished he rose from her bed and stalked from the room. She had cried for hours.

Axiana felt dizzy. She opened her eyes to see bright lights dancing before her vision. 'Breathe slowly,' advised Bison. 'You'll pass out else. And we don't want that, do we?'

Pain flared once more, reaching new heights. 'There's blood! There's blood!' wailed Pharis.

'Of course there's blood,' snapped Bison. 'Just stay calm, girl. Go and fetch some more water!'

Axiana moaned. Bison leaned in to her. 'Try to think of something else,' he said. 'One of my wives used to chant. You know any chants?'

Anger replaced the pain in Axiana, roaring up like a forest fire. 'You oaf! You stupid . . .' Suddenly she let fly with a stream of coarse and obscene swear words, in both Drenai and Ventrian, words she had heard but had never before uttered; would never have believed herself capable of uttering. It was, as she had always believed, the language of the gutter. Bison was completely unfazed.

'My third wife used to talk like that,' he said. 'It's as good as a chant,' he added, brightly.

511

Axiana sagged against him, exhausted. All the years of nobility, the education and the instilled belief that nobles were a different species to mere mortals, peeled away from her, like the layers of an onion. She was an animal now, sweating, grunting and moaning; a creature without pride. Tears welled as the pain soared to fresh heights. 'I can't stand it!' she whispered. 'I can't!'

'Course you can. You're a brave girl. Course you can.' She swore at him again, repeating the same word over and over.

'That's good,' he said, with a grin. Her head sagged against his shoulder. His hand pushed back the sweat-drenched hair from her brow. More than anything else this one small gesture restored her courage. She was not alone. The pain eased momentarily.

'Where is Ulmenetha?' she asked Bison.

'She'll be here when she wakes. I don't know why she's still sleeping. Nogusta thinks it's magick of some kind. But I'm here. You can trust old Bison.'

Pharis leaned in and wiped her face, then offered her more water. Axiana drank gratefully.

The morning wore on, the sun passing noon and drifting slowly across the sky. For a time Bison lifted her once more to a kneeling position, but the cramps returned, and by mid-afternoon she was sitting once more with her back against the fallen tree. Her strength was almost gone, and she was floating in pain, semiconscious. She remembered her mother, the wan young face, the eyes dark circled. She had died in childbirth. Her son born dead, her body torn, her life blood draining away. Axiana had been six years old. Her nurse had brought her in to say goodbye. But her mother had been delirious, and had not recognized her. She had called out a name, screamed it loud. No-one knew who she was calling for.

She had been buried on a bright summer afternoon, her son beside her.

'I am going to die like her,' thought Axiana.

'No, you're not,' said Bison.

'I didn't . . . mean to say that . . . aloud,' whispered Axiana.

'You're not going to die, girl. In a little while I'll lay your son on your breast, and the sunlight will touch you both.'

'My . . . son.' The thought was a strange one. For the duration of her pregnancy Axiana had thought only of the *baby* inside her. Skanda's baby. Skanda's child. An object created by a virtual rape which had changed her young life.

My son is waiting to be born.

512

'I can see the head,' said Pharis. 'The baby is coming!'

Bison wiped away the sweat from Axiana's face. 'Do not push,' he said. 'Not yet.'

She heard the advice, but the urge to propel the obstruction from her body was overpowering. 'I can't . . . stop myself!' she told him, taking a deep breath.

'No!' he thundered. 'The head is not engaged fully.' Her face reddened with the effort of pushing. 'Pant!' he ordered her. 'Pant. Like this!' Pushing out his tongue he made quick shallow breaths.

'I'm not . . . a . . . dog!' she hissed at him.

'You'll damage the child if you don't. His head is soft. Now pant, damn you!' Summoning Pharis to support the queen's shoulders Bison moved back to observe the birth. The head was almost clear, and one shoulder. Then he saw the umbilical cord, tight around the baby's neck like a blue-grey serpent, choking the life away. His fingers were too thick and clumsy to dislodge it. Fear touched him then. Twice before he had observed this phenomenon. The first time a surgeon had cut the cord. The baby had lived, but the woman had died, for the afterbirth had not come away cleanly, remaining inside to rot and poison the blood. The second time the cord had effectively strangled the infant. 'Don't push!' he told the queen. Taking a deep breath Bison supported the infant's head with his left hand then, as gently as he could eased the little finger of his right hand under the cord. Twice it slipped back into place, but the third time he hooked it, drawing it carefully over the head.

With the threat removed Bison called out. 'Now you can push! Push like the Devil!'

Axiana grunted, then cried out as the baby slid clear into Bison's hands. The babe's face and body were covered in grease and blood. Swiftly Bison tied the umbilical cord, then cut it. Then he wiped the child's nostrils and mouth, clearing its airways. The babe's tiny arm moved, then it drew in its first breath.

A thin wail sounded into the forest.

Bison heard the sound of running feet outside the roofless tent. 'Stay back!' he yelled. He swung to Pharis. 'Get some fresh water.' Moving forward on his knees he laid the babe on Axiana's breast. Her arms went around it. Pharis was staring open mouthed at the tiny, wrinkled creature in the queen's arms. 'Get water, girl,' said Bison. 'You'll have plenty of time to gawp later.'

Pharis scrambled up and ran from the tent.

Axiana smiled at Bison. Then she began to sob. The old man kissed her brow. 'You did well,' he said, gruffly.

'So did you,' said Ulmenetha, from behind him.

Bison sucked in a deep breath and released his hold on the queen. Glancing up at the priestess he forced a grin. 'Well, if you really want to thank me . . .' he began.

Ulmenetha raised her hand to silence him. 'Do not spoil this moment, Bison,' she said, not unkindly. 'Go back to your friends. I will finish what you have done so well.' Bison sighed and pushed himself to his feet. He was tired now. Bone weary.

He wanted to say something to the queen, something to show how much these last few hours had meant to him; how proud he was of her, and how he would never forget what had happened here. He wanted to say he was privileged to have attended her.

But Ulmenetha had moved past him, and the queen was lying back with her eyes closed, her arms holding the infant king.

Bison walked silently from the tent.

Bakilas sat in the starlight, his pale body naked, the water burns on his ankles and feet healing slowly, the blisters fading. His three companions were sitting close by. Drasko's burns were more severe, but the bleeding had stopped. His horse had fallen as they forded the river, and only swift work by Lekor and Mandrak had saved him. They had hauled him clear, but the river water had penetrated the black armour, and was scorching the skin of his chest, belly and arms. Drasko's mood was not good as he sat with the group.

Pelicor's physical death, and return to the Great Void, had been amusing. The warrior had always been stupid and Bakilas had never felt any kinship with him. But the destruction of Nemor upon the bridge had cast a pall over the company. They had watched the huge old man charge the mounted warrior, and had felt their brother's terror as he fell through the flames and plummeted into the raging river. They had experienced the pain of his burns as the acid water ate away his skin and dissolved his flesh and bones.

Even with the probable success of Anharat's Great Spell bringing the Illohir back to the earth, it would still take hundreds of years for Pelicor and Nemor to build the psychic energy necessary to take form once more. Two of his brothers had become Windborn, and the enemy remained untouched. It was most galling.

Yet, at least, they now knew the source of the magick hurled against them. The blond-haired child. This, in itself, led to other questions. How could a child of such tender years master the power of *halignat*?

'What do we do now, brother?' asked Drasko.

'Do?' countered Bakilas. 'Nothing has changed. We find the child and return it to Anharat.'

Drasko idly rubbed at the healing wound on his shoulder. 'With respect, I disagree. We are all warriors here, and in battle can face any ten humans. But this is not a battle. Two of our number have returned to the Other Place, their forms lost to them. And we are no closer to completing our mission.'

'They will have to fight us,' said Bakilas. 'They cannot run for ever. And once we face them they will die.'

'I am not so sure,' said Mandrak. 'They may be old, but did you feel the power of their spirits? These men are warrior born. There is no give in them. Such men are dangerous.'

Bakilas was surprised. 'You think they can stand against the Krayakin?'

Mandrak shrugged. 'Ultimately? Of course not. But we are not invincible, brother. Others of us may lose our forms before this mission is done.'

Bakilas considered his words, then turned to the fourth of the group. 'What do you say, Lekor?'

The thin-faced warrior looked up. 'I agree with Mandrak,' he said, his voice deep as distant thunder. 'I too saw the spirits at the bridge. These men will not die easily. They will choose their own battleground, and we have no choice but to follow them. Then there is the question of the sorcery. Who is the power behind the child?'

The night breeze shifted. Mandrak's nostrils flared. With one smooth move he threw himself to his right, and rolled to his feet alongside where his armour lay. The others had moved almost as swiftly, and when the men emerged from the tree line the naked Krayakin were waiting for them, swords in hands.

There were a dozen men in the group, all roughly dressed in homespun clothing, and jerkins of animal skins. The leader, a large man with a forked black beard, wore a helm fashioned from a wolf's head. Three of the men had bows drawn, the others held knives or swords and one was hefting a curved sickle. 'Well, what have we here?' said the leader. 'Four naked knights on a moonlight tryst. Perverse, if you ask me.' His men chuckled obediently.

'Put down your swords, gentlemen,' he told the Krayakin. 'You are outnumbered, and once we have divested you of your horses and gold we will let you go.'

Bakilas spoke, but not to the man. 'Kill them all – save for the leader,' he said.

Instantly the four Krayakin warriors leapt at the startled men. One bowman loosed a shaft, but Bakilas's sword flashed in the night air, snapping the arrow in two. Then he was among the robbers, his sword cleaving left and right. One man died, his neck severed, a second fell to the ground, his chest gaping open. Mandrak blocked a savage cut from the leader's sword, then stepped inside and hammered a straight left to the man's face, breaking his nose. The leader staggered. Mandrak leaned back, then leapt, his right foot thundering against the leader's chin. The man went down as if poleaxed. Drasko killed two men, then lanced his sword through the back of another as the man turned to run.

Within moments the battle was over. Four survivors had fled into the forest, and seven men lay dead upon the grass. Bakilas moved to the unconscious leader, flipping the man with his foot. The leader grunted and struggled to sit up. Still dazed he rubbed his chin. Then, incongruously he cast around for his fallen helm. Setting it upon his head he pushed himself to his feet. He saw the dead men lying where they had fallen. He tried to run, but Mandrak was quicker, grabbing him by his jerkin and hurling him to the ground. 'What are you going to do with me?' he wailed.

Bakilas stepped up to the man, hauling him to his feet. 'We need to contact our leader,' he said, softly. 'You can help us with that task.'

'Anything,' said the man. 'Just ask.'

Bakilas took hold of the man's shirt and ripped it open, exposing his naked chest. He traced a line down the skin, locating the man's sternum. Slamming his fingers into the man's chest he split the skin beneath the breast bone. His hand drove in like a blade, then opened for his long fingers to encircle the still beating heart. With one wrench he tore the organ free. Letting the body sink to the grass he held up the dripping heart. 'Anharat!' he called. 'Speak to your brothers!'

The heart rose from Bakilas's hand and burst into a bright flame which soared up above the clearing. Then it coalesced into a ball and slowly dropped to hover above the warriors.

'I am here,' said a voice that whispered like a cold wind across a graveyard.

The Krayakin sat in a circle around the flame. 'Two of our company are Windborn once more,' said Bakilas. 'We would appreciate your guidance.'

'The child is born,' said the voice of Anharat. 'The route to the sea is cut off, and they must journey south. I am marching with the army to the city of Lem. There we will sacrifice the child. His blood will flow upon my own altar.'

'What of the wizard who is helping them?' asked Drasko.

'There is no wizard. The soul of Kalizkan possessed the child, but he is now gone to the Halls of the Dead. He will not return. Continue south. I have also returned a *gogarin* to the forest ahead of them. They will not pass him.'

'We need no help, brother,' said Bakilas. 'And a *gogarin* could kill them all – the babe included.'

'They will not be foolish enough to attempt to pass the beast,' said Anharat. 'Not once they know it is there. And I shall see that they do.'

'You are taking a great risk, Anharat. What if it does kill the babe?'

'I have already begun the Spell,' said the voice of the Demon Lord. 'It hangs in the air awaiting only the death of the third king. If the babe is killed before the time of sacrifice there will still be enough power released to bring back more than two-thirds of the Illohir. Now find them, and bring the babe to my altar.'

The flame faded, becoming thick, black smoke, which drifted in the air before slowly dispersing.

'The city of Lem,' said Drasko. 'Not a place of good omens.'

'Let us ride, brothers,' said Bakilas.

Nogusta drew rein at the mouth of the great canyon, and for several moments all his fears and tensions disappeared, swamped by the awesome beauty before him. The ancient map had shown a canyon here, and a trade road winding through it, but nothing etched on paper could have prepared Nogusta for the sheer majesty before him. Towering peaks, cloaked with trees and crowned by snow, deep valleys, full of lush grass and glittering streams and rivers, filled his field of vision.

The road continued along a wide ridge, steadily climbing and twisting around a mountain. At each curve a new panorama greeted him. The canyon was colossal.

Nogusta rode on, lost in the natural splendour of this high country. He felt young again, clean air filling his lungs, long-forgotten dreams rising from the dusty halls of his memory. This was a place for a man to live!

Starfire too seemed to be enjoying the ride. The great black gelding had been increasing in strength for some days now and, though still a shadow of his former self, the horse was swiftly recovering from the lung infection that had condemned him to the slaughterhouse. Nogusta dismounted and walked to the rim, staring down at the forest and river below. What were the dreams of men when compared to this, he wondered?

The wagon was an hour behind him, and he found himself growing angry. How had he become chained to this doomed quest? The answers were obvious, but offered little comfort. For life to have meaning a man needed a code to live by. Without it he was just a small, greedy creature following his whims and desires to the detriment of those around him. Nogusta's code was iron. And it meant he could not ride away and leave his friends and the others to the fate that so obviously awaited them somewhere along the road.

He had told the boy, Conalin, his reasons for helping the queen were selfish – and so they were. He remembered the day his father had taken the family to the Great Museum in Drenan. They had viewed the exhibits, the ancient swords and statues, the gilded scrolls and the many bones, and at last his father had led them to the Sickle Lake, and there they had sat, eating a lunch of bread and cold roast meat. It was his tenth birthday. He had asked his father about the heroes, whose lives were celebrated at the museum. He had wondered what made them stand and die for their beliefs. His father's answer had been long-winded, and much of it had passed over the boy's head. But there was one, striking, visual memory. His father had taken his mother's hand mirror and placed it in Nogusta's hand. 'Look into it, and tell me what you see,' he said. Nogusta had seen his own reflection, and told him so.

'Do you like what you see?' his father had asked. It was a strange question. He was seeing himself.

'Of course I do. It's me!'

Then his father said: 'Are you proud of what you see?' Nogusta couldn't answer that. His father smiled. 'That is the true secret that carries a hero to deeds other men can only envy. You must always be able to look in a mirror and feel pride. When faced with peril you ask yourself, if I run, or hide, or beg or plead for life, will I still be able to look into a mirror and feel pride?'

Stepping into the saddle Nogusta rode on. The ridge road dipped steeply and Starfire's hoofs slipped on the stone. Riding with care the black warrior reached the canyon floor, and an old stone bridge that crossed the river. He was riding under the trees now, and stopped to examine the map once more. There was a second bridge marked, some 3 or 4 miles to the south-east. He decided to examine it before heading back to the wagon. There were still patches of snow upon the hillsides, and the air was cool as he heeled Starfire forward. The old road ran alongside a steep incline, then disappeared round the flanks of the hill.

Knowing he could see more of the land from higher ground Nogusta took hold of the pommel and ran the gelding up the slope. Starfire was breathing heavily as he crested the hill and Nogusta paused to allow the gelding to catch his breath.

Then he saw the cabin, set back in the trees, its walls built of natural stone, its roof covered with earth. Climbing ivy clung to the walls, and flowering shrubs had been set beneath the windows. The area around the cabin was well tended, and smoke drifted lazily from the stone chimney. Nogusta hesitated. He did not want to bring danger to any innocent mountain folk, but equally they would know the mountains and be able to advise him on the best route to Lem. Touching heels to Starfire he rode forward, but the horse grew nervous as they cleared the trees, and backed away.

Nogusta spoke soothingly to the animal, stroking the long black neck. Once in the clearing before the cabin he could see why Starfire was reluctant to approach the house. Partly hidden by a tall flowering shrub lay a blood-drenched body. He saw it was that of a man – or rather the remains of a man. The corpse was in two halves. Dismounting and holding on to the reins Nogusta approached it, kneeling to examine the tracks around it. The earth was hard, and little could be seen. The man was around twenty years of age. In his right hand there was a rusty sword. He had known then that he was under attack, and had faced his killer. Ragged talon marks showed across his chest and belly. He had literally been cut in half at the stomach by one violent slashing blow. Nogusta glanced to the right. Blood had spattered the ground at least 20 feet from the scene of death. No bear could have done this. Still holding on to the reins Nogusta moved to the cabin. The door had been caved in, the thick timbers smashed to shards. To the right the door frame had been torn away, and a section of wall caved in. Within the main room lay the partially consumed body of a woman.

Looping the reins over a fence rail Nogusta entered the cabin. He had seen great horror in his life, from the murder of his wife and family, to the victims of sacked cities, and the awesome, bloody aftermath of great battles. But there was here, in this grim tableau, a sadness that touched him deeply. The cabin was old, but had been lovingly restored by this young couple. They had turned a deserted ruin into a home. They had planted bright flowers, some of them inappropriate to forest soil, blooms that would never take root, but would wither and die here. This young couple were not expert, but they were romantic and hard working. Eventually they might have made a good living here. But something had come upon them. Something unexpected and deadly. The man had taken his sword and tried to defend his love. He had failed, and had died knowing his failure.

The woman had hidden behind a strong locked door, and had seen it smashed to shards. The beast had been too large to pass through the doorway, and had caved in the wall. The woman had tried to run through to the back of the house. Talons had swept across her back, ripping her apart. Death for both of them had been mercifully swift.

Nogusta returned to the sunlight and scanned the clearing. The blood was almost dry, but the attack on these people was very recent. He gazed at the tree line. There was a broken sapling there. Nogusta ran across the clearing. Here the earth was softer and he saw the footprint. Three times as long as that of a man, flaring wide at the toes. Talons had made deep gouges in the earth. The sapling, as thick as a man's arm, had been snapped cleanly, and a large bush had been uprooted by the charging beast. Back across the clearing Starfire whinnied. He pawed at the ground, his ears flat to his skull. Nogusta moved to the horse, unlooping the reins. The breeze shifted. Starfire reared suddenly. Taking hold of the pommel Nogusta vaulted to the saddle. He felt heat flare against his chest, and realized the talisman he wore was beginning to glow.

Beyond the cabin, to the north he saw tall trees swaying, and heard the splintering of wood. A hideous screeching began, and the ground trembled beneath the horse. Swinging Starfire he let the horse have its head. Starfire needed no urging, and launched himself into a run. Behind them something colossal burst from the undergrowth. Nogusta could not risk glancing back, as Starfire was galloping over rough ground towards the trees. But he could hear the beast bearing down upon them with terrible speed. Ducking under a low branch he headed for the road, urging the gelding on. Starfire was tired now, but his hoofs pounded the ground and he quickened. Nogusta rode down the incline at breakneck pace, Starfire slithering to his haunches. Only brilliant horsemanship kept Nogusta from being hurled from the saddle. Then they were on flat ground and riding towards the ridge road. Here Nogusta swung Starfire once more.

There was no sign of pursuit, and the talisman was no longer glowing.

What kind of an animal was strong enough to cut a man in half, fast enough to chase a horse as swift as Starfire, and evil enough to cause a reaction in his talisman?

Nogusta had no answer.

All he knew was that this beast stood between the wagon and the bridge.

And there was no other known route to safety.

Axiana was sleeping as the wagon slowly lumbered along the old road. Ulmenetha laid her now slender hand on the queen's brow. Axiana's life force was strong, radiating from her. The priestess leaned back against a pillow of empty sacks and stared up at the blue sky. The sensation of waking from her long life with Kalizkan had been disorientating in the extreme. The old wizard had told her that time had no meaning where they sat, but she had not understood it fully until she woke. It was as if she had slept for decades. The memories of the flight from the palace seemed to belong to another life, a distant existence. Ulmenetha had struggled to recall them. Equally she could not quite remember the fat, frightened woman she had been.

The girl, Pharis, was holding the infant, and the child Sufia was asleep beside her.

'Isn't he beautiful?' said Pharis. 'So small, so sweet.'

'He is beautiful,' agreed Ulmenetha. 'And so are you.' The girl glanced up, confused. Her face was thin, pinched and dirty, and her filthy hair hung in greasy rat's tails. Her clothes were rags and there were sores upon her bony shoulders. 'I am not mocking you, Pharis,' said Ulmenetha. 'You have great love within you, and that is a virtue of great beauty. Be sure to support the babe's head, for his neck is not strong.'

'I will,' she said, happily. 'I am holding a king!'

'You are holding an infant. Titles are bestowed by men, and no title would concern him now. What he needs is love and his mother's milk.'

Ulmenetha glanced back to where Kebra and Conalin were riding behind the wagon. The boy was riding close to Kebra, listening to the bowman. With the talent Kalizkan had inspired in her Ulmenetha could see so much more than the naked eye would allow. Conalin had been starved of affection all his life, and had never known the love of a father. Kebra was a quiet, lonely man, frightened to commit himself to a wife and family. The two were perfect for one another. She transferred her gaze to Dagorian. The young officer was well to the rear, leading the five spare horses. He was full of fear, and fighting to maintain his courage.

You should have remained a priest, thought Ulmenetha, for you are a gentle soul.

Rising she climbed across to sit beside Bison. He glanced at her and gave a crooked smile. 'How's my boy doing?' he asked.

'He is sleeping. Where did you learn to birth a child?'

'Here and there. The camp followers always used to call for me when a babe was due. Only ever had one die on me. Cord strangled it. Almost happened with our little prince. Apart from that, though, the camp whores thought I was a good-luck omen at a birth.'

The wagon emerged onto open ground and in the distance Ulmenetha could see the awesome majesty of the canyon. 'How did you get so thin?' asked Bison.

'It is a long story. How did you get so ugly?' She said it with a smile and Bison chuckled.

'I was born ugly,' he said, 'but I was also born strong. I'm still strong. Stronger than most men half my age.'

'How old are you?'

'Fifty,' he lied.

'You are sixty-six,' she said, 'and I see no reason to be ashamed of the fact. And you are quite right, you are stronger than most men half your age. You are also a better man than you like to admit. So let's have no more stupidity.'

'Well, I am stupid,' he said. 'Always have been. Nogusta and Kebra they talk about things I don't understand. Honour and such like. Philosophy. Goes over my head like a flight of geese. I'm just a soldier. I don't know anything else. I don't want to know anything else. I eat when I'm hungry, piss when my bladder's full, and rut when I can afford the price. That's all life is for me. And it's all I want.'

'That is just not true,' said Ulmenetha. 'You have friends, and you stand by them. You have ideals, and you live by those. You are not terribly honest, but you are loyal.' She fell silent and studied his profile, then focused as Kalizkan had taught her. Vivid images appeared in her mind, bright with colour. Random scenes from Bison's life sped across her vision. Honing her concentration she slowed them. Most were what she would have expected, lust or violence, drunkenness or debauchery. But, here and there, she found more edifying scenes. She spoke again. 'Six years ago you came upon four men raping a woman. You saved her, and received two stab wounds which almost killed you.'

'How do you know that? Did Kebra tell you?'

'No-one needed to tell me. I know many things now, Bison. I can see more clearly than I ever have before. In fact, more clearly than I would wish to. What is your greatest dream?'

'I don't have dreams.'

'When you were a child. What did you dream of?'

'Flying like a bird,' he said, with a wide, gap-toothed grin. 'I'd spread my wings and soar through the sky, feel the wind in my face. I'd be free.'

The child, Sufia, came climbing over the backrest. 'Did you really have wings?' she asked Bison, as she scrambled onto his lap.

'I had great big wings,' he said. 'White wings, and I flew over mountains.'

'I'd like big wings,' said Sufia. 'I'd like white wings. Will you take me flying with you?'

'I don't fly any more,' he said, ruffling her blond hair. 'When you get old and fat you lose your wings.' He glanced at Ulmenetha. 'Isn't that right?'

'Sometimes,' she agreed.

Sufia snuggled up against Bison, holding on to his heavy, black woollen jerkin. He glanced at Ulmenetha. 'Children like me. They're not so bright, are they?'

'Children can make mistakes,' she agreed. 'But, in the main, they know a protector.' Ulmenetha gazed fondly down upon the child. Her heart was weak, and, under normal circumstances, she would be unlikely to reach puberty. Reaching out she laid her hand on Sufia's head, and, for the first time, released the power that Kalizkan had taught her. 'There is a force in all of us,'

523

Kalizkan had told her. 'The Chiatze call it *tshi*. It is invisible, and yet terribly potent. It maintains our lives and our health. It helps us to repair damaged tissue.'

'Why did it not work for you?' she asked.

'Man is not intended to be immortal, Ulmenetha. The cancer came on too fast, and too powerfully. However, mastery of the *tshi* is an invaluable tool for a healer.'

Ulmenetha focused her energies, flowing her own *tshi* into the child.

'Your hand is very hot,' said Sufia. 'It's nice.'

Ulmenetha relaxed as she felt the child's fluttering heart grow stronger. It was not healed as yet, but it would be.

'I preferred you with more meat on you,' said Bison. 'But you do look younger.' He was about to speak again but Ulmenetha gave him a warning glance.

'Remember,' she said, 'no more stupidities.'

'If you don't ask you don't get,' he said, with a grin.

Up ahead she saw Nogusta walking his horse towards them. Ulmenetha could sense his concern. The black warrior was a powerful man, not given to despair and negative thoughts. But now his spirits were at a low ebb. Dagorian, Kebra and Conalin rode around the wagon to meet him. Bison hauled on the reins. Swiftly Nogusta told them of the killings at the cabin, and the beast that had pursued him.

'Did you get a look at it?' asked Bison.

'No,' said Nogusta. 'Had I waited a heartbeat longer I would have been as dead as the two lovers I found.'

'You're sure it wasn't just a bear?' said Bison.

'If so it is the mother of all bears. But no, I do not think it a creature of this world. Nothing I know of – or have heard of – could cut a grown man in half with one sweep.'

'What do we do then?' asked Dagorian. 'Find another way through?'

Nogusta drew in a deep breath. 'I do not see that we can. Firstly the maps do not show a second route. Secondly – even if there are other routes – if the beast was sent against us specifically there may be others of his kind guarding them. And last, but by no means least, we do not have the strength or the weapons to fight, on open ground, the warriors trailing us. And they must be getting close now.'

'Well, this is all very jolly,' snapped Bison. 'What more bastard luck can we expect? An outbreak of plague among us?'

'What choices do we have?' asked Kebra. 'We can't go back, we can't go forward, and if we stay here the Krayakin will kill us. For once I'm in agreement with Bison – luck seems to be running against us.'

'We are still alive,' said Nogusta. 'And we do have choices. The question is, which one gives us the best hope of success.'

'We cannot go back,' said Ulmenetha. 'Therefore we must face the beast.'

'With what?' queried Bison.

'With magick and with lances,' she said.

'I like the sound of the magick part,' said Bison.

'What do you have in mind, lady?' asked Kebra.

'Explanations will need to wait. One group of the Krayakin are less than two hours behind us. Ride back to the trees and fashion three long lances. Make sure the wood is stout and strong.'

Kebra swung his horse and rode back to the woods. Dagorian followed him, but Nogusta hesitated.

'Take the wagon on into the canyon, but do not leave the main road,' Ulmenetha ordered Bison. He glanced at Nogusta for confirmation. The black man nodded. Then he too rode to the woods.

'If you can kill it with magick,' said Bison, 'why do we need lances?'

'I cannot *kill* it,' she told him. 'What I can do is cast a spell that masks our scent and renders us almost invisible.'

'*Almost* invisible?'

'If the beast is close he will see a disturbance in the air around us – like a heat haze.'

'I don't want to go near any beasts,' wailed Sufia. Bison lifted her to his shoulder.

'No beast can get you while old Bison is here,' he said. 'I'll bite his head off.'

'You haven't got any front teeth,' she pointed out.

'No, but I've got tough old gums,' he said, with a chuckle.

The lances they cut were around 8 feet long, strong but unwieldy. Nogusta and Kebra strapped knives to the tips, and Nogusta added more twine around the lower haft, creating a hand grip. Dagorian's lance was more primitive, 7 feet in length the wood sharpened to a jagged point. As the wagon rolled slowly along the ridge road Nogusta and Kebra rode ahead, the bases of their lances resting on the saddle stirrups. There was little conversation.

Axiana, Pharis and Sufia sat in the wagon, Conalin with them, his horse tied to the rear.

'I could have cut a lance,' said the boy.

'You don't have the skill with horses yet,' said Bison. 'When horses get frightened they take a deal of handling. You couldn't do that and wield a lance.' Conalin was unconvinced, but he said no more.

The light was fading as they neared the lower road. Nogusta and Kebra drew rein and the black warrior turned his mount and rode back to the wagon. He was about to ask when Ulmenetha needed to cast her spell, but she signalled him to silence. He was momentarily confused. Then she asked him. 'How is your chest?'

'My chest? It is fine.'

'No sensation of heat? How strange, for there should be.'

For a moment he thought she had lost her senses. Then he felt the talisman glowing. Ulmenetha touched her lips then her ear. Nogusta understood immediately. They were being observed, and overheard.

'I am feeling much better,' he said. 'I think it must have been a spring chill.'

'Spring chill?' said Bison. 'What the . . . ?' Ulmenetha's hand came down upon his in a sharp pinch.

'Do not speak,' she said, softly. Bison cast a glance at Nogusta and was about to disobey Ulmenetha when Kebra's horse suddenly reared, half pitching the bowman from the saddle. Dropping his lance Kebra clung to the pommel. The horse backed away.

Upon the road ahead a glowing figure had appeared, almost 7 feet high, black wings spreading from its shoulders, like a massive cloak fluttering in the breeze. The face was dark, wide at the brow, narrow at the chin, an inverted black triangle with a wide gash of a mouth, and high slanted eyes, burning like coals.

'It is only an image,' whispered Ulmenetha. But Nogusta did not hear her. He drew a throwing knife and hurled it with all his might. The blade flashed through the dusk air, cutting through the apparition and clattering to the road beyond.

'You cannot harm me, human,' said the demon. The black wings spread wide and it rose into the air, floating close to the wagon. The creature peered inside, his gaze fixed to the babe carried by Axiana. Sufia screamed and buried herself under some blankets. The horses were growing uneasy. The demonic creature hovered for a moment, then drew back. 'It is not necessary for you all to die,' he said. 'What will it achieve? Can you stop me? No. Why then do you struggle on? Behind you – oh so close behind you – are my Krayakin. Ahead is a *gogarin*. Do you need me to explain the nature of such creatures? Or do the legends persist?'

'It was a beast with six legs,' said Nogusta. 'It was said to weigh as much as three tall horses.'

'Five would be closer,' said the apparition. He floated close to Nogusta, the burning eyes glittering. 'Yes, you look like him,' he said, and Nogusta could feel the hatred in the voice. 'The last of his mongrel line.' He moved away again. 'But I was speaking of the *gogarin*. It is a creature unlike all others upon this earth. Eternally hungry it will eat anything that lives and breathes. Nothing can approach it, for it radiates terror. Strong men fall to their knees at its approach, spilling their urine to drench their leggings. You cannot defeat it with your pitiful spears. I watched you flee from it earlier today. You, at least, understand what I am saying. Your heart was beating like a war drum – and that was without seeing the beast. Soon you will see it. And then you will all die.'

'What is the alternative you offer?' asked Nogusta.

'Merely life. For you have already lost. Had you the smallest chance of success I might offer riches, or perhaps even an extra hundred years of youth. I know that would appeal to your bald friend. But I need offer nothing more. The babe is mine. Leave it and its mother by the roadside. Then you can travel on to wherever you choose. My Krayakin will not harm you, and I will draw the *gogarin* back from this place. You also have my word that no harm will befall the queen.'

'I do not believe you,' said the warrior.

'I do not blame you for that,' the apparition told him, 'but it is the truth. I can also say that I will not be displeased should you reject my offer. You cannot stop me taking the babe, and it will give me great pleasure to see you die, Nogusta. Your ancestor – of cursed memory – visited a great evil upon my people, ripping their souls from the joys of this planet, and consigning them to an eternity of *Nothing*. No breath, no touch of flesh upon flesh, no hunger, no pain, no emotion – no life!' The apparition fell silent for a moment, and seemed to be struggling to contain his anger. 'Ride on,' he said, at last. 'Ride on and die for me. But do you really wish to take your friends to their deaths? They do not carry your blood guilt. They did not betray their race. Do they not deserve a chance to live?'

'My friends can speak for themselves,' said Nogusta.

The winged demon floated close to Bison. 'Do you wish to live?' he asked him. Ignoring the demon Bison lifted his buttocks from the driver's seat and broke wind thunderously.

'By Heaven, that's better,' he said. 'Are we moving on, or what?'

'I think we should,' said Ulmenetha, 'the stench is over-powering.'

'It was those wild onions,' said Bison, apologetically.

'Not from you . . . fool!' she snapped.

The demon drew back and hovered before Nogusta. Starfire whinnied and backed away. Nogusta calmed him. 'I would like to stay to watch you die,' said the apparition. 'But the body I have chosen waits for me some miles back – with the Ventrian army. Be assured, however, your passing will be painful. Not as painful, you understand, as I made it for your family. You should have seen them trying to flee the flames. Your wife was running along a corridor, her hair and her dress ablaze. Her screams were delightful. Her flesh burned like a great candle.'

There was a sudden gust of wind, and the apparition dis-appeared.

'That was Anharat, the Demon Lord,' said Ulmenetha. 'He it was who possessed Kalizkan, and brought such evil to the city.'

Nogusta did not respond at first. His face was streaked with sweat, and his face was set. When he did speak his voice was colder than the tomb. 'He killed my family. He watched them burn.'

'He has killed many families. Thousands upon thousands,' said Ulmenetha. 'His evil is colossal.' Nogusta took a deep, calming breath.

'What did he mean about my ancestor?'

'He was talking about Emsharas – his own brother. He it was who cast the first Great Spell.'

'His brother? Are you saying that my ancestor was a demon?'

'I have no answers for you, Nogusta. Little is known of Emsharas, save that he is considered the Father of Healers, and that his magick was holy. He was certainly of the Illohir, the Windborn.'

'Then I have demon blood in my veins?'

'Forget about demons!' she snapped. 'That is not important now. Why do you think he came to us? It was to instil fear, to cause torment and disquiet. You must overcome such thoughts.

Any anger or rage you feel will only add to our danger, increasing the chances of the *gogarin* to sense our presence.'

'I understand,' said Nogusta. 'Let us move on.'

'When we reach the foot of the slope,' said Ulmenetha, 'you must ride close to the wagon. The spell will only extend a few feet. We must be as quiet as possible.' Nogusta nodded, then rode ahead and retrieved his lance and the thrown dagger.

'Can we kill this *gogarin* if necessary?' Bison asked Ulmenetha.

'I don't know.'

'Could he really give me another hundred years of youth?'

'I don't know that either. Does it matter?'

'Nice thought,' said Bison, lifting the reins and snapping them down to the backs of the waiting team. They lurched forward and the wagon moved slowly on down towards the canyon floor.

In the distance storm clouds were gathering, and a rumble of thunder echoed over the mountains.

At the foot of the slope Ulmenetha climbed down from the wagon and kicked off her shoes, feeling the soft earth beneath her feet. Relaxing she drew on the power of the land. The magick here was weak, and this surprised her. It was as if the flow was being blocked. She wondered then if Anharat's power had affected the magick. Surely not. Squatting down she dug her hand into the earth. Her fingers struck something hard and flat. She smiled with relief. They were upon the old trade road. Over the centuries earth had covered the flagstones, and it was these buried stones that blocked her. Stepping from the old road she walked to a grove of nearby trees. The magick here was strong and ancient, and she drew upon it, feeling it flow through her legs, and up through the veins and arteries, swelling and surging. It was almost too strong, like fine wine, and she reached out to hold fast to the trunk of a tree.

Thunder rumbled to the south. Moving away from the trees she strode to the front of the wagon, and positioned herself to the left of the team. Nogusta, Kebra and Dagorian rode in close upon her command. Raising her hand she cast the spell. It was not especially difficult to create, but once created it needed to be held in place. The air around the wagon shimmered. Ulmenetha glanced back. She could no longer see the others. Reaching up she ran her hand along the sleek, near invisible, neck of the horse beside her, and curled her fingers around the bridle. 'Let no-one speak from now until I give the word,' she said. 'Let us go!'

She heard the reins slap upon the backs of the team, and, holding to the bridle she walked on towards the forest. The soft footfalls of the horses seemed as loud to her as the distant thunder, and the soft creaking of the wagon wheels swelled in her mind. Be calm, she warned herself, the thunder and the wind in the trees will mask the sounds.

The sky darkened, the storm moving over the forest. Lightning flashed, lighting up the forest road. A horse snorted in fear, and she heard Kebra soothe it with soft, whispered words. Ahead was the slope down which Nogusta had fled the beast. The wagon continued on, slowly.

Rain began to slash down from the heavy clouds above. Ulmenetha welcomed it. The sound covered them like a blanket.

Holding to the spell she walked on.

From above came the sound of splintering wood, and a high screeching cry that tore against Ulmenetha's ear drums, causing her knees to tremble. She dragged back on the bridle, halting the team. The screeching continued. One of the horses whinnied in terror. The screeching died away instantly, and a terrible silence followed. Ulmenetha glanced up the slope. Trees were swaying there. Fear threatened to swamp her, but she held fast to the spell.

Lightning flashed. Two of the horses snorted and stamped their hooves.

Some 30 feet above the wagon a huge, wedge shaped head emerged from the trees. Ulmenetha could see only the silhouette against the dark sky, but even above the lashing wind she could hear it snuffling, sucking in the scents of the forest, seeking out its prey.

The rain eased, and a break in the clouds allowed moonlight to bathe the scene. Ulmenetha stood very still, staring up at the great head. From the serpentine shape she had expected it to be scaled like a reptile. But it was not. Its skin was corpse white and almost translucent, and she could see the large bones of its neck pushing against the skin. The pale head twisted on its long neck, and she found herself staring into a slanted blue eye as large as a man's head. The pupil was round and black, and horribly human. The *gogarin* stared unblinking down towards the road. Then the head withdrew into the trees, and she heard again the splintering of wood as its enormous bulk crashed back through the forest. Tugging on the bridle she urged the wagon on, following the road around the base of the slope.

The storm swept on towards the north, the rain dying away.

Breaks in the cloud cover came more often now, and the company kept moving towards the distant bridge and safety.

For an hour they plodded on. Ulmenetha was tired now, and finding it difficult to maintain the spell. The flagstones beneath the earth of the road did not allow her to replenish her power, and twice the spell faltered. She halted the team and softly called out to Nogusta.

'Does your talisman glow?'

'No,' came the response.

'I must draw power from the land. I need to leave the road.'

Releasing the bridle she ran to the roadside. Immediately the wagon and the surrounding riders became visible. Ulmenetha sank to her knees, pushing her hands into the earth. Unlike before the power seeped slowly, and she felt the tension rise in her. Her fear slowed the flow even more. She fought for calm, but it eluded her. 'Be swift!' called Nogusta. 'The talisman grows warm!'

Ulmenetha sucked in a deep breath, and sent up a swift prayer. The energy she sought had touched her blood, but it was not enough! Rising she ran towards the wagon and took hold of the bridle once more. She could hear the beast's approach now, as it crashed through the undergrowth. Fear made her falter on the third line of the spell, and she began it again.

The magick surged from her, flowing over the wagon and riders.

In the bright moonlight the *gogarin* emerged from the trees to the road ahead. Now they could all see it fully. It was over 20 feet long. Nogusta had earlier described it as having six legs, but Ulmenetha saw that this was not quite so. The hind and middle legs were powerful and treble jointed, but the limbs at the beast's shoulders were more like long arms, equipped with murderous talons, each as long as a cavalry sabre. Rearing up on its hind legs it sniffed the night breeze. One of the spare horses, tied to the rear of the wagon, reared in terror, snapping its reins. Turning, it galloped from the road, and into the forest.

The *gogarin* reacted with sickening speed, dropping to all six limbs and propelling itself forward with incredible power. Ulmenetha stood stock still as it raced towards the wagon. Then it veered after the horse. Its mighty shoulder struck a young tree, uprooting it. Then it was gone behind them.

The horse galloped on, then Ulmenetha heard its death cry.

She could not move, and stood trembling beside the team.

Nogusta dismounted and carefully felt his way to her side. 'We must move,' he whispered. Ulmenetha did not reply. Yet even through her terror she maintained the spell. Nogusta led her to the front of the wagon and lifted her to the seat beside the near invisible Bison. Remounting his horse Nogusta rode to the head of the team and reached down for the bridle. At his encouragement the horses moved forward.

Ulmenetha could not stop the trembling in her hands. Her eyes were tight shut, and she almost cried out as Bison's large hand reached out and patted her leg. He leaned in to her and whispered. 'Big whoreson wasn't he.'

His voice was so calm, and the strength of the man seemed to flow with the sound. Ulmenetha felt herself growing calmer. She swung on her seat, gazing fearfully back down the trail. The wagon was moving very slowly, and, with every moment that passed the priestess expected to see the huge, white form of the *gogarin* lumbering out behind them.

They covered another half mile. Slowly the road began to rise, and they climbed to a second ridge road. The wagon filled almost two thirds of it. The horses were tired, and twice Bison was forced to lash them with the reins, forcing them on. The power was almost gone from Ulmenetha now. She tried to draw fresh strength from the mountains, but the old stone would not surrender its magick.

Licking her finger she raised it to the wind. It was blowing from behind them. Their scent could no longer carry back to the forest. With relief she let fall the spell.

'By Heaven, that's better,' whispered Bison.

The ridge road levelled out and Bison paused the team, allowing them to catch their breath. The moon was shining brightly now, and the forest was far below them.

A thin piping cry came from the back of the wagon, as the hungry babe awoke. Bison swore and swung round. Axiana was unbuttoning her dress. The babe's cries echoed in the mountains. The queen tore at the last two buttons, exposing her left breast. The infant calmed down and began to suckle. Bison swore again, and pointed back to the forest.

Far behind them the *gogarin* had emerged from the trees and was moving swiftly along the road.

Nogusta leapt from the saddle. 'Everyone out of the wagon!' he yelled. 'Kebra, help me unhitch the horses.' The bowman urged his horse forward, then dismounted. He did not even try to release the traces, but drew his dagger and cut them clear. Dagorian edged his horse around the wagon, then jumped down to assist him. Pharis helped the queen down, while Conalin swept up little Sufia and climbed over the side. Bison scrambled into the back of the wagon, picking up food sacks and blankets and hurling them to the roadside.

The giant glanced back down the steep incline. The *gogarin* was running towards them. It seemed small at this distance, a white hound against the moonlit grey of the rock road. The team clattered clear. Nogusta climbed to stand alongside Bison. In his hand was the heavy lance, tipped with a razor sharp throwing knife.

'You know what needs to be done,' said Nogusta. Bison looked into his friend's pale blue eyes.

'I know. Let me take the spear.'

'No! The talisman will protect me from the terror it radiates. Now get down – and set the wagon rolling on my signal.'

Bison jumped to the roadside and summoned Kebra and Dagorian. 'What is he doing?' asked the young officer, as Nogusta settled himself in the back of the wagon.

'He's going to ram it,' said Bison. Stepping back he dropped down behind the front wheels, judging the line which the wagon would follow once they started it down the slope. There was a slight curve to the right some 60 yards ahead. That would be the point where – if they misjudged the speed – the wagon would roll over the edge and plunge hundreds of feet down the mountainside. Sweat beaded Bison's brow and he wiped his sleeve across his face.

'Get ready!' shouted Nogusta. The three men put their shoulders to the vehicle.

On the rear of the wagon Nogusta hefted the lance. He too could see the curve in the road, and was trying to judge the speed of the approaching beast. There was little room for error here. If the wagon rolled too fast it would reach the curve before the *gogarin*, and Nogusta would die uselessly. If too late the wagon might not have picked up enough speed to hurl the creature out over the abyss. Nogusta's mouth was dry, and his heart was beating fast.

'Start her moving,' he called. The three men threw their weight against the wagon. It did not budge.

'The brake is on!' shouted Bison. Nogusta ran to the headboard

533

and vaulted to the driver's seat, pulling the brake clear. The wagon jolted forward. Nogusta almost fell, but then righted himself and ran back to the rear, taking up his lance. Valuable seconds had been lost.

'Push harder!' he commanded. The wagon began to gather speed. The *gogarin* rounded the curve, and saw the rumbling wagon approaching. Rearing up on its hind legs it let out a hideous screech. Nogusta felt the wave of terror strike him like a physical blow. It ripped through his mind and belly, and he screamed and fell to his knees. In all his life he had never known fear such as this. The spear dropped from his trembling fingers and he wanted to fall with it, burying his head in his hands, and squeezing shut his eyes. He could feel the talisman warm upon his skin, but it offered no help. In that moment, when despair threatened to unman him, he saw again the face of his wife, and remembered the Demon Lord's words, of how she had run through the flames. Anger came to his rescue, flaring in his belly and burning into his brain. Grabbing the lance he surged to his feet.

The wagon was almost upon the beast. The *gogarin* reared up high, then dropped to all six limbs, and charged. Nogusta braced himself for the impact. At the last second the *gogarin* reared again, its talons lashing out. The wooden side of the wagon exploded. Then the full weight of the vehicle struck the beast. Lance extended, Nogusta was catapulted forward. The dagger strapped to the lance sliced into the beast, the weapon driving deep into its shoulder. Nogusta's weight powered it on, the wood plunging deeper still. Then it snapped. Nogusta's flying body struck the *gogarin*'s neck, then sailed on to collide with the cliff wall. Searing pain burst through his shoulder as he fell to the road and slid towards the edge. His legs went over the side and he scrabbled for a hand hold. Glancing down he saw pine trees far below. His shoulder was numb, and there was no strength in his left hand. Fear touched him, but he quelled it, and relaxed. Then he slowly hauled himself back up to the ridge.

The *gogarin* had been driven to the lip of the road, and the beast was flailing at its wooden enemy, its sweeping talons ripping at the wagon, smashing it to shards. Nogusta pushed himself to his feet, staggered, then drew his sword and prepared to attack.

Bison came running into sight carrying a lance, followed by Kebra and Dagorian. The bowman sent a shaft slamming into the *gogarin*'s neck. Then Bison scrambled over the remains of the wagon and hurled himself at the beast. As the *gogarin* swung to meet this new attack its right hind foot slipped on the rock. The beast staggered, and tried to right itself. Bison's spear slammed against its chest, barely breaking the skin. But the giant's weight tipped the balance, and the lance propelled the creature back. The *gogarin* fell, tumbling through the air. Twice it crashed against the mountainside, then it soared clear and plunged through the branches of a tall pine, snapping the tree in two.

Bison leapt clear as the ruined wagon slid over the edge. He ran to Nogusta. 'Are you all right?' he asked.

The black man groaned as he tried to move his left shoulder. 'Just bruised, I hope,' he said. 'Is it dead?' Bison peered over the edge.

'I can't see it,' he said. 'But nothing could have survived that fall.'

Antikas Karios was not a man usually given to regrets. Life was life, and a man made the best of it. Yet, strangely, on this misty morning, as he sat on the stone wall of the old bridge, he found himself haunted by the ghosts of lost dreams. He had never before given much thought to the opinions of other men, or their criticisms of him. They had called him cruel, vengeful and merciless. The insults were never said to his face, but Antikas had heard them nonetheless, and had believed himself immune to them. No strong man would be affected by the sneers of lesser beings. As his father used to say, 'A lion is always followed by jackals.'

Antikas Karios had been a man with a mission, single-mindedly following a narrow road. There had been no time for introspection. No time for the casual niceties. No time for friendship. His mind and his time had been fully occupied with thoughts of freeing Ventria from the aggressor.

Not so now, as he gazed into the mist that rolled across the hills. Here in this lonely country there was time for little else but introspection.

He had been waiting by this bridge for two days now, directed here by the spirit of the sorcerer Kalizkan. 'Why do you not lead me directly to them?' he had asked.

'This is where you will be needed most.'

'Wherever they are they will be in peril. My sword could sway the balance.'

'Trust me, Antikas. Wait at the bridge. They will be with you in two days.' The spirit had left him then, and Antikas Karios had waited.

At first the beauty of the mountains had been pleasant to the eyes, and he felt calm, and ready to give his life to the cause of the queen. But as the hours passed on that first day he had found himself reappraising his life. It happened without conscious thought. He was sitting on the bridge, and he suddenly thought of Kara, and the plans they had made to build a home by the sea. Sweet, soft, gentle Kara. He had made her many promises, and had kept none of them. It was not that he had meant to lie. But the war with the Drenai had taken precedence. She should have understood that.

Dreams of love and family had been washed away in a tidal wave of patriotism, and then replaced by the dream of independence. Now both dreams were dust.

During the last five years memories of Kara had come often to him, but, as busy as he was, it had been easy to suppress them. Always there were plans and schemes that required his attention. But here, during these two, lonely, soul searching days, he had found it increasingly difficult to avoid his guilt.

He remembered the last time he had seen her.

'It was not cruelty or vengeance,' he said, aloud. 'She brought humiliation upon me. What then could she expect?' The words hung in the air, and echoed, unconvincingly, in his mind. Kara had written to him, ending their engagement. She had, she wrote, waited three years. She pointed out that Antikas had promised to return home within one year. He had not done so. Nor had he written for more than eight months. It was obvious that he no longer loved her, and she had now fallen in love with a young nobleman from a neighbouring estate. They were to be married within the month.

And married they were. Antikas had arrived late for the ceremony. He had approached them both as they walked hand in hand from the church, garlands of flowers around their necks. He had removed his heavy riding glove and had struck the groom across the face with it. The duel had taken place that evening and Antikas killed him.

That night he had been summoned to Kara's home. He found her sitting in a darkened room, the lanterns unlit, heavy velvet curtains blocking out the moonlight. A single candle burned on a small table, and by its flickering light he saw her, a heavy blanket wrapped around her slender frame. Antikas remembered how hard his heart had felt, and how he had decided to make no apology for her loss. Hers was the blame, not his. He was planning to make her aware of this. But she did not rail at him. She merely looked up in the gloom and stared at his face. There was no hatred in her, he realized, merely a great sadness. In the candlelight she looked exquisitely beautiful, and he had found himself wondering how he could ever have left her for so long. In his arrogance he believed that she had never truly loved the other man, but had accepted his offer knowing that Antikas would come for her. Now he had, and, if she begged him, he would take her back, despite the humiliation. He was prepared to be forgiving. But this scene was not what he had expected. Tears, yes. Anger? Of course. But this eerie silence was intolerable.

'What is it you want of me, lady?' he said.

Her voice when it came was a faint whisper. 'You are . . . an evil man . . . Antikas. But you will hurt us . . . no longer.' Her eyes held to his for a moment more, then they closed and her head sagged back. For a moment only he thought she had swooned. Then he saw the pool of blood around the base of the chair. Stepping forward he wrenched the blanket from her. Both her wrists were cut, and her clothes were drenched in blood. Still wearing her wedding dress and her garland, she had died without another word.

Antikas tried to push away the memory, but it clung to him like a poisoned vine. 'It was not evil,' he said. 'She should have waited for me. Then it would not have happened. I am not to blame.'

Who then do we blame? The thought leapt unbidden from his subconscious.

It had not ended there. Her brother had challenged Antikas. He too had died. Antikas had tried to disarm the boy, to wound him and stop the duel. But his attack had been ferocious and sustained, and, when the moment came, Antikas had responded with instinct rather than intent, his blade sinking into his opponent's heart.

Antikas Karios rose from the wall and turned to gaze down into the rushing water below. He saw the broken branch of an old oak floating there, drifting fast. It stuck for a moment against a jutting rock, then twisted free and continued on its way. Further down the bank a brown bear ambled out of the woods and waded into the water. Antikas watched it. Twice its paw splashed down. On the third time it caught a fish, propelling it out to the bank. The fish flopped against the earth, its tail thrashing wildly. The bear left the river and devoured the fish.

Antikas swung away and walked to where his horse was cropping grass. From his saddlebag he took the last of his rations.

Thoughts of Kara intruded as he ate, but this time he suppressed them, concentrating instead on the escape from Usa. Kalizkan's spirit had taken him first to an old church by the south wall, and there he had directed him to a secret room behind the altar. By the far wall was an ancient chest. It was not locked. The hinges were almost rusted through. One snapped as Antikas opened the lid. Inside were three scabbarded short swords, each wrapped in linen. Antikas removed them.

'These are the last of the Storm Swords,' said Kalizkan, 'created when the world was younger. They were fashioned by Emsharas the Sorcerer, for use against the demonic Krayakin.'

Antikas had carried them from the city to where the army was camped beyond. There he had obtained a horse and supplies and had ridden out into the mountains.

On his first night he had unwrapped one of the swords. The pommel was inset with a blue jewel, heavy and round, held in place by golden wire. The tang was covered by a wooden grip, wrapped in a pale, greyish white skin, while the upwardly curved quillons were deeply engraved with gold lettering. The scabbard was simple, and without adornment. Slowly Antikas drew the sword forth.

'Do not touch the blade!' warned the voice of Kalizkan. In the moonlight the blade was black, and, at first, Antikas believed it to be of tarnished silver. But, as he turned it, he saw the moon reflected brilliantly on its dark surface.

'What is the metal?' he asked Kalizkan.

'Not metal, child. Enchanted ebony,' replied the sorcerer. 'I don't know how he did it. It can cut through stone, yet it is made of wood.'

'Why is it called a Storm Sword?'

'Stand up and hold the flat of your hand just above the blade.'

Antikas did so. Colours swept along the ebony, then white blue lightning lanced up into his palm. In surprise he leapt back, dropping the sword. The point vanished into the earth, and only the curved quillons prevented the blade sinking from sight. Antikas drew it clear. Not a mark of mud had stained the sword. Once again he held his hand over it. Lightning danced to his skin.

There was no pain. The sensation was curious, and he noticed that the hairs on the back of his hand were tingling.

'What causes the small lightning?' he asked Kalizkan.

'I wish I knew. Emsharas was Windborn. He knew far more than any human sorcerer.'

'A demon? Yet he made swords to fight demons? Why would that be?'

'You have a penchant for asking questions I cannot answer. Whatever his reasons Emsharas allied himself with the Three Kings, and he it was who cast the Great Spell that banished all demons from the earth.'

'Including himself?'

'Indeed so.'

'That makes no sense,' said Antikas. 'He betrayed more than his own people, he betrayed his entire race. What could induce a man to commit such an act?'

'He was not a man, he was – as you rightly say – a demon,' said Kalizkan. 'And who can know the minds of such creatures? Certainly not I, for I was foolish enough to trust one, and paid for it with my life.'

'I loathe mysteries,' said Antikas.

'I have always been rather partial to them,' admitted Kalizkan. 'But to attempt an answer to your question, perhaps it was simply hatred. He and his brother, Anharat, were mortal enemies. Anharat desired the destruction of the human race. Emsharas set out to thwart him. You know the old adage, the enemy of my enemy must be my friend? Therefore Emsharas became a friend to humans.'

'It is not convincing,' said Antikas. 'There must have been some among his people that he loved – and yet he caused their destruction also.'

'He did not destroy them – merely banished them from the earth. But if we are questioning motivations, did you not cause the destruction of the one you loved?'

Antikas was shocked. 'That was entirely different,' he snapped.

'I stand corrected.'

'Let us talk of more relevant matters,' said the swordsman. 'These warriors I am to fight are Krayakin, yes?'

'They are indeed – the greatest fighters ever to walk the earth.'

'They have not met me yet,' Antikas pointed out.

'Trust me, my boy, they will not be quaking in their boots.'

'They ought to,' said Antikas. 'Now tell me about them.'

Antikas was sitting once more on the bridge wall when the riders emerged from the mist. The black warrior, Nogusta, was leading them. Antikas could see the queen, sitting side saddle, her horse led by a tall, slim, blond-haired woman in a flowing blue robe. Behind them came the man, Bison. Antikas had last seen him tied to the whipping post, on the day that Nogusta slew Cerez. A small, fair-haired child was seated before him. Behind the giant came two more youngsters, riding double, a red-haired boy of around fourteen and a wand-thin girl with long dark hair. Then he saw Dagorian. The officer was holding a small bundle in his arms. Bringing up the rear was the bowman, Kebra.

Nogusta saw him and left the group, cantering his horse down the shallow slope.

'Good morning to you,' said Antikas, rising and offering a bow. 'I am pleased to see you alive.'

Nogusta dismounted and moved closer, his expression unreadable. Antikas spoke again. 'I am not here as an enemy, black man.'

'I know.'

Antikas was surprised. 'Kalizkan told you about me?'

'No. I had a vision.' Slowly the group filed to the bridge. Nogusta waved them on, and they rode past the two swordsmen. Antikas bowed deeply to Axiana, who responded with a smile. She looked wan and terribly weary.

'Is the queen sick?' he asked Nogusta, after she had passed.

'The birth was not easy, and she lost blood. The priestess healed her, but she will need time to recover fully.'

'Is the child strong?'

'He is strong,' said Nogusta. 'It is our hope that he remains that way. You know that we are followed?'

Antikas nodded. 'By the Krayakin. Kalizkan told me. I will remain here and bar their path.'

Nogusta smiled for the first time. 'Not even you can defeat four such warriors. Even with the black swords.'

'It was a good vision you had,' said Antikas. 'Would you care to share it with me?' Nogusta shook his head. 'Ah,' said Antikas, with a wide grin, 'I am to die then. Well, why not? It is something I've not done before. Perhaps I shall enjoy the experience.'

Nogusta remained silent for a moment. Dagorian, Kebra and Bison came running back across the bridge to stand alongside him. 'What is he doing here?' said Dagorian, his face flushed and angry.

'He is here to help us,' said Nogusta.

'That's not likely,' hissed Dagorian. 'He sent assassins after me. He is in league with the enemy.'

'Such indiscipline in your ranks, Nogusta,' said Antikas. 'Perhaps that is why you never gained a commission.'

'Shall I break his neck?' asked Bison.

'How novel,' muttered Antikas, 'an ape that speaks.' Bison surged forward. Nogusta threw out his arm. The effort of blocking the giant made him wince, as his injured shoulder flared with fresh pain.

'Calm down,' he said. 'There is no treachery here. Antikas Karios is one of us. Understand that. The past is of no consequence. He is here to defend the bridge and buy us time. Let there be no more insults.' He turned to Antikas. 'The Krayakin will come tonight. They do not like the sun, and will wait for the clouds to clear and the moon to shine bright. There will be four of them. But riding with them will be a unit of Ventrian cavalry, sent by the demon who inhabits Malikada.'

'You say I cannot defeat them alone? Will you then stand with me?'

'I would like nothing more.'

'No,' said Dagorian, suddenly. 'Your shoulder is injured. I have watched you ride. You are in great pain and your movements are slow and sluggish. I will stay.'

'I too,' said Kebra.

Nogusta shook his head. 'We cannot risk everything on one encounter. There are only four of the Krayakin directly behind us. Four more are out there, moving to cut us off. We need to put distance between us. Antikas Karios has chosen to defend this bridge. Dagorian has offered to stand beside him. That is how it will be.' He swung to Kebra. 'You and Bison ride on with the others. Keep heading south. About a mile ahead the road branches. Take the route to the left. You will pass over the highest ridge. Move with care, for it will be cold and treacherous. I will join you soon.'

The two men moved away and Nogusta sat down on the bridge wall and rubbed his injured shoulder. Ulmenetha's newfound magick had knitted the broken collar bone, and he could feel himself healing fast. But not fast enough to be of use to the two men who would guard the bridge.

'Bring out the black swords,' he told Antikas. The swordsman moved to his horse and lifted clear the bundle tied to the rear of the saddle. Warning Nogusta and Dagorian to beware of the blades he unwrapped them. They were identical save for the crystal jewels in the pommels. One was blue, the second white as fresh fallen snow, the third crimson. The blue blade Antikas took for himself. Nogusta waited for Dagorian. The young officer chose the sword with the white pommel. Nogusta accepted the last.

'There is little I can say to advise you,' he told Dagorian. 'Stay close to Antikas Karios, guard his back as best you can.'

'You have seen the coming fight, haven't you?'

'Glimpses of it only. Do not ask me about the outcome. You are a good man, Dagorian. Few would have the courage to face the warriors coming against you.'

'This is all very touching, black man,' said Antikas, 'but why don't you ride on? I will take Dagorian under my wing, as it were.'

'I don't need your protection,' snapped Dagorian.

'You Drenai are so touchy. It comes from lacking any sense of true nobility, I expect.' Antikas strode back to his horse, mounted and rode past them down the bridge.

'Are you sure he can be trusted?' asked Dagorian. Nogusta nodded.

'Do not be fooled by his manner. He is a man of great honour, and he carries a burden of shame. He is also frightened. What you are seeing is merely a mask. He is of the old Ventrian nobility, and he is drawing on its values in order to face a terrible enemy.'

Dagorian sat alongside the black swordsman. 'I never wanted to be a soldier,' he said.

'You told me, you wanted to be a priest. Well, think on this, my friend, is it not a priest's duty to keep a lantern lit against the dark? Is it not his purpose to stand against evil in all its forms?'

'That is true,' agreed Dagorian.

'Then today you are a priest, for the demons are coming. They seek the blood of innocence.'

Dagorian smiled. 'I did not need encouragement, but I thank you for it anyway.'

Nogusta rose. 'When your mission here is done, head south, follow the high road. You will see the ghost city of Lem in the distance. We will meet you there.'

Dagorian said nothing, but he gave a knowing smile. Then he held out his hand. Nogusta clasped it firmly. Then he mounted Starfire and rode away.

Nogusta walked his horse to the far end of the bridge. Ulmenetha stepped in front of his horse.

'Did you tell him?' she asked.

'No,' he told her, sadly.

'Why? Does he not have a right to know?'

'Would he fight the better if he did?' he countered.

As the others rode away Dagorian took a deep breath then stared around the bridge. Built of stone it was around 80 feet across and 20 wide. He had seen it on two of Nogusta's maps. Once it must have had a name, for it was a fine structure, carefully constructed. But it was lost to history now, as was the name of the river it spanned. Built when Lem was a thriving city it must have cost a fortune, he thought, picturing the hundreds of men who had laboured here. There had once been statues at both ends of the bridge, but only the plinths remained. It was as Nogusta had said, 'History forgets us all eventually.' Walking to the bridge wall he looked down at the river bank. A stone arm jutted from the mud. Dagorian strolled down to it, pushing the earth away, and exposing a marble shoulder. The head was missing. Casting around he saw a section of a stone leg, covered by weeds. Someone had toppled the statues. He wondered why.

He drank from the river then climbed back to the bridge. 'Time for a little work, Drenai,' said Antikas.

The area around the north of the bridge was heavy with rocks and boulders. Dagorian and Antikas laboured for two hours, rolling large stones onto the bridge to impede enemy horses. The two men spoke little as they worked, for Dagorian remained uneasy in the presence of the hawk-eyed Ventrian. This man had planned to kill him, and had been instrumental in the destruction of the Drenai army, and the murder of the king. Now he was to stand beside him against a terrible foe. The thought was not a pleasant one.

Antikas cut several large sections of brush and used his horse to drag them to the bridge, wedging thick branches into the stone side supports, and angling them to jut out over the rocks. At last satisfied he carefully led his horse through the obstacles, tethering him at the far end of the bridge alongside Dagorian's mount.

'That is all we can do,' he told the young officer. 'Now we wait.' Dagorian nodded and moved away from the man to sit on the bridge wall. The mist was clearing now, and the sun shone clearly in a sky of pale blue.

'We should practise,' said Antikas.

'I need no practice,' snapped Dagorian. Antikas Karios said nothing for a moment, then he stepped in close.

'Your hatred means less than nothing to me, Drenai,' he said, softly. 'But your petulance is irritating.'

'You are a murderer and a traitor,' said Dagorian. 'It should be enough that I am prepared to stand beside you. I don't need to talk to you, and I certainly have no wish to engage in a meaningless training drill. I already know how to fight.'

'Is that so?' Antikas drew his sword. 'Observe!' he ordered. Lifting a thick piece of wood he held the black sword to it. The blade slid through the old wood like a hot knife through butter. 'You and I,' said Antikas, softly, 'will be fighting alongside one another. One clumsy sweep, one careless move and one of us could kill the other. How many times, in close order battle, have comrades accidentally caused injury to one another?'

It was true and Dagorian knew it. Pushing himself from the wall he drew his own blade. 'What do you suggest?' he asked.

'Which side do you wish to defend, the left or the right?'

'The right.'

'Very well, take up your position, and let us rehearse some simple moves.' The two men walked out onto the bridge. 'The enemy will be forced to advance on foot, clambering over the rocks and brush. We will wait for them, and engage them here,' he said. 'No matter what happens you must stay on my right. Do not cross over. Now you are less skilful than I, so at no time try to move to my defence. If I move to yours I will call out, so that you know where I am.'

For a while they practised moves, rehearsed signals and discussed strategies. Then they broke off to eat from Dagorian's ration of dried beef. They sat in silence on the rocks, each lost in his own thoughts.

'I have never fought a demon,' said Dagorian, at last. 'I find the thought unsettling.'

'It is just a name,' said Antikas. 'Nothing more. They walk, they talk, they breathe. And we have the weapons to kill them.'

'You sound very sure.'

'And you are not?'

Dagorian sighed. 'I do not want to die,' he admitted. 'Does that sound cowardly?'

'No man *wants* to die,' responded Antikas. 'But if thoughts of survival enter your mind during the fight, death will be certain. It is vital for a warrior to suspend imagination during a battle. What if I get stabbed, what if I am crippled, what if I die? These thoughts impair a warrior's skills. The enemy will come. We will kill them. That is all you need to focus upon.'

'Easier said than done,' Dagorian told him.

Antikas gave a thin smile. 'Do not be frightened by death, Dagorian, for it comes to all men. For myself I would sooner die young and strong, than become a toothless, senile old man talking of the wonders of my youth.'

'I do not agree. I would like to live to see my children and grandchildren grow. To know love and the joys of family.'

'Have you ever loved?' asked Antikas.

'No. I thought . . .' he hesitated. 'I thought I loved Axiana, but it was a dream, an ideal. She looked so fragile, lost almost. But no, I have never loved. You?'

'No,' answered Antikas, the lie sticking in his throat, the memory of Kara, burning in his mind.

'Do demons love, do you think?' asked Dagorian, suddenly. 'Do they wed and have children? I suppose they must.'

'I have never given it much thought,' admitted Antikas. 'Kalizkan told me that Emsharas the Great Sorcerer fell in love with a human woman, and she bore him children. He was a demon.'

'All I know of him is that he cast the Great Spell thousands of years ago.'

'Yes, and that I find curious,' said Antikas. 'According to Kalizkan he banished his entire race to a world of nothing, empty and void. Hundreds of thousands of souls ripped from the earth to float for eternity without form. Can there have ever been a crime worse than that?'

'You call it a crime? I don't understand. Humanity was saved by the action.'

'Humanity yes, but Emsharas was not human. Why then did he do it? Why not cast a spell that would banish *humanity* into a void, and leave the earth for his own people? It makes no sense.'

'It must have made sense to him. Perhaps it was that his people were evil.'

'Come now,' snapped Antikas, 'that makes even less sense. If we are to judge his actions as good, then we must accept that he was not evil. Why then should he have been the only good demon in the world? What of the Dryads who lived to protect the forest, or the Krandyl who preserved the fields and meadows? These also are creatures of legend, spirit beings, demons.'

Dagorian suddenly laughed and shook his head. 'What is so amusing?' asked Antikas.

'You do not find it amusing that two men sitting on a bridge and waiting for death can debate the actions of a sorcerer who died thousands of years ago? It is the kind of conversation I would expect to have sitting in the library at Drenan.' His laughter faded away. 'I don't care why he did it. What does it matter now? To us?'

'Are you determined to be morbid all day?' countered Antikas. 'If so you will be a less than merry companion. You do not have to stay here, Dagorian. There are no chains.'

'Why do you stay?' asked the younger man.

'I like to sit on bridges,' Antikas told him. 'It calms my soul.'

'Well I am staying because I'm too frightened not to,' said Dagorian. 'Can you understand that?'

'No,' admitted Antikas Karios.

'A few days ago I attacked five Ventrian lancers. I thought I was going to die. But my blood was up and I charged them. Then Nogusta and Kebra came to my aid and we won.'

'Yes, yes,' interrupted Antikas. 'I saw you had Vellian's horse. But what is the point of this tale?'

'The point?' said Dagorian, his face twisting in anguish. 'The point is that the fear never went away. Every day it grows. There are demons pursuing us. Unbeatable and unholy. And where are we headed? To a ghost city with no hope of rescue. I could not take the fear any more. So here I am. And look at me! Look at my hands!' Dagorian held out his hands, which were trembling uncontrollably. 'So humour me, Antikas Karios. Tell me why you are here on this cursed bridge?'

Antikas leaned forward, his hand snaking out, the palm lashing against Dagorian's cheek. The sound of the slap hung in the air. Dagorian surged to his feet, hand scrabbling for his sword. 'Where is your fear now?' said Antikas, softly. The softly spoken words cut through Dagorian's fury, and he stood, hand on sword hilt, staring into the dark, cruel eyes of Antikas Karios. The Ventrian spoke again. 'It is gone, is it not, your fear? Swamped by rage.'

'Yes, it is gone,' said Dagorian, coldly. 'What was your point?'

'You were right to stay here, Dagorian. A man would have to be a contortionist to both face his fear and flee from it.' Antikas stood and walked to the side of the bridge, leaning upon it and staring down into the water below. 'Come and look,' he said. The Drenai officer joined him.

'What am I looking at?'

'Life,' answered Antikas. 'It starts high in the mountains with the melting of the snow. Small streams bubbling together, merging, flowing down to join larger rivers, then out to the warm sea. There the sun shines upon the water and it rises as vapour and floats back over the mountains, falling as rain or snow. It is a circle, an endless beautiful circle. Long after we are gone, and the children of our grandchildren are gone, this river will still flow all the way to the sea. We are very small creatures, Dagorian, with very small dreams.' He turned to the young officer and smiled. 'Look at your hands. They are no longer shaking.'

'They will – when the Krayakin come.'

'I don't think so,' said Antikas.

His experience within the body form of Kalizkan had given the Demon Lord, Anharat, great insights into the workings of human mechanisms. Unable to halt the cancer spreading through the sorcerer's body Anharat had allowed all the mechanisms to fail, then using magick to maintain the illusion of life. Not so with this body form!

With Malikada slain and departed Anharat repaired the pierced heart, and kept it pumping, the nutrients in the blood feeding the cells and keeping the form alive – after a fashion. The spell needed to be maintained at all times. If the magick ceased to flow the body would decay immediately. This was not, however, a problem, for the spell was a small one. He had more difficulty with the autonomic responses, like breathing and blinking, but, upon experimentation overcame them. Using Kalizkan's corpse had been an effort, especially when corruption and decay accelerated. More and more power had been needed to maintain a cloak spell over the disgusting form. Now, however, he merely needed to keep the blood flowing, and air filling the lung sacs. There were also advantages to this new method. Senses of taste, touch and smell were incredibly heightened.

Anharat sat now in his tent, sipping a goblet of fine wine, swilling it around his mouth and savouring the taste. Although he preferred his own natural form Anharat considered keeping this one for a few years in order to fully appreciate the pleasures of human flesh. They were so much more exquisite than he could have imagined. Perhaps it was because the humans were so short-lived, he thought, a gift of nature to creatures who were in existence for a few, brief heartbeats. Emsharas had discovered these pleasures, and now Anharat understood them. No wonder his brother had spent so much time with the black woman.

Outside the tent he could hear the sounds of the army settling down for night camp, the rattling of pans and dishes as the men lined up for food, the smell of wood smoke from the fires, and the laughter of soldiers listening to tall tales.

He had dispensed with his undead guards. Their blank, uncomprehending stares had unnerved the officers. Equally he had withdrawn the Entukku from the city, allowing the terrified populace to return to a semblance of normality before the army marched. Thousands had died in the riots, and none of the surviving humans had the least notion of what had caused their own murderous rages. Curiously the Entukku, who normally thrived on terror and pain, had gorged themselves equally on the waves of remorse that had billowed forth. These humans were a constant source of all kinds of nourishment.

Anharat could hardly wait to experiment further upon them.

A faint glow shone on the walls of the tent behind him. His skin prickled, and he swung towards the light, his hands opening, the first words of an incantation upon his lips. A pale figure was forming. Anharat saw that it was merely an image, for the legs of the figure were merging with the iron brazier, filled with hot coals. He relaxed, his curiosity aroused. Was Kalizkan returned?

Then the light began to fade and the features of a man appeared. Anharat's rage grew and he began to tremble. His face twisted and he stepped forward, aching to rip his talons through the heart of the figure. The newcomer was dressed in robes of white. His skin was black, his eyes pale blue. Upon his brow he wore a circlet of gold. 'Greetings, my brother,' he said.

Anharat was almost too angry to speak, but he fought for control. If he could hold the image here for a while he could concoct a search spell that would follow it back to its source. 'Where have you been hiding, Emsharas?' he asked.

'Nowhere,' answered the figure.

'You lie, brother. For I was sentenced to exist in the hell of Nowhere, with all the creatures of the Illohir. And you were not there. Nor were you among the humans, for I have searched for you these last four thousand years.'

'I did not hide, Anharat,' said the figure, softly. 'Nor was it –

nor is it – my intention for our people to exist in a void for ever.'

'I care nothing for your intentions, traitor. Did you know that I have destroyed your descendants?'

'Not all of them. One remains.'

'I will see him dead, and I will have the babe. Then your evil will be undone. The people of the Illohir will walk free upon the earth.'

'Aye, they will,' said Emsharas. 'But they will not be able to drink the water or the wine, nor will they laze under the sun.'

Anharat's mind was working furiously, and the search spell was almost complete. 'So, brother, will you not tell me where you have been all these centuries? Have you been enjoying life as a human? Have you tasted fine wines and bedded great beauties?'

'I have done none of these things, Anharat. Where do you think I found the power for the Great Spell?'

'I neither know, nor care,' lied Anharat.

'Oh, you care, brother, for you know that you and I were almost equally matched, and yet I discovered a source of power hitherto unknown. You could use it too. I will willingly tell it to you – if you will help me complete my work.'

'Complete . . . ? What new horror do you have in mind for the Illohir, brother? Perhaps we could create chains of fire to torture our people down the ages?'

'I offer them a world where they can lie in the sun and swim in the rivers and lakes. A world of their own.'

'Really? How kind you are, Emsharas. Perhaps though you would explain why they are not already there. And why we have waited so long for this little discussion.'

'I did not have the power to complete the Spell. I needed you, Anharat.'

Anharat's finger jabbed out, and the completed search spell flowed around Emsharas, bathing him in a blue light. 'Now I will find you,' hissed Anharat. 'I will find you and I will destroy you. I swear it! But first I will kill the third king, and complete the prophecy.'

Emsharas smiled. '*My* prophecy,' he said. 'I left it for you, brother. And it is a true one. Upon the death of the third king the Illohir will rise again. We will speak soon.'

With that the figure vanished.

Anharat closed his eyes and fastened to the search spell. He felt it grow weaker and weaker, as if coming to him across a vast distance. Then it was gone.

The Demon Lord returned to his wine and drank deeply. In all his thousands of years held captive in the void he had used every known spell to locate Emsharas, sending search spells out through the universe. Yet there was nothing. It was as if Emsharas had never been.

And now, with the hour of Anharat's triumph approaching, his brother had returned.

Anharat could have endured threats, but Emsharas had made none. And what did he mean by denying that he had been hiding? A tiny seed of doubt seeped into Anharat's mind. His brother never lied. Refilling his goblet Anharat drank again, recalling again the words of Emsharas. 'Oh, you care, brother, for you know that you and I were almost equally matched, and yet I discovered a source of power hitherto unknown. You could use it too. I will willingly tell it to you – if you will help me complete my work.' What source of power? Anharat moved to the pallet bed and lay down. *Tell* it to you. That's what Emsharas had said. Not *give* it to you. Not tell you where it *is*. The secret power source was not then an object, like a talisman, but something that could be passed on with words alone. It was impossible.

And yet . . . they *had* been almost equally matched. Where then had his brother found the power to banish an entire race?

There would be time to ponder the question. For now Anharat wished to see his victory draw closer. Allowing his mind to relax, his dark spirit floated free and flew over the mountains towards the stone bridge.

Chapter Ten

Antikas Karios removed his red cloak and neatly folded it, laying it upon the stone work of the bridge. Then he tied his long hair into a tight pony-tail and began moving through a series of routines designed to stretch his back and shoulders and hips. At the beginning the movements were slow, graceful and balletic. Then they grew more swift, becoming a dance, full of leaps and turns. Dagorian watched the man with a growing sense of sadness. Such a dance, he thought, should be to celebrate life and youth, not as a prelude to violence and death.

The sun was falling below the western mountains, and the violet sky was streaked with golden clouds. Antikas strolled across to where Dagorian waited. 'What a beautiful sunset,' he said.

The young officer did not reply. A line of ten riders had appeared from the woods, and were moving towards the bridge. As they cleared the tree line four more riders appeared, tall men, wearing black armour and full-faced helms.

The Ventrian captain rode his horse to the first of the obstacles, then called out to Antikas. 'Give way for the emperor's riders.'

'Which emperor would that be?' Antikas responded.

'Give way, Antikas Karios, you cannot stand against all of us. And I have no orders for your arrest.' The captain shifted nervously on his horse, and continually glanced back towards the black armoured Krayakin.

'I fear I cannot comply, captain,' said Antikas. 'You see I am a servant of the infant king, and I have been ordered to hold this bridge. Might I suggest that you and your men ride away, for you are wrong –' his voice hardened. '– I *can* stand against you. More than that, I can promise you that any man who steps upon this bridge will die.'

The captain licked his dry lips. 'This is madness,' he said. 'What is your purpose here?'

'I have already told you my purpose. Now attack – or be gone!'

The captain dragged back on the reins and wheeled his horse. Dagorian could see that none of the Ventrian soldiers seemed willing to enter the fray. Such was the awesome – and justified – reputation of the man facing them. Still they dismounted and drew their swords, for they were brave men and disciplined.

'Remember,' whispered Antikas, 'stay to the right.'

'I shall.'

'Are your hands trembling?'

'No.'

'Good. That is of some relief to me – for I cannot really take ten men alone.' He grinned at Dagorian then drew both his swords, one of shining steel, one darker than the pit, and stepped up to take his place on the left.

The bridge was wide enough for four warriors to walk abreast and still leave room to swing a sword. The Ventrians advanced slowly, picking their way through the rocks. Antikas stood very still. As they got closer he suddenly leapt at them with an ear-splitting battle cry. His steel sword swept out slashing through a soldier's throat, then the black blade sliced through the chest of a second man, killing him instantly. The Ventrians surged forward. Three made it past the swordsman. Dagorian jumped forward. The black blade licked out and a man died. A sword pierced Dagorian's shoulder. He fell back. The swordsman stumbled over a rock and lost his balance. Dagorian killed him with a straight thrust to the heart. Then Dagorian was struck again, this time by the third soldier. He felt as if he had been kicked by a horse, and could not, at first, locate the wound. Ignoring it he leapt to the attack, blocking a wild cut and sending a riposte that swept through the man's ribs. He fell without a sound.

Dagorian looked up to see Antikas battling furiously, his blades a blur as he cut and parried. There was blood on his face and left arm, but five men were down. Only the captain and one other remained.

Antikas ran at them – and they turned and fled.

They did not get far.

The four warriors of the Krayakin blocked the bridge. Two of them stepped forward and slew the fleeing soldiers.

'Hardly sporting,' called out Antikas Karios. 'Do you often kill your own men?'

'You fight well, human,' came a muffled voice. 'And I see you have found a Storm Sword. It should be an interesting encounter.'

'All at once – or one at a time. I care not,' said Antikas.

The sound of laughter greeted his challenge. Then the tallest of the warriors stepped forward. 'I like you, human,' he said. 'But there is blood running into your eyes. Move back and tie a scarf around your brow. I will await you.'

Antikas grinned then backed away to where Dagorian was sitting with his back to the bridge wall. 'Taking a rest, Drenai?' he asked. Then his smile faded as he saw the blood soaking Dagorian's tunic.

'Do not concern yourself with me,' said Dagorian, with a weak smile. 'Do as he bid.' Antikas had been cut just above his left eyebrow. The gash was around 2 inches long and blood was dripping into his eye. With his dagger he slashed through his shirt sleeve, then ripped it clear. Tearing a strip from it he bound his brow.

'Terrible thing to do to a good shirt,' he said. 'My tailor would be most annoyed.'

Then he rose and glanced down at Dagorian. 'Don't go away,' he said. 'I shall be back soon.'

'I don't think I'm going anywhere,' said Dagorian. 'Take the Storm Sword. I have a feeling you'll need it.'

Armed with the two black blades Antikas strode back to the centre of the bridge. 'What is your name?' he asked the tall warrior.

'I am Golbar,' replied the Krayakin.

'Come then, Golbar, let us dance a jig.'

'Bear with me, human,' said Golbar, removing his gauntlets. Slowly he removed the black armour, unbuckling the breastplate and the shoulder guards, the greaves and the forearm protectors. Lastly he removed his helm. His hair was white, his eyes dark, his skin pale. Drawing his sword he turned to one of his comrades, who threw him a second. He caught it cleanly and advanced across the stones. Antikas watched his movements. They were quick and graceful.

Antikas attacked, and as their swords met lightning crackled from the blades. The attack was parried with ease and Antikas

553

only just managed to avoid a murderous riposte that further sliced the ruined satin shirt. The Krayakin came at him with bewildering speed and Antikas found himself fighting for his life. Never had he faced a more skilful opponent, nor met a man with reflexes as fast as this Krayakin. Antikas parried and blocked with increasing desperation, and slowly he was forced further back along the bridge. Anger touched him then, for the Krayakin was toying with him. Twice he had an opportunity to lance a thrust through the human's guard, and twice he merely sliced small cuts in his opponent's chest.

'You are very good,' said Golbar, conversationally, while still attacking. 'Not the best I ever killed, but close. Do let me know when you are ready to die.'

Antikas did not answer. Despite his increasing weariness and desperate battle for survival he had been reading his opponent's moves, seeking out a weakness. The man was ambidextrous – as indeed was Antikas – but he favoured the right, and sought to kill with thrusts rather than cleaving cuts. Antikas leapt back.

'I am ready now,' he said. The Krayakin attacked. Instead of backing away Antikas moved suddenly forward. As he had expected Golbar sent a lightning thrust with his right hand blade. Antikas swayed to the right, his enemy's sword glancing along his ribs. Ignoring the pain he slammed the black blade through the Krayakin's chest, spearing the heart. Golbar's dark eyes widened in pain and shock, his swords falling from his hands. Without a word he fell back to the stone of the bridge.

Antikas moved forward to face the remaining three.

'Who gets to strip next?' he asked.

'No-one,' came the response. 'Golbar always had a taste for the dramatic.'

Hefting their swords they came at him together. Antikas watched them, determined to take at least one more with him.

The moon was shining now over the mountains, and a cool breeze was whispering over the bridge. It would be so easy to sprint back to his horse and ride from here, ready to fight another day. He cast a quick glance at Dagorian. The young officer was sitting very still, his hands locked over the terrible wound in his belly. He had a sudden desire to tell him why he had chosen to fight on this bridge, to speak of redemption, and the loss of Kara. But there was no time.

The Krayakin were picking their way through the debris. Antikas tensed, ready to attack them.

A colossal, white form burst from the undergrowth, smashing aside trees as it came. It thundered towards the bridge, letting forth a terrifying screech. Antikas stared disbelievingly at the monstrous form, with its huge, wedge-shaped head and gaping jaws. It was moving at great speed. Blood was streaming from a wound high in the beast's shoulder, and Antikas could see a broken lance jutting there.

The three Krayakin swung round as the beast bore down upon them. There was nowhere to run, save to hurl themselves into the river. They stood their ground, dwarfed by the monstrosity looming over them. One Krayakin tried to attack, but a sweep from a taloned arm tore his head from his shoulders. The wedge-head lunged down, fastening to the shoulder of a second warrior, lifting him high. The Krayakin plunged his sword deep into the beast's neck. The beast's head flicked and the warrior sailed out over the river, splashing down into the torrent and disappearing below the waves. The third Krayakin had run in and lanced his sword deep into the fish-white belly of the beast, ripping a great wound, from which gushed a prodigious amount of blood. Talons ripped into the knight, smashing through his armour. He was hurled back against the stone supports of the bridge, his sword wrenched from his hand. The beast's head lunged at him. He tried to avoid it, but the terrible teeth caught him in the mid-section, ripping him apart.

The monster reared up and the stone work trembled as it let out a howl of pain. The wound in its belly ripped further open, spilling its entrails to the bridge. Twisting its head it saw Antikas standing alone at the centre of the bridge. It made two faltering steps towards him, then stumbled sideways. The side bridge supports crumbled under its weight and it toppled into the rushing river.

Antikas moved to the edge, staring down. The body was moving slowly out of sight, towards the distant falls.

Remembering Kalizkan's warning about the near miraculous healing powers of the Krayakin Antikas ran to the first body and heaved both sections into the river. He paused at the second, and stared down at the decapitated head. The helm visor was still closed. Antikas flipped it open and found himself staring into glowing eyes, that were alive and full of hatred. The mouth moved, but without vocal cords no sound issued forth. Antikas picked up the head and tossed it into the water, then rolled the body after it. Lastly he moved to the armourless body of Golbar. This too he fed to the river.

Returning to Dagorian he slumped down beside the dying officer. 'How do you feel?' he asked.

'There is no pain, but I can no longer move my legs. I am dying, Antikas.'

'Yes, you are. But we won, Drenai.'

'Perhaps. Then again, perhaps we merely delayed the inevitable. There are four more Krayakin, and the Ventrian army has closed off the road to the sea.'

'Let tomorrow take care of itself, Dagorian. You fought well, and bravely. It was an honour to stand beside you. I do not know much about your religion. Is there a Hall of Heroes contained in it?'

'No.'

'Then you should convert to mine, my friend. In it you will find a palace full of young virgins ready to obey your every whim. There will be wine and song and endless sunshine.'

'It . . . sounds . . . very fine,' whispered Dagorian.

'I will say a prayer for your spirit, Drenai, and that prayer will shine above you like a lantern. Follow it to the palace that awaits me. I will see you there.' Antikas reached across and closed the dead eyes. Then he scabbarded the Storm Swords and walked slowly back to the horses. The cut on his ribs was stinging now as the blood clotted over it. He stepped into the saddle and gazed back along the bridge.

Then he fulfilled his promise and sent a prayer-light to shine for Dagorian.

Swinging the horses he rode after the others.

The cave was deep, and curved like a horn. The biting wind could not reach them here and the group huddled around two fires. Nogusta stood apart from the others, heavy of heart. He had not lied to Dagorian. He had not *seen* him die. Yet he had known that the young man would not survive the encounter on the bridge, for in the vivid flashes of the future which had come to him there had been no sign of the officer.

Kebra moved from the fire and stood beside him. 'How long before we come down from this mountain?' he asked.

'Some time late tomorrow.'

'I have fed the last of the grain to the horses, but they need rest, Nogusta, and good grass and water.'

Nogusta unrolled the parchment map, and held it up so that they could both see it in the firelight. 'Tomorrow we will reach the highest point. It will be bitterly cold and the road will be ice covered and treacherous. After that we begin the long descent to the five valleys and Lem.'

'The fires will not last the night,' said Kebra, 'and it will be below freezing in here without them.' They had gathered wood in the last valley, and Bison had also tied several bundles of dried timber from the smashed wagon. It was these which were burning now.

'Then we will be cold,' said Nogusta. 'Though not as cold as Dagorian.'

'You think we should have stayed?'

Nogusta shook his head. 'The other Krayakin are close by.'

'What have you seen?'

'Too much,' said Nogusta, sadly. 'The Gift is more of a curse than ever. I see, but I cannot change what I see. Dagorian asked me if he was to die. I did not tell him. I think he knew nonetheless. He was a good man, Kebra, a man who should have lived to build, to sire children and teach them the virtues of honesty, courage and honour. He should not be lying dead on a forgotten bridge.'

'We will not forget him,' said the silver-haired bowman.

'No, we will not. And what does that count for? We are old men, you and I. Our time is passing. And when I look back over my life I wonder whether it has been for good or ill. I have fought for most of my life. I defended the Drenai cause, even though most of my comrades either feared me or loathed me for the colour of my skin. Then I took part in the invasion of Ventria, and saw the destruction of an ancient empire. All for the vanity of one arrogant man. What will I say to the Keeper of the Book when I stand before him? What excuses shall I offer for my life?'

Kebra looked closely at his friend, and he thought carefully before speaking. 'This is probably not the time to consider it,' he said, at last. 'Despair touches you, and there is no comfort to be found in melancholy. You have in your life rescued many, and risked yourself for others. You do so now. Such deeds will also be recorded. I am not a philosopher, Nogusta, but there are things I know. If your Gift sees us fail, and the child is destined to fall into the hands of evil, no matter what we do, will you ride then away and leave him to his fate? No you will not. Even if death and defeat are inevitable. No more will I. No-one can ask more of us than that.'

Nogusta smiled. He would have reached out and embraced the man, save that Kebra was not tactile, and disliked being touched. 'My father once told me that if a man could count true friends on the fingers of one hand then he was blessed beyond riches. I have been blessed, Kebra.'

'I too. Now get a little rest. I will keep watch for a while.'

'Listen for a single horse, for Antikas Karios will be trying to find us.'

'I have to say that I do not like the man,' admitted Kebra. 'His arrogance sticks in my throat.'

Nogusta smiled again. 'Reminds you of us some twenty years ago, doesn't he?'

Kebra nodded and walked to the mouth of the cave. Sitting back from the wind he looked out over the peaks and shivered. They were thousands of feet above the valley floor, and the clouds looked close enough to touch. Drawing his cloak about him he leaned back against the wall. Dagorian's death had saddened him also. He had liked the young man. His fear had been great, his courage greater still. He would have raised fine sons, thought Kebra.

The rocks were cold and he lifted his hood into place. Fine sons. The thought saddened him. What kind of a father would I have been? he wondered. He would never know. And, unlike Bison or Nogusta, there was no chance that he had sired children with any of the whores he had encountered through thirty years of campaigning, for he had never coupled with any of them. He had, of course, visited the brothels with both his comrades, but upon reaching the quiet of the bedroom he had merely paid the girls to sit and talk with him. To make love one had to touch, and Kebra could not even bear the thought of it. Flesh upon flesh? He shuddered.

From out of the past the memory came. It caught him unawares, for he had long ago buried it beyond the reaches of his imagination. The dark walls of the barn, the huge hairy hands of his father, the pain and the terror, and the threats of death if ever he spoke of it. He blinked and focused his gaze on the mountain peaks.

Conalin crept up to sit alongside him, a blanket wrapped tight around his thin shoulders. 'I brought your bow and arrows,' said the boy.

'Thank you – but I don't think we'll need them tonight.' He glanced down at the boy, seeing the fear in his eyes.

'Antikas Karios and Dagorian held the bridge. Antikas will be coming soon.'

'How do you know?'

'Nogusta had a vision. His visions are always true.'

'You said Antikas will be coming. What about Dagorian?'

There was no other way to say it. 'He died for us,' said Kebra. 'He fought like a man, and he died like a man.'

'I don't want to die,' said Conalin, miserably.

'But you will, one day,' observed Kebra. He chuckled suddenly. 'I had an old uncle, and he used to say, "Only one thing in life is certain, son, you won't get out of it alive." He lived every day to the full. He was a man who loved life. He was a soldier for a while, then a merchant, and lastly a farmer. He never did anything brilliantly, but he always gave it his best. I liked him – and he once did me a great service.'

'What did he do?'

'He killed my father.'

Conalin was shocked. 'And that was a service?'

'Indeed it was. Sadly he killed him too late, but that was not his fault.' He fell silent for a moment. Conalin wanted to ask him other questions, but he saw the sadness in the old man's eyes. Then Kebra spoke again. 'What would you like to be, Conalin?'

'Married to Pharis,' answered the boy, instantly.

'Yes, I know that. But what career do you desire?'

Conalin thought about it. 'Something to do with horses. That's what I'd really like.'

'A good occupation. Nogusta has similar plans. Once his family were renowned for their horses. But his wife and all of his kin were murdered, the great house burned to the ground, the stables destroyed. The herd escaped into the mountains. Nogusta has a dream of returning to the family estate and rebuilding it. He says that deep in the mountains there are many valleys, and that the herd will have grown now. He plans to find them.'

Conalin's eyes were shining now. 'I'd like to do that. Would he let me, do you think?'

'You would have to ask him.'

'Could you not ask him for me?'

'I could,' agreed Kebra, 'but that is not the way it should be. A strong man makes his own way in the world. He does not ask others to do that which he fears himself.'

Conalin moved out of the wind. He was a little too close to Kebra now, and the bowman felt uncomfortable. 'I will ask him,' said the boy. 'Will you be there with us?'

'I might be – if the Source wills it.'

The boy's excited expression suddenly faded. 'What is wrong?' asked Kebra.

'What is the point of talking about horses? We are going to die here.'

'We've made it this far,' Kebra pointed out. 'And I have yet to see the enemy who could defeat Nogusta. And as for Bison . . . well, he is the strongest man I ever knew, and he has more heart than any ten demons. No, Conalin, do not dismiss them so lightly. They may be old, but they are canny.'

'What about you?'

'Me? I am quite simply the finest archer ever to walk the earth. I could hit a fly's testicles from thirty paces.'

'Do flies have testicles?' asked Conalin.

'Not when I'm close by,' answered Kebra, with a smile.

Antikas Karios reached the cave just before midnight. His beard was caked with ice, as was his horse's mane, and both he and his mount were mortally weary. For the last 2 miles he had been swaying in the saddle, and fighting to stay awake.

Kebra stepped out into the biting wind, taking hold of the horse's bridle and leading him into the cave. It took Antikas two attempts before he could summon the energy to dismount. Nogusta approached him.

'Sit by the fire and warm yourself,' he said.

'Horse first,' muttered Antikas. From the back of his saddle he untied a thick bundle of wood and handed it to Nogusta. 'I thought the fuel might be running low,' he said. Dragging off his gauntlets Antikas rubbed life back into his cold fingers, then began to unsaddle the chestnut gelding. His movements were stiff and slow.

'Let me help you,' said Kebra, lifting the saddle clear and laying it over a rock. Antikas did not thank him, but moved to the saddlebags. His cold, swollen fingers fumbled at the buckles, but, at last he opened them, taking out a body brush and a cloth. Returning to the horse he rubbed the animal dry then, with deep circular strokes, brushed him. Conalin watched with interest. He had seen Kebra and Nogusta do the same some hours before, when they had first arrived at the cave. 'Why is it so important for the horse to have a brushed coat?' he whispered to the bow-man.

'Grooming is not just about the coat,' answered Kebra. 'That horse is cold and tired. The brush helps to improve the circulation of blood, and tones the muscles.'

Antikas stepped back from the horse, cleaned the brush and returned it to his saddlebag. Then he removed his crimson cloak and laid it over the gelding's back. It was then that the others saw the dried blood on his torn, satin shirt. Ulmenetha rose from the first of the fires and bade Antikas to remove his shirt. He did so with great difficulty. Satin fibres had stuck to his wounds, and as he pulled the shirt clear the small cuts in his chest and the long, jagged slice along his ribs began to bleed once more. Sitting him down by the fire Ulmenetha examined the wounds. The smaller cuts she could heal immediately without stitches, but the wound caused by Golbar's last thrust first needed more traditional treatment. Nogusta handed Antikas a cup of broth, which he accepted gratefully. As Ulmenetha prepared her needle and thread Antikas stared around the firelit cave. The ape, Bison, was asleep by the far wall. Alongside him, huddled close for warmth was a young girl and a child. Beyond them the queen was sitting in the shadows, holding her babe close to her breast. Antikas saw that the child was feeding, and looked away guiltily.

'Stand up,' ordered Ulmenetha. Antikas did so. The priestess came to her knees, and began to stitch the wound, beginning first at the centre, drawing the flaps of skin together. Antikas looked across at Nogusta, and their eyes met.

'He died well,' said Antikas.

'I know.'

'Good, for I am too tired to discuss it further.' He winced as Ulmenetha drew tight the centre stitch. 'You are not knitting a rug, woman,' he snapped.

'I'll wager you did not whine so when the Krayakin faced you,' she responded. Antikas grinned, but said nothing. Three more stitches were inserted, then Ulmenetha laid a slender hand over the wound, and began to chant in a low voice. Antikas glanced down at the priestess, then gave a questioning look to Nogusta. The black man had turned away and was untying the bundle of wood.

Antikas felt a tingling sensation begin in the wound, heat flaring from it. It was mildly uncomfortable, but not at all painful. After some minutes Ulmenetha removed her hand, then, with a small knife, cut the stitches and pulled them clear. Antikas touched the cut. It was almost healed. More than this he felt curiously rejuvenated, as if he had slept for several hours.

'You are very talented, lady,' he said.

'You should see me knitting a rug,' she answered, rising to stand before him. She repeated the Healing Prayer on the smaller chest wounds, then reached up to pull clear the blood-stained satin strip around his brow. 'Bend your head,' she ordered him. Antikas obeyed.

As she healed the cut she spoke again. 'You are a lucky man, Antikas. Had the blow been two inches lower you would have lost an eye.'

'Strangely, the more I practise the luckier I get,' he said.

Ulmenetha stepped back from him, and appraised her work. Satisfied she moved back to the fire and sat down. 'Had you remained at the bridge you might have saved Dagorian,' he said. Ulmenetha shook her head.

'His internal injuries were far beyond my powers.' So saying she turned away from him. Kebra handed him a clean, folded tunic of off-white wool. Antikas thanked him. Lifting it to his nose he smiled. 'Scented rosewood,' he said. 'How civilized. You are a man after my own heart.'

'Probably not,' said Kebra.

Antikas slipped on the shirt. The arms were too long, and he folded back the cuffs. 'Well, Nogusta,' he said, 'what now? What do your visions tell you?'

'We go to the ghost city,' answered Nogusta. 'That is all I can say. I do not yet know the outcome of this quest. But all questions will be answered in Lem.'

The child sleeping beside Bison suddenly cried out and sat up. The girl beside her awoke, and took her in her arms. 'What is wrong, Sufia?' she asked, stroking the child's blond hair.

'I had a dream. Demons in my dream. They were eating me up.' The child began to cry. Then she saw Antikas, and her eyes widened.

'Hello,' said Antikas, giving her his best smile. Sufia let out a wail and buried her head in Pharis's chest. 'I've always had a way with children,' said Antikas, drily.

The noise awoke Bison, who gave a great yawn, then belched loudly. He too saw Antikas, and looked around for Dagorian. Rising he scratched at his groin then moved to the fire, where he belched again. 'Killed 'em all, did you?' he asked Antikas.

'One of them. A huge beast came from the forest and slaughtered the others.'

Fear showed in Bison's face. 'Is it still alive?'

'No. It fell into the river and drowned.'

'Well, that's a relief,' said Bison. 'Almost makes up for the fact that you survived. Where is the lad, Dagorian?'

'He died.'

Bison absorbed the information without comment, then swung to Kebra. 'Is there any broth left?'

'No, Antikas ate the last of it.'

'What about the biscuits?'

'A few left,' said Kebra. 'But we are saving them for the morning. The children can have them for breakfast.'

Antikas removed his sword belt, and laid it beside him. 'There are four more Krayakin,' he said. 'Believe me, Nogusta, that is four too many. I fought one. He had a sense of honour, and removed his armour to fight me. He was faster than any man I have ever known. I am not sure I could defeat another, and I certainly could not defeat more than one.'

'What then do you suggest?' asked Nogusta.

'I have no suggestions. What I am saying is that I treated them too lightly. I thought of them merely as men, and there is no man more skilled than I. But they are not men. Their reflexes are astonishing, and their strength prodigious.'

'And yet we must face them,' said Nogusta. 'We have no choice.'

'Whatever you say,' said Antikas. He stretched out beside the fire, then glanced up at Bison. 'We could always send him against them,' he said. 'His body odour would fell an ox.'

Bison glared at him. 'I'm beginning to *really* dislike you, little man,' he said.

Breakfast was a sorry affair, with the last of the oatcake biscuits being shared by Sufia, Pharis and Conalin. Pharis offered hers to the queen, but Axiana smiled and shook her head. Bison grumbled about starvation as he saddled the horses.

As she finished her food little Sufia climbed onto Ulmenetha's lap. 'Did you sleep well, in the end, little one?' asked the priestess.

'Yes. I didn't dream no more. It's very cold,' she added, snuggling close. The last of the wood had long burnt away, and the temperature in the cave was dropping fast.

'We are going down into the valleys today,' Ulmenetha told her. 'It will be much warmer there.'

'I'm still hungry.'

'We are all hungry.' Sufia gave a nervous glance across at Antikas. 'He looks like a demon,' she said. Antikas heard her and gave her a grin. She scowled at him from the perceived safety of Ulmenetha's lap.

'I am not a demon,' said Antikas. 'I am earth born, as you are.'

'What does that mean?' Sufia asked the priestess.

'It means that we come from the earth, whereas demons are born of the wind. We are solid. We can touch things. Demons are like the wind. They can blow against us, but they cannot live and breathe as we do.'

Pharis came and sat alongside them. 'If that is true, how can the Krayakin fight us? Are they not solid?'

'There is an old story,' said Antikas, 'that my father used to tell. It is part of Ventrian history and myth. Once there were two Windborn gods, great and powerful. They floated above the earth, and watched the deer and the lion, the eagle and the lamb. They were envious of them, and their ability to walk the land. These gods had many Windborn subjects, and they too looked upon the earth with jealousy. One day the two gods – who did not like one another . . .'

'Why didn't they like one another?' asked Sufia.

'That's not important. Anyway . . .'

'I think it is important,' said Pharis. 'Why would gods not like one another?'

Antikas suppressed his irritation. 'Very well, let us say that one of the gods was evil, the other good. One was a lord of chaos and destruction, while the other loved the light, and delighted to see things grow. They were like night and day.'

'All right,' said Pharis. 'I can understand that. Go on.'

'Thank you. One day these gods decided to use their great power to cast a spell that would allow their people, the Illohir, to take on fleshly forms. These spirit beings floated down to the earth, and wherever they landed they drew matter to themselves, creating bodies that could walk upon the earth.'

'How did they do that?' asked Sufia.

'I don't know how they did it,' snapped Antikas.

'I do,' said Ulmenetha. 'All matter is made up of tiny molecules – so tiny that the human eye cannot see them. They literally drew these molecules to them, like so many bricks and built their bodies.'

'There,' said Antikas to Sufia. 'Does that satisfy you?'

The child looked mystified. Axiana, who had been listening to the tale, walked across to them, the babe asleep in her arms. Antikas rose and bowed to her. She responded with a smile. 'I too heard this story,' she said, softly. 'There is great beauty in it. Some of the Windborn landed in forests, and drew their strength from the trees. They became Dryads, protectors of woodland, their souls entwined with the trees they loved. Others came down in the mountains, building their forms from the rocks and stones. These were the High Trolls. Some groups emerged near living creatures, like wolves. Because they drew particles from everything around them they became Shape-Shifters, manlike during the day, but becoming wolves at night. All over the world the Illohir took on different forms, and rejoiced in their new-found freedom.'

'Did any become birds?' asked Sufia.

'I expect that they did,' said Axiana.

'That means Bison is a demon,' said Sufia, 'because he once had big white wings and flew over mountains.'

'Must have been *really* big wings,' said Antikas.

Conalin joined them. 'If they were all so happy why did they start a war with people?'

Ulmenetha answered him. 'They weren't *all* happy. Some of the Windborn had landed in places that were . . . unclean. Battlefields, graveyards, scenes of violence or terror. What they drew into themselves was dark and fearsome. These became the Hollow Tooths, who suck blood from sleepers. Or the Krayakin, who live for war and slaughter.'

'And these were the ones who started the war?' persisted Conalin.

Antikas took up the story again. 'Yes. The real problem was in the nature of the spell which brought the Windborn to the earth. They were . . . are . . . creatures of spirit, and though they could build their bodies with magick, they could not hold them together for long. They could not feed as we do, and, as the years passed, some of the Illohir began to wither away, and return to the air. Those that remained needed to find a new source of nourishment. *We* were that nourishment. The Illohir began to feed on human emotions. The Dryads, the fauns, and other creatures of the forest found they could draw energy from human happiness and joy. That is why there are so many stories of wild celebration involving fauns and humans. Fauns were said to have invented wine, to further enhance human joy. But the darker demons fed on terror and dismay – as you saw back in Usa. It was said that the fear and pain inspired in a human tortured to death could feed a demon for years. And because they had magick – which gave them domination over us – they treated us like cattle, as a food source. Mankind suffered through many centuries under their rule, until at last three human kings rebelled against them. The war was long and terrible, the battles many.'

'How did we win?' asked Conalin.

'No-one really knows,' Antikas told him, 'for it was so long ago, and there are so many legends. However, Kalizkan told me that Emsharas the Sorcerer – himself a demon – betrayed his own people and cast a great spell that banished all his brethren from the earth. He made them Windborn again, and locked them away in a great void.'

'And now they are coming back,' said Conalin.

Nogusta stepped forward. 'It is time to ride,' he said.

For the first hour they rode in single file along the narrowing ridge road, Nogusta leading, followed by Kebra and Conalin. Ulmenetha was walking, and holding to the bridle of the queen's mount. Behind her came Bison, also walking, and leading the horse ridden by Pharis and Sufia. Antikas Karios rode at the rear, leading the two spare horses. The wind was cold, hissing over jagged rocks, whipping snow into their faces.

By noon they had reached the highest point and Nogusta drew rein, scanning the road ahead. It dipped gently, curving round a mountain towards an area of high timber several hundred feet below them. From here Nogusta could see a waterfall and a river emptying into a wide lake. Ducking his head against the wind he urged Starfire on. The road widened, and Antikas Karios rode past the others, drawing rein alongside the black warrior.

'We need to rest the horses,' shouted Antikas. Nogusta nodded and pointed to the distant falls.

'I'll scout the area,' said Antikas, and rode on ahead.

There were patches of ice on the road, and the queen's horse slipped. Axiana lurched in the saddle, and found herself staring down into a deep abyss. Grabbing the saddle pommel with her free hand she righted herself in the saddle. The sudden jerk woke the babe. But, safe and warm in his blanket, he went straight back to sleep.

Kebra spotted movement in the trees below. Several small deer

566

moved out of the trees. Taking his bow he also rode alongside Nogusta. 'I'll see you at the falls,' he said, and followed Antikas Karios down the mountain.

They journeyed on for another hour before reaching the falls. It was still cold here, for they were several thousand feet above the valley floor, but the thick stand of trees dispersed the wind, and there was enough dead wood to light a good fire. Kebra returned with a deer, which he had already skinned and quartered, and soon the smell of roasting meat filled the air.

Nogusta ate swiftly, then walked away from the group to stand at the edge of the falls. Antikas Karios joined him there. 'I see you ride the king's horse,' he said. 'I thought it was dying.'

'It had a lung infection caused by poor stabling.'

'It was a fine beast once,' said Antikas. 'But it is old now.'

'Old it may be, Antikas, but it will outrun any horse among the Ventrian cavalry, and it would ride through the fires of Hell for a rider it trusted.'

'Trusted? It is just a horse, black man. No more, no less. A beast of burden.'

Nogusta did not reply. 'I think it is time to tell me what you have seen,' said the Ventrian.

Nogusta swung back towards him. 'You want to know if you live or die?'

'No. Time will tell about that. But you are carrying a great weight. I can tell. It might be better if you shared it.'

Nogusta thought about it for a moment. 'My Gift,' he said, at last, 'is not precise. If it were I would have saved my family from massacre. What I see are sudden, vivid scenes. You remember the king's birthday celebrations? I was talking to Dagorian. I saw him fighting you in the final of the sabres. I could not see if he was winning or losing. The vision lasted a heartbeat only. But then I saw him beside you again, on a bridge. He was sitting against the wall, badly wounded. I had no way of knowing where that bridge was, or when in the future the event would take place. All I knew was that Dagorian would probably die alongside you. Indeed, you may have been the one to cause the wound.'

'I understand,' said Antikas. 'So now tell me what else you have seen.'

For a moment Nogusta did not speak, and stood staring out over the lake. 'I have seen the death of a friend,' he said, at last, dropping his voice. 'And the question that haunts me is this, can

I change his destiny? Could I have prevented Dagorian from standing on that bridge with you? And if I had would you have won alone?'

'Probably not. Dagorian took out three soldiers. Ten would have been too many – even for me.'

'That is what I thought,' said Nogusta. 'Which could mean that, although I could change the future and save my friend, by doing so I might bring about the return of the demons.'

'Alternatively, by changing the future you might bring about the opposite,' Antikas pointed out. 'Have you ever tried to alter events, based on your visions?'

Nogusta nodded. 'I saw a wagon crushing a child to death outside an inn. I knew the inn, and I could tell the event was to happen just before dusk. I went to the area, seeking out the child. I waited at the inn. She came on the second day, and I spoke with her. I told her to beware of running out in front of wagons. I went every day for a week, and we talked often. Then, one afternoon, she was running towards me when I saw a wagon turn the corner. I shouted to her, and she stopped running. The wagon missed her.'

'Then you can alter the future for the good,' said Antikas.

Nogusta shook his head. 'No. I thought I had accomplished the task. The following day she was struck by another wagon and killed. But that was not the worst of it. She was running to meet *me*, because she enjoyed our conversations. Had I not sought her out she might never have been outside the inn at all.'

'It is all very complicated,' said Antikas. 'I am glad that I do not have visions. I do have one observation, however. The Demon Lord needs to sacrifice the babe in order to bring about the end of the Spell. If the child were to die before the sacrifice the Spell would be thwarted.'

'That has occurred to me,' admitted Nogusta.

'And what conclusion did you reach?'

'Whatever destiny holds in store for me it will not be as a killer of children. What the Demon Lord plans is evil. I do not believe that the way to fight great evil is to commit a lesser one. My role now is to protect the child. That I will do.'

'You are very rigid in your thinking,' Antikas pointed out. 'Kill one babe to save the world? It seems a small price to pay.'

'It is not a question of scale,' said Nogusta. 'If it were then ten thousand babes would be a small price for such a great reward. It is a question of right and wrong. That child may prove to be one of the greatest men ever born, a peacemaker and a builder, a prophet or a philosopher. Who can say what wonders he may bring about?'

Antikas chuckled. 'More likely he will be another Skanda, full of vanity and arrogance.'

'Is that your advice then, Antikas Karios, to kill the child?'

'Answer me this first,' responded the Ventrian. 'If your vision told you that the babe was certain to fall into the clutches of the Demon Lord, would you reconsider?'

'No. I will defend it to the last drop of my blood. Now answer my question.'

'I am no longer a general, Nogusta. I am merely a man. You are in command here. As long as you live I will follow your orders, and I too will defend the child to the last.'

'And if I do not live, and you survive me?'

'I will do whatever I think is right by my own principles. Does that satisfy you?'

'Of course.'

Antikas smiled and began to turn away. Then he stopped. 'You are a romantic, Nogusta, and an idealist. I have often wondered how men like you find happiness in such a corrupt and selfish world.'

'Perhaps one day you will find out,' Nogusta told him.

Antikas returned to the camp. Conalin was rubbing down the horses, while Bison sat by the fire eating roast meat, the juices running down his chin and staining his already filthy tunic. Antikas moved to where Axiana was sitting with Ulmenetha and the young girl, Pharis. The priestess was holding the sleeping babe, and the queen was daintily picking at her food.

'A far cry from palace banquets,' observed Antikas, making a deep bow.

'And yet very welcome, sir,' she told him. Axiana's dark eyes met his gaze. 'We thank you for coming to our assistance.'

'My pleasure, highness.'

As Antikas moved away Ulmenetha leaned in to the queen. 'Do you trust him, child?' she asked.

'He is a Ventrian noble,' she replied, as if that answered the question. Reaching out she took back her son, and held him close to her, carefully supporting his head. His tiny hand flapped out from the blanket. 'Look at his finger nails,' she said, 'how small and perfect they are. So tiny. So beautiful.' She gazed down into his face. 'How could anyone wish to hurt him?'

Ulmenetha gave no answer. Stretching out upon the cold ground she released her spirit and flew high above the trees. The fierce winds were merely a sound here, and they shrieked around her, as if angry that they could not buffet her spirit. Like a shaft of light she sped south, searching the land for sign of the Krayakin.

Her spirit soared over woodland and valleys, over tiny settlements and farms. Nowhere could she find evidence of the black-armoured riders. She moved north, back over the canyon and along the Great River. The army of Ventria was marching here, in columns of threes, cavalry riding on the flanks. Ulmenetha drew away from them, afraid that the Demon Lord would sense her spirit.

Back over the canyon she flew, until, far below, she saw the camp-site.

Pain struck her like an arrow, claws digging into her spirit flesh. Instantly she produced the fire of *halignat*, which blazed around her. The claws withdrew, but she could sense a presence close by. Hovering in the air she gazed around her, but could see nothing.

'Show yourself,' she commanded.

Just outside the white fire, so close that it shocked her, a figure materialized. It was that of a man, with ghost-white hair, and a pale face. His eyes were blue and large, his mouth thin lipped and cruel. 'What do you want of me?' she asked him.

'Nothing,' he told her. 'I want only the child.'

'You cannot have him.'

He smiled then. 'Six of my brothers have returned to the great void. You and your companions have done well, and have acted with great courage. I admire that. I always have. But you cannot survive, woman.'

'We have survived so far,' she pointed out.

'By flight. By running into the wilderness. Think about where you are heading. To a ghost city, whose walls have long since crumbled. A stone shell offering no sanctuary. And what is behind you? An army who will reach the city by dusk tomorrow. Where then will you run?'

Ulmenetha could think of no answer. 'You seek to protect a flower in a blizzard,' he said. 'And you are ready to die to do so. But the flower will perish. That is its destiny.'

'That is *not* its destiny,' she told him. 'You and your kind have great powers. But they have not prevailed so far. As you say six of your brothers have gone. The rest of you will follow. Nogusta is a great warrior. He will kill you.'

'Ah, yes, the descendant of Emsharas. The last descendant. An old man, tired and spent. He will defeat the Krayakin and the army of Anharat? I think not.'

Ulmenetha remembered the Demon Lord's words as he floated above the wagon. He had looked at Nogusta and said, 'Yes, you look like him, the last of his mongrel line.' Ulmenetha smiled and looked into the eyes of the Krayakin. 'Do you not find it strange that the descendant of Emsharas should be here now, defying you as his ancestor defied you? Does it not cause you concern? Does it not have a feeling of destiny at work?'

'Yes, it does,' he admitted. 'But it will not alter the outcome. He has no magick. He is not a sorcerer. All his gifts stem from the talisman he wears. It can turn aside spells, but cannot deflect a sword blade.'

'Your evil will not conquer,' she said.

He seemed genuinely surprised. 'Evil? Why is it you humans always speak of evil as something that exists outside of yourselves? Do your cattle think of you as evil because you devour them? Do the fish of the ocean see you as evil? Such arrogance. You are no different to the cattle, and we are not evil for feeding upon you. You wish to hear my view of evil? The actions of Emsharas, banishing his people to a soulless hell, void of sound and smell, of taste and joy. I see our return as no more than simple justice.'

'I will not debate with you, demon,' she told him, and yet she did not move away.

'Not *will not*, woman. *Cannot!* By what right do you deny us a chance at life under the moon and stars?'

'I do not deny you,' she said. 'But by what right do you seek to kill a child?'

'Kill? Another interesting concept. Do you believe in the soul?'

'I do.'

'Then we kill nothing. All we do is end the mortal existence of humans. Their souls go on. And since their mortal existence is fragile and short-lived anyway, what have we really taken from them?'

'Your kind are immortal. You can never know the value of what you so casually remove from others. Death is alien to you. Yes, I believe in the soul, but I do not know if it is immortal. All

I know is the pain you cause to those who are left behind. The misery and the despair.'

He smiled again. 'These things you speak of are our food source.'

'There is no point in this conversation,' she told him.

'Wait! Do not go yet!'

In that moment, as she looked into his eyes, Ulmenetha saw a moment of panic. Why did he want her to stay? Could it be she was reaching him, in some indefinable way. She relaxed and prepared to talk on. Then, though he tried to hide it, she saw the triumph in his eyes. And she knew! She was the only one among the group who could use magick. His only purpose was to detain her.

Spinning away from him she sped for her body.

It was too late. Three Krayakin burst from the bushes and charged into the camp.

Drasko stepped into the clearing, Mandrak to his left, Lekor to his right. Their swords were in their hands, and Drasko felt the long forgotten surging of battle fever in his veins. The bald giant who had killed Nemor ran at him. Drasko spun and plunged his sword through the man's ribs, then backhanded him across the face, hurling the giant to the ground.

On the far side of the fire a hawk-eyed swordsman leapt to his feet. Drasko saw that he carried two Storm Swords. Beyond him a silver-haired man had rolled to his left, coming up with a bow, and notching an arrow to the string. Opening his hand Drasko tossed a small, black crystal globe across the clearing, then closed his eyes.

The explosion was deafening, and Drasko's eyes, even through tightly closed lids, were hurt by the blinding light which followed. Opening his eyes he saw that the swordsman had been hurled across the clearing and was lying, stunned, beside a tall pine. The bowman was sprawled some distance from him. The queen had also been caught by the blast, and was lying unconscious by the bushes, the babe beside her. A red-headed youngster came running from the trees, grabbing the hand of a skinny girl and dragging her away. Drasko had no interest in them.

He turned towards the queen. At that moment the blond-haired woman lying beside her lunged to her feet. The holy fire of *halignat* burst around his helm. He staggered back. The priestess advanced, holy fire blazing from her fingers. Instantly all was confusion. A fireball enveloped Mandrak, who fell back into the undergrowth. Then Lekor hurled a knife, that spun through the air, slamming hilt first into the woman's temple. She dropped to her knees, the fire extinguished. The stunned swordsman was stirring, and Drasko turned once more to where the queen lay unconscious.

Flipping open the visor of his helm he looked for the baby. It was nowhere in sight. The shock was immense. The infant could not have vanished. He knew enough of humans to know that newborn babes could not crawl! He glanced around. The giant human had also gone, and where he had fallen there was now only a bright red stain of blood upon the grass.

'The bald one has the child,' he told the others. 'Find him, kill him, and then return here.'

Lekor and Mandrak turned and ran back through the undergrowth, following a grisly trail of blood.

Drasko moved towards the swordsman. The man was on his knees now, sucking in great gulps of air.

'Gather your swords and face me,' said Drasko. 'It is long since I killed a Storm Swordsman.'

'Then face me, demon,' came a voice from behind.

Drasko spun on his heel and saw the black warrior, Nogusta standing by the camp-fire. He too held a Storm Sword. 'Very well, old one,' said Drasko. 'You shall be – as you humans say – the appetizer before the main course.'

Behind him Antikas Karios fell once more, then rolled to his side, his vision swimming.

Drasko leapt to meet Nogusta. The black man moved in, then swayed away from a wild cut. Their swords met, and lightning flared from the blades. The sound of clashing swords filled the clearing with savagely discordant music. As his vision cleared Antikas Karios watched the warriors circle one another, their blades shimmering in the sunlight, lightning leaping up from every exchange. He knew what Nogusta was going through, and, worse, he knew the end result.

Drasko knew also that the old man was tiring. Always a careful fighter he took no chances. The moment a swordsman went for the kill, was also the most dangerous time. If such an attack was mis-timed a fatal riposte could follow. Therefore Drasko fought on, making no attempt to end the contest, merely waiting for the tiring old man to leave an opening.

Nogusta leapt back, then stumbled, his fatigue obvious. From the ground Antikas watched him. A slow smile began as he recalled the fight with Cerez. Nogusta was trying the same tactic. It worked. Drasko suddenly leapt to the attack. Nogusta swayed away from the thrust. But not fast enough. The blade slammed home in his shoulder, smashing the bone, and emerging at the back. Then his own Storm Sword swept across and down, striking Drasko's sword arm at the elbow. The enchanted blade slid through armour, flesh and bone, severing the limb in one strike. Drasko screamed in pain. The severed arm flopped to the ground, and the black man stood stock still facing his enemy, the sword jutting from his shoulder.

'Time,' said Nogusta, 'to return from whence you came.'

Drawing a dagger with his left hand Drasko lunged. But the Storm Sword flashed in a glittering arc beheading the warrior cleanly. As the body fell Nogusta staggered, then fell to his knees beside it. Flipping his sword he held it dagger fashion, plunging it into Drasko's heart.

Antikas Karios came to his feet and stumbled to where Nogusta knelt. 'Let me help you,' he said.

'No. Follow the trail. Bison has the babe.'

Antikas began to run through the trees. He had seen Bison stabbed. The wound was mortal. And Bison's sword was still lying where it fell.

Unarmed and dying he was the only hope now for the child.

Bison stumbled on, his body racked by spasms of pain. Sweat dripped into his eyes as he ran. Sufia's arms were around his neck, and she was crying. He couldn't remember picking her up. He did, however, remember picking up the baby and staggering into the wood. It was all so confusing. He glanced down. There was blood on the baby's head. For a moment he was worried. Then he realized that the blood was his, and that the child was unhurt. Relieved he moved on. Why am I running? he thought, suddenly. Why am I hurting? His shoulder struck a tree trunk and he spun and almost fell. Regaining his balance he pushed on.

The Krayakin had come. One of them had stabbed him, then struck him on the temple. He had never felt such a blow in his life.

The ground was sloping upwards now. He struggled to the top of a rise and stood, breathing heavily. Then he began to cough. He could feel warm liquid in his throat, choking him. He spewed it out, then gasped for air. Sufia pulled back in his arms and stared at him, her blue eyes wide and fearful. 'Your mouth is bleeding,' she cried.

He couldn't remember being hit in the mouth. He coughed again. Blood dribbled to his chin. Dizziness swamped him. 'They're coming!' shouted the child. Bison swung round.

Two Krayakin in black armour were walking purposefully towards him, black swords in their hands. Holding firmly to the babe and the child Bison pushed on. He had no idea where he was going. All he knew was that he had to carry the children to safety.

But where was safety?

Emerging from the tree line he saw a towering cliff face, and a narrow ledge winding along the face. Blinking sweat from his eyes he struggled on.

'Where are we going?' asked Sufia. Bison did not answer. He felt weak and disoriented, and his breath was coming now in short, painful gasps. I've been wounded before, he told himself. I always heal. I'll heal again. Glancing back he saw the Krayakin reach the top of the rise some 70 yards behind him. Where is Nogusta, he wondered. And Kebra.

They'll be coming! Then I can rest for a while. Nogusta can stitch my wound. Blood was pooling in his boot, and his leggings were drenched. So much blood. He stumbled on. The ledge was narrow here, no more than 3 feet wide. He looked down over the edge. They were impossibly high. Below him Bison could see wispy clouds clinging to the side of the abyss, and through them he could just make out a tiny river flowing through the base of the canyon. 'We are above the clouds,' he told Sufia. 'Look!' But she clung to his shoulder, her head buried against his neck. 'Above the clouds,' he said again. He swayed and almost fell. The baby began to cry. Bison focused his mind on movement and continued along the ledge.

Another coughing spasm shook him, and this time there was a rush of blood, that exploded from his mouth in a crimson spray. Sufia was crying again. Bison stopped moving. The ledge ended here, in a blank, grey wall of rock. Gently he laid the baby on the ledge, then pulled Sufia's arms from around his neck.

'Old Bison needs a rest,' he said. 'You . . . look after the baby for me.'

He was on his knees, but couldn't remember falling. 'There's lots of blood,' wailed Sufia.

'Look . . . after the baby. There's a good girl.' Bison crawled to the edge and gazed down again. 'Never . . . been this high,' he told her.

'What about when you had wings?' she asked.

'Big . . . white . . . wings,' he said. He looked back along the ledge. The Krayakin must be close now, but he could not see them yet.

I don't want to die! The thought was a terrible one, and far too frightening to contemplate. I'm not going to die, he told himself. I'll be fine. A few stitches. The sun was shining, but it was cold here on this exposed face. The cold wind felt good. The wind had been cold back at Mellicane. It was winter then, a hard, harsh winter. The rivers had frozen solid and no-one had expected an army to march through the raging blizzards. But the Drenai had, crossing mountains and lakes of ice. The Ventrian army had been surprised at Mellicane. That's where I got my medal, he remembered. The medal he had sold for a night with a fat whore.

She was a good whore, though, he recalled.

He sat with his back to the cliff, a great wave of weariness covering him like a warm blanket. Sleep, that was what he needed. Healing sleep. When he woke up the wound would be mending. That priestess, she can heal me. A few days' rest and I'll be good as new. Where is Nogusta? Why has he left me alone here?

The baby wailed. Bison thought it best to pick him up, but he didn't seem to have the strength. Sufia screamed and pointed back along the ledge. The two Krayakin were in sight now, moving in single file along the narrow finger of rock.

Twisting round Bison scrabbled at the rock face, dragging himself to his feet. So this is how it ends, he thought. And this time there was no fear. He glanced at Sufia. The child was terrified. Bison forced a smile. 'Don't you worry . . . little one,' he said. 'No-one's going . . . to hurt you. You just . . . look after . . . the little prince until . . . Nogusta comes.'

'What are you going to do?' she asked him.

The Krayakin were closer now. The ledge had widened, and they were advancing together.

Bison pushed at the rock wall, and stood blocking their way.

'Did you know,' he told them, 'that I have wings? Big white wings? I fly . . . over . . . mountains.'

Suddenly he launched himself at them, spreading his arms wide. The Krayakin had nowhere to run. In desperation they stabbed at him, plunging their blades into his chest. With a last desperate lunge he hurled his weight forward, into the cold metal that clove through his heart. Dying, he clamped his huge arms to their armour and propelled them over the edge.

Sufia looked out, and saw them spiralling away, down and down, Bison with outstretched arms, falling into the white, wispy clouds.

Antikas Karios had arrived just in time to see them fall. He ran to Sufia and knelt beside her.

'He got his wings back,' she said, her eyes bright with wonder. 'Big, white wings.'

Little Sufia put her arms around Antikas Karios's neck. Instinctively his own arm curled around her. Then he looked down at the baby. This was the source of all their problems, this tiny package of flesh, soft bone and tissue. It was crying still, thin piping wails that echoed from the rocks. It would be so easy to choke off that sound. The baby's neck was so slender that Antikas could crush the life from it by merely pinching the flesh between his thumb and index finger.

The world would be safe from the demons. His hand reached down. As his finger touched the baby's cheek its head turned towards it, mouth open, seeking to suckle. 'Got to look after the baby,' Sufia whispered into his ear.

'What?'

'That's what Bison said before he flew away.'

He pondered what to do. If he killed the baby, then he would have to kill Sufia too. He could toss them both from the ledge and say he had arrived too late to help them. His thoughts turned to Bison. The grotesque old man had run for almost half a mile, with a wound that should have killed him instantly. Then he had carried two Krayakin to their deaths. He had shown enormous courage, and in that moment Antikas realized that, were he now to kill the child, it would sully the memory of Bison's deed. Gathering up the baby he walked back along the ledge, and down the slope to the camp-site. Kebra and the queen were still unconscious, and Conalin and Pharis were sitting by the fire, hand in hand. The girl looked up as Antikas walked into the camp. Her thin face broke into a wide smile. Surging to her feet she ran to him, lifting Sufia clear. The little girl immediately began to tell her of Bison's wings.

Ulmenetha was sitting beside Nogusta. Antikas walked over to them. Nogusta was looking twenty years older, a grey sheen covering the ebony of his features. His pale blue eyes were tired beyond description. The black sword still jutted from his shoulder.

'Can you remove the sword?' Ulmenetha asked Antikas. Laying the baby on the grass he took hold of the hilt. Nogusta gritted his teeth.

'Brace yourself,' said Antikas, setting his boot against Nogusta's chest. With one savage wrench he dragged the blade clear. Nogusta cried out, then sagged against Ulmenetha. Holding her hands over the entry and exit wounds she began to chant.

Antikas moved away from them to where Kebra lay. Kneeling beside him he felt for the man's pulse. It was firm and strong. Conalin appeared alongside him. 'He is just sleeping,' said the boy. 'Ulmenetha has already prayed over him.'

'Good,' said Antikas.

'Did you see Bison's wings?' asked Conalin.

'No.' He gazed up at the boy, angry now. 'There were no wings,' he snapped. 'Such stories are for children who cannot deal with the harsh realities of life. A brave man gave his life to save others. He fell thousands of feet and his dead body was smashed upon the rocks below.'

'Why did he do it?'

'Why indeed? Go away and leave me, boy.'

Conalin walked back to the fire, and the waiting Pharis. Antikas pushed himself to his feet and made his way to the water's edge, where he drank deeply.

The death of Bison had moved him in a way he had difficulty understanding. The man was an animal, ill bred and uncultured, uncouth and coarse. Yet when the Krayakin had attacked he had been the first to tackle them, and had, without doubt, saved the children. He had gone willingly to his death. All his life Antikas had been taught that nobility lay in the blood line. Nobles and peasants, thinking beings and near animals. Only the nobility were said to understand the finer points of honour and chivalry.

The manner of Bison's sacrifice was unsettling. Axiana was a Ventrian princess, her child the son of the man who had spurned Bison's services. Bison owed them nothing, but gave them everything.

It was more than unsettling. It was galling.

In Ventrian history heroes had always been noblemen, full of courage and virtue. They were never belching, groin-scratching simpletons. A thought struck him, and he smiled. Maybe they were. Conalin had asked him if Bison had grown wings. If they survived this quest the story would grow. Antikas would tell it. Sufia would tell it. And the story to be believed would be the child's. And why? Because it was more satisfying to believe that heroes never die, that somehow they live on, to return in another age. In a hundred years the real Bison would be remembered not at all. He would become golden haired and handsome, perhaps the bastard son of a Ventrian noble. Antikas glanced at the sleeping queen. Most likely he would also, in future legends, become Axiana's lover and the father of the babe he saved.

Antikas returned to the camp. Nogusta was sleeping now. Axiana was awake and feeding the child. Ulmenetha signalled for Antikas to join her. 'The wound is a bad one,' she said. 'I have done what I can, but he is very weak, and may still die.'

'I would lay large odds against that, lady. The man is a fighter.'

'And an old man devastated not just by a wound, but by grief. Bison was his friend, and he knew his friend was to die.'

Antikas nodded. 'I know this. What would you have me do?'

'You must lead us to Lem.'

'What is so vital about the ghost city? What is it we seek among the ruins?'

'Get us there and you will see,' said Ulmenetha. 'We can wait another hour, then I will wake the sleepers.'

As she turned her head he saw the angry, swollen bruise upon her temple, and remembered the knife hilt laying her low. 'That was a nasty blow,' he said. 'How are you feeling?'

She smiled wearily. 'I feel a little nauseous, but I will live, Antikas Karios. I have the maps here. Perhaps you would like to study them.' He took them from her and unrolled the first. Ulmenetha leaned in. 'The Ventrian army are moving from here,' she said, stabbing her finger at the map, 'and they have swept out in a sickle formation, expecting us to make for the sea. Within the next two days they will have secured all the roads leading to Lem.'

'There is no proper scale to this map,' he said. 'I cannot tell how far we are from the ruins.'

'Less than forty miles,' she told him. 'South and west.'

'I will think on a route,' he said. He glanced at Axiana, who was sitting just out of earshot. 'It would have been better for the world had Bison jumped with the babe,' he said, softly.

'Not so,' she told him. 'The Demon Lord has already begun the

Great Spell. The child's death will complete it, with or without a sacrifice.'

Antikas felt suddenly chill. He looked away, and remembered his fingers reaching for the babe's throat.

'Well,' he said, at last, 'that, at least, adds a golden sheen to the old man's death.'

'Such a deed needs no sheen,' she told him.

'Perhaps not,' he agreed. He left her then and moved to the fire. Little Sufia was sitting quietly with Conalin and Pharis. She scampered over to Antikas. 'Will he fly back to us?' she asked him. 'I keep looking in the sky.'

Antikas took a deep breath, and he looked at Conalin.

'He will fly back one day,' he told the child, 'when he is most needed.'

Chapter Eleven

Nogusta was only vaguely aware that he was riding a horse. Someone was sitting behind him, holding him in the saddle. He opened his eyes and saw that the company was moving slowly across a verdant valley. Up ahead Antikas Karios was riding Starfire. Nogusta felt a stab of irritation, but then remembered he had commanded the Ventrian to take his horse. Starfire was a spirited animal, and Nogusta was in no condition to ride him.

He glanced down at the hands supporting him. They were slender and feminine. Patting the hands he whispered, 'Thank you.'

'Do you need to stop and rest?' Ulmenetha asked him.

'No.' His vision swam and he leaned back into the woman.

Bison was gone, and the pain of loss struck him savagely. He swayed in the saddle and felt Ulmenetha's arms holding him firmly. Then he drifted into dreams of the past. The day passed in a haze. When they stopped to rest the horses Kebra helped him down. Nogusta did not know where he was, only that the sun was warm on his face, the grass cool against his back. It was blissful here, and he wanted to sleep for ever. From somewhere close came the cry of an infant. Then he heard a child singing a song. He seemed to remember the child had been killed by a wagon, but obviously this was not so. He was relieved – as if a burden had been lifted from him.

At some point he was fed a thick soup. He remembered the taste, but could not recall who had fed him, nor why he had not fed himself.

Then he saw his father. They were all sitting in the main room of the house, his brothers and sisters, his mother, and his old aunt. 'I shall show you some magick,' his father said, rising from the old horse hide chair he cherished. He had lifted the talisman from around his neck. The chain was long, the gold glinting in the lantern light. Father walked to the eldest of Nogusta's brothers and tried to loop the chain over his head. But the chain shrank, and would not pass over the boy's skull. Each of the brothers in turn marvelled at the magick. Then he came to Nogusta. The chain slid easily over his head, the talisman settling to his chest.

'What is the trick?' asked his eldest brother.

'There is no trick,' said father. 'The talisman has chosen. That is all.'

'That is not fair,' said the eldest. 'I am the heir. It should be mine.'

'I was not the heir,' father pointed out. 'Yet it chose me.'

'How does it choose?' asked the youngest brother.

'I do not know. But the man who made it was our ancestor. He was greater than any king.'

That night, alone in their room, his eldest brother had struck him in the face. 'It should have been mine,' he said. 'It was a trick because father loves you more.'

Nogusta could still feel the pain of the blow. Only now, for some strange reason that he could not fathom, the pain was emanating from his shoulder.

He was riding again, and he opened his eyes to see the stars shining in the night sky. A new moon hung like a sickle over the mountains, just like on his talisman. He almost expected to see a golden hand reach out to encircle it. High above him an owl glided by on white wings.

White wings . . .

'Poor Bison,' he said, aloud.

'He is at peace,' said a voice. The voice confused Nogusta. Somehow Ulmenetha had transformed into Kebra.

'How did you do that?' he mumbled. Then he slept again, and awoke beside a camp-fire. Kebra had become Ulmenetha again, and her hand was upon his wound. She was chanting softly.

A figure floated before his vision, blurred and indistinct, and Nogusta fell away into a deep dream.

He was sitting in the Long Meadow back at home, and he could hear his mother singing in the kitchen. A tall man was sitting beside him, a black man, but one he did not know.

'This was a peaceful time for you,' said the man.

'It was the best of times,' Nogusta told him.

'If you survive you must come back and rebuild. The descendants of your herds are back in the mountains. There are great stallions there, and the herds are strong.'

'The memories are too painful.'

'Yes they are painful, but there is peace here, if you seek it.'

He looked at the man. 'Who are you?'

'I am Emsharas. And you are the last of my human line.'

'You cast the Great Spell.'

'I began it. It is not complete yet.'

'Will the child die?'

'All of Man's children die, Nogusta. It is their weakness – and their strength. There is great power in death. Rest now, for you have one last test before you.'

Nogusta opened his eyes. The glorious light of a new dawn was edging over the mountains. He groaned as he sat up. Kebra grinned at him.

'Welcome back, my brother,' he said. There were tears in Kebra's eyes as he leaned forward, and, for the first time, embraced Nogusta.

Anharat's anger had cooled now, as he sat in his tent, listening to the reports from his scouts. The renegades had crossed the last bridge before Lem, and were now less than 12 miles from the ruins. A five-man scouting party had attacked them, but Antikas Karios had killed two, a third being shot from the saddle by a bowman. 'Bring in the survivors,' ordered Anharat.

Two burly scouts entered the tent, then threw themselves to the floor, touching their brows to the rug at Anharat's feet.

'Up!' he commanded. The men rose, their expressions fearful. 'Tell me what you saw.' Both men began speaking at once, then glanced at one another. 'You,' said Anharat, pointing to the man on the left. 'Speak.'

'They were coming down a long slope, my lord. Antikas Karios was leading them. He was followed by a white-haired man, then by the queen and her servant. There was a small child, and two youngsters. And a black man with a bandage around his chest. There was blood on it. Captain Badayen thought we could surprise them with a sudden charge. So that's what we did. He was the first to die. Antikas Karios wheeled his horse and charged us! The captain went down, then Malik. Then the bowman shot an arrow through the throat of Valis. So me and Cupta turned our horses and galloped off. We thought it best to report what we'd seen.'

Anharat looked deep into the man's dark eyes. They both expected death. The Demon Lord wished he could oblige them. But morale among the humans was low. Most of them had friends and family back in the tortured city of Usa, and they did not understand why they were pursuing a small group across a wilderness. Added to this Anharat had noticed a great wariness among his officers when they spoke to him. At first it had confused him, for even while inhabiting the decaying body of Kalizkan, the Warmth Spell had maintained the popularity the sorcerer had enjoyed. The same spell had little effect on Malikada's men. This, he reasoned, at last, was because Malikada had never been popular. He was feared. This was not a wholly undesirable state of affairs, but with morale suffering Anharat would gain no added support from these humans by butchering two hapless scouts.

'You acted correctly,' he told the men. 'Captain Badayen should not have charged. He should have ridden ahead, as ordered and held the last bridge. You are blameless. Had the captain survived I would have hanged him. Go and get some food.'

The men stood blinking in disbelief. Then they bowed and swiftly backed from the tent. Anharat gazed at his officers, sensing their relief. What curious creatures these humans are, he thought.

'Leave me now,' he told them.

No-one moved. Not a man stirred. All stood statue still, not a flickering muscle, not the blink of an eyelid. As if from a great distance Anharat heard the gentle tinkling music of wind chimes. He spun around to see Emsharas standing by the tent entrance. His brother was wearing a sky-blue robe, and a gold circlet adorned his brow. It was no vision! Emsharas was here in the flesh.

A cold fury grew within Anharat, and he began to summon his power. 'Not wise, brother,' said Emsharas. 'You need all your strength for the completion of the Spell.'

It was true. 'What do you want here?' demanded Anharat.

'Peace between us – and the salvation of our people,' said Emsharas.

'There will never be peace between you and I. You betrayed us all. I will hate you until the stars burn out and die, and the universe returns to the dark.'

'I have never hated you, Anharat. Not now, not ever. But I ask you – as I asked you once before – to consider your actions. The Illohir could never have won. We are few, they are many. Their curious minds grow with each passing generation. The secrets of magick will not be held from them for ever. Where then shall we be? What must we become, save dusty legends from their past? We opened the gateways, you and I. We brought the Illohir to this hostile world. We did not kill when we were Windborn, we did not lust after terror and death.'

Anharat gave a derisive laugh. 'And we knew no pleasures, save those of the intellect. We knew no joys, Emsharas.'

'I disagree. We saw the birthing of stars, we raced upon the cosmic storm winds. There was joy there. Can you not see that we are alien to this planet? It conspires against us. The waters burn our skin, the sunlight saps our strength. We cannot feed here, unless it be from the emotions of humans. We are parasites on this world. Nothing more.'

Emsharas stepped further into the tent, and looked closely at the frozen officers. 'Their dreams are different from ours. We will never live among them. And one day they will destroy us all.'

'They are weak and pitiful,' said Anharat, his hand slowly moving towards the dagger at his belt. It would need no magick to plunge a dagger into his brother's heart. Then he too would be cast into Nowhere.

'I offer a new world for our people,' said Emsharas.

'Tell me the source of your power,' whispered Anharat, his fingers curling around the dagger hilt.

Emsharas swung to face him. 'Why have you not already guessed it?' he countered. 'All the clues are there, in the failure of your search spells, and the nature of the Great Spell itself.'

'You found a place to hide. That is all I know.'

'No, Anharat. I am not hiding.'

'You liar! I see you standing before me, drawing breath.'

'Indeed you can. Tonight I opened a gateway, Anharat, to bring me through to you. But where is *tonight*? It is four thousand years in the past and I am with the army of the Three Kings, and tomorrow you and I will fight above the battlefield. You will lose. Then I will prepare myself for the Great Spell. You can help me complete it. Our people can have a world of their own!'

'This is the world I want!' snarled Anharat, drawing the

dagger. Leaping forward he slashed the blade at his brother. Emsharas swayed aside. His form shimmered.

And he was gone.

Bakilas sat quietly in the dark. The Illohir had no need of sleep. There was no necessity to regenerate tissue. All was held in place by magick fuelled by feeding. The Lord of the Krayakin needed no rest. He was waiting in this place only because his horse was weary.

Truth to tell he had not been surprised when his brothers had been defeated. This quest was flawed from the beginning. The priestess was right. It was no coincidence that a descendant of Emsharas should be guarding the baby. There was some grand strategy here, whose significance was lost on Bakilas.

What do I do now? he wondered. Where do I go?

He stood and walked to the brow of the hill and gazed down on the ruins of Lem. He could remember when this city had been like a jewel, shimmering in the night with a hundred thousand lights.

He gazed up at the stars, naming them in his mind, recalling the times when, formless, he had visited them. In that moment he wished he had never been offered the gift of flesh.

Anharat and Emsharas had brought it to the Illohir. The Twins, the gods of glory. Their power combined had created the link between wind and earth. They had been the first. Emsharas had taken human form, while Anharat had chosen wings. The Krayakin had followed.

Who could have guessed then that the gift was also a curse?

True the sunlight had caused great pain, and the water of the rivers had been deadly, but there were so many other pleasures to be enjoyed, and an eternity in which to enjoy them.

Until Emsharas betrayed them all.

Even now, after 4,000 years of contemplation, Bakilas could not begin to understand his reasons. Nor what had become of him. Where could an Illohir hide? Even now Bakilas could sense all his brothers in the void of Nowhere. Emsharas had shone like the largest star. It was impossible not to know his whereabouts. Bakilas could feel the powerful, pulsing presence of Anharat at his camp a few miles away. Equally, had Anharat been Windborn, he could have felt his spirit across the universe. Where then did Emsharas dwell?

One day the answer will become clear, he thought. One day, when the universe ends and the Illohir die with it.

Bakilas shivered. Death. To cease to be. It was a terrifying thought. Humans could not begin to comprehend the true fear of mortality. They lived always with the prospect of death. They understood its inevitability. A few short seasons and they were gone. Worse yet they tasted death throughout their few heart-beats of existence. Every passing year brought them fresh lines and wrinkles, and the slow erosion of their strength. Their skin sagged, their bones dried out, until toothless and senile they flopped into their graves. What could they know of immortal fear?

Not one of the Illohir had ever known death.

Bakilas recalled the Great Birthing in the Coming of Light, when the first chords of the Song of the Universe rang out across the dark. It was a time of discovery and harmony, a time of comradeship. It was life. Sentient and curious. Everything was born at that time, the stars and then the planets, the oceans of lava, and finally the great seas.

There had been joys then of a different kind; the increase of knowledge and awareness. But there had been no pain, no disappointments, no tragedies. Absolute serenity had been enjoyed – endured? – by all the Illohir. Only with the coming of the flesh did the contrasts begin. How could one know true joy until one had tasted true despair? Contrast was everything. Which was why the Illohir lusted after the life of *form*.

Bakilas moved back from the hilltop and drew his sword. Moving silently alongside the sleeping horse he beheaded it with one terrible sweep of his blade. As the beast fell Bakilas tore out its heart and held it up to the night sky, calling upon Anharat.

The heart burst into flame.

'I am glad that you called upon me, brother,' said the voice of Anharat. 'Emsharas has returned.'

'I do not sense him.'

'His powers are great. But he is here. He seeks to prevent our destiny.'

'But why?' asked Bakilas. 'You and he are the Twins. Since time began you were One in all things.'

'We are One no longer,' snapped Anharat. 'I will defeat him. I will hold his spirit in the palm of my hand and I will torment it until the end of time.'

Bakilas said nothing. He sensed a joy in Anharat that had been missing since the betrayal. He was *pleased* that Emsharas had returned! How curious! Bakilas had felt Anharat's pain, and his

587

sense of loss. His hatred of Emsharas had become all consuming. Throughout the centuries he had never given up the hunt for his brother, sending search spell after search spell. His hatred was almost as strong as his love had been. A thought came to Bakilas then. Perhaps hatred and love were, in some ways, the same. Both echoed an intense need in Anharat. His existence without Emsharas had been hollow and empty. Even now the Demon Lord dreamed only of holding his brother's spirit in his hand. Hatred and love. Indistinguishable.

'You must go into Lem,' said Anharat. 'Hide there until the time to strike! When the babe dies, and my power swells, I will find Emsharas and there will be a reckoning.'

Nayim Pallines had always disliked Antikas Karios, though he had wisely kept this information to himself for several years. He had known Kara since childhood, and was one of the guests at her wedding. He had seen her radiant joy, and had envied the look of love she gave her husband as the vows were made, and the ceremonial cord had been looped about their wrists.

Two days later both were dead, the husband slain by the killer Antikas Karios, Kara dead by her own hand. Love, Nayim knew, was far too precious to be so casually destroyed. When the tragedies occurred his dislike of Antikas Karios turned to hatred.

And yet, as a colonel in the Royal Lancers he had been obliged to serve this man, to take his orders, and to bow before him. It had been hard.

But today – with the help of the Source, and the courage of the fifty men riding behind him – he would put an end to both the hatred and the object of it. His scouts had spotted them 3 miles from the ruins of Lem, and Nayim was less than half a mile behind them.

Soon they would see the pursuing riders. Nayim could picture it. The fleeing group would lash at their mounts in a last, desperate attempt to evade capture. But their tired horses would soon be overhauled by the powerful mounts of the lancers. Nayim half hoped that Antikas Karios would beg for his life. Yet even as the thought occurred he knew it would not be so. Antikas, for all his vileness, was a man of courage. He would attack them all.

Nayim was no more than a capable swordsman. He would have to be sure to hang back when the attack began. While not afraid to die he did not wish to miss the capture of Antikas Karios.

His sergeant, Olion, rode alongside him, his white cape fluttering in the breeze. There was a mud stain upon the cape. Olion was a superb horseman, and a fine soldier, but incapable of smartness, no matter what disciplinary measures were taken against him. The high, curved helm of bronze and the ceremonial cape had been designed to add grandeur to the armour of the Lancers. But for Olion, short, stocky, and round shouldered, his face endlessly marked by angry red spots, the end result was comic.

Nayim glanced at the man as he rode alongside. Yet another boil was showing on the nape of Olion's neck. 'The lads are worried, sir,' said the sergeant. 'I don't like the mood.'

'Are you telling me that fifty men are frightened of tackling one swordsman?'

'It's not about them, sir. In fact they'll be relieved to see a little action. No, it's not that, sir.'

'Spit it out, man. You'll not lose your head for it.'

'I could, sir, if you take my meaning?'

Nayim understood perfectly. His face hardened. 'I do indeed. Therefore it will be better to say nothing. Ride up to the top of the slope there and see if you can see them yet.'

'Yes, sir.' Olion galloped off towards the south-east. Nayim glanced back. His men were riding in columns of twos behind him, the butts of their lances resting on their stirrups. Signalling them to continue at their present pace he flicked his heels and rode after Olion.

At the top of the slope he hauled in his mount, and found himself gazing over the distant, ruined city of Lem. Said to be one of the greatest cities ever built it was now a place of ghosts and lost memories. The huge walls had been eroded by time, brought down by earthquakes, many of the stones removed to build houses at the far end of the valley. What remained of the north wall stood before the ghost city like a row of broken teeth.

Then he saw the riders, still around a half mile ahead. At this distance he could not make out individuals, but he could see that their horses were tiring, and they were still some way from the city. Once his men caught up they would ride them down within minutes.

'Be swift and say what you have to say,' he told Olion. 'For then we must do our duty.'

'This is all wrong, sir. The men know it. I know it. I mean, what happened back in the city? There are thousands dead, by all accounts. That's where we ought to be. And why bring the whole army into this wilderness? There's no-one to fight, sir. So why are we here?'

'We are here because we are ordered to be,' said Nayim, anxious to capture the runaways.

'And what about supplies, sir? According to the quartermaster we only have enough food to bring us to Lem. What are we supposed to do then? We've not even been put on half rations. Come the day after tomorrow there'll be no food at all for three thousand men. It's madness!'

'I'll tell you what madness is, Olion, it is a soldier in the army of Malikada who starts spouting mutinous words.' Nayim tried to make the threat sound convincing, but he could not. He shared the man's concern. 'Listen,' he said, in a more conciliatory tone. 'We will do our duty here, then return the prisoners to Malikada. We saw the tracks of elk a few miles back. Once we have the prisoners secured you can lead a unit after them. Then at least we'll eat well tonight.'

'Yes, sir,' said the man, dubiously.

Nayim cast a nervous glance back. The lancers were almost within earshot. 'I take it there is something else? Make it quick!'

'Why is the queen running away? Malikada is her cousin. They have always been close, so it's said. And why would a general like Antikas Karios be helping her?'

'I don't know. Perhaps we shall ask Antikas when we take him.'

As the troops drew reins behind him Nayim raised his arm. 'Follow me!' he shouted.

Picking up the pace he cantered his mount along the old road, swiftly closing the distance between himself and the fleeing riders. A red-headed youngster riding the last horse looked back, then kicked his mount into a run.

Now the chase was on. Nayim drew his sabre. He could see Antikas Karios now, riding a huge black gelding. The man swung his horse, and, for a moment, Nayim thought he would charge them. Instead he galloped back to the rear of his group, urging them on. Nayim gently drew back on his reins, allowing some of his men to overtake him.

The silver-haired bowman swung in the saddle, sending a shaft flashing towards him. Nayim swayed and ducked. He heard a man cry out behind him. Glancing back he saw the arrow jutting from a rider's shoulder.

Nayim was anxious to catch the runaways before they entered the ruins, for once there Antikas and the others could dismount and take cover. They would not last long, but it would cost him men. One of the reasons why Nayim was a popular commander was that he was careful with the lives of his soldiers. No reckless charges, no seeking after glory. He was a professional soldier who always thought out his strategies.

They were closing fast now. Up ahead Antikas Karios was now leading a second horse upon which sat a young woman in a blue dress. It was with some surprise that Nayim recognized the queen. He had always seen her in gowns of silk and satin, looking like a goddess from myth. Now she was merely a woman on a slow horse.

Only around 40 yards separated them now. Antikas would have no time to seek cover, for they would catch him at the city walls!

Suddenly one of his men shouted a warning. Nayim soon saw why.

Armed men were pouring from the ruins of the city, forming a deep fighting line before the broken gates. They were Drenai soldiers, wearing full-faced helms and sporting long, red cloaks. Hundreds of them, moving smoothly into place with the easy discipline of veterans. Nayim could scarce believe his eyes.

The Drenai army had been destroyed. How then could this be?

Then he realized with shock that he was charging down towards them. Hauling on the reins he held up his arm. All around him his men slowed their mounts.

The fleeing group rode towards the fighting line, which parted smoothly before them, allowing them access to the city.

Ordering his men to wait Nayim rode slowly forward. 'Where is your commander?' he called out. Silence greeted his words. He scanned the line, calculating numbers. There were close to a thousand men in sight. It was inconceivable!

The line parted once more and a tall, thin old man walked out to stand before him.

Nayim felt a sudden chill touch him, as he gazed into the cold eyes of the White Wolf.

As soon as he rode past the old city wall Conalin jumped down from his horse and ran back, scrambling up a jutting stump of stone and squatting down to watch the soldiers. They looked terrifyingly impressive in their bronze breastplates, full-faced bronze helms and crimson cloaks. Their spears were held steady, and their shields presented a strong wall between Conalin and those who had sought to kill him. For the first time in his young life he felt utterly safe. What force on earth could penetrate such a wall of men. He wanted to leap up and dance, to shout his scorn at the waiting Ventrian riders. They looked so puny now. Conalin glanced up at the blue sky, and felt a cool breeze upon his face.

He was safe – and the world was beautiful.

Pharis scrambled up to sit beside him. He took her hand. 'Look at them!' he said. 'Are they not the most wonderful soldiers you ever saw?'

'Yes,' she agreed, 'but where did they come from? Why are they here?'

'Who cares? We get to live, Pharis. We get to have that house in Drenan.' Conalin fell silent, for the old general was talking to the Ventrian lancer. Conalin strained to hear their words, but they were speaking softly.

Nayim dismounted and approached Banelion, offering a respectful bow, which the old man acknowledged with a brief nod. 'We are instructed by the Lord Malikada to return the queen to her palace,' said Nayim. 'We have no quarrel with you, sir.'

'The queen and her son travel with me to Drenan,' said the White Wolf. 'There she will be safe.'

'Safe? You think I mean to do her harm?'

Banelion looked into the young man's eyes. 'What you do or do not do is entirely your own affair. Malikada – or the beast who inhabits Malikada – intends to kill the babe. This I know. This I shall prevent.'

Nayim was taken aback by the words, but, on reflection, was not surprised by them. If Malikada wished to seize the throne then he would certainly see that all rivals were put to the sword. 'Let us assume, sir, for the sake of argument, that you are correct in your assessment. By my judgement you have less than a thousand men here, and no cavalry. A half a day to the north is the Ventrian army. We are three times your number. And we were trained by you, sir. You cannot prevail.'

Banelion gave a mirthless smile that chilled the younger man. 'I have followed your recent career with interest, Nayim Pallines. You are an efficient, courageous and disciplined officer. Had I remained with the army I would have secured promotion for you. But you are wrong, young man. Armies fight best when they have something to fight for, something they believe in. In such instances numerical advantage is lessened considerably. Do you believe in what you are fighting for, Nayim? Do you believe that two armies should fight over whether a child is put to the knife?'

'I believe in doing my duty, sir.'

'Then go back to the Beast, and prepare to die for him. But do not be deceived, Nayim, you are not following Malikada. Malikada is dead. A Demon Lord has possessed his body.'

'With respect, sir, you do not expect me to believe that?'

The White Wolf shrugged. Nayim bowed once more and returned to his horse. 'The army will be here by sunset, sir. It is my hope that you will reconsider your position.' Swinging his horse he rode back to his men, then led them north.

The White Wolf watched them go, then gave the order to stand down. The troops broke formation and laid down their spears and shields, removing their helms. On the broken wall Conalin watched them, a sick sense of dread flowing through him.

Old men! They were all old men, grey haired or bald. Where moments before had been an invincible force, he now saw them shuffling around on what he perceived to be arthritic limbs, slowly lowering themselves to the ground. Conalin felt betrayed by them. Pharis saw his anger and reached out to him.

'What is it, Con?'

He did not reply, could not reply. Emotions surged within him. He jumped down from the wall and walked to his horse. Taking it by the bridle he led it further into the ruins. There was only one building mostly intact, a huge structure built from white marble, and it was here that the other horses had been tethered. A flight of cracked steps led to a huge, arched doorway. Conalin stepped inside. There was an enormous chamber within, with a high domed roof, part of which had collapsed. Fallen stones littered the remains of the mosaic which had once decorated the entire floor. There was no furniture here, but against the far wall were several broken benches. Light was streaming into the building through high, arched windows. Fragments of coloured glass still clung to some of the frames.

Conalin saw his companions at the far end of the chamber, sitting upon a raised octagonal dais. Kebra saw him and smiled. Conalin strode to where the bowman sat. 'They are all old men,' he said, bitterly.

'They were our comrades,' said Kebra. 'Most of them are younger than Bison.'

'And Bison's dead,' snapped Conalin. Instantly he regretted it, for he saw the pain in Kebra's eyes. 'I'm sorry,' he said, swiftly. 'I didn't mean it like that. It's just . . . they looked so strong when we first saw them.'

'They *are* strong,' said Kebra. 'And they have the White Wolf to lead them. He has never lost a battle.'

'We should ride on,' said the boy. 'Leave the old men to fight.'

Kebra shook his head. 'This will be the final battle, Con. Here, in this ruined place. I will not run any further.'

Conalin sat beside the bowman, his shoulders bowed. 'I wish I had never come with you,' he said.

'I am glad that you did. You have taught me a great deal.'

'I have? What could I teach you?'

Kebra gave a sad smile. 'I have always wondered what it would be like to have a son, a boy I could be proud of; someone I could watch grow into manhood. You have shown me what it could have been like. And you are quite right, there is no reason for you to stay here. There is nothing you can do. Why not take Pharis and Sufia, and some supplies and head off into the hills. If you head west you will eventually reach the sea. I will give you money. I do not have much, but it will help.'

The thought of leaving touched Conalin like the cool breeze that follows a storm, blowing away his anger and his fear. He and Pharis would be safe. And yet, in that moment, it wasn't enough. 'Why can you not come with us? One man won't make a difference.'

'These are my friends,' said Kebra. 'A true man does not desert his friends in time of need.'

'You think I am not a man?' asked Conalin.

'No, no! I am sorry for the way that sounded. You will be a fine man. But you are young yet, and war is not for . . .' He was going to say children, but as he looked into Conalin's young face he saw the man there, waiting to be born. 'I do not want to see you hurt, Con,' he said, lamely.

'Nor I you. I think I will stay.'

Kebra cleared his throat and held out his hand. Conalin looked embarrassed, but he gripped it firmly. 'I am proud of you,' said Kebra.

They sat in pleasant silence for a while and Conalin gazed around the enormous building. 'What was this place?' he asked.

'I don't know,' admitted Kebra. 'But it has the feel of a temple, don't you think?'

'I have never been in one,' said Conalin. Sufia was sitting on the floor close by, rubbing at the stones with the ragged sleeve of her dress.

'There's pictures on the floor,' she said, happily.

Ulmenetha moved to her side, kneeling down. 'They are called mosaics,' she told the child. 'They are created with lots of coloured stones.'

'Come look!' Sufia called out to Conalin. He did so. There was no way of telling what the original mosaic had depicted, for many of the coloured stones had been shattered by falling masonry from the ceiling, the rest covered by the dust of centuries. There was a tiny patch of blue, and a line of red. It could have been a flower, or a section of sky.

'It's very pretty,' he told her.

'I shall clean it all up,' she said, with the confidence of the very young, and began to scrub at a tiny section.

'It will take you weeks,' he said, staring around the vast temple.

'Weeks,' she repeated. 'That's all right.' She rubbed at the stones for a few more seconds then sat back. 'I'm hungry now.'

Conalin picked her up, and kissed her cheek. 'Then let us find you some food,' he said. Perching her on his shoulders he walked back out into the sunlight. Pharis was sitting on the steps. Off to the left was a line of seven wagons. Cookfires had been lit close by, and the three of them moved off in search of a meal.

As they approached the cookfires an elderly soldier called out to them. The man had a wicked scar upon his face, and a black patch over what had once been his right eye. Beside him was a trestle table, stacked with pewter plates. 'You look in need of something hot and savoury,' he said. Moving to a huge, black cooking pot he ladled thick stew into three deep plates and handed them to the youngsters. 'Take some spoons,' he said, 'but bring them back, with the plates, when you're finished. Then I've some honey cakes for you.'

Conalin thanked the man. The soup was thick and nourishing, though with too much salt for the boy's liking. But he was famished, and consumed it with relish. The old soldier did not wait for them to return the utensils, but came over with a plate of honey cakes. Sufia grabbed two, then looked anxiously up at Conalin, waiting for a rebuke. When none came she happily devoured them.

'Why did you come here?' Conalin asked the soldier.

'White Wolf brought us,' said the man.

'Yes, but why?'

'He didn't say. Just offered us twenty gold pieces a man. Said there might be a battle.'

'There will be,' said Conalin.

'Good. Wouldn't want to come all this way for nothing,' said the soldier. Collecting the plates and spoons he moved away. Moments later other soldiers began to file past the cookfires, and soon the area was crowded. Everyone seemed at ease, and many of the soldiers took time to speak with the youngsters. Conalin was confused.

'They seem to be looking forward to fighting,' he said to Pharis. 'I don't understand it.'

'It is what they do,' replied the girl. 'It is what they are. We should take some food back to the queen.'

'Can I carry it?' asked Sufia.

'Of course you can, little one.'

'I won't spill any,' she promised. 'Not even a drop.'

Axiana watched as four veteran soldiers erected Banelion's tent at the far end of the temple. Simple furniture was carried in, a hinged bed, several canvas-backed chairs and a folding table. Then they swept the floor inside and laid simple rugs upon it. Not once did the men look at her. It was as if she was invisible. While they were working the youngsters returned. The blonde child, Sufia, brought her a bowl of soup. She thanked her with a smile, and turned away from the soldiers while she ate.

Some distance away Antikas Karios and Kebra were sitting beside the sleeping figure of Nogusta. The black man's wounds were healing, but his continuing weakness was a source of concern.

As Axiana finished her meal the tall, slim, armoured figure of Banelion entered the temple, followed by two soldiers carrying a wooden chest. The White Wolf approached the queen and bowed low. 'I am pleased to see you safe, your highness,' he said. 'My tent is yours, and I took the liberty of bringing some spare clothes for you.' Gesturing the men forward he had the chest placed on the dais before her, and opened. The first item she saw was a dress of sky blue satin. 'I do not have an eye for fashion, your highness,' said Banelion, 'but I borrowed these from a noble lady in Marain. It is a small town, and there was little to choose from.'

'It was kind of you, sir, and I thank you.' Ulmenetha appeared alongside her, taking the sleeping baby from the queen's arms.

Axiana reached out and stroked the dress. It was wonderfully soft. Then she noticed – against the clean pure satin – how dirty her hands were. For the first time in days she felt embarrassment.

'There is an antechamber just beyond where the tent is placed,' said Banelion. 'There is a spring there. Some of my men have prepared a fire, and warmed some water. When you are ready you and your maidservant can refresh yourselves. I brought a small amount of scented oil with me to perfume the water.'

Before Axiana could reply another soldier entered, carrying a rough made crib, and a small, woven mattress. Setting it beside the queen he placed the mattress within it. 'Best I could do in the time, my lady,' he said, with a bow. Ulmenetha placed the babe within it. The child settled contentedly on the mattress, his sleep undisturbed.

The unexpected kindness left Axiana close to tears. She smiled at the soldier. 'You are most kind.' The man blushed and backed away.

The White Wolf gazed down at the babe, a far-away look in his eye. Then he straightened. 'There are some clothes for an infant at the bottom of the chest,' he said.

'You seem to have thought of everything,' said Axiana. 'I am most grateful. But tell me, how is it that you are here in our hour of need? We are a long way from the sea.'

He glanced at Ulmenetha. 'First Kalizkan appeared to me in a dream, then this lady came. She told me of your peril, and the threat to your son. She asked me to bring my men to this city. I did so willingly. And, if it is humanly possible I shall take you on to Drenan.'

Axiana sat quietly for a moment, gathering her thoughts. For the last few days she had been like a straw in the wind, swept along without the benefit of choice. Her life as a queen had meant less than nothing in the wilderness, and she had given birth to her child while kneeling in the mud like a peasant. But, here and now, was the moment of decision. Was she still a queen? Would her son live to find his destiny. She looked into the pale eyes of the White Wolf and saw the strength there, the iron will that had carried Skanda to a score of victories. 'And if I do not wish to go to Drenan?' she said, at last.

'Drenan would be safest,' he said.

'You swore an oath to Skanda. Do you accept his son as his rightful heir?'

'I do, lady.'

'Then I ask you again, as the mother to the king, what if I do not wish to go to Drenan?'

She knew this was difficult for him. Continued war between the two nations was more than likely. If Axiana remained in Ventria the Drenai would almost certainly declare independence. If she went to Drenan the Ventrians would find another emperor. At least with her and the child in Drenan the Drenai would have legitimate cause to reinvade Ventria. She held to his iron gaze without flinching. He smiled. 'If not Drenan,' he said, 'then I will escort you to wherever you wish to travel. You are not my hostage, your highness, nor my prisoner. I am your servant, and will do whatever you bid.'

Axiana rose. 'I will think on what you have said, general. But first I would like to bathe and lay aside these garments of travel.' He bowed and one of the soldiers stepped forward to lead the queen and Ulmenetha towards the antechamber.

The White Wolf strode to where Nogusta lay. Antikas Karios and Kebra rose. Banelion gave Antikas a cold look, then knelt beside the wounded warrior. Nogusta opened his eyes as Banelion took his hand. 'Am I always to rescue you, my boy?' he said, fondly.

'It would seem so. It is good to see you, general.' Nogusta's smile faded. 'Bison didn't make it.'

'I know. The priestess showed me his death in a dream. It was valiant, and no less than I would have expected from him. He was an obdurate man, and I liked him not at all. But he had heart. I admired that.'

Nogusta relaxed and closed his eyes. 'It is not over, general. There are three thousand Ventrians riding with the Demon Lord. They think he is Malikada.'

'I wish he was,' said Banelion, sourly. 'I'd have dearly loved to slit his treacherous throat.'

'A feeling I am sure he would have reciprocated,' said Antikas Karios. The White Wolf ignored him.

'I am not troubled by the numbers of the enemy,' he told Nogusta. 'I am more concerned that they are being duped. Ulmenetha tells me that if the Demon Lord is successful the soldiers riding with him will – like Malikada – be possessed and destroyed. It is bad enough having to kill men in a good cause. But those Ventrians are going to die for the wrong reasons.'

'Good of you to concern yourself,' said Antikas, his words edged with sarcasm.

Once again Banelion ignored him. 'Rest now,' he told Nogusta. 'Regain your strength. I will do all that needs to be done.' Then he rose and his pale eyes rested, for a moment, on Antikas. 'I watched you fight alongside Dagorian on the bridge,' he said. 'I loved that boy, and it was good of you to say that prayer for him. I am not a religious man, but I would like to think that a light did appear for him, and lead him to your palace.' Without waiting for a response he strode away, calling his soldiers after him.

'He hates me, yet he praises me,' whispered Antikas. 'Truly he is a strange man.'

'Maybe he does, maybe he doesn't,' said Kebra. 'One rarely knows what the White Wolf is thinking. That's what makes him the best. There's never been a general like him.'

'You think he genuinely cares about what happens to the Ventrian troops?'

'Oh yes,' Kebra told him. 'He does not revel in slaughter. There is no battle madness in him.'

Antikas looked down. Nogusta was sleeping again. He knelt beside the black man and looked closely at his face. A thin sheen of sweat lay upon the skin, and snow white bristles were showing on his shaven head. 'It is easy to forget how old he is,' said Antikas, with a sigh. He looked up and smiled at Kebra. 'I watched him fight Cerez, and I marvelled at his skill. I thought him to be around forty years of age. Had I known he was this old I would have bent my knee to him.'

Glancing down once more he saw the talisman on Nogusta's chest begin to glow, the silver moon in the golden hand, shining like a tiny lantern.

'What does that mean?' asked Antikas.

'Evil is near,' said Kebra, lifting his hand and making the sign of the Protective Horn.

The White Wolf stood outside the ruins and once more cast his eyes over the landscape. There was a line of hills to the left and right, thinly covered by trees and brush, but the ground was flat and uncluttered between the hills. The Ventrian army was mainly cavalry, and he pictured all possible lines of attack.

He glanced back at the ruins. They could, of course, decline a pitched battle here, and move around the ruins, coming at him from all sides, but he thought this unlikely. Cavalry could not operate effectively in the ruins themselves, and by spreading themselves thin they would hand the advantage to the Drenai foot soldiers. No, the best chance of victory for the enemy lay in a direct frontal assault, seeking to sunder the line and scatter the defenders.

Banelion summoned his officers to him, and began to give out orders. They listened without comment, then moved back to their men.

The sun was sinking towards the mountain peaks, and there was perhaps an hour before dusk.

Ulmenetha walked out to stand alongside the old man. 'How is Nogusta?' he asked.

'A little better, I think.'

'Good. It is bad enough that Dagorian had to die. I dearly want Nogusta to survive.'

'Did you mean what you said to the queen?' she asked him, her frank blue eyes meeting his iron gaze.

'I always mean what I say,' he told her. 'I think she would be safer in Drenan, but I am her servant, and it is not for me to gainsay her wishes.'

'But you do foresee problems if she decides to remain in Ventria?'

'Of course. The Drenai nobles will either elect a new king, or declare for a new republic. As for the Ventrians – will they accept Skanda's heir, without an army to back his claim? I doubt it.' He raised his arm and gestured to the surrounding land. 'But then the mountains will still be here, and the rivers will run to the sea. It does not matter to Nature who rules or who dies. However, these are problems for another day.'

'Indeed they are,' she agreed. 'I have not thanked you for coming to our aid. I do so now. My gratitude is more than my words can convey.'

'You needn't thank me, lady. All my life has been occupied by thoughts of duty and responsibility. I am too old to change now.'

'Even so you have pledged most of your fortune to the men who now follow you. Not many would have done that.'

'I think you would be surprised at *how* many would do exactly that. It has become fashionable to believe that all actions have a cynical base. That's what comes of believing the lies of politicians. I have lived long, Ulmenetha, and I have seen much. There is among many people a desire to help others. Perhaps it is this which binds us all together. Dagorian and Bison gave their lives to protect the mother and child. They did it willingly, with no thought of profit.'

600

'You say that, and yet your men have followed you here for the promise of gold. Is this not at odds with your philosophy?'

'Not at all. I offered them the gold because a soldier is worth his pay. But had I been penniless and asked them to follow me, most would have. Now let us speak of more pressing matters. I have seen your magick, but not your power. Is there any way in which you might help us tonight?'

'I cannot kill,' she explained. 'Land magick is of a healing nature. If I drew fire from the land and used it against the Ventrians the power would vanish from me instantly.'

'I was not thinking about using it against a human foe,' he said.

'There is nothing I can do to hurt Anharat. He is too powerful.'

Banelion fell silent, staring out once more over the battle-ground. 'There is no doubt that we can withstand their charges,' he said. 'They will impale themselves on our spears, seeking to break through. They will not succeed. But I would like to avoid unnecessary casualties.'

'I do not see how that can be achieved,' she admitted.

'I think I do,' he told her, 'but I do not know whether your power can achieve it.'

Nogusta awoke just before dusk. His mouth was dry and his left shoulder throbbed with pain. He winced as he sat up. The interior of the temple was gloomy now, save for two lanterns which burned in a tent by the far wall. Nogusta pushed himself to his feet, and, for a moment, felt light headed and dizzy. Twenty feet away Conalin was sitting on some rubble, drinking water from a pottery cup. Nogusta called him over.

The black man sat down as the boy moved alongside. 'I want you to take Bison's sword,' he said.

'Why?'

'If the enemy breaks through then we will be the last line of defence.'

Conalin gazed up at the black warrior, noting his weakness. 'I'll get you some water,' he said. The boy ran off to the antechamber and returned with a full cup of cool, clear water. Nogusta drank gratefully. Then he handed Conalin the scabbarded short sword. The boy flipped the belt around his waist, but it was too big. Using his dagger Nogusta made a new hole and shortened the sword belt. Conalin buckled it into place.

'Draw it,' said Nogusta. The boy did so.

'It is heavier than I thought,' said Conalin.

'Remember it is a stabbing blade, not a cleaver. When your enemy is close thrust towards the heart. Let me see you practise.' Conalin made several clumsy lunges. 'That's good,' said Nogusta. 'We'll make a fine swordsman of you, given time. But thrust off your lead foot. That will put your body weight behind the movement.'

Conalin grinned, and tried again. This time the thrust was smooth and swift. He looked at Nogusta. 'Your talisman is glowing,' he said.

'I know.'

Pharis and Sufia ran in to the doorway of the temple. 'They're here! So many!' shouted Pharis. They ran back outside.

Conalin went to join them, but Nogusta called him back. 'I want you to wait with me,' he said, softly.

'I just wanted to see them.'

'It is important that you stay.' Nogusta turned away from the boy and climbed to the octagonal dais, then sat back upon the stone altar placed there. 'This is one of the oldest buildings anywhere in the world. Most of the city was built after it. Like the palace back in Usa it was said to have been erected in a single night by a giant. I don't believe it, of course, but it is a pretty tale when heard in full.' He took a deep breath. 'This wound is bothersome,' he said.

'Why do you not want to see the battle?' asked Conalin, stepping up to the dais. 'Antikas, Kebra and Ulmenetha are all there. Why should we not go?'

'I have seen battles, Conalin. I had hoped never to see another. Kebra tells me you want to work with horses. Is that right?'

'Yes, I do.'

'It is my plan to return to the northern mountains of Drenan and find the descendants of the herds my father raised. I will rebuild our house. It was set in a beautiful location. My wife loved it there, especially in spring, when the fruit trees were in blossom.'

'Did she die?'

'Yes, she died. All my family died. I am the last of my line.' He could see that the boy was anxious to leave, and decided to distract him. 'Would you like to see some magick?' he asked.

'Yes.'

Carefully Nogusta lifted the talisman from around his neck and looped it over the boy's head. It settled neatly into place around his neck. 'Where is the magick?' said the boy.

602

Nogusta was surprised, but did not show it. Pharis and the child had returned looking for Conalin. He called them over. 'Try to place it around Sufia's neck,' he said. Conalin lifted the talisman clear, but when he tried to put it on the child he found that the golden chain was too short by several inches.

'I don't understand,' he said.

'Put it back on me,' said Nogusta. The boy stepped forward, and found, to his amazement, that it was still too short. 'It is yours now,' said the warrior. 'It has chosen you.' Softly he spoke the words his father had used. 'A man greater than kings wore this charm and while you wear it make sure that your deeds are always noble.'

'How do I do that?' asked Conalin.

'A good question. Follow your heart. Listen to what it tells you. Do not steal or lie, do not speak or act with malice or hatred.'

'I will try,' promised the boy.

'And you will succeed, for you are chosen. This talisman has been in my family for many generations. Always it chooses its owner. One day, when your sons are near grown you will play the magick game, and you will see it choose again.'

'Why didn't you keep it?' asked Conalin. 'You are still young enough to sire sons. You could take a wife.'

'It is done,' said Nogusta. 'And I am pleased. You are a fine lad, brave and intelligent. If you wish to come back to Drenan with me we will build the house together. Then we can hunt the horses.'

'Will Kebra come too?'

'I hope that he will.'

From outside came the sound of war horns blaring. Axiana emerged from her tent, wearing a shimmering dress of blue satin. Her dark hair was drawn up, and a string of pearls had been braided there. Pharis gasped to see her. The queen approached Nogusta. She was holding the sleeping babe close to her chest.

'If I am to die,' she said, 'I shall die *looking* like a queen.'

Conalin felt heat upon his chest. The talisman was glowing with a bright light now. A sudden vision came to him. A man in black armour moving through the ruins.

'What did you see?' asked Nogusta.

'The last of the Krayakin is coming,' said Conalin.

'He will soon be here,' said the warrior.

'You knew?'

603

'It was the last of my visions. You now have the gift. Use it wisely.'

'You cannot beat him. You are wounded and weak.'

'A great evil is coming,' said Nogusta. 'You will need all your courage. Never lose heart. You hear me, boy? Never lose heart!'

The Ventrian cavalry appeared on the hills on either side, lancers in their white cloaks and curved bronze helms, light cavalry with wicker shields and wooden spears, mounted archers in garish red shirts, and heavily armoured swordsmen in black cloaks and breastplates of burnished bronze.

The Drenai soldiers waited. Not a man moved. They stood silently their spears pointing towards the sky, their long, rectangular shields held to their sides.

The White Wolf glanced to left and right, and felt a surge of pride in the fighting men who stood ready. The sun was dipping low now, the sky golden, the mountains crowned with fire. At the centre of the Ventrians came Anharat-Malikada, riding a white stallion. He raised his arm, ready to order the attack.

'Prepare!' bellowed the White Wolf. A thousand shields swept up, and a thousand spears dropped down to face the enemy. The movement was perfectly co-ordinated.

The Ventrians rode slowly down from the hills, creating a fighting wedge.

Anharat galloped his horse to the front of the line, then drew rein.

From the highest point of the ruined wall Ulmenetha watched him. Her concentration grew as she summoned the power of the land, feeling it swell inside her. Her body began to shake, and she felt her heart beating faster and faster. Still the power flowed into her. Pain, terrible pain burst in her head and she cried out. But even through the pain she continued to draw on the power of the earth. Tears flowed, and her vision misted. Raising her arms she released the fire of *halignat*.

A huge ball of white flame flew from her hands screeching above the Drenai defenders, and passing through the Ventrian riders. Not one of them was harmed, though their horses reared in panic. The blazing *halignat* swept on, curling around Anharat, swelling into a white globe that hid him from his army. Slowly the *halignat* faded away. Anharat's horse was unharmed, and the Demon Lord laughed aloud.

'I am safe,' he told the officers around him. 'Attack now, and kill them all!'

But no-one moved. Anharat looked at the closest man. His eyes were wide, and he was staring in horror. 'What is it, man?' he said. He looked at the others. They were all staring at him. Several made the sign of the Protective Horn.

Then he saw the White Wolf walking towards him. Antikas Karios was beside him, and the silver-haired bowman, Kebra. 'There is the enemy!' he shouted, lifting his arm to point at the three warriors. Only then did he see what had terrified his men. The flesh of his hand was grey and rotting. The *halignat* had burned away the spell, and the body of Malikada was decaying fast.

'He is not Malikada,' he heard Antikas shout. 'He is a demon. Look at him!'

All around Anharat riders were pulling away.

The sun fell behind the mountains, and the moon shone in the darkening sky.

Anharat suddenly laughed, and spread his dead arms wide. The body of Malikada burst open, the clothes ripping and falling away. The head fell back, then split from the brow to the chin, and black smoke billowed up into the night sky. Slowly it solidified, forming two wide black wings around a powerful body. The wings began to beat, and the grotesque beast flew above the waiting armies.

Kebra reacted first, notching an arrow to his bow, and sending a shaft flashing into the sky. It pierced Anharat's side, but did not stop his flight.

He flew on over the ruined walls towards the ancient temple.

Antikas Karios ran to the nearest horseman and dragged him to the ground. Then he vaulted into the saddle and kicked the horse into a run. He thundered through the Drenai line and into the ghost city. The winged beast hovered above the temple.

His taloned hand gestured towards the ground. Red fire leapt up, flames 20 feet high encircling the building. Antikas Karios tried to ride through them, but the horse reared and turned away. Antikas leapt to the ground and tried to run through the flames. His shirt caught fire and he fell back, hurling himself to the ground and rolling through the dirt. Two soldiers ran to him, covering him with their cloaks and beating out the flames.

Antikas glanced up and saw the winged demon land upon a high window and disappear into the temple.

Nogusta stood on the dais and gazed around the temple. Some 30 feet to his left was the queen's tent, and beyond that the entrance to the antechamber. Two hundred feet ahead of him were the main doors. He glanced up at the high, arched window above the doors. From here would come the winged terror.

The queen emerged from her tent. Nogusta smiled at her. Carrying the babe she walked to the dais. There was in her movement now a renewed pride and strength, and her bearing was once more regal. Nogusta bowed.

'I thank you for your service to me,' she said. 'And I apologize for any apparent lack of gratitude upon the journey.'

'Stay close to the dais, your highness,' he told her. 'The last hour is upon us.' Pharis and Sufia were sitting close by. Nogusta ordered them to move to the far wall.

'Where do you want me?' asked Conalin.

'Stand before the queen. The beast will come from that high window.'

Conalin looked up fearfully, but then strode to the dais and took up his position.

Nogusta drew the Storm Sword and stepped from the dais. At that moment a figure in black armour moved from the shadows behind the queen's tent. He too held a sword.

'We meet at last,' said Bakilas, removing his helm. 'I commend your bravery.'

Nogusta swayed, and reached out to steady himself. He took a deep breath, and his vision swam.

'You are sick, human,' said Bakilas. 'Stand aside. I have no wish to kill you.'

Nogusta's vision cleared. He wiped the sweat from his eyes. 'Then leave,' he said.

'I cannot do that. My Lord Anharat requires a sacrifice.'

'And I am here to prevent it,' said Nogusta. 'So, come forward and die.'

Beaten back by the pillars of flame surrounding the building Antikas Karios stood with the White Wolf and his men. Ulmenetha ran to stand alongside them. 'Is there nothing your magick can do?' hissed Antikas.

'Nothing,' she said, her voice echoing her despair. Antikas swore, then ran for the horses. Starfire was still saddled and the warrior heeled him back towards the temple. The White Wolf stepped into his path and grabbed the bridle.

'No horse will run into those flames – and even if it did, both horse and rider would be burned to a cinder.'

'Get out of my way!'

'Wait!' shouted Ulmenetha. 'Fetch water. There may yet be something we can do.'

Several soldiers ran and collected buckets of water. Under Ulmenetha's direction they doused the gelding. Antikas pulled off his cloak, and this too was drenched. The priestess reached up and took hold of Antikas's hand. 'Listen to me. I shall lower the temperature around you, but I will not be able to hold the spell for long. You must ride through at full gallop. Even then . . .' her words tailed away.

'Do what you can,' he said, drawing his sword.

'The horse will swerve and throw you into the flames!' said Banelion.

Antikas grinned. 'Nogusta told me he would ride through the fires of Hell. Now we will see.' Tugging on the reins he rode the giant gelding back 50 yards, then swung again to face the flames. Swirling his dripping cloak around his shoulders he waited for Ulmenetha's signal.

She gestured towards him, and he felt a terrible chill sweep over him. With a loud battle cry he kicked Starfire into a run. The gelding powered forward, his steel shod hooves striking sparks from the stone.

Soldiers scattered ahead of him. Antikas continued to shout his battle cries as Starfire reached full gallop. As they came closer to the pillars of fire he felt the horse begin to slow. 'On Great Heart!' he shouted. 'On!'

The gelding responded to his call.

And the flames engulfed them.

Bakilas was about to attack when suddenly flames burst around the temple, and a fierce glow shone through the windows bathing the temple in crimson light. Then came the beating of giant wings and Nogusta saw the monstrous form of Anharat glide down from an upper window. The wings beat furiously as his huge form descended, and a great wind blew across the temple sending up a dust storm, and exposing the mosaic at the centre of the floor. It was a surreal sight, for the exposed mosaic depicted a winged creature, with long talons, and blood-red eyes – the mirror image of the creature now hovering above it.

Conalin stood on the dais, the queen and her babe behind him. The boy wanted to run, but in that moment remembered the bravery of Dagorian and the courage of Bison. He drew his sword and stood his ground, tiny against the monstrous creature before him. The beast's talons scrabbled on the mosaic floor and his wings stretched out a full 20 feet in both directions. He gazed at Conalin through blood-red eyes. 'It is fitting that I find you all in my own temple,' he said. He looked beyond the boy, his gaze fixing on Axiana. 'Your work is done, my queen,' he said. 'You have delivered salvation for my people.'

Nogusta was about to attack the beast, but felt a cold blade against his throat. Bakilas spoke. 'You have done all that you can, human. And I respect you for it. Lay down your sword.' Nogusta's blade flashed up, knocking away the Krayakin's sword. He lunged at the black-armoured warrior, but Bakilas sidestepped and parried the Storm Sword, sending a riposte that slammed into Nogusta's ribs. As the blade plunged home, and terrible pain tore through him, Nogusta reached out and grabbed Bakilas's sword arm. Then, with the last of his strength he rammed his own blade into Bakilas's belly. The Krayakin cried out, then fell back, pulling Nogusta with him. They both fell to the ground. Nogusta struggled to rise, but his legs failed him, and he slumped down. Bakilas reared over him, dragging his sword clear of Nogusta's body. Then he rose unsteadily and advanced towards the dais.

Anharat moved towards Conalin, who stood on the dais, holding Bison's sword before him.

'You have only moments to live, child,' said Anharat. 'I shall tear out your heart.'

He started to move, when suddenly there came the sound of distant chimes. Dust motes hung in the air, and the boy stood unblinking before him.

Time stood still and the shining figure of Emsharas appeared on the dais, next to the statue-still queen and the frozen, armoured figure of Bakilas.

'You are in time to see my victory, brother,' said Anharat.

'Indeed I am, brother. And tell me what you will achieve?'

'I will undo your spell, and the Illohir will walk upon the earth.'

'And they will be consigned to the void, one by one. It may take centuries, but in the end you will all be returned to the place that is Nowhere,' said Emsharas.

'And where will you be?' roared Anharat. 'What place of pleasure have you found that you have not shared with your people?'

'You still do not see, Anharat,' said Emsharas, sadly. 'Do you truly not know what became of me? Think, my brother. What could prevent you finding me? We are twin souls. Since the dawn of time we have been together. Where could I go that you could not feel my soul?'

'I have no time for riddles,' said Anharat. 'Tell me, and then be gone!'

'Death,' said Emsharas. 'When I cast the Great Spell in that tomorrow that is already four thousand years past, I shall power it with my life force. I shall die. Indeed, in this time I am already dead. That is why you could not find me. Why you will never find me. From tomorrow I will no longer exist!'

'Dead?' echoed Anharat. 'That is impossible. We cannot die!'

'But we can,' said Emsharas. 'We can surrender our souls to the universe. And when we do so the power we release is colossal. It was that power which dragged the Illohir from the surface of this planet and held them in the limbo that is Nowhere. But it was only the first step, Anharat. Not even my death could propel our people to the world I found, a world where we can take form, and eat and drink, and know the joy of true life.'

'No,' said Anharat, 'you cannot be dead! I will not have it. I . . . I will not believe it!'

'I do not lie, brother. You know that. But it was the only way I could think of to save our people, and give them a chance of life in the pleasure of the flesh. I did not want to leave you, Anharat. You and I were a part of each other. Together we were One.'

'Aye, we were!' shouted Anharat. 'But now I do not need you. Go then and die! And leave me to my victory! I hate you, brother, more than anything under the stars!'

The shining figure of Emsharas seemed to fade under the power of Anharat's rage, and his voice when he spoke again was distant. 'I am sorry that you hate me, for I have always loved you. And I know how much you want to thwart me, but think on this: With all the power you have amassed what have you achieved? The Krayakin are returned to the void, the *gogarin* is dead, and an army awaits you outside the temple. Once you have killed the child you will need all your power to draw back the Illohir. After that you will be merely a sorcerer. The army will kill you, and all across the world mankind will unite against our people. But you will have thwarted me. You will have made my death useless and unnecessary. It will be your final victory.'

'Then that will be enough for me!' roared Anharat.

'Will it?' asked Emsharas. 'Our people have two destinies, and both are in your hands, my brother. They can pass to a world of light, or they can return to the void. The choice is yours. My death alone could not complete the spell. But yours will. If you choose to be the third king to die then our people shall know joy. But whatever your choice I shall not remain to see it. We will never speak again. Goodbye, my twin!'

Emsharas stepped back and vanished. Anharat stood very still, and a great emptiness engulfed him. He realized in that moment what Bakilas had sensed the day before. His hatred of Emsharas was almost identical to his love. Without Emsharas there was nothing. There never had been. Throughout the last four thousand years thoughts of Emsharas, and the revenge he would know, had filled his mind. But he had never desired his brother's death. Not to lose him for all time.

'I love you too, my brother,' he said. He looked around the temple, and saw that the humans were still frozen. Against the wall a young girl had her arms around a child, and upon the dais a teenage boy stood holding a sword. Behind him the queen had turned away, shielding her baby with her body. Bakilas was close by, his sword raised. The black warrior was lying sprawled beside the dais, his blood pooling on the mosaic floor.

Anharat blinked and remembered the journeys upon the cosmic winds, when he and Emsharas had been as one, twin souls, inseparable.

To die? The thought filled him with terror. To lose eternity? And yet what joy would there be in immortality now?

Then the music of the chimes began to fade, and the humans started to move.

Conalin watched the beast as it landed on the mosaic floor. 'You have only moments to live, child,' said Anharat. 'I shall tear out your heart.' The beast seemed to flicker for a moment, then it moved slowly forward, towering above the boy. Suddenly it dropped down, arms outstretched, its huge dark head lunging forward. Conalin leapt, plunging the sword deep into the thick, black neck. The talons swept down and settled over Conalin's shoulder. But they did not pierce the skin. Gently the beast pushed Conalin aside. Cream-coloured ichor spilled from the wound as the sword was torn free. Anharat dragged himself up onto the dais. Conalin hacked at his back, the blade slashing open the skin. The demon crawled past the queen and hauled himself up onto the altar. Twisting he spread his wings and lay back. Conalin jumped up and holding his sword with both hands drove it down into Anharat's chest. The boy stared down into the demon's eyes. Only then did he realize that the creature had made no move to attack him.

Confused, Conalin released the sword. Anharat's taloned fingers curled round the hilt. But he made no attempt to draw it forth.

'Emsharas!' whispered the demon.

A black shadow moved alongside Conalin. He swung to see the armoured knight moving towards the queen. 'No!' he shouted. With no weapon he sprang at the knight. A mailed fist hit him with a back handed blow that spun him from his feet.

Bakilas struggled on, the Storm Sword still thrust deep in his belly. Clinging to life he raised his blade. Axiana backed away. 'Do not harm my son,' she pleaded. Twenty feet away Nogusta pushed himself to his knees and drew a knife. His arm snapped forward. The blade flashed through the air, plunging deep into Bakilas's left eye. The Krayakin staggered back, then dragged the knife clear, hurling it to the floor. Nogusta tried to draw another. Then he passed out.

The sound of galloping hoofs filled the air. Bakilas turned to see a horseman with a cloak of fire bearing down upon him. Desperately he swung towards the queen and made one last attempt to reach her. Antikas Karios lifted the Storm Sword high and threw it with all his strength. The blade scythed through the air and slammed through Bakilas's neck. The Krayakin crumpled and fell across the body of Anharat.

Casting aside the blazing cloak Antikas leapt from Starfire. The horse's mane was aflame and the warrior smothered the fire with his hands. The gelding was burned across the lower body, and his legs were blistered and bleeding. Antikas himself had injuries to his arms and hands, and the skin over his cheek bone showed a vivid red burn.

Upon the dais Anharat's body began to glow with a brilliant, blinding light which filled the temple. Temporarily blinded Antikas fell to his knees, his hands over his face.

Behind him he could hear the pounding of feet, and guessed the pillars of fire had vanished.

Hands grabbed him, hauling him upright. He opened his eyes. At first he could see only vague shapes. But then he saw the face of the White Wolf swim into focus.

'That was a fine ride,' said Banelion. Antikas gazed upon the altar. There was no sign now of the Demon Lord, nor of the dead Krayakin. Both had vanished.

Conalin ran to where Nogusta lay, and knelt down beside him. 'I killed it,' he said. 'I killed the beast!'

Nogusta gave a weak smile. 'You did well, my friend. I . . . am proud of you.' He took the boy's hand and lifted it to the talisman. 'What . . . do . . . you see?' he asked, his voice weak and fading.

Conalin closed his eyes. 'I see a strange land, with purple mountains. The Krayakin are there. They are bewildered.'

'What . . . else?'

'I see a woman. She is tall and black and beautiful.'

Nogusta leaned against the boy. 'I . . . see her too,' he said. Kebra ran forward and threw himself down by Nogusta's side.

'Don't you dare die on me!' he said.

Nogusta released Conalin's hand and gripped Kebra's arm. 'No . . . choice,' he whispered. 'Take Starfire . . . back to the mountains.'

'Ulmenetha!' shouted Kebra.

'I am here,' she said. Conalin moved back and allowed the priestess to kneel beside the dying man.

'You can heal him,' said Kebra. 'Lay your hands on him.'

'I cannot heal him,' she said. 'Not now.'

Kebra looked down into Nogusta's dead eyes. 'Oh no,' he said. 'You can't leave me like this! Nogusta!' Tears fell to his cheeks. 'Nogusta!' Ulmenetha leaned over and closed the bright blue eyes. Kebra hugged the body to him, cradling the head. Ulmenetha moved back, and, as Conalin tried to reach Kebra she took hold of his arm and drew him away.

'Leave them together for a little while,' she said.

'I just wanted to tell him what I saw. He found his wife. On a world with two moons.'

'I know.' Ulmenetha walked to where Starfire was standing. The horse was shivering, and in great pain. She stroked his neck, then went to work on his wounds, healing the blisters and the burns. The worst of the wounds was in his right eye, which was almost blinded. But this too she healed.

Antikas approached her. 'He is a great horse,' he said. 'Nogusta was right.'

'Let me heal your burns,' she said, reaching up towards his blistered face. He shook his head.

'I will carry the pain. It will remind me of what we lost here today.'

She smiled up at him. 'That sounds dangerously like humility, Antikas Karios.'

He nodded. 'Yes it does. How depressing. Do you think it will wear off?'

'I hope not,' she told him.

'I will see that it does not,' he said. Offering her a bow he turned and walked back to the queen.

The White Wolf stood silently gazing down at Kebra and Nogusta, his expression unreadable. Then he moved to the queen's side. 'Where would you like to go, highness?' he asked, his voice weary.

'Back to Usa,' she said. 'And I would like you and your men to help me restore order in the city, and bring peace to the land. Will you do this for me, Banelion?'

'I will, highness.'

Stepping forward she summoned Antikas Karios. He bowed deeply. 'Will you swear allegiance to me, and promise to defend the rights of my son?'

'With my life,' he told her.

'Then you will take command of the Ventrian army.'

Lastly she called Conalin to her. 'What is it I can do for you?' she asked. 'Name it and it is yours.'

'Kebra and I are going to Drenan,' he said. 'We are going to find Nogusta's horses and rebuild his house.'

'I shall see you have gold for the journey,' she said. Conalin bowed then walked to where Pharis was sitting with Sufia.

'Will you come with me to Drenan?' he asked them. Pharis took his hand.

'Where you are I will be,' she said. 'Always.'

'And me! And me!' said Sufia.

Kebra walked out into the night, grief overwhelming him. Ulmenetha stepped out of the shadows and took his arm. 'He knew he was to die,' she said. 'He saw it. But he saw something else, something incredible. He wanted me to tell you. He was descended from Emsharas, and that meant he was part Illohir. As was Ushuru, for they were cousins. He saw himself walking with her in a strange land, under a violet sky. The Krayakin were

613

there, and Dryads and Fauns and many other Illohir. I think he saw it as some kind of paradise.'

Kebra said nothing, and gazed up at the bright stars. 'I know the pain you are feeling,' said Ulmenetha. 'I too have lost loved ones. But the three of you saved us all. None of you will ever be forgotten.'

Kebra turned on her. 'Do you think I care about fame? They were my family. I loved them. I feel their loss as if someone has cut them from me. I wish I had died with them.'

Ulmenetha was silent for a moment. Conalin came out of the temple, holding hands with Pharis and little Sufia. The child broke away and ran to Kebra, who was weeping once more. She reached up and took his hand.

'Don't be sad,' she said. 'Please don't be sad.' Then she too began to cry. Kebra dropped down beside her.

'Sometimes,' he said, 'it is good to be sad.' He brushed her blond hair back from her eyes. Conalin came alongside him and laid a hand on his shoulder.

'You are not alone, Kebra,' said Ulmenetha. 'You have a family to raise. Conalin and Pharis and Sufia. And I shall come with you for a while, for I have an urge to run over mountain trails and see the wild flowers grow.'

'We will find Nogusta's horses,' said Conalin. 'And we will rebuild his house.'

Kebra smiled. 'He would like that.'

HERO IN THE SHADOWS

Introduction

Waylander is a character I am hugely fond of. Hard to say why. Perhaps it is because he is – as the Bible says – 'strong in the broken places'.

The first Waylander novel appeared in 1986. He proved an endearing and popular character. For years afterwards I received mail from readers asking when the next adventure would be published. In response to that I wrote *Waylander II: In the Realm of the Wolf.*

To be honest I felt he had gone as far as he wanted to go, and I had no plans to wheel him out into the spotlight again. I have always disliked series that go on too long. There is something magical about seeing a section of a life and then watching the hero ride away. We don't know where he's going. We don't know who he'll meet.

When Shane rides away, at the end of the book and film, the boy calls out, 'Come back, Shane.' A part of us wants him to, but a stronger part knows that his work is done. The hero appears when needed, and then departs.

Pushing a series too far creates the danger of risibility.

Years ago I remember watching a TV series called *The Rifleman*, starring Chuck Connors. It ran for years. It was about a peace-loving Kansas farmer and his cute blond kid. As the years flowed by they had to keep changing the kid. Every episode would begin with a little headline under the picture, something like 'Kansas 1876'. It was always 1876. Villains would ride in, and the reluctant rifleman would have to deal with them. One of

617

the events which caused the demise of the series was brought about by a fan. He had watched every episode and taken notes. The peace-loving Kansas farmer had killed around ninety people and wounded around a hundred and forty in the long, single summer of 1876. He had been wounded forty times, almost always in the left arm. He had been knocked unconscious more often than all the heavyweight boxers of the twentieth century. The credibility of *The Rifleman* vanished almost overnight.

I didn't want that to happen to Waylander.

But I couldn't stop thinking about him. Where had he gone after the events of *Waylander II*? Did he find the peace he so desired? I thought of his life and I wondered, would he have to face a reckoning for past misdeeds? Or would the good that he had tried to do outweigh them? After a while I realized I was being haunted by the ghost of Waylander. His story was incomplete.

There was still one last great adventure. All I had to do was find it.

DG
2002

Prologue

Mercenary captain Camran Osir reined in his mount at the crest of the hill and swung in the saddle to stare back down the forest trail. The twelve men under his command rode from the trees in single file, and paused while he scanned the horizon. Removing his iron helm, Camran ran his fingers through his long blond hair, enjoying, momentarily, the warm breeze evaporating the sweat on his scalp. He glanced at the captive girl on the horse beside him. Her hands were tied, her dark eyes defiant. He smiled at her, and saw her blanch. She knew he was going to kill her, and that her passing would be painful. He felt the warmth of blood pulsing in his loins. Then the feeling passed. His blue eyes narrowed as he gazed over the valley, seeking sign of pursuit.

Satisfied that no-one was following, Camran tried to relax. He was still angry, of course, but calmed himself with the thought that his riders were ill-educated brutes, with little understanding of civilized behaviour.

The raid had gone well. There were only five men in the little farming settlement, and these had been killed quickly, with no wounds or losses among his own men. Some of the women and children had managed to escape into the woods, but three young women had been taken. Enough, at least, to satisfy the carnal urges of his riders. Camran himself had captured the fourth, the dark-haired girl on the sway-backed horse beside him. She had tried to run, but he had ridden her down, leaping from his horse and bearing her to the ground. She had fought silently, without panic, but one blow to the chin had rendered her unconscious, and he had thrown her over his saddle. There was blood now upon her pale cheek, and a purple bruise was showing on the side of her neck. Her faded yellow dress was torn at the shoulder and had flapped down, almost exposing her breast. Camran jerked his thoughts from her soft skin, turning his mind to more urgent concerns.

Yes, the raid had gone well. Until that idiot Polian had incited the others to set fire to the old farmhouse. Wanton destruction of property was anathema to a man of breeding like Camran. It was criminally wasteful. Peasants could always be replaced, but good buildings should be treated with respect. And the farmhouse was a good building, soundly constructed by a man who cared about quality work. Camran had been furious – not only with them, but with himself. For instead of merely killing the captured women he had allowed his needs to override his common sense. He had taken his time, enjoying the screams of the first, luxuriating in the desperate pleading of the second, and the subsequent cries of agony of the third. With each of them dead he had turned his attentions to the dark-haired girl. She had not pleaded, or made a sound after returning to consciousness to find her hands and ankles bound. She was to be the richest harvest; her cries, when they came, would be the purest and sweetest.

The smoke had billowed over him just as he was unwrapping his ivory-handled skinning knives. Swinging round, he saw the fires. Leaving the bound girl where she lay, he ran back to the scene. Polian was grinning as Camran came alongside him. He was still grinning as he died, Camran's dagger plunging between his ribs, skewering his heart.

This sudden act of savagery cowed the men. 'Did I not tell you?' he thundered. 'Never property! Not unless directly ordered. Now, gather supplies and let's be gone.'

Camran had returned to the young woman. He thought of killing her, but there would be no pleasure in it now, no slow, pounding joy as he watched the light of life fade from her eyes. Gazing down at the six small skinning knives in their silk-lined canvas pouch, he felt the dead weight of disappointment dragging at him. Carefully he rolled the pouch, tying it with black ribbon. Then he hauled the girl to her feet, cut the ropes around her ankles and lifted her to the dead Polian's mount. Still she said nothing.

As Camran rode away he gazed back at the burning building, and a deep sense of shame touched him. The farmhouse had not been built speedily, but with great patience, the timbers lovingly fashioned, the joints fitting to perfection. Even the window-frames had been carved and embellished. Destroying such a place was an act of sacrilege. His father would have been ashamed of him.

Camran's sergeant, the hulking Okrian, rode alongside him. 'Wasn't in time to stop them, sir,' he said.

Camran saw the fear in the man's eyes. 'It is what happens when one is forced to deal with scum,' said Camran. 'Let's hope there are better men available when we reach Qumtar. We'll earn little commission from Panagyn with only eleven men.'

'We'll get more, sir. Qumtar is crawling with fighters seeking employment with one or other of the Houses.'

'*Crawling* is probably an apt description. Not like the old days, is it?'

'Nothing ever is,' said Okrian, and the two men rode in silence, each lost in thoughts of the past. Camran remembered the invasion of Drenai lands eighteen years earlier, when he had been a junior officer in the army of Vagria, serving under Kaem. It had been, Kaem had promised, the dawn of a new empire. And, for a time, it was true. They crushed all armies sent against them, forcing the greatest of the Drenai generals, Egel, into the vastness of Skultik Forest, and besieging the last fortress, Dros Purdol. But that had been the high point of the campaign. Under the command of the giant Karnak, Purdol had held, and Egel had broken from Skultik, descending upon the Vagrian army like a storm. Kaem himself had been slain by the assassin Waylander, and within two years Drenai forces had invaded Vagria. And it had not ended there. Arrest warrants were issued against many of the best Vagrian officers, charging them with crimes against the populace. It was laughable. What crime was there in killing your enemies, whether they be soldiers or farmers? But many officers were taken and hanged.

Camran had escaped north into the lands of the Gothir, but even here agents of the Drenai continued to hunt him. So he had drifted east, across the sea into Ventria and beyond, serving in numerous armies and mercenary bands.

At thirty-seven he was now in charge of recruitment for House Bakard, one of the four ruling Houses of Kydor. There was no outright war for them to fight. Not yet. But each of the Houses was gathering soldiers, and there were many skirmishes in the wild lands.

News from home rarely reached Kydor, but Camran had been

delighted to hear of the death of Karnak some years previously. Assassinated as he led a parade. Wonderful! Killed, apparently, by a woman wielding the bow of the legendary Waylander.*

Jerking his mind once more to the present, Camran gazed back at his recruits. They were still frightened now, and anxious to please, hoping that when they made camp Camran would let them have the girl. He would soon dash those hopes. His plan was to use her, skin her, and leave the men to bury the body. He glanced once more at her, and smiled. She looked at him coolly and said nothing.

Just before dusk Camran swung from the trail and selected a camp-site. As the men unsaddled their mounts he took the girl deeper into the forest. She made no resistance as he pushed her to the ground, and she did not cry out as he took her. As he was reaching his climax he opened his eyes and found her staring at his face, expressionless. This not only removed any pleasure from the rape; it also ruined his erection. Anger roared through him. Drawing his knife, he laid the edge on her throat.

'The Grey Man will kill you,' she said, slowly, no trace of fear in her voice. The words carried certainty and he paused.

'The Grey Man? Some demon of the night, perhaps? A protector of peasants?'

'He is coming,' she said.

He felt the prickle of fear on the nape hairs of his neck. 'I suppose he is a giant, or some such?'

She did not reply. A movement came from the bushes to his left. Camran surged to his feet, heart pounding. But it was Okrian.

'The men were wondering if you'd finished with her,' said the sergeant, his small eyes focusing on the peasant girl.

'No, I have not,' said Camran. 'Maybe tomorrow.'

The sergeant shrugged and walked back to the camp-fire. 'One more day of life,' Camran told the girl. 'Are you going to thank me?'

'I am going to watch you die,' she said.

Camran smiled, then punched her in the face, hurling her back to the ground. 'Stupid peasant,' he said.

But her words kept coming back to him, and the following morning's ride found him constantly scanning the back trail. His neck was beginning to ache. Camran was about to heel his horse forward when he took one last look back. For a heartbeat only, he saw a shadow moving into the trees some half a mile down the

*From *Waylander II: In the Realm of the Wolf* (1993)

622

trail. He blinked. Was it a horseman, or merely a wandering deer? He could not be sure. Camran swore softly, then summoned two of his riders. 'Go back down the trail. There may be a man following. If there is, kill him.'

The men swung their mounts and rode away. Camran glanced at the girl. She was smiling.

'What's happening, sir?' asked Okrian, nudging his horse alongside Camran's mount.

'Thought I saw a rider. Let's move on.'

They rode through the afternoon, stopping for an hour to walk the horses, then made camp in a sheltered hollow, close to a stream. There was no sign of the two men Camran had sent out. He summoned Okrian to him. The big mercenary eased himself down alongside his captain and Camran told him about the girl's warning. 'Grey Man?' he said. 'Never heard of him. But, then, I don't know this area of Kydor well. If he is following, the boys will get him. Tough lads.'

'Then where are they?'

'Probably dawdling somewhere. Or, if they caught him, they're probably having a little fun with him. Perrin is said to be somewhat of an artist when it comes to the Blood Eagle. The men say he can open a man's ribs, pin the guts back with twigs, and still leave the poor bastard alive for hours. Now, what about the girl, sir? The men could use a little diversion.'

'Aye, take her,' said Camran.

Okrian hauled her up by her hair and dragged her back to the camp-fire. A cheer went up from the nine men gathered there. Okrian hurled her towards them. The first man rose and grabbed her as she half fell. 'Let's see a little flesh,' he shouted, tearing at her dress.

Suddenly the girl spun on her heel, slamming her elbow into the man's face, crushing his nose. Blood spurted over his moustache and beard and he staggered back. The sergeant came up behind the girl, curling his arms around her and dragging her back into a tight embrace. Her head snapped back into his face, striking him on the cheekbone. He grabbed her hair and savagely twisted her head. The first man drew a dagger and advanced towards her. 'You puking bitch,' he snarled, 'I'm going to cut you bad. Not enough so we can't enjoy you, you little whore. But enough to make you scream like a gutted pig.'

The girl, unable to move, stared with undisguised malevolence at the knifeman. She did not beg or cry out.

Suddenly there was a crunching thud. The knifeman stopped, his expression bemused. Slowly he reached up with his left hand. As he did so he fell to his knees. His questing finger touched the black-feathered bolt jutting from the base of his skull. He tried to speak, but no words flowed. Then he pitched to his face.

For a few heartbeats no-one moved. The sergeant hurled the girl to the ground, and drew his sword. Another man, closer to the trees, grunted in shock and pain as a bolt speared his chest. He fell back, tried to rise, then gave out a gurgling scream as he died.

Camran, sword in hand, ran back to the fire, then charged into the undergrowth, his men fanning out around him.

All was silent, and there was no sign of an enemy.

'Make for open ground!' shouted Camran. The men ran back to their horses, saddling them swiftly. Camran grabbed the girl, forcing her to mount, then clambered up behind her and rode from the hollow.

Clouds drifted across the moon as the men raced through the forest. In the darkness they were forced to slow their flight. Camran saw a break in the trees, and angled his mount towards it, emerging on to a hillside. Okrian came close behind. As the other men broke through Camran counted them. Including himself and his sergeant, eight men were now clear of the trees. Flicking his gaze around the milling group he counted again. The killer had taken another victim during the flight.

Okrian removed his black leather helm and rubbed his hand across his balding pate. 'Shem's balls,' he said. 'We've lost five men and we've seen no-one!'

Camran glanced around. They were in a circle of clear ground, but to progress in any direction they would have to re-enter the forest.

'We'll wait for the dawn,' said Camran, dismounting. Dragging the girl from the saddle, he swung her round. 'Who is this Grey Man?' he asked. She did not reply and he slapped her hard. 'Talk to me, you bitch,' he hissed, 'or I'll cut open your belly and strangle you with your entrails!'

'He owns all the valley,' she said. 'My brother, and the other men you killed, farmed for him.'

'Describe him.'

'He is tall. His hair is long, mostly grey.'

'An old man?'

'He does not move like an old man,' she said. 'But, yes, he is old.'

'And how did you know he would be coming?'

'Last year five men attacked a settlement north of the valley. They killed a man and his wife. The Grey Man followed them. When he returned he sent out a wagon and the bodies were brought back and displayed in the market square. Outlaws do not trouble us now. Only foreigners such as yourself would bring evil to the Grey Man's land.'

'Does he have a name?' asked Camran.

'He is the Grey Man,' she said. 'That is all I know.'

Camran moved away from her, and stared back at the shadow-haunted trees. Okrian joined him. 'He can't be everywhere at once,' whispered Okrian. 'Much will depend on which way we choose to travel. We were heading east, so perhaps we should change our plans.'

The mercenary captain drew a map from the pocket of his saddlebag and opened it out on the ground. They had been heading towards the eastern border and Qumtar, but now all Camran wished to see was an end to the tree-line. On open ground the assassin could not overcome eight armed men. He studied the map in the moonlight. 'The nearest edge of the forest is to the north-east,' he said. 'Around two miles away. Once it is light we'll make for it.' Okrian nodded, but did not reply.

'What are you thinking?'

The sergeant took a deep breath, then rubbed his hand across his face. 'I was remembering the attack. Two crossbow bolts, one close upon the other. No time to reload. So, either there's two men or it must be a double-winged weapon.'

'If there'd been two men we'd have seen some sign as we rushed the undergrowth,' said Camran. 'They couldn't both have avoided us.'

'Exactly. So it is one man, who uses a double crossbow. One man – one skilled assassin who, having already killed the first two we sent, can then take out three tough men without being seen.'

'I take it there is a point to this?' muttered Camran.

'There was a man, years ago, who used such a weapon. Some say he was killed. Others claim he left the lands of the Drenai and bought himself a palace in Gothir territory. But perhaps he came instead to Kydor.'

Camran laughed. 'You think we are being hunted by Waylander the Slayer?'

'I hope not.'

'Gods, man, we're two thousand miles from Gothir. No, this is just another hunter using a similar weapon. Whoever he is, we're ready for him now,' said Camran. 'Put two men on watch and tell the rest to get some sleep.'

Camran moved to the girl, retied her hands and feet, then settled down on the ground. He had served in six campaigns and knew how important it was to rest whenever possible. Sleep did not come instantly. Instead he lay in the darkness thinking about what Okrian had said.

Waylander. Even the name made him shiver. A legend back in the days of his youth, Waylander the Slayer was said to be a demon in human form. Nothing could stop him; not walls or armed guards, not spells. It was said that the terrifying priests of the Dark Brotherhood had hunted him. All had died. Werebeasts, created by a Nadir shaman, were sent after him. Even these he had slain.

Camran shivered. Get a grip on yourself, he thought. Back then Waylander was said to be a man in his late thirties. If he was following them now he would have to be a man close to sixty, and an old man could not kill and move as this one did.

No, he decided, it could not be Waylander. With that thought he slept.

He awoke suddenly and sat up. A shadow moved across him. Hurling himself to his right he ducked and scrabbled for his sword. Something struck him on the brow and he pitched back. Okrian shouted a battle cry and sprinted forward. Camran surged to his feet, sword in hand. Clouds covered the moon once more, but not before Camran saw a shadowy figure merge into the darkness of the trees.

'Who was on watch?' shouted Camran. 'By the gods I'll cut his bastard eyes out!'

'No point in that,' said Okrian, pointing to a sprawled figure. Blood was pooling around the man. His throat had been slashed open. Another dead man was hunched by a boulder. 'You've been wounded,' he said. Blood was dripping from a shallow cut in Camran's brow.

'I ducked at the right moment,' said the captain, 'otherwise his blade would have opened my throat.' He glanced at the sky. 'Another hour and it will be light.' Pulling a handkerchief from his pocket he held it to the bleeding wound on his brow.

'I think I cut him,' said Okrian. 'But he moved fast.'

Camran continued to dab at his wound, but the blood was flowing freely. 'You'll have to stitch it,' he told Okrian.

'Yes, sir.' The hulking sergeant moved to his horse, removing a medicine pouch from his saddlebag. Camran sat very still as Okrian went to work. He glanced at the four other surviving conscripts, sensing their fear. Even as the sun rose there was no lessening of tension. For now they had to ride back into the forest.

The sky was clear and bright as Camran stepped into the saddle, the hostage girl seated before him. He swung to his men. 'If he attacks in daylight we'll kill him,' he said. 'If not we'll be clear of the trees soon. He'll stop following us then. He'll not tackle six armed men on open ground.'

His words did not convince them. But, then, they didn't convince him either. They moved slowly towards the trees, found the trail, then picked up the pace, Camran in the lead, Okrian just behind him. They rode for half an hour. Okrian glanced back to see two riderless horses. He shouted an alarm. Panic touched them all then and they began to ride faster, lashing their horses.

Camran emerged from the trees and hauled on the reins. He was sweating now, and could feel his heart beating wildly. Okrian and the other two surviving men drew their swords.

A rider on a dark horse moved slowly from the trees, his long black cloak drawn closely around him. The four warriors sat very still as he approached. Camran blinked back sweat. The man's face was strong, and somehow ageless. He could have been anywhere from his thirties to his fifties. His grey hair, lightly streaked with black, was shoulder-length, held back from his face by a black silk band tied about his brow. He was expressionless, but his dark eyes focused on Camran.

He rode to within ten feet of them, then drew back on the reins, waiting.

Camran felt the sting of salt sweat upon his cut brow. His lips were dry and he licked them. One grey-haired man against four warriors. The man could not survive. Why, then, the terrible fear causing Camran's belly to cramp?

In that moment the girl threw herself from the saddle. Camran tried to grab her, missed and swung back to face the rider. In that briefest of moments the rider's cloak flickered. His arm came up. Two crossbow bolts slammed into the riders on either side of Okrian. The first pitched from the saddle, the second slumped forward, sliding over his horse's neck. Okrian heeled his mount forward and charged at the rider. Camran followed, his sabre extended. The man's left hand flashed forward. A shining streak of silver light sped through the air, punching through Okrian's left eye-socket and into his brain. His body tipped back, his blade flying from his hand. Camran's sabre lanced out towards the assassin, but the man swayed in the saddle, the blade missing him by mere inches. Camran swung his mount.

Something struck him in the throat. Suddenly he couldn't breathe. Dropping his sword, his hand came up. Grabbing the hilt of the throwing knife, he dragged it clear of his flesh. Blood bubbled over his tunic. His horse reared, dumping him on the grass. As he lay there, choking on his own blood, a face appeared above his own.

It was the girl.

'I told you,' she said.

The dying man watched in horror as her bound hands lifted the blood-drenched throwing knife, raising it above his face. 'This is for the women,' she said.

And the blade swept down.

Chapter One

Waylander swayed in the saddle, the weight of weariness and pain bearing down on him, washing away the anger. Blood from the gash in his left shoulder had flowed over his chest and stomach, but this had halted now. The wound in his side, however, was still bleeding. He felt light-headed, and gripped the saddle pommel, taking slow, deep breaths.

The village girl was kneeling by the dead raider. He heard her say something, then watched as she took up his throwing knife in her bound hands and rammed it into the man's face over and over again. Waylander looked away, his vision blurring.

Fifteen years ago he would have hunted down these men and emerged without a scratch. Now his wounds throbbed and, with the fury gone, he felt empty, devoid of emotion. With great care he dismounted. His legs almost gave way, but he kept hold of the pommel and sagged against the steeldust gelding. Anger at his weakness flared, giving him a little strength. Reaching into his saddlebag he pulled out a small pouch of blue linen and moved to a nearby boulder. His fingers were trembling as he opened it. He sat quietly for a few heartbeats, breathing deeply, then unfastened his black cloak, letting it drop back to drape over the boulder. The girl came alongside him. Blood had splashed onto her face, and into her long, dark hair. Waylander drew his hunting knife and cut the ropes binding her wrists. The skin beneath was raw and bleeding.

Twice he tried to sheath his blade, but his vision was misting, and he placed the knife on the boulder beside him. The girl peered at his torn leather tunic shirt, and the bloodstains upon it. 'You are hurt,' she said. Waylander nodded. Unbuckling his belt, he reached up with his right hand and tried to pull his shirt over his head. But there was no strength left. Swiftly she stepped in, lifting the garment clear. There were two wounds, a shallow cut from the top of his left shoulder and down past the collarbone, and a deeper puncture wound that had entered just above his left hip and exited at the back. Both holes were plugged with tree moss, but blood was still oozing. Waylander reached for the crescent needle embedded in the blue linen pouch. As his fingers touched it darkness swept over him.

When first he opened his eyes he wondered why the needle was shining so brightly, and why it was floating before his eyes. Then he realized he was staring at the crescent moon in a clear night sky. His cloak had been laid over him, and beneath his head was a pillow fashioned from a folded blanket. A fire was burning close by, and he could smell the savoury scent of woodsmoke. As he tried to move, pain erupted in his shoulder, stitches stretching against tortured flesh. He sagged back.

The girl moved alongside him, stroking his hair from his sweat-drenched brow.

Waylander closed his eyes and slept again, floating in a sea of dreams. A giant creature with the face of a wolf bore down upon him. He shot two crossbow bolts into its mouth. A second came at him. With no weapons to hand, he leapt at the beast, his hands grasping for its throat. It shifted and changed, becoming a slender woman whose neck snapped as his hands gripped hard. He cried out in agony, then looked around. The first dead beast had also changed. It had become a small boy, lying dead in a meadow of spring flowers. Waylander looked at his hands. They were covered in blood, which flowed up over his arms, covering his chest and neck, streaming over his face and into his mouth, choking him. He spat it out, struggling for breath, and staggered to a nearby stream, hurling himself into it, trying to wash the blood from his face and body.

A man was sitting on the bank. 'Help me!' called Waylander.

'I cannot,' said the man. He stood and turned away, and Waylander saw two crossbow bolts jutting from his back.

The terrible dreams continued, dreams of blood and death.

When he awoke it was still dark, but he felt stronger. Moving with care to protect the stitches, he rolled to his right and pushed himself to a sitting position. The second wound above his hip flared with pain and he grunted.

'Are you feeling better?' the girl asked him.

'A little. Thank you for helping me.'

She laughed.

'What is so amusing?' he asked.

'You rode after thirteen men and suffered these wounds to come to my rescue. And you thank *me*? You are a strange man, Lord. Are you hungry?' He realized that he was. In fact, he was ravenous. She took a stick and rolled three large clay balls from the fire. Cracking open the first with a sharp blow she knelt down and examined the contents. Looking up at him, she smiled.

It was a pretty smile, he thought. 'What do you have there?' he asked.

'Pigeons. I killed them yesterday. They are a little too fresh, but there was no other food. My uncle taught me how to cook them in clay, but I have not tried it in years.'

'Yesterday? How long have I been sleeping?'

'On and off for three days.'

Satisfied that the first pigeon was cooked, she cracked open the other two balls. The smell of roasted meat filled the air. Waylander felt almost sick with hunger. They waited impatiently until the meat had cooled, then devoured the birds. The flavour was strong, the texture not unlike aged beef.

'Who is Tanya?' she asked.

He looked at her, and his eyes were cold. 'How do you know that name?'

'You cried out in your sleep.'

He did not answer at first, and she did not press him. Instead she built up the fire and sat quietly, a blanket around her shoulders. 'She was my first wife,' he said at last. 'She died. Her grave is a long way from here.'

'Did you love her greatly?'

'Aye. Greatly. You are very curious.'

'How else does one find out what one wishes to know?'

'I cannot argue with that.' She was about to speak, but he raised his hand. 'And let that be an end to questions on this matter,' he said.

'As you will, Lord.'

'I am not a lord. I am a landowner.'

'Are you very old? Your hair is grey, and there are lines on your face. But you move like a young man.'

'What is your name?' he asked her.

631

'Keeva Taliana.'

'Yes, I am old, Keeva Taliana. Older than sin.'

'Then how is it that you could kill all those men? They were young and strong and fierce as devils.'

Suddenly he felt weary again. She was instantly full of concern. 'You must drink lots of water,' she said. 'My uncle told me that. Loss of blood, lots of water.'

'A wise man, your uncle. Did he also teach you to use your elbow as a weapon?'

'Yes. He taught me many things. None of which was terribly useful when the raiders came.'

Fetching a canteen from a saddle on the ground close by, she held it out to him. Waylander took it from her and drank deeply. 'Do not be so sure,' he said. 'You are alive. The others are not. You stayed cool and you used your mind.'

'I was lucky,' she said, a note of anger in her voice.

'Yes, you were. But you planted the seed of fear in the leader. For that he kept you alive.'

'I don't understand.'

'You told him the Grey Man was coming.'

'You were there?'

'I was there when he told his sergeant what you had said. I was about to slay them both when the sergeant grabbed you by the hair and dragged you back to the fire. That caught me out of position. Had you not crushed that man's nose I would not have had time to come to your aid. So, yes, you were lucky. But you made the best use of that luck.'

'I did not see you or hear you,' she said.

'Neither did they.' Then he lay back and slept again.

When he awoke she was snuggled down alongside him, sleeping peacefully. It was pleasant to be this close to another human being, and he realized he had been alone too long. Easing himself away from her, he rose to his feet and pulled on his boots. As he did so, a group of crows detached themselves from the bodies of the dead and rose into the air, cawing raucously. The sound woke Keeva. She sat up, smiled at him, then moved away behind the boulders. Waylander saddled two of the horses she had tethered, the effort causing his wounds to throb.

He was still angry about the first wound to his shoulder. He should have guessed the leader would send out a rearguard. They almost had him. The first had been crouched on a tree branch above the trail, the second hiding in the bushes. Only the scraping of the first man's boot upon the bark above had alerted him. Bringing up his crossbow he had sent a bolt into the man as he leapt. It had entered at the belly, slicing up through the heart. He had fallen almost on top of Waylander, his sword slashing across his shoulder. Luckily the man was dead as the blow struck, and there was no real force in it. The second man had lunged from the bushes, a single-bladed axe in his hand. The steeldust gelding had reared, forcing the attacker back. In that moment Waylander sent the second bolt through the man's forehead. You are getting old and slow, he chided himself. Two clumsy assassins and they almost had you.

It had probably been this anger that had led him to attack their camp – a need to prove to himself that he could still move as he once had. Waylander sighed. He had been lucky to escape with his life. Even so, one of the men had managed to slam a blade into his hip. An inch or so higher and he would have been disembowelled, a few inches lower and the blade would have sliced the femoral artery, killing him for sure.

Keeva returned, smiling and waving as she came. He felt a touch of guilt. He had not known, at first, that the raiders had a captive. He had hunted them purely because they raided his lands. Her rescue, though it gave him great pleasure, was merely a fluke, a fortunate happenstance.

Keeva rolled the blankets and tied them to the back of her saddle. Then she brought him his cloak and weapons. 'Do you have a name, Lord?' she asked. 'Apart from the Grey Man.'

'I am not a lord,' he said again, ignoring her question.

'Yes, Grey Man,' she said, with an impudent smile. 'I will remember that.'

How resilient the young are, he thought. Keeva had witnessed death and destruction, had been raped and abused, and was now miles from home in the company of a stranger. Yet she could still smile. Then he looked into her dark eyes, and saw beneath the smile the traces of sorrow and fear. She was making a great effort to appear carefree, to charm him. And why not? he thought. She is a peasant girl with no rights, save those her master allows her. And these were few. If Waylander were to rape and kill her, there would be no inquest and few questions asked. In essence he owned her as if she were a slave. Why would she not seek to please him?

'You are safe with me,' he said.

'I know that, Lord. You are a good man.'

'No, I am not. But you can trust my words. No further harm

will come to you, and I will see you safely home.'

'I do trust your words, Grey Man,' she replied. 'My uncle said that words were just noises in the air. Trust deeds, he told me, not words. I will not be a burden to you. I will help with your wounds as we travel.'

'You are not a burden, Keeva,' he said softly, then heeled his horse forward. She rode alongside him.

'I told them you were coming. I told them you would kill them. But I didn't really believe it. I just wanted them to know fear as I knew fear. Then you came. And they were terrified. It was wonderful.'

They rode for several hours, heading south and west, until they came to an old stone road leading to a secluded fishing settlement on the banks of a wide, flowing river. There were some forty houses, many of them stone-built. The people here looked prosperous, thought Keeva. Even the children playing close by boasted tunics without patches or any sign of wear, and all wore shoes. The Grey Man was recognized instantly and a crowd gathered. The village headman, a small, portly man with thinning blond hair, pushed his way through them. 'Welcome, sir,' he said, with a deep bow. Keeva could see fear in the man's eyes, and felt the nervous tension emanating from the small crowd. The Grey Man dismounted.

'Jonan, isn't it?'

'Yes, sir. Jonan,' answered the little headman, bowing once more.

'Well, be at ease, Jonan, I am merely passing through. I need some food for the rest of the journey, and my companion needs a change of clothing and a warm cloak.'

'It will be done instantly, sir. You are most welcome to wait in my home, where my wife will prepare some refreshment. Let me show you the way.' The little man bowed once more and turned towards the crowd. He gestured once at them, and they all bowed. Keeva climbed down from the tall horse and followed the two men. The Grey Man did not show any evidence of his wounds, save that there was still dried blood on his ripped tunic.

Jonan's house was of sand-fired brick, the frontage decorated with blackened timbers, the roof covered by red terracotta tiles. Jonan led them into a long living room. At the northern end was a large fireplace, also built with brick, and before it were set several deep leather chairs and a low table. The floor was of polished timber, adorned with attractive rugs, beautifully crafted from

Chiatze silk. The Grey Man eased himself into a chair, resting his head against the high back-rest. A young blonde woman entered. She smiled nervously at Keeva and curtsied to the Grey Man. 'We have ale, sir,' she said, 'or wine. Whatever pleases you.'

'Just some water, thank you,' he replied.

'We have apple juice, if that would be preferable?'

He nodded. 'That would be very fine.'

The headman shifted from foot to foot. 'May I sit, sir?' he asked.

'It is your house, Jonan. Of course you may sit.'

'Thank you.' He sank into the chair opposite. Keeva, unnoticed, sat down cross-legged upon a rug. 'It is a great pleasure and an honour to see you, sir,' continued Jonan. 'Had we known you were coming we could have prepared a feast in your honour.'

The woman returned, bringing a goblet of apple juice for the Grey Man and a tankard of ale for Jonan. As she backed away she glanced down at Keeva and silently gestured for her to follow. Keeva rose from the floor and walked from the room, through the hall beyond and into a long kitchen. The woman of the house was flustered, but she offered Keeva a seat at a pine table and filled a clay cup with juice. Keeva drank it.

'We did not know he was coming,' said the woman nervously, sitting down opposite Keeva. She ran her fingers through her long, blond hair, pushing it back from her eyes, and tying it at the nape of her neck.

'It is not an inspection,' said Keeva softly.

'No? You are sure?'

'I am sure. Some raiders attacked my village. He hunted them down and killed them.'

'Yes, he is a terrible killer,' said the woman, her hands trembling. 'Has he harmed you?'

Keeva shook her head. 'He rescued me from them. He is taking me home.'

'I thought my heart would stop beating when he rode in.'

'He owns this village too?' asked Keeva.

'He owns all the lands of the Crescent. Bought them six years ago from Lord Aric, though he has been here only once in that time. We send him his taxes. In full,' she added quickly. Keeva did not respond to this. Surely no community paying full taxes could afford so many fine clothes, furniture and Chiatze rugs. Nor would they be so nervous concerning inspections. But, then, withholding taxes was, in her limited experience, a way of life among farmers and fishermen. Her brother had always managed to squirrel away one sack of grain in twenty to sell at market in order to supply small luxuries to his family, like new shoes, or a better-made bed for himself and his wife.

'My name is Conae,' said the woman, relaxing a little.

'Keeva.'

'Did the raiders kill many in your village?'

'Five men and three women.'

'So many? How awful.'

'They came in at dusk. Some of the women managed to run, taking the children with them. The men tried to fight. It was over very quickly.' Keeva shuddered at the memory.

'Was your husband among them?'

'I am not married. I was living in Carlis with my uncle, and when he died last year I went to work for my brother. He was killed. So was his wife. And they burned down our house.'

'You poor girl,' said Conae.

'I am alive,' said Keeva.

'Were you close to your brother?'

'He was a hard man and he treated me like a slave. His wife was little better.'

'You could stay here,' said Conae. 'There are more young men than young girls and a pretty creature like you could find a good husband.'

'I am not looking for a husband,' said Keeva. 'Not yet,' she added, seeing the concern on Conae's face. They sat in uncomfortable silence for a little while, then Conae smiled awkwardly and rose. 'I'll fetch you some clothes,' she said. 'For your journey.'

As Conae left the room Keeva leant back in the chair. She was tired now, and very hungry. Am I evil not to mourn Grava's death? she wondered, picturing his broad face, and his small, cold eyes. He was a brute and you hated him, she told herself. It would be hypocrisy to pretend grief. Pushing herself to her feet, she moved across the kitchen, cutting herself a slab of bread and pouring another cup of apple juice. In the silence she could hear the conversation from the living room. Chewing the bread, she moved closer to the wall. There was a closed wooden hatch, crafted so that food could be passed from the kitchen. Putting her eye to the crack, she saw the Grey Man rise from his chair. Jonan stood also.

'There are bodies in the woods to the north-east,' said the Grey

Man. 'Send out some men to bury them, and gather whatever weapons and coin they were carrying. These you can keep. You will also find horses. These will be brought to me at my house.'

'Yes, sir.'

'One other thing, Jonan. Your profits from smuggling are nothing to do with me. Taxes on goods shipped in from Chiatze lands are subject to the Duke's laws not mine. You should bear in mind, however, that punishment for smugglers is severe indeed. I am reliably informed that the Duke's inspectors will be sent out in the next month.'

'You are mistaken, sir. We don't . . .' His words tailed away as he met the Grey Man's gaze.

'If the inspectors find you guilty you will all be hanged. Then who will bring in the fish and pay me my taxes? Are you all blind here? You are a fishing settlement and yet your children wear clothes of the best wool, your women boast brooches of silver, and your own house has three rugs that would cost a year's profit from a good fishing vessel. If there are any old clothes left in this village I suggest you find them. And when the inspectors arrive make sure they are worn.'

'It will be as you say, sir,' said Jonan miserably.

Keeva pulled away from the hatch as Conae returned with a dress of blue wool, a pair of high-laced ankle-length shoes, and a brown woollen cloak lined with rabbit fur. Keeva put them on. The dress was a little loose, the shoes a perfect fit.

Jonan called out for the women and they both returned to the living room. The Grey Man was on his feet. Reaching into a pouch by his side, he gave Jonan several small silver coin, in payment for the clothes.

'That is not necessary, sir,' said Jonan.

Ignoring him, the Grey Man turned to Conae. 'Thank you for your hospitality, lady.'

Conae curtsied.

The horses were outside, the saddlebags bulging with food for the journey. The Grey Man helped Keeva to mount, then stepped into the saddle.

Without a word of farewell he rode from the settlement, Keeva following.

Chapter Two

They rode in silence for a little while and Keeva saw that the Grey Man's face was stern. She guessed he was angry. Even so, she noted that he studied the lands as he rode, always alert and watchful. Clouds obscured the sun and a little light rain began to fall. Keeva lifted her hood into place and drew her new fur-lined cloak about her.

The rain passed swiftly, sunlight spearing through a break in the clouds. The Grey Man angled his horse up a shallow slope and paused at the top. Keeva drew alongside. 'How are your wounds?' she asked him.

'Almost healed,' he said.

'In such a short time? I don't think so.'

He shrugged and, satisfied the way was clear of danger, heeled the steeldust forward.

Throughout the long afternoon they rode steadily, once more entering the forest. An hour before dusk the Grey Man found a camp-site beside a stream and set a fire. 'Are you angry with the villagers for cheating you?' asked Keeva, as the flames licked at the dry wood.

'No. I am angry at their stupidity.' He looked at her. 'You were listening?'

She nodded. The Grey Man's face softened. 'You are a canny girl, Keeva. You remind me of my daughter.'

'Does she live with you?'

'No, she lives far away in another land. I have not seen her in several years. She is married now to an old friend of mine. They had two sons, last I heard.'

'You have grandsons.'

'In a manner of speaking. She is my adopted daughter.'

'Do you have children of your own?'

He fell silent for a moment, and in the firelight she saw a look of deep sadness touch him. 'I had children, but they . . . died,' he said. 'Let us see what food Jonan's wife prepared for us.' Rising smoothly he moved to the saddlebags, returning with a hunk of ham and some freshly baked bread. They ate in silence. Keeva gathered more dry wood and fed the fire. The clouds had returned, but the night was not cold.

The Grey Man removed his shirt. 'Time to draw these stitches,' he said.

'The wounds cannot have healed,' she told him sternly. 'The stitches should remain for at least ten days. My uncle . . .'

'. . . was a very wise man,' said the Grey Man. 'But see for yourself.'

Keeva moved closer to him and examined the wounds. He was right. The skin had healed, and already scar tissue had formed. Taking his hunting knife, she carefully cut through the twine, pulling each stitch clear. 'I have never heard of anyone healing this fast,' she said, as he pulled on his shirt. 'Do you know magic?'

'No. But once I was healed by a monster. It changed me.'

'A monster?'

He grinned at her. 'Aye, a monster. Seven feet tall, with a single eye in the centre of his forehead – an eye that had two pupils.'

'You are making fun of me,' she chided him.

The Grey Man shook his head. 'No, I am not. His name was Kai. He was a freak of nature – a man beast. I was dying and he laid his hands upon me and all my wounds closed, healed in a heartbeat. Ever since then I have known no sickness, no winter chills, no fevers, no boils. I think even time has slowed for me, for by now I should be spending my days sitting in a comfortable chair with a blanket around my knees. He was a fine man, Kai.'

'What happened to him?'

He shrugged. 'I don't know. Perhaps he is happy somewhere, perhaps he is dead.'

'You have lived an interesting life,' she said.

'How old are you?' he asked her.

'Seventeen.'

'Kidnapped by raiders, and taken away into the forest. There are some in years to come who will hear of this tale and say, "You have lived an interesting life." What will you say to them?'

Keeva smiled. 'I shall agree – and they will envy me.'

He laughed then, the sound full of good humour. 'I like you, Keeva,' he said. Then, he added wood to the fire, stretched out and covered himself with a blanket.

'I like you too, Grey Man,' she said.

He did not answer, and she saw that he was already asleep.

She looked at his face in the firelight. It was strong – the face of a fighter – and yet she could detect no cruelty there.

Keeva slept, and woke with the dawn. The Grey Man was already up. He was sitting by the stream and splashing water to his face. Then, using his hunting knife, he shaved away the black and silver stubble from his chin and cheeks. 'Did you sleep well?' he asked, as he returned to the fire.

'Yes,' she told him. 'No dreams. It was wonderful.' He looked so much younger without the stubble, a man perhaps in his late thirties. She wondered momentarily how old he was. Forty-five? Fifty-five? Surely not older.

'We should be at your settlement by noon,' he said.

Keeva shivered, remembering the murdered women. 'There is nothing there for me. I was staying with my brother and his wife. They are both dead, the farmhouse burned.'

'What will you do?'

'Go back to Carlis and seek work.'

'Are you trained in some craft or skill?'

'No, but I can learn.'

'I can offer you employment at my home,' he said.

'I will not be your mistress, Grey Man,' she told him.

He smiled broadly. 'Have I *asked* you to be my mistress?'

'No, but why else are you offering to take me to your palace?'

'Do you think so little of yourself?' he countered. 'You are intelligent and brave. I also think you are trustworthy and would be loyal. I have one hundred and thirty servants at my home, administering often to more than fifty guests. You would clean rooms, prepare beds for those guests, and help in the kitchens. For this I will pay you two silvers a month. You will have your own room and one day a week free of all duties. Think on it.'

'I accept,' she said.

'Then let it be so.'

'Why do you have so many guests?'

'My home – my palace, as you call it – houses several libraries, an infirmary and a museum. Scholars come from all over Kydor

640

to study there. There is also a separate centre in the South Tower for students and physicians to analyse medicinal herbs and their uses, and three further halls have been set aside for the treatment of the sick.'

Keeva remained silent for a while, then she looked into his eyes. 'I am sorry,' she said.

'Why would you apologize? You are an attractive young woman, and I can understand why you would fear unwelcome advances. You do not know me. Why should I be trusted?'

'I trust you,' she told him. 'Can I ask you a question?'

'Of course.'

'If you have a palace why are your clothes so old, and why do you ride out alone to protect your lands? Think of all you could lose.'

'Lose?' he asked.

'All your wealth.'

'Wealth is a small thing, Keeva, tiny like a grain of sand. It seems large only to those who do not possess it. You talk of *my* palace. It is not mine. I built it, I live within it. Yet one day I will die and the palace will have another owner. Then he will die. And so it goes on. A man *owns* nothing but his life. He holds items briefly in his hand. If they are made of metal or stone they will surely outlive him and be owned by someone else for a short time. If they are cloth he will – with luck – outlive them. Look around you, at the trees and the hills. According to Kydor law, they are mine. You think the trees care that they are mine? Or the hills? The same hills that were bathed in sunlight when my earliest ancestor walked the earth. The same hills that will still be covered in grass when the last man turns to dust.'

'I see that,' said Keeva, 'but with all your wealth you can have everything you want for the rest of your life. Every pleasure, every joy is available to you.'

'There is not enough gold in all the world to supply what I want,' he said.

'And what is that?'

'A clean conscience,' he said. 'Now, do you wish to return to the settlement to see your brother buried?'

The conversation was obviously over. Keeva shook her head. 'No. I don't want to go there.'

'Then we will push on. We should reach my home by dark.'

Cresting a hill, they began the slow descent on to a wide plain. As far as the eye could see there were ruins everywhere. Keeva drew rein and stared out over the plain. In some places there were merely a few white stones, in others the shapes of buildings could still be seen. Towards the west, against a granite cliff-face there were the remains of two high towers, which had crumbled at the base and crashed to the ground like felled trees.

'What was this place?' she asked.

The Grey Man gazed over the ruins. 'An ancient city called Kuan-Hador. No-one knows who built it, or why it fell. Its history is lost in the mists of time.' He looked at her and smiled. 'I expect the people here once believed they owned the hills and the trees,' he said.

They rode down on to the plain. Some way to the west Keeva saw a mist rolling between the jagged ruins. 'Speaking of mists,' she said, pointing it out to her companion. Waylander halted his horse and glanced to the west. Keeva rode alongside. 'Why are you loading your crossbow?' she asked him, as his hands slid two bolts into the grooves in the small black weapon.

'Habit,' he said, but his expression was stern, his dark eyes wary. Angling his horse towards the south-east, away from the mist, he rode away.

Keeva followed him and swung in the saddle to stare back at the ruins. 'How strange,' she said. 'The mist is gone.'

He, too, glanced back, then unloaded his weapon, slipping the bolts back into the quiver at his belt. He saw her looking at him.

'I do not like this place,' she said. 'It feels . . . dangerous,' she concluded lamely.

'You have good instincts,' he told her.

Matze Chai parted the painted silk curtains of his palanquin and gazed with undisguised malevolence at the mountains. Sunlight was filtering through the clouds and shining brightly upon the snow-capped peaks. The elderly man sighed and pulled shut the curtains. As he did so his dark, almond-shaped eyes focused on the back of his slender hand, seeing again the brown liver spots of age staining the dry skin.

The Chiatze merchant reached for a small, ornate wooden box and removed a tub of sweet-smelling lotion, which he applied carefully to his hands, before leaning back against his cushions and closing his eyes.

Matze Chai did not hate mountains. Hatred would mean giving in to passion, and passion, in Matze's view, indicated an uncivilized mind. He loathed what the mountains represented,

642

what the Philosopher termed the Mirrors of Mortality. The peaks were eternal, never changing, and when a man gazed upon them his own ephemeral nature was exposed to the light; the frailty of his flesh apparent. And frail it was, he thought, regarding his coming seventieth birthday with a mixture of disquiet and apprehension.

He leant forward and slid back a panel in the wall, revealing a rectangular mirror. Matze Chai gazed upon his reflection. The thinning hair, drawn tightly across his skull and braided at the nape of his neck, was as black as in his youth. But a tiny line of silver at the hairline meant that he would need to have the dye reapplied soon. His slender face showed few lines, but his neck was sagging, and even the high collar of his scarlet and gold robes could no longer disguise it.

The palanquin lurched to the right, as one of the eight bearers, weary after six hours of labour, slipped on a loose stone. Matze Chai reached up and rang the small golden bell bolted to the embossed panel by the window. The palanquin stopped smoothly and was lowered to the ground.

The door was opened by his *Rajnee*, Kysumu. The small warrior extended his hand. Matze Chai took it and stepped through the doorway, his long robes of heavily embroidered yellow silk trailing to the rocky path. He glanced back. The six soldiers of his guard sat their mounts silently. Beyond them the second team of bearers climbed down from the first of the three wagons. Dressed in livery of red and black, the eight men marched forward to replace the tired first team, who trudged silently back to the wagon.

Another liveried servant ran forward, bearing a silver goblet. He bowed before Matze Chai and offered him the watered wine. The merchant took the goblet, sipping the contents. 'How much longer?' he asked the man.

'Captain Liu says we will camp at the foot of the mountains, sir. The scout has found a suitable site. He says it is an hour from here.'

Matze Chai drank a little more, then returned the goblet, still half full, to the servant. Climbing back into the palanquin he settled himself down on his cushions. 'Join me, Kysumu,' he said.

The warrior nodded, pulled his sword and scabbard from the sash of his long grey robes, and climbed inside, seating himself opposite the merchant. The eight bearers took hold of the cushioned poles, raising them to waist height. At a whispered command from the lead bearer they then hefted the poles to their shoulders. Inside the palanquin Matze Chai gave a satisfied sigh. He had trained the two teams well, paying attention to every detail. Travel by palanquin was usually not dissimilar to sailing a small boat on choppy water. The cabin lurched from side to side and within minutes those with delicate constitutions would begin to feel queasy. Not so for those who travelled with Matze Chai. His teams were made up of eight men of equal height, trained for hours every day back in Namib. They were well paid, well fed, powerful young labourers; men of little imagination but great strength.

Matze Chai leant back in his cushions, transferring his gaze to the slim, dark-haired young man seated opposite him. Kysumu sat silently, his three-foot-long curved sword on his lap, his coal-black slanted eyes returning Matze Chai's gaze. The merchant had grown to like the little swordsman, for he spoke rarely and radiated calm. There was never a hint of tension about him.

'How is it you are not wealthy?' Matze Chai asked him.

'Define wealth,' answered Kysumu, his long face, as ever, expressionless.

'The ability to purchase whatever one desires, whenever one desires it.'

'Then I am wealthy. All I desire is a little food and water each day. These I can pay for.'

Matze Chai smiled. 'Then let me rephrase the question: how is it that your renowned skills have not supplied you with plentiful amounts of gold and coin?'

'Gold does not interest me.'

Matze Chai already knew this. It explained why Kysumu was the most highly prized *Rajnee* in all the lands of the Chiatze. All men knew that the swordsman could not be bought, and thus would never betray the nobleman who hired him. Yet it was baffling, for among the Chiatze nobility loyalty always came at a price, and it was perfectly acceptable for warriors and body-guards like Kysumu to change allegiance when better offers were made. Intrigue and treachery were endemic to the Chiatze way of life – indeed, among politicians of all races. Which made it even more curious that Kysumu was revered among the treacherous nobility for his honesty. They did not laugh behind his back, or mock his 'stupidity'. Even though it highlighted, in glorious colour, their own lack of morals. What a strange race we are, thought Matze Chai.

Kysumu had closed his eyes and was breathing deeply. Matze Chai looked at him closely. No more than five and a half feet tall, slightly round-shouldered, the man looked more like a scholar or a priest. His long face and slightly downturned mouth gave him a look of melancholy. It was an ordinary face, not handsome, not ugly. The only distinctive feature was a small purple birthmark on his left eyebrow. Kysumu's eyes opened and he yawned.

'Have you ever visited the lands of Kydor?' asked the merchant.

'No.'

'They are an uncivilized people, and their language is hard on both the ear and the mind. It is guttural and coarse. Not musical in any way. Do you speak any foreign tongues?'

'A few,' said Kysumu.

'The people here are offshoots from two empires, the Drenai and the Angostin. Both languages have the same base.' Matze Chai was just beginning to outline the history of the land, when the palanquin came to a sudden stop. Kysumu opened the panelled door and leapt lightly to the ground. Matze Chai rang the small bell and the palanquin was lowered to the rocks. Not smoothly, which irritated him. He climbed out to berate the bearers, then saw the group of armed men barring the way. He scanned them. There were eleven warriors, all armed with swords and clubs, though two carried longbows.

Matze Chai flicked a glance back to his six guards, who had all edged their horses forward. They were looking nervous, and this added to Matze's irritation. They were supposed to be fighters. They were *paid* to be fighters.

Lifting his yellow robes to keep the dust from the hem, Matze Chai moved towards the armed men. 'Good day to you,' he said. 'Why have you stopped my palanquin?'

A bearded man stepped forward. He was tall and broad-shouldered, a longsword in his hand, two long, curved knives sheathed in his thick belt. 'This is a toll road, Slant-eye. No-one passes here without payment.'

'And what is the payment?' asked Matze Chai.

'For a rich foreigner like you? Twenty in gold.' Movement came from left and right as a dozen more men emerged from behind rocks and boulders.

'The toll seems excessive,' said Matze Chai. He turned to Kysumu and spoke in Chiatze. 'What do you think?' he asked. 'They are robbers and they outnumber us.'

'Do you wish to pay them?'

'Do you believe they will merely take twenty in gold?'

'No. Once we accede to their demands they will demand more.'

'Then I do not wish to pay them.'

'Return to your palanquin,' said Kysumu softly, 'and I will clear the path.'

Matze Chai returned his gaze to the bearded leader. 'I suggest,' he said, 'that you step aside. This man is Kysumu, the most feared *Rajnee* among the Chiatze. And you are, at this moment, only heartbeats from death.'

The tall leader laughed. 'He may be all you say, Slant-eye, but to me he's just another vomit-coloured dwarf ripe for the taking.'

'I fear you are making a mistake,' said Matze Chai, 'but, then, all actions have consequences and a man must have the courage to face them.' He gave an abrupt bow, which in Chiatze would have been insulting, and turned away, walking slowly back to his palanquin. He glanced back, and saw Kysumu walk forward to stand before the leader. Two robbers advanced from the group to stand alongside the bearded man. For a moment only Matze Chai doubted the wisdom of this course of action. Kysumu seemed suddenly tiny and innocuous against the brute power of the round-eye robber and his men.

The leader's sword came up. Kysumu's blade flashed into the air.

Moments later, with four men dead, the rest of the robbers scattering and running away into the rocks, Kysumu wiped clean his sword and returned to the palanquin. He was not out of breath, neither was his face flushed. He looked, as always, serene and at peace. Matze Chai's heart was beating wildly, but he fought to keep his face expressionless. Kysumu had moved with almost inhuman speed, cutting, slashing, spinning like a dancer into the midst of the robbers. At the same moment his six guards had charged their horses into the second group, and they, too, had run for cover. All in all, a most satisfactory outcome, and one that justified the expense of hiring guards.

'Do you believe they will come back?' asked Matze Chai.

'Perhaps,' said Kysumu, with a shrug. Then he stood quietly waiting for orders. Matze Chai summoned a servant and asked Kysumu if he wished to partake of some watered wine. The swordsman refused. Matze Chai accepted a goblet, intending to take a sip. Instead he half drained it.

'You did well, *Rajnee*,' he said.

'We should be moving from here,' replied Kysumu.

'Indeed so.'

The cabin of the palanquin felt like a sanctuary as Matze Chai settled himself down on his cushions. Lightly striking the bell to signal the bearers to move on, he closed his eyes. He felt safe, secure, and almost immortal. Opening his eyes, he glanced out through the window and saw the setting sun blaze its dying light over the mountain peaks. Reaching up, he drew the curtains closed, his good humour evaporating.

They made camp an hour later, and Matze Chai sat in his palanquin while his servants unloaded his night-time furniture from the wagons, assembling his gold-lacquered bed, and spreading upon it his satin sheets and thick goose-down quilt. After this they raised the poles and frame of his blue and gold silk tent, spreading out the black canvas sheet upon the ground, then unrolling his favourite silk rug to cover it. Lastly his two favourite chairs, both inlaid with gold and deeply cushioned with padded velvet, were placed in the tent entrance. When finally Matze Chai climbed from the palanquin the camp was almost prepared. His sixteen bearers were sitting together round two camp-fires set in a jumble of boulders, two of the six guards had taken up sentry positions to patrol the perimeter, and his cook was busy preparing a light supper of spiced rice and dried fish.

Matze Chai moved across the campground to his tent and sank gratefully into his chair. He was tired of living like a frontier nomad, at the mercy of the elements, and longed for the journey to be over. Six weeks of this harsh existence had drained his energy.

Kysumu was sitting cross-legged upon the ground close by, a section of parchment, pinned to a board of cork, resting on his knees. Using a shaped piece of charcoal Kysumu was sketching a tree. Matze Chai watched the little swordsman. Every evening he would fetch his leather folder from the supply wagon, take a fresh section of parchment, and sketch for an hour. Usually trees or plants, Matze Chai had noted.

Matze Chai had many such drawings in his own home, by some of the greatest Chiatze masters. Kysumu was talented, but by no means exceptional. His compositions lacked, in Matze Chai's opinion, the harmony of emptiness. Kysumu's work had too much passion. Art should be serene, devoid of human emotion. Stark and simple, it should encourage meditation. Even so,

Matze Chai decided, he should – at journey's end – offer to purchase one of the sketches. It would be impolite not to do so.

A servant brought him a cup of scented tisane and, with the temperature dropping, laid a fur-lined robe around Matze Chai's thin shoulders. Then two of the bearers, using forked wooden poles, carried an iron brazier, glowing with coals, into Matze Chai's tent, setting it down on a pewter base plate, to prevent cinders singeing the expensive rugs.

The incident with the robbers had proved spiritually uplifting. As the mountains spoke silently of the fleeting nature of man, the sudden peril had brought to the fore just how much Matze Chai enjoyed life. It made him aware of the sweetness of the air he breathed, and of the feel of silk upon his skin. Even the tisane he now sipped was almost unbearably fine upon the tongue.

Despite the discomforts of travel Matze Chai was forced to admit that he now felt better than he had in years. Wrapping himself in the fur-lined cloak he settled back and found himself thinking of Waylander. It had been six years since last they met, back in Namib. At that time, Matze Chai had recently returned from Drenan, where he had, upon Waylander's instruction, purchased a skull from the Great Library. Waylander had then sold his home and journeyed north and east, seeking a new land and a new life.

Such a restless soul, thought Matze Chai. But, then, Waylander was a man on a mission that could never be completed, a quest born in despair and longing. At first Matze Chai had believed Waylander to be seeking redemption for past sins. This was only partly true. No, what the Grey Man sought was an impossibility.

An owl hooted close by, breaking Matze Chai's concentration.

Kysumu finished his sketch, and replaced it in the leather folder. Matze Chai beckoned him to sit in the second chair. 'It occurs to me,' he said, 'that had the remaining robbers not panicked and run you would have been overwhelmed.'

'Indeed,' said Kysumu.

'Or, if my guards had not attacked the second group at just that instant, they could have run at the palanquin and killed me.'

'They could have,' agreed the swordsman.

'But you did not think it likely?'

'I did not think of it at all,' said Kysumu.

Matze Chai suppressed a smile, but allowed the feeling of warm satisfaction to flow through him. Kysumu was a delight. The ideal companion. He did not gush or chatter, or ask endless

648

questions. He was, in truth, harmony itself. They sat thus for a little while. Then food was brought and they ate quietly.

At the conclusion of the meal Matze Chai rose from his chair. 'I shall sleep now,' he said. Kysumu rose, pushed his sword and scabbard into the sash around his robes, and strolled from the camp.

The captain of Matze Chai's guards, a young man named Liu, approached his master and bowed deeply. 'Might I enquire, Lord, where the *Rajnee* is going?'

'I would imagine he is seeking out the robbers, in the event that they might be following,' Matze Chai told him.

'Should some of the men not go with him, Lord?'

'I do not believe he has need of them.'

'Yes, Lord,' said Liu, bowing and backing away.

'You did well today, Liu,' said Matze Chai. 'I shall mention it to your father upon our return.'

'Thank you, Lord.'

'You were frightened, though, were you not, before the fighting began?'

'Yes, Lord. Did it show?'

'I am afraid that it did. Try to exhibit a little more control of your expressions should any similar incidents occur.'

The Grey Man's palace had initially both surprised and disappointed Keeva. Darkness had fallen as they arrived. They had ridden slowly up a dirt road through thick woods, emerging on to open ground and an area of well-trimmed lawn, bisected by a wide stone avenue. There were no fountains or statues. Two spear-wielding guards were patrolling the front of a long, flat, single-storey building around two hundred feet long. There were few windows to be seen, and even these were dark. The only light Keeva could see came from four large brass lanterns hanging in the wide, marble-pillared entrance. It looks like a mausoleum, thought Keeva, as the Grey Man rode his horse forward.

The black doors opened and two young men ran out to meet them. Both wore grey livery. Weary now, Keeva dismounted. The servants led the horses away, and the Grey Man beckoned her to follow him inside. An elderly man was waiting for them, a tall, stooping figure, white-haired and long-faced. He, too, was wearing grey, an ankle-length tunic of fine wool. At the shoulder the image of a tree had been beautifully embroidered in black satin. He bowed to the Grey Man. 'You look tired, sir,' he said, his voice deep and low. 'I shall have a hot bath prepared.'

'Thank you, Omri. This young woman will be joining the staff. Have a room prepared for her.'

'Of course, sir.'

Without a word of farewell the Grey Man strode away across the marble-tiled hallway. He had said little since they had moved away from the ruins, and Keeva wondered if she had said, or done, something to annoy him. She felt confused and uncertain, and gazed around at the velvet hangings, the ornate rugs and the walls adorned by fine paintings.

'Follow me, girl,' said Omri.

'I have a name,' she said, an edge of irritation in her voice.

Omri paused, then turned slowly.

She expected an angry response, but he merely smiled. 'My apologies, young woman. Of course you have. So let us not keep it a secret. Pray share it with me.'

'I am Keeva.'

'Well, that was easily settled, Keeva. *Now* will you follow me?'

'Yes.'

'Good.' He moved across the hall, and turned right into a broad corridor, which led to a wide staircase that descended into shadow. Keeva paused at the top. She had no wish at all to spend the night in this ugly, flat dwelling. But to go underground? What kind of man would spend his wealth building a home burrowed under the earth? she wondered.

The servant Omri was a little ahead of her now and Keeva moved swiftly down the carpeted stairs. The whole building seemed dark and dingy, occasional lanterns casting sinister shadows to the walls. Within minutes Keeva felt hopelessly lost within a gloomy labyrinth. 'How can you live here?' she asked Omri, her voice echoing in the bleak corridor. 'It is an awful place.'

He laughed with genuine amusement. It was a good sound and she found herself warming to the man. 'It is surprising what one can become used to,' he told her. They passed several doors before Omri took a lantern from the wall and halted before a narrow doorway. Lifting the latch he stepped inside. Keeva followed him. Omri moved to the centre of the small room, took a candle from an oval table-top, and held the wick to the lantern flame. Once it was lit he replaced it in a bronze holder shaped like an open flower. Keeva looked around. There was a bed against the wall, a simple piece, unadorned and crafted from pine. Beside it was a small cabinet, upon which was placed another candle in a bronze holder. Heavy curtains covered the far wall. 'Get a little rest,' Omri told her. 'I will send someone to you tomorrow morning early to explain your duties.'

'What is it that you do here?' she asked him, her words tumbling out in her anxiety not to be left alone.

'I am Omri, the steward. Are you all right? You seem to be trembling.'

With a great effort Keeva smiled. 'I am well. Truly.'

Omri paused and ran his thin hands through his thinning grey hair. 'I know that he fought and killed the men who attacked your settlement, and that you were captured by them, and treated . . . badly. But this is a good house, Keeva. You are safe here.'

'How could you know all that happened?' she asked.

'One of our guests is a Chiatze priestess. She can see over great distances.'

'She practises magic?'

'I do not know if it is magic. There are no spells cast. She merely closes her eyes. But it is, I must admit, beyond my understanding. Now, get some rest.'

Keeva heard his footsteps echoing along the corridor. Safe she might be, but she was determined to stay in this awful place not one heartbeat longer than necessary. Never before had Keeva been afraid of the dark, but here, in this underground palace, she found herself staring at the little candle, pitifully grateful for its flickering light.

Weary from the long ride, she removed the cloak, dangling it over the back of a chair, then slipped out of her dress. The bed was comfortable, the mattress firm, the blankets clean, the pillow soft and yielding. Keeva closed her eyes and slipped into a dream-filled sleep. She saw again the Grey Man ride from the forest to confront the raiders, but this time when he came to rescue her his face was bleached of all colour. He took her by the arm and led her to a wide hole in the ground, dragging her in. She screamed – and woke, heart pounding. The candle had guttered and gone out, leaving the room in total darkness. Keeva rolled from the bed and scrabbled for the door latch, dragging it open. In the corridor a distant lantern was still burning. Taking the second candle from the bedside cabinet she ran to the lantern and lit the wick from its flame. Then she returned to her room, and sat quietly, berating herself for her fear.

'In life,' her uncle had told her, 'there are two kinds of people: those who run from their fears, and those who overcome them.

Fear is like a coward. If you back away it becomes a fearsome bully who will beat you into the ground. Face him and he shrinks to a tiny noisy insect.'

Steeling herself, she blew out the candle and, lying down, pulled the blankets back into place. I will not give in to night terrors, she told herself. I will not panic, Uncle.

This time she slept more peacefully, and when she awoke there was the faintest of lights within the room. Sitting up, she saw that the light emanated from a crack in the heavy curtains of the far wall. Rising from the bed, Keeva crossed the room and drew back the curtains. Sunlight flooded in – and she found herself staring out across the brilliantly blue Bay of Carlis, the morning sun glittering on the waves. Tiny fishing-boats dotted the water, their white sails gleaming in the light. Above them gulls swooped and dived. Astonished now, Keeva opened the wooden-framed glass doors and stepped out on to a curved balcony. All around her, on different levels, were similar balconies, most larger, some smaller, but all looked out over the beauty of the bay.

She was not underground at all. The Grey Man's white marble palace had been built on the side of a sloping cliff, and she had entered at the top, unable to see its true magnificence.

Keeva glanced down. Below the balcony she saw terraced gardens and walkways and steps angling down towards the distant beach, where a wooden ramp extended into the sea. A dozen sailing-boats were moored there, sails furled. Returning her gaze to the palace itself, she saw that two towers had been erected to the north and south, huge structures, each with its own terraces.

Everywhere gardeners were already at work among the scores of flower-beds, some clearing away dead plants, others sweeping leaves from the paths and gathering them into sacks slung over their shoulders. Still more were planting fresh border flowers or dead-heading the many rosebushes.

Keeva was so entranced by the beauty of the scene that she failed to hear the gentle tapping at her door, or the creaking of the latch as it opened.

'I think perhaps you should come inside and dress yourself,' said a voice. Keeva whirled and saw a young woman with braided blond hair. She was carrying a neat pile of folded clothes. The woman grinned at her. 'The priests might catch sight of you, and what would happen to their vows then?'

'Priests?' asked Keeva, stepping inside and accepting the clothes from the woman.

'Chiatze foreigners. They are studying the ancient books that the Gentleman keeps in the library of the North Tower.'

Keeva took a white cotton blouse from the pile, shook it out, then slipped it over her head. The material was very soft – like a summer breeze upon the skin. She shivered with pleasure, then stepped into the long grey skirt. It had a belt of silvered leather, and a bright silver buckle. 'These are mine?' she asked.

'Yes.'

'They are wonderful.' Keeva reached up and touched the embroidered tree on the right shoulder of her blouse. 'What does this represent?' she asked.

'It is the Gentleman's mark.'

'The Grey Man?'

'In public we call him the Gentleman, since he is not a lord and far too powerful to be merely a landowner or a merchant. Omri says you came in with him last night. Did you bed him?'

Keeva was shocked. 'No, I did not. And you are very rude to ask such a question.'

The blonde woman laughed. 'Life is very different here, Keeva. We speak freely and think freely – except in front of the Gentleman's guests. He is a very unusual man. None of us is beaten, and he does not use the young women as his personal slaves.'

'Then perhaps I shall like it here,' said Keeva. 'What is your name?'

'I am Norda, and you will be working with my team in the North Tower. Are you hungry?'

'Yes.'

'Then let us get some breakfast. You have a great deal to learn today. The palace is like a rabbit warren and most of the new servants get lost.'

Some minutes later, after what was for Keeva a bewildering journey through endless corridors and several sets of stairs, the two women emerged on to a wide, paved terrace. A long breakfast table was covered with a score of deep dishes containing cooked meats, vegetables, smoked fish, cheeses and fruits. Fresh-baked bread had been set at one end, and flagons of water and fruit juices at the other. Keeva followed Norda's lead and took a plate, heaping it with bread, a slab of butter and some smoked fish. Then they walked to a table by the terrace wall and sat down to eat.

'Why did you ask if I'd slept with the Grey Man?'

'The Gentleman!' corrected Norda.

'Yes, the Gentleman.'

'There is great harmony here between the servant girls. The Gentleman does not play favourites – and neither does Omri. Had the Gentleman bedded you it would have caused discord. Many of the young women would like to . . . enchant him.'

'He is a strikingly attractive man – but he is very old,' said Keeva.

Norda laughed again. 'Age has little to do with it,' she said. 'He is handsome, strong – and immensely rich. The woman who captures his heart would never want for anything, even if she had ten lives to live.'

'From what you say it is surprising he has taken no wife,' observed Keeva.

'Oh, he has taken many.' Norda leaned in close, dropping her voice. 'Gold wives.'

'He *pays* for his pleasures?' asked Keeva, astonished.

'Always. Isn't that weird? Most of the girls here would rush to his rooms at the merest gesture from him. Yet he sends his carriage to bring whores from the town. Oh, fancily dressed and bedecked with jewels, but whores nonetheless. For the last year his favourite has been Lalitia – a red-headed strumpet from the capital.' Norda's face reddened, and Keeva saw her pale blue eyes grow cold.

'You obviously don't like her.'

'Nobody *likes* Lalitia. She rides around in a gilded carriage, with liveried servants whom she treats abominably. In her house she has been known to thrash the maids when the mood takes her. She is a vile creature.'

'What does he see in her?' asked Keeva.

Norda laughed aloud. 'Oh, you'll recognize it when you lay eyes on her. Loathe her as I do, even I have to admit she is astonishingly beautiful.'

'I would have thought him a better judge of people,' offered Keeva.

'You don't know much about men, do you?' said Norda, with a quick smile. 'When Lalitia passes by you can hear the sounds of jaws striking the ground. Strong men, bright men, scholarly men, even priestly men all fall under the spell of her beauty. They see what they want to see. Women, on the other hand, see her for what she is – a whore. And not as young as she pretends. I'd say she was closer to forty than the twenty-five she claims.'

Other servants had begun to arrive, gathering their food and finding places to sit and eat. A young man in a grey mailshirt approached them. Removing his helm he smiled at Norda. 'Good morning,' he said. 'Will you introduce me to the newcomer?'

Norda smiled. 'Keeva, this is Emrin, the guard sergeant. He thinks he's more handsome than he is and will do everything in his power to lure you to his bed. It is, sadly, his nature. Do not judge him too harshly.'

Keeva glanced up at the man. He had a round, good-looking face and blue eyes. His hair was light blond, short and tightly curled. Emrin extended his hand and Keeva shook it. 'Do not believe everything Norda says about me,' he told her. 'I am really a gentle soul, seeking the perfect partner for my heart.'

'Surely you found him the first time you looked in a mirror,' said Keeva, with a sweet smile.

'Sadly that is true,' said Emrin, with disarming honesty. Taking her hand he kissed it, then turned his attention to Norda. 'Be sure to tell your new friend what a great lover I am,' he said.

'I will,' said Norda. She glanced at Keeva. 'The best ten heart-beats I've ever experienced.' Both women laughed.

'I think I should leave,' Emrin said, 'while I have a modicum of dignity left.'

'Too late,' said Keeva. The man grinned and moved away.

'Neatly done,' said Norda. 'He will pursue you with even greater vigour.'

'Not something I desire,' Keeva told her.

'Oh, don't rule him out,' said Norda. 'As he says, he really is quite good in bed. Not the best I have known, but more than adequate.'

Keeva burst into laughter, and Norda joined in.

'So who was the best?'

She knew it was the wrong question as soon as she spoke: the good humour faded from Norda's face. 'I am sorry,' said Keeva, swiftly.

'Don't be,' Norda told her, laying her hand over Keeva's. 'Now we'd better finish breakfast for there is much to do. There are several more guests due to arrive today, and one of them is a Chiatze. Believe me, there is no race so fussy.'

Chapter Three

Using long, lazy strokes Waylander swam through the cold water. He could feel the warmth of the sun on the skin of his back, and he dived deep, through shoals of silver-backed fish, which scattered before him. Rolling and twisting, he felt a surge of joy. Here there was silence and – almost – contentment. Relaxing, he let his body float upward towards the sun. Breaking clear of the surface, he drew in a deep breath, tossed back his head to clear the hair from his eyes and trod water while he gazed around the bay.

At the harbour opposite, a dozen ships were unloading their cargoes, while anchored further out on the bay were twenty more, waiting for the signal to dock. Twenty-eight of the ships flew under the flag of the Tree. His ships.

It seemed incredible to Waylander that a man, like himself, without a great understanding of the subtleties of commerce should have become so ridiculously wealthy. No matter how much he spent now – or, indeed, gave away – more gold flowed in. Matze Chai, and other merchants, had invested Waylander's money well. But even his own ventures had paid handsomely. It is all a grand nonsense, he thought, as he floated in the water. He had lost track of the number of ships he now owned. Somewhere above three hundred. Then there were the mines – emerald, diamond, ruby, gold and silver – scattered from the hinterlands of Ventria to the eastern Vagrian mountains.

He swung in the water and gazed up at the white marble palace. He had commissioned it six years ago following an idle conversation with a young architect who had talked passionately about the overwhelming and delightful problems of construction, and of his dream to create a marvel. 'Why should we always seek out flat ground?' asked the young man. 'Where is the wonder in that? Great buildings should make an observer gasp.'

Three years in construction, the White Palace was indeed a wonder, though the young architect had not lived to see it finished. A nobleman from House Kilraith, he had been stabbed to death one night by assassins from a rival House. Such was life among the nobles of Kydor.

Waylander swam for the beach and emerged on to the white sand. His steward Omri left his seat beneath the olive tree and walked out to meet him, a long linen towel folded over his arm. 'Was the swim beneficial, sir?' he asked, extending the towel and draping it over Waylander's shoulders.

'It was refreshing,' said Waylander. 'And now I am ready for the pressing matters of the day.'

'The Lady requests an audience with you, sir,' said Omri, 'when you have the time.'

Waylander looked at the older man closely. 'Is something bothering you, Omri?'

'Were you aware she is a mystic?'

'No, but it is not surprising. I have known many priests with Talent.'

'I find it unsettling,' admitted Omri. 'I rather feel she can read my thoughts.'

'Are your thoughts so terrible?' asked Waylander, with a smile.

'Occasionally, sir,' admitted Omri, straight-faced. 'But that is not the point. They are *my* thoughts.'

'Indeed so. What else requires my attention?'

'We have received a message from Lord Aric saying he will visit in ten days on his way to the Winter Palace.'

'He needs more money,' said Waylander.

'I fear so, sir.'

Dry now, Waylander moved into the shade of the olive tree and pulled on a black silk shirt and a pair of soft leather leggings. Tugging on his boots, he sat back and gazed once more over the bay. 'Did the Lady say why she wished to see me?'

'No, sir. But she did tell me of your fight with the raiders.'

Waylander caught the note of criticism in the old man's voice. 'It is too fine a day to be chided, Omri,' he said.

'You take great risks, sir. Largely unnecessary risks. We have thirty guards here, and a dozen tough foresters. They could have been sent after the robbers.'

'Very true. But I was close by.'

'And you were bored,' said the old man. 'You always ride off into the wilderness when you are bored. I have come to the conclusion that you do not enjoy being rich. It is, I must say, hard to understand.'

'It is a terrible thing, boredom,' said Waylander. 'It has come to me over the years that wealth and tedium are great bedfellows. When one is rich there is nothing to strive for. Every pleasure I desire is available to me.'

'Obviously not every one, sir, otherwise you would not be bored.'

Waylander laughed. 'That is true. Now, enough of this soul-searching, my friend. What other news is there?'

'Two retainers from House Bakard were murdered in Carlis two days ago, supposedly by men hired by House Kilraith. There is great tension in the town. The merchant Vanis has requested an increase to his loan. He claims to have lost two ships in a storm and is unable to meet his debt payments. Also . . .' Omri pulled a slip of parchment from the pocket of his grey robe and perused it. '. . . the surgeon Mendyr Syn has asked if you would be prepared to hire three extra students, at a cost of six silvers a month, to assist him. There are now no spare beds in the infirmary and Mendyr has been working for fifteen hours a day trying to aid the sick.' Omri folded the parchment, returning it to his pocket. 'Oh, yes, and . . . er . . . Lady Lalitia has invited you to attend a celebration of her birthday in three days.'

Waylander sat in the shade, staring out at the fishermen casting their nets in the bay. 'Call in the loan on Vanis,' he said. 'This is the third time in a year he has furnished an excuse for non-payment. His debts have not prevented him buying three racing stallions and extending his eastern estate. Increase the funds to Mendyr Syn and tell him he should have requested help much earlier. And send a message to Lady Lalitia that I will be delighted to attend her celebration. Purchase a diamond pendant from Calicar and have it delivered to her on the day.'

'Yes, sir. Might I point out two things? Point one: Vanis has many friends in House Kilraith. Foreclosing his debt will bankrupt him and be seen as a slight upon the House.'

'If he has that many friends,' said Waylander, 'let them pay his debts. Now, what was the second point?'

'If memory serves me correctly is this not the third birthday that Lady Lalitia has had in the past fifteen months?'

Waylander laughed. 'Yes, it is. Make it a *small* diamond pendant.'

'Yes, sir. By the way, the young woman you brought in has been put to work with Norda's team. Do you wish for any special treatment towards her?'

'Give her a little leeway for she has suffered much. She is a strong girl, but even so she has witnessed the murder of her family, been treated cruelly and threatened with death. It would be remarkable were she to suffer no after-effects. Watch her closely and give her a little support. If she does not prove to be a good worker, dismiss her.'

'Very well, sir. And what message shall I send the Chiatze Lady?'

'No message, Omri. I will go and see her presently.'

'Yes, sir. Would it be considered a discourtesy to ask her how long she and her retainers plan to stay?'

'I am more interested to know why they came here – and how,' said Waylander.

'*How*, sir?'

'A priestess in robes of embroidered silk, with three retainers, appears at our gates. Where was the carriage? Where were the horses? From where did they come? They did not stay in Carlis.'

'Obviously they walked from elsewhere,' said Omri.

'And yet attracted little dust to their clothing, and showed no sign of weariness.'

Omri made the Sign of the Protective Horn. 'Regardless of the discourtesy, sir, I would gratefully appreciate knowledge of their departure date.'

'I do not believe there is any need to fear them, Omri. I sense no evil in her.'

'That is good to hear, sir. But some of us have little choice concerning what we fear. I have always been a frightened man. I don't know why.'

Waylander laid his hand on the old man's shoulder. 'You are a gentle soul and a good man,' he said. 'You care about people and their happiness. That is rare.'

Omri looked embarrassed. 'I would have liked to have been more . . . manly, shall we say? I was a terrible disappointment to my father.'

'Most of us are,' said Waylander. 'Had my father seen what I have done with my life he would have burned with shame. But that is neither here nor there. We live in the *now*, Omri. And *now* you are a steward, valued and respected – even loved by those who serve under you. It should be enough.'

'Perhaps,' said Omri, 'but then you are loved and respected by those who serve you. Is it enough for you?'

Waylander gave a rueful smile, but did not reply. Moving away, he climbed the terrace steps towards the North Tower.

Minutes later he reached the top of the circular stair to the largest of the library rooms. It had originally been designed as a large state room, but as his collection of ancient scrolls and books grew, so too did the need for added space. There were now five smaller libraries within the palace, as well as the huge museum in the South Tower. Pushing open the door, he stepped inside and bowed to the slender woman sitting at the long, oval table, scrolls spread out around her. He found himself marvelling once more at her beauty, the pale gold of her flawless skin, and her finely boned Chiatze features. Even the shaven head only emphasized her exquisite good looks. She seemed almost too frail to bear the weight of the heavy robes of red and gold silk adorning her body.

'What are you studying, Lady?' he asked.

She looked up. Her slanted eyes were not the deep chestnut of the Chiatze, but tawny gold, flecked with blue. They were disconcerting eyes that seemed to stare deep into the recesses of his soul. 'I have been reading this,' she said, her gloved hand lightly touching an ancient scroll of dry and faded parchment. 'It is, I am told, a fifth-generation copy of the sayings of a writer named Missael. He was one of the most extraordinary men of the New Order, following the destruction of the Elder Races. Some believe his verses contain prophecies for the future.' She smiled. 'But, then, words are so imprecise. Some of these verses could mean anything.'

'Then why do you study them?'

'Why does one study at all?' she countered. 'For greater knowledge, and with it greater understanding. Missael tells how the old world was destroyed by lust, greed, fear and hatred. Did mankind learn from the destruction?'

'Mankind does not have a single set of eyes,' said Waylander. 'A million eyes see too much and absorb too little.'

'Ah, you are a philosopher.'

'A poor one at best.'

'From your words you believe mankind cannot change for the better, evolve and develop into a finer species?'

'Individuals can evolve and change, Lady. This I have seen. But gather together any large group and within a few heartbeats you can have a howling mob, intent on murder and destruction. No, I do not believe mankind will ever change.'

'That may be true,' she agreed, 'but it leaves the taste of defeat and despair. I cannot countenance such a philosophy. Please sit.'

Drawing up a chair, he reversed it and sat opposite her. 'Your rescue of the girl, Keeva, does you credit,' she said, her voice low, almost musical.

'I did not at first know they had taken a hostage,' he admitted.

'Even so. She now has a life – and a destiny – that would otherwise have been robbed from her. Who knows what she may achieve, Waylander?'

'Not a name I use now,' he told her. 'And not one by which I am known by any in Kydor.'

'No-one shall hear it from me,' she told him. 'So, tell me, why did you ride after the bandits?'

'They attacked my lands and my people. What other reason did I need?'

'Perhaps you needed to prove to yourself that you are still the man you were. Perhaps, beneath the hard, worldly exterior, you felt for the pain and the loss of the villagers, and were determined that those evil men would never again cause such distress. Or perhaps you were thinking of your first wife, Tanya, and how you were not present when the raiders came to kill her and murder your children.'

His voice hardened. 'You asked to see me, Lady. Your messenger said it was a matter of some importance.'

She sighed, then looked once more into his eyes. When she spoke her voice was softer, the tone regretful. 'It distresses me to have caused you pain, Grey Man. Forgive me.'

'Let us understand one another,' he said coldly. 'I try to hold my pain in a private place. Not entirely successfully. You opened a window to it. I would consider it a courtesy if you did not open it again.'

'You have my word upon it.' She sat silently for a moment, her golden eyes holding to his gaze. 'It is sometimes difficult for me, Grey Man. You see, nothing is hidden from me. When I meet someone for the first time I see all. Their lives, their memories, their angers and pains are all laid bare to me. I try to close myself to myriad images and emotions, but that is painful and exhausting. So, in the main, I absorb them. It is why I avoid crowds, for it is like being trapped under an avalanche of roaring emotion. So let me say again that I am sorry to have offended you. You have been most kind to me and my followers.'

Waylander spread his hands. 'It is forgotten,' he said.

'That is most generous of you.'

'And the matter you wished to speak of?'

She averted her eyes. 'This is not easy for me,' she said, 'for I need to ask your forgiveness a second time.'

'I have already said—'

'No, not for my earlier words. In coming here I may have placed you in some . . . danger. My followers and I are being hunted. It is possible – though I hope unlikely – that we will be found. I felt obliged to inform you of this, and to offer, with genuine intent, to leave immediately, should you desire it.'

'You have broken some Chiatze law?' he asked.

'No, we are not law-breakers. We are seekers of knowledge.'

'Then who hunts you, and why?'

Now her eyes met his. 'Bear with me, Grey Man, while I explain why I cannot yet tell you. As I have already shown, your thoughts and memories are known to me. They blaze from you like the rays of the sun, and like those rays they radiate out over the land. All human thoughts do this. The world is awash with them. Far beyond this palace there are minds attuned to such thoughts, seeking out a resonance that will lead them to me. If I told you the names of those hunting me they would form part of your thinking. And merely by thinking them you might alert those who seek to kill me.'

Waylander smiled. 'Since I do not understand the ways of magickers let us move on,' he said. 'Why did you come here?'

'Partly because you are here,' she said simply, then fell silent.

'And the other part?'

'That is even more complicated.'

Waylander laughed. 'More complicated than magical enemies who can read thoughts over great distances? It is a bright morning, with a fresh breeze and a blue sky. I am fresh from a cooling swim. My mind is clear. Speak on, Lady.'

'This is not the only world, Grey Man.'

'I know. There are many lands.'

'That is not what I meant. We dwell at this time in Kydor. But there are other Kydors, an infinite number of them. Just as there

662

are an infinite number of Drenai worlds. Many have identical histories, many are different. In some the assassin Waylander killed the Drenai king and the land was overrun by Vagrian forces. In others he killed the king and the Drenai won. In some he did not kill the king and there was no war. You follow?'

Waylander's good humour seeped away. 'I murdered the king. For money. It was unforgivable. But it happened. I cannot change it. No-one can change it.'

'It happened *here*,' she said softly. 'But there are other worlds. An infinite number. Somewhere, at this moment, in the vastness of space there is another woman, sitting with a tall man. The scene is exactly as this one, save perhaps that the woman is wearing a blue robe and not one of gold. The man may be bearded, or dressed differently. But she is still me, and he is still you. And the land they dwell in is called Kydor.'

Waylander took a deep breath. 'He is not me. I am me.'

'I am sure *he* is saying exactly that.'

'And he is right,' said Waylander. 'He might also be about to ask the point of this conversation. What does it matter if there are two Waylanders, or two hundred, if they never meet or interact?'

'A good question. I have seen some of these worlds. In all of them, no matter what the outcome, the man known as Waylander has a part to play.'

'Not in this world, Lady. Not any longer.'

'We shall see. Do you wish us to go?'

'I will think on it,' he told her, rising from his chair.

'That is kind of you. One other small matter . . .'

'Yes?'

'You did not ask Keeva how she killed the pigeons she cooked for you.'

'No, I did not.' He gave a wry smile. 'I had other matters on my mind.'

'Of course. She used your crossbow. She missed with the first bolt, but then killed all three – the last as it took flight.'

'Impressive,' he said.

'I thought that it would interest you.'

He paused in the doorway. 'In all your studies have you come across anything about the ruins to the west?'

'Why do you ask?'

'I was there yesterday. I . . . did not like the feel of the place. And yet I have passed through it many times. Something today was different.'

'You felt in danger?'

He smiled. 'I felt fear, and yet all I saw was a mist.'

'I know that the ruins are five thousand years old,' she said. 'Perhaps you sensed the spirit of someone long dead. But if I find anything of interest I will call upon you, Grey Man,' she told him.

'It is probably nothing. But it was too warm for a mist, and it seemed to be flowing against the breeze. Had the girl not been with me I would have investigated the phenomenon. I do not like mysteries.'

Then he turned and was gone.

As the Grey Man left the library a small door opened and a slender, round-shouldered man stepped into the presence of the priestess. Like her he was shaven-headed, and wearing an ankle-length robe. It was of white wool, with matching gloves and boots of thin, pale grey leather. His tawny eyes cast a nervous glance towards the outer door. 'I do not like him,' he said. 'He is a savage just like them.'

'No, Prial,' she said. 'There are similarities, but he does not have their cruelty.'

'He is a killer.'

'Yes, he is a killer,' she agreed. 'And he knew you were beyond the door.'

'How could that be? I scarcely even allowed myself to breathe.'

'He knew. He has an unconscious talent for these matters. It is, I think, why he has survived so long.'

'And yet he did not know one of the raiders was hiding in a tree above him?'

The priestess smiled. 'No, he did not. But he had strung his crossbow minutes before, and was holding it ready when the man leapt. As I said, it is an unconscious talent.'

'I thought for a moment you were going to tell him,' said Prial.

She shook her head. 'I am hoping still that I do not have to. Perhaps they will not find us before we have completed our mission.'

'You believe that?'

'I *want* to believe it.'

'As do I, Ustarte. But time is short, and we still have not found the way. I have scanned over two hundred tomes. Menias and Corvidal have at least equalled me in this, and there are still more than a thousand to study. Has it occurred to you that these people have long forgotten the truth of Kuan-Hador?'

'They cannot entirely have forgotten,' said Ustarte. 'Even the name of the land remains similar. We have come across references to demons and monsters, and heroes who fought them. Fragments, mostly, but somewhere there will be a clue.'

'How soon will the gateway begin to open?' he asked her.

'Within days rather than weeks. But the creatures of the mist are already here. The Grey Man sensed their evil.'

'And now the deaths will begin,' said Prial sadly.

'Yes, they will,' she admitted. 'And we must continue our search with hope in our hearts.'

'I am fast losing hope, Ustarte. How many worlds must we see fall before we admit we are too weak to save them?'

The priestess sighed and rose from her chair, the heavy silk gown rustling as she moved. 'This one world *did* defeat them three thousand years ago. They drove them back through the gateways. Despite the power of their sorcery, and the allies they brought with them, they were beaten back. Even the *Kriaz-nor* could not save them.'

Prial did not look her in the eyes. 'Five years we have been searching and have found nothing. Now we have – perhaps – a few days. Then they will send an *Ipsissimus* and he will sense our presence.'

'He is already here,' she said softly.

Prial shivered. 'You have seen him?'

'There is a cloak-spell around him. I cannot see him, but I can sense his power. He is close.'

'Then we must flee while we have the opportunity.'

'He does not yet know we are here, Prial. There is some power left in me. I also know how to cloak our presence.'

He stepped forward, taking her gloved hand in his and raising it to his lips. 'I know that, Ustarte. But you cannot stand against an *Ipsissimus*. If he has not found us it is because he is not yet looking for us. When he does he will kill us.' Prial began to tremble, and she felt his gloved fingers close tightly about her hand.

She watched him closely, and saw him take a deep, shuddering breath. 'I am calm,' he told her. 'Truly I am.' Then he pulled away from her, embarrassed by his show of weakness. 'These clothes chafe me,' he complained. Opening his robe he pushed it back from his shoulders. Ustarte moved behind him, scratching her fingers through the thick grey fur of his back and shoulders.

His tawny eyes closed, and he grunted with pleasure, his terror subsiding.

But it would return, she knew.

Keeva was tense and more than a little angry as she reached the unusual buildings set aside for the Grey Man. Despite Norda's directions, she had lost herself twice in the maze of corridors and stairs, and had emerged on a lower level, only to see that the building she sought was one storey above and to the right. Climbing a set of stone steps, which cut through a rockery, she finally arrived at the entrance. She stood for a moment, surprised by what she saw. The Grey Man's dwelling place was set back into the cliff, the stone facing roughly fashioned and blending with the natural rock around it. This made it virtually invisible from the bay side of the palace. It looked stark and unprepossessing – not the home of a rich man at all.

Her disquiet grew. Keeva had told the Grey Man she would not be his mistress, but now, within a day, he had summoned her to his rooms. Keeva's anger subsided, and she felt a sudden sadness. For a little while today she had allowed herself to believe she might be happy here. She liked Norda, and the other girls of the team had been friendly. They all spoke highly of old Omri, and the atmosphere among them had been full of good humour. Ah, well, she thought, best get it over. Stepping forward she tapped on the door.

The Grey Man opened it. He was dressed in the same manner as when first she had seen him, dark leggings over riding boots, and a shirt of thin, supple leather. He wore no rings, or chains of gold, and his clothes boasted no brooches and no embroidery. He beckoned her inside. 'Come through,' he said, swinging away from her and strolling into the main living area. It was a rectangular room with only two hide-covered chairs and an old rug. There were no shelves or cabinets, and the fireplace was bare of ornament. A pile of logs was set beside it and a blackened iron poker. The Grey Man wandered through the room and out through a door at the rear. Keeva followed him, expecting to see a bedroom. Her anger began to rise once more.

She crossed the doorway and paused, surprised. It was no bedroom. The thirty-foot wall on the left was panelled with pine, and upon it hung many weapons: longbows, crossbows, Chiatze war darts, swords, knives of all descriptions, some small, others long and double-edged. The right-hand wall was set with six lanterns, their light casting flickering shadows over an array of wooden frames and curious apparatus. Targets had been placed around the room, some round, others crafted from straw, string and old clothing into the forms of men.

The Grey Man moved to a bench table from which he took his crossbow. Loading it with two bolts, he carried it back to Keeva. Then he pointed at the round target some twenty feet away. 'Direct two bolts into the centre,' he told her.

Keeva's arm came up, her hand settling into the worn pistol grip, her fingers on the two bronze triggers. As she had learnt when shooting at the pigeons, the weapon was front heavy, and as the triggers were depressed it tipped slightly downward. Adjusting for this, she loosed both bolts. They flew across the room, slamming into the small red centre of the target. The Grey Man said nothing. Relieving her of the weapon, he moved to the target, retrieving the bolts. Returning the crossbow to the bench he took up two throwing blades. They were diamond-shaped and around four inches in length. There were no hilts, but grooves had been cut into the metal for greater grip.

'Handle this with care,' he said, passing her a blade. 'It is very sharp.' She took it gingerly. It was heavier than it appeared. 'It is not just about direction and speed,' he told her, 'but about spin. The blade must reach its target point first.' He pointed to a nearby straw man. 'Hit that.'

'Where?'

'In the throat.'

Her hand came up, the arm snapping forward. The blade struck the throat area hilt first then bounced away. 'I see what you mean,' she said. 'Can I have the second?' He passed it to her. This time the blade sliced home through the straw man's chin. 'Damn!' she swore.

'Not bad,' he said. 'You have a good eye and excellent co-ordination. That is rare.'

'In a woman, you mean?'

'In anyone.' Moving to the straw target he extracted the blade, picked up the second from the floor and returned to her side. 'Turn your back to the target,' he said. Keeva did so. The Grey Man handed her a blade. 'At my command spin and throw – aiming for the chest.'

He stepped back from her. 'Now,' he said softly. Keeva whirled, the blade slashing through the air to cannon from the target's shoulder and strike the far wall. Sparks flashed briefly from the stone.

'Again,' he said, offering her the second blade. This time it thumped home – once more in the shoulder, but closer to the chest.

'Why are we doing this?' she asked.

'Because we can,' he answered, with a smile. 'You are very talented. With a little work you could be exceptional.'

'If I wanted to spend my life throwing knives,' she observed.

'You told me you had no craft, but were willing to learn. Skilled marksmen can earn a good living at market fairs and celebration days. Not one man in a hundred could have brought down three pigeons in four shots with an unfamiliar weapon. Not one in a thousand could have achieved it without some rudimentary training. In short, like me, you are a freak of nature. Mind and body in harmony. The gauging of distance, the balancing of weight, the power of the throw – all these require precise judgement. For some it takes a lifetime to acquire. For others it can be learnt in a matter of moments.'

'But I missed the chest. Twice.'

'Try again,' he said, gathering up the fallen blade.

She spun – and sent it hurtling into the target.

'Straight through the heart,' he said. 'Trust me. With training you can be among the best.'

'I do not know that I want to be skilled with weapons,' she told him. 'I loathe men of war, their posturing, their arrogance and their endless cruelties.'

Removing the knives from the target the Grey Man took them to the bench and began to clean them with a soft cloth. Placing them in sheaths of black leather he turned again to Keeva. 'I was once a farmer. I lived with a woman I adored. We had three children, a boy of seven and two babes. One day, when I was out hunting, a group of men came to my farm. Nineteen men. Mercenaries seeking employment between wars.' He fell silent for a moment. 'I rarely speak of this, Keeva, but today it is strong in my mind.' He took a deep breath. 'The men tied my Tanya to a bed then – after a little time – killed her. They also killed my children. Then they left.

'When I rode out that morning I recall the sound of laughter in the air. My wife and my son were playing a chasing game in the meadow, my babes were asleep in their cots. When I returned all was silence, and there was blood upon the walls. So I, too, loathe the men of war and their cruelty.'

His face was terribly calm, and there was no sign of the

emotional struggle Keeva guessed was raging below the surface. 'And that is when you became a hunter of men?' she said.

The Grey Man ignored the question. 'My point is that there will always be vile men, just as there will always be men of kindness and compassion. It should have no bearing on whether you choose to develop your talents. This world is a troubled, savage place. It would, however, be even more ghastly if only evil men took the time to master weapons.'

'Was your wife skilled with weapons?' she asked.

'No. And before you ask, it would have made no difference had she been the finest archer in the land. Nineteen killers would have overpowered her and the result would have been the same.'

'Did you go after them, Grey Man?' she asked softly.

'Yes. It took many years, and in that time some of them committed other foul deeds. Others married, settled down and raised families of their own. But I found them all. Every one.'

It was suddenly quiet in the room, the air heavy. Keeva watched the Grey Man. His gaze seemed far away, and upon his face was a look of infinite sadness. In that moment she understood this grim and gloomy dwelling place, set alongside the gleaming white marble of his palace. The Grey Man had no home, for the home of his heart had been destroyed a long time ago. She glanced around at the targets of straw and the array of weapons upon the walls. When she looked back she met his gaze. 'I do not wish to learn this craft,' she said. 'I am sorry if that disappoints you.'

'People long ago ceased to disappoint me, Keeva Taliana,' he told her, with a rueful smile. 'But let me ask you this: how did you feel when you killed the raider captain?'

'I do not want to talk about it.'

'I understand.'

'Do you? You have been a killer so long I wonder if you do.' She reddened as she realized what she had said. 'I'm sorry if that sounds disrespectful, Grey Man. I do not mean it to be. You saved my life and I will be for ever in your debt. But what I mean is that I do not want to experience again the feelings I had when I killed Camran. What I did was needless. He was dying anyway. All I did was to inflict a little more agony. If I had the time again I would merely have walked away from him. What hurts and angers me is that, in those few heartbeats, I allowed myself to be dragged down in the filth of his evil. I became him. You understand?'

669

He smiled sadly. 'I understood *that* long before you were born, Keeva, and I respect what you say. Now you had better return to your duties.'

Yu Yu Liang was not a happy man. A little distance away the arguments were still raging among the dozen survivors and Yu Yu struggled to hear what they were saying. His understanding of the round-eye tongue was merely fair, and he found that many of the words and phrases sailed by him before his ears could catch them and his mind translate them. He was concentrating hard, for he knew it was only a matter of time before someone pointed an accusing finger at him.

Sitting on the rock, his stolen sword in his lap, the former ditch-digger did his best to look silently ferocious – like the warrior he pretended to be. Yu Yu had only been with the group for three days. In that time he had heard many fine promises from the now dead leader, Rukar, about life on the road, and the riches to be made from passing merchants. Instead Rukar had been cut down by the *Rajnee* and Yu Yu had moved faster than ever in his twenty-three years to escape the swinging swords of the charging horsemen.

Truth to tell, he felt a little stab of pride that it had been a Chiatze who had cowed them – a true *Rajnee*. Not a fraud with a stolen blade. Yu Yu shivered. Six years of training before a *Rajnee* could own a blood-tempered blade, and a further five years of philosophical study before he was allowed to fight. But only the very, very best were allowed to wear the grey robes and black sash sported by the man who killed Rukar. As soon as Yu Yu had seen him he had carefully eased himself to the back of the second group and was primed to flee the moment the horsemen charged.

The reality was that Rukar had been a dead man from the moment the *Rajnee* approached him.

'One little swordsman,' someone said, 'and you all run like frightened rabbits.' Yu Yu understood the word *rabbits* and guessed the moment of truth was approaching.

'I didn't notice you standing up to him,' another man pointed out.

'I was caught up in the rush,' the first responded. 'It was like being in a stampede. If I hadn't run I'd have been crushed to death.'

'I thought we had our own Chiatze *Rajnee*,' put in a third

voice. 'Where in Shem's balls was *he* when we needed him?'

Here it comes, thought Yu Yu Liang miserably. He turned his bearded face towards the twelve men in the group and glowered. 'Well, he ran past me like his arse was on fire,' someone observed. A ripple of laughter sounded.

Yu Yu rose slowly to his feet, his double-handed sword glinting as he swept it left and right in what he hoped might look a menacing fashion. Plunging the blade into the ground dramatically, he drew himself up to his full height. 'Any man think me afraid?' he asked, lowering his voice. 'Do you?' he thundered, leaping forward and stabbing his finger at the nearest, who, surprised by the suddenness of the move, fell backwards. 'Or you?' No-one spoke. Yu Yu breathed an inner sigh of relief. 'I am Yu Yu Liang!' he shouted. 'Feared from Blood River to shores of Jian Seas. I kill you all!' he bellowed.

In that instant he saw their faces change, from surprise to stark horror. It was very satisfying. Suddenly one of them scrambled to his feet and ran towards the south. Immediately the others followed, leaving behind their meagre possessions. Yu Yu laughed and threw his hands in the air. 'Rabbits!' he shouted after them. He expected the men to retreat a little distance, but they carried on running. Surely I cannot have been that terrifying, he thought. Must have been the firelight glinting on the muscles of my arms and shoulders, he reasoned, looking down and clenching his fists. Ten years of ditch-digging had honed his upper body beautifully. This warrior life is really not so hard, thought Yu Yu. Bluff and bravado could achieve wonders.

Even so, their reaction was unusual, to say the least. He squinted into the distance, looking for signs of their return. 'I am Yu Yu Liang,' he shouted again, keeping his voice gruff. Then he laughed, and swung back to where he had left his sword.

Standing quietly in the firelight was the little grey-garbed swordsman.

Yu Yu's heart skipped a beat. He leapt backwards, his heel landing in the fire. He swore and jumped forward, then scrabbled for the sword, yanking it from the ground and waving it furiously back and forth, while at the same time shouting a battle cry. It would have been more impressive, he realized, had it not burst forth in a shrill falsetto.

The *Rajnee* stood very still, watching him. He had not drawn his sword. Yu Yu, still holding his sword aloft, glared at him. 'I am Yu Yu Liang . . .' he began, this time in Chiatze.

'Yes, I heard,' said the swordsman. 'Are you left-handed?'

'Left-handed?' echoed Yu Yu, bemused. 'No, I am not left-handed.'

'Then you are holding the sword incorrectly,' observed the *Rajnee*. Moving past Yu Yu he glanced towards the south.

'Are you going to fight me?' Yu Yu asked him.

'Do you wish me to?'

'Isn't that why you came here?'

'No. I came to see if the robbers were planning another attack. Obviously they are not. Where did you find the sword?'

'It has been in my family for generations,' said Yu Yu.

'May I see it?'

Yu Yu was about to hand it to the man. Then he jumped back again, slashing it through the empty air. 'You seek to trick me?' he shouted. 'Very clever!'

The *Rajnee* shook his head. 'I am not trying to trick you,' he said quietly. 'Farewell.'

As he turned away Yu Yu called out after him. 'Wait!' The *Rajnee* halted and glanced back. 'I found it after a battle,' Yu Yu said. 'So I took it. The owner didn't care. Most of his head was missing.'

'You are a long way from home, Yu Yu Liang. Is it your ambition to be a robber?'

'No! I want to be a hero. A great fighter. I want to strut through the market towns and hear people say, "There he is. That's——"'

'Yes, yes,' said the *Rajnee*, 'Yu Yu Liang. Well, all journeys begin with a single step, and at least you have mastered the strutting. Now I suggest you follow me.' With that he walked away.

Yu Yu sheathed his sword, and looped the baldric over his shoulder. Then, grabbing the carrysack containing his meagre possessions, he ran to catch up with the departing *Rajnee*.

The man said nothing at first, as Yu Yu marched along beside him, but after walking for almost an hour the *Rajnee* paused. 'Beyond those trees is the camp of my master, the merchant Matze Chai.' Yu Yu nodded sagely and waited. 'Should anyone recognize you what will you tell them?'

Yu Yu thought about this for a moment. 'That I am your pupil, and you are teaching me to be a great hero.'

'Are you an imbecile?'

'No, I am a ditch-digger.'

The *Rajnee* turned towards him and sighed. 'Why did you come to this land?' he asked.

Yu Yu shrugged. 'I don't really know. I was heading west when I found the sword, then I decided to swing north-east.'

Yu Yu felt uncomfortable under the man's dark gaze and the silence grew. 'Well,' he said, at last, 'what are you thinking?'

'We will talk in the morning,' said Kysumu. 'There is much to consider.'

'Then I am your pupil?'

'You are *not* my pupil,' said Kysumu. 'If you are recognized you will tell the truth. You will say you are not a robber and that you were merely travelling with them.'

'Why was I travelling with them?'

'What?'

'If they ask.'

The *Rajnee* took a deep breath. 'Just tell them about your desire to strut.' Then he strode away towards the camp-fires.

Chapter Four

The first of the outlaws drifted back to the fading camp-fire, moving in warily, terrified that the grey-robed *Rajnee* would be hiding somewhere close by, ready to leap out and rip their lives from them with his wickedly curved sword. They had seen Rukar's body opened from shoulder to belly, his entrails spilling out, and had no wish to share his grisly fate.

Satisfied that the swordsman had gone, one of the men gathered up some dead wood, throwing it on to the fire. Flames licked out, the light spreading.

'What happened to Yu Yu?' said another man, searching the ground for signs of a struggle.

'He must have run,' said another. 'There's no blood.'

Within an hour nine men had gathered around the fire. Three were still hiding out on the plain. It was growing colder, and a fine mist had begun to seep across the land, swirling like pale smoke.

'Where did you hide, Kym?' someone asked.

'There are some ruined walls. I lay down behind one.'

'Me too,' said another. 'Must have been a big settlement here once.'

'It was a city,' said Kym, a small man with sandy hair and buck teeth. 'I remember my grandfather used to tell stories about it, great stories. Monsters and demons. Wonderful stuff. Me and my brother used to lie in bed and listen to them. We'd be terrified.' The man laughed. 'Then we wouldn't be able to sleep and our mother would start shouting at Grandfather for scaring us. Then the following night we'd beg him to tell us more.'

'So what was this place then?' asked Bragi, a stoop-shouldered figure with thinning black hair.

'It was called Guanador, I think,' said Kym. 'Grandfather said there was a great war and the entire city was destroyed.'

'Where did the monsters come in?' put in another man.

Kym shrugged. 'There were magickers, and they had great black hounds with teeth of sharpened iron. Then there were the man-bears, eight feet tall with talons like sabres.'

'How come they got beat, then?' asked Bragi.

'I don't know,' said Kym. 'It's only a story.'

'I hate stories like that,' said Bragi. 'Don't make any sense. Who beat 'em, anyway?'

'I don't know! Wish I'd never mentioned it.'

The mist thickened and edged into the camp. 'Man, it's cold,' said Bragi, taking up a blanket and wrapping it around his shoulders.

'You're always complaining about something,' said a power-fully built man with a shaven head and a forked beard.

'A pox on you, Canja,' snapped Bragi.

'He's right, though,' said someone else. 'It is damned cold. It's this mist. Feels like ice.' Rising from the ground, the men sought out more wood, building up the fire. Then they sat, wrapped in their blankets.

'It's worse than winter,' said Kym.

Moments later the cold was forgotten as a terrible scream echoed in the night. Kym swore and drew his sword. Canja leapt to his feet, dagger in hand, and peered out past the fire. The mist was so thick that he could see no more than a few feet.

'I bet it's that *Rajnee*,' he said. 'He's out there.'

Canja moved a little way into the mist. Kym was watching him.

A curious noise began. The men looked at one another, then clambered to their feet.

'What the Hell is that?' whispered one. It sounded like scratch-ing on the rocky ground just beyond the line of their sight.

The mist was even thicker now, flowing across the fire, causing it to hiss and splutter. Then came a sickening sound, followed by a grunt. Kym swung round to see Canja tottering back towards the fire. Blood was gouting from a huge hole in his chest. His mouth was open, but no sound came forth. Then something white closed around the dying man's head, wrenching it from his body. Bragi spun on his heel and ran several steps in the opposite

675

direction. A huge white form loomed from the mist, and a taloned arm swept down. Bragi's face disappeared in a crimson spray. Talons ripped into his belly, hurling him high into the air.

Kym screamed, and backed away to the fire, dragging out a blazing brand, which he waved around in front of him. 'Get away!' he shouted. 'Get away!'

Something cold curled around his ankle. He glanced down to see a white serpent slithering over his boot. He leapt back – straight into the fire. Flames licked around his leggings. The pain was terrible, but even through it he could see huge white forms approaching the blaze on every side.

Dropping the brand, Kym drew his dagger and turned the point towards his throat. Closing his eyes he rammed it into his jugular.

Something struck him in the back, and he fell from the fire. Gurgling on his life blood he felt sharp teeth rip into his side.

And the mist closed over him.

Kysumu was sitting on the ground, cross-legged, his back against the tree. He was not asleep but in a meditation trance, which served to revitalize his tired muscles. It took many minutes to establish the trance, for the snoring of Yu Yu Liang beside him was a constant irritant, rather like the buzzing of an insect around one's face on a summer's day.

Many years of training served Kysumu well, for he calmly put aside all thoughts of Yu Yu and honed his concentration. Once established he released it in a blaze of emptiness, holding only to the image of a blue flower, bright and ethereal against a backdrop of endless black space, unlit by stars. Slowly – so slowly – he began mentally to recite the Mantra of the *Rajnee*. Thirteen words, set in a child's rhyme.

Ocean and star,
Each am I
Broken my wings
And yet I fly.

With each repeated verse Kysumu grew calmer, his mind expanding, feeling the blood flowing through his veins, the tension easing from his body. One hour of this every day and Kysumu had little need of sleep.

Yet tonight something was disturbing his trance. It was not the

676

sleeping Yu Yu, or even the growing cold. Kysumu was hardened to extremes of cold or heat. He struggled to hold the trance, but it receded from him. He became aware of the scabbarded sword in his lap. It seemed to be vibrating gently under his fingers.

Kysumu's dark eyes flicked open. He glanced about the camp. The night had turned very cold and a mist was seeping through the trees. One of the horses whinnied in fear. Kysumu took a deep breath, then glanced down at his sword. The oval bronze fist-guard was glowing. The *Rajnee* placed his slender hand over the leather-wrapped hilt and drew the sword from its black-lacquered scabbard. The blade was shining with a bright blue light so powerful that it hurt the eyes to gaze upon it. Rising to his feet the swordsman saw that Yu Yu Liang's stolen sword was also shining.

Suddenly a sentry screamed. Kysumu threw aside his scabbard and ran across the camp, cutting round the back of the supply wagon. No-one was there. But the mist was rising now and Kysumu heard a crunching noise from within it. Dropping into a crouch, he examined the ground. Something wet touched his fingers. By the brilliant light of the sword he saw that it was blood.

'Awake!' he shouted. 'Awake!'

Something moved beyond the mist. Kysumu had the merest glimpse of a colossal white figure. Then it disappeared. The mist rolled over his legs. Icy cold touched his skin. Instinctively Kysumu leapt back. His sword slashed down. As it touched the mist, blue lightning rippled through the air, crackling and hissing. A deep, angry growl sounded from close by. Kysumu jumped forward, plunging his sword into the mist. Once more blue lightning sparked, and thunder boomed over the camp.

Another guard yelled from somewhere to the left. Kysumu glanced back to see Yu Yu Liang hacking and slashing at the mist, lightning blazing from his sword. The guard was on the ground, close to the edge of the trees. Something white was wrapped around his foot, dragging him from the camp. Kysumu sprinted across the clearing. The guard was screaming at the top of his voice. As Kysumu reached him he saw what appeared to be the tail of a great white worm looped around the man's ankle. He hacked at it, cutting deeply into the albino flesh. Yu Yu Liang appeared alongside him. With a high-pitched cry he slammed his blade into the worm. It released the guard, who scrabbled back to the relative safety of the camp. The worm slid back into the mist.

Yu Yu bellowed a battle cry and gave chase. Kysumu's left hand snaked out, grabbing the collar of Yu Yu's wolfskin jerkin, yanking him back. Yu Yu's legs shot into the air and he landed heavily.

'Stay with me,' said Kysumu calmly.

'You could have just asked me!' grumbled Yu Yu, rubbing furiously at his bruised backside.

Kysumu backed away to the centre of the camp. The guards and bearers had all gathered here, and were gazing fearfully at the mist, and listening in silent horror to the strange sounds, clicking and tapping just out of vision.

The mist swirled up. Kysumu cut his sword into it. Blue lightning flashed once more, and weird howls of pain could be heard from within the fog.

Yu Yu appeared alongside him. 'What is this?' asked Yu Yu, swinging his sword.

Kysumu ignored him. Two of the horses screamed and went down. 'Stay here! Keep the mist back,' said Kysumu, turning and running across the clearing. The mist parted before him. Something moved to his left. Kysumu dived to his right, rolling and coming to his feet in one smooth motion. A long taloned arm slashed down towards his face. Kysumu swayed back, and sent the glittering sword straight through the limb. There was a howl of agony, and – for a heartbeat only – Kysumu saw a ghastly face, with huge protruding red eyes and wickedly curved fangs. Then it was gone, back into the mist.

The sky began to lighten, the mist flowing back towards the trees.

Within moments the sun shone above the mountains, and the clearing was calm. Two of the horses were dead, their bellies ripped open. Of the missing sentry there was no sign.

As sunlight bathed the scene Kysumu's sword ceased to shine, fading back to silver steel.

On the ground at his feet the taloned arm continued to writhe. Then, as sunlight touched it, the skin blistered and turned black, peeling away from grey bone. Smoke rose from it, the stench filling the air.

Kysumu walked back across the clearing. Yu Yu Liang joined him.

'Whatever they were,' said Yu Yu happily, 'they were no match for two *Rajnee*.'

Matze Chai opened the flap of his tent and stepped out into the open. 'What is the meaning of this noise?' he asked.

678

'We were attacked,' said Kysumu quietly. 'One man is dead and we lost two horses.'

'Attacked? The robbers came back?'

'No, not robbers,' Kysumu told him. 'I think we should move from here. And swiftly.'

'As you wish, *Rajnee*.' Matze Chai leaned forward and peered at Yu Yu Liang. 'And who is this – this person?'

'I am Yu Yu Liang. And I helped fight the demons.' Yu Yu raised his sword and puffed out his chest. 'When the demons came we leapt and cut—' he began excitedly.

'Stop!' said Matze Chai, raising a slender hand. Yu Yu fell silent. 'Stand still and say nothing.' Matze Chai turned his attention to Kysumu. 'You and I will continue this conversation in my palanquin once we are on our way.' Casting a malevolent glance at Yu Yu the merchant disappeared back inside his tent. Kysumu walked away.

Yu Yu ran after him. 'I didn't know these swords could shine like that.'

'Neither did I.'

'Oh. I thought you could explain it to me. We make a good team, though, hey?'

Kysumu wondered briefly if he had committed some great sin in a former life, and Yu Yu was a punishment for it. He glanced up into the taller man's bearded face, then walked away without a word.

'Good team,' he heard Yu Yu say.

Walking back across the camp Kysumu could find no trace of the severed arm, but on the edge of the woods he found many tracks of three-toed taloned feet. Liu, the young captain of the guard, approached him. The man's eyes were frightened and he cast nervous glances into the woods. 'I heard your pupil say they were demons.'

'He is not my pupil.'

'Ah, forgive me, sir. But you think they were demons?'

'I have never before seen a demon,' said Kysumu softly. 'But we can discuss it once we are on the road and away from these woods.'

'Yes, sir. Whatever they were it was fortunate that your – your friend was on hand to aid us with his shining sword.'

'He is not my friend,' said Kysumu. 'But, yes, it was fortunate.'

Matze Chai sat in his palanquin, the silk curtains drawn shut. 'You think they were demons?' he asked the little swordsman.

'I can think of no alternative. I cut the limb from one and it burned in the sunlight as if in a furnace.'

'I have not heard of demons in this part of the world but, then, my knowledge of Kydor is limited. My client said nothing of them when he invited me here.' Matze Chai fell silent. He had once used a sorcerer to summon a demon and kill a business rival. The rival had been found the following morning with his heart torn out. Matze Chai had never really known whether the supernatural was genuinely involved, or whether the sorcerer had merely hired a killer. The sorcerer himself had been impaled two years later, following an attempted coup against the Gothir emperor. It was said that a horned demon had appeared within the palace and killed several guards. Could it be, he wondered, that one of Matze's many enemies had hired a magicker to send the creatures in the mist to kill him? He dismissed the thought almost immediately. The murdered sentry had been at the far end of the camp, furthest from his tent, as had the butchered horses. Surely a spell aimed at Matze Chai himself would have focused upon the tent where he lay? A random incident, then, but a disquieting one. 'Liu tells me that your sword shone like the brightest moonlight. I have not heard of this before. Are the swords of the *Rajnee* magical?'

'I had not thought them to be,' said Kysumu.

'Can you think of an explanation?'

'The rituals of the *Rajnee* are ancient. Each sword is blessed with one hundred and forty-four incantations. The iron ore is blessed before smelting, the steel is blessed, the armourer-priest tempers it with his own blood after three days of fasting and prayer. Finally it is laid upon the temple altar at Ri-ashon, and all the monks join together in that most holy of places to give the sword its name and its final blessing. The swords of the *Rajnee* are unique. No-one knows the origins of many of the incantations, and some are spoken in a language no longer understood, even by the priests who utter them.'

Matze Chai sat silently as Kysumu spoke. It was the longest speech he had heard from the normally laconic swordsman. 'I am not an expert in military matters,' said Matze Chai, 'but it seems to me that the swords of the *Rajnee* must have been created originally for a purpose other than merely battling enemy swordsmen. Why else would they display such mystical properties when demons are close?'

'I agree,' said Kysumu. 'It is a matter I must ponder upon.'

'While you do so, might you explain the appearance of the loud oaf in the foul-smelling wolfskin?' asked Matze Chai.

'He is a ditch-digger,' answered the *Rajnee*, his face expressionless.

'We were aided by a ditch-digger?'

Kysumu nodded. 'With a stolen *Rajnee* sword.'

Matze Chai looked into the swordsman's face. 'How was it that you happened upon him?'

'He was one of the robbers who attacked us. I went to their camp. The rest ran away, but he stood his ground.'

'Why was it that you did not slay him?'

'Because of the sword.'

'You feared it?' asked Matze Chai, his surprise making him momentarily forget his manners.

Kysumu seemed untroubled by the remark. 'No, I did not fear it. When a *Rajnee* dies his sword dies with him. It shivers and cracks, the blade shattering. The sword is linked to the soul of the bearer, and travels with him to the world beyond.'

'Then perhaps he stole it from a living *Rajnee* who still hunts for it.'

'No. Yu Yu did not lie when he said he took it from the body of a dead *Rajnee*. I would have known. I believe the sword chose him. It also led him to this land and, ultimately, to our camp-site.'

'You believe the swords are sentient?'

'I cannot explain it to you, Matze Chai. I underwent five years of intensive study before I began to grasp the concept. So let me say this, by way of explanation. You have wondered since we met why I accepted this assignment. You came to me because you were told I was the best. But you did not expect me to agree to journey from the lands of the Chiatze. Not so?'

'Indeed,' agreed Matze Chai.

'I had many requests to consider. As I was taught, I went to the holy place and sat, with my sword in my lap, to meditate, to request the guidance of the Great One. And then, when my mind was purged of all selfish desire, I considered the many offers. When I came to yours I felt the sword grow warm in my hands. I knew then that I had to journey to Kydor.'

'Does the sword then yearn for peril?' asked Matze Chai.

'Perhaps. But I believe it merely shows the *Rajnee* a path towards the will of the Great One.'

'And these paths inevitably carry you towards evil?'

'Yes,' said Kysumu.

681

'Hardly a comforting thought,' said Matze Chai, deciding he had no wish to elicit further explanation. He disliked excitement, and this journey had already contained too many incidents. Now, it seemed, the mere presence of Kysumu guaranteed further adventure.

Pushing thoughts of demons and swords from his mind he closed his eyes, picturing his garden and the scented, flowering trees. The image calmed him.

From outside the palanquin came a raucous noise. The ditch-digger was singing in a loud, horrible discordant voice. Matze Chai's eyes snapped open. The song was in a broad northern Chiatze dialect, and concerned the physical endowments and unnatural body hair of a young pleasure-woman. A small pain began behind Matze Chai's left eye.

Kysumu rang the bell and the palanquin came to a smooth halt. The *Rajnee* opened the door and leapt lightly to the ground. The singing stopped.

Matze Chai heard the loud oaf say, 'But the next verse is really funny.'

Lalitia was a woman not easily surprised. She had learnt all there was to know about men by the time she was fourteen, and her capacity for surprise had been exhausted long before that. Orphaned and living on the streets of the capital at the age of eight, she had learnt to steal, to beg, to run and to hide. Sleeping on the sand beneath the wharf timbers, she had sometimes huddled in the dark and watched the cut-throats drag victims to the water's edge before knifing them viciously and hurling the bodies into the surf. She had listened as the cheap tavern whores plied their trade, rutting with their customers in the moon shadows. On many occasions she was close by when the officers of the watch came round to collect their bribes from the tavern women, before taking it in turns to enjoy free sport with them.

The red-headed child learnt swiftly. By the age of twelve she was leading a gang of juvenile cutpurses, operating throughout the market squares, paying out a tenth of their earnings to the watch, ensuring they were never caught.

For two years Lalitia – Sly Red, as she was known then – hoarded her own takings, hiding the coin where no-one would find it. She spent her spare time crouched in alleyways watching the rich enjoying their meals in the finer taverns, noting the way the great ladies moved and spoke, the languid grace they displayed, the faint air of boredom they assumed when in the company of men. Their backs were always straight, their movements slow, smooth and assured. Their skin was creamy white, untanned – indeed, untouched – by the sun. In summer they wore wide-brimmed hats, with gossamer veils. Sly Red watched, absorbed their movements, carefully storing them in the vaults of memory.

At fourteen her luck had run out. While running from a merchant, whose money pouch strings she had neatly sliced, she slipped on a piece of rotten fruit and fell heavily to the cobbles. The merchant had held her until the watch soldiers arrived, and they had dragged her away.

'Can't help you this time, Red,' said one of them. 'You just robbed Vanis, and he's an important man.'

The magistrate had sentenced her to twelve years. She served three in a rat-infested dungeon before being summoned one day to the office of the gaol captain, a young officer named Aric. He was slim and cold-eyed, even handsome in a vaguely dissolute manner. 'I saw you walking by the far wall this morning,' he told the seventeen-year-old girl. 'You do not appear to be a peasant.'

Sly Red had been using her hour of daylight to practise the movements she had observed among the great ladies of the capital. She said nothing to the captain. 'Come closer, let me look at you,' he said. She stepped forward. He moved in – then recoiled. 'You have lice,' he said.

'Aye,' she said huskily, 'and fleas. I think the bath in my apartment is out of order. Perhaps you could assign a servant to repair it.'

He grinned at her. 'Of course, my lady. You should have brought it to my attention sooner.'

'I would have,' she said, adopting a languid pose, 'but there are so many calls upon my time.'

Aric summoned the guard and had her returned to her cell. An hour later two soldiers came to collect her. She was marched through the prison to a private wing, and brought to a bathroom. In it was a bronze hip tub, brimming with perfumed water. Two female prisoners were waiting beside it. The male guards ordered her to disrobe and she removed the filthy dress she wore and stepped into the tub. One of the women poured warm water over her greasy red hair, then massaged a sweet-smelling soap into it. The other woman began to scrub her skin. The feeling was exquisite and Sly Red closed her eyes. Tension seeped from her muscles.

When the bath was completed, her hair dried, combed and braided, she was dressed in a green gown of faded satin.

The larger of the two women leant in to her. 'Don't get too used to this, dearie,' she whispered. 'Not one of his girls lasts more than a week. He is easily bored.'

Sly Red lasted a year, and at eighteen was given a full pardon. Aric at first amused himself with her, then began teaching her the more esoteric secrets of noble behaviour. The pardon was hard-earned, for Aric's carnal desires were wide-ranging and sometimes painful. In return for the pardon Sly Red agreed to become a plaything for men Aric needed to impress, or rivals he desired to exploit, or enemies he was determined to destroy. In the years that followed Lalitia, as Sly Red became, found men only too eager to surrender their secrets. It seemed that arousal loosened tongues and brains in equal measure. Bright and brilliant men became like children, anxious to please. Secrets long hidden spilled out as they sought to impress her with their cleverness. Stupid men!

In his own way Aric had been good to her, allowing her to keep the gifts her lovers bestowed. Within a few years Lalitia was close to wealthy. Aric even gave his blessing when she married the old merchant Kendar. He died within a year. Lalitia was overjoyed. Now she could have the life she had always desired. Kendar's wealth should have been enough for two lifetimes. Except that Kendar's wealth had been bogus. He died massively in debt, and once more Lalitia found herself surviving on her wits and her physical charms.

Her second husband had the bad grace not to die, despite being over seventy when she married him. This had necessitated drastic action. The thought of poisoning him occurred to her, but she dismissed it. He was a pleasant enough man, even kind. Instead Lalitia fed him a diet spiced with powerfully aphrodisiac herbs, acquired at great cost. When he finally expired, the surgeon summoned to pronounce him dead could not fail to remark that he had never seen a happier corpse.

Lalitia was now truly rich.

And set about becoming poor with a speed that beggared belief. She began with a series of investments in merchant enterprises, all of which failed, then bought land, which she was convinced would multiply in value. It fell sharply. One day her dressmaker sent a message to say that no further clothes would be forthcoming unless all bills were paid. Lalitia was amazed to discover she had no funds to cover the debt.

She had contacted Aric, who once more made use of her services.

Now, at thirty-five, she had funds, a fine house in Carlis, and a lover so rich he could probably buy the whole of Kydor and not notice the difference.

Leaning back on the satin pillow she gazed at the tall, powerfully built man standing by the window. 'Did I thank you for the diamond pendant, Grey Man?' she asked.

'I believe that you did,' he told her. 'Quite eloquently. So, tell me, why do you not wish to attend my banquet?'

'I have not been feeling well these last few days. It would be better for me to rest, I think.'

'You seemed well a few moments ago,' he observed drily.

'That is because you are such an exquisite lover. Where did you learn such skills?'

He did not answer, but transferred his gaze back out of the window. Compliments slid from him like water from slate. 'Do you love me?' she asked him. 'Even a little?'

'I am fond of you,' he said.

'Then why do you never tell me anything about yourself? You have been coming to me for two years now and I don't even know your real name.'

He turned his dark gaze towards her. 'Nor I yours,' he said. 'It does not matter. I must be going.'

'Be careful,' she said suddenly, surprising herself.

He looked at her closely. 'Of what?'

She was flustered. 'There is some talk in the town . . . You have enemies,' she concluded lamely.

'Vanis the merchant? Yes, I know.'

'He could . . . hire men to kill you.'

'Indeed. Are you sure you will not attend my banquet?'

She nodded. As always he walked across the room without any farewells. The door closed behind him.

Stupid! Stupid! Stupid! she railed at herself. She had heard from Aric that Vanis was considering assassination. With his creditor dead Vanis would stave off bankruptcy. Aric had warned her to say nothing. 'It should be a surprising evening,' he had said, 'the rich peasant slaughtered in his own palace. Quite a memorable event, I would think.'

At first Lalitia had been annoyed, for now the gifts would cease, but she knew, after two years, there was no hope of the Grey Man proposing marriage. And she already knew he was seeing another courtesan in the south of the town. Soon he would stop coming to her. But, as the day wore on, she couldn't stop thinking about his demise.

Aric had always been good to her, but she knew that if she betrayed him he would have no hesitation in ordering her killed. And yet she had almost risked it. Almost told the Grey Man that the killers were waiting.

'I do not love him,' she said aloud. Lalitia had never loved anyone. Why then, she wondered, did she want to save him? Partly, she thought, it was that he never sought to possess her. He paid for his pleasure, was never cruel or dismissive, never judgemental or dominating. He did not seek to question her life, or offer her advice.

She rose from the bed and walked naked to the window where he had stood only moments before. She watched him ride the steeldust gelding through the open gates, and the heavy weight of sadness bore down on her.

Aric called him the rich peasant, but there was nothing of the peasant about the man. He radiated power and purpose. There was something elemental about him. Unyielding.

Lalitia smiled suddenly. 'I do not think they will kill you, Grey Man,' she whispered.

The words, and the accompanying lift to her spirits, astonished her.

Life, it seemed, still had the capacity to surprise.

Keeva had never attended a Noble Gathering, though as a child she had seen the elaborate carriages of the wealthy, and caught glimpses of the ladies in their silks and satins as they attended such events. Now she stood by the western wall of the Great Hall, a silver tray in her hands, bearing a selection of delicately crafted pastries, some filled with cheese, others with spiced meats. She was one of forty servants moving among the Grey Man's two hundred guests.

Never had Keeva seen so much satin, so many jewels: golden bangles encrusted with precious stones, ear-rings that sparkled in the light cast by a hundred lanterns, dresses or tunics embroidered with pearls and edged with silver, glittering tiaras, and even shoes decorated with rubies, emeralds and diamonds.

A young nobleman and his lady paused before her. The man was wearing a short cape edged with sable, over a red satin jacket embroidered with gold thread. He reached out and took a pastry. 'These are wonderful. You should try them, dearheart,' he said to the woman beside him.

'I'll try a taste of yours,' she said, her white satin gown rustling as she moved in closer to her lover. He grinned at her and placed a small portion of the pastry between his teeth. She laughed, leant in and took it from him with a kiss. Keeva stood very still, aware that she was invisible to them. It was a curious feeling. Not once did their eyes meet hers, and they moved away into the crowd without ever registering her presence. Other guests flowed by, some pausing to take a pastry, others merely moving towards the dance floor. Her tray empty, Keeva edged around the wall and down the short staircase to the long kitchens.

Norda was there, refilling goblets with fine wine. 'When does the Grey Man arrive?' asked Keeva.

'Later,' she said.

'But it is his Gathering.'

'He is here already,' said Norda. 'Have you not noticed a steady stream of people moving through to the Small Hall beyond?'

Keeva had, but had not thought about it. The young sergeant, Emrin, was stationed at the rear door and Keeva was determined not to be seen looking at him. She wished to give the man no reason to pursue his interest in her.

'Most of the nobles and merchants here this evening will be seeking some favour from the Gentleman,' said Norda, 'so, for the first three hours, he sits in the Walnut Room and receives them. Omri is with him, and he will be writing down their requests.'

'So many people wanting favours,' said Keeva. 'He must be very well loved.'

Norda's laughter pealed out. 'Idiot,' she said, as she took up her tray and moved back to the stairs.

Keeva was confused, and she glanced around and saw some of the other girls smiling. Embarrassed, though she did not know why, Keeva refilled her tray and returned to the Great Hall.

Twenty musicians were playing now, the music fast and lively, and dancers whirled on the polished floor. It was warm in the hall, but all the wide doors leading to the terrace were open, and a fresh sea breeze was filtering into the room.

For another hour the dancing continued, and the hall was filled with the sounds of music and laughter. Keeva's arms began to ache from holding the tray. Few people were now eating. Norda moved carefully around the edge of the hall. 'Time to exchange that tray for refreshments,' she said.

Keeva followed her downstairs. 'Why did you call me an idiot?' she asked, as the blonde woman began to fill crystal glasses with wine.

'He is not loved,' said Norda. 'He is hated by them all.'

'But why, if he grants them favours?'

'That is why. Do you know nothing about the nobility?'

'Obviously not.'

Norda paused in her work. 'He is a foreigner and immensely wealthy. They envy him, and envy always leads to hatred. It doesn't matter what he does, they will always hate him. Last year when there was a failure of the crops in the east the Gentleman sent two hundred tons of grain to be distributed among the starving. A fine deed, yes?'

'Of course.'

'Well, this fine deed prevented the cost of grain from soaring, and thus reduced the profits the nobles and merchants could have made. You think they would thank him for that?' Norda smiled. 'You'll learn, Keeva. Nobles are a different breed.' Her smile faded, and her eyes became cold and angry. 'I wouldn't piss on one if he was on fire.'

'I do not know any,' said Keeva.

'Best to keep it that way,' replied Norda, her voice softening. 'They bring nothing but grief to the likes of us. We'd better get back.'

Carrying a tray of drinks, Keeva returned to the Great Hall, and began moving through the throng. The musicians had ceased playing briefly, and were partaking of refreshments, and most of the nobles had gathered in small groups. They were chatting and laughing, and the mood was a happy one. There was still no sign of the Grey Man, though Keeva saw the one noble she did recognize: Lord Aric of House Kilraith. Resplendent in a grey and black striped tunic shirt of heavy silk, edged with silver braid, he was standing close to the terrace, talking to the young woman Keeva had earlier seen taking the pastry from the mouth of her companion. The two were laughing, and Keeva saw Aric whisper something in the woman's ear. He was a handsome man, slim and elegant, his features fine, though his nose a little long, thought

688

Keeva. He looked younger than she remembered, his hair uniformly dark. Keeva seemed to recall that he had had grey in his hair when he had ridden through the settlement last year. And his face had seemed puffier. He has probably dyed the hair, she thought, and lost a little weight. It suited him.

Just behind them stood a black-bearded man, tall and broad-shouldered with deep-set eyes. He was wearing an ankle-length robe of deep blue velvet edged with silver thread. In his right hand was a long staff, topped with an ornate twist of silver. The man was standing quietly, holding the hand of a young, blond-haired boy around eight years of age. Keeva moved towards them. The tall bearded man stepped away from the shadows of the terrace doorway and Keeva felt his gaze upon her. It was a shock, for she had become used to being invisible to these people. His eyes were dark and large beneath hooded lids.

'Drink, sir?' she said.

The tall man nodded. His face was broad, made even wider by the heavy black beard. He released the boy's hand and took a crystal goblet filled with red wine. 'I much prefer it white,' he said, his voice low. He smiled at her and held up the goblet. Immediately colour began to drain from it, becoming first a bright scarlet, then a deep pink, until, at last, it looked as clear as water. Keeva blinked. The man chuckled, then sipped the changed wine. 'Excellent,' he said.

She glanced down at the silent boy. His bright blue eyes met hers and he gave a shy smile. 'Can I fetch something for your son?' she asked the bearded man.

He smiled and ruffled the boy's hair. 'He is my nephew and my page, not my son. And, yes, that would be most kind.'

'We have cordials made from apples, or pears or peaches,' she told the boy. 'Which would you prefer?'

The child glanced up into the face of the bearded man, who turned to Keeva. 'He is very shy, but I know that he likes pear juice. Let me relieve you of your tray while you fetch it.'

Instantly the tray floated up from Keeva's hands, hovering in the air, before lowering itself down to a small side-table. Keeva clapped her hands in delight, and the small boy smiled.

'Come now, my friend,' said the Lord Aric. 'You must save your entertainments for those who will most appreciate them.'

Keeva moved swiftly downstairs, filled a goblet with cooled pear juice and returned to the ballroom. The boy accepted the drink with a smile of thanks and sipped the contents.

Lord Aric took the bearded man by the arm and led him away towards the centre of the hall. A breath of breeze whispered through the terrace doorway. Keeva sighed with relief, for her clothes were sticking to her in the heat. Not only was it a warm summer night, but the lantern flames and the hundreds of bodies in the hall were producing almost intolerable warmth.

In the centre of the hall Lord Aric ordered two servants to pull a table across the floor. Then he sprang upon it and lifted his arms in the air. 'My friends,' he called out, 'by your leave, I have brought a little entertainment to amuse you. I ask you to offer your warmest greetings to Eldicar Manushan, recently arrived from our Angostin homeland.' With that he reached down, and the tall bearded man took his hand and climbed to the table. The nobles and their ladies politely applauded. Aric leapt down from the table and Eldicar Manushan gazed out over their faces. 'It is a trifle warm, dear people,' he told them. 'I can see that some of the ladies are feeling faint, and that their wrists will soon begin to burn from overuse of their fans. So let me begin with a small rearrangement of the weather.' Laying the long staff at his feet he clasped his hands together, raised them high, then opened his fingers and drew his arms apart. What appeared to Keeva to be a white mist floated from his palms, and rose into the air.

Eldicar made a circular motion with his hand, and the mist rolled itself into a ball and began to grow. With a gesture he made it float across the room to where a small group of noblewomen were fanning themselves. As it hovered above them their faces changed, and they squealed with delight. The ball split into two. One remained above the women, the other bobbed in the air, then floated to another group. Each time it stopped it split itself, though neither of the globes lost any size.

People underneath them began to applaud, while those they had not yet reached looked mystified. Keeva watched as one of the globes spun gently towards her. As it came close she felt suddenly cool, as if a breeze, filtered over snow, was blowing through the room. It was both refreshing and exhilarating. Soon there were white globes all around the Great Hall, and the temperature had dropped dramatically.

All conversation ceased. Eldicar Manushan lowered his arms. 'Now,' he said, 'the entertainment can begin. But first, my friends, let me thank you for your welcome. It is extremely gratifying to see such grace, beauty and culture so far from home.' He bowed to them, and they applauded the compliment with great

690

enthusiasm. 'Might I also thank Lord Aric for his courtesy and his generosity in inviting me to share his home during my stay in Kydor.' Again they applauded. 'And now,' he said, 'a little entertainment to amuse you. What you are about to see are images. They cannot touch you. They cannot see you. So please do not be alarmed. Especially when you notice there is a huge black bear among you!' He suddenly pointed to the western wall.

A massive form reared there, and a bloodcurdling roar sounded from it. Those closest to the ferocious animal screamed and backed away. In an instant the bear dropped to all fours and broke into a dozen pieces. Each of the pieces then bounded out on to the dance floor, and Keeva saw that they were all black rabbits. Laughter echoed around the hall – most loudly from those terrified only moments before. Eldicar Manushan clapped his hands, and the rabbits became blackbirds, which flew into the air and out through the terrace doorway.

A lion bounded in. People scattered, but without real fear now. Rising on its hind legs it pawed at the air, and growled menacingly. Then it padded around the room. A young woman reached out as it loped by, her hand sinking into the beast and passing through it. The lion turned towards her and reared up. She cried out – but the lion shattered, becoming a flock of golden doves, which circled the room.

The crowd cried out for more, but Eldicar Manushan merely bowed. 'I have promised Lord Aric to reserve my finest – shall we say? – tricks for the Duke's Feast at the Winter Palace in eight days. It was merely my duty tonight to whet your appetite. I thank you for your applause.' He bowed again, and this time the clapping was thunderous.

Climbing down from the table he retrieved his staff and walked back to where Keeva and the boy were standing. Taking another goblet he twirled it in his hands before sipping the wine. Then he glanced at Keeva. 'Did you enjoy the entertainment?' he asked her.

'I did, sir. I will be sorry to miss the Duke's Feast. What is your page's name?'

'His name is Beric. He is a good boy, and I thank you for your kindness to him.' Raising her hand to his lips he kissed it. At that moment there was a stir from the far side of the hall. Dressed in a black satin tunic shirt, dark leggings and boots, the Grey Man made his entrance. He was immediately seen by several women, who smiled and curtsied. He bowed, exchanged pleasantries and moved across the room.

Keeva watched him, and was struck by the easy, confident way in which he greeted his guests. He stood out from them by his lack of adornment. He wore no brooches or rings, and no gold or silver glistened from his tunic. Even so, he looked every inch the lord of the palace, she thought. Around him the other men seemed as flamboyant as peacocks.

Moving from group to group he made his way to the far end of the hall, where Keeva stood holding her tray. Lord Aric and his friend, Eldicar Manushan, stepped forward and greeted him.

'I am sorry to have missed your display,' the Grey Man told the magicker.

'I do apologize, sir,' he said, with a bow. 'It was remiss of me to begin while you were not present. However, you will see something far greater at the Duke's Feast.'

The music began again, and dancers took to the floor. Several of the guests approached the Grey Man. Keeva could no longer hear the conversation, but she watched his face as he listened to them. He was attentive, though his eyes had a faraway look, and it seemed to Keeva that he was not enjoying the festivities.

At that moment Keeva's attention was caught by a young noble edging closer to the Grey Man. He looked tense, and there was sweat upon his brow, despite the cool breeze still emanating from the white globes that hung above the revellers. Then Keeva saw a second man detach himself from a nearby group, and also move towards the Grey Man. Their movements seemed furtive and Keeva found her heart beating faster.

The Grey Man was talking to a young woman in a red gown as the first of the men came up behind him. Keeva saw something glitter in the man's hand. Before she could cry out a warning the Grey Man spun on his heel, his left arm blocking a knife thrust, his right hand, fingers extended, slamming into the assassin's throat. The man gagged and fell to his knees, the long-bladed knife clattering to the floor. The second man ran in, knife raised, but collided with the woman in the red dress, who was trying to back away from the scene. The assassin pushed her aside and she fell heavily. The music had stopped now, and all the dancers were standing staring at the knifeman. Keeva saw the guard, Emrin, run at the assassin, but the Grey Man waved him back. The assassin stood very still, knife extended towards his intended victim. 'Well,' said the Grey Man, 'are you intending to earn your pay?'

'I do this for the honour of House Kilraith!' shouted the young noble, charging forward.

The Grey Man sidestepped, slapped away the knife arm, and tripped the young man, who sprawled headlong to the stone floor. He hit hard, but rolled and came to his knees. The Grey Man moved in and kicked the knife from the assassin's hand. The young noble surged to his feet, and ran for the terrace. 'Let him go,' the Grey Man ordered Emrin and two other guards who had joined him.

Turning his attention to the first of the assassins, the Grey Man knelt by the still body. Keeva glanced down. The man's bladder had released its contents, which had stained the expensive grey leggings he wore. His eyes were open, staring sightlessly up at the ornate ceiling. The Grey Man rose and turned to Emrin. 'Remove the body,' he said. Then he strolled from the room.

'An unusual man,' said Eldicar Manushan.

Recovering from her shock, Keeva glanced down at little Beric, who was staring wide-eyed at the dead man.

'It is all right,' she said, kneeling and putting her arms around his slim shoulders. 'There is no danger.'

'Will he be all right?' asked Beric, his voice trembling. 'He is very still.'

'They will take care of him,' Keeva assured him. 'Perhaps you should leave.'

'I shall take him to his room,' said Eldicar. 'Once again my thanks to you.' Taking the boy by the hand the magicker walked across the hall and vanished into the crowd.

The musicians, not knowing what to do, started to play once more, but the music faded away when no-one moved. Then the first of the nobles began to leave the area.

Within minutes the Great Hall was deserted and Keeva and the other servants cleared away goblets, tankards and dishes, before returning with mops, buckets and cleaning cloths. By the time they had finished there was no sign that hundreds of guests had danced and dined there.

In the kitchens, as they washed the dishes and cutlery, Keeva listened to the other girls talking about the failed assassination. She learnt that the two young men were nephews of the merchant Vanis, but no-one had any idea why they should seek to kill the Gentleman. The girls talked about how lucky the Gentleman had been, and how fortunate that his blow had killed the first assassin.

As the dawn was breaking Keeva made her way to her room. She was tired, but her mind whirled with the events of the night, and she sat for a while upon her balcony, watching the sunlight gleaming like gold upon the waters of the bay.

How had he known he was in danger? she wondered. With the noise of the music there was no way he could have heard the man move up behind him. Yet his arm had been moving to block the blow even as he turned. His movements had been unhurried and smooth. Picturing the scene again, she shivered. There was no doubt in Keeva's mind that the death blow to the young man's throat had not been, as the other girls believed, a fortunate strike. It had been delivered coldly and with deadly intent, in a move that spoke of long practice.

What are you, Grey Man? she mused.

Waylander left the Great Hall and strode down the second-level corridor leading to the South Tower. As he turned the first corner he pushed aside a velvet hanging and pressed a stud on the panelled wall beyond. There was a faint creak as the panel opened. Stepping through he pulled it shut behind him and stood in the near-total darkness. Then, without hesitation, he began to descend the hidden steps. He was angry now, and made no attempt to stifle it. He knew both the young men who had attacked him, had spoken to them on several occasions while they had been in the company of their uncle, the merchant Vanis. They were not of great intelligence, nor were they stupid. To all intents and purposes they were merely pleasant young nobles who should have been considering a lifetime of possibilities.

Instead one was lying in a darkened room waiting for someone to collect his body and place it in the cold ground to feed worms and maggots. And his shade would be wandering the Void, frightened and alone. The second was somewhere out in the night, contemplating his next move, and probably not realizing that he was facing death.

Waylander descended the steps, counting them as he went. One hundred and fourteen had been cut into the cliff, and as he reached the hundredth he saw the faintest gleam of moonlight dappling the lower wall.

He paused at the hedge that disguised the lower entrance, then edged his way around it and stepped across the rocks leading to the winding path. The sky was clear, the night warm. He glanced

694

up at the windows and terrace of the Great Hall far above. There were still people there but they would be leaving soon.

As indeed would he.

Tomorrow he would see Matze Chai and reveal his plans. The Chiatze would be horrified, he knew. The thought lifted him briefly. Matze Chai was one of the few people Waylander both trusted and liked. The merchant had arrived just before the Gathering. Waylander had sent Omri to show Matze Chai the suite of rooms assigned to him, and to convey Waylander's apologies for not being present to greet him. Omri had returned looking flustered and annoyed.

'Were the rooms to his liking?' Waylander had asked.

'He indicated they would *suffice*,' answered Omri. 'He then had one of his servants move around the suite wearing a white glove, which he used to see if there was any dust upon the shelves.'

Waylander laughed aloud. 'That is Matze Chai,' he said.

'I did not find it amusing, sir. In fact, it was extremely annoying. Other servants stripped the satin sheets from the bed examining it for bugs, while still more appeared with cloths and began cleaning and perfuming the bedroom. All the while your friend sat upon the balcony, saying nothing to me, but relaying his instructions through the captain of his guard. You told me that Matze Chai speaks our language perfectly, and yet he did not say a word to me. Most discourteous. I wish you had been there, sir. Perhaps he would have acted in a more civilized manner.'

'You dislike him?' asked Waylander.

'I do, sir.'

'Trust me, Omri, once you get to know him you will *detest* him.'

'What is it, may I ask, that *you* like about him?'

'A question I ask myself constantly,' answered Waylander, with a smile.

'I do not doubt it, sir, but – if you don't mind me saying – that is no answer.'

'A full answer would only confuse you more, my friend. So let me say this. There is only one fact that I know for certain about Matze Chai. His name is not Matze Chai. He is an invention. My guess is that Matze was low born, and clawed his way up from the lowest levels of Chiatze society, reinventing himself at every stage.'

'You mean he is a fraud?'

695

'No, far from it. Matze is like a living work of art. He has transformed something he perceived as base into a flawless Chiatze noble. I doubt he even allows himself to remember his origins.'

Waylander walked on through the moonlight, angling towards his own quarters. He paused at the edge of the cliff and stared out at the dark sea. The moon was reflected there, broken and shimmering upon the gentle waves. He stood in silence as a sea breeze blew gently across his face, and wished that he had been as successful as Matze in reinventing himself.

He gazed at the two moons, the high perfect light in the sky, and the fragmented twin upon the waves. As he did so he recalled the words of the seer: 'When you close your eyes and think of your son, what do you see?'

'I look down upon his dead face. He is lying on the meadow and there are spring flowers around his head.'

'You will not know happiness until you look *up* into his face,' the old man had told him.

The words had been meaningless then, and were meaningless now. The boy was dead, murdered, and buried. Waylander would never be able to look up into his face. Unless the seer had been talking about picturing him in some spiritual paradise high above the stars. Waylander took a deep breath, then moved on along the cliff path.

Ahead were a series of terraces, covered by flowers and screened by scented bushes. Waylander slowed, then stopped. 'Come out, boy,' he said wearily.

The young blond noble rose from behind a bush. In his hand was a golden-hilted shortsword – a light ceremonial blade, worn at official functions. 'Did you learn nothing from your brother's death?' asked Waylander.

'You killed him?'

'Aye, I killed him,' said Waylander coldly. 'I crushed his throat and he choked to death on the floor. As he died he pissed himself. That is what happens. That is the reality. He is gone – and for what?'

'For honour,' said the young man. 'He died for the honour of the family.'

'Where are your wits?' snapped Waylander. 'I loaned your uncle money, and when he could not repay I loaned him more. I did this because he made me promises – promises he failed to keep. Whose is the dishonour? Now your brother is dead. And all

696

so that fat Vanis can avoid financial ruin. A man of his stupidity faced ruin anyway.' Waylander stepped in close to the young man. 'I do not want to have to kill you, boy. The last time we met you talked of your engagement to a young woman you adored. You spoke of love and a small estate by the coast. Think on it. If you walk away now I will take this matter no further. If you do not you will certainly die, for I offer no second chances to my enemies.'

He looked into the young man's eyes, and saw the fear there, and also the pride. 'I do love Sanja,' said the noble. 'But the estate I spoke of belongs – belonged – to my uncle. Without it I have nothing to offer her.'

'Then I shall give it to you as a wedding gift,' said Waylander softly, knowing even as he spoke that it was to no avail.

Anger shone in the noble's eyes. 'I am of House Kilraith!' he snapped. 'I do not need your pity, peasant!' He leapt forward, the sword slashing through the air. Waylander moved in to meet him, throwing up his left arm to block the blow at the noble's wrist, and curling his right hand up and behind the sword arm, clamping to it and dragging it back. The noble screamed, the sword dropping from his fingers as his arm snapped. Waylander pushed him away and swept up the fallen blade. The young man fell heavily and rolled to his knees. As he started to rise he felt the cold iron point of the blade against his throat. 'Don't kill me,' he begged.

A great sadness descended on Waylander as he looked into the frightened blue eyes. He took a deep breath. 'Too late,' he said. The blade plunged home, slashing through the jugular. Blood gouted from the severed vein and the noble fell back, his legs kicking out. Waylander let fall the sword and, turning his back, walked the last few steps to his quarters.

Another man was waiting there, sitting quietly, cross-legged upon the ground. He wore a pale grey, chequered robe, and a long Chiatze blade, scabbarded, was resting in his lap. He was a small man, round-shouldered, his face thin. He looked up as Waylander approached. 'You are a hard man,' he said.

'So they say,' replied Waylander coldly. 'What do you want?'

The Chiatze rose, pushing his scabbarded sword into the black sash at his waist. 'Matze Chai will be returning to his home soon. It is my desire to stay in Kydor. He said you might have need of a *Rajnee*. I see now that you do not.'

'Why do you wish to stay?' asked Waylander. 'Is there not employment enough within Chiatze lands?'

'There is a mystery I must solve,' the *Rajnee* told him.

Waylander shrugged. 'You are welcome here as long as you wish to stay,' he said. 'If you arrived with Matze Chai you will already have been given lodging. But I can offer no work for a swordsman.'

'That is most kind, Grey Man.' The *Rajnee* sighed. 'I must, however, inform you that I am carrying a . . . a burden.'

At that moment, from the path behind them, came a cry of shock and surprise. Waylander turned. A stocky, bearded Chiatze ran into view carrying a long, curved sword. He was wearing a roughly made garment fashioned from wolfskin. 'There's a body!' he said, his voice shrill. 'On the path. Had his throat cut!' He peered around at the surrounding vegetation. 'There are assassins,' he added. 'They could be anywhere. We should get inside. Call the guards!'

'This,' said the *Rajnee*, 'is Yu Yu Liang, the burden of which I spoke.'

'We fought demons together,' said Yu Yu.

Waylander glanced at the *Rajnee*. 'Demons?'

The man nodded. 'That is part of the mystery.'

'Come inside,' said Waylander, moving past the man and opening the door to his quarters.

Moments later they were seated by the fire, the room bathed in the glow of lanterns and firelight. Yu Yu Liang sat on a rug, while the other two men occupied the only chairs in the room. 'The man who owns palace should give you better rooms,' Yu Yu told Waylander. 'I walk through palace. Much silver and gold, and velvet and silk. Probably he is rich bastard, and mean with money?'

'This man *is* the owner of the palace,' said the *Rajnee* in Chiatze.

Yu Yu glanced around the bare walls and grinned. 'And I am the emperor of the world.'

'You mentioned demons,' said Waylander. Briefly, and with no hint of melodrama, the *Rajnee* told him of the attack, the coming of the mist, and the strange creatures who walked within its depths. Waylander listened intently.

'The arm! Tell him about the arm!' said Yu Yu.

'I cut a limb from one of the creatures. The skin was pale, white grey. When sunlight touched it the flesh began to burn. Within a few heartbeats it had vanished entirely.'

'I have not heard of any such creatures in Kydor,' Waylander told him, 'nor any attacks of the kind you describe. I do recall reading about swords of bright light. I cannot remember the tome, but it is in the North Library. I will search for it tomorrow.' He looked into the *Rajnee*'s dark eyes. 'What is your name, swordsman?'

'I am Kysumu.'

'I have heard of you. You are welcome in my home.'

Kysumu bowed, and said nothing.

'Recently I saw such a mist as you describe,' said Waylander. 'I sensed there was evil in it. We will discuss the mystery further when I have searched my library.'

Kysumu rose. Yu Yu scrambled to his feet beside him. He tugged at Kysumu's robe. 'What about assassins?' he asked.

'The dead man *was* the assassin,' said Kysumu.

'Oh.'

Kysumu sighed. He bowed again to Waylander. 'I will send your guards to fetch the body.'

Waylander nodded, then walked away from the two men, entering a lantern-lit room at the rear of the building.

Chapter Five

Matze Chai slept without dreams, and awoke feeling refreshed and invigorated. The suite of rooms assigned to him had been decorated with sublime taste, the colours of the walls delightfully matched in pastel shades of pale lime and pink. Works of art by the most famous and sought-after Chiatze artists adorned the walls, and the hand-painted silk curtains filtered the morning light, allowing Matze Chai to appreciate the beauty of the dawn without the harshness of the sun's glare upon his delicate eyes.

The furniture was exquisite, embellished with gold leaf, the bed wide and firm beneath a silken canopy. Even the pot beneath the bed, which Matze had used three times during the night, was embellished with gold. Such elegance almost made the trip worthwhile. Matze Chai rang the golden bell alongside his bed. The door opened and a servant stepped inside, a young man employed by Matze for the last two years. He couldn't remember his name.

The servant offered Matze Chai a goblet of cool water, but he waved it away. The young man left the room and returned with a ceramic bowl filled with warmed, scented water. Matze Chai sat up and the servant pulled back the covers. The old merchant relaxed as the boy helped him remove his night-shirt and hair-cap, allowing his mind to wander as the servant gently sponged and dried his skin. The boy then opened a pot of sweet-smelling cream.

'Not too much,' warned Matze Chai. The servant did not answer, for Matze Chai did not allow conversation so early in the

day. Instead he lightly smoothed the cream into the dry skin of
Matze Chai's shoulders and arms. After this he pulled loose the
long ivory pins in Matze Chai's hair, applied fresh oils, then skilfully combed and brushed the hair, drawing it back into a tight
bun at the crown, before slipping the ivory locking pins into
place.

A second servant entered, bearing a tray on which sat a small
silver tisane pot and a ceramic cup. Setting the tray by the bedside, the second servant moved to a large wardrobe, taking from
it a heavy gown of yellow silk, beautifully embroidered with gold
and blue songbirds. Matze Chai stood and stretched out his arms.
The servant expertly slipped the gown over them, moving to the
rear to button the upper portion of the garment, before attaching
the lower section to ivory hooks at Matze Chai's waist. Swinging
the golden sash around his master's waist, the servant tied it, then
stepped back with a bow.

'I shall take my tisane upon the balcony,' said Matze Chai.
Instantly the first servant moved to the curtains, drawing them
aside. The second gathered up a wide-brimmed hat of artfully
fashioned straw.

Matze Chai stepped out on to the balcony and sat down on a
curved wooden bench, leaning his back against a large, embroidered cushion. The air was fresh and Matze believed he could
detect salt in it. The light, however, was bright and unpleasant,
and he gestured to the man holding the hat. He ran forward and
placed it on Matze's head, angling it so that his face was in partial shadow, before tying it under his chin.

The stone of the balcony was cold under the merchant's feet.
Glancing down, he wiggled his toes. Brief moments later one of
the men knelt down and placed fur-lined slippers upon his feet.

Matze Chai sipped his tisane and decided that all was well with
the world on this fine day. Waving his hand, he dismissed the servants and sat quietly in the morning sunshine. The breeze was
fresh and cool, the sky a clear, cloudless blue.

He heard movement behind him, and the merest touch of irritation disturbed his tranquillity. Liu, the young captain of his
guard, moved into sight and bowed deeply. He said nothing,
waiting for his master's permission to speak.

'Well?' asked Matze Chai.

'The master of the house requests an audience, Lord. His servant, Omri, suggests that he could attend you presently.'

Matze Chai leant back against his cushion. For all that he was a round-eyed *gajin* Waylander's manners were perfect. 'Convey to the servant that I would be honoured to entertain my old friend,' he said.

Liu bowed again, but did not depart immediately. Irritation once more touched Matze Chai, but he did not show it. He looked quizzically at the young soldier.

'One more matter, Lord, that you should be made aware of. There was an attempt on your . . . old friend's life last night. At the ball. Two men with knives attacked him.'

Matze Chai gave the briefest of nods, then waved his hand to dismiss the soldier. Was there ever a time, he wondered, when someone was not attempting to kill Waylander? One would have thought they would have learnt by now. His cup was empty and he looked for a servant to refill it, then remembered he had dismissed them. And his golden bell was all the way across the room by the bedside. He sighed. Then, glancing round to see that he was not observed, he filled the cup. Matze Chai smiled. To serve oneself was quite liberating. But not civilized, he chided himself. Even so his good mood was restored and he waited patiently for Waylander to arrive.

A different servant ushered him in, removed the pot of tisane and the empty cup, then departed without a word. Matze Chai rose from his chair and offered a deep bow to his client, who responded in similar fashion before seating himself.

'It is good to see you, my friend,' said Waylander. 'I understand your journey was not without excitement.'

'It was – regrettably – not as dull as one would have liked,' agreed Matze Chai.

Waylander laughed. 'You don't change, Matze Chai,' he said, 'and I cannot tell you what a delight that is.' The smile faded. 'I apologize for asking you to make this journey, but I needed to see you.'

'You are leaving Kydor,' said Matze Chai.

'I am indeed.'

'Where to now? Ventria?'

Waylander shook his head. 'Across the western ocean.'

'The ocean? But why? There is nothing there – save the end of the world. It is where the stars flow into the sea. There is no land, no civilization. And even if there is land it will be barren and empty. Your wealth would be meaningless there.'

'It is meaningless *here*, Matze Chai.'

The elderly merchant sighed. 'You have never been content to be rich, Dakeyras. This, in some strange way I have yet to fathom, is why you *are* rich. You care nothing for wealth. What is it, then, that you desire?'

'I wish I could answer that,' said Waylander. 'All I can say is that this life is not for me. I have no taste for it.'

'What is it that you wish me to do?'

'You already manage one sixth of all my ventures, and hold two fifths of my wealth. I shall give you letters to all merchants with whom I have business dealings. These will inform them that, from the time they receive my instructions, you will speak for me. I shall also tell them that if they do not hear from me within five years then all my ventures and capital become yours.'

Matze Chai was aghast at the thought. He struggled to come to terms with what Waylander offered. Already wealthy, Matze Chai would become instantly the richest man in all of Chiatze. What would there be left to strive for?

'I cannot accept this,' he said. 'You must reconsider.'

'You can always give it all away,' said Waylander. 'But whatever you choose I shall sail from this world and not return.'

'Are you truly so unhappy, my old friend?' asked Matze Chai. 'Will you do as I ask?'

Matze Chai sighed again, deeply. 'I will,' he said.

Waylander rose, then smiled. 'I will tell your servants to prepare your second pot of tisane,' he said. 'They really should have brought it by now.'

'I am served by cretins,' admitted Matze Chai, 'but, then, if I did not employ them their stupidity would see them starve in the streets.'

After Waylander had left Matze Chai sat lost in thought. He had long ago ceased to be surprised by his fondness for his *gajin* client. When Waylander had first come to him, all those years ago, Matze Chai had been merely curious about the man. That curiosity led him to engage the old seer. Matze had sat upon the silken rug at the centre of the temple's inner sanctum and watched as the elderly priest cast the bones.

'Will this man be a danger to me?'

'Not if you do not betray him.'

'Is he evil?'

'All men carry evil within them, Matze Chai. The question is imprecise.'

'What, then, can you tell me of him?'

'He will never be content, for his deepest desire is unattainable.

703

Yet he will become rich, and make you rich. Is that enough for you, merchant?'

'What is this unattainable desire?'

'Deep in his heart, far below the level of conscious thought, he is desperate to save his family from terror and death. This unconscious desire drives him on, forces him to seek out danger, to pit himself against the might of violent men.'

'Why is it unattainable?'

'His family are already dead, slain in a mindless orgy of lust and depravity.'

'Surely,' said Matze Chai, 'he knows they are dead.'

'Of course. As I said, it is an unconscious desire. A part of his soul has never accepted that he was too late to save them.'

'But he will make me rich?'

'Oh, yes, Matze Chai, he will make you richer than you could ever dream possible. Be sure, however, that you recognize the riches when you have them.'

'I am sure that I will.'

The stooping servant, Omri, was waiting in the corridor outside Matze Chai's apartments. As Waylander stepped out he bowed briefly. 'Lord Aric is waiting to see you, sir, along with the magicker, Eldicar Manushan,' he said. 'I have had refreshments served to them in the Oak Room.'

'I was expecting him,' said Waylander, his expression cold.

'I must say that he looks well. I believe he has dyed his hair.'

Together the two men walked back along the corridor, and up two sets of stairs. 'The bodies have been removed, sir. Emrin had them loaded on to a wagon and has driven it into Carlis. He will make a report to the watch officer, but I expect there will be an official inquiry. The incident, I should imagine, is the talk of Carlis. One of the young men was due to be wed next week. You even received an invitation to the ceremony.'

'I know. He and I spoke of it last night, but he was in no mood to listen.'

'A shocking incident,' said Omri. 'Why did they do it? What did they have to gain?'

'*They* had nothing to gain. They were sent by Vanis.'

'That is disgraceful,' said Omri. 'We must inform the watch officer. You should lay charges against him.'

'That will not be necessary,' said Waylander. 'I do not doubt that Lord Aric has a plan to resolve the situation.'

'Ah, I see. A plan that no doubt involves money.'

'No doubt.'

They moved on in silence, emerging into a wide, arched hallway on the upper floor.

As they reached the doors of carved oak Omri stepped back. 'I have to say, sir,' he said, in a low voice, 'that I am not comfortable in the presence of this magicker. There is something about the man that I find disturbing.'

'You are a good judge of character, Omri. I shall bear that in mind.'

Waylander pushed open the doors and entered the Oak Room.

The room, panelled with oak, had been designed in the shape of an octagon. Rare weapons from many nations hung on the walls, a battleaxe and several hunting bows from Vagria, spears and curved scimitars from Ventria. Angostin broadswords, daggers and shields vied with tulwars, lances, pikes and several embossed crossbows. Four armour trees had been placed around the room, boasting ornate helms, breastplates and shields. The furniture consisted of twelve deep chairs and three cushion-covered couches, set upon a scattering of Chiatze rugs of hand-dyed silk. The room was lit by sunlight streaming through the high-arched, east-facing windows.

Lord Aric was seated on a couch below the window, his booted feet resting on a low table. Opposite him was the magicker, Eldicar Manushan, his blond page standing beside him. Neither man rose as Waylander entered, but Aric waved his hand and gave a broad smile. 'Good morning, my friend,' he called. 'I am so glad you could find time to join us.'

'You are up early, Lord Aric,' said Waylander. 'I have always been led to believe it was considered uncivilized for a noble to rise before noon – unless a hunt was in the offing.'

'Indeed so,' agreed Aric, 'but, then, we have pressing matters to discuss.'

Waylander sat down and stretched out his legs. The door opened and Omri entered, bearing a tray on which was set a large silver pot of tisane and three cups. The men sat in silence as he filled the cups then departed. Waylander sipped the brew. It was camomile sweetened with mint and a little honey. He closed his eyes, enjoying the taste upon his tongue. Then he glanced at Aric. The slim noble was doing his best to appear at ease, but there was an underlying tension in him. Transferring his gaze to the black-bearded magicker, Waylander saw no sign of unease. Eldicar Manushan was drinking his tisane quietly, apparently lost in thought. Waylander caught the eye of the little blond boy, who smiled nervously.

The silence grew, and Waylander made no attempt to disturb it.

'Last night was most unfortunate,' said Aric at last. 'The two boys were well liked and neither of them had ever been in any kind of trouble.'

Waylander waited.

'Parellis – the blond boy – is . . . was a second cousin to the Duke. In fact, I understand that the Duke had agreed to stand alongside Parellis at his wedding. It is one of the reasons the Duke decided to bring the Winter Court to Carlis. You see the complications that are beginning to arise.'

'No,' said Waylander.

Aric seemed momentarily bewildered. Then he forced a smile. 'You have killed a relative of the ruler of Kydor.'

'I killed two assassins. Is this against the law in Carlis?'

'No, of course not, my friend. As to the first killing there were hundreds of witnesses. No problems there. But the second . . . Well,' he said, spreading his hands, 'no-one saw that. It is my understanding that there was only one weapon – a ceremonial sword belonging to Parellis. This would indicate you dispossessed him of that weapon and killed him with it. That being so, it could be argued that you killed an unarmed man, which, according to the law, is murder.'

'Well,' said Waylander easily, 'the inquiry will establish the facts then make a judgement. I will abide by that.'

'Would that it were so easy,' said Aric. 'The Duke is not a forgiving man. Had both boys been killed in the ballroom I think even he would have been forced to accept the outcome. But I fear that the relatives of Parellis will seek to have you arrested.'

Waylander gave a thin smile. 'Unless?'

'Ah, well, this is where I can help, my dear friend. As one of the leading nobles in House Kilraith, and the chief magistrate of Carlis, I can mediate between the factions. I would suggest some reparation to the bereaved family – merely as a gesture of regret over the incident. Say . . . twenty thousand gold crowns to the mother of the boys, and the cancelling of the debts owed by their uncle, the grieving Vanis. In this way the matter will be solved before the arrival of the Duke.'

'It touches me that you would go to such lengths on my behalf,' said Waylander. 'I am most grateful.'

'Oh, think nothing of it! It is what friends are for.'

'Indeed. Well, let us make it thirty thousand gold crowns for the mother. I understand she has two other younger sons and that the family is not as wealthy as once they were.'

'And Vanis?'

'By all means let the debt be cancelled,' said Waylander. 'It was a piffling sum.' He rose and gave a bow to Aric. 'And now, my friend, you must excuse me. Much as I enjoy your company I have other pressing matters of my own to attend to.'

'Of course, of course,' said Aric, rising from his seat and offering his hand. Waylander shook it, nodded to the magicker, then left the room.

As the door closed Aric's smile vanished. 'Well, that was simply done,' he said coldly.

'You would have preferred it to be difficult?' asked Eldicar Manushan softly.

'I would have preferred to see him squirm a little. There is nothing quite so stomach-churning as a peasant with wealth. It offends me that I am forced to deal with him. In the old days he would have been dispossessed by his betters, his wealth used by those who understood the nature of power and its uses.'

'I can see how much it must grieve you,' said the magicker, 'to come to this man and beg for scraps from his table.'

All colour drained from Aric's thin face. 'How dare you?'

Eldicar laughed. 'Come, come, my friend, what else can it be called? Each year for the past five years this rich peasant has paid your gambling debts, the mortgage on your two estates, settled your tailor's accounts and enabled you to live in the style and manner of a noble. Did he do this of his own volition? Did he come running to your house and say, "My dear Aric, I have heard how fortune has fled you, so please allow me to pay all your debts?" No, he did not. You came to him.'

'I leased him land!' stormed Aric. 'It was a business arrangement.'

'Aye, business. And all the monies you have received since then? Including the five thousand crowns you requested last night?'

'This is intolerable! Beware, Eldicar, my patience is not limitless.'

'Neither is mine,' said Eldicar, his voice suddenly sibilant. 'Shall I ask for the return of the gift *I* gave you?'

Aric blinked. His mouth opened. He sat down heavily. 'Oh, come now, Eldicar, there is no need for us to argue. I intended no disrespect.'

The magicker leant forward. 'Then remember this, Aric. You are mine. Mine to use, mine to reward, and mine to dispose of if I see fit. Tell me that you understand this.'

'I do. I do understand. I am sorry.'

'That is good. Now, tell me what you observed during our meeting with the Grey Man.'

'Observed? What was there to observe? He came in, agreed to all my demands and left.'

'He did not just agree,' said Eldicar. 'He *raised* the sum.'

'I know that. The size of his fortune is a matter of legend. Money means little to him, obviously.'

'Do not underestimate this man,' said Eldicar.

'I do not understand that. I just plucked him like a chicken – and he offered no resistance.'

'The game is not over yet. You have just seen a man who can mask his anger brilliantly. His only slip was to show his contempt by raising the amount of the extortion. This Grey Man is formidable, and I am not yet ready to have him as an enemy. So when this game moves on you will take no action.'

'Moves on?'

Eldicar Manushan gave a small smile. 'Soon you will come to me with news and we will speak of it again.' Eldicar pushed himself to his feet. 'But for now I wish to explore this palace. I like it. It will suit me well.' Rising from his chair he reached out, took the hand of his page, and walked from the room.

There were those who believed fat Vanis the merchant was incapable of regret. Always jovial, he would talk often of the stupidity of those who insisted on reliving past mistakes; of worrying over them and examining them from every angle. 'You cannot change the past,' he would say. 'Learn from your mistakes and move on.'

And yet Vanis was forced to admit to himself a tiny feeling of regret – even sadness – at the death of his two stupid nephews. This was, of course, assuaged by the news from Aric that all debts had been cancelled and that an extra fortune in gold would soon be in the hands of his sister, Parla. The money would be passed immediately to Vanis for investment, since Parla was even less intelligent than her departed children.

Thoughts of the gold, and what he would do with it, filled his mind, submerging the hint of sadness beneath a cascade of anticipated pleasures. Perhaps now he would be able to interest the courtesan Lalitia. For some reason she had rebuffed all his advances.

Vanis heaved his considerable bulk from the couch and wandered to the window, gazing down at the guards patrolling the walled perimeter of his house. Pushing open the window he stepped out on to the balcony. The stars were bright in a clear sky, and a three-quarter moon hung just above the tree tops. It was a fine night, warm yet not cloying. Two guard dogs loped across the paved entrance path, disappearing into the undergrowth. Ferocious creatures, they made him shiver, and he hoped all the downstairs doors were locked. He had no wish to find one of the beasts padding along his corridors during the night.

The iron gates to his home were chained shut and Vanis relaxed a little.

Despite his own philosophy he found himself thinking back over the mistakes of the past months. He had taken the Grey Man lightly, believing he would not dare to push the matter of the debts. After all, Vanis was highly connected within House Kilraith, and the Grey Man – being a foreigner – needed all the friends he could find in order to operate his business interests in Carlis. The miscalculation had proved costly. Vanis should have guessed that matters would not be so easily resolved when the debts had been lodged with the Merchants Guild, the promises of repayment written down and witnessed.

He moved back inside and poured himself a cup of Lentrian Fire, an amber spirit he had found to be more potent than the finest wines.

It was not his fault that the boys were dead. Had the Grey Man not threatened to ruin him none of this would have happened. *His* was the blame.

Vanis had another drink and walked across to the western window. From here he could see the distant palace of the Grey Man across the bay, shining white in the moonlight. Once more he moved out on to the balcony, checking on the guards. A blond crossbowman was sitting on the lower branches of an oak, his eyes trained on the garden wall. Below him two more guards were patrolling, and Vanis saw one of the black hunting dogs padding across the open ground. The merchant moved back inside and sank into a deep leather seat alongside the flask of Lentrian Fire.

Aric had laughed at Vanis's insistence on hiring bodyguards. 'He is a merchant like you, Vanis. You think he would risk himself by hiring killers to hunt you down? If any were captured – and named him – he would lose everything. We'd have his palace and whatever of his fortune rests hidden in the palace vaults. By Heaven, it is almost worth hoping that he *does* send assassins.'

'Easy for you to say, Aric. Did you hear about his hunting down of the raiders who attacked his lands? Thirty of them, it is said. And he killed them all.'

'Nonsense,' sneered Aric. 'There were around a dozen, and I don't doubt that the Grey Man had most of his guards with him. It is just a lie put about to enhance the Grey Man's reputation.'

'A lie, eh? I suppose it was a lie that he killed Jorna with a single blow to the neck and then slew Parellis with his own sword. As I understand it, he did not even break sweat.'

'Two stupid boys,' said Aric. 'Gods, man, I could have done the same. What possessed you to use such simpletons?'

'It was an error,' said Vanis. 'I thought they were planning to surprise him in the grounds of his palace. I did not expect them to make the attempt at a ball in front of a hundred witnesses!'

'Ah, well, it is over now,' said Aric smoothly. 'The Grey Man gave in without a struggle. Not even a raised word. Have you thought what you will do with Parla's fifteen thousand?'

'Thirty thousand,' corrected Vanis.

'Minus my commission, of course,' said Aric.

'There are those who might feel that your commission is a little excessive, my friend,' said Vanis, struggling to control his anger.

Aric laughed. 'There are also those who believe that, as chief magistrate of Carlis, I should be investigating what caused those two hitherto exemplary boys to commit such a deed. Are you one of those?'

'You have made your point,' muttered Vanis. 'Fifteen thousand it is.'

Even now, some hours later, the conversation left a bad taste in his mouth.

Vanis finished a third cup of Lentrian Fire, and heaved himself once more to his feet. Moving somewhat unsteadily across the room, he pulled open the door and staggered to his bedchamber. The satin sheets on his bed had been pulled back and Vanis peeled off his robe and slippers and sat down heavily, his head spinning. He fell back on to the pillow and yawned.

A shadowy figure moved to the bedside. 'Your nephews are waiting for you,' said a soft voice.

Three hours after dawn a servant brought a tray of fresh-baked bread and soft cheese to the bedroom of the merchant Vanis. There was no reply to his gentle tapping, and he knocked louder. Thinking his master in a deep sleep the servant returned to the kitchens. Half an hour later he tried again. The door was still locked, and no sound came from inside.

He reported this to the head manservant, who, with a duplicate key, opened the door.

The merchant Vanis was lying back on blood-drenched sheets, his throat cut, a small, curved knife held in his right hand.

Within the hour the chief magistrate, Lord Aric, was at the property, along with the dark-bearded Eldicar Manushan, two officers of the watch and a young surgeon. The magicker ordered the little page-boy, dressed now in a tunic of black velvet, to wait outside the door. 'Not a scene to be witnessed by a child,' Eldicar told him. The boy nodded and stood outside with his back to the wall.

'It seems fairly obvious,' said the surgeon, stepping back from the body. 'He cut his own throat and died within a few heart-beats. The knife, as you can see, is very sharp. There is only the one cut – a deep slash that opened the jugular.'

'Strange that he removed his robe first, don't you think?' offered Eldicar Manushan, pointing to the garment on the floor by the bed.

'Why strange?' asked Aric. 'He was getting into bed.'

'To die,' said the magicker. 'Not to sleep. This means he knew his body would be found. Let us face it, gentlemen, Vanis was not a handsome man. Bald, monstrously fat and ugly would be an accurate description. Yet he disrobes, sits down upon white satin sheets and ensures he will be found in the most disgusting of positions. One would have thought he would have left his clothes on. A second thought concerns the wound itself. Very messy and painful. It takes a man of great courage to open his throat. Just as effective would be to open the arteries at the wrist.'

'Yes, yes, yes,' said the surgeon. 'This is all very interesting. But what we have here is a man dead in a locked bedroom, the instrument of his demise in his hand. We will never know what was going on in his mind at the time of his death. I understand his beloved nephews were killed only days ago. His brain was obviously unhinged by grief.'

Eldicar Manushan laughed, the sound horribly contrasting to the bloody scene within the room. 'Unhinged? Indeed he must have been. For he was so frightened of the thought of being killed he surrounded his house with guards and dogs. Then, once he was safe, he cut his throat. I would agree that sounds unhinged.'

'You believe he was murdered, sir?' asked the young surgeon, icily.

The magicker walked to the window and gazed down at the grounds below the balcony. He swung back. 'If he was murdered, young man, then he would have to have been killed by a man who could move in utter silence through a screen of guards and vicious dogs, scale a wall, commit the deed and depart without being seen or scented.'

'Precisely,' said the surgeon, turning to Lord Aric. 'I shall send for the morgue wagon, my lord, and prepare a report.'

With that the young man bowed to Aric, nodded towards Eldicar Manushan, and left the room.

Aric looked at the grotesque bloated body upon the bed, then swung to the two officers of the watch. 'Go and question the servants and the guards. See if anyone heard or saw anything – no matter how inconsequential it may have seemed at the time.'

The men saluted and walked away. Eldicar Manushan moved from the window and pushed shut the bedroom door. 'Would you like to know what really happened?' he asked softly.

'He killed himself,' whispered Aric. 'No-one could have got to him.'

'Let us ask him.'

Eldicar stepped to the bedside and laid his hand upon the dead merchant's brow. 'Hear me,' whispered the magicker. 'Return from the Void and flow once more into this ruined shell. Come back to the world of pain. Come back to the world of light.'

The bloated body spasmed, and a choking, gargling noise came from the throat. The body began to tremble violently. Eldicar thrust his fingers into the man's mouth and dragged out a rolled-up ball of parchment. Hissing breath blew from the dead man's lung, and the remnants of his blood bubbled from the wound in his throat.

'Speak, Vanis,' ordered Eldicar Manushan.

'Grey . . . Man . . .' croaked the corpse. The body sagged back,

712

arms and legs twitching. Eldicar Manushan clapped his hands twice. 'Return to the pit,' he said coldly. All movement ceased.

The magicker glanced at the ashen face of Lord Aric, then lifted the wet ball of parchment he had pulled from the merchant's throat. He opened it and spread it on the bedside table.

'What is it?' whispered Aric, taking a scented handkerchief from his pocket and holding it to his nose.

'It appears to be the contract for the debt the Grey Man waived. It contains all the promises made by Vanis for repayment.' Eldicar laughed again. 'One might say that Vanis was forced to eat his words before his demise.'

'I shall have him arrested!'

'Do not be a fool. I told you the game was not yet over. What evidence will you offer against him? Will you say that the dead man spoke to you? I do not wish that to happen. Great events will soon be upon us, Aric. The dawn of a new age. This matter is closed. As the surgeon said, Vanis took his life in a moment of terrible grief.'

'How did the Grey Man do it? The guards, the dogs . . .'

'What do we know of him?'

'Very little. He came here some years ago from the south. He has business interests in all the great trading nations, Gothir, Chiatze, Drenan, Ventria. He owns a huge fleet of merchant vessels.'

'And no-one knows where he comes from?'

'No – not for sure. Lalitia enjoys his favours, but when I spoke with her she said he never talks about his past. She believes he has been a soldier, though she does not know with which army, and he speaks with knowledge about all the countries with which he has dealings.'

'A wife, children?' asked Eldicar.

'No. Lalitia says he once spoke of a woman who died. But he has been bedding Lalitia for more than a year now, and still she has managed to elicit no useful information.'

'Then I fear it will remain a mystery,' said the magicker. 'For within a few days the Grey Man will be gone from this world – as indeed will many others.'

Just before dawn a blond-haired man wearing a red shirt, embroidered with the coiled snake emblem of Vanis the merchant, rowed a small boat to the edge of the beach below Waylander's palace. Stepping into the shallow water he dragged the boat free of the tide then walked up the steps and through the terraced gardens. As he approached the rooms of the Grey Man he pulled a black skull-cap from his head. The blond hair came away with it. Pushing open the door of his rooms Waylander returned the skull-cap to a hidden drawer at the rear of an old wooden cabinet, then stripped off his clothing. The red shirt he rolled into a ball and tossed into the fireplace, atop the dried logs. Taking a small tinder box from beside the hearth he struck flint and lit the fire.

Waylander's mood was dark and he felt the heaviness of guilt upon him, though he did not know why. Vanis deserved to die. He was a liar, a cheat and a would-be murderer who had caused the death of two innocent boys. In any civilized society he would have been placed on trial and executed, Waylander told himself.

So why the guilt? The question nagged at him.

Was it, perhaps, because the kill had been so easy? Moving through to the small kitchen, he poured himself some water and drank deeply. Yes, it had been easy. Always the miser, Vanis had hired cheap guards, getting one of his servants to conduct the negotiations. There was no guard commander, the men having been hired singly from the taverns and docks, and told to patrol the grounds. It was after dark when Waylander, dressed as a guard, had scaled the wall and made his way to the tall oak some twenty feet from the house. Once there he had sat quietly in plain sight, crossbow in hand, watching the wall. One by one the hired men moved below him, occasionally glancing up and waving. The dog handler had also been hired independently, but in order for his dogs not to savage the guards he had walked the beasts around the grounds, letting them pick up the scent of every man dressed in a red tunic shirt. Thus when the man was on his rounds Waylander climbed down, chatted to him and patted the dogs, who sniffed at his boots, then ignored him.

After that it had been simplicity itself, waiting in the tree until the depths of the night, then scaling the wall and hiding patiently behind the velvet curtains alongside the merchant's bed.

He had not made Vanis suffer. The kill had been swift – one fast sweep and he had sliced the knife through the merchant's jugular. There was no time for Vanis to make a sound and he fell back on the bed, his blood pumping to the satin sheets. As a last flourish Waylander thrust the crumpled contract deep into the dead man's throat. Moving to the balcony he waited for the guards to pass, then climbed down to the gardens below.

Once over the wall he had strolled through the near-deserted streets of Carlis, climbed into the small boat he had left moored in the harbour, and rowed across the bay.

It was while in the boat that the guilt had come. He had not recognized the emotion at first, putting it down to the same malaise he had been suffering for months now; a dissatisfaction at his life of riches and plenty. But it was far more than that.

Yes, Vanis had deserved to die, but in killing him Waylander had returned, albeit briefly, to a way of life that had once filled him with contempt and shame: the dark days when he had been Waylander the Slayer, a killer for hire. He knew at that moment why the guilt was growing. The deed had reminded him of an innocent, unarmed man, whose murder by Waylander sparked a terrible war and the death of thousands.

There is no comparison, he tried to tell himself, between a Drenai king and a fat, murderous merchant.

Stepping naked into the dawn's golden light, Waylander made his way around the terrace to where a small waterfall was bubbling over the rocks. Wading into the shallow pool below it, he stood under the cascading water, half hoping that it would wash away the bitterness of his memories. No man could reshape the past, he knew. If it could be done he would ride back to the little farm and save Tanya and the children from the raiders. In his nightmares he still saw her tied to the bed, the gaping, bloody wound in her belly. In reality she had been dead when he found her, but in his dreams she was alive and crying for help. Her blood had flowed across the floor, up the walls and over the ceiling. Crimson drops fell like rain upon the room. 'Save me!' she would cry. And he would scrabble at the blood-drenched ropes, unable to untie the knots. Always he would wake trembling, his body bathed in sweat.

The waterfall flowed over him, cold and refreshing, washing the dried blood from his hands.

Leaving the water, he sat down on a white marble boulder, allowing the sun to dry him. A man could always make excuses for his actions, he thought, seeking some sense of self-worth for his stupidities or meanness of spirit. Ultimately, however, a man's actions were his own, and he would have to answer for them at the Court of the Soul.

What will you say? he wondered. What excuses will you offer?

It was true that had the raiders not killed his family Dakeyras would never have become Waylander. Had he not become

Waylander he would not have taken the life of the last Drenai king. Perhaps then the terrible war with Vagria would never have happened. Hundreds of villages and towns would not have been burned, and scores of thousands would never have died.

Guilt merged with sorrow as he sat in the sunshine. It seemed incredible now to Waylander that he had once been a Drenai officer, in love with a gentle woman who wanted nothing more than to raise a family on a farm she could call her own. He could hardly even recall the thoughts and dreams of that young man. One fact was certain. The young Dakeyras would never have donned a disguise to butcher an unarmed man in his bed.

Waylander shivered at the thought.

He had, over the years, tried to change his life so many times. He had allowed himself to care for another woman, Danyal, and had helped her to raise the two orphan girls, Miriel and Krylla. After the Vagrian War he had built a cabin high in the mountains, and assumed the life of the peaceful Dakeyras, a family man. He had almost grown content. After Danyal died in a riding accident he had raised the girls alone. Krylla wed a young man and they moved away to a distant land to build a farm and start a family.

Then the killers had come into the mountains. Dakeyras had no idea why Karnak, the ruler of the Drenai, should send assassins after him. It made no sense. Until the day he discovered that Karnak's son had unwittingly caused the death of Krylla during a drunken chase. Terrified that this action would result in Waylander seeking revenge, Karnak took precipitate action. Assassins were despatched to kill him. They failed. They died. And the days of death and blood had returned.

Eventually Waylander moved to the distant Gothir city of Namib, where he tried to rebuild his life. Once more assassins came for him. He led them deep into the forests outside the city, killing three and capturing the fourth. Instead of executing the last man he made a deal with him. Karnak had offered a fortune in gold for the head of Waylander. Proof of the killing would come with the handing over of his famed double-winged crossbow. One of the dead assassins bore a passing resemblance to Waylander, so he cut the head from the corpse and placed it in a sack. Then he gave his crossbow to the survivor. 'With these you will become rich,' he said. 'Is our business concluded?'

'Aye, it is,' said the man, who returned to Drenan and pocketed his reward. The skull and crossbow had then been exhibited in the Marble Museum.

Once more Waylander had journeyed to far places, choosing the distant realm of Kydor and attempting to immerse himself in a life of riches and plenty.

Yet now he had become the assassin once more. Not through necessity but through false pride.

It was not a pleasant thought.

Perhaps, he thought, when the ship comes in ten days' time, and I journey across the ocean, I will find a life that does not involve violence and death. A world without people, a vast land of soaring mountains and trickling streams. I could be content there, he decided.

Deep inside he could almost hear the mocking laughter.

You will always be Waylander the Slayer. It is your nature.

Ustarte the Priestess stood by the window. Far below her she could see the Grey Man sitting beside the waterfall. Even from here she could feel his shame. She turned from the window. Her three shaven-headed acolytes waited silently at the table. Their thoughts were troubled, their emotions strong. Prial was the most fearful, for he was the most imaginative. He was remembering the cage and the whips of fire. His heart was beating wildly.

The powerful, brooding Menias also felt fear, but it was leavened by frustration and anger. He hated the Masters with all of his being, and dreamt of the day he could Change and tear into them, ripping the flesh from their bones. He had not wanted to escape through the gateway. He had urged them all to remain and fight on.

Corvidal was the calmest of the three, but then he was the most content. All he desired was to be in the company of Ustarte. The priestess felt his love, and though she could not return it in the way he desired she still found great joy in it, for it had freed him from the hatred that still chained Menias. The simple fact that love could conquer hate gave Ustarte hope.

'Do we go?' asked the golden-eyed Prial.

'Not yet.'

'But we have failed,' said Menias, the shortest and heaviest of the three. 'We should go home, find others who have survived, and continue the fight.'

Ustarte returned to the table, her heavy red silk gown rustling as she moved. The dark-eyed, slender Corvidal rose and drew back her chair. She glanced into his gentle face and smiled her thanks as she sat down. How could she tell Menias that none of

717

the others had survived, that she had felt their death even from beyond the gateway. 'I cannot just leave these people to the fate awaiting them.'

They sat in silence once more. Then Prial spoke. 'The gateways are opening. The killers in the mist have already been seen. The *Kriaz-nor* will follow soon. The puny weapons of this world will not stop them, Ustarte. I have no wish to view the horrors to come.'

'And yet the people of this world defeated them three thousand years ago,' she said.

'They had greater weapons then,' said Menias, his voice deep and low.

She felt the frustration in him, and the anger. 'Where did they gain the knowledge for such weapons?' she countered. 'And where are those weapons now?'

'How can we know?' put in Corvidal. 'The legends speak of fantastic gods, demons and heroes. There is no history of that period in this world. Only fable.'

'And yet there are clues,' said Ustarte. 'All the legends speak of a war among the gods. That suggests to me that there was discord in Kuan-Hador, and that at least some of them sided with humanity. How else could they have created the swords of light? How else could they have won? Yes, we have failed in our attempt to prevent the opening of the gates, and we have failed so far in our search to discover what happened to the weapons humanity used to win the first war. However, we must go on.'

'It is too late for this world, Ustarte,' said Prial. 'I say we should use the last of the power to open a gateway.'

Ustarte considered his words, then shook her head. 'What power remains in me I will use to aid those who will fight the enemy. I will not run.'

'And who will fight?' asked Menias. 'Who will stand against the *Kriaz-nor*? The Duke and his soldiers? They will be cut down – or worse. They will be captured and Joined. Other nobles will be seduced by promises of riches or extended life, or power within the new order. Humans are so easily corrupted.'

'I think the Grey Man will fight,' she said.

'One human?' asked the astonished Menias. 'We risk our lives because of your faith in one human?'

'There will be more than one,' she said. 'There is another clue that links the legends. All the stories speak of the return of the heroes. They die, and yet people believe they will come again when the need is upon the land. It is my belief that those who aided humanity subtly Joined the heroes they used, so that when the evil returned their descendants would have the power to combat it.'

'With respect, Great One,' said Corvidal, 'that is a hope not a belief. There is not a shred of true evidence to substantiate such a hypothesis.'

'It is more than a hope, Corvidal. We know the power of Joining for that is how we exist. We also know that *our* rulers ensure that no Joining can ever sire – or bear – children. They dare not risk creating beings who could decide their own destiny. But I think this is what the Ancients did, enhancing their human allies and allowing the talents to be passed from generation to generation. We see it around us even now. Nadir shamen who can meld man and wolf into fearsome creatures. Source Priests whose spirits can soar and whose powers can heal terrible diseases. We know from our studies that before the coming of the Ancients mankind had few of these gifts. The Ancients imbued certain members of the human race with them. The Ancients told their allies that, in times to come, if the evil returned, these powers would flower again. Hence the legends of the return of kings and heroes. I sense it in the Grey Man.'

'He is merely a killer,' said Prial dismissively.

'He is more than that. There is a nobility of spirit in him, and a power not found in ordinary men.'

'I am not convinced,' said Prial. 'I stand with Corvidal on this issue. You are risking our lives on a forlorn hope.'

Seeing that they were all in agreement she bowed her head. 'I will open a gateway for you all to leave,' she said, sadly.

'And yet you will stay?' asked Corvidal softly.

'I will.'

'Then I will stay with you, Great One.'

Menias and Prial glanced at one another. Then Prial spoke. 'I will stay until the arrival of the *Kriaz-nor*. But I have no wish to throw away my life needlessly.'

'And you, Menias?' asked the priestess.

He shrugged his powerful shoulders. 'Where you are, Great One, there shall I be.'

Yu Yu Liang cleared his throat and spat into the sea. He was miserable. It seemed to him that his quest to become a hero was not all he had anticipated. As a ditch-digger he received a small

719

amount of coin at the end of the week, which he would use on food, alcohol, lodging and pleasure-women. There was always enough food, never enough women and far too much alcohol. But, looking back, it had not been as unpleasant a life as it had seemed while he was living it.

Picking up a flat rock, Yu Yu threw it far out over the waves. It struck once, skimmed for another twenty feet, then disappeared below the surface.

He sighed. Now he had a sharp sword, no money, no women, and was sitting in the sunshine of a foreign land wondering why he had travelled this far. He had not intended to leave the lands of the Chiatze. His first thought had been to strike out for the mountains to the west and join a band of robbers. Then he had come upon the battlefield, and the dead *Rajnee*. He recalled the moment when he had first seen the sword. It was jutting from the earth just behind a bush. Sunlight had glanced from the blade as Yu Yu was robbing the corpse. The *Rajnee* was carrying no coin, and Yu Yu had pushed himself to his feet and walked to the sword. It was quite beautiful, the blade gleaming, the long, two-handed hilt wondrously fashioned and leatherbound. The pommel was of silver, embossed with a mountain flower. Reaching out, Yu Yu drew the sword from the earth.

He then forgot his original purpose and decided to head northeast, filled with a desire to see foreign lands. It was most peculiar, and sitting in the sunshine of the Bay of Carlis he could not, for the life of him, remember just why he had thought it was such a fine idea.

Two days later something even more mysterious occurred. He came upon a merchant who was travelling in a cart with two pretty daughters and a retarded son. The wheel had come off the cart and the group were sitting by the roadside. In his new life as a robber and an outlaw Yu Yu should have stolen the man's gold, ravished his daughters and left the scene richer and more relaxed. Indeed this had been his plan, and he had marched forward, adopting what he considered to be a menacing expression. Then, to show his intent, he grasped the hilt of the sword, ready to draw it and terrify his victims.

An hour later he had repaired the cart, and escorted the merchant to his home village some six miles to the east. For this he received a fine meal, a kiss on the cheek from both daughters, and a small sack of supplies from the merchant's wife. You are too stupid to be a robber, he had told himself, as he resumed his journey.

And now that stupidity had brought him to Kydor, a land where men bearing Chiatze features stood out like . . . like . . . he struggled for a simile, but could only come up with 'warts on a whore's arse'. This was not entirely pleasing and he stopped thinking of similes. However, the point was a good one. How could a Chiatze warrior become a robber in a land where he would be instantly identified wherever he went? It was a nonsense.

At that moment a young, blond-haired woman emerged on to the small beach. To Yu Yu's surprise she ignored him and began to remove her dress and undergarments. Once naked she ran across the sand and dived into the water. Coming to the surface she swam in long, easy strokes, curving round to approach Yu Yu's position. Treading water, she threw back her head, and swept her hands through her wet hair. 'Why are you not swimming?' she called out to him. 'Are you not hot sitting there in wolf fur?'

Yu Yu admitted that he was. She laughed and swung away, swimming out into deeper water.

As swiftly as he could Yu Yu struggled out of his clothes and hurled himself into the sea, landing on his belly, which was painful. Not, however, as unpleasant as what followed. He sank like a stone. Thrashing his arms wildly, he fought for the surface. His head broke clear and he sucked in a great gulp of air. For a moment he bobbed in the water, but then he breathed out and disappeared once more beneath the cold water.

Panic swept through him. Something grabbed his hair, hauling him up. He struggled wildly, and broke through the surface once more.

'Take a deep breath and hold it,' the woman ordered him. Yu Yu did so, and bobbed alongside her. 'It is the air in your lungs that lets you float.'

Reassured by her presence, Yu Yu relaxed a little. What she said was true. As long as he held air in his chest he floated.

'Now lean back,' she said. 'I will support you.' As she floated alongside him he felt her arms below his spine and he gratefully dropped back into them. Glancing to his right he found himself staring at a pair of perfect breasts. Air whooshed from his lungs and he sank. Her arms pushed him back to the surface and he spluttered for a while. 'What kind of an idiot leaps into the sea when he cannot swim?' she asked.

'I am Yu Yu Liang,' he managed to say, between great gulps of air.

721

'Well, let me teach you, Yu Yu Liang,' she said.

The next few minutes were a joy as she taught him a rudimentary stroke that allowed him to pull himself through the water. The sun was warm upon his back, the water cool upon his body. Finally she bade him make his way to the shallow water close to the beach. Then he watched as she waded back to where she had laid her clothes. Yu Yu followed her.

She climbed up the rocks to where a small waterfall cascaded down to the beach and washed the salt from her body. Yu Yu gazed on her beauty, almost awestruck. Then he scrambled up and also washed himself. They returned to the beach and the woman sat down on a rock, to let her body dry in the sunshine.

'You came in with the lord Matze Chai,' she said.

'I am . . . bodyguard,' said Yu Yu. The excitement caused by her nakedness made Yu Yu feel light-headed. His grasp of the round-eye tongue, feeble at best, came close to deserting him.

'I hope you fight better than you swim,' she said.

'I am great fighter. I have fought demons. I fear nothing.'

'My name is Norda,' she said. 'I work in the palace. All the servants have heard the stories of the demons in the mist. Is it true? Or were they merely robbers?'

'Demons, yes,' said Yu Yu. 'I cut arm from one and it burn. Then . . . gone. Nothing left. I did this.'

'Truly?' she asked him.

Yu Yu sighed. 'No. Kysumu cut arm. But I would have if closer.'

'I like you, Yu Yu Liang,' she said, with a smile. Rising to her feet, she dressed and wandered away back up the rocks to the path.

'I like you too,' he called. She turned and waved, then was gone.

Yu Yu sat for a while, then realized he was growing hungry. Putting on his clothes he thrust his scabbarded sword into his belt and walked back up the hill. Perhaps, he thought, life in Kydor will not be so unpleasant.

Kysumu was sitting on the balcony of their room. He was sketching the outline of the cliffs and town across the bay. He glanced up as Yu Yu entered. 'I've had a great time,' said Yu Yu. 'I swam with a girl. She was beautiful, with golden hair and breasts like melons. Beautiful breasts. I am a great swimmer.'

'I saw,' said Kysumu. 'However, if you wish to be a *Rajnee* you must put aside carnal desires, and concentrate on the spiritual, the journey of the soul towards true humility.'

Yu Yu thought about this, then decided Kysumu was making a joke. He didn't understand it, but laughed out of politeness. 'I am hungry,' he said.

Elphons, Duke of Kydor, angled his grey charger down the slope towards the grasslands of the Eiden Plain. Behind him came his aides and his personal bodyguard of forty lancers. At fifty-one Elphons had found the long journey from the capital tiring. A man of great physical strength, the Duke had lately been plagued by sharp pains in his joints, most especially in the elbows, ankles and knees, which were now swollen and tender. He had hoped that the journey from the damp and cold of the capital to the warmer climes around Carlis would relieve the problem, but so far there had been little change. He was also experiencing difficulty at times with his breathing.

He glanced back at the convoy of five heavy wagons, the first carrying his wife and her three ladies-in-waiting. His fifteen-year-old son, Niallad, was riding alongside the convoy, the sun glinting on his new armour. Elphons sighed and heeled his horse onward.

The weather had been clement during their mountain passage, but as they made their way slowly down towards the plain the temperature rose. At first it was a pleasant warmth, after the cold mountain winds, but now it was becoming intolerable. Sweat trickled down the Duke's broad face. He lifted his gold-embossed iron helm from his head and pushed back his hood of silver mail rings, exposing thick, unruly grey hair.

The slim, balding aide, Lares, rode alongside the Duke. 'Uncommonly hot, sire,' he said, pulling the stopper from his leather canteen and pouring water on to a linen handkerchief. This he passed to Elphons, who wiped it over his face and grey-streaked beard. Instantly the hot breeze felt cool against his skin. Unclipping his heavy red cloak he passed it to Lares.

Far below, Elphons saw the wagons of the merchant convoy enter the deep woods bordering the long Lake of Cepharis. His mood soured. They had first caught sight of the convoy earlier that morning, as a dustcloud on the horizon. Slowly they had gained on it, and were now a mere half-mile behind them. Elphons had been looking forward to arriving at the lake, divesting himself of his armour and swimming in the cool water, and did not relish the thought of sharing it with two score wagoners and their families. As always the young Lares was in tune with his master's thoughts. 'I could ride down and get them to move on, sire,' he said.

It was a tempting thought, but Elphons pushed it aside. The wagoners would be no less hot than he, and the lake was common ground. It would be enough for the Duke and his retainers to ride close and wait patiently. The wagoners would get the message and move on more swiftly. Even so, it meant that before the day was over the Duke and his retainers would be eating dust thrown up by the convoy.

Elphons patted the sleek neck of his charger. 'You are tired, Osir,' he said to the horse, 'and I fear I am not as light as once I was.' The horse snorted and tossed its head.

The Duke touched heels to the animal's flanks and began once more the long descent. A solitary cloud drifted momentarily between the sun and the land and Elphons enjoyed a few seconds of relief from the heat.

Then it was gone. With the prospect of the lake looming, Elphons drained the last of the water from his canteen, and swung in the saddle to watch his wagons making their slow and careful descent. There was scree upon the road and if not handled with skill a wagon could slide off and smash into shards on the rocky slope.

His wife, the silver-haired Aldania, waved at him, and he grinned back. As she smiled she looked young again, he thought, and infinitely desirable. Twenty-two years they had been wed, and he still marvelled at his luck in winning her. The only daughter of Orien, the last but one king of the Drenai, she had fled her own lands during the war against Vagria. Elphons had been merely a knight at that time, and had met her in the Gothir capital of Gulgothir. Under any normal circumstances a romance between a princess and a knight would have been short-lived, but with her brother King Niallad slain by an assassin, and the Drenai empire in ruins, there were few suitors for her hand. And after the war, when the Drenai declared for a republic, she was even less sought-after. The new ruler, the fat giant Karnak, made it clear that Aldania would not be welcome back home. So Elphons had won her heart and her hand, bringing her to Kydor and enjoying twenty-two years of great joy.

Thoughts of his good fortune made him forget burning heat and painful joints, and he rode for some time lost in the memories of their years together. She was everything he could have wished for: a friend, a lover, and a wise adviser in times of crisis. There was only one area in which he could offer any criticism. The raising of their son. It was the only subject on which they rowed. She doted on Niallad, and would hear no words said against him.

Elphons loved the boy, but he worried for him. He was too fearful. The Duke twisted in the saddle and glanced back. Niallad waved at him. Elphons smiled and returned the wave. If I could turn back the years, thought the Duke, I would throttle that damned story-teller. Niallad had been around six years of age when he had learned the full story of the death of his uncle, the Drenai king. He had suffered nightmares for months, believing that the evil Waylander was hunting him. For most of the summer the boy had taken to creeping into his parents' bedroom and climbing into bed between them.

Elphons had finally summoned the Drenai ambassador, a pleasant man with a large family of his own. He had sat with Niallad and explained how the monstrous Waylander had been hunted down and how his head had been cut off. The head had been brought to Drenan, where, stripped of skin, it had been displayed in the museum, alongside the assassin's infamous crossbow.

For a while the boy's nightmares ceased. But then news had come of the theft of the crossbow, and the murder of Karnak, the Drenai ruler.

Even now, nine years later, Niallad would not travel without bodyguards. He hated crowds and would avoid large gatherings when he could. On state occasions, when Elphons forced him to attend, he would stay close to his father, eyes wide with fear, sweat upon his face. No-one mentioned it, of course, but all saw it.

Elphons returned his attention to the trail. He was almost at the foot of the slope. Shading his eyes he stared ahead at the wooded lake a quarter of a mile ahead. There was no-one swimming. How curious, he thought. They must have pushed on. Hardy men, these wagoners. And yet they had women and children with them. One would have thought they would have appreciated a cooling swim. Perhaps they realized the Duke was close behind and were nervous about stopping. He hoped this was not the reason.

Lares moved alongside him and waved the troop of twenty

soldiers forward. They cantered past the Duke and rode ahead to scout the woods.

Sadly such precautions were necessary. There had been three attempts on the Duke's life in the last two years. Such was the Angostin way. A man held power only as long as his strength and his guile held out. And his luck, thought Elphons. The four major Houses of Kydor were involved in an uneasy truce, but disputes broke out often, and battles were fought. Only last year Lord Panagyn of House Rishell had waged a short and bloody war against Lord Ruall of House Loras, and Lord Aric of House Kilraith. There were three battles, all indecisive, but Panagyn had lost an eye in the third, while Ruall's two brothers were both killed in the second. Lord Shastar, of the smaller House Bakard, had now broken his treaty with Panagyn and allied himself with Aric and Ruall, which suggested a new war was looming. This was why, Elphons believed, Panagyn had sent assassins against him. Angostin law stated that the Duke's forces could not be used in disputes between Houses. However, if the Duke was dead, his three thousand soldiers would likely join Panagyn. The man, though a brute, was a fighting soldier, and highly regarded by the troops. With them he could win a civil war and make himself Duke.

Sooner or later I will have to kill Panagyn, he thought, for if he ever slays me he will see my son murdered on the same day. Elphons found the fear of such an outcome weighed heavily upon him. Niallad was not ready to rule. Perhaps he never would be. The thought made him shiver. He looked up at the sky. 'Just give me five more years,' he prayed to the Source. In that time Niallad *might* change.

The Duke drew rein as his cavalrymen fanned out and entered the wood. Within moments they were galloping their mounts away from the trees and back to the convoy. The captain, a young man named Korsa, dragged his mount to a halt before him. 'There has been a massacre, my lord,' he said, forgetting to salute.

Elphons stared hard into the young man's ashen face. 'Massacre? What are you talking about?'

'They are all dead, sire. Butchered!'

Elphons heeled the charger into a run, his forty lancers swinging their mounts and following him.

The wagons were all drawn up within the trees some fifty feet from the water's edge, but there were no horses. Blood was everywhere, splashed against tree-trunks, pooling on the earth.

Elphons drew his longsword and gazed around the scene. Lares and Korsa dismounted, while the other cavalrymen, weapons in their hands, sat nervously awaiting a command.

A cold winter wind blew across the lake. Elphons shivered. Then he climbed down from his mount and walked to the water's edge. Amazingly there was ice upon the water. It was melting fast. He scooped some into his hand. The mud beneath his feet crunched as he moved. Sheathing his sword he walked back to where Lares and Korsa were examining the traces of an over-turned wagon. Blood was smeared upon the smashed wood, and a blood trail, like the crimson slime of a giant worm, could be seen leading away from the wagons and deeper into the trees. Several bushes had been uprooted.

Elphons turned to one of the soldiers. 'Ride out and keep the wagons back from here,' he said. Gratefully the man swung his horse and rode away.

Melting ice was everywhere. The Duke scanned the ground. It was badly churned, but he found a clear imprint just beyond the wagon. It was like the mark of a bear, only longer and thinner: four-toed and taloned.

In the space of a few moments something had descended upon forty wagoners and their families, killed them and their horses and dragged them away into the woods. It couldn't have happened without a sound. There must have been screams of terror and pain. Yet, only a few hundred yards away, Elphons had heard nothing. And how could ice form in this cloying heat?

Elphons followed the blood trails for a little way. Dead birds littered the ground, frost upon their feathers.

Lares crossed the blood-covered ground. The young man was trembling. 'What are your orders, sire?'

'If we skirt the lake to the north how long till we reach Carlis?'

'By dusk, sire.'

'Then that is what we shall do.'

'I cannot understand how we heard nothing. We had the woods in sight all the time.'

'Sorcery was used here,' said the Duke, making the Sign of the Protective Horn. 'Once my family is safe in Carlis I'll return with Aric's forces and a Source priest. Whatever evil is here will be destroyed. I swear it.'

It was still early when Waylander strolled into the North Tower library, climbing the cast-iron spiral staircase to the Antiquities section on the third floor. The three acolytes of the priestess Ustarte were sitting at the central table, examining tomes and parchment scrolls. They did not look up as he entered.

Strange men, he thought. Despite the thick stone of the tower the heat was already rising within the chamber, and yet they were garbed in heavy grey-hooded robes, silk scarves around their necks, and each wore thin grey gloves. Waylander did not acknowledge them as he moved past, but he felt their eyes upon his back. He allowed himself a wry smile. He had never been loved by priests.

Waylander paused and scanned the shelves. More than three thousand documents were stored here, ancient skinbound volumes, fading parchments, even tablets of clay and stone. Some were beyond deciphering, but still drew scholars from as far afield as Ventria and the distant Angostin homeland.

His search would have been so much easier had the old librarian, Cashpir, not succumbed to a fever and taken to his bed. His knowledge of the library was phenomenal, and it was through him that Waylander had gathered so many of the precious tomes. He tried to recall the day he had read of the shining swords. There had been a storm raging, the sky black and heavy. He had sat where the priests were now, reading under lantern-light. For three days he had been racking his mind for any bright shard of memory.

He glanced towards the open window, and the new wooden shutters. Then it came to him.

The old shutters had been leaking, and water had splashed to the shelves close by, damaging the documents stored there. Waylander and Cashpir had moved some of the scrolls to the table. It was one of these he had been idly scanning. The area of the shelf closest to the window was still empty. Waylander walked across the chamber to the small office used by Cashpir. The place was a mess, scrolls scattered everywhere, and he could hardly see the leather-topped desk beneath the mass of books and parchment. Cashpir had an amazing mind, but no talent whatsoever for organization.

Waylander walked round the desk and sat down, picking through the parchments that lay there, recalling what had pricked his original interest on the day of the storm. One of the scrolls had told of giant creatures, melded from men and beasts. Waylander himself had been hunted by just such creatures twenty years before – sent to kill him by a Nadir shaman.

He studied the scrolls, examining each one before laying it on the floor at his feet. Finally he lifted a yellowing parchment and recognized it immediately. The ink had faded badly in places and one section of the parchment had been stained by fungus. Cashpir had treated the rest with a preservative solution of his own design. Waylander took the scroll back into the main library and walked to the window. In the sunlight he read the opening lines.

Of the glory that was Kuan-Hador there are only ruins now, stark and jagged, testimony to the fruitless arrogance of man. There are no signs of the God-Kings, no shadows of the Mist Warriors cast by the harsh sunlight. The history of the city is gone from the world, as indeed are the stories of its heroes and villains. All that remains are a few contradictory oral legends, garbled tales of creatures of fire and ice, and warriors with swords of shining light who stood against demons shaped from both men and beasts.

Having visited the ruins one can understand the birth of such legends. There are fallen statues that appear to have the heads of wolves and the bodies of men. There are the remains of great arches, built, as far as one can ascertain, for no purpose. One arch, named by the Historian Ventaculus as the Hador Folly, is carved from a sheer cliff of granite. It is the most curious piece, for when one examines it one finds that the pictographic carvings upon the inner arch pillars vanish into the rock, almost as if the cliff had grown over it like moss.

I have copied separately many of the pictographs, and several of my colleagues have spent decades trying to decipher the complex language contained in them. So far complete success has eluded us. What is apparent is that Kuan-Hador was unique in the ancient world. Its methods of architecture, the skill of its artisans, are apparent nowhere else. Many of the stones still standing are blackened by fire, and it is likely that the city was destroyed in a great conflagration, perhaps as the result of a war with neighbouring civilizations. Few artefacts have been recovered from Kuan-Hador, though the King of Symilia has in his possession a mirror of silver that never tarnishes. This, he claims, was recovered from the site.

Waylander paused in his reading. There followed a series of descriptions of site examinations and a suggested layout of the city. Bored by the scholarly writing Waylander skimmed through the text until he came to the concluding paragraphs.

As is ever the case when a civilization falls, tales abound that it was evil. Nomads who inhabit the areas that once were the realm of Kuan-Hador talk of human sacrifice and the summoning of demons. There is no doubt that the city boasted great magickers. I suspect, from the statues and those pictographs we have been partly able to decipher, that the rulers of Kuan-Hador did indeed have some understanding of the vile art of meld-magic. It is entirely probable that more recent examples of this abhorrent practice – among the Nadir and other barbaric peoples – are legacies of Kuan-Hador.

I have listed separately some of the oral legends pertaining to the fall of Kuan-Hador. The one most told concerns the return of the shining swords. Among the nomads of the Varnii – distant relatives of the Chiatze – the shamen speak a succession of doggerel verses at season feasts. The first and last verse read:

But seek ye not the Men of Clay,
Who buried lie in crafted night,
Their shining swords are put away,
Their eyes are closed against the light.

Death must await these Men of Clay,
Who stand in rows of ghostly white,
And will until that dreadful day,
When they awake to one last fight.

A more complete translation can be found in Appendix 5. The Historian Ventaculus produced an appealing essay on the song, claiming it to be a metaphor for the death and resurrection of those of heroic virtue, a faith system not unusual among warrior peoples.

Waylander put the scroll back in its rightful place on the shelf and strolled from the library. Minutes later he emerged on to the central terrace outside the Banquet Hall. Kysumu was waiting there, standing by the balustrade and staring out over the bay and the sea beyond. As Waylander approached the little swordsman turned. He bowed deeply. Waylander returned the compliment.

'I have found little,' he told the *Rajnee*. 'There are stories of an ancient city that once ruled this land. Apparently it was destroyed by warriors with shining swords.'

'A city of demons,' said Kysumu.

'So it is said.'

'They are returning.'

'That is quite a leap of imagination,' said Waylander. 'The city fell around three thousand years ago. The scroll I examined was written a thousand years ago. One attack on a merchant and his bodyguards is too little to convince me.'

'I also discovered a scroll,' said Kysumu. 'It talked of nomads avoiding the ruins because their legends say the demons were not all slain, but had escaped through a gateway to another world, one day to return.'

'Even so, the evidence is small.'

'Perhaps,' said Kysumu. 'But when I see birds flying south I know winter is coming. They do not need to be *large* birds, Grey Man.'

Waylander smiled. 'Let us say you are correct, and the demons of Kuan-Hador are returning. What is your plan?'

'I have no plan. I will fight them. I am *Rajnee*.'

'Matze Chai tells me you believe your sword brought you here.'

'It is not a belief, Grey Man, it is a fact. And now that I am here I know it is right. How far are the ruins from the palace?'

'Less than a day's ride.'

'Will you loan me a horse?'

'I'll do better than that,' said Waylander. 'I'll take you myself.'

If one fact of life was incontrovertible for Yu Yu Liang it was that one golden ounce of good luck was invariably followed by several pounds of bad. Usually, in his experience, falling upon him from a great height. Or, as his mother would say, 'When the emperor's parade passes by, the horse-turd collectors are not far behind.'

The blond-haired Norda had left his bed only moments before, and Yu Yu was happier than he had been in months. This was despite the initial criticism offered by the woman. 'You are not in a race,' she had whispered to him, as he clung to her.

He had paused, his heart pounding wildly. 'A race?' he managed to say, between great gulps of air.

'Be slow. We have plenty of time.'

If Nashda, the crippled god of all labourers, had appeared in his room offering him immortality at that moment it could not have been sweeter. First, there was this beautiful woman lying beneath him, her golden legs around his hips. Second, there was not a queue of impatient ditch-diggers outside the door shouting for him to hurry. Third, as far as he knew, this glorious creature desired no money from him. Which was fortuitous since he had no money. And now to be told he had plenty of time . . . Could Heaven be any sweeter?

He took her advice. There were many new joys to discover, and some obstacles to overcome. Kissing a woman who still had all her teeth was surprisingly pleasant. Almost as pleasant as the fact that there was no sand-glass on the table beside the bed, swiftly trickling his time away.

If life could get better than this, Yu Yu Liang did not know how.

The first indications that there was a price to be paid for such pleasure came just after she left, when he pulled on his harsh, woollen shirt. His upper back tingled with pain from the scratches to his skin. She had also bitten his ear, which had been most pleasurable at the time, but now throbbed a little.

Even so Yu Yu was whistling a merry tune as he stepped from the room – to find himself facing three of the Grey Man's guards.

The first, a stocky man with tightly curled golden hair, was staring at him malevolently. 'You have made a bad mistake, you slant-eyed pig,' he said. 'You think you can come here and force yourself on our women?'

In Yu Yu's village there had been a Source temple, and many of the children had attended school there. They had no wish to learn the tongue of the round-eye, but the priests had supplied two meals a day, and for this it was worth putting in a little study. Yu Yu had been a quick learner, but lack of practice since then meant he needed a little time to translate complicated sentences. Apparently he had committed some kind of error and was being accused of stealing a woman's one-eyed pig. He looked into the man's face and saw the hatred there, then flicked his gaze to the man on either side. Both were staring at him through narrowed eyes. 'Well, now you are going to learn a little lesson,' continued the first man. 'We're going to teach you to stick with your own kind. Understand, yellow man?'

Despite having no knowledge of the pig theft, Yu Yu understood only too well the lesson they were about to deliver.

'I said, do you understand?'

The man's hatred turned briefly to shock, and then to blank emptiness as Yu Yu's left fist cannoned into his nose. He was already unconscious as the right cross followed. The guard hit the floor, blood seeping from his nostrils. A second guard lunged forward. Yu Yu butted him full in the face then brought his knee up into the man's groin.

The guard gave a strangled cry of pain and sagged against the Chiatze. Yu Yu pushed him away and downed him with a left hook to the jaw.

'You give lessons too?' Yu Yu asked the last guard.

The man shook his head vehemently. 'I didn't want to be here,' he said. 'It wasn't my idea.'

'I don't steal pigs,' said Yu Yu, then stalked away down the corridor, his good mood evaporating. There were scores of guards in the Grey Man's palace and when next they came it would be in greater numbers. This meant, at best, a bad beating.

Yu Yu had suffered such beatings before, blows and kicks raining in on him. The last such attack, just over a year ago, had almost killed him. His left arm had been broken in three places. Several ribs had been snapped, one of which had pierced his lung. It took months to recover, months of hardship and hunger. Unable to work he had been reduced, at first, to begging for rice at the poorhouse. Finally he had journeyed back to the Source temple. Some of the priests still remembered him, and he had been welcomed warmly. They tended his broken bones, and fed him. When his strength returned he journeyed back to the site of his beating and sought out singly each of the eight men involved in the attack. And he thrashed them. The last had been the most difficult. Shi Da was six and a half feet tall, heavily muscled and supremely tough. It had been his kicks that had snapped Yu Yu's ribs. Yu Yu had given a lot of thought to challenging Shi Da. It was a matter of honour that a challenge should be made, but the timing had to be exactly right.

So Yu Yu had walked up behind him in the Chong tavern and thwacked a heavy iron bar across the back of the man's head. As he slumped forward Yu Yu struck him twice more. Shi Da had fallen to his knees, barely conscious. 'I challenge you to man-to-man combat,' said Yu Yu, in the time-honoured fashion. 'Do you accept?'

A low garbled grunt of incomprehension came from the giant.

'I shall take that as a yes,' said Yu Yu. Then he kicked Shi Da in the jaw. Shi Da had hit the floor hard, then slowly rolled to his knees. Amazingly the big man climbed to his feet. Panicked, Yu Yu had dropped the iron bar and rushed in smashing blows left and right into Shi Da's face. Shi Da landed one clumsy punch before pitching sideways to the floor.

In his relief Yu Yu felt magnanimous and only kicked the unconscious man a few times. It was a mistake. He should have knelt by him and beaten him to death. When Shi Da recovered he put out the word that he would cut Yu Yu Liang's heart from his body and feed it to his dogs.

That was the day when Yu Yu decided upon an outlaw's life in the mountains.

Now, in a foreign land, he had made more enemies. And he still did not know why. With a little more time to work on the translation Yu Yu realized that the man had called *him* a slant-eyed pig, and that the problem was, in fact, not about theft, but about making love to the blonde woman. It seemed peculiar to Yu Yu that the shape of his Chiatze eyes, or the golden colour of his skin, should preclude him from forming friendships with Kydor women. And why would he want to stick with his own kind? It was a mystery. Yu Yu had been a ditch-digger for nine years and had never met another ditch-digger he found remotely attractive.

Except for Pan Jian.

She was the only female ditch-digger he had ever known. A monstrous woman with huge arms and a flat round face that boasted several chins, two of which sported large, matching warts. One evening, when drunk and broke, he had propositioned her.

'Pay me a compliment,' she told him, 'and I'll think about it.'

Yu Yu stared at her through bleary eyes, searching for some evidence of femininity. 'You have nice ears,' he said at last.

Pan Jian had laughed. 'That will do,' she told him, and they had rutted in a ditch.

She had been dismissed two days later for arguing with the foreman. It was a short argument. He pointed out he had seen cows with smaller and more attractive arses than hers, and she had broken his jaw.

As Yu Yu climbed the stairs to the upper level he found himself remembering her fondly. Although making love to her was like clinging to the back of a greased hippo, the ride had been enjoyable, and he had discovered in Pan Jian an unexpected tenderness. Afterwards she had talked of her life, and her hopes and her dreams. It had been a gentle night, of balmy soft breezes and a bright hunter's moon. Pan Jian had spoken of finding a small place near the Great River and starting a business, cutting rushes and weaving hats and baskets. Her hands were as big as shovels and Yu Yu had great difficulty picturing her creating delicate articles from straw. But he said nothing. 'And I'd like a dog,' she said. 'One of those small dogs that the magistrate has with him. A white one.'

'They are very expensive,' said Yu Yu.

'But they are so pretty.' Her voice was wistful, and suddenly in the moonlight her face did not seem ugly to him at all.

'Have you ever had a dog?' he asked.

'Yes. It was a mongrel. Very friendly. Followed me everywhere. She was a lovely dog. Big brown eyes.'

'She died?'

'Yes. You remember that awful winter four years ago? The famine?'

Yu Yu had shivered. He remembered, all right. Thousands had died of starvation.

'I had to eat her,' said Pan Jian.

Yu Yu nodded sympathetically. 'How did she taste?'

'Pretty good,' said Pan Jian. 'But a bit stringy.' Lifting one enormous leg, she pointed down at her fur-edged boot. 'This was her,' she said, stroking the fur. 'I made them so I wouldn't forget her.'

Yu Yu smiled as he recalled the moment. That was always the way with women, he thought. No matter how tough they seemed they were cursed with sentimentality.

Emerging into the entrance hallway, Yu Yu saw the Grey Man and Kysumu walking out into the sunshine. He hurried across to join them. 'Are we going somewhere?' he asked.

'Do you ride?' asked the Grey Man.

'I am a great rider,' said Yu Yu.

Kysumu stepped in. 'Have you ever ridden a horse?'

'No.'

The Grey Man laughed, but there was no mockery in the sound. 'I have a grey mare famous for her gentle and patient nature. She will teach you how to ride.'

'Where are we going?' asked Yu Yu.

'We are hunting demons,' said Kysumu.

'My day is complete,' said Yu Yu Liang.

They rode for some hours. Initially Yu Yu felt comfortable in the deep saddle. It was exhilarating being so high above the ground.

Until, that is, they reached small inclines or depressions where the horses picked up the pace. Yu Yu was bounced painfully around on the saddle. The Grey Man dropped back and dismounted, adjusting Yu Yu's stirrups, which were, he said, a little high. 'It is not easy to find the rhythms of the trot,' he said, 'but it will come.'

It could not come soon enough for Yu Yu. After two hours of riding his buttocks were bruised and painful.

Instead of moving directly to the ruins the Grey Man led them along a ridge of high ground overlooking the Eiden Plain. From here an observer could make out the original lines of Kuan-Hador, depressions in the land, showing where mighty walls once stood. From this height the lines of streets could also be seen, linking the edges of ruined buildings. Further to the east, where the city had once abutted the granite cliffs, there were the remains of two round towers, one seeming to have snapped across the middle, huge stones littering the ground for two hundred feet.

The ruins covered a vast area, vanishing into the distance. 'This was once a *huge* city,' said Kysumu. 'I have never seen the like.'

'It was called Kuan-Hador,' said the Grey Man. 'According to some historians, more than two hundred thousand people lived here.'

'What happened to them?' asked Yu Yu, drawing alongside.

'No-one knows,' the Grey Man told him. 'Many of the ruins show signs of fire damage, so I would guess it fell during a war.'

Kysumu half drew his sword. The steel shone in the sunlight, but not with the glittering blue radiance it had displayed during the demonic attack.

'It looks peaceful now,' said Yu Yu Liang.

The Grey Man heeled the steeldust forward and rode out on to the slope. The horses placed their hoofs warily on the scree-covered trail, moving with care. At the rear Yu Yu was growing hot, and undid the brass clasp of his wolfskin cloak, intending to place it over his saddle pommel. The wolfskin fluttered up, alarming the grey mare, who reared and leapt from the trail directly on to the steep slope below. Immediately she began to slide, dropping her haunches. 'Keep her head up!' yelled the Grey Man.

Yu Yu did his best – and the descent continued at breakneck speed. The mare fought for balance on the sliding scree, righted herself then, still panicked, began to run. Yu Yu clung on in frightened desperation as the descent continued in a cloud of

736

dust. He was almost unseated twice as the mare lurched. Dropping the reins, Yu Yu grabbed the saddle pommel.

The grey mare slowed and stood on trembling legs, steam snorting from her nostrils. Gingerly Yu Yu patted her neck, then gathered up the reins. As the dust cleared he saw they had reached the plain. Turning in the saddle he saw the Grey Man and Kysumu high above, still picking their way down the slope. Yu Yu's heart was thudding in his chest, and he felt light-headed.

Some minutes later the Grey Man rode up. 'You should step down now and let the mare rest,' he said.

Yu Yu nodded, tried to move, and let out a grunt. 'I can't,' he said. 'My legs won't work. They seem to be stuck to saddle.'

'The muscles of your inner thigh have been overstretched,' said the Grey Man. 'It is a common problem for new riders.' He dismounted then moved alongside Yu Yu. 'Just topple and I will catch you.'

With another grunt Yu Yu leant to his left. The Grey Man took hold of his arm and eased him down. Once on flat ground Yu Yu felt a little better, but it was difficult to walk. Rubbing his tortured muscles he grinned up at the Grey Man. 'My cloak frightened her,' he said.

'She is none the worse for it,' said the Grey Man. 'But this must be a lucky day for you. If she had fallen and rolled that pommel would have ruptured your spleen.'

Kysumu rode up, carrying Yu Yu's cloak. 'Did you see my ride?' asked Yu Yu.

The grey-garbed *Rajnee* nodded. 'It was very impressive,' he said, stepping from the saddle. He half drew his sword again, gazing at the blade. It remained silver steel, with not a hint of unearthly radiance.

'Maybe they have gone,' said Yu Yu hopefully.

'We shall see,' answered Kysumu.

Having tethered the horses the Grey Man and Kysumu began to scout the ruins. Yu Yu, his thighs still throbbing, wandered to the remains of what had once been a large house, and sat down upon a ruined wall. It was hot here, and the events of the day – the love-making, the fight, and the wild ride down the slope – had sapped his energy. He yawned and glanced around for the others. The Grey Man was some way to the east, climbing over a pile of ruins. Yu Yu could not see Kysumu.

Removing his sword-belt he lay down in the shade, rolled his cloak for a pillow, and dozed.

He awoke with a start as Kysumu climbed over the low wall.

Yu Yu felt curiously disorientated. Rising to his feet he stared around the ruins. 'Where is he?' he asked.

'The Grey Man has ridden further to the east to scout the woods.'

'No, not him. The man with the golden robe.' Yu Yu walked to the wall and peered out over the plain.

'You were dreaming,' said Kysumu.

'I suppose I must have been,' agreed Yu Yu. 'He was asking me questions and I had no answers.'

Kysumu pulled the stopper from a leather water-bag and drank sparingly. Then he passed it to Yu Yu.

'No demons, then?' said Yu Yu happily.

'No, but there is something here. I can feel it.'

'Something . . . evil?' asked Yu Yu nervously.

'I cannot tell. It is like a whisper in my soul.'

Kysumu sat quietly, eyes closed. Yu Yu drank more water, then glanced up at the fading sun. It would be dusk soon, and he had no wish to be in these ruins once night had fallen.

'Why do you want to find these demons anyway?' he asked the *Rajnee*.

Kysumu's face twitched. His dark eyes opened. 'Do not disturb me when I am meditating,' he said, without anger. 'It is painful.'

Yu Yu apologized, feeling foolish.

'You were not to know,' said Kysumu. 'But to answer your question I do not *want* to find demons. I am *Rajnee*. I swore an oath to stand against evil wherever I found it. This is the way of the *Rajnee*. What we experienced in the camp of Matze Chai was evil. Of that there is no doubt. And that is why my sword brought me here.' He looked closely at Yu Yu. 'It is why you are here too.'

'I don't want to fight evil,' said Yu Yu. 'I want to be rich and happy.'

'I thought you wanted to strut through marketplaces with people pointing at you and saying your name with pride.'

'That too.'

'Such respect has to be earned, Yu Yu. Were you a good ditch-digger?'

'I was a great—'

'Yes, yes,' interrupted Kysumu. 'Now think about the question, and answer it with seriousness.'

'I was good,' said Yu Yu. 'I worked hard. My foreman praised me. When times were tough I would always be employed ahead of other men. I was not lazy.'

'You were respected as a ditch-digger?'

'I was. But I was also paid for being a ditch-digger. Who will pay me for being a hero and fighting demons?'

'The payment is greater than a mountain of gold, Yu Yu. And more beautiful than the richest gems. Yet you cannot touch it, or hold it. It swells the heart and feeds the soul.'

'It doesn't feed the body, though, does it?' said Yu Yu.

'No, it does not,' agreed Kysumu. 'But think back to how you felt when we fought the demons in the camp of Matze Chai, when the sun came up and the mist departed. You recall how your heart swelled with pride, because you had stood your ground and survived?'

'That was good,' agreed Yu Yu. 'Almost as good as making love to Norda.'

Kysumu sighed.

Yu Yu walked to the edge of the broken wall. 'I cannot see the Grey Man. Why did he go off on his own?'

'He is a solitary man,' said Kysumu. 'He works better alone.'

The sun dipped below the western ridges. 'Well, I hope he gets back soon. I do not want to spend a night here.' Yu Yu picked up his cloak and shook it out, then swirled it around his shoulders. 'What is a *pria-shath*?' he asked.

Kysumu's face registered shock. 'Where did you hear that word?'

'The golden man in my dream. He asked if I was a *pria-shath*.'

'And you have never heard it before?'

Yu Yu shrugged. 'I don't think so.'

'What else did he ask?'

'I don't remember. It is all very hazy now.'

'Try to think,' said Kysumu.

Yu Yu sat down and scratched his beard. 'He asked me a lot of questions, and I didn't know the answers to any of them. There was something about the stars, but I don't recall exactly. Oh . . . and he told me his name . . . Qin someone . . .'

'Qin Chong?'

'Yes. How did you know?'

'Later. Keep thinking of the dream.'

'I told him I was a ditch-digger, and I didn't know what he was talking about. Then he said, "You are the *pria-shath*." That was when you woke me. What is a *pria-shath*?'

'A Lantern Bearer,' said Kysumu. 'He was seeking me. That must be why the sword brought me here. I shall contact this spirit myself. It means going into a trance. You must stand guard over me.'

'Guard? What happens if the demons come? You will wake, yes?'

'It depends on how deep the trance. Now do not speak again.' With that Kysumu dipped his head and closed his eyes.

The last of the sunlight blazed up from behind the mountains, then darkness descended upon the Eiden Plain.

Yu Yu sat miserably upon a broken wall, and longed for a return to the lands of the Chiatze, with a good shovel in his hands and a deep ditch waiting to be dug. He wished in that moment he had never found the *Rajnee* sword, and had stayed on to face the wrath of the giant, Shi Da.

'You have brought me nothing but trouble,' he said, glancing down at the sword in his lap.

Then he swore.

A soft blue light began to glow along the length of the blade.

Chapter Six

Leaving the steeldust tethered close to the lake, Waylander moved cautiously among the abandoned wagons, examining the tracks. The wagons had come over the pass and been drawn up here to rest the horses. Some of the footprints in the mud were of small feet, and several had run to the water's edge. A pair of shoes and a yellow shirt had been laid on a rock, indicating that at least one youngster had been preparing for a swim. The ground was too churned for Waylander to be exactly sure of what had happened next, save that the adults had herded together, pulling back towards the lake. Blood splashes to nearby trees and large stains upon the dead grass showed what happened next. They had been slaughtered – killed by huge creatures whose taloned feet left deep impressions in the earth.

The grass itself might have proved a mystery, had Kysumu not already told him of the immense cold that accompanied the coming of the mist. It was frost-damaged by temperatures far below freezing.

Waylander moved warily across the killing ground, examining the hoofprints of riders who had come upon the scene later. Twenty, maybe thirty riders had entered the wood, and left in the same direction. All around the site were the bodies of scores of birds. He found a dead fox in the bushes to the north of the wagons. There were no marks upon it.

Venturing deeper into the woods he followed the trail of dead birds and ice-scorched grass, coming at last to what he believed to be the point of origin. It was a perfect circle, some thirty feet in diameter. Waylander walked around it, picturing as best he could what must have happened here. An icy mist had formed in the spot, then rolled towards the west as if driven by a fierce breeze. Everything in its path had died, including the wagoners and their families.

But where then were the remains of the bodies, the discarded bones, the shredded clothing?

Backtracking towards the wagons, he stopped and examined an area where bushes had been crushed, or torn from the ground. Blood had seeped into the earth. This was where one of the dead horses had been dragged. Waylander found more deep imprints of taloned feet close by. One creature had killed the horse and torn it from its traces, pulling it deeper into the woods. The blood trail stopped suddenly. Waylander squatted down, his fingers tracing the indented earth. The horse had been dragged to this point, and then had lost all bodyweight. Yet it had not been devoured here. Even if the demon had been ten feet tall it could not have consumed an entire horse. And there were no signs that others of the creatures had gathered around to share in a feast. There were no split and discarded bones, no guts or offal.

Waylander rose and re-examined the surrounding area. The tracks of taloned feet just beyond this point were all heading in one direction, towards the lake. The demons, having slaughtered the wagoners and their horses, had returned to where he now stood – and vanished. As incredible as it seemed, there was no other explanation. They had returned from wherever they had come, taking the bodies with them.

The light was beginning to fail. Waylander returned to the steeldust and stepped into the saddle.

What had caused the demons to materialize in the first place? Surely it could not have been chance that they had happened upon a convoy. As far as he knew, there had been two attacks, one upon Matze Chai and his men, the second upon these unfortunate wagoners. Both parties contained large numbers of men and horses.

Or, looked at from another viewpoint, a great deal of food.

Waylander headed the steeldust away from the woods, and began the long ride around the lake. In the years he had dwelt in Kydor there had been no such attacks. Why now?

The sun was setting behind the mountains as he skirted the lake. A feeling of unease grew within him as he headed towards the distant ruins. Lifting his crossbow he slid two bolts into place.

When the sword began to shine Yu Yu Liang had been frightened. Now, an hour later, he would give anything he possessed to be merely frightened. Clouds had obscured the moon and stars and the only light came from the blade in his hands. From beyond the ruined walls, and all around him, he could hear stealthy sounds. Sweat dripped into Yu Yu's eyes as he strained to see beyond the jagged stonework. Twice he had tried to wake Kysumu, the second time shaking him roughly. It was like trying to rouse the dead.

Yu Yu's mouth was dry. He heard a scratching upon the stony ground to his left and swung towards it, raising his sword high. As the light shone he saw a dark shadow disappear behind the rocks. A low growl came from somewhere close by, the sound echoing in the night air. Yu Yu was petrified now. His hands began to tremble, and he was gripping the sword hilt so power-fully that he could hardly feel his fingers. They are just wild dogs, he told himself. Scavenging for scraps. Nothing to fear.

Wild dogs that could make the *Rajnee* blade shine?

With a trembling hand he wiped sweat from his eyes and glanced back towards the horses. They were tethered within the ruin. The grey mare was also shivering with terror, her eyes wide, her ears flat back against her skull. Kysumu's bay gelding was pawing the ground nervously. From here Yu Yu could just make out the line of hills, and the slope he had ridden down only a few hours before. If he was to run to the mare and clamber into the saddle he could make that ride again, and be clear of these ruins within moments.

The thought was like cool water to a man dying of thirst.

He flicked a glance to the seated Kysumu. His face, as ever, was calm. Yu Yu swore loudly, feeling his anger rise. 'Only an idiot goes seeking demons,' he said, his voice sounding shrill.

High above him the clouds parted briefly, and moonlight bathed the ghostly city of Kuan-Hador. In that sudden light Yu Yu saw several dark shapes scatter to hide among the rocks. As he tried to focus upon them the clouds gathered once more. Yu Yu licked his lips and backed across the ruin to stand alongside Kysumu.

'Wake up!' he shouted, nudging the man with his foot.

The moon shone once more. Again the dark shapes scattered.

But they were closer now. Yu Yu rubbed his sweating palms on the sides of his leggings and took up his sword once more, swinging it left and right to loosen the muscles of his shoulders. 'I am Yu Yu Liang!' he shouted. 'I am a great swordsman and I fear nothing!'

'*I can taste your fear,*' came a sibilant voice. Yu Yu leapt backwards, catching his leg on the low wall and falling over it. He scrambled to his feet.

At that moment a huge black form came hurtling towards him, its great jaws open, long fangs snapping for his face. Yu Yu swung the sword. It slashed into the beast's neck, slicing through flesh and bone and exiting in a bloody spray. The creature's dead body cannoned into him, hurling him from his feet. Yu Yu hit the ground hard, rolled to his knees, then surged to his feet. Smoke began to ooze from the carcass alongside him, and a terrible stench filled the air.

Five more of the beasts came padding towards the ruin, clambering over the broken stones, and forming a circle around him. Yu Yu saw that they were hounds, but of a kind he had never seen before. Their shoulders were bunched with muscle, their heads huge. Their eyes were upon him, and he sensed a feral intelligence within their baleful gaze.

To his left the grey mare suddenly reared, dragged her reins loose of the rock and leapt over the wall. The bay gelding followed her lead and the two horses galloped away towards the hills. The huge hounds ignored them.

The voice came again, and he realized it was somehow speaking inside his head. '*Your order has fallen a long way since the Great Battle. My brothers will be pleased to hear of your decline. The mighty* Riaj-nor, *who once were lions, are now frightened monkeys with bright swords.*'

'You show yourself,' said Yu Yu, 'and this monkey will cut your poxy head from your poxy shoulders.'

'*You cannot see me? Better and better.*'

'No, but *I* can see you, creature of darkness,' came the voice of Kysumu. The little *Rajnee* stepped up alongside Yu Yu. 'Cloaked in shadow you stand just out of harm's way.' Yu Yu glanced at Kysumu and saw that he was staring towards the eastern wall. He squinted, trying to make out a figure there, but he could see nothing.

The demon hounds began to move. Kysumu had still not drawn his sword.

744

'I see there are still lions in this world. But lions can also die.'

The hounds rushed in. Kysumu's blade flashed left and right. Two of the beasts fell, writhing upon the stones. A third struck Yu Yu, fangs closing upon his shoulder. With a cry of pain Yu Yu rammed his sword deep into the beast's belly. In its agony the hound opened its jaws, letting out a ferocious howl. Yu Yu tore the blade clear and brought it down upon the hound's skull. The sword clove through bone and wedged itself. Desperately Yu Yu tried to haul it clear. The last two beasts rushed at him. Kysumu's sword sliced through the neck of the first, but the second leapt for Yu Yu's throat.

In that instant a black bolt materialized in the creature's skull, a second lancing through its neck. The hound fell at Yu Yu's feet. Freeing his sword Yu Yu swung round to see the Grey Man upon his steeldust gelding, a small crossbow in his hand.

'Time to go,' said the Grey Man softly, pointing towards the east.

A thick mist was moving across the ancient city, a wall of fog rolling slowly towards them. The Grey Man swung the gelding and galloped away. Yu Yu and Kysumu followed him. The pain in Yu Yu's shoulder was intense now, and he could feel blood flowing down his left arm. Even so he ran swiftly.

Far ahead he saw the Grey Man still riding away. 'A pox on you, bastard!' he shouted.

Glancing back, he saw that the wall of mist was closer, moving faster than he could run. Kysumu also glanced back. Yu Yu staggered and almost fell. Kysumu dropped back to take his arm. 'Just a little further,' said Kysumu.

'We . . . can't . . . outrun it.'

Kysumu said nothing, and the two men moved on in the darkness. Yu Yu heard hoofbeats and looked up to see the Grey Man riding back towards them, leading the grey mare and the bay gelding. Kysumu helped Yu Yu into the saddle, then ran to his own mount.

The mist was very close now, and Yu Yu could hear bestial sounds emanating from it.

The grey mare needed no urging and took off at speed, Yu Yu clinging to the saddle pommel. She was panting heavily by the time they reached the slope, but panic gave her greater strength and she fought her way up the steep incline.

A little ahead the Grey Man swung the steeldust, gazing back down towards the plain.

The mist was swirling at the foot of the slope – but not advancing. Yu Yu swayed in the saddle. He felt Kysumu's hand upon his arm, then passed into darkness.

The tall, blue-garbed surgeon, Mendyr Syn, replaced the poultice on the shoulder of the unconscious man and sighed. 'I have never seen a wound reacting like this,' he told Waylander. 'It is a simple bite, yet the flesh is peeling back rather than sealing itself. It is worse now than when you brought him in.'

'I can see that,' said Waylander. 'What can you do?'

The middle-aged man shrugged, then moved to a wash-basin and began to scrub his hands. 'I have bathed it in *lorassium*, which is usually effective against any infection, but the blood does not clot. In fact, were it not impossible, I would say that whatever is in the wound is eating away at the flesh.'

'He is dying, then?'

'I believe he is. His heart is labouring. He is losing body heat. He will not last the night. By rights he should be dead already, but he is a tough man.' Wiping his hands on a clean towel, he glanced down at the grey-faced Yu Yu Liang. 'You say it was a hound that bit him?'

'Yes.'

'I hope it was killed.'

'It was.'

'I can only assume there was some kind of poison in the bite. Perhaps it had eaten something and some rancid meat was caught between its teeth.' Pinching the bridge of his long nose, the surgeon sat down beside the dying man. 'I can do nothing for him,' he said, exasperation in his voice.

'I'll sit with him,' said Waylander. 'You should get some rest. You look exhausted.'

Mendyr Syn nodded. He glanced up at Waylander. 'I am sorry,' he said. 'You have been most kind to me in my research and my one chance to repay you is ending in failure.'

'You do not need to repay me. You have helped many who needed it.'

As the surgeon rose the door opened and the shaven-headed priestess, Ustarte, entered the room, followed by Kysumu. She dipped her head towards Waylander, and then to Mendyr Syn. 'Please pardon my intrusion,' she said, looking into the surgeon's pale blue eyes. 'I thought I might be of some assistance. However, I do not wish to offend.'

'I am not an arrogant man, Lady,' said Mendyr Syn. 'If there is anything you can do for this man I would be grateful.'

'That is most gracious,' she said, moving past him to the bedside. Her gloved hand lifted the poultice clear and she examined the festering wound. 'I will need a metal dish,' she said, 'and more light.' Mendyr Syn left the room, returning with a copper bowl and a second lantern, which he placed by the bedside. 'It may be too late to save him,' she continued. 'Much will depend on the power of his body and the strength of his spirit.'

Dipping her hand into a pocket at the front of her red silk robe, Ustarte drew forth a gold-rimmed circle of blue crystal some three inches in diameter. 'Bring a chair and sit beside me,' she told Mendyr Syn. The surgeon did so. Ustarte leant across him, placing her hand over the copper bowl. Flames sprang up within it, burning without fuel. Then she handed the blue crystal to Mendyr Syn. 'Look upon the wound through this,' she said.

Mendyr Syn held the crystal to his eye – then jerked back. 'By Missael!' he whispered. 'What magic is this?'

'The worst kind,' she told him. 'He has been bitten by a *Kraloth*. This is the result.'

Waylander stepped forward. 'May I see?' he asked. Mendyr Syn gave him the crystal. He leant over the wound, and lifted the crystal. Scores of luminous maggots were devouring the flesh, their bodies swelling as they fed. Ustarte drew a long, sharp pin from the sleeve of her robe, offering it to Mendyr Syn. 'Use this,' she said. 'Pierce the centre of each maggot then drop them into the fire.' With that she rose from her chair and turned to Waylander. 'The merest scratch inflicted by the teeth or talons of a *Kraloth* is generally fatal. Tiny eggs are deposited in the wound, and these swiftly become the maggots you saw.'

'And the removal of the maggots will give him a chance?' asked Waylander.

'It is a beginning,' she said. 'When the wound is clean I will show Mendyr Syn how to prepare a new poultice. This will destroy any eggs still present in the bite. You should know, however, that it is possible that some of the maggots may have moved deeper within his body, devouring his flesh from within. He may awake, or he may not. If he does he may be blind – or insane.'

'It seems that you know a great deal about the enemy we faced,' he said softly.

'Too much and too little,' she told him. 'We will speak after I have aided Mendyr Syn.'

'We will be outside, upon the terrace,' said Waylander. Bowing to the priestess, he spun on his heel and left the room.

Kysumu followed him and the two men walked along a wide corridor leading to a terraced flower garden overlooking the bay. The night was clear, and the first hint of a new dawn tinged the sky. Waylander wandered to the marble balustrade and stared out over the gleaming water. 'What did you learn from your trance?' he asked Kysumu.

'Nothing,' admitted the *Rajnee*.

'Yet you are convinced a spirit of a dead *Rajnee* came to your friend?'

'Yes.'

'It makes no sense to me,' said Waylander. 'Why would a dead *Rajnee* contact a labourer yet not appear to one of his own?'

'That is a question I have pondered upon,' admitted Kysumu.

Waylander glanced at the little swordsman. 'And this troubles you?'

'Of course. I also feel great shame for putting Yu Yu in such danger.'

'He chose to stand his ground,' said Waylander. 'He could have run.'

'Indeed. It amazes me that he did not.'

'Would you have run?' asked Waylander, quietly.

'No. But, then, I am *Rajnee*.'

'Tonight I saw a frightened man, with a shining sword, battling demons to protect a friend. What would you call him?'

Kysumu smiled, then offered a deep bow. 'I would say he has a *Rajnee* heart,' he said simply.

The two men sat together in silence for another hour, each lost in his own thoughts. Slowly the sky lightened, and birdsong filled the air. Waylander leant back in his seat, weariness heavy upon him. He closed his eyes and dozed. Immediately he fell into dreams, swirling colours that drew him down.

He awoke with a start as the red-robed priestess moved out on to the terrace. 'Is he dead?' he asked.

'No, he will recover, I think.'

'Then you found all the . . . eggs?'

'I had help,' she said, seating herself alongside him. 'His soul was being guarded, and power flowed from within him.'

748

'Qin Chong,' said Kysumu softly.

Ustarte glanced across at him. 'I do not know the name of the spirit. I could not commune with him.'

'It was Qin Chong,' said Kysumu. 'In legend he is named as the first of the *Rajnee*. He appeared to Yu Yu in the ruins. But not to me,' he added wistfully.

'Nor me,' she said. 'What can you tell me of him?'

'Very little. His deeds are lost among fables, oral tales expanded upon or invented. Depending which story you read, he fought dragons, evil gods, giant worms beneath the earth. He had a sword of fire called *Pien'chi*, and he was known as the Potter.'

'Do the legends say how he died?'

'Yes, in a dozen different ways, by fire, by sword, dragged down into the sea. One story has him walking down into the underworld to rescue his love, and never returning. Another even has him sprouting wings and soaring to the heavens. One has the gods appearing at his death and turning him into a mountain to watch over his people.'

Ustarte fell silent. 'Perhaps Yu Yu can tell us more when he wakes.'

'I would like to hear more of these *Kraloth*,' said Waylander. 'What are they?'

'They are meld-hounds,' Ustarte told him. 'Artificial creations born of dark magic. They are very powerful, and ordinary weapons cannot harm them ...' she looked into his eyes and gave a wan smile '. . . unless they pierce the skull or the upper neck. As you know, their bite brings a painful death. They are led by a *Bezha* – a Houndmaster.'

'I caught a glimpse of him,' said Kysumu, 'but only the eyes.'

'He would have been wearing the robe of night,' Ustarte told him. 'It is true-black and reflects no light. The eye, therefore, cannot see it.'

'Why are they here?' asked Waylander.

'They are the advance guard of two terrible enemies. My followers and I had hoped to prevent their coming. We failed.'

'What enemies?' put in Kysumu.

'Anharat's demons – and the sorcerers of Kuan-Hador.'

'I have read the legends of Anharat,' said Kysumu. 'The Lord of Demons. I recall he was cast from the world after a war. I believe he had a brother who aided humankind.'

'The brother was Emsharas,' said Ustarte, 'and it is true that he sided with humanity. Great were the heroes who fought against

Anharat. Mighty men, men of principle and courage. These were the men of Kuan-Hador.'

'I do not understand,' put in Kysumu. 'If these men were heroes, why do we fear their return?'

'Man never learns lessons from the past,' she said. 'It is his curse. My people and I have been trying to discover some evidence of the Great War. What we have found is that there was not one war but two. The first – let us call it the Demon War – saw great horror and devastation. Only when Emsharas aided the humans did the tide begin to turn. But that aid carried within it the seeds of Kuan-Hador's downfall. In order to defeat the enemy the rebel demon lord, Emsharas, gave the lords of Kuan-Hador instruction in the most arcane secrets of meld-magic. Warriors were enhanced, blended with the power of beasts; panthers, lions, wolves and bears. And they won. Anharat's demon legions were expelled from the world. Kuan-Hador was mankind's saviour.'

'How then did they become evil?' asked Kysumu.

'By taking one small step at a time towards the dark,' she answered. 'For a little while the world knew peace and tranquillity, under the city's benevolent rule. The people of Kuan-Hador were proud of what they had achieved. Yet it had cost them greatly. They asked other nations to help bear that cost, and huge amounts of gold and silver were despatched to the city. The following year they asked for more. Several nations refused. The proud lords of Kuan-Hador decided that this refusal was an affront to the world's saviours, and sent their armies to plunder those nations. Kuan-Hador had moved from benevolent rule to tyranny. They had saved mankind, therefore – so they believed – they had earned the right to rule. Nations that rose against them were considered treacherous, and were crushed mercilessly by the *Kriaz-nor*, the meld-legions. This was the beginning of the second war – what is now termed the Great War. At first it was man against man. Kuan-Hador was powerful, yet it was but a city state and its resources were finite. By this time Emsharas was gone from the world, but his descendants aided the rebels. Slowly they began to force back the *Kriaz-nor* legions. In desperation the rulers of Kuan-Hador allied themselves with Anharat, opening portals to allow his demon warriors to return to the world.' She fell silent and stood staring out over the bay.

'Yet they were still defeated,' said Kysumu.

'Yes, they were,' she said softly. 'The rebels created their own

750

legions – the *Riaj-nor*, men of noble hearts and great courage, wielding weapons of power. The *Rajnee* are the last embers of that fine order, and it seems, Kysumu, that of them all only you have been drawn here. Where once were legions there is now only a single warrior and a wounded labourer.' She sighed, then continued her tale. 'The Great War ended here, the survivors of Kuan-Hador retreating through a portal to another world. The city was destroyed by fire, and a sorcerer – or, perhaps, a group of sorcerers – laid powerful spells upon the portal, sealing it against the return of the enemy. These spells have endured the passing of the centuries. Now they are fading. The gateway will soon open fully, allowing legions of *Kriaz-nor* to invade this land. At the moment it is merely flickering, and only a few can cross. The sorcerers who once protected it are long dead, as are the original *Riaj-nor*. There is now no power in this world to defeat them if they come in force, which is why I had hoped to replicate the original spell and cast it once more. But there are no clues to be found. There are riddles, verses and garbled legends, none of which is helpful. My last hope now rests with Yu Yu and the spirit of Qin Chong.' She swung to Kysumu. 'It seems that the *Rajnee* swords retain their magic. Why, then, are more of your comrades not here to fight?'

'Few now hold fully to the old ways,' he said, sadly. 'Most *Rajnee* are now merely bodyguards, seeking to earn riches. They will not heed the call of the swords, nor journey to foreign lands.'

'And what of you, Grey Man?' she asked. 'Will you fight the demon lords?'

'Why should I?' he countered, his voice edged with bitterness. 'It is just another war – just another group of greedy men seeking to take what does not belong to them. And they will hold it for just so long as they are strong enough to resist the next group of greedy men who desire to take it from them.'

'This one is different,' she said softly. 'If they win, the world will know the nature of true terror. Children dragged from their mothers' arms to be melded into beasts, or have their organs removed in order to prolong the lives of the rulers. Thousands butchered in the name of arcane science. Magic of the most horrific kind will become commonplace.'

When Waylander spoke his voice was cold. 'During the Vagrian Wars babes were torn from their mothers' arms to have their heads smashed against walls of stone. Children were slaughtered and men slain in their thousands. Women were raped and mutilated. This was done by men. A grieving mother would not care whether her babe was destroyed by magic or by might. No, I have had my fill of wars, Lady.'

'Then think of it as a battle against evil,' she said.

'Look at me,' he said. 'Do I have a shining sword? You know my life, Lady. Does it seem to you that I have been a warrior of the light?'

'No,' she told him, 'you have also walked the path of evil, which gives you greater understanding of its nature. Yet you overcame it. You fought the darkness, and gave the Drenai people hope by recovering the Armour of Bronze. Now a greater evil looms.'

'How is it that you know so much about this evil?' he asked her.

'Because I was born of it,' she said. Her gloved hands moved to her high collar, pulling loose the hooks that held it. With a sudden wrench she opened the silken robe, letting it drop to the terrace. The morning sunlight shone upon her slim body, highlighting the striped fur of gold and black that covered her skin. Both men stood very still as she peeled off one of her gloves and raised the hand high. The fur ended at her wrists, but her fingers seemed unnatural and oddly shortened. She flexed the hand and long silver claws emerged from sheaths at her fingertips. 'I am a Joining, Grey Man. A failed experiment. It was intended that I should be a new form of *Kraloth* – a killing machine of great strength and speed. Instead the magic, which created this monstrosity of a body, also enhanced my mind. You are looking upon the future of mankind. Do you find it beautiful?'

Waylander said nothing, for there was nothing to say. Her face was human, and indescribably beautiful, but her body was feline, the joints crooked.

Kysumu stepped up behind the naked priestess, and raised her robe from the floor. Ustarte smiled her thanks and drew the garment around her. 'My followers and I came through the gateway. Six were killed in the attempt. We came to save this world. Will you help us?'

'I am not a general, Lady. I am an assassin. I have no armies. You want me to ride out alone against a horde of demons? For what? Honour and a swift death?'

'You would not be alone,' said Kysumu softly.

'I am always alone,' said Waylander. With that he strolled from the terrace.

*

He stared hard at the armour. It shone brightly in the lantern-light as if crafted from moonlight. The winged helm was gleaming, and he could see his reflection in the closed visor. The chainmail attached to the nape was impossibly delicate, light glittering from it as if from a hundred diamonds. The cuirass was beautifully fashioned, and engraved with runes he could not read.

'It would look fine upon you, sir,' said the armourer, his voice echoing in the high, domed hall.

'I do not want it,' said Waylander, swinging away and walking down a long, crooked corridor. He turned left then right, pushing open a door and stepping into another hall.

'Try it on,' said the armourer, removing the bright helm from its place on the armour tree and offering it to him.

Waylander did not reply. Angry now, he turned on his heel, moved back through the doorway and stood in the shadowed corridor. Then he walked on. Everywhere there were turnings and soon he lost all sense of direction. He came upon a set of stairs, and climbed and climbed. At the top, exhausted, he sat down. A doorway faced him, but he was reluctant to enter. He knew instinctively what he would find. And yet there was nowhere else to go. With a deep sigh he pushed open the door and gazed upon the armour tree.

'Why do you not want it?' asked the armourer.

'Because I am not worthy to wear it,' he told the man.

'No-one is,' said the armourer.

The scene faded, and Waylander found himself seated beside a fast-flowing stream. The sky was bright and blue, the water fresh and cool. Cupping his hands he drank from the stream then sat back, leaning his shoulders against the trunk of a weeping willow, whose branches trailed all around him. It was peaceful here, and he wished he could stay for ever.

'Evil carries a price,' said a voice.

He glanced to his right. Just beyond the trailing branches stood a cold-eyed man. There was blood upon his face and his hands. He knelt by the stream to wash. But instead of the blood being cleansed the entire stream turned crimson, and began to bubble and steam. The willow branches darkened, the leaves falling away. The tree groaned. Waylander moved away from it, and the bark split, disgorging hordes of insects, which crawled over the dead wood.

'Why are you doing this?' Waylander asked the man.

'It is my nature,' he answered.

'Evil carries a price,' said Waylander, stepping forward. A knife appeared in his hand and he sliced it through the man's throat in one smooth motion. Blood sprayed from the wound, and the man fell back. The body disappeared. Waylander stood very still. His hands were drenched in blood. He moved to the stream to wash them, and the stream turned crimson and began to bubble and hiss.

'Why are you doing this?' asked a voice.

Surprised, Waylander turned, and saw a man beside the dying willow.

'It is my nature,' he told him – as the gleaming knife appeared in the newcomer's hand . . .

He awoke with a start. Pushing himself from the chair he walked out into the sunlight. He had slept for less than two hours, and he felt disoriented. Strolling down to the beach he found Omri waiting there, fresh white towels folded nearby, a pitcher of cool water and a goblet ready on the small wooden table.

'You look dreadful, sir,' said the white-haired servant. 'Perhaps you should forgo your swim and have some breakfast.'

Waylander stripped off his clothing. Wading into the cool water he flung himself forward and began to swim. His head cleared, but he couldn't shake himself from the mood the dreams had left. Turning, he headed back for the beach with long, easy strokes, then walked up to the waterfall and cleansed the salt and sand from his body.

Omri handed him a towel. 'I brought fresh clothes while you were swimming, sir,' he said.

Waylander towelled himself dry, then pulled on a shirt of soft white silk, and a pair of thin leather leggings. 'Thank you, my friend,' he said. Omri smiled, then poured a goblet of water, which Waylander drank.

Norda came running down the steps, curtsying to the Grey Man. 'There is a large party of horsemen coming up the hill, sir,' she said. 'There are knights and lancers and bowmen. Lord Aric is at the head. Emrin thinks the Duke is riding with them.'

'Thank you, Norda,' said Omri. 'We shall be there presently.'

The girl curtsied once more, then ran back up the steps. Omri glanced at his employer. 'Are we in some trouble, sir?' he enquired.

'Let us find out,' said Waylander, tugging on his boots.

'Might I suggest a shave first, sir?' offered Omri.

Waylander rubbed a hand over the black and silver bristles on his chin. 'Doesn't pay to keep a duke waiting,' he said, with a smile.

The two men strolled up the terrace steps side by side. 'Mendyr Syn said to tell you that the Chiatze warrior is sleeping more easily now. His heartbeat has steadied, and the wound is healing.'

'Good. He is a brave man.'

'Might I enquire how he came by the wound?' asked Omri.

Waylander glanced at the man, and saw the fear in his eyes. 'He was bitten by a large hound.'

'I see. The servants are all talking about a massacre in the woods by the lake. Apparently the Duke came upon the scene, and is now leading a company of soldiers to investigate.'

'Is that all the servants are saying?' asked Waylander, as they mounted the steps.

'No, sir. They are saying that there are demons abroad in the land. Is it true?'

'Yes,' said Waylander. 'It is true.'

Omri held his hand over his chest, made the Sign of the Protective Horn, and asked no more questions.

'Have you ever met the Duke?' Waylander asked Omri.

'Yes, sir. Three times.'

'Tell me of him.'

'He is a powerful man, both in mind and in body. He is a good ruler, fair and not capricious. He was originally of House Kilraith, but once he became Duke he renounced, as is the custom, all claims to leadership of Kilraith, the title passing to Aric. He is married to a Drenai princess and has several children, but only one son. The marriage is said to be happy.'

'A long time since I heard the words *Drenai princess*,' said Waylander. 'There are no kings in Drenan now.'

'No, sir, not now,' agreed Omri. 'The Duke's wife, Aldania, was the sister of King Niallad. He was murdered by a foul assassin just before the Vagrian War. After the war, so the story goes, the despot Karnak refused to allow her to come home. He forfeited all her estates and monies and issued a decree of banishment. So she married Elphons and came to Kydor.'

They reached the entrance hall. Beyond the double doors, Waylander could see horses and men waiting in the sunshine. Ordering Omri to organize refreshments for the riders, he walked into the long reception room. Lord Aric was there, wearing breastplate and helm. The black-bearded magicker Eldicar Manushan was standing by the far wall, his blond page beside him. A youth, dressed in dark riding clothes, and wearing a chainmail shoulder-guard, was standing close by. His face was familiar, thought Waylander. He felt a small knot of tension form in his belly as he realized why. This was the grandson of Orien, and the nephew of Niallad, the Drenai king. For a moment only, Waylander saw again the tortured features of the dying monarch. Pushing the memory away he focused on the heavy-set man sprawled in the wide leather chair. The Duke was powerfully built, with great breadth of shoulder and massive forearms. He glanced up at Waylander, his cold eyes locking to the Grey Man's dark gaze.

Waylander offered the seated man a bow. 'Good morning, my lord, and welcome to my home.'

The Duke nodded curtly, and beckoned Waylander to the seat opposite.

'The day before yesterday,' said the Duke, 'some forty wagoners and their families were murdered less than two hours' ride from here.'

'I know,' said Waylander. 'I rode over the ground late yesterday.'

'Then you will also know that the killers were . . . shall we say? . . . not of this world?'

Waylander nodded. 'They were demons. There were some thirty of them. They move upright and the distance between the tracks suggests that the smallest is around eight feet tall.'

'It is my intention to find their lair and destroy them,' said the Duke.

'You will not find it, my lord.'

'And why is that?'

'I followed the tracks. The demons appeared in a circle some two hundred paces from the wagons. They disappeared in another circle, taking the bodies with them.'

'Ah,' said Eldicar Manushan, stepping forward, 'a Third Level manifestation, then. A powerful spell must have been cast in that area.'

'You have come across such . . . spells before?' asked the Duke.

'Sadly, yes, sire. They are known as portal-spells.'

'Why Third Level?' asked Waylander.

Eldicar Manushan turned towards him. 'According to the Ancients' texts, there are three levels of gateway magic. The Third

756

Level opens on to the world of Anharat and his demons, but summons only mindless blood-feeders, such as the beast described by our host. The Second Level allows, it is said, the summoning of powerful individual demons, who can be directed against specific enemies.'

'And the First Level?' asked the Duke.

'A First Level spell would summon one of Anharat's companion demons – or even Anharat himself.'

'I understand little of magic and its uses,' snapped the Duke. 'It has always sounded like babble to me. But a Third Level spell is what brought these demons, yes?'

'Yes, sire.'

'And how was this done?'

Eldicar Manushan spread his hands. 'Once again, sire, we have only the words of the Ancients, as stored in sacred text. Many thousands of years ago man and demon co-existed on this world. The demons followed a great sorcerer god called Anharat. There was a war, which Anharat lost. He and all his followers were expelled from the earth, banished to another dimension. This very land, which now prospers under your rule, was instrumental in defeating Anharat. It was then called Kuan-Hador, and its people were versed in great magic. With the banishing of Anharat and his legions Kuan-Hador began an age of great enlightenment. However, Anharat still had followers among the more savage tribes, and these banded together to destroy Kuan-Hador, butchering its people and plunging the world into a new age of darkness and desolation.'

'Yes, yes,' said the Duke, 'I have always liked stories, but I would appreciate it if you would leap across the centuries and tell me about the demons who attacked the wagoners.'

'Of course, sire. My apologies,' said Eldicar Manushan. 'It is my belief that one of the spells used in the original battle against Kuan-Hador has been – somehow – reactivated, opening a Third Level portal. It may be that it was cast again by a sorcerer, or merely recharged by a natural event, lightning, for example, striking an altar stone where the spell was first spoken.'

'Can you reverse this spell?' asked the Duke.

'If we can find the source of it, my lord, I believe that I can.'

The Duke returned his attention to Waylander. 'I am told that a party of your friends was attacked recently by these demons, but that two of the party had magical blades which held the beasts at bay. Is this true?'

'That is my understanding,' said Waylander.

'I would like to see these men.'

'One is severely wounded, my lord,' Waylander told him. 'I will send for the other.' A servant was despatched, and some minutes later Kysumu entered the room. He bowed low to the Duke, and also to Waylander, then stood silently, his face impassive.

'It would be a great help, my lord,' said Eldicar Manushan, 'were I able to examine the sword. I could then, perhaps, identify which spells were cast upon the blade.'

'Give him your sword,' ordered the Duke.

'No man touches a *Rajnee* blade,' said Kysumu softly, 'save the one for whom it was forged.'

'Yes, yes,' said the Duke, 'I am also a great believer in tradition. But these are extraordinary circumstances. Hand it over.'

'I cannot,' said Kysumu.

'This is senseless,' said the Duke, without raising his voice. 'I can call fifty men to this room. Then they will take the sword from you.'

'Many will die,' said Kysumu calmly.

'You threaten me?' said the Duke, leaning forward in his chair.

Waylander rose and moved to stand before Kysumu. 'I have always found,' he said, 'in circumstances like these, that there is a subtle difference between a threat and a promise. I have read of these *Rajnee* blades. They are linked to the warriors who hold them. When a warrior dies his blade shatters and turns black. Perhaps the same would happen if he allowed Eldicar Manushan to take it from him. If that proves to be the case then we will have lost one of only two weapons proved to be of use against the demons.'

The Duke rose from his chair and stepped close to the small swordsman. 'Do you believe that your blade would become useless if handled by another?'

'It is more than belief,' said Kysumu. 'It is knowledge. I have seen it. Three years ago a *Rajnee* surrendered to an opponent and offered his sword. The blade splintered as soon as the opponent took hold of the hilt.'

'If this is true,' said Lord Aric suddenly, 'how is it that your companion carries such a blade? He is not *Rajnee*, nor was the blade fashioned for him.'

'The blade chose him,' said Kysumu.

Aric laughed. 'Then it must be a more fickle blade. Let us send for that and Eldicar Manushan can examine it.'

'No,' said Kysumu. 'The sword now belongs to Yu Yu Liang. He is my pupil, and, since he is still unconscious, I speak for him. The blade will not be examined or touched by anyone.'

'This is getting us nowhere,' said the Duke. 'I have no wish to use force here.' He looked at Kysumu. 'And I certainly have no desire to bring about either the death of a brave man or the destruction of such a powerful weapon. We are riding out to locate the source of the demon magic. Will you come with us, and aid us with your sword?'

'Of course.'

The Duke turned to Waylander. 'I would be obliged if you would offer hospitality to my son, Niallad, and his guards.'

The sound of the name struck Waylander like a dagger blade, but his face remained calm, and he bowed. 'It will be my pleasure, my lord.'

'But, Father, I want to ride with you,' said the youth.

'It would be folly to risk both myself and my heir,' said the Duke softly. 'We do not yet know the nature of the enemy. No, my son, you will remain here. Gaspir and Naren will stay with you. You will be safe.' The youth bowed, his expression downcast.

Eldicar Manushan approached him. 'Perhaps you would be kind enough to look after my page, Beric,' he asked. 'He is a good boy, but he becomes nervous when we are apart.'

Niallad looked down at the golden-haired page, and smiled ruefully. 'Do you swim, Beric?' he asked.

'No, sir,' answered the boy. 'But I like to sit by the water.'

'Then we will go to the beach while our elders and betters perform their manly tasks.' The sarcasm hung heavily in the air, and Waylander saw the Duke flush with embarrassment.

'Time to be on our way,' said the Duke.

As the men filed from the room Eldicar Manushan paused before Waylander.

'The *Rajnee* was bitten, I understand. How is the wound?'

'Healing.'

'Strange. Such wounds are usually fatal. You must have a highly skilled surgeon.'

'I do. He found translucent worms in the bite. Most unusual.'

'A clever man. Is he a mystic also?'

'I do not believe that he is. He used an ancient artefact, a blue crystal. With this he could see the infestation.'

'Ah! I have heard of such . . . artefacts. Very rare.'

'So I understand.'

Eldicar Manushan stood silently for a moment. 'Lord Aric informs me that there is a priestess currently in residence at the palace. She is said to have the gift of far-sight. I would very much like to meet her.'

'Sadly she left yesterday,' said Waylander. 'I believe she is returning to Chiatze lands.'

'How disappointing.'

'Are there sharks, Uncle?' asked the blond page, tugging at Eldicar Manushan's robe. Waylander gazed down at the boy's upturned face, and saw the love and trust the child had for the magicker.

Eldicar Manushan knelt by the boy. 'Sharks, Beric?'

'In the bay. Niallad is planning to swim.'

'No, there are no sharks.' The boy smiled happily and Eldicar drew him into a brief hug.

'I already told him that,' said Niallad, moving across the room. 'They prefer cooler, deeper water.'

Two soldiers entered the room, tough men with grim faces. Niallad grinned as he saw them. 'These are my bodyguards, Gaspir and Naren,' he said. 'There are no finer fighters in all of Kydor.'

'Is your life in danger?' asked Waylander.

'Always,' said Niallad. 'It is the curse of my family to be hunted by assassins. My uncle was the king of the Drenai. Did you know that?' Waylander nodded. 'He was killed by a cowardly traitor,' continued the young man. 'Shot through the back while he was praying.'

'Praying can be a perilous business,' said Eldicar Manushan.

The youth looked at him quizzically. 'Murder should not be the subject of jests, sir,' he said.

'I was not jesting, young man,' answered Eldicar Manushan. With a bow he turned and left the room.

Niallad watched him go. 'I will not be assassinated,' he told Waylander. 'Gaspir and Naren will see to that.'

'We will indeed, young sir,' said Gaspir, the taller of the men. He turned to Waylander. 'Which is the safest beach?' he asked.

'I shall have my manservant, Omri, show you,' said Waylander. 'And I will have fresh towels and cool drinks served there.'

'Most kind,' said Gaspir.

'When will Uncle Eldicar be back?' asked the blond page.

'I do not know, boy,' Waylander told him, 'but it might be after dark.'

'Where shall I stay? I do not like the dark.'

'I shall have a room prepared for you that shines with light, and someone to sit with you until he returns.'

'Could it be Keeva?' asked the youngster. 'I like her.'

'It shall be Keeva,' Waylander promised.

Chapter Seven

Waylander watched the Duke and his soldiers ride away from the palace, then moved back out on to the terrace. The sunshine was bright against his tired eyes, but the breeze from the bay felt good upon his face. Omri joined him there and Waylander gave him various instructions. The white-haired manservant bowed and walked away.

Waylander continued down the steps, past the waterfall, across the rock garden and on to his spartan accommodation. The door was open. He moved to the porch then closed his eyes. He felt calm, and sensed no danger. Pushing the door further open, he stepped inside. The priestess Ustarte was seated by the hearth, her gloved hands folded on her lap, her high-collared red silk robe buttoned to the chin. She rose as he entered. 'I am sorry for the impertinence of entering your home-place,' she said, bowing her head.

'You are welcome here, Lady.'

'Why did you tell Eldicar Manushan that I had left?'

'You know why.'

'Yes,' she admitted. 'But how did you know he was the enemy?'

Moving past her, he poured himself a goblet of water. 'Tell me of him,' he said, ignoring her question.

'I do not know him, though I know his masters. He is an *Ipsissimus* – a sorcerer of great power. I have felt the emanations of his power for some time now. He has crossed the gateway for two reasons. First, in order to establish allies in this world, and, second, to break the Great Spell, which prevents their armies from crossing over.'

'Is he a king of some kind?'

'No, merely a servant of the Council of Seven. Believe me, that makes him more powerful than many kings of your world. Are you aware that he knew you were lying?'

'Of course.'

'Then why did you do it?'

Waylander ignored the question. 'Are you strong enough to withstand his power?'

'No. Not directly.'

'Then you and your companions should leave the palace. Find somewhere to hide – or return whence you came.'

'I cannot leave now.'

Waylander lifted the water jug and left the building, hurling the stale liquid to the flower garden and refilling the jug from the waterfall. Returning to the main room, he offered the priestess a drink. She shook her head and he filled his own goblet. 'What is it that Eldicar Manushan can offer to potential allies here?' he asked.

'Have you looked closely at Aric?'

'He seems fitter and leaner.'

'Younger?'

'I see,' said Waylander. 'Is it real, or an illusion?'

'It is real, Grey Man. Some servant of Aric's will have died perhaps to supply it, but it is real. The Seven long ago mastered the art of enhancement and regeneration, just as they mastered the vileness of Joining.'

'If I killed this magicker, would it aid you in keeping the gateway sealed?'

'Perhaps. But you cannot kill him.'

'There is no-one I cannot kill, Lady. That is my curse.'

'I know of your talent, Grey Man. But I mean what I say: Eldicar Manushan cannot be killed. You could put a bolt through his heart, or cut off his head and he would not die. Slice off his arm and another will grow. The Seven and their servants are immortal and virtually invulnerable.'

'Virtually?'

'The use of spells is dangerous. The summoning of Third Level demons carries few perils. Once made flesh they exist merely to feed. But the summoning of specific demons of the First and Second Levels carries great danger. Such a demon must have a death. If it cannot succeed against the intended victim, then it will turn against the sorcerer who summoned it. If Eldicar Manushan was to summon a First Level demon, and that demon was thwarted, then Eldicar would be dragged back into the realm of Anharat and torn to pieces.'

'That seems a good weakness to exploit,' said Waylander.

'It would be. But that is why Eldicar Manushan has the boy with him. He is his *loachai*, his familiar. Eldicar Manushan casts his spells *through* the child. If anything were to go wrong the child would be slain.'

Waylander swore softly. Crossing the room, he sat down in the hide chair beside the hearth. Weariness lay heavy upon him. Ustarte sat opposite him.

'Can he read minds as well as you?' he asked her.

'I do not believe so.'

'Yet he knew I was lying about your departure?'

She nodded. 'He would have sensed it. As I said, he is an *Ipsissimus* and his power is very great. But it is finite. He can summon demons, create illusions, enhance youth and strength. He can regenerate himself if wounded.' She looked at him closely. 'I sense your confusion,' she said softly. 'What is it?'

'The boy,' said Waylander. 'He obviously loves his uncle. In turn Eldicar Manushan seems fond of him. It is hard to believe the boy is merely a tool.'

'And because of this you doubt whether the *Ipsissimus* can be truly evil? I do understand that, Grey Man. You humans are wonderful creatures. You can show compassion and love that is awe-inspiring, and hatred of such power and vileness it could darken the sun itself. What you find hard to accept is that such extremes are in each and every one of you. You gaze upon the works of evil men and you tell yourselves that they *must* be monsters, inhuman and different. Because to accept that they are just like you would threaten the foundations of your existence. Can you not see that you are an example of this, Grey Man? In your hatred and your lust for vengeance you became what you hunted; savage and uncaring, callous and indifferent to suffering. How much further might you have travelled had you not met the priest Dardalion, and been touched by his purity of soul? Eldicar Manushan is not a monster. He is a man. He can laugh and know joy. He can hug a child and feel the warmth of human love. And he can order the death of thousands without regret. He can torture and kill, and rape and maim. It will not touch him.

'Yes, he may love the boy, but he loves power more. The spells of Eldicar Manushan are great, but when cast through a *loachai* they become enhanced. The boy is a vessel, a source of untapped spiritual energy.'

'You are sure of this?'

'I sense both their energies, the *Ipsissimus* and the *loachai*. When joined together they are terrifyingly strong.' She rose from the chair. 'And now you must ride with the Duke, Grey Man,' she said.

'I think I will stay here and sleep for a while,' he told her. 'There must be a hundred men with the Duke. He has no need of me.'

'No, but Kysumu has. Eldicar Manushan will fear the shining sword. He will see the *Rajnee* dead if he can. Kysumu needs you, Waylander.'

'This is not my fight,' he said, though he knew, even as he spoke, that he could not leave Kysumu to his fate.

'Yes, it is, Waylander. It always was,' she said, moving away towards the door.

'What does that mean?' he asked her.

'This is a time for heroes,' she said softly. 'Even shadow warriors once touched by evil.'

He watched her cross the threshold and draw the door closed behind her. With a soft curse he pushed himself to his feet and walked through to his armoury. From a chest at the rear of the room he removed a heavy linen sack. Placing it on a worktop he opened it, drawing forth a black leather shoulder-guard, reinforced by black mail rings. Returning to the chest he lifted two other wrapped items, followed by a sword-belt hung with two empty scabbards. Carefully he unwrapped the shortswords. Each had a round fist-guard of black iron beneath claw-shaped dark quillons. The bright blades gleamed with oil. Taking up a soft cloth he wiped them clean, careful to avoid the razor-sharp edges. Buckling the sword-belt to his lean waist he slipped the swords into the scabbards.

His baldric, hung with throwing knives, was looped over the back of a chair. Fetching it, he removed each of the six diamond-shaped blades and honed them before slipping them back into place. Donning the chainmail shoulder-guard, he slipped the baldric over his head. Lastly he took up his small, double-winged crossbow and a quiver of twenty bolts.

He strode from his rooms, climbing the steps to the upper buildings and the stable.

Will you ever learn? he asked himself.

765

Yu Yu Liang awoke to see sunshine streaming through a high-arched window. It was bright upon the white coverlet of his bed. He sighed, and felt a pang of deep regret. His shoulder was painful, though he could not remember why, but the sharpness of it meant he was back in the world of the flesh. Sadness filled his mind, as the feel of the sun and the whisper of a sea breeze leeched away the exquisite harmony he had come to value so highly. A figure loomed over him, the face thin and ascetic, the nose long and curved. 'How are you feeling?' asked the man. The noise was yet another intrusion, and Yu Yu felt the joy of the past years with Qin Chong slipping away. The question was asked again.

'I am flesh again,' responded Yu Yu. 'It saddens me.'

'Flesh? I was talking about your wound, young man.'

'My wound?'

'In your shoulder. You were bitten. The Gentleman and your Chiatze companion brought you. You have been injured, young man. You have been unconscious for around fourteen hours.'

'Hours?' Yu Yu closed his eyes. It was incomprehensible. On his journeys he had seen the birth of worlds, and the fall of stars; great empires rising from the mists of savagery before being swallowed by the oceans. He became aware of a dull, throbbing pain in his left shoulder. 'Why am I back?' he asked.

The man looked concerned. 'You were bitten last night by a demon beast,' he said slowly. 'But the wound is clean now. You are recovering well. I am Mendyr Syn, the surgeon. And you are resting in the palace of Dakeyras, the Gentleman.'

Bitten last night.

Yu Yu groaned as he struggled to sit. Instantly Mendyr Syn's hands came down on his good shoulder. 'Lie still. You will break the stitches.'

'No. I must sit up,' muttered Yu Yu.

Mendyr Syn transferred his grip to Yu Yu's right biceps, assisting him. 'This is not wise, young man. You are very weak.' The surgeon adjusted the pillows behind the wounded man and Yu Yu sagged back to them.

'Where is Kysumu?'

'He has gone with the Duke and his men. He will be back shortly, I don't doubt. How does the wound feel?'

'Painful.'

Mendyr Syn filled a goblet with cool water and held it to Yu

Yu's lips. It tasted divine as it slipped down his parched throat. Resting his head back against the pillow he closed his eyes once more and drifted into a dreamless sleep. When he awoke the sunshine no longer lit the bed, but was shining brightly against the far wall.

The room was empty and Yu Yu was thirsty again. Pushing back the covers, he tried to swing his legs from the bed.

'Stay where you are, yellow man,' said a voice. 'You are in no condition to get up.'

Another figure loomed over him. He looked up into the man's face, noting the swollen nose and the two discoloured eyes. It was the golden-haired guard sergeant who had accosted him so many years ago. It was all so confusing. 'What is it you need?' asked the man.

'Some water,' said Yu Yu. The sergeant filled a goblet and sat on the bed, offering it to Yu Yu, who took it with his right hand and drank deeply. 'Thank you.' He struggled to think. So many scenes were whirling inside his head – like a bag of pearls without a string. Closing his eyes he began slowly and carefully to thread the thoughts. He had left the lands of the Chiatze after thrashing Shi Da. Then he had met the robbers, and later Kysumu. Together they had come . . . For a moment he drifted. Then he recalled the palace and the mysterious Grey Man. His eyes flared open. 'Where is my sword?'

'You won't need a sword for a while,' said the sergeant. 'But it is there by the wall.'

'Pass it to me, please.'

'Of course.'

'Touch only scabbard,' warned Yu Yu. The guard hefted the weapon and laid it by Yu Yu's side. Then he returned to his chair by the door. 'Why are you here?' asked Yu Yu.

'The Gentleman ordered me to guard you.' He smiled. 'He obviously thinks you have enemies.'

'Are you one of them?'

The man sighed. 'Yes, I am. I'll be honest. I don't like you, yellow man. But I take my pay from the Gentleman. He treats me well, and in return I obey his orders. Fully. I don't much care if you live or die, but not one of your – other – enemies will reach you while I live.'

Yu Yu smiled. 'May you live long,' he said.

'Is it true you were attacked by demon hounds?'

The jagged memories filtered back, the ruins and the moonlight, the black hounds moving stealthily through the shadows. 'Yes, true.'

'What were they like?'

'Make wolves look like piglets,' answered Yu Yu, with an involuntary shudder.

'You were frightened?'

'Big fear. How is your nose?'

'Painful.' The man shrugged. 'I should have remembered my father's advice: if you're going to fight then fight. Don't talk. You hit hard, yellow man.'

'My name is Yu Yu.'

'I am Emrin.'

'Pleased for to meet with you,' said Yu Yu.

'Don't be too pleased. It is my intention to pay you back just as soon as you are fit and strong.'

Yu Yu smiled, then slept again. When he awoke there was no sunlight. Emrin had lit a lantern and hung it by the far wall. The soldier was dozing in his chair. Yu Yu was hungry and looked around the room for something to eat. There was nothing. Carefully he swung his legs over the side of the bed and, using his scabbarded sword as a support, pushed himself to his feet. His legs were a little unsteady.

Emrin woke. 'What do you think you are doing?' he asked.

'I am going to find food,' said Yu Yu.

'The kitchen is two floors down. You'd never make it. Wait for a while. One of the girls will be bringing supper in an hour or so.'

'I don't like lying here,' said Yu Yu. 'I don't like being . . . weak.' Suddenly his legs gave way and he slumped back down to the bed. He swore in Chiatze.

'All right,' said Emrin. 'I'll assist you. But you can't go wandering about the palace naked.' Striding across the room he gathered up Yu Yu's clothes and tossed them to the bed. Yu Yu managed to pull on his leggings and Emrin helped him into his wolfskin boots. There was no way Yu Yu could lift his injured left arm to put on his shirt, so, bare-chested and supported by Emrin, he made his way to the door.

'You are heavier than you look, yellow man,' said Emrin.

'And you not as strong as you look, Broken Nose,' countered Yu Yu.

Emrin chuckled and pulled open the door. Slowly they made their way down the corridor towards the stairs.

A few minutes after they had gone a small globe of bright light materialized outside the door to Yu Yu's room. Cold air emanated from it. A layer of frost covered the carpet. The globe swelled, forming a white, icy mist that swirled and grew until it reached from floor to ceiling. A shuffling sound emanated from the mist, and two enormous creatures stepped clear of it. They were bone-white and hairless. One ducked its head and entered the room, its massive arm lashing out at the bed. The frame split as the bed crashed into the far wall. The second lowered its head, its small red eyes staring malevolently down the corridor. A third beast slithered from the mist, a scaled white serpent with a long flat head. The head swayed from side to side just above the carpet, snuffling air through four slitted nostrils. Then it began an undulating glide along the corridor towards the stairs.

The mist rolled back across the other beasts.

And flowed along the corridor, following the serpent.

The kitchen was some fifty feet long and twenty wide, boasting several large, stone-dressed iron ovens. Shelves lined the north wall, upon which were placed stacks of plates, jugs and cups. There were five huge, and splendidly crafted, glass-fronted cabinets containing engraved crystal goblets and dishes. Below the shelves were cupboards filled with cooking utensils and cutlery. There were two main doors, one set against the eastern wall, leading to the stairs and the South Tower, the other opening on to a broad winding staircase that emerged on to the main banqueting hall.

There were no windows, and despite a hidden series of chimneys that carried away much of the heat from the ovens, the kitchen could become intolerably warm when large amounts of cooked food were being prepared and a score of servants were scurrying around.

Even now, with the servants abed and only two lanterns burning, it still retained some of the heat produced in the preparing of the evening meals some two hours before. Keeva moved to a drawer and took out a knife, then opened the pantry door and removed a round crusty loaf, a slab of honey-roasted ham, and a dish of butter, which she placed on the long, marble-topped table.

'That is a *meat* knife,' said Norda, with a laugh. 'Do you know nothing, farm girl?'

Keeva pushed out her tongue at her, and continued clumsily to carve slices from the loaf. 'A knife is a knife,' she said. 'If it is sharp it will cut bread.'

Norda rolled her eyes in mock horror. 'There are fish knives, bread knives, meat knives, carving knives, shell knives, fruit knives, cheese knives. You'll have to learn them, you know, if you are ever to wait table at the Gentleman's banquets.'

Keeva ignored her, lifted the top from the butter dish and smeared a slab over her bread.

'Oh, yes,' said Norda, 'and there are butter knives.'

'What a complete waste of metal,' mocked Keeva.

Norda laughed again. 'Knives are like men: each has a different purpose. Some are great hunters, some are great lovers.'

'Ssh! Not in front of the boy!'

Norda laughed again. 'He is asleep. It is so like children. First they want to play, then they get hungry, and by the time you've brought them to the kitchen and prepared some food they are fast asleep and you are left with a mountain of bread.' The women gazed at the small blond boy, asleep on the bench, his head resting on his arm. 'So sweet,' whispered Norda. 'One day he'll be a ladies' man. You can tell. Those baby-blue eyes will melt the hardest heart. They'll be slipping out of their dresses faster than you can say *knife*.'

'Maybe he won't be like that,' said Keeva. 'Maybe he'll fall in love with one woman, get married and have a fine family.'

'True,' agreed Norda. 'He might turn out dull.'

'Oh, you are incorrigible!' Keeva cut some cold ham, placed it between two slices of buttered bread and took a huge bite.

'That's disgusting!' cried Norda. 'And now you've got butter on your chin.'

Keeva wiped her chin with her arm, then licked the butter from it. 'Too good to waste,' she said, laughing at Norda's expression of disgust. 'Now show me these wondrous knives.'

The blonde woman moved to a pine drawer and gathered up two handfuls of bone-handled blades. These she arranged on the table before Keeva. They ranged in size from about eight inches long and fearsomely sharp to two inches with rounded tips. One was curved like a tulwar, ending in two prongs. 'What is that?' she asked.

'It is for cheese. First you cut a chunk, then you reverse the blade and pierce it with the prongs.'

'They are very beautiful,' said Keeva, examining the ornately carved bone handles.

The door at the far end of the kitchen was pushed open and Keeva saw Emrin enter. He was supporting Yu Yu Liang. The

Chiatze's face was grey with exhaustion, but he gave a wide smile when he saw Norda. Emrin was not so pleased, his handsome mouth becoming a grim line.

'Ah, my day brightens!' said Yu Yu. 'Two beautiful women – and some food!' Emrin released his arm and Yu Yu tottered, holding his balance only by leaning on his scabbarded sword. Emrin stomped to the long table, drew his hunting knife and sliced himself several pieces of meat. Norda ran to Yu Yu's side and helped him to the table.

'My two favourite men,' she said.

'You have too many favourites,' barked Emrin.

Norda turned to Keeva and gave a wink. 'He fought for me, you know. Isn't that gallant?'

'I didn't fight for you,' snapped Emrin. 'I fought *because* of you. There is a difference.'

'And doesn't he look handsome with his war wounds?' continued Norda. 'Those dark brooding eyes, that big, swollen nose.'

'Stop it, Norda!' ordered Keeva. She moved round the table and took Emrin's arm. 'I, for one, am proud of you.'

'For what?' asked Norda. 'For ramming his nose into Yu Yu's fist?'

'Oh shut up!' said Keeva. 'He has spent today guarding Yu Yu, and has even now helped him down to the kitchen. It takes a man to be able to put aside his anger for the sake of duty.'

'Aye, he is good man,' said Yu Yu. 'I like him. Everybody like him. Now can we eat?'

'You are shivering!' said Norda, moving round behind Yu Yu. 'You shouldn't be up, you foolish man!' A cold breeze filtered through the far doorway. Keeva ran to the door, pushing it shut and dropping the latch, while Norda fetched a blanket, which she draped over Yu Yu's shoulders.

'I had not realized it gets so cool in here,' said Emrin. But the women ignored him and continued to fuss over the wounded man, preparing him food and a goblet of peach juice.

Emrin wandered away from the table. He could hear sounds on the stairs beyond the second door. He strolled towards it. It opened just as he reached it. The elderly Omri entered, followed by two warriors and a young man. Omri nodded towards Emrin then called out to Keeva to bring some food for Niallad and his bodyguards.

The Duke's son halted by the sleeping child, and grinned down at him. 'I think we tired him out at the beach,' he said.

Keeva carved a dozen thick slices of cold ham, divided it on to three platters and offered it to the newcomers, who sat at the table and began to eat. The young noble thanked her, but the two guards merely tore into the meat. One of them, the taller of the two, a heavily bearded man with deep-set brown eyes, glanced at Yu Yu's sword, resting on the table top. The hilt was black and unadorned, as was the lacquered wooden scabbard. 'Doesn't look anything special to me,' he said, reaching out towards it.

'Don't touch it,' said Yu Yu.

'Or what?' snapped the man aggressively, his hand still moving.

'Do as he says, Gaspir,' ordered the young noble. 'It is his blade, after all.'

'Yes, sir,' said Gaspir, casting a malevolent glance at Yu Yu. 'It is all rubbish anyway. Magic swords!'

The boy Beric awoke and sat up. He blinked and stretched – then suddenly screamed. Keeva followed his gaze. A white mist was swirling under the far door. Yu Yu saw it, and muttered a curse. He groaned as he reached for his sword, dragging it from the scabbard. The blade was glowing with a shimmering blue light. Yu Yu tried to stand, but fell against the table.

'What is going on?' shouted Omri, his face grey with fear.

'Demons . . . are here,' said Yu Yu, levering himself up. Blood began to soak through the bandage on his shoulder.

Omri backed away from the mist, towards the door through which he had entered only moments before. Emrin saw that the old man was trembling uncontrollably. 'Steady, my friend,' he whispered.

'Must get out,' said Omri.

The mist was rising steadily now, the temperature dropping fast. Gaspir and Naren also moved back from the table, blades in hand. Keeva reached out and hefted a long carving knife, balancing it in her hand.

'We have to run!' cried Omri, his voice quavering. Emrin swung towards him. The old man turned and moved towards the other door. Emrin was about to follow him when he saw a faint, swirling mist seeping beneath the frame. Omri was almost at the door. The guard sergeant shouted after him: 'Don't, Omri! The mist . . .'

He was too late. Omri yanked at the latch. As the door swung inward white mist enveloped the old man. A massive taloned arm slashed out, crunching through bone and sending a bloody spray across the dining table. A second blow smashed Omri's skull to shards.

Emrin hurled himself at the door, slamming it shut and dropping the latch – even as Omri's lifeless body hit the floor. There was a thundering crash, and a panel on the door split. Emrin drew his own sword and backed away towards the centre of the room.

Another crash came from the second door. Yu Yu staggered forward, then fell. Emrin grabbed his arm, hauling him to his feet. The page, Beric, had ceased his screaming, and was now cowering on the bench. Keeva ran to him. She reached out for him, but he squirmed away and ran back to where the others waited. The youth, Niallad, drew his dagger, then placed his hand on the little boy's shoulder. 'Be brave, Beric. We will protect you,' he said, but his voice was fearful, his hands trembling. The page crouched down and crept under the table. Norda was already there, her hands over her face.

Icy mist swirled across the stone floor. The right-hand door gave way and a wall of mist swept across the room. Yu Yu's sword came up. Blue lightning lanced through the mist, leaping and crackling. A terrible cry of pain came from within the icy fog.

'Lift up your sword!' Yu Yu told Emrin. The guard sergeant did so, and Yu Yu touched his own blade to it. Instantly blue fire flowed from one weapon to the other. 'You too!' Yu Yu ordered Gaspir and Naren. Their blades also began to flicker. 'It will not last long,' said Yu Yu. 'Attack now!'

For a moment only they hesitated, then Emrin charged the mist, swinging his sword into it. Lightning crackled – and the mist retreated further. Gaspir and Naren joined him. A huge white form leapt from the mist, cannoning into the black-bearded Gaspir, who was hurled from his feet. Naren panicked and tried to run. As the bodyguard turned the beast swung its arm. Keeva saw Naren arch backwards, talons punching through his back and exiting from his chest. Blood exploded from the dying man's mouth. Emrin ran in, slamming his sword into the beast's belly, and ripping the blade up through its chest. It let out a bellow of pain and hurled Naren's body away. Then it turned on Emrin. Keeva lifted her arm and hurled the carving knife across the room. As the beast loomed over Emrin the blade slashed into its eye-socket, plunging deep. At that moment Yu Yu Liang staggered forward and swung the *Rajnee* sword. It sliced deep into the hairless white neck, cutting through muscle and bone. The

773

great beast toppled sideways, striking the table and overturning it.

The mist shrank back, sliding across the floor and vanishing under the far doorway.

The temperature in the room began to rise. Gaspir pushed himself to his feet and gathered up his sword. It was no longer gleaming. A faint and fading blue light still shone on Yu Yu's blade. Yu Yu had fallen to his knees and was breathing heavily. The wound in his shoulder had opened up badly. Blood had soaked through the bandage and was flowing over his bare chest. Emrin moved to his side. 'Hold on, yellow man,' he said softly. 'Let me get you to a chair.'

Yu Yu had no strength left and he sagged against Emrin. Keeva and Norda helped the sergeant to lift him and seat him at the table.

'Are those things gone?' asked Niallad, gazing at the dark stairwells.

'The sword isn't shining,' said Keeva. 'I think they have. But they may be back.'

The young noble looked at her and forced a smile. 'That was a magnificent throw,' he said. 'I've rarely seen a carving knife put to better use.'

Keeva said nothing. She was staring down at the lifeless body of the old man, Omri. A kind and gentle man, he deserved better than to die this way.

'What do we do now?' asked Gaspir. 'Do we leave or stay?'

'We stay . . . for a while,' said Yu Yu. 'Here we can defend. Only . . . two entrances.'

'I agree,' said Gaspir. 'In fact, I can't think of anything that would make me climb either of those stairwells.'

Even as he spoke a distant scream echoed eerily. Then another.

'People are dying up there,' said Emrin. 'We should help them!'

'My job is to guard the Duke's son,' said Gaspir. 'But if you want to charge up those stairs feel free to do so.' The black-bearded bodyguard glanced down at the near-unconscious Yu Yu. 'Though without the magic of his sword I doubt you'll last ten heartbeats.'

'I have to go,' said Emrin. He started to head towards the door.

'Don't!' called out Keeva.

'It is what I am paid for! I am the guard sergeant!'

Keeva moved round the table. 'Listen to me, Emrin. You are a brave man. We've all seen that. But with Yu Yu so badly hurt

774

there is no way we could hold them off without you. You must stay here. The Grey Man told you to protect Yu Yu. You can't do that from upstairs.'

More screams sounded from above. Emrin stared at the shadowed doorway. 'Trust me,' whispered Keeva, taking his arm. His face had a haunted look as the screams continued from the floors above. 'You cannot help them,' she said. Then she turned towards Gaspir. 'We need to barricade the doors. Overturn the far cabinets and push them against the door. Emrin and I will block this one.'

'I don't take orders from serving wenches,' snapped Gaspir.

'It was not an order,' Keeva told him, masking her anger, 'and I apologize if it sounded like one. But the doors need to be blocked, and it will take a strong man to move those cabinets.'

'Do as she says,' put in Niallad. 'I'll help you.'

'You'd better be quick,' warned Keeva. 'Yu Yu's sword is beginning to shine again.'

Chapter Eight

Chardyn, the Source priest, was renowned for his blistering sermons. His charismatic personality and powerful booming voice could fill any hall and bring a host of converts to the Source. As an orator he was without peer, and would, in any just world, have been promoted to abbot many years before. Yet despite his awesome skill one small impediment had stunted his career, one tiny irrelevance used against him by men with small minds.

He didn't believe in the Source.

Once he had, two decades ago, when, full of youth and fire, he had chosen the path of priesthood. Oh, he had believed then. His faith had been strong through war and disease, through poverty and famine. And when his mother had fallen ill he had journeyed home knowing that through his prayers the Source would heal her. He had arrived at the family estate, rushed to her bedside, and called upon the Source to bless His servant and touch his mother with His healing hand. Then he had ordered a celebration feast to be prepared for that night, when they would all give thanks for the coming miracle.

His mother had died just before dusk, in appalling pain and coughing up blood. Chardyn had sat with her, staring at her dead face. Then he had walked downstairs, where the servants were setting fine silver cutlery at the celebration table. In a sudden burst of fury Chardyn had overturned the tables, scattering dishes and plates. The servants had fled his anger.

He had run out into the night, and screamed his rage at the stars.

Chardyn stayed for the funeral, and even made the Soul Journey prayer at the graveside, when his mother's body was laid alongside that of her husband, and the two children who had died in infancy. Then he had journeyed to the Nicolan monastery, where his old teacher, Parali, was the abbot. The old man had welcomed him with a hug, and a kiss upon the cheek.

'I grieve for your loss, my boy,' he said.

'I called upon the Source and He did not answer me.'

'Sometimes He does not. Or if He does He answers in a way we do not like. But, then, we are His servants, not He ours.'

'I no longer believe in Him,' admitted Chardyn.

'You have seen death before,' Parali reminded him. 'You have watched babes die. You have buried children and their parents. How is it that your faith remained strong during these dread times?'

'She was my mother. He should have saved her.'

'We are born, we live a brief time, and then we die,' said Parali. 'That is the way of life. I knew your mother well. She was a fine woman and, it is my belief, she now resides in Paradise. Be grateful for her life, and her love.'

'Grateful?' stormed Chardyn. 'I organized a celebration feast to give thanks to the Source for her recovery. I was made to look like an idiot. Well, I will be an idiot no longer. If the Source exists then I curse Him, and want no more to do with Him.'

'You will leave the priesthood?'

'Yes.'

'Then I pray you will find peace and joy.'

Chardyn had spent a year working on a farm. It was back-breaking toil for little reward, and he came to miss the small luxuries he had taken for granted as a priest, the comfort of life in a temple, the abundance of food, the times of quiet meditation.

One night, after a day of cutting and binding straw for the winter feed, Chardyn had been sitting with the other workers around the Feast Fire, listening to them talk. They were simple folk, and before they ate the roasted meat they gave thanks to the Source for the plentiful harvest. The previous year, following a failed crop, they had given thanks to the Source for their lives. In that moment Chardyn had realized that religion was what crooked gamblers dubbed a 'no lose proposition'. In times of plenty thank the Source, in times of famine thank the Source. When someone survived a plague it was down to divine inter-vention. When someone died of the plague they had been taken to glory. Praise the Source! Faith, it seemed, regardless of its obvious cosmic stupidity, brought happiness and contentment. Why then should Chardyn labour on a farm when he could be adding to the happiness and contentment of the world by preaching the faith? It would certainly add massively to his own happiness and contentment to be living once more in a fine house and attended by skilled servants.

So he had donned the blue robes and journeyed across Kydor, taking up a position at the small temple in the centre of Carlis. Within weeks his sermons had trebled the congregation. Two years later, the coffers swelled by donations, a new temple had been designed, twice the size of the old. Three years after that even this imposing building struggled to contain the masses who came to hear Chardyn.

The adulation of the congregation was in sharp contrast to the low regard in which the church authorities held him. Parali had seen to that. Yet it did not rankle unduly. Chardyn now lived in a large house, with many servants. He had also managed to put away a sizeable sum to indulge his taste for fine foods, expensive wines and soft women.

Indeed, he was as content as a man could be. Or, rather, he had been until this morning, when riders from the Duke had arrived demanding his presence on an expedition to exorcize demons from the ancient ruins in the valley. Chardyn had no experience of demons. Nor did he wish to acquire any. However, it would not be wise to refuse the Duke's summons, so he had swiftly gathered several scrolls dealing with the subject of exorcism and had joined the riders.

The sun was unbearably hot as the company rode down the hillside towards the valley. Up ahead Chardyn could see the Duke and his aides, riding with Lord Aric and the magicker Eldicar Manushan. Behind them came fifty bowmen, twenty heavily armoured lancers, and fifty cavalrymen armed with long sabres.

Once they reached flat ground Chardyn pulled the first of the scrolls from his saddlebag and began to peruse it, trying to memorize the incantations. It was far too complex and he put it away. The second scroll involved the use of holy water, of which he had none, so this, too, was thrust back into the saddlebag. The third spoke of the laying on of hands to remove demonic possession from someone suffering fits. Chardyn resisted the temptation to swear, screwed up the scroll and threw it to the ground.

He rode on, listening to the talk of the men around him. They were nervous and frightened – emotions he began to share as they spoke of the massacred wagoners, and of the attack upon the Grey Man and his Chiatze companions.

A lancer rode alongside him. 'I am glad you are with us, sir,' he said. 'I have heard you speak. You are blessed by the Source and a true holy man.'

'Thank you, my son,' said Chardyn.

The lancer removed his silver helm and bowed his head. Chardyn leant over, placing his hand on the man's hair. 'May the Source bless you and keep you from all harm.' Other soldiers began bunching around the priest, but he waved them away. 'Come, come, my friends, wait until we have reached our destination.' He smiled at them, exuding a bonhomie and confidence he did not feel.

Chardyn had never before visited the ruins of Kuan-Hador and was surprised by the vast distance they covered. The Duke led the riders deep into the ruins, then dismounted. The soldiers followed his lead. A picket line was set up, the horses tethered. Then the bowmen were ordered to take up positions on the camp's perimeter. Chardyn moved across to where the Duke was conversing with Aric, Eldicar Manushan, and a short, slender Chiatze warrior wearing a long grey robe. 'This is where the last attack took place,' said the Duke, removing his helm and running his fingers through his thick black and grey hair. 'Can you sense any evil here?' he asked Chardyn.

The priest shook his head. 'It seems merely a warm day, my lord.'

'What of you, magicker? Do you sense anything?'

'Sensing evil is not my forte, my lord,' said Eldicar Manushan, glancing at Chardyn, who met his eyes and saw amusement there. Something akin to mockery, he thought. Eldicar Manushan swung to the little Chiatze warrior. 'Does your blade shine?' he asked.

The man half drew his sword, then thrust it back into the black scabbard. 'No. Not yet.'

'Perhaps you should move around the ruins,' said the magicker. 'See if the evil is present elsewhere.'

'Let him stay close for the time being,' said the Duke. 'I do not know how swiftly the mist can appear, but I do know the creatures within it killed the wagoners in a matter of heartbeats.'

Eldicar Manushan bowed. 'As you wish, sire.'

The sound of a galloping horse came to them. Chardyn turned

and saw the Grey Man riding his mount across the valley. He heard Lord Aric curse softly, and noted that the amused look had vanished from Eldicar Manushan's face. Chardyn felt his own good humour rise. He had once gone to the Grey Man for a contribution to the new temple, and had received a thousand gold pieces – without even a request for the Grey Man's name to be added to the roll of honour, or the altar table to be named after him. 'The Source will bless you, sir,' Chardyn had told him.

'Let us hope not,' said the Grey Man. 'Those of my friends He has blessed so far are all dead.'

'You are not a believer, sir?'

'The sun will still rise whether I believe or not.'

'Why, then, are you giving us a thousand gold pieces?'

'I like your sermons, priest. They are lively and thought-provoking, and they encourage people to love one another and to be kind and compassionate. Whether the Source exists or not, these are values to be cherished.'

'Indeed so, sir. Then why not make it two thousand?'

The Grey Man had smiled. 'Why not five hundred?'

Chardyn had chuckled then. 'The thousand is ample, sir. I was but jesting.'

The Grey Man dismounted, tethered his horse, and strolled across to the little group. He moved, Chardyn noted, with an easy grace that spoke of confidence and power. He was wearing a dark chainmail shoulder-guard over a black leather shirt, leggings and boots. Two shortswords were strapped to his waist, and over his shoulder was slung a small double-winged crossbow. There was not a glint of shining metal upon him, and even the chainmail had been dyed black. Though Chardyn had chosen the priesthood he had been raised in a military family. No soldier, in his experience, would pay extra to have his armour dulled. Most wanted to stand out, to shine in battle. The Grey Man's garb achieved the exact opposite. Chardyn flicked a glance at the steel-dust gelding. The stirrups and bridle, and even the straps on the saddlebags, were dulled. Interesting, he thought.

The Grey Man nodded towards Chardyn, and gave a courteous bow to the Duke.

'Your company was not requested,' said the Duke, 'but I thank you for taking the trouble to join us.'

If the Grey Man registered the mild rebuke he did not show it. He glanced at the screen of archers. 'If the mist appears it will swamp them,' he said. 'They will need to be more closely grouped. They also need to be told to shoot swiftly at first sight of a black hound. Their bite carries vile poison.'

'My men are well trained,' said Lord Aric. 'They can look after themselves.'

The Grey Man shrugged. 'So be it.' Tapping the Chiatze warrior on the arm, he led him deeper into the ruins, where they sat in close conversation.

'He is an arrogant man,' snapped Aric.

'With much to be arrogant about,' put in Chardyn.

'What does *that* mean?' asked Aric.

'Exactly what it says, my lord. He is a man of power – and not just due to his wealth. You can see it in his every movement and gesture. He is, as my father would have said, a man of dangerous ashes.'

The Duke laughed. 'It is a long time since I heard that phrase. But I tend to agree.'

'I have never heard it at all, sire,' said Aric. 'It sounds meaningless.'

'It's from an old tale,' said the Duke. 'There was an outlaw named Karinal Bezan. A deadly man who killed a great many people, most of them in one-on-one combat. He was arrested and sentenced to be burnt at the stake. When the executioner stepped forward and applied the torch to the tinder Karinal managed to get one hand free. He grabbed the man and dragged him into the flames and they died together, the man screaming and Karinal's laughter ringing above the roar of the blaze. Some time after that the phrase "You can burn him – but walk wide around the ashes" came into use to describe a certain kind of man. Our friend is just such a man. With that in mind, I suggest you move your men closer to the camp and pass on his warnings about the black hounds.'

'Yes, sire,' said Aric, struggling to control his anger.

The Duke rose and stretched. 'And you, sir,' he said to Chardyn, 'should walk among the men and offer them the blessing of the Source. They are far too nervous, and it will stiffen their resolve.'

And who will stiffen mine? thought Chardyn.

Kysumu listened quietly as Waylander told him of his conversation with the priestess. The *Rajnee* tapped the black hilt of his sword. 'There is no proof that he is the enemy. If there was I would slay him.'

'Ustarte says he cannot be killed.'

'You believe that?'

Waylander shrugged. 'I find it hard to believe he could survive a bolt through his heart, but then he is a magicker, and such powers are beyond my understanding.'

Kysumu glanced round at the archers, taking up fresh positions. 'If the mist comes, many will die here,' he said softly. Waylander nodded, and watched as the priest, Chardyn, strolled among the men, administering blessings. 'You think Eldicar Manushan plans to kill us all?'

'I don't know what he plans,' said Waylander. 'But Ustarte says he is looking for allies, so perhaps not.'

Kysumu looked into Waylander's dark eyes. 'Why are you here, Grey Man?' he asked.

'I have to be somewhere.'

'That is true.'

'And what of you, *Rajnee*? What makes you desire to fight demons?'

'I have no desire any longer to fight anything,' said Kysumu. 'When I was young I wanted to be a great swordsman. I wanted fame and riches.' He gave a brief smile. 'I was like Yu Yu. I wanted people to bow down before me as I passed.'

'But not now?'

'Such are the thoughts of the young. Pride is everything, status must be fought for. It is all empty and meaningless. It is ephemeral. Like the leaf on the oak tree. "Look at me, I am the greenest leaf, the biggest leaf, the finest leaf. None of the other leaves has my majesty." Yet autumn beckons, and winter mocks all the leaves, the great and the green, the small and the stunted.'

'I understand that,' said Waylander, 'but it is also an argument against waiting here to fight demons. What difference will it make if we fight or we run, if we win or we lose?'

'Fame is fleeting,' said Kysumu, 'but love and hate are eternal. I may be but a small leaf in the wind of history, but I will stand against evil wherever I find it, no matter the cost. The demon I slay will not descend upon the home of a farmer and murder his family. The bandit who falls beneath my sword will never again rape or kill or plunder. If my death saves a single soul from pain and anguish then it is a price worth paying.'

Chardyn clambered across the broken rocks and approached them. 'Would you like a blessing?' he asked. Waylander shook his head, but Kysumu rose and bowed. Chardyn laid his hand upon the *Rajnee*'s head. 'May the Source cherish you and keep you from all harm,' he whispered. Kysumu thanked him, and sat down once more. 'May I join you?' asked Chardyn. Waylander gestured for him to sit. 'You think the demons will come?' the priest enquired.

'Do you have a spell ready if they do?' asked Waylander.

Chardyn leant forward. 'No,' he admitted, with a wry smile. 'My knowledge of demons and exorcism is – shall we say? – severely limited.'

'I admire your honesty,' said Waylander. 'However, if you can't fight them you should leave. If they come it will be no place for an unarmed man.'

'I cannot leave,' said Chardyn, 'though I would dearly love to follow that advice. My presence helps the men.' He smiled, but Waylander saw the fear in his eyes. 'And perhaps – if the demons do come – I can hurl one of my sermons at them.'

'If the mist comes stay close to us, priest,' said Waylander.

'Now *that* is advice I will take.'

They sat in silence for a while, then Eldicar Manushan strolled over to them. He halted before Waylander. 'Will you walk with me?' he asked.

'Why not?' replied Waylander, rising smoothly. The magicker picked his way through the broken rocks until they were a little way from the others.

'I think you have misread me,' said Eldicar Manushan. 'I am not evil, nor do I seek to do you harm.'

'I am glad you have told me,' said Waylander. 'It will save me so many sleepless nights of worry.'

Eldicar Manushan laughed with genuine good humour. 'I like you, Grey Man. Truly. And there is no need for us to be enemies. I can offer you your deepest desires. It is within my power.'

'I think not,' said Waylander. 'I have no desire to be young again.'

The magicker seemed momentarily puzzled. 'Normally I would find that hard to believe,' he said at last. 'Though not in this instance. Are you so unhappy with life that you yearn to see an end to it?'

'Why do you desire my friendship?' countered Waylander.

'Look about you,' said Eldicar, gesturing towards the soldiers. 'Frightened men, small men, malleable men, the world is made up of such men as these. They live to be conquered and ruled. Look at them cowering behind ancient stones, praying that their insignificant lives will be allowed to continue past this night. If they were animals they would be sheep. You, on the other hand, are a predator, a superior being.'

'Like yourself?' asked Waylander.

'I have always loathed false modesty, so, yes, like myself. You are rich, and therefore powerful in this world. You could be useful to Kuan-Hador.'

Waylander laughed softly, and gazed around at the broken stones. '*This*,' he said, 'is Kuan-Hador.'

'It was destroyed *here*,' said Eldicar Manushan. 'This is merely one reality. Kuan-Hador is eternal. And she will prevail. This world was once ours. It will be again. When that happens it would be preferable for you to be our friend, Dakeyras.'

'*If* that happens,' said Waylander.

'It will happen. It will be bloody and many will die. But it will happen.'

'I think this is the point where you tell me what happens if I decide not to be your friend,' observed Waylander.

Eldicar Manushan shook his head. 'You do not need to hear threats from me, Grey Man. As I said, you are a predator. You are also highly intelligent. I merely ask you to consider my offer of friendship.'

Clasping his hands behind his back, Eldicar Manushan walked back to the Duke and his officers.

The afternoon was hot and clammy, heavy rainclouds obscuring the sun. Elphons, Duke of Kydor, struggled to appear relaxed. A little way to the west the Grey Man was stretched out on the ground, apparently asleep. The little Chiatze swordsman was sitting cross-legged nearby, eyes closed. The priest Chardyn was restlessly pacing back and forth, occasionally stopping to peer out over the ruins.

The men seemed a little more at ease, though Elphons knew their mood was fragile at best. Like himself, they had never fought demons.

'Will our swords cut demon flesh?' he had asked Eldicar Manushan.

The magicker spread his hands. 'It is said that the skin of a demon is like toughened leather, my lord. But, then, there are many kinds of demon.'

'You think they will come?'

'If they do it will be after dusk,' said Eldicar Manushan.

The Duke pushed himself to his feet and approached the priest, Chardyn, who was pacing to and fro. The man looked frightened, he thought, which was not an encouraging sign. Priests should always be serene. 'I hear you have filled the new temple with worshippers,' said the Duke. 'I must attend one of your services.'

'Most kind, my lord. But, yes, the faithful grow ever more powerful in Carlis.'

'Religion is a good thing,' said the Duke. 'It keeps the poor content.'

Chardyn smiled. 'You believe that is its only purpose?'

The Duke shrugged. 'Who can say? For myself I have never witnessed a miracle, nor has the Source ever spoken to me. But I am a soldier, first and foremost. I tend to believe what I can see and touch. I have little time for faith.'

'You have never prayed?'

The Duke chuckled. 'Once I was surrounded by Zharn tribesmen and my sword broke. I said a prayer then, I can tell you.'

'It was obviously answered, for here you stand.'

'I leapt at them and rammed the broken blade through the throat of the first man. As the others closed in, my men regrouped and scattered them. So tell me of your faith. From where does it spring?'

Chardyn looked away. 'I realized the truth about the Source many years ago,' he said softly. 'Nothing I have learnt since has changed my mind.'

'It must be comforting to have faith at times like this,' said the Duke. He glanced down and saw that the Grey Man was awake. 'Only an old soldier would be able to sleep before a battle,' he said, with a smile.

The Grey Man moved to his feet. 'If they come it won't be a *long* battle,' he said.

The Duke nodded. 'You mean the ice? I saw the dead birds in the woods. Frozen to death. I am hoping our archers will strike many down before they reach us. Then – if the Source is with us,' he added, with a glance at Chardyn, 'we can finish the rest with swords.'

'Always good to have a plan,' said the Grey Man.

'You disagree?'

The Grey Man shrugged. 'The tracks I saw were of creatures far bigger than bears. Forget demons, my lord. If twenty bears were to rush this camp how many would be brought down by your archers? And how many would be killed by your swordsmen?'

'I take your point, sir, but you must understand mine. I am the lord of these lands. It is my duty to protect its citizens. I have no choice but to face this evil, and hope that strength and courage will hold the day.'

The Grey Man turned towards the western peaks. 'We'll know soon enough,' he said, as the sun began to sink below the mountain-tops.

As darkness fell upon the valley a small bright spark flickered behind a half-shattered column of stone. Dust swirled around it, and moisture from the air was drawn to it. Slowly it took shape, as the molecules of earth, air and water melded to the spark of fire. A form began to materialize, tall and thin, naked under the new moonlight. The skin, at first speckled, became scaled and grey. Arms stretched from the form, and a flowing hooded robe of darkness cloaked it. The thin lipless mouth opened, dragging in air, filling the new lungs.

Niaharzz became aware, aware of the warm air around him, the soft earth beneath his feet, the silken robe upon the naked grey skin of his shoulders. The membrane over his eyes slid back and he blinked. For a moment he could not move, for the exquisite joy of material existence was strong upon him, causing his limbs to tremble.

When at last he felt confident of movement he stretched his legs and stepped to the edge of the stone column, peering round it. Some thirty paces to the east he could see the humans. Lifting his head, he tasted the air in his nostrils. The scent of flesh caused his belly to tighten, but the heady aroma of fear among these pale, pink creatures made him shudder with desire. Instinctively his mouth opened, exposing pointed fangs. Memories of a glorious past flooded him, trembling females exuding the dizzying perfume of terror, younglings, their soft bones yielding sweet marrow.

Niaharzz quelled his hunger and leant back against the stone.

Once he had been a god, stalking the earth and feeding where he chose. Now he was a servant, fed only when his masters allowed it. And as long as they controlled the gateways he would remain a slave to their ambitions.

Still, food was food . . .

Niaharzz flipped his hood of darkness over his head, drawing it like a veil over his face. Then he moved to the far side of the rock and sought out the warrior with the bright sword of death. He was sitting on a stone, the vile weapon in his hands. Another human stood close by, tall and garbed in black. Niaharzz watched him. This one was dangerous too. He could feel it – though he sensed no magic emanating from him.

Take no risks, he told himself. In spirit form Niaharzz was immortal, but clothed in flesh he could die like any of these primitive creatures. Stay away from the sword, he warned himself. Do not let them see you.

Crouching down, he extended his hand. Seven sparks leapt from his fingers, and began to dance and swirl in the shadows of the column, forming into huge *Kraloth* hounds, their massive jaws dripping venom.

Niaharzz toyed with directing them at the swordsman, but he had already seen the man destroy several of his beauties the night before. No, the Ice Giants could rend and tear the man. His *Kraloth* would sacrifice their lives to kill the humans carrying the weapons of far-death. He gestured to the hounds, and they slunk away, keeping to the shadows, moving silently ever closer to the archers.

The sword in Kysumu's lap began to glow. The *Rajnee* climbed to a rock and held the blade aloft. 'The enemy is close!' he shouted.

Men scrambled to their feet, soldiers drawing their swords and hefting their shields, archers notching arrows to bowstrings. Chardyn peered out among the shadow-haunted ruins. 'There!' he bellowed, pointing to the west.

The first of the giant black hounds charged at the archers. Shafts flew at it, most hissing by its hurtling black form. One struck it high on the back and glanced clear without marking the skin.

'Neck or head!' shouted Waylander. Six more hounds came in sight, moving at great speed. The first beast reached the broken wall behind which the archers crouched. It leapt, clearing the barrier in one bound, its curved fangs closing upon the face of a bowman. The crunching of bone that followed made Chardyn feel sick.

All was pandemonium now as the *Kraloth* leapt among the archers.

'Kill the hounds,' Waylander ordered Kysumu. 'I'll find the Houndmaster.'

Kysumu sprinted across the ruins, his sword blazing. The Grey Man vanished into the shadows.

Chardyn stood alone.

In the distance he saw a wall of mist seeping across the valley.

The smell of blood in the air caused Niaharzz to tremble with hunger. Now is not the time to feed, he told himself. Later, when the Ice Giants had finished the slaughter. Though he hoped to be able to drag at least one live victim clear of the mist before the flesh froze. Meat should slide around the mouth, its juices rich and savoury, not break into icy pieces as fangs closed upon it.

Niaharzz moved silently to the edge of the broken column and risked a glance. The small warrior with the shining sword was among the archers now, but he was hampered by the crush of bodies; men panicking and attempting to flee. Even so, he had killed two of the hounds, curse him! Offset against this more than a dozen of the archers were down, most of them dead, but two were screaming.

The sound was delicious. It was almost as good as feeding. Niaharzz filtered the raw emotions, various degrees of terror, ranging from stomach-tightening fear to bowel-loosening panic. He blinked, a sense of shock touching his soul. Amid all the fear there was an emotion subtly different. Powerful, yes, but not sweet to the senses . . . He knew he had sensed it before, thousands of years ago, when last he had walked these night-dark lands. Niaharzz focused on the emotion, separating it from those flowing from the carnage.

Then it came to him.

It was rage. But not the boiling, extravagant rage of the fighting man. No, this was cold, controlled – and close.

Niaharzz did not move.

There was a man close by. Very close! He guessed it to be the tall man he had seen standing with the swordsman. Fear touched Niaharzz. It was not an entirely unpleasant feeling, for it made him more aware of the joys of physical reality. Very, very slowly he turned his head.

The man was some twenty paces to the right. He was searching the shadows, and facing away from Niaharzz.

It was so long since Niaharzz had felt his fangs close upon living flesh, the warm blood running down his throat.

Keeping his night-cloak around him he drew on his power, then raised his feet from the ground, floating silently in the shadows. The man took several steps towards a jagged wall, then turned again. Now his back was towards Niaharzz.

The *Bezha* floated towards the man, his arms extending, talons sliding from his fingers.

'Time to die,' said the man softly.

Niaharzz barely had time to register the words before the man spun on his heel, right hand extended. Something dark leapt from the small weapon in his hand.

There was no time to flee the prison of flesh, no time even to cry out against the cruel injustice of such a fate.

The bolt smashed through his skull, skewering the brain . . .

The body disappeared instantly, the black cloak floating for a moment on the wind, seeming no heavier than a grass seed. Waylander reached out and grabbed it.

Back among the ruins the remaining four *Kraloth* burst into flames, their bodies dwindling until they became little more than dancing sparks above the stones. They flickered for a few heartbeats and then were gone.

The cloak in Waylander's hands felt insubstantial. It seemed to roll under his fingers like liquid. More peculiar was the weird sensation as he tried to examine it. His gaze slid away from it, focusing on the rocks, or on his wrists, but never able to fasten to the garment itself.

'The mist is coming!' shouted Chardyn.

Waylander glanced towards the west and saw the white wall rolling towards him. Swiftly he rolled the cloak, wedged it into his belt before loping back to where the frightened soldiers were bunching together.

'Archers, stand firm!' bellowed the Duke, drawing his longsword and moving among the men.

Eldicar Manushan strode out from the group and climbed to a jutting rock. The mist swept on. The magicker raised his right arm and held it aloft, palm extended towards the mist. Then he began to chant, his voice ringing out. The mist slowed. Kysumu stepped alongside Waylander, his shining sword extended. Waylander glanced down at him. The man seemed utterly calm. The priest Chardyn eased himself behind the two men.

'Shouldn't you be praying?' asked Waylander.

Chardyn forced a smile. 'Somehow this does not feel like a day for hypocrites,' he said.

The temperature began to drop as the mist came closer. Eldicar Manushan continued to chant, his voice ringing with confidence and great power. Lord Aric had also drawn his sword now and was standing alongside the Duke and his swordsmen. The surviving archers had notched arrows to their bows and were waiting tensely.

The mist slowed to a halt immediately before the magicker, but flowed on past him on both sides. Still his voice continued to chant. Then he jerked suddenly and almost lost his balance on the stone. The chant died away. Instantly the mist swept over him. Just as it did so Waylander saw a massive form descend on the magicker, a taloned arm sweeping out, ripping through Eldicar Manushan's chest. Waylander saw the magicker's right arm slashed in two and ripped from his body, just as the mist closed over him.

'So much for magic,' he said.

Kysumu leapt towards the mist. His gleaming blade touched it, and blue lightning crackled and flashed. A huge white form towered over the little *Rajnee*. Waylander sent a bolt into its eye. The massive head jerked backwards. Kysumu slashed a vicious cut through the beast's chest, then spun on his heel to flash a reverse slice through its neck as it fell.

Ice was forming on the stones now. The mist swept on. Waylander and Chardyn moved in behind Kysumu. The sounds of screaming men and crunching bone came from all around now as the ice beasts fell upon the soldiers of Kydor.

A white serpent reared up from the ground at Waylander's feet. His sword slashed down, barely breaking the skin above the flat skull. Kysumu's blade sliced through the neck. As it did so it glanced from the blade of Waylander's weapon. Instantly blue fire flowed along Waylander's sword, and the mist retreated. For a moment only, Waylander stood staring at the shining blade. 'The magic can be transferred,' he said. 'Now we have a chance!' He glanced at Kysumu. 'We must get to the Duke!' Kysumu understood instantly and the two men, followed by the priest, charged into the mist towards the sounds of battle. Kysumu cut down another of the huge creatures, then clambered over a low rock wall. The Duke and several heavily armoured swordsmen were battling bravely. Kysumu leapt in, touching his blade to the Duke's longsword. Instantly the Duke's sword blazed bright. The mist fell back a little, and the Chiatze moved from warrior to warrior, charging their blades with blue magic.

The voice of Eldicar Manushan came faintly through the mist, once more chanting. Louder and louder came the chant. The mist began to shrink, pulling back from the survivors, growing smaller and smaller until it was no more than the size of a large stone.

Eldicar Manushan strode from the rocks, still maintaining his chant. He held out his right hand and the small globe of mist floated up to it. He tossed it into the air. There was a sudden clap of thunder and a brilliant white light.

And the mist was gone.

Waylander sheathed his blade and looked hard at the magicker. There was no sign of a serious wound upon him, though his right sleeve was shorn away and his tunic slashed open. There was no blood upon the ruined cloth.

The Duke stepped forward, pulling his ice-covered helm from his head and dropping it to the ground. 'Well done, magicker,' he said. 'I thought you had been killed.'

'Merely knocked from my feet, my lord.'

'Are they destroyed?'

'They will not return to this place. I have closed the portal.'

'We owe you a great debt, Eldicar,' said the Duke, clapping the man on the shoulder. He gazed around at the sprawled bodies. Thirty men had been killed, twelve others wounded. 'Damn, but it was close,' he said. The shining sword in his hands began to fade until it gleamed only as steel in the moonlight. 'My thanks to you, Chiatze,' he told Kysumu, 'though it would have been good to have known about this trick a little earlier.'

'I did not know myself,' said Kysumu.

The Duke swung away and moved among the wounded, organizing aid for them.

Waylander approached Eldicar Manushan. 'For a moment there I thought you had been killed,' he said.

'Yes, it seemed likely.'

'I thought your arm had been torn from your body, but I see it was only your sleeve.'

'I was lucky,' said Eldicar. 'As indeed were you. You killed a *Bezha*. That is no mean feat, Grey Man. How were you able to do that?'

Waylander gave a cold smile. 'One day I might show you,' he said.

Eldicar Manushan chuckled. 'Let us hope not,' he said. The

smile faded. 'Perhaps we can talk later.' With a courteous bow he moved away, and began to assist Chardyn with the wounded.

Waylander stood for a moment. The temperature was rising again, but there was still ice upon the ground. He shivered and strode across to where Kysumu was standing. The little Chiatze sheathed his sword. 'Do you believe they have gone for good?' asked the *Rajnee*.

Waylander shrugged. 'They have or they haven't.'

'Did you see the magicker fall?'

'Yes.'

'He was all but torn in half.'

'I know.'

'The priestess was right then. He cannot be killed.'

'It would appear so,' agreed Waylander. Suddenly weary, he sat down on a broken wall. Lord Aric, divested now of his armour, walked over to join them. He offered Waylander a canteen of water. Waylander accepted it and drank deeply, then passed it to Kysumu, who declined it.

'I have never seen the like,' said Aric. 'I thought we were finished for certain. Without that sword of yours we would have been. My thanks to you, *Rajnee*.' Kysumu bowed. A little way to the left a man screamed in pain, the sound ebbing away and ending abruptly. Aric looked back. 'Victory has a high price,' he said.

'It usually does,' agreed Waylander, pushing himself to his feet. 'I am riding home. I shall send wagons for the wounded. Those injured by the hounds will need swift attention. Any who can ride should follow on and I will see that Mendyr Syn is waiting for them.' With that he strode across the killing ground to where the horses were tethered. Kysumu followed and they rode from the ruins.

Clouds drifted across the moon as the two riders reached the slope, and they made the climb carefully and in silence. By the time they reached higher ground the sky had cleared, but still they rode on without speaking. Waylander was lost in thought. If the demons had been summoned by Eldicar Manushan why, then, did he defeat them? And if the demons were his creatures why did they attack him? Something was missing here, and it galled Waylander that he could not fasten to it. He replayed the events in his mind: Eldicar standing on the rock, his voice booming and confident, the mist slowing and even beginning to recede.

Then Eldicar had faltered, his confidence draining away, the spell evaporating. Talons had ripped into him. Only the accidental discovery of the true power of Kysumu's blade had saved the Duke and his men.

Two hours later, still having reached no conclusions, Waylander rode his horse through the last of the trees and on to the long path leading to the upper palace. It was close to dawn, and he saw more than a hundred people milling outside the double doors. Many torches and lanterns had been lit, and his guards, led by Emrin, had placed themselves between the palace and the crowd. Many of the soldiers had swords drawn.

Emrin came running from the group as the riders approached. 'What is happening?' asked Waylander.

'Demons attacked the palace, sir,' said Emrin. 'Two men are dead, but nineteen more people are missing, including the surgeon, the foreign priestess and her followers – and your friend Matze Chai. The demons came at us in the Long Kitchens, killing Omri and one of the Duke's bodyguards – Naren, I think he was called.'

'And the Duke's son?' asked Waylander.

'He is fine, sir. We killed one demon – Yu Yu and I. Then the mist withdrew into the palace. We stayed where we were for a long while. We heard many screams.' Emrin took a deep breath and looked away. 'I did not investigate.' He looked back at Waylander, awaiting censure.

'When did you leave the kitchens?'

'About an hour ago. Yu Yu's sword was not shining, so we crept up the stairs and along to the banquet hall. We saw nothing – save that there was ice upon the walls of the outer corridor. Then we made our way to the lawns here. We found what you see, most of the servants and guests had fled. There are more down on the beach – about forty.'

'You went there – through the palace?' asked Waylander.

'Yes, sir.'

'That took courage, Emrin. Did you see any sign of the mist?'

'No, sir. But I didn't stop to investigate. I ran back through the banquet hall and out on to the terrace. I didn't stop running until I reached the beach.'

'How many of Matze Chai's servants are among the missing?'

'Ten, sir, according to the captain of his guard.'

'Fetch him.'

Emrin bowed, then turned and moved back through the crowd. Waylander saw Keeva sitting close to the trees. The page-boy was asleep, his blond head resting against her shoulder.

Moments later Emrin led the Chiatze captain to Waylander. The man bowed deeply to both Waylander and Kysumu.

'Tell me of the attack,' said Waylander.

The man glanced at Kysumu and spoke rapidly in Chiatze. The *Rajnee* turned to Waylander. 'The captain regrets that his command of the Kydor language is not sufficient to describe in detail the events. He asks if you would permit me to translate for him.'

'You may tell me in your own tongue,' said Waylander in excellent Chiatze.

The captain bowed even more deeply. 'I am Liu, noble sir. It is my honour to be captain of Matze Chai's troops. It is also my great shame that I could not reach my master in his time of peril. I was sleeping, noble sir, when a scream awoke me. I rose, pulled on my robe, and opened the door to seek out the cause of the cry. At first I could see nothing, but I felt the cold immediately. I knew what it was, sir, for it attacked our camp. I buckled on my breast-plate, took up my sword and tried to reach the suite of my master. But the mist was already there, filling the corridor. It came for me – and I ran, noble sir. I heard other doors opening behind me, and I heard . . . I heard . . .' He fell silent. 'I heard people being killed,' he said. 'I did not look back. I could not have saved them.'

Waylander thanked the man then unclipped the crossbow from his belt and loaded two bolts. Without a word to the others he walked towards the double doors. Emrin swore softly then followed, sword in hand. Waylander paused in the doorway and looked back at Emrin. 'Do not follow me. You are needed here,' he said. 'Send ten wagons to the old ruins, and ensure there are plenty of bandages and a good amount of fresh water. The Duke's men have also suffered losses against the demons.'

Waylander pushed open the doors and walked into the darkness beyond. Kysumu strolled after him.

For almost an hour the Grey Man stalked the deserted corridors, pushing open doors, striding down stairwells, through halls and storage areas. He made no attempt to move stealthily, and it seemed to Kysumu that his companion was disappointed that they found no monsters. His anger, though controlled, was apparent in every movement.

Finally they reached the Long Kitchens. The body of Omri lay in a pool of congealing blood alongside that of the bodyguard Naren. The Grey Man knelt beside the old retainer. 'You deserved better than this,' he said. Omri's face was frozen in a mask of terror, and his eyes were wide open. For a little while the Grey Man remained beside the body, then he rose. 'He was a frightened man,' he told Kysumu. 'He abhorred violence. It terrified him. But he was a deep well when it came to kindness and compassion. You'd have to ride far to find any who would speak ill of him.'

'Such men are rare,' observed Kysumu. 'You valued him. That is good.'

'Of course I valued him. There would be no civilization without men like Omri. They care, and in caring they create all that is good. It was Omri who urged me to allow Mendyr Syn to create his hospital here. Before that Omri was raising funds for two schools in Carlis. He spent his life working for the good of others. And this was his reward – to be ripped apart by some mindless beast.'

The Grey Man swore softly, then moved away to examine the room. On the panelled floor close by there was a large stain, as if oil had seeped into the wood. Around eight feet long, it was all that remained of the creature who had killed Omri. A long-bladed carving knife lay beside the stain. The blade was pitted with rust, the bone handle singed as if from fire.

The two men left the scene and climbed to the first level of the South Tower. Here were the hospital wards of Mendyr Syn. Several of the twenty beds in the first ward had been upturned, and there was blood upon the floor. The room was still cold and there were no bodies. Moving to the second level, they found even greater chaos. Blood had sprayed to the walls and ceiling. Many of the beds were smashed.

Kysumu pointed to a bed by the far window. A body was lying within it, untouched. The Grey Man moved across the panelled floor and stood by the bedside. The occupant, an elderly woman, was dead, her hands folded across her chest. Waylander examined her. Rigor mortis was well under way.

'She has been dead for more than just a few hours,' said Kysumu. 'Probably late yesterday afternoon.'

'Yes,' agreed the Grey Man, gazing around at the smashed beds and blood-smeared walls.

'I once went into the ruins of a house destroyed by an

earthquake,' said Kysumu. 'Everything was smashed. But a perfect egg was sitting in a broken plate.'

'These demons are obviously not interested in the dead,' said the Grey Man, 'unless they have killed them themselves. There were more than thirty people here,' he continued, 'not counting Mendyr Syn and his three helpers. Thirty souls sent screaming to the Void.'

The third level, the medical library, showed no sign of ice damage. The door to the office of Mendyr Syn was open, many of his papers scattered upon the two desks. The Grey Man searched the room, finding Ustarte's gold-ringed blue crystal below a pile of papers. Tucking it into his pocket, he left the office and continued up the stairs to the guest suites. Here the corridor carpets were wet, the walls cold.

Opening the door to Matze Chai's suite, the Grey Man moved across the silk Chiatze rugs and through into the bedroom. The first of the dawn light was filtering through the pale blinds. For the first time since the search had begun Kysumu saw the Grey Man relax. A low chuckle sounded from him.

Matze Chai opened his eyes and yawned. He glanced at the bedside table. 'Where is my tisane?' he asked.

'It will be a little late this morning,' said the Grey Man.

'Dakeyras? What is happening?' Matze Chai sat up, his pale blue nightcap falling from his head, revealing the carefully tied net that held his lacquered hair in place.

'I am sorry to disturb your rest, my dear friend,' said the Grey Man softly, 'but we feared you were dead. The demons came to the palace last night. Many people were killed. I shall leave you now and send your servants to you.'

'Most kind,' said Matze Chai.

The Grey Man left the room.

Kysumu bowed to Matze Chai and followed him. 'His life is charmed,' observed Kysumu.

'It is a great relief to me,' said the Grey Man. 'Matze Chai is a good friend – perhaps my only friend. He is incorruptible and loyal. It would have hurt me deeply had he been among the slain.'

'Why did he survive, do you think?' asked Kysumu.

The Grey Man shrugged. 'Who can say? Matze always takes a sleeping draught. Perhaps it lowered his heart rate and they did not sense him. Or maybe, since the creatures feed on flesh, they sought out younger meat. Matze may be a fine man, but there's precious little fat on those old bones.'

'I am glad to see your mood has lifted a little,' said Kysumu.

'Not by much,' said the Grey Man. 'You go back to the lawns. Tell Emrin to fetch Matze's servants.'

'Where will you go?'

'To the North Tower.'

'We have not searched that yet. You think it safe?'

'The demons have gone. I can feel it.'

The Grey Man slipped the bolts from his crossbow, returning them to the quiver by his side. Without another word he strode off.

Chapter Nine

Waylander kept moving until he was out of sight of the *Rajnee* then sat down on a velvet-covered bench seat in the corridor. His relief at the survival of Matze Chai was overwhelming, and he could feel his hands trembling. Leaning back against the wall, he took several deep, calming breaths. The death of Mendyr Syn and Omri saddened him greatly, but he had known them for only a short while. Matze Chai had been part of his life for three decades, a solid anchor he could always rely upon. He had not, however, realized until this day how much he cared for the old man.

But with the relief came a deeper anger, a cold and terrible resentment against the arrogant cruelty of men who were willing to visit such terror on innocent victims. Ultimately, he knew, wars were never about simple issues like right and wrong. They were launched by men who lusted after power. They did not care about the victims like Omri or Mendyr Syn. They lived for fame, and all the empty, fruitless joys it brought. One man like Omri was worth ten thousand of such killers, he thought.

Having recovered his composure Waylander moved on at a lope, scaling the stairs of the North Tower two at a time. He slowed when he reached the first level. Shelves had been torn from the walls, and manuscripts, scrolls and leatherbound volumes were scattered across the floor. Kneeling, he touched his hand to the carpet. It was wet and cold. To the left were two eight-foot stains upon the floor. Dark blood was spattered around them. Ustarte's followers, it seemed, had fought well.

Treading carefully through the debris he reached the second stairwell and climbed once more. As he turned a corner he saw the body of a huge, golden wolf, its belly ripped open, its golden eyes glazing. The body twitched as he approached and it tried to raise its head. Then it slumped down and died.

Climbing past the dead beast he came across two more bodies, those of the acolytes who had followed Ustarte. Waylander struggled to remember their names. Prial was one. He was lying upon his back, his chest open, ribs splayed. The other lay close by. Huge talon marks were on his back, and the lower part of his spine was jutting from his body.

Waylander stepped over them. The door to Ustarte's apartments had been torn from its hinges. He moved into the doorway and scanned the room. Furniture had been hurled against the walls, the ornate carpet was ripped in places, and there was blood upon the floor and walls. There was no sign of Ustarte. Waylander moved to the window. Upon the sill was a bloody smear. Leaning out, he looked down. Two floors below was a balcony. A patch of blood showed on the balustrade.

Retracing his steps he returned to the stairs. The body of the golden wolf had vanished. In its place lay the third of Ustarte's acolytes.

Waylander walked to the front of the palace, where Emrin was anxiously waiting.

'The palace is clear,' said Waylander. 'Tell the servants they can return to their rooms.'

'Yes, sir. Quite a few have left your service. They have gone to Carlis. Even those who remain are frightened.'

'I don't blame them. Send some men to fetch the bodies from the Long Kitchens and the North Tower library. And set the servants tasks to take their minds from their fear. Tell them all there will be an extra month's salary to compensate for the terror they have endured.'

'Yes, sir. They will be most grateful. Did you find the priestess?'

'She and her people are dead.' Waylander looked into the young man's eyes. 'With Omri gone I need someone to manage the household. That role is yours for now. Your salary is doubled.'

'Thank you, sir.'

'No need to thank me. It is an arduous duty and you will earn your pay. Have the wagons left?'

'Yes, sir. I also sent riders to the hospital in Carlis, where

Mendyr Syn's two assistants are working. They should be here soon to help with the wounded.'

Waylander moved across to where Yu Yu Liang was sitting with his back to a tree. Keeva was beside him, her arm still around the shoulders of the blond page. The boy looked up at Waylander and gave a nervous smile.

'Were you very frightened?' Waylander asked the boy.

'Yes, sir. Is my uncle safe?'

'He was when last I saw him.' He turned his attention to Yu Yu. 'How are you feeling?' he asked.

'Like I want to be ditch-digger again,' said Yu Yu. 'Like I could throw this puking sword in sea and go home.'

'You can do that,' said Waylander. 'You are a free man.'

'Later,' said Yu Yu, 'but first we have to find Men of Clay.'

Many of the servants were reluctant to return to the palace, but as the boldest of them moved through the doors most of the others followed. Another fifteen joined the thirty who had already quit the Grey Man's service and journeyed to Carlis.

Waylander walked out through the banquet hall and found Kysumu sitting cross-legged on the terrace stones. The *Rajnee's* arms were extended outwards, his head bowed. Waylander moved silently past him, leaving the warrior to his meditation.

The sun was high now in a clear blue sky, shining down upon the myriad colours of the flowers in the terraced gardens. The scent of roses filled the air. It made the events of the night seem like a dream. Waylander strolled down to his apartments. The door was open, and there was a crimson smear upon the frame.

Inside the priestess Ustarte lay naked in one corner. Blood from a number of wounds to her flanks, arms and legs was seeping through her striped fur. Waylander knelt beside her. She was unconscious. Stretching her out on her back he examined the wounds. They were deep. Waylander drew the blue crystal from his pocket, slowly moving it over the tears in her flesh. He could see no sign of the flesh-eating maggots. Finding his medicine bag he took from it a curved needle and began to stitch the largest of the jagged rips in her side. Her golden eyes opened and locked to his gaze. Then they closed once more. Waylander continued his work. Her fur was not soft, like that of a cat. It was wiry and thick, the muscles beneath supple and immensely strong. Indeed she was far stronger than the slim form suggested. There was further evidence of this when he tried to lift her, to carry her to his bed. She weighed at least as much as two tall men. Unable to move her, Waylander fetched a pillow and some blankets and laid them on a chair close by. Then, using old cloths, he mopped up the blood around her. Wiping his hands clean, he lifted her head and slipped the pillow under it. Then he covered her with the blankets.

Having done all he could, Waylander left the building, pulled shut the door and walked to the waterfall. Stripping off his clothes he stood beneath the cold water.

Refreshed, he returned to his rooms. He found a fresh shirt and leggings, dressed and returned to the priestess. Her breathing was shallow, her face ashen. Her eyes opened and she tried to speak, the effort causing her to wince. 'Don't talk,' he said softly. 'Rest now. I will fetch you some water.' He filled a goblet, raised her head and held it to her lips. She drank a little then sank back. 'Sleep,' he said. 'Nothing will harm you.' He was aware even as he said it that he could, in truth, make no such guarantees, but the words were out before he could stop them.

He walked to the door and sat down on the step. The fishermen were out in the bay, the white sails of their boats bright in the sunlight. Waylander leaned back against the door frame.

Eldicar Manushan had been torn apart battling the demons in the ruins. He could not, surely, at the same time, have summoned more monsters to attack the palace. Waylander considered the attack. There had been three targets, Mendyr Syn, Yu Yu Liang and Ustarte. Since Yu Yu and the *Rajnee* sword had been in the hospital building, the death of the surgeon may have been merely a tragic coincidence. Anger flickered in his weary frame. Life was full of such meaningless tragedies.

His first wife Tanya and his three children had died because a group of raiders had decided to head south-east rather than south-west. Coincidentally he had chosen that day to hunt venison, rather than stay and rebuild the south pasture fence. 'You have no time for self-pity,' he said, aloud, pushing the awful scenes from his mind.

He truly did not care whether Kydor stood or fell. War was a grisly fact of life, and one that he was powerless to alter. But the enemy had brought death to *his* house, and *that* he did care about. Demons had been unleashed within the palace. Omri had been a gentle, kind man. Talons had torn his chest open. Mendyr Syn had devoted his life to the care of others. His last moments had been to witness his patients ripped apart.

Until now this had not been Waylander's war.

Now it was.

Leaning his head back against the door frame he closed his eyes. Sunlight was warm upon his face. A soft breeze whispered against his skin. He was almost asleep when he heard soft footfalls on the steps. His dark eyes flicked open and he drew a diamond-shaped knife from its sheath.

Keeva appeared, carrying a tray of food. Waylander pushed himself to his feet, and stood blocking the doorway. 'Emrin asked me to bring you some breakfast,' she said.

'Was it you who hurled the carving knife at the beast?' he asked.

'Yes. How did you know?'

'I saw it upon the floor. Where did you aim for?'

'The eye.'

'Did you hit it?'

'Yes. It went in to the hilt.'

'Excellent.' He looked at her closely. 'I want you to do something for me,' he said.

'Of course.'

'I want it done quietly. No-one must know. No-one at all.'

'You can trust me, Grey Man. I owe you my life.'

'Go to the North Tower and the rooms of the priestess Ustarte. Let no-one see you. Gather some of her clothes and gloves. Do not forget the gloves. Put them in a sack and bring them here.'

'She is still alive?'

Waylander stepped back into the apartments, beckoning her to follow him. Keeva paused in the doorway and gazed down on the sleeping priestess. One arm was outside the blankets. Keeva moved closer and stared down at the exposed, fur-covered limb and the sharp claws extending from the short, stubby fingers. She recoiled instantly. 'Sweet Heaven! What is she?'

'Someone who has been badly wounded,' he said softly. 'No-one must know she has survived the attack. You understand?'

'Is she a demon?'

'I do not know what she is, Keeva, but I believe there is no evil in her. Will you trust me on this?'

'I trust you, Grey Man. Will she live?'

'I have no way of knowing. The wounds are deep, and there may be internal bleeding. But I will do what I can.'

Ustarte opened her eyes. Her vision swam, then focused on the rough wrought ceiling above her. Her mouth was dry, and she became aware of pain. It grew from a dull, throbbing ache to needles of fire in her side and back. She groaned.

Instantly a figure appeared above her. Lifting her head he held a goblet of water to her lips. She drank sparingly at first, allowing the cool liquid to ease its way down her parched throat. The swirling began in her belly and she quelled it. Must not Change now, she thought, an edge of panic seeping into her mind. Looking up into the Grey Man's face she read his thoughts instinctively. He was concerned for her. 'I will live,' she whispered. 'If I do not . . . become the beast.' She caught an image in his mind of a golden wolf, dying on the stairs of the library. Sorrow flowed over her and tears welled in her eyes. 'They died for me,' she whispered.

'Aye, they did,' he said. The tears flowed on to her cheeks and she began sobbing. She felt his hands upon her shoulders. 'Be calm, Ustarte! You will tear the stitches. There will be time for grief later.'

'They trusted me,' she said. 'I betrayed them.'

'You betrayed no-one. You did not summon the demons.'

'I could have opened a portal and taken them to safety.'

'Now you are making me angry,' he said, but the hand stroking her head was still gentle. 'There is no-one living who would not change some aspect of the past if they could, to avoid a hurt or a tragedy. We make mistakes. It is just the grim game of life. Your people followed you because they loved and believed in you. You were seeking to prevent a great evil. Yes, they died to protect you. And they did it willingly. It is for you to make that sacrifice worthwhile by surviving, as they wanted you to survive. You hear me?'

'I hear you, Grey Man. But we have lost. The gateway will open, and the evil of Kuan-Hador will return.'

'Maybe so – maybe not. We still live. I have had many enemies, Ustarte, powerful enemies. Some commanded nations, others armies, others demons. They are all dead and I still live. And while I live I will not accept defeat.'

Closing her eyes, she tried to flow with the pain. Ustarte felt the blanket being lifted from her. The Grey Man was studying her wounds. 'They are healing well,' he said. 'Why will this Change be dangerous for you?'

'I become larger. The stitches will tear open. If this begins to happen you must . . . kill me. I will no longer be Ustarte. And what I become will . . . slaughter you in its agony. You understand?'

'Yes. Rest now.'

For a human it would have been sound advice, but Ustarte knew that if she did not stay conscious the swirling would begin again and she would metamorphose. She lay very still. Her thoughts began to drift. Several times she almost lost the focus. She saw again the breeding pens, felt again the terrible fear she had known. The crippled girl, dragged from her home and brought underground to the ceaseless horror of the pens. Sharp knives cutting into her flesh, noxious liquids being forced down her throat. Each time she vomited more of the fluid was poured into her mouth. Spells were cast, sharper than knives, hotter than fire, colder than ice.

Then the awful day when her frail body was merged with the beast. Its terror and rage swamped her, as its molecules flowed within her human frame. The pain was indescribable, every muscle swelling and cramping. The child was swept away in a sea of blackness. But she had clung on to her individuality, despite the roaring of the beast in her mind. Sensing her presence, the beast had calmed.

Strange dreams followed. She felt herself running on all fours, her great limbs powering her across the plain at terrible speed. Then the leap to the back of the deer, her fangs closing on its neck, dragging it down, warm blood filling her mouth. She almost lost herself in the blood-memory – but she clutched the tiny spark that was Ustarte.

She remembered the day she became aware of voices. 'This new *Kraloth* does not conform, Lord. It sleeps twenty hours, and when awake seems confused. We have noted tremors in the muscles of its hind legs, and occasional spasms.'

'Kill it,' came a second voice, harsh and cold.

'Aye, Lord.'

The thought of dying flooded Ustarte with a burst of energy, and her spirit flowed up from the dark recesses of the bestial body. She felt again the pull of the flesh, the power of the muscles in her four limbs. Her eyes opened. She reared up, trying to speak. A low, guttural growl rippled from her throat. Her paws struck at the iron bars of the cage. A man in a green tunic pushed a long stick through the bars. Something sharp and bright upon the end of it stabbed into her flesh. Fire flowed into her flanks.

Instinctively she knew it was poison. How she dealt with it remained a mystery to her to this day. She could only assume that the merging had created in her an unforeseen talent, enhancing her lymphatic pathways in such a way that she could draw the poison into her system, breaking it down into component parts and subtly changing it.

She had dropped to her haunches, waiting silently until the poison was dispersed harmlessly. Now she became aware of the thoughts of the three men in the room. One was waiting to go home to his family. Another was thinking of a missed meal. The third was considering murder.

Even as she linked to the thought she felt the man close his mind to her. A golden spell lanced through the bars, flowing over her body with whips of fire. She writhed under this new pain.

So desperate was she to escape it that she fled deep within the bestial body, allowing the beast control. It raged around the cage, slashing its great paws at the bars, bending them. Still the pain increased. Ustarte tried to flee again, surging up through the body, as if trying to claw her way free of the tortured flesh.

And in that moment she found the key that would save her life.

The beast withdrew. The spirit of Ustarte swelled. The body fell to the floor of the cage, writhing and Changing.

When she awoke she was resting in a bed. Her body was no longer quite that of the beast, but neither was it human. Her shoulders and torso were covered in thick, striped fur, her fingers were tipped with retractable talons. 'You are a mystery to me, child,' said a voice. Turning her head, she saw the third man sitting beside the bed. He was wonderfully handsome, his hair golden, his eyes a summer blue. The eyes of a kindly uncle, she thought. Yet there was no kindness in him. 'But we will learn to solve it.'

Two days later she had been taken to a stockaded palace-prison high in the mountains. Here there were other mutations, man-beasts and were-creatures, the subjects of failed experiments. There was a serpent with the face of a child. It was kept in a domed cage of thin wire mesh, and fed on live rats. The creature did not speak, but at night it would make music, high and keening. The sound would tear at Ustarte's soul every night for the five years she was imprisoned in that awful place.

Unspeakable acts were committed against her body, and she in turn was trained to kill and feed. For two years she refused to kill a human. For two years Deresh Karany, the golden-haired sorcerer, subjected her to dreadful pain. Ultimately the torture broke her resistance, and she learnt to obey. Her first kill had been a young woman, her next a powerful man with only one arm. After that she learnt not to remember the faces and forms of her victims. Time and again Deresh Karany would force her to Change, and once in the bestial form she would be directed against some hapless human. Her long fangs and terrible talons would rip into the frail flesh, tearing off limbs, lapping up blood and crunching brittle bones.

She was a good *Kraloth*, obedient and trustworthy. Not once – in either of her forms – did she turn on her jailers. Not even a growl. Her obedience was instantaneous. And day by day they grew more complacent about her. They thought they had her beaten. She could read it in their thoughts. Never, since that first day back in the city, had she let them know of her other powers. She was careful not to betray her talent. Ustarte knew that Deresh Karany sensed them. Once he had walked towards her with a dagger in his hand. His thoughts were clear. *I am going to ram this blade into your throat.*

'Good morning, my lord,' she said.

'Good morning, Ustarte.' He sat beside her. 'I am very pleased with you.'

I am going to kill you!

'Thank you, my lord. What do you require of me?'

He had smiled and sheathed the dagger. 'The creatures in this place are unique; twin forming is so rare. How does it feel when you shift from one form to the other?'

'It is painful, Lord.'

'Which form gives you the most pleasure?'

'Neither gives me pleasure, Lord. In this, my near-human form, I derive some satisfaction from study, from the beauty of the sky. In *Kraloth* guise I glory in power and strength and the taste of flesh.'

'Yes,' he said, nodding, 'the beast has no perception of abstracts. How then do you control it?'

'I cannot fully control it, Lord. It is wild and savage. It obeys me because it knows I can deny it existence, but it constantly seeks ways to overcome me.'

'The spirit of the tiger remains alive?'

'I believe so.'

'Interesting.' He fell silent and seemed lost in thought. Then he met her gaze. 'Back in the city I sensed you reaching out and touching my mind. You recall this?'

She had waited for this moment, and knew it would be dangerous to offer a complete lie. 'Yes, Lord. It was most mysterious.

It was like flowing up from a deep sleep. Suddenly I heard distant voices, though I knew they were not real sounds.'

'And this has not happened since?'

'No, Lord.'

'Let me know if it does.'

'I will, Lord.'

'You are doing well, Ustarte. We are all proud of you.'

'Thank you, Lord. That is most pleasing to me.'

One day, as she strolled in semi-human form, she saw that the small postern gate was unlocked. She stood in the doorway gazing out upon the mountain path leading to the forest. Reaching out with her mind, she sensed the watchers close by, reading their thoughts. The door had been left open for her. Concentrating, she pushed her talent further. Five more guards were hidden behind the rocks some fifty paces from the postern gate. They were armed with spears and two held a strong net.

Ustarte turned away and walked back to the main exercise area.

As the months passed they trusted her more and more. She was used to assist in the training of others like herself. Prial was brought to the prison in chains. He was in his wolf form then, snapping and biting at the guards. Ustarte reached out with her talent, feeling his rage and terror. '*Be calm,*' she whispered into his mind. '*Be patient, for our time is coming.*'

Waylander sat with the sleeping priestess for a while. Her breathing was even, but the gleam of perspiration on her face showed that her temperature was rising. Moving to the kitchen he filled a bowl with cool water and returned to her side. Taking a cloth he placed it in the water, squeezed out the excess liquid and laid it on her brow. She stirred and the golden eyes opened. 'Feels good,' she whispered. Gently he dabbed the cloth to her cheeks. She slept again.

Waylander rose from the floor and stretched. Then he stood very still and listened. Walking swiftly to the window he drew the shutters closed, then stepped out through the door and into the sunshine, pulling closed the door behind him.

Eldicar Manushan and the page, Beric, were crossing the terrace garden and walking along the path to his apartments. The magicker was wearing a pale blue tunic shirt of glimmering silk. His legs were bare, and he wore no boots or shoes. His page was clad only in a loincloth, and he was carrying towels across his shoulder.

'Good day to you, Dakeyras,' said the magicker, with a broad smile.

'And to you. Where are you heading?'

'To the beach. Beric has become fond of it.'

The blond page looked up at his uncle and grinned. 'The water is very cold,' he said.

'You have taken a wrong turn,' said Waylander. 'Go back to the tall yellow rose and turn right. The steps there will take you to the sea.'

Eldicar Manushan glanced at the rough-cut walls of Waylander's apartments. 'I understand you live here,' he said. 'You are a most curious man. You build a palace of great style and beauty and yet live in little more than a cave on a cliff wall. Why is that?'

'I sometimes ask myself the same question,' said Waylander.

'Can we go to the sea now, Uncle?' put in the boy. 'It is getting very hot.'

'You go down, Beric. I will join you presently.'

'Don't be long,' said the child, running back down the path.

'The young have such energy,' observed Eldicar Manushan, moving into the shade of a flowering tree and seating himself on a rock.

'And innocence,' added Waylander.

'Yes. It is always a cause of sadness when it passes. I did not take a wrong turn, Dakeyras. I wanted to speak with you.'

'I am here. Speak.'

'I am sorry for the death of your people. It was not my doing.'

'Just an unfortunate coincidence,' said Waylander.

Eldicar sighed. 'I will not lie to you. My people have formed an alliance with . . . another powerful group. Such is the way of war. What I am saying is that *I* did not bring the beasts to your palace.'

'What is it you seek here?' asked Waylander. 'This is not rich land.'

'Perhaps not. But it is ours. It was once ruled by my people. We were temporarily defeated by force of arms. We retreated. Now we are coming back. There is nothing overtly evil in this. It is just human. We want what is ours by right, and are willing to fight for it. The question for you is, is this your fight? You are not a native of Kydor. You have a fine palace, servants and the freedom only riches can supply. That will not change. You are a strong and deadly man, but whether for us or against us you can make no discernible difference to the outcome.'

'Then why concern yourself with my friendship?'

'Partly because I like you,' the magicker smiled, 'and partly because you killed the *Bezha*. Not many men could have done that. Our cause is not unjust, Dakeyras. This *was* our land, and it is the way of man to fight for what he believes is just. You agree?'

Waylander shrugged. 'It is said that this land was once below the sea. Does the sea own it? Men hold what they are strong enough to hold. If you can take this land, then take it. But I will think on what you have said.'

'Don't take too long,' advised Eldicar Manushan. He turned to follow his page to the beach, then swung back. 'Did you find the body of the priestess?'

'I found the body of a creature not human,' said Waylander.

Eldicar Manushan stood silently for a moment. 'She was a Joining. A failed experiment, full of bitterness and hatred. My own lord, Deresh Karany, invested much time and passion in her training. She betrayed him.'

'And he sent the demons?'

Eldicar spread his hands. 'I am only a servant. I do not know all my master's plans.' He strolled away.

Waylander sat for some time outside the apartments. He was a hunter, trained to follow his prey and kill it. This situation was far more subtle, and infinitely more dangerous.

Added to which there was another player in the game, who had not yet shown himself.

Who was Deresh Karany?

During the next three days life in the palace began to return to a semblance of normality. The servants were still nervous, and many purchased ward-charms from stallholders in Carlis, hanging them upon the doors of their rooms, or around their necks. The temple was filled daily with new converts, all anxious to be blessed by Chardyn and the three other priests.

Chardyn himself spent hours every day poring over scrolls and learning, as best he could, the ancient spells said to be useful against demonic possession and manifestation. He also removed an ornate box, hidden below the altar. From this he took two items: a golden ring with a carved carnelian stone at the centre, and a talismanic necklet, both said to have been blessed by the great Dardalion, first Abbot of the Thirty. 'You are a hypocrite,' he told himself, as he looped the necklet over his head.

In the palace hospital many of the wounded soldiers died in agony, despite the use of the crystal supplied to the two surgeons by Waylander. Neither of the men was as skilled as Mendyr Syn. But others survived. They were visited daily by the Duke, and offered encouragement. The crippled were assured they would receive good pensions and parcels of land back near the capital.

Little was seen of Waylander during this time, and all callers to the palace were greeted by Emrin, who informed them that the Gentleman was not in residence.

In the Winter Palace, on the far side of the bay, the Duke began preparations for the celebration feast. The lords of Kydor, Panagyn of House Rishell, Ruall of House Loras, and Shastar of House Bakard, all arrived in Carlis and were given sumptuous suites in three of the towers. Lord Aric, of House Kilraith, occupied the fourth tower. Invitations to the feast were sent to all the heads of the minor noble families, and a handful of wealthy merchants, including the Grey Man.

There was great excitement among the invited, for those who had already seen the wondrous talents of Eldicar Manushan had spread the word. And the magicker had promised a night to remember for all the guests.

A little to the west of the Grey Man's apartments was a sheltered ledge, hidden from the palace above by a jutting overhang. Here there were several bench seats, created from split logs, surrounding the sanded stump of a huge tree. The Grey Man was stretched out on one of the benches. To his right sat Ustarte the priestess, dressed now in a green robe of silk. Her face was still grey and her eyes reflected both weariness and pain. On the bench opposite sat Yu Yu Liang and Kysumu.

Yu Yu's shoulder was healing fast, but he found himself wishing he was back in his hospital bed. Ustarte had tried to question him about his experiences with the spirits of the original *Riajnor*. Yu Yu found it hard now to remember all that he had been told. Much of it was beyond him anyway, and he hadn't understood it even when it was being relayed to him by the spirit of Qin Chong. There was a feeling of tension in the air. The Grey Man was stretched out on his side, resting on one elbow, but his face was stern, his eyes locked to Yu Yu's face. It was most disconcerting. The priestess was disappointed, and only Kysumu seemed relaxed and at ease. Yu Yu guessed this was merely an outward show.

810

'I am sorry,' he said in Chiatze. 'I remember the tall man coming to me. I remember he called me *pria-shath*, which Kysumu said means Lantern Bearer. Then he took my hand and we flew. High through clouds and under stars. And all the time he was talking to me. I thought I was remembering it, but when I awoke it started slipping away. Sometimes things come back to me – like when I remembered about how the magic of the swords could be passed on. But most of it is gone.'

The Grey Man swung his legs to the ground and sat up. 'When I spoke to you in the grounds of the palace,' he said, 'you told me we had to find the Men of Clay. You remember?'

'Yes, the Men of Clay. I remember that.'

'Who are they?'

'They wait in the Dome. That's what he told me. They wait for the Lantern Bearer.'

'And where is the Dome?'

'I don't know. I can't think any more.' Yu Yu was feeling agitated now.

Kysumu laid a hand on his arm. 'Stay calm, Yu Yu. All will be well.'

'I don't see how,' muttered Yu Yu. 'I am an idiot.'

'You are the Chosen, the *pria-shath*. That is why you were drawn here,' said Kysumu. 'So sit calmly and let us continue to seek the truth. You agree?'

Yu Yu leant back and closed his eyes. 'Yes, I agree. But my mind is emptying. I can feel it all washing away.'

'It will come back. Qin Chong told you that you must find the Men of Clay, who live in a place called the Dome. He said these Men of Clay were waiting for the Lantern Bearer. Did you see the Men of Clay in your travels with Qin Chong?'

'Yes! Yes, I did. It was after a great battle. There were thousands of warriors – men like you, Kysumu, in robes, some of grey, some white and some crimson. They knelt and prayed on the battlefield and then they drew lots. Certain of the warriors then moved away from the others. They walked into the hills. Qin Chong was with them. He was with them *and* with me, if you take my meaning. And he said, "These are the Men of Clay."'

'This is good,' said Kysumu. 'What else did Qin Chong say to you?'

'He said I must find them. At the Dome. Then we floated again, over hills and valleys, and across a bay, and we sat in a little wood, and he told me of his life, and asked about mine. I told him I dug ditches and foundations, and he said that was an honourable occupation. Which, of course, it is, for without foundations you couldn't—'

'Yes, yes,' said Kysumu, allowing his irritation to show. 'But let us return to the Men of Clay. Did he mention them again?'

'No, I don't think so.'

The Grey Man leant forward. 'When they drew lots how many men moved away into the hills with Qin Chong?'

'Several hundred, I would think,' said Yu Yu.

'And the black man,' said Ustarte.

Yu Yu blinked in surprise and stared at the ailing priestess. 'Yes, how did you know? I had almost forgotten myself.'

'My wounds have sapped my powers – but not completely,' she said. 'Tell us of him.'

'He was a wizard, I think. His skin was very dark. He was tall and well built. He wore a blue robe, and carried a long white staff, curved at the top. At least I think he was a wizard. He was related to someone famous. Grandson, or great-grandson. Something like that.'

'Emsharas,' put in Ustarte.

'That's it!' said Yu Yu. 'Grandson of Emsharas, who was also a wizard.'

'Far more than a wizard,' said Ustarte. 'He was a lord of demons. According to legend, he rebelled against his brother, Anharat, and aided the humans of Kuan-Hador in the first Demon War. Through his power the warriors of Kuan-Hador defeated the demons, casting them from this dimension. That was in the days when Kuan-Hador was a symbol of purity and courage. When Kuan-Hador fell into evil ways and a second war broke out, the few descendants of Emsharas took arms against the empire. There were many battles. Nothing is known of the fate of Emsharas's descendants.'

'We seem to be no closer to an answer,' said Kysumu.

'I think that we are,' observed the Grey Man. He turned to Yu Yu. 'The last battle you saw was at the city of Kuan-Hador?'

'Yes.'

'In which direction did the Men of Clay walk?'

'South . . . south-west, maybe. A southerly direction anyway.'

'That area is mostly forest now,' said the Grey Man. 'It covers a vast area on the way to Qumtar. Do you remember any landmarks?'

Yu Yu shook his head. 'Just a lot of hills.'

812

'We must travel there,' said the Grey Man. To his right Ustarte gave a low moan. Her head sagged back against the headrest of the bench. The Grey Man moved swiftly to her side. 'Help me with her,' he told Kysumu. Together, and with great effort, they lifted the priestess, carrying her back to the apartments and laying her on the bed.

Her golden eyes opened. 'I . . . need a little . . . rest,' she whispered.

The men left her and returned to where Yu Yu waited. 'How is your wound?' the Grey Man asked him.

'Better.'

'Can you ride?'

'Of course. I am a great rider.'

'You and Kysumu should head back to the ruins, then strike out towards the south.'

'What are we looking for?' asked Yu Yu.

'Anything that looks familiar to you. The Men of Clay walked away from the battlefield. Did they walk far? More than a day, for example? Did they make camp?'

'No, I don't think so. I think the hills were close to the burning city.'

'Then you must find those hills. I will join you in a day or two.'

Kysumu stepped in close to the Grey Man. 'What if the demons come back? You will not have our swords to protect you.'

'One concern at a time, my friend,' said the Grey Man. 'Emrin will see that you have two good mounts and a week's supplies. Tell no-one where you are heading.'

Lord Aric of House Kilraith stepped past the two guards at the door, and led Eldicar Manushan through to the rear apartments, where a third guard politely relieved Aric of his ruby-pommelled dagger. Lord Panagyn of House Rishell was lounging in an armchair, his booted feet resting on a glass table-top. A big, ugly man, with iron-grey hair and a large bulbous nose, his face was given a hint of glamour by the silver patch he wore over his left eye.

'Greetings, cousin,' said Aric amiably. 'I trust you are comfortable?'

'As comfortable as any man sitting in the fortress of his enemy.'

'Always so suspicious, cousin. You will not die here. Allow me to introduce my friend, Eldicar Manushan.'

The broad-shouldered magicker bowed. 'A pleasure, my lord.'

'So far the pleasure is all yours,' grunted Panagyn, swinging his legs from the table. 'If you are looking for an alliance with House Rishell, Aric, you can forget it. You were behind the treacherous turncoat Shastar. Had he not switched sides I would have killed Ruall, as I killed his brothers.'

'Indeed so,' said Aric. 'And you are quite right. I did convince Shastar to change sides.'

'You admit it, you dog!'

'Yes, I do.' Aric sat down opposite the astonished man. 'But all that is in the past. There are far greater prizes in our grasp now. We have battled one another to gain control of larger areas of Kydor. Larger areas of a tiny nation. But suppose for a moment we could conquer the lands of the Chiatze, and the Gothir. And beyond. Drenan, Vagria, Lentria. Suppose that we could be kings of great empires.'

Panagyn chuckled, the sound rich with mockery. 'Oh, yes, cousin,' he said. 'And we could fly over our empires on the backs of winged pigs. I do believe I saw a feathered pig swooping past my window as I arrived.'

'I don't blame you for your cynicism, Panagyn,' said Aric. 'I will even give you another opportunity for jest. Not only can we rule these empires, but we will never die. We will be immortal like gods.' He fell silent for a moment, then smiled. 'You wish to make another jest?'

'No – but I would appreciate you offering me a taste of the narcotic you have obviously been imbibing.'

Aric laughed. 'How is your eye?'

'It hurts, Aric. How do you think it feels? An arrow cut through it, and I had to pluck out both shaft and orb.'

'Then perhaps a small demonstration would aid our negotiation,' said Aric. He turned to Eldicar Manushan. The magicker raised his hand. From the tip of his index finger a blue flame leapt into the air, closing in on itself and swirling, like a tiny, glowing ball.

'What is this?' asked Panagyn. Suddenly the ball sped across the room, flowing through the silver eye-patch. Panagyn fell back with a groan. He swore loudly and scrabbled for his dagger.

'No need for that,' said Eldicar Manushan. 'Stay calm and wait for the pain to pass. The result will surprise you, my lord. The pain should be receding now. What do you feel?'

'An itching in the socket,' muttered Panagyn. 'It feels like something is lodged there.'

'As indeed something is,' said Eldicar. 'Remove your eye-patch.'

814

Panagyn did so. The socket had been stitched tight. Eldicar Manushan touched his finger to the sealed lids. The skin peeled back, the muscles of the lids swelling with new life. 'Open your eye,' ordered the magicker.

Panagyn obeyed him. 'Sweet Heaven!' he whispered. 'I have my sight. It is a miracle.'

'No, merely magic,' said Eldicar, looking at him closely. 'And I didn't quite get the colour right. The iris is a deeper blue in your right eye.'

'Gods, man, I care nothing for the colour,' said Panagyn. 'To be free of pain – and to have two good eyes.' Rising from his chair, he walked to the balcony and stared out over the bay. He swung back to the two men. 'How have you done this?'

'It would take rather an age to explain, my lord. But essentially your body regenerated itself. Eyes are really quite simple. Bones take a little more expertise. Had you, for example, lost an arm it would have taken several weeks – and more than two dozen spells – to regrow. Now, if you will, my lord, take a close look at your cousin.'

'Good to be able to take a *close* look at anything,' said Panagyn. 'What am I looking for?'

'Does he seem well to you?'

'You mean apart from dyeing his hair and beard?'

'It is not dye,' said Eldicar Manushan. 'I have given him back some ten years or so. He is now a man in his early thirties, and could remain so for several hundred years. Perhaps more.'

'By the gods, he does seem younger,' whispered Panagyn. 'And you could do this for me?'

'Of course.'

'And what do you require in return? The soul of my first-born?' Panagyn forced a laugh, but his eyes showed no humour.

'I am not a demon, Lord Panagyn. I am a man, just as you are. What I require is your friendship, and your loyalty.'

'And this will make me a king?'

'In time. I have an army waiting to enter this land. I do not wish them to have to fight as soon as they arrive. Far better to enter a land that is friendly, that will be a base for expansion. You have upwards of three thousand fighting men. Aric can summon close to four thousand. I do not wish for a battle so early.'

'Where is this army coming from?' asked Panagyn. 'The lands of the Chiatze?'

'No. A gateway will open not thirty miles from here. One

815

thousand of my men will pass through it. It will take time to bring the whole army through. Perhaps a year. Perhaps a little more. But once our base here is established we will conquer the lands of the Chiatze, and beyond. The ancient realm will be restored. And you will be rewarded beyond any dream you can envisage.'

'And what of the others, the Duke, Shastar and Ruall?' asked Panagyn. 'Are they to be included in our venture?'

'Sadly, no,' said Eldicar Manushan. 'The Duke is a man with no understanding of avarice, and no desire for conquest. Shastar and Ruall are loyal to him, and will follow where he leads. No, initially the land of Kydor will be shared between you and your cousin.'

'They are to die, then?' said Panagyn.

'Indeed. Does that trouble you, my lord?'

'Everybody dies,' replied Panagyn, with a smile.

'Not everybody,' observed Aric.

In the nights that followed the attack on the palace many of the servants found difficulty in sleeping. Alone in their rooms as night fell, they would light lanterns and recite prayers. If sleep did come it was light, the merest sound of wind against the window-frames enough to have them wake in a cold sweat. Not so for Keeva, who slept more deeply than she had in years. Deep, dreamless sleep, from which she awoke feeling refreshed and invigorated.

And she knew why. When the demons had come she had not cowered in a corner, but taken up a weapon and used it. Yes, she had been afraid, but the fear had not overcome her. She remembered her uncle, and pictured his face as they sat on the riverbank. 'You'll hear people say that pride is a sin. Ignore them. Pride is vital. Not excessive pride, mind you. That is merely arrogant stupidity. No, being proud of yourself is what counts. Do nothing that is mean and spiteful, petty or cruel. And never give way to evil, no matter what the cost. Be proud, girl. Stand tall.'

'Is that how you have lived your life, Uncle?'

'No. That's why I know how important it is.'

Keeva smiled at the memory, as she sat by the bed of the priestess. Ustarte was sleeping peacefully. Keeva heard the Grey Man enter and glanced up at him. He was dressed all in black, the clothes very fine. He beckoned to her and she followed him into the weapons room. 'Ustarte is in danger,' he said.

'She seems to be recovering well.'

'Not from her wounds. She has enemies. Soon they will come for her.' He paused, his dark eyes locking to her gaze.

'What do you want me to do?' she asked.

'What do you want to do?' he countered.

'I don't understand you.'

'You have a choice of two paths, Keeva. One carries you back up the steps to the palace and your room, the other will take you to places you may not want to go.' He gestured towards the far bench. Upon it was laid a pair of soft leather leggings and a double-shouldered hunting jerkin. Beside the clothes was a belt bearing a bone-handled knife.

'These are for me?'

'Only if you want them.'

'What are you saying, Grey Man? Speak plainly.'

'I need someone to take Ustarte from here to a place of – relative – safety. It must be someone with wit and courage, someone who will not panic when the chase begins. I am not asking you to do this, Keeva. I do not have that right. If you choose to return to your room I will think none the worse of you.'

'Where is this place of safety?'

'About a day's ride from here.' He moved in closer to her. 'Give it some thought. I will be with Ustarte.'

Keeva stood alone in the weapons room. Stepping forward, she laid her hand on the hunting jerkin. The leather was soft and lightly oiled. Drawing the hunting knife from its sheath, she hefted it. It was perfectly balanced, and double-edged. Conflicting thoughts assailed her. She owed her life to the Grey Man, and the debt lay heavy upon her. Equally she loved life in the palace. Proud as she was of her part in the fight against the demons, Keeva had no wish to face any further dangers. She had been lucky in the raid upon the village. Camran could have killed her straight away. That luck had doubled with the coming of the Grey Man. But, surely, there was a limit to one person's luck? Keeva felt she would cross that limit were she to agree to escort the priestess.

'What should I do, Uncle?' she whispered.

There was no answer from the dead, but Keeva remembered his oft-repeated advice.

'*When in doubt, do what is right, girl.*'

Chapter Ten

Waylander moved to the bedside. Ustarte's golden eyes were open. He sat beside her. 'You were wrong to do that,' she said, her voice almost a whisper.

'I gave her a choice.'

'No, you didn't. She owes you her life. She will feel obliged to do as you ask.'

'I know, but I don't have too many choices,' he admitted.

'You could become a friend to Kuan-Hador,' she reminded him.

He shook his head. 'I would have remained neutral, but they brought death to my house and to my people. I cannot forgive that.'

'It is more than that,' she said.

He laughed then, with genuine good humour. 'I forget for a moment that you can read minds.'

'And speak with spirits,' she reminded him.

His smile faded. On the first night he had tended her Ustarte had woken and told him that the spirit of Orien, the Battle King of the Drenai, had appeared to her. It had shaken Waylander, for the same spirit had appeared to him years before, offering him the chance to redeem himself by finding the Armour of Bronze.*

'Has he come to you again?'

'No. He harbours no ill-will towards you. He wanted you to know that.'

'He should. I killed his son.'

*From the novel *Waylander* (1986)

818

'I know,' she said sadly. 'You were a different man then, and almost beyond redemption. But the goodness in you fought back. He has forgiven you.'

'Strangely, that is harder to bear than hate,' he said.

'That is because you cannot forgive yourself.'

'Can you read the minds of spirits?' he asked her.

'No – but I liked him.'

'He was a king,' said Waylander, 'a great king. He saved the Drenai, and forged a nation. When he was old, his sight failing, he abdicated in favour of his son, Niallad.'

'I know this from your own memories,' she said. 'He hid the Armour of Bronze. You found it.'

'He asked me to. How could I refuse?'

'Some men would have. And now he has asked a second favour of you.'

'It makes no sense to me. Finding the Armour of Bronze helped the Drenai overcome a great enemy. But going to a feast? Why would a dead king care about a feast?'

'He did not say. But I think you will be in danger if you go. You know that?'

'I know.'

Keeva moved in from the weapons room. Waylander turned to see her standing in the doorway. She was wearing the dark shirt and leggings and a pair of fringed riding boots. The hunting knife was belted at her waist. Her long dark hair was pulled back from her face and tied in a pony-tail. Waylander rose from the bedside. 'The clothes fit well,' he said. Moving past her he walked to a cabinet on the far wall of the weapons room. Opening it, he withdrew a small double-winged crossbow. Calling out to Keeva he carried the weapon to a bench. Under the light of a lantern he examined the crossbow, lightly oiling the bolt grooves. As Keeva came alongside he passed the weapon to her. 'I had this made for my daughter, Miriel,' he said, 'but she preferred the more traditional hunting bow. It is considerably lighter than my own bow and the killing range is no more than fifteen paces.'

Keeva hefted the bow. It was T-shaped, when viewed either vertically or horizontally, the grip projecting down from the centre of the weapon. The rear of the crossbow was fluted back, and shaped so that it settled snugly over the wrist. There were no bronze triggers. Two black studs had been set into the grip.

Waylander handed the girl two black bolts. 'Load the lower groove first,' he advised. Keeva struggled with the action. The centre of the lower bowstring was hidden inside the mechanism. 'Let me show you,' he said.

On the underside of the bow was a catch. Waylander flicked it open and pulled it down. This engaged the lower bowstring, drawing it back into view. Slipping his fingers into the groove he cocked the weapon, then slid a bolt into place. Snapping the catch, he handed the weapon to Keeva. Extending her arm, she loosed the centre bolt into a nearby target. He watched her reload it. She still struggled with the lower section. 'Do not leave it loaded for too long,' he said, 'for it will weaken the wings. When you get time, practise loading and unloading. It will become easier.'

'I do not want it to become *easier*,' she told him. 'I will take Ustarte to this place you spoke of, but then you can have this weapon back. I told you once before I do not want to be a killer. That remains true.'

'I understand that, and I am grateful to you,' he said. 'I will be with you late tomorrow. After that you will be free of any obligation to me.'

Finding a stick of charcoal and a section of parchment he drew two diamond shapes, the first with a diagonal line across it running left to right, the second right to left. 'Skirt the ruins of Kuan-Hador to the south-west and head into the mountains. Follow the main road for around a mile. You will come to a fork in the road. Take the left fork and continue until you see a lightning-blasted tree. Ride on, keeping your eyes on the trunks of the trees you pass. Each time you see these symbols change direction according to the line through the diamond, left to right or right to left. You will come to a cliff-face. If you have followed the symbols correctly you will be close to a deep cleft in the rocks. Dismount and lead the horses into that cleft. Inside you will find a deep cave with a freshwater pool. There are supplies there, and grain for the horses.'

Keeva slipped the bolts from the crossbow and loosed the strings. 'I heard the priestess say you would be in danger at the Feast. Why go?'

'Why indeed?' he observed.

'You had best be wary.'

'I am *always* wary.'

Niallad, son of the mighty Duke Elphons, and blood heir to the vanished throne of Drenan, stood naked before a full-length mirror disliking what he saw. The slender face, with its large blue eyes and full mouth, seemed to him to be that of a girl. There was no real sign yet of facial hair. His shoulders and arms were still skinny, despite the many weeks of hard physical labour he had pushed himself to complete. His chest, also hairless, carried no flesh and his ribs could clearly be seen. He looked nothing like the powerhouse that was his father.

And the fears he carried would not go away. When surrounded by crowds he would start to sweat, his palms becoming clammy, his heart beating wildly. His dreams were always of darkness, an unfamiliar maze of corridors, and the stealthy footfalls of an assassin who was never seen.

Turning away from the mirror Niallad went to the chest beneath the window and opened it, pulling forth a grey tunic and dark leggings. Dressing, he pulled on his calf-length riding boots and strapped his dagger-belt to his waist. Then came a light tapping at the door. 'Come in,' he called.

The bodyguard, Gaspir, stepped inside. He pointed at the dagger-belt. 'No weapons, young lord,' he said. 'Your father's orders.'

'Yes, of course. A hall full of enemies and we carry no weapons.'

'Only the friends of the Duke are invited,' said Gaspir.

'Panagyn is no friend, and I do not trust Aric.'

The broad-shouldered bodyguard shrugged. 'Even if Panagyn were an enemy he would be a fool to attempt an assassination in a hall filled with the Duke's supporters. Put your mind at rest. Tonight is a celebration.'

'Are there many people here?' asked Niallad, trying not to show his fear.

'Only about a hundred so far, but they are still arriving.'

'I shall be down presently,' said Niallad. 'Is the food being served?'

'Aye, it looks enticing.'

'Then go down and eat, Gaspir. I will see you in a little while.'

The guard shook his head. 'You are in my charge, young lord. I will wait outside.'

'I thought you said there was no danger.'

The man stood his ground for a moment, then nodded. 'It will be as you say,' he replied at last, 'but I will watch for you. Do not be too long, sir.'

Alone now in the sanctuary of his rooms, Niallad felt the panic building. It was not even that he expected to be attacked. His mind knew it was entirely improbable. And yet he could not suppress the fear. His uncle had been in his own garden when the assassin, Waylander, shot him in the back. His own garden! With the king murdered, the country in a state of near-anarchy, the Vagrian army had poured across the border, burning towns and cities and butchering thousands.

Niallad sat down on the bed, closed his eyes, and took several deep, calming breaths. I will stand up, he thought, and walk slowly out on to the gallery. I will not look down at the mass of people. I will turn left and descend the stairs . . .

. . . into the heaving mass.

His heartbeat quickened once more. This time it was accompanied by anger. I will not be cowed by this fear, he promised himself. Rising, he marched across the room and pulled open the door. Immediately he heard the noise from below, the chattering, the laughter, the sounds of cutlery on dishes, all mixed together creating a discordant and vaguely threatening hum. Niallad walked to the banister rail at the edge of the gallery and looked down. At least a hundred and fifty people were already present. His father and mother were seated almost exactly below him, their chairs raised on a circular dais. Lord Aric was standing close by, as was the magicker, Eldicar Manushan, and little Beric. The boy looked up and saw him. Niallad smiled and waved. The men around the Duke also glanced up. Niallad nodded to them, and stepped back from the edge. In the far corner he saw the portly priest Chardyn talking to a group of women. And there, by the terrace arch, the Grey Man, standing alone. He was wearing a sleeveless jerkin of brushed grey silk, over a black shirt and leggings. His long black and silver hair was held back from his face by a slender black headband. He wore no ornaments or jewellery. No rings adorned his fingers. As if sensing eyes upon him, the Grey Man glanced up, saw Niallad, and raised his goblet. Niallad walked down the stairs towards him. He did not know the man well, but there was space around him, and the beckoning safety of the terrace beyond.

The bottom of the stairwell had been recently closed off by an archway and two doors. A guard stood inside the porch. He bowed as Niallad approached the door. The porchway blocked much of the sound from the hall and Niallad toyed with the thought of engaging the guard in conversation for a while, putting off the dread moment when he must step through and face the throng. But the man lifted the lock-bar and pushed open the doors. Niallad stepped through and walked across to where the Grey Man stood.

'Good evening to you, sir,' said Niallad politely. 'I trust you are enjoying my father's celebration.'

'It was courteous of him to invite me,' said the Grey Man, extending his hand. Niallad shook it.

Up close he saw that the Grey Man's clothes were not entirely free of adornment. His belt had a beautiful, and unusual, buckle of polished iron, shaped like an arrowhead. The same design had been used on the outer rim of his calf-length boots.

The sound of rasping metal from behind caused Niallad to spin round. At a nearby table a chef was sharpening his carving knife. Niallad felt panic looming. The Grey Man spoke. 'I do not like crowds,' he said softly. 'They make me uneasy.'

Niallad struggled for calm. Was the man mocking him? 'Why is that?' he heard himself say.

'Probably because I've spent too long in my own company, riding the high country. I like the peace I find there. The meaningless chatter of these events grates on my nerves. Would you like to take some air with me on the terrace?'

'Yes, of course,' said Niallad gratefully. They stepped out through the archway and on to the paved stone beyond. The night was cool, the sky clear. Niallad could smell the sea. He felt himself becoming calmer. 'I suppose,' he said, 'that such problems with crowds dissipate after a while as one becomes more accustomed to them.'

'That is mostly the way with problems of this nature,' agreed the Grey Man. 'The trick is to allow oneself to *become* accustomed.'

'I don't follow you.'

'If you were faced with a snarling dog, what would you do?'

'Stand very still,' said Niallad.

'And if it attacked?'

'If I was armed I would try to kill it. If not I would shout loudly and kick at it.'

'What would happen were you to run from it?'

'It would chase and bite me. That is the way with dogs.'

'That is also the way with fear,' said the Grey Man. 'You can't run from it. It will follow, snapping at your heels. Most fears recede if you face them down.'

A servant came out on to the terrace, bearing a tray upon which were crystal goblets filled with watered wine. Niallad took one and thanked the man, who bowed and departed. 'Rare to see a nobleman thank a servant,' said the Grey Man.

'Is that a criticism?'

'No. A compliment. Are you staying long in Carlis?'

'A few weeks only. My father wanted to meet with the lords of the four Houses. He is trying to avert another war.'

'Let us hope he succeeds.'

At that moment Gaspir strode out on to the terrace. He bowed. 'Your father is asking for you, young lord,' he said. Niallad offered his hand to the Grey Man, who shook it.

'Thank you for your company, sir,' said Niallad. The Grey Man bowed.

Niallad strolled away. Somehow the conversation with the Grey Man had settled his nerves, but his heart began to beat faster as he entered the throng. 'Face it down,' he told himself. 'It is merely a growling dog, and you are a man. You only have to be here for a while, then you can return to the sanctuary of your room.'

Niallad walked on, his expression grim and determined.

Waylander watched the youth make his way across the hall. The bodyguard Gaspir was following him closely. Elsewhere he saw Eldicar Manushan moving among the crowds, smiling and chatting to people. Waylander saw that his long robe seemed to shimmer and change colour as he moved. At first sight it was silver grey, but the folds glinted at times with subtle shades of pink and red, lemon yellow and gold. Waylander's gaze flowed over the hall. There had been changes since last he had been here. The stairwells were now closed off, and the arches leading to the library boasted heavy doors of oak. He preferred the previous style. It was more open and inviting.

A servant offered him a drink, but he refused, and strolled into the hall. He could see the boy, Niallad, talking with his father and the tall, slim Lord Ruall. The lad seemed ill at ease once more and Waylander could see the gleam of sweat upon his face.

Reaching the new door to the library, Waylander tried to open it, but it was locked from the other side. Eldicar Manushan strolled over to him. 'Your garb is most elegant, sir,' he said. 'Your lack of adornment makes most men here look like peacocks. Including me,' he added, with a grin.

'An unusual robe,' observed Waylander.

'It is my favourite,' said Eldicar. 'It is woven from the silk of a rare worm. Heat and light bring about changes in colour. In bright sunshine the robe becomes golden. It is a delightful piece.' Stepping in close, the magicker lowered his voice. 'Have you considered what we spoke about?'

'I have thought on it.'

'Will you be a friend to Kuan-Hador?'

'I think not.'

'Ah, that is a shame. But it is also a worry for another day. Enjoy your evening.' The magicker's hand tapped lightly on Waylander's back. In that moment Waylander felt a sudden chill. His senses sharpened, his heartbeat quickened. Eldicar moved away back into the crowd.

The thought came to him that he should leave this place.

Waylander walked back towards the terrace. He saw Niallad, climbing the stairs. He was moving slowly, as if at ease, but Waylander could sense the tension in him. Niallad reached the gallery, then turned to his right, entering his room. Sadness touched Waylander.

'Such a grim face for so lively an evening,' said the priest Chardyn.

'I was thinking of the past,' Waylander told him.

'Not a pleasant past, it seems.'

Waylander shrugged. 'If a man lives long enough he will gather bad memories among the good.'

'That is true, my friend. Though some are worse than others. It is worth remembering that the Source is ever forgiving.'

Waylander laughed. 'We are alone here, priest. No-one else can hear us. You do not believe in the Source.'

'What makes you think that?' asked Chardyn, dropping his voice.

'You stood your ground against the demons – and that makes you a brave man, but you had no spells, no belief that your god was stronger than the evil to come. I knew a Source priest once. He had faith. I know it when I see it.'

'And you, sir?' queried Chardyn. 'Do you have faith?'

'Oh, I believe, priest. I do not want to, but I believe.'

'Then why did the Source not strike down the demons as I prayed he would?'

Waylander smiled. 'Who is to say he did not?'

'Eldicar Manushan destroyed them, and though I may not be holy myself I also know holiness when I see it.'

'You think the Source only uses good men for his purposes? I have seen differently. I knew a man once, a killer and a robber. He had, to all intents and purposes, the morals of a gutter rat. This man gave his life for me, and before that had helped to save a nation.'

Chardyn smiled. 'Who can say for certain that it was the Source who inspired him? Where were the miracles, the light in the sky, the glowing angels?'

Waylander shrugged. 'My father told me a story once, about a man who lived in a valley. A great storm rose up and the river overflowed. The valley began to flood. A horseman rode by the man's small house and said to him, "Come, ride with me, for your house will soon be under water." The man told him that he needed no help, for the Source would save him. As the waters rose the man took refuge on his roof. Two swimmers came by and called out to him, "Jump into the water. We will help you reach dry land." Again he waved them away, saying that the Source would protect him. As he sat perched on his chimney, thunder filling the sky, a boat came by. "Jump in," called the boatman. Again the man refused. Moments later the water swept him away and he drowned.'

'What is the point of this story?' asked Chardyn.

'The man's spirit appeared before the Source. The man was angry. "I believed in you," he said, "and you failed me." The Source looked at him and said, "But, my son, I sent a rider, two swimmers and a boat. What more did you want?"'

Chardyn smiled. 'I like that. I shall use it in one of my sermons.' Then he fell silent.

Within the hall Eldicar Manushan, Lord Aric and Lord Panagyn had moved to the stair doors. A guard opened them and they moved through. Elsewhere Waylander saw other guests quietly leaving the hall. Most were followers of Panagyn. His expression hardened. His heart began to beat faster and a sense of danger rose in him. Moving to the terrace doors he saw a squad of soldiers marching through the gardens.

The five-man squad climbed the steps to the terrace. Waylander took the priest by the arm and drew the surprised man out into the night. The guards ignored them, and pushed shut the heavy doors, dropping a crossbar into place before marching off.

'What are you doing?' asked Chardyn. 'How will we get back in?'

'Trust me, priest, you do not *want* to go back in.' Waylander leant in close. 'I don't often offer advice,' he said, 'but were I you I would leave this place *now*.'

'I don't understand.'

'All exits from the hall have been blocked. The stairs are sealed off. That is no longer a banqueting hall, priest. It is a killing ground.'

Without another word Waylander walked away into the night.

Reaching the western postern gate he paused and glanced back at the palace, silhouetted against the night sky. Anger flared in him, but he quelled it. Everyone in that lower hall was destined for death. They would be slaughtered like cattle.

Is that why you wanted me there, Orien? he wondered. *So that I could die for killing your son?*

He dismissed the thought even as it came to him. There had been no malice in the old king. Waylander had murdered his son, and yet the old man had given him the chance to find the Armour of Bronze and, at least in part, redeem himself for his past sins. So why had he come to Ustarte? There was no mystical armour to find, no great and perilous quest to undertake. Waylander had attended the gathering, which was all that had been asked of him.

Then why did you want me here?

Into his mind came the face of a frightened youth, a boy who feared crowds and lived in terror of assassination. Orien's grandson.

With a soft curse Waylander turned and ran back towards the palace.

Within the hall a trumpet sounded, and all conversation ceased. Lord Aric and Eldicar Manushan appeared at the North Gallery rail above the throng.

'My dear friends,' said Aric. 'Now comes a moment you have all anticipated with great relish – as indeed have I. Our friend Eldicar Manushan will entertain you with wonders beyond description.'

Thunderous applause broke out, and the magicker raised his hands.

With all the doors closed the temperature in the great room began to rise. As he had at Waylander's palace, the magicker created small swirling globes of white mist, which floated and danced above the spectators, cooling the air and bringing applause.

A huge, black-maned lion appeared in the centre of the hall,

827

and rushed towards the revellers. Several screams sounded – followed by a rush of relieved laughter as the lion became a flock of small blue songbirds, which rose up towards the rafters. The audience clapped wildly. The birds circled the hall, then gathered together, merging into the form of a small flying dragon, with golden scales and a long snout with flaring nostrils. It swooped upon the crowd, sending out a roaring blaze of fire, which engulfed the spectators by the western wall. Once more screams were followed by laughter and applause as the victims saw that not a single scorch had blemished the beauty of their satin robes and silken jackets.

On the dais the Duke Elphons clapped politely, then reached out and took the hand of his wife, Aldania, sitting beside him. A tall, slim man to the Duke's left leant in to his lord and whispered something. Elphons smiled and nodded.

At that moment Eldicar Manushan's voice boomed, 'Dear friends, I thank you for your gracious applause, and now offer a climax to the evening's entertainment, which I am sure will make what has gone before seem trivial in the extreme.'

Dark plumes of smoke began to form in the centre of the hall, twisting and snaking, braiding together like copulating serpents. The braid broke in a dozen places, and huge dark hounds leapt out, snarling, their massive fangs dripping venom. The last of the smoke floated close to the seats of the Duke and his lady. It rose up before them, forming a dark doorway, through which stepped a swordsman. He wore an ornate helm, created from layered strips of black metal, and a black silk, ankle-length tunic, split at the waist. He carried two swords, long and curved, the blades so dark they seemed to have been carved from the night sky. A third sword, scabbarded, was thrust into the black silk sash around his waist.

Stepping forward he bowed to the Duke – then flung one of his swords into the air. The second followed it. Swiftly he drew the third, and this, too, he sent spinning into the air, just as the first blade returned to his hand. He began to leap and twirl, while juggling the blades. Meanwhile the twelve black hounds moved stealthily towards the spectators.

Faster and faster the swordsman spun the blades.

What happened next was so swift that few registered the act. The swordsman's hand flicked out. One of the swords flew straight into the chest of Lord Ruall. Instantly the second lanced through the throat of Elphons, Duke of Kydor. The third plunged through the heart of Lady Aldania.

For a moment only, there was silence in the hall.

Then the first of the hounds leapt, its great fangs ripping out the throat of a reveller.

'Enjoy a taste of true magic!' bellowed Lord Aric.

More smoke billowed, and a score of *Kraloth* rushed from it. The crowd panicked and tried to beat their way through the barred doors. Again the smoke came. Now there were some fifty demonic hounds.

They rushed into the crowd, their long fangs ripping and tearing at the silk- and satin-clad nobles. Aric watched from the gallery, his eyes gleaming. It was incredible! He saw one young man run across the hall and try to jump to the stair rail. A *Kraloth* leapt at him, jaws closing on his leg. The noble clung desperately to the rail. The *Kraloth* fell back to the hall floor, taking the lower part of the man's leg with him. Aric tapped Lord Panagyn on the shoulder, pointing out the scene. Blood gouting from the severed limb, the noble had almost managed to haul himself on to the stairs. Aric gestured to the bodyguard Gaspir, who was standing close by. The man ran along the gallery, and down the stairs. Just as the noble believed he had reached safety Gaspir came alongside. The young man reached out to Gaspir, seeking help. The black-bearded bodyguard grabbed him, tipping him back into the hall. As his body struck the floor a *Kraloth* leapt upon him, ripping away his face.

All across the hall there were similar scenes. Aric gloried in them. He swung to make a comment to Eldicar Manushan, and saw that the magicker had withdrawn from the gallery rail and was sitting on a bench with his page. He seemed lost in thought.

Aric stared down at the dead Duke. His one complaint was that the man had died too swiftly. Pompous bastard! He should have been made to watch all his followers scream and die.

At that moment Aric saw movement on the East Gallery. The youth, Niallad, had emerged from his room and was standing at the rail, staring in horror at the blood-letting below.

Aric looked around for Gaspir. The bodyguard was standing with one of Panagyn's men. They, too, had seen the boy. Gaspir glanced towards Aric for confirmation. Aric nodded. Gaspir drew his dagger.

Niallad's mind reeled at the sights before him. The sound of screaming filled his ears. The hall was awash with blood and corpses. A severed arm was draped over one of the food tables, dripping gore on to bone-white plates. Huge black hounds were leaping on the terrified survivors. Niallad saw a man hammering at one of the doors, shouting to be let out. One hound leapt upon his back, massive teeth crunching down on his skull.

Niallad gazed down and saw his parents, slain where they sat. A black-garbed swordsman approached his father's body, reached out, then pulled a sword from the body. The corpse of Duke Elphons toppled sideways.

'Murderer!' screamed Niallad. The warrior looked up, then transferred his gaze to Eldicar Manushan, who was now leaning on the North Gallery banister rail, watching the carnage below. Beside him stood Lords Aric and Panagyn.

Niallad could not, at that moment, comprehend why these men were standing idly by. He felt giddy and sick and began to lose all sense of reality. Then he saw Gaspir and another man moving towards him.

'They have killed my father, Gaspir,' he said.

'They have killed you too,' said his bodyguard.

Niallad saw the knives in their hands. He backed away into his room. His legs were trembling. All his young life he had feared just such a moment as this. And now it was upon him. Curiously the terror faded away, replaced by a cold anger. His limbs ceased to tremble and he ran to his bed, where he had discarded his dagger-belt. His fingers curled around the carved ebony hilt, pulling the weapon clear. Then he swung to face the men.

'I thought you were my friend, Gaspir,' he said, and felt a surge of pride that there was no fear in his voice.

'I *was* your friend,' said Gaspir, 'but I serve Lord Aric. I will kill you swiftly, boy. I'll not throw you to the beasts.'

Gaspir stepped closer. The other man edged away to the right.

'Why are you doing this?' asked Niallad.

'There's little point in such a question,' said the Grey Man, stepping through the balcony doorway. 'You might just as well ask a rat why it spreads disease. It does it because it is a rat. It knows no other way.'

The two assassins hesitated. Gaspir glanced at the Grey Man, who was standing unarmed, his thumbs resting in his belt. 'Kill the boy,' he ordered the second man, then advanced on the Grey Man. His intended victim did not back away. His right hand moved to his ornate belt buckle. In that fraction of a heartbeat Gaspir saw the arrowhead-shaped centre of the buckle slide clear. The Grey Man's hand flicked out. Blinding white light exploded in Gaspir's right eye-socket, lancing fire through his skull. He fell back.

Niallad saw the Grey Man step in swiftly, grab Gaspir's knife arm and twist it savagely. The long blade fell clear. The Grey Man caught the falling blade by the hilt, and flipped it. His arm rose and fell. There was a grunt from Niallad's left. The second assassin staggered, Gaspir's blade lodged in his neck. Even so he raised his own knife and lunged at Niallad. The youth sidestepped and, without thinking, slammed his own dagger through the man's chest, piercing the heart. He dropped without a sound.

Gaspir was on his knees groaning, one hand over the bleeding wound in his eye. The Grey Man slapped his hand away, and tore the throwing knife clear. Gaspir gave a cry of pain and fell back. The Grey Man coolly sliced his blade across Gaspir's throat. Ignoring the dying man, who continued to writhe on the floor, he walked across to Niallad.

'My parents are dead,' said Niallad.

'I know,' said the Grey Man, moving past the boy and making for the door. Gently he pushed it shut. He swung back to Niallad. 'Breathe slowly,' he said, 'and look into my eyes.'

Niallad did so. 'Now, listen to me. If you are going to survive you must understand your position. You are no longer the son of the mightiest man in the realm. You are, from this moment, an outlaw. They will hunt you and try to kill you. You are a man alone. You must learn to think like one. Strap on that dagger-belt, and follow me.'

Lord Shastar of House Bakard, his shirt torn away, blood seeping from the clawmarks on his naked back, sat huddled against the western wall, watching the black hounds ripping flesh from the bodies – some of which were still living.

Shastar sat very still, aware that the slightest movement could alert the creatures to his presence. Across from him he could see the bodies of the Duke and his wife, the dead Ruall lying beside them.

The black-garbed warrior who had killed them was standing silently, arms folded across his chest.

A massive hound padded across to where Shastar sat. He did not move. The beast's nostrils flared, its huge head so close to Shastar's own that he could smell the beast's foetid breath. Shastar closed his eyes, waiting for the fangs to rip away at him. Just then a dying woman close by let out a groan. The hound leapt upon her, and Shastar heard the sound of crunching bones.

Voices sounded close by. Opening his eyes he saw the magicker, Eldicar Manushan, strolling among the corpses. As he reached each hound he lightly touched it. With each touch one of the creatures disappeared, until at last the hall was eerily silent.

'Gods, what a mess,' he heard someone say. Shastar glanced to his right to see Lord Aric, picking his way across the marble floor, careful to avoid the pools of blood and severed limbs. Shastar watched, as if in a dream. He could hardly believe this was happening. How could a cultured man like Aric have been responsible for such a massacre? He had known Aric for years. They had hunted together, discussed art and poetry. There had been no indication of the monster dwelling within him.

Shastar watched as the magicker walked around the hall, staring down at the bodies. He saw him reach the East Gallery stairs. Aric moved across to the body of Duke Elphons, dragging it from the ornate, high-backed chair. The lord of House Kilraith then tore the cape from the Duke's shoulders and wiped blood from the chair before sitting down and surveying the hall. Eldicar Manushan joined him. 'There is no sign of the Grey Man,' he said.

'What? He must be here.'

At that moment a shadow fell across Shastar. He looked up to see the black-garbed warrior who had killed the Duke looming over him. The man's features were Chiatze, though his eyes were golden. He leaned in close. Shastar saw that his pupils were elongated, like those of a cat.

'This one lives,' said the warrior. Reaching down he grabbed Shastar by the arm and hauled him to his feet. The strength in the man's grip surprised Shastar. The warrior was slim and not tall, yet the heavy-set lord of House Bakard was dragged upright in an instant.

'Well, well,' said Eldicar Manushan, striding forward, 'I never cease to be surprised by the vagaries of war.' He looked into Shastar's face. 'Have you any idea of the odds against surviving an attack by so many *Kraloth*? Millions to one.' Stepping in close he looked at the wounds on Shastar's back. 'Hardly a scratch, though the wounds will still be fatal if left untreated.'

'Why have you done this?' asked Shastar.

'I can assure you it wasn't for pleasure,' said Eldicar Manushan. 'I take no joy in such enterprises. But, you see, there are only two ways to deal with potential enemies: make them allies or kill them. I just did not have the time to make so many alliances. However, since you have so luckily escaped death, I feel obliged to give you the opportunity of serving my cause. I can heal your wounds, give you back your youth, and promise you centuries of life.'

'We don't need him!' shouted Aric.

'I say who we need, mortal,' hissed Eldicar Manushan. 'What say you, Lord Shastar?'

'If an alliance with you means joining forces with a worm like Aric I'll have to decline,' said Shastar.

'You really should reconsider,' said Eldicar gently. 'Death is terribly final.'

Shastar smiled – then lunged at the magicker. His right hand curled around Eldicar Manushan's dagger, dragging it from its sheath and ramming the blade into the magicker's chest. Eldicar Manushan staggered back, then righted himself. Taking hold of the hilt he slowly pulled the weapon clear. Blood dripped from the blade. Eldicar Manushan held the dagger out before him and released it. Instead of falling to the floor it hovered in the air. 'That really hurt,' he said, aggrieved. 'But I understand your anger. Rest in peace.'

The blade spun and swept into Shastar's chest, slipping between the ribs and plunging into his heart.

Shastar grunted then fell to his knees. He too tried to pull the dagger clear, but then pitched face first to the floor. 'Such a shame,' said the magicker. 'I liked the man. He had honour and courage. Now . . . where were we? Ah, yes, the Grey Man.' He glanced up at the East Gallery. 'Your men are taking rather a long time to complete a simple task, Aric.'

Lord Aric rose from the Duke's chair and ordered two of the guards to fetch Gaspir. Moments later one of the men called from the gallery, 'My lord, Gaspir and Valik are dead. There is no sign of the boy. They must have escaped to the gardens and the beach.'

'Find them!' roared Aric.

'Good advice,' muttered Eldicar Manushan. 'It would be greatly advisable to find him – before he finds you.'

Eldicar Manushan crouched down by the body of the dead Shastar and pulled his dagger clear, wiping the blade on the dead man's leggings. Sheathing the dagger, he noted that the hem of his shimmering robe was stained with blood. With a sigh he picked his way through the corpse-strewn hall and opened the stair door.

Climbing to the gallery he found Beric still sitting on the bench. Taking the boy's hand he led him back through to their own suite of rooms.

'It is time for the communion,' said Beric.

'I know.'

Eldicar sat down on a wide couch, the boy beside him. The magicker, still holding the boy's hand, closed his eyes and tried to relax. Communion did not come easily, for first he had to mask his feelings. He had not wanted this massacre, believing it unnecessary. Most of the people present would not have been a threat to the plans of Kuan-Hador. He could have engineered it so that only the Duke and his closest allies were killed. He did not want such thoughts in his mind once communion was established. Deresh Karany did not tolerate criticism.

Eldicar concentrated on thoughts of his childhood, and the small sailboat his father had built for him on the lake. Good days, when the Talent was imprecise and unskilled, and he had dreamed of becoming a healer.

He felt the first sharp tug in his mind. It was most painful, as if the flesh of his brain was being teased by a talon.

'*Not a great success, Eldicar Manushan,*' came the voice of Deresh Karany.

'*Nor yet a failure, Lord. The Duke and his allies are dead.*'

'*The Grey Man lives, as do the two sword-bearers.*'

'*I have sent eight Kriaz-nor to intercept the sword-bearers. Two squads, one led by Three-swords, the other by Striped-claw.*'

'*Commune with both squads. Tell them they have three days.*'

'*Yes, Lord.*'

'*And what of the traitor, Ustarte?*'

'*I believe her to be alive and hidden in the palace of the Grey Man. A troop of Lord Aric's soldiers are already on their way.*'

'*I would appreciate her being taken alive.*'

'*That is the instruction they have. I would be happier if more Kriaz-nor could be sent.*'

'*More will come when the gateway finally collapses. Until then you must use Anharat's creatures. Tell me, why did you offer the man Shastar his life?*'

'*He had courage.*'

'*He was a potential enemy. You have a soft heart, Eldicar. Do not allow it to interfere with the orders you have been given. We are great because we obey. We do not question.*'

'*I understand, Lord.*'

'*I hope that you do. I risked my reputation to speak up for you following the débâcle at Parsha-noor. It would hurt me if you proved unworthy of my trust. When you have found the priestess commune again.*'

'*Yes, Lord.*'

Eldicar groaned as the link was severed. 'Your nose is bleeding,' said Beric. Eldicar pulled a handkerchief from the pocket of his robe, and dabbed at it. His head was pounding.

'You should lie down,' said Beric.

'I shall,' said Eldicar, pushing himself to his feet and walking through to his bedroom.

Lying back on the satin coverlet of his bed, his head upon the soft pillow, he thought of the débâcle at Parsha-noor.

Eldicar had given the enemy an extra day to consider surrender. An extra day! They had refused, and Deresh Karany had arrived at the battlefield. He sent a First Level demon to rip out the heart of the enemy king, and a host of *Kraloth* to terrorize the city-dwellers. Oh, they had surrendered fast enough then, Eldicar recalled. When they finally opened the gates to their conquerors Deresh Karany ordered twenty-six thousand of the citizens – one in three of the city-dwellers – to be put to death. Another ten thousand had been shipped back to Kuan-Hador to be Joined.

The extra day had seen Eldicar censured before the Seven. Only the mitigating plea from Deresh Karany had saved him from impalement.

The bleeding stopped.

Eldicar closed his eyes and dreamed of sailboats.

'All in all a fine night's work,' said Lord Panagyn, peeling away the silver eye-patch and staring around the blood-drenched hall. 'Ruall, Shastar and Elphons are dead, with most of their captains and supporters.' He stared at the dead Aldania. 'Shame about the woman. I always admired her.'

Aric summoned two of his guards and ordered them to gather work parties to clear the bodies. He was not a happy man. Panagyn clapped him on the shoulder. 'Why so glum, cousin? So the boy got away. He won't get far.'

'It is not the boy who concerns me,' said Aric. 'It is the Grey Man.'

'I've heard of him. A rich merchant, and your largest creditor.' Panagyn chuckled. 'You always did love to live above your means, cousin.'

'He is a deadly man. He killed Vanis. Came into his house while it was surrounded by guards and cut his throat.'

'I heard it was suicide.'

'You heard wrong.'

'Well, you have fifty men scouring the town for him. So relax. Enjoy the victory.'

Aric stalked across the hall, past the silent, black-garbed warrior who had killed the Duke. The man was sitting quietly by the stairs, arms folded, eyes closed. He did not look up as Aric passed. Climbing the stairs, Aric moved to Niallad's room. Panagyn came in behind him. Aric knelt by the body of Gaspir. 'Stabbed through the eye, then had his throat cut,' said Panagyn.

Aric could not have cared less. He walked through to the balcony. He gazed out over the moonlit garden towards the wrought-iron gate leading to the private beach. From here he could see the blazing torches and lanterns of the searchers. There had been no boats upon the beach, which meant that the fugitives would have to swim the bay. There was no other escape route. The front of the palace had been swarming with guards.

The Grey Man had not been seen there.

'Take a look at this,' said Panagyn. Aric turned to see the Lord of House Rishell kneeling by the second body. He pointed at the knife jutting from the man's neck. It had an ornate handle of carved ivory. 'Wasn't this Gaspir's knife?'

'Aye,' said Aric, puzzled.

Panagyn glanced back at the other body. 'So the Grey Man killed Gaspir, took away his knife and stabbed my nephew through the neck before he could kill the boy. No, that would have taken too long. He took the knife and *threw* it.' Panagyn smiled. 'I see what you mean by deadly. Have to admire skill like that, though.'

'You are taking the death of your relative very well,' snapped Aric. 'I commend the manner in which you are hiding your grief.'

Panagyn ruffled the dead man's hair. 'He was a good lad. Not very bright, though.' Rising, he moved to a nearby table and poured a goblet of wine. 'And it is hard to be sad on a night when almost all of one's enemies have been killed.'

'Well, *all* of mine are not yet dead,' said Aric.

'*All* of them never will be, cousin. That is the penalty for being a ruler.' Panagyn drained the wine. 'I think I shall take to my bed. It has been a long – and rewarding – night. You should get some rest. There is much to do tomorrow.'

'I will rest – when they have found the Grey Man,' said Aric.

Back in the hall the bodies were being cleared away. Aric descended the stairs and walked out into the night. A line of men bearing torches was climbing up from the beach. Aric waited. His captain, a thin, hatchet-faced man named Shad, approached. He gave a brief bow. 'No sign of them on the beach, Lord. I have sent out boats to search the water, and riders to scour the opposite shoreline. We are also organizing a house-to-house search through the town.'

'They could not have made it to the White Palace in this time,' said Aric. 'Are you certain no unauthorized guest left the hall?'

'There was one, Lord. The priest Chardyn. The guards assumed his name had been mistakenly omitted from the list.'

'I don't care about the priest.'

'There was no-one else, Lord. The second squad reported that there was another man with the priest when they closed the western doors. From the description it was the Grey Man. He must have walked around to the rear of the palace and scaled the wall to the boy's room.'

'That much we already know,' said Aric. 'What happened *then* is what we must find out.'

'They must have gone to the beach, Lord. The tide was in so they could not have skirted the cliffs. We will find them. It will be light soon. If they are swimming in the bay the boatmen will catch them. Do you wish for them to be taken alive?'

'No, just kill them. But bring me the heads.'

'Yes, Lord.'

Aric strode back into the palace. There was a growing stench in the hall, but it faded as he climbed the stairs. Pausing at the top, he looked down, remembering the screams and cries of the dying. The pleasure he experienced had quite surprised him. Thinking back now, he found his previous joy disconcerting. He had never seen himself as a cruel man. As a child he had even hated hunting. It was most puzzling.

Panagyn had mentioned the death of Aldania. Aric paused. He had always liked the Duke's wife. She had been most kind to him. Why, then, did he feel nothing at her passing? Not the tiniest touch of guilt or regret. You are just tired, he told himself. There is nothing wrong with you.

Aric opened the door to his apartments. It was dark inside. The servants had not lit his lanterns. He was momentarily irritated – until he recalled that the servants had been ordered to leave the

837

hall for Eldicar's performance. After that, in the chaos that had followed the slaughter, it was not surprising that they had forgotten their duties.

Moving through the main room, he walked to the balcony and stared out once more over the gardens and the distant beach. There were many boats drawn up now on the sand, and he could see the commandeered fishing boats heading back towards their moorings. Obviously the Grey Man and the boy had not chosen to swim the bay. Where, then, were they?

In that moment he heard a whisper of sound from behind. As he turned he saw a dark figure loom out of the shadows. Something glittering and bright flashed for his face. Aric hurled himself backwards. His legs thudded against the balcony balustrade and he toppled over it, striking his head on a jutting stone.

Darkness swamped him.

Aric became aware of the taste of blood in his mouth. He tried to move, but something was pulling at his arm. He opened his eyes. His face was resting against bare earth, his left arm wedged into the branches of a flowering bush. He dragged it clear, and groaned as pain shot through his side. Lying still for a moment he gathered his thoughts.

Someone had been in his room. He had been attacked and had fallen twenty feet from the balcony. The bush had broken his fall, but it felt as if he had snapped a rib. Pushing himself to his knees he saw that blood had stained the earth beneath him. Panicked now, Aric searched for signs of a wound. A drop of blood dripped to his hand. It was coming from his face. Gingerly he lifted his fingers to his jaw. It was wet and sore. He remembered the flashing blade. It had cut him along the jawline from just below the ear all the way to the chin.

With a grunt of pain Aric levered himself to his feet and staggered along the path, emerging at the front of the palace. Two guards were standing nearby. Seeing him, they ran forward and helped him back into the palace.

Within minutes he was in his rooms once more. Eldicar Manushan came to him there and examined his wounds. 'You have two cracked ribs, and your left wrist is sprained,' he said.

'What about my face? Will it be badly scarred?'

'I shall deal with that presently. What happened?'

'I was attacked. Here, in this very room.'

Eldicar moved out on to the balcony, then returned. 'There is a narrow ledge from your balcony to that of the Duke's son,' he said. 'The Grey Man did not flee the palace. He merely climbed along to your apartments and waited for the hunt to die down.'

'He could have killed me,' whispered Aric.

'He almost did. Had that cut been a hair's breadth lower it would have opened your jugular. A formidable opponent. He hides where no-one would think of looking, in the very heart of his enemy's fortress.' Eldicar sighed. 'Such a shame he would not join us.'

Aric lay quietly on the bed, feeling nauseous. Eldicar spoke again: 'You were very lucky, Aric. The enhancements to your body enabled you to react with far greater speed than the average human. That allowed you – just – to avoid your throat being cut. It also helped your body absorb the impact of the fall.'

'What else do these . . . *enhancements* do, Eldicar?'

'What do you mean?'

'I seem to have . . . changed in other ways. To have lost . . . something.'

'You have lost nothing you will need as a servant of Kuan-Hador. Now, let me seal that cut.'

As the ride progressed Keeva's tension grew. From the start she had realized this was not going to be an easy task. Most of the horses shied away from Ustarte, nostrils flaring, ears flat against their skulls. There was something about her scent that frightened them. Finally Emrin had brought out an old, sway-backed mare. She was almost blind, and allowed Ustarte to approach. Emrin lifted a saddle from a nearby rail. 'I cannot ride in the usual fashion,' said Ustarte. Emrin stood still, confused. 'My legs are . . . deformed,' she told him. His expression changed to one of embarrassment.

'Perhaps a *shabraque* would be more suitable,' he said. 'We have several, though they are not comfortable for a long ride. But you will be able to sit sideways upon old Grimtail. Will that suit, Lady?'

'You are very kind. I am sorry to put you to this trouble.'

'No trouble, I assure you.' Emrin moved to the back of the stable and returned with a leopardskin *shabraque* which he fastened around the pony's neck and belly. He swung to Keeva, who was already sitting upon a tall chestnut gelding. 'I have packed supplies for around three days, and two sacks of grain for the mounts.'

'We must be swift,' said Ustarte suddenly. 'There are riders heading up from the town.'

Emrin tried to lift Ustarte to the pony. He failed. 'Your . . . robes must be very heavy,' he said. The soldier searched around the barn, returning with a three-legged stool. Ustarte stepped on to it, then carefully sat down on the mare's back.

'Keep hold of her mane, Lady. Keeva will take the reins. And you had better carry the stool with you for when you want to mount again.'

Keeva heeled the chestnut forward. Leaning down, she took up the reins of the pony. It did not move. Emrin slapped the beast lightly on the rump and the two mounts walked out into the moonlit yard. In the distance Keeva caught sight of a troop of riders cresting a hill some half a mile away.

Now, an hour later, the two women had covered very little ground. The pony kept stopping and standing stubbornly in place for several minutes at a time, breathing heavily. Its dark flanks were already wet with sweat. Ustarte seemed untroubled. 'They are not following yet,' she said. 'They are searching the palace.'

'If we were being chased by a cripple with a crutch he would have overtaken us by now,' said Keeva.

'The pony is old and tired. I think I shall walk for a while.' Ustarte slipped from the mare's back. Keeva dismounted alongside her, and the two women moved off into the darkness of the trees.

They walked in silence for another hour, then Ustarte stopped. Keeva heard her sigh. She saw tears on the face of the priestess. 'What is wrong?' she asked.

'The killing has begun.'

'At the palace?'

'No, at the Duke's Feast. The *Ipsissimus* has summoned demons into the hall. The people there are being slaughtered. It is vile!'

'The Grey Man?' asked Keeva, fear swelling.

'He is not there. But he is close by.' Ustarte placed the stool she was carrying on the ground and sat down. 'He is scaling the wall behind the palace, and climbing into a room. Now he waits.'

'What of the riders who came looking for you?'

'They are gathering their mounts and preparing to follow. One of the servants said they had seen us at the stables.'

'Then we must ride. On fast horses they could be upon us in less than an hour.'

Using the stool, Ustarte mounted the pony and they set off once more. The old mare seemed to have gathered strength, and for a little while they made good time. But as they reached the scree slopes above the ruins of Kuan-Hador the beast stumbled. Ustarte climbed down and placed her ear against the pony's flanks. 'Her heart is labouring. She cannot go any further carrying me.'

'We cannot escape on foot,' said Keeva. 'There is still too far to go.'

'I know,' answered Ustarte softly.

Tossing aside the stool the priestess removed her grey gloves. Slowly she undressed, the moonlight gleaming upon the striped fur of her back and flanks. Passing the robe, gloves and soft leather shoes to Keeva she said, 'You ride on. I will meet you where the trail forks on the mountain road.'

'I cannot leave you here,' objected Keeva. 'I made a promise to the Grey Man.'

'You must,' said Ustarte. 'I will deal with the men following, and I will be at the road to meet you. Now go swiftly, for I must prepare. Go!'

Keeva leaned over to take the reins of the pony. 'Leave her,' said Ustarte. 'There is one more service she must provide.' Keeva was about to argue when Ustarte leapt towards the chestnut. Panicked by her scent the big gelding reared, then sprang away down the slope.

Ustarte moved to the old pony. 'I am sorry, my dear,' she said. 'You deserve better than this.' Her talons slashed through the pony's throat. Blood spurted. The mare tried to rear but Ustarte was holding the reins. As the blood pumped out through the severed artery the pony's front legs buckled. Ustarte lay down alongside her, pushing her face into the gaping wound. Swiftly she drank.

Her body writhed and twisted, muscles swelling.

Though not an expert horsewoman Keeva did not panic as the gelding raced down the slope. With one hand on the reins, the other grasping the saddle pommel, she held on grimly. The gelding, only momentarily panicked by the scent of Ustarte's fur, calmed down swiftly, and by the time they reached the first bend in the trail he was moving at a trot. Keeva gently tugged on the reins, halting the animal. She stroked the long sleek neck, and whispered soothing words, then swung in the saddle to stare back up the slope.

She was angry now. The Grey Man had asked her to see Ustarte safely away from danger, and now the priestess was going back alone to face the enemy. Keeva swung the gelding and began the long ride back to where she had last seen Ustarte.

It took some time, for the slope was steep. When finally she came upon the scene there was no sign of the beast-woman. The little pony lay dead upon the trail, her throat torn out, blood pooling on the stones. From some distance away Keeva heard a fearful roar. The gelding tensed. Keeva patted his neck. The distant roar came again, accompanied by the screams of terrified horses.

Keeva sat very still, and fear was strong upon her. A part of her wanted to ride on and aid the priestess, but the greater part desired nothing more than to flee, putting as great a distance as possible between herself and the dreadful sounds. In that moment she knew there was no *right* answer to the problem. If she rode to what she thought was Ustarte's rescue, and was captured, she would not be able to keep her promise to the Grey Man. If she followed Ustarte's orders and rode on, leaving the priestess to her fate, she would also be betraying the Grey Man's trust. Struggling for calm Keeva recalled the last words Ustarte had used. *'I will deal with the men following, and I will be at the road to meet you. Now go swiftly, for I must prepare. Go!'*

She did not say she would *try to* deal with the men, but that she *would* deal with them. Keeva gazed down at the dead pony. Ustarte had said she must prepare, and part of that preparation had been to kill the beast. Keeva dismounted and knelt by the body. Blood had spread out across the trail. Just beyond it Keeva saw a blood print on the stone. It was of a huge padded paw. Moving to it, she recognized it as that of a great cat.

All was silence now. There were no more screams in the distance, no echoes of terror.

Keeva backed away to the gelding and stepped into the saddle. She guided her mount down the slope and on to the plain, skirting the moonlit ruins of Kuan-Hador and the shimmering lake beyond.

Two hours later, with the dawn approaching, she halted at a fork on the mountain road and dismounted, leading the gelding into the trees. Tethering the horse, she walked back on to the slope and sat down on a rock. From here she could see the shadow-haunted plain below. A few clouds were drifting across the night sky, casting fast-moving shadows over the land. Keeva saw a movement on the plain, and tried to focus upon it. Something was moving at speed. A wolf, perhaps?

She had only seen it for an instant, but she knew it was no wolf. Clouds obscured the moonlight and Keeva sat quietly waiting for them to pass. She heard sounds upon the trail below her and, for a fraction of a heartbeat, saw a huge striped beast leave the path and enter the trees. The gelding whinnied in fear as the wind blew the scent of the creature across its nostrils. Keeva ran back to the horse, and lifted the small crossbow from the saddle pommel. Swiftly she loaded it.

A low growl came from the undergrowth, a rumbling, deep-throated sound that spoke of massive lungs. Keeva levelled the crossbow towards the sound. Then there was silence.

The dawn light filtered through the trees. The undergrowth parted.

And Ustarte stepped out. Blood was smeared across her face and arms. Pointing the crossbow to the ground Keeva released both bolts, then ran to Ustarte. 'Are you hurt?' she asked.

'Only my soul,' said Ustarte sadly. 'Do not fear, Keeva, the blood is not mine.'

Staying downwind of the frightened gelding, Ustarte made her way deeper into the trees, following the sound of running water. Keeva stayed with her, and saw there were tears on Ustarte's face. Reaching the water, the priestess crouched down and eased her crooked body into the stream. When all the blood was washed away she climbed once more to the bank. She stared down at her deformed hands and began to weep. Keeva sat beside her saying nothing.

'I wanted,' said Ustarte, at last, 'to keep this world free from the evil of Kuan-Hador. Now I have added to it. My people are dead – and I have killed.'

'They were hunting us,' said Keeva.

'They were obeying the orders of their lord. How good it would be to believe that those who died under my claws were evil men. But I felt their thoughts as I leapt among them. There were husbands there, thinking of wives and children they would never see again. Such is the nature of evil, Keeva. It corrupts us all. We cannot fight it and stay pure.'

Keeva returned to her horse and fetched Ustarte's red silk gown. She helped the priestess to dress. 'We must get to the cave,' said Keeva. Leading the gelding, Ustarte following some ten paces behind, she made her way through the trees watching for the carved signs left by the Grey Man.

They climbed for just under an hour, reaching the cliff-face and finding the cleft just as the Grey Man had described it. Inside there was a large chamber. A number of boxes had been piled there. Two lanterns were set atop the boxes. They were not needed yet, for light was streaming in from above, through a crack in the upper wall.

Keeva removed the saddle from the gelding and brushed him down. Then she fed him with the grain Emrin had supplied. At the rear of the cave, running water trickled down, forming a small pool at the base before flowing on down through a fissure in the floor. When the gelding had finished the grain she tethered him close to the pool, so that he could drink when he chose.

Ustarte had stretched herself out on the floor and was sleeping.

Keeva walked out into the morning sunlight. The trail outside was rocky scree, and she could see no sign of their passing. She sat back against the cliff-face and watched the branches of nearby oaks rustling in the breeze. A pair of wood pigeons flew by, their wings making a slapping sound. She looked up and smiled, feeling some of the tension drain from her body.

A red hawk swooped down from the skies, its long talons ripping into one of the pigeons. The wings folded and it dropped to the rocks. The hawk landed alongside the still-twitching body. Talons gripped it, the curved beak ripping into the living flesh.

Weariness flowed over Keeva, and she leant back and closed her eyes. She dozed for a while in the sunshine, and dreamt of her uncle. She was nine again, and the townspeople had dragged the old witch to a stake in the marketplace. Keeva had been out buying apples, which her uncle intended to use for a pie. She had watched the crowd baying at the witch, spitting at her and striking her with sticks. There was blood on the woman's face.

They had hauled her to the stake, tied her securely, then placed bundles of dry kindling all around her. After dousing her with oil they set fire to the kindling. Her screams were terrible.

Keeva had dropped the apples and run all the way home. Her uncle had hugged her, stroking her hair. 'She was an evil woman,' he said. 'She poisoned her entire family to gain an inheritance.'

'But they were laughing as she burned.'

'Aye, I expect they were. That's the nature of evil, Keeva. It breeds. It is born in every hateful thought, every spiteful word, every greedy deed. The crowd hated her, and in hating her they drew just a touch of evil into themselves. In some it will fade away. In others it will find a place to seed.'

The child Keeva had not understood. But she had remembered.

Keeva opened her eyes. The sun was almost at noon, and she rose and stretched.

Inside the cave Ustarte was awake, sitting quietly in the shadows.

'Are they still following?' asked Keeva.

'No, some returned to Carlis with their dead and wounded. Others are waiting at the White Palace to arrest the Grey Man. But they will come again.'

'Does the Grey Man know they are at the palace?'

'Yes.'

Keeva sighed. 'Good. Then he will avoid them.'

'No, he won't,' said Ustarte. 'He is already there. His anger is very great, but his mind is cool.' Ustarte closed her golden eyes. 'The hunters are closing in on the sword-bearers,' she said.

'You mean Yu Yu and his friend?'

'Yes. They are being pursued by two squads of *Kriaz-nor*, one from the south, one from the north.'

'What are *Kriaz-nor*?' asked Keeva.

'They are meld-creatures like myself. Faster, stronger and more deadly than almost any human.'

'Almost?'

Ustarte gave a wan smile. 'Nothing that walks or breathes is more deadly than the Grey Man.'

Keeva saw tears once more upon the face of the priestess. 'And that saddens you?'

'Of course. Within the darkness of the Grey Man's soul a small light flickers, all that remains of a good and kindly man. I asked him to fight for us, and fight he will. If that light goes out it will be my fault.'

'It will not go out,' said Keeva, putting her hand on Ustarte's shoulder. 'He is a hero. My uncle told me that heroes have special souls that are blessed by the Source. He was a wise man, my uncle.'

Ustarte smiled. 'I pray that your uncle was right.'

Chapter Eleven

Niallad sat quietly on the ledge, his back against the cliff-face, the white surf crashing upon the rocks several hundred feet below. The Grey Man was sitting motionless beside him, his face calm, no suggestion of tension in him. They had been sitting here now for two hours. The sun had been up for some time, and Niallad's clothes were almost dry.

The events of the night before kept replaying in his mind. The death of his parents, the treachery of Gaspir, the rescue by the Grey Man. It all seemed somehow unreal. How could his father be dead? He was the strongest, most vital man in the duchy. Niallad saw again his mother lying sprawled on the floor. A dreadful emptiness assailed him and he felt tears welling. The Grey Man touched his arm. Blinking, Niallad turned his head. The Grey Man lifted a finger to his lips and shook his head. No sound. Niallad nodded and glanced up. Some ten feet above them was an overhang of rock. From beyond that they could hear the guards talking outside the Grey Man's apartments.

'This is stupid,' he heard one of the guards say. 'He's not going to come back here, is he? I mean, the place has been searched. A few weapons, some old clothes. Nothing to risk your life for.'

Niallad could not help but agree. He could not understand why they had come here. After killing Aric, the Grey Man had led Niallad to the beach. There were now several boats beached there, left by the soldiers who had been searching the bay. Niallad had helped the Grey Man push out a small boat until it bobbed upon the water. Then they had climbed in and rowed across the bay. When they reached a spot some two hundred yards from the beach below the White Palace the Grey Man had slipped into the water and begun to swim. Niallad had followed him.

Upon reaching the beach the Grey Man had gestured to Niallad to remain silent, and climbed slowly to this spot. Everything about the man until then had spoken of purpose. But once they had reached here he had just sat down, and now the hours were drifting past. Niallad had no idea what he was waiting for.

Time moved on. Niallad's left leg was cramped and he stretched it out.

'About time,' he heard a guard say. 'Thought you'd forgotten all about us.'

'Gren got to talking to a blonde serving maid. Nice piece. Very tasty.'

'Speaking of tasty, I hope there's some breakfast left.'

'Any word on the runaways?' someone asked.

'I'll say there has been. Being stuck down here you missed all the excitement, lads. One search party was attacked by a wild beast. Three dead, five wounded.'

'Our lads?'

'Only one, old Pikka. Had his head stove in. The others were from House Rishell. Word from town is that the Duke's dead and most of his people. Sorcery,' he added, dropping his voice.

'What happened to the Duke?'

'Demons, they say. Appeared in the hall. Killed everybody. The Grey Man summoned them, apparently. Shad says not to talk about it. Lord Aric's going to be the new Duke. Once they've found the body of the Duke's son.'

'The Grey Man? That's what you get when you let foreigners come in and start acting like lords.'

'He always was a weird bastard,' said another voice. 'And he almost killed Lord Aric last night. Cut him right along the jaw-line. Missed his throat by no more than a sparrow's dick. Shad's questioning the steward now. He's a tough lad, but I reckon you'll hear him screaming before long. Best eat your breakfast quick. I tell you there's nothing like hearing a man scream to make you lose your appetite.'

Niallad heard the first two guards moving away. The others fell silent for a few moments. Then one said, 'Reckon that Norda would be great in bed.'

'That's true, Gren. Until Marja finds out, and cuts off your prick.'

'Don't even joke about it!' said the other, with feeling. 'She would, you know.'

Niallad turned towards the Grey Man. But he was gone.

The youth was shocked and stared around. He had heard nothing, not a whisper of cloth against the rocks. He sat still, wondering what to do. Then he heard a grunt from above, followed by a heavy thud. Looking up, he saw the Grey Man lean over the overhang.

'Traverse to the left and climb up,' he said.

Niallad did so, hauling himself over the top. The two guards were both dead. The Grey Man was dragging one body inside the door of a crudely fashioned building. Niallad just stood there. Only moments ago these men had been talking about a pretty woman. Now they would talk to no-one ever again. In that moment Niallad realized the Grey Man had been waiting for the guards to change, so that when he killed them he could be sure they would not be discovered for some time. The man was chilling! Niallad had always believed Gaspir to be one of the toughest men he had ever known. But he was merely a leaf, ripped from the tree by the fury of the Grey Man's storm. Now other leaves had fallen. Niallad could still hear the voices of the guards in his mind, ordinary men, dreaming ordinary dreams.

The Grey Man dragged the second corpse inside, then returned with a bucket of water and doused the blood on the ground. 'Come inside,' he said, his voice cool.

On leaden legs Niallad stepped across the threshold. The bodies were to the right of the door. The Grey Man pushed it closed and led Niallad into a long, dark windowless room. He lit two lanterns, hanging them on the wall, and Niallad saw that the room was hung with weapons, and targets had been placed around it, some round, as if for archery, others shaped into the forms of men.

'They think you were responsible for the massacre,' said Niallad.

'It is no surprise. Murder and lies usually go together.'

'I thought you had killed Aric.'

'So did I, boy. The rug moved under my feet as I lunged at him. Perhaps I'm getting too old for this kind of life.'

The Grey Man stripped off his silk jerkin, leggings and boots, hurling them to a nearby bench. From a chest set against one wall he drew out a leather hunting shirt, buckskin leggings and knee-length moccasins. Dressing swiftly he strapped on a sword-belt then looped a baldric, with seven throwing knives, over his shoulder. He glanced back at Niallad. 'Get out of those clothes,' he said. He delved into the chest once more and produced a second shirt of dark leather, which he tossed to Niallad.

'Why did you save me?' asked Niallad.

The Grey Man stood silently for a moment. 'To pay a debt, boy,' he said at last.

'My name is Niallad. Please be so kind as to use it.'

'Very well, Niallad. Get out of those clothes and find yourself a weapon that suits you. I would suggest a shortsword, but there are several sabres. Also choose a hunting knife.'

'A debt to whom?'

The Grey Man paused. 'This is no time for questions.'

'I am the Duke's son . . .' Niallad hesitated, seeing again his father's corpse. 'I am the Duke of Kydor,' he continued, his voice trembling. 'I have seen you kill four men tonight. I want to know why I am here, and what are your intentions.'

The Grey Man moved to a bench and sat down. He rubbed a hand across his face and Niallad saw how tired he was. He was not young, and there were dark rings below his eyes. 'It was my intention,' said the Grey Man, 'to board a ship and leave this land, to find a place where there were no wars, no murders, no scheming politicians, no greed. *That* was my intention. Instead I am about to be hunted once more. Why did I save you? Because a ghost came to a friend of mine. Because you are young and I knew you feared assassination. Because I am a fool, and somewhere deep inside me there is still a semblance of honour. Take your pick. As to my intentions towards you? I have none. Now, choose a weapon and let us leave more questions until we are away from here.'

'Who was the ghost?' persisted Niallad.

'Your grandfather, Orien the Battle King.'

'Why would he come to you?'

'He didn't. As I said, he came to a friend.' The Grey Man placed his hand on Niallad's shoulder. 'I know this has been a terrible night for you but, believe me, it could get worse. We do not have the time to talk now. Later, when we are away from here, I will answer what questions you have. All right?'

The Grey Man moved away. Niallad removed his tunic and donned the shirt. It was too large, but it felt comfortable. He walked around the room, examining the weapons on display. He chose a sabre with a blued blade and a fist-guard of black-stained brass. It was beautifully balanced. Finding the scabbard and belt, he tried to put it on. But the belt was too large. 'Here,' said the Grey Man, tossing him a baldric with a scabbard ring attached. Niallad settled it into place and slipped the scabbard through the reinforced leather loop.

'What do we do now?' asked Niallad.

'We live or we die,' said the Grey Man.

Emrin's head sagged forward. Blood was dripping from his mouth. His upper body was a sea of pain. 'I don't seem to be hearing any more smart remarks,' said Shad. His fist thundered against the side of Emrin's head. The chair to which he was tied swayed and fell to the floor. 'Get him up!' ordered Shad. Rough hands grabbed him. He felt sick as he was wrenched upright.

Shad's fingers took hold of Emrin's hair, yanking his head back. 'You want to say something funny now, Emrin?' he asked. Emrin's left eye was closed, but he stared silently into Shad's hatchet face. He wanted to summon up the courage for another insult, but there was nothing left. 'You see, lads, he wasn't so tough.'

'I don't . . . know anything,' whispered Emrin. Shad's fist slammed into his face, rocking his head back.

Emrin spat out a broken tooth and sagged forward once more. Shad yanked his head back. 'I no longer care if you know anything, Emrin. I've always hated you. Did you know that? Strutting around, fine as you like, with the Grey Man's money in your pockets. Buying the pretty girls, looking down on us *common* soldiers. So you know what I'm going to do? I'm going to beat you to death. I'm going to watch you suffocate on your own blood. What do you think of that?'

'Hey, come on, Shad,' put in another soldier, 'there's no call for that.'

'You can shut your mouth! If you're that squeamish wait outside.'

Emrin's heart sank as he heard the rasp of the door latch being lifted.

'Now what shall we do first to entertain you, Emrin?' asked Shad. 'Perhaps we should cut off your fingers. Or maybe . . .' Emrin felt the touch of a dagger against his groin. For the first time he screamed, the sound echoing around the ceiling of the Oak Room.

Hurling himself back against the chair Emrin tipped it and crashed to the floor, struggling furiously with his bonds. 'Pick him up,' ordered Shad. The two remaining guards moved to the chair.

From his position on the floor Emrin saw the door open. The Grey Man stepped inside, a small double-winged crossbow in his hand.

'Cut him loose,' said the Grey Man, 'and I shall let you live.' His voice was calm and conversational. The three soldiers in the room backed away, drawing their weapons.

It was Shad who spoke first. 'Big of you,' he said. 'But that weapon only has two bolts. There are three of us.'

The Grey Man's arm extended. A bolt sliced through the air, punching into Shad's throat. He stumbled back then fell to his knees, choking on his own blood. 'Now there are two of you,' said the Grey Man. 'Cut him loose.'

The guards cast nervous glances at the dying Shad. One drew a knife and slashed through the ropes binding Emrin to the chair. Then he dropped the weapon and backed away to the wall. The other man followed his lead. The Grey Man walked past Emrin to the mortally wounded Shad. The man was weakly trying to pull the bolt from his throat. The Grey Man wrenched it clear. Blood spurted from the wound. Gagging and choking Shad rolled to the floor. His legs kicked out and he died.

Emrin forced himself to his knees and tried to stand. He staggered. The Grey Man caught him. 'Steady yourself. Take a few deep breaths. I need you to be able to ride.'

'Yes, sir,' mumbled Emrin.

A young man appeared at Emrin's side. He saw that it was the Duke's son, Niallad. 'Let me help you,' he said. Emrin leant in to him.

'Go to the stable,' said the Grey Man. 'Saddle two mounts and the steeldust. I will see you there presently.'

Supported by the youth, Emrin moved through the doorway. The body of the guard who had left the room was lying on the rug. His throat had been cut. Supported by Niallad, Emrin made it to the main doors and out into the sunlight. The fresh air helped to revive him, and by the time they reached the stables he was walking unsupported.

Norda was waiting there, with several small sacks of supplies.

She ran to Emrin. 'Oh my poor dear,' she said, reaching up and stroking his bruised and swollen face.

'Not . . . so pretty, eh?'

'You look good to me,' she said, 'but you'd best be seeing to your horses. The Gentleman wants his steeldust saddled. He told me that.' She took his hand. 'Now, you listen to me, Emrin, the Gentleman is a fine man, but he has many enemies. You look after him.'

Suddenly, despite all his pain, Emrin laughed. 'Me? Look after *him*? Ah, Norda, what a thought!'

The Grey Man strode from the palace and along the gravel-covered path. Norda curtsied as she saw him. Emrin saw that his face was grim. 'Can you ride?' asked the Grey Man.

'I can, sir.'

Niallad came from the stables, leading three saddled horses, two roans and the steeldust gelding. The Grey Man stepped into the saddle and called to Norda, 'My thanks to you, girl.' Norda curtsied. 'And tell Matze Chai to return home.'

'I will, sir.'

Emrin walked to the first of the roans and hauled himself painfully into the saddle, then followed the Grey Man and the youth as they rode towards the trees.

They had been riding in silence for almost an hour when Emrin heard the youth say, 'The guards will raise the alarm. How soon before we are followed?'

'We have a little time,' answered the Grey Man.

The youth was silent for a moment. 'You killed them, didn't you?' he said at last.

'Yes, I killed them.'

'You told them you would let them live if they cut him loose. What kind of a man are you?'

Emrin winced as he heard the question.

The Grey Man did not answer it. Swinging his horse, he rode back to Emrin. 'Head west towards the forest, keeping the ruins to the south. If you see mist keep clear of it. I will catch up with you before dusk.'

'Yes, sir.' As the Grey Man rode back along the trail Emrin called, 'And thank you!' Heeling his horse, he moved up alongside the young man.

Niallad was flushed and angry. 'He has no concern for human life,' he said.

'He had concern for yours – and mine,' said Emrin. 'That'll do for me.'

'You condone what he did?'

Emrin hauled on the reins and swung in the saddle to face the young noble. 'Look at me!' he said fiercely, struggling to control his anger. 'Those men were about to beat me to death. You think I care that they are dead? When I was a lad a group of us thought it would be great sport to go on a deer hunt. We had our new spears, and a couple of us had hunting bows. Seven of us, there were. We went into the mountains and soon came upon tracks. As we were closing in on our quarry we moved into some dense undergrowth. Suddenly, out of nowhere, a huge grizzly reared up. One of my friends – an idiot named Steff – loosed a shaft into it. Only two of us made it down from the mountain.'

'What has this to do with the Grey Man?' asked Niallad.

'If you anger a bear don't be surprised if it rips your guts out!' snapped Emrin.

Three-swords was hot, the sun beating down on his lacquered black hair while not a breath of breeze stirred against his ankle-length tunic of black silk. He stood quietly, his hands resting on the hilts of two curved swords, scabbarded at his sides. A third sword hung between his shoulder-blades, his ornate helm tied to the hilt. The *Kriaz-nor* scanned the clearing then moved swiftly across it and into the shadows of the trees, closely followed by his three black-garbed companions.

Once in the shade Three-swords paused, enjoying the respite from the harsh sun. His golden eyes scanned the trail. Irritation touched him. They should have been given a hunt-hound, for despite his tracking skills they had lost the trail three times so far. It was most galling. Deresh Karany had given them three days to kill the sword-bearers, and two were almost gone. If they failed to complete the task in the time allotted it was likely that one of the four would be executed. Three-swords knew he was unlikely to be the one chosen, but with Deresh Karany nothing was certain.

He glanced back at his squad. Most likely it would be Stone-four, he thought. Fresh from the Stone training pen, he had yet to earn a fighting name. He had talent, though, as his apprentice name showed. He had finished fourth of fifty in the Pen rankings for that year. Three-swords ordered his companions to remain where they were, then carefully scouted further along the deer trail that led south through the trees. The ground was hard. Three-swords moved on. He heard the sound of water trickling over rocks and moved through the undergrowth towards it. Here the ground was softer, and between two bushes he saw hoof-prints, and alongside the water the deep impression left by a boot.

Calling out to his soldiers, Three-swords waited for them to join him. 'Maybe half a day, maybe less,' he said, his golden gaze focusing on the boot-print. 'Edges are drying out and crumbling.' The hulking, round-shouldered Iron-arm ambled forward. Pulling his scabbard from the black sash around his thick waist, Iron-arm dropped to his knees then bent over, sniffing at the print. Closing his eyes, he screened out the scents of his three companions. A male fox had urinated in the bushes close by, the musky smell all but masking the delicate aroma left by the humans. Opening his eyes, he looked into the grim features of his captain, Three-swords. 'One is very tired,' he said. 'The one with drying blood upon him. The other one – the *Riaj-nor* – is strong.'

'He is not *Riaj-nor*,' said Three-swords. 'Their order has died out. I am told they now have pale imitations calling themselves *Rajnee*. They have gone soft in this world. It happens.'

'Not to us,' said Stone-four.

Three-swords looked at the powerfully built young warrior. 'Until idiots start thinking that,' he said. Stone-four gave a low growl. His shoulders hunched. Three-swords stepped in close to the angry *Kriaz-nor*. 'You think you are ready to face me? You think you have the skill? Make the challenge, sheep turd! Make it – and I will take your head and eat your heart.'

For a moment it seemed that Stone-four would draw his sword. His hand hovered over the black hilt. Then he relaxed.

'Wise,' said Three-swords. 'Now you might live long enough to earn a name.'

'We should have them by nightfall,' said Iron-arm. 'If we push hard.'

'Better to reach them at midnight,' said Long-stride, the tallest of the quartet. His face was long and heavily bearded, his eyes deep-set, the pupils slitted. 'They'll be deep asleep.'

'I'd sooner kill them in combat,' said Stone-four.

'That's because you're young,' said Long-stride amiably. 'They taste better if they die relaxed. Is that not so, Three-swords?'

'Aye, it is true. Rage or fear stiffens the muscles. Don't know why. Midnight it is. We shall rest here for an hour.'

Three-swords moved away and sat by the stream. The

854

powerful Iron-arm joined him. 'No sign of Striped-claw's squad. They must be near as close as us.'

'Maybe closer,' said Three-swords, dipping his hand into the stream and scooping water to his thin mouth.

Iron-arm dropped his voice. 'Then why agree to wait until midnight? You want Striped-claw to be first?'

Three-swords smiled. 'I do not like Striped-claw. Too much cat in him. One of these days I'll have to eat his heart. I'll wager it will taste bad.'

'So why allow him the glory of the kill?'

'All the stories talk of the great skill of the *Riaj-nor* and the deadly spell-poisons of their blades. If Striped-claw overcomes such a blade, and takes the heart of the warrior who carries it, I will be disappointed. But I shall shrug and live with it.'

'You don't think that he will?'

Three-swords thought about the question. 'Striped-claw – though a ferociously good swordsman – is foolhardy and reckless. It would neither surprise me nor break my heart to hear of him being cut down by a *Riaj-nor*.'

'You said these warriors were but pale imitations,' put in Iron-arm.

'I said that is what I have been told. I prefer to withhold judgement until I have seen for myself.'

Three-swords pulled the two scabbards from his waist sash and laid them on the ground. Then he stretched out on his side and closed his eyes.

Yes, Striped-claw would arrive first. He would rush in and engage the humans without any thought of their talents, relying on his own blistering speed and skill. With luck he would suffer hugely for it. Then his men would finish the humans and Three-swords and his squad could join them for the ritual feast. It was a good thought.

He lay quietly, allowing his body to relax.

It was good to be wandering this land. For nine years Three-swords had travelled with the army, surrounded by hundreds of fellow *Kriaz-nor*, sleeping with nine others in a crowded tent, marching in formation or attacking cities. In this land the sky seemed larger, and Three-swords found that he enjoyed the freedom his mission offered.

He dozed for a while, and then became aware that he was dreaming. He could see himself standing by a cabin, a stream running nearby, his children playing near the trees. He sat up, cursing inwardly. From where does such stupidity spring? he asked himself.

'Bad dream?' asked Iron-arm.

'No.' Three-swords pushed up the sleeve of his black silk tunic and gazed down on the fine wolf fur that covered his forearm. 'It will be good when the army comes through,' he said. 'I miss the life. Do you?'

Iron-arm shrugged. 'I don't miss Sky-dagger's snoring, or the smell of Tree-nine's feet.'

Three-swords rose and slid the two scabbards back into his sash. 'I am tired of this place,' he said. 'We will not wait until midnight.'

Kysumu tethered the horses and fed them the last of the grain. The sun was setting as he moved back into the camp-site and prepared a small fire. Yu Yu was already asleep, his head resting on his cloak, his knees drawn up like a child. Kysumu gazed around at the trees, their trunks glowing in the light of the dying sun, and wished he had brought his charcoal and parchment. Instead he closed his eyes and tried for meditation. Yu Yu rolled on to his back and began to snore softly.

Kysumu sighed. For the first time in many years he felt somehow lost, adrift from his centre. Meditation would not come. An insect buzzed around his face and he brushed it away. He knew what was wrong, and the very moment that the seeds of his disquiet had been sown. Knowledge made it no easier to accept. Kysumu found himself thinking back to the years of training, but most of all his thoughts returned to the Star Lily, and the Night of Bitter Sweetness.

The Night was a mystery. All the students had heard of it, but none knew what it meant. Those *Rajnee* who had passed through it were sworn to secrecy.

Kysumu had joined the temple when he was thirteen, determined to become the greatest *Rajnee*. He had worked tirelessly, studying by day and night, absorbing the teachings, enduring the hardships. Not once did he complain of the bitter cold in the cell during winter, or the stifling heat of summer. At sixteen he had been sent to work on a poor farm for a season, to learn the life of the lowliest workers. He had toiled all season, working fifteen hours a day on arid land, rewarded with a bowl of thin soup and a hunk of bread. His bed was a straw mat beneath a lean-to. He had suffered with boils and dysentery. His teeth became loose. But he had endured.

His mentor had been pleased with him. A legend among the *Rajnee*, Mu Cheng was known as the Eye of the Storm. He had left the service of the emperor to serve ten years as a temple tutor. Every time Kysumu felt he could not go on he would think of the disdain in the eyes of Mu Cheng, and in that thought would find the courage to persevere. It was Mu Cheng who first taught Kysumu the Way of the Blade. This was the hardest of lessons, for Kysumu had spent years controlling himself, steeling his body against hardships, driving it often beyond its limits. This very control stopped him from becoming the swordsman he desired to be. In combat, Mu Cheng told him, the Way of the Blade was emptiness and surrender. Not surrender to an enemy, but the surrender of control, in order that the trained body could react instantly without thought. No fear, no anger, no imagination. The sword, said Mu Cheng, is not an extension of the man. The man must become an extension of the sword.

Two more years of strenuous physical work followed. By the end Kysumu was fast, his sword work dazzling. Mu Cheng announced himself satisfied, though pointed out there was much learning still to come.

Then came the Night of Bitter Sweetness.

Mu Cheng had taken him to a small palace in the foothills overlooking the Great River. It was a beautiful structure, with delicately fashioned towers, emblazoned with elegant statues, its walls plastered and painted red and gold, its gardens immaculate, pathways wending around shimmering fountains, beds of flowers in full bloom. The scent of roses, jasmine and honeysuckle hung in the air.

Mu Cheng led the bewildered Kysumu inside. In a large room a table had been laid, and an assortment of food was on display. The two men sat on gold-embossed chairs with satin cushions. For six years the student had dined on maize and boiled fish, hard bread and salted biscuits. On occasions he had tasted honey, but these were rare. On the table before him were pastries, cured meats, cheeses – delicacies of every description. Kysumu gazed upon them. Mu Cheng produced a small phial from his pocket and poured the contents into a crystal goblet. 'Drink this,' he said. Kysumu did so. For a moment nothing happened. Then the most exquisite feeling began to seep into Kysumu's body. He began to laugh. 'What is this?' he asked.

'It is a mixture of seed oils and extracts. How do you feel?'

Mu Cheng's voice sounded strange, as if the words were

floating around inside Kysumu's head, booming and fading. 'I feel . . . wonderful.'

'That is its purpose,' he heard Mu Cheng say. 'Now, eat.'

Kysumu tasted one of the pastries. It was exquisite. His body all but screamed with delight. He ate another, and another. Never in his life had he experienced such pleasure. Mu Cheng poured him a goblet of wine. As the evening progressed Kysumu almost passed out with joy. Such was his rapture that he failed to notice that Mu Cheng ate nothing, and merely drank water.

As the light began to fail two young women appeared, bringing lanterns which they hung on brass hooks. Kysumu watched them, noting the way their robes of silk clung to their bodies. They departed and another young woman entered. Her hair was black, drawn back from her face and held in place by a delicate net of silver threads. Her eyes were large and lustrous. She sat beside Kysumu, and, reaching out, pushed her fingers through his hair. At her touch he trembled and turned to look into her face. Her skin was pale and flawless, her lips red and moist. She took him by the hand and drew him to his feet.

'Go with her,' said Mu Cheng.

Kysumu followed the woman willingly, to a circular chamber and a large bed covered with satin sheets. Incense was burning, the scent heady and strong. The woman stood before him. Her hand went to a brooch at her shoulder. As she removed it her robe slipped away, as if it was made of liquid, flowing down over her body and pooling at her feet. Kysumu gazed with undisguised longing at her nakedness. She took his hands and raised them to her breasts. Kysumu moaned. His knees felt weak, his legs trembling. She drew him to the bed and undressed him. 'Who are you?' he asked huskily.

'I am the Star Lily,' she told him. These were the only words he would ever hear her say.

During the next few hours, until he fell into a contented sleep, the young *Rajnee* discovered the true meaning of ecstasy.

As the dawn was breaking Kysumu awoke to the sound of birdsong beyond the window. His body was aching, his head pounding. He sat up and groaned. The events of the night came back to him and he felt a surge of joy that swept away his headache. He looked around for the woman, but she was gone.

Rising from the bed, he dressed himself and walked through the palace until he found the scene of last night's feast.

Mu Cheng was still there. Upon the table was a goblet of water and a loaf of black bread.

'Join me for breakfast,' said Mu Cheng.

Kysumu sat. 'Will they be bringing more food?'

'This *is* our food.'

'Will the Star Lily be joining us?'

'She has gone.'

'Gone? Where?'

'Back to the world, Kysumu.'

'I do not understand.'

'You have two choices now. To be a *Rajnee* or to be a wandering warrior, selling your sword and living among men and women.'

'Why have you done this to me?'

'It is not hard, student, to forswear pleasures you have never experienced. There is no strength in that. Now you truly know all that the world can offer. The memory of this night will always be with you, dark and seductive, tugging at your resolve. In many ways this is the greatest test for a *Rajnee*. It is why it is called the Night of Bitter Sweetness.'

Mu Cheng had been right. In the years that followed Kysumu would often dream of the Star Lily and her flawless skin. Yet he had resisted the urge to find her, or to seek anyone like her. He did this in order to be the best *Rajnee* he could be.

Yet here he sat, unable to commune with the spirit of the greatest *Rajnee* to walk the earth. Instead that spirit had chosen to visit a lascivious ditch-digger with a stolen sword.

It was this that stopped Kysumu from reaching the required level of non-concentration required for meditation. The thought rankled.

Yu Yu Liang sat up and stretched, then pushed himself to his feet. To Kysumu's surprise he began to move through a series of muscle-loosening exercises.

'Where did you learn those?' asked Kysumu. Yu Yu ignored him, and continued to exercise. The *Rajnee* sat quietly as the ditch-digger began to dance through the elaborate steps of the Heron and Leopard, a series of ritualistic motions interspersed with moments of utter stillness. At the conclusion Yu Yu drew his sword and began a second series of exercises, thrusting, blocking, leaping and twirling. Kysumu's surprise turned to astonishment. As the exercises continued, Yu Yu became more and more supple, his speed increasing, until the blade moved like a blur.

Finally he stopped, sheathed the sword, and strolled across to Kysumu, squatting down before him. 'You know who I am?' asked the voice of Yu Yu Liang.

'You are Qin Chong, the first of the *Rajnee*.'

'I am.'

'I have tried to reach you. You did not hear me.'

'I heard you. But I needed all my energy to commune with the *pria-shath*. He tells me you are skilled with that blade. May the Source make that a golden truth, for the enemy is upon us.'

Chapter Twelve

Even as he spoke, four black-garbed warriors stepped from the shadows, moving into the clearing, their dark, curved swords in their hands. Kysumu rose and drew his own blade.

Qin Chong, in the body of Yu Yu Liang, drifted towards the centre of the clearing, his movements unhurried, his sword arm by his side, the blade trailing on the hard-packed ground.

Kysumu relaxed his body into the Way of the Sword, the great emptiness in which there was no fear, no exultation, merely a sense of quiet harmony. The four warriors spread out. Kysumu noted the way they moved. All were perfectly in balance. Kysumu sensed great strength in them, and guessed they would be fast. He could feel their confidence.

They did not rush in, and Kysumu observed they were deferring to the largest warrior. His robe of black silk, slashed to the waist, bore a silver brooch, shaped like the claw of a lion. Perhaps it was a badge of rank among the *Kriaz-nor*, thought Kysumu. The leader moved to face Qin Chong, who still stood quietly, his blade trailing.

Then he darted forward, his speed awesome. Kysumu blinked – and almost lost the Way. No human could move that fast! The dark sword lanced at Qin Chong's face. His own blade parried it, and the two fighters spun away. The *Kriaz-nor* attacked again and again. The other three warriors stood by silently. The two swords clashed repeatedly, setting up a discordant yet almost rhythmic music in the clearing. Sparks flew from the blades. Never in his life had Kysumu seen such brilliant swordplay. It was as if the two warriors had choreographed each move, practising it for years. The blades moved faster than Kysumu's eyes could follow, glittering in the new moonlight. The fighters spun away once more. There was blood on the wolfskin jerkin worn by Qin Chong. Then the swords clashed again in a whirlwind of shrieking steel. Neither of the swordsmen had spoken, and the struggle continued with renewed ferocity. Kysumu saw blood spray from the *Kriaz-nor*'s face as Qin Chong's blade nicked the skin of his cheekbone. The *Kriaz-nor* leapt back. 'I shall be proud to eat your heart,' he said. 'You are worthy.'

Qin Chong did not reply. The *Kriaz-nor* attacked again. Qin Chong leapt to his right, the sword of Yu Yu Liang flashing in a tight arc. The *Kriaz-nor* staggered for several steps, then turned. His belly opened, his entrails spilling out. With a strangled cry he tried to make one last charge, but Qin Chong stepped in to meet him, parrying his blade and sending a vicious cut into the *Kriaz-nor*'s neck, half severing the head. The huge warrior toppled to the ground.

For a moment all was stillness. Kysumu transferred his gaze to the other three warriors. Without their leader they seemed unsure, confidence draining from them. Suddenly one of them screamed a battle cry and ran at Kysumu. The little *Rajnee* did not wait to meet the charge, but stepped in. The *Kriaz-nor*'s blade swept down. Kysumu sidestepped, his own sword slashing up through the sword arm. The *Kriaz-nor*'s sword flew through the air, the hand still grasping the hilt. The warrior drew a serrated dagger and leapt at the *Rajnee*, who plunged his blade deep into the *Kriaz-nor*'s chest. A grunt of surprise and pain came from the warrior. Kysumu looked into the man's slitted golden eyes and watched the light of life fade from them. Dragging clear his sword, the *Rajnee* moved to stand alongside Qin Chong. The remaining two *Kriaz-nor* faded back into the forest.

'More will join them,' said Qin Chong. 'Let us ride.'

Sheathing his blade, he ran to the horses. Kysumu followed him. Swiftly they saddled their mounts and rode from the clearing. Pushing the horses hard for several miles, they came at last to a small valley. Qin Chong cut away from the trail and dismounted. Kysumu joined him. Qin Chong led the two geldings back to the trail and slapped their rumps. Both beasts headed off towards the south. Ducking back into the trees, Qin Chong beckoned Kysumu to follow him, then ran down a wooded slope and into a fast-flowing stream. Wading along it for almost a quarter of a mile Qin Chong halted alongside an old oak. There was an overhanging branch almost ten feet above the stream. Removing his sword and scabbard Qin Chong hurled it to the bank beyond the tree, then turned to Kysumu. 'Cup your hands,' he ordered. Kysumu did so. Qin Chong placed his right foot in the cup, then launched himself upwards. His hands grabbed at the branch and he hauled himself over it. Curling his legs around the bough he hung upside down, extending his arms towards Kysumu. The *Rajnee* threw his own sword to the bank, then leapt, caught hold of Qin Chong's wrists, then drew himself up until he could reach the branch.

Once back on firm ground Qin Chong headed south-east, climbing ever higher until they reached a small cave created by a sheet of overhanging rock. Here he sat, breathing heavily. Kysumu squatted down alongside him. Blood was still seeping from a shallow wound high on Qin Chong's chest.

'The *pria-shath* was right,' said Qin Chong. 'You do know how to use your blade. It was fortunate, however, that your opponent was panicked and frightened.'

'I have never seen warriors who can move at such speed,' admitted Kysumu.

'The advantages of the meld,' Qin Chong told him.

'How was it that you could make Yu Yu's body match them?'

'In all animals muscles work in rhythmic harmony, sharing the load. A man lifts a cup to his lips. He does not use *all* his strength to do this. Only a few of the muscles in his arm will be needed. If he lifts a rock he will use more. Imagine a muscle as being, say, twenty men. If you have to raise the rock ten times then the first time two of the men will do it, the second time two more, and so on. But it is possible – though not wise – to engage all of the men at once. This is what I did, though Yu Yu will not thank me when he wakes.' He smiled. 'Ah, but I have enjoyed this last moment of the flesh, the scent of the forest, the feeling of cool air in my lungs.'

'You will feel it again, surely, when we find the Men of Clay? You will return to aid us.'

'I will not return, Kysumu. These are my last moments in the world.'

'There is so much I want to ask you.'

'There is only one question that burns in your heart, swordsman. Why were you not chosen to be the *pria-shath*?'

'Can you tell me?'

'Better for you to discover the truth yourself,' said Qin Chong. 'Farewell, Kysumu.'

With that he closed his eyes, and was gone.

Niallad was dreaming about his father. They were hawking in the high country close to the castle. His father's bird, the legendary Eera, had brought down three hares. Niallad's bird, young and newly trained, had flown to a nearby tree and would not come down at his call.

'You must have patience,' said his father, as they sat together. 'Bird and man never form a friendship. It is a partnership. As long as you feed him he will stay with you. He will not, however, offer you loyalty or friendship.'

'I thought he liked me. He dances whenever I come close.'

'We shall see.'

They had waited for some hours, and then the hawk had flown away, never to return.

Niallad awoke. For a heartbeat he felt warm and secure in his father's love. Then, with terrible ferocity, reality smote him and he groaned aloud. He sat up, his heart breaking. Emrin was asleep on the ground close by. The Grey Man was seated upon a rock close to the horses. He did not look round. His figure was silhouetted by the bright moon and Niallad guessed he was staring back over the moonlit plain, seeking signs of pursuit. He had rejoined them some hours before, leading them to this high, lonely place, bordering the trees. The Grey Man had said little to him.

The young man rose from his blanket and strolled to where the Grey Man sat. 'May I join you?' he asked. The Grey Man nodded. Niallad sat alongside him on the flat rock. 'I am sorry for my words earlier. It was ungrateful of me. Without you I would have been killed by a man I trusted. And Emrin would be dead.'

'You were not wrong,' said the Grey Man. 'I am a killer. Did you have a bad dream?'

'No, a good one.'

'Ah, yes. They can hurt worse than fire on the soul.'

'I cannot believe my father is dead,' said Niallad. 'I thought he would either live for ever or die swinging his great sword and cleaving his enemies.'

'When it comes, death is usually sudden,' said the Grey Man.

They sat in silence for a while. Niallad found himself calmed by the Grey Man's presence. 'I trusted Gaspir,' said the boy at last. 'He had the ability to make me lose my fear. He seemed so strong. So loyal. I shall never trust anyone again.'

'Do not even think that,' warned the Grey Man. 'There are people who are worthy of trust. If you become suspicious of everyone you will never have true friends.'

'Do you have friends?'

The Grey Man looked at him and smiled. 'No. Therefore I speak from experience.'

'What do you think will happen now?'

'They'll be more careful who they send after us. Tough men, trackers, foresters.'

'Demons?' asked the boy, trying to disguise his fear.

'Aye, and demons,' agreed the Grey Man.

'We are beaten, aren't we? Panagyn and Aric have thousands of men. I have nothing. If I was to make it back to the capital I wouldn't know where to go.'

'The armies mean nothing without men to lead them,' said the Grey Man. 'When I have you in a place of safety I shall return. Then we will see.'

'You would go back to Carlis? Why?'

The Grey Man did not answer, but pointed down to the plain below. In the distance Niallad could see a line of riders. 'Wake Emrin,' ordered the Grey Man. 'It is time to be moving.'

Yu Yu groaned as he awoke. He felt as if a herd of oxen had spent the night walking across his body. With a grunt of pain he struggled up. Kysumu was at the mouth of the cave, his sword in his lap. 'I don't want to be a hero,' grumbled Yu Yu.

'You have been asleep for hours,' said Kysumu wearily. The little *Rajnee* rose and padded away from the cave. Yu Yu pushed himself to his knees and groaned again. Glancing down, he saw the fresh stitches in the new wound to his shoulder. 'Every time I fight I get hurt,' he said, though Kysumu was nowhere in sight. 'Every time. And when a great hero takes over my body *he* gets hurt. I'm tired of my body getting hurt. Once we find the Men of Clay I'm going home. I'm going to dig ditches.' He thought about it for a moment, remembering the threat to his life. 'No, first I'm going to sneak into Shi Da's house and cut his throat. *Then* I'll dig ditches.'

'You are talking to yourself,' said Kysumu, returning to the cave with a double handful of dark berries. He offered them to

Yu Yu, who sat down and ate gratefully. They did no more than dent the edge of his appetite.

'Qin Chong came to me,' said Kysumu.

'I know. I was there. Here. Whatever! He was very complimentary about my strength and speed. We fought well, hey? Cut his bastard head off.'

'You fought well,' agreed Kysumu. 'But now there are six more *Kriaz-nor* closing in on us.'

'Six? That's a lot,' said Yu Yu. 'Don't know if I could kill six.'

'*You* couldn't kill one,' said Kysumu, an edge of irritation in his voice.

'I know why you are angry. Qin Chong wouldn't tell you why you weren't the *pria-shath*.'

Kysumu sighed. 'You are correct, Yu Yu. All my life I have struggled to be the perfect *Rajnee*, to be worthy of the name, and to uphold the standards set by men like Qin Chong. I could have been rich, the owner of a palace, the lord of a province. I could have wed the Star Lily.'

'The Star Lily?' queried Yu Yu.

'It is not important. I have eschewed all riches and remained a humble swordsman. What more could I have done to be worthy?'

'I don't know,' said Yu Yu. 'I haven't done any of these things. But, then, I didn't want to be the *pria-shath*.' He wandered out of the cave, seeking more berries and finding a bush some sixty paces away. They were not quite ripe, but they tasted heavenly. Yu Yu had no idea why Kysumu longed to be the *pria-shath*. What was so great about being hunted and hungry, with killers on your trail? As far as Yu Yu was concerned he wished Kysumu *had* been the *pria-shath*. Having stripped the bush Yu Yu turned – and stopped in his tracks. The cave was set into the side of a domed hill. Yu Yu stared at it, remembering his spirit journeys with Qin Chong. As fast as his bruised limbs would carry him he hurried back to the cave. 'We are here,' he told Kysumu. 'This is it! This is the hill of the Men of Clay.'

'You are sure?'

'Certain.'

The two men moved to the open air, scanning the hillside. 'How do we enter?' asked Kysumu.

'I don't know.'

Slowly they traversed the base. No trees grew upon the hillside, and there were no openings of any kind, save for the cave in which they had rested. Kysumu climbed to the top, scanning the surrounding ground. Then he returned to where Yu Yu waited.

'I can see no sign of an entrance,' said Kysumu.

They walked back to the cave and Kysumu began to examine the grey walls. They were seamless. Yu Yu waited outside. He, too, was mystified. In his dream he had seen the *Riaj-nor* walking to this hillside and vanishing inside. He did not recall there being a cave, nor indeed an overhang like the one above, jutting from the hillside like a lean-to roof.

He walked back to the berry bush and stared at the overhang and the land below it. He had been a ditch-digger and a builder for most of his adult life, and he knew a little about the movement of soil. It seemed to him then that the area around the cave mouth could have eroded, exposing the cave. Kysumu joined him. 'I can find nothing,' he said.

Yu Yu ignored him, and walked to the rock face, just to the left of the cave mouth. His body was still aching, but he reached up, found a handhold and slowly began to climb. Had he not been so bruised and weary the climb would have been easy. As it was he was grunting as he hauled himself over the lip of the overhang. 'Up here!' he called, beckoning Kysumu to follow him. The little *Rajnee* scaled the face swiftly. There was a slab of stone, some six feet high and four feet wide, set vertically into the hillside.

'It looks like a door,' said Kysumu, pushing at it. It did not budge.

Yu Yu did not answer. He was staring towards the tree line, where six warriors had emerged.

Kysumu saw them too. 'At least they don't have bows,' he muttered. 'Perhaps I can kill them as they climb.'

Yu Yu stepped towards the rock door, extending his hand. As his fingers touched the stone it shimmered. Just like a pebble falling into a pond. Tiny waves rippled out. Yu Yu stared at the ripples, then he reached out. His hand passed through the door as if through a cold fog. He gestured to Kysumu, who was watching the advancing *Kriaz-nor*. 'I have found the way in,' he said, pointing to the cold stone.

'What are you talking about?'

Yu Yu swung back – to see that the entrance was solid stone once more.

'Take my hand,' said Yu Yu.

'We have you now, little men!' shouted a *Kriaz-nor*, running forward and scrambling up towards them. Kysumu's blade swept into the air.

Yu Yu touched the stone once more, and, as the ripples began, grabbed Kysumu's arm and dragged him through the fog.

On the other side they stood in pitch darkness.

'Oh, this is wonderful!' said Yu Yu. 'What now?' Immediately a score of lanterns flared. Kysumu narrowed his eyes against the sudden glare. As his vision acclimatized he saw that they were standing in a short tunnel, leading to a vast domed hall. Releasing Yu Yu's hand, Kysumu moved to the end of the tunnel. Within the hall, standing in ranks, were several hundred dazzlingly white, full-sized clay figures. Each of the figures was of a *Riaj-nor* swordsman. They were magnificently cast and sculpted. Towards the front of the silent army three of the figures lay broken. A section of rock had fallen from the roof, shattering them. Kysumu picked up a section of a fragmented head and examined it. He had never seen such quality of workmanship. Reverently replacing it on the ground he moved through the ghostly ranks, gazing upon their faces. Such nobility. Such humanity. Kysumu was awestruck. He felt he could see modest heroism in every face. These were the great ones, who had fought a colossal evil for the benefit of mankind. Kysumu's heart swelled. He felt immensely privileged merely to gaze upon their features.

Yu Yu sat down, leaning his back against the wall and closing his eyes.

After a while Kysumu came back and sat alongside him. 'What do we do now?' he asked.

'You do as you please,' said Yu Yu. 'I need to rest.' Stretching out, he laid his head on his arm and fell asleep.

Kysumu rose. He could not take his eyes from the grim Men of Clay. Every face was different, though each wore the same armour, ornate helms that flared out to protect the neck, torso protectors that seemed to have been created from coins, perfectly round and held together by small rings. Each of the warriors was also clothed in a full-length tunic, split to the waist at front and back. Their swords were like his own, long and slightly curved. Kysumu strolled through the ranks again, wondering which of these men was Qin Chong.

The lanterns burned brightly. Kysumu examined one, and saw that it carried no oil, no fuel of any kind. A globe of glass sat upon a small cup, white light radiating from its centre.

Slowly he walked around the domed hall. On one side he

found hundreds of small golden items laid on a wide rocky shelf. Some were rings, others brooches or wrist bangles, scattered and piled one upon another. There were pendants, ornaments and tiny good-luck figures shaped in the form of animals, dogs, cats, even the head of a bear. Mystified, Kysumu returned to where Yu Yu slept. He did not try to wake him. Yu Yu was exhausted.

A dull thumping sound echoed through the hall. Kysumu guessed that the *Kriaz-nor* had climbed to the overhang and were seeking a way through. They will not move that rock, he thought. But sooner or later he and Yu Yu would have to leave this place and face them.

He stared once more at the Men of Clay. 'Well, we have found you, my brothers,' he said. 'But what happens now?'

Matze Chai sat quietly, waiting for the interrogation to begin. He had heard of the massacre at the Winter Palace, and knew that Waylander was now, once more, a hunted man. What he did not know was why he had been summoned to the Oak Room of Waylander's home.

The captain of his guard, young Liu, was standing at his master's right-hand side. Opposite sat the magicker Eldicar Manushan, and two men who had been introduced as Lords Aric and Panagyn. Matze instantly found himself disliking both of them. Aric had the look of a contented weasel, while Panagyn's face was flat and brutal. A slender blond-haired little boy stood beside the magicker. Despite himself Matze found himself warming to the little lad, which was most strange since he loathed children.

The silence grew. Finally Eldicar Manushan spoke. 'It is my understanding that the individual known as the Grey Man is one of your clients.'

Matze said nothing, but he held the magicker's gaze, and maintained an expression of icy disdain.

'Is it your intention to answer none of my questions?' asked the magicker.

'I was not aware that it was a question,' said Matze. 'It seemed to me a statement of fact. There is no secret concerning my visit. I organize the financial dealings of the Grey Man, as you call him, within the lands of the Chiatze.'

'My apologies, Matze Chai,' said Eldicar, with a thin smile. 'By what name do you know this man?'

'I know him as Dakeyras.'

'Where is he from?'

'Some land in the far south-west. Drenan or Vagria. It is not my business to enquire too deeply into the background of my clients. I am retained to make their finances grow. That is my talent.'

'Are you aware that your client and a vile sorceress caused the death of more than a hundred people, including the Duke and his lady?'

'If you say so,' answered Matze, pulling a perfumed handkerchief from his red silk sleeve. Delicately he dabbed it to his nose.

'We do say it, you slant-eyed horse turd,' snapped Lord Panagyn.

Matze did not look at the man, but kept his gaze firmly on the face of the magicker.

'Your client has also kidnapped the heir to the Duchy, dragged him from the palace amid the slaughter.'

'An amazingly gifted man, obviously,' said Matze. 'And yet, apparently, not very intelligent.'

'Why is that?' asked Eldicar.

'He summons demons to wipe out the Duke and all his followers, yet somehow fails to kill the two most powerful lords. Instead of slaying them – a feat he could accomplish with ease – he decides to kidnap the Duke's son and, thus burdened, rushes off into the night, leaving his enemies alive and in possession of his castle, his lands and a great deal of his wealth. Hard to imagine what he thought he was achieving. Remarkably stupid.'

'What are you insinuating?' snarled Aric.

'I would have thought that was obvious,' said Matze. 'My client, as you well know, was not responsible for the murders. He had no reason to kill the Duke, and certainly would not resort to summoning demons if he could. So stop playing stupid games. I do not care who rules this realm, or who summoned the demons. I am supremely uninterested in such matters. I am a merchant. My interests lie in commerce.'

'Very well, Matze Chai,' said Eldicar smoothly. 'Let us put aside questions of guilt and innocence. We need to find the Grey Man, and we need you to tell us all you know about him.'

'My clients require from me a great deal of discretion,' Matze told him. 'I do not gossip about their affairs.'

'I am not sure that you realize the peril of your predicament, sir,' said Eldicar, his voice hardening. 'The Grey Man is our enemy, and must be found. The more we know about him the easier the task. It would be better for you to speak freely than to have the words wrung from you. And, believe me, I have the power to tear the words from you in between screams of agony.' Eldicar smiled and leant back in his chair. 'However, let us put aside such thoughts for a moment and examine ways in which you might reconsider your position and become my friend.'

'Friendship is always welcome,' said Matze.

'You are an old man, close to death. Would you like to be young again?'

'Who would not?'

'A small demonstration then – as a gesture of good faith.' Eldicar lifted his hand. A fist-sized globe of shimmering blue smoke appeared. It sped from his fingers, flowing into the nostrils and mouth of the startled Liu. The Chiatze guard fell to his knees, choking. Blue smoke exploded from his lungs and he gasped, taking in great gulps of air. The smoke flowed around Matze Chai. The merchant tried to hold his breath, but the smoke clung to his face. At the last he inhaled. A tingling sensation seeped through his limbs. He felt his heart beat faster, his muscles swelling with new life. Energy roared within him. He felt strong again. His vision cleared, and he found he could see with greater clarity than he had for years. He turned to Liu. The young captain had regained his feet. Matze's expression hardened as he saw Liu's dark hair was showing grey at the temples.

'How does it feel, Matze Chai?' asked Eldicar Manushan.

'It feels very fine,' answered Matze coldly. 'However, it would have been good manners to ask my captain if he objected to losing some of his youth.'

'I have given you twenty years, merchant. I can give you twenty more. You can be young and virile once more. You can enjoy your wealth in a manner denied to you for decades. Are you now willing to be my friend?'

Matze took a deep breath. 'My client is unique, magicker. Some men are talented painters and sculptors, others can grow any kind of bloom, in any kind of climate. You are obviously skilled in the arcane arts. But my client is a master of only one skill, one terrible talent. He is a killer. In all my long and – thus far – remarkably uneventful life I have neither known nor heard of anyone to match him. He has fought demons, and magickers, and were-beasts. He is still here.' Matze Chai gave a thin smile. 'But then I think you already realize this. He was supposed to have died in your massacre, and he did not. Now you believe you are hunting him. It is an illusion. He is hunting you. You are already dead men. I do not desire friendship with dead men.'

Eldicar looked at him in silence. 'It is time to know pain, Matze Chai,' he said. As he spoke he raised his hand and pointed to Liu. The officer's dagger slid from its sheath, spun, and plunged through Liu's right eye-socket. He fell without a sound.

Matze sat silently, his hands upon his lap as the guards moved in.

Three-swords stepped back from the rock door. Iron-arm continued to beat at the stone with the pommel of his sword. 'Enough,' said Three-swords. 'It will not budge.'

'How, then, did they pass through?'

'I do not know. But we have searched the hillside and this is the only way out. So we wait.'

The two *Kriaz-nor* climbed down to join the others. Long-stride was sitting down in the cave mouth, Stone-four beside him. The two survivors of Striped-claw's group were standing apart. Three-swords called them to him. They were both fresh from the Pens. It was stupid of Striped-claw to have chosen them for this task, but entirely predictable. Striped-claw liked to impress, and Pen-younglings were easier to impress than seasoned warriors. 'Tell me of the fight,' said Three-swords.

One of the warriors began to speak. 'Striped-claw told us to stand back while he made the kill. Then he fought the one in the wolfskin. It was very fast. The human moved like a *Kriaz-nor*. Great speed. Then Striped-claw went down. It was then that Hill-six attacked the second man. He died.'

'Then you ran?'

'Yes, sir.'

Three-swords stepped back from the pair and drew one of his swords. In one move of dazzling speed he beheaded the speaker. The second warrior turned to run, but Three-swords was upon him within a few paces, his blade slashing through the back of the *Kriaz-nor*'s neck. Turning, he strolled back to Iron-arm. 'Fresh meat,' he said. 'But leave the hearts. I do not want the blood of cowards flowing in my veins.'

At that moment the ground began to vibrate. Three-swords almost lost his footing.

'Earthquake!' shouted Stone-four.

A dull sound like distant thunder boomed across the clearing. A dislodged boulder rolled past them.

'It is coming from inside the hill,' said Iron-arm.

Another boulder moved, falling upon the overhang and bouncing out to crash to the ground close by. 'Back to the tree line,' ordered Three-swords. Iron-arm ran to one of the bodies and, hauling it behind him, followed his three comrades back to the safety of the trees.

Yu Yu felt stronger when he awoke, his bruised body refreshed. Kysumu was sitting cross-legged beside him, eyes closed and deep in a meditation trance. Yu Yu sat up and stared out over the white ranks of the ghostly army.

Leaving Kysumu, he strolled among the clay figures, looking at faces, seeking out Qin Chong. But he was nowhere to be found. At last Yu Yu came upon the broken figures. Kneeling, he pieced together what he could of the heads. As he half completed the second, sadness touched him. In his hands he held the features of the *Riaj-nor* who had befriended him in his dreams. 'What do I do now?' he whispered. 'I am here.' There was no answer. Yu Yu placed the broken pieces on the ground and sat back. Kysumu should have been the *pria-shath*. He was a trained *Rajnee*.

Yu Yu moved back to Kysumu and waited for the trance to end. Within minutes Kysumu opened his eyes. 'Are you feeling stronger?' asked the swordsman.

'Yes,' answered Yu Yu miserably.

'Did Qin Chong come to you in your sleep?'

'No.'

'Do you have any idea of what to do now?'

'No, I don't!' snapped Yu Yu. 'I don't know how statues can help us.' Pushing himself to his feet he walked away from the swordsman, anxious to avoid further questioning. Yu Yu had never felt so useless. He wandered around the walls, coming at last to the ledge scattered with golden ornaments. In his mind's eye he saw the warriors lining up here, placing their trinkets upon the rock. He picked up a small golden ring, then let it drop. In his vision he had seen warriors march into the depths of the hill. Now there were only statues. Where were the warriors? Had they been covered with clay? The broken head of Qin Chong's statue had been hollow, and there were no bones or scraps of hair within it, so that seemed unlikely. What, then, was the purpose behind these statues? Yu Yu strained at the thought until his head hurt. '*You must wake the Men of Clay,*' Qin Chong had told him.

'Wake up!' bellowed Yu Yu.

'What are you shouting for?' Kysumu called out.

Yu Yu did not reply. Unable to think of an answer he turned back to the ledge. His gaze fell upon a threaded rod of gold some four inches long. Beside it was a circular stand, with a hole at the centre. Yu Yu picked up the stand and inserted the rod into the hole, screwing it tight. The top of the rod was hooked, like a shepherd's crook.

'What are you doing?' asked Kysumu, coming alongside.

'Nothing,' said Yu Yu. 'Amusing myself. Something should hang from this hook.'

'We have more important matters to decide,' said Kysumu.

'I know.' Yu Yu continued to probe among the ornaments, finally finding a small golden bell with a ring at the crest. 'This is it,' he said, carefully hooking the bell to the rod. 'Pretty.'

'Yes, it is pretty,' said Kysumu, with a sigh. Yu Yu flicked the bell. A small chime sounded. The bell continued to swing, and the next chime was louder than the first. The sound began to reverberate through the domed hall, growing louder and louder. The rock wall began to vibrate, ornaments tumbling from it. Kysumu tried to say something, but Yu Yu could not hear him. Yu Yu's ears were hurting and he covered them with his hands.

Dust fell from the domed ceiling, and cracks appeared in the walls. The bell was now booming louder than thunder. Yu Yu felt sick. He staggered back from the ledge and fell to his knees. Kysumu had also covered his ears, and was squatting down, a look of intense pain upon his features.

The clay statues were trembling now. Yu Yu saw tiny cracks appear in the nearest figure, spreading out like a spider's web. And still the terrible tolling of the bell continued. Pain roared inside Yu Yu's head.

And he passed out.

Chapter Thirteen

Kysumu rolled to his knees. Blood was dripping from his nose. The noise was so incredible now that it had transcended mere sound. Everything hurt: ears, eyes, fingertips, belly. Every joint pulsed with pain. Kysumu forced himself to his feet and fell against the ledge, where the bell was still vibrating. Reaching out, the swordsman closed his hand around the tiny object. Instantly the tolling ceased. Kysumu staggered, then fell. He could scarcely breathe. Dust was everywhere, like a fog. Lifting the collar of his robe, he held it over his mouth. His ears were still ringing, his hands trembling.

Only then did he see the shining lights gleaming through the cracks that criss-crossed the statues. He blinked and tried to focus. It was as if the sun itself was trapped within the clay. The cracks of light widened, clay falling away. As the dust settled Kysumu saw that most of the statues were now bathed in golden light. The domed hall blazed with brightness. Kysumu closed his eyes against it, and where, only moments before, he had covered his ears, now he held his hands over his face. He waited for a few heartbeats, then opened his fingers. Light still blazed against his closed lids, and he waited again. Finally the brilliance faded. Kysumu let fall his hands and opened his eyes.

The Men of Clay were gone. Standing in the hall were several hundred living, breathing *Riaj-nor*.

Kysumu rose and approached them. They waited in silence. He bowed deeply. 'I am Kysumu,' he said, in formal Chiatze. 'Is Qin Chong among you?'

A young man stepped forward. He was wearing a full-length tunic of silver satin, his sword thrust into a black silk sash around his waist. He removed his helm and neglected to bow to Kysumu. 'Qin Chong did not survive the transformation.' Kysumu looked into the man's eyes. The pupils were black slits surrounded by gold. In that moment Kysumu felt as if he had been stabbed through the soul. His heart sank. These were not men at all. They were creatures just like the *Kriaz-nor*.

'I am Ren Tang,' said the warrior. 'Are you the *pria-shath*?'

'No,' said Kysumu, turning away. 'The bell rendered him unconscious.'

Ren Tang strode to where Yu Yu lay. Other warriors gathered in silence around him. Then Ren Tang nudged Yu Yu with his foot. 'Behold the great one, the *pria-shath*,' he said. 'We have crossed the centuries to aid a human monkey in wolfskin.' Some of the men chuckled. Kysumu knelt beside Yu Yu and saw that he, too, had bled from the nose. He rolled him on to his back. Yu Yu groaned. Kysumu hauled him to a seated position.

'I feel sick,' muttered Yu Yu. He opened his eyes, then jerked as he saw the warriors milling around. He swore loudly.

'You did it, Yu Yu,' said Kysumu. 'You brought the Men of Clay back to life.'

'It takes no great intellect to ring a bell,' sneered Ren Tang.

'I spoke with Qin Chong,' said Kysumu, his voice cold. 'He was a man of great power and strength. He also understood courtesy and the need for good manners.'

Ren Tang's feral eyes locked to Kysumu's gaze. 'First, *human*, Qin Chong was not a *man*. He was, as we are, *Riaj-nor*. Second, I care nothing for your opinions. We drew lots to see which of us would fight for you humans when the gateway spell began to fail. It is enough that we will fight for you. Do not expect more.'

'It is not important,' said Yu Yu, climbing to his feet. 'I don't care whether they treat me with respect. Qin Chong sent them here to fight. So let them fight.' He looked into Ren Tang's eyes. 'Do you know who you are supposed to fight, and where?'

'You are the *pria-shath*,' said Ren Tang, contempt in his voice. 'We await your orders.'

'Very well,' said Yu Yu. 'Why don't you take some of your fighters and go outside? There were some enemy warriors out there earlier.'

Ren Tang put on his helmet and tied it below his chin. Taking several of the warriors with him he strode down the tunnel, returning moments later. 'We cannot get out,' he said. 'The stone door will not budge.'

'Is that right, Buttock Brain?' said Yu Yu. 'One simple order and already you fail.'

For a moment Ren Tang stood stock still. Then his sword flashed into the air, the point hovering over Yu Yu's throat. 'You dare insult me?'

'What insult?' snarled Yu Yu. 'You wait thousands of years and your first act is to draw your sword against the only person who can lead you out of this tomb. What animal did they join you with? A goat?'

Ren Tang snarled. The sword lanced forward. Kysumu's blade blocked it.

A low growl came from Ren Tang, and his eyes glittered in the lantern-light. 'You cannot beat me, human,' he said. 'I could cut out your heart before you could move.'

'Show me,' said Kysumu quietly.

Another warrior stepped from the ranks. 'Enough of this,' he said. 'Ren Tang, put away your sword. You too, human.' He was taller than most of the *Riaj-nor* and slightly round-shouldered. His armour was the same as that of the others – ornate helm and a torso guard of gold coins – but his ankle-length tunic was of heavy crimson silk. 'I am Song Xiu,' he said, offering a respectful bow to both Kysumu and Yu Yu. He looked at Ren Tang, who stepped back, sheathing his sword.

'Why are you so angry?' Yu Yu asked Ren Tang.

The warrior swung away from him and walked back into the ranks of the *Riaj-nor*. Song Xiu spoke for him. 'He is angry because yesterday we won a great victory. After all the years of struggle and suffering. We thought it was over, and that we would have a chance to know peace. To rest and lie in the sunshine. To send for the pleasure girls and rut and get drunk. It was a glorious day. But then the black wizard told us that the spell would one day falter, and Qin Chong asked all the *Riaj-nor* to draw lots to see which of us would leave the world we knew and enter the long sleep. Now we are here, to fight again and die for a cause that is not our own. Ren Tang is not alone in feeling angry, human. We only agreed because Qin Chong said he would lead us. But he is dead. He fought his way across two continents, facing and overcoming dangers you could not possibly imagine. Only to die from a rockfall inside a hollow hill. You expect us to be less than angry?'

Yu Yu shrugged. 'You didn't want to be here. I didn't want to be here. But we *are* here. So let's leave this place. I need to breathe fresh air.'

Yu Yu strode along the tunnel to the rock door and stretched out his hand. Instead of passing through it his fingers touched solid rock. 'Oh, it just gets better,' muttered Yu Yu. He kicked the stone. Cracks flowed across it. The door shivered and broke, collapsing to the overhang and falling to the trail below. Yu Yu gave a proud grin and swung to Kysumu. 'Nobody told me how to do that,' he said. 'I just did it myself! Good, hey?' Then he stepped out into the light. Kysumu followed him, then the *Riaj-nor*. The warriors milled around, turning their faces up to the sunlight. Two of them approached the body of the dead *Kriaz-nor*. One knelt down and dipped his finger in the gaping wound at the warrior's neck. Lifting his hand he licked blood from the finger. 'Recent kill,' he said. Peeling a strip of flesh from the body he put it in his mouth and chewed upon it. Then he spat it out. 'Tastes of fear,' he said.

Kysumu walked away from the group and stood staring into the distance. Yu Yu joined him. 'Are you all right, *Rajnee*?'

'Look at them, Yu Yu. All my life I have dreamt of being as great as these. And what are they? Part animal, part man – and as vile as those we fight against. I thought to find great heroes. Instead . . .' His voice tailed away.

'They are here,' said Yu Yu. 'They endured a spell that left them dead for centuries, so that they could protect a new generation. Doesn't that make them heroes?'

'How could you understand?' snapped Kysumu.

'Being a ditch-digger, you mean?'

'No, no,' said Kysumu, reaching out and gripping Yu Yu's shoulder. 'There is no dishonour in that. What I meant was that all my life I have denied myself pleasure. No fine foods, strong drink, women, gambling. I possess nothing but my robes, my sword and my sandals. I did this because I believed in the order of the *Rajnee*. My life had a noble purpose. But it has all been based on a falsehood. To win that war our ancestors merely duplicated the enemy. No honour, no holding to principles. What does that make of my life?'

'You have honour and principles,' said Yu Yu. 'You are a great man. It doesn't matter about the past. You are who you are, regardless of it. When I first began to dig trenches they told us the foundations needed to be four feet deep. When the first earthquake hit, all our new buildings crumbled. Foundations should have been six feet deep, you see. All that digging just to make an unsafe house. But it didn't make me a bad digger. I was a great digger. A legend among diggers,' he added.

At that moment Song Xiu and Ren Tang approached them. 'What are your orders, *Pria-shath*?' asked the crimson-clad Song Xiu.

'Do you know how to make the gateway stay closed?' asked Yu Yu.

'Of course. The spell was cast using the power of *Riaj-nor* blades,' said Song Xiu. 'We must assemble at the gateway and hold our swords against it.'

'That is all we have to do?' asked Yu Yu, astonished. 'Just walk up to the gateway and tap it with a sword? We could have done that!'

'It will take more than two,' said Ren Tang.

'How many?' asked Kysumu.

Song Xiu shrugged. 'Ten, twenty, all of them. I do not know. But it will all be for nothing if the gateway is fully open. We must reach it before that event, while it is still blue.'

'Blue?' queried Yu Yu.

'I watched the first spell cast,' said Song Xiu. 'It began with what appeared to be white lightning searing across the opening. Then the colour deepened, becoming at first pale blue like a winter sky, then darker. At the last it was silver, like a sword blade. Then the light faded, the silver turned to grey and we were standing before a wall of solid rock. After the Men of Clay were chosen we were told that as the spell degrades it will flow through the colours in reverse. If it reaches white the spell is finished. If we can restore it to silver the gateway will seal itself.'

'Then we'd better get started,' said Yu Yu.

Eldicar Manushan felt sick. The communion had been more painful than usual but, then, it had been prolonged almost beyond endurance. Yet it was Deresh Karany's torture of Matze Chai that had turned his stomach. The old man had been far tougher than anyone could have expected, considering his effete lifestyle. The boils sprouting on his flesh, the open, cancerous wounds had failed to break him. Blinding head pain had weakened his resolve, the fat maggots chewing upon his wounds bringing him even closer to the edge. But it was the leprosy that had sent him spinning into Deresh Karany's control. The old man was fastidious to the point of obsession. The thought of his own skin decaying and falling away had been too much for him.

'*It was good that you gave him those extra twenty years, Eldicar. He would not have survived the pain without the gift.*'

'*Indeed not, my lord.*'

'*You seem to be suffering.*'

'*The communion is always painful.*'

'*So do you think there is anything more to be learned from the merchant?*'

'*I believe not, my lord.*'

'*Still, it is enough. The Grey Man is an assassin once known as Waylander. It is almost amusing. Niallad has lived his whole life in fear of meeting this man, and now he is travelling with him.*'

Eldicar's head felt as if it would burst. He sagged against the cellar wall. '*You must try to be tougher, Eldicar. Take note of the wonderful display shown by the Chiatze. Very well, I will let you go.*'

Freedom from pain made Eldicar cry aloud. He sank to his knees. The cellar was cold. He sat down, resting his back against the wall. Tied to a chair close by was the unconscious Matze Chai. He was naked, his body a mass of festering sores, his skin showing the white blotches of leprosy. Maggots crawled upon his bony thighs.

I wanted to be a healer, thought Eldicar. With a sigh he pushed himself to his feet and walked to the door. He glanced back at the dying man. There was no-one here, save for himself and the prisoner. No guard outside the unlocked door. Deresh Karany had evinced no further interest in the man. Turning back Eldicar moved to Matze Chai's side. Taking a deep breath he laid his hands on the merchant's blood-encrusted face. Deresh Karany's spells were powerful and destroying the leprosy was the hardest task. It was deep-rooted. Eldicar worked silently, his mind focused. First he killed the maggots and healed the boils. The merchant groaned and began to wake. Eldicar placed him in a deep sleep then continued. Concentrating all his power into his hands Eldicar pulsed life-giving energy into Matze's veins. Eyes closed, he sought out all pockets of the disease, slowly eradicating them.

Why are you doing this? he asked himself. There was no rational answer. Perhaps, he thought, it will add one fragrant lily to the rancid lake of my life. Stepping back he gazed down at the sleeping man. Matze's skin gleamed with health. 'You did not come out of this too badly, Matze Chai,' he said. 'You still have your twenty years.'

Pulling shut the door behind him, Eldicar climbed the stone stairs to the first level and moved through to the Oak Room. Beric was sitting by the far window. Lord Aric was lounging on a couch nearby. 'Where is Panagyn?' asked Eldicar.

'He is preparing to ride out in search of the Grey Man,' said Aric. 'I think he is looking forward to the hunt. Did you learn anything from the slant-eye?'

'Yes. The Grey Man is an assassin called Waylander.'

'I have heard of him,' said Aric. 'I wish you'd let me observe the torture.'

'Why?' asked Eldicar wearily.

'It would have been amusing, and I am bored.'

'I am sorry to hear that, my friend,' said Eldicar. 'Perhaps you should visit Lady Lalitia.'

'Aye, I think I will,' said Aric, his mood momentarily brightening.

The small group had made camp in a wooded hollow close to the crest of a hill overlooking the Eiden Plain. Waylander was standing alone, staring out over the ruins of Kuan-Hador. Behind him the priestess Ustarte was sleeping. Emrin and Niallad were skinning three hares Keeva had killed that morning.

'It looks so peaceful in the moonlight,' said Keeva. Waylander nodded. 'You look tired,' she added.

'I am tired.' He forced a smile. 'I am too old for this.'

'I have never understood wars,' said Keeva. 'What do they achieve?'

'Nothing of worth,' he said. 'Mostly it comes down to mortality and the fear of death.'

'Fear of death makes men kill one another? That is beyond me.'

'Not the soldiers, Keeva, the leaders, the men who desire power. The more powerful they perceive themselves to be, the more god-like they become in their own eyes. Fame then becomes a kind of immortality. The leader cannot die. His name will echo down the centuries. It is all nonsense. They die anyway and turn to dust.'

'You really *are* tired,' she said, hearing the weary contempt in his words. 'Why don't you get some rest?'

Ustarte awoke and called out to them. Waylander strolled to

where the priestess was sitting. Keeva followed him. 'How are you feeling?' asked Waylander.

'Stronger,' she said, with a smile, 'and not just because of the sleep. Yu Yu Liang has found the Men of Clay.'

'And?'

'The *Riaj-nor* have returned. Already they are marching towards the gateway. Three hundred of them. When they reach it the power of their swords will seal it for another millennium.' Her smile faded. 'But it will be close. The *Ipsissimus* has been directing a dispersal spell against the gateway for days. If he succeeds, and the gateway spell is broken, no force in this world will bring it back.'

'You have magic,' said Emrin, moving in. 'Can you not . . . cast your own spell against the magicker?'

'I have very few spells, Emrin. I have a talent for far-sight and once I could move freely between worlds. That power is almost gone. I do not know why. I think it was part of the meld-magic that created me, and the magic is fading. But, no, I cannot fight the *Ipsissimus*. We must just hope that the *Riaj-nor* can save us.'

Climbing clumsily to her feet, she took Waylander by the arm. 'Come, walk with me.'

They moved away from the group. Behind them Keeva started a small fire, and she and Emrin sat quietly beside it, preparing the hares. Niallad stood up and wandered away into the woods.

'They tortured Matze Chai,' Ustarte told Waylander. 'I only saw glimpses of it. He was extraordinarily brave.'

'Glimpses?'

'There is a cloak-spell over the magicker and his *loachai*. I cannot *see* events around them. But I did fasten to the thoughts of Matze Chai.'

'He is still alive?' asked Waylander softly.

'Yes, he lives. There is something else. The *loachai* then healed Matze, bringing him back from the point of death.'

'So his master could torture him again?'

'I don't think so. It was as if the cloak-spell parted for a heartbeat and I caught just a glimpse of his thoughts – more an echo of his emotions. He was saddened and sickened by the torture. His healing of Matze Chai was a tiny act of rebellion. It is mysterious. I feel there is some fact we have overlooked. Something vital. It is like a nagging thought just below the level of consciousness.'

'I have the same feeling,' said Waylander. 'It has been bothering me ever since the battle with the demons. I saw the magicker ripped apart. But just before that I saw him falter. His spell was working, the mist was receding. Then he seemed to lose all confidence. His voice stammered. The mist swept over him. I watched his arm torn from his body. Yet, moments later, his voice rang out again, and he conquered the demons.'

'An *Ipsissimus* has great power,' said Ustarte.

'Then why did he lose it for those few heartbeats? And why did he not have his *loachai* with him? Surely that goes against what you told me about a magicker and his *loachai*. The boy is supposed to be Eldicar's shield.'

'The boy was with Keeva and Yu Yu at the time,' said Ustarte. 'Perhaps when the demons attacked them Eldicar sensed his peril. That could be why he lost concentration.'

'It still makes no sense,' insisted Waylander. 'He leaves his *shield* behind, and when the *shield* is in danger *he* gets ripped apart? No. If the *loachai* had been sent against the demons, and his master was threatened, it would be understandable. You told me that the master is the one with the real power, and he directs it through his *loachai*. Therefore if the master was threatened the link to his servant could be severed, leaving the *loachai* defenceless. But that was not what happened. It was Eldicar who fought the demons.'

Ustarte considered his words. 'He cannot be the *loachai*,' said Ustarte. 'You say the boy is around eight years old? No child could summon the power of an *Ipsissimus*, no matter how gifted. Nor do I believe anyone of that age would radiate such consummate evil.'

'Beric is a fine boy,' said Niallad, moving out of the darkness. 'I like him greatly. There is no evil in him.'

'I like him too,' said Waylander, 'but something is not right here. Eldicar told me he did not summon the demons to my home. I believed him. He spoke of Deresh Karany.'

'I know this man,' said Ustarte, her voice cold. 'He is vile beyond all imaginings. But he is a grown man. I would have sensed it had there been more than one *Ipsissimus*.' She turned to Niallad. 'You must pardon my intrusion, but I am reading your thoughts, and I need to see events through your memories. Think back to the night your parents were killed.'

'I don't want to do that,' said Niallad, backing away.

'I am sorry,' said Ustarte, 'but it is vital. Please, Niallad.' The young man stood very still. He took a deep breath, and

Waylander saw that he was gathering his strength. Then Niallad nodded to Ustarte and closed his eyes.

'Now I see,' whispered Ustarte. 'The boy is there. You see him. He is standing alongside the magicker.'

'Yes, I remember. What point are you making?'

'Think back. How did he seem to you?'

'He was just standing there, watching.'

'Watching the slaughter?'

'I suppose so.'

'His face shows no emotion. Not shock, not surprise, not horror?'

'He is just a child,' said Niallad. 'He probably didn't understand what was happening. He is a wonderful boy.'

Ustarte swung and looked across at Keeva and Emrin. 'All of you are smitten by the boy. Even Matze Chai, as he faced torture, could think only good thoughts of Beric. This is not natural, Grey Man,' she said. She returned her gaze to Niallad. 'Think back now over all the times you have been with Beric. I need to see the events myself.'

'It is not that often,' said Niallad. 'The first time was in the Grey Man's palace. He and I went to the beach.'

'What did you do there?'

'I swam, Beric sat on the sand.'

'He did not swim?'

Niallad smiled. 'No, I teased him about it and threatened to carry him into the water. I reached down but he grabbed on to a rock and I could not lift him.'

'I do not see a rock in your memory,' said Ustarte.

'There must have been. I almost tore my back trying to prise him away.'

Ustarte reached out and took Niallad by the arm. 'Picture his face, as well as you can. Look at it closely. I need to see it! Every detail.' She stood very still, and Waylander saw her jerk, as if stung. She backed away from Niallad, her eyes wide with fear. 'He is not a child,' she whispered. 'He has become a meld-creature.' Waylander moved alongside her.

'Tell me!' he said.

'Your suspicions were correct, Grey Man. Eldicar Manushan is the *loachai*. The one who appears as a child is Deresh Karany – the *Ipsissimus*.'

'It cannot be,' whispered Niallad. 'You are wrong!'

'No, Niallad. He is radiating a charm-spell. All who come close

884

are deceived by it. It is fine protection. Who would suspect a golden-haired and beautiful child?'

Ustarte walked away, lost in fearful memories. She had crossed a gateway between worlds to escape Deresh Karany's evil. And now he was here – and all her hopes of victory seemed suddenly frail, as insubstantial as woodsmoke.

She should have known he would come. She should have guessed it would be in a different form. Deresh Karany had become obsessed with the mysterious magic of the meld. He had realized through Ustarte that the possibilities went far beyond the mere physical. The correct balance could enhance the powers of the mind. Already virtually immortal, Deresh desired more. Conducting increasingly grisly experiments on his hapless captives, he sought the key that would unlock the secrets of the meld.

Ustarte had become his passion. She shuddered at the memory. He worked on her endlessly, seeking to find the source of her ability to change form. One day he had her strapped to a table. Sharp knives opened her flesh, and Deresh removed one of her kidneys, replacing it with a spell-charged organ taken from a failed meld. The pain had been indescribable and only Ustarte's great strength had saved her from madness. As she lay in her cell recovering she felt the organ stir within her, like a living creature. Tendrils slid from it, probing along the muscles of her back and into her lungs. Ustarte had gone into a terrible spasm. Her life was being drawn from her, and in her panic she threw herself into the change. The creature within her was crushed, but one tiny tendril broke off and fled deep into Ustarte's skull, nestling against the base of her brain. There it died. Poison seeped from its corpse, hot and burning. Tiger-Ustarte roared furiously, slashing her great paws against the walls of the cell, ripping out great chunks of plaster. Then, as she had with the first poison used on her, Ustarte absorbed it into her system, breaking it down, rendering it harmless. It could no longer kill her, but it did change her.

When Ustarte awoke, back in her own form, she felt different. Faintly dizzy and nauseous she had sat upon the floor, amid the ruins of the furniture torn to shreds by her tiger self. Suddenly her mind opened, and she heard the thoughts of every man and creature within the prison. Simultaneously. The shock made her scream, but she did not hear it. Her mind was full to bursting. Resisting panic, she tried to focus, creating compartments of the mind, which she closed against the tumultuous roar. The most powerful of the thoughts would not be shut out, for they were born of agony.

And they were coming from Prial. Two of Deresh Karany's assistants were experimenting on him.

Anger flooded through Ustarte, and a pulsing, volcanic rage began to build. Rising from the floor she focused on the men – and reached out. The air around her seemed to shiver and part. A fraction of a heartbeat later she found herself standing alongside the torturers within one of the meld-rooms on the other side of the prison. Ustarte's talons ripped through the throat of the first man. The second tried to run, but she leapt upon his back, bearing him to the ground. His head struck the stone floor, shattering the bones of his face.

Ustarte freed Prial.

'How did you . . . ?' whispered Prial. 'You . . . appeared from the air.' There was blood upon his fur, and several implements were still embedded in his flesh. Gently Ustarte eased them clear.

'We are leaving now,' said Ustarte.

'The time has come?'

'It has come.'

Closing her eyes she pulsed a message to all of the meld-creatures within the prison. Then she disappeared.

The apartments of Deresh Karany were empty, and she recalled that he had gone to the city to meet with the Council of Seven. Deresh had plans to open a gateway between worlds and invade once more an ancient realm that had defeated them so many years before.

From outside came the sound of splintering timbers and screaming men. Ustarte walked to the window and saw the creatures of the meld swarming across the exercise ground. Guards were fleeing in terror. They did not get far.

An hour later Ustarte led the one hundred and seventy prisoners out into the countryside, high into the forested mountain slopes.

'They will hunt us down,' said Prial. 'We have nowhere to go.'

His words were proved true within days, when *Kriaz-nor* troops and hunt-hounds began scouring the forest.

The escapees fought well, and for a time enjoyed some small victories. But gradually they were whittled down, and forced further into the high country. Some of the prisoners took off on their own, moving still higher into the snow, others were sent by Ustarte in groups to seek freedom to the east or the south.

Disfigured and malformed as they were, she warned them to avoid the haunts of men.

On the last morning, as several hundred *Kriaz-nor* were climbing towards their camp, Ustarte gathered the remaining twenty followers around her. 'Stay close to me,' she ordered her people, 'and follow when I move.' Reaching out she pictured the gateway as she had seen it in Deresh Karany's thoughts.

The air rippled. Ustarte threw out her arms. 'Now!' she cried, just as the *Kriaz-nor* burst upon the camp. Ustarte stepped forward. Bright lights in a score of colours flickered around her. As they faded she found herself standing within a green clearing in the shadow of a line of tall cliffs. The sun was shining brightly in a clear blue sky. Only nine of her followers made it through with her. Startled *Kriaz-nor* warriors were standing close by. Ahead was a huge stone arch, cut into the cliff. Beneath the arch the rock was glowing, ripples of blue lightning flashing across it. The *Kriaz-nor* rushed at them. Ustarte leapt towards the arch. Prial, Menias, Corvidal and Sheetza, a young girl with the scaled skin of a lizard, ran with her. The others charged the *Kriaz-nor*.

Throwing out her arms, Ustarte summoned all of her power. For an instant only the rock before her faded, and through it she saw moonlight over a series of ghostly ruins. As it began to fade she, and the last of her followers, stepped through.

Behind her the gateway closed, only bare rock remaining.

Sheetza stumbled and fell. Ustarte saw that a knife was embedded in her back. The deformed girl was unconscious. Ustarte drew out the blade and threw it aside. Then she laid her hands over the wound, sealing it. Sheetza's heart was no longer beating. Concentrating her power Ustarte set the girl's blood flowing. Sheetza opened her eyes. 'I thought I was stabbed,' she said, her voice sibilant. 'But there is no pain. Are we safe now?'

'We are safe,' said Ustarte, feeling for the girl's pulse. There was none. Only Ustarte's magic kept the blood flowing. She was, in effect, already dead.

In the distance Ustarte saw a glimmering lake. The small group made their way to it. Corvidal went for a swim with Sheetza. The girl moved through the water with the grace of a dolphin. When she emerged she was laughing. She sat down at the water's edge and splashed Menias. He ran forward and grabbed her and they both fell into the water.

Ustarte moved away from them. Prial came and sat with her. 'Maybe some of the others got away,' he said.

Ustarte did not answer. She was watching Sheetza. 'I didn't know you were also a healer,' he said.

'I am not. Sheetza is dying. Her heart was pierced.'

'But she is swimming,' said Prial.

'When the magic fades she will pass away. A few hours. A day. I don't know.'

'Oh, Great One! Why are we so cursed? Did we commit some vile sins in a past life?'

That night Ustarte sat talking with Sheetza. The priestess could feel the magic in the girl fading. She tried to add more power to it, but to no avail. Sheetza grew sleepy and lay down. 'What will we do in this world, Great One?' asked Sheetza.

'We will save it,' answered Ustarte. 'We will thwart the foul plans of Deresh Karany.'

'Will the people here accept me?'

'When they know you they will love you, Sheetza, as we love you.' Sheetza had smiled, and fallen asleep. Some time in the night, as Ustarte lay beside her, the lizard girl finally died.

Still lost in thought, Ustarte did not notice Waylander move alongside – not until he laid his hand on her shoulder.

'I was very arrogant to believe I could stand against Deresh Karany and the Seven,' she said. 'Arrogant and stupid.'

'Rather let us say brave and unselfish,' said Waylander. 'But do not judge yourself yet. Tomorrow Emrin and Keeva will take the lad over the high passes and try to make it to the capital. Once they are safely on the road I shall put your magicker's immortality to the test.'

'You must not go against him, Grey Man.'

'I don't have a choice.'

'We all have choices. Why throw your life away needlessly? He cannot die.'

'It is not about him, Ustarte. These men have killed my people, and tortured my friend. What kind of a man would I be if I did not fight them?'

'I do not want to see you die,' she said. 'I have seen too much death already.'

'I have lived long, Ustarte. Perhaps too long. Many better men are now below ground. Death does not frighten me. But even if I were to accept what you say about the folly of hunting Deresh Karany, there is one fact I cannot ignore. Matze Chai is still their prisoner. And I do not desert my friends.'

Chapter Fourteen

Lord Aric of House Kilraith lounged back in the carriage and stared idly out of the window at the houses along the Avenue of Pines. There were few people on the streets of Carlis. The massacre of the Duke and his followers had been shocking enough, but to learn that demons were responsible had terrified the population. Most stayed behind locked doors, rediscovering the delights of prayer. Several hundred families were congregated within the temple, believing its walls would keep out all evil spirits. They were hoping for an appearance from Chardyn, but the priest had wisely gone into hiding.

The carriage moved on through the deserted town.

Aric's mood was not good. As he had told Eldicar Manushan, he was bored. It was impolite of the man to have forbidden him to see the torture of the Chiatze. There was something about screams of pain that cut through the malaise Aric had been suffering for some while.

His spirits lifted a little as he thought of Lalitia, remembering the slim, red-haired girl he had discovered in the prison. She had courage and ambition, and a body she had soon learnt how to use. Those had been good days, he thought.

Aric had been lord of the Crescent then, enjoying a fine life on the taxes he received from the farmers and fishermen. But not so fine as some of the other nobles, notably Ruall, whose income was ten times that of Aric. One night, at the old Duke's palace in Masyn, Aric had taken part in a gambling tourney. He had won twenty thousand gold pieces. Ruall had been the biggest loser.

From being moderately wealthy Aric had suddenly become, in his own eyes at least, rich. He had spent like a man with ten hands, and within a year had debts at least the equal of the money he had won. So he gambled again, and this time lost heavily. The more he lost, the greater he gambled.

He had been saved from destitution only by the death of the old Duke and the accession of Elphons. This, in turn, allowed Aric to assume the lordship of Kilraith. With the new funds from taxes he was able at least to maintain the interest on his debts.

The arrival of the Grey Man had been his salvation. He had leased the mysterious stranger the lands of the Crescent, against ten years of taxation. It should have been enough to allow Aric freedom from debt. And it would have – had he not accepted Ruall's wager of forty thousand gold pieces on a single horse-race. Aric had been delighted for, though the two horses were evenly matched, Aric had already paid a stable-boy to feed Ruall's thoroughbred a potion that would seriously affect its stamina. The potion had worked better than expected, and the horse had died during the night. So Ruall had substituted another racing mount. Aric could not object. The new horse had beaten Aric's racer by half a length.

The memory still galled, and was made only slightly less bitter by the recollection of Ruall's death, the look of surprise as the black sword sliced into him, and the expression of dreadful agony as life fled from him.

Aric recalled the night Eldicar Manushan had appeared at his door, the beautiful child beside him. It had been almost midnight. Aric had been mildly drunk, and his head was pounding. He swore at the servant who announced the visitors, hurling his goblet at the man and missing him by a yard. The black-bearded magicker had strolled into the Long Room, bowed once, then approached the bleary-eyed noble. 'I see that you are suffering, my lord,' he said. 'Let us remove that head pain.' He had reached out and touched Aric on the brow. It was as if a cooling breeze was flowing inside Aric's head. He felt wonderful. Better than he had in years.

The boy had fallen asleep on a couch, and he and Eldicar had talked long into the night.

It was around dawn when the magicker first mentioned immortality. Aric had been sceptical. Who would not be? Eldicar leant forward and asked him if he wanted proof.

'If you can supply it, of course.'

'The servant you threw the goblet at, is he valuable to you?'

'Why do you ask?'

'Would it distress you were he to die?'

'Die? Why would he die?'

'He is not a young man. He will die when I steal what remains of his life, and give it to you,' said Eldicar.

'You are jesting, surely.'

'Not at all, Lord Aric. I can make you young and strong in a matter of minutes. But the life force I will give you must come from somewhere.'

Looking back, Aric could not remember why he had hesitated. What possible difference could the death of a servant make to the world? And yet, he recalled, he had wondered if the man had a family. Baffling. As the dawn came up, Eldicar moved to a cabinet and took a small, ornately embellished mirror. He approached Aric, holding the mirror before the nobleman's face. 'Look at yourself. See what is.' Aric saw the sagging face, the hooded eyes, all the signs of age and a life of mild debauchery. 'Now see what could be,' said Eldicar softly. The image in the mirror shimmered and changed. Aric had sighed with genuine regret as he looked upon the man he had once been, hawkishly handsome and clear-eyed. 'Is the servant important to you?' whispered Eldicar.

'No.'

An hour later the youth and vitality he had been promised had become a reality. The servant died in his bed.

'He did not have a great deal of life left,' said Eldicar. 'We will need to find someone else soon.'

Aric had been too delighted to care about such matters.

The carriage trundled on, turning right into Merchants Square. Aric saw the sign for the Starlight tavern, a brightly painted shield showing a woman's head surrounded by stars. He remembered his first meeting with Rena there. She had served him his food, and curtsied prettily. Not a very bright woman, he recalled, but she had been warm in bed, and she had loved him. He had taken her on as the housekeeper of a comfortable villa he owned just outside Carlis, on the shores of Willow Lake. She had borne him a daughter, a delightful child, curly-haired and precocious. She would perch on Aric's lap and demand stories of olden times, of fairies and magic.

The carriage slowed as it climbed the hill. The driver cracked his whip and the two horses lurched into the traces. Aric settled back into the deep horsehair-filled leather seat.

Rena had been crying about something on that final day. Aric couldn't remember what. She had taken to crying a lot in the last few months. Women, thought Aric, could be so selfish. She should have realized that, with his new youth and vigour, he would need other outlets. The plump, docile Rena had been entirely adequate for the tired, middle-aged man he had been. But she was not equipped to dance the night away in gowns of satin, or to attend the various banquets and functions that Aric now gloried in. She was, after all, merely a low-born housekeeper. Then he remembered why she had been crying. Yes, he had tried to explain this to her. She had prattled on about his promise of marriage. She should have realized that such a promise from an ageing, poverty-stricken noble should not have been held against the young and powerful man he had become. A different man had made that promise. But she did not have the wit to understand, and had begun to wail. He had warned her to be quiet. She took no notice. So he had strangled her. It was a most satisfying experience, he recalled. Looking back, he wished he had made it last a little longer.

Under different circumstances Aric would have raised the child himself, but with the need to plan for the Duke's assassination he had had no time. Anyway Eldicar Manushan had pointed out that the girl's life force would prove far more efficacious than the servant whose death had provided Aric with his first taste of immortality. 'Being of your own blood she will supply years of youth and health.'

Aric had no doubt that it was true. He had stood in the child's bedroom as she lay sleeping and felt the tremendous surge of vitality that flowed into him as she died.

The carriage came to a halt and Aric climbed out. He strode to the front door, which was opened by a large middle-aged woman. She curtsied and led him through to a beautifully furnished room. Lalitia, wearing a simple dress of green silk, was sitting beneath a lantern, reading.

'Wine for our guest,' she told the fat woman. Aric strolled across the room, kissed Lalitia's hand, then seated himself on a couch opposite her.

As he looked at her, noting the whiteness of her neck and the beautiful curve of her breasts, he found himself thinking of how it would feel to slide a dagger through that green dress. He pictured it flowering with blood. Eldicar should have let him see the Chiatze tortured. He had been thinking about the music of screams all day. And he had no more use for Lalitia. So there was no reason why he should not kill her.

'You seem in good humour, my lord,' said Lalitia.

'I am, my sweet. I feel . . . immortal.'

There was something in Aric's manner that caused a tremor of fear in Lalitia. She couldn't quite pin down the reason. He seemed relaxed, but his eyes were glittering strangely. 'It was a great relief to me that you survived the massacre,' she said. 'It must have been terrifying.'

'No,' he said. 'It was exhilarating. To see so many enemies die at one time. I wish I could do it again.'

Now the fear was really growing. 'So you will be the new Duke,' said Lalitia.

'For a while,' he said, rising and drawing his dagger.

Lalitia sat very still.

'I am so bored, Red,' he said conversationally. 'So little seems to pique my interest of late. Would you scream for me?'

'Not for you or any man,' she said. Aric moved in closer. Lalitia rolled away from him, her hand dipping down behind a satin cushion and emerging holding a thin-bladed knife.

'Ah, Red, you were always such a delight!' said Aric. 'I am not bored at all now.'

'Come any closer and you'll never be bored again,' she told him.

The door behind Lalitia opened and the Source priest Chardyn entered. Aric smiled as he saw him. 'So this is where you've been hiding, priest? Who would have thought it? My men have searched the houses of your congregation. They didn't think to check the homes of local whores.'

The burly priest stood very quietly for a moment. 'What has become of you, Aric?' he asked.

'Become of me? What a ridiculous question. I am younger, stronger and immortal.'

'Last year I visited you at Willow Lake. You seemed content. You were playing with a child, I recall.'

'My daughter. A sweet creature.'

'I was not aware you had a daughter. Where is she now?'

'She died.'

'Did you grieve?' asked Chardyn, his voice low and compelling.

'Grieve? I suppose that I must have.'

'Did you grieve?' asked Chardyn again.

Aric blinked. The man's voice was almost hypnotic. 'How dare you question me?' he blustered. 'You are a hunted – criminal. Yes, a traitor!'

'Why did you not grieve, Aric?'

'Stop this!' shouted the noble, stepping back.

'What have they done to you, my boy? I saw you with that child. You clearly loved her.'

'Loved?' Aric was nonplussed. He turned away, his dagger forgotten. 'Yes, I . . . seem to remember that I felt . . .'

'What did you feel?'

Aric swung back. 'I don't want to talk about this, priest. Look, leave now and I will not report that I have seen you. Just go. I need to . . . to talk with Red.'

'You need to talk with *me*, Aric,' said Chardyn. Aric stared at the powerfully built priest, and found himself looking into the man's deep, dark eyes. He could not look away. Chardyn's gaze seemed to hold him trapped. 'Tell me about the child. Why did you not grieve?'

'I . . . don't know,' admitted Aric. 'I asked Eldicar . . . on the night of the killings. I couldn't understand why I reacted in the way that I did. I felt . . . nothing. I asked if I had lost something when he gave me my – my youth.'

'What did he say?'

'He said I had lost nothing. No, that's not quite right. He said I had lost nothing that would be of value to Kuan-Hador.'

'And now you want to kill Lalitia?'

'Yes. It would amuse me.'

'Think back, Aric. Think of the man sitting with his child by that lake. Would it have amused him to kill Lalitia?'

Aric tore his gaze away from the priest and sat down, staring at the dagger in his hand. 'You are confusing me, Chardyn,' he said, and became aware of a pounding pain in his head. Placing the dagger on the table before him he began to rub his temples.

'What was your daughter's name?'

'Zarea.'

'Where is her mother?'

'She died too.'

'How did she die?'

'I strangled her. She would not stop crying, you see.'

'Did you kill your daughter too?'

'No. Eldicar did that. Her life force was very strong. It gave me greater youth and strength. Surely you can see how good I look.'

'I see far more than that,' said Chardyn.

Aric looked up and saw Lalitia staring at him, an expression of revulsion on her face. Chardyn came closer, sitting alongside Aric on the couch. 'You once told me that Aldania had been kind to you. Do you remember?'

'Yes. My mother had died and she invited me to the castle in Masyn. She sat and hugged me as I wept.'

'Why did you weep?'

'My mother had died.'

'Your daughter died. Did you weep?'

'No.'

'Do you remember how you felt when your mother died?' asked Chardyn.

Aric looked inside himself. He could *see* the man he had once been, and *watch* the tears flow. But he no longer had any inkling as to why the man was crying. It was most peculiar. 'You were right, Aric,' said Chardyn softly. 'You did lose something. Or rather Eldicar Manushan stole it from you. You have lost all understanding of humanity, compassion, kindness and love. You are no longer human. You have murdered a woman who loved you, and agreed to the killing of a child you adored. You have taken part in an unholy massacre, which saw the brutal slaying of Aldania, who was kind to you.'

'I – I am immortal now,' said Aric. 'That is what is important.'

'Yes, you are immortal. Immortal and bored. You were not bored that day by the lake. You were laughing. It was a good sound. You were happy. No-one had to die to bring you amusement. Can you not see how they have tricked you? They have given you longer life, and yet removed all the emotions you needed to *enjoy* that greater life.'

Aric's head was bursting. He pressed his hands to his temples. 'Stop this, Chardyn. It is killing me! My head is on fire.'

'I want you to think of Zarea, and that day by the lake,' said Chardyn. 'I want you to hold to it, to feel her tiny arms around your neck, the sound of happy childish laughter ringing in your ears. Can you hear it, Aric? Can you?'

'I can hear it.'

'Just before we all went inside she was cuddling you. She said something to you. You remember?'

'Yes.'

'Say it.'

'I don't want to.'

'Say it, Aric.'

'She said, "I love you, Papa!"'

'And what did you reply?'

'I told her I loved her too.' Aric gave a groan and fell back, his eyes squeezed shut. 'I can't think . . . the pain . . . !'

'It is the spell upon you, Aric. It is fighting to stop you remembering. Do you want to remember how it felt to be human?'

'Yes!'

Chardyn opened his collar and lifted clear the golden necklet he wore. A talisman hung from it, a piece of jade in the shape of a tear-drop. Runes had been cut into the surface. 'This was blessed by the Abbot Dardalion,' said Chardyn. 'It is said to ward off spells and cure disease. I do not know, in truth, if it carries magic or is merely a trinket. But, if you are willing, I will place it around your neck.'

Aric stared at the jade. A part of him wanted to push it away, to ram his dagger into the bearded throat of the priest. Another part wanted to remember how he felt when his daughter told him she loved him. He sat very still, then he looked into Chardyn's eyes. 'Help me!' he said. Chardyn looped the necklet over Aric's head.

Nothing happened. The pain came again, almost blinding him, and he cried out. He felt Chardyn take his hand and lift it to the jade tear-drop. 'Hold to it,' said the priest. 'And think of Zarea.'

I love you, Papa!

From deep below the pain came a rush of emotion, swamping Aric's mind. He felt again his daughter's arms around his neck, her soft hair rubbing on his cheek. For a moment pure joy filled him. Then he saw himself standing by the little girl's bed, revelling in the theft of her life force. He cried out and began to sob. Lalitia and Chardyn sat silently as the nobleman wept. Slowly the sobbing faded away. Aric gave a groan and snatched up the dagger, turning the point towards his own throat.

Chardyn's hand swept up, grabbing Aric's wrist. 'No!' shouted the priest. 'Not this way, Aric! You were weak, yes, to desire such gifts. But you did not kill your woman. Not the real you. You were under a spell. Don't you see? They used you.'

'I stood and laughed as Aldania died,' said Aric, his voice trembling. 'I joyed in the butchery. And I killed Rena and Zarea.'

'Not you, Aric,' repeated Chardyn. 'The magicker is the real evil. Put down the dagger, and help us find a way to destroy him.'

Aric relaxed and Chardyn released his hand. The lord of Kilraith rose slowly to his feet and turned to Lalitia. 'I am so sorry, Red,' he told her. 'At least I *can* apologize to you. I can never ask forgiveness from the others.' He swung to Chardyn. 'I thank you, priest, for returning to me that which was stolen from me. I cannot help you, though. The guilt is too great.' Chardyn was about to speak, but Aric held up his hand. 'I hear what you say about Eldicar, and there is truth in it. But I made the choice. I allowed him to kill a man to feed my vanity. Had I been stronger my Rena and little Zarea would still be alive. I cannot live like this.'

Moving past them he went to the door and opened it. Without a backward glance he strolled out into the night. Climbing into his carriage he bade the driver take him to Willow Lake.

Once there he dismissed the man and walked past the deserted villa and out to the moonlit shores. He sat down by the jetty, and pictured again the glorious day when he and his daughter had laughed and played in the sunshine.

Then he cut his throat.

Lord Panagyn had always believed himself immune to fear. He had fought battles and faced enemies all his adult life. Fear was for lesser men. Thus it was that he did not at first recognize the trembling in his belly, or the first tugs of panic pulling at his mind.

He ran headlong through the forest, his arms thrashing aside the overhanging vegetation, ignoring the twigs and thin branches that snapped back against his face. He stopped by a gnarled oak to catch his breath. Sweat had soaked his face, and his close-cropped iron-grey hair lay damp against his skull. Looking around he was no longer sure where he was in relation to the trail. But that did not matter now. Staying alive was all that counted. Unused to running, his legs were cramped and painful, and he sank to his haunches. His scabbard caught against a tree root, ramming the hilt of his cavalry sabre against his ribs. Panagyn grunted with pain, and shifted to his left, lifting the scabbard clear.

A cool breeze filtered through the trees. He wondered if any of his men had survived. He had seen some of them run, throwing aside their crossbows and trying to make it back to the cliffs. Surely Waylander could not have killed them all! It was not humanly possible. One man could not slay twelve skilled fighting men!

'Do not treat this man lightly,' Eldicar Manushan had warned him. 'He is a skilled killer. According to Matze Chai, he is the finest assassin this world has seen.'

'You want him brought in alive or dead?' Panagyn had asked.

'Just kill him,' said Eldicar. 'Be advised that there is a woman with him gifted with far-sight. I shall surround you and your men with a cloak-spell that will prevent her from sensing you. But this will not prevent Waylander, or any of the others, from seeing you with their eyes. You understand?'

'Of course. I am not an idiot.'

'Sadly, in my experience, that is exactly the phrase most used by idiots. As to the priestess, we would prefer her to be taken alive, but this may not be possible. She is a Joining – a were-creature. She can become a tiger. Once in that form you will have to kill her. If you can take her while in her semi-human guise, bind her wrists and ankles and blindfold her.'

'What of the others?'

'Kill them all. They are of no use.'

Panagyn had chosen his twelve men with care. They had all fought beside him in a score of battles. Cool men, hardy and tough, they would not panic or run. Equally they would think nothing of killing captives.

So where had it gone wrong? he wondered.

He had guessed rightly that Waylander would seek to escape over the high roads and had led his men in a fast ride to an area called Parsitas Rocks. There they had left the horses and scaled the towering cliff-face, emerging above the escapees. From here they moved through the forest, taking up positions on both sides of the trail and preparing their crossbows. Far below, Panagyn had seen the riders, and glimpsed the shaven-headed priestess walking just behind them. Panagyn ordered his men to shoot high, killing the riders and allowing the walking priestess to be taken alive.

Panagyn himself had crouched down alongside one of the bowmen on the left of the trail, ducking behind a thick bush. Here he waited in silence, listening for the sound of hoofbeats upon the hard-packed trail. Time drifted by. A trickle of sweat ran down Panagyn's cheek. He did not move to brush it away, wanting to risk no sound. The clip-clopping of walking horses drifted to him. He glanced at the bowman, who raised his weapon to his shoulder.

Then came a thud and a crash from the opposite side of the

trail. Someone cried out. The sound was followed by a choking gurgle. Then silence. Panagyn risked a glance. One of his men came running from the bushes. Panagyn saw him swing and raise his crossbow. A small black bolt flowered from the man's brow. He staggered back, loosing his own shaft into the air. Then he fell, the body twitching for a few moments.

A man to Panagyn's right screamed and reared up, fingers scrabbling at a bolt jutting from his neck. The warrior beside Panagyn twisted, bringing his crossbow to bear. Panagyn saw something streak through the air. The crossbowman pitched to his right. Panagyn did not see where the bolt had struck him. Panicked by the unseen killer, others of Panagyn's men rose from their hiding places, shooting at shadows. Another man went down, this time with a bolt through the eye. The remaining men threw aside their bows and fled.

Lurching to his feet, Panagyn ran into the trees, his arms flailing at the undergrowth as he blundered through bushes. He scrambled up the hillside, half slid down a steep incline and kept moving until his lungs could take no more.

Now, as he sat by the tree, he started to regain a little composure. If he could just get back to the cliffs, and climb down to the horses . . .

Pushing himself to his feet he started to turn. His foot caught in a tree root and he stumbled. It saved his life. A black bolt slammed into the oak. Panagyn hurled himself to the right and darted away into the trees. He scrambled over the lip of a rise, then half slid down the slope, emerging on to the trail. Several riders were sitting motionless upon their mounts, and Panagyn saw the shaven-headed priestess close by. No-one moved.

Panagyn backed away, drawing his sword.

A black-clad figure stepped into sight, long black and silver hair held back from his head by a leather headband. In his hand was a small double-winged crossbow. From the other side of the trail came four of his men. Their hands were raised. A dark-haired woman walked behind them. She, too, was carrying a small crossbow.

Panagyn switched his gaze back to Waylander. The man's face was set and grim, and Panagyn could read his own imminent death in Waylander's eyes. 'Face me like a man!' challenged Panagyn, in desperation.

'No,' said Waylander. The crossbow came up.

'Do not shoot!' ordered Niallad. Panagyn flicked a glance at the young man, who had heeled his horse forward.

'This is not some game, Niallad,' said Waylander. 'This man is a traitor who took part in the killing of your parents. He deserves to die.'

'I know that,' replied Niallad, 'but he is a lord of Kydor and should not be shot down like some common bandit. Have you no understanding of the chivalric code? He has challenged you.'

'The chivalric code?' said Waylander. 'Did he use the chivalric code when the demons came? You think he and his killers were hiding here to offer us a challenge?'

'No,' said Niallad, 'they were not. And I accept that Panagyn is a disgrace to all that nobles should hold dear. But I will not be a disgrace, or party to a disgrace. If you will not accept his challenge then let me fight him.'

Waylander gave a rueful smile. 'Very well . . . my lord, it will be as you say. I'll kill him in the time-honoured fashion.' Handing his crossbow to Niallad, the assassin moved into open space and drew one of his shortswords.

Panagyn grinned. 'Well, Waylander,' he said, 'you're good at shooting men from ambush. Let's see how you fare against an Angostin swordsman.'

Chapter Fifteen

As he moved, Waylander loosened the muscles of his shoulders. Panagyn was a large man, and his cavalry sabre was custom-made, heavier than the standard issue and some six inches longer. He guessed that the man would attack with a sudden charge, relying on brute strength to force his opponent back. The fact that he had agreed to this duel surprised Waylander. Codes of chivalry were largely for the story-tellers and bards to sing of. Enemies should be slain with the minimum of effort. He had learnt this during close to forty years of combat and danger. The knowledge had been hard-won.

So why are you doing it? he wondered, as Panagyn also began to work on the muscles of his shoulders, swinging the sabre left and right.

Then it came to him. There *ought* to be such codes, and the world would be a lesser place if the young, like Niallad, failed to believe in them. Perhaps, given time, he could make such codes a reality within Kydor. Waylander doubted it.

You are getting old and soft, he told himself.

Panagyn charged. Instead of stepping back, Waylander leapt to meet him, blocking a savage cut and ramming his head into Panagyn's face, crushing his nose. The burly nobleman staggered back. Waylander lunged. Panagyn blocked desperately, then backed away. Waylander circled him. Panagyn dragged out a dagger and flung it at Waylander. As he ducked, the nobleman rushed in. Waylander dropped to the ground, then kicked out, catching Panagyn below the right knee, just as the man's weight was coming down on it. Panagyn fell heavily. Waylander rolled to his feet and sent a slashing blow that cannoned from the top of Panagyn's head, opening his scalp. With a cry of rage and pain Panagyn charged again. This time Waylander stepped swiftly to his left, slamming the shortsword into Panagyn's belly. The blade sank deep. Waylander grabbed the hilt with both hands, tipping the sword and driving it up into Panagyn's heart. The nobleman sagged against him.

'This is for Matze Chai,' said Waylander. 'Now rot in Hell!'

Panagyn toppled to the ground. Putting his foot on the dead man's chest, Waylander tore his sword loose and cleaned the blade on Panagyn's embroidered tunic.

Stepping back, he turned towards the horses – and stopped.

Niallad was sitting very still, the crossbow pointed at Waylander. 'He called you by a name, Grey Man,' said the boy, his face pale. 'It is an old word meaning stranger or foreigner. Tell me that is all he meant. Tell me that you are not the traitor who killed my uncle.'

'Put up that weapon, boy,' said Emrin. 'He is the man who saved your life.'

'Tell me!' shouted Niallad.

'What is it you want to hear?' asked Waylander.

'I want the truth.'

'The truth? All right, I'll tell you the truth. Yes, I am Waylander the Slayer and, yes, I did kill the king. I killed him for money. It is a deed that has haunted me all my life since. There is no way to make amends when you kill the wrong man. So, if you want to use that weapon on me, do so. It is your right!'

Waylander stood very still and stared at the crossbow in the youth's hand. This was the weapon he had used to kill the king, the crossbow which had sent so many to their death. In that frozen moment of time Waylander thought how fitting it would be to be killed by this weapon, loosed by the only blood relative of the innocent king whose murder had plunged the world into chaos. He relaxed and waited.

At that moment the wind changed. Ustarte had moved closer and her scent drifted across the nostrils of Niallad's horse. It reared. Niallad was thrown back in the saddle. His hand involuntarily squeezed the bronze trigger of the crossbow. The bolt slammed into Waylander's chest. He half turned, took three faltering steps then fell to the grass close to the body of Panagyn.

Ustarte reached his side first, turning him and pulling the bolt clear.

'I didn't mean to shoot!' said Niallad.

Keeva and Emrin dismounted and ran towards the fallen man. Ustarte waved them back. 'Leave him to me,' said Ustarte. Putting her arms beneath the unconscious Waylander, she lifted him with ease and carried him into the forest.

When he opened his eyes he was lying on a bed of leaves. Ustarte was squatting beside him. Waylander's hand went to his chest. 'I thought he had killed me,' he said.

'He did,' Ustarte told him, her voice heavy with sadness.

Kysumu stared out over the ruins of Kuan-Hador. The sun was setting, and the plain below seemed immensely peaceful. Moving away from the warriors of the *Riaj-nor*, he squatted down and drew his sword. A great sadness was upon him. It lay like a boulder on his heart.

He remembered his teacher Mu Cheng, the Eye of the Storm, and the long years of training. Mu Cheng had tried, with great patience, to show Kysumu the secrets of the Way of the Sword, how to release control and become a living weapon. The sword, Mu Cheng had said, is not an extension of the man. The man must become the extension of the sword. No emotion, no fear, no excitement. Calm, and in harmony, the *Rajnee* did his duty, no matter the cost. Kysumu had tried. He had struggled with every fibre of his being to master the Way. His swordsmanship was beyond excellent, but it could not reach the sublime skill shown by Mu Cheng. 'It will come one day,' Mu Cheng had told him. 'And on that day you will be the perfect *Rajnee*.'

Two years later Kysumu had accepted the role of bodyguard to the merchant Lu Fang. He soon discovered why Lu Fang needed a *Rajnee* bodyguard: the man was amoral to the point of evil. His ventures included forced prostitution, slavery, and the distribution of deadly narcotics. Upon learning this, Kysumu had climbed the stairs to Lu Fang's apartments and informed him that he could no longer be his bodyguard.

Lu Fang had railed at him. 'You gave me your promise, *Rajnee*,' he said. 'And now you will leave me unprotected?'

'I will stay until noon tomorrow,' Kysumu told him. 'You will send your servants out in the morning to find other protectors. Then I leave.'

Lu Fang had cursed him, but the curses were just empty sounds to the young *Rajnee*. There was no honour to be gained in defending a man like Lu Fang. He walked from the apartments to the balcony beyond. Two hooded and masked figures were stealthily climbing the stairs. Kysumu moved to block them, his sword raised. Both men hesitated. 'Leave now,' said Kysumu, 'and you live.'

The men glanced at one another. Both carried thin-bladed daggers, but neither had a sword. They backed down the stairs, Kysumu following them. As they reached the last step they turned and ran.

Another figure moved into sight.

It was Mu Cheng.

As Kysumu stood now, overlooking the Eiden Plain, and the ghostly ruins of the ancient city, he remembered his shock at the condition of his former master. Mu Cheng's eyes had been red-rimmed, and there was stubble upon his cheeks. His robes were dirty, but the sword he held was clean. It shone brightly in the lantern-light.

'Step aside, pupil,' said Mu Cheng. 'The villain will die tonight.'

'I have told him I can no longer serve him,' said Kysumu. 'I leave him at noon tomorrow.'

'I have promised he will die tonight. Step aside.'

'I cannot, master. You know this. Until noon I am his *Rajnee*.'

'Then I cannot save you,' said Mu Cheng. The attack was incredibly swift. Kysumu barely blocked it. The two swordsmen had then engaged in a blisteringly fast series of encounters. Kysumu could never recall quite when it happened. But somewhere within that fight he had discovered the Way of the Sword. He had relinquished control. His blade moved faster and faster, casting bewildering patterns of light in the air. Mu Cheng had been forced back until, at the last, Kysumu's sword cut through his chest. The Eye of the Storm died without a word. His sword fell to the carpeted floor, the blade shattering into a hundred shards.

Kysumu stared down at the dead face of a man he had loved.

The voice of Lu Fang came from the balcony above. 'Are they dead? Are they gone?'

'They are gone,' said Kysumu, striding from the house.

Two days later Lu Fang had been stabbed to death in a market square.

Now Kysumu looked back and wondered just why he had

longed to be a *Rajnee*. Around him he could hear the coarse, gutter language of the *Riaj-nor*. What a fool I have been, he thought. Everything I was taught was based on lies. I have wasted my life trying to be as great as the original heroes of legend. And now I find they are part beast, part man, and have no honour in them.

Yu Yu Liang approached, squatting down beside him. 'They will come, you think, the demons?' he asked.

'They will come.'

'You are still sad?'

Kysumu nodded.

'I've been thinking about what you said, Kysumu. I think you are wrong.'

'Wrong?' Kysumu gestured towards the warriors. 'You believe they are great and mystic heroes?'

'I don't know. But I was talking to Song Xiu, and he was saying that the meld affects the body in a number of ways. One of them is that no *Riaj-nor* can sire children.'

'What is your point, Yu Yu?' snapped Kysumu.

'Whatever you think of them they *did* defeat the enemy. But once they were all dead – of old age or whatever – who could replace them? Ordinary men did not have the strength or the speed. So the elders had to find special men. Men like you, Kysumu. It is not about a lie. It is not about trickery. It doesn't matter that the original warriors were Joinings. The order of the *Rajnee* has always been . . . pure. That is why they have inspired our people for centuries. I know I am not putting this well. I am no debater. You were raised to believe in stories about a great warrior people. Well, they are great warriors. They did fight and die for us. You were then taught to believe in the *Rajnee* code. It is a good code. You do not swear, you do not lie, you do not steal, you do not cheat. You fight for what you believe in, and never give in to evil. What is wrong with that?'

'Nothing is wrong with it, Yu Yu. It just isn't based on truth.'

Yu Yu sighed and pushed himself to his feet. Song Xiu and Ren Tang walked across to join them.

'The gateway is an hour's march from here,' said Song Xiu. 'It will be guarded. One of our scouts picked up the trail of a small group of *Kriaz-nor*. It is my belief they saw our arrival, and will have communicated it to their masters.'

'There are going to be demons among those ruins,' said Yu Yu. 'They will come in a mist. Big black dogs and white bear creatures and serpents.'

'We have fought them before,' said Ren Tang.

'So have I – and I'm not looking forward to doing it again,' said Yu Yu.

'And you shouldn't,' said Kysumu, his voice gentle. 'You have fulfilled your part in this, Yu Yu. You were chosen to find the Men of Clay and you have done this. But from now on other skills will be required. You should make your way back to the coast.'

'I can't leave now,' said Yu Yu.

'There is nothing more you can do. I do not mean this unkindly, but you are not a swordsman. You are not *Rajnee*. Many of us – perhaps all of us – will die upon that plain. It is what we were trained for. You have great courage, Yu Yu. But now is the time for other skills to come into play. You understand? I want you to live. I want you to . . . go home and find a wife. Have a family.'

Yu Yu was quiet. Then he shook his head. 'I may not be a swordsman,' he said, with great dignity, 'but I am the *priashath*. I brought these men to this place. I will lead them to the gateway.'

'Ha!' said Ren Tang. 'I like you, human.' Throwing his arm around Yu Yu's shoulder he kissed his cheek. 'You stay close to me. I'll teach you how to use that demon-sticker.'

'Time to march,' said Song Xiu.

Yu Yu Liang, the Chiatze ditch-digger, led the fighting men of the *Riaj-nor* down on to the Eiden Plain.

As they reached the ruins a mist began to form ahead of them.

Norda was quite sure she was dreaming. At first she had been frightened, but now she relaxed, wondering where the dream would take her next. She rather hoped it would involve Yu Yu Liang.

The first part of the dream had been very real. Eldicar Manushan had sent for her, and told her that Beric had need of someone to sit with him while Eldicar himself was engaged in other duties. This was no hardship, for Beric was a delightful boy. Norda had been a little surprised to hear that Beric was waiting for her in the North Tower library. It was getting late, and in Norda's experience little boys tended to dislike dark, cold places.

Norda had climbed the circular stair, and been surprised to find four dark-garbed swordsmen in the library room below the tower. She had paused, sudden fear flooding her system. Such . . .

creatures as these had been the talk of the palace for days now, with their cat-like eyes and their haughty manner.

The first of them had bowed to her and offered her a sharp-toothed smile. His arm swept out, beckoning her to mount the stairs.

At this point Norda had no idea it was a dream. She climbed the stairs to the tower, and found Beric lounging on a wide couch. He was wearing only a white robe, belted at the waist. The tower room was chilly, a cold breeze whispering from the open balcony. Norda shivered. 'You must be cold,' she said to the boy.

'Yes, Norda,' he said sweetly. She was filled with the urge to hug him, and crossed the room to sit beside him. He snuggled into her. That was when she first realized that she was dreaming. Norda felt light-headed as he moved in close, and awash with feelings of love and contentment. It was really quite exquisite. She gazed down at his beautiful face, and saw that it was swelling at the temples, large blue veins pulsing across the stretching skin of his brow. His eyes grew smaller under heavy brows, the blue changing, becoming tawny gold. He seemed to be smiling, but she saw that, in reality, his lips were being dragged back across his cheeks, as his teeth grew longer and thicker, overlapping each other. His face was but inches from her own, and Norda frowned as it changed. She still felt great love for the boy, even though he was obviously a boy no longer. Norda regretted the cheese and bread she had eaten for supper, and the goblet of red wine with which she had washed it down. Cheese and wine always made her dream. But how odd that Beric should feature. Normally Norda dreamt of more potent men – men like Yu Yu Liang and Emrin. Even the Grey Man had figured in the more erotic dreams.

'You are not so pretty now, Beric,' said Norda, reaching up to stroke the pallid grey skin of his face. Her fingers brushed against his now dark hair. It was more like a pelt. His own, taloned, hand moved across her shoulder. She glanced down and saw that the skin of his arm was scaled and grey.

Something touched her leg. Norda saw that it was a long, scaled tail, with what seemed to be a claw growing from the base. She laughed.

'What is amusing, my dear?' asked the creature.

'Your tail,' she said. 'Long tails.' Then she laughed again. 'Emrin has a long tail. Yu Yu's tail is shorter and thicker. They don't have claws on them, though. I'll not drink that Lentrian wine again, that's for sure.'

'No, you won't,' said the creature.

The tail slid up over her belly, the claw pricking at the skin.

'That hurts,' said Norda, surprised. 'I've never felt pain in a dream before.'

'You never will again,' said Deresh Karany. The claw ripped into her.

Eldicar Manushan climbed the stairs and tapped lightly at the door. When he entered he gave one glance to the shapeless husk that only moments before had been a vibrant, friendly young woman. The desiccated corpse had been carelessly flung into a corner.

Deresh Karany was standing by the balcony window, staring out into the night.

Eldicar found the melded form repugnant, and realized that Deresh had let fall the charm-spell. 'Are you refreshed, Lord?' asked Eldicar.

Deresh turned slowly. His legs were twisted, the knees reversed, the feet splayed. The long tail, resting on the carpeted floor, gave him balance. His grey face twisted towards Eldicar. 'Invigorated, my friend. No more. Her essence was very powerful. It gave me a vision. Panagyn and Aric are dead. The Grey Man will be coming here. He thinks to kill us.'

'And the gateway, Lord?'

'The *Riaj-nor* are battling to reach it.' Deresh Karany moved clumsily towards the couch. His taloned feet hooked into a rug and he half slipped. 'How I loathe this form!' he hissed. 'When the gateway is open, and this land is ours, I shall find a way to reverse this . . . this foulness.'

Eldicar said nothing. Deresh Karany had become obsessed with the twin-meld, and acquiring the ability to change at will. As far as Eldicar could see, he had succeeded admirably. Deresh could assume the perfect body of a golden-haired child, or this powerful monstrosity, part lizard, part lion. This second form suited his personality perfectly.

'What are you thinking, Eldicar?' asked Deresh Karany suddenly.

'I was thinking of the problems of the meld, Lord,' replied Eldicar. 'You have mastered the twin forms. I don't doubt you will find a way to make the larger form more . . . attractive to the eye.'

'Aye, I will. Have you set the guards in place?'

'Yes, Lord. Three-swords and his group will be patrolling the lower access points, and Panagyn's soldiers are watching the grounds and the other entrances. If Waylander does come he will be captured or killed. But surely he is no threat to us. He cannot kill us.'

'He could kill you, Eldicar,' said Deresh. 'I might decide not to revive you. Tell me, how did it feel to have your arm ripped off by Anharat's demons?'

'It was agonizing, Lord.'

'And that, my dear Eldicar, is why I don't want Waylander to reach me. He cannot kill me, but he can cause me pain. I do not like pain.'

Except in others, thought Eldicar, remembering the sharp hurts of the many communions, and Deresh Karany's dismissive contempt of his own suffering. Deresh had always insisted upon communion, rather than conversation. He claimed that he did not want to risk being overheard. But there had been many occasions when no-one had been close enough to eavesdrop. Even then Deresh had demanded communion. Some part of him revelled in the pain it caused Eldicar. How I hate you! he thought.

In that moment he felt a great warmth settle over him. He looked into the crooked features of his master and smiled. He knew it was the charm-spell, yet he was unable to resist its power. Deresh Karany was his friend. He loved Deresh Karany, and would die for him.

'Even Waylander will be unable to resist the spell,' said Eldicar. 'He will love you as I do.'

'Perhaps, but we will give him to Anharat anyway.'

'One of his demons, you mean, Lord?' Eldicar could not keep the fear from his voice.

'No. You will help me prepare for the Summoning.'

Even through the comforting warmth of the charm-spell Eldicar felt panic rising. 'Surely, Lord, we do not need Anharat to kill one mortal. Will he not be insulted by being summoned for such a small task?'

'Perhaps he will,' agreed Deresh, 'but then again even the Lord of Demons must enjoy feeding occasionally. An added advantage will be to remind Anharat who is the master and who is the servant.' Deresh saw the growing terror in Eldicar and laughed. It was an ugly sound. 'Fear not, Eldicar, there is a good reason for using Anharat. Ustarte is with Waylander. She knows several ward-spells. She will most certainly lay one upon him. Now, if I was to summon a lesser demon and her ward-spell proved effective, that demon would turn on me – or, rather, on you as my *loachai*. There is no ward-spell that can turn back Anharat. Once loosed against a victim he is unstoppable.'

There was truth in that, Eldicar knew. Equally the Summoning would take a great deal of power. His heart sank as he realized what was coming.

'Pick ten of the servants,' said Deresh. 'Young ones, preferably female. Bring them here, two at a time.'

'Yes, Lord.'

As Eldicar Manushan left the tower he tried to think of lakes and sailboats.

But there was no refuge there.

Yu Yu stumbled – just as a huge white-furred creature broke through the line before him. Song Xiu leapt across his path, sending his sword slashing through the creature's neck. It roared and lashed out. Song Xiu grabbed Yu Yu, hauling him out of the demon's reach. Ren Tang and Kysumu both stabbed the beast, which fell writhing to the ground. More demons swept through the breach. Yu Yu clove his blade through the neck of a serpent. Kysumu half decapitated a black *Kraloth* hound as it leapt towards his throat.

Then the mist faded back. The *Riaj-nor* regrouped. Yu Yu glanced around. It seemed to him that they had lost around forty of their number. And they had covered barely half a mile. The *Riaj-nor* fought with a savagery Yu Yu could scarcely believe. There were no war cries, no exhortations, no screams from the wounded and dying. Merely blinding webs of dazzling blue light from the mystical blades as they ripped and tore into the flesh of the demonic army opposing them.

Kysumu had been right. This was no place for Yu Yu. He knew that now. He was merely a clumsy, slow human. Several of the *Riaj-nor* had died protecting him, and both Song Xiu and Ren Tang watched over him constantly.

'Thank you,' said Yu Yu, in the brief lull.

Ren Tang grinned at him. 'It is our duty to protect the *pria-shath*,' he said.

'I feel like a fool,' Yu Yu told him.

Song Xiu stepped in. 'You are not a fool, Yu Yu Liang. You are a brave man, and you fight well. With a touch of the meld you could be very good.'

'They are coming again,' said Kysumu.

'Then let us not keep them waiting,' said Ren Tang.

The *Riaj-nor* swept forward. The mist rolled towards and around them. Winged creatures appeared overhead, throwing barbed darts down upon the fighting men. The *Riaj-nor* drew daggers from their belts and hurled them up at the demons. They fell from the sky to be stabbed to death. One warrior tore a dart from his shoulder and leapt, grabbing a creature by the ankle. Huge black wings flapped furiously, but the combined weight bore both of them down. The *Riaj-nor* stabbed the dart through the creature's bony chest. As it died its talons ripped across the *Riaj-nor*'s throat. Blood sprayed over Yu Yu. Swinging round, he hacked off the demon's head.

Ren Tang went down. Yu Yu leapt across his fallen body, delivering a mighty blow to the chest of the bear-like beast that had downed him. The blade sank deep. The creature bellowed in pain and fell back. Ren Tang rose to his feet. There was blood on his face, and a flap of skin was hanging from his temple.

The fighting was furious now. The demons were above them and all around them. But still the *Riaj-nor* drove forward into the mass.

More than half of the Men of Clay were dead, but the demon hordes were thinning now.

Yu Yu was close to exhaustion. Ice was clinging to his wolfskin jerkin. He tripped and fell across the body of a dead *Riaj-nor*. Kysumu hauled him to his feet.

The mist parted.

A warm breeze blew across the ruins.

And the demons vanished.

Song Xiu put his arm around Yu Yu and pointed to a line of cliffs. 'There is the gateway,' he said.

Yu Yu peered through the gloom. He could see a flickering blue light against the grey stone. But it was not the light that caught his attention.

It was the two hundred black-garbed *Kriaz-nor* warriors who were moving out to form a defensive line.

Yu Yu swore. 'After all we've been through you'd think we deserved a bit of luck,' he grumbled.

'This is luck,' said Ren Tang. 'You can't feast on the hearts of demons.'

Yu Yu looked at him, but made no response. Despite the attempted lightness of his tone, Ren Tang looked bone weary. Song Xiu leant on his sword and swung to assess the remaining warriors. Yu Yu did the same. There were just over a hundred *Riaj-nor* left standing, and many were wounded.

'Can we beat them?' asked Yu Yu.

'We don't have to beat them,' said Song Xiu. 'We just have to get through them and reach the gateway.'

'We can do that, though, hey?'

'It is why we came,' said Song Xiu.

'Let's do it,' said Ren Tang. 'And then I want to find a town and a tavern and a fat-arsed woman. Maybe two.'

'Taverns or women?' asked another warrior.

'Taverns,' admitted Ren Tang. 'I'm a little too tired to want more than one woman.' Putting aside his sword, he lifted the bloody flap of skin back into place, pressing his hand against the wound.

Song Xiu moved alongside him, drawing a curved needle from a small pouch tucked into his waist sash. Swiftly he stitched the upper section of the wound. 'Well,' he said, 'if you don't want both women I'll take one.'

'Aye,' answered Ren Tang, with a quick grin. 'So let us not waste any more time. Let's sweep away these ugly vermin, then get drunk.'

'Agreed,' said Song Xiu, with a brief smile. Then he took a deep breath and swung to Yu Yu. 'I heard what your friend told you earlier. He was wrong then, but his words are right at this time. You cannot come with us on this last fight. We will not be able to protect you. And once we break through we will not be able to protect ourselves.'

'What do you mean?'

'As our swords touch the gateway they will simply cease to be. They will be absorbed by the spell that was placed there.'

'Then you will all be killed,' said Yu Yu.

'But the gateway will be closed,' pointed out the *Riaj-nor*.

'I will not stay behind,' insisted Yu Yu.

Ren Tang stepped in. 'Listen to me. Despite my hatred of them, I have to admit these *Kriaz-nor* are great fighters. We *cannot* battle them *and* look after you. Yet if you come we will be forced to try to protect you. You see the predicament? Your presence will lessen our chance of success.'

'Do not be sad, Yu Yu,' said Song Xiu. 'It was for people like you that Qin Chong and I, and the others, surrendered our humanity. It is pleasing to me that you are here. For it shows that we did not take this path in vain. Your friend Kysumu can come with us. He will represent humans in this encounter. It is what he wants. He has no true love of life. He knows no fears, as he knows no joys. That is why he can never be the hero you are. And that, my friend, is why *you* were the *pria-shath*. Without fear there can be no courage. You have fought beside us, ditch-digger, and we are proud to have known you.' He held out his hand. Yu Yu blinked back tears as he shook it. 'Now we must fulfil our destiny,' said Song Xiu.

The *Riaj-nor* formed a fighting line, Ren Tang, Song Xiu and Kysumu at the centre.

Yu Yu stood by wretchedly as they walked slowly towards the ancient enemy.

Waylander looked into Ustarte's golden eyes. 'You are telling me that I am dying? I feel fine. There is no pain.'

'And no heartbeat,' said Ustarte sadly.

Waylander sat up and felt for his pulse. She was right. There was nothing. 'I do not understand.'

'It is a talent I did not know I had until we crossed the gateway. One of my companions, a lovely child named Sheetza, was stabbed. Her heart, too, had stopped beating. I healed the wound – as I have yours – and sent a surge of my power into her blood, causing it to continue to flow through the body. She lived for some hours, but then, as the spell faded, she died. You have a few hours left, Waylander. I am sorry.'

Keeva stepped forward from where she had been standing in the shadows of the trees. 'There must be something you can do,' she said, dropping to her knees beside the Grey Man.

'How many hours?' Waylander asked.

'Ten – perhaps twelve at the most,' Ustarte told him.

'The boy must not know,' said Waylander, rising to his feet. He walked back through the trees to where Emrin and Niallad were sitting by the trail.

As Niallad saw him he scrambled to his feet. 'I did not mean to shoot,' he said.

'I know. It barely pierced the skin. Come, walk with me.'

Niallad stood very still, fear showing on his face. 'I will not harm you, Niallad. We need to talk.' Waylander led the boy to a cluster of rocks beside a fast-flowing stream, and there they sat as the sun sank below the mountains. 'Evil creeps up on a man,' said Waylander. 'He starts out on a mission he believes is just, and with every killing he darkens his soul just a little more. He

913

lives neither in the day nor in the night. And eventually this man of twilight, this . . . Grey Man finally steps into the dark. As a young man I tried to live a decent life. Then one day I arrived home to find my family butchered. My wife, Tanya, my son, my two baby girls. I set out to hunt down the nineteen men who had taken part in the raid. It took me almost twenty years to find them all. I killed every one. I made them suffer, as Tanya had suffered. They all died in dreadful agony. I look back on the torturer I became and I barely recognize the man. His heart was stone. He turned his back on almost everything of value. I cannot tell you now why he . . . I accepted the contract to kill the king. It no longer matters why. The simple fact is that I did accept, and I did kill him. And in killing him I became as evil as the men who murdered my family. I tell you all this not to excuse myself or to ask for forgiveness. Forgiveness is not yours to give. I tell you simply because it may help you in your own life. You fear being weak. I see that fear in you. But you are not weak, Niallad. One of the men who slaughtered your parents was in your power, and you upheld the chivalric code. That is strength of a kind I never possessed. Hold to that, Niallad. Hold to the light. Keep that code in your heart with every decision you make. And when, one day, you are faced with a rival, or an enemy, make sure you do nothing that would bring you shame.'

With that Waylander rose and the two walked back to the horses. Waylander gathered up his bow and loaded it. He called the four prisoners to him. They shuffled forward uncertainly. 'You are free to go,' he said. 'If I see you again you die. Now get out of my sight.'

The four men stood for a moment, then one walked away into the forest. The others waited to see if Waylander would shoot him. When he did not the others followed. Waylander approached Emrin. 'There should be no pursuit now,' he said. 'Their horses are far away. So take the high road and bring Niallad and Keeva to the capital. If the lad is strong enough he will win over the other nobles and become the Duke. I want you to stand beside him.'

'I will, sir. Where are you going?'

'Where you can't follow, Emrin.'

'No, but I can,' said Keeva.

Waylander turned to her. 'You told me you did not wish to become a killer. I respect that, Keeva Taliana. If you walk with me now you will have to use that bow.'

'There is no time for debate now,' said Keeva grimly. 'I shall come with you to stop the magicker. Just in case – for any reason – you are unable to do so.'

'Then let it be so,' he said. 'And now we must go. We have some hard riding to do.'

'There is no need to ride,' said Ustarte. 'Come, stand with me, and I shall take you where you wish to go.'

Waylander and Keeva moved alongside her.

Niallad called out. 'For what it is worth, Grey Man, I do forgive you. And I thank you for all you have done for me.'

Ustarte raised her hands. The air shimmered before her. Then she stepped from sight, Waylander and Keeva disappearing with her.

Chapter Sixteen

The massive nave of the temple was thronged with people; mothers holding fast to their children, husbands staying close to their loved ones. Hundreds of the citizens of Carlis had taken refuge here: workers, merchants, tanners and clerics all huddled together. A few soldiers were with them, men who had been ordered to watch for the renegade priest Chardyn.

Priests moved among the crowds, offering blessings, leading prayers.

The corpse of an elderly man lay by one of the walls, the face covered by a cloak. His heart had failed. The body was a reminder of the perils that awaited them outside. Fear was almost palpable, and conversations were held in hushed whispers. The topic was the same everywhere. Would the hallowed walls keep out the demons? Were they safe within this holy place?

A white-robed figure moved into sight, climbing the steps to the high altar. A cry went up from the crowd as they recognized Chardyn. People began to cheer. Relief swept through the crowd.

Chardyn stood in full sight of them all and spread his arms. 'My children!' he bellowed. Several soldiers moved forward. Chardyn looked down at them. 'Stand where you are!' he thundered.

Such was the power in his voice that the soldiers stopped, and glanced at one another. The crowd would tear to pieces any who tried to harm the priest. The soldiers relaxed.

'The Duke is dead,' said Chardyn, transferring his gaze to the crowd. 'He was slain by sorcery. And now demons stalk the land. You know this. You know that a magicker summoned

916

Hell-hounds to kill and to maim. That is why you are here. But let me ask you this: do you think these walls might protect you? These walls were built by *men*.' He fell silent, his eyes scanning the silent congregation. Then he pointed at a large man standing at the centre of the throng. 'I see you, Benae Tarlin! You and your team constructed the south wall. What power do you possess that will hold back demons? What magic did you invest in these stones? What ward-spells did you cast?' He waited for an answer. The crowd swung to stare at the hulking man, who reddened and said nothing. 'The answer is none!' roared Chardyn. 'They are merely walls of stone. Cold, lifeless stone. And so, you might ask, where is the sanctuary against the evil that is outside? Where can we hide to be safe?' He paused and allowed the silence to grow.

'Where is anyone safe from evil?' he said at last. 'The answer is nowhere. You cannot run from evil. It will find you. You cannot hide from evil. It will burrow down to the deepest place in your heart and it will discover you.'

'And what of the Source?' shouted a man. 'Why does He not protect us?'

'Aye, what of the Source?' responded Chardyn. 'Where is He in our hour of need? Well, He is here, my friends. He is ready. He waits with a shield of thunder and a spear of lightning. He waits.'

'What is he waiting for?' came another shout, this time from the stone-mason Chardyn had picked out earlier.

'He is waiting for *you*, Benae Tarlin,' answered Chardyn. 'He is waiting for you, and he is waiting for me. At the palace of the Grey Man there is a magicker, a man who summons demons. He has bewitched the lords Aric and Panagyn, and arranged the massacre of many of our leading citizens. He now rules Carlis, and soon, perhaps, all of Kydor. One man. One vile and evil man. One man who believes that the murder of a group of nobles will cow and terrorize an entire population. Is he right? Of course he is. Here we are, cowering behind walls of stone. And the Source waits. He waits to see if we have the courage to believe. If we have the faith to act. Every week we assemble here and we sing songs of the Source, of His greatness and His power. Do we believe them? We do when times are good. You listen to sermons about the heroes of the Source, of the Abbot Dardalion and the Thirty, his warrior priests. My, but they make great listening, do they not? A few men who, with courage and faith, set themselves against a terrible enemy. Did they cower behind walls and ask the Source to fight for them? No, for the Source was *within* them.

The Source fed their courage, their spirit, their strength. That same Source is within *us*, my friends.'

'Well, I don't feel it!' called Benae Tarlin.

'Nor can you while you hide,' Chardyn told him. 'Your son slipped down that cliff last year, and you climbed down to the ledge to rescue him. He clung to your back and you felt you did not have the strength to carry him clear. We have talked of this, Benae. You prayed for the strength to bring your son to safety. And you did so. Did you sit upon that cliff and call out for the Source to raise your boy on a magical cloud? No. You set off in faith and your faith was rewarded.

'I tell you now that the Source waits. He waits with power greater than any magicker. You want to see that power – then walk with me to the palace of the Grey Man. We will find the magicker. And we will destroy him.'

'If we march with you,' asked another man, 'do you promise the Source will be with us?'

'With us and within us,' said Chardyn. 'I pledge it upon my life.'

Three-swords was standing by the window, looking out over the bay, when he caught what seemed to be a flash of light on one of the lower terraces. He stepped out on to the balcony and peered at the area below. Two human guards were walking down the steps. They were heading in the direction from which the light came. Three-swords relaxed and went back into the library.

Iron-arm was stretched out on a long bench. Stone-four and Long-stride were sitting at the base of the stairs. There had been no screams from the upper chamber for some time. Three-swords did not like the sound of screams, especially from young females. He had little stomach for cruelty. In battle you fought an enemy and killed it. You did not set out to make it suffer. Iron-arm strolled across to join him. 'The magicker is on his way back,' said Iron-arm. Three-swords nodded. He had not yet scented the man, but Iron-arm was never wrong. Then Three-swords caught the scent. It was faintly acrid, the scent of fear.

The black-bearded magicker came up the stairs and stopped. He stared at the circular steps leading to the upper chamber. Then he moved to a seat and slumped down, rubbing his eyes. 'All is quiet out there,' he said to Three-swords.

The warrior knew he was merely making conversation in a bid to delay his return to Deresh Karany. 'So far,' said Three-swords.

Iron-arm rose suddenly and strode to the window. 'Blood,' he said, opening his mouth and drawing in a hiss of air over his tongue. 'Human blood.' Three-swords and Long-stride joined him instantly.

Three-swords closed his eyes and breathed in deeply. Yes. He could just taste it on the air. He turned to Eldicar Manushan. 'At least one man is bleeding heavily.'

'Two,' said Iron-arm. 'And there is something else.' His broad nostrils flared. 'It is very faint. But ... yes ... big cat. Lion, maybe. No. Not a lion – a meld.'

'Ustarte!' whispered Eldicar Manushan. He backed away from the window, then swung to Stone-four and Long-stride. 'Get out there. Find her. Kill anyone with her.'

'It might be better to stay together,' said Three-swords.

'This Waylander must not reach the tower,' said Eldicar Manushan. 'Do as I say.'

'Move warily,' Three-swords told Long-stride and Stone-four. 'This human is a hunter and a canny fighter. He uses a crossbow that shoots two bolts.'

The two warriors descended the staircase. Eldicar Manushan sat down. The smell of fear was strong on him now, and Three-swords joined Iron-arm at the window. 'The cat-woman is sick,' said Iron-arm, 'or weak. I cannot tell which. She is out of sight, just below those gardens. She has not moved.'

'Can you scent any humans?'

'No – only the wounded or dead. I would think they are dead, for there is no movement or sound from them.'

From where they stood they saw Long-stride and Stone-four emerge into the gardens. Stone-four was moving swiftly, but Long-stride tapped him on the shoulder, ordering him to slow down.

'They won't surprise Long-stride,' said Iron-arm. 'He's careful.'

Three-swords did not answer. He glanced back at Eldicar Manushan. Why was the man so terrified?

He strolled across to where the magicker sat. 'What is it that I do not know?' he asked.

'I don't know what you mean.'

'What is happening here, Eldicar? Why were so many women killed? Why are you so frightened?'

Eldicar licked his lips, then rose and moved in close to Three-swords. 'If the human gets through,' he whispered, 'Deresh Karany will perform the Summoning.'

'So he will use a demon to kill him. He has done this before.'

'Not any demon,' said Eldicar. 'He plans to summon Anharat himself.'

Three-swords said nothing. What was there to say? The arrogance of these humans was beyond his understanding. He saw Iron-arm looking at him quizzically, and he knew why.

He is scenting my fear now, thought Three-swords.

As the air shimmered around her Keeva felt an icy wind swirl over her body. Bright colours exploded before her eyes. Then, as if a curtain had opened, she saw the moonlit apartments of the Grey Man appear before her. The ground shifted under her feet and she half staggered. Ustarte gave out a low moan and sank to the ground. Instantly Waylander knelt by her. 'What is wrong?'

'I am . . . exhausted. It . . . takes great energy. I will be fine.' Ustarte stretched herself out. 'So . . . little power left,' she whispered. She closed her eyes. Waylander moved towards the door of his apartments, and two guards appeared on the pathway to the right. One was holding a hunting bow, an arrow notched to the string. The second carried a spear. Both men froze as they took in the scene.

Keeva raised her crossbow. 'Put down your weapons,' she said.

For a moment it seemed they would obey her, but then the bowman drew back on the string. A bolt from Waylander's weapon slammed into his chest. He grunted and fell back, his arrow slashing through the air, missing Keeva by inches. The spearman charged at Keeva. Instinctively she pressed both trigger studs on her crossbow. One bolt struck the spearman in the mouth, smashing his teeth, the second entered his skull between the eyes. His charge faltered and he dropped the spear. His hand went to his mouth. Then, as if his bones had turned to water, his body crumpled and he fell at Keeva's feet.

She looked round for the Grey Man, but he had entered the apartments. She transferred her gaze to the dead man, and felt sick. The other guard groaned. Rolling to his stomach, he tried to crawl away. Keeva crossed the ground and stood over him. 'Lie still,' she told him. 'No-one is going to harm you further.'

Kneeling by his side, she put a hand to his shoulder, to help him turn on to his back. He relaxed at her touch and she looked into his eyes. He was young and beardless, with large brown eyes. Keeva smiled at him. He seemed about to say something. Then a bolt smashed into the side of his head, crunching through the temple.

Fury swept through Keeva and she swung on the Grey Man. 'Why?' she hissed.

'Look at his hand,' said Waylander.

Keeva glanced down. Moonlight shone upon the dagger blade. 'You do not know that he was going to use it,' she said.

'I did not know that he wasn't,' Waylander told her. Moving past her, he wrenched the bolt clear of the soldier's head, cleaned it on the man's tunic, and slipped it back into his quiver. 'We do not have time for lessons, Keeva Taliana,' he said. 'We are surrounded by enemies who will seek to take our lives. To hesitate is to die. Learn fast – or you will not survive the night.'

Behind them Ustarte called out weakly. Waylander knelt by her. 'There are *Kriaz-nor* within the tower. The wind is off the sea and they will scent the blood.'

'How many can you sense?' he asked.

'Four. There is something else. I cannot quite fasten to it. There has been murder done and there is a tremor in the air. Magic is being cast, but for what purpose I cannot tell.'

Waylander took her hand. 'How soon before you can walk?'

'A few moments more. My limbs are trembling. I have no strength yet.'

'Then rest,' said Waylander, rising and moving to Keeva. 'I have something for you that will give you an edge,' he said.

Ustarte called out again. 'Two *Kriaz-nor* are moving down the terrace steps.'

Long-stride moved warily. He had not yet drawn his sword. There would be time for that. For now he was using all his senses. He could smell the blood, and the sour odour of urine. The bladders of the dead had emptied. The scent of the meld-woman was also strong, and Long-stride could detect within it an unhealthy aroma. The woman was sick. Stone-four was moving too fast, and was some paces ahead now. Irritated, Long-stride caught up with him. 'Wait!' he ordered.

Stone-four obeyed him and they moved stealthily around the corner. Some fifteen paces ahead of them, sitting upon a rock, was a dark-garbed human. In his left hand he held a double-winged crossbow. Beyond him lay the cat-woman. 'Let me kill him,' said Stone-four. 'I want to win a name!'

Long-stride nodded, and continued to sniff at the air.

Stone-four stepped towards the human. 'Your weapon looks formidable,' he said. 'Why don't you show me how formidable?'

'Come a little closer,' said the human, his voice calm.

'Surely this range is adequate,' replied Stone-four.

'Aye, it is adequate. Did you wish to draw your sword?'

'I will not need it, human. I shall remove your heart with my hands.'

The human rose. 'I am told you are very fast, and that bows are useless against you. Is this true?'

'It is true.'

'Let us find out,' said the man, his voice suddenly cold. Long-stride felt the beginning of apprehension as he heard the man's tone, but Stone-four was tensed and ready. The bow came up. Stone-four's right hand swept up, snatching the bolt from mid-air. Instantly a second bolt followed the first. Stone-four moved with lightning speed, catching this with his left hand. He grinned widely and glanced at Long-stride. 'Easy!' he said. Before Long-stride could warn his comrade the human's right hand flashed out. The throwing knife sped through the air, slamming into Stone-four's throat. The *Kriaz-nor*, his windpipe severed, took two faltering steps towards the human, then toppled face-first to the ground.

Long-stride drew his sword. 'You have any more tricks to play, human?' he asked.

'Only one,' said the man, drawing a shortsword.

'And what might that be?'

Long-stride heard a whisper of movement behind him. Spinning on his heel, he scanned the area. Nothing was there. Low bushes and rocks that could not hide a human. Then he saw something so weird that he did not at first register what it was. A crossbow suddenly extended from low to the ground. Long-stride blinked. He could not focus properly on the area around it. The weapon tilted and, in that fraction of a heartbeat, Long-stride saw a slim hand upon the weapon. Two bolts slashed towards him. His sword swept up blocking the first. The second slammed into his chest, burying itself deep into his lungs. A sword blade plunged into his back. Long-stride arched, then swung, his own sword slicing the air. But the human had not crept up behind him as he had thought. The man was still standing some fifteen paces away. He had hurled the sword! Long-stride felt all strength seeping away. Letting fall his blade, he walked stiffly to a rock and sat down heavily. 'You are very skilful, human,' he said. 'How did you make the crossbow shoot?'

'He didn't,' said a female voice.

Long-stride looked towards his left and saw a woman's head

appear, floating in the air. Then an arm came into sight, sweeping upwards, as if pushing a cloak aside. Then it came to him. 'A *Bezha* cloak,' he said, slipping from the rock.

Pain roared through him as he fell, and he realized his weight had come down upon the sword jutting from his back, driving it deeper. He struggled to rise, but there was no power left in his limbs. His face was resting against a cold flagstone.

It felt surprisingly pleasant.

Waylander and Keeva helped Ustarte inside the apartments. 'I just need to rest for an hour or so,' said the priestess. 'Leave me here. Do what you have to do.'

Keeva reloaded her crossbow and walked to the doorway. 'Do you have a plan?' she asked Waylander.

He smiled at her. 'Always.'

'How are you feeling?'

The smile faded. 'I've felt better.'

She looked into his face. Dark rings showed under his eyes, and his skin was pallid, the cheeks sunken. 'I'm sorry,' she whispered. 'I don't know what else to say.'

'No-one lives for ever, Keeva. Are you ready?'

'I am.'

Waylander moved out into the darkness, and ran along the path, cutting left towards the waterfall. Keeva followed him. He clambered up the rocks and entered a dark opening. He waited for her there and took her hand. 'These steps lead up into the palace,' he said. 'Once we are there I want you to make your way to the stairs underneath the library. Cover yourself with the cloak then climb the stairs until you can see into it. Do nothing more until I make my move. You understand this?'

'I understand.'

Still holding her hand he climbed the stairs. The darkness was total. At the top he paused, listening. There was no sound from beyond and he slid open the panel leading to the corridor outside the Great Hall. Lanterns had been lit here, but there was no sign of people. Waylander released her hand. 'Be lucky, Keeva,' he said, then moved away swiftly.

Keeva was suddenly fearful. All the time he had been with her she had felt somehow protected. Now alone, she found her hands trembling.

'Be strong,' she told herself, then ran along the corridor towards the library stairs.

'I cannot see them,' said Eldicar Manushan, staring out over the terraced gardens. Three-swords did not answer. He exchanged glances with Iron-arm. The huge warrior nodded. Three-swords turned away. He had always liked Long-stride. The warrior was reliable and cool under pressure. He would be hard to replace. 'What can be taking them so long?' asked Eldicar Manushan. 'Are they eating his heart, do you think?'

'They are not eating anything,' said Three-swords. 'They are dead.'

'Dead?' responded the magicker, his voice rising. 'They are *Kriaz-nor*. How can they be dead?'

'We die too, magicker. We are not invulnerable. This assassin is obviously everything you feared. Are you sure he is human, and not meld?'

Eldicar Manushan wiped sweat from his face. 'I don't know what he is, but he killed a *Bezha*. I was there. A little while ago he entered a house, surrounded by guards and killer dogs. He killed the merchant who lived there and then left. No-one saw him.'

'Perhaps he knows magic,' said Iron-arm.

'I would have sensed it,' said Eldicar. 'No, he is just a man.'

'Well,' continued Iron-arm, '*just a man* has killed two *Kriaz-nor*. And now he is coming to kill you.'

'Be quiet!' stormed Eldicar, swinging round and staring out over the balcony. He gazed down at the ground some fifty feet below and watched for any sign of movement on the steps. Dark clouds obscured the moon and lightning flashed over the bay, followed some seconds later by a rolling boom of thunder. Rain began to lash down, hissing against the white walls of the palace. Eldicar could see little now, and moved to the shelter of the balcony doorway.

Back in the library Three-swords was just about to pour a goblet of water, when he paused, nostrils flaring. Iron-arm had also caught the scent. Three-swords carefully replaced the goblet on the table and turned, his golden gaze raking the room and the wrought-iron stairs leading up to it. He could see nothing, but he knew someone was close. Iron-arm moved stealthily along the wall.

Three-swords strolled casually towards the stairs, then darted forward. As he did so a crossbow appeared from thin air, and loosed a bolt. Three-swords swayed to one side. The bolt flashed by him. A second followed the first. Three-swords' arm swept up. The point of the bolt gashed the back of his hand, before careering across the library and clattering against the shelves. Three-swords leapt down the stairs, grabbing the outstretched arm. With one heave he threw the assassin back over his shoulder and into the room. The archer landed heavily. Three-swords spun and ran up the stairs. The assassin had come to his knees, although that was not what Three-swords saw. He saw a head and one arm, and a disembodied foot. Reaching out, he tore away the *Bezha* cloak with one hand, while dragging the assassin to his feet with the other. He was about to rip out the man's throat when he saw that he held a slim young woman. She kicked him, but he ignored it and turned towards Eldicar Manushan.

'This is not your Waylander,' he said. 'It is a female.'

'Well, kill her,' shouted Eldicar.

The woman drew a dagger from its sheath. Three-swords absently batted it from her hand. 'Stop struggling,' he said. 'It is beginning to annoy me.'

'What are you waiting for?' said Eldicar. 'Kill her.'

'I have already killed one woman for you, magicker. I did not relish that task, but I did it. It still sits badly with me. I am a warrior, not a woman-killer.'

'Then you do it,' Eldicar ordered Iron-arm.

'That's my captain,' said Iron-arm. 'Where he goes I follow.'

'You insolent dogs! I'll kill her myself!' Eldicar pulled his dagger from his belt and took one step away from the balcony door. At that moment something dark moved into sight behind him. A hand hooked into the collar of his robe, dragging him back. His hips hit the balcony rail and his body cartwheeled over the edge. Iron-arm sprang towards the balcony. There was no-one there. He glanced up.

Through the lashing rain he saw a dark figure scaling the wall, heading towards the upper balcony of the library tower.

Iron-arm looked down. Fifty feet below the magicker lay spreadeagled on the stones. Moving back into the room, Iron-arm headed for the upper stairs.

Three-swords stopped him. 'Trust me, my friend, you do not want to go up there.' He looked down at the woman in his grasp, then released her. She half fell. Three-swords saw a swelling on the side of her face, and her left eye was closing fast. 'Sit down,' he said, 'and drink some water. What is your name?'

'Keeva Taliana.'

'Well, Keeva Taliana, have your drink and gather your strength. Then, were I you, I would leave this tower.'

Eldicar Manushan lay very still. Pain threatened to engulf him, but he concentrated his powers, blocking the agony. Fighting for calm, he sent his spirit flowing through his broken body. He had landed heavily on his back, but, thankfully, his spine was not severed. His right hip was smashed, and his left leg broken in three places, his left wrist fractured. His head had missed the stone of the path, striking the soft earth of a flower-bed beside it. Otherwise his neck might have been broken. There were some internal injuries, but quietly and carefully Eldicar healed them. Occasionally the pain would burst through his defences, but he held it back and continued to direct power to his injuries, accelerating the healing. He could do little about the broken bones in such a short time, but he swelled and stiffened the muscles around them, forcing them back into position.

The rain pounded down upon him as he lay there. Lightning speared across the sky. By its light he saw Waylander scaling the wall. He had almost reached the upper balcony. Despite his broken bones Eldicar felt a wave of relief sweep over him. He would not now have to be in the room when Anharat was summoned. Even better, the Lord of Demons could not be summoned through *him*.

Carefully Eldicar rolled to his stomach and pushed himself to his knees. Sharp pain flared in his ruined hip, but the muscles around it held firm. Rising to his feet, he let out a groan as his broken leg twisted, a jagged shard biting into the cramped muscles of his calf. Bending down he forced the bone back into place with his thumbs, then tightened the muscles once more.

Taking a deep breath he put weight on the injured limb. It held. Almost all of his talent had been used, and Eldicar knew he had to find a place of safety where he could rest and recoup his power. Slowly he inched his way towards the palace, entering a corridor opposite the Oak Room. It came to him then that he did not want to remain in this place. He wanted to go home. If he could just make it to the stables and saddle a horse he could ride for the gateway and never again be forced to serve monsters like Deresh Karany. Eldicar thought of the family house beside the lake, the cool breezes flowing over the snow-capped mountains.

He paused as pain swamped him.

I should never have come, he thought. This venture has ruined me. He saw again the contempt in the *Kriaz-nor*'s eyes as he called for the death of the girl, and remembered the night of horror when the *Kraloth* had ripped into the nobles of Kydor.

'I am not an evil man,' he whispered. 'The cause was just.'

He tried to hold to the teachings of his youth, about the greatness of Kuan-Hador, and its divine purpose to bring peace and civilization to all peoples. Peace and civilization? Desiccated corpses were strewn around Deresh Karany, who was summoning the Lord of Demons.

'I am going home,' said Eldicar Manushan.

He limped towards the main doors and dragged them open, stepping out into the storm-swept night.

And came face to face with an angry crowd, led by the priest Chardyn.

There were many conflicting thoughts and emotions within the Source priest Chardyn as he led the townspeople up the hill towards the White Palace. First and foremost was a terrible fear. Righteous anger had led him to make his speech at the temple, allied to an underlying belief that an army of common folk would prove a match for a few score soldiers and a magicker.

But when the march began many of the townspeople had drifted away. And when the storm came even more hung back. And so it was that Chardyn arrived at the White Palace leading a bedraggled group of around a hundred people, many of them women.

He had promised them that the Source would show His power. He had pledged a shield of thunder and a spear of lightning. Well, he had the thunder and the lightning – and with it the sheeting rain that had drenched his followers, cooling their ardour.

Very few of the people with him had weapons. They had not come to fight. They had come to witness the miracle. The stonemason, Benae Tarlin, was carrying an iron spear, and, to his right, Lalitia was holding her dagger. Benae had asked Chardyn to bless the spear, and the priest had solemnly laid his hands upon it, and in a loud voice had intoned, 'This is a weapon of righteousness. May it blaze with the Light of the Source!' That had been back in Carlis, and the crowd had cheered mightily. What Chardyn had noticed was that the spear was old and dull, the point pitted with rust.

The small crowd crested the hill and saw the palace. 'When will we see the magic?' asked Benae Tarlin.

Chardyn did not answer. His white robes were soaked and he felt a great weariness upon him. His own anger had long since been replaced by a feeling of impending doom. All he knew was that he would enter the palace and do his best to wring the throat of Eldicar Manushan. He marched on, Lalitia beside him.

'I hope you are right about the Source,' she said.

As they came closer the doors of the palace opened, and Eldicar Manushan stepped out to meet them.

Chardyn saw him, and hesitated. Thunder rumbled above them, and Chardyn could feel the fear in the crowd swelling. Eldicar Manushan looked at him. 'What do you want here?' he called.

'I am here, in the name of the Source, to put an end to your evil,' replied Chardyn, aware that his normally powerful voice lacked conviction.

Eldicar moved out from the doorway. The crowd fell back. 'Leave here now,' boomed the magicker, 'or I shall summon demons to destroy you all!'

Benae Tarlin backed away from Chardyn. Lalitia swore and stepped in. 'Give me that!' she hissed, snatching the iron spear from the stone-mason's hand. Spinning on her heel Lalitia took two running steps towards Eldicar Manushan and launched the weapon.

The surprised magicker threw up his arm but the spear plunged into his belly. He staggered and almost fell. Then he grabbed the iron haft with both hands, dragging it clear. 'I cannot die!' he shouted.

Thunder boomed as he spoke – and a blast of lightning tore down from the sky. The iron spear in Eldicar's hand exploded in a tremendous flash of white light. The magicker's body was hurled high into the air. The force of the explosion threw Lalitia from her feet. Chardyn ran to her, helping her up. Then he walked slowly towards the charred body of Eldicar Manushan. One arm was completely gone and a part of the man's chest had been torn open. A blackened section of the iron haft had crashed through Eldicar's face and was jutting from the rear of his skull.

As Chardyn stood there he saw the body twitch. One hand opened and closed. The leg jerked. Eldicar's eyes flared open. Blood bubbled from his ruined chest, but the wound began to close.

Lalitia dropped to her knees beside the magicker and rammed her dagger into his throat, severing the jugular. Blood pumped out. Eldicar's eyes stayed open for a little while, wide and terrified. Then they closed, and all movement ceased.

Benae Tarlin moved alongside Chardyn, and then the other townspeople crowded around.

'All praise to the Source!' someone said.

'The spear of lightning,' said another.

Chardyn looked up from the charred corpse and saw people staring at him, their faces awestricken. Benae Tarlin took his hand and kissed it. Chardyn realized that the crowd were waiting for him to say something; some grand words, something memorable to match the occasion. But he had nothing to say.

He turned away from them and began the long walk back to Carlis.

Lalitia came alongside him, taking his arm. 'Well, you are a saint now, my friend,' she said. 'A man of miracles.'

'It was no miracle. He was struck by lightning in a storm,' said Chardyn. 'And I am a fraud.'

'How can you say that? You promised them the Source would strike him down. He was struck down. Why do you continue to doubt?'

Chardyn gave a sigh. 'I am a liar and a charlatan. You – though I love you dearly – are a whore and a thief. You think the Source would work his wonders through people like us?'

'Perhaps that is the real miracle,' she said.

The fingers of Waylander's left hand were cramping as he eased himself up the wall, reaching for the cracks where the sections of marble dressing joined. The cracks were thin, no more than half an inch wide in places. Rain swept over him, making the handholds slippery. Waylander paused and opened and closed his left fist, trying to keep the fingers supple. Then he pushed on.

A figure appeared on the balcony just above him. Waylander froze. Lightning flashed over the bay and the assassin saw in its fierce light a nightmare face. Hideously stretched at the temples, the head was triangular, with huge almond-shaped eyes. The texture of the grey skin was scaly, like that of a serpent. Then the creature moved back from the balcony and into the tower beyond. Waylander gripped one of the stone balcony rails and hauled himself up. Lifting the crossbow from the clip at his belt, he vaulted the rail then dived into the room.

Something bright flashed by his face. He rolled to his right. A second burning missile flew past. Coming to his knees, bow raised, he saw the creature's hand come up. A ball of fire appeared in the palm. Waylander shot swiftly. The bolt slammed through the fiery globe, embedding itself in the shoulder of the creature. It leapt forward, then spun, its huge tail raking out. Waylander threw himself to his left. A sharp claw missed him by inches. He shot again. The bolt sliced through the creature's face. It reared up, then fell heavily. Waylander notched the upper string of his bow and slipped another bolt into place.

The creature lay still.

Suddenly Waylander felt immense pity for it, and a powerful yearning to befriend the beast. He knew, in that instant, that it could not be evil, that it desired only love and friendship. He could not believe that he had come here to kill it. The creature rose slowly and turned. Waylander relaxed. Then his eyes fell upon the bodies around the walls. In the corner he saw a dried-out husk. Braided golden hair clung to the skull. He knew the style of the braid. The corpse had once been Norda.

He looked back at the creature. Never in his life had he known such love as he felt now. From somewhere deep in his mind he recalled Ustarte telling him about the charm-spell used by Deresh Karany. The creature was closer now. Its tail swept round, the claw glinting in the lantern-light.

'Will you die for me?' asked the creature sweetly.

'Not tonight,' said Waylander. With a huge effort of will he raised his weapon and touched the trigger. The bolt tore through the creature's neck. Deresh Karany gave a terrible cry. The spell broke.

Waylander dropped the crossbow and drew a throwing knife, which he hurled into Deresh Karany's chest. The creature screamed and rushed at him. Talons snaked out. Waylander dropped to his knees and flung himself to the right. The tail lashed at him, throwing him against an oak table. Waylander came to his feet and drew his shortsword. The tail swept up. Waylander's blade cut deep into it. A high-pitched scream sounded from Deresh Karany, who backed away, his tail oozing blood to the floor. 'You cannot kill me, mortal,' he said.

'But I can bring you a world of pain,' answered Waylander. Another knife sliced through the air, plunging deep into the creature's biceps.

Deresh Karany backed away once more, and began to chant. Waylander had never before heard the language. It was guttural and harsh, yet powerfully rhythmic. The air in the room grew colder as the chanting grew louder. The walls began to vibrate. Shelves came crashing down. Realizing that the creature was summoning a demon, Waylander hurled himself at him. Deresh Karany spun, his blood-smeared tail whiplashing out.

The assassin was thrown across the room. He landed hard, striking his head against the wall. Groggy now, he struggled to rise. A bright light was forming by the far wall. The stone began to ripple. In desperation Waylander drew another knife and hurled it with all his might. It hammered into Deresh Karany's outstretched hand. Waylander heard him grunt with pain. For a moment only the chanting ceased. Then it began again. The cold intensified. Waylander shivered. Fear swelled within him. Not fear of death, or even fear of failure. But fear itself, undiluted and pure. He felt the unseen presence of something so primal, so powerful, that all his strength and guile were as nothing against it. Like a blade of grass trying to withstand a hurricane.

His limbs trembled. Deresh Karany screeched with laughter, the sound bizarre and insane. 'You can feel it, can't you?' he shouted. 'Where are your knives now, little man? Here is one for you!' The *Ipsissimus* pulled the throwing knife from the flesh of his face and tossed it towards Waylander. It clattered on the floor close by. Plucking the other blades from his flesh, he casually threw them down. 'Quick, gather them up,' he said. 'I will enjoy watching you use them against the greatest of demons, the Lord of the Pit. Do you feel honoured? Your soul is to be devoured by Anharat himself!'

The air around Waylander vibrated. Terror, pure and undiluted, swept through him, and he felt a desperate need to escape this place.

'Why not run?' mocked Deresh Karany. 'If you are fast enough his wings will not be able to catch you!'

Waylander hefted his sword, anger coming to his aid. He was still unsteady on his feet, but he prepared himself for one last attack.

A dark figure appeared in the rippling wall, then ducked down and stepped into the room. Its skin was black and scaled, its head round, its ears long and pointed. As it entered it raised itself up until it stood more than ten feet tall, its head just below the rafters. Black wings stretched out, touching the walls on either side. Fire burned in the demon's eye-sockets and flames flickered from its wide mouth. A sickening odour filled the room. Waylander recognized it. It was the stench of decaying flesh.

'I summoned thee, Anharat,' said Deresh Karany.

'For what purpose, human?' came the response. As it spoke, fire billowed from the gaping mouth, curling up against the skin of its face. The words hung in the cold air, echoing around the rafters.

'To kill my enemy.'

The Demon Lord's burning eyes fastened on Waylander. Ponderously he advanced across the room. As his taloned feet touched the ornate rugs the cloth burst into flame. Smoke rose around the creature.

Waylander flipped the shortsword, catching it by the blade as he prepared to hurl it into the breast of the demon.

The beast paused. Its head arched back and it began to laugh. Flames roared from its mouth, the sound causing the room to tremble. Waylander threw the sword. As it left his hand it burst into flame then flew up to plunge into one of the rafters. The Demon Lord swung to face Deresh Karany. 'Ah, but this is a good moment!' he said. 'I have always loathed humans, Deresh Karany, but you I hold in utter contempt. Did I not warn you that this gateway would be protected? Did I not tell you that only the death of three kings would open the portals? Did you listen? No. Hundreds of my people have been slain, and now you have the effrontery to call upon Anharat to kill a single human.'

'You must obey, Demon!' shouted Deresh Karany. 'I have followed all the ancient rituals. To the last detail. Ten deaths I have given you, and the incantations were perfect. You have no choice but to accept my order.'

'Oh, this is exquisite! You are a skilled sorcerer, Deresh Karany. You know all the laws governing the Summoning. And what, pray, is the prime law?'

'There must be a death. That is the price! And there he is, Anharat. Kill him, and the ritual is complete.'

'And how many times can a man be killed?' asked the Demon Lord, moving slowly towards Deresh Karany until he towered over the *Ipsissimus*. Waylander stood silently by. Deresh Karany tried to back away. The wall stopped him.

'I don't understand,' he said, his voice shaking. 'Kill him – and go!'

'I cannot kill him, mortal. For he is already dead. His heart no longer beats. His body stands only because a magicker laid a spell upon it.'

'No. This cannot be!' shouted Deresh. 'You are trying to trick me!'

'The prime law,' said Anharat. 'There must be a life.' His huge arm snaked out. Sharp talons crunched through Deresh Karany's body, hauling him into the air. As Waylander watched, the Demon Lord tore open the sorcerer's chest, ripping out his heart. Yet still Deresh struggled. 'Even better,' said Anharat. 'You have mastered the art of regeneration. You will wish you had not. For now it may take a hundred years for you to die.' A blast of flame roared from the demon's mouth, engulfing the beating heart in his hand. Ponderously he turned and moved back to the rippling wall. Deresh Karany was still struggling as Anharat ducked down and stepped through.

As the portal closed Waylander heard one last despairing scream.

Then there was silence.

Kysumu had never fought better in his life. He was the representative of humanity in a battle to save his world, and pride flooded his muscles with a power he had never before experienced. *This* was what he had been waiting for his entire life. To be the instrument of good against evil, to be the hero. He was unstoppable, and fought beside the *Riaj-nor* with a chilling ferocity.

At first they clove deep into the superior ranks of the *Kriaz-nor*, driving towards the great arch. It was a curious sight and, even as he battled, Kysumu found it wondrous. Above him the sky was lit by moon and stars, and yet sunshine was beaming through the gateway, casting a golden light upon the stark ruins of Kuan-Hador. Intermittently dark-blue lightning would ripple across the opening, filling the air with an acrid smell.

The *Riaj-nor* had hacked and cut their way forward. Four warriors burst through the *Kriaz-nor* lines and sprinted towards the gateway. A dozen *Kriaz-nor* gave chase. As the grey-garbed warriors reached the portal they hurled their blades towards the golden light. As the swords crossed the opening they flared with a brilliance that dazzled the eye. Blue lightning tore across the huge arch. To Kysumu it seemed fractionally darker than before, but still the sunlight from another world streamed through. Unarmed now, the four *Riaj-nor* had turned and flung themselves at their enemies. They were cut down in moments.

That had been almost an hour ago.

Now the lightning was pale, and within its flare Kysumu could see white streaks. Only around thirty of the *Riaj-nor* were still fighting, and though they had taken a terrible toll on the enemy they were still outnumbered two to one. Ren Tang had fallen moments before, cut down by two *Kriaz-nor*. As he fell, his chest pierced, he reached out and pulled one of the warriors in close, ripping out his throat with his teeth.

The sound of thunder rumbled from some distance away, as a storm broke over the Bay of Carlis. The wind changed and a light rain began to fall over the ruins. Kysumu's grey robes were saturated with blood, and now the rain made the ground slippery beneath his feet. Yet still he fought with controlled frenzy. Two more *Riaj-nor* forced a way past the enemy, running at the gateway and throwing their swords towards it. As the blades disappeared the white streaks faded, the lightning becoming a blue so deep that the sunlight could no longer shine through. Three *Kriaz-nor* fighters peeled back from the battle, killing the unarmed warriors, and taking up positions directly in front of the gateway, ready to cut down any who broke through.

Song Xiu killed two warriors, then darted through the gap. Kysumu ducked under a slashing blade, disembowelled the wielder, then ran after him. But before they could reach the gateway a group of *Kriaz-nor* cut them off. Back to back Kysumu and Song Xiu struggled to defend themselves. The remaining *Riaj-nor* swept forward to aid them. Many were killed.

Only a dozen made it, forming a defensive circle. They were exhausted now.

'It would take no more than one – maybe two blades,' said Song Xiu, during a momentary lull in the fighting. He swore and cast an angry glance at the stone arch. They were so close now that their faces, and those of their enemies, were bathed in blue light. One warrior tried to fling his sword over the heads of the *Kriaz-nor*. It spun towards the gateway, but an enemy warrior leapt and caught it by the hilt. The blade shivered and broke.

Song Xiu stared venomously at the remaining *Kriaz-nor*, who were standing now some ten feet away. They were equally weary. 'One last charge,' said Song Xiu. A movement caught Kysumu's eye. He glanced to the left.

Low to the ground, moving behind a ruined wall, was a crawling figure. Kysumu saw the edge of a wolfskin jerkin. Suddenly Yu Yu Liang surged to his feet, sprinting towards the gateway. The three *Kriaz-nor* stationed there ran to block his way.

Yu Yu leapt at them, his sword cleaving through the air.

'Now!' shouted Song Xiu.

The *Riaj-nor* charged. Kysumu lost sight of Yu Yu and joined

934

Song Xiu and the others. They threw themselves at the enemy. The *Kriaz-nor* did not give ground, nor could the weary attackers force them back.

The battle was being fought as if in a dream, the movements of the warriors slow and sluggish. Finally both sides fell back and stared malevolently at each other. There were only eight attackers still standing, and fourteen *Kriaz-nor*.

In the lull Kysumu looked around for Yu Yu. He knew what he would see.

His body lay close to the gateway. His sword arm had been severed. The *Rajnee* blade lay beside it. Kysumu felt sick with grief. Then he saw the body twitch. The *Kriaz-nor* guarding the gateway had moved forward to stand with their comrades. None of them could see Yu Yu.

Kysumu watched as Yu Yu rolled to his side. There was a ghastly wound in his belly, and his entrails had spilled out. Even so, he began to crawl, leaving a bloody smear upon the rocks. Reaching out with his left hand, Yu Yu gathered up the fallen sword. He groaned as he did so. One of the *Kriaz-nor* swung round. Yu Yu flung the blade into the gateway.

There was a searing burst of brightness, accompanied by a high-pitched hum that made the ground vibrate. The blue lightning ceased to crackle. Instead a silver sheen covered the gateway.

The *Kriaz-nor* turned suddenly and raced towards the arch. Thirteen made it through, but as the last warrior crossed it the silver became grey rock. At first it seemed that the warrior had merely stopped in the gateway, but then his body slid down the stone and flopped to its back. He had been cut in half.

Kysumu ran to where Yu Yu lay. Gently he turned him. Yu Yu's eyes were open.

'Oh, my friend,' said Kysumu, tears flowing, 'you closed the gateway.'

Yu Yu could not hear him, and Kysumu gazed down into the dead face. He hugged Yu Yu to him and sat rocking back and forth. Song Xiu moved to his side and sat down. For a while he was silent as Kysumu wept. Then he spoke. 'He was a good man,' he said.

Kysumu kissed Yu Yu's brow, then laid him back on the ground. 'It makes no sense to me,' said Kysumu, brushing away his tears. 'He could have lived. He didn't want to be the *priashath*. He didn't want to fight demons and die. So why? Why did he throw away his life?'

'He did not *throw* it away, human. He *gave* it. For you, for me, for this land. Why do you think he was chosen? If the Source had wanted the best swordsman he might have picked you. But He didn't. He wanted a man. An ordinary man.' Song Xiu chuckled. 'A ditch-digger with a stolen sword. And look what that ditch-digger achieved.'

'It just makes me sad,' said Kysumu, reaching down and stroking Yu Yu's face.

'It makes me proud,' said Song Xiu. 'I shall find his soul in the Void, and we will walk together.'

Kysumu looked into the warrior's face. Song Xiu's hair was grey, his face ageing. 'What is happening to you?'

'I am dying,' said Song Xiu. 'We are out of time.'

Kysumu swung round and saw that the other *Riaj-nor* were all stretched out on the ground, unmoving. 'Why?' asked Kysumu.

'We should have died thousands of years ago,' Song Xiu told him, his voice no more than a whisper. 'We knew when we returned that there would be only days left to us. Yu Yu Liang made it worth the price we paid.'

Song Xiu lay down. His hair was white now, the skin of his face as dry as parchment. Kysumu moved to him. 'I am so sorry,' he said. 'I . . . misjudged you. All of you. I have been a fool. Forgive me!'

The *Riaj-nor* did not answer. A breeze blew across the ruins. Song Xiu's body shivered and turned to dust.

Kysumu sat for a while, lost in thoughts and bittersweet memories. Then he took his sword and dug out a grave for Yu Yu Liang. He covered it with stones, then sheathed his weapon and walked away from the ruins of Kuan-Hador.

Waylander gathered up his crossbow, and his knives, and moved down the stairs to the lower library. Keeva was sitting there, but there was no sign of the two warriors.

'They left,' said Keeva, rising and putting her arms around the Grey Man. 'How are you feeling?'

'Like death,' he told her, with a wry grin.

'I heard the . . . demon,' she said. 'I have never been more terrified. Not even when Camran took me from the village.'

'That seems a long time ago now,' he replied. Taking her hand Waylander made his way down to the terrace steps where he found Ustarte waiting.

'The gateway is closed,' she told him. 'Yu Yu Liang died to seal it. Kysumu survived.'

Waylander glanced around him, seeking the body of Eldicar Manushan. 'He is dead,' said Ustarte.

'Truly dead?' queried Waylander. 'I would have thought the fall would have killed him.'

'He had some regenerative powers. They could not withstand being struck by a bolt of lightning.'

'So it is over,' said Waylander wearily. 'That is good. Where is Matze?'

'He is still tied in the cellar. Keeva can release him. You and I have to go to the stables.'

'Why there?'

'I have one last gift for you, my friend.'

Waylander smiled. 'I can feel death approaching, Ustarte. My blood is flowing sluggishly and your spell is wearing off. I do not think this is a time for gifts.'

'Trust me, Grey Man.'

Taking his arm she led him back into the palace.

Keeva ran down to the cellar to free Matze Chai. The old man was naked and tied to a chair. He looked up as she entered, and stared at her quizzically.

'I am here to free you,' she told him. 'The Grey Man has killed the sorcerer.'

'Of course he has,' said Matze. 'And what, pray, possessed you to come to me without bearing any clothing for me to wear? Does a little peril make people lose all sense of good manners? Untie me, then go to my rooms and fetch a suitable robe and some soft shoes.'

Keeva shook her head and smiled. 'My apologies, Lord,' she said, with a bow. 'Is there anything else you require?'

Matze nodded. 'If any of my servants have survived you can tell them to prepare a sweet tisane.'

The dawn was breaking as Keeva made her way to the stables. She found Ustarte sitting on a stone bench under a willow tree. The two *Kriaz-nor* warriors were beside her. There was no sign of the Grey Man. 'Where is he?' she asked.

'He is gone, Keeva. I opened a portal for him.'

'Where did you send him?'

'Where he always wanted to be.'

Keeva sat down. A great sadness settled upon her. 'It is hard to believe,' she said, 'that there is no Grey Man. He seemed somehow . . . immortal, unbeatable.'

'And he is, my dear,' Ustarte told her. 'He is only gone from this world. Waylander will never truly die. Men like him are eternal. Somewhere, even as we speak, there is another Grey Man, preparing to face his destiny.'

Keeva glanced at the two warriors, then back at the priestess. 'And what of you? Where will you go?'

'We do not belong here, Keeva. Now that I am no longer using most of my power to thwart Deresh Karany I have enough energy to take us home.'

'You will go back to the land of Deresh Karany?'

'The fight is over for you – but not for me. I cannot rest while the evil that spawned Deresh Karany still thrives.'

Keeva turned to the warriors. 'And you will help her?'

'I think that we will,' said Three-swords.

Epilogue

Using a stiff broom Tanya swept the dust from the hard-packed clay floor. As much rose around her as was pushed out through the door. Dakeyras had carved designs in the clay, and around the hearth he had created a mosaic with coloured stones from the streambed. Last year's crop had barely supplied them with enough coin to last the year, but Dakeyras had promised that with the first profits from the farm a real floor would be laid.

Tanya was looking forward to such a time, though, as she gazed upon the mosaic, she felt a stab of anticipated regret. She had been pregnant with the twins when Dakeyras had returned from the stream with the sack of stones. Six-year-old Gellan had been with him, full of excitement. 'I found all the red stones, Mama. I picked them all,' he said. 'Isn't that right, Father?'

'You did well, Gil,' said Dakeyras.

'You also soaked your new leggings,' Tanya told the boy.

'You can't take stones from a streambed without getting wet,' said Dakeyras.

'That's right, Mama. And it was fun getting wet. I almost caught a fish with my hands.' Tanya gazed into the boy's bright-blue eyes. He grinned at her and her heart melted. 'All right,' she said, 'you are forgiven. But why do we need a sack of stones?'

For the next two days Dakeyras and Gellan had worked on the rectangular mosaic. Tanya remembered it fondly; the laughter and the joy, Gellan squealing with delight, Dakeyras, his face smeared with clay, tickling him. And when they had finished she recalled them stripping off their clothing and having a race to the stream, which Dakeyras let the boy win. Those were good days.

Tanya put down her broom and stood in the doorway. Gellan was out in the meadow with his wooden sword, the twins were asleep in their crib and Dakeyras had gone out hunting for venison. The day was quiet, the sun bright in a sky dotted with puffballs of white cloud. They looked like sheep grazing on a field of blue, she thought.

It would be good to have venison. Supplies were low, and though the town storekeeper extended them credit Tanya was loath to fall further into debt.

People had been kind. But, then, Dakeyras was a popular man. Everyone remembered him as the officer whose prompt action had saved the community from the Sathuli raid. He had fought with distinction, and he, and his friend Gellan – after whom they had named their son – had been awarded medals. Gellan had remained with the army. Tanya often wondered whether Dakeyras regretted becoming a farmer.

His commanding officer had come to see Tanya the day after Dakeyras said he wanted to resign his commission, telling her that he felt her husband was making a grave mistake. 'He is that rarest of animals, a natural fighting man but also a thinker. The men revere him. He could go far, Tanya.'

'I did not ask him to leave the service, sir,' she said. 'It was his own decision.'

'That is a shame,' he told her. 'I had hoped it was your idea, and that I could persuade you to change your mind.'

'I would be happy with him whether he was a soldier, a farmer, a baker . . . But he told me that he had to leave the service.'

'Did he say why? Was he unhappy?'

'No, sir. He was too happy.'

'I don't understand.'

'I can say no more. It would not be right.'

He had still been confused when he left. How could Tanya have told him what Dakeyras confided to her? The fighting and the killing, which dismayed most men, had begun to fill Dakeyras with a savage delight. 'If I stay,' he said, 'I will become someone I do not want to be.' In the end his commanding officer had convinced Dakeyras to take a year's sabbatical, while still holding his commission. That year was almost up.

Tanya walked out into the sunshine and untied the ribbon that held her long blond hair in place. Shaking out the dust, she moved to the well, and slowly drew up a bucket. Reaching out, she dragged it over until it rested on the stone wall. She drank deeply, then splashed water to her face.

'Riders, Mama!' shouted Gellan.

Tanya turned towards the north and saw a line of horsemen making their way down the slope. She wondered if they might be soldiers, but soon saw that, although they were heavily armed, they were not from the Drenai garrison.

She walked back towards the house and waited for them by the porch.

The first of the men, riding a tall bay, drew rein. He had a long face and deep-set eyes. Tanya, who liked most people, found herself vaguely repelled by him. She glanced at the other riders. They were unshaven, their clothes dirty. Alongside the lead rider was a man with Nadir features, high cheekbones and slanted eyes. No-one spoke.

'If you would like to water your horses,' said Tanya, 'you may use the stream. It is a little further back into the trees.'

'We didn't come for water,' said the long-faced man. He stared at her, his eyes glittering. Tanya felt both anger and fear as his gaze flowed over her. 'You are a pretty thing, farm girl. I like a woman with good breasts. I think you can supply what we need.'

'You had better leave,' she said. 'My husband . . . and his friends . . . will be back soon. You are not welcome here.'

'We are not welcome anywhere,' said the rider. 'Now, you can do this easy or hard. Best to know that I gutted the last woman who chose hard.'

Tanya stood very still. One of the twins began to cry for food, the sound high and keening. Little Gellan had moved closer. 'What do they want, Mama?' he called.

The long-faced man turned towards the Nadir. 'Kill the brat!' he said.

A blast of cold air swept across the riders. Horses reared and were brought under control. Tanya turned her head, and saw another horseman. She had not heard him approach. The riders were all staring at him.

'Where the Hell did he come from?' she heard someone ask.

'From the back of the house,' said Long-face. 'Where else?'

Tanya stared hard at the newcomer. There was something familiar about him. He was old, his face masked by grey stubble. And he looked tired. Dark rings circled his eyes. He heeled his horse forward, and Tanya saw that in his left hand he held a small black crossbow.

'What do you want here?' asked Long-face.

'I know you,' said the newcomer. 'I know all of you.' Shock rippled through Tanya as she heard his voice, though she didn't know why. He moved his mount closer to Long-face. 'You are Bedrin, known as the Stalker. You are a man with no redeeming features. There is nothing I have to say to you.' The crossbow came up, and Long-face pitched from the saddle, a bolt through his brain. 'As for the rest of you,' continued the rider, 'there are some who can still find redemption.'

Tanya saw the Nadir draw his sword and heel his horse forward. A crossbow bolt slammed through into his throat, and he, too, fell to the ground, his horse cantering past the man, who continued to talk. There was no hint of emotion in his voice. He might as well have been discussing the weather. The seventeen remaining riders sat their mounts, almost mesmerized by this deadly, grey-faced stranger.

'It is fitting that Kityan should join his master,' he said, casually reloading the crossbow. 'He lived for torture, to inflict pain on others.' He glanced at the remaining raiders. 'But you,' he said, pointing at a broad-shouldered young man, 'you, Maneas, have better dreams. Back in Gothir, at the village of the Nine Oaks, there is a girl. You wanted to marry her, but her father gave her to another. You were heartbroken when you rode away. Would it help to know that her husband will drown this summer? She will be alone. If you return to her you will sire two sons and a daughter.'

'How do you know this?' asked the young man. 'Are you a wizard?'

'You can think of me as a prophet,' said the man. 'For I know what is, and what will be. I have seen the future. If you kill this woman and her children, Maneas, you will still go home. You will still wed Leandra, and she will bear you the three children I spoke of. And then one night this woman's husband will find you. He will have been searching for nine years. He will take you into the woods and put out your eyes. Then he will stake you to the ground and build a fire upon your belly.' Tanya saw all colour drain from the young man's face.

The newcomer's hand swept out, pointing to a thin, middle-aged man. 'And you, Patris. No matter what happens here today you will leave this band and journey to Gulgothir. You will seek to fulfil a dream you have had since childhood, to begin a business, designing jewellery for the nobles, wonderfully wrought

942

rings and brooches. You will discover that what you thought of as talent is, in fact, genius. You will find happiness and wealth and fame in Gulgothir. But if this woman dies her man will find you. He will cut off your hands, and your body will be discovered impaled upon a sharp stake.'

He fell silent, and they waited. Finally he spoke again. 'The luckiest of you will survive for nineteen years. But many of those years will be lived in terror. You will hear of the murders of your comrades. One by one. Every day you will stare into the faces of strangers, wondering if the faceless killer is one of them. And one day he will be. This is the truth.

'Now it is time to make a choice. Ride from here and live. Or stay, and know the endless torment of the damned.'

For a moment no-one moved. Then the young Maneas swung his horse and galloped back towards the north. One by one the others followed until only a swarthy, round-shouldered man remained. 'And what of me, prophet?' he asked. 'Is there some happiness I can find?'

'There is *now*, Lodrian. Now you can journey to Lentria. You will find a village and, short of coin, you will seek employment. A young widow will ask you to repair her roof. And your life will change.'

'Thank you,' said Lodrian. He looked down at Tanya. 'I am sorry for the fear we caused you.' Then he rode away.

The rider slowly dismounted. Tanya saw him stumble as he did so, dropping his crossbow to the ground. He took several steps towards Gellan then fell to his knees. Tanya ran to his side, putting her arms around his shoulders. 'You are ill, sir,' she said. 'Let me help you.'

The man swayed and, with difficulty, Tanya lowered him to the ground. He lay back, his head surrounded by the fading spring flowers of the meadow. He looked into her eyes.

'Do I know you, sir?' she asked.

'No. We have . . . never met. But I knew a woman once, who was . . . like you.'

'My husband will be home soon. He will help me get you to a bed. We will send for the surgeon.'

His voice was weaker. 'I will not be alive when he returns.'

She took his hand and kissed it. 'You saved us,' she said, tears in her eyes. 'There must be something we can do for you!'

'Let me see the boy,' he whispered. Tanya called out to Gellan and the child moved forward nervously. The man looked up at him. Tanya saw him relax, and upon his face appeared a look of utter contentment. He smiled at the boy. Then his eyes closed, his head lolling to one side. Tanya sat beside him, holding his hand.

After a while the child spoke. 'Is he sleeping, Mama?'

'No, Gil, he is dead.'

The sound of a galloping horse came to her. Fear flared and she spun round. But the raiders had not returned. The rider was Dakeyras. He leapt from the saddle.

'What happened here?' he asked. She told him of the raiders, and of the arrival of the grey-faced man.

'They were going to kill us all. I know it,' she concluded. 'He saved our lives, Dak. I'm sure I've seen him somewhere. Do you recognize him?'

Dakeyras knelt by the body. 'He looks familiar,' he said. 'Perhaps he was a soldier.'

Little Gellan ran to him. 'He killed the bad men, Father. And he made the others ride away. Then he lay down and died.'

The sound of a baby's cry came from the house. Tanya rose and went to feed it.

Dakeyras walked to where the stranger's crossbow was lying on the ground, and lifted it. It was perfectly balanced, and beautifully made. Extending his arm, Dakeyras loosed both bolts. They flew exactly where he aimed them, slamming into the fence post twenty paces to his left.

Tanya walked out into the sunlight, holding one of the twins to her breast.

Her husband was holding the bow.

She shivered suddenly.

'Are you all right?' he asked.

'Someone just walked over my grave,' she said.